RUDYARD KIPLING

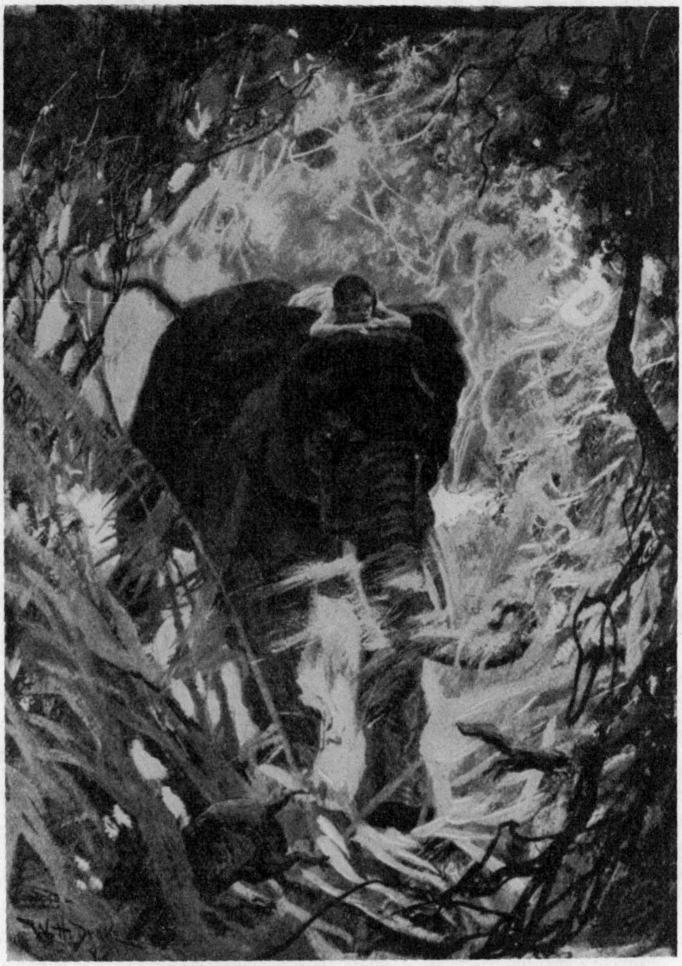

"LITTLE TOOMAI LAID HIMSELF DOWN CLOSE TO THE GREAT NECK, LEST A SWINGING BOUGH SHOULD SWEEP HIM TO THE GROUND."

RUDYARD KIPLING

Selected Works

THE JUNGLE BOOK

THE SECOND JUNGLE BOOK

JUST SO STORIES FOR LITTLE CHILDREN

PUCK OF POOK'S HILL

CAPTAINS COURAGEOUS

STALKY & CO.

KIM

PLAIN TALES FROM THE HILLS

SHORT STORIES

GRAMERCY BOOKS
NEW YORK • AVENEL

This 1995 edition is published by Gramercy Books,
distributed by Random House Value Publishing, Inc.,
40 Engelhard Avenue,
Avenel, New Jersey 07001.

Random House
New York • Toronto • London • Sydney • Auckland

Printed and bound in the United States

Library of Congress Cataloging-in-Publication Data
Kipling, Rudyard, 1865-1936
[Selections. 1995]
Selected works / Rudyard Kipling.
p. cm.
ISBN 0-517-11827-0
1. India—Social life and customs—Literary collections
I. Title
PR4852 1995 94-24680
828'.809—dc20 CIP

10 9 8 7 6 5 4 3 2 1

Contents

Foreword

More than a hundred years ago, a great event was taking place in Bombay, India. It was the birth of a literary legend, a legend by the name of Rudyard Kipling. When Dickens, Chekhov, and Twain are being lauded as the best tale-spinners of time, Kipling is most assuredly included in that revered circle of giants. In fact, many consider him to be the greatest storyteller ever to have lived.

Kipling wrote with compassion and sensitivity, which may have been nurtured and developed from his troubled times as a child. At the tender age of six Kipling was sent by his parents, along with his younger sister, Trix, to England to be raised in proper English fashion and at the same time protected from the dangerous climate that prevailed throughout India. Being separated from his parents at such a young age and being subjected to the care of an elderly, military, and evangelistic couple, the child was lonely and miserable. The pain was further accentuated by the harsh punishment inflicted on him. This traumatic chapter of his life was vividly brought in focus in his story "Baa, Baa Black Sheep."

As a youth, Kipling attended a military school; this turned out to be a travesty. He could not conform to the school's rigid standards and restraints. Ironically, Kipling later earned a deep and sincere respect for the military. His school days, however, served as the source for the uproarious tales of *Stalky and Co.*

At the age of seventeen Kipling returned to India in the capacity of a journalist, taking a job as a reporter with the *Lahore Civil and Military Gazette,* a major newspaper in northwest India. It was his career as a journalist that became a major force in the evolution of Kipling's literary talents. At the age of twenty-two Kipling introduced *Plain Tales from the Hills.* In this series of tales, he gave a view of India that people had not been exposed to. He had made an impression. Shortly thereafter, Kipling was famous in England and was becoming known worldwide.

It was the freshness and simple genius of his writing, matched with the frankness and discipline of a journalist set in the relatively mysterious and active frontier of India, that spurred Kipling to classic heights in literature. He was a writer for all types of people of every age and every place, and he has proved to be a writer of all time. Kipling followed up two years later, in 1891, with his novel *The Light That Failed.* It was written in response to critics who said his narratives were strictly limited to short pieces.

Kipling rounded out the century with the *Jungle Books, Captains Courageous,* and *Stalky and Co.* The *Jungle Books* epitomized the universal appeal of the author, with the endearing characters of Mowgli, Rikki-tikki-tavi, and Baloo the Bear, which won the hearts of children and adults alike. Kipling loved children and their imaginations, and in 1902 he presented the *Just So Stories,* which included the tales of how the leopard got his spots, how the camel got his hump, how the whale got his throat, and how the alphabet was made. The stories feature illustrations by the author, showing another facet of his creativity. This set of stories was preceded in 1901 by Kipling's work of triump, *Kim.* He earned international acclaim with this full-length work of fiction about a young white boy growing up in India. In 1906 *Puck of Pook's*

Hill tells about exciting moments in English history, as Puck confronts two children with some very interesting people, including the Roman legion.

The turn of the century, however, seemed to mark a change in the life of Rudyard Kipling. He was becoming more and more the imperialist. Although he was always rich and successful, his popularity at times was in question. He was doing war correspondent pieces, and his writing seemed to be increasingly polemical. After his son was killed in the war in 1915, his writings took an even gloomier tone.

His writings seemed to spark controversy everywhere he turned—whether to the Canadians, British, German, Russians, Irish, or Americans. His reference to Queen Victoria in *The Widow at Windsor* made her so irate that she banned Kipling from the country for a short while and vetoed his hopes of becoming Poet Laureate. He lost the position once again, after the ban was lifted, when it was thought that his attitudes would be an embarrassment internationally. However, he won the Nobel Prize in 1907—the first Englishman to do so.

Although many people were hypercritical of Kipling's ultraimperialism, his writings, primarily his earlier Indian works, were read with excitement and interest then as they are today.

Kipling once said that "one's own heart is the best place in which to store the few things of life that really matter." With the stories presented here in *Rudyard Kipling: Illustrated,* we are indeed fortunate that he has shared with us some of the things that mattered.

GEORGE GESNER

New York

1981

The Jungle Book

CONTENTS

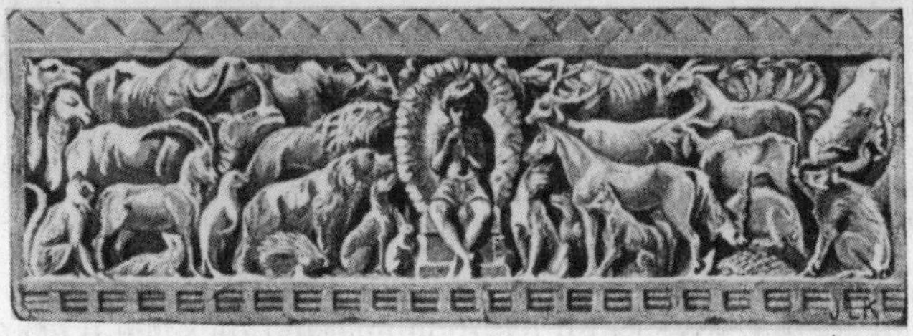

Mowgli's Brothers

Now Rann, the Kite, brings home the night
    That Mang, the Bat, sets free—
The herds are shut in byre and hut,
    For loosed till dawn are we.
This is the hour of pride and power,
    Talon and tush and claw.
Oh, hear the call!—Good hunting all
    That keep the Jungle Law!

Night-Song in the Jungle

It was seven o'clock of a very warm evening in the Seeonee hills when Father Wolf woke up from his day's rest, scratched himself, yawned, and spread out his paws one after the other to get rid of the sleepy feeling in the tips. Mother Wolf lay with her big gray nose dropped across her four tumbling, squealing cubs, and the moon shone into the mouth of the cave where they all lived. "Augrh!" said Father Wolf, "it is time to hunt again"; and he was going to spring downhill when a little shadow with a bushy tail crossed the threshold and whined: "Good luck go with you, O Chief of the Wolves; and good luck and strong white teeth go with the noble children, that they may never forget the hungry in this world."

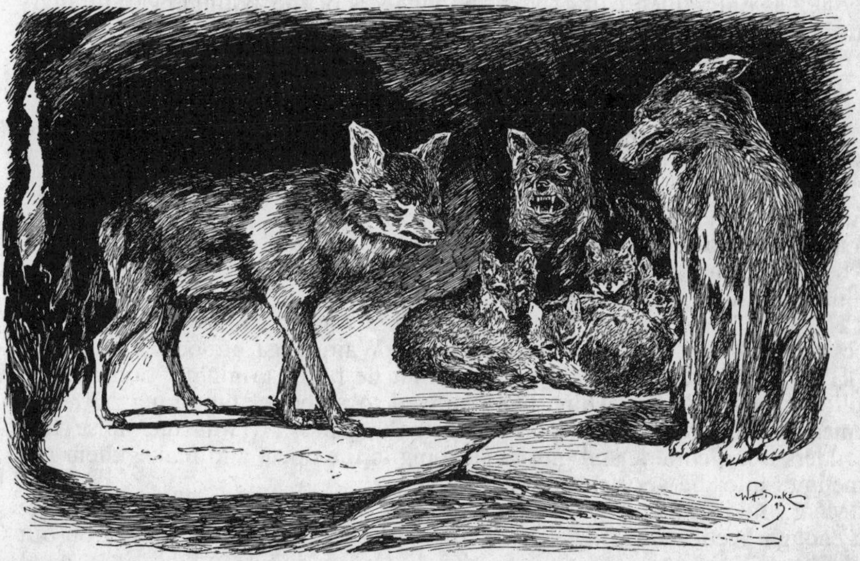

"'GOOD LUCK GO WITH YOU, O CHIEF OF THE WOLVES.'"

It was the jackal–Tabaqui, the Dish-licker–and the wolves of India despise Tabaqui because he runs about making mischief, and telling tales, and eating rags and pieces of leather from the village rubbish-heaps. They are afraid of him too, because Tabaqui, more than any one else in the jungle, is apt to go mad, and then he forgets that he was ever afraid of any one, and runs through the forest biting everything in his way. Even the tiger hides when little Tabaqui goes mad, for madness is the most disgraceful thing that can overtake a wild creature. We call it hydrophobia, but they call it *dewanee*–the madness–and run.

"Enter, then, and look," said Father Wolf, stiffly; "but there is no food here."

"For a wolf, no," said Tabaqui; "but for so mean a person as myself a dry bone is a good feast. Who are we, the Gidur-log [the Jackal People], to pick and choose?" He scuttled to the back of the cave, where he found the bone of a buck with some meat on it, and sat cracking the end merrily.

"All thanks for this good meal," he said, licking his lips. "How beautiful are the noble children! How large are their eyes! And so young too! Indeed, indeed, I might have remembered that the children of kings are men from the beginning."

Now, Tabaqui knew as well as any one else that there is nothing so unlucky as to compliment children to their faces; and it pleased him to see Mother and Father Wolf look uncomfortable.

Tabaqui sat still, rejoicing in the mischief that he had made, and then he said spitefully:

"Shere Khan, the Big One, has shifted his hunting-grounds. He will hunt among these hills during the next moon, so he has told me."

Shere Khan was the tiger who lived near the Waingunga River, twenty miles away.

"He has no right!" Father Wolf began angrily. "By the Law of the Jungle he has no right to change his quarters without fair warning. He will frighten every head of game within ten miles; and I–I have to kill for two, these days."

"His mother did not call him Lungri [the Lame One] for nothing," said Mother Wolf, quietly. "He has been lame in one foot from his birth. That is why he has only killed cattle. Now the villagers of the Waingunga are angry with him, and he has come here to make *our* villagers angry. They will scour the jungle for him when he is far away, and we and our children must run when the grass is set alight. Indeed, we are very grateful to Shere Khan!"

"Shall I tell him of your gratitude?" said Tabaqui.

"Out!" snapped Father Wolf. "Out, and hunt with thy master. Thou hast done harm enough for one night."

"I go," said Tabaqui, quietly. "Ye can hear Shere Khan below in the thickets. I might have saved myself the message."

Father Wolf listened, and in the dark valley that ran down to a little river, he heard the dry, angry, snarly, singsong whine of a tiger who has caught nothing and does not care if all the jungle knows it.

"The fool!" said Father Wolf. "To begin a night's work with that noise! Does he think that our buck are like his fat Waingunga bullocks?"

"H'sh! It is neither bullock nor buck that he hunts to-night," said Mother Wolf; "it is Man." The whine had changed to a sort of humming purr that seemed to roll from every quarter of the compass. It was the noise that bewilders wood-cutters, and gipsies sleeping in the open, and makes them run sometimes into the very mouth of the tiger.

"Man!" said Father Wolf, showing all his white teeth. "Faugh! Are there not enough beetles and frogs in the tanks that he must eat Man–and on our ground too!"

The Law of the Jungle, which never orders anything without a reason, forbids every beast to eat Man except when he is killing to show his children how to kill, and then he must hunt outside the hunting-grounds of his pack or tribe. The real reason for this is that man-killing means, sooner or later, the arrival of white men on elephants, with guns, and hundreds of brown men with gongs and rockets and torches. Then everybody in the jungle suffers. The reason the beasts give among themselves is that Man is the weakest and most defenseless of all living things, and it is unsportsmanlike to touch him. They say too—and it is true—that man-eaters become mangy, and lose their teeth.

The purr grew louder, and ended in the full-throated "Aaarh!" of the tiger's charge.

Then there was a howl—an untigerish howl—from Shere Khan. "He has missed," said Mother Wolf. "What is it?"

Father Wolf ran out a few paces and heard Shere Khan muttering and mumbling savagely, as he tumbled about in the scrub.

"The fool has had no more sense than to jump at a wood-cutters' camp-fire, so he has burned his feet," said Father Wolf, with a grunt. "Tabaqui is with him."

"Something is coming uphill," said Mother Wolf, twitching one ear. "Get ready."

The bushes rustled a little in the thicket, and Father Wolf dropped with his haunches under him, ready for his leap. Then, if you had been watching, you would have seen the most wonderful thing in the world—the wolf checked in mid-spring. He made his bound before he saw what it was he was jumping at, and then he tried to stop himself. The result was that he shot up straight into the air for four or five feet, landing almost where he left ground.

"Man!" he snapped. "A man's cub. Look!"

Directly in front of him, holding on by a low branch, stood a naked brown baby who could just walk—as soft and as dimpled a little thing as ever came to a wolf's cave at night. He looked up into Father Wolf's face and laughed.

"Is that a man's cub?" said Mother Wolf. "I have never seen one. Bring it here."

A wolf accustomed to moving his own cubs can, if necessary, mouth an egg without breaking it, and though Father Wolf's jaws closed right on the child's back not a tooth even scratched the skin, as he laid it down among the cubs.

"How little! How naked, and—how bold!" said Mother Wolf, softly. The baby was pushing his way between the cubs to get close to the warm hide. "Ahai! He is taking his meal with the others. And so this is a man's cub. Now, was there ever a wolf that could boast of a man's cub among her children?"

"I have heard now and again of such a thing, but never in our pack or in my time," said Father Wolf. "He is altogether without hair, and I could kill him with a touch of my foot. But see, he looks up and is not afraid."

The moonlight was blocked out of the mouth of the cave, for Shere Khan's great square head and shoulders were thrust into the entrance. Tabaqui, behind him, was squeaking: "My Lord, my Lord, it went in here!"

"Shere Khan does us great honor," said Father Wolf, but his eyes were very angry. "What does Shere Khan need?"

"My quarry. A man's cub went this way," said Shere Khan. "Its parents have run off. Give it to me."

Shere Khan had jumped at a wood-cutter's camp-fire, as Father Wolf had said, and was furious from the pain of his burned feet. But Father Wolf knew that the mouth of the cave was too narrow for a tiger to come in by. Even where he was, Shere Khan's shoulders and fore paws were cramped for want of room, as a man's would be if he tried to fight in a barrel.

"The Wolves are a free people," said Father Wolf. "They take orders from the Head of the Pack, and not from any striped cattle-killer. The man's cub is ours–to kill if we choose."

"Ye choose and ye do not choose! What talk is this of choosing? By the Bull that I killed, am I to stand nosing into your dog's den for my fair dues? It is I, Shere Khan, who speak!"

The tiger's roar filled the cave with thunder. Mother Wolf shook herself clear of the cubs and sprang forward, her eyes, like two green moons in the darkness, facing the blazing eyes of Shere Khan.

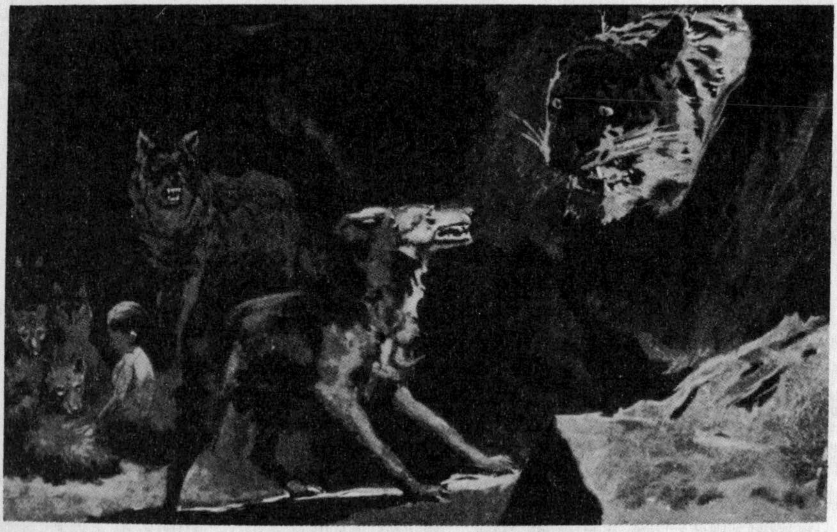

"THE TIGER'S ROAR FILLED THE CAVE WITH THUNDER."

"And it is I, Raksha [the Demon], who answer. The man's cub is mine, Lungri–mine to me! He shall not be killed. He shall live to run with the Pack and to hunt with the Pack; and in the end, look you, hunter of little naked cubs–frog-eater–fish-killer, he shall hunt *thee!* Now get hence, or by the Sambhur that I killed (*I* eat no starved cattle), back thou goest to thy mother, burned beast of the jungle, lamer than ever thou camest into the world! Go!"

Father Wolf looked on amazed. He had almost forgotten the days when he won Mother Wolf in fair fight from five other wolves, when she ran in the Pack and was not called the Demon for compliment's sake. Shere Khan might have faced Father Wolf, but he could not stand up against Mother Wolf, for he knew that where he was she had all the advantage of the ground, and would fight to the death. So he backed out of the cave-mouth growling, and when he was clear he shouted:

"Each dog barks in his own yard! We will see what the Pack will say to this fostering of man-cubs. The cub is mine, and to my teeth he will come in the end, O bush-tailed thieves!"

Mother Wolf threw herself down panting among the cubs, and Father Wolf said to her gravely:

"Shere Khan speaks this much truth. The cub must be shown to the Pack. Wilt thou still keep him, Mother?"

"Keep him!" she gasped. "He came naked, by night, alone and very hungry; yet he was not afraid! Look, he has pushed one of my babes to one side already. And that lame butcher would have killed him, and would have run off to the Waingunga while the villagers here hunted through all our lairs in revenge! Keep him? Assuredly I will keep him. Lie still, little frog. O thou

Mowgli,—for Mowgli, the Frog, I will call thee,—the time will come when thou wilt hunt Shere Khan as he has hunted thee!"

"But what will our Pack say?" said Father Wolf.

The Law of the Jungle lays down very clearly that any wolf may, when he marries, withdraw from the Pack he belongs to; but as soon as his cubs are old enough to stand on their feet he must bring them to the Pack Council, which is generally held once a month at full moon, in order that the other wolves may identify them. After that inspection the cubs are free to run where they please, and until they have killed their first buck no excuse is accepted if a grown wolf of the Pack kills one of them. The punishment is death where the murderer can be found; and if you think for a minute you will see that this must be so.

Father Wolf waited till his cubs could run a little, and then on the night of the Pack Meeting took them and Mowgli and Mother Wolf to the Council Rock—a hilltop covered with stones and boulders where a hundred wolves could hide. Akela, the great gray Lone Wolf, who led all the Pack by strength and cunning, lay out at full length on his rock, and below him sat forty or more wolves of every size and color, from badger-colored veterans who could handle a buck alone, to young black three-year-olds who thought they could. The Lone Wolf had led them for a year now. He had fallen twice into a wolf-trap in his youth, and once he had been beaten and left for dead; so he knew the manners and customs of men.

There was very little talking at the Rock. The cubs tumbled over one another in the center of the circle where their mothers and fathers sat, and now and again a senior wolf would go quietly up to a cub, look at him carefully, and return to his place on noiseless feet. Sometimes a mother would push her cub far out into the moonlight, to be sure that he had not been overlooked. Akela from his rock would cry: "Ye know the Law—ye know the Law! Look well, O Wolves!"

At last—and Mother Wolf's neck-bristles lifted as the time came—Father Wolf pushed "Mowgli, the Frog," as they called him, into the center, where he sat laughing and playing with some pebbles that glistened in the moonlight.

Akela never raised his head from his paws, but went on with the monotonous cry, "Look well!" A muffled roar came up from behind the rocks—the voice of Shere Khan crying, "The cub is mine; give him to me. What have the Free People to do with a man's cub?"

Akela never even twitched his ears. All he said was, "Look well, O Wolves! What have the Free People to do with the orders of any save the Free People? Look well!"

There was a chorus of deep growls, and a young wolf in his fourth year flung back Shere Khan's question to Akela: "What have the Free People to do with a man's cub?"

Now the Law of the Jungle lays down that if there is any dispute as to the right of a cub to be accepted by the Pack, he must be spoken for by at least two members of the Pack who are not his father and mother.

"Who speaks for this cub?" said Akela. "Among the Free People, who speaks?" There was no answer, and Mother Wolf got ready for what she knew would be her last fight, if things came to fighting.

Then the only other creature who is allowed at the Pack Council—Baloo, the sleepy brown bear who teaches the wolf cubs the Law of the Jungle; old Baloo, who can come and go where he pleases because he eats only nuts and roots and honey—rose up on his hind quarters and grunted.

"The man's cub—the man's cub?" he said. "*I* speak for the man's cub. There is no harm in a man's cub. I have no gift of words, but I speak the truth. Let him run with the Pack, and be entered with the others. I myself will teach him."

"We need yet another," said Akela. "Baloo has spoken, and he is our teacher for the young cubs. Who speaks besides Baloo?"

A black shadow dropped down into the circle. It was Bagheera, the Black Panther, inky black all over, but with the panther markings showing up in certain lights like the pattern of watered silk. Everybody knew Bagheera, and nobody cared to cross his path; for he was as cunning as Tabaqui, as bold as the wild buffalo, and as reckless as the wounded elephant. But he had a voice as soft as wild honey dripping from a tree, and a skin softer than down.

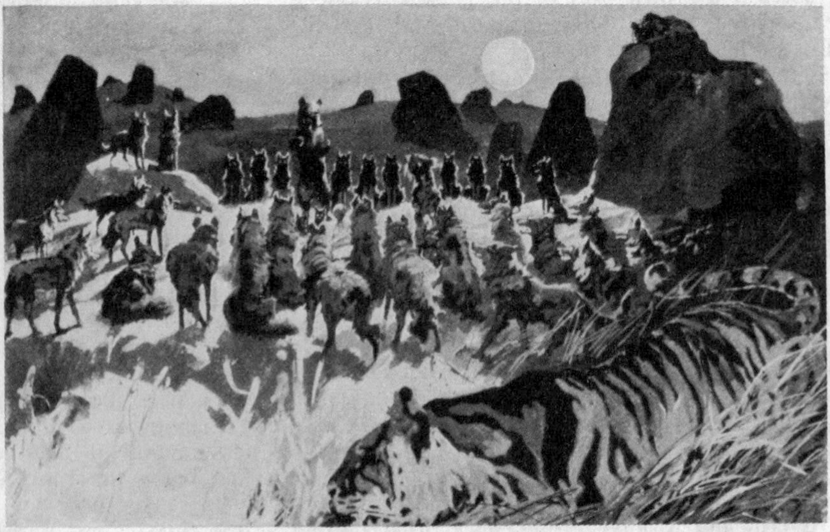

THE MEETING AT THE COUNCIL ROCK.

"O Akela, and ye, the Free People," he purred, "I have no right in your assembly; but the Law of the Jungle says that if there is a doubt which is not a killing matter in regard to a new cub, the life of that cub may be bought at a price. And the Law does not say who may or may not pay that price. Am I right?"

"Good! good!" said the young wolves, who are always hungry. "Listen to Bagheera. The cub can be bought for a price. It is the Law."

"Knowing that I have no right to speak here, I ask your leave."

"Speak then," cried twenty voices.

"To kill a naked cub is shame. Besides, he may make better sport for you when he is grown. Baloo has spoken in his behalf. Now to Baloo's word I will add one bull, and a fat one, newly killed, not half a mile from here, if ye will accept the man's cub according to the Law. Is it difficult?"

There was a clamor of scores of voices, saying: "What matter? He will die in the winter rains. He will scorch in the sun. What harm can a naked frog do us? Let him run with the Pack. Where is the bull, Bagheera? Let him be accepted." And then came Akela's deep bay, crying: "Look well–look well, O Wolves!"

Mowgli was still playing with the pebbles, and he did not notice when the wolves came and looked at him one by one. At last they all went down the hill for the dead bull, and only Akela, Bagheera, Baloo, and Mowgli's own wolves were left. Shere Khan roared still in the night, for he was very angry that Mowgli had not been handed over to him.

"Ay, roar well," said Bagheera, under his whiskers; "for the time comes when this naked thing will make thee roar to another tune, or I know nothing of Man."

"It was well done," said Akela. "Men and their cubs are very wise. He may be a help in time."

"Truly, a help in time of need; for none can hope to lead the Pack forever," said Bagheera.

Akela said nothing. He was thinking of the time that comes to every leader of every pack when his strength goes from him and he gets feebler and feebler, till at last he is killed by the wolves and a new leader comes up—to be killed in his turn.

"Take him away," he said to Father Wolf, "and train him as befits one of the Free People."

And that is how Mowgli was entered into the Seeonee wolf-pack for the price of a bull and on Baloo's good word.

Now you must be content to skip ten or eleven whole years, and only guess at all the wonderful life that Mowgli led among the wolves, because if it were written out it would fill ever so many books. He grew up with the cubs, though they of course were grown wolves almost before he was a child, and Father Wolf taught him his business, and the meaning of things in the jungle, till every rustle in the grass, every breath of the warm night air, every note of the owls above his head, every scratch of a bat's claws as it roosted for a while in a tree, and every splash of every little fish jumping in a pool, meant just as much to him as the work of his office means to a business man. When he was not learning he sat out in the sun and slept, and ate, and went to sleep again; when he felt dirty or hot he swam in the forest pools; and when he wanted honey (Baloo told him that honey and nuts were just as pleasant to eat as raw meat) he climbed up for it, and that Bagheera showed him how to do.

Bagheera would lie out on a branch and call, "Come along, Little Brother," and at first Mowgli would cling like the sloth, but afterward he would fling himself through the branches almost as boldly as the gray ape. He took his place at the Council Rock, too, when the Pack met, and there he discovered that if he stared hard at any wolf, the wolf would be forced to drop his eyes, and so he used to stare for fun.

At other times he would pick the long thorns out of the pads of his friends, for wolves suffer terribly from thorns and burs in their coats. He would go down the hillside into the cultivated lands by night, and look very curiously at the villagers in their huts, but he had a mistrust of men because Bagheera showed him a square box with a drop-gate so cunningly hidden in the jungle that he nearly walked into it, and told him it was a trap.

He loved better than anything else to go with Bagheera into the dark warm heart of the forest, to sleep all through the drowsy day, and at night see how Bagheera did his killing. Bagheera killed right and left as he felt hungry, and so did Mowgli—with one exception. As soon as he was old enough to understand things, Bagheera told him that he must never touch cattle because he had been bought into the Pack at the price of a bull's life. "All the jungle is thine," said Bagheera, "and thou canst kill everything that thou art strong enough to kill; but for the sake of the bull that bought thee thou must never kill or eat any cattle young or old. That is the Law of the Jungle." Mowgli obeyed faithfully.

And he grew and grew strong as a boy must grow who does not know that he is learning any lessons, and who has nothing in the world to think of except things to eat.

Mother Wolf told him once or twice that Shere Khan was not a creature to be trusted, and that some day he must kill Shere Khan; but though a young wolf would have remembered that advice every hour, Mowgli forgot it because he was only a boy—though he would have called himself a wolf if he

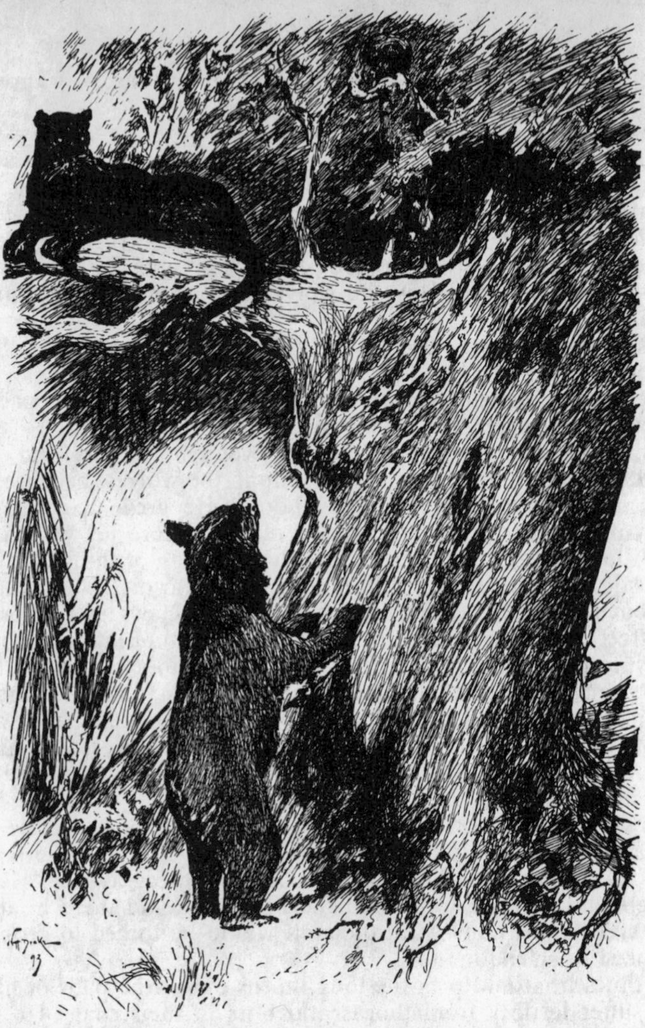

"BAGHEERA WOULD LIE OUT ON A BRANCH AND CALL, 'COME ALONG, LITTLE BROTHER.'"

had been able to speak in any human tongue.

Shere Khan was always crossing his path in the jungle, for as Akela grew older and feebler the lame tiger had come to be great friends with the younger wolves of the Pack, who followed him for scraps, a thing Akela would never have allowed if he had dared to push his authority to the proper bounds. Then Shere Khan would flatter them and wonder that such fine young hunters were content to be led by a dying wolf and a man's cub. "They tell me," Shere Khan would say, "that at Council ye dare not look him between the eyes"; and the young wolves would growl and bristle.

Bagheera, who had eyes and ears everywhere, knew something of this, and once or twice he told Mowgli in so many words that Shere Khan would kill him some day; and Mowgli would laugh and answer: "I have the Pack and I have thee; and Baloo, though he is so lazy, might strike a blow or two for my sake. Why should I be afraid?"

It was one very warm day that a new notion came to Bagheera—born of something that he had heard. Perhaps Ikki, the Porcupine, had told him; but he said to Mowgli when they were deep in the jungle, as the boy lay with his head on Bagheera's beautiful black skin: "Little Brother, how often have I told thee that Shere Khan is thy enemy?"

"As many times as there are nuts on that palm," said Mowgli, who, naturally, could not count. "What of it? I am sleepy, Bagheera, and Shere Khan is all long tail and loud talk, like Mao, the Peacock."

"But this is no time for sleeping. Baloo knows it, I know it, the Pack know it, and even the foolish, foolish deer know. Tabaqui has told thee too."

"Ho! ho!" said Mowgli. "Tabaqui came to me not long ago with some rude talk that I was a naked man's cub, and not fit to dig pig-nuts; but I caught Tabaqui by the tail and swung him twice against a palm-tree to teach him better manners."

"That was foolishness; for though Tabaqui is a mischief-maker, he would have told thee of something that concerned thee closely. Open those eyes, Little Brother! Shere Khan dares not kill thee in the jungle for fear of those that love thee; but remember, Akela is very old, and soon the day comes when he cannot kill his buck, and then he will be leader no more. Many of the wolves that looked thee over when thou wast brought to the Council first are old too, and the young wolves believe, as Shere Khan has taught them, that a man-cub has no place with the Pack. In a little time thou wilt be a man."

"And what is a man that he should not run with his brothers?" said Mowgli. "I was born in the jungle; I have obeyed the Law of the Jungle; and there is no wolf of ours from whose paws I have not pulled a thorn. Surely they are my brothers!"

Bagheera stretched himself at full length and half shut his eyes. "Little Brother," said he, "feel under my jaw."

Mowgli put up his strong brown hand, and just under Bagheera's silky chin, where the giant rolling muscles were all hid by the glossy hair, he came upon a little bald spot.

"There is no one in the jungle that knows that I, Bagheera, carry that mark–the mark of the collar; and yet, Little Brother, I was born among men, and it was among men that my mother died–in the cages of the King's Palace at Oodeypore. It was because of this that I paid the price for thee at the Council when thou wast a little naked cub. Yes, I too was born among men. I had never seen the jungle. They fed me behind bars from an iron pan till one night I felt that I was Bagheera, the Panther, and no man's plaything, and I broke the silly lock with one blow of my paw, and came away; and because I had learned the ways of men, I became more terrible in the jungle than Shere Khan. Is it not so?"

"Yes," said Mowgli; "all the jungle fear Bagheera–all except Mowgli."

"Oh, *thou* art a man's cub," said the Black Panther, very tenderly; "and even as I returned to my jungle, so thou must go back to men at last,–to the men who are thy brothers,–if thou art not killed in the Council."

"But why–but why should any wish to kill me?" said Mowgli.

"Look at me," said Bagheera; and Mowgli looked at him steadily between the eyes. The big panther turned his head away in half a minute.

"*That* is why," he said, shifting his paw on the leaves. "Not even I can look thee between the eyes, and I was born among men, and I love thee, Little Brother. The others they hate thee because their eyes cannot meet thine; because thou art wise; because thou hast pulled out thorns from their feet–because thou art a man."

"I did not know these things," said Mowgli, sullenly; and he frowned under his heavy black eyebrows.

"What is the Law of the Jungle? Strike first and then give tongue. By thy very carelessness they know that thou art a man. But be wise. It is in my heart that when Akela misses his next kill,–and at each hunt it costs him more to pin the buck,–the Pack will turn against him and against thee. They will hold a jungle Council at the Rock, and then–and then . . . I have it!"

said Bagheera, leaping up. "Go thou down quickly to the men's huts in the valley, and take some of the Red Flower which they grow there, so that when the times comes thou mayest have even a stronger friend than I or Baloo or those of the Pack that love thee. Get the Red Flower."

By Red Flower Bagheera meant fire, only no creature in the jungle will call fire by its proper name. Every beast lives in deadly fear of it, and invents a hundred ways of describing it.

"The Red Flower?" said Mowgli. "That grows outside their huts in the twilight. I will get some."

"There speaks the man's cub," said Bagheera, proudly. "Remember that it grows in little pots. Get one swiftly, and keep it by thee for time of need."

"Good!" said Mowgli. "I go. But art thou sure, O my Bagheera"—he slipped his arm round the splendid neck, and looked deep into the big eyes—"art thou sure that all this is Shere Khan's doing?"

"By the Broken Lock that freed me, I am sure, Little Brother."

"Then, by the Bull that bought me, I will pay Shere Khan full tale for this, and it may be a little over," said Mowgli; and he bounded away.

"That is a man. That is all a man," said Bagheera to himself, lying down again. "Oh, Shere Khan, never was a blacker hunting than that frog-hunt of thine ten years ago!"

Mowgli was far and far through the forest, running hard, and his heart was hot in him. He came to the cave as the evening mist rose, and drew breath, and looked down the valley. The cubs were out, but Mother Wolf, at the back of the cave, knew by his breathing that something was troubling her frog.

"What is it, Son?" she said.

"Some bat's chatter of Shere Khan," he called back. "I hunt among the plowed fields tonight"; and he plunged downward through the bushes, to the stream at the bottom of the valley. There he checked, for he heard the yell of the Pack hunting, heard the bellow of a hunted Sambhur, and the snort as the buck turned at bay. Then there were wicked, bitter howls from the young wolves: "Akela! Akela! Let the Lone Wolf show his strength. Room for the leader of our Pack! Spring, Akela!"

The Lone Wolf must have sprung and missed his hold, for Mowgli heard the snap of his teeth and then a yelp as the Sambhur knocked him over with his fore foot.

He did not wait for anything more, but dashed on; and the yells grew fainter behind him as he ran into the crop-lands where the villagers lived.

"Bagheera spoke truth," he panted, as he nestled down in some cattle-fodder by the window of a hut. "To-morrow is one day for Akela and for me."

Then he pressed his face close to the window and watched the fire on the hearth. He saw the husbandman's wife get up and feed it in the night with black lumps; and when the morning came and the mists were all white and cold, he saw the man's child pick up a wicker pot plastered inside with earth, fill it with lumps of red-hot charcoal, put it under his blanket, and go out to tend the cows in the byre.

"Is that all?" said Mowgli. "If a cub can do it, there is nothing to fear"; so he strode around the corner and met the boy, took the pot from his hand, and disappeared into the mist while the boy howled with fear.

"They are very like me," said Mowgli, blowing into the pot, as he had seen the woman do. "This thing will die if I do not give it things to eat"; and he dropped twigs and dried bark on the red stuff. Half-way up the hill he met Bagheera with the morning dew shining like moonstones on his coat.

"Akela has missed," said the panther. "They would have killed him last night, but they needed thee also. They were looking for thee on the hill."

"I was among the plowed lands. I am ready. Look!" Mowgli held up the fire-pot.

"Good! Now, I have seen men thrust a dry branch into that stuff, and presently the Red Flower blossomed at the end of it. Art thou not afraid?"

"No. Why should I fear? I remember now–if it is not a dream–how, before I was a wolf, I lay beside the Red Flower, and it was warm and pleasant."

All that day Mowgli sat in the cave tending his fire-pot and dipping dry branches into it to see how they looked. He found a branch that satisfied him, and in the evening when Tabaqui came to the cave and told him, rudely enough, that he was wanted at the Council Rock, he laughed till Tabaqui ran away. Then Mowgli went to the Council, still laughing.

Akela the Lone Wolf lay by the side of his rock as a sign that the leadership of the Pack was open, and Shere Khan with his following of scrap-fed wolves walked to and fro openly, being flattered. Bagheera lay close to Mowgli, and the fire-pot was between Mowgli's knees. When they were all gathered together, Shere Khan began to speak–a thing he would never have dared to do when Akela was in his prime.

"He has no right," whispered Bagheera. "Say so. He is a dog's son. He will be frightened."

Mowgli sprang to his feet. "Free People," he cried, "does Shere Khan lead the Pack? What has a tiger to do with our leadership?"

"Seeing that the leadership is yet open, and being asked to speak–" Shere Khan began.

"By whom?" said Mowgli. "Are we *all* jackals, to fawn on this cattle-butcher? The leadership of the Pack is with the Pack alone."

There were yells of "Silence, thou man's cub!" "Let him speak; he has kept our law!" And at last the seniors of the Pack thundered: "Let the Dead Wolf speak!"

When a leader of the Pack has missed his kill, he is called the Dead Wolf as long as he lives, which is not long, as a rule.

Akela raised his old head wearily:

"Free People, and ye too, jackals of Shere Khan, for twelve seasons I have led ye to and from the kill, and in all that time not one has been trapped or maimed. Now I have missed my kill. Ye know how that plot was made. Ye know how ye brought me up to an untried buck to make my weakness known. It was cleverly done. Your right is to kill me here on the Council Rock now. Therefore I ask, 'Who comes to make an end of the Lone Wolf?' For it is my right, by the Law of the Jungle, that ye come one by one."

There was a long hush, for no single wolf cared to fight Akela to the death. Then Shere Khan roared: "Bah! What have we to do with this toothless fool? He is doomed to die! It is the man-cub who has lived too long. Free People, he was my meat from the first. Give him to me. I am weary of this man-wolf folly. He has troubled the jungle for ten seasons. Give me the man-cub, or I will hunt here always, and not give you one bone! He is a man–a man's child, and from the marrow of my bones I hate him!"

Then more than half the Pack yelled: "A man–a man! What has a man to do with us? Let him go to his own place."

"And turn all the people of the villages against us?" snarled Shere Khan. "No; give him to me. He is a man, and none of us can look him between the eyes."

Akela lifted his head again, and said: "He has eaten our food; he has slept with us; he has driven game for us; he has broken no word of the Law of the Jungle."

"Also, I paid for him with a bull when he was accepted. The worth of a bull is little, but Bagheera's honor is something that he will perhaps fight for," said Bagheera in his gentlest voice.

"A bull paid ten years ago!" the Pack snarled. "What do we care for bones ten years old?"

"Or for a pledge?" said Bagheera, his white teeth bared under his lip.

"Well are ye called the Free People!"

"No man's cub can run with the people of the jungle!" roared Shere Khan. "Give him to me."

"He is our brother in all but blood," Akela went on; "and ye would kill him here. In truth, I have lived too long. Some of ye are eaters of cattle, and of others I have heard that, under Shere Khan's teaching, ye go by dark night and snatch children from the villager's doorstep. Therefore I know ye to be cowards, and it is to cowards I speak. It is certain that I must die, and my life is of no worth, or I would offer that in the man-cub's place. But for the sake of the Honor of the Pack,—a little matter that, by being without a leader, ye have forgotten,—I promise that if ye let the man-cub go to his own place, I will not, when my time comes to die, bare one tooth against ye. I will die without fighting. That will at least save the Pack three lives. More I cannot do; but, if ye will, I can save ye the shame that comes of killing a brother against whom there is no fault—a brother spoken for and bought into the Pack according to the Law of the Jungle."

"He is a man—a man—a man!" snarled the Pack; and most of the wolves began to gather round Shere Khan, whose tail was beginning to switch.

"Now the business is in thy hands," said Bagheera to Mowgli. "*We* can do no more except fight."

Mowgli stood upright—the fire-pot in his hands. Then he stretched out his arms, and yawned in the face of the Council; but he was furious with rage and sorrow, for, wolf-like, the wolves had never told him how they hated him.

"Listen, you!" he cried. "There is no need for this dog's jabber. Ye have told me so often to-night that I am a man (though indeed I would have been a wolf with you to my life's end) that I feel your words are true. So I do not call ye my brothers any more, but *sag* [dogs], as a man should. What ye will do, and what ye will not do, is not yours to say. That matter is with *me;* and that we may see the matter more plainly, I, the man, have brought here a little of the Red Flower which ye, dogs, fear."

He flung the fire-pot on the ground, and some of the red coals lit a tuft of dried moss that flared up as all the Council drew back in terror before the leaping flames.

Mowgli thrust his dead branch into the fire till the twigs lit and crackled, and whirled it above his head among the cowering wolves.

"Thou art the master," said Bagheera, in an undertone. "Save Akela from the death. He was ever thy friend."

Akela, the grim old wolf who had never asked for mercy in his life, gave one piteous look at Mowgli as the boy stood all naked, his long black hair tossing over his shoulders in the light of the blazing branch that made the shadows jump and quiver.

"Good!" said Mowgli, staring around slowly, and thrusting out his lower lip. "I see that ye are dogs. I go from you to my own people—if they be my own people. The jungle is shut to me, and I must forget your talk and your companionship; but I will be more merciful than ye are. Because I was all but your brother in blood, I promise that when I am a man among men I will not betray ye to men as ye have betrayed me." He kicked the fire with his foot, and the sparks flew up. "There shall be no war between any of us and the Pack. But here is a debt to pay before I go." He strode forward to where Shere Khan sat blinking stupidly at the flames, and caught him by the tuft on his chin. Bagheera followed close, in case of accidents. "Up, dog!" Mowgli cried. "Up, when a man speaks, or I will set that coat ablaze!"

Shere Khan's ears lay flat back on his head, and he shut his eyes, for the blazing branch was very near.

"This cattle-killer said he would kill me in the Council because he had not killed me when I was a cub. Thus and thus, then, do we beat dogs when we are men! Stir a whisker, Lungri, and I ram the Red Flower down thy gullet!" He beat Shere Khan over the head with the branch, and the tiger whimpered and whined in an agony of fear.

"Pah! Singed jungle-cat—go now! But remember when next I come to the Council Rock, as a man should come, it will be with Shere Khan's hide on my head. For the rest, Akela goes free to live as he pleases. Ye will *not* kill him, because that is not my will. Nor do I think that ye will sit here any longer, lolling out your tongues as though ye were somebodies, instead of dogs whom I drive out—thus! Go!"

The fire was burning furiously at the end of the branch, and Mowgli struck right and left round the circle, and the wolves ran howling with the sparks burning their fur. At last there were only Akela, Bagheera, and perhaps ten wolves that had taken Mowgli's part. Then something began to hurt Mowgli inside him, as he had never been hurt in his life before, and he caught his breath and sobbed, and the tears ran down his face.

"What is it? What is it?" he said. "I do not wish to leave the jungle, and I do not know what this is. Am I dying, Bagheera?"

"No, Little Brother. Those are only tears such as men use," said Bagheera. "Now I know thou art a man, and a man's cub no longer. The jungle is shut indeed to thee henceforward. Let them fall, Mowgli; they are only tears." So Mowgli sat and cried as though his heart would break; and he had never cried in all his life before.

"Now," he said, "I will go to men. But first I must say farewell to my mother"; and he went to the cave where she lived with Father Wolf, and he cried on her coat, while the four cubs howled miserably.

"Ye will not forget me?" said Mowgli.

"Never while we can follow a trail," said the cubs. "Come to the foot of the hill when thou art a man, and we will talk to thee; and we will come into the crop-lands to play with thee by night."

"Come soon!" said Father Wolf. "Oh, wise little Frog, come again soon; for we be old, thy mother and I."

"Come soon," said Mother Wolf, "little naked son of mine; for, listen, child of man, I loved thee more than ever I loved my cubs."

"I will surely come," said Mowgli; "and when I come it will be to lay out Shere Khan's hide upon the Council Rock. Do not forget me! Tell them in the jungle never to forget me!"

The dawn was beginning to break when Mowgli went down the hillside alone to the crops to meet those mysterious things that are called men.

Hunting-Song of the Seeonee Pack

As the dawn was breaking the Sambhur belled
    Once, twice, and again!

And a doe leaped up—and a doe leaped up
From the pond in the wood where the wild deer sup.
This I, scouting alone, beheld,
    Once, twice, and again!

As the dawn was breaking the Sambhur belled
    Once, twice, and again!
And a wolf stole back—and a wolf stole back
To carry the word to the waiting Pack;
And we sought and we found and we bayed on his track
    Once, twice, and again!

As the dawn was breaking the Wolf-pack yelled
Once, twice, and again!
Feet in the jungle that leave no mark!
Eyes that can see in the dark—the dark!
Tongue—give tongue to it! Hark! O Hark!
Once, twice, and again!

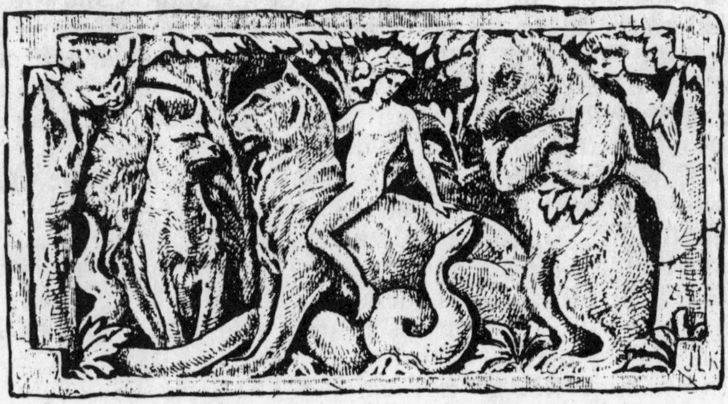

Kaa's Hunting

His spots are the joy of the Leopard: his horns are the Buffalo's pride—
Be clean, for the strength of the hunter is known by the gloss of his hide.

If ye find that the Bullock can toss you, or the heavy-browed Sambhur can gore;
Ye need not stop work to inform us: we knew it ten seasons before.

Oppress not the cubs of the stranger, but hail them as Sister and Brother,
For though they are little and fubsy, it may be the Bear is their mother.

"There is none like to me!" says the Cub in the pride of his earliest kill;
But the Jungle is large and the Cub he is small. Let him think and be still.

Maxims of Baloo.

ALL THAT IS told here, happened some time before Mowgli was turned out of the Seeonee wolf-pack. It was in the days when Baloo was teaching him the Law of the Jungle. The big, serious, old brown bear was delighted to have so quick a pupil, for the young wolves will only learn as much of the Law of the Jungle as applies to their own pack and tribe, and run away as soon as they can repeat the Hunting Verse: "Feet that make no noise; eyes that can see in the dark; ears that can hear the winds in their lairs, and sharp white teeth—all these things are the marks of our brothers except Tabaqui and the Hyena, whom we hate." But Mowgli, as a man-cub, had to learn a great deal more than this. Sometimes Bagheera, the Black Panther, would come lounging through the jungle to see how his pet was getting on, and would purr with his head against a tree while Mowgli recited the day's lesson to Baloo. The boy could climb almost as well as he could swim, and swim almost as well as he could run; so Baloo, the Teacher of the Law, taught him the Wood and

Water laws: how to tell a rotten branch from a sound one; how to speak politely to the wild bees when he came upon a hive of them fifty feet aboveground; what to say to Mang, the Bat, when he disturbed him in the branches at midday; and how to warn the water-snakes in the pools before he splashed down among them. None of the Jungle People like being disturbed, and all are very ready to fly at an intruder. Then, too, Mowgli was taught the Strangers' Hunting Call, which must be repeated aloud till it is answered, whenever one of the Jungle People hunts outside his own grounds. It means, translated: "Give me leave to hunt here because I am hungry"; and the answer is: "Hunt, then, for food, but not for pleasure."

All this will show you how much Mowgli had to learn by heart, and he grew very tired of repeating the same thing a hundred times; but, as Baloo said to Bagheera one day when Mowgli had been cuffed and had run off in a temper: "A man's cub is a man's cub, and he must learn *all* the Law of the Jungle."

"But think how small he is," said the Black Panther, who would have spoiled Mowgli if he had had his own way. "How can his little head carry all thy long talk?"

"Is there anything in the jungle too little to be killed? No. That is why I teach him these things, and that is why I hit him, very softly, when he forgets."

"Softly! What dost thou know of softness, old Iron-feet?" Bagheera grunted. "His face is all bruised to-day by thy–softness. Ugh!"

"Better he should be bruised from head to foot by me who love him than that he should come to harm through ignorance," Baloo answered, very earnestly. "I am now teaching him the Master Words of the Jungle that shall protect him with the Birds and the Snake People, and all that hunt on four feet, except his own pack. He can now claim protection, if he will only remember the Words, from all in the jungle. Is not that worth a little beating?"

"Well, look to it then that thou dost not kill the man-cub. He is no tree-trunk to sharpen thy blunt claws upon. But what are those Master Words? I am more likely to give help than to ask it"–Bagheera stretched out one paw and admired the steel-blue ripping-chisel talons at the end of it–"Still I should like to know."

"I will call Mowgli and he shall say them–if he will. Come, Little Brother!"

"My head is ringing like a bee-tree," said a sullen voice over their heads, and Mowgli slid down a tree-trunk, very angry and indignant, adding, as he reached the ground: "I come for Bagheera and not for *thee,* fat old Baloo!"

"That is all one to me," said Baloo, though he was hurt and grieved. "Tell Bagheera, then, the Master Words of the Jungle that I have taught thee this day."

"Master Words for which people?" said Mowgli, delighted to show off. "The jungle has many tongues. *I* know them all."

"A little thou knowest, but not much. See, O Bagheera, they never thank their teacher! Not one small wolfling has come back to thank old Baloo for his teachings. Say the Word for the Hunting People, then,–great scholar!"

"We be of one blood, ye and I," said Mowgli, giving the words the Bear accent which all the Hunting People of the Jungle use.

"Good! Now for the Birds."

Mowgli repeated, with the Kite's whistle at the end of the sentence.

"Now for the Snake People," said Bagheera.

The answer was a perfectly indescribable hiss, and Mowgli kicked up his feet behind, clapped his hands together to applaud himself, and jumped on Bagheera's back, where he sat sideways, drumming with his heels on the glossy skin and making the worst faces that he could think of at Baloo.

"There–there! That was worth a little bruise," said the Brown Bear, tenderly. "Some day thou wilt remember me." Then he turned aside to tell Bagheera how he had begged the Master Words from Hathi, the Wild Elephant, who knows all about these things, and how Hathi had taken Mowgli down to a pool to get the Snake Word from a water-snake, because Baloo could not pronounce it, and how Mowgli was now reasonably safe against all accidents in the jungle, because neither snake, bird, nor beast would hurt him.

"No one then is to be feared," Baloo wound up, patting his big furry stomach with pride.

"Except his own tribe," said Bagheera, under his breath; and then aloud to Mowgli: "Have a care for my ribs, Little Brother! What is all this dancing up and down?"

Mowgli had been trying to make himself heard by pulling at Bagheera's shoulder-fur and kicking hard. When the two listened to him he was shouting at the top of his voice: "And *so* I shall have a tribe of my own, and lead them through the branches all day long."

"What is this new folly, little dreamer of dreams?" said Bagheera.

"Yes, and throw branches and dirt at old Baloo," Mowgli went on. "They have promised me this, ah!"

"Whoof!" Baloo's big paw scooped Mowgli off Bagheera's back, and as the boy lay between the big fore paws he could see the bear was angry.

"Mowgli," said Baloo, "thou hast been talking with the Bandar-log–the Monkey People."

Mowgli looked at Bagheera to see if the panther was angry too, and Bagheera's eyes were as hard as jade-stones.

"Thou hast been with the Monkey People–the gray apes–the people without a Law–the eaters of everything. That is great shame."

"When Baloo hurt my head," said Mowgli (he was still down on his back), "I went away, and the gray apes came down from the trees and had pity on me. No one else cared." He snuffled a little.

"The pity of the Monkey People!" Baloo snorted.

"The stillness of the mountain stream! The cool of the summer sun! And then, man-cub?"

"And then–and then they gave me nuts and pleasant things to eat, and they–they carried me in their arms up to the top of the trees and said I was their blood-brother, except that I had no tail, and should be their leader some day."

"They have *no* leader," said Bagheera. "They lie. They have always lied."

"They were very kind, and bade me come again. Why have I never been taken among the Monkey People? They stand on their feet as I do. They do not hit me with hard paws. They play all day. Let me get up! Bad Baloo, let me up! I will go play with them again."

"Listen, man-cub," said the bear, and his voice rumbled like thunder on a hot night. "I have taught thee all the Law of the Jungle for all the Peoples of the Jungle–except the Monkey Folk who live in the trees. They have no Law. They are outcasts. They have no speech of their own, but use the stolen words which they overhear when they listen and peep and wait up above in the branches. Their way is not our way. They are without leaders. They have no remembrance. They boast and chatter and pretend that they are a great people about to do great affairs in the jungle, but the falling of a nut turns their minds to laughter, and all is forgotten. We of the jungle have no dealings with them. We do not drink where the monkeys drink; we do not go where the monkeys go; we do not hunt where they hunt; we do not die where they die. Hast thou ever heard me speak of the Bandar-log till to-day?"

"No," said Mowgli in a whisper, for the forest was very still now that Baloo had finished.

"The Jungle People put them out of their mouths and out of their minds.

They are very many, evil, dirty, shameless, and they desire, if they have any fixed desire, to be noticed by the Jungle People. But we do *not* notice them even when they throw nuts and filth on our heads."

He had hardly spoken when a shower of nuts and twigs spattered down through the branches; and they could hear coughings and howlings and angry jumpings high up in the air among the thin branches.

"The Monkey People are forbidden," said Baloo, "forbidden to the Jungle People. Remember."

"Forbidden," said Bagheera; "but I still think Baloo should have warned thee against them."

"I–I? How was I to guess he would play with such dirt. The Monkey People! Faugh!"

A fresh shower came down on their heads, and the two trotted away, taking Mowgli with them. What Baloo had said about the monkeys was perfectly true. They belonged to the tree-tops, and as beasts very seldom look up, there was no occasion for the monkeys and the Jungle People to cross one another's path. But whenever they found a sick wolf, or a wounded tiger or bear, the monkeys would torment him, and would throw sticks and nuts at any beast for fun and in the hope of being noticed. Then they would howl and shriek senseless songs, and invite the Jungle People to climb up their trees and fight them, or would start furious battles over nothing among themselves, and leave the dead monkeys where the Jungle People could see them.

They were always just going to have a leader and laws and customs of their own, but they never did, because their memories would not hold over from day to day, and so they settled things by making up a saying: "What the Bandar-log think now the Jungle will think later"; and that comforted them a great deal. None of the beasts could reach them, but on the other hand none of the beasts would notice them, and that was why they were so pleased when Mowgli came to play with them, and when they heard how angry Baloo was.

They never meant to do any more,–the Bandar-log never mean anything at all,–but one of them invented what seemed to him a brilliant idea, and he told all the others that Mowgli would be a useful person to keep in the tribe, because he could weave sticks together for protection from the wind; so, if they caught him, they could make him teach them. Of course Mowgli, as a wood-cutter's child, inherited all sorts of instincts, and used to make little play-huts of fallen branches without thinking how he came to do it. The Monkey People, watching in the trees, considered these huts most wonderful. This time, they said, they were really going to have a leader and become the wisest people in the jungle–so wise that every one else would notice and envy them. Therefore they followed Baloo and Bagheera and Mowgli through the jungle very quietly till it was time for the midday nap, and Mowgli, who was very much ashamed of himself, slept between the panther and the bear, resolving to have no more to do with the Monkey People.

The next thing he remembered was feeling hands on his legs and arms,–hard, strong little hands,–and then a swash of branches in his face; and then he was staring down through the swaying boughs as Baloo woke the jungle with his deep cries and Bagheera bounded up the trunk with every tooth bared. The Bandar-log howled with triumph, and scuffled away to the upper branches where Bagheera dared not follow, shouting: "He has noticed us! Bagheera has noticed us! All the Jungle People admire us for our skill and our cunning!" Then they began their flight; and the flight of the Monkey People through tree-land is one of the things nobody can describe. They have their regular roads and cross-roads, uphills and downhills, all laid out from fifty to seventy or a hundred feet aboveground, and by these they can travel even at night if necessary.

Two of the strongest monkeys caught Mowgli under the arms and swung off with him through the tree-tops, twenty feet at a bound. Had they been alone they could have gone twice as fast, but the boy's weight held them back. Sick and giddy as Mowgli was he could not help enjoying the wild rush, though the glimpses of earth far down below frightened him, and the terrible check and jerk at the end of the swing over nothing but empty air brought his heart between his teeth.

His escort would rush him up a tree till he felt the weak topmost branches crackle and bend under them, and, then, with a cough and a whoop, would fling themselves into the air outward and downward, and bring up hanging by their hands or their feet to the lower limbs of the next tree. Sometimes he could see for miles and miles over the still green jungle, as a man on the top of a mast can see for miles across the sea, and then the branches and leaves would lash him across the face, and he and his two guards would be almost down to earth again.

So, bounding and crashing and whooping and yelling, the whole tribe of Bandar-log swept along the tree-roads with Mowgli their prisoner.

For a time he was afraid of being dropped; then he grew angry, but he knew better than to struggle; and then he began to think. The first thing was to send back word to Baloo and Bagheera, for, at the pace the monkeys were going, he knew his friends would be left far behind. It was useless to look down, for he could see only the top sides of the branches, so he stared upward and saw, far away in the blue, Rann, the Kite, balancing and wheeling as he kept watch over the jungle waiting for things to die. Rann noticed that the monkeys were carrying something, and dropped a few hundred yards to find out whether their load was good to eat. He whistled with surprise when he saw Mowgli being dragged up to a tree-top, and heard him give the Kite call for "We be of one blood, thou and I." The waves of the branches closed over the boy, but Rann balanced away to the next tree in time to see the little brown face come up again. "Mark my trail!" Mowgli shouted. "Tell Baloo of the Seeonee Pack, and Bagheera of the Council Rock."

"In whose name, Brother?" Rann had never seen Mowgli before, though of course he had heard of him.

"Mowgli, the Frog. Man-cub they call me! Mark my tra–il!"

The last words were shrieked as he was being swung through the air, but Rann nodded, and rose up till he looked no bigger than a speck of dust, and there he hung, watching with his telescope eyes the swaying of the tree-tops as Mowgli's escort whirled along.

"They never go far," he said, with a chuckle. "They never do what they set out to do. Always pecking at new things are the Bandar-log. This time, if I have any eyesight, they have pecked down trouble for themselves, for Baloo is no fledgling and Bagheera can, as I know, kill more than goats."

Then he rocked on his wings, his feet gathered up under him, and waited.

Meanwhile, Baloo and Bagheera were furious with rage and grief. Bagheera climbed as he had never climbed before, but the branches broke beneath his weight, and he slipped down, his claws full of bark.

"Why didst thou not warn the man-cub!" he roared to poor Baloo, who had set off at a clumsy trot in the hope of overtaking the monkeys. "What was the use of half slaying him with blows if thou didst not warn him?"

"Haste! O haste! We–we may catch them yet!" Baloo panted.

"At that speed! It would not tire a wounded cow. Teacher of the Law, cub-beater–a mile of that rolling to and fro would burst thee open. Sit still and think! Make a plan. This is no time for chasing. They may drop him if we follow too close."

"*Arrula! Whoo!* They may have dropped him already, being tired of carrying him. Who can trust the Bandar-log? Put dead bats on my head! Give me black bones to eat! Roll me into the hives of the wild bees that I may be stung to death, and bury me with the hyena; for I am the most miserable of bears! *Arulala! Wahooa!* O Mowgli, Mowgli! Why did I not warn thee against the Monkey Folk instead of breaking thy head? Now perhaps I may have knocked the day's lesson out of his mind, and he will be alone in the jungle without the Master Words!"

Baloo clasped his paws over his ears and rolled to and fro, moaning.

"At least he gave me all the Words correctly a little time ago," said Bagheera, impatiently. "Baloo, thou hast neither memory nor respect. What would the jungle think if I, the Black Panther, curled myself up like Ikki, the Porcupine, and howled?"

"What do I care what the jungle thinks? He may be dead by now."

"Unless and until they drop him from the branches in sport, or kill him out of idleness, I have no fear for the man-cub. He is wise and well-taught, and, above all, he has the eyes that make the Jungle People afraid. But (and it is a great evil) he is in the power of the Bandar-log, and they, because they live in trees, have no fear of any of our people." Bagheera licked his one fore paw thoughtfully.

"Fool that I am! Oh fat, brown, root-digging fool that I am!" said Baloo, uncoiling himself with a jerk. "It is true what Hathi, the Wild Elephant, says: *'To each his own fear'*; and they, the Bandar-log, fear Kaa, the Rock Snake. He can climb as well as they can. He steals the young monkeys in the night. The mere whisper of his name makes their wicked tails cold. Let us go to Kaa."

"What will he do for us? He is not of our tribe, being footless and with most evil eyes," said Bagheera.

"He is very old and very cunning. Above all, he is always hungry," said Baloo, hopefully. "Promise him many goats."

"He sleeps for a full month after he has once eaten. He may be asleep now, and even were he awake, what if he would rather kill his own goats?" Bagheera, who did not know much about Kaa, was naturally suspicious.

"Then in that case, thou and I together, old hunter, may make him see reason." Here Baloo rubbed his faded brown shoulder against the panther, and they went off to look for Kaa, the Rock Python.

They found him stretched out on a warm ledge in the afternoon sun, admiring his beautiful new coat, for he had been in retirement for the last ten days changing his skin, and now he was very splendid—darting his big blunt-nosed head along the ground, and twisting the thirty feet of his body into fantastic knots and curves, and licking his lips as he thought of his dinner to come.

"He has not eaten," said Baloo, with a grunt of relief, as soon as he saw the beautifully mottled brown and yellow jacket. "Be careful, Bagheera! He is always a little blind after he has changed his skin, and very quick to strike."

Kaa was not a poison snake—in fact he rather despised the Poison Snakes for cowards; but his strength lay in his hug, and when he had once lapped his huge coils round anybody there was no more to be said. "Good hunting!" cried Baloo, sitting up on his haunches. Like all snakes of his breed Kaa was rather deaf, and did not hear the call at first. Then he curled up ready for any accident, his head lowered.

"Good hunting for us all," he answered. "Oho, Baloo, what dost thou do here? Good hunting, Bagheera. Once of us at least needs food. Is there any news of game afoot? A doe now, or even a young buck? I am as empty as a dried well."

"We are hunting," said Baloo, carelessly. He knew that you must not hurry Kaa. He is too big.

"Give me permission to come with you," said Kaa. "A blow more or less is nothing to thee, Bagheera or Baloo, but I—I have to wait and wait for days in a wood-path and climb half a night on the mere chance of a young ape. *Pss naw!* The branches are not what they were when I was young. Rotten twigs and dry boughs are they all."

"Maybe thy great weight has something to do with the matter," said Baloo.

"I am a fair length—a fair length," said Kaa, with a little pride. "But for all that, it is the fault of this new-grown timber. I came very near to falling on my last hunt—very near indeed—and the noise of my slipping, for my tail was not tight wrapped round the tree, waked the Bandar-log, and they called me most evil names."

" 'Footless, yellow earthworm,' " said Bagheera under his whiskers, as though he were trying to remember something.

"Sssss! Have they ever called me *that?"* said Kaa.

"Something of that kind it was that they shouted to us last moon, but we never noticed them. They will say anything—even that thou hast lost all thy teeth, and dare not face anything bigger than a kid, because (they are indeed shameless, these Bandar-log)—because thou art afraid of the he-goats' horns," Bagheera went on sweetly.

Now a snake, especially a wary old python like Kaa, very seldom shows that he is angry; but Baloo and Bagheera could see the big swallowing muscles on either side of Kaa's throat ripple and bulge.

"The Bandar-log have shifted their grounds," he said, quietly. "When I came up into the sun today, I heard them whooping among the tree-tops."

"It—it is the Bandar-log that we follow now," said Baloo; but the words stuck in his throat, for this was the first time in his memory that one of the Jungle People had owned to being interested in the doings of the monkeys.

"Beyond doubt, then, it is no small thing that takes two such hunters—leaders in their own jungle, I am certain—on the trail of the Bandar-log," Kaa replied, courteously, as he swelled with curiosity.

"Indeed," Baloo began, "I am no more than the old, and sometimes very foolish, Teacher of the Law to the Seeonee wolf-cubs, and Bagheera here—"

"Is Bagheera," said the Black Panther, and his jaws shut with a snap, for he did not believe in being humble. "The trouble is this, Kaa. Those nut-stealers and pickers of palm-leaves have stolen away our man-cub, of whom thou hast perhaps heard."

"I heard some news from Ikki (his quills make him presumptuous) of a man-thing that was entered into a wolf-pack, but I did not believe. Ikki is full of stories half heard and very badly told."

"But it is true. He is such a man-cub as never was," said Baloo. "The best and wisest and boldest of man-cubs. My own pupil, who shall make the name of Baloo famous through all the jungles; and besides, I—we—love him, Kaa."

"Ts! Ts!" said Kaa, shaking his head to and fro. "I also have known what love is. There are tales I could tell that—"

"That need a clear night when we are all well fed to praise properly," said Bagheera, quickly. "Our man-cub is in the hands of the Bandar-log now, and we know that of all the Jungle People they fear Kaa alone."

"They fear me alone. They have good reason," said Kaa. "Chattering, foolish, vain—vain, foolish, and chattering—are the monkeys. But a man-thing in their hands is in no good luck. They grow tired of the nuts they pick, and throw them down. They carry a branch half a day, meaning to do great things with it, and then they snap it in two. That manling is not to be envied. They called me also—'yellow fish,' was it not?"

"Worm—worm—earthworm," said Bagheera; "as well as other things which I cannot now say for shame."

"We must remind them to speak well of their master. *Aaa-sssh!* We must help their wandering memories. Now, whither went they with thy cub?"

"The jungle alone knows. Toward the sunset, I believe," said Baloo. "We had thought that thou wouldst know, Kaa."

"I? How? I take them when they come in my way, but I do not hunt the Bandar-log—or frogs—or green scum on a water-hole, for that matter."

"Up, up! Up, up! *Hillo! Illo! Illo!* Look up, Baloo of the Seeonee Wolf Pack!"

Baloo looked up to see where the voice came from, and there was Rann, the Kite, sweeping down with the sun shining on the upturned flanges of his wings. It was near Rann's bedtime, but he had ranged all over the jungle looking for the bear, and missed him in the thick foliage.

"What is it?" said Baloo.

"I have seen Mowgli among the Bandar-log. He bade me tell you. I watched. The Bandar-log have taken him beyond the river to the Monkey City—to the Cold Lairs. They may stay there for a night, or ten nights, or an hour. I have told the bats to watch through the dark time. That is my message. Good hunting, all you below!"

"Full gorge and a deep sleep to you, Rann!" cried Bagheera. "I will remember thee in my next kill, and put aside the head for thee alone, O best of kites!"

"It is nothing. It is nothing. The boy held the Master Word. I could have done no less," and Rann circled up again to his roost.

"He has not forgotten to use his tongue," said Baloo, with a chuckle of pride. "To think of one so young remembering the Master Word for the birds while he was being pulled across trees!"

"It was most firmly driven into him," said Bagheera. "But I am proud of him, and now we must go to the Cold Lairs."

They all knew where that place was, but few of the Jungle People ever went there, because what they called the Cold Lairs was an old deserted city, lost and buried in the jungle, and beasts seldom use a place that men have once used. The wild boar will, but the hunting-tribes do not. Besides, the monkeys lived there as much as they could be said to live anywhere, and no self-respecting animal would come within eye-shot of it except in times of drouth, when the half-ruined tanks and reservoirs held a little water.

"It is half a night's journey—at full speed," said Bagheera. Baloo looked very serious. "I will go as fast as I can," he said, anxiously.

"We dare not wait for thee. Follow, Baloo. We must go on the quick-foot—Kaa and I."

"Feet or no feet, I can keep abreast of all thy four," said Kaa, shortly.

Baloo made one effort to hurry, but had to sit down panting, and so they left him to come on later, while Bagheera hurried forward, at the rocking panther-canter. Kaa said nothing, but, strive as Bagheera might, the huge Rock Python held level with him. When they came to a hill-stream, Bagheera gained, because he bounded across while Kaa swam, his head and two feet of his neck clearing the water, but on level ground Kaa made up the distance.

"By the Broken Lock that freed me," said Bagheera, when twilight had fallen, "thou art no slow-goer."

"I am hungry," said Kaa. "Besides, they called me speckled frog."

"Worm—earthworm, and yellow to boot."

"All one. Let us go on," and Kaa seemed to pour himself along the ground, finding the shortest road with his steady eyes, and keeping to it.

In the Cold Lairs the Monkey People were not thinking of Mowgli's friends at all. They had brought the boy to the Lost City, and were very pleased with themselves for the time. Mowgli had never seen an Indian city before, and though this was almost a heap of ruins it seemed very wonderful and splendid. Some king had built it long ago on a little hill. You could still trace the stone causeways that led up to the ruined gates where the last splinters of wood hung to the worn, rusted hinges. Trees had grown into and out of the walls; the battlements were tumbled down and decayed, and wild creepers hung out of the windows of the towers on the walls in bushy hanging clumps.

A great roofless palace crowned the hill, and the marble of the courtyards and the fountains was split and stained with red and green, and the very cobblestones in the courtyard where the king's elephants used to live had been thrust up and apart by grasses and young trees. From the palace you could see the rows and rows of roofless houses that made up the city, looking like empty honeycombs filled with blackness; the shapeless block of stone that had been an idol in the square where four roads met; the pits and dimples at street corners where the public wells once stood, and the shattered domes of temples with wild figs sprouting on their sides.

The monkeys called the place their city, and pretended to despise the Jungle People because they lived in the forest. And yet they never knew what the buildings were made for nor how to use them. They would sit in circles on the hall of the king's council-chamber, and scratch for fleas and pretend to be men; or they would run in and out of the roofless houses and collect pieces of plaster and old bricks in a corner, and forget where they had hidden them, and fight and cry in scuffling crowds, and then break off to play up and down the terraces of the king's garden, where they would shake the rose-trees and the oranges in sport to see the fruit and flowers fall. They explored all the passages and dark tunnels in the palace and the hundreds of little dark rooms; but they never remembered what they had seen and what they had not, and so drifted about in ones and twos or crowds, telling one another that they were doing as men did. They drank at the tanks and made the water all muddy, and then they fought over it, and then they would all rush together in mobs and shout: "There are none in the jungle so wise and good and clever and strong and gentle as the Bandar-log." Then all would begin again till they grew tired of the city and went back to the tree-tops, hoping the Jungle People would notice them.

Mowgli, who had been trained under the Law of the Jungle, did not like or understand this kind of life. The monkeys dragged him into the Cold Lairs late in the afternoon, and instead of going to sleep, as Mowgli would have done after a long journey, they joined hands and danced about and sang their foolish songs.

One of the monkeys made a speech, and told his companions that Mowgli's capture marked a new thing in the history of the Bandar-log, for Mowgli was going to show them how to weave sticks and canes together as a protection against rain and cold. Mowgli picked up some creepers and began to work them in and out, and the monkeys tried to imitate; but in a very few minutes they lost interest and began to pull their friends' tails or jump up and down on all fours, coughing.

"I want to eat," said Mowgli. "I am a stranger in this part of the jungle. Bring me food, or give me leave to hunt here."

Twenty or thirty monkeys bounded away to bring him nuts and wild pawpaws; but they fell to fighting on the road, and it was too much trouble to go back with what was left of the fruit. Mowgli was sore and angry as well as hungry, and he roamed through the empty city giving the Strangers' Hunting Call from time to time, but no one answered him, and Mowgli felt that he had reached a very bad place indeed.

"All that Baloo has said about the Bandar-log is true," he thought to himself. "They have no Law, no Hunting Call, and no leaders–nothing but foolish words and little picking, thievish hands. So if I am starved or killed here, it will be all my own fault. But I must try to return to my own jungle. Baloo will surely beat me, but that is better than chasing silly rose-leaves with the Bandar-log."

But no sooner had he walked to the city wall than the monkeys pulled him back, telling him that he did not know how happy he was, and pinching him to make him grateful. He set his teeth and said nothing, but went with the shouting monkeys to a terrace above the red sandstone reservoirs that were half full of rain-water. There was a ruined summer-house of white marble in the center of the terrace, built for queens dead a hundred years ago. The domed roof had half fallen in and blocked up the underground passage from the palace by which the queens used to enter; but the walls were made of screens of marble tracery—beautiful, milk-white fretwork, set with agates and cornelians and jasper and lapis lazuli, and as the moon came up behind the hill it shone through the openwork, casting shadows on the ground like black-velvet embroidery.

Sore, sleepy, and hungry as he was, Mowgli could not help laughing when the Bandar-log began, twenty at a time, to tell him how great and wise and strong and gentle they were, and how foolish he was to wish to leave them. "We are great. We are free. We are wonderful. We are the most wonderful people in all the jungle! We all say so, and so it must be true," they shouted. "Now as you are a new listener and can carry our words back to the Jungle People so that they may notice us in future, we will tell you all about our most excellent selves."

Mowgli made no objection, and the monkeys gathered by hundreds and hundreds on the terrace to listen to their own speakers singing the praises of the Bandar-log, and whenever a speaker stopped for want of breath they would all shout together: "This is true; we all say so."

Mowgli nodded and blinked, and said "Yes" when they asked him a question, and his head spun with the noise. "Tabaqui, the Jackal, must have bitten all these people," he said to himself, "and now they have the madness. Certainly this is *dewanee*—the madness. Do they never go to sleep? Now there is a cloud coming to cover that moon. If it were only a big enough cloud I might try to run away in the darkness. But I am tired."

That same cloud was being watched by two good friends in the ruined ditch below the city wall, for Bagheera and Kaa, knowing well how dangerous the Monkey People were in large numbers, did not wish to run any risks. The monkeys never fight unless they are a hundred to one, and few in the jungle care for those odds.

"I will go to the west wall," Kaa whispered, "and come down swiftly with the slope of the ground in my favor. They will not throw themselves upon *my* back in their hundreds, but—"

"I know it," said Bagheera. "Would that Baloo were here; but we must do what we can. When that cloud covers the moon I shall go to the terrace. They hold some sort of council there over the boy."

"Good hunting," said Kaa, grimly, and glided away to the west wall. That happened to be the least ruined of any, and the big snake was delayed a while before he could find a way up the stones.

The cloud hid the moon, and as Mowgli wondered what would come next he heard Bagheera's light feet on the terrace. The Black Panther had raced up the slope almost without a sound, and was striking—he knew better than to waste time in biting—right and left among the monkeys, who were seated round Mowgli in circles fifty and sixty deep. There was a howl of fright and rage, and then as Bagheera tripped on the rolling, kicking bodies beneath him, a monkey shouted: "There is only one here! Kill him! Kill!" A scuffling mass of monkeys, biting, scratching, tearing, and pulling, closed over Bagheera, while five or six laid hold of Mowgli, dragged him up the wall of the summer-house, and pushed him through the hole of the broken dome. A man-trained boy would have been badly bruised, for the fall was a good ten feet, but Mowgli fell as Baloo had taught him to fall, and landed light.

"Stay there," shouted the monkeys, "till we have killed thy friend. Later we will play with thee, if the Poison People leave thee alive."

"We be of one blood, ye and I," said Mowgli, quickly giving the Snake's

Call. He could hear rustling and hissing in the rubbish all round him, and give the Call a second time to make sure.

"Down hoods all," said half a dozen low voices. Every old ruin in India becomes sooner or later a dwelling-place of snakes, and the old summer-house was alive with cobras. "Stand still, Little Brother, lest thy feet do us harm."

Mowgli stood as quietly as he could, peering through the openwork and listening to the furious din of the fight round the Black Panther–the yells and chatterings and scufflings, and Bagheera's deep, hoarse cough as he backed and bucked and twisted and plunged under the heaps of his enemies. For the first time since he was born, Bagheera was fighting for his life.

"Baloo must be at hand; Bagheera would not have come alone," Mowgli thought; and then he called aloud: "To the tank, Bagheera! Roll to the water-tanks! Roll and plunge! Get to the water!"

Bagheera heard, and the cry that told him Mowgli was safe gave him new courage. He worked his way desperately, inch by inch, straight for the reservoirs, hitting in silence.

Then from the ruined wall nearest the jungle rose up the rumbling war-shout of Baloo. The old bear had done his best, but he could not come before. "Bagheera," he shouted, "I am here! I climb! I haste! *Ahuwora!* The stones slip under my feet! Wait my coming, O most infamous Bandar-log!"

He panted up the terrace only to disappear to the head in a wave of monkeys, but he threw himself squarely on his haunches, and spreading out his fore paws, hugged as many as he could hold, and then began to hit with a regular *bat-bat-bat,* like the flipping strokes of a paddle-wheel.

A crash and a splash told Mowgli that Bagheera had fought his way to the tank, where the monkeys could not follow. The panther lay gasping for breath, his head just out of water, while the monkeys stood three deep on the red stone steps, dancing up and down with rage, ready to spring upon him from all sides if he came out to help Baloo. It was then that Bagheera lifted up his dripping chin, and in despair gave the Snake's Call for protection,– "We be of one blood, ye and I,"–for he believed that Kaa had turned tail at the last minute. Even Baloo, half smothered under the monkeys on the edge of the terrace, could not help chuckling as he heard the big Black Panther asking for help.

Kaa had only just worked his way over the west wall, landing with a wrench that dislodged a coping-stone into the ditch. He had no intention of losing any advantage of the ground, and coiled and uncoiled himself once or twice, to be sure that every foot of his long body was in working order.

All that while the fight with Baloo went on, and the monkeys yelled in the tank round Bagheera, and Mang, the Bat, flying to and fro, carried the news of the great battle over the jungle, till even Hathi, the Wild Elephant, trumpeted, and, far away, scattered bands of the Monkey Folk woke and came leaping along the tree-roads to help their comrades in the Cold Lairs, and the noise of the fight roused all the day-birds for miles round.

Then Kaa came straight, quickly, and anxious to kill. The fighting strength of a python is in the driving blow of his head, backed by all the strength and weight of his body. If you can imagine a lance, or a battering-ram, or a hammer, weighing nearly half a ton driven by a cool, quiet mind living in the handle of it, you can imagine roughly what Kaa was like when he fought. A python four or five feet long can knock a man down if he hits him fairly in the chest, and Kaa was thirty feet long, as you know. His first stroke was delivered into the heart of the crowd round Baloo–was sent home with shut mouth in silence, and there was no need of a second. The monkeys scattered with cries of "Kaa! It is Kaa! Run! Run!"

Generations of monkeys had been scared into good behavior by the stories their elders told them of Kaa, the night-thief, who could slip along the branches as quietly as moss grows, and steal away the strongest monkey that ever lived; of old Kaa, who could make himself look so like a dead branch or a rotten stump that the wisest were deceived till the branch caught them, and then–

Kaa was everything that the monkeys feared in the jungle, for none of them knew the limits of his power, none of them could look him in the face, and none had ever come alive out of his hug. And so they ran, stammering with terror, to the walls and the roofs of the houses, and Baloo drew a deep breath of relief. His fur was much thicker than Bagheera's, but he had suffered sorely in the fight. Then Kaa opened his mouth for the first time and spoke one long hissing word, and the far-away monkeys, hurrying to the defense of the Cold Lairs, stayed where they were, cowering, till the loaded branches bent and crackled under them. The monkeys on the walls and the empty houses stopped their cries, and in the stillness that fell upon the city Mowgli heard Bagheera shaking his wet sides as he came up from the tank.

Then the clamor broke out again. The monkeys leaped higher up the walls; they clung round the necks of the big stone idols and shrieked as they skipped along the battlements; while Mowgli, dancing in the summer-house, put his eye to the screen work and hooted owl-fashion between his front teeth, to show his derision and contempt.

"Get the man-cub out of that trap; I can do no more," Bagheera gasped. "Let us take the man-cub and go. They may attack again."

"They will not move till I order them. Stay you sssso!" Kaa hissed, and the city was silent once more. "I could not come before, Brother, but I *think* I heard thee call"–this was to Bagheera.

"I–I may have cried out in the battle," Bagheera answered. "Baloo, art thou hurt?"

"I am not sure that they have not pulled me into a hundred little bearlings," said Baloo, gravely shaking one leg after the other. "Wow! I am sore. Kaa, we owe thee, I think, our lives–Bagheera and I."

"No matter. Where is the manling?"

"Here, in a trap. I cannot climb out," cried Mowgli. The curve of the broken dome was above his head.

"Take him away. He dances like Mao, the Peacock. He will crush our young," said the cobras inside.

"Hah!" said Kaa, with a chuckle, "he has friends everywhere, this manling. Stand back, Manling; and hide you, O Poison People. I break down the wall."

Kaa looked carefully till he found a discolored crack in the marble tracery showing a weak spot, made two or three light taps with his head to get the distance, and then lifting up six feet of his body clear of the ground, sent home half a dozen full-power, smashing blows, nose-first. The screenwork broke and fell away in a cloud of dust and rubbish, and Mowgli leaped through the opening and flung himself between Baloo and Bagheera–an arm round each big neck.

"Art thou hurt?" said Baloo, hugging him softly.

"I am sore, hungry, and not a little bruised; but, oh, they have handled ye grievously, my Brothers! Ye bleed."

"Others also," said Bagheera, licking his lips and looking at the monkey-dead on the terrace and round the tank.

"It is nothing, it is nothing if thou art safe, O my pride of all little frogs!" whimpered Baloo.

"Of that we shall judge later," said Bagheera, in a dry voice that Mowgli did not at all like. "But here is Kaa, to whom we owe the battle and thou owest thy life. Thank him according to our customs, Mowgli."

Mowgli turned and saw the great python's head swaying a foot above his own.

"So this is the manling," said Kaa. "Very soft is his skin, and he is not so unlike the Bandar-log. Have a care, Manling, that I do not mistake thee for a monkey some twilight when I have newly changed my coat."

"We be of one blood, thou and I," Mowgli answered. "I take my life from thee, to-night. My kill shall be thy kill if ever thou art hungry, O Kaa."

"All thanks, Little Brother," said Kaa, though his eyes twinkled. "And what may so bold a hunter kill? I ask that I may follow when next he goes abroad."

"I kill nothing–I am too little–but I drive goats toward such as can use them. When thou art empty come to me and see if I speak the truth. I have some skill in these [he held out his hands], and if ever thou art in a trap, I may pay the debt which I owe to thee, to Bagheera, and to Baloo, here. Good hunting to ye all, my masters."

"Well said," growled Baloo, for Mowgli had returned thanks very prettily. The python dropped his head lightly for a minute on Mowgli's shoulder. "A brave heart and a courteous tongue," said he. "They shall carry thee far through the jungle, Manling. But now go hence quickly with thy friends. Go and sleep, for the moon sets, and what follows it is not well that thou shouldst see."

The moon was sinking behind the hills and the lines of trembling monkeys huddled together on the walls and battlements looked like ragged, shaky fringes of things. Baloo went down to the tank for a drink, and Bagheera began to put his fur in order, as Kaa glided out into the center of the terrace and brought his jaws together with a ringing snap that drew all the monkeys' eyes upon him.

"The moon sets," he said. "Is there yet light to see?"

From the walls came a moan like the wind in the tree-tops: "We see, O Kaa!"

"Good!" Begins now the Dance–the Dance of the Hunger of Kaa. Sit still and watch."

He turned twice or thrice in a big circle, weaving his head from right to left. Then he began making loops and figures of eight with his body, and soft, oozy triangles that melted into squares and five-sided figures, and coiled mounds, never resting, never hurrying, and never stopping his low, humming song. It grew darker and darker, till at last the dragging, shifting coils disappeared, but they could hear the rustle of the scales.

Baloo and Bagheera stood still as stone, growling in their throats, their neck-hair bristling, and Mowgli watched and wondered.

"Bandar-log," said the voice of Kaa at last, "can ye stir foot or hand without my order? Speak!"

"Without thy order we cannot stir foot or hand, O Kaa!"

"Good! Come all one pace nearer to me."

The lines of the monkeys swayed forward helplessly, and Baloo and Bagheera took one stiff step forward with them.

"Nearer!" hissed Kaa, and they all moved again.

Mowgli laid his hands on Baloo and Bagheera to get them away, and the two great beasts started as though they had been waked from a dream.

"Keep thy hand on my shoulder," Bagheera whispered. "Keep it there, or I must go back–must go back to Kaa. *Aah!*"

"It is only old Kaa making circles on the dust," said Mowgli; "let us go"; and the three slipped off through a gap in the walls to the jungle.

"*Whoof!*" said Baloo, when he stood under the still trees again. "Never more will I make an ally of Kaa," and he shook himself all over.

"He knows more than we," said Bagheera, trembling. "In a little time, had I stayed, I should have walked down his throat."

"Many will walk that road before the moon rises again," said Baloo. "He will have good hunting–after his own fashion."

"But what was the meaning of it all?" said Mowgli, who did not know anything of a python's powers of fascination. "I saw no more than a big snake making foolish circles till the dark came. And his nose was all sore. Ho! Ho!"

"Mowgli," said Bagheera, angrily, "his nose was sore on *thy* account; as my ears and sides and paws, and Baloo's neck and shoulders are bitten on *thy* account. Neither Baloo nor Bagheera will be able to hunt with pleasure for many days."

"It is nothing," said Baloo; "we have the man-cub again."

"True; but he has cost us most heavily in time which might have been spent in good hunting, in wounds, in hair,–I am half plucked along my back,–and last of all, in honor. For, remember, Mowgli, I, who am the Black Panther, was forced to call upon Kaa for protection, and Baloo and I were both made stupid as little birds by the Hunter-Dance. All this, Man-cub, came of thy playing with the Bandar-log."

"True; it is true," said Mowgli, sorrowfully. "I am an evil man-cub, and my stomach is sad in me."

"*Mf!* What says the Law of the Jungle, Baloo?"

Baloo did not wish to bring Mowgli into any more trouble, but he could not tamper with the Law, so he mumbled, "Sorrow never stays punishment. But remember, Bagheera, he is very little."

"I will remember; but he has done mischief; and blows must be dealt now. Mowgli, hast thou anything to say?"

"Nothing. I did wrong. Baloo and thou art wounded. It is just."

Bagheera gave him half a dozen love-taps; from a panther's point of view they would hardly have waked one of his own cubs, but for a seven year-old boy they amounted to as severe a beating as you could wish to avoid. When it was all over Mowgli sneezed, and picked himself up without a word.

"Now," said Bagheera, "jump on my back, Little Brother, and we will go home."

One of the beauties of Jungle Law is that punishment settles all scores. There is no nagging afterward.

Mowgli laid his head down on Bagheera's back and slept so deeply that he never waked when he was put down by Mother Wolf's side in the home-cave.

Road-song of the Bandar-log

Here we go in a flung festoon,
Half-way up to the jealous moon!
Don't you envy our pranceful bands?
Don't you wish you had extra hands?
Wouldn't you like if your tails were–*so*–
Curved in the shape of a Cupid's bow?
    Now you're angry, but–never mind,
    Brother, thy tail hangs down behind!

Here we sit in a branchy row,
Thinking of beautiful things we know;
Dreaming of deeds that we mean to do,
All complete, in a minute or two–
Something noble and grand and good,
Won by merely wishing we could.
    Now we're going to–never mind,
    Brother, thy tail hangs down behind!

All the talk we ever have heard
Uttered by bat or beast or bird–
Hide or fin or scale or feather–
Jabber it quickly and all together!
Excellent! Wonderful! Once again!
Now we are talking just like men.
    Let's pretend we are . . . never mind,
    Brother, thy tail hangs down behind!
    This is the way of the Monkey-kind.

Then join our leaping lines that scumfish through the pines,
That rocket by where, light and high, the wild-grape swings.
By the rubbish in our wake, and the noble noise we make,
Be sure, be sure, we're going to do some splendid things!

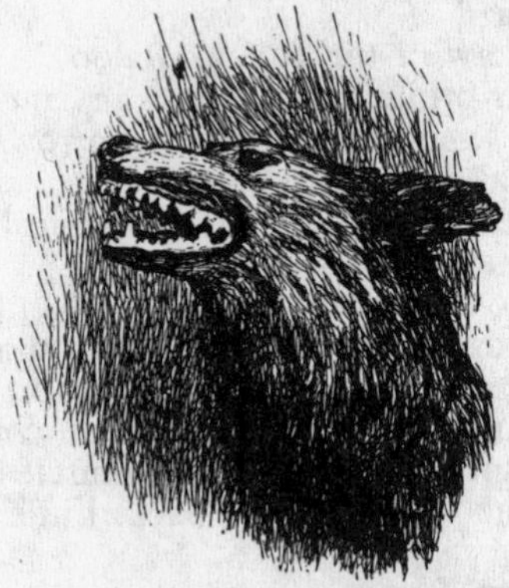

"Tiger! Tiger!"

What of the hunting, hunter bold?
    Brother, the watch was long and cold.
What of the quarry ye went to kill?
    Brother, he crops in the jungle still.
Where is the power that made your pride?
    Brother, it ebbs from my flank and side.
Where is the haste that ye hurry by?
    Brother, I go to my lair–to die.

NOW WE MUST go back to the last tale but one. When Mowgli left the wolf's cave after the fight with the Pack at the Council Rock, he went down to the plowed lands where the villagers lived, but he would not stop there because it was too near to the jungle, and he knew that he had made at least one bad enemy at the Council. So he hurried on, keeping to the rough road that ran down the valley, and followed it at a steady jog-trot for nearly twenty miles, till he came to a country that he did not know. The valley opened out into a great plain dotted over with rocks and cut up by ravines. At one end stood a little village, and at the other the thick jungle came down in a sweep to the grazing-grounds, and stopped there as though it had been cut off with a hoe. All over the plain, cattle and buffaloes were grazing, and when the little boys in charge of the herds saw Mowgli they shouted and ran away, and the yellow pariah dogs that hang about every Indian village barked. Mowgli walked on, for he was feeling hungry, and when he came to the village gate he saw the big thorn-bush that was drawn up before the gate at twilight, pushed to one side.

"Umph!" he said, for he had come across more than one such barricade in his night rambles after things to eat. "So men are afraid of the People of the Jungle here also." He sat down by the gate, and when a man came out he stood up, opened his mouth, and pointed down it to show that he wanted food. The man stared, and ran back up the one street of the village shouting for the priest, who was a big, fat man dressed in white, with a red and yellow mark on his forehead. The priest came to the gate, and with him at least a hundred people, who stared and talked and shouted and pointed at Mowgli.

"They have no manners, these Men Folk," said Mowgli to himself. "Only the gray ape would behave as they do." So he threw back his long hair and frowned at the crowd.

"What is there to be afraid of?" said the priest. "Look at the marks on his arms and legs. They are the bites of wolves. He is but a wolf-child run away from the jungle."

Of course, in playing together, the cubs had often nipped Mowgli harder than they intended, and there were white scars all over his arms and legs. But he would have been the last person in the world to call these bites; for he knew what real biting meant.

"*Arré! Arré!*" said two or three women together. "To be bitten by wolves, poor child! He is a handsome boy. He has eyes like red fire. By my honor, Messua, he is not unlike thy boy that was taken by the tiger."

"Let me look," said a woman with heavy copper rings on her wrists and ankles, and she peered at Mowgli under the palm of her hand. "Indeed he is not. He is thinner, but he has the very look of my boy."

The priest was a clever man, and he knew that Messua was wife to the richest villager in the place. So he looked up at the sky for a minute, and said solemnly: "What the jungle has taken the jungle has restored. Take the boy into thy house, my sister, and forget not to honor the priest who sees so far into the lives of men."

"By the Bull that bought me," said Mowgli to himself, "but all this talking is like another looking-over by the Pack! Well, if I am a man, a man I must become."

The crowd parted as the woman beckoned Mowgli to her hut, where there was a red lacquered bedstead, a great earthen grain-chest with curious raised patterns on it, half a dozen copper cooking-pots, an image of a Hindu god in a little alcove, and on the wall a real looking-glass, such as they sell at the country fairs.

She gave him a long drink of milk and some bread, and then she laid her hand on his head and looked into his eyes; for she thought perhaps that he might be her real son come back from the jungle where the tiger had taken him. So she said: "Nathoo, O Nathoo!" Mowgli did not show that he knew the name. "Dost thou not remember the day when I gave thee thy new shoes?" She touched his foot, and it was almost as hard as horn. "No," she said, sorrowfully; "those feet have never worn shoes, but thou art very like my Nathoo, and thou shalt be my son."

Mowgli was uneasy, because he had never been under a roof before; but as he looked at the thatch, he saw that he could tear it out any time if he wanted to get away, and that the window had no fastenings. "What is the good of a man," he said to himself at last, "if he does not understand man's talk? Now I am as silly and dumb as a man would be with us in the jungle. I must learn their talk."

It was not for fun that he had learned while he was with the wolves to imitate the challenge of bucks in the jungle and the grunt of the little wild pig. So as soon as Messua pronounced a word Mowgli would imitate it almost perfectly, and before dark he had learned the names of many things in the hut.

There was a difficulty at bedtime, because Mowgli would not sleep under anything that looked so like a panther-trap as that hut, and when they shut the door he went through the window. "Give him his will," said Messua's husband. "Remember he can never till now have slept on a bed. If he is indeed sent in the place of our son he will not run away."

So Mowgli stretched himself in some long, clean grass at the edge of the field, but before he had closed his eyes a soft gray nose poked him under the chin.

"Phew!" said Gray Brother (he was the eldest of Mother Wolf's cubs). "This is a poor reward for following thee twenty miles. Thou smellest of wood-smoke and cattle–altogether like a man already. Wake, Little Brother; I bring news."

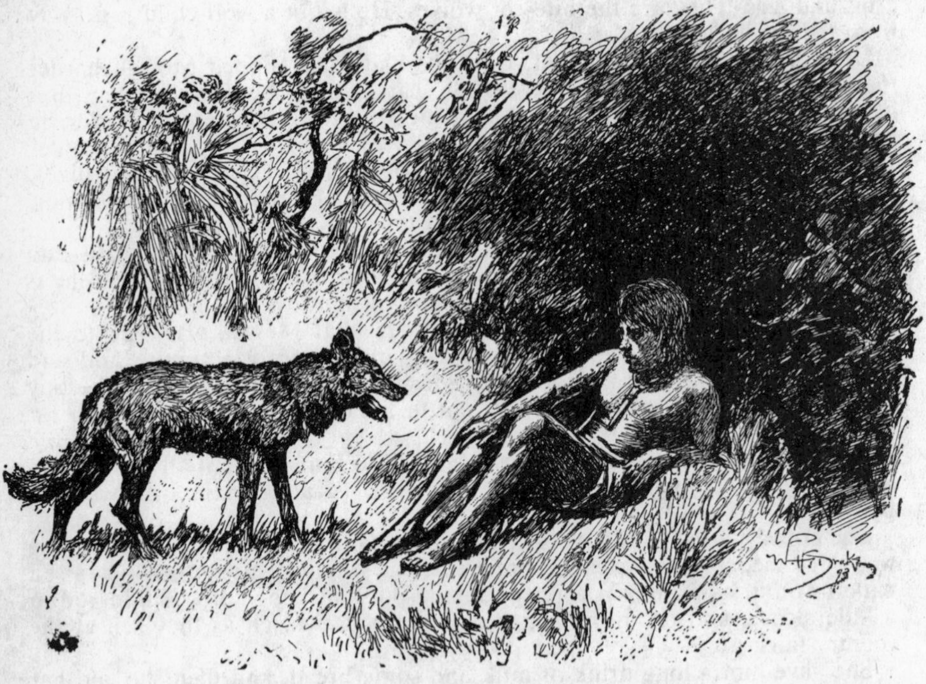

"'WAKE, LITTLE BROTHER; I BRING NEWS.'"

"Are all well in the jungle?" said Mowgli, hugging him.

"All except the wolves that were burned with the Red Flower. Now, listen. Shere Khan has gone away to hunt far off till his coat grows again, for he is badly singed. When he returns he swears that he will lay thy bones in the Waingunga."

"There are two words to that. I also have made a little promise. But news is always good. I am tired to-night,–very tired with new things, Gray Brother,–but bring me the news always."

"Thou wilt not forget that thou art a wolf? Men will not make thee forget?" said Gray Brother, anxiously.

"Never. I will always remember that I love thee and all in our cave; but also I will always remember that I have been cast out of the Pack."

"And that thou mayest be cast out of another pack. Men are only men, Little Brother, and their talk is like the talk of frogs in a pond. When I come down here again, I will wait for thee in the bamboos at the edge of the grazing-ground."

For three months after that night Mowgli hardly ever left the village gate, he was so busy learning the ways and customs of men. First he had to wear a cloth round him, which annoyed him horribly; and then he had to learn about money, which he did not in the least understand, and about plowing, of which he did not see the use. Then the little children in the village made him very angry. Luckily, the Law of the Jungle had taught him to keep his temper, for in the jungle, life and food depend on keeping your temper; but when they made fun of him because he would not play games or fly kites, or because he mispronounced some word, only the knowledge that it was unsportsmanlike to kill little naked cubs kept him from picking them up and breaking them in two.

He did not know his own strength in the least. In the jungle he knew he was weak compared with the beasts, but in the village, people said he was as strong as a bull.

And Mowgli had not the faintest idea of the difference that caste makes between man and man. When the potter's donkey slipped in the clay-pit, Mowgli hauled it out by the tail, and helped to stack the pots for their journey to the market at Khanhiwara. That was very shocking, too, for the potter is a low-caste man, and his donkey is worse. When the priest scolded him, Mowgli threatened to put him on the donkey, too, and the priest told Messua's husband that Mowgli had better be set to work as soon as possible; and the village head-man told Mowgli that he would have to go out with the buffaloes next day, and herd them while they grazed. No one was more pleased than Mowgli; and that night, because he had been appointed a servant of the village, as it were, he went off to a circle that met every evening on a masonry platform under a great fig-tree. It was the village club, and the head-man and the watchman and the barber (who knew all the gossip of the village), and old Buldeo, the village hunter, who had a Tower musket, met and smoked. The monkeys sat and talked in the upper branches, and there was a hole under the platform where a cobra lived, and he had his little platter of milk every night because he was sacred; and the old men sat around the tree and talked, and pulled at the big *huqas* (the water-pipes) till far into the night. They told wonderful tales of gods and men and ghosts; and Buldeo told even more wonderful ones of the ways of beasts in the jungle, till the eyes of the children sitting outside the circle bulged out of their heads. Most of the tales were about animals, for the jungle was always at their door. The deer and the wild pig grubbed up their crops, and now and again the tiger carried off a man at twilight, within sight of the village gates.

Mowgli, who naturally knew something about what they were talking of, had to cover his face not to show that he was laughing, while Buldeo, the Tower musket across his knees, climbed on from one wonderful story to another, and Mowgli's shoulders shook.

Buldeo was explaining how the tiger that had carried away Messua's son was a ghost-tiger, and his body was inhabited by the ghost of a wicked old money-lender, who had died some years ago. "And I know that this is true," he said, "because Purun Dass always limped from the blow that he got in a riot when his account-books were burned, and the tiger that I speak of *he* limps, too, for the tracks of his pads are unequal."

"Ture, true; that must be the truth," said the graybeards, nodding together.

"Are all these tales such cobwebs and moon-talk?" said Mowgli. "That tiger limps because he was born lame, as every one knows. To talk of the soul of a money-lender in a beast that never had the courage of a jackal is child's talk."

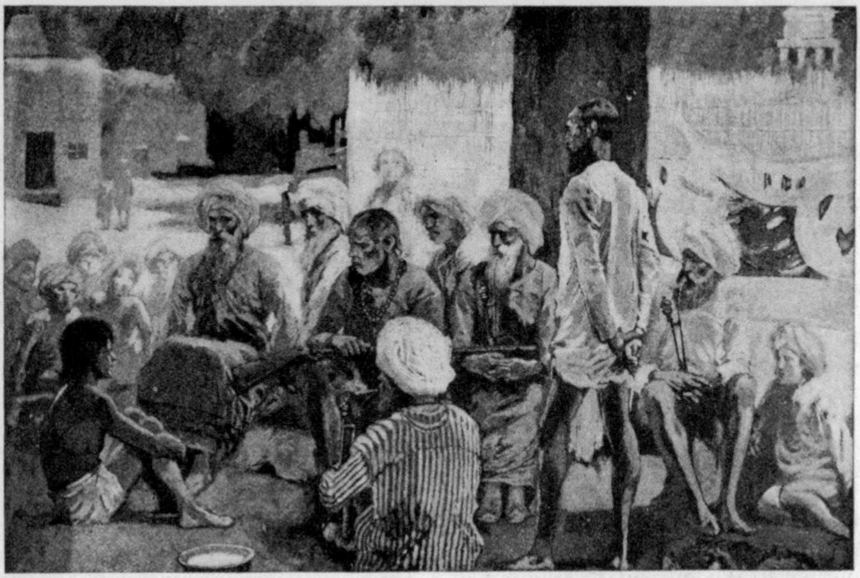

"'ARE ALL THESE TALES SUCH COBWEBS AND MOONTALK?' SAID MOWGLI."

Buldeo was speechless with surprise for a moment, and the head-man stared.

"Oho! It is the jungle brat, is it?" said Buldeo. "If thou art so wise, better bring his hide to Khanhiwara, for the Government has set a hundred rupees [$30] on his life. Better still, do not talk when thy elders speak."

Mowgli rose to go. "All the evening I have lain here listening," he called back over his shoulder, "and, except once or twice, Buldeo has not said one word of truth concerning the jungle, which is at his very doors. How, then, shall I believe the tales of ghosts and gods and goblins which he says he has seen?"

"It is full time that boy went to herding," said the head-man, while Buldeo puffed and snorted at Mowgli's impertinence.

The custom of most Indian villages is for a few boys to take the cattle and buffaloes out to graze in the early morning, and bring them back at night; and the very cattle that would trample a white man to death allow themselves to be banged and bullied and shouted at by children that hardly come up to their noses. So long as the boys keep with the herds they are safe, for not even the tiger will charge a mob of cattle. But if they straggle to pick flowers or hunt lizards, they are sometimes carried off. Mowgli went through the village street in the dawn, sitting on the back of Rama, the great herd bull; and the slaty-blue buffaloes, with their long, backward-sweeping horns and savage eyes, rose out of their byres, one by one, and followed him, and Mowgli made it very clear to the children with him that he was the master. He beat the buffaloes with a long, polished bamboo, and told Kamya, one of the boys, to graze the cattle by themselves, while he went on with the buffaloes, and to be very careful not to stray away from the herd.

An Indian grazing-ground is all rocks and scrub and tussocks and little ravines, among which the herds scatter and disappear. The buffaloes generally keep to the pools and muddy places, where they lie wallowing or basking in the warm mud for hours. Mowgli drove them on to the edge of the plain where the Waingunga River came out of the jungle; then he dropped from Rama's neck, trotted off to a bamboo clump, and found Gray Brother. "Ah," said Gray Brother, "I have waited here very many days. What is the meaning of this cattle-herding work?"

"It is an order," said Mowgli. "I am a village herd for a while. What news of Shere Khan?"

"He has come back to this country, and has waited here a long time for thee. Now he has gone off again, for the game is scarce. But he means to kill thee."

"Very good," said Mowgli. "So long as he is away do thou or one of the brothers sit on that rock, so that I can see thee as I come out of the village. When he comes back wait for me in the ravine by the *dhâk*-tree in the center of the plain. We need not walk into Shere Khan's mouth."

Then Mowgli picked out a shady place, and lay down and slept while the buffaloes grazed round him. Herding in India is one of the laziest things in the world. The cattle move and crunch, and lie down, and move on again, and they do not even low. They only grunt, and the buffaloes very seldom say anything, but get down into the muddy pools one after another, and work their way into the mud till only their noses and staring china-blue eyes show above the surface, and there they lie like logs. The sun makes the rocks dance in the heat, and the herd-children hear one kite (never any more) whistling almost out of sight overhead, and they know that if they died, or a cow died, that kite would sweep down, and the next kite miles away would see him drop and follow, and the next, and the next, and almost before they were dead there would be a score of hungry kites come out of nowhere. Then they sleep and wake and sleep again, and weave little baskets of dried grass and put grasshoppers in them; or catch two praying-mantises and make them fight; or string a necklace of red and black jungle-nuts; or watch a lizard basking on a rock, or a snake hunting a frog near the wallows. Then they sing long, long songs with odd native quavers at the end of them, and the day seems longer than most people's whole lives, and perhaps they make a mud castle with mud figures of men and horses and buffaloes, and put reeds into the men's hands, and pretend that they are kings and the figures are their armies, or that they are gods to be worshiped. Then evening comes, and the children call, and the buffaloes lumber up out of the sticky mud with noises like gunshots going off one after the other, and they all string across the gray plain back to the twinkling village lights.

Day after day Mowgli would lead the buffaloes out to their wallows, and

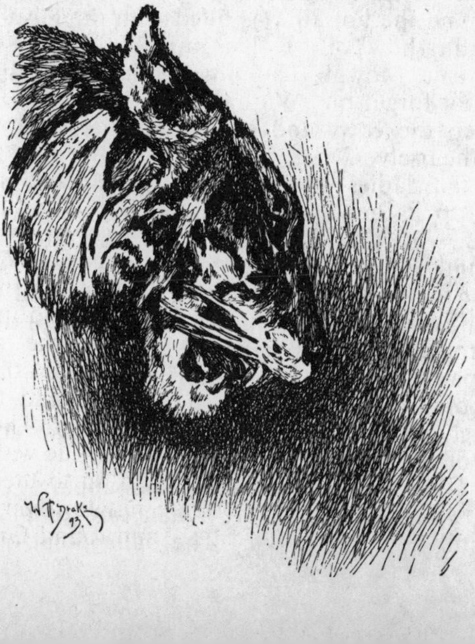

day after day he would see Gray Brother's back a mile and a half away across the plain (so he knew that Shere Khan had not come back), and day after day he would lie on the grass listening to the noise round him, and dreaming of old days in the jungle. If Shere Khan had made a false step with his lame paw up in the jungles by the Waingunga, Mowgli would have heard him in those long still mornings.

At last a day came when he did not see Gray Brother at the signal place, and he laughed and headed the buffaloes for the ravine by the *dhâk*-tree, which was all covered with golden-red flowers. There sat Gray Brother, every bristle on his back lifted.

"He has hidden for a month to throw thee off thy guard. He crossed the ranges last night with Tabaqui, hot-foot on thy trail," said the wolf, panting.

Mowgli frowned. "I am not afraid of Shere Khan, but Tabaqui is very cunning."

"Have no fear," said Gray Brother, licking his lips a little. "I met Tabaqui in the dawn. Now he is telling all his wisdom to the kites, but he told *me* everything before I broke his back. Shere Khan's plan is to wait for thee at the village gate this evening–for thee and for no one else. He is lying up now in the big dry ravine of the Waingunga."

"Has he eaten to-day, or does he hunt empty?" said Mowgli, for the answer meant life or death to him.

"He killed at dawn,–a pig,–and he has drunk too. Remember, Shere Khan could never fast even for the sake of revenge."

"Oh! Fool, fool! What a cub's cub it is! Eaten and drunk too, and he thinks that I shall wait till he has slept! Now, where does he lie up? If there were but ten of us we might pull him down as he lies. These buffaloes will not charge unless they wind him, and I cannot speak their language. Can we get behind his track so that they may smell it?"

"He swam far down the Waingunga to cut that off," said Gray Brother.

"Tabaqui told him that, I know. He would never have thought of it alone." Mowgli stood with his finger in his mouth, thinking. "The big ravine of the Waingunga. That opens out on the plain not half a mile from here. I can take the herd round through the jungle to the head of the ravine and then sweep down–but he would slink out at the foot. We must block that end. Gray Brother, canst thou cut the herd in two for me?"

"Not I,perhaps–but I have brought a wise helper." Gray Brother trotted off and dropped into a hole. Then there lifted up a huge gray head that Mowgli knew well, and the hot air was filled with the most desolate cry of all the jungle–the hunting-howl of a wolf at midday.

"Akela! Akela!" said Mowgli, clapping his hands. "I might have known that thou wouldst not forget me. We have a big work in hand. Cut the herd in two, Akela. Keep the cows and calves together, and the bulls and the plow-buffaloes by themselves."

The two wolves ran, ladies'-chain fashion, in and out of the herd, which snorted and threw up its head, and separated into two clumps. In one the cow-buffaloes stood, with their calves in the center, and glared and pawed, ready, if a wolf would only stay still, to charge down and trample the life out of him. In the other the bulls and the young bulls snorted and stamped; but, though they looked more imposing, they were much less dangerous, for they had no calves to protect. No six men could have divided the herd so neatly.

"What orders!" panted Akela. "They are trying to join again."

Mowgli slipped on to Rama's back. "Drive the bulls away to the left, Akela. Gray Brother, when we are gone hold the cows together, and drive them into the foot of the ravine."

"How far?" said Gray Brother, panting and snapping.

"Till the sides are higher than Shere Khan can jump," shouted Mowgli. "Keep them there till we come down." The bulls swept off as Akela bayed, and Gray Brother stopped in front of the cows. They charged down on him, and he ran just before them to the foot of the ravine, as Akela drove the bulls far to the left.

"Well done! Another charge and they are fairly started. Careful, now—careful, Akela. A snap too much, and the bulls will charge. *Hujah!* This is wilder work than driving blackbuck. Didst thou think these creatures could move so swiftly?" Mowgli called.

"I have—have hunted these too in my time," gasped Akela in the dust. "Shall I turn them into the jungle?"

"Ay, turn! Swiftly turn them. Rama is mad with rage. Oh, if I could only tell him what I need of him to-day!"

The bulls were turned to the right this time, and crashed into the standing thicket. The other herd-children, watching with the cattle half a mile away, hurried to the village as fast as their legs could carry them, crying that the buffaloes had gone mad and run away.

But Mowgli's plan was simple enough. All he wanted to do was to make a big circle uphill and get at the head of the ravine, and then take the bulls down it and catch Shere Khan between the bulls and the cows, for he knew that after a meal and a full drink Shere Khan would not be in any condition to fight or to clamber up the sides of the ravine. He was soothing the buffaloes now by voice, and Akela had dropped far to the rear, only whimpering once or twice to hurry the rear-guard. It was a long, long circle, for they did not wish to get too near the ravine and give Shere Khan warning. At last Mowgli rounded up the bewildered herd at the head of the ravine on a grassy patch that sloped steeply down to the ravine itself. From that height you could see across the tops of the trees down to the plain below; but what Mowgli looked at was the sides of the ravine, and he saw with a great deal of satisfaction that they ran nearly straight up and down, and the vines and creepers that hung over them would give no foothold to a tiger who wanted to get out.

"Let them breathe, Akela," he said, holding up his hand. "They have not winded him yet. Let them breathe. I must tell Shere Khan who comes. We have him in the trap."

He put his hands to his mouth and shouted down the ravine,—it was almost like shouting down a tunnel,—and the echoes jumped from rock to rock.

After a long time there came back the drawling, sleepy snarl of a full-fed tiger just awakened.

"Who calls?" said Shere Khan, and a splendid peacock fluttered up out of the ravine, screeching.

"I, Mowgli. Cattle-thief, it is time to come to the Council Rock! Down—hurry them down, Akela. Down, Rama, down!"

The herd paused for an instant at the edge of the slope, but Akela gave tongue in the full hunting-yell, and they pitched over one after the other just as steamers shoot rapids, the sand and stones spurting up round them. Once started, there was no change of stopping, and before they were fairly in the bed of the ravine Rama winded Shere Khan and bellowed.

"Ha! Ha!" said Mowgli, on his back. "Now thou knowest!" and the torrent of black horns, foaming muzzles, and staring eyes whirled down the ravine like boulders in flood-time; the weaker buffaloes being shouldered out to the sides of the ravine where they tore through the creepers. They knew what the business was before them—the terrible charge of the buffalo-herd, against which no tiger can hope to stand. Shere Khan heard the thunder of their hoofs, picked himself up, and lumbered down the ravine, looking from side to side for some way of escape, but the walls of the ravine were straight, and he had to keep on, heavy with his dinner and his drink, willing to do anything rather than fight. The herd splashed through the pool he had just left, bellowing till the narrow cut rang. Mowgli heard an answering bellow from the foot of the ravine, saw Shere Khan turn (the tiger knew if the worst came to the worst it was better to meet the bulls than the cows with their calves), and then Rama tripped, stumbled, and went on again over something soft, and, with the bulls at his heels, crashed full into the other herd, while the weaker buffaloes were lifted clean off their feet by the shock of the meeting. That charge carried both herds out into the plain, goring and stamping and snorting. Mowgli watched his time, and slipped off Rama's neck, laying about him right and left with his stick.

"Quick, Akela! Break them up. Scatter them, or they will be fighting one another. Drive them away, Akela. *Hai,* Rama! *Hai! hai! hai!* my children. Softly now, softly! It is all over."

Akela and Gray Brother ran to and fro nipping the buffaloes' legs, and though the herd wheeled once to charge up the ravine again, Mowgli managed to turn Rama, and the others followed him to the wallows.

Shere Khan needed no more trampling. He was dead, and the kites were coming for him already.

"Brothers, that was a dog's death," said Mowgli, feeling for the knife he always carried in a sheath round his neck now that he lived with men. "But he would never have shown fight. His hide will look well on the Council Rock. We must get to work swiftly."

A boy trained among men would never have dreamed of skinning a ten-foot tiger alone, but Mowgli knew better than any one else how an animal's skin fitted on, and how it can be taken off. But it was hard work, and Mowgli slashed and tore and grunted for an hour, while the wolves lolled out their tongues, or came forward and tugged as he ordered them.

Presently a hand fell on his shoulder, and looking up he saw Buldeo with the Tower musket. The children had told the village about the buffalo stampede, and Buldeo went out angrily, only too anxious to correct Mowgli for not taking better care of the herd. The wolves dropped out of sight as soon as they saw the man coming.

"What is this folly?" said Buldeo, angrily. "To think that thou canst skin a tiger! Where did the buffaloes kill him? It is the Lame Tiger, too, and there is a hundred rupees on his head. Well, well, we will overlook thy letting the herd run off, and perhaps I will give thee one of the rupees of the reward when I have taken the skin to Khanhiwara." He fumbled in his waist-cloth for flint and steel, and stooped down to singe Shere Khan's whiskers. Most native hunters singe a tiger's whiskers to prevent his ghost haunting them.

"Hum!" said Mowgli, half to himself as he ripped back the skin of a fore paw. "So thou wilt take the hide to Khanhiwara for the reward, and perhaps give me one rupee? Now it is in my mind that I need the skin for my own use. Heh! old man, take away that fire!"

"What talk is this to the chief hunter of the village? Thy luck and the stupidity of thy buffaloes have helped thee to this kill. The tiger has just fed, or he would have gone twenty miles by this time. Thou canst not even skin him properly, little beggar-brat, and forsooth I, Buldeo, must be told not to singe his whiskers. Mowgli, I will not give thee one anna of the reward, but only a very big beating. Leave the carcass!"

"By the Bull that bought me," said Mowgli, who was trying to get at the shoulder, "must I stay babbling to an old ape all noon? Here, Akela, this man plagues me."

Buldeo, who was still stooping over Shere Khan's head, found himself sprawling on the grass, with a gray wolf standing over him, while Mowgli went on skinning as though he were alone in all India.

"Ye-es," he said, between his teeth. "Thou art altogether right, Buldeo. Thou wilt never give me one anna of the reward. There is an old war between this lame tiger and myself–a very old war, and–I have won."

To do Buldeo justice, if he had been ten years younger he would have taken his chance with Akela had he met the wolf in the woods, but a wolf who obeyed the orders of this boy who had private wars with man-eating tigers was not a common animal. It was sorcery, magic of the worst kind, thought Buldeo, and he wondered whether the amulet round his neck would

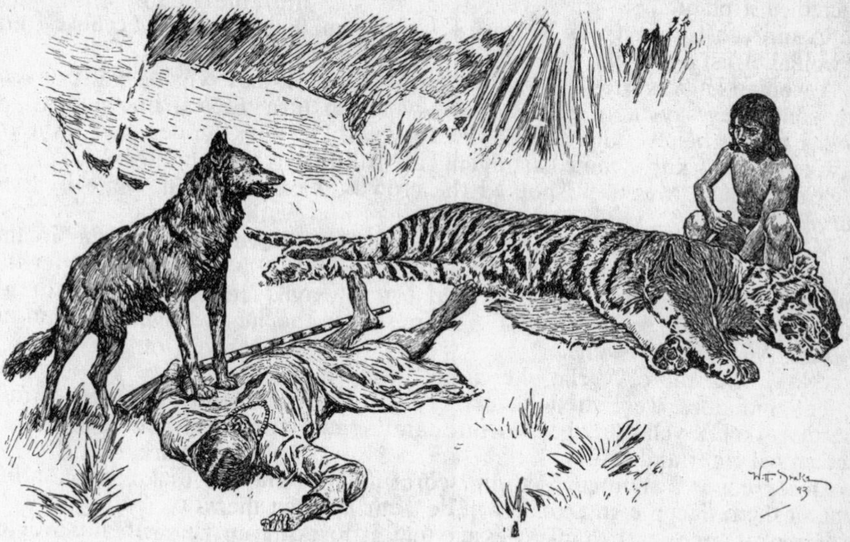

"BULDEO LAY AS STILL AS STILL, EXPECTING EVERY MINUTE TO SEE MOWGLI TURN INTO A TIGER, TOO."

protect him. He lay as still as still, expecting every minute to see Mowgli turn into a tiger, too.

"Maharaj! the Great King," he said at last, in a husky whisper.

"Yes," said Mowgli, without turning his head, chuckling a little.

"I am an old man. I did not know that thou wast anything more than a herd-boy. May I rise up and go away, or will thy servant tear me to pieces?"

"Go, and peace go with thee. Only, another time do not meddle with my game. Let him go, Akela."

Buldeo hobbled away to the village as fast as he could, looking back over his shoulder in case Mowgli should change into something terrible. When he got to the village he told a tale of magic and enchantment and sorcery that made the priest look very grave.

Mowgli went on with his work, but it was nearly twilight before he and the wolves had drawn the great gay skin clear of the body.

"Now we must hide this and take the buffaloes home! Help me to herd them, Akela."

The herd rounded up in the misty twilight, and when they got near the village Mowgli saw lights, and heard the conches and bells in the temple blowing and banging. Half the village seemed to be waiting for him by the gate. "That is because I have killed Shere Khan," he said to himself; but a shower of stones whistled about his ears, and the villagers shouted: "Sorcerer! Wolf's brat! Jungle-demon! Go away! Get hence quickly, or the priest will turn thee into a wolf again. Shoot, Buldeo, shoot!"

The old Tower musket went off with a bang, and a young buffalo bellowed in pain.

"More sorcery!" shouted the villagers. "He can turn bullets. Buldeo, that was *thy* buffalo."

"Now what is this?" said Mowgli, bewildered, as the stones flew thicker.

"They are not unlike the Pack, these brothers of thine," said Akela, sitting down composedly. "It is in my head that, if bullets mean anything, they would cast thee out."

"Wolf! Wolf's cub! Go away!" shouted the priest, waving a sprig of the sacred *tulsi* plant.

"Again? Last time it was because I was a man. This time it is because I am a wolf. Let us go, Akela."

A woman–it was Messua–ran across to the herd, and cried: "Oh, my son, my son! They say thou art a sorcerer who can turn himself into a beast at will. I do not believe, but go away or they will kill thee. Buldeo says thou art a wizard, but I know thou hast avenged Nathoo's death."

"Come back, Messua!" shouted the crowd. "Come back, or we will stone thee."

Mowgli laughed a little short ugly laugh, for a stone had hit him in the mouth. "Run back, Messua. This is one of the foolish tales they tell under the big tree at dusk. I have at least paid for thy son's life. Farewell; and run quickly, for I shall send the herd in more swiftly than their brickbats. I am no wizard, Messua. Farewell!

"Now, once more, Akela," he cried. "Bring the herd in."

The buffaloes were anxious enough to get to the village. They hardly needed Akela's yell, but charged through the gate like a whirlwind, scattering the crowd right and left.

"Keep count!" shouted Mowgli, scornfully. "It may be that I have stolen one of them. Keep count, for I will do your herding no more. Fare you well, children of men, and thank Messua that I do not come in with my wolves and hunt you up and down your street."

He turned on his heel and walked away with the Lone Wolf; and as he looked up at the stars he felt happy. "No more sleeping in traps for me, Akela. Let us get Shere Khan's skin and go away. No; we will not hurt the

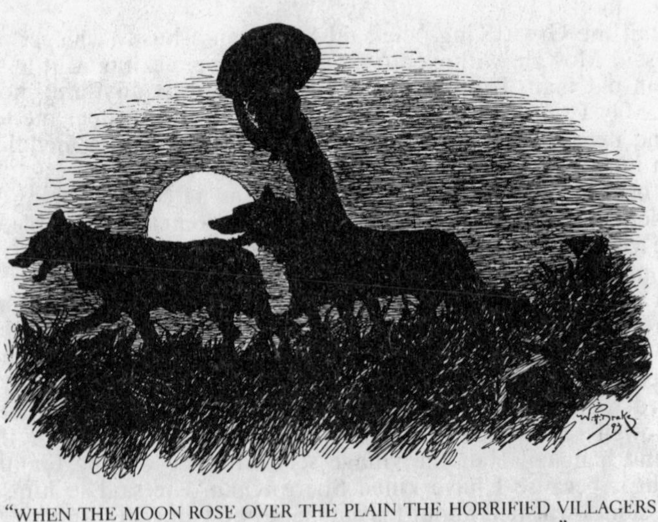

"WHEN THE MOON ROSE OVER THE PLAIN THE HORRIFIED VILLAGERS SAW MOWGLI, WITH TWO WOLVES AT HIS HEELS."

village, for Messua was kind to me."

When the moon rose over the plain, making it look all milky, the horrified villagers saw Mowgli, with two wolves at his heels and a bundle on his head, trotting across at the steady wolf's trot that eats up the long miles like fire.

Then they banged the temple bells and blew the conches louder than ever; and Messua cried, and Buldeo embroidered the story of his adventures in the jungle, till he ended by saying that Akela stood up on his hind legs and talked like a man.

The moon was just going down when Mowgli and the two wolves came to the hill of the Council Rock, and they stopped at Mother Wolf's cave.

"They have cast me out from the Man Pack, Mother," shouted Mowgli, "but I come with the hide of Shere Khan to keep my word." Mother Wolf walked stiffly from the cave with the cubs behind her, and her eyes glowed as she saw the skin.

"I told him on that day, when he crammed his head and shoulders into this cave, hunting for thy life, Little Frog—I told him that the hunter would be the hunted. It is well done."

"Little Brother, it is well done," said a deep voice in the thicket. "We were lonely in the jungle without thee," and Bagheera came running to Mowgli's bare feet. They clambered up the Council Rock together, and Mowgli spread the skin out on the flat stone where Akela used to sit, and pegged it down with four slivers of bamboo, and Akela lay down upon it, and called the old call to the Council, "Look—look well, O Wolves!" exactly as he had called when Mowgli was first brought there.

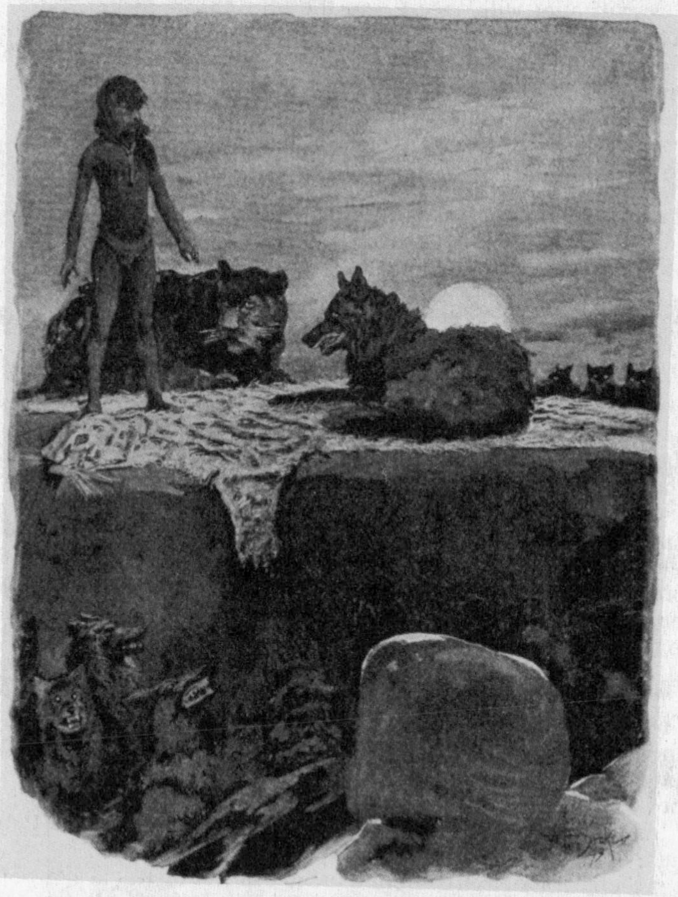

"THEY CLAMBERED UP ON THE COUNCIL ROCK TOGETHER, AND MOWGLI SPREAD THE SKIN OUT ON THE FLAT STONE."

Ever since Akela had been deposed, the Pack had been without a leader, hunting and fighting at their own pleasure. But they answered the call from habit, and some of them were lame from the traps they had fallen into, and some limped from shot-wounds, and some were mangy from eating bad food, and many were missing; but they came to the Council Rock, all that were left of them, and saw Shere Khan's striped hide on the rock, and the huge claws dangling at the end of the empty, dangling feet. It was then that Mowgli made up a song without any rhymes, a song that came up into his throat all by itself, and he shouted it aloud, leaping up and down on the rattling skin, and beating time with his heels till he had no more breath left, while Gray Brother and Akela howled between the verses.

"Look well, O Wolves. Have I kept my word?" said Mowgli when he had finished; and the wolves bayed "Yes," and one tattered wolf howled:

"Lead us again, O Akela. Lead us again, O Man-cub, for we be sick of this lawlessness, and we would be the Free People once more."

"Nay," purred Bagheera, "that may not be. When ye are full-fed, the madness may come upon ye again. Not for nothing are ye called the Free People. Ye fought for freedom, and it is yours. Eat it, O Wolves."

"Man Pack and Wolf Pack have cast me out," said Mowgli. "Now I will hunt alone in the jungle."

"And we will hunt with thee," said the four cubs.

So Mowgli went away and hunted with the four cubs in the jungle from that day on. But he was not always alone, because years afterward he became a man and married.

But that is a story for grown-ups.

Mowgli's Song

That He Sang at the Council Rock When He Danced on Shere Khan's Hide

The Song of Mowgli–I, Mowgli, am singing. Let the jungle listen to the things I have done.
Shere Khan said he would kill–would kill! At the gates in the twilight he would kill Mowgli, the Frog!
He ate and he drank. Drink deep, Shere Khan, for when wilt thou drink again? Sleep and dream of the kill.
I am alone on the grazing-grounds. Gray Brother, come to me! Come to me, Lone Wolf, for there is big game afoot.
Bring up the great bull-buffaloes, the blue-skinned herd-bulls with the angry eyes. Drive them to and fro as I order.
Sleepest thou still, Shere Khan? Wake, O wake! Here come I, and the bulls are behind.
Rama, the King of the Buffaloes, stamped with his foot. Waters of the Waingunga, whither went Shere Khan?
He is not Ikki to dig holes, nor Mao, the Peacock, that he should fly. He is not Mang, the Bat, to hang in the branches. Little bamboos that creak together, tell me where he ran?
Ow! He is there. *Ahoo!* He is there. Under the feet of Rama lies the Lame One! Up, Shere Khan! Up and kill! Here is meat; break the necks of the bulls!
Hsh! He is asleep. We will not wake him, for his strength is very great. The

kites have come down to see it. The black ants have come up to know it. There is a great assembly in his honor.
Alala! I have no cloth to wrap me. The kites will see that I am naked. I am ashamed to meet all these people.
Lend me thy coat, Shere Khan. Lend me thy gay striped coat that I may go to the Council Rock.
By the Bull that bought me I have made a promise–a little promise. Only thy coat is lacking before I keep my word.
With the knife–with the knife that men use–with the knife of the hunter, the man, I will stoop down for my gift.
Waters of the Waingunga, bear witness that Shere Khan gives me his coat for the love that he bears me. Pull, Gray Brother! Pull, Akela! Heavy is the hide of Shere Khan.
The Man Pack are angry. They throw stones and talk child's talk. My mouth is bleeding. Let us run away.
Through the night, through the hot night, run swiftly with me, my brothers. We will leave the lights of the village and go to the low moon.
Waters of the Waingunga, the Man Pack have cast me out. I did them no harm, but they were afraid of me. Why?
Wolf Pack, ye have cast me out too. The jungle is shut to me and the village gates are shut. Why?
As Mang flies between the beasts and the birds so fly I between the village and the jungle. Why?
I dance on the hide of Shere Khan, but my heart is very heavy. My mouth is cut and wounded with the stones from the village, but my heart is very light because I have come back to the jungle. Why?
These two things fight together in me as the snakes fight in the spring. The water comes out of my eyes; yet I laugh while it falls. Why?
I am two Mowglis, but the hide of Shere Khan is under my feet.
All the jungle knows that I have killed Shere Khan. Look–look well, O Wolves!
Ahae! My heart is heavy with the things that I do not understand.

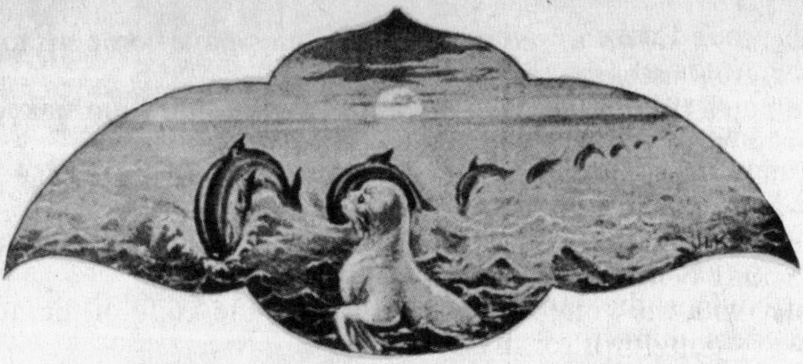

The White Seal

Oh! hush thee, my baby, the night is behind us,
 And black are the waters that sparkled so green.
The moon, o'er the combers, looks downward to find us
 At rest in the hollows that rustle between.
Where billow meets billow, there soft be thy pillow;
 Ah, weary wee flipperling, curl at thy ease!
The storm shall not wake thee, nor shark overtake thee,
 Asleep in the arms of the slow-swinging seas.

Seal Lullaby.

ALL THESE THINGS happened several years ago at a place called Novastoshnah, or North East Point, on the Island of St. Paul, away and away in the Bering Sea. Limmershin, the Winter Wren, told me the tale when he was blown on to the rigging of a steamer going to Japan, and I took him down into my cabin and warmed and fed him for a couple of days till he was fit to fly back to St. Paul's again. Limmershin is a very odd little bird, but he knows how to tell the truth.

Nobody comes to Novastoshnah except on business, and the only people who have regular business there are the seals. They come in the summer months by hundreds and hundreds of thousands out of the cold gray sea; for Novastoshnah Beach has the finest accommodation for seals of any place in all the world.

Sea Catch knew that, and every spring would swim from whatever place he happened to be in—would swim like a torpedo-boat straight for Novastoshnah, and spend a month fighting with his companions for a good place on the rocks as close to the sea as possible. Sea Catch was fifteen years old, a huge gray fur-seal with almost a mane on his shoulders, and long, wicked dogteeth. When he heaved himself up on his front flippers he stood more than four feet clear of the ground, and his weight, if anyone had been bold enough to weigh him, was nearly seven hundred pounds. He was scarred all over with the marks of savage fights, but he was always ready for just one fight more. He would put his head on one side, as though he were afraid to look his enemy in the face; then he would shoot it out like lightning, and when the big teeth were firmly fixed on the other seal's neck, the other seal might get away if he could, but Sea Catch would not help him.

Yet Sea Catch never chased a beaten seal, for that was against the Rules of the Beach. He only wanted room by the sea for his nursery; but as there were forty or fifty thousand other seals hunting for the same thing each spring, the whistling, bellowing, roaring, and blowing on the beach was something frightful.

From a little hill called Hutchinson's Hill you could look over three and a half miles of ground covered with fighting seals; and the surf was dotted all over with the heads of seals hurrying to land and begin their share of the fighting. They fought in the breakers, they fought in the sand, and they fought on the smooth-worn basalt rocks of the nurseries; for they were just as stupid and unaccommodating as men. Their wives never came to the island until late in May or early in June, for they did not care to be torn to pieces; and the young two-, three-, and four-year-old seals who had not begun housekeeping went inland about half a mile through the ranks of the fighters and played about on the sand-dunes in droves and legions, and rubbed off every single green thing that grew. They were called the holluschickie,—the bachelors,—and there were perhaps two or three hundred thousand of them at Novastoshnah alone.

Sea Catch had just finished his forty-fifth fight one spring when Matkah, his soft, sleek, gentle-eyed wife came up out of the sea, and he caught her by the scruff of the neck and dumped her down on his reservation, saying gruffly: "Late, as usual. Where *have* you been?"

It was not the fashion for Sea Catch to eat anything during the four months he stayed on the beaches, and so his temper was generally bad. Matkah knew better than to answer back. She looked around and cooed: "How thoughtful of you. You've taken the old place again."

"I should think I had," said Sea Catch. "Look at me!"

He was scratched and bleeding in twenty places; one eye was almost blind, and his sides were torn to ribbons.

"Oh, you men, you men!" Matkah said, fanning herself with her hind flipper. "Why can't you be sensible and settle your places quietly? You look as though you had been fighting with the Killer Whale."

"I haven't been doing anything *but* fight since the middle of May. The beach is disgracefully crowded this season. I've met at least a hundred seals from Lukannon Beach, house-hunting. Why can't people stay where they belong?"

"I've often though we should be much happier if we hauled out at Otter Island instead of this crowded place," said Matkah.

"Bah! Only the holluschickie go to Otter Island. If we went there they would say we were afraid. We must preserve appearances, my dear."

Sea Catch sunk his head proudly between his fat shoulders and pretended to go to sleep for a few minutes, but all the time he was keeping a sharp lookout for a fight. Now that all the seals and their wives were on the land you could hear their clamor miles out to sea above the loudest gales. At the lowest counting there were over a million seals on the beach,—old seals, mother seals, tiny babies, and holluschickie, fighting, scuffling, bleating, crawling, and playing together,—going down to the sea and coming up from it in gangs and regiments, lying over every foot of ground as far as the eye could reach, and skirmishing about in brigades through the fog. It is nearly always foggy at Novastoshnah, except when the sun comes out and makes everything look all pearly and rainbow-colored for a little while.

Kotick, Matkah's baby, was born in the middle of that confusion, and he was all head and shoulders, with pale, watery blue eyes, as tiny seals must be; but there was something about his coat that made his mother look at him very closely.

"Sea Catch," she said, at last, "our baby's going to be white!"

"Empty clam-shells and dry seaweed!" snorted Sea Catch. "There never has been such a thing in the world as a white seal."

"I can't help that," said Matkah; "there's going to be now"; and she sang the low, crooning seal-song that all the mother seals sing to their babies:

You mustn't swim till you're six weeks old,
  Or your head will be sunk by your heels;

And summer gales and Killer Whales
    Are bad for baby seals.

Are bad for baby seals, dear rat,
    As bad as bad can be;
But splash and grow strong,
And you can't be wrong,
    Child of the Open Sea!

Of course the little fellow did not understand the words at first. He paddled and scrambled about by his mother's side, and learned to scuffle out of the way when his father was fighting with another seal, and the two rolled and roared up and down the slippery rocks. Matkah used to go to sea to get things to eat, and the baby was fed only once in two days; but then he ate all he could, and throve upon it.

The first thing he did was to crawl inland, and there he met tens of thousands of babies of his own age, and they played together like puppies, went to sleep on the clean sand, and played again. The old people in the nurseries took no notice of them, and the holluschickie kept to their own grounds, so the babies had a beautiful playtime.

When Matkah came back from her deep-sea fishing she would go straight to their playground and call as a sheep calls for a lamb, and wait until she heard Kotick bleat. Then she would take the straightest of straight lines in his direction, striking out with her fore flippers and knocking the youngsters head over heels right and left. There were always a few hundred mothers hunting for their children through the playgrounds, and the babies were kept lively; but, as Matkah told Kotick, "So long as you don't lie in muddy water and get mange; or rub the hard sand into a cut or scratch; and so long as you never go swimming when there is a heavy sea, nothing will hurt you here."

Little seals can no more swim than little children, but they are unhappy till they learn. The first time that Kotick went down to the sea a wave carried him out beyond his depth, and his big head sank and his little hind flippers flew up exactly as his mother had told him in the song, and if the next wave had not thrown him back again he would have drowned.

After that he learned to lie in a beach-pool and let the wash of the waves just cover him and lift him up while he paddled, but he always kept his eye open for big waves that might hurt. He was two weeks learning to use his flippers; and all that while he floundered in and out of the water, and coughed and grunted and crawled up the beach and took cat-naps on the sand, and went back again, until at last he found that he truly belonged to the water.

Then you can imagine the times that he had with his companions, ducking under the rollers; or coming in on top of a comber and landing with a swash and a splutter as the big wave went whirling far up the beach; or standing up on his tail and scratching his head as the old people did; or playing "I'm the King of the Castle" on slippery, weedy rocks that just stuck out of the wash. Now and then he would see a thin fin, like a big shark's fin, drifting along close to shore, and he knew that that was the Killer Whale, the Grampus, who eats young seals when he can get them; and Kotick would head for the beach like an arrow, and the fin would jig off slowly, as if it were looking for nothing at all.

Late in October the seals began to leave St. Paul's for the deep sea, by families and tribes, and there was no more fighting over the nurseries, and the holluschickie played anywhere they liked. "Next year," said Matkah to Kotick, "you will be a holluschickie; but this year you must learn how to catch fish."

They set out together across the Pacific, and Matkah showed Kotick how to sleep on his back with his flippers tucked down by his side and his little nose just out of the water. No cradle is so comfortable as the long, rocking swell of the Pacific. When Kotick felt his skin tingle all over, Matkah told him he was learning the "feel of the water," and that tingly, prickly feelings meant bad weather coming, and he must swim hard and get away.

"In a little time," she said, "you'll know where to swim to, but just now we'll follow Sea Pig, the Porpoise, for he is very wise." A school of porpoises were ducking and tearing through the water, and little Kotick followed them as fast as he could. "How do you know where to go to?" he panted. The

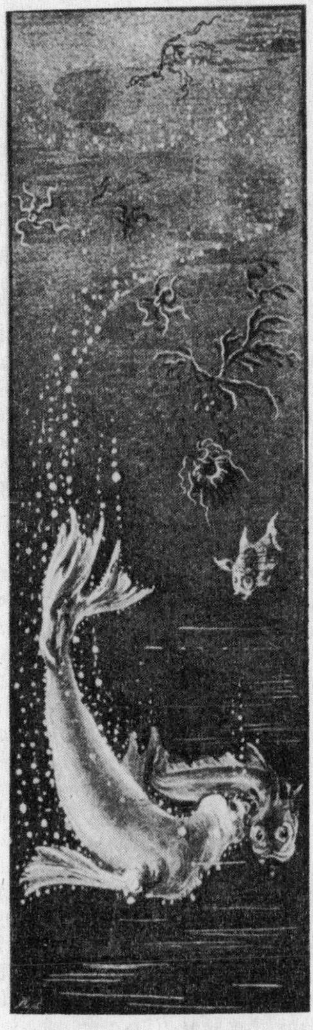

"TEN FATHOMS DEEP."

leader of the school rolled his white eyes, and ducked under. "My tail tingles, youngster," he said. "That means there's a gale behind me. Come along! When you're south of the Sticky Water [he meant the Equator], and your tail tingles, that means there's a gale in front of you and you must head north. Come along! The water feels bad here."

This was one of very many things that Kotick learned, and he was always learning. Matkah taught him how to follow the cod and the halibut along the under-sea banks, and wrench the rockling out of his hole among the weeds; how to skirt the wrecks lying a hundred fathoms below water, and dart like a rifle-bullet in at one porthole and out at another as the fishes ran; how to dance on the top of the waves when the lightning was racing all over the sky, and wave his flipper politely to the Stumpy-tailed Albatross and the Man-of-war Hawk as they went down the wind; how to jump three or four feet clear of the water, like a dolphin, flippers close to the side and tail curved; to leave the flying-fish alone because they are all bony; to take the shoulder-piece out of a cod at full speed ten fathoms deep; and never to stop and look at a boat or a ship, but particularly a row boat. At the end of six months, what Kotick did not know about deep-sea fishing was not worth the knowing, and all that time he never set flipper on dry ground.

One day, however, as he was lying half asleep in the warm water somewhere off the Island of Juan Fernandez, he felt faint and lazy all over, just as human people do when the spring is in their legs, and he remembered the good firm beaches of Novastoshnah seven thousand miles away; the games his companions played, the smell of the seaweed, the seal-roar, and the fighting. That very minute he turned north, swimming steadily, and as he went on he met scores of his mates, all bound for the same place, and they said: "Greeting, Kotick! This year we are all holluschickie, and we can dance the Fire-dance in the breakers off Lukannon and play on the new grass. But where did you get that coat?"

Kotick's fur was almost pure white now, and though he felt very proud of it, he only said: "Swim quickly! My bones are aching for the land." And so they all came to the beaches where they had been born and heard the old seals, their fathers, fighting in the rolling mist.

That night Kotick danced the Fire-dance with the yearling seals. The sea is full of fire on summer nights all the way down from Novastoshnah to Lukannon, and each seal leaves a wake like burning oil behind him, and a flaming flash when he jumps, and the waves break in great phosphorescent streaks and swirls. Then they went inland to the holluschickie grounds, and rolled up and down in the new wild wheat, and told stories of what they had done while they had been at sea. They talked about the Pacific as boys would talk about a wood that they had been nutting in, and if any one had understood them, he could have gone away and made such a chart of that ocean as never was. The three- and four-year-old holluschickie romped down from Hutchinson's Hill, crying: "Out of the way, youngsters! The sea is deep, and you don't know all that's in it yet. Wait till you've rounded the Horn. Hi, you yearling, where did you get that white coat?"

"I didn't get it," said Kotick; "it grew." And just as he was going to roll the speaker over, a couple of black-haired men with flat red faces came from behind a sand-dune, and Kotick, who had never seen a man before, coughed and lowered his head. The holluschickie just bundled off a few yards and sat staring stupidly. The men were no less than Kerick Booterin, the chief of the seal-hunters on the island, and Patalamon, his son. They came from the little village not half a mile from the seal nurseries, and they were deciding what seals they would drive up to the killing-pens (for the seals were driven just like sheep), to be turned into sealskin jackets later on.

"Ho!" said Patalamon. "Look! There's a white seal!"

Kerick Booterin turned nearly white under his oil and smoke, for he was an Aleut, and Aleuts are not clean people. Then he began to mutter a prayer. "Don't touch him, Patalamon. There has never been a white seal since–since I was born. Perhaps it is old Zaharrof's ghost. He was lost last year in the big gale."

"I'm not going near him," said Patalamon. "He's unlucky. Do you really think he is old Zaharrof come back? I owe him for some gulls' eggs."

"Don't look at him," said Kerick. "Head off that drove of four-year-olds. The men ought to skin two hundred to-day, but it's the beginning of the season, and they are new to the work. A hundred will do. Quick!"

Patalamon rattled a pair of seal's shoulder-bones in front of a herd of holluschickie and they stopped dead, puffing and blowing. Then he stepped near, and the seals began to move, and Kerick headed them inland, and they never tried to get back to their companions. Hundreds and hundreds of thousands of seals watched them being driven, but they went on playing just the same. Kotick was the only one who asked questions, and none of his companions could tell him anything, except that the men always drove seals in that way for six weeks or two months of every year.

"I am going to follow," he said, and his eyes nearly popped out of his head as he shuffled along in the wake of the herd.

"The white seal is coming after us," cried Patalamon. "That's the first time a seal has ever come to the killing-grounds alone."

"Hsh! Don't look behind you," said Kerick. "It *is* Zaharrof's ghost! I must speak to the priest about this."

The distance to the killing-grounds was only half a mile, but it took an hour to cover, because if the seals went too fast Kerick knew that they would get heated and then their fur would come off in patches when they were skinned. So they went on very slowly, past Sea-Lion's Neck, past Webster House, till they came to the Salt House just beyond the sight of the seals on the beach. Kotick followed, panting and wondering. He thought that he was at the world's end, but the roar of the seal nurseries behind him sounded as loud as the roar of a train in a tunnel. Then Kerick sat down on the moss and pulled out a heavy pewter watch and let the drove cool off for thirty minutes, and Kotick could hear the fog-dew dripping from the brim of his cap. Then ten or twelve men, each with an iron-bound club three or four feet long, came up, and Kerick pointed out one or two of the drove that were bitten by their companions or were too hot, and the men kicked those aside with their heavy boots made of the skin of a walrus's throat, and then Kerick said: "Let go!" and then the men clubbed the seals on the head as fast as they could.

Ten minutes later little Kotick did not recognize his friends any more, for their skins were ripped off from the nose to the hind flippers—whipped off and thrown down on the ground in a pile.

That was enough for Kotick. He turned and galloped (a seal can gallop very swiftly for a short time) back to the sea, his little new mustache bristling with horror. At Sea-Lion's Neck, where the great sea-lions sit on the edge of the surf, he flung himself flipper over-head into the cool water, and rocked there, gasping miserably. "What's here?" said a sea-lion, gruffly; for as a rule the sea-lions keep themselves to themselves.

"Scoochnie! Ochen scoochnie!" ("I'm lonesome, very lonesome!"), said Kotick. "They're killing *all* the holluschickie on *all* the beaches!"

The sea-lion turned his head inshore. "Nonsense," he said; "your friends are making as much noise as ever. You must have seen old Kerick polishing off a drove. He's done that for thirty years."

"It's horrible," said Kotick, backing water as a wave went over him, and steadying himself with a screw-stroke of his flippers that brought him up all standing within three inches of a jagged edge of rock.

"Well done for a yearling!" said the sea-lion, who could appreciate good swimming. "I suppose it *is* rather awful from your way of looking at it; but if you seals will come here year after year, of course the men get to know of it, and unless you can find an island where no men ever come, you will always be driven."

"Isn't there any such island?" began Kotick.

"I've followed the *poltoos* [the halibut] for twenty years, and I can't say I've found it yet. But look here—you seem to have a fondness for talking to your betters; suppose you go to Walrus Islet and talk to Sea Vitch. He may know something. Don't flounce off like that. It's a six-mile swim, and if I were you I should haul out and take a nap first, little one."

Kotick thought that that was good advice, so he swam round to his own beach, hauled out, and slept for half an hour, twitching all over, as seals will. Then he headed straight for Walrus Islet, a little low sheet of rocky island almost due northeast from Novastoshnah, all ledges of rock and gulls' nests, where the walrus herded by themselves.

He landed close to old Sea Vitch—the big, ugly, bloated, pimpled, fat-necked, long-tusked walrus of the North Pacific, who has no manners except when he is asleep—as he was then, with his hind flippers half in and half out of the surf.

"Wake up!" barked Kotick, for the gulls were making a great noise.

"Hah! Ho! Hmph! What's that?" said Sea Vitch, and he struck the next walrus a blow with his tusks and waked him up, and the next struck the next, and so on till they were all awake and staring in every direction but the right one.

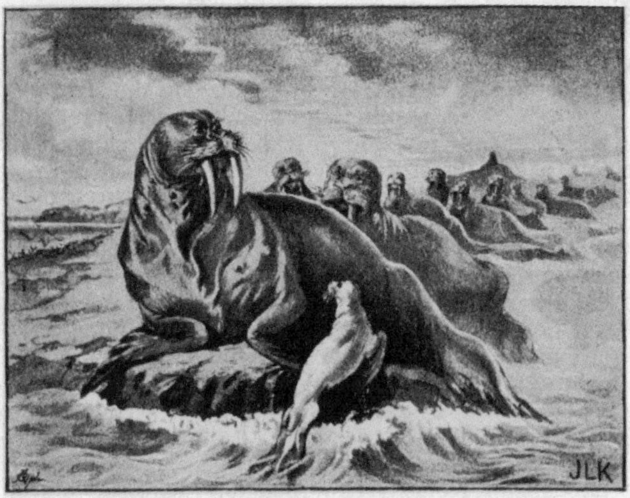

"THEY WERE ALL AWAKE AND STARING IN EVERY DIRECTION BUT THE RIGHT ONE."

"Hi! It's me," said Kotick, bobbing in the surf and looking like a little white slug.

"Well! May I be—skinned!" said Sea Vitch, and they all looked at Kotick as you can fancy a club full of drowsy old gentlemen would look at a little boy. Kotick did not care to hear any more about skinning just then; he had seen enough of it; so he called out: "Isn't there any place for seals to go where men don't ever come?"

"Go and find out," said Sea Vitch, shutting his eyes. "Run away. We're busy here."

Kotick made his dolphin-jump in the air and shouted as loud as he could: "Clam-eater! Clam-eater!" He knew that Sea Vitch never caught a fish in his life, but always rooted for clams and seaweeds; though he pretended to be a very terrible person. Naturally the Chickies and the Gooverooskies and the Epatkas, the Burgomaster Gulls and the Kittiwakes and the Puffins, who are always looking for a chance to be rude, took up the cry, and—so Limmerskin told me—for nearly five minutes you could not have heard a gun fired on Walrus Islet. All the population was yelling and screaming: "Clam-eater! *Stareek* [old man]!" while Sea Vitch rolled from side to side grunting and coughing.

"*Now* will you tell?" said Kotick, all out of breath.

"Go and ask Sea Cow," said Sea Vitch. "If he is living still, he'll be able to tell you."

"How shall I know Sea Cow when I meet him?" said Kotick, sheering off.

"He's the only thing in the sea uglier than Sea Vitch," screamed a burgomaster gull, wheeling under Sea Vitch's nose. "Uglier, and with worse manners! *Stareek!*"

Kotick swam back to Novastoshna, leaving the gulls to scream. There he found that no one sympathized with him in his little attempts to discover a quiet place for the seals. They told him that men had always driven the holluschickie—it was part of the day's work—and that if he did not like to see ugly things he should not have gone to the killing-grounds. But none of the other seals had seen the killing, and that made the difference between him and his friends. Besides, Kotick was a white seal.

"What you must do," said old Sea Catch, after he had heard his son's adventures, "is to grow up and be a big seal like your father, and have a nursery on the beach, and then they will leave you alone. In another five years you ought to be able to fight for yourself." Even gentle Matkah, his mother, said: "You will never be able to stop the killing. Go and play in the sea, Kotick." And Kotick went off and danced the Fire-dance with a very heavy little heart.

That autumn he left the beach as soon as he could, and set off alone because of a notion in his bullet-head. He was going to find Sea Cow, if there was such a person in the sea, and he was going to find a quiet island with good firm beaches for seals to live on, where men could not get at them. So he explored and explored by himself from the North to the South Pacific, swimming as much as three hundred miles in a day and a night. He met with more adventures than can be told, and narrowly escaped being caught by the Basking Shark, and the Spotted Shark, and the Hammerhead, and he met all the untrustworthy ruffians that loaf up and down the high seas, and the heavy polite fish, and the scarlet-spotted scallops that are moored in one place for hundreds of years, and grow very proud of it; but he never met Sea Cow, and he never found an island that he could fancy.

If the beach was good and hard, with a slope behind it for seals to play on, there was always the smoke of a whaler on the horizon, boiling down blubber, and Kotick knew what *that* meant. Or else he could see that seals had once visited the island and been killed off, and Kotick knew that where men had come once they would come again.

He picked up with an old stumpy-tailed albatross, who told him that Kerguelen Island was the very place for peace and quiet, and when Kotick went down there he was all but smashed to pieces against some wicked black cliffs in a heavy sleet-storm with lightning and thunder. Yet as he pulled out against the gale he could see that even there had once been a seal nursery. And it was so in all the other islands that he visited.

Limmershin gave a long list of them, for he said that Kotick spent five seasons exploring, with a four months' rest each year at Novastoshnah, where the holluschickie used to make fun of him and his imaginary islands. He went to the Gallapagos, a horrid dry place on the Equator, where he was nearly baked to death; he went to the Georgia Islands, the Orkneys, Emerald Island, Little Nightingale Island, Gough's Island, Bouvet's Island, the Crossets, and even to a little speck of an island south of the Cape of Good Hope. But everywhere the People of the Sea told him the same things. Seals had come to those islands once upon a time, but men had killed them all off. Even when he swam thousands of miles out of the Pacific, and got to a place called Cape Corientes (that was when he was coming back from Gough's Island), he found a few hundred mangy seals on a rock, and they told him that men came there too.

That nearly broke his heart, and he headed round the Horn back to his own beaches; and on his way north he hauled out on an island full of green trees, where he found an old, old seal who was dying, and Kotick caught fish for him and told him all his sorrows. "Now," said Kotick, "I am going back to Novastoshnah, and if I am driven to the killing-pens with the holluschickie I shall not care."

The old seal said: "Try once more. I am the last of the Lost Rookery of Masafuera, and in the days when men killed us by the hundred thousand there was a story on the beaches that some day a white seal would come out of the north and lead the seal people to a quiet place. I am old and I shall never live to see that day, but others will. Try once more."

And Kotick curled up his mustache (it was a beauty), and said: "I am the only white seal that has ever been born on the beaches, and I am the only seal, black or white, who ever thought of looking for new islands."

That cheered him immensely; and when he came back to Novastoshnah that summer, Matkah, his mother, begged him to marry and settle down, for he was no longer a holluschick, but a full-grown sea-catch, with a curly white mane on his shoulders, as heavy, as big, and as fierce as his father. "Give me another season," he said. "Remember, Mother, it is always the seventh wave that goes farthest up the beach."

Curiously enough, there was another seal who thought that she would put off marrying till the next year, and Kotick danced the Fire-dance with her all down Lukannon Beach the night before he set off on his last exploration.

This time he went westward, because he had fallen on the trail of a great shoal of halibut, and he needed at least one hundred pounds of fish a day to keep him in good condition. He chased them till he was tired, and then he curled himself up and went to sleep on the hollows of the ground-swell that sets in to Copper Island. He knew the coast perfectly well, so about midnight, when he felt himself gently bumped on a weed bed, he said: "Hm, tide's running strong tonight," and turning over under water opened his eyes slowly and stretched. Then he jumped like a cat, for he saw huge things nosing about in the shoal water and browsing on the heavy fringes of the weeds.

"By the Great Combers of Magellan!" he said, beneath his mustache. "Who in the Deep Sea are these people?"

They were like no walrus, sea-lion, seal, bear, whale, shark, fish, squid, or scallop that Kotick had ever seen before. They were between twenty and thirty feet long, and they had no hind flippers, but a shovel-like tail that looked as if it had been whittled out of wet leather. Their heads were the most foolish-looking things you ever saw, and they balanced on the ends of their tails in deep water when they weren't grazing, bowing solemnly to one another and waving their front flippers as a fat man waves his arm.

"Ahem!" said Kotick. "Good sport, gentlemen?" The big things answered by bowing and waving their flippers like the Frog-Footman. When they began feeding again Kotick saw that their upper lip was split into two pieces, that they could twitch apart about a foot and bring together again with a whole bushel of seaweed between the splits. They tucked the stuff into their mouths and chumped solemnly.

"Messy style of feeding that," said Kotick. They bowed again, and Kotick began to lose his temper. "Very good," he said. "If you do happen to have an extra joint in your front flipper you needn't show off so. I see you bow gracefully, but I should like to know your names." The split lips moved and twitched, and the glassy green eyes stared; but they did not speak.

"Well!" said Kotick, "you're the only people I've ever met uglier than Sea Vitch–and with worse manners."

Then he remembered in a flash what the Burgomaster Gull had screamed to him when he was a little yearling at Walrus Islet, and he tumbled backward in the water, for he knew that he had found Sea Cow at last.

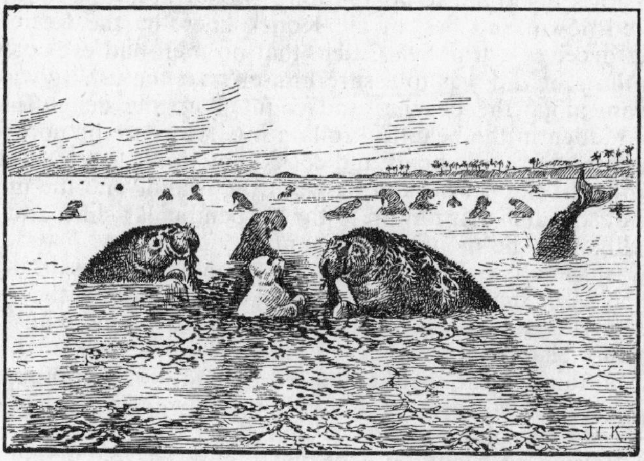

"HE HAD FOUND SEA COW AT LAST."

The sea cows went on schlooping and grazing, and chumping in the weed, and Kotick asked them questions in every language that he had picked up in his travels; and the Sea People talk nearly as many languages as human beings. But the Sea Cow did not answer, because Sea Cow cannot talk. He has only six bones in his neck where he ought to have seven, and they say under the sea that that prevents him from speaking even to his companions; but, as you know, he has an extra joint in his fore flipper, and by waving it up and down and about he makes what answers to a sort of clumsy telegraphic code.

By daylight Kotick's mane was standing on end and his temper was gone where the dead crabs go. Then the Sea Cow began to travel northward very slowly, stopping to hold absurd bowing councils from time to time, and Kotick followed them, saying to himself: "People who are such idiots as these are would have been killed long ago if they hadn't found out some safe island; and what is good enough for the Sea Cow is good enough for the Sea Catch. All the same, I wish they'd hurry."

It was weary work for Kotick. The herd never went more than forty or fifty miles a day, and stopped to feed at night, and kept close to the shore all the time; while Kotick swam round them, and over them, and under them, but he could not hurry them up one half-mile. As they went farther north they held a bowing council every few hours, and Kotick nearly bit off his mustache with impatience till he saw that they were following up a warm current of water, and then he respected them more.

One night they sank through the shiny water–sank like stones–and, for the first time since he had known them, began to swim quickly. Kotick followed, and the pace astonished him, for he never dreamed that Sea Cow was anything of a swimmer. They headed for a cliff by the shore, a cliff that ran down into deep water, and plunged into a dark hole at the foot of it, twenty fathoms under the sea. It was a long, long swim, and Kotick badly wanted fresh air before he was out of the dark tunnel they led him through.

"My wig!" he said, when he rose, gasping and puffing, into open water at the farther end. "It was a long dive, but it was worth it."

The sea cows had separated, and were browsing lazily along the edges of the finest beaches that Kotick had ever seen. There were long stretches of smooth worn rock running for miles, exactly fitted to make seal nurseries, and there were playgrounds of hard sand, sloping inland behind them, and there were rollers for seals to dance in, and long grass to roll in, and sand-dunes to climb up and down, and best of all, Kotick knew by the feel of the water, which never deceives a true Sea Catch, that no men had ever come there.

The first thing he did was to assure himself that the fishing was good, and then he swam along the beaches and counted up the delightful low sandy islands half hidden in the beautiful rolling fog. Away to the northward out to sea ran a line of bars and shoals and rocks that would never let a ship come within six miles of the beach; and between the islands and the mainland was a stretch of deep water that ran up to the perpendicular cliffs, and somewhere below the cliffs was the mouth of the tunnel.

"It's Novastoshnah over again, but ten times better," said Kotick. "Sea Cow must be wiser than I thought. Men can't come down the cliffs, even if there were any men; and the shoals to seaward would knock a ship to splinters. If any place in the sea is safe, this is it."

He began to think of the seal he had left behind him, but though he was in a hurry to go back to Novastoshnah, he thoroughly explored the new country, so that he would be able to answer all questions.

Then he dived and made sure of the mouth of the tunnel, and raced through to the southward. No one but a sea cow or a seal would have dreamed of there being such a place, and when he looked back at the cliffs even Kotick could hardly believe that he had been under them.

He was six days going home, though he was not swimming slowly; and when he hauled out just above Sea-Lion's Neck the first person he met was the seal who had been waiting for him, and she saw by the look in his eyes that he had found his island at last.

But the holluschickie and Sea Catch, his father, and all the other seals, laughed at him when he told them what he had discovered, and a young seal about his own age said: "This is all very well, Kotick, but you can't come from no one knows where and order us off like this. Remember we've been fighting for our nurseries, and that's a thing you never did. You preferred prowling about in the sea."

The other seals laughed at this, and the young seal began twisting his head from side to side. He had just married that year, and was making a great fuss about it.

"I've no nursery to fight for," said Kotick. "I want only to show you all a place where you will be safe. What's the use of fighting?"

"Oh, if you're trying to back out, of course I've no more to say," said the young seal, with an ugly chuckle.

"Will you come with me if I win?" said Kotick; and a green light came into his eyes, for he was very angry at having to fight at all.

"Very good," said the young seal, carelessly. "*If* you win, I'll come."

He had no time to change his mind, for Kotick's head darted out and his teeth sunk in the blubber of the young seal's neck. Then he threw himself back on his haunches and hauled his enemy down the beach, shook him, and knocked him over. Then Kotick roared to the seals: "I've done my best for you these five seasons past. I've found you the island where you'll be safe, but unless your heads are dragged off your silly necks you won't believe. I'm going to teach you now. Look out for yourselves!"

Limmershin told me that never in his life—and Limmershin sees ten thousand big seals fighting every year—never in all his little life did he see anything like Kotick's charge into the nurseries. He flung himself at the biggest sea-catch he could find, caught him by the throat, choked him and bumped him and banged him till he grunted for mercy, and then threw him aside and attacked the next. You see, Kotick had never fasted for four months as the big seals did every year, and his deep-sea swimming-trips kept him in perfect condition, and, best of all, he had never fought before. His curly white mane stood up with rage, and his eyes flamed, and his big dogteeth glistened, and he was splendid to look at.

Old Sea Catch, his father, saw him tearing past, hauling the grizzled old seals about as though they had been halibut, and upsetting the young bachelors in all directions; and Sea Catch gave one roar and shouted: "He may be a fool, but he is the best fighter on the Beaches. Don't tackle your father, my son! He's with you!"

Kotick roared in answer, and old Sea Catch waddled in, his mustache on end, blowing like a locomotive, while Matkah and the seal that was going to marry Kotick cowered down and admired their men-folk. It was a gorgeous fight, for the two fought as long as there was a seal that dared lift up his head, and then they paraded grandly up and down the beach side by side, bellowing.

At night, just as the Northern Lights were winking and flashing through the fog, Kotick climbed a bare rock and looked down on the scattered nurseries and the torn and bleeding seals. "Now," he said, "I've taught you your lesson."

"My wig!" said old Sea Catch, boosting himself up stiffly, for he was fearfully mauled. "The Killer Whale himself could not have cut them up worse. Son, I'm proud of you, and what's more, *I'll* come with you to your island–if there is such a place."

"Hear you, fat pigs of the sea! Who comes with me to the Sea Cow's tunnel? Answer, or I shall teach you again," roared Kotick.

There was a murmur like the ripple of the tide all up and down the beaches. "We will come," said thousands of tired voices. "We will follow Kotick, the White Seal."

Then Kotick dropped his head between his shoulders and shut his eyes proudly. He was not a white seal any more, but red from head to tail. All the same he would have scorned to look at or touch one of his wounds.

A week later he and his army (nearly ten thousand holluschickie and old seals) went away north to the Sea Cow's tunnel, Kotick leading them, and the seals that stayed at Novastoshnah called them idiots. But next spring when they all met off the fishing-banks of the Pacific, Kotick's seals told such tales of the new beaches beyond Sea Cow's tunnel that more and more seals left Novastoshnah.

Of course it was not all done at once, for the seals need a long time to turn things over in their minds, but year by year more seals went away from Novastoshnah, and Lukannon, and the other nurseries, to the quiet, sheltered beaches where Kotick sits all the summer through, getting bigger and fatter and stronger each year, while the holluschickie play round him, in that sea where no man comes.

Lukannon

This is the great deep-sea song that all the St. Paul seals sing when they are heading back to their beaches in the summer. It is a sort of very sad seal National Anthem.

I met my mates in the morning (and oh, but I am old!)
Where roaring on the ledges the summer ground-swell rolled;
I heard them lift the chorus that dropped the breakers' song—
The beaches of Lukannon—two million voices strong!

The song of pleasant stations beside the salt lagoons,
The song of blowing squadrons that shuffled down the dunes,
The song of midnight dances that churned the sea to flame—
The beaches of Lukannon—before the scalers came!

I met my mates in the morning (I'll never meet them more!);
They came and went in legions that darkened all the shore.
And through the floam-flecked offing as far as voice could reach
We hailed the landing-parties and we sang them up the beach.

The beaches of Lukannon—the winter-wheat so tall—
The dripping, crinkled lichens, and the sea-fog drenching all!
The platforms of our playground, all shining smooth and worn!
The beaches of Lukannon—the home where we were born!

I meet my mates in the morning, a broken, scattered band.
Men shoot us in the water and club us on the land;
Men drive us to the Salt House like silly sheep and tame,
And still we sing Lukannon—before the sealers came.

Wheel down, wheel down to southward; oh, Gooverooska go!
And tell the Deep-Sea Viceroys the story of our woe;
Ere, empty as the shark's egg tempest flings ashore,
The beaches of Lukannon shall know their sons no more!

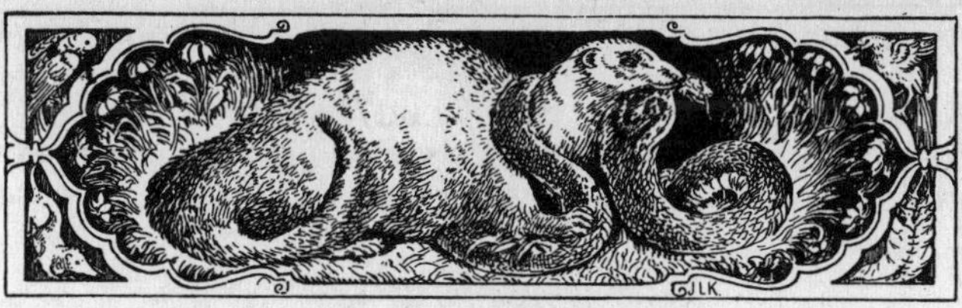

"Rikki-tikki-tavi"

At the hole where he went in
Red-Eye called to Wrinkle-Skin.
Hear what little Red-Eye saith:
"Nag, come up and dance with death!"

Eye to eye and head to head,
(Keep the measure, Nag.)
This shall end when one is dead;
(At thy pleasure, Nag.)
Turn for turn and twist for twist—
(Run and hide thee, Nag.)
Hah! The hooded Death has missed
(Woe betide thee, Nag!)

THIS IS THE story of the great war that Rikki-tikki-tavi fought single-handed, through the bath-rooms of the big bungalow in Segowlee cantonment. Darzee, the tailor-bird, helped him, and Chuchundra, the muskrat, who never comes out into the middle of the floor, but always creeps round by the wall, gave him advice; but Rikki-tikki did the real fighting.

He was a mongoose, rather like a little cat in his fur and his tail, but quite like a weasel in his head and his habits. His eyes and the end of his restless nose were pink; he could scratch himself anywhere he pleased, with any leg, front or back, that he chose to use; he could fluff up his tail till it looked like a bottle-brush, and his war-cry as he scuttled through the long grass, was: *"Rikk-tikk-tikki-tikki-tchk!"*

One day, a high summer flood washed him out of the burrow where he lived with his father and mother, and carried him, kicking and clucking, down a roadside ditch. He found a little wisp of grass floating there, and clung to it till he lost his senses. When he revived, he was lying in the hot sun on the middle of a garden path, very draggled indeed, and a small boy was saying: "Here's a dead mongoose. Let's have a funeral."

"No," said his mother; "let's take him in and dry him. Perhaps he isn't really dead."

They took him into the house, and a big man picked him up between his finger and thumb and said he was not dead but half choked; so they wrapped him in cotton-wool, and warmed him, and he opened his eyes and sneezed.

"Now," said the big man (he was an Englishman who had just moved into the bungalow); "don't frighten him, and we'll see what he'll do."

It is the hardest thing in the world to frighten a mongoose, because he is eaten up from nose to tail with curiosity. The motto of all the mongoose family is, "Run and find out"; and Rikki-tikki was a true mongoose. He looked at the cotton-wool, decided that it was not good to eat, ran all round the table, sat up and put his fur in order, scratched himself, and jumped on the small boy's shoulder.

"Don't be frightened, Teddy," said his father. "That's his way of making friends."

"Ouch! He's tickling under my chin," said Teddy.

Rikki-tikki looked down between the boy's collar and neck, snuffed at his ear, and climbed down to the floor, where he sat rubbing his nose.

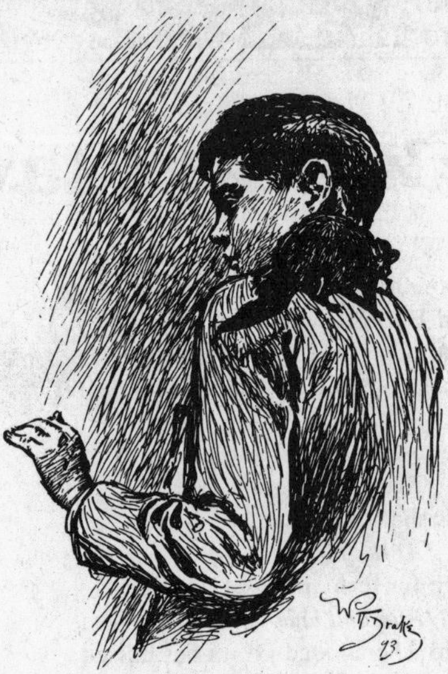

"RIKKI-TIKKI LOOKED DOWN BETWEEN THE BOY'S COLLAR AND NECK."

"Good gracious," said Teddy's mother, "and that's a wild creature! I suppose he's so tame because we've been kind to him."

"All mongooses are like that," said her husband. "If Teddy doesn't pick him up by the tail, or try to put him in a cage, he'll run in and out of the house all day long. Let's give him something to eat."

They gave him a little piece of raw meat. Rikki-tikki liked it immensely, and when it was finished he went out into the veranda and sat in the sunshine and fluffed up his fur to make it dry to the roots. Then he felt better.

"There are more things to find out about in this house," he said to himself,

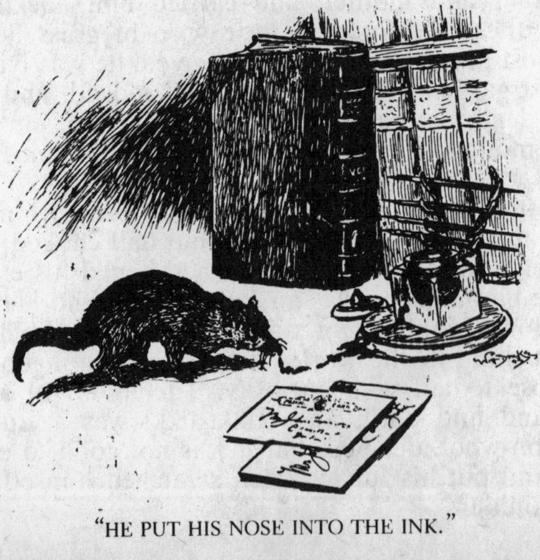

"HE PUT HIS NOSE INTO THE INK."

"than all my family could find out in all their lives. I shall certainly stay and find out."

He spent all that day roaming over the house. He nearly drowned himself in the bath-tubs, put his nose into the ink on a writing-table, and burned it on the end of the big man's cigar, for he climbed up in the big man's lap to see how writing was done. At nightfall he ran into Teddy's nursery to watch how kerosene lamps were lighted, and when Teddy went to bed Rikki-tikki climbed up too; but he was a restless companion, because he had to get up and attend to every noise all through the night, and find out what made it. Teddy's mother and father came in, the last thing, to look at their boy, and Rikki-tikki was awake on the pillow. "I din't like that," said Teddy's mother; "he may bite the child." "He'll do no such thing," said the father. "Teddy's

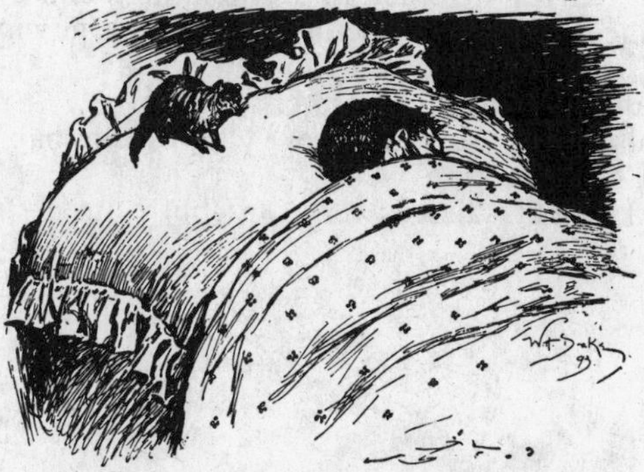

"RIKKI-TIKKI WAS AWAKE ON THE PILLOW."

safer with that little beast than if he had a bloodhound to watch him. If a snake came into the nursery now–"

But Teddy's mother wouldn't think of anything so awful.

Early in the morning Rikki-tikki came to early breakfast in the veranda riding on Teddy's shoulder, and they gave him banana and some boiled egg; and he sat on all their laps one after the other, because every well-brought-up

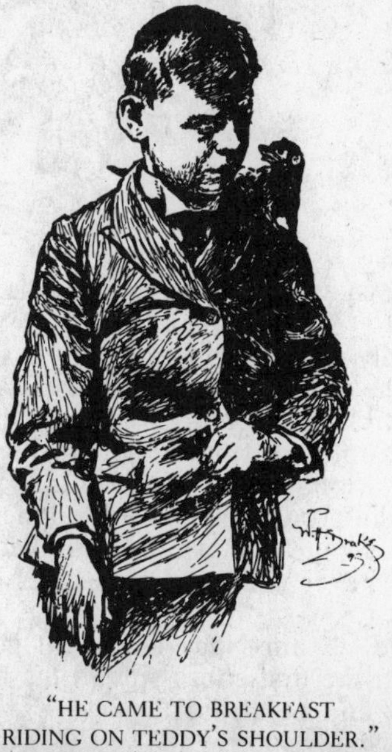

"HE CAME TO BREAKFAST
RIDING ON TEDDY'S SHOULDER."

mongoose always hopes to be a house-mongoose some day and have rooms to run about in, and Rikki-tikki's mother (she used to live in the General's house at Segowlee) had carefully told Rikki what to do if ever he came across white men.

Then Rikki-tikki went out into the garden to see what was to be seen. It was a large garden, only half cultivated, with bushes as big as summer-houses of Marshal Niel roses, lime and orange trees, clumps of bamboos, and thickets of high grass. Rikki-tikki licked his lips. "This is a splendid hunting-ground," he said, and his tail grew bottle-bushy at the thought of it, and he scuttled up and down the garden, snuffing here and there till he heard very sorrowful voices in a thorn-bush.

It was Darzee, the tailor-bird, and his wife. They had made a beautiful nest by pulling two big leaves together and stitching them up the edges with fibers, and had filled the hollow with cotton and downy fluff. The nest swayed to and fro, as they sat on the rim and cried.

"What is the matter?" asked Rikki-tikki.

"We are very miserable," said Darzee. "One of our babies fell out of the nest yesterday and Nag ate him."

"H'm!" said Rikki-Tikki, "that is very sad—but I am a stranger here. Who is Nag?"

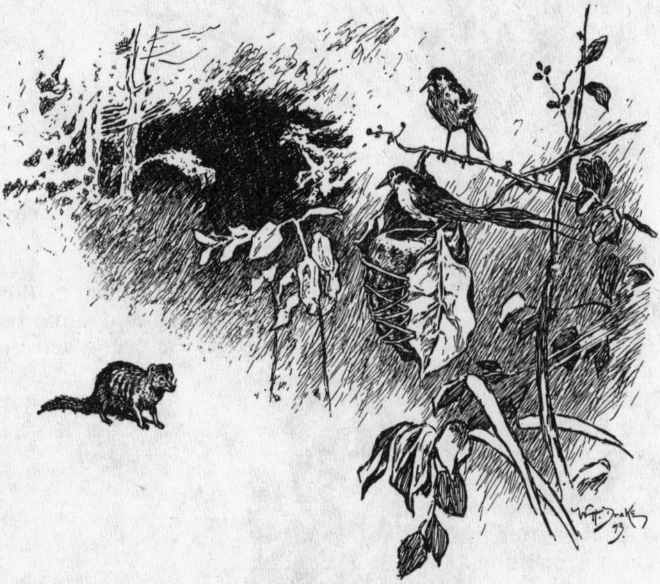

"'WE ARE VERY MISERABLE,' SAID DARZEE."

Darzee and his wife only cowered down in the nest without answering, for from the thick grass at the foot of the bush there came a low hiss—a horrid cold sound that made Rikki-tikki jump back two clear feet. Then inch by inch out of the grass rose up the head and spread hood of Nag, the big black cobra, and he was five feet long from tongue to tail. When he had lifted one-third of himself clear of the ground, he stayed balancing to and fro exactly as a dandelion-tuft balances in the wind, and he looked at Rikki-tikki with the wicked snake's eyes that never change their expression, whatever the snake may be thinking of.

"Who is Nag?" he said. "*I* am Nag. The great god Brahm put his mark upon all our people when the first cobra spread his hood to keep the sun off Brahm as he slept. Look, and be afraid!"

He spread out his hood more than ever, and Rikki-tikki saw the spectacle-mark on the back of it that looks exactly like the eye part of a hook-and-eye fastening. He was afraid for the minute; but it is impossible for a mongoose to stay frightened for any length of time, and though Rikki-tikki had never met a live cobra before, his mother had fed him on dead ones, and he knew that all a grown mongoose's business in life was to fight and eat snakes. Nag knew that too, and at the bottom of his cold heart he was afraid.

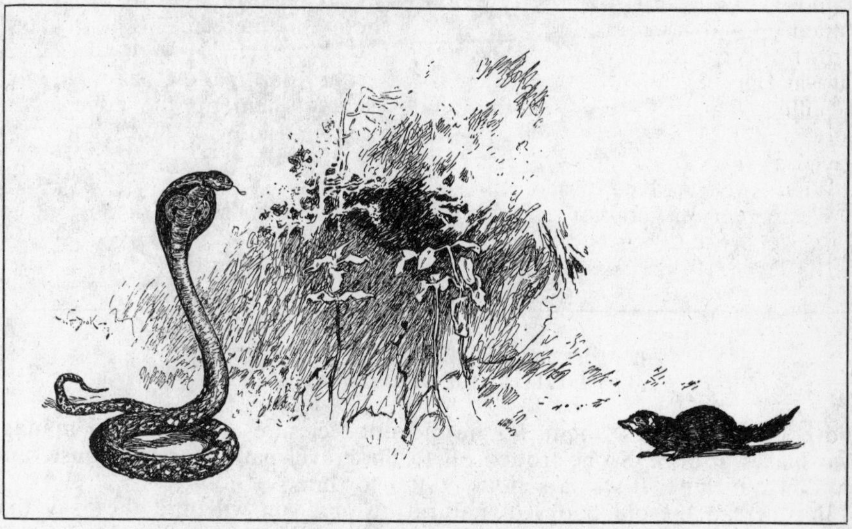

"'I AM NAG,' SAID THE COBRA. 'LOOK AND BE AFRAID.'"

"Well," said Rikki-tikki, and his tail began to fluff up again, "marks or no marks, do you think it is right for you to eat fledglings out of a nest?"

Nag was thinking to himself, and watching the least little movement in the grass behind Rikki-tikki. He knew that mongooses in the garden meant death sooner or later for him and his family; but he wanted to get Rikki-tikki off his guard. So he dropped his head a little, and put it on one side.

"Let us talk," he said. "You eat eggs. Why should not I eat birds?"

"Behind you! Look behind you!" sang Darzee.

Rikki-tikki knew better than to waste time in staring. He jumped up in the air as high as he could go, and just under him whizzed by the head of Nagaina, Nag's wicked wife. She had crept up behind him as he was talking, to make an end of him; and he heard her savage hiss as the stroke missed. He came down almost across her back, and if he had been an old mongoose he would have known that then was the time to break her back with one bite; but he was afraid of the terrible lashing return-stroke of the cobra. He bit, indeed, but did not bite long enough, and he jumped clear of the whisking tail, leaving Nagaina torn and angry.

"Wicked, wicked Darzee!" said Nag, lashing up as high as he could reach toward the nest in the thorn-bush; but Darzee had built it out of reach of snakes, and it only swayed to and fro.

Rikki-tikki felt his eyes growing red and hot (when a mongoose's eyes grow red, he is angry), and he sat back on his tail and hind legs like a little kangaroo, and looked all around him, and chattered with rage. But Nag and Nagaina had disappeared into the grass. When a snake misses its stroke, it never says anything or gives any sign of what it means to do next. Rikki-tikki

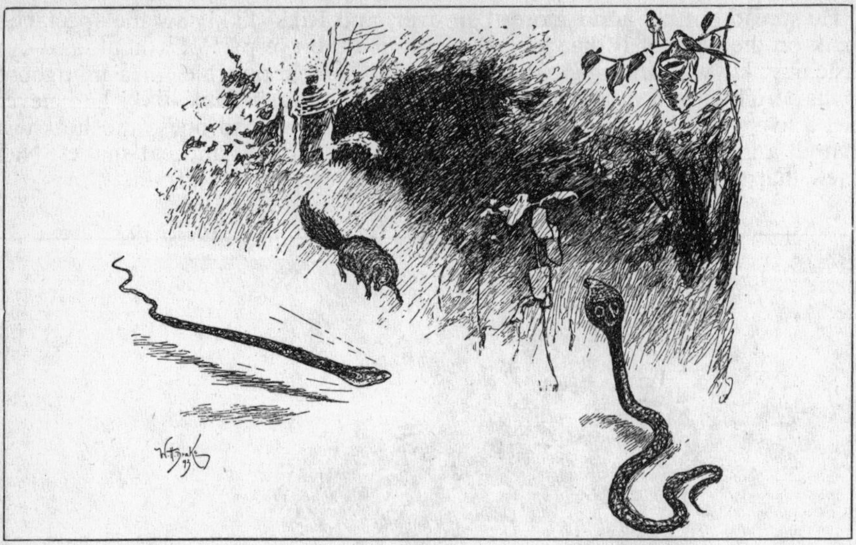

"HE JUMPED UP IN THE AIR, AND JUST UNDER HIM WHIZZED BY THE HEAD OF NAGAINA."

did not care to follow them, for he did not feel sure that he could manage two snakes at once. So he trotted off to the gravel path near the house, and sat down to think. It was a serious matter for him.

If you read the old books of natural history, you will find they say that when the mongoose fights the snake and happens to get bitten, he runs off and eats some herb that cures him. That is not true. The victory is only a matter of quickness of eye and quickness of foot,–snake's blow against mongoose's jump,–and as no eye can follow the motion of a snake's head when it strikes, that makes things much more wonderful than any magic herb. Rikki-tikki knew he was a young mongoose, and it made him all the more pleased to think that he had managed to escape a blow from behind. It gave him confidence in himself, and when Teddy came running down the path, Rikki-tikki was ready to be petted.

But just as Teddy was stooping, something flinched a little in the dust, and a tiny voice said: "Be careful. I am death!" It was Karait, the dusty brown snakeling that lies for choice on the dusty earth; and his bite is as dangerous as the cobra's. But he is so small that nobody thinks of him, and so he does the more harm to people.

Rikki-tikki's eyes grew red again, and he danced up to Karait with the peculiar rocking, swaying motion that he had inherited from his family. It looks very funny, but it is so perfectly balanced a gait that you can fly off from it at any angle you please; and in dealing with snakes this is an advantage. If Rikki-tikki had only known, he was doing a much more dangerous thing than fighting Nag, for Karait is so small, and can turn so quickly, that unless Rikki bit him close to the back of the head, he would get the return-stroke in his eye or lip. But Rikki did not know: his eyes were all red, and he rocked back and forth, looking for a good place to hold. Karait struck out. Rikki jumped sideways and tried to run in, but the wicked little dusty gray head lashed within a fraction of his shoulder, and he had to jump over the body, and the head followed his heels close.

Teddy shouted to the house: "Oh, look here! Our mongoose is killing a snake"; and Rikki-tikki heard a scream from Teddy's mother. His father ran out with a stick, but by the time he came up, Karait had lunged out once too far, and Rikki-tikki had sprung, jumped on the snake's back, dropped his head far between his fore legs, bitten as high up the back as he could get hold, and rolled away. That bite paralyzed Karait, and Rikki-tikki was just going to eat him from the tail, after the custom of his family at dinner, when he remembered that a full meal makes a slow mongoose, and if he wanted all his strength and quickness ready, he must keep himself thin.

He went away for a dust-bath under the castor-oil bushes, while Teddy's father beat the dead Karait. "What is the use of that?" thought Rikki-tikki. "I have settled it all"; and then Teddy's mother picked him up from the dust and hugged him, crying that he had saved Teddy from death, and Teddy's father said that he was a providence, and Teddy looked on with big scared eyes. Rikki-tikki was rather amused at all the fuss, which, of course, he did not understand. Teddy's mother might just as well have petted Teddy for playing in the dust. Rikki was thoroughly enjoying himself.

That night, at dinner, walking to and fro among the wine-glasses on the table, he could have stuffed himself three times over with nice things; but he remembered Nag and Nagaina, and though it was very pleasant to be patted and petted by Teddy's mother, and to sit on Teddy's shoulder, his eyes would get red from time to time, and he would go off into his long war-cry of "*Rikk-tikk-tikki-tikki-tchk!*"

Teddy carried him off to bed, and insisted on Rikki-tikki sleeping under his chin. Rikki-tikki was too well bred to bite or scratch, but as soon as Teddy was asleep he went off for his nightly walk around the house, and in the dark he ran up against Chuchundra, the muskrat, creeping round by the wall.

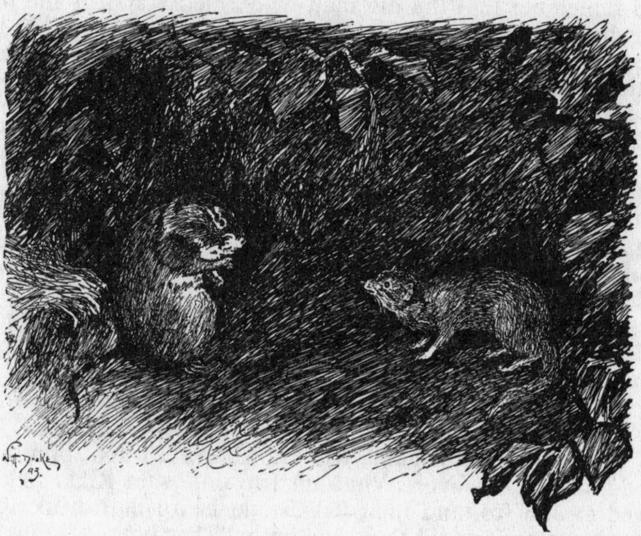

"IN THE DARK HE RAN UP AGAINST CHUCHUNDRA, THE MUSKRAT."

Chuchundra is a broken-hearted little beast. He whimpers and cheeps all the night, trying to make up his mind to run into the middle of the room, but he never gets there.

"Don't kill me," said Chuchundra, almost weeping. "Rikki-tikki, don't kill me."

"Do you think a snake-killer kills muskrats?" said Rikki-tikki scornfully.

"Those who kill snakes get killed by snakes," said Chuchundra, more sorrowfully than ever. "And how am I to be sure that Nag won't mistake me for you some dark night?"

"There's not the least danger," said Rikki-tikki; "but Nag is in the garden, and I know you don't go there."

"My cousin Chua, the rat, told me–" said Chuchundra, and then he stopped.

"Told you what?"

"H'sh! Nag is everywhere, Rikki-tikki. You should have talked to Chua in the garden."

"I didn't–so you must tell me. Quick, Chuchundra, or I'll bite you!"

Chuchundra sat down and cried till the tears rolled off his whiskers. "I am a very poor man," he sobbed. "I never had spirit enough to run out into the middle of the room. H'sh! I mustn't tell you anything. Can't you *hear,* Rikki-tikki?"

Rikki-tikki listened. The house was as still as still, but he thought he could just catch the faintest *scratch-scratch* in the world,–a noise as faint as that of a wasp walking on a window pane,–the dry scratch of a snake's scales on brickwork.

"That's Nag or Nagaina," he said to himself; "and he is crawling into the bath-room sluice. You're right, Chuchundra; I should have talked to Chua."

He stole off to Teddy's bath-room, but there was nothing there, and then to Teddy's mother's bath-room. At the bottom of the smooth plaster wall there was a brick pulled out to make a sluice for the bath-water, and as Rikki-tikki stole in by the masonry curb where the bath is put, he heard Nag and Nagaina whispering together outside in the moonlight.

"When the house is emptied of people," said Nagaina to her husband, "*he* will have to go away, and then the garden will be our own again. Go in quietly, and remember that the big man who killed Karait is the first one to bite. Then come out and tell me, and we will hunt for Rikki-tikki together."

"But are you sure that there is anything to be gained by killing the people?" said Nag.

"Everything. When there were no people in the bungalow, did we have any mongoose in the garden? So long as the bungalow is empty, we are king and queen of the garden; and remember that as soon as our eggs in the melon-bed hatch (as they may to-morrow), our children will need room and quiet."

"I had not thought of that," said Nag. "I will go, but there is no need that we should hunt for Rikki-tikki afterward. I will kill the big man and his wife; and the child if I can, and come away quietly. Then the bungalow will be empty, and Rikki-tikki will go."

Rikki-tikki tingled all over with rage and hatred at this, and then Nag's head came through the sluice, and his five feet of cold body followed it. Angry as he was, Rikki-tikki was very frightened as he saw the size of the big cobra. Nag coiled himself up, raised his head, and looked into the bath-room in the dark, and Rikki could see his eyes glitter.

"Now, if I kill him here, Nagaina will know; and if I fight him on the open floor, the odds are in his favor. What am I to do?" said Rikki-tikki-tavi.

Nag waved to and fro, and then Rikki-tikki heard him drinking from the biggest water-jar that was used to fill the bath. "That is good," said the snake. "Now, when Karait was killed, the big man had a stick. He may have that stick still, but when he comes in to bathe in the morning he will not have a stick. I shall wait here till he comes. Nagaina–do you hear me?–I shall wait here in the cool till daytime."

There was no answer from outside, so Rikki-tikki knew Nagaina had gone away. Nag coiled himself down, coil by coil, round the bulge at the bottom of the water-jar, and Rikki-tikki stayed still as death. After an hour he began to move, muscle by muscle, toward the jar. Nag was asleep, and Rikki-tikki looked at his big back, wondering which would be the best place for a good hold. "If I don't break his back at the first jump," said Rikki, "he can still fight; and if he fights–O Rikki!" He looked at the thickness of the neck below the hood, but that was too much for him; and a bite near the tail would only make Nag savage.

"It must be the head," he said at last; "the head above the hood; and, when I am once there, I must not let go."

Then he jumped. The head was lying a little clear of the water-jar, under the curve of it; and, as his teeth met, Rikki braced his back against the bulge of the red earthenware to hold down the head. This gave him just one second's purchase, and he made the most of it. Then he was battered to and fro as a rat is shaken by a dog–to and fro on the floor, up and down, and round in great circles; but his eyes were red, and he held on as the body cartwhipped over the floor, upsetting the tin dipper and the soap-dish and the fresh-brush, and banged against the tin side of the bath. As he held he closed his jaws tighter and tighter, for he made sure he would be banged to death, and, for the honor of his family, he preferred to be found with his teeth locked. He was dizzy, aching, and felt shaken to pieces when something went off like a thunderclap just behind him; a hot wind knocked him senseless and red fire singed his fur. The big man had been wakened by the noise, and had fired both barrels of a shot-gun into Nag just behind the hood.

Rikki-tikki held on with his eyes shut, for now he was quite sure he was dead; but the head did not move, and the big man picked him up and said: "It's the mongoose again, Alice; the little chap has saved *our* lives now." Then Teddy's mother came in with a very white face, and saw what was left of Nag, and Rikki-tikki dragged himself to Teddy's bedroom and spent half the rest of the night shaking himself tenderly to find out whether he really was broken into forty pieces, as he fancied.

When morning came he was very stiff, but well pleased with his doings. "Now I have Nagaina to settle with, and she will be worse than five Nags, and there's no knowing when the eggs she spoke of will hatch. Goodness! I must go and see Darzee," he said.

Without waiting for breakfast, Rikki-tikki ran to the thorn-bush where Darzee was singing a song of triumph at the top of his voice. The news of Nag's death was all over the garden, for the sweeper had thrown the body on the rubbish-heap.

"Oh, you stupid tuft of feathers!" said Rikki-tikki, angrily. "Is this the time to sing?"

"Nag is dead–is dead–is dead!" sang Darzee. "The valiant Rikki-tikki caught him by the head and held fast. The big man brought the bang-stick and Nag fell in two pieces! He will never eat my babies again."

"All that's true enough; but where's Nagaina?" said Rikki-tikki, looking carefully round him.

"Nagaina came to the bath-room sluice and called for Nag," Darzee went on; "and Nag came out on the end of a stick–the sweeper picked him up on the end of a stick and threw him upon the rubbish-heap. Let us sing about the great, the red-eyed Rikki-tikki!" and Darzee filled his throat and sang.

"If I could get up to your nest, I'd roll all your babies out!" said Rikki-tikki. "You don't know when to do the right thing at the right time. You're safe enough in your nest there, but it's war for me down here. Stop singing a minute, Darzee."

"For the great, the beautiful Rikki-tikki's sake I will stop," said Darzee. "What is it, O Killer of the terrible Nag!"

"Where is Nagaina, for the third time?"

"On the rubbish-heap by the stables, mourning for Nag. Great is Rikki-tikki with the white teeth."

"Bother my white teeth! Have you ever heard where she keeps her eggs?"

"In the melon-bed, on the end nearest the wall, where the sun strikes nearly all day. She had them there weeks ago."

"And you never thought it worth while to tell me? The end nearest the wall, you said?"

"Rikki-tikki, you are not going to eat her eggs?"

"Not eat exactly; no. Darzee, if you have a grain of sense you will fly off to the stables and pretend that your wing is broken, and let Nagaina chase you away to this bush. I must get to the melon-bed, and if I went there now she'd see me."

Darzee was a feather-brained little fellow who could never hold more than one idea at a time in his head; and just because he knew that Nagaina's children were born in eggs like his own, he didn't think at first that it was fair to kill them. But his wife was a sensible bird, and she knew that cobra's eggs meant young cobras later on; so she flew off from her nest, and left Darzee to keep the babies warm, and continue his song about the death of Nag. Darzee was very like a man in some ways.

She fluttered in front of Nagaina by the rubbish-heap, and cried out, "Oh, my wing is broken! The boy in the house threw a stone at me and broke it." Then she fluttered more desperately than ever.

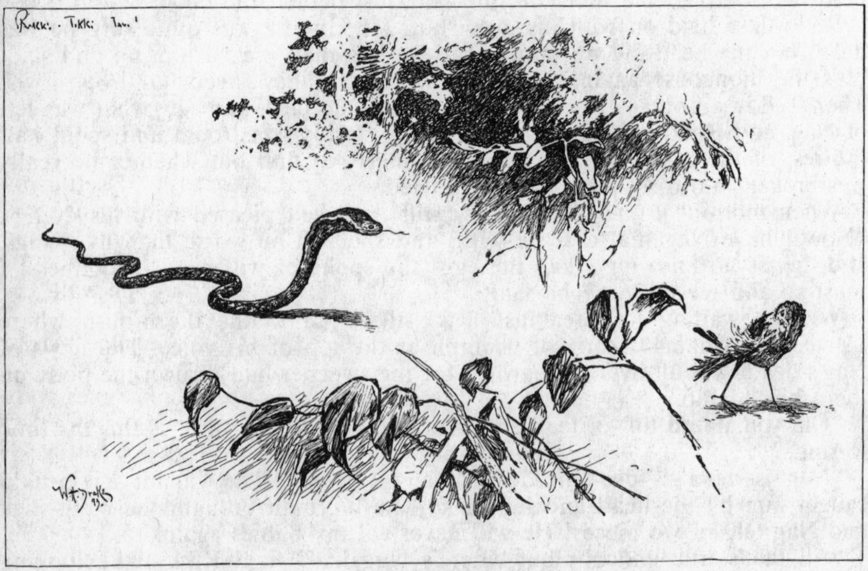

"DARZEE'S WIFE PRETENDS TO HAVE A BROKEN WING."

Nagaina lifted up her head and hissed, "You warned Rikki-tikki when I would have killed him. Indeed and truly, you've chosen a bad place to be lame in." And she moved toward Darzee's wife, slipping along over the dust.

"The boy broke it with a stone!" shrieked Darzee's wife.

"Well! It may be some consolation to you when you're dead to know that I shall settle accounts with the boy. My husband lies on the rubbish-heap this morning, but before night the boy in the house will lie very still. What is the use of running away? I am sure to catch you. Little fool, look at me!"

Darzee's wife knew better than to do *that,* for a bird who looks at a snake's eyes gets so frightened that she cannot move. Darzee's wife fluttered on, piping sorrowfully, and never leaving the ground, and Nagaina quickened her pace.

Rikki-tikki heard them going up the path from the stables, and he raced for the end of the melon-patch near the wall. There, in the warm litter about the melons, very cunningly hidden, he found twenty-five eggs, about the size of a bantam's eggs, but with whitish skin instead of shell.

"I was not a day too soon," he said; for he could see the baby cobras curled up inside the skin, and he knew that the minute they were hatched they could each kill a man or a mongoose. He bit off the tops of the eggs as fast as he could, taking care to crush the youhg cobras, and turned over the litter from time to time to see whether he had missed any. At last there were only three eggs left, and Rikki-tikki began to chuckle to himself, when he heard Darzee's wife screaming:

"Rikki-tikki, I led Nagaina toward the house, and she has gone into the veranda, and–oh, come quickly–she means killing!"

Rikki-tikki smashed two eggs, and tumbled backward down the melon-bed with the third egg in his mouth, and scuttled to the veranda as hard as he could put foot to the ground. Teddy and his mother and father were there at early breakfast; but Rikki-tikki saw that they were not eating anything. They sat stone-still, and their faces were white. Nagaina was coiled up on the matting by Teddy's chair, within easy striking distance of Teddy's bare leg, and she was swaying to and fro singing a song of triumph.

"Son of the big man that killed Nag," she hissed, "stay still. I am not ready yet. Wait a little. Keep very still, all you three. If you move I strike, and if you do not move I strike. Oh, foolish people, who killed my Nag!"

Teddy's eyes were fixed on his father, and all his father could do was to whisper, "Sit still, Teddy. You mustn't move. Teddy, keep still."

Then Rikki-tikki came up and cried: "Turn round, Nagaina; turn and fight!"

"All in good time," said she, without moving her eyes. "I will settle my account with *you* presently. Look at your friends, Rikki-tikki. They are still and white; they are afraid. They dare not move, and if you come a step nearer I strike."

"Look at your eggs," said Rikki-tikki, "in the melon-bed near the wall. Go and look, Nagaina."

The big snake turned half around, and saw the egg on the veranda. "Ah-h! Give it to me," she said.

Rikki-tikki put his paws one on each side of the egg, and his eyes were blood-red. "What price for a snake's egg? For a young cobra? For a young king-cobra? For the last–the very last of the brood? The ants are eating all the others down by the melon-bed."

Nagaina spun clear around, forgetting everything for the sake of the one egg; and Rikki-tikki saw Teddy's father shoot out a big hand, catch Teddy by the shoulder, and drag him across the little table with the tea-cups, safe and out of reach of Nagaina.

"Tricked! Tricked! Tricked! *Rikk-tck-tck!*" chuckled Rikki-tikki. "The boy is safe, and it was I–I–I that caught Nag by the hood last night in the bathroom." Then he began to jump up and down, all four feet together, his head close to the floor. "He threw me to and fro, but he could not shake me off. He was dead before the big man blew him in two. I did it. *Rikki-tikki-tck-tck!* Come then, Nagaina. Come and fight with me. You shall not be a widow long."

Nagaina saw that she had lost her chance of killing Teddy, and the egg lay between Rikki-tikki's paws. "Give me the egg, Rikki-tikki. Give me the last of my eggs, and I will go away and never come back," she said, lowering her hood.

"Yes, you will go away, and you will never come back; for you will go to the rubbish-heap with Nag. Fight, widow! The big man has gone for his gun! Fight!"

Rikki-tikki was bounding all round Nagaina, keeping just out of reach of her stroke, his little eyes like hot coals. Nagaina gathered herself together, and flung out at him. Rikki-tikki jumped up and backward. Again and again and again she struck, and each time her head came with a whack on the matting of the veranda and she gathered herself together like a watch-spring. Then Rikki-tikki danced in a circle to get behind her, and Nagaina spun round to keep her head to his head, so that the rustle of her tail on the matting sounded like dry leaves blown along by the wind.

He had forgotten the egg. It still lay on the veranda, and Nagaina came nearer and nearer to it, till at last, while Rikki-tikki was drawing breath, she caught it in her mouth, turned to the veranda steps, and flew like an arrow down the path, with Rikki-tikki behind her. When the cobra runs for her life, she goes like a whiplash flicked across a horse's neck.

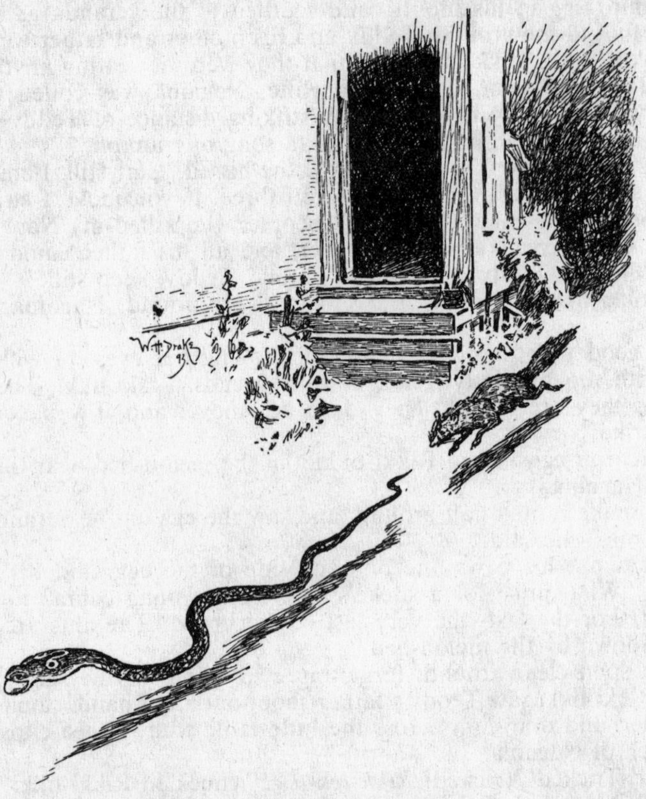

"NAGAINA FLEW DOWN THE PATH, WITH RIKKI-TIKKI BEHIND HER."

Rikki-tikki knew that he must catch her, or all the trouble would begin again. She headed straight for the long grass by the thorn-bush, and as he was running Rikki-tikki heard Darzee still singing his foolish little song of triumph. But Darzee's wife was wiser. She flew off her nest as Nagaina came along, and flapped her wings about Nagaina's head. If Darzee had helped they might have turned her; but Nagaina only lowered her hood and went on. Still, the instant's delay brought Rikki-tikki up to her, and as she plunged into the rat-hole where she and Nag used to live, his little teeth were clenched on her tail, and he went down with her–and very few mongooses, however wise and old they may be, care to follow a cobra into its hole. It was dark in the hole; and Rikki-tikki never knew when it might open out and give Nagaina room to turn and strike at him. He held on savagely, and struck out his feet to act as brakes on the dark slope of the hot, moist earth.

Then the grass by the mouth of the hole stopped waving, and Darzee said: "It is all over with Rikki-tikki! We must sing his death-song. Valiant Rikki-tikki is dead! For Nagaina will surely kill him underground."

So he sang a very mournful song that he made up all on the spur of the minute, and just as he got to the most touching part the grass quivered again, and Rikki-tikki, covered with dirt, dragged himself out of the hole leg by leg, licking his whiskers. Darzee stopped with a little shout. Rikki-tikki shook some of the dust out of his fur and sneezed. "It is all over," he said. "The widow will never come out again." And the red ants that live between the grass stems heard him, and began to troop down one after another to see if he had spoken the truth.

Rikki-tikki curled himself up in the grass and slept where he was–slept and slept till it was late in the afternoon, for he had done a hard day's work.

"Now," he said, when he awoke, "I will go back to the house. Tell the Coppersmith, Darzee, and he will tell the garden that Nagaina is dead."

The Coppersmith is a bird who makes a noise exactly like the beating of a little hammer on a copper pot; and the reason he is always making it is because he is the town-crier to every Indian garden, and tells all the news to everybody who cares to listen. As Rikki-tikki went up the path, he heard his "attention" notes like a tiny dinner-gong; and then the steady *"Ding-dong-tock!* Nag is dead–*dong!* Nagaina is dead! *Ding-dong-tock!"* That set all the birds in the garden singing, and the frogs croaking; for Nag and Nagaina used to eat frogs as well as little birds.

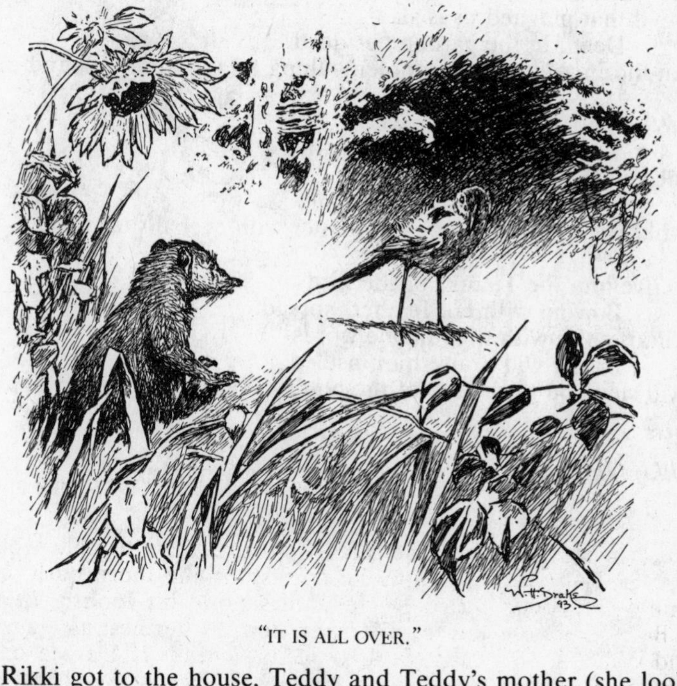

"IT IS ALL OVER."

When Rikki got to the house, Teddy and Teddy's mother (she looked very white still, for she had been fainting) and Teddy's father came out and almost cried over him; and that night he ate all that was given him till he could eat no more, and went to bed on Teddy's shoulder, where Teddy's mother saw him when she came to look late at night.

"He saved our lives and Teddy's life," she said to her husband. "Just think, he saved all our lives."

Rikki-tikki woke up with a jump, for all the mongooses are light sleepers.

"Oh, it's you," said he. "What are you bothering for? All the cobras are dead; and if they weren't, I'm here."

Rikki-tikki had a right to be proud of himself; but he did not grow too proud, and he kept that garden as a mongoose should keep it, with tooth and jump and spring, and bite, till never a cobra dared show its head inside the walls.

Darzee's Chaunt

(Sung in Honor of Rikki-Tikki-Tavi)

Singer and tailor am I—
    Doubled the joys that I know—
Proud of my lilt through the sky,
    Proud of the house that I sew—
Over and under, so weave I my music—so weave I the house that I sew.

Sing to your fledglings again
    Mother, oh lift up your head!
Evil that plagued us is slain,
    Death in the garden lies dead.
Terror that hid in the roses is impotent—flung on the dung-hill and dead!

Who hath delivered us, who?
    Tell me his nest and his name.
Rikki, the valiant, the true,
    Tikki, with eyeballs of flame.
Rik-tikki-tikki, the ivory-fanged, the hunter with eyeballs of flame.

Give him the Thanks of the Birds,
    Bowing with tail-feathers spread!
Praise him with nightingale words—
    Nay, I will praise him instead.
Hear! I will sing you the praise of the bottle-tailed Rikki, with eyeballs of red!

(Here Rikki-tikki interrupted, and the rest of the song is lost.)

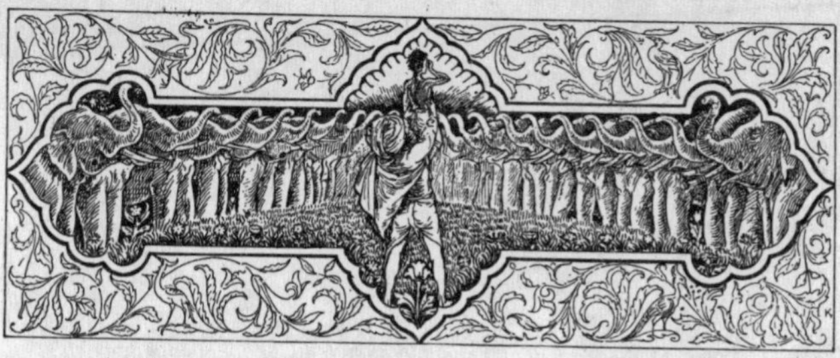

Toomai of the Elephants

I will remember what I was, I am sick of rope and chain—
  I will remember my old strength and all my forest affairs.
I will not sell my back to man for a bundle of sugar-cane,
  I will go out to my own kind, and the wood-folk in their lairs.

I will go out until the day, until the morning break,
  Out to the winds' untainted kiss, the waters' clean caress;
I will forget my ankle-ring and snap my picket-stake.
  I will revisit my lost loves, and playmates masterless!

KALA NAG, WHICH means Black Snake, had served the Indian Government in every way that an elephant could serve it for forty-seven years, and as he was fully twenty years old when he was caught, that makes him nearly seventy—a ripe age for an elephant. He remembered pushing; with a big leather pad on his forehead, at a gun stuck in deep mud, and that was before the Afghan war of 1842, and he had not then come to his full strength. His mother, Radha Pyari,—Radha the darling,—who had been caught in the same drive with Kala Nag, told him, before his little milk tusks had dropped out, that elephants who were afraid always got hurt: and Kala Nag knew that that advice was good, for the first time that he saw a shell burst he backed, screaming, into a stand of piled rifles, and the bayonets pricked him in all his softest places. So, before he was twenty-five, he gave up being afraid, and so he was the best-loved and the best-looked-after elephant in the service of the Government of India. He had carried tents, twelve hundred pounds' weight of tents, on the march in Upper India: he had been hoisted into a ship at the end of a steam-crane and taken for days across the water, and made to carry a mortar on his back in a strange and rocky country very far from India, and had seen the Emperor Theodore lying dead in Magdala, and had come back again in the steamer entitled, so the soldiers said, to the Abyssinian war medal. He had seen his fellow-elephants die of cold and epilepsy and starvation and sunstroke up at a place called Ali Musjid, ten years later; and afterward he had been sent down thousands of miles south to haul and pile big baulks of teak in the timber-yards at Moulmein. There he had half killed an insubordinate young elephant who was shirking his fair share of the work.

After that he was taken off timber-hauling, and employed, with a few score other elephants who were trained to the business, in helping to catch wild elephants among the Garo hills. Elephants are very strictly preserved by the Indian Government. There is one whole department which does nothing else but hunt them, and catch them, and break them in, and send them up and down the country as they are needed for work.

Kala Nag stood ten fair feet at the shoulders, and his tusks had been cut

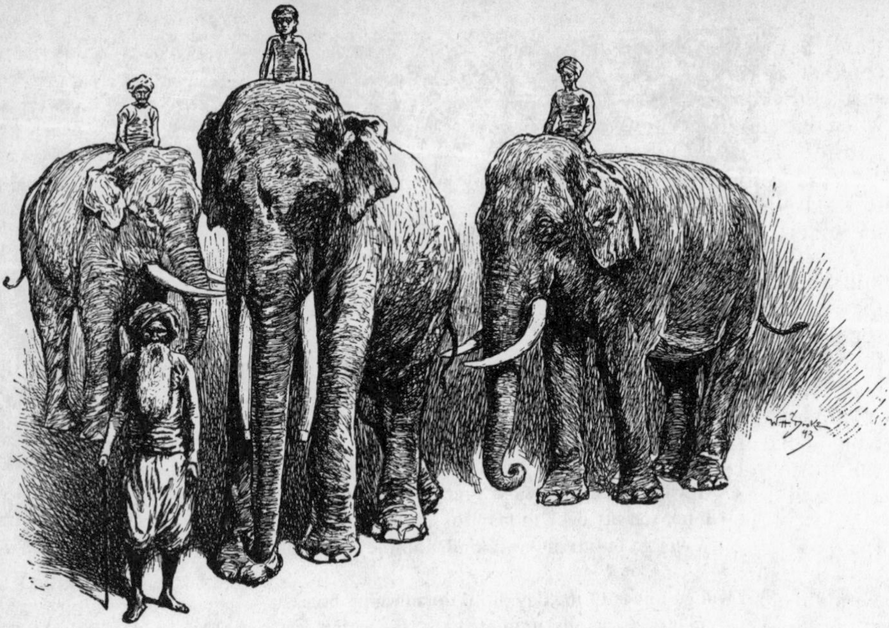

"KALA NAG WAS THE BEST-LOVED ELEPHANT IN THE SERVICE."

off short at five feet, and bound round the ends, to prevent them splitting, with bands of copper; but he could do more with those stumps than any untrained elephant could do with the real sharpened ones.

When, after weeks and weeks of cautious driving of scattered elephants across the hills, the forty or fifty wild monsters were driven into the last stockade, and the big drop-gate, made of tree-trunks lashed together, jarred down behind them, Kala Nag, at the word of command, would go into that flaring, trumpeting pandemonium (generally at night, when the flicker of the torches made it difficult to judge distances), and, picking out the biggest and wildest tusker of the mob, would hammer him and hustle him into quiet while the men on the backs of the other elephants roped and tied the smaller ones.

There was nothing in the way of fighting that Kala Nag, the old wise Black Snake, did not know, for he had stood up more than once in his time to the charge of the wounded tiger, and, curling up his soft trunk to be out of harm's way, had knocked the springing brute sideways in mid-air with a quick sickle-cut of his head, that he had invented all by himself; and knocked him over, and kneeled upon him with his huge knees till the life went out with a gasp and a howl, and there was only a fluffy striped thing on the ground for Kala Nag to pull by the tail.

"Yes," said Big Toomai, his driver, the son of Black Toomai who had taken him to Abyssinia, and grandson of Toomai of the Elephants who had seen him caught, "there is nothing that the Black Snake fears except me. He has seen three generations of us feed him and groom him, and he will live to see four."

"He is afraid of *me* also," said Little Toomai, standing up to his full height of four feet, with only one rag upon him. He was ten years old, the eldest son of Big Toomai, and, according to custom, he would take his father's place on Kala Nag's neck when he grew up, and would handle the heavy iron *ankus,* the elephant-goad that had been worn smooth by his father, and his grandfather, and his great-grandfather. He knew what he was talking of; for he had been born under Kala Nag's shadow, had played with the end of his trunk before he could walk, had taken him down to water as soon as he could walk, and Kala Nag would no more have dreamed of disobeying his shrill little orders than he would have dreamed of killing him on that day when Big Toomai carried the little brown baby under Kala Nag's tusks, and told him to salute his master that was to be.

"Yes," said Little Toomai, "he is afraid of *me,"* and he took long strides up to Kala Nag, called him a fat old pig, and made him lift up his feet one after the other.

"Wah!" said Little Toomai, "thou art a big elephant," and he wagged his fluffy head, quoting his father. "The Government may pay for elephants, but they belong to us mahouts. When thou art old, Kala Nag, there will come some rich Rajah, and he will buy thee from the Government, on account of thy size and thy manners, and then thou wilt have nothing to do but to carry gold earrings in thy ears, and a gold howdah on thy back, and a red cloth covered with gold on thy sides, and walk at the head of the processions of the King. Then I shall sit on thy neck, O Kala Nag, with a silver *ankus,* and men will run before us with golden sticks, crying, 'Room for the King's elephant!' That will be good, Kala Nag, but not so good as this hunting in the jungles."

"Umph!" said Big Toomai. "Thou art a boy, and as wild as a buffalo-calf. This running up and down among the hills is not the best Government service. I am getting old, and I do not love wild elephants. Give me brick elephant-lines, one stall to each elephant, and big stumps to tie them to safely, and flat, broad roads to exercise upon, instead of this come-and-go camping. Aha, the Cawnpore barracks were good. There was a bazaar close by, and only three hours' work a day."

Little Toomai remembered the Cawnpore elephant-lines and said nothing. He very much preferred the camp life, and hated those broad, flat roads, with the daily grubbing for grass in the forage-reserve, and the long hours when

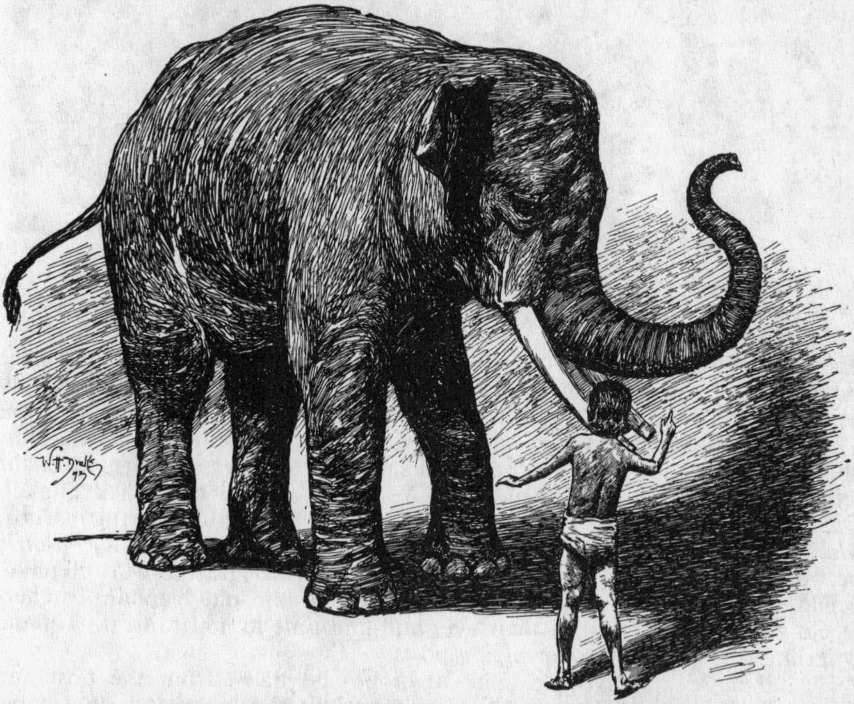

"'HE IS AFRAID OF ME,' SAID LITTLE TOOMAI, AND HE MADE KALA NAG LIFT UP HIS FEET ONE AFTER THE OTHER."

there was nothing to do except to watch Kala Nag fidgeting in his pickets.

What Little Toomai liked was to scramble up bridle-paths that only an elephant could take; the dip into the valley below; the glimpses of the wild elephants browsing miles away; the rush of the frightened pig and peacock under Kala Nag's feet; the blinding warm rains, when all the hills and valleys smoked; the beautiful misty mornings when nobody knew where they would camp that night; the steady, cautious drive of the wild elephants, and the mad rush and blaze and hullaballoo of the last night's drive, when the elephants poured into the stockade like boulders in a landslide, found that they could not get out, and flung themselves at the heavy posts only to be driven back by yells and flaring torches and volleys of blank cartridge.

Even a little boy could be of use there, and Toomai was as useful as three boys. He would get his torch and wave it, and yell with the best. But the really good time came when the driving out began, and the Keddah, that is, the stockade, looked like a picture of the end of the world, and men had to make signs to one another, because they could not hear themselves speak.

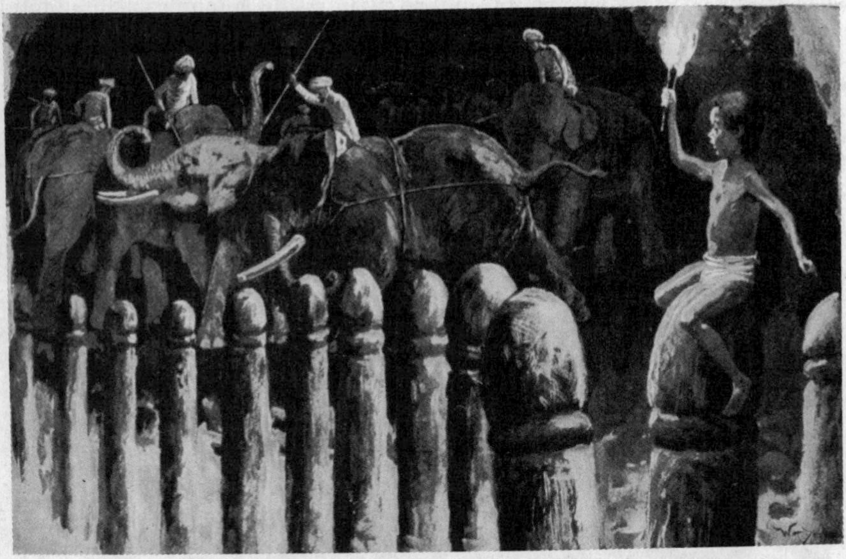

"HE WOULD GET HIS TORCH AND WAVE IT, AND YELL WITH THE BEST."

Then Little Toomai would climb up to the top of one of the quivering stockade-posts, his sun-bleached brown hair flying loose all over his shoulders, and he looking like a goblin in the torch-light; and as soon as there was a lull you could hear his high-pitched yells of encouragement to Kala Nag, above the trumpeting and crashing, and snapping of ropes, and groans of the tethered elephants. *"Maîl, maîl, Kala Nag!* (Go on, go on, Black Snake!) *Dant do!* (Give him the tusk!) *Somalo! Somalo!* (Careful, careful!) *Maro! Mar!* (Hit him, hit him!) Mind the post! *Arre! Arre! Hai! Yai! Kya-a-ah!"* he would shout, and the big fight between Kala Nag and the wild elephant would sway to and fro across the Keddah, and the old elephant-catchers would wipe the sweat out of their eyes and find time to nod to Little Toomai wriggling with joy on the top of the posts.

He did more than wriggle. One night he slid down from the post and slipped in between the elephants, and threw up the loose end of a rope, which had dropped, to a driver who was trying to get a purchase on the leg of a kicking young calf (calves always give more trouble than full-grown animals). Kala Nag saw him, caught him in his trunk, and handed him up to Big Toomai, who slapped him then and there, and put him back on the post.

Next morning he gave him a scolding, and said: "Are not good brick elephant-lines and a little tent-carrying enough, that thou must needs go elephant-catching on thy own account, little worthless? Now those foolish hunters, whose pay is less than my pay, have spoken to Petersen Sahib of the matter." Little Toomai was frightened. He did not know much of white men, but Petersen Sahib was the greatest white man in the world to him. He was the head of all the Keddah operations—the man who caught all the elephants for the Government of India, and who knew more about the ways of elephants than any living man.

"What—what will happen?" said Little Toomai.

"Happen! the worst that can happen. Petersen Sahib is a madman. Else why should he go hunting these wild devils? He may even require thee to be an elephant-catcher, to sleep anywhere in these fever-filled jungles, and at last to be trampled to death in the Keddah. It is well that this nonsense ends safely. Next week the catching is over, and we of the plains are sent back to our stations. Then we will march on smooth roads, and forget all this hunting. But, son, I am angry that thou shouldst meddle in the business that belongs to these dirty Assamese jungle-folk. Kala Nag will obey none but me, so I must go with him into the Keddah, but he is only a fighting elephant, and he does not help to rope them. So I sit at my ease, as befits a mahout,—not a mere hunter,—a mahout, I say, and a man who gets a pension at the end of his service. Is the family of Toomai of the Elephants to be trodden underfoot in the dirt of a Keddah? Bad one! Wicked one! Worthless son! Go and wash Kala Nag and attend to his ears, and see that there are no thorns in his feet; or else Petersen Sahib will surely catch thee and make thee a wild hunter—a follower of elephant's foot-tracks, a jungle-bear. Bah! Shame! Go!"

Little Toomai went off without saying a word, but he told Kala Nag all his grievances while he was examining his feet. "No matter," said Little Toomai, turning up the fringe of Kala Nag's huge right ear. "They have said my name to Petersen Sahib, and perhaps—and perhaps—and perhaps—who knows? Hai! That is a big thorn that I have pulled out!"

The next few days were spent in getting the elephants together, in walking the newly caught wild elephants up and down between a couple of tame ones, to prevent them from giving too much trouble on the downward march to the plains, and in taking stock of the blankets and ropes and things that had been worn out or lost in the forest.

Petersen Sahib came in on his clever she-elephant Pudmini; he had been paying off other camps among the hills, for the season was coming to an end, and there was a native clerk sitting at a table under a tree, to pay the drivers their wages. As each man was paid he went back to his elephant, and joined the line that stood ready to start. The catchers, and hunters, and beaters, the men of the regular Keddah, who stayed in the jungle year in and year out, sat on the backs of the elephants that belonged to Petersen Sahib's permanent force, or leaned against the trees with their guns across their arms, and made fun of the drivers who were going away, and laughed when the newly caught elephants broke the line and ran about.

Big Toomai went up to the clerk with Little Toomai behind him, and Machua Appa, the head-tracker, said in an undertone to a friend of his, "There goes one piece of good elephant-stuff at least. 'Tis a pity to send that young jungle-cock to moult in the plains."

Now Petersen Sahib had ears all over him, as a man must have who listens to the most silent of all living things—the wild elephant. He turned where he was lying all along on Pudmini's back, and said, "What is that? I did not know of a man among the plain-drivers who had wit enough to rope even a dead elephant."

"This is not a man, but a boy. He went into the Keddah at the last drive, and threw Barmao there the rope, when we were trying to get that young calf with the blotch on his shoulder away from his mother."

Machua Appa pointed at Little Toomai, and Petersen Sahib looked, and Little Toomai bowed to the earth.

"He throw a rope? He is smaller than a picket-pin. Little one, what is thy name?" said Petersen Sahib.

Little Toomai was too frightened to speak, but Kala Nag was behind him, and Toomai made a sign with his head, and the elephant caught him up in his trunk and held him level with Pudmini's forehead, in front of the great Petersen Sahib. Then Little Toomai covered his face with his hands, for he was only a child, and except where elephants were concerned, he was just as bashful as a child could be.

"Oho!" said Petersen Sahib, smiling underneath his mustache, "and why didst thou teach thy elephant *that* trick? Was it to help thee steal green corn from the roofs of the houses when the ears are put out to dry?"

"Not green corn, Protector of the Poor,—melons," said Little Toomai, and all the men sitting about broke into a roar of laughter. Most of them had taught their elephants that trick when they were boys. Little Toomai was hanging eight feet up in the air, and he wished very much that he were eight feet underground.

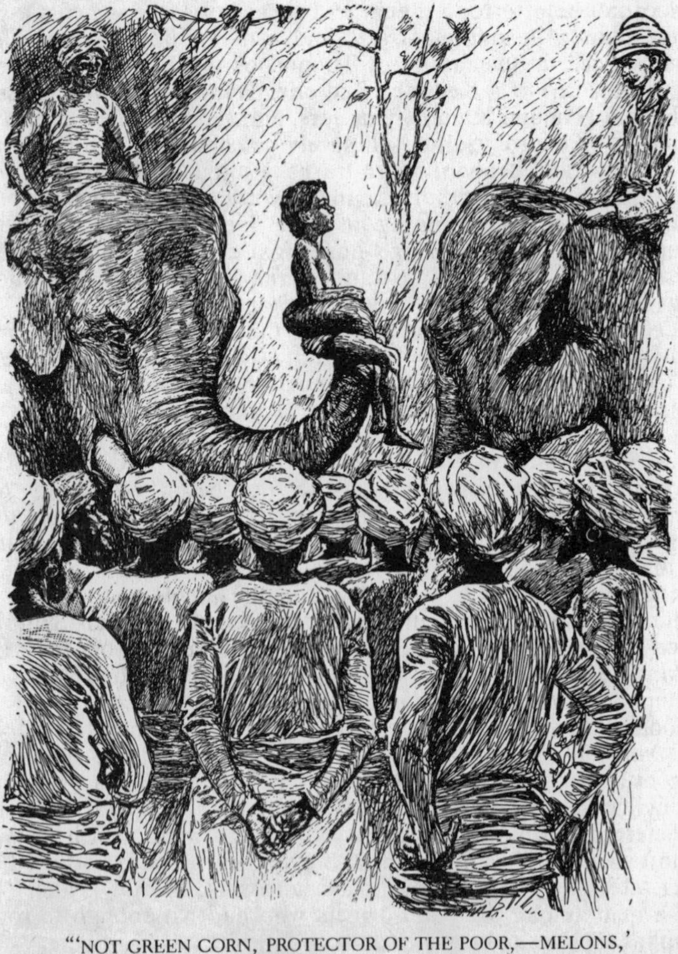

"'NOT GREEN CORN, PROTECTOR OF THE POOR,—MELONS,' SAID LITTLE TOOMAI."

"He is Toomai, my son, Sahib," said Big Toomai, scowling. "He is a very bad boy, and he will end in a jail, Sahib."

"Of that I have my doubts," said Petersen Sahib. "A boy who can face a full Keddah at his age does not end in jails. See, little one, here are four annas to spend in sweetmeats because thou has a little head under that great thatch of hair. In time thou mayest become a hunter too." Big Toomai scowled more than ever. "Remember, though, that Keddahs are not good for children to play in," Petersen Sahib went on.

"Must I never go there, Sahib?" asked Little Toomai, with a big gasp.

"Yes." Petersen Sahib smiled again. "When thou hast seen the elephants dance. That is the proper time. Come to me when thou hast seen the elephants dance, and then I will let thee go into all the Keddahs."

There was another roar of laughter, for that is an old joke among elephant-catchers, and it means just never. There are great cleared flat places hidden away in the forest that are called elephants' ballrooms, but even these are found only by accident, and no man has ever seen the elephants dance. When a driver boasts of his skill and bravery the other drivers say, "And when didst *thou* see the elephants dance?"

Kala Nag put Little Toomai down, and he bowed to the earth again and went away with his father, and gave the silver four-anna piece to his mother, who was nursing his baby-brother, and they all were put up on Kala Nag's back, and the line of grunting, squealing elephants rolled down the hill-path to the plains. It was a very lively march on account of the new elephants, who gave trouble at every ford, and who needed coaxing or beating every other minute.

Big Toomai prodded Kala Nag spitefully, for he was very angry, but Little Toomai was too happy to speak. Petersen Sahib had noticed him, and given him money, so he felt as a private soldier would feel if he had been called out of the ranks and praised by his commander-in-chief.

"What did Petersen Sahib mean by the elephant-dance?" he said, at last, softly to his mother.

Big Toomai heard him and grunted. "That thou shouldst never be one of these hill-buffaloes of trackers. *That* was what he meant. Oh you in front, what is blocking the way?"

An Assamese driver, two or three elephants ahead, turned round angrily, crying: "Bring up Kala Nag, and knock this youngster of mine into good behavior. Why should Petersen Sahib have chosen *me* to go down with you donkeys of the rice-fields? Lay your beast alongside, Toomai, and let him prod with his tusks. By all the Gods of the Hills, these new elephants are possessed, or else they can smell their companions in the jungle."

Kala Nag hit the new elephant in the ribs and knocked the wind out of him, as Big Tooomai said, "We have swept the hills of wild elephants at the last catch. It is only your carelessness in driving. Must I keep order along the whole line?"

"Hear him!" said the other driver. "*We* have swept the hills! Ho! ho! You are very wise, you plains-people. Any one but a mud-head who never saw the jungle would know that *they* know that the drives are ended for the season. Therefore all the wild elephants tonight will–but why should I waste wisdom on a river-turtle?"

"What will they do?" Little Toomai called out.

"*Ohé,* little one. Art thou there? Well, I will tell thee, for thou hast a cool head. They will dance, and it behooves thy father, who has swept *all* the hills of *all* the elephants, to double-chain his pickets to-night."

"What talk is this?" said Big Toomai. "For forty years, father and son, we have tended elephants, and we have never heard such moonshine about dances."

"Yes; but a plains-man who lives in a hut knows only the four walls of his hut. Well, leave thy elephants unshackled to-night and see what comes; as for their dancing, I have seen the place where—*Bepree-Bap!* how many windings has the Dihang River? Here is another ford, and we must swim the calves. Stop still, you behind there."

And in this way talking and wrangling and splashing through the rivers, they made their first march to a sort of receiving-camp for the new elephants; but they lost their tempers long before they got there.

Then the elephants were chained by their hind legs to their big stumps of pickets, and extra ropes were fitted to the new elephants, and the fodder was piled before them, and the hill-drivers went back to Petersen Sahib through the afternoon light, telling the plains-drivers to be extra careful that night, and laughing when the plains-drivers asked the reason.

Little Toomai attended to Kala Nag's supper, and as evening fell, wandered through the camp, unspeakably happy, in search of a tom-tom. When an Indian child's heart is full, he does not run about and make a noise in an irregular fashion. He sits down to a sort of revel all by himself. And Little Toomai had been spoken to by Petersen Sahib! If he had not found what he wanted I believe he would have burst. But the sweetmeat-seller in the camp lent him a little tom-tom—a drum beaten with the flat of the hand—and he sat down, cross-legged, before Kala Nag as the stars began to come out, the tom-tom in his lap, and he thumped and he thumped and he thumped, and the more he thought of the great honor that had been done to him, the more he thumped, all alone among the elephant-fodder. There was no tune and no words, but the thumping made him happy.

The new elephants strained at their ropes, and squealed and trumpeted from time to time, and he could hear his mother in the camp hut putting his small brother to sleep with an old, old song about the great God Shiv, who once told all the animals what they should eat. It is a very soothing lullaby, and the first verse says:

> Shiv, who poured the harvest and made the winds to blow,
> Sitting at the doorways of a day of long ago,
> Gave to each his portion, food and toil and fate,
> From the King upon the *guddee* to the Beggar at the gate.
>   All things made he—Shiva the Preserver.
>   Mahadeo! Mahadeo! he made all,—
>   Thorn for the camel, fodder for the kine,
>   And mother's heart for sleepy head, O little son of mine!

Little Toomai came in with a joyous *tunk-a-tunk* at the end of each verse, till he felt sleepy and stretched himself on the fodder at Kala Nag's side.

At last the elephants began to lie down one after another as is their custom, till only Kala Nag at the right of the line was left standing up; and he rocked slowly from side to side, his ears put forward to listen to the night wind as it blew very slowly across the hills. The air was full of all the night noises that, taken together, make one big silence—the click of one bamboo-stem against the other, the rustle of something alive in the undergrowth, the scratch and squawk of a half-waked bird (birds are awake in the night much more often than we imagine), and the fall of water ever so far away. Little Toomai slept for some time, and when he waked it was brilliant moonlight, and Kala Nag was still standing up with his ears cocked. Little Toomai turned, rustling in the fodder, and watched the curve of his big back against half the stars in heaven, and while he watched he heard, so far away that it sounded no more than a pinhole of noise pricked through the stillness, the "hoot-toot" of a wild elephant.

All the elephants in the lines jumped up as if they had been shot, and their grunts at last waked the sleeping mahouts, and they came out and drove in the picket-pegs with big mallets, and tightened this rope and knotted that till all was quiet. One new elephant had nearly grubbed up his picket, and Big Toomai took off Kala Nag's leg-chain and shackled that elephant fore foot to hind foot, but slipped a loop of grass-string round Kala Nag's leg, and told him to remember that he was tied fast. He knew that he and his father and his grandfather had done the very same thing hundreds of times before. Kala Nag did not answer to the order by gurgling, as he usually did. He stood still, looking out across the moonlight, his head a little raised and his ears spread like fans, up to the great folds of the Garo hills.

"Look to him if he grows restless in the night," said Big Toomai to Little Toomai, and he went into the hut and slept. Little Toomai was just going to sleep, too, when he heard the coir string snap with a little "tang," and Kala Nag rolled out of his pickets as slowly and as silently as a cloud rolls out of the mouth of a valley. Little Toomai pattered after him, barefooted, down the road in the moonlight, calling under his breath, "Kala Nag! Kala Nag! Take me with you, O Kala Nag!" The elephant turned without a sound, took three strides back to the boy in the moonlight, put down his trunk, swung him up to his neck, and almost before Little Toomai had settled his knees, slipped into the forest.

There was one blast of furious trumpeting from the lines, and then the silence shut down on everything, and Kala Nag began to move. Sometimes a tuft of high grass washed along his sides as a wave washes along the sides of a ship, and sometimes a cluster of wild-pepper vines would scrape along his back, or a bamboo would creak where his shoulder touched it; but between those times he moved absolutely without any sound, drifting through the thick Garo forest as though it had been smoke. He was going uphill, but though Little Toomai watched the stars in the rifts of the trees, he could not tell in what direction.

Then Kala Nag reached the crest of the ascent and stopped for a minute, and Little Toomai could see the tops of the trees lying all speckled and furry under the moonlight for miles and miles, and the blue-white mist over the river in the hollow. Toomai leaned forward and looked, and he felt that the forest was awake below him—awake and alive and crowded. A big brown fruit-eating bat brushed past his ear; a porcupine's quills rattled in the thicket, and in the darkness between the tree-stems he heard a hog-bear digging hard in the moist warm earth, and snuffing as it digged.

Then the branches closed over his head again, and Kala Nag began to go down into the valley—not quietly this time, but as a runaway gun goes down a steep bank—in one rush. The huge limbs moved as steadily as pistons, eight feet to each stride, and the wrinkled skin of the elbow-points rustled. The undergrowth on either side of him ripped with a noise like torn canvas, and the saplings that he heaved away right and left with his shoulders sprang back again, and banged him on the flank, and great trails of creepers, all matted together, hung from his tusks as he threw his head from side to side and plowed out his pathway. Then Little Toomai laid himself down close to the great neck, lest a swinging bough should sweep him to the ground, and he wished that he were back in the lines again.

The grass began to get squashy, and Kala Nag's feet sucked and squelched as he put them down, and the night mist at the bottom of the valley chilled Little Toomai. There was a splash and a trample, and the rush of running water, and Kala Nag strode through the bed of a river, feeling his way at each step. Above the noise of the water, as it swirled round the elephant's legs, Little Toomai could hear more splashing and some trumpeting both up-stream and down—great grunts and angry snortings, and all the mist about him seemed to be full of rolling wavy shadows.

"*Ai!*" he said, half aloud, his teeth chattering. "The elephant-folk are out to-night. It *is* the dance, then."

Kala Nag swashed out of the water, blew his trunk clear, and began another climb; but this time he was not alone, and he had not to make his path. That was made already, six feet wide, in front of him, where the bent jungle-grass was trying to recover itself and stand up. Many elephants must have gone that way only a few minutes before. Little Toomai looked back, and behind him a great wild tusker with his little pig's eyes glowing like hot coals, was just lifting himself out of the misty river. Then the trees closed up again, and they went on and up, with trumpetings and crashings, and the sound of breaking branches on every side of them.

At last Kala Nag stood still between two tree-trunks at the very top of the hill. They were part of a circle of trees that grew round an irregular space of some three or four acres, and in all that space, as Little Toomai could see, the ground had been trampled down as hard as a brick floor. Some trees grew in the center of the clearing, but their bark was rubbed away, and the white wood beneath showed all shiny and polished in the patches of moonlight. There were creepers hanging from the upper branches, and the bells of the flowers of the creepers, great waxy white things like convolvuluses, hung down fast asleep; but within the limits of the clearing there was not a single blade of green—nothing but the trampled earth.

The moonlight showed it all iron-gray, except where some elephants stood upon it, and their shadows were inky black. Little Toomai looked, holding his breath, with his eyes starting out of his head, and as he looked, more and more and more elephants swung out into the open from between the tree-trunks. Little Toomai could count only up to ten, and he counted again and again on his fingers till he lost count of the tens, and his head began to swim. Outside the clearing he could hear them crashing in the undergrowth as they worked their way up the hillside; but as soon as they were within the circle of the tree-trunks they moved like ghosts.

There were white-tusked wild males, with fallen leaves and nuts and twigs lying in the wrinkles of their necks and the folds of their ears; fat slow-footed she-elephants, with restless, little pinky-black calves only three or four feet high running under their stomachs; young elephants with their tusks just beginning to show, and very proud of them; lanky, scraggy old-maid elephants, with their hollow anxious faces, and trunks like rough bark; savage old bull-elephants, scarred from shoulder to flank with great weals and cuts of bygone fights, and the caked dirt of their solitary mud-baths dropping from their shoulders; and there was one with a broken tusk and the marks of the full-stroke, the terrible drawing scrape, of a tiger's claws on his side.

They were standing head to head, or walking to and fro across the ground in couples, or rocking and swaying all by themselves—scores and scores of elephants.

Toomai knew that so long as he lay still on Kala Nag's neck nothing would happen to him; for even in the rush and scramble of a Keddah-drive a wild elephant does not reach up with his trunk and drag a man off the neck of a tame elephant; and these elephants were not thinking of men that night. Once they started and put their ears forward when they heard the chinking of a leg-iron in the forest, but it was Pudmini, Petersen Sahib's pet elephant, her chain snapped short off, grunting, snuffling up the hillside. She must have broken her pickets, and come straight from Petersen Sahib's camp; and Little Toomai saw another elephant, one that he did not know, with deep rope-galls on his back and breast. He, too, must have run away from some camp in the hills about.

At last there was no sound of any more elephants moving in the forest, and Kala Nag rolled out from his station between the trees and went into the middle of the crowd, clucking and gurgling, and all the elephants began to talk in their own tongue, and to move about.

Still lying down, Little Toomai looked down upon scores and scores of broad backs, and wagging ears, and tossing trunks, and little rolling eyes. He heard the click of tusks as they crossed other tusks by accident, and the dry rustle of trunks twined together, and the chafing of enormous sides and shoulders in the crowd, and the incessant flick and *hissh* of the great tails. Then a cloud came over the moon, and he sat in black darkness; but the quiet, steady hustling and pushing and gurgling went on just the same. He knew that there were elephants all round Kala Nag, and that there was no chance of backing him out of the assembly; so he set his teeth and shivered. In a Keddah at least there was torch-light and shouting, but here he was all alone in the dark, and once a trunk came up and touched him on the knee.

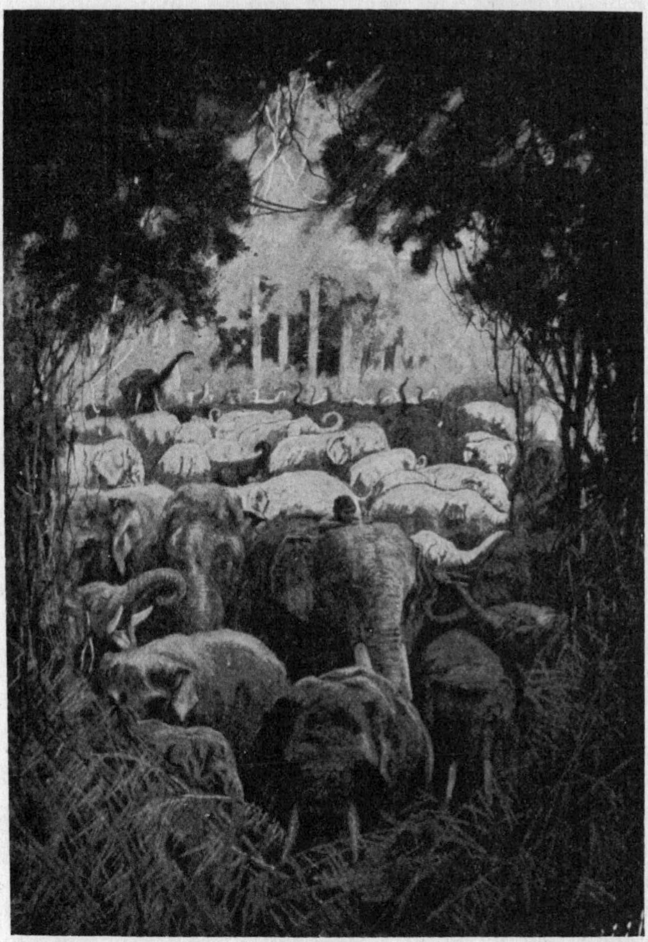

"LITTLE TOOMAI LOOKED DOWN UPON SCORES AND SCORES OF BROAD BACKS."

Then an elephant trumpeted, and they all took it up for five or ten terrible seconds. The dew from the trees above spattered down like rain on the unseen backs, and a dull booming noise began, not very loud at first, and Little Toomai could not tell what it was; but it grew and grew, and Kala Nag lifted up one fore foot and then the other, and brought them down on the ground–one-two, one-two, as steadily as trip-hammers. The elephants were stamping altogether now, and it sounded like a war-drum beaten at the mouth of a cave. The dew fell from the trees till there was no more left to fall, and the booming went on, and the ground rocked and shivered, and Little Toomai put his hands up to his ears to shut out the sound. But it was all one gigantic jar that ran through him—this stamp of hundreds of heavy feet on the raw earth. Once or twice he could feel Kala Nag and all the others surge forward a few strides, and the thumping would change to the crushing sound of juicy green things being bruised, but in a minute or two the boom of feet on hard earth began again. A tree was creaking and groaning somewhere near him. He put out his arm and felt the bark, but Kala Nag moved forward, still tramping, and he could not tell where he was in the clearing. There was no sound from the elephants, except once, when two or three little calves squeaked together. Then he heard a thump and a shuffle, and the booming went on. It must have lasted fully two hours, and Little Toomai ached in every nerve; but he knew by the smell of the night air that the dawn was coming.

The morning broke in one sheet of pale yellow behind the green hills, and the booming stopped with the first ray, as though the light had been an order. Before Little Toomai had got the ringing out of his head, before even he had shifted his position, there was not an elephant in sight except Kala Nag, Pudmini, and the elephant with the rope-galls, and there was neither sign nor rustle nor whisper down the hillsides to show where the others had gone.

Little Toomai stared again and again. The clearing, as he remembered it, had grown in the night. More trees stood in the middle of it, but the undergrowth and the jungle-grass at the sides had been rolled back. Little Toomai stared once more. Now he understood the trampling. The elephants had stamped out more room—had stamped the thick grass and juicy cane to trash, the trash into slivers, the slivers into tiny fibers, and the fibers into hard earth.

"Wah!" said Little Toomai, and his eyes were very heavy. "Kala Nag, my lord, let us keep by Pudmini and go to Petersen Sahib's camp, or I shall drop from thy neck."

The third elephant watched the two go away, snorted, wheeled round, and took his own path. He may have belonged to some little native king's establishment, fifty or sixty or a hundred miles away.

Two hours later, as Petersen Sahib was eating early breakfast, his elephants, who had been double-chained that night, began to trumpet, and Pudmini, mired to the shoulders, with Kala Nag, very foot-sore, shambled into the camp.

Little Toomai's face was gray and pinched, and his hair was full of leaves and drenched with dew; but he tried to salute Petersen Sahib, and cried faintly: "The dance—the elephant-dance! I have seen it, and—I die!" As Kala Nag sat down, he slid off his neck in a dead faint.

But, since native children have no nerves worth speaking of, in two hours he was lying very contentedly in Petersen Sahib's hammock with Petersen Sahib's shooting-coat under his head, and a glass of warm milk, a little brandy, with a dash of quinine inside of him, and while the old hairy, scarred hunters of the jungles sat three-deep before him, looking at him as though he were a spirit, he told his tale in short words, as a child will, and wound up with:

"Now, if I lie in one word, send men to see, and they will find that the elephant-folk have trampled down more room in their dance-room, and they will find ten and ten, and many times ten, tracks leading to that dance-room. They made more room with their feet. I have seen it. Kala Nag took me, and I saw. Also Kala Nag is very leg-weary!"

Little Toomai lay back and slept all through the long afternoon and into the twilight, and while he slept Petersen Sahib and Machua Appa followed the track of the two elephants for fifteen miles across the hills. Petersen Sahib had spent eighteen years in catching elephants, and he had only once before found such a dance-place. Machua Appa had no need to look twice at the clearing to see what had been done there, or to scratch with his toe in the packed, rammed earth.

"The child speaks truth," said he. "All this was done last night, and I have counted seventy tracks crossing the river. See, Sahib, where Pudmini's leg-iron cut the bark of that tree! Yes; she was there too."

They looked at each other, and up and down, and they wondered; for the ways of elephants are beyond the wit of any man, black or white, to fathom.

"Forty years and five," said Machua Appa, "have I followed my lord, the elephant, but never have I heard that any child of man had seen what this child has seen. By all the Gods of the Hills, it is—what can we say?" and he shook his head.

When they got back to camp it was time for the evening meal. Petersen Sahib ate alone in his tent, but he gave orders that the camp should have two sheep and some fowls, as well as a double-ration of flour and rice and salt, for he knew that there would be a feast.

Big Toomai had come up hot-foot from the camp in the plains to search for his son and his elephant, and now that he had found them he looked at them as though he were afraid of them both. And there was a feast by the blazing campfires in front of the lines of picketed elephants, and Little Toomai was the hero of it all; and the big brown elephant-catchers, the trackers and drivers and ropers, and the men who know all the secrets of breaking the wildest elephants, passed him from one to the other, and they marked his forehead with blood from the breast of a newly killed jungle-cock, to show that he was a forester, initiated and free of all the jungles.

And at last, when the flames died down, and the red light of the logs made the elephants look as though they had been dipped in blood too, Machua Appa, the head of all the drivers of all the Keddahs—Machua Appa, Petersen Sahib's other self, who had never seen a made road in forty years: Machua Appa, who was so great that he had no other name than Machua Appa—leaped to his feet, with Little Toomai held high in the air above his head, and shouted: "Listen, my brothers. Listen, too, you my lords in the lines there, for I, Machua Appa, am speaking! This little one shall no more be called Little Toomai, but Toomai of the Elephants, as his great-grandfather was called before him. What never man has seen he has seen through the long night, and the favor of the elephant-folk and of the Gods of the Jungles is with him. He shall become a great tracker; he shall become greater than I, even I, Machua Appa! He shall follow the new trail, and the stale trail, and the mixed trail, with a clear eye! He shall take no harm in the Keddah when he runs under their bellies to rope the wild tuskers; and if he slips before the feet of the charging bull-elephant that bull-elephant shall know who he is and shall not crush him. *Aihai!* my lords in the chains,"—he whirled up the line of pickets,—"here is the little one that has seen your dances in your hidden places—the sight that never man saw! Give him honor, my lords! *Salaam karo,* my children. Make your salute to Toomai of the Elephants! Gunga Pershad, ahaa! Hira Guj, Birchi Guj, Kuttar Guj, ahaa! Pudmini, thou hast seen him at the dance, and thou too, Kala Nag, my pearl among elephants! ahaa! Together! To Toomai of the Elephants. *Barrao!*"

And at that last wild yell the whole line flung up their trunks till the tips touched their foreheads, and broke out into the full salute—the crashing trumpet-peal that only the Viceroy of India hears, the Salaamut of the Keddah.

But it was all for the sake of Little Toomai, who had seen what never man had seen before—the dance of the elephants at night and alone in the heart of the Garo hills!

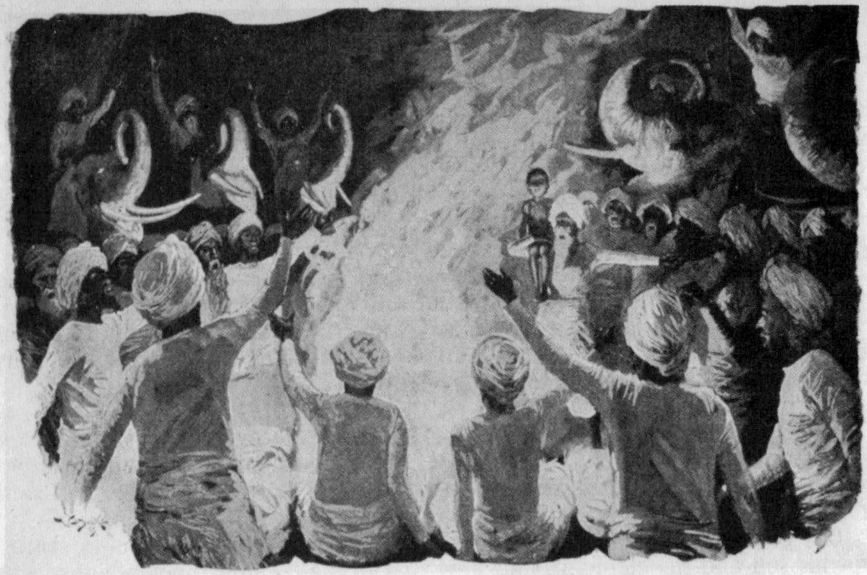

"'TO TOOMAI OF THE ELEPHANTS. *BARRAO!*'"

Shiv and the Grasshopper

(The Song That Toomai's Mother Sang to the Baby)

Shiv, who poured the harvest and made the winds to blow,
Sitting at the doorways of a day of long ago,
Gave to each his portion, food and toil and fate,
From the King upon the *guddee* to the Beggar at the gate.
All things made he—Shiva the Preserver.
Mahadeo! Mahadeo! he made all,—
Thorn for the camel, fodder for the kine,
And mother's heart for sleepy head, O little son of mine!

Wheat he gave to rich folk, millet to the poor,
Broken scraps for holy men that beg from door to door;
Cattle to the tiger, carrion to the kite,
And rags and bones to wicked wolves without the wall at night.
Naught he found too lofty, none he saw too low—
Parbati beside him watched them come and go;
Thought to cheat her husband, turning Shiv to jest—
Stole the little grasshopper and hid it in her breast.
So she tricked him, Shiva the Preserver.
Mahadeo! Mahadeo! turn and see.
Tall are the camels, heavy are the kine,
But this was least of little things, O little son of mine!

When the dole was ended, laughingly she said,
"Master, of a million mouths is not one unfed?"

Laughing, Shiv made answer, "All have had their part,
Even he, the little one, hidden 'neath thy heart."
From her breast she plucked it, Parbati the thief,
Saw the Least of Little Things gnawed a new-grown leaf!
Saw and feared and wondered, making prayer to Shiv,
Who hath surely given meat to all that live.
All things made he—Shiva the Preserver.
Mahadeo! Mahadeo! he made all,—
Thorn for the camel, fodder for the kine,
And mother's heart for sleepy head, O little son of mine!

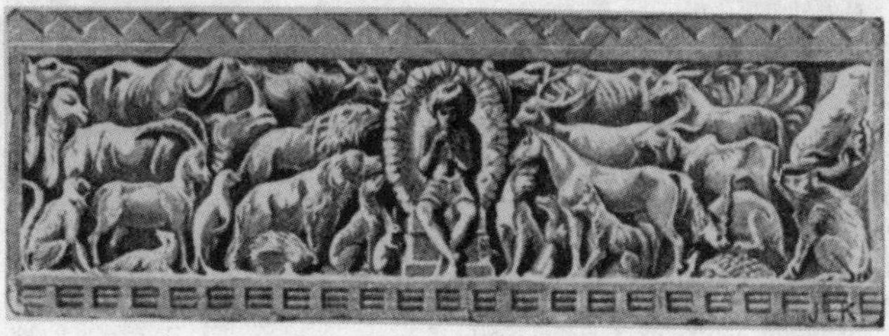

Her Majesty's Servants

You can work it out by Fractions or by simple Rule of Three,
But the way of Tweedle-dum is not the way of Tweedle-dee.
You can twist it, you can turn it, you can plait it till you drop,
But the way of Pilly-Winky's not the way of Winkie-Pop!

IT HAD BEEN raining heavily for one whole month—raining on a camp of thirty thousand men, thousands of camels, elephants, horses, bullocks, and mules, all gathered together at a place called Rawal Pindi, to be reviewed by the Viceroy of India. He was receiving a visit from the Amir of Afghanistan—a wild king of a very wild country; and the Amir had brought with him for a bodyguard eight hundred men and horses who had never seen a camp or a locomotive before in their lives—savage men and savage horses from somewhere at the back of Central Asia. Every night a mob of these horses would be sure to break their heel-ropes, and stampede up and down the camp through the mud in the dark, or the camels would break loose and run about and fall over the ropes of the tents, and you can imagine how pleasant that was for men trying to go to sleep. My tent lay far away from the camel lines, and I thought it was safe; but one night a man popped his head in and shouted, "Get out, quick! They're coming! My tent's gone!"

I knew who "they" were; so I put on my boots and waterproof and scuttled out into the slush. Little Vixen, my fox-terrier, went out through the other side; and then there was a roaring and a grunting and bubbling, and I saw the tent cave in, as the pole snapped, and begin to dance about like a mad ghost. A camel had blundered into it, and wet and angry as I was, I could not help laughing. Then I ran on, because I did not know how many camels might have got loose, and before long I was out of sight of the camp, plowing my way through the mud.

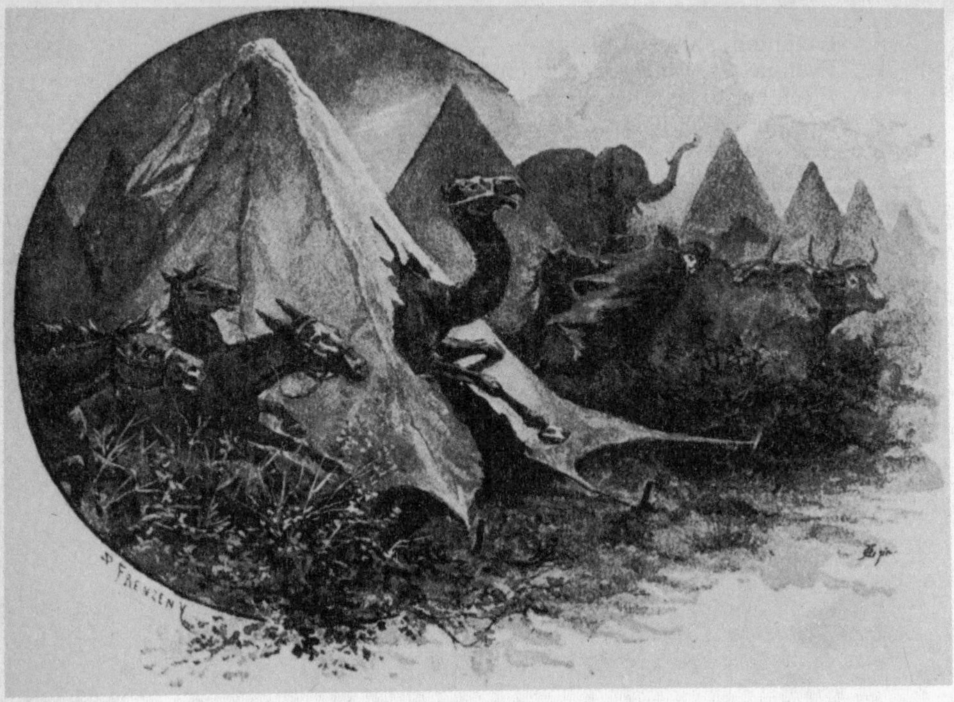

"A CAMEL HAD BLUNDERED INTO MY TENT."

At last I fell over the tail-end of a gun, and by that knew I was somewhere near the Artillery lines where the cannon were stacked at night. As I did not want to plowter about any more in the drizzle and the dark, I put my waterproof over the muzzle of one gun, and made a sort of wigwam with two or three rammers that I found, and lay along the tail of another gun, wondering where Vixen had got to, and where I might be.

Just as I was getting ready to sleep I heard a jingle of harness and a grunt, and a mule passed me shaking his wet ears. He belonged to a screw-gun battery, for I could hear the rattle of the straps and rings and chains and things on his saddle-pad. The screw-guns are tidy little cannon made in two pieces, that are screwed together when the time comes to use them. They are taken up mountains, anywhere that a mule can find a road, and they are very useful for fighting in rocky country.

Behind the mule there was a camel, with his big soft feet squelching and slipping in the mud, and his neck bobbing to and fro like a strayed hen's. Luckily, I knew enough of beast language–not wild-beast language, but camp-beast language, of course–from the natives to know what he was saying.

He must have been the one that flopped into my tent, for he called to the mule, "What shall I do? Where shall I go? I have fought with a white thing that waved, and it took a stick and hit me on the neck." (That was my broken tentpole, and I was very glad to know it.) "Shall we run on?"

"Oh, it was you," said the mule, "you and your friends, that have been disturbing the camp? All right. You'll be beaten for this in the morning; but I may as well give you something on account now."

I heard the harness jingle as the mule backed and caught the camel two kicks in the ribs that rang like a drum. "Another time," he said, "you'll know better than to run through a mule-battery at night, shouting 'Thieves and fire!' Sit down, and keep your silly neck quiet."

The camel doubled up camel-fashion, like a two-foot rule, and sat down whimpering. There was a regular beat of hoofs in the darkness, and a big troop-horse cantered up as steadily as though he were on parade, jumped a gun-tail, and landed close to the mule.

"It's disgraceful," he said, blowing out his nostrils. "those camels have racketed through our lines again—the third time this week. How's a horse to keep his condition if he isn't allowed to sleep? Who's here?"

"I'm the breech-piece mule of number two gun of the First Screw Battery," said the mule, "and the other's one of your friends. He's waked me up too. Who are you?"

"Number Fifteen, E troop, Ninth Lancers—Dick Cunliffe's horse. Stand over a little, there."

"Oh, beg your pardon," said the mule. "It's too dark to see much. Aren't these camels too sickening for anything? I walked out of my lines to get a little peace and quiet here."

"My lords," said the camel humbly, "we dreamed bad dreams in the night, and we were very much afraid. I am only a baggage-camel of the 39th Native Infantry, and I am not so brave as you are, my lords."

"Then why the pickets didn't you stay and carry baggage for the 39th Native Infantry, instead of running all round the camp?" said the mule.

"They were such very bad dreams," said the camel. "I am sorry. Listen! What is that? Shall we run on again?"

"Sit down," said the mule, "or you'll snap your long legs between the guns." He cocked one ear and listened. "Bullocks!" he said; "gun-bullocks. On my word, you and your friends have waked the camp very thoroughly. It takes a good deal of prodding to put up a gun-bullock."

I heard a chain dragging along the ground, and a yoke of the great sulky white bullocks that drag the heavy siege-guns when the elephants won't go any nearer to the firing, came shouldering along together; and almost stepping on the chain was another battery-mule, calling wildly for "Billy."

"That's one of our recruits," said the old mule to the troop-horse. "He's calling for me. Here, youngster, stop squealing; the dark never hurt anybody yet."

The gun-bullocks lay down together and began chewing the cud, but the young mule huddled close to Billy.

"Things!" he said; "fearful and horrible things, Billy! They came into our lines while we were asleep. D'you think they'll kill us?"

"I've a very great mind to give you a number one kicking," said Billy. "The idea of a fourteen-hand mule with your training disgracing the battery before this gentleman!"

"Gently, gently!" said the troop-horse. "Remember they are always like this to begin with. The first time I ever saw a man (it was in Australia when I was a three-year-old) I ran for half a day, and if I'd seen a camel I should have been running still."

Nearly all our horses for the English cavalry are brought to India from Australia, and are broken in by the troopers themselves.

"True enough," said Billy. "Stop shaking, youngster. The first time they put the full harness with all its chains on my back, I stood on my force legs and kicked every bit of it off. I hadn't learned the real science of kicking then, but the battery said they had never seen anything like it."

"But this wasn't harness or anything that jingled," said the young mule. "You know I don't mind that now, Billy. It was Things like trees, and they fell up and down the lines and bubbled; and my head-rope broke, and I couldn't find my driver, and I couldn't find you, Billy, so I ran off with—with these gentlemen."

"H'm!" said Billy. "As soon as I heard the camels were loose I came away on my own account, quietly. When a battery—a screw-gun mule calls gun-bullocks gentlemen, he must be very badly shaken up. Who are you fellows on the ground there?"

The gun-bullocks rolled their cuds, and answered both together: "The seventh yoke of the first gun of the Big Gun Battery. We were asleep when the camels came, but when we were trampled on we got up and walked away. It is better to lie quiet in the mud than to be disturbed on good bedding. We told your friend here that there was nothing to be afraid of, but he knew so much that he thought otherwise. Wah!"

They went on chewing.

"That comes of being afraid," said Billy. "You get laughed at by gun-bullocks. I hope you like it, young'un."

The young mule's teeth snapped, and I heard him say something about not being afraid of any beefy old bullock in the world; but the bullocks only clicked their horns together and went on chewing.

"Now, don't be angry *after* you've been afraid. That's the worst kind of cowardice," said the troop-horse. "Anybody can be forgiven for being scared in the night, *I* think, if they see things they don't understand. We've broken out of our pickets, again and again, four hundred and fifty of us, just because a new recruit got to telling tales of whip-snakes at home in Australia till we were scared to death of the loose ends of our head-ropes."

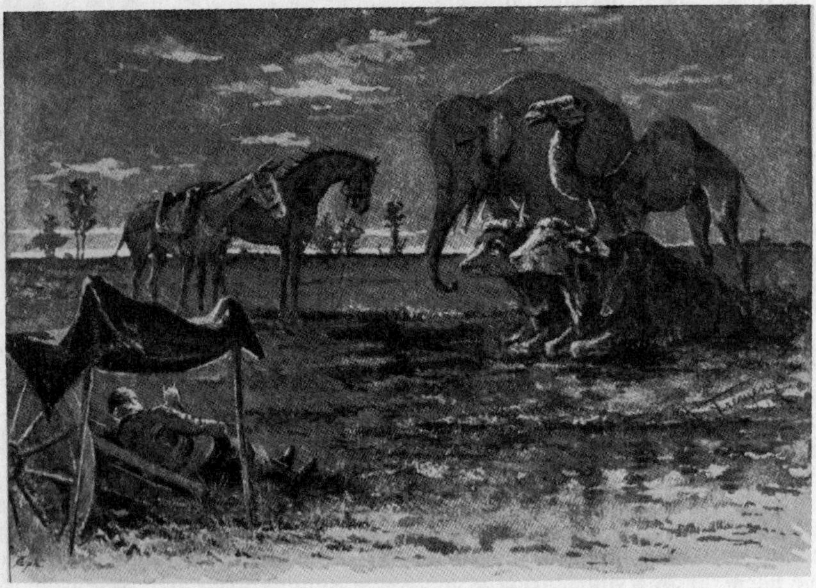

"'ANYBODY CAN BE FORGIVEN FOR BEING SCARED IN THE NIGHT,' SAID THE TROOP-HORSE."

"That's all very well in camp," said Billy; "I'm not above stampeding myself, for the fun of the thing, when I haven't been out for a day or two; but what do you do on active service?"

"Oh, that's quite another set of new shoes," said the troop-horse. "Dick Cunliffe's on my back then, and drives his knees into me, and all I have to do is to watch where I am putting my feet, and to keep my hind legs well under me, and be bridle-wise."

"What's bridle-wise?" said the young mule.

"By the Blue Gums of the Back Blocks," snorted the troop-horse, "do you mean to say that you aren't taught to be bridle-wise in your business? How can you do anything, unless you can spin round at once when the rein is pressed on your neck? It means life or death to your man, and of course that's life or death to you. Get round with your hind legs under you the instant you feel the rein on your neck. If you haven't room to swing round, rear up a little and come round on your hind legs. That's being bridle-wise."

"We aren't taught that way," said Billy the mule stiffly. "We're taught to obey the man at our head: step of when he says so, and step in when he says so. I suppose it comes to the same thing. Now, with all this fine fancy business and rearing, which must be very bad for your hocks, what do you *do?*"

"That depends," said the troop-horse. "Generally I have to go in among a lot of yelling, hairy men with knives,–long shiny knives, worse than the farrier's knives,–and I have to take care that Dick's boot is just touching the next man's boot without crushing it. I can see Dick's lance to the right of my right eye, and I know I'm safe. I shouldn't care to be the man or horse that stood up to Dick and me when we're in a hurry."

"Don't the knives hurt?" said the young mule.

"Well, I got one cut across the chest once, but that wasn't Dick's fault–"

"A lot I should have cared whose fault it was, if it hurt!" said the young mule.

"You must," said the troop-horse. "If you don't trust your man, you may as well run away at once. That's what some of our horses do, and I don't blame them. As I was saying, it wasn't Dick's fault. The man was lying on the ground, and I stretched myself not to tread on him, and he slashed up at me. Next time I have to go over a man lying down I shall step on him–hard."

"H'm!" said Billy; "it sounds very foolish. Knives are dirty things at any time. The proper thing to do is to climb up a mountain with a well-balanced saddle, hang on by all four feet and your ears too, and creep and crawl and wriggle along, till you come out hundreds of feet above any one else, on a ledge where there's just room enough for your hoofs. Then you stand still and keep quiet,–never ask a man to hold your head, young'un,–keep quiet while the guns are being put together, and then you watch the little poppy shells drop down into the tree-tops ever so far below."

"Don't you ever trip?" said the troop-horse.

"They say that when a mule trips you can split a hen's ear," said Billy. "Now and again *per-haps* a badly packed saddle will upset a mule, but it's very seldom. I wish I could show you our business. It's beautiful. Why, it took me three years to find out what the men were driving at. The science of the thing is never to show up against the sky-line, because, if you do, you may get fired at. Remember that, young 'un. Always keep hidden as much as possible, even if you have to go a mile out of your way. I lead the battery when it comes to that sort of climbing."

"Fired at without the chance of running into the people who are firing!" said the troop-horse, thinking hard. "I couldn't stand that. I should want to charge, with Dick."

"Oh no, you wouldn't; you know that as soon as the guns are in position *they'll* do all the charging. That's scientific and neat; but knives–pah!"

The baggage-camel had been bobbing his head to and fro for some time past, anxious to get a word in edgeways. Then I heard him say, as he cleared his throat, nervously:

"I–I–I have fought a little, but not in that climbing way or that running way."

"No. Now you mention it," said Billy, "you don't look as though you were made for climbing or running–much. Well, how was it, old Hay-bales?"

"The proper way," said the camel. "We all sat down–"

"Oh, my crupper and breastplate!" said the troop-horse under his breath. "Sat down?"

"We sat down–a hundred of us," the camel went on, "in a big square, and

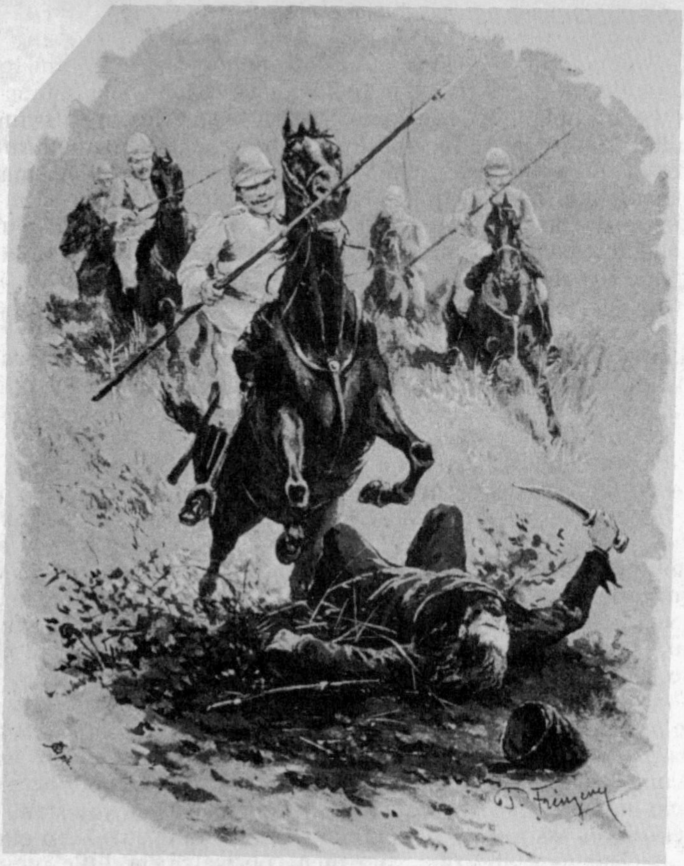

"'THE MAN WAS LYING ON THE GROUND, AND I STRETCHED MYSELF NOT TO TREAD ON HIM, AND HE SLASHED UP AT ME.'"

the men piled our packs and saddles outside the square, and they fired over our backs, the men did, on all sides of the square."

"What sort of men? Any men that came along?" said the troop-horse. "They teach us in riding-school to lie down and let our masters fire across us, but Dick Cunliffe is the only man I'd trust to do that. It tickles my girths, and, besides, I can't see with my head on the ground."

"What does it matter who fires across you?" said the camel. "There are plenty of men and plenty of other camels close by, and a great many clouds of smoke. I am not frightened then. I sit still and wait."

"And yet," said Billy, "you dream bad dreams and upset the camp at night. Well! well! Before I'd lie down, not to speak of sitting down, and let a man fire across me, my heels and his head would have something to say to each other. Did you ever hear anything so awful as that?"

There was a long silence, and then one of the gun-bullocks lifted up his big head and said, "This is very foolish indeed. There is only one way of fighting."

"Oh, go on," said Billy. "*Please* don't mind me. I suppose you fellows fight standing on your tails?"

"Only one way," said the two together. (They must have been twins.) "This is that way. To put all twenty yoke of us to the big gun as soon as Two Tails trumpets." ("Two Tails" is camp slang for the elephant.)

"What does Two Tails trumpet for?" said the young mule.

"To show that he is not going any nearer to the smoke on the other side.

Two tails is a great coward. Then we tug the big gun all together—*Heya—Hullah! Heeyah! Hullah! We* do not climb like cats nor run like calves. We go across the level plain, twenty yoke of us, till we are unyoked again, and we graze while the big guns talk across the plain to some town with mud walls, and pieces of the wall fall out, and the dust goes up as though many cattle were coming home."

"Oh! And you choose that time for grazing do you?" said the young mule.

"That time or any other. Eating is always good. We eat till we are yoked up again and tug the gun back to where Two Tails is waiting for it. Sometimes there are big guns in the city that speak back, and some of us are killed, and then there is all the more grazing for those that are left. This is Fate—nothing but Fate. None the less, Two Tails is a great coward. That is the proper way to fight. We are brothers from Hapur. Our father was a sacred bull of Shiva. We have spoken."

"Well, I've certainly learned something tonight," said the troop-horse. "Do you gentlemen of the screw-gun battery feel inclined to eat when you are being fired at with big guns, and Two Tails is behind you?"

"About as much as we feel inclined to sit down and let men sprawl all over us, or run into people with knives. I never heard such stuff. A mountain ledge, a well-balanced load, a driver you can trust to let you pick your own way, and I'm your mule; but the other things—no!" said Billy, with a stamp of his foot.

"Of course," said the troop-horse, "every one is not made in the same way, and I can quite see that your family, on your father's side, would fail to understand a great many things."

"Never you mind my family on my father's side," said Billy angrily; for every mule hates to be reminded that his father was a donkey. "My father was a Southern gentleman, and he could pull down and bite and kick into rags every horse he came across. Remember that, you big brown Brumby!"

Brumby means wild horse without any breeding. Imagine the feelings of Sunol if a carhorse called her a "skate," and you can imagine how the Australian horse felt. I saw the white of his eye glitter in the dark.

"See here, you son of an imported Malaga jackass," he said between his teeth, "I'd have you know that I'm related on my mother's side to Carbine, winner of the Melbourne Cup, and where *I* come from we aren't accustomed to being ridden over roughshod by any parrot-mouthed, pig-headed mule in a pop-gun peashooter battery. Are you ready?"

"On your hind legs!" squealed Billy. They both reared up facing each other, and I was expecting a furious fight, when a gurgly, rumbly voice called out of the darkness to the right—"Children, what are you fighting about there? Be quiet."

Both beasts dropped down with a snort of disgust, for neither horse nor mule can bear to listen to an elephant's voice.

"It's Two Tails!" said the troop-horse. "I can't stand him. A tail at each end isn't fair!"

"My feelings exactly," said Billy, crowding into the troop-horse for company. "We're very alike in some things."

"I suppose we've inherited them from our mothers," said the troop-horse. "It's not worth quarreling about. Hi! Two Tails, are you tied up?"

"Yes," said Two Tails, with a laugh all up his trunk. "I'm picketed for the night. I've heard what you fellows have been saying. But don't be afraid. I'm not coming over."

The bullocks and the camel said, half aloud: "Afraid of Two Tails—what nonsense!" And the bullocks went on: "We are sorry that you heard, but it is true. Two Tails, why are you afraid of the guns when they fire?"

"Well," said Two Tails, rubbing one hind leg against the other, exactly like a little boy saying a piece, "I don't quite know whether you'd understand."

"We don't, but we have to pull the guns," said the bullocks.

"I know it, and I know you are a good deal braver than you think you are. But it's different with me. My battery captain called me a Pachydermatous Anachronism the other day."

"That's another way of fighting, I suppose?" said Billy, who was recovering his spirits.

"*You* don't know what that means, of course, but I do. It means betwixt and between, and that is just where I am. I can see inside my head what will happen when a shell bursts; and you bullocks can't."

"I can," said the troop-horse. "At least a little bit. I try not to think about it."

"I can see more than you, and I *do* think about it. I know there's a great deal of me to take care of, and I know that nobody knows how to cure me when I'm sick. All they can do is to stop my driver's pay till I get well, and I can't trust my driver."

"Ah!" said the troop-horse. "That explains it. I can trust Dick."

"You could put a whole regiment of Dicks on my back without making me feel any better. I know just enough to be uncomfortable, and not enough to go on in spite of it."

"We do not understand," said the bullocks.

"I know you don't. I'm not talking to you. You don't know what blood is."

"We do," said the bullocks. "It is red stuff that soaks into the ground and smells."

The troop-horse gave a kick and a bound and a snort.

"Don't talk of it," he said. "I can smell it now, just thinking of it. It makes me want to run—when I haven't Dick on my back."

"But it is not here," said the camel and the bullocks. "Why are you so stupid?"

"It's vile stuff," said Billy. "I don't want to run, but I don't want to talk about it."

"There you are!" said Two Tails, waving his tail to explain.

"Surely. Yes, we have been here all night," said the bullocks.

Two Tails stamped his foot till the iron ring on it jingled. "Oh, I'm not talking to *you.* You can't see inside your heads."

"No. We see out of our four eyes," said the bullocks. "We see straight in front of us."

"If I could do that and nothing else you wouldn't be needed to pull the big guns at all. If I was like my captain—he can see things inside his head before the firing begins, and he shakes all over, but he knows too much to run away—if I was like him I could pull the guns. But if I were as wise as all that I should never be here. I should be a king in the forest, as I used to be, sleeping half the day and bathing when I liked. I haven't had a good bath for a month."

"That's all very fine," said Billy; "but giving a thing a long name doesn't make it any better."

"H'sh!" said the troop-horse. "I think I understand what Two Tails means."

"You'll understand better in a minute," said Two Tails angrily. "Now, just you explain to me why you don't like *this!*"

He began trumpeting furiously at the top of his trumpet.

"Stop that!" said Billy and the troop-horse together, and I could hear them stamp and shiver. An elephant's trumpeting is always nasty, especially on a dark night.

"I sha'n't stop," said Two Tails. "Won't you explain that, please? *Hhrrmph! Rrrt! Rrrmph! Rrrhha!"* Then he stopped suddenly, and I heard a little whimper in the dark, and knew that Vixen had found me at last. She knew as well as I did that if there is one thing in the world the elephant is more afraid of than another it is a little barking dog; so she stopped to bully Two Tails in his pickets, and yapped round his big feet. Two Tails shuffled and squeaked. "Go away, little dog!" he said. "Don't snuff at my ankles, or I'll kick at you. Good little dog–nice little doggie, then! Go home, you yelping little beast! Oh, why doesn't someone take her away? She'll bite me in a minute."

"Seems to me," said Billy to the troop-horse, "that our friend Two Tails is afraid of most things. Now, if I had a full meal for every dog I've kicked across the parade-ground, I should be as fat as Two Tails nearly."

I whistled, and Vixen ran up to me, muddy all over, and licked my nose, and told me a long tale about hunting for me all through the camp. I never let her know that I understood beast talk, or she would have taken all sorts of liberties. So I buttoned her into the breast of my overcoat, and Two Tails shuffled and stamped and growled to himself.

"Extraordinary! Most extraordinary!" he said. "It runs in our family. Now, where has that nasty little beast gone to?"

I heard him feeling about with his trunk.

"We all seem to be affected in various ways," he went on, blowing his nose. "Now, you gentlemen were alarmed, I believe, when I trumpeted."

"Not alarmed, exactly," said the troop-horse, "but it made me feel as though I had hornets where my saddle ought to be. Don't begin again."

"I'm frightened of a little dog, and the camel here is frightened by bad dreams in the night."

"It is very lucky for us that we haven't all got to fight in the same way," said the troop-horse.

"What I want to know," said the young mule, who had been quiet for a long time–"what *I* want to know is, why we have to fight at all."

"Because we are told to," said the troop-horse, with a snort of contempt.

"Orders," said Billy the mule; and his teeth snapped.

"Hukm hai!" (It is an order), said the camel with a gurgle; and Two Tails and the bullocks repeated, *"Hukm hai!"*

"Yes, but who gives the orders?" said the recruit-mule.

"The man who walks at your head–Or sits on your back–Or holds the nose-rope–Or twists your tail," said Billy and the troop-horse and the camel and the bullocks one after the other.

"But who gives them the orders?"

"Now you want to know too much, young 'un," said Billy, "and that is one way of getting kicked. All you have to do is to obey the man at your head and ask no questions."

"He's quite right," said Two Tails. "I can't always obey, because I'm betwixt and between; but Billy's right. Obey the man next to you who gives the order, or you'll stop all the battery, besides getting a thrashing."

The gun-bullocks got up to go. "Morning is coming," they said. "We will go back to our lines. It is true that we see only out of our eyes, and we are not very clever; but still, we are the only people to-night who have not been afraid. Good night, you brave people."

Nobody answered, and the troop-horse said, to change the conversation, "Where's that little dog? A dog means a man somewhere near."

"Here I am," yapped Vixen, "under the guntail with my man. You big, blundering beast of a camel you, you upset our tent. My man's very angry."

"Phew!" said the bullocks. "He must be white?"

"Of course he is," said Vixen. "Do you suppose I'm looked after by a black bullock-driver?"

"Huah! Ouach! Ugh!" said the bullocks. "Let us get away quickly."

They plunged forward in the mud, and managed somehow to run their yoke on the pole of an ammunition-wagon, where it jammed.

"Now you *have* done it," said Billy calmly. "Don't struggle. You're hung up till daylight. What on earth's the matter?"

The bullocks went off into the long hissing snorts that Indian cattle give, and pushed and crowded and slued and stamped and slipped and nearly fell down in the mud, grunting savagely.

"You'll break your necks in a minute," said the troop-horse. "What's the matter with white men? I live with 'em."

"They–eat–us! Pull!" said the near bullock: the yoke snapped with a twang, and they lumbered off together.

I never knew before what made Indian cattle so afraid of Englishmen. We eat beef–a thing that no cattle-driver touches–and of course the cattle do not like it.

"May I be flogged with my own pad-chains! Who'd have thought of two big lumps like those losing their heads?" said Billy.

"Never mind. I'm going to look at this man. Most of the white men, I know, have things in their pockets," said the troop-horse.

"I'll leave you, then. I can't say I'm overfond of 'em myself. Besides, white men who haven't a place to sleep in are or more than likely to be thieves, and I've a good deal of Government property on my back. Come along, young 'un, and we'll go back to our lines. Good-night, Australia! See you on parade to-morrow, I suppose. Good-night, old Hay-bale!–try to control your feelings, won't you? Good-night, Two Tails! If you pass us on the ground to-morrow, don't trumpet. It spoils our formation."

Billy the mule stumped off with the swaggering limp of an old campaigner, as the troop-horse's head came nuzzling into my breast, and I gave him biscuits; while Vixen, who is a most conceited little dog, told him fibs about the scores of horses that she and I kept.

"I'm coming to the parade to-morrow in my dog-cart," she said. "Where will you be?"

"On the left hand of the second squadron. I set the time for all my troop, little lady," he said politely. "Now I must go back to Dick. My tail's all muddy, and he'll have two hours' hard work dressing me for the parade."

The big parade of all the thirty thousand men was held that afternoon, and Vixen and I had a good place close to the Viceroy and the Amir of Afghanistan, with his high big black hat of astrakhan wool and the great diamond star in the center. The first part of the review was all sunshine, and the regiments went by in wave upon wave of legs all moving together, and guns all in a line, till our eyes grew dizy. Then the cavalry came up, to the beautiful cavalry canter of "Bonnie Dundee," and Vixen cocked her ear where she sat on the dog-cart. The second squadron of the lancers shot by, and there was the troop-horse, with his tail like spun silk, his head pulled into his breast, one ear forward and one back setting the time for all his squadron, his legs going as smoothly as waltz-music. Then the big guns came by, and I saw Two Tails and two other elephants harnessed in line to a forty-pounder siege-gun while twenty yoke of oxen walked behind. The seventh pair had a new yoke, and they looked rather stiff and tired. Last came the screw-guns, and Billy the mule carried himself as though he commanded all the troops, and his harness was oiled and polished till it winked. I gave a cheer all by myself for Billy the mule, but he never looked right or left.

The rain began to fall again, and for a while it was too misty to see what the troops were doing. They had made a big half-circle across the plain, and were spreading out into a line. That line grew and grew and grew till it was three-quarters of a mile long from wing to wing–one solid wall of men, horses, and guns. Then it came on straight toward the Viceroy and the Amir, and as it got nearer the ground began to shake, like the deck of a steamer when the engines are going fast.

Unless you have been there you cannot imagine what a frightening effect this steady come-down of troops has on the spectators, even when they know it is only a review. I looked at the Amir. Up till then he had not shown the shadow of a sign of astonishment or anything else; but now his eyes began to get bigger and bigger, and he picked up the reins on his horse's neck and looked behind him. For a minute it seemed as though he were going to draw his sword and slash his way out through the English men and women in the carriages at the back. Then the advance stopped dead, the ground stood still, the whole line saluted, and thirty bands began to play all together. That was the end of the review, and the regiments went off to their camps in the rain; and an infantry band struck up with–

The animals went in two by two,
Hurrah!
The animals went in two by two,
The elephant and the battery mu-
l', and they all got into the Ark,
For to get out of the rain!

Then I heard an old, grizzled, long-haired Central Asian chief, who had come down with the Amir, asking questions of a native officer.

"Now," said he, "in what manner was this wonderful thing done?"

And the officer answered, "There was an order, and they obeyed."

"But are the beasts as wise as the men?" said the chief.

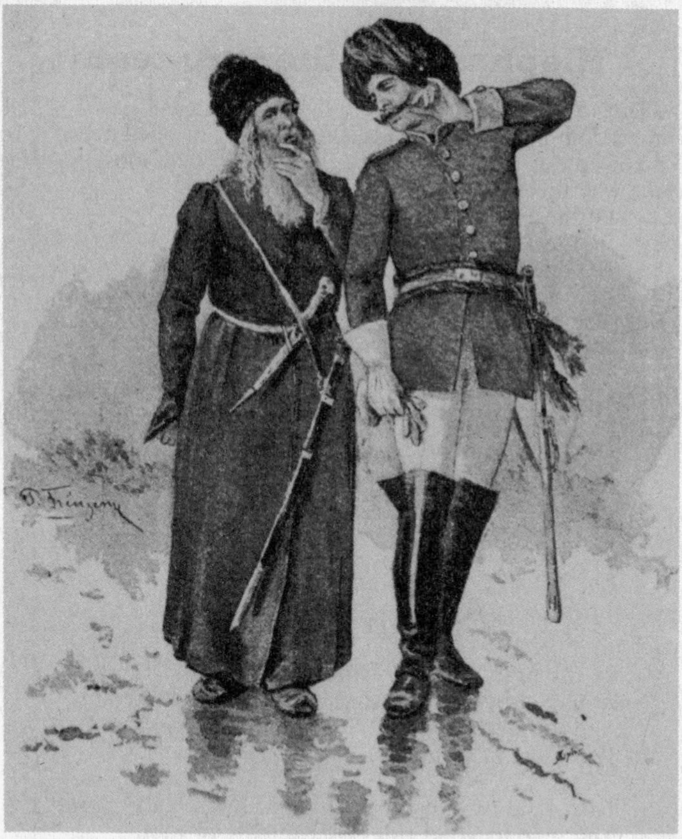

"THEN I HEARD AN OLD, GRIZZLED, LONG-HAIRED, CENTRAL ASIAN CHIEF ASKING QUESTIONS OF A NATIVE OFFICER."

"They obey, as the men do. Mule, horse, elephant, or bullock, he obeys his driver, and the driver his sergeant, and the sergeant his lieutenant, and the lieutenant his captain, and the captain his major, and the major his colonel, and the colonel his brigadier commanding three regiments, and the brigadier his general, who obeys the Viceroy, who is the servant of the Empress. Thus it is done."

"Would it were so in Afghanistan!" said the chief; "for there we obey only our own wills."

"And for that reason," said the native officer, twirling his mustache, "your Amir whom you do not obey must come here and take orders from our Viceroy."

Parade-song of the Camp Animals

Elephants of the Gun-team

We lent to Alexander the strength of Hercules,
The wisdom of our foreheads, the cunning of our knees;
We bowed our necks to service; they ne'er were loosed again,–
Make way there, way for the ten-foot teams
Of the Forty-Pounder train!

Gun-Bullocks

Those heroes in their harness avoid a cannon-ball,
And what they know of powder upsets them one and all;
Then *we* come into action and tug the guns again,–
Make way there, way for the twenty yoke
Of the Forty-Pounder train!

Cavalry Horses

By the brand on my withers, the finest of tunes
Is played by the Lancers, Hussars, and Dragoons,
And it's sweeter than "Stables" or "Water" to me,
The Cavalry Canter of "Bonnie Dundee"!

Then feed us and break us and handle and groom,
And give us good riders and plenty of room,
And launch us in column of squadrons and see
The way of the war-horse to "Bonnie Dundee"!

Screw-Gun Mules

As me and my companions were scrambling up a hill,
The path was lost in rolling stones, but we went forward still;
For we can wriggle and climb, my lads, and turn up everywhere,
And it's our delight on a mountain height, with a leg or two to spare!

Good luck to every sergeant, then, that lets us pick our road;
Bad luck to all the driver-men that cannot pack a load:
For we can wriggle and climb, my lads, and turn up everywhere,
And it's our delight on a mountain height with a leg or two to spare!

Commissariat Camels

We haven't a camelty tune of our own
To help us trollop along,
But every neck is a hairy trombone
(*Rtt-ta-ta-ta!* is a hairy trombone!)
And this is our marching song:
Can't! Don't! Sha'n't! Won't!
Pass it along the line!
Somebody's pack has slid from his back,
Wish it were only mine!
Somebody's load has tipped off in the road—
Cheer for a halt and a row!
Urrr! Yarrh! Grr! Arrh!
Somebody's catching it now!

All the Beasts Together

Children of the Camp are we,
Serving each in his degree;
Children of the yoke and goad,
Pack and harness, pad and load.
See our line across the plain,
Like a heel-rope bent again.
Reaching, writhing, rolling far,
Sweeping all away to war!
While the men that walk beside,
Dusty, silent, heavy-eyed,
Cannot tell why we or they
March and suffer day by day.
Children of the Camp are we,
Serving each in his degree;
Children of the yoke and goad,
Pack and harness, pad and load.

The Second Jungle Book

"Now these are the Laws of the Jungle,
  and many and mighty are they;
But the head and the hoof of the Law
  and the haunch and the hump is—Obey!"

CONTENTS

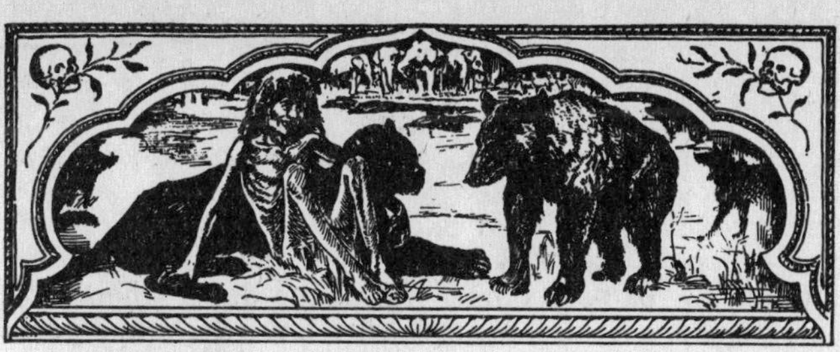

How Fear Came

The stream is shrunk—the pool is dry,
And we be comrades, thou and I;
With fevered jowl and sunken flank
Each jostling each along the bank;
And, by one drouthy fear made still,
Foregoing thought of quest or kill.
Now 'neath his dam the fawn may see
The lean Pack-wolf as cowed as he,
And the tall buck, unflinching, note
The fangs that tore his father's throat.
The pools are shrunk—the streams are dry,
And we be playmates, thou and I,
Till yonder cloud—Good Hunting!—loose
The rain that breaks the Water Truce.

THE LAW OF the Jungle—which is by far the oldest law in the world—has arranged for almost every kind of accident that may befall the Jungle People, till now its code is as perfect as time and custom can make it. If you have read the other book about Mowgli, you will remember that he spent a great part of his life in the Seeonee Wolf-Pack, learning the Law from Baloo, the Brown Bear; and it was Baloo who told him, when the boy grew impatient at the constant orders, that the Law was like the Giant Creeper, because it dropped across every one's back and no one could escape. "When thou hast lived as long as I have, Little Brother, thou wilt see how all the Jungle obeys at least one Law. And that will be no pleasant sight," said Baloo.

This talk went in at one ear and out at the other, for a boy who spends his life eating and sleeping does not worry about anything till it actually stares him in the face. But, one year, Baloo's words came true, and Mowgli saw all the Jungle working under the Law.

It began when the winter Rains failed almost entirely, and Ikki, the Porcupine, meeting Mowgli in a bamboo-thicket, told him that the wild yams were drying up. Now everybody knows that Ikki is ridiculously fastidious in his choice of food, and will eat nothing but the very best and ripest. So Mowgli laughed and said, "What is that to me?"

"Not much *now,*" said Ikki, rattling his quills in a stiff, uncomfortable way, "but later we shall see. Is there any more diving into the deep rock-pool below the Bee-Rocks, Little Brother?"

"No. The foolish water is going all away, and I do not wish to break my head," said Mowgli, who, in those days, was quite sure that he knew as much as any five of the Jungle People put together.

"That is thy loss. A small crack might let in some wisdom." Ikki ducked quickly to prevent Mowgli from pulling his nose-bristles, and Mowgli told

Baloo what Ikki had said. Baloo looked very grave, and mumbled half to himself: "If I were alone I would change my hunting-grounds now, before the others began to think. And yet—hunting among strangers ends in fighting; and they might hurt the Man-cub. We must wait and see how the *mohwa* blooms."

That spring the *mohwa* tree, that Baloo was so fond of, never flowered. The greeny, cream-colored, waxy blossoms were heat-killed before they were born, and only a few bad-smelling petals came down when he stood on his hind legs and shook the tree. Then, inch by inch, the untempered heat crept into the heart of the Jungle, turning it yellow, brown, and at last black. The green growths in the sides of the ravines burned up to broken wires and curled films of dead stuff; the hidden pools sank down and caked over, keeping the last least footmark on their edges as if it had been cast in iron; the juicy-stemmed creepers fell away from the trees they clung to and died at their feet; the bamboos withered, clanking when the hot winds blew, and the moss peeled off the rocks deep in the Jungle, till they were as bare and as hot as the quivering blue boulders in the bed of the stream.

The birds and the monkey-people went north early in the year, for they knew what was coming; and the deer and the wild pig broke far away to the perished fields of the villages, dying sometimes before the eyes of men too weak to kill them. Chil, the Kite, stayed and grew fat, for there was a great deal of carrion, and evening after evening he brought the news to the beasts, too weak to force their way to fresh hunting-grounds, that the sun was killing the Jungle for three days' flight in every direction.

Mowgli, who had never known what real hunger meant, fell back on stale honey, three years old, scraped out of deserted rock-hives—honey black as a sloe, and dusty with dried sugar. He hunted, too, for deep-boring grubs under the bark of the trees, and robbed the wasps of their new broods. All the game in the Jungle was no more than skin and bone, and Bagheera could kill thrice in a night, and hardly get a full meal. But the want of water was the worst, for though the Jungle People drink seldom they must drink deep.

And the heat went on and on, and sucked up all the moisture, till at last the main channel of the Waingunga was the only stream that carried a trickle of water between its dead banks; and when Hathi, the wild elephant, who lives for a hundred years and more, saw a long, lean blue ridge of rock show dry in the very center of the stream, he knew that he was looking at the Peace Rock, and then and there he lifted up his trunk and proclaimed the Water Truce, as his father before him had proclaimed it fifty years ago. The deer, wild pig, and buffalo took up the cry hoarsely; and Chil, the Kite, flew in great circles far and wide, whistling and shrieking the warning.

By the Law of the Jungle it is death to kill at the drinking-places when once the Water Truce has been declared. The reason of this is that drinking comes before eating. Every one in the Jungle can scramble along somehow when only game is scarce; but water is water, and when there is but one source of supply, all hunting stops while the Jungle People go there for their needs. In good seasons, when water was plentiful, those who came down to drink at the Waingunga—or anywhere else, for that matter—did so at the risk of their lives, and that risk made no small part of the fascination of the night's doings. To move down so cunningly that never a leaf stirred; to wade knee-deep in the roaring shallows that drown all noise from behind; to drink, looking backward over one shoulder, every muscle ready for the first desperate bound of keen terror; to roll on the sandy margin, and return, wet-muzzled and well plumped out, to the admiring herd, was a thing that all tall-antlered young bucks took a delight in, precisely because they knew that at any moment Bagheera or Shere Khan might leap upon them and bear them down. But now all that life-and-death fun was ended, and the Jungle People came up, starved and weary, to the shrunken river,—tiger, bear, deer, buffalo, and pig, all together,–drank the fouled waters, and hung above them, too exhausted to move off.

The deer and the pig had tramped all day in search of something better than dried bark and withered leaves. The buffaloes had found no wallows to be cool in, and no green crops to steal. The snakes had left the Jungle and come down to the river in hope of finding a stray frog. They curled round wet stones, and never offered to strike when the nose of a rooting pig dislodged them. The river-turtles had long ago been killed by Bagheera, cleverest of hunters, and the fish had buried themselves deep in the dry mud. Only the Peace Rock lay across the shallows like a long snake, and the little tired ripples hissed as they dried on its hot side.

It was here that Mowgli came nightly for the cool and the companionship. The most hungry of his enemies would hardly have cared for the boy then. His naked hide made him seem more lean and wretched than any of his fellows. His hair was bleached to tow color by the sun; his ribs stood out like the ribs of a basket, and the lumps on his knees and elbows, where he was used to track on all fours, gave his shrunken limbs the look of knotted grass-stems. But his eye, under his matted forelock, was cool and quiet, for Bagheera was his adviser in this time of trouble, and told him to go quietly, hunt slowly, and never, on any account, to lose his temper.

"It is an evil time," said the Black Panther, one furnace-hot evening, "but it will go if we can live till the end. Is thy stomach full, Man cub?"

"There is stuff in my stomach, but I get no good of it. Think you, Bagheera, the Rains have forgotten us and will never come again?"

"Not I! We shall see the *mohwa* in blossom yet, and the little fawns all fat with new grass. Come down to the Peace Rock and hear the news. On my back, Little Brother."

"This is no time to carry weight. I can still stand alone, but–indeed we be no fatted bullocks, we too."

Bagheera looked along his ragged, dusty flank and whispered: "Last night I killed a bullock under the yoke. So low was I brought that I think I should not have dared to spring if he had been loose. *Wou!*"

Mowgli laughed. "Yes, we be great hunters now," said he. "I am very bold–to eat grubs," and the two came down together through the crackling undergrowth to the river-bank and the lace-work of shoals that ran out from it in every direction.

"The water cannot live long," said Baloo, joining them. "Look across. Yonder are trails like the roads of Man."

On the level plain of the further bank the stiff jungle-grass had died standing, and, dying, had mummied. The beaten tracks of the deer and the pig, all heading toward the river, had striped that colorless plain with dusty gullies driven through the ten-foot grass, and, early as it was, each long avenue was full of first-comers hastening to the water. You could hear the does and fawns coughing in the snuff-like dust.

Up-stream, at the bend of the sluggish pool round the Peace Rock, and Warden of the Water Truce, stood Hathi, the wild elephant, with his sons, gaunt and gray in the moonlight, rocking to and fro–always rocking. Below him a little were the vanguard of the deer; below these, again, the pig and the wild buffalo; and on the opposite bank, where the tall trees came down to the water's edge, was the place set apart for the Eaters of Flesh–the tiger, the wolves, the panther, and the bear, and the others.

"We are under one Law, indeed," said Bagheera, wading into the water and looking across at the lines of clicking horns and starting eyes where the deer and the pig pushed each other to and fro. "Good hunting, all you of my blood," he added, lying down at full length, one flank thrust out of the shallows; and then, between his teeth, "But for that which is the Law it would be *very* good hunting."

The quick-spread ears of the deer caught the last sentence, and a frightened whisper ran along the ranks. "The Truce! Remember the Truce!"

"Peace there, peace!" gurgled Hathi, the wild elephant. "The Truce holds, Bagheera. This is no time to talk of hunting."

"Who should know better than I?" Bagheera answered, rolling his yellow eyes up-stream. "I am an eater of turtles—a fisher of frogs. *Ngaayah!* Would I could get good from chewing branches!"

"*We* wish so, very greatly," bleated a young fawn, who had only been born that spring, and did not at all like it. Wretched as the Jungle People were, even Hathi could not help chuckling; while Mowgli, lying on his elbows in the warm water, laughed aloud, and beat up the scum with his feet.

"Well spoken, little bud-horn," Bagheera purred. "When the Truce ends that shall be remembered in thy favor," and he looked keenly through the darkness to make sure of recognizing the fawn again.

Gradually the talking spread up and down the drinking-places. One could hear the scuffling, snorting pig asking for more room; the buffaloes grunting among themselves as they lurched out across the sand-bars, and the deer telling pitiful stories of their long foot-sore wanderings in quest of food. Now and again they asked some question of the Eaters of Flesh across the river, but all the news was bad, and the roaring hot wind of the Jungle came and went between the rocks and the rattling branches, and scattered twigs and dust on the water.

"The men-folk, too, they die beside their plows," said a young sambhur. "I passed three between sunset and night. They lay still, and their bullocks with them. We also shall lie still in a little."

"The river has fallen since last night," said Baloo. "O Hathi, hast thou ever seen the like of this drought?"

"It will pass, it will pass," said Hathi, squirting water along his back and sides.

"We have one here that cannot endure long," said Baloo; and he looked toward the boy he loved.

"I?" said Mowgli indignantly, sitting up in the water. "I have no long fur to cover my bones, but—but if *thy* hide were taken off, Baloo—"

Hathi shook all over at the idea, and Baloo said severely:

"Man-cub, that is not seemly to tell a Teacher of the Law. *Never* have I been seen without my hide."

"Nay, I meant no harm, Baloo; but only that thou art, as it were, like the cocoanut in the husk, and I am the same cocoanut all naked. Now that brown husk of thine—" Mowgli was sitting cross-legged, and explaining things with his forefinger in his usual way, when Bagheera put out a paddy paw and pulled him over backward into the water.

"Worse and worse," said the Black Panther, as the boy rose sputtering. "First, Baloo is to be skinned, and now he is a cocoanut. Be careful that he does not do what the ripe cocoanuts do."

"And what is that?" said Mowgli, off his guard for the minute, though that is one of the oldest catches in the Jungle.

"Break thy head," said Bagheera quietly, pulling him under again.

"It is not good to make a jest of thy teacher," said the bear, when Mowgli had been ducked for the third time.

"Not good! What would ye have? That naked thing running to and fro makes a monkey-jest of those who have once been good hunters, and pulls the best of us by the whisker for sport." This was Shere Khan, the Lame Tiger, limping down to the water. He waited a little to enjoy the sensation he made among the deer on the opposite bank; then he dropped his square, frilled head and began to lap, growling: "The Jungle has become a whelping-ground for naked cubs now. Look at me, Man-cub!"

Mowgli looked—stared, rather—as insolently as he knew how, and in a minute Shere Khan turned away uneasily. "Man-cub this, and Man-cub that," he rumbled, going on with his drink, "the cub is neither man nor cub, or he would have been afraid. Next season I shall have to beg his leave for a drink. *Aurgh!*"

"That may come, too," said Bagheera, looking him steadily between the eyes. "That may come, too–Faugh, Shere Khan!–what new shame has thou brought here?"

The Lame Tiger had dipped his chin and jowl in the water, and dark oily streaks were floating from it down-stream.

"Man!" said Shere Khan coolly, "I killed an hour since." He went on purring and growling to himself.

The line of beasts shook and wavered to and fro, and a whisper went up that grew to a cry: "Man! Man! He has killed Man!" Then all looked toward Hathi, the wild elephant, but he seemed not to hear. Hathi never does anything till the time comes, and that is one of the reasons why he lives so long.

"At such a season as this to kill Man! Was no other game afoot?" said Bagheera scornfully, drawing himself out of the tainted water, and shaking each paw, cat-fashion, as he did so.

"I killed for choice–not for food." The horrified whisper began again, and Hathi's watchful little white eye cocked itself in Shere Khan's direction. "For choice," Shere Khan drawled. "Now come I to drink and make me clean again. Is there any to forbid?"

Bagheera's back began to curve like a bamboo in a high wind, but Hathi lifted up his trunk and spoke quietly.

"Thy kill was from choice?" he asked; and when Hathi asks a question it is best to answer.

"Even so. It was my right and my Night. Thou knowest, O Hathi." Shere Khan spoke almost courteously.

"Yes, I know," Hathi answered; and, after a little silence, "Hast thou drunk thy fill?"

"For to-night, yes."

"Go, then. The river is to drink, and not to defile. None but the Lame Tiger would so have boasted of his right at this season when–when we suffer together–Man and Jungle People alike. Clean or unclean, get to thy lair, Shere Khan!"

The last words rang out like silver trumpets, and Hathi's three sons rolled forward half a pace, though there was no need. Shere Khan slunk away, not daring to growl, for he knew–what every one else knows–that when the last comes to the last, Hathi is the Master of the Jungle.

"What is this right Shere Khan speaks of?" Mowgli whispered in Bagheera's ear. "To kill Man is *always* shameful. The Law says so. And yet Hathi says–"

"Ask him. I do not know, Little Brother. Right or no right, if Hathi had not spoken I would have taught that lame butcher his lesson. To come to the Peace Rock fresh from a kill of Man–and to boast of it–is a jackal's trick. Besides, he tainted the good water."

Mowgli waited for a minute to pick up his courage, because no one cared to address Hathi directly, and then he cried: "What is Shere Khan's right, O Hathi?" Both banks echoed his words, for all the People of the Jungle are intensely curious, and they had just seen something that none, except Baloo, who looked very thoughtful, seemed to understand.

"It is an old tale," said Hathi; "a tale older than the Jungle. Keep silence along the banks, and I will tell that tale."

There was a minute or two of pushing and shouldering among the pigs and the buffalo, and then the leaders of the herds grunted, one after another, "We wait," and Hathi strode forward till he was nearly knee-deep in the pool by the Peace Rock. Lean and wrinkled and yellow-tusked though he was, he looked what the Jungle knew him to be—their master.

"Ye know, children," he began, "that of all things ye most fear Man"; and there was a mutter of agreement.

"This tale touches thee, Little Brother," said Bagheera to Mowgli.

"I? I am of the Pack—a hunter of the Free People," Mowgli answered. "What have I to do with Man?"

"And ye do not know why ye fear Man?" Hathi went on. "This is the reason. In the beginning of the Jungle, and none know when that was, we of the Jungle walked together, having no fear of one another. In those days there was no drought, and leaves and flowers and fruit grew on the same tree, and we ate nothing at all except leaves and flowers and grass and fruit and bark."

"I am glad I was not born in those days," said Bagheera. "Bark is only good to sharpen claws."

"And the Lord of the Jungle was Tha, the First of the Elephants. He drew the Jungle out of deep waters with his trunk; and where he made furrows in the ground with his tusks, there the rivers ran; and where he struck with his foot, there rose ponds of good water; and when he blew through his trunk,—thus,—the trees fell. That was the manner in which the Jungle was made by Tha; and so the tale was told to me."

"It has not lost fat in the telling," Bagheera whispered, and Mowgli laughed behind his hand.

"In those days there was no corn or melons or pepper or sugar-cane, nor were there any little huts such as ye have all seen; and the Jungle People knew nothing of Man, but lived in the Jungle together, making one people. But presently they began to dispute over their food, though there was grazing enough for all. They were lazy. Each wished to eat where he lay down, as sometimes we can do now when the spring rains are good. Tha, the First of the Elephants, was busy making new jungles and leading the rivers in their beds. He could not walk in all places: therefore he made the First of the Tigers the master and the judge of the Jungle, to whom the Jungle People should bring their disputes. In those days the First of the Tigers ate fruit and grass with the others. He was as large as I am, and he was very beautiful, in color all over like the blossom of the yellow creeper. There was never stripe nor bar upon his hide in those good days when this the Jungle was new. All the Jungle People came before him without fear, and his word was the Law of all the Jungle. We were then, remember ye, one people.

"Yet upon a night there was a dispute between two bucks—a grazing-quarrel such as ye now settle with the horns and the fore feet—and it is said that as the two spoke together before the First of the Tigers lying among the flowers, a buck pushed him with his horns, and the First of the Tigers forgot that he was the master and judge of the Jungle, and, leaping upon that buck, broke his neck.

"Till that night never one of us had died, and the First of the Tigers, seeing what he had done, and being made foolish by the scent of the blood, ran away into the marshes of the North, and we of the Jungle, left without a judge, fell to fighting among ourselves; and Tha heard the noise of it and came back. Then some of us said this and some of us said that, but he saw the dead buck among the flowers, and asked who had killed, and we of the Jungle would not tell because the smell of the blood made us foolish. We ran to and fro in circles, capering and crying out and shaking our heads. Then Tha gave an order to the trees that hang low, and to the trailing creepers of the Jungle, that they should mark the killer of the buck so that he should know him again, and he said, 'Who will now be master of the Jungle People?' Then up leaped the Gray Ape who lives in the branches, and said, 'I will now be master of the Jungle.' At this Tha laughed, and said, 'So be it,' and went away very angry.

"Children, ye know the Gray Ape. He was then as he is now. At the first he made a wise face for himself, but in a little while he began to scratch and to leap up and down, and when Tha came back he found the Gray Ape hanging, head down, from a bough, mocking those who stood below; and they mocked him again. And so there was no Law in the Jungle–only foolish talk and senseless words.

"Then Tha called us all together and said: 'The first of your masters has brought Death into the Jungle, and the second Shame. Now it is time there was a Law, and a Law that ye must not break. Now ye shall know Fear, and when ye have found him ye shall know that he is your master, and the rest shall follow.' Then we of the Jungle said, 'What is Fear?' And Tha said, 'Seek till ye find.' So we went up and down the Jungle seeking for Fear, and presently the buffaloes–"

"Ugh!" said Mysa, the leader of the buffaloes, from their sand-bank.

"Yes, Mysa, it was the buffaloes. They came back with the news that in a cave in the Jungle sat Fear, and that he had no hair, and went upon his hind legs. Then we of the Jungle followed the herd till we came to that cave, and Fear stood at the mouth of it, and he was, as the buffaloes had said, hairless, and he walked upon his hinder legs. When he saw us he cried out, and his voice filled us with the fear that we have now of that voice when we hear it, and we ran away, tramping upon and tearing each other because we were afraid. That night, so it was told to me, we of the Jungle did not lie down together as used to be our custom, but each tribe drew off by itself–the pig with the pig, the deer with the deer; horn to horn, hoof to hoof,–like keeping to like, and so lay shaking in the Jungle.

"Only the First of the Tigers was not with us, for he was still hidden in the marshes of the North, and when word was brought to him of the Thing we had seen in the cave, he said: 'I will go to this Thing and break his neck.' So he ran all the night till he came to the cave; but the trees and the creepers on his path, remembering the order that Tha had given, let down their branches and marked him as he ran, drawing their fingers across his back, his flank, his forehead, and his jowl. Wherever they touched him there was a mark and a stripe upon his yellow hide. *And those stripes do his children wear to this day!* When he came to the cave, Fear, the Hairless One, put out his hand and called him 'The Striped One that comes by night,' and the First of the Tigers was afraid of the Hairless One, and ran back to the swamps howling."

Mowgli chuckled quietly here, his chin in the water.

"So loud did he howl that Tha heard him and said, 'What is the sorrow?' And the First of the Tigers, lifting up his muzzle to the new-made sky, which is now so old, said: 'Give me back my power, O Tha. I am made ashamed before all the Jungle, and I have run away from a Hairless One, and he has called me a shameful name.' 'And why?' said Tha. 'Because I am smeared with the mud of the marshes,' said the First of the Tigers. 'Swim, then, and roll on the wet grass, and if it be mud it will wash away,' said Tha; and the First of the Tigers swam, and rolled and rolled upon the grass, till the Jungle ran round and round before his eyes, but not one little bar upon all his hide was changed, and Tha, watching him, laughed. Then the First of the Tigers said, 'What have I done that this comes to me?' Tha said, 'Thou hast killed the buck, and thou hast let Death loose in the Jungle, and with Death has come Fear, so that the people of the Jungle are afraid one of the other, as thou art afraid of the Hairless One.' The First of the Tigers said, 'They will never fear me, for I knew them since the beginning.' Tha said, 'Go and see.' And the First of the Tigers ran to and fro, calling aloud to the deer and the pig and the sambhur and the porcupine and all the Jungle Peoples, and they all ran away from him who had been their judge, because they were afraid.

"Then the First of the Tigers came back, and his pride was broken in him, and, beating his head upon the ground, he tore up the earth with all his feet and said: 'Remember that I was once the Master of the Jungle. Do not forget me, O Tha! Let my children remember that I was once without shame or fear!' And Tha said: 'This much I will do, because thou and I together saw the Jungle made. For one night in each year it shall be as it was before the buck was killed–for thee and for thy children. In that one night, if ye meet the Hairless One–and his name is Man–ye shall not be afraid of him, but he shall be afraid of you, as though ye were judges of the Jungle and masters of all things. Show him mercy in that night of his fear, for thou hast known what Fear is.'

"Then the First of the Tigers answered, 'I am content'; but when next he drank he saw the black stripes upon his flank and his side, and he remembered the name that the Hairless One had given him, and he was angry. For a year he lived in the marshes, waiting till Tha should keep his promise. And upon a night when the Jackal of the Moon [the Evening Star] stood clear of the Jungle, he felt that his Night was upon him, and he went to that cave to meet the Hairless One. Then it happened as Tha promised, for the Hairless One fell down before him and lay along the ground, and the First of the Tigers struck him and broke his back, for he thought that there was but one such Thing in the Jungle, and that he had killed Fear. Then, nosing above the kill, he heard Tha coming down from the woods of the North, and presently the voice of the First of the Elephants, which is the voice that we hear now–"

The thunder was rolling up and down the dry, scarred hills, but it brought no rain–only heat-lightning that flickered along the ridges–and Hathi went on: "*That* was the voice he heard, and it said: 'Is this thy mercy?' The First of the Tigers licked his lips and said: 'What matter? I have killed Fear.' And Tha said: 'O blind and foolish! Thou hast untied the feet of Death, and he will follow thy trail till thou diest. Thou hast taught Man to kill!'

"The First of the Tigers, standing stiffly to his kill, said: 'He is as the buck was. There is no Fear. Now I will judge the Jungle Peoples once more."

"And Tha said: 'Never again shall the Jungle Peoples come to thee. They shall never cross thy trail, nor sleep near thee, nor follow after thee, nor browse by thy lair. Only Fear shall follow thee, and with a blow that thou canst not see he shall bid thee wait his pleasure. He shall make the ground to open under thy feet, and the creeper to twist about thy neck, and the tree-trunks to grow together about thee higher than thou canst leap, and at the last he shall take thy hide to wrap his cubs when they are cold. Thou hast shown him no mercy, and none will he show thee.'

"The First of the Tigers was very bold, for his Night was still on him, and he said: 'The Promise of Tha is the Promise of Tha. He will not take away my Night?' And Tha said: 'The one Night is thine, as I have said, but there is a price to pay. Thou hast taught Man to kill, and he is no slow learner.'

"The First of the Tigers said: 'He is here under my foot, and his back is broken. Let the Jungle know I have killed Fear.'

"Then Tha laughed, and said: 'Thou hast killed one of many, but thou thyself shalt tell the Jungle–for thy Night is ended.'

"So the day came; and from the mouth of the cave went out another Hairless One, and he saw the kill in the path, and the First of the Tigers above it, and he took a pointed stick–"

"They throw a thing that cuts now," said Ikki, rustling down the bank; for Ikki was considered uncommonly good eating by the Gonds–they called him Ho-Igoo–and he knew something of the wicked little Gondee axe that whirls across a clearing like a dragon-fly.

"It was a pointed stick, such as they put in the foot of a pit-trap," said

Hathi, "and throwing it, he struck the First of the Tigers deep in the flank. Thus it happened as Tha said, for the First of the Tigers ran howling up and down the Jungle till he tore out the stick, and all the Jungle knew that the Hairless One could strike from far off, and they feared more than before. So it came about that the First of the Tigers taught the Hairless One to kill—and ye know what harm that has since done to all our peoples—through the noose, and the pitfall, and the hidden trap, and the flying stick, and the stinging fly that comes out of white smoke [Hathi meant the rifle], and the Red Flower that drives us into the open. Yet for one night in the year the Hairless One fears the Tiger, as Tha promised, and never has the Tiger given him cause to be less afraid. Where he finds him, there he kills him, remembering how the First of the Tigers was made ashamed. For the rest, Fear walks up and down the Jungle by day and by night."

"Ahi! Aoo!" said the deer, thinking of what it all meant to them.

"And only when there is one great Fear over all, as there is now, can we of the Jungle lay aside our little fears, and meet together in one place as we do now."

"For one night only does Man fear the Tiger?" said Mowgli.

"For one night only," said Hathi.

"But I—but we—but all the Jungle knows that Shere Khan kills Man twice and thrice in a moon."

"Even so. *Then* he springs from behind and turns his head aside as he strikes, for he is full of fear. If Man looked at him he would run. But on his one Night he goes openly down to the village. He walks between the houses and thrusts his head into the doorway, and the men fall on their faces and there he does his kill. One kill in that Night."

"Oh!" said Mowgli to himself, rolling over in the water. *"Now* I see why it was Shere Khan bade me look at him! He got no good of it, for he could not hold his eyes steady, and—and I certainly did not fall down at his feet. But then I am not a man, being of the Free People."

"Umm!" said Bagheera deep in his furry throat. "Does the Tiger know his Night?"

"Never till the Jackal of the Moon stands clear of the evening mist. Sometimes it falls in the dry summer and sometimes in the wet rains—this one Night of the Tiger. But for the First of the Tigers, this would never have been, nor would any of us have known fear."

The deer grunted sorrowfully, and Bagheera's lips curled in a wicked smile. "Do men know this—tale?" said he.

"None know it except the tigers, and we, the elephants—the children of Tha. Now ye by the pools have heard it, and I have spoken."

Hathi dipped his trunk into the water as a sign that he did not wish to talk.

"But—but—but," said Mowgli, turning to Baloo, "why did not the First of the Tigers continue to eat grass and leaves and trees? He did but break the buck's neck. He did not *eat.* What led him to the hot meat?"

"The trees and the creepers marked him, Little Brother, and made him the striped thing that we see. Never again would he eat their fruit; but from that day he revenged himself upon the deer, and the others, the Eaters of Grass," said Baloo.

"Then *thou* knowest the tale. Heh? Why have I never heard?"

"Because the Jungle is full of such tales. If I made a beginning there would never be an end to them. Let go my ear, Little Brother."

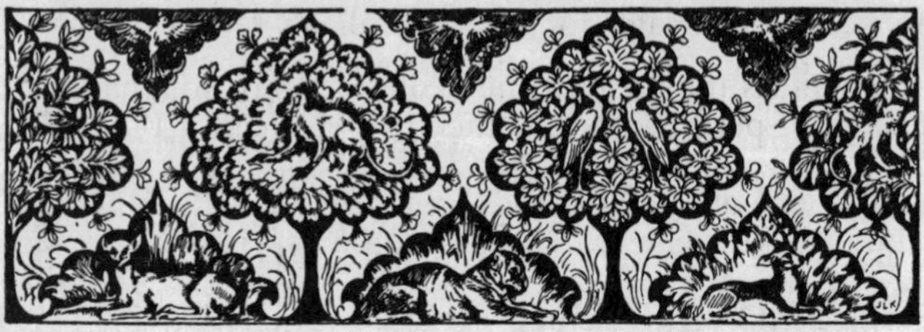

The Law of the Jungle

Just to give you an idea of the immense variety of the Jungle Law, I have translated into verse (Baloo always recited them in a sort of sing-song) a few of the laws that apply to the wolves. There are, of course, hundreds and hundreds more, but these will do for specimens of the simpler rulings.

Now this is the Law of the Jungle—as old and as true as the sky;
And the Wolf that shall keep it may prosper, but the Wolf that shall break it must die.
As the creeper that girdles the tree-trunk the Law runneth forward and back—
For the strength of the Pack is the Wolf, and the strength of the Wolf is the Pack.

Wash daily from nose-tip to tail-tip; drink deeply, but never too deep;
And remember the night is for hunting, and forget not the day is for sleep.

The Jackal may follow the Tiger, but, Cub, when thy whiskers are grown,
Remember the Wolf is a hunter—go forth and get food of thine own.

Keep peace with the Lords of the Jungle—the Tiger, the Panther, and Bear;
And trouble not Hathi the Silent, and mock not the Boar in his lair.

When Pack meets Pack in the Jungle, and neither will go from the trail,
Lie down till the leaders have spoken—it may be fair words shall prevail.

When ye fight with a Wolf of the Pack, ye must fight him alone and afar,
Lest others take part in the quarrel, and the Pack be diminished by war.

The Lair of the Wolf is his refuge, and where he has made him his home,
Not even the Head Wolf may enter, not even the Council may come.

The Lair of the Wolf is his refuge, but where he has digged it too plain,
The Council shall send him a message, and so he shall change it again.

If ye kill before midnight, be silent, and wake not the woods with your bay,
Lest ye frighten the deer from the crops, and thy brothers go empty away.

Ye may kill for yourselves, and your mates, and your cubs as they need, and ye can;
But kill not for pleasure of killing, and *seven times never kill Man.*

If ye plunder his Kill from a weaker, devour not all in thy pride,
Pack-Right is the right of the meanest; so leave him the head and the hide.

The Kill of the Pack is the meat of the Pack. Ye must eat where it lies;
And no one may carry away of that meat to his lair, or he dies.

The Kill of the Wolf is the meat of the Wolf. He may do what he will,
But, till he has given permission, the Pack may not eat of that Kill.

Cub-Right is the right of the Yearling. From all of his Pack he may claim
Full-gorge when the killer has eaten; and none may refuse him the same.

Lair-Right is the right of the Mother. From all of her year she may claim
One haunch of each kill for her litter, and none may deny her the same.

Cave-Right is the right of the Father–to hunt by himself for his own;
He is freed of all calls to the Pack; he is judged by the Council alone.

Because of his age and his cunning, because of his gripe and his paw,
In all that the Law leaveth open, the word of the Head Wolf is Law.

Now these are the Laws of the Jungle, and many and mighty are they;
But the head and the hoof of the Law and the haunch and the hump is–Obey!

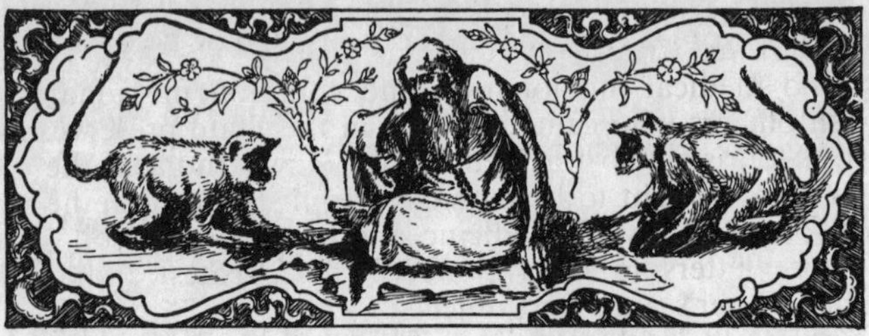

The Miracle of Purun Bhagat

The night we felt the earth would move
    We stole and plucked him by the hand,
Because we loved him with the love
    That knows but cannot understand.

And when the roaring hillside broke,
    And all our world fell down in rain,
We saved him, we the Little Folk;
    But lo! he does not come again!

Mourn now, we saved him for the sake
    Of such poor love as wild ones may.
Mourn ye! Our brother will not wake,
    And his own kind drive us away!

Dirge of the Langurs.

THERE WAS ONCE a man in India who was Prime Minister of one of the semi-independent native States in the northwestern part of the country. He was a Brahmin, so high-caste that caste ceased to have any particular meaning for him; and his father had been an important official in the gay-colored tag-rag and bobtail of an old-fashioned Hindu Court. But as Purun Dass grew up he felt that the old order of things was changing, and that if any one wished to get on in the world he must stand well with the English, and imitate all that the English believed to be good. At the same time a native official must keep his own master's favor. This was a difficult game, but the quiet, close-mouthed young Brahmin, helped by a good English education at a Bombay University, played it coolly, and rose, step by step, to be Prime Minister of the kingdom. That is to say, he held more real power than his master, the Maharajah.

When the old king—who was suspicious of the English, their railways and telegraphs—died, Purun Dass stood high with his young successor, who had been tutored by an Englishman; and between them, though he always took care that his master should have the credit, they established schools for little girls, made roads, and started State dispensaries and shows of agricultural implements, and published a yearly blue-book on the "Moral and Material Progress of the State," and the Foreign Office and the Government of India were delighted. Very few native States take up English progress altogether, for they will not believe, as Purun Dass showed he did, that what was good for the Englishman must be twice as good for the Asiatic. The Prime Minister became the honored friend of Viceroys and Governors, and Lieutenant-Governors, and medical missionaries, and common missionaries, and hard-riding English officers who came to shoot in the State preserves, as well as of whole hosts of tourists who traveled up and down India in the cold weather, showing how things ought to be managed. In his spare time he would endow scholarships for the study of medicine and manufactures on strictly English lines, and write letters to the "Pioneer," the greatest Indian daily paper, explaining his master's aims and objects.

At last he went to England on a visit, and had to pay enormous sums to the priests when he came back; for even so high-caste a Brahmin as Purun Dass lost caste by crossing the black sea. In London he met and talked with every one worth knowing–men whose names go all over the world–and saw a great deal more than he said. He was given honorary degrees by learned universities, and he made speeches and talked of Hindu social reform to English ladies in evening dress, till all London cried, "This is the most fascinating man we have ever met at dinner since cloths were first laid."

When he returned to India there was a blaze of glory, for the Viceroy himself made a special visit to confer upon the Maharajah the Grand Cross of the Star of India–all diamonds and ribbons and enamel; and at the same ceremony, while the cannon boomed, Purun Dass was made a Knight Commander of the Order of the Indian Empire; so that his name stood Sir Purun Dass, K. C. I. E.

That evening, at dinner in the big Viceregal tent, he stood up with the badge and the collar of the Order on his breast, and replying to the toast of his master's health, made a speech few Englishmen could have bettered.

Next month, when the city had returned to its sunbaked quiet, he did a thing no Englishman would have dreamed of doing; for, so far as the world's affairs went, he died. The jeweled order of his knighthood went back to the Indian Government, and a new Prime Minister was appointed to the charge of affairs, and a great game of General Post began in all the subordinate appointments. The priests knew what had happened and the people guessed; but India is the one place in the world where a man can do as he pleases and nobody asks why; and the fact that Dewan Sir Purun Dass, K. C. I. E., had resigned position, palace, and power, and taken up the begging-bowl and ocher-colored dress of a Sunnyasi or holy man, was considered nothing extraordinary. He had been, as the Old Law recommends, twenty years a youth, twenty years a fighter,–though he had never carried a weapon in his life,–and twenty years head of a household. He had used his wealth and his power for what he knew both to be worth; he had taken honor when it came his way; he had seen men and cities far and near, and men and cities had stood up and honored him. Now he would let these things go, as a man drops the cloak he no longer needs.

Behind him, as he walked through the city gates, an antelope skin and brass-handled crutch under his arm, and a begging-bowl of polished brown *coco-de-mer* in his hand, barefoot, alone, with eyes cast on the ground–behind him they were firing salutes from the bastions in honor of his happy successor. Purun Dass nodded. All that life was ended; and he bore it no more ill-will or good-will than a man bears to a colorless dream of the night. He was a Sunnyasi–a houseless wandering mendicant, depending on his neighbors for his daily bread; and so long as there is a morsel to divide in India neither priest nor beggar starves. He had never in his life tasted meat, and very seldom eaten even fish. A five-pound note would have covered his personal expenses for food through any one of the many years in which he had been absolute master of millions of money. Even when he was being lionized in London he had held before him his dream of peace and quiet–the long, white, dusty Indian road, printed all over with bare feet, the incessant, slow-moving traffic, and the sharp-smelling wood smoke curling up under the fig-trees in the twilight, where the wayfarers sit at their evening meal.

When the time came to make that dream true the Prime Minister took the proper steps, and in three days you might more easily have found a bubble in the trough of the long Atlantic seas than Purun Dass among the roving, gathering, separating millions of India.

At night his antelope skin was spread where the darkness overtook him—sometimes in a Sunnyasi monastery by the roadside; sometimes by a mud pillar shrine of Kala Pir, where the Jogis, who are another misty division of holy men, would receive him as they do those who know what castes and divisions are worth; sometimes on the outskirts of a little Hindu village, where the children would steal up with the food their parents had prepared; and sometimes on the pitch of the bare grazing-grounds, where the flame of his stick fire waked the drowsy camels. It was all one to Purun Dass—or Purun Bhagat, as he called himself now. Earth, people, and food were all one. But unconsciously his feet drew him away northward and eastward; from the south to Rohtak; from Rohtak to Kurnool; from Kurnool to ruined Samanah, and then up-stream along the dried bed of the Gugger river that fills only when the rain falls in the hills, till one day he saw the far line of the great Himalayas.

Then Purun Bhagat smiled, for he remembered that his mother was of Rajput Brahmin birth, from Kulu way—a Hill-woman, always homesick for the

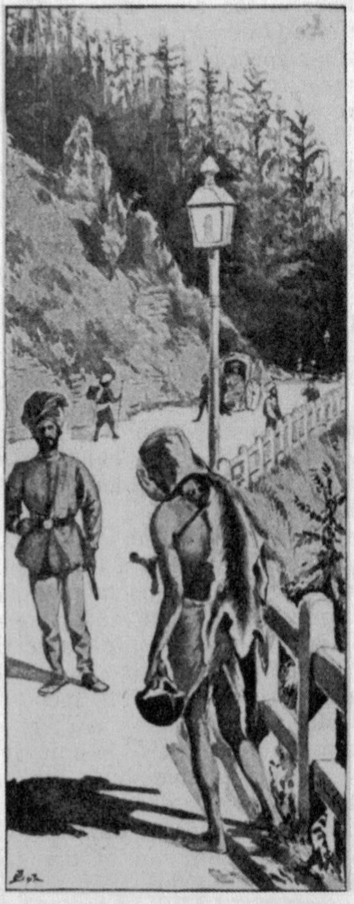

snows–and that the least touch of Hill blood draws a man at the end back to where he belongs.

"Yonder," said Purun Bhagat, breasting the lower slopes of the Sewaliks, where the cacti stood up like seven-branched candlesticks–"yonder I shall sit down and get knowledge"; and the cool wind of the Himalayas whistled about his ears as he trod the road that led to Simla.

The last time he had come that way it had been in state, with a clattering cavalry escort, to visit the gentlest and most affable of Viceroys; and the two had talked for an hour together about mutual friends in London, and what the Indian common folk really thought of things. This time Purun Bhagat paid no calls, but leaned on the rail of the Mall, watching that glorious view of the Plains spread out forty miles below, till a native Mohammedan policeman told him he was obstructing traffic; and Purun Bhagat salaamed reverently to the Law, because he knew the value of it, and was seeking for a Law of his own. Then he moved on, and slept that night in an empty hut at Chota Simla, which looks like the very last end of the earth, but it was only the beginning of his journey.

He followed the Himalaya-Thibet road, the little ten-foot track that is blasted out of solid rock, or strutted out on timbers over gulfs a thousand feet deep; that dips into warm, wet, shut-in valleys, and climbs out across bare, grassy hill-shoulders where the sun strikes like a burning-glass; or turns through dripping, dark forests where the tree-ferns dress the trunks from head to heel, and the pheasant calls to his mate. And he met Thibetan herdsmen with their dogs and flocks of sheep, each sheep with a little bag of borax on his back, and wandering wood-cutters, and cloaked and blanketed Lamas from Thibet, coming into India on pilgrimage, and envoys of little solitary Hill-states, posting furiously on ring-streaked and piebald ponies, or the cavalcade of a Rajah paying a visit; or else for a long, clear day he would see nothing more than a black bear grunting and rooting below in the valley. When he first started, the roar of the world he had left still rang in his ears, as the roar of a tunnel rings long after the train has passed through; but when he had put the Mutteeanee Pass behind him that was all done, and Purun Bhagat was alone with himself, walking, wondering, and thinking, his eyes on the ground, and his thoughts with the clouds.

One evening he crossed the highest pass he had met till then–it had been a two days' climb–and came out on a line of snow peaks that banded all the horizon–mountains from fifteen to twenty thousand feet high, looking almost near enough to hit with a stone, though they were fifty or sixty miles away. The pass was crowned with dense, dark forest–deodar, walnut, wild cherry, wild olive, and wild pear, but mostly deodar, which is the Himalayan cedar; and under the shadow of the deodars stood a deserted shrine to Kali–who is Durga, who is Sitala, who is sometimes worshiped against the smallpox.

Purun Bhagat swept the stone floor clean, smiled at the grinning statue, made himself a little mud fireplace at the back of the shrine, spread his antelope skin on a bed of fresh pine-needles, tucked his *bairagi*–his brass-handled crutch–under his armpit, and sat down to rest.

Immediately below him the hillside fell away, clean and cleared for fifteen hundred feet, where a little village of stone-walled houses, with roofs of beaten earth, clung to the steep tilt. All round it the tiny terraced fields lay out like aprons of patchwork on the knees of the mountain, and cows no bigger than beetles grazed between the smooth stone circles of the threshing-floors. Looking across the valley, the eye was deceived by the size of things, and could not at first realize that what seemed to be low scrub, on the opposite mountain-flank, was in truth a forest of hundred-foot pines. Purun Bhagat saw an eagle swoop across the gigantic hollow, but the great bird dwindled to a dot ere it was half-way over. A few bands of scattered clouds strung up and down the valley, catching on a shoulder of the hills, or rising up and dying out when they were level with the head of the pass. And "Here shall I find peace," said Purun Bhagat.

Now, a Hill-man makes nothing of a few hundred feet up or down, and as soon as the villagers saw the smoke in the deserted shrine, the village priest climbed up the terraced hillside to welcome the stranger.

When he met Purun Bhagat's eyes–the eyes of a man used to control thousands–he bowed to the earth, took the begging-bowl without a word, and returned to the village, saying, "We have at last a holy man. Never have I seen such a man. He is of the Plains–but pale-colored–a Brahmin of the Brahmins." Then all the housewives of the village said, "Think you he will stay with us?" and each did her best to cook the most savory meal for the Bhagat. Hill-food is very simple, but with buckwheat and Indian corn, and rice and red pepper, and little fish out of the stream in the valley, and honey from the flue-like hives built in the stone walls, and dried apricots, and turmeric, and wild ginger, and bannocks of flour, a devout woman can make good things, and it was a full bowl that the priest carried to the Bhagat. Was he going to stay? asked the priest. Would he need a *chela*–a disciple–to beg for him? Had he a blanket against the cold weather? Was the food good?

Purun Bhagat ate, and thanked the giver. It was in his mind to stay. That was sufficient, said the priest. Let the begging-bowl be placed outside the shrine, in the hollow made by those two twisted roots, and daily should the Bhagat be fed; for the village felt honored that such a man–he looked timidly into the Bhagat's face–should tarry among them.

That day saw the end of Purun Bhagat's wanderings. He had come to the place appointed for him–the silence and the space. After this, time stopped, and he, sitting at the mouth of the shrine, could not tell whether he were alive or dead; a man with control of his limbs, or a part of the hills, and the clouds, and the shifting rain and sunlight. He would repeat a Name softly to himself a hundred hundred times, till, at each repetition, he seemed to move more and more out of his body, sweeping up to the doors of some tremendous discovery; but, just as the door was opening, his body would drag him back, and, with grief, he felt he was locked up again in the flesh and bones of Purun Bhagat.

Every morning the filled begging-bowl was laid silently in the crutch of the roots outside the shrine. Sometimes the priest brought it; sometimes a Ladakhi trader, lodging in the village, and anxious to get merit, trudged up the path; but, more often, it was the woman who had cooked the meal overnight; and she would murmur, hardly above her breath: "Speak for me before the gods, Bhagat. Speak for such a one, the wife of so-and-so!" Now and then some bold child would be allowed the honor, and Purun Bhagat would hear him drop the bowl and run as fast as his little legs could carry him, but the Bhagat never came down to the village. It was laid out like a map at his feet. He could see the evening gatherings, held on the circle of the threshing-floors because that was the only level ground; could see the wonderful unnamed green of the young rice, the indigo blues of the Indian corn, the dock-like patches of buckwheat, and, in its season, the red bloom of the amaranth, whose tiny seeds, being neither grain nor pulse, make a food that can be lawfully eaten by Hindus in time of fasts.

When the year turned, the roofs of the huts were all little squares of purest gold, for it was on the roofs that they laid out their cobs of the corn to dry. Hiving and harvest, rice-sowing and husking, passed before his eyes, all embroidered down there on the many-sided plots of fields, and he thought of them all, and wondered what they all led to at the long last.

Even in populated India a man cannot a day sit still before the wild things run over him as though he were a rock; and in that wilderness very soon the wild things, who knew Kali's Shrine well, came back to look at the intruder. The *langurs,* the big gray-whiskered monkeys of the Himalayas, were, naturally, the first, for they are alive with curiosity; and when they had upset the begging-bowl, and rolled it round the floor, and tried their teeth on the brass-handled crutch, and made faces at the antelope skin, they decided that the human being who sat so still was harmless. At evening, they would leap down from the pines, and beg with their hands for things to eat, and then swing off

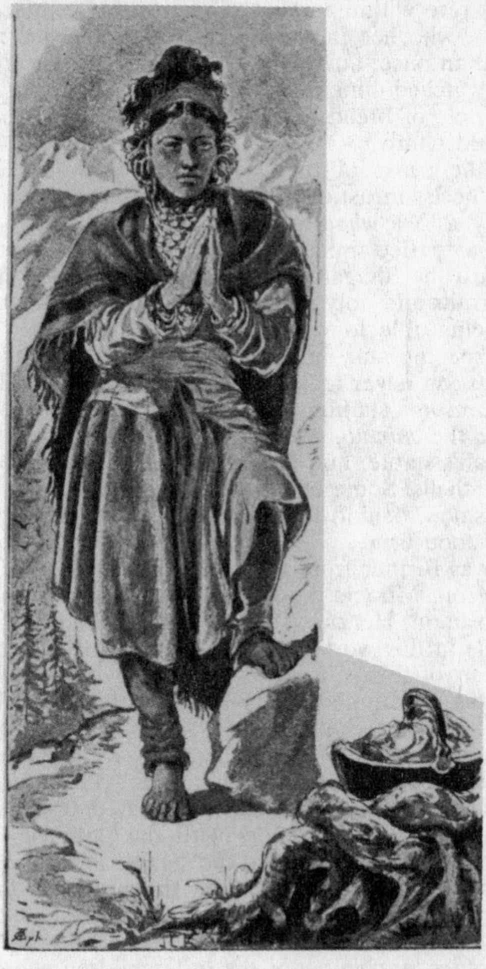

in graceful curves. They liked the warmth of the fire, too, and huddled round it till Purun Bhagat had to push them aside to throw on more fuel; and in the morning, as often as not, he would find a furry ape sharing his blanket. All day long, one or other of the tribe would sit by his side, staring out at the snows, crooning and looking unspeakably wise and sorrowful.

After the monkeys came the *barasingh,* that big deer which is like our red deer, but stronger. He wished to rub off the velvet of his horns against the cold stones of Kali's statue, and stamped his feet when he saw the man at the shrine. But Purun Bhagat never moved, and little by little, the royal stag ended up and nuzzled his shoulder. Purun Bhagat slid one cool hand along the hot antlers, and the touch soothed the fretted beast, who bowed his head, and Purun Bhagat very softly rubbed and raveled off the velvet. Afterward, the *barasingh* brought his doe and fawn—gentle things that mumbled on the holy man's blanket—or would come alone at night, his eyes green in the fire-flicker, to take his share of fresh walnuts. At last, the musk-deer, the shyest and almost the smallest of the deerlets, came, too, her big rabbity ears erect; even brindled, silent *mushick-nabha* must needs find out what the light in the shrine meant, and drop her moose-like nose into Purun Bhagat's lap, coming and going with the shadows of the fire. Purun Bhagat called them all "my brothers," and his low call of *"Bhai! Bhai!"* would draw them from the forest at noon if they were within earshot. The Himalayan black bear, moody and suspicious–Sona, who has the V-shaped white mark under his chin–passed that way more than once; and since the Bhagat showed no fear, Sona showed no anger, but watched him, and came closer, and begged a share of the caresses, and a dole of bread or wild berries. Often, in the still dawns, when the Bhagat would climb to the very crest of the pass to watch the red day walking along the peaks of the snows, he would find Sona shuffling and grunting at his heels, thrusting a curious fore-paw under fallen trunks, and bringing it away with a *whoof* of impatience; or his early steps would wake Sona where he lay curled up, and the great brute, rising erect, would think to fight, till he heard the Bhagat's voice and knew his best friend.

Nearly all hermits and holy men who live apart from the big cities have the reputation of being able to work miracles with the wild things, but all the miracle lies in keeping still, in never making a hasty movement, and, for a long time, at least, in never looking directly at a visitor. The villagers saw the outline of the *barasingh* stalking like a shadow through the dark forest behind the shrine; saw the *minaul,* the Himalayan pheasant, blazing in her best colors before Kali's statue; and the *langurs* on their haunches, inside, playing with the walnut shells. Some of the children, too, had heard Sona singing to himself, bear-fashion, behind the fallen rocks, and the Bhagat's reputation as miracle-worker stood firm.

Yet nothing was further from his mind than miracles. He believed that all things were one big Miracle, and when a man knows that much he knows something to go upon. He knew for a certainty that there was nothing great and nothing little in this world; and day and night he strove to think out his way into the heart of things, back to the place whence his soul had come.

So thinking, his untrimmed hair fell down about his shoulders, the stone slab at the side of the antelope skin was dented into a little hole by the foot of his brass-handled crutch, and the place between the tree-trunks, where the begging-bowl rested day after day, sunk and wore into a hollow almost as smooth as the brown shell itself; and each beast knew his exact place at the fire. The fields changed their colors with the seasons; the threshing-floors filled and emptied, and filled again and again; and again and again, when winter came, the *langurs* frisked among the branches feathered with light snow, till the mother-monkeys brought their sad-eyed little babies up from the warmer valleys with the spring. There were few changes in the village. The priest was older, and many of the little children who used to come with the begging-bowl sent their own children now; and when you asked of the villagers how long their holy man had lived in Kali's Shrine at the head of the pass, they answered, "Always."

Then came such summer rains as had not been known in the Hills for many seasons. Through three good months the valley was wrapped in cloud and soaking mist–steady, unrelenting downfall, breaking off into thunder-shower after thunder-shower. Kali's Shrine stood above the clouds, for the most part, and there was a whole month in which the Bhagat never saw his village. It was packed away under a white floor of cloud that swayed and shifted and rolled on itself and bulged upward, but never broke from its piers–the streaming flanks of the valley.

All that time he heard nothing but the sound of a million little waters, overhead from the trees, and underfoot along the ground, soaking through the pine-needles, dripping from the tongues of draggled fern, and spouting in newly torn muddy channels down the slopes. Then the sun came out, and drew forth the good incense of the deodars and the rhododendrons, and that far-off, clean smell which the Hill people call "the smell of the snows." The hot sunshine lasted for a week, and then the rains gathered together for their last downpour, and the water fell in sheets that flayed off the skin of the ground and leaped back in mud. Purun Bhagat heaped his fire high that night, for he was sure his brothers would need warmth; but never a beast came to the shrine, though he called and called till he dropped asleep, wondering what had happened in the woods.

It was in the black heart of the night, the rain drumming like a thousand drums, that he was roused by a plucking at his blanket, and stretching out, felt the little hand of a *langur*. "It is better here than in the trees," he said sleepily, loosening a fold of blanket; "take it and be warm." The monkey caught his hand and pulled hard. "Is it food, then?" said Purun Bhagat. "Wait awhile, and I will prepare some." As he kneeled to throw fuel on the fire the *langur* ran to the door of the shrine, crooned, and ran back again, plucking at the man's knee.

"What is it? What is thy trouble, Brother?" said Purun Bhagat, for the *langur's* eyes were full of things that he could not tell. "Unless one of thy caste be in a trap–and none set traps here–I will not go into that weather. Look, Brother, even the *barasingh* comes for shelter!"

The deer's antlers clashed as he strode into the shrine, clashed against the grinning statue of Kali. He lowered them in Purun Bhagat's direction and stamped uneasily, hissing through his half-shut nostrils.

"Hai! Hai! Hai!" said the Bhagat, snapping his fingers. "Is *this* payment for a night's lodging?" But the deer pushed him toward the door, and as he did so Purun Bhagat heard the sound of something opening with a sigh, and two slabs of the floor draw away from each other, while the sticky earth below smacked its lips.

"Now I see," said Purun Bhagat. "No blame to my brothers that they did not sit by the fire to-night. The mountain is falling. And yet–why should I go?" His eye fell on the empty begging-bowl, and his face changed. "They have given me good food daily since–since I came, and, if I am not swift, to-morrow there will not be one mouth in the valley. Indeed, I must go and warn them below. Back there, Brother! Let me get to the fire."

The *barasingh* backed unwillingly as Purun Bhagat drove a pine torch deep into the flame, twirling it till it was well lit. "Ah! ye came to warn me," he said, rising. "Better than that we shall do; better than that. Out, now, and lend me thy neck, Brother, for I have but two feet."

He clutched the bristling withers of the *barasingh* with his right hand, held the torch away with his left, and stepped out of the shrine into the desperate night. There was no breath of wind, but the rain nearly drowned the flare as the great deer hurried down the slope, sliding on his haunches. As soon as they were clear of the forest more of the Bhagat's brothers joined them. He heard, though he could not see, the *langurs* pressing about him, and behind them the *uhh! uhh!* of Sona. The rain matted his long white hair into ropes; the water splashed beneath his bare feet, and his yellow robe clung to his frail old body, but he stepped down steadily, leaning against the *barasingh*. He was no longer a holy man, but Sir Purun Dass, K. C. I. E., Prime Minister of no small State, a man accustomed to command, going out to save life. Down the steep, plashy path they poured all together, the Bhagat and his brothers, down and down till the deer's feet clicked and stumbled on the wall of a threshing-floor, and he snorted because he smelt Man. Now they were at the head of the one crooked village street, and the Bhagat beat with his crutch on the barred windows of the blacksmith's house as his torch blazed up in the shelter of the eaves. "Up and out!" cried Purun Bhagat; and he did not know his own voice, for it was years since he had spoken aloud to a man.

"The hill falls! The hill is falling! Up and out, oh, you within!"

"It is our Bhagat," said the blacksmith's wife. "He stands among his beasts. Gather the little ones and give the call."

It ran from house to house, while the beasts, cramped in the narrow way, surged and huddled round the Bhagat, and Sona puffed impatiently.

The people hurried into the street–they were no more than seventy souls all told–and in the glare of the torches they saw their Bhagat holding back the terrified *barasingh,* while the monkeys plucked piteously at his skirts, and Sona sat on his haunches and roared.

"Across the valley and up the next hill!" shouted Purun Bhagat. "Leave none behind! We follow!"

When the people ran as only Hill folk can run, for they knew that in a landslip you must climb for the highest ground across the valley. They fled, splashing through the little river at the bottom, and panted up the terraced fields on the far side, while the Bhagat and his brethren followed. Up and up the opposite mountain they climbed, calling to each other by name–the roll-call of the village–and at their heels toiled the big *barasingh,* weighted by the failing strength of Purun Bhagat. At last the deer stopped in the shadow of a deep pine-wood, five hundred feet up the hillside. His instinct, that had warned him of the coming slide, told him he would be safe here.

Purun Bhagat dropped fainting by his side, for the chill of the rain and that fierce climb were killing him; but first he called to the scattered torches ahead, "Stay and count your numbers"; then, whispering to the deer as he saw the lights gather in a cluster: "Stay with me, Brother. Stay–till–I–go!"

There was a sigh in the air that grew to a mutter, and a mutter that grew to a roar, and a roar that passed all sense of hearing, and the hillside on which the villagers stood was hit in the darkness, and rocked to the blow. Then a note as steady, deep, and true as the deep C of the organ drowned everything for perhaps five minutes, while the very roots of the pines quivered to it. It died away, and the sound of the rain falling on miles of hard ground and grass changed to the muffled drum of water on soft earth. That told its own tale.

Never a villager–not even the priest–was bold enough to speak to the Bhagat who had saved their lives. They crouched under the pines and waited till the day. When it came they looked across the valley and saw that what had been forest, and terraced field, and track-threaded grazing-ground was one raw, red, fan-shaped smear, with a few trees flung head-down on the scarp. That red ran high up the hill of their refuge, damming back the little river, which had begun to spread into a brick-colored lake. Of the village, of the road to the shrine, of the shrine itself, and the forest behind, there was not trace. For one mile in width and two thousand feet in sheer depth the mountain-side had come away bodily, planed clean from head to heel.

And the villagers, one by one, crept through the wood to pray before their Bhagat. They saw the *barasingh* standing over him, who fled when they came near, and they heard the *langurs* wailing in the branches, and Sona moaning up the hill; but their Bhagat was dead, sitting cross-legged, his back against a tree, his crutch under his armpit, and his face turned to the northeast.

The priest said: "Behold a micracle after a miracle, for in this very attitude must all Sunnyasis be buried! Therefore where he now is we will build the temple to our holy man."

They built the temple before a year was ended–a little stone-and-earth shrine–and they called the hill the Bhagat's Hill, and they worship there with lights and flowers and offerings to this day. But they do not know that the saint of their worship is the late Sir Purun Dass, K. C. I. E., D. C. L., Ph. D., etc., once Prime Minister of the progressive and enlightened State of Mohiniwala, and honorary or corresponding member of more learned and scientific societies than will ever do any good in this world or the next.

A Song of Kabir

Oh, light was the world that he weighed in his hands!
Oh, heavy the tale of his fiefs and his lands!
He has gone from the *guddee* and put on the shroud,
And departed in guise of *bairagi* avowed!

Now the white road to Delhi is mat for his feet,
The *sal* and the *kikar* must guard him from heat;
His home is the camp, and the waste, and the crowd–
He is seeking the Way as *bairagi* avowed!

He has looked upon Man, and his eyeballs are clear
(There was One; there is One, and but One, saith Kabir);
The Red Mist of Doing has thinned to a cloud–
He has taken the Path for *bairagi* avowed!

To learn and discern of his brother the clod,
Of his brother the brute, and his brother the God.
He has gone from the council and put on the shroud
("Can ye hear?" saith Kabir), a *bairagi* avowed!

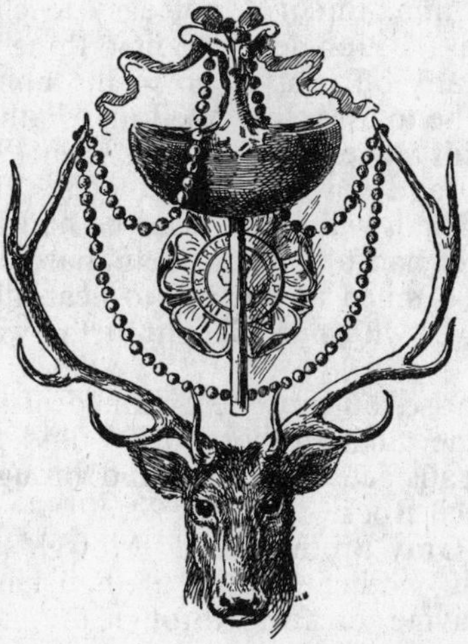

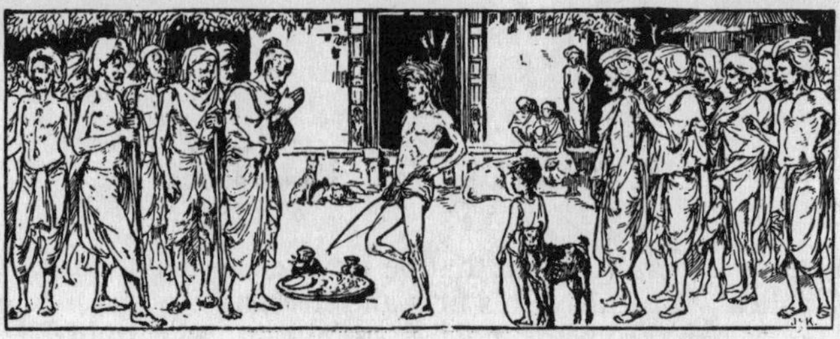

Letting in the Jungle

Veil them, cover them, wall them round—
    Blossom, and creeper, and weed—
Let us forget the sight and the sound,
    The smell and the touch of the breed!

Fat black ash by the altar-stone,
    Here is the white-foot rain,
And the does bring forth in the fields unsown,
    And none shall affright them again;
And the blind walls crumble, unknown, o'erthrown,
    And none shall inhabit again!

YOU WILL REMEMBER, if you have read the tales in the first Jungle Book, that, after Mowgli had pinned Shere Khan's hide to the Council Rock, he told as many as were left of the Seeonee Pack that henceforward he would hunt in the Jungle alone; and the four children of Mother and Father Wolf said that they would hunt with him. But it is not easy to change one's life all in a minute—particularly in the Jungle. The first thing Mowgli did, when the disorderly Pack had slunk off, was to go to the home-cave, and sleep for a day and a night. Then he told Mother Wolf and Father Wolf as much as they could understand of his adventures among men; and when he made the morning sun flicker up and down the blade of his skinning-knife,—the same he had skinned Shere Khan with,—they said he had learned something. Then Akela and Gray Brother had to explain their share of the great buffalo-drive in the ravine, and Baloo toiled up the hill to hear all about it, and Bagheera scratched himself all over with pure delight at the way in which Mowgli had managed his war.

It was long after sunrise, but no one dreamed of going to sleep, and from time to time, during the talk, Mother Wolf would throw up her head, and sniff a deep snuff of satisfaction as the wind brought her the smell of the tiger-skin on the Council Rock.

"But for Akela and Gray Brother here," Mowgli said, at the end, "I could have done nothing. Oh, mother, mother! if thou hadst seen the black herd-bulls pour down the ravine, or hurry through the gates when the Man-Pack flung stones at me!"

"I am glad I did not see that last," said Mother Wolf, stiffly. "It is not *my* custom to suffer my cubs to be driven to and fro like jackals. *I* would have taken a price from the Man-Pack; but I would have spared the woman who gave thee the milk. Yes, I would have spared her alone."

"Peace, peace, Raksha!" said Father Wolf, lazily. "Our Frog has come back again—so wise that his own father must lick his feet; and what is a cut, more or less, on the head? Leave Men alone." Baloo and Bagheera both echoed: "Leave Men alone."

Mowgli, his head on Mother Wolf's side, smiled contentedly, and said that, for his own part, he never wished to see, or hear, or smell Man again.

"But what," said Akela, cocking one ear–"but what if men do not leave thee alone, Little Brother?"

"We be *five,"* said Gray Brother, looking round at the company, and snapping his jaws on the last word.

"We also might attend to that hunting," said Bagheera, with a little *switch-switch* of his tail, looking at Baloo. "But why think of men now, Akela?"

"For this reason," the Lone Wolf answered: "when that yellow thief's hide was hung up on the rock, I went back along our trail to the village, stepping in my tracks, turning aside, and lying down, to make a mixed trail in case one should follow us. But when I had fouled the trail so that I myself hardly knew it again, Mang, the Bat, came hawking between the trees, and hung up above me. Said Mang, 'The village of the Man-Pack, where they cast out the Man-cub, hums like a hornet's nest.' "

"It was a big stone that I threw," chuckled Mowgli, who had often amused himself by throwing ripe paw-paws into a hornet's nest, and racing off to the nearest pool before the hornets caught him.

"I asked of Mang what he had seen. He said the Red Flower blossomed at the gate of the village, and men sat about it carrying guns. Now *I* know, for I have good cause,"–Akela looked down at the old dry scars on his flank and side,–"that men do not carry guns for pleasure. Presently, Little Brother, a man with a gun follows our trail–if, indeed, he be not already on it."

"But why should he? Men have cast me out. What more do they need?" said Mowgli, angrily.

"Thou art a man, Little Brother," Akela returned. "It is not for *us,* the Free Hunters, to tell thee what thy brethren do, or why."

He had just time to snatch up his paw as the skinning-knife cut deep into the ground below. Mowgli struck quicker than an average human eye could follow, but Akela was a wolf; and even a dog, who is very far removed from the wild wolf, his ancestor, can be waked out of deep sleep by a cart-wheel touching his flank, and can spring away unharmed before that wheel comes on.

"Another time," Mowgli said quietly, returning the knife to its sheath, "speak of the Man-Pack and of Mowgli in *two* breaths–not one."

"Phff! That is a sharp tooth," said Akela, snuffing at the blade's cut in the earth, "but living with the Man-Pack has spoiled thine eye, Little Brother. I could have killed a buck while thou wast striking."

Bagheera sprang to his feet, thrust up his head as far as he could, sniffed, and stiffened through every curve in his body. Gray Brother followed his example quickly, keeping a little to his left to get the wind that was blowing from the right, while Akela bounded fifty yards up wind, and, half crouching, stiffened too. Mowgli looked on enviously. He could smell things as very few human being could, but he had never reached the hair-trigger-like sensitiveness of a Jungle nose; and his three months in the smoky village had set him back sadly. However, he dampened his finger, rubbed it on his nose, and stood erect to catch the upper scent, which, though it is the faintest, is the truest.

"Man!" Akela growled, dropping on his haunches.

"Buldeo!" said Mowgli, sitting down. "He follows our trail, and yonder is the sunlight on his gun. Look!"

It was no more than a splash of sunlight, for a fraction of a second, on the brass clamps of the old Tower musket, but nothing in the Jungle winks with just that flash, except when the clouds race over the sky. Then a piece of mica, or a little pool, or even a highly polished leaf will flash like a heliograph. But that day was cloudless and still.

"I knew men would follow," said Akela, triumphantly. "Not for nothing have I led the Pack."

The four cubs said nothing, but ran down hill on their bellies, melting into the thorn and underbrush as a mole melts into a lawn.

"Where go ye, and without word?" Mowgli called.

"H'sh! We roll his skull here before mid-day!" Gray Brother answered.

"Back! Back and wait! Man does not eat Man!" Mowgli shrieked.

"Who was a wolf but now? Who drove the knife at me for thinking he might be Man?" said Akela, as the four wolves turned back sullenly and dropped to heel.

"Am I to give a reason for all I choose to do?" said Mowgli, furiously.

"That is Man! There speaks Man!" Bagheera muttered under his whiskers. "Even so did men talk round the King's cages at Oodeypore. We of the Jungle know that Man is wisest of all. If we trusted our ears we should know that of all things he is most foolish." Raising his voice, he added, "The Man-cub is right in this. Men hunt in packs. To kill one, unless we know what the others will do, is bad hunting. Come, let us see what this Man means toward us."

"We will not come," Gray Brother growled. "Hunt alone, Little Brother. *We* know our own minds. That skull would have been ready to bring by now."

Mowgli had been looking from one to the other of his friends, his chest heaving and his eyes full of tears. He strode forward to the wolves, and, dropping on one knee, said: "Do I not know my mind? Look at me!"

They looked uneasily, and when their eyes wandered, he called them back again and again, till their hair stood up all over their bodies, and they trembled in every limb, while Mowgli stared and stared.

"Now," said he, "of us five, which is leader?"

"Thou art leader, Little Brother," said Gray Brother, and he licked Mowgli's foot.

"Follow, then," said Mowgli, and the four followed at his heels with their tails between their legs.

"This comes of living with the Man-Pack," said Bagheera, slipping down after them. "There is more in the Jungle now than Jungle Law, Baloo."

The old bear said nothing, but he thought many things.

Mowgli cut across noiselessly through the Jungle, at right angles to Buldeo's path, till, parting the undergrowth, he saw the old man, his musket on his shoulder, running up the trail of overnight at a dog-trot.

You will remember that Mowgli had left the village with the heavy weight of Shere Khan's raw hide on his shoulders, while Akela and Gray Brother trotted behind, so that the triple trail was very clearly marked. Presently Buldeo came to where Akela, as you know, had gone back and mixed it all up. Then he sat down, and coughed and grunted, and made little casts round and about into the Jungle to pick it up again, and all the time he could have thrown a stone over those who were watching him. No one can be so silent as a wolf when he does not care to be heard; and Mowgli, though the wolves thought he moved very clumsily, could come and go like a shadow. They ringed the old man as a school of porpoises ring a steamer at full speed, and as they ringed him they talked unconcernedly, for their speech began below the lowest end of the scale that untrained human beings can hear. [The other end is bounded by the high squeak of Mang, the Bat, which very many people cannot catch at all. From that note all the bird and bat and insect talk takes on.]

"This is better than any kill," said Gray Brother, as Buldeo stooped and peered and puffed. "He looks like a lost pig in the Jungles by the river. What does he say?" Buldeo was muttering savagely.

Mowgli translated. "He says that packs of wolves must have danced round me. He says that he never saw such a trail in his life. He says he is tired."

"He will be rested before he picks it up again," said Bagheera coolly, as he slipped round a tree-trunk, in the game of blindman's-buff that they were playing. *"Now,* what does the lean thing do?"

"Eat or blow smoke out of his mouth. Men always play with their mouths," said Mowgli; and the silent trailers saw the old man fill and light and puff at a water-pipe, and they took good note of the smell of the tobacco, so as to be sure of Buldeo in the darkest night, if necessary.

Then a little knot of charcoal-burners came down the path, and naturally halted to speak to Buldeo, whose fame as a hunter reached for at least twenty miles round. They all sat down and smoked, and Bagheera and the others came up and watched while Buldeo began to tell the story of Mowgli, the Devil-child, from one end to another, with additions and inventions. How he himself had really killed Shere Khan; and how Mowgli had turned himself into a wolf, and fought with him all the afternoon, and changed into a boy again and bewitched Buldeo's rifle, so that the bullet turned the corner, when he pointed it at Mowgli, and killed one of Buldeo's own buffaloes; and how the village, knowing him to be the bravest hunter in Seeonee, had sent him out to kill this Devil-child. But meantime the village had got hold of Messua and her husband, who were undoubtedly the father and mother of this Devil-child, and had barricaded them in their own hut, and presently would torture them to make them confess they were witch and wizard, and then they would be burned to death.

"When?" said the charcoal-burners, because they would very much like to be present at the ceremony.

Buldeo said that nothing would be done till he returned, because the village wished him to kill the Jungle Boy first. After that they would dispose of Messua and her husband, and divide their lands and buffaloes among the village. Messua's husband had some remarkably fine buffaloes, too. It was an excellent thing to destroy wizards, Buldeo thought; and people who entertained Wolf-children out of the Jungle were clearly the worst kind of witches.

But, said the charcoal-burners, what would happen if the English heard of it? The English, they had heard, were a perfectly mad people, who would not let honest farmers kill witches in peace.

Why, said Buldeo, the head-man of the village would report that Messua and her husband had died of snake-bite. *That* was all arranged, and the only thing now was to kill the Wolf-child. They did not happen to have seen anything of such a creature?

The charcoal-burners looked round cautiously, and thanked their stars they had not; but they had no doubt that so brave a man as Buldeo would find him if any one could. The sun was getting rather low, and they had an idea that they would push on to Buldeo's village and see that wicked witch. Buldeo said that, though it was his duty to kill the Devil-child, he could not think of letting a party of unarmed men go through the Jungle, which might produce the Wolf-demon at any minute, without his escort. He, therefore, would accompany them, and if the sorcerer's child appeared—well, he would show them how the best hunter in Seeonee dealt with such things. The Brahmin, he said, had given him a charm against the creature that made everything perfectly safe.

"What says he? What says he? What says he?" the wolves repeated every few minutes; and Mowgli translated until he came to the witch part of the story, which was a little beyond him, and then he said that the man and woman who had been so kind to him were trapped.

"Does Man trap Man?" said Bagheera.

"So he says. I cannot understand the talk. They are all mad together. What have Messua and her man to do with me that they should be put in a trap;

and what is all this talk about the Red Flower? I must look to this. Whatever they would do to Messua they will not do till Buldeo returns. And so–" Mowgli thought hard, with his fingers playing round the haft of the skinning-knife, while Buldeo and the charcoal-burners went off very valiantly in single file.

"I am going hot-foot back to the Man-Pack," Mowgli said at last.

"And those?" said Gray Brother, looking hungrily after the brown backs of the charcoal-burners.

"Sing them home," said Mowgli with a grin; "I do not wish them to be at the village gates till it is dark. Can ye hold them?"

Gray Brother bared his white teeth in contempt. We can head them round and round in circles like tethered goats–if I know Man."

"That I do not need. Sing to them a little, lest they be lonely on the road, and, Gray Brother, the song need not be of the sweetest. Go with them. Bagheera, and help make that song. When the night is shut down, meet me by the village–Gray Brother knows the place."

"It is no light hunting to work for a Man-cub. When shall I sleep?" said Bagheera, yawning, though his eyes showed that he was delighted with the amusement. "Me to sing to naked men! But let us try."

He lowered his head so that the sound would travel, and cried a long, long, "Good hunting"–a midnight call in the afternoon, which was quite awful enough to begin with. Mowgli heard it rumble, and rise, and fall, and die off in a creepy sort of whine behind him, and laughed to himself as he ran through the Jungle. He could see the charcoal-burners huddled in a knot; old Buldeo's gun-barrel waving, like a banana-leaf, to every point of the compass at once. Then Gray Brother gave the *Ya-la-hi! Yalaha!* call for the buck-driving, when the Pack drives the nilghai, the big blue cow, before them, and it seemed to come from the very ends of the earth, nearer, and nearer, and nearer, till it ended in a shriek snapped off short. The other three answered, till even Mowgli could have vowed that the full Pack was in full cry, and then they all broke into the magnificent Morning-song in the Jungle, with every turn, and flourish, and grace-note, that a deep-mouthed wolf of the Pack knows. This is a rough rendering of the song, but you must imagine what it sounds like when it breaks the afternoon hush of the Jungle:

One moment past our bodies cast
    No shadow on the plain;
Now clear and black they stride our track,
    And we run home again.
In morning hush, each rock and bush
    Stands hard, and high, and raw:
Then give the Call: *"Good rest to all*
    That keep the Jungle Law!"

Now horn and pelt our peoples melt
    In covert to abide;
Now, crouched and still, to cave and hill
    Our Jungle Barons glide.
Now, stark and plain, Man's oxen strain,
    That draw the new-yoked plow;
Now, stripped and dread, the dawn is red
    Above the lit *talao.*

Ho! Get to lair! The sun's aflare
    Behind the breathing grass:
And creaking through the young bamboo
    The warning whispers pass.

By day made strange, the woods we range
With blinking eyes we scan;
While down the skies the wild duck cries:
"The Day—the Day to Man!"

The dew is dried that drenched our hide,
Or washed about our way;
And where we drank, the puddled bank
Is crisping into clay.
The traitor Dark gives up each mark
Of stretched or hooded claw;
Then hear the Call: *"Good rest to all
That keep the Jungle Law!"*

But no translation can give the effect of it, or the yelping scorn the Four threw into every word of it, as they heard the trees crash when the men hastily climbed up into the branches, and Buldeo began repeating incantations and charms. Then they lay down and slept, for, like all who live by their own exertions, they were of a methodical cast of mind; and no one can work well without sleep.

Meantime, Mowgli was putting the miles behind him, nine to the hour, swinging on, delighted to find himself so fit after all his cramped months among men. The one idea in his head was to get Messua and her husband out of the trap, whatever it was; for he had a natural mistrust of traps. Later on, he promised himself, he would pay his debts to the village at large.

It was at twilight when he saw the well-remembered grazing-grounds, and the *dhak*-tree where Gray Brother had waited for him on the morning that he killed Shere Khan. Angry as he was at the whole breed and community of Man, something jumped up in his throat and made him catch his breath when he looked at the village roofs. He noticed that every one had come in from the fields unusually early, and that, instead of getting to their evening cooking, they gathered in a crowd under the village tree, and chattered, and shouted.

"Men must always be making traps for men, or they are not content," said Mowgli. "Last night it was Mowgli—but that night seems many Rains ago. To-night it is Messua and her man. To-morrow, and for very many nights after, it will be Mowgli's turn again."

He crept along outside the wall till he came to Messua's hut, and looked through the window into the room. There lay Messua, gagged, and bound hand and foot, breathing hard, and groaning: her husband was tied to the gaily painted bedstead. The door of the hut that opened into the street was shut fast, and three or four people were sitting with their backs to it.

Mowgli knew the manners and customs of the villagers very fairly. He argued that so long as they could eat, and talk, and smoke, they would not do anything else; but as soon as they had fed they would begin to be dangerous. Buldeo would be coming in before long, and if his escort had done its duty, Buldeo would have a very interesting tale to tell. So he went in through the window, and, stooping over the man and the woman, cut their thongs, pulling out the gags, and looked round the hut for some milk.

Messua was half wild with pain and fear (she had been beaten and stoned all the morning), and Mowgli put his hand over her mouth just in time to stop a scream. Her husband was only bewildered and angry, and sat picking dust and things out of his torn beard.

"I knew—I knew he would come," Messua sobbed at last. "Now do I *know* that he is my son!" and she hugged Mowgli to her heart. Up to that time Mowgli had been perfectly steady, but now he began to tremble all over, and that surprised him immensely.

"Why are these thongs? Why have they tied thee?" he asked, after a pause.

"To be put to the death for making a son of thee–what else?" said the man, sullenly. "Look! I bleed."

Messua said nothing, but it was at *her* wounds that Mowgli looked, and they heard him grit his teeth when he saw the blood.

"Whose work is this?" said he. "There is a price to pay."

"The work of all the village. I was too rich. I had too many cattle. *Therefore* she and I are witches, because we gave thee shelter."

"I do not understand. Let Messua tell the tale."

"I gave thee milk, Nathoo; dost thou remember?" Messua said timidly. "Because thou wast my son, whom the tiger took, and because I loved thee very dearly. They said that I was thy mother, the mother of a devil, and therefore worthy of death."

"And what is a devil?" said Mowgli. "Death I have seen."

The man looked up gloomily, but Messua laughed. "See!" she said to her husband, "I knew–I said that he was no sorcerer. He is my son–my son!"

"Son or sorcerer, what good will that do us?" the man answered. "We be as dead already."

"Yonder is the road to the Jungle"–Mowgli pointed through the window. "Your hands and feet are free. Go now."

"We do not know the Jungle, my son, as–as thou knowest," Messua began. "I do not think that I could walk far."

"And the men and women would be upon our backs and drag us here again," said the husband.

"H'm!" said Mowgli, and he tickled the palm of his hand with the tip of his skinning-knife; "I have no wish to do harm to any one of this village–*yet*. But I do not think they will stay thee. In a little while they will have much else to think upon. Ah!" he lifted his head and listened to shouting and trampling outside. "So they have let Buldeo come home at last?"

"He was sent out this morning to kill thee," Messua cried. "Didst thou meet him?"

"Yes–we–I met him. He has a tale to tell; and while he is telling it there is time to do much. But first I will learn what they mean. Think where ye would go, and tell me when I come back."

He bounded through the window and ran along again outside the wall of the village till he came within ear-shot of the crowd round the peepul-tree. Buldeo was lying on the ground, coughing and groaning, and every one was asking him questions. His hair had fallen about his shoulders; his hands and legs were skinned from climbing up trees, and he could hardly speak, but he felt the importance of his position keenly. From time to time he said something about devils and singing devils, and magic enchantment, just to give the crowd a taste of what was coming. Then he called for water.

"Bah!" said Mowgli. "Chatter–chatter! Talk, talk! Men are blood-brothers of the *Bandar-log*. Now he must wash his mouth with water; now he must blow smoke; and when all that is done he has still his story to tell. They are very wise people–men. They will leave no one to guard Messua till their ears are stuffed with Buldeo's tales. And–I grow as lazy as they!"

He shook himself and glided back to the hut. Just as he was at the window he felt a touch on his foot.

"Mother," said he, for he knew that tongue well, "what dost *thou* here?"

"I heard my children singing through the woods, and I followed the one I loved best. Little Frog, I have a desire to see that woman who gave thee milk," said Mother Wolf, all wet with the dew.

"They have bound and mean to kill her. I have cut those ties, and she goes with her man through the Jungle."

"I also will follow. I am old, but not yet toothless." Mother Wolf reared herself up on end, and looked through the window into the dark of the hut.

In a minute she dropped noiselessly, and all she said was: "I gave thee thy first milk; but Bagheera speaks truth: Man goes to Man at the last."

"Maybe," said Mowgli, with a very unpleasant look on his face; "but to-night I am very far from that trail. Wait here, but do not let her see."

"*Thou* wast never afraid of *me,* Little Frog," said Mother Wolf, backing into the high grass, and blotting herself out, as she knew how.

"And now," said Mowgli, cheerfully, as he swung into the hut again, "they are all sitting round Buldeo, who is saying that which did not happen. When his talk is finished, they say they will assuredly come here with the Red–with fire and burn you both. And then?"

"I have spoken to my man," said Messua. "Kanhiwara is thirty miles from here, but at Kanhiwara we may find the English–"

"And what Pack are they?" said Mowgli.

"I do not know. They be white, and it is said that they govern all the land, and do not suffer people to burn or beat each other without witnesses. If we can get thither to-night, we live. Otherwise we die."

"Live, then. No man passes the gates to-night. But what does *he* do?" Messua's husband was on his hands and knees digging up the earth in one corner of the hut.

"It is his little money," said Messua. "We can take nothing else."

"Ah, yes. The stuff that passes from hand to hand and never grows warmer. Do they need it outside this place also?" said Mowgli.

The man stared angrily. "He is a fool, and no devil," he muttered. "With the money I can buy a horse. We are too bruised to walk far, and the village will follow us in an hour."

"I say they will *not* follow till I choose; but the horse is well thought of, for Messua is tired." Her husband stood up and knotted the last of the rupees into his waist-cloth. Mowgli helped Messua through the window, and the cool night air revived her, but the Jungle in the starlight looked very dark and terrible.

"Ye know the trail to Kanhiwara?" Mowgli whispered.

They nodded.

"Good. Remember, now, not to be afraid. And there is no need to go quickly. Only–only there may be some small singing in the Jungle behind you and before."

"Think you we would have risked a night in the Jungle through anything less than the fear of burning? It is better to be killed by beasts than by men," said Messua's husband; but Messua looked at Mowgli and smiled.

"I say," Mowgli went on, just as though he were Baloo repeating an old Jungle Law for the hundredth time to a foolish cub–"I say that not a tooth in the Jungle is bared against you; not a foot in the Jungle is lifted against you. Neither man nor beast shall stay you till ye come within eye-shot of Kanhiwara. There will be a watch about you." He turned quickly to Messua, saying, "*He* does not believe, but thou wilt believe?"

"Ay, surely, my son. Man, ghost, or wolf of the Jungle, I believe."

"*He* will be afraid when he hears my people singing. Thou wilt know and understand. Go now, and slowly, for there is no need of any haste. The gates are shut."

Messua flung herself sobbing at Mowgli's feet, but he lifted her very quickly with a shiver. Then she hung about his neck and called him every name of blessing she could think of, but her husband looked enviously across his fields, and said: "*If* we reach Kanhiwara, and I get the ear of the English, I will bring such a lawsuit against the Brahmin and old Buldeo and the others as shall eat the village to the bone. They shall pay me twice over for my crops untilled and my buffaloes unfed. I will have a great justice."

Mowgli laughed. "I do not know what justice is, but–come next Rains and see what is left."

They went off toward the Jungle, and Mother Wolf leaped from her place of hiding.

"Follow!" said Mowgli; "and look to it that all the Jungle knows these two are safe. Give tongue a little. I would call Bagheera."

The long, low howl rose and fell, and Mowgli saw Messua's husband flinch and turn, half minded to run back to the hut.

"Go on," Mowgli called cheerfully. "I said there might be singing. The call will follow up to Kanhiwara. It is Favor of the Jungle."

Messua urged her husband forward, and the darkness of the Jungle shut down on them and Mother Wolf as Bagheera rose up almost under Mowgli's feet, trembling with delight of the night that drives the Jungle People wild.

"I am ashamed of thy brethren," he said, purring.

"What? Did they not sing sweetly to Buldeo?" said Mowgli.

"Too well! Too well! They made even *me* forget my pride, and, by the Broken Lock that freed me, I went singing through the Jungle as though I were out wooing in the spring! Didst thou not hear us?"

"I had other game afoot. Ask Buldeo if he liked the song. But where are the Four? I do not wish one of the Man-Pack to leave the gates to-night."

"What need of the Four, then?" said Bagheera, shifting from foot to foot, his eyes ablaze, and purring louder than ever. "I can hold them, Little Brother. Is it killing at last? The singing and the sight of the men climbing up the trees have made me very ready. What is Man that we should care for him—the naked brown digger, the hairless and toothless, the eater of earth? I have followed him all day—at noon—in the white sunlight. I herded him as the wolves herd buck. I am Bagheera! Bagheera! Bagheera! As I dance with my shadow, so danced I with those men. Look!" The great panther leaped as a kitten leaps at a dead leaf whirling overhead, struck left and right into the empty air, that sung under the strokes, landed noiselessly, and leaped again and again, while the half purr, half growl gathered head as steam rumbles in a boiler. "I am Bagheera—in the Jungle—in the night, and all my strength is in me. Who shall stay my stroke? Man-cub, with one blow of my paw I could beat thy head flat as a dead frog in the summer!"

"Strike, then!" said Mowgli, in the dialect of the village, *not* the talk of the Jungle, and the human words brought Bagheera to a full stop, flung back on haunches that quivered under him, his head just at the level of Mowgli's. Once more Mowgli stared, as he had stared at the rebellious cubs, full into the beryl-green eyes till the red glare behind their green went out like the light of a lighthouse shut off twenty miles across the sea; till the eyes dropped, and the big head with them—dropped lower and lower, and the red rasp of a tongue grated on Mowgli's instep.

"Brother—Brother—Brother!" the boy whispered, stroking steadily and lightly from the neck along the heaving back: "Be still, be still! It is the fault of the night, and no fault of thine."

"It was the smells of the night," said Bagheera penitently. "This air cries aloud to me. But how dost *thou* know?"

Of course the air round an Indian village is full of all kinds of smells, and to any creature who does nearly all his thinking through his nose, smells are as maddening as music and drugs are to human beings. Mowgli gentled the panther for a few minutes longer, and he lay down like a cat before a fire, his paws tucked under his breast, and his eyes half shut.

"Thou art of the Jungle and *not* of the Jungle," he said at last. "And I am only a black panther. But I love thee, Little Brother."

"They are very long at their talk under the tree," Mowgli said, without noticing the last sentence. "Buldeo must have told many tales. They should come soon to drag the woman and her man out of the trap and put them into the Red Flower. They will find that trap sprung. Ho! ho!"

"Nay, listen," said Bagheera. "The fever is out of my blood now. Let them find *me* there! Few would leave their houses after meeting me. It is not the first time I have been in a cage; and I do not think they will tie *me* with cords."

"Be wise, then," said Mowgli, laughing; for he was beginning to feel as reckless as the panther, who had glided into the hut.

"Pah!" Bagheera grunted. "This place is rank with Man, but here is just such a bed as they gave me to lie upon in the King's cages at Oodeypore. Now I lie down." Mowgli heard the strings of the cot crack under the great brute's weight. "By the Broken Lock that freed me, they will think they have caught big game! Come and sit beside me, Little Brother; we will give them 'good hunting' together!"

"No; I have another thought in my stomach. The Man-Pack shall not know what share I have in the sport. Make thine own hunt. I do not wish to see them."

"Be it so," said Bagheera. "Ah, now they come!"

The conference under the peepul-tree had been growing noisier and noisier, at the far end of the village. It broke in wild yells, and a rush up the street of men and women, waving clubs and bamboos and sickles and knives. Buldeo and the Brahmin were at the head of it, but the mob was close at their heels, and they cried, "The witch and the wizard! Let us see if hot coins will make them confess! Burn the hut over their heads! We will teach them to shelter wolf-devils! Nay, beat them first! Torches! More torches! Buldeo, heat the gun-barrels!"

Here was some little difficulty with the catch of the door. It had been very firmly fastened, but the crowd tore it away bodily, and the light of the torches streamed into the room where, stretched at full length on the bed, his paws crossed and lightly hung down over one end, black as the Pit, and terrible as a demon, was Bagheera. There was one half-minute of desperate silence, as the front ranks of the crowd clawed and tore their way back from the threshold, and in that minute Bagheera raised his head and yawned—elaborately, carefully, and ostentatiously—as he would yawn when he wished to insult an equal. The fringed lips drew back and up; the red tongue curled; the lower jaw dropped and dropped till you could see half-way down the hot gullet; and the gigantic dog-teeth stood clear to the pit of the gums till they rang together, upper and under, with the snick of steel-faced wards shooting home round the edges of a safe. Next instant the street was empty; Bagheera had leaped back through the window, and stood at Mowgli's side, while a yelling, screaming torrent scrambled and tumbled one over another in their panic haste to get to their own huts.

"They will not stir till day comes," said Bagheera quietly. "And now?"

The silence of the afternoon sleep seemed to have overtaken the village, but, as they listened, they could hear the sound of heavy grain-boxes being dragged over earthen floors and set down against doors. Bagheera was quite right; the village would not stir till daylight. Mowgli sat still, and thought, and his face drew darker and darker.

"What have I done?" said Bagheera, at last, coming to his feet, fawning.

"Nothing but great good. Watch them now till the day. I sleep." Mowgli ran off into the Jungle, and dropped like a dead man across a rock, and slept and slept the day round, and the night back again.

When he waked, Bagheera was at his side, and there was a newly-killed buck at his feet. Bagheera watched curiously while Mowgli went to work with his skinning-knife, ate and drank, and turned over with his chin in his hands.

"The man and the woman are come safe within eye-shot of Kanhiwara," Bagheera said. "Thy lair mother sent the word back by Chil, the Kite. They found a horse before midnight of the night they were freed, and went very quickly. Is not that well?"

"That is well," said Mowgli.

"And thy Man-Pack in the village did not stir till the sun was high this morning. Then they ate their food and ran back quickly to their houses."

"Did they, by chance, see thee?"

"It may have been. I was rolling in the dust before the gate at dawn, and I may have made also some small song to myself. Now, Little Brother, there is nothing more to do. Come hunting with me and Baloo. He has new hives that he wishes to show, and we all desire thee back again as of old. Take off that look which makes even me afraid! The man and woman will not be put into the Red Flower, and all goes well in the Jungle. Is it not true? Let us forget the Man-Pack."

"They shall be forgotten in a little while. Where does Hathi feed to-night?"

"Where he chooses. Who can answer for the Silent One? But why? What is there Hathi can do which we cannot?"

"Bid him and his three sons come here to me."

"But, indeed, and truly, Little Brother, it is not–it is not seemly to say 'Come,' and 'Go,' to Hathi. Remember, he is the Master of the Jungle, and before the Man-Pack changed the look on thy face, he taught thee the Master-words of the Jungle."

"That is all one. I have a Master-word for him now. Bid him come to Mowgli, the Frog, and if he does not hear at first, bid him come because of the Sack of the Fields of Bhurtpore."

"The Sack of the Fields of Bhurtpore," Bagheera repeated two or three times to make sure. "I go. Hathi can but be angry at the worst, and I would give a moon's hunting to hear a Master-word that compels the Silent One."

He went away, leaving Mowgli stabbing furiously with his skinning-knife into the earth. Mowgli had never seen human blood in his life before till he had seen, and–what meant much more to him–smelled Messua's blood on the thongs that bound her. And Messua had been kind to him, and, so far as he knew anything about love, he loved Messua as completely as he hated the rest of mankind. But deeply as he loathed them, their talk, their cruelty, and their cowardice, not for anything the Jungle had to offer could he bring himself to take a human life, and have that terrible scent of blood back again in his nostrils. His plan was simpler but much more thorough; and he laughed to himself when he thought that it was one of old Buldeo's tales told under the peepul-tree in the evening that had put the idea into his head.

"It *was* a Master-word," Bagheera whispered in his ear. "They were feeding by the river, and they obeyed as though they were bullocks. Look, where they come now!"

Hathi and his three sons had arrived in their usual way, without a sound. The mud of the river was still fresh on their flanks, and Hathi was thoughtfully chewing the green stem of a young plantain-tree that he had gouged up with his tusks. But every line in his vast body showed to Bagheera, who could see things when he came across them, that it was not the Master of the Jungle speaking to a Man-cub, but one who was afraid coming before one who was not. His three sons rolled side by side, behind their father.

Mowgli hardly lifted his head as Hathi gave him "Good hunting." He kept him swinging and rocking, and shifting from one foot to another, for a long time before he spoke, and when he opened his mouth it was to Bagheera, not to the elephants.

"I will tell a tale that was told to me by the hunter ye hunted to-day," said Mowgli. "It concerns an elephant, old and wise, who fell into a trap, and the sharpened stake in the pit scarred him from a little above his heel to the crest of his shoulder, leaving a white mark." Mowgli threw out his hand, and as Hathi wheeled the moonlight showed a long white scar on his slaty side, as though he had been struck with a red-hot whip. "Men came to take him from the trap," Mowgli continued, "but he broke his ropes, for he was strong, and went away till his wound was healed. Then came he, angry, by night to the fields of those hunters. And I remember now that he had three sons. These things happened many, many Rains ago, and very far away—among the fields of Bhurtpore. What came to those fields at the next reaping, Hathi?"

"They were reaped by me and by my three sons," said Hathi.

"And to the plowing that follows the reaping?" said Mowgli.

"There was no plowing," said Hathi.

"And to the men that live by the green crops on the ground?" said Mowgli.

"They went away."

"And to the huts in which the men slept?" said Mowgli.

"We tore the roofs to pieces, and the Jungle swallowed up the walls," said Hathi.

"And what more?" said Mowgli.

"As much good ground as I can walk over in two nights from the east to the west, and from the north to the south as much as I can walk over in three nights, the Jungle took. We let in the Jungle upon five villages; and in those villages, and in their lands, the grazing-ground and the soft crop-grounds, there is not one man to-day who takes his food from the ground. That was the Sack of the Fields of Bhurtpore, which I and my three sons did; and now I ask, Man-cub, how the news of it came to thee?" said Hathi.

"A man told me, and now I see even Buldeo can speak truth. It was well done, Hathi with the white mark; but the second time it shall be done better, for the reason that there is a man to direct. Thou knowest the village of the Man-Pack that cast me out? They are idle, senseless, and cruel; they play with their mouths, and they do not kill the weaker for food, but for sport. When they are full-fed they would throw their own breed into the Red Flower. This I have seen. It is not well that they should live here any more. I hate them!"

"Kill, then," said the youngest of Hathi's three sons, picking up a tuft of grass, dusting it against his fore legs, and throwing it away, while his little red eyes glanced furtively from side to side.

"What good are white bones to me?" Mowgli answered angrily. "Am I the cub of a wolf to play in the sun with a raw head? I have killed Shere Khan, and his hide rots on the Council Rock; but—but I do not know whither Shere Khan is gone, and my stomach is still empty. Now I will take that which I can see and touch. Let in the Jungle upon that village, Hathi!"

Bagheera shivered, and cowered down. He could understand, if the worst came to the worst, a quick rush down the village street, and a right and left blow into a crowd, or a crafty killing of men as they plowed in the twilight, but this scheme for deliberately blotting out an entire village from the eyes of man and beast frightened him. Now he saw why Mowgli had sent for Hathi. No one but the long-lived elephant could plan and carry through such a war.

"Let them run as the men ran from the fields of Bhurtpore, till we have the rain-water for the only plow, and the noise of the rain on the thick leaves for the pattering of their spindles—till Bagheera and I lair in the house of the Brahmin, and the buck drink at the tank behind the temple! Let in the Jungle, Hathi!"

"But I—but we have no quarrel with them, and it needs the red rage of great pain ere we tear down the places where men sleep," said Hathi, doubtfully.

"Are ye the only eaters of grass in the Jungle? Drive in your peoples. Let the deer and the pig and the nilghai look to it. Ye need never show a hand's-breadth of hide till the fields are naked. Let in the Jungle, Hathi!"

"There will be no killing? My tusks were red at the Sack of the Fields of Bhurtpore, and I would not wake that smell again."

"Nor I. I do not wish even their bones to lie on the clean earth. Let them go and find a fresh lair. They cannot stay here. I have seen and smelled the blood of the woman that gave me food—the woman whom they would have killed but for me. Only the smell of the new grass on their door-steps can take away that smell. It burns in my mouth. Let in the Jungle, Hathi!"

"Ah!" said Hathi. "So did the scar of the stake burn on my hide till we watched the villages die under in the spring growth. Now I see. Thy war shall be our war. We will let in the Jungle!"

Mowgli had hardly time to catch his breath–he was shaking all over with rage and hate–before the place where the elephants had stood was empty, and Bagheera was looking at him with terror.

"By the Broken Lock that freed me!" said the Black Panther at last. "Art *thou* the naked thing I spoke for in the Pack when all was young? Master of the Jungle, when my strength goes, speak for me–speak for Baloo–speak for us all! We are cubs before thee! Snapped twigs under foot! Fawns that have lost their doe!"

The idea of Bagheera being a stray fawn upset Mowgli altogether, and he laughed and caught his breath, and sobbed and laughed again, till he had to jump into a pool to make himself stop. Then he swam round and round, ducking in and out of the bars of the moonlight like the frog, his namesake.

By this time Hathi and his three sons had turned, each to one point of the compass, and were striding silently down the valleys a mile away. They went on and on for two days' march–that is to say, a long sixty miles–through the Jungle; and every step they took, and every wave of their trunks, was known and noted and talked over by Mang and Chil and the Monkey People and all the birds. Then they began to feed, and fed quietly for a week or so. Hathi and his sons are like Kaa, the Rock Python. They never hurry till they have to.

At the end of that time–and none knew who had started it–a rumor went through the Jungle that there was better food and water to be found in such and such a valley. The pig–who, of course, will go to the ends of the earth for a full meal–moved first by companies, scuffling over the rocks, and the deer followed, with the small wild foxes that live on the dead and dying of the herds; and the heavy-shouldered nilghai moved parallel with the deer, and the wild buffaloes of the swamps came after the nilghai. The least little thing would have turned the scattered, straggling droves that grazed and sauntered and drank and grazed again; but whenever there was an alarm some one would rise up and soothe them. At one time it would be Sahi the Porcupine, full of news of good feed just a little further on; at another Mang would cry cheerily and flap down a glade to show it was all empty; or Baloo, his mouth full of roots, would shamble alongside a wavering line and half frighten, half romp it clumsily back to the proper road. Very many creatures broke back or ran away or lost interest, but very many were left to go forward. At the end of another ten days or so the situation was this. The deer and the pig and the nilghai were milling round and round in a circle of eight or ten miles radius, while the Eaters of Flesh skirmished round its edge. And the center of that circle was the village, and round the village the crops were ripening, and in the crops sat men on what they call *machans*–platforms like pigeon-perches, made of sticks at the top of four poles–to scare away birds and other stealers. Then the deer were coaxed no more. The Eaters of Flesh were close behind them, and forced them forward and inward.

It was a dark night when Hathib and his three sons slipped down from the Jungle, and broke off the poles of the *machans* with their trunks; they fell as a snapped stalk of hemlock in bloom falls, and the men that tumbled from them heard the deep gurgling of the elephants in their ears. Then the vanguard of the bewildered armies of the deer broke down and flooded into the village grazing-grounds and the plowed fields; and the sharp-hoofed, rooting wild pig came with them, and what the deer left the pig spoiled, and from time to time an alarm of wolves would shake the herds, and they would rush to and fro desperately, treading down the young barley, and cutting flat the banks of the irrigating channels. Before the dawn broke the pressure on the outside of the circle gave way at one point. The Eaters of Flesh had fallen back and left an open path to the south, and drove upon drove of buck fled along it. Others, who were bolder, lay up in the thickets to finish their meal next night.

But the work was practically done. When the villagers looked in the morning they saw their crops were lost. And that meant death if they did not get away, for they lived year in and year out as near to starvation as the Jungle was near to them. When the buffaloes were sent to graze the hungry brutes found that the deer had cleared the grazing-grounds, and so wandered into the Jungle and drifted off with their wild mates; and when twilight fell the three or four ponies that belonged to the village lay in their stables with their heads beaten in. Only Bagheera could have given those strokes, and only Bagheera would have thought of insolently dragging the last carcass to the open street.

The villagers had no heart to make fires in the fields that night, so Hathi and his three sons went gleaning among what was left; and where Hathi gleans there is no need to follow. The men decided to live on their stored seed-corn until the rains had fallen, and then to take work as servants till they could catch up with the lost year; but as the grain-dealer was thinking of his well-filled crates of corn, and the prices he would levy at the sale of it, Hathi's sharp tusks were picking out the corner of his mud house, and smashing open the big wicker-chest, leeped with cow-dung, where the precious stuff lay.

When that last loss was discovered, it was the Brahmin's turn to speak. He had prayed to his own Gods without answer. It might be, he said, that, unconsciously, the village had offended some one of the Gods of the Jungle, for, beyond doubt, the Jungle was against them. So they sent for the head man of the nearest tribe of wandering Gonds–little wise, and very black hunters, living in the deep Jungle, whose fathers came of the oldest race in India–the aboriginal owners of the land. They made the Gond welcome with what they had, and he stood on one leg, his bow in his hand, and two or three poisoned arrows stuck through his top-knot, looking half afraid and half contemptuously at the anxious villagers and their ruined fields. They wished to know whether his Gods–the Old Gods–were angry with them, and what sacrifices should be offered. The Gond said nothing, but picked up a trail of the *Karela,* the vine that bears the bitter wild gourd, and laced it to and fro across the temple door in the face of the staring red Hindu image. Then he pushed with his hand in the open air along the road to Kanhiwara, and went back to his Jungle, and watched the Jungle people drifting through it. He knew that when the Jungle moves only white men can hope to turn it aside.

There was no need to ask his meaning. The wild gourd would grow where they had worshiped their God, and the sooner they saved themselves the better.

But it is hard to tear a village from its moorings. They stayed on as long as any summer food was left to them, and they tried to gather nuts in the Jungle, but shadows with glaring eyes watched them, and rolled before them even at midday; and when they ran back afraid to their walls, on the tree trunks they had passed not five minutes before the bark would be stripped and chiseled with the stroke of some great taloned paw. The more they kept to their village, the bolder grew the wild things that gamboled and bellowed on the grazing-grounds by the Waingunga. They had no time to patch and plaster the rear walls of the empty byres that backed on to the Jungle; the wild pig trampled them down, and the knotty-rooted vines hurried after and threw their elbows over the new-won ground, and the coarse grass bristled behind the vines like the lances of a goblin army following a retreat. The unmarried men ran away first, and carried the news far and near that the village was doomed. Who could fight, they said, against the Jungle, or the Gods of the Jungle, when the very village cobra had left his hole in the platform under the peepul-tree? So their little commerce with the outside world shrunk as the trodden paths across the open grew fewer and fainter. At last the nightly trumpetings of Hathi and his three sons ceased to trouble them; for they had no more to be robbed of. The crop on the ground and the seed in the ground had been taken. The outlying fields were already losing their shape, and it was time to throw themselves on the charity of the English at Kanhiwara.

Native fashion, they delayed their departure from one day to another till the first Rains caught them and the unmended roofs let in a flood, and the grazing-ground stood ankle deep, and all life came on with a rush after the heat of the summer. Then they waded out, men, women, and children, through the blinding hot rain of the morning, but turned naturally for one farewell look at their homes.

They heard, as the last burdened family filed through the gate, a crash of falling beams and thatch behind the walls. They saw a shiny, snaky black trunk lifted for an instant, scattering sodden thatch. It disappeared, and there was another crash, followed by a squeal. Hathi had been plucking off the roofs of the huts as you pluck water-lilies, and a rebounding beam had pricked him. He needed only this to unchain his full strength, for of all things in the Jungle the wild elephant enraged is the most wantonly destructive. He kicked backward at a mud wall that crumbled at the stroke, and, crumbling, melted to yellow mud under the torrent of rain. Then he wheeled and squealed, and tore through the narrow streets, leaning against the huts right and left, shivering the crazy doors, and crumpling up the eaves; while his three sons raged behind as they had raged at the Sack of the Fields of Bhurtpore.

"The Jungle will swallow these shells," said a quiet voice in the wreckage. "It is the outer wall that must lie down," and Mowgli, with the rain sluicing over his bare shoulders and arms, leaped back from a wall that was settling like a tired buffalo.

"All in good time," panted Hathi. "Oh, but my tusks were red at Bhurtpore! To the outer wall, children! With the head! Together! Now!"

The four pushed side by side; the outer wall bulged, split, and fell, and the villagers, dumb with horror, saw the savage, clay-streaked heads of the wreckers in the ragged gap. Then they fled, houseless and foodless, down the valley, as their village, shredded and tossed and trampled, melted behind them.

A month later the place was a dimpled mound, covered with soft, green young stuff; and by the end of the Rains there was the roaring Jungle in full blast on the spot that had been under plow not six months before.

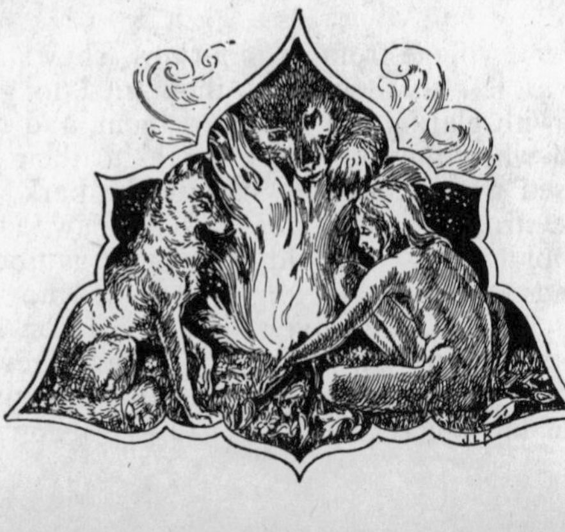

Mowgli's Song Against People

I will let loose against you the fleet-footed vines–
I will call in the Jungle to stamp out your lines!
The roofs shall fade before it,
The house-beams shall fall,
And the *Karela,* the bitter *Karela,*
Shall cover it all!

In the gates of these your councils my people shall sing,
In the doors of these your garners the Bat-folk shall cling;
And the snake shall be your watchman,
By a hearthstone unswept;
For the *Karela,* the bitter *Karela,*
Shall fruit where ye slept!

Ye shall not see my strikers; ye shall hear them and guess;
By night, before the moon-rise, I will send for my cess,
And the wolf shall be your herdsman
By a landmark removed,
For the *Karela,* the bitter *Karela,*
Shall seed where ye loved!

I will reap your fields before you at the hands of a host;
Ye shall glean behind my reapers for the bread that is lost;
And the deer shall be your oxen
By a headland untilled,
For the *Karela,* the bitter *Karela,*
Shall leaf where ye build!

I have untied against you the club-footed vines,
I have sent in the Jungle to swamp out your lines!
The trees–the trees are on you!
The house-beams shall fall,
And the *Karela,* the bitter *Karela,*
Shall cover you all!

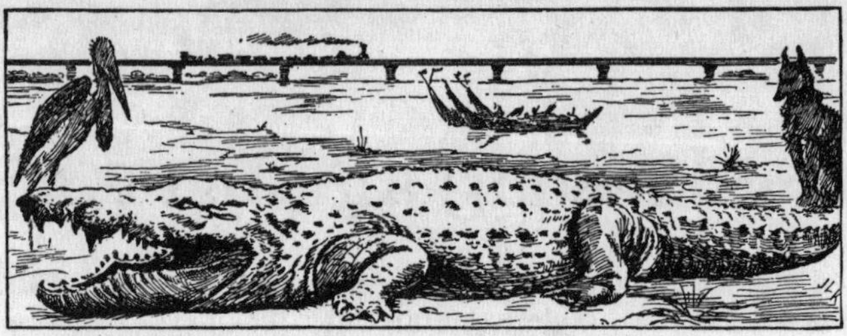

The Undertakers

When ye say to Tabaqui, "My Brother!" when ye call the Hyena to meat,
Ye may cry the Full Truce with Jacala—the Belly that runs on four feet.

—Jungle Law.

RESPECT THE AGED!"

It was a thick voice—a muddy voice that would have made you shudder—a voice like something soft breaking in two. There was a quaver in it, a croak and a whine.

"Respect the aged! O Companions of the River—respect the aged!"

Nothing could be seen on the broad reach of the river except a little fleet of square-sailed, wooden-pinned barges, loaded with building-stone, that had just come under the railway bridge, and were driving down-stream. They put their clumsy helms over to avoid the sand-bar made by the scour of the bridge-piers, and as they passed, three abreast, the horrible voice began again:

"O Brahmins of the River—respect the aged and infirm!"

A boatman turned where he sat on the gun-wale, lifted up his hand, said something that was not a blessing, and the boats creaked on through the twilight. The broad Indian river, that looked more like a chain of little lakes than a stream, was as smooth as glass, reflecting the sandy-red sky in mid-channel, but splashed with patches of yellow and dusky purple near and under the low banks. Little creeks ran into the river in the wet season, but now their dry mouths hung clear above water-line. On the left shore, and almost under the railway bridge, stood a mud-and-brick and thatch-and-stick village, whose main street, full of cattle going back to their byres, ran straight to the river, and ended in a sort of rude brick pier-head, where people who wanted to wash could wade in step by step. That was the Ghaut of the village of Mugger-Ghaut.

Night was falling fast over the fields of lentils and rice and cotton in the low-lying ground yearly flooded by the river; over the reeds that fringed the elbow of the bend, and the tangled low jungle of the grazing-grounds behind the still reeds. The parrots and crows, who had been chattering and shouting over their evening drink, had flown inland to roost, crossing the out-going battalions of the flying-foxes; and cloud upon cloud of water-birds came whistling and "honking" to the cover of the reed-beds. There were geese, barrel-headed and black-backed, teal, widgeon, mallard, and sheldrake, with curlews, and here and there a flamingo.

A lumbering Adjutant-crane brought up the rear, flying as though each slow stroke would be his last.

"Respect the aged! Brahmins of the River—respect the aged!"

The Adjutant half turned his head, sheered a little in the direction of the voice, and landed stiffly on the sand-bar below the bridge. Then you saw what a ruffianly brute he really was. His back view was immensely respectable, for he stood nearly six feet high, and looked rather like a very proper bald-headed person. In front it was different, for his Ally Sloper-like head and neck had not a feather to them, and there was a horrible raw-skin pouch on his neck under his chin—a hold-all for the things his pickaxe beak might steal. His legs were long and thin and skinny, but he moved them delicately, and looked at them with pride as he preened down his ashy-gray tail-feathers, glanced over the smooth of his shoulder, and stiffened into "Stand at attention."

A mangy little Jackal, who had been yapping hungrily on a low bluff, cocked up his ears and tail, and scuttered across the shallows to join the Adjutant.

He was the lowest of his caste—not that the best of jackals are good for much, but this one was peculiarly low, being half a beggar, half a criminal—a cleaner-up of village rubbish-heaps, desperately timid or wildly bold, everlastingly hungry, and full of cunning that never did him any good.

"Ugh!" he said, shaking himself dolefully as he landed. "May the red mange destroy the dogs of this village! I have three bites for each flea upon me, and all because I looked—only looked, mark you—at an old shoe in a cow-byre. Can I eat mud?" He scratched himself under his left ear.

"I heard," said the Adjutant, in a voice like a blunt saw going through a thick board—"I *heard* there was a new-born puppy in that same shoe."

"To hear is one thing; to know is another," said the Jackal, who had a very fair knowledge of proverbs, picked up by listening to men round the village fires of an evening.

"Quite true. So, to make sure, I took care of that puppy while the dogs were busy elsewhere."

"They were *very* busy," said the Jackal. "Well, I must not go to the village hunting for scraps yet awhile. And so there truly was a blind puppy in that shoe?"

"It is here," said the Adjutant, squinting over his beak at his full pouch. "A small thing, but acceptable now that charity is dead in the world."

"Ahai! The world is iron in these days," wailed the Jackal. Then his restless eye caught the least possible ripple on the water, and he went on quickly: "Life is hard for us all, and I doubt not that even our excellent master, the Pride of the Ghaut and the Envy of the River—"

"A liar, a flatterer, and a Jackal were all hatched out of the same egg," said the Adjutant to nobody in particular; for he was rather a fine sort of a liar on his own account when he took the trouble.

"Yes, the Envy of the River," the Jackal repeated, raising his voice. "Even he, I doubt not, finds that since the bridge has been built good food is more scarce. But on the other hand, though I would by no means say this to his noble face, he is so wise and so virtuous—as I, alas! am not—"

"When the Jackal owns he is gray, how black must the Jackal be!" muttered the Adjutant. He could not see what was coming.

"That *his* food never fails, and in consequence—"

There was a soft grating sound, as though a boat had just touched in shoal water. The Jackal spun round quickly and faced (it is always best to face) the creature he had been talking about. It was a twenty-four-foot crocodile, cased in what looked like treble-riveted boiler-plate, studded and keeled and crested; the yellow points of his upper teeth just overhanging his beautifully fluted lower jaw. It was the blunt-nosed Mugger of Mugger-Ghaut, older than any man in the village, who had given his name to the village; the demon of the ford before the railway bridge came—murderer, man-eater, and local fetish in one. He lay with his chin in the shallows, keeping his place by an almost invisible rippling of his tail, and well the Jackal knew that one stroke of that same tail in the water could carry the Mugger up the bank with the rush of a steam-engine.

"Auspiciously met, Protector of the Poor!" he fawned, backing at every word. "A delectable voice was heard, and we came in the hopes of sweet conversation. My tailless presumption, while waiting here, led me, indeed, to speak of thee. It is my hope that nothing was overheard."

Now the Jackal had spoken just to be listened to, for he knew flattery was the best way of getting things to eat, and the Mugger knew that the Jackal had spoken for this end, and the Jackal knew that the Mugger knew, and the Mugger knew that the Jackal knew that the Mugger knew, and so they were all very contented together.

The old brute pushed and panted and grunted up the bank, mumbling, "Respect the aged and infirm!" and all the time his little eyes burned like coals under the heavy, horny eyelids on the top of his triangular head, as he shoved his bloated barrel-body along between his crutched legs. Then he settled down, and, accustomed as the Jackal was to his ways, he could not help starting, for the hundredth time, when he saw how exactly the Mugger imitated a log adrift on the bar. He had even taken pains to lie at the exact angle a naturally stranded log would make with the water, having regard to the current of the season at the time and place. All this was only a matter of habit, of course, because the Mugger had come ashore for pleasure; but a crocodile is never quite full, and if the Jackal had been deceived by the likeness he would not have lived to philosophize over it.

"My child, I heard nothing," said the Mugger, shutting one eye. "The water was in my ears, and also I was faint with hunger. Since the railway bridge was built my people at my village have ceased to love me; and that is breaking my heart."

"Ah, shame!" said the Jackal. "So noble a heart, too! But men are all alike, to my mind."

"Nay, there are very great differences indeed," the Mugger answered gently. "Some are as lean as boat-poles. Others again are fat as young ja– dogs. Never would I causelessly revile men. They are of all fashions, but the long years have shown me that, one with another, they are very good. Men, women, and children–I have no fault to find with them. And remember, child, he who rebukes the World is rebuked by the World."

"Flattery is worse than an empty tin can in the belly. But that which we have just heard is wisdom," said the Adjutant, bringing down one foot.

"Consider, though, their ingratitude to this excellent one," began the Jackal tenderly.

"Nay, nay, not ingratitude!" the Mugger said. "They do not think for others; that is all. But I have noticed, lying at my station below the ford, that the stairs of the new bridge are cruelly hard to climb, both for old people and young children. The old, indeed, are not so worthy of consideration, but I am grieved–I am truly grieved–on account of the fat children. Still, I think, in a little while, when the newness of the bridge has worn away, we shall see my people's bare brown legs bravely splashing through the ford as before. Then the old Mugger will be honored again."

"But surely I saw marigold wreaths floating off the edge of the Ghaut only this noon," said the Adjutant.

Marigold wreaths are a sign of reverence all India over.

"An error–an error. It was the wife of the sweetmeat-seller. She loses her eyesight year by year, and cannot tell a log from me–the Mugger of the Ghaut. I saw the mistake when she threw the garland, for I was lying at the very foot of the Ghaut, and had she taken another step I might have shown her some little difference. Yet she meant well, and we must consider the spirit of the offering."

"What good are marigold wreaths when one is on the rubbish-heap?" said the Jackal, hunting for fleas, but keeping one wary eye on his Protector of the Poor.

"True, but they have not yet begun to make the rubbish-heap that shall carry *me.* Five times have I seen the river draw back from the village and make new land at the foot of the street. Five times have I seen the village rebuilt on the banks, and I shall see it built yet five times more. I am no faithless, fish-hunting Gavial, I, at Kasi to-day and Prayag to-morrow, as the saying is, but the true and constant watcher of the ford. It is not for nothing, child, that the village bears my name, and 'he who watches long,' as the saying is, 'shall at last have his reward.' "

"*I* have watched long–very long–nearly all my life, and my reward has been bites and blows," said the Jackal.

"Ho! ho! ho!" roared the Adjutant.

"In August was the Jackal born;
The Rains fell in September;
'Now such a fearful flood as this,'
Says he, 'I can't remember!' "

There is one very unpleasant peculiarity about the Adjutant. At uncertain times he suffers from acute attacks of the fidgets or cramp in his legs, and though he is more virtuous to behold than any of the cranes, who are all immensely respectable, he flies off into wild, cripple-stilt war-dances, half opening his wings and bobbing his bald head up and down; while for reasons best known to himself he is very careful to time his worst attacks with his nastiest remarks. At the last word of his song he came to attention again, ten times adjutaunter than before.

The Jackal winced, though he was full three seasons old, but you cannot resent an insult from a person with a beak a yard long, and the power of driving it like a javelin. The Adjutant was a most notorious coward, but the Jackal was worse.

"We must live before we can learn," said the Mugger, "and there is this to say: Little jackals are very common, child, but such a mugger as I am is not common. For all that, I am not proud, since pride is destruction; but take notice, it is Fate, and against his Fate no one who swims or walks or runs should say anything at all. I am well contented with Fate. With good luck, a keen eye, and the custom of considering whether a creek or a backwater has an outlet to it ere you ascend, much may be done."

"Once I heard that even the Protector of the Poor made a mistake," said the Jackal viciously.

"True; but there my Fate helped me. It was before I had come to my full growth–before the last famine but three (by the Right and Left of Gunga, how full used the streams to be in those days!). Yes, I was young and unthinking, and when the flood came, who so pleased as I? A little made me very happy then. The village was deep in flood, and I swam above the Ghaut and went far inland, up to the rice-fields, and they were deep in good mud. I remember also a pair of bracelets (glass they were, and troubled me not a little) that I found that evening. Yes, glass bracelets; and, if my memory serves me well, a shoe. I should have shaken off both shoes, but I was hungry. I learned better later. Yes. And so I fed and rested me; but when I was ready to go to the river again the flood had fallen, and I walked through the mud of the main street. Who but I? Came out all my people, priests and women and children, and I looked upon them with benevolence. The mud is not a good place to fight in. Said a boatman, 'Get axes and kill him, for he is the Mugger of the ford.' 'Not so,' said the Brahmin. 'Look, he is driving the flood before him! He is the godling of the village.' Then they threw many flowers at me, and by happy thought one led a goat across the road."

"How good–how very good is goat!" said the Jackal.

"Hairy—too hairy, and when found in the water more than likely to hide a cross-shaped hook. But that goat I accepted, and went down to the Ghaut in great honor. Later, my Fate sent me the boatman who had desired to cut off my tail with an axe. His boat grounded upon an old shoal which you would not remember."

"We are not *all* jackals here," said the Adjutant. "Was it the shoal made where the stone-boats sank in the year of the great drouth—a long shoal that lasted three floods?"

"There were two," said the Mugger; "an upper and a lower shoal."

"Ay, I forgot. A channel divided them, and later dried up again," said the Adjutant, who prided himself on his memory.

"On the lower shoal my well-wisher's craft grounded. He was sleeping in the bows, and, half awake, leaped over to his waist—no, it was no more than to his knees—to push off. His empty boat went on and touched again below the next reach, as the river ran then. I followed, because I knew men would come out to drag it ashore."

"And did they do so?" said the Jackal, a little awe-stricken. This was hunting on a scale that impressed him.

"There and lower down they did. I went no further, but that gave me three in one day—well-fed *manjis* (boatmen) all, and, except in the case of the last (then I was careless), never a cry to warn those on the bank."

"Ah, noble sport! But what cleverness and great judgment it requires!" said the Jackal.

"Not cleverness, child, but only thought. A little thought in life is like salt upon rice, as the boatmen say, and I have thought deeply always. The Gavial, my cousin, the fish-eater, has told me how hard it is for him to follow his fish, and how one fish differs from the other, and how he must know them all, both together and apart. I say that is wisdom; but, on the other hand, my cousin the Gavial, lives among his people. *My* people do not swim in companies, with their mouths out of the water, as Rewa does; nor do they constantly rise to the surface of the water, and turn over on their sides, like Mohoo and little Chapta; nor do they gather in shoals after flood, like Batchua and Chilwa."

"All are very good eating," said the Adjutant, clattering his beak.

"So my cousin says, and makes a great to-do over hunting them, but they do not climb the banks to escape his sharp nose. *My* people are otherwise. Their life is on the land, in the houses, among the cattle. I must know what they do, and what they are about to do; and, adding the tail to the trunk, as the saying is, I make up the whole elephant. Is there a green branch and an iron ring hanging over a doorway? The old Mugger knows that a boy has been born in that house, and must some day come down to the Ghaut to play. Is a maiden to be married? The old Mugger knows, for he sees the men carry gifts back and forth; and she, too, comes down to the Ghaut to bathe before her wedding, and—he is there. Has the river changed its channel, and made new land where there was only sand before? The Mugger knows."

"Now, of what use is that knowledge?" said the Jackal. "The river has shifted even in my little life." Indian rivers are nearly always moving about in their beds, and will shift, sometimes, as much as two or three miles in a season, drowning the fields on one bank, and spreading good silt on the other.

"There is no knowledge so useful," said the Mugger, "for new land means new quarrels. The Mugger knows. Oho! the Mugger knows. As soon as the water has drained off, he creeps up the little creeks that men think would not hide a dog, and there he waits. Presently comes a farmer saying he will plant cucumbers here, and melons there, in the new land that the river has given him. He feels the good mud with his bare toes. Anon comes another, saying he will put onions, and carrots, and sugar-cane in such and such places. They meet as boats adrift meet, and each rolls his eye at the other under the big blue turban. The old Mugger sees and hears. Each calls the other 'Brother,' and they go to mark out the boundaries of the new land. The Mugger hurries with them from point to point, shuffling very low through the mud. Now they begin to quarrel! Now they say hot words! Now they pull turbans! Now they lift up their *lathis* (clubs), and, at last, one falls backward into the mud, and the other runs away. When he comes back the dispute is settled, as the iron-bound bamboo of the loser witnesses. Yet they are not grateful to the Mugger. No, they cry 'Murder!' and their families fight with sticks, twenty a side. My people are good people–upland Jats–Malwais of the Bêt. They do not give blows for sport, and, when the fight is done, the old Mugger waits far down the river, out of sight of the village, behind the *kikar*-scrub yonder. Then come they down, my broad-shouldered Jats–eight or nine together under the stars, bearing the dead man upon a bed. They are old men with gray beards, and voices as deep as mine. They light a little fire–ah! how well I know that fire!–and they drink tobacco, and they nod their heads together forward in a ring, or sideways toward the dead man upon the bank. They say the English Law will come with a rope for this matter, and that such a man's family will be ashamed, because such a man must be hanged in the great square of the Jail. Then say the friends of the dead, 'Let him hang!' and talk is all to do over again–once, twice, twenty times in the long night. Then says one, at last, 'The fight was a fair fight. Let us take blood-money, a little more than is offered by the slayer, and we will say no more about it.' Then do they haggle over the blood-money, for the dead was a strong man, leaving many sons. Yet before *amratvela* (sunrise) they put the fire to him a little, as the custom is, and the dead man comes to me, and *he* says no more about it. Aha! my children, the Mugger knows–the Mugger knows–and my Malwah Jats are a good people!"

"They are too close–too narrow in the hand for my crop," croaked the Adjutant. "They waste not the polish on the cow's horn, as the saying is; and, again, who can glean after a Malwai?"

"Ah, I–glean–*them,*" said the Mugger.

"Now, in Calcutta of the South, in the old days," the Adjutant went on, "everything was thrown into the streets, and we picked and chose. Those were dainty seasons. But to-day they keep their streets as clean as the outside of an egg, and my people fly away. To be clean is one thing; to dust, sweep, and sprinkle seven times a day wearies the very Gods themselves."

"There was a down-country jackal had it from a brother, who told me, that in Calcutta of the South all the jackals were as fat as otters in the Rains," said the Jackal, his mouth watering at the bare thought of it.

"Ah, but the white-faces are there–the English, and they bring dogs from somewhere down the river, in boats–big fat dogs–to keep those same jackals lean," said the Adjutant.

"They are, then, as hard-hearted as these people? I might have known. Neither earth, sky, nor water shows charity to a jackal. I saw the tents of a white-face last season, after the Rains, and I also took a new yellow bridle to eat. The white-faces do not dress their leather in the proper way. It made me very sick."

"That was better than my case," said the Adjutant. "When I was in my third season, a young and a bold bird, I went down to the river where the big boats come in. The boats of the English are thrice as big as this village."

"He has been as far as Delhi, and says all the people there walk on their heads," muttered the Jackal. The Mugger opened his left eye, and looked keenly at the Adjutant.

"It is true," the big bird insisted. "A liar only lies when he hopes to be believed. No one who had not seen those boats *could* believe this truth."

"*That* is more reasonable," said the Mugger. "And then?"

"From the insides of this boat they were taking out great pieces of white stuff, which, in a little while, turned to water. Much split off, and fell about on the shore, and the rest they swiftly put into a house with thick walls. But a boatman, who laughed, took a piece no larger than a small dog, and threw it to me. I–all my people–swallow without reflection, and that piece I swallowed as is our custom. Immediately I was afflicted with an excessive cold which, beginning in my crop, ran down to the extreme end of my toes, and deprived me even of speech, while the boatmen laughed at me. Never have I felt such cold. I danced in my grief and amazement till I could recover my breath, and then I danced and cried out against the falseness of this world; and the boatmen derided me till they fell down. The chief wonder of the matter, setting aside that marvelous coldness, was that there was nothing at all in my crop when I had finished my lamentings!"

The Adjutant had done his very best to describe his feelings after swallowing a seven-pound lump of Wenham Lake ice, off an American ice-ship, in the days before Calcutta made her ice by machinery; but as he did not know what ice was, and as the Mugger and the Jackal knew rather less, the tale missed fire.

"Anything," said the Mugger, shutting his left eye again–"*anything* is possible that comes out of a boat thrice the size of Mugger-Ghaut. My village is not a small one."

There was a whistle overhead on the bridge, and the Delhi Mail slid across, all the carriages gleaming with light, and the shadows faithfully following along the river. It clanked away into the dark again; but the Mugger and the Jackal were so well used to it that they never turned their heads.

"Is that anything less wonderful than a boat thrice the size of Mugger-Ghaut?" said the bird, looking up.

"I saw that built, child. Stone by stone I saw the bridge-piers rise, and when the men fell off (they were wondrous sure-footed for the most part–but *when* they fell) I was ready. After the first pier was made they never thought to look down the stream for the body to burn. There, again, I saved much trouble. There was nothing strange in the building of the bridge," said the Mugger.

"But that which goes across, pulling the roofed carts! That is strange," the Adjutant repeated.

"It is, past any doubt, a new breed of bullock. Some day it will not be able to keep its foothold up yonder, and will fall as the men did. The old Mugger will then be ready."

The Jackal looked at the Adjutant, and the Adjutant looked at the Jackal. If there was one thing they were more certain of than another, it was that the engine was everything in the wide world except a bullock. The Jackal had watched it time and again from the aloe-hedges by the side of the line, and the Adjutant had seen engines since the first locomotive ran in India. But the Mugger had only looked up at the thing from below, where the brass dome seemed rather like a bullock's hump.

"M–yes, a new kind of bullock," the Mugger repeated ponderously, to make himself quite sure in his own mind; and "Certainly it is a bullock," said the Jackal.

"And again it might be–" began the Mugger pettishly.

"Certainly–most certainly," said the Jackal, without waiting for the other to finish.

"What?" said the Mugger angrily, for he could feel that the others knew more than he did. "What might it be? *I* never finished my words. You said it was a bullock."

"It is anything the Protector of the Poor pleases. I am *his* servant–not the servant of the thing that crosses the river."

"Whatever it is, it is white-face work," said the Adjutant; "and for my own part, I would not lie out upon a place so near to it as this bar."

"You do not know the English as I do," said the Mugger. "There was a white-face here when the bridge was built, and he would take a boat in the evenings and shuffle with his feet on the bottom-boards, and whisper: 'Is he here? Is he there? Bring me my gun.' I could hear him before I could see him—each sound that he made—creaking and puffing and rattling his gun, up and down the river. As surely as I had picked up one of his workmen, and thus saved great expense in wood for the burning, so surely would he come down to the Ghaut, and shout in a loud voice that he would hunt me, and rid the river of me—the Mugger of Mugger-Ghaut! *Me!* Children, I have swum under the bottom of his boat for hour after hour, and heard him fire his gun at logs; and when I was well sure he was wearied, I have risen by his side and snapped my jaws in his face. When the bridge was finished he went away. All the English hunt in that fashion, except when they are hunted."

"Who hunts the white-faces?" yapped the Jackal excitedly.

"No one now, but I have hunted them in my time."

"I remember a little of that Hunting. I was young then," said the Adjutant, clattering his beak significantly.

"I was well established here. My village was being builded for the third time, as I remember, when my cousin, the Gavial, brought me word of rich waters above Benares. At first I would not go, for my cousin, who is a fish-eater, does not always know the good from the bad; but I heard my people talking in the evenings, and what they said made me certain."

"And what did they say?" the Jackal asked.

"They said enough to make me, the Mugger of Mugger-Ghaut, leave water and take to my feet. I went by night, using the littlest streams as they served me; but it was the beginning of the hot weather and all streams were low. I crossed dusty roads; I went through tall grass; I climbed hills in the moonlight. Even rocks did I climb, children—consider this well. I crossed the tail of Sirhind, the waterless, before I could find the set of the little rivers that flow Gunga-ward. I was a month's journey from my own people and the river that I knew. That was very marvelous!"

"What food on the way?" said the Jackal, who kept his soul in his little stomach, and was not a bit impressed by the Mugger's land travels.

"That which I could find—*cousin,*"said the Mugger slowly, dragging each word.

Now you do not call a man a cousin in India unless you think you can establish some kind of blood-relationship, and as it is only in old fairy-tales that the Mugger ever marries a jackal, the Jackal knew for what reason he had been suddenly lifted into the Mugger's family circle. If they had been alone he would not have cared, but the Adjutant's eyes twinkled with mirth at the ugly jest.

"Assuredly, Father, I might have known," said the Jackal. A Mugger does not care to be called a father of jackals, and the Mugger of Mugger-Ghaut said as much—and a great deal more which there is no use in repeating here.

"The Protector of the Poor has claimed kinship. How can I remember the precise degree? Moreover, we eat the same food. He has said it," was the Jackal's reply.

That made matters rather worse, for what the Jackal hinted at was that the Mugger must have eaten his food on that land march fresh and fresh every day, instead of keeping it by him till it was in a fit and proper condition, as every self-respecting mugger and most wild beasts do when they can. Indeed, one of the worst terms of contempt along the River-bed is "eater of fresh meat." It is nearly as bad as calling a man a cannibal.

"That food was eaten thirty seasons ago," said the Adjutant quietly. "If we talk for thirty seasons more it will never come back. Tell us, now, what happened when the good waters were reached after thy most wonderful land journey. If we listened to the howling of every jackal the business of the town would stop, as the saying is."

The Mugger must have been grateful for the interruption, because he went on, with a rush:

"By the Right and Left of Gunga! when I came there never did I see such waters!"

"Were they better, then, than the big flood of last season?" said the Jackal.

"Better! That flood was no more than comes every five years–a handful of drowned strangers, some chickens, and a dead bullock in muddy water with cross-currents. But the season I think of, the river was low, smooth, and even, and, as the Gavial had warned me, the dead English came down, touching each other. I got my girth in that season–my girth and my depth. From Agra, by Etawah and the broad waters by Allahabad–"

"Oh, the eddy that set under the walls of the fort at Allahabad!" said the Adjutant. "They came in there like widgeon to the reeds, and round and round they swung–thus!"

He went off into his horrible dance again, while the Jackal looked on enviously. He naturally could not remember the terrible year of the Mutiny they were talking about. The Mugger continued:

"Yes, by Allahabad one lay still in the slack-water and let twenty go by to pick one; and, above all, the English were not cumbered with jewelry and nose-rings and anklets as my women are nowadays. To delight in ornaments is to end with a rope for necklace, as the saying is. All the muggers of all the rivers grew fat then, but it was my Fate to be fatter than them all. The news was that the English were being hunted into the rivers, and by the Right and Left of Gunga! we believed it was true. So far as I went south I believed it to be true; and I went down-stream beyond Monghyr and the tombs that look over the river."

"I know that place," said the Adjutant. "Since those days Monghyr is a lost city. Very few live there now."

"Thereafter I worked up-stream very slowly and lazily, and a little above Monghyr there came down a boatful of white-faces–alive! They were, as I remember, women, lying under a cloth spread over sticks, and crying aloud. There was never a gun fired at us the watchers of the fords in those days. All the guns were busy elsewhere. We could hear them day and night inland, coming and going as the wind shifted. I rose up full before the boat, because I had never seen white-faces alive, though I knew them well–otherwise. A naked white child kneeled by the side of the boat, and, stooping over, must needs try to trail his hands in the river. It is a pretty thing to see how a child loves running water. I had fed that day, but there was yet a little unfilled space within me. Still, it was for sport and not for food that I rose at the child's hands. They were so clear a mark that I did not even look when I closed; but they were so small that though my jaws rang true–I am sure of that–the child drew them up swiftly, unhurt. They must have passed between tooth and tooth–those small white hands. I should have caught him crosswise at the elbows; but, as I said, it was only for sport and desire to see new things that I rose at all. They cried out one after another in the boat, and presently I rose again to watch them. Their boat was too heavy to push over. They were only women, but he who trusts a woman will walk on duckweed in a pool, as the saying is: and by the Right and Left of Gunga, that is truth!"

"Once a woman gave me some dried skin from a fish," said the Jackal. "I had hoped to get her baby, but horse-food is better than the kick of a horse, as the saying is. What did thy woman do?"

"She fired at me with a short gun of a kind I have never seen before or since. Five times, one after another" (the Mugger must have met with an old-fashioned revolver); "and I stayed open-mouthed and gaping, my head in the smoke. Never did I see such a thing. Five times, as swiftly as I wave my tail–thus!"

The Jackal, who had been growing more and more interested in the story, had just time to leap back as the long tail swung by like a scythe.

"Not before the fifth shot," said the Mugger, as though he had never dreamed of stunning one of his listeners—"not before the fifth shot did I sink, and I rose in time to hear a boatman telling all those white women that I was most certainly dead. One bullet had gone under a neckplate of mine. I know not if it is there still, for the reason I cannot turn my head. Look and see, child. It will show that my tale is true."

"I?" said the Jackal. "Shall an eater of old shoes, a bone-cracker, presume to doubt the word of the Envy of the River? May my tail be bitten off by blind puppies if the shadow of such a thought has crossed my humble mind. The Protector of the Poor has condescended to inform me, his slave, that once in his life he has been wounded by a woman. That is sufficient, and I will tell the tale to all my children, asking for no proof."

"Over-much civility is sometimes no better than over-much discourtesy, for, as the saying is, one can choke a guest with curds. I do *not* desire that any children of thine should know that the Mugger of Mugger-Ghaut took his only wound from a woman. They will have much else to think of if they get their meat as miserably as does their father."

"It is forgotten long ago! It was never said! There never was a white woman! There was no boat! Nothing whatever happened at all."

The Jackal waved his brush to show how completely everything was wiped out of his memory, and sat down with an air.

"Indeed, very many things happened," said the Mugger, beaten in his second attempt that night to get the better of his friend. (Neither bore malice, however. Eat and be eaten was fair law along the river, and the Jackal came in for his share of plunder when the Mugger had finished a meal.) "I left that boat and went up-stream, and, when I had reached Arrah and the backwaters behind it, there were no more dead English. The river was empty for a while. Then came one or two dead, in red coats, not English, but of one kind all—Hindus and Purbeeahs—then five and six abreast, and at last, from Arrah to the North beyond Agra, it was as though whole villages had walked into the water. They came out of little creeks one after another, as the logs come down in the Rains. When the river rose they rose also in companies from the shoals they had rested upon; and the falling flood dragged them with it across the fields and through the jungle by the long hair. All night, too, going North, I heard the guns, and by day the shod feet of men crossing fords, and that noise which a heavy cart-wheel makes on sand under water; and every ripple brought more dead. At last even I was afraid, for I said: 'If this thing happen to men how shall the Mugger of Mugger-Ghaut escape?' There were boats, too, that came up behind me without sails, burning continually, as the cotton-boats sometimes burn, but never sinking."

"Ah!" said the Adjutant. "Boats like those come to Calcutta of the South. They are tall and black, they beat up the water behind them with a tail, and they—"

"Are thrice as big as my village. *My* boats were low and white; they beat up the water on either side of them, and were no larger than the boats of one who speaks truth should be. They made me very afraid, and I left water and went back to this my river, hiding by day and walking by night, when I could not find little streams to help me. I came to my village again, but I did not hope to see any of my people there. Yet they were plowing and sowing and reaping, and going to and fro in their fields, as quietly as their own cattle."

"Was there still good food in the river?" said the Jackal.

"More than I had any desire for. Even I—and I do not eat mud—even I was tired, and, as I remember, a little frightened of this constant coming down of the silent ones. I heard my people say in my village that all the English were dead; but those that came, face-down, with the current were *not* English, as my people saw. Then my people said that it was best to say nothing at all, but to pay the tax and plow the land. After a long time the river cleared, and those that came down it had been clearly drowned by the floods, as I could well see; and, though it was not so easy then to get food, I was heartily glad of it. A little killing here and there is no bad thing–but even the Mugger is sometimes satisfied, as the saying is."

"Marvelous! Most truly marvelous!" said the Jackal. "I am become fat through merely hearing about so much good eating. And afterward what, if it be permitted to ask, did the Protector of the Poor do?"

"I said to myself–and by the Right and Left of Gunga! I locked my jaws on that vow–I said I would never go roving any more. So I lived by the Ghaut, very close to my own people, and I watched over them year after year; and they loved me so much that they threw marigold wreaths at my head whenever they saw it lift. Yes, and my Fate has been very kind to me, and the river is good enough to respect my poor and infirm presence; only–"

"No one is all happy from his beak to his tail," said the Adjutant sympathetically. "What does the Mugger of Mugger-Ghaut need more?"

"That little white child which I did not get," said the Mugger, with a deep sigh. "He was very small, but I have not forgotten. I am old now, but before I die it is my desire to try one new thing. It is true they are a heavy-footed, noisy, and foolish people, and the sport would be small, but I remember the old days above Benares, and, if the child lives, he will remember still. It may be he goes up and down the bank of some river, telling how he once passed his hands between the teeth of the Mugger of Mugger-Ghaut, and lived to make a tale of it. My Fate has been very kind, but that plagues me sometimes in my dreams–the thought of the little white child in the bows of that boat." He yawned, and closed his jaws. "And now I will rest and think. Keep silent, my children, and respect the aged."

He turned stiffly, and shuffled to the top of the sand-bar, while the Jackal drew back with the Adjutant to the shelter of a tree stranded on the end nearest the railway bridge.

"That was a pleasant and profitable life," he grinned, looking up inquiringly at the bird who towered above him. "And not once, mark you, did he think fit to tell me where a morsel might have been left along the banks. Yet I have told *him* a hundred times of good things wallowing down-stream. How true is the saying, 'All the world forgets the Jackal and the Barber when the news has been told!' Now he is going to sleep! *Arrh!*"

"How can a Jackal hunt with a Mugger?" said the Adjutant coolly. "Big thief and little thief; it is easy to say who gets the pickings."

The Jackal turned, whining impatiently, and was going to curl himself up under the tree-trunk, when suddenly he cowered, and looked up through the draggled branches at the bridge almost above his head.

"What now?" said the Adjutant, opening his wings uneasily.

"Wait till we see. The wind blows from us to them, but they are not looking for us–those two men."

"Men, is it? My office protects me. All India knows I am holy." The Adjutant, being a first-class scavenger, is allowed to go where he pleases, and so this one never flinched.

"I am not worth a blow from anything greater than an old shoe," said the Jackal, and listened again. "Hark to that footfall!" he went on. "That was no country leather, but the shod foot of a white-face. Listen again! Iron hits iron up there! It is a gun! Friend, those heavy-footed, foolish English are coming to speak with the Mugger."

"Warn him, then. He was called Protector of the Poor by some one not unlike a starving Jackal but a little time ago."

"Let my cousin protect his own hide. He has told me again and again there is nothing to fear from the white-faces. They must be white-faces. Not a villager of Mugger-Ghaut would dare to come after him. See, I said it was a gun! Now, with good luck, we shall feed before daylight. He cannot hear well out of water, and—this time it is not a woman!"

A shiny barrel glittered for a minute in the moonlight on the girders. The Mugger was lying on the sand-bar as still as his own shadow, his fore feet spread out a little, his head dropped between them, snoring like a—mugger.

A voice on the bridge whispered: "It's an odd shot—straight down almost—but as safe as houses. Better try behind the neck. Golly! what a brute! The villagers will be wild if he's shot, though. He's the *deota* (godling) of these parts."

"Don't care a rap," another voice answered; "he took about fifteen of my best coolies while the bridge was building, and it's time he was put a stop to. I've been after him in a boat for weeks. Stand by with the Martini as soon as I've given him both barrels of this."

"Mind the kick, then. A double four-bore's no joke."

"That's for him to decide. Here goes!"

There was a roar like the sound of a small cannon (the biggest sort of elephant-rifle is not very different from some artillery), and a double streak of flame, followed by the stinging crack of a Martini, whose long bullet makes nothing of a crocodile's plates. But the explosive bullets did the work. One of them struck just behind the Mugger's neck, a hand's breadth to the left of the backbone, while the other burst a little lower down, at the beginning of the tail. In ninety-nine cases out of a hundred a mortally wounded crocodile can scramble to deep water and get away; but the Mugger of Mugger-Ghaut was literally broken into three pieces. He hardly moved his head before the life went out of him, and he lay as flat as the Jackal.

"Thunder and lightning! Lightning and thunder!" said the miserable little beast. "Has the thing that pulls the covered carts over the bridge tumbled at last?"

"It is no more than a gun," said the Adjutant, though his very tail-feathers quivered. "Nothing more than a gun. He is certainly dead. Here come the white-faces."

The two Englishmen had hurried down from the bridge and across to the sand-bar, where they stood admiring the length of the Mugger. Then a native with an axe cut off the big head, and four men dragged it across the spit.

"The last time that I had my hand in a Mugger's mouth," said one of the Englishmen, stooping down (he was the man who had built the bridge), "it was when I was about five years old—coming down the river by boat to Monghyr. I was a Mutiny baby, as they call it. Poor mother was in the boat, too, and she often told me how she fired dad's old pistol at the beast's head."

"Well, you've certainly had your revenge on the chief of the clan—even if the gun has made your nose bleed. Hi, you boatman! Haul that head up the bank, and we'll boil it for the skull. The skin's too knocked about to keep. Come along to bed now. This was worth sitting up all night for, wasn't it?"

. . . . .

Curiously enough, the Jackal and the Adjutant made the very same remark not three minutes after the men had left.

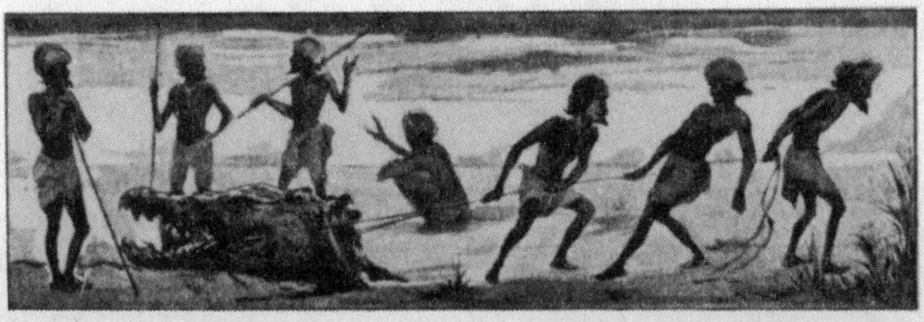

A Ripple Song

Once a ripple came to land
    In the golden sunset burning–
Lapped against a maiden's hand,
    By the ford returning.

Dainty foot and gentle breast–
Here, across, be glad and rest.
"Maiden, wait," the ripple saith;
"Wait awhile, for I am Death!"

"Where my lover calls I go–
    Shame it were to treat him coldly–
'T was a fish that circled so,
    Turning over boldly."

Dainty foot and tender heart,
Wait the loaded ferry-cart.
"Wait, ah, wait!" the ripple saith;
"Maiden, wait, for I am Death!"

"When my lover calls I haste–
    Dame Disdain was never wedded!"
Ripple-ripple round her waist,
    Clear the current eddied.

Foolish heart and faithful hand,
Little feet that touched no land.
Far away the ripple sped,
Ripple–ripple–running red!

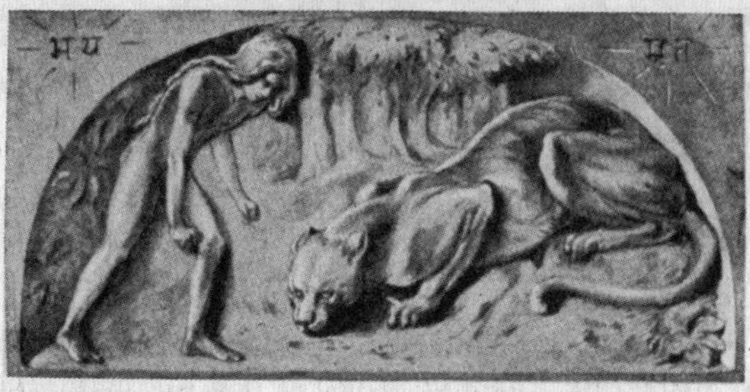

The King's Ankus

These are the Four that are never content, that have never been filled since the Dews began—
Jacala's mouth, and the glut of the Kite, and the hands of the Ape, and the Eyes of Man.

—Jungle Saying.

KAA, THE BIG Rock Python, had changed his skin for perhaps the two hundredth time since his birth; and Mowgli, who never forgot that he owed his life to Kaa for a night's work at Cold Lairs, which you may perhaps remember, went to congratulate him. Skin-changing always makes a snake moody and depressed till the new skin begins to shine and look beautiful. Kaa never made fun of Mowgli any more, but accepted him, as the other Jungle People did, for the Master of the Jungle, and brought him all the news that a python of his size would naturally hear. What Kaa did not know about the Middle Jungle, as they call it,—the life that runs close to the earth or under it, the boulder, burrow, and the tree-bole life,—might have been written upon the smallest of his scales.

That afternoon Mowgli was sitting in the circle of Kaa's great coils, fingering the flaked and broken old skin that lay all looped and twisted among the rocks just as Kaa had left it. Kaa had very courteously packed himself under Mowgli's broad, bare shoulders, so that the boy was really resting in a living arm-chair.

"Even to the scales of the eyes it is perfect," said Mowgli, under his breath, playing with the old skin. "Strange to see the covering of one's own head at one's own feet!"

"Aye, but I lack feet," said Kaa; "and since this is the custom of all my people, I do not find it strange. Does thy skin never feel old and harsh?"

"Then go I and wash, Flathead; but, it is true, in the great heats I have wished I could slough my skin without pain, and run skinless."

"I wash, and *also* I take off my skin. How looks the new coat?"

Mowgli ran his hand down the diagonal checkerings of the immense back. "The Turtle is harder-backed, but not so gay," he said judgmatically. "The Frog, my name-bearer, is more gay, but not so hard. It is very beautiful to see—like the mottling in the mouth of a lily."

"It needs water. A new skin never comes to full color before the first bath. Let us go bathe."

"I will carry thee," said Mowgli; and he stooped down, laughing, to lift the middle section of Kaa's great body, just where the barrel was thickest. A man might just as well have tried to heave up a two-foot water-main; and Kaa lay still, puffing with quiet amusement. Then the regular evening game began—the boy in the flush of his great strength, and the Python in his sumptuous new skin, standing up one against the other for a wrestling-match—a trial of eye and strength. Of course, Kaa could have crushed a dozen Mowglis if he had let himself go; but he played carefully, and never loosed one tenth of his power. Ever since Mowgli was strong enough to endure a little rough handling, Kaa had taught him this game, and it suppled his limbs as nothing else could. Sometimes Mowgli would stand lapped almost to his throat in Kaa's shifting coils, striving to get one arm free and catch him by the throat. Then Kaa would give way limply, and Mowgli, with both quick-moving feet, would try to cramp the purchase of that huge tail as it flung backward feeling for a rock or a stump. They would rock to and fro, head to head, each waiting for his chance, till the beautiful, statue-like group melted in a whirl of black-and-yellow coils and struggling legs and arms, to rise up again and again. "Now! now! now!" said Kaa, making feints with his head that even Mowgli's quick hand could not turn aside. "Look! I touch thee here, Little Brother! Here, and here! Are thy hands numb? Here again!"

The game always ended in one way–with a straight, driving blow of the head that knocked the boy over and over. Mowgli could never learn the guard for that lightning lunge, and, as Kaa said, there was not the least use in trying.

"Good hunting!" Kaa grunted at last; and Mowgli, as usual, was shot away half a dozen yards, gasping and laughing. He rose with his fingers full of grass, and followed Kaa to the wise snake's pet bathing-place–a deep, pitchy-black pool surrounded with rocks, and made interesting by sunken tree-stumps. The boy slipped in, Jungle-fashion, without a sound, and dived across; rose, too, without a sound, and turned on his back, his arms behind his head, watching the moon rising above the rocks, and breaking up her reflection in the water with his toes. Kaa's diamond-shaped head cut the pool like a razor, and came out to rest on Mowgli's shoulder. They lay still, soaking luxuriously in the cool water.

"It is *very* good," said Mowgli at last, sleepily. "Now, in the Man-Pack, at this hour, as I remember, they laid them down upon hard pieces of wood in the inside of a mud-trap, and, having carefully shut out all the clean winds, drew foul cloth over their heavy heads, and made evil songs through their noses. It is better in the Jungle."

A hurrying cobra slipped down over a rock and drank, gave them "Good hunting!" and went away.

"Sssh!" said Kaa, as though he had suddenly remembered something. "So the Jungle gives thee all that thou hast ever desired, Little Brother?"

"Not all," said Mowgli, laughing; "else there would be a new and strong Shere Khan to kill once a moon. Now, I could kill with my own hands, asking no help of buffaloes. And also I have wished the sun to shine in the middle of the Rains, and the Rains to cover the sun in the deep of summer; and also I have never gone empty but I wished that I had killed a goat; and also I have never killed a goat but I wished it had been buck; nor buck but I wished it had been nilghai. But thus do we feel, all of us."

"Thou hast no other desire?" the big snake demanded.

"What more can I wish? I have the Jungle, and the favor of the Jungle! Is there more anywhere between sunrise and sunset?"

"Now, the Cobra said–" Kaa began.

"What cobra? He that went away just now said nothing. He was hunting."

"It was another."

"Hast thou many dealings with the Poison People? I give them their own path. They carry death in the fore-tooth, and that is not good–for they are so small. But what hood is this thou hast spoken with?"

Kaa rolled slowly in the water like a steamer in a beam sea. "Three or four moons since," said he, "I hunted in Cold Lairs, which place thou hast not forgotten. And the thing I hunted fled shrieking past the tanks and to that house whose side I once broke for thy sake, and ran into the ground."

"But the people of Cold Lairs do not live in burrows." Mowgli knew that Kaa was talking of the Monkey People.

"This thing was not living, but seeking to live," Kaa replied, with a quiver of his tongue. "He ran into a burrow that led very far. I followed, and having killed, I slept. When I waked I went forward."

"Under the earth?"

"Even so, coming at last upon a White Hood [a white cobra], who spoke of things beyond my knowledge, and showed me many things I had never before seen."

"New game? Was it good hunting?" Mowgli turned quickly on his side.

"It was no game, and would have broken all my teeth; but the White Hood said that a man—he spoke as one that knew the breed—that a man would give the breath under his ribs for only the sight of those things."

"We will look," said Mowgli. "I now remember that I was once a man."

"Slowly—slowly. It was haste killed the Yellow Snake that ate the sun. We two spoke together under the earth, and I spoke of thee, naming thee as a man. Said the White Hood (and he is indeed as old as the Jungle): 'It is long since I have seen a man. Let him come, and he shall see all these things, for the least of which very many men would die.' "

"That *must* be new game. And yet the Poison People do not tell us when game is afoot. They are an unfriendly folk."

"It is *not* game. It is—it is—I cannot say what it is."

"We will go there. I have never seen a White Hood, and I wish to see the other things. Did he kill them?"

"They are all dead things. He says he is the keeper of them all."

"Ah! As a wolf stands above meat he has taken to his own lair. Let us go."

Mowgli swam to bank, rolled on the grass to dry himself, and the two set off for Cold Lairs, the deserted city of which you may have heard. Mowgli was not the least afraid of the Monkey People in those days, but the Monkey People had the liveliest horror of Mowgli. Their tribes, however, were raiding in the Jungle, and so Cold Lairs stood empty and silent in the moonlight. Kaa led up to the ruins of the queen's pavilion that stood on the terrace, slipped over the rubbish, and dived down the half-choked staircase that went underground from the center of the pavilion. Mowgli gave the snake-call—"We be of one blood, ye and I,"—and followed on his hands and knees. They crawled a long distance down a sloping passage that turned and twisted several times, and at last came to where the root of some great tree, growing thirty feet overhead, had forced out a solid stone in the wall. They crept through the gap, and found themselves in a large vault, whose domed roof had been also broken away by tree-roots so that a few streaks of light dropped down into the darkness.

"A safe lair," said Mowgli, rising to his firm feet, "but over far to visit daily. And now what do we see?"

"Am I nothing?" said a voice in the middle of the vault; and Mowgli saw something white move till, little by little, there stood up the hugest cobra he had ever set eyes on—a creature nearly eight feet long, and bleached by being in darkness to an old ivory-white. Even the spectacle-marks of his spread hood had faded to faint yellow. His eyes were as red as rubies, and altogether he was most wonderful.

"Good hunting!" said Mowgli, who carried his manners with his knife, and that never left him.

"What of my city?" said the White Cobra, without answering the greeting. "What of the great, the walled city—the city of a hundred elephants and twenty thousand horses, and cattle past counting—the city of the King of Twenty Kings? I grow deaf here, and it is long since I heard their war-gongs."

"The Jungle is above our heads," said Mowgli. "I know only Hathi and his sons among elephants. Bagheera has slain all the horses in one village, and–what is a King?"

"I told thee," said Kaa softly to the Cobra–"I told thee, four moons ago, that thy city was not."

"The city–the great city of the forest whose gates are guarded by the King's towers–can never pass. They builded it before my father's father came from the egg, and it shall endure when my son's sons are as white as I! Salomdhi, son of Chandrabija, son of Viyeja, son of Yegasuri, made it in the days of Bappa Rawal. Whose cattle are *ye?*"

"It is a lost trail," said Mowgli, turning to Kaa. "I know not his talk."

"Nor I. He is very old. Father of Cobras, there is only the Jungle here, as it has been since the beginning."

"Then who is *he,*" said the White Cobra, "sitting down before me, unafraid, knowing not the name of the King, talking our talk through a man's lips? Who is he with the knife and the snake's tongue?"

"Mowgli they call me," was the answer. "I am of the Jungle. The Wolves are my people, and Kaa here is my brother. Father of Cobras, who art thou?"

"I am the Warden of the King's Treasure. Kurrun Raja builded the stone above me, in the days when my skin was dark, that I might teach death to those who came to steal. Then they let down the treasure through the stone, and I heard the song of the Brahmins my masters."

"Umm!" said Mowgli to himself. "I have dealt with one Brahmin already, in the Man-Pack, and–I know what I know. Evil comes here in a little."

"Five times since I came here has the stone been lifted, but always to let down more, and never to take away. There are no riches like these riches–the treasures of a hundred kings. But it is long and long since the stone was last moved, and I think that my city has forgotten."

"There is no city. Look up. Yonder are roots of the great trees tearing the stones apart. Trees and men do not grow together," Kaa insisted.

"Twice and thrice have men found their way here," the White Cobra answered savagely; "but they never spoke till I came upon them groping in the dark, and then they cried only a little time. But *ye* come with lies, Man and Snake both, and would have me believe the city is not, and that my wardship ends. Little do men change in the years. But *I* change never! Till the stone is lifted, and the Brahmins come down singing the songs that I know, and feed me with warm milk, and take me to the light again, I–I–*I,* and no other, am the Warden of the King's Treasure! The city is dead, ye say, and here are the roots of the trees? Stoop down, then, and take what ye will. Earth has no treasure like to these. Man with the snake's tongue, if thou canst go alive by the way that thou hast entered at, the lesser Kings will be thy servants!"

"Again the trail is lost," said Mowgli, coolly. "Can any jackal have burrowed so deep and bitten this great White Hood? He is surely mad. Father of Cobras, I see nothing here to take away."

"By the Gods of the Sun and Moon, it is the madness of death upon the boy!" hissed the Cobra. "Before thine eyes close I will allow thee this favor. Look thou, and see what man has never seen before!"

"They do not well in the Jungle who speak to Mowgli of favors," said the boy, between his teeth; "but the dark changes all, as I know. I will look, if that please thee."

He stared with puckered-up eyes round the vault, and then lifted up from the floor a handful of something that glittered.

"Oho!" said he, "this is like the stuff they play with in the Man-Pack: only this is yellow and the other was brown."

He let the gold pieces fall, and moved forward. The floor of the vault was buried some five or six feet deep in coined gold and silver that had burst from the sacks it had been originally stored in, and, in the long years, the metal had packed and settled as sand packs at low tide. On it and in it, and rising through it, as wrecks lift through the sand, were jeweled elephant-howdahs of embossed silver, studded with plates of hammered gold, and adorned with carbuncles and turquoises. There were palanquins and litters for carrying queens, framed and braced with silver and enamel, with jade-handled poles and amber curtain-rings; there were golden candlesticks hung with pierced emeralds that quivered on the branches; there were studded images, five feet high, of forgotten gods, silver with jeweled eyes; there were coats of mail, gold inlaid on steel, and fringed with rotted and blackened seed-pearls; there were helmets, crested and beaded with pigeon's-blood rubies; there were shields of lacquer, of tortoise-shell and rhinoceros-hide, strapped and bossed with red gold and set with emeralds at the edge; there were sheaves of diamond-hilted swords, daggers, and hunting-knives; there were golden sacrificial bowls and ladles, and portable altars of a shape that never see the light of day; there were jade cups and bracelets; there were incense-burners, combs, and pots for perfume, henna, and eye-powder, all in embossed gold; there were nose-rings, armlets, head-bands, finger-rings, and girdles past any counting; there were belts, seven fingers broad, of square-cut diamonds and rubies, and wooden boxes, trebly clamped with iron, from which the wood had fallen away in powder, showing the pile of uncut star-sapphires, opals, cat's-eyes, sapphires, rubies, diamonds, emeralds, and garnets within.

The White Cobra was right. No mere money would begin to pay the value of this treasure, the sifted pickings of centuries of war, plunder, trade, and taxation. The coins alone were priceless, leaving out of count all the precious stones; and the dead weight of the gold and silver alone might be two or three hundred tons. Every native ruler in India to-day, however poor, has a hoard to which he is always adding; and though, once in a long while, some enlightened prince may send off forty or fifty bullock-cart loads of silver to be exchanged for Government securities, the bulk of them keep their treasure and the knowledge of it very closely to themselves.

But Mowgli naturally did not understand what these things meant. The knives interested him a little, but they did not balance so well as his own, and so he dropped them. At last he found something really fascinating laid on the front of a howdah half buried in the coins. It was a three-foot ankus, or elephant-goad–something like a small boat-hook. The top was one round

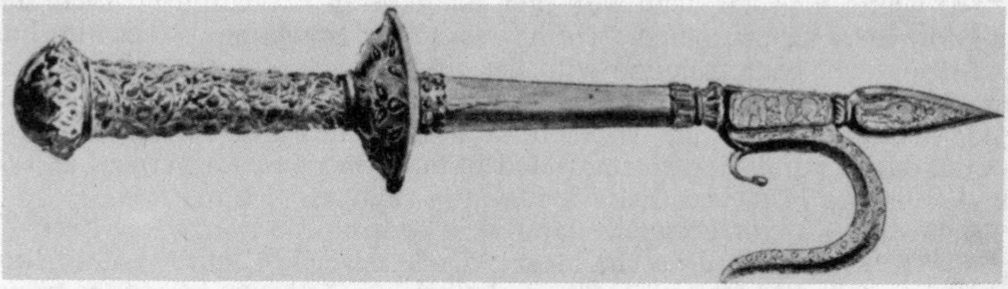

shining ruby, and twelve inches of the handle below it were studded with rough turquoises close together, giving a most satisfactory grip. Below them was a rim of jade with a flower-pattern running round it–only the leaves were emeralds, and the blossoms were rubies sunk in the cool, green stone. The rest of the handle was a shaft of pure ivory, while the point–the spike and hook–was gold-inlaid steel with pictures of elephant-catching; and the pictures attracted Mowgli, who saw that they had something to do with his friend Hathi the Silent.

The White Cobra had been following him closely.

"Is this not worth dying to behold?" he said. "Have I not done thee a great favor?"

"I do not understand," said Mowgli. "The things are hard and cold, and by no means good to eat. But this"–he lifted the ankus–"I desire to take away, that I may see it in the sun. Thou sayest they are all thine? Wilt thou give it to me, and I will bring thee frogs to eat?"

The White Cobra fairly shook with evil delight. "Assuredly I will give it," he said. "All that is here I will give thee–till thou goest away."

"But I go now. This place is dark and cold, and I wish to take the thorn-pointed thing to the Jungle."

"Look by thy foot! What is that there?"

Mowgli picked up something white and smooth. "It is the bone of a man's head," he said quietly. "And here are two more."

"They came to take the treasure away many years ago. I spoke to them in the dark, and they lay still."

"But what do I need of this that is called treasure? If thou wilt give me the ankus to take away, it is good hunting. If not, it is good hunting none the less. I do not fight with the Poison People, and I was also taught the Master-word of thy tribe."

"There is but one Master-word here. It is mine!"

Kaa flung himself forward with blazing eyes. "Who bade me bring the Man?" he hissed.

"I surely," the old Cobra lisped. "It is long since I have seen Man, and this Man speaks our tongue."

"But there was no talk of killing. How can I go to the Jungle and say that I have led him to his death?" said Kaa.

"I talk not of killing till the time. And as to thy going or not going, there is the hole in the wall. Peace, now, thou fat monkey-killer! I have but to touch thy neck, and the Jungle will know thee no longer. Never Man came here that went away with the breath under his ribs. I am the Warden of the Treasure of the King's City!"

"But, thou white worm of the dark, I tell thee there is neither king nor city! The Jungle is all about us!" cried Kaa.

"There is still the Treasure. But this can be done. Wait a while, Kaa of the Rocks, and see the boy run. There is room for great sport here. Life is good. Run to and fro a while, and make sport, boy!"

Mowgli put his hand on Kaa's head quietly.

"The white thing has dealt with men of the Man-Pack until now. He does not know me," he whispered. "He has asked for this hunting. Let him have it." Mowgli had been standing with the ankus held point down. He flung it from him quickly, and it dropped crossways just behind the great snake's hood, pinning him to the floor. In a flash, Kaa's weight was upon the writhing body, paralyzing it from hood to tail. The red eyes burned, and the six spare inches of the head struck furiously right and left.

"Kill!" said Kaa, as Mowgli's hand went to his knife.

"No," he said, as he drew the blade; "I will never kill again save for food. But look you, Kaa!" He caught the snake behind the hood, forced the mouth open with the blade of the knife, and showed the terrible poison-fangs of the upper jaw lying black and withered in the gum. The White Cobra had outlived his poison, as a snake will.

"Thuu" ("It is dried up"),[1] said Mowgli; and motioning Kaa away, he picked up the ankus, setting the White Cobra free.

"The King's Treasure needs a new Warden," he said gravely. "Thuu, thou hast not done well. Run to and fro and make sport, Thuu!"

"I am ashamed. Kill me!" hissed the White Cobra.

[1] Literally, a rotted out tree-stump.

"There has been too much talk of killing. We will go now. I take the thorn-pointed thing, Thuu, because I have fought and worsted thee."

"See, then, that the thing does not kill thee at last. It is Death! Remember, it is Death! There is enough in that thing to kill the men of all my city. Not long wilt thou hold it, Jungle Man, nor he who takes it from thee. They will kill, and kill, and kill for its sake! My strength is dried up, but the ankus will do my work. It is Death! It is Death! It is Death!"

Mowgli crawled out through the hole into the passage again, and the last that he saw was the White Cobra striking furiously with his harmless fangs at the stolid golden faces of the gods that lay on the floor, and hissing, "It is Death!"

They were glad to get to the light of day once more; and when they were back in their own Jungle and Mowgli made the ankus glitter in the morning light, he was almost as pleased as though he had found a bunch of new flowers to stick in his hair.

"This is brighter than Bagheera's eyes," he said delightedly, as he twirled the ruby. "I will show it to him; but what did the Thuu mean when he talked of death?"

"I cannot say. I am sorrowful to my tail's tail that he felt not thy knife. There is always evil at Cold Lairs–above ground or below. But now I am hungry. Dost thou hunt with me this dawn?" said Kaa.

"No; Bagheera must see this thing. Good hunting!" Mowgli danced off, flourishing the great ankus, and stopping from time to time to admire it, till he came to that part of the Jungle Bagheera chiefly used, and found him drinking after a heavy kill. Mowgli told him all his adventures from beginning to end, and Bagheera sniffed at the ankus between whiles. When Mowgli came to the White Cobra's last words, the Panther purred approvingly.

"Then the White Hood spoke the thing which is?" Mowgli asked quickly.

"I was born in the King's cages at Oodeypore, and it is in my stomach that I know some little of Man. Very many men would kill thrice in a night for the sake of that one big red stone alone."

"But the stone makes it heavy to the hand. My little bright knife is better; and–see! the red stone is not good to eat. Then *why* would they kill?"

"Mowgli, go thou and sleep. Thou hast lived among men, and–"

"I remember. Men kill because they are not hunting;–for idleness and pleasure. Wake again, Bagheera. For what use was this thorn-pointed thing made?"

Bagheera half opened his eyes–he was very sleepy–with a malicious twinkle.

"It was made by men to thrust into the head of the sons of Hathi, so that the blood should pour out. I have seen the like in the street of Oodeypore, before our cages. That thing has tasted the blood of many such as Hathi."

"But why do they thrust into the heads of elephants?"

"To teach them Man's Law. Having neither claws nor teeth, men make these things–and worse."

"Always more blood when I come near, even to the things the Man-Pack have made," said Mowgli, disgustedly. He was getting a little tired of the weight of the ankus. "If I had known this, I would not have taken it. First it was Messua's blood on the thongs, and now it is Hathi's. I will use it no more. Look!"

The ankus flew sparkling, and buried itself point down thirty yards away, between the trees. "So my hands are clean of Death," said Mowgli, rubbing his palms on the fresh, moist earth. "The Thuu said Death would follow me. He is old and white and mad."

"White or black, or death or life, *I* am going to sleep, Little Brother. I cannot hunt all night and howl all day, as do some folk."

Bagheera went off to a hunting-lair that he knew, about two miles off. Mowgli made an easy way for himself up a convenient tree, knotted three or four creepers together, and in less time than it takes to tell was swinging in a hammock fifty feet above ground. Though he had no positive objection to strong daylight, Mowgli followed the custom of his friends, and used it as little as he could. When he waked among the very loud-voiced peoples that live in the trees, it was twilight once more, and he had been dreaming of the beautiful pebbles he had thrown away.

"At least I will look at the thing again," he said, and slid down a creeper to the earth; but Bagheera was before him. Mowgli could hear him snuffing in the half light.

"Where is the thorn-pointed thing?" cried Mowgli.

"A man has taken it. Here is the trail."

"Now we shall see whether the Thuu spoke truth. If the pointed thing is Death, that man will die. Let us follow."

"Kill first," said Bagheera. "An empty stomach makes a careless eye. Men go very slowly, and the Jungle is wet enough to hold the lightest mark."

They killed as soon as they could, but it was nearly three hours before they finished their meat and drink and buckled down to the trail. The Jungle People know that nothing makes up for being hurried over your meals.

"Think you the pointed thing will turn in the man's hand and kill him?" Mowgli asked. "The Thuu said it was Death."

"We shall see when we find," said Bagheera, trotting with his head low. "It is single-foot" (he meant that there was only one man), "and the weight of the thing has pressed his heel far into the ground."

"Hai! This is as clear as summer lightning," Mowgli answered; and they fell into the quick, choppy trail-trot in and out through the checkers of the moonlight, following the marks of those two bare feet.

"Now he runs swiftly," said Mowgli. "The toes are spread apart." They went on over some wet ground. "Now why does he turn aside here?"

"Wait!" said Bagheera, and flung himself forward with one superb bound as far as ever he could. The first thing to do when a trail ceases to explain itself is to cast forward without leaving your own confusing foot-marks on the ground. Bagheera turned as he landed, and faced Mowgli, crying, "Here comes another trail to meet him. It is a smaller foot, this second trail, and the toes turn inward."

Then Mowgli ran up and looked. "It is the foot of a Gond hunter," he said. "Look! Here he dragged his bow on the grass. That is why the first trail turned aside so quickly. Big Foot hid from Little Foot."

"That is true," said Bagheera. "Now, lest by crossing each other's tracks we foul the signs, let each take one trail. I am Big Foot, Little Brother, and thou art Little Foot, the Gond."

Bagheera leaped back to the original trail, leaving Mowgli stooping above the curious narrow track of the wild little man of the woods.

"Now," said Bagheera, moving step by step along the chain of footprints, "I, Big Foot, turn aside here. Now I hide me behind a rock and stand still, not daring to shift my feet. Cry thy trail, Little Brother."

"Now, I, Little Foot, come to the rock," said Mowgli, running up his trail. "Now, I sit down under the rock, leaning upon my right hand, and resting my bow between my toes. I wait long, for the mark of my feet is deep here."

"I also," said Bagheera, hidden behind the rock. "I wait, resting the end of the thorn-pointed thing upon a stone. It slips, for here is a scratch upon the stone. Cry thy trail, Little Brother."

"One, two twigs and a big branch are broken here," said Mowgli, in an undertone. "Now, how shall I cry *that?* Ah! It is plain now. I, Little Foot, go away making noises and tramplings so that Big Foot may hear me." He moved away from the rock pace by pace among the trees, his voice rising in the distance as he approached a little cascade. "I—go—far—away—to—where—the—noise—of—falling—water—covers—my—noise; and—here—I—wait. Cry thy trail, Bagheera, Big Foot!"

The panther had been casting in every direction to see how Big Foot's trail led away from behind the rock. Then he gave tongue:

"I come from behind the rock upon my knees, dragging the thorn-pointed thing. Seeing no one, I run. I, Big Foot, run swiftly. The trail is clear. Let each follow his own. I run!"

Bagheera swept on along the clearly marked trail, and Mowgli followed the steps of the Gond. For some time there was silence in the Jungle.

"Where art thou, Little Foot?" cried Bagheera. Mowgli's voice answered him not fifty yards to the right.

"Um!" said the panther, with a deep cough. "The two run side by side, drawing nearer!"

They raced on another half mile, always keeping about the same distance, till Mowgli, whose head was not so close to the ground as Bagheera's, cried: "They have met. Good hunting—look! Here stood Little Foot, with his knee on a rock—and yonder is Big Foot indeed!"

Not ten yeards in front of them, stretched across a pile of broken rocks, lay the body of a villager of the district, a long, small-feathered Gond arrow through his back and breast.

"Was the Thuu so old and so mad, Little Brother?" said Bagheera gently. "Here is one death, at least."

"Follow on. But where is the drinker of elephant's blood—the red-eyed thorn?"

"Little Foot has it—perhaps. It is single-foot again now."

The single trail of a light man who had been running quickly and bearing a burden on his left shoulder, held on round a long, low spur of dried grass, where each footfall seemed, to the sharp eyes of the trackers, marked in hot iron.

Neither spoke till the trail ran up to the ashes of a camp-fire hidden in a ravine.

"Again!" said Bagheera, checking as though he had been turned into stone.

The body of a little wizened Gond lay with its feet in the ashes, and Bagheera looked inquiringly at Mowgli.

"That was done with a bamboo," said the boy, after one glance. "I have used such a thing among the buffaloes when I served in the Man-Pack. The Father of Cobras—I am sorrowful that I made a jest of him—knew the breed well, as I might have known. Said I not that men kill for idleness?"

"Indeed, they killed for the sake of the red and blue stones," Bagheera answered. "Remember, I was in the King's cages at Oodeypore."

"One, two, three, four tracks," said Mowgli, stooping over the ashes. "Four tracks of men with shod feet. They do not go so quickly as Gonds. Now, what evil had the little woodman done to them? See, they talked together, all five, standing up, before they killed him. Bagheera, let us go back. My stomach is heavy in me, and yet it heaves up and down like an oriole's nest at the end of a branch."

"It is not good hunting to leave game afoot. Follow!" said the panther. "Those eight shod feet have not gone far."

No more was said for fully an hour, as they worked up the broad trail of the four men with shod feet.

It was clear, hot daylight now, and Bagheera said, "I smell smoke."

"Men are always more ready to eat than to run," Mowgli answered, trotting in and out between the low scrub bushes of the new Jungle they were exploring. Bagheera, a little to his left, made an indescribable noise in his throat.

"Here is one that has done with feeding," said he. A tumbled bundle of gay-colored clothes lay under a bush, and round it was some spilt flour.

"That was done by the bamboo again," said Mowgli. "See! that white dust is what men eat. They have taken the kill from this one,–he carried their food,–and given him for a kill to Chil, the Kite."

"It is the third," said Bagheera.

"I will go with new, big frogs to the Father of Cobras, and feed him fat," said Mowgli to himself. "The drinker of elephant's blood is Death himself–but still I do not understand!"

"Follow!" said Bagheera.

They had not gone half a mile further when they heard Ko, the Crow, singing the death-song in the top of a tamarisk under whose shade three men were lying. A half-dead fire smoked in the center of the circle, under an iron plate which held a blackened and burned cake of unleavened bread. Close to the fire, and blazing in the sunshine, lay the ruby-and-turquoise ankus.

"The thing works quickly; all ends here," said Bagheera. "How did *these* die, Mowgli? There is no mark on any."

A Jungle-dweller gets to learn by experience as much as many doctors know of poisonous plants and berries. Mowgli sniffed the smoke that came up from the fire, broke off a morsel of the blackened bread, tasted it, and spat it out again.

"Apple of Death," he coughed. "The first must have made it ready in the food for *these,* who killed him, having first killed the Gond."

"Good hunting, indeed! The kills follow close," said Bagheera.

"Apple of Death," is what the Jungle call thorn-apple or dhatura, the readiest poison in all India.

"What now?" said the panther. "Must thou and I kill each other for yonder red-eyed slayer?"

"Can it speak?" said Mowgli, in a whisper. "Did I do it a wrong when I threw it away? Between us two it can do no wrong, for we do not desire what men desire. If it be left here, it will assuredly continue to kill men one after another as fast as nuts fall in a high wind. I have no love to men, but even I would not have them die six in a night."

"What matter? They are only men. They killed one another and were well pleased," said Bagheera. "That first little woodman hunted well."

"They are cubs none the less; and a cub will drown himself to bite the moon's light on the water. The fault was mine," said Mowgli, who spoke as though he knew all about everything. "I will never again bring into the Jungle strange things–not though they be as beautiful as flowers. This"–he handled the ankus gingerly–"goes back to the Father of Cobras. But first we must sleep, and we cannot sleep near these sleepers. Also we must bury *him,* lest he run away and kill another six. Dig me a hole under that tree."

"But, Little Brother," said Bagheera, moving off to the spot, "I tell thee it is no fault of the blood-drinker, T e trouble is with men."

"All one," said Mowgli. "Dig the hole deep. When we wake I will take him up and carry him back."

. . . . .

Two nights later, as the White Cobra sat mourning in the darkness of the vault, ashamed, and robbed, and alone, the turquoise ankus whirled through the hole in the wall, and clashed on the floor of golden coins.

"Father of Cobras," said Mowgli (he was careful to keep the other side of the wall), "get thee a young and ripe one of thine own people to help thee guard the King's Treasure so that no man may come away alive any more."

"Ah-ha! It returns, then. I said the thing was Death. How comes it that thou art still alive?" the old Cobra mumbled, twining lovingly round the ankus-haft.

"By the Bull that bought me, I do not know! That thing has killed six times in a night. Let him go out no more."

The Song of the Little Hunter

Ere Mor the Peacock flutters, ere the Monkey People cry,
    Ere Chil the Kite swoops down a furlong sheer,
Through the Jungle very softly flits a shadow and a sigh–
    He is Fear, O Little Hunter, he is Fear!
Very softly down the glade runs a waiting, watching shade,
    And the whisper spreads and widens far and near;
And the sweat is on thy brow, for he passes even now–
    He is Fear, O Little Hunter, he is Fear!

Ere the moon has climbed the mountain, ere the rocks are ribbed with light,
    When the downward-dipping trails are dank and drear,
Comes a breathing hard behind thee–*snuffle-snuffle* through the night–
    It is Fear, O Little Hunter, it is Fear!
On thy knees and draw the bow; bid the shrilling arrow go;
    In the empty, mocking thicket plunge the spear;
But thy hands are loosed and weak, and the blood has left thy cheek–
    It is Fear, O Little Hunter, it is Fear!

When the heat-cloud sucks the tempest, when the slivered pine-trees fall,
    When the blinding, blaring rain-squalls lash and veer;
Through the war-gongs of the thunder rings a voice more loud than all–
    It is Fear, O Little Hunter, it is Fear!
Now the spates are banked and deep; now the footless boulders leap–
    Now the lightning shows each littlest leaf-rib clear–
But thy throat is shut and dried, and thy heart against thy side
    Hammers: Fear, O Little Hunter–this is Fear!

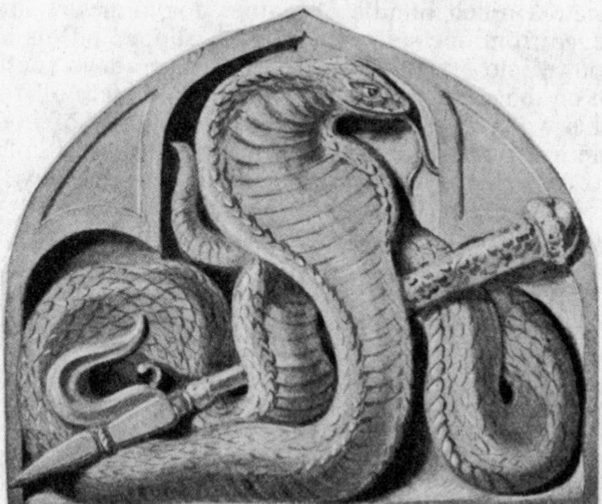

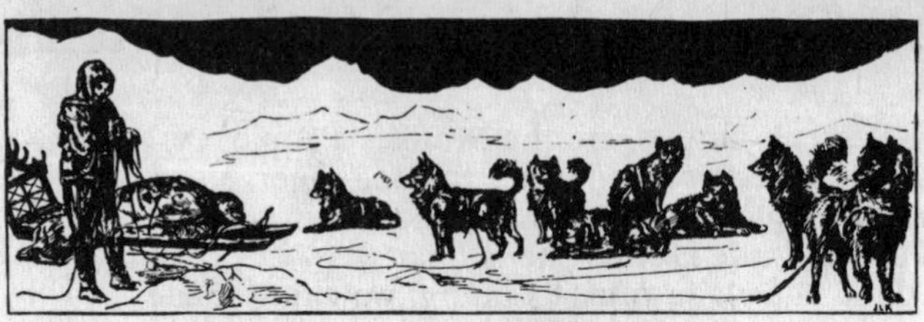

Quiquern

The People of the Eastern Ice, they are melting like the snow—
They beg for coffee and sugar; they go where the white men go.
The People of the Western Ice, they learn to steal and fight;
They sell their furs to the trading post; they sell their souls to the white.
The People of the Southern Ice, they trade with the whaler's crew;
Their women have many ribbons, but their tents are torn and few.
But the People of the Elder Ice, beyond the white man's ken—
Their spears are made of the narwhal-horn, and they are the last of the Men!
—*Translation.*

"HE HAS OPENED his eyes. Look!"

"Put him in the skin again. He will be a strong dog. On the fourth month we will name him."

"For whom?" said Amoraq.

Kadlu's eyes rolled round the skin-lined snow-house till it fell on fourteen-year-old Kotuko sitting on the sleeping-bench, making a button out of walrus ivory. "Name him for me," said Kotuko, with a grin. "I shall need him one day."

Kadlu grinned back till his eyes were almost buried in the fat of his flat cheeks, and nodded to Amoraq, while the puppy's fierce mother whined to see her baby wriggling far out of reach in the little sealskin pouch hung above the warmth of the blubber-lamp. Kotuko went on with his carving, and Kadlu threw a rolled bundle of leather dog-harnesses into a tiny little room that opened from one side of the house, slipped off his heavy deerskin hunting-suit, put it into a whalebone-net that hung above another lamp, and dropped down on the sleeping-bench to whittle at a piece of frozen seal-meat till Amoraq, his wife, should bring the regular dinner of boiled meat and blood-soup. He had been out since early dawn at the seal-holes, eight miles away, and had come home with three big seal. Halfway down the long, low snow passage or tunnel that led to the inner door of the house you could hear snappings and yelpings, as the dogs of his sleigh-team, released from the day's work, scuffled for warm places.

When the yelpings grew too loud Kotuko lazily rolled off the sleeping-bench, and picked up a whip with an eighteen-inch handle of springy whalebone, and twenty-five feet of heavy, plaited thong. He dived into the passage, where it sounded as though all the dogs were eating him alive; but that was no more than their regular grace before meals. When he crawled out at the far end half a dozen furry heads followed him with their eyes as he went to a sort of gallows of whale-jawbones, from which the dog's meat was hung; split off the frozen stuff in big lumps with a broad-headed spear; and stood, his whip in one hand and the meat in the other. Each beast was called by name, the weakest first, and woe betide any dog that moved out of his turn; for the tapering lash would shoot out like thonged lightning, and flick away an inch or so of hair and hide. Each beast growled, snapped, choked once over his portion, and hurried back to the protection of the passage, while the boy stood upon the snow under the blazing Northern Lights and dealt out justice. The last to be served was the big black leader of the team, who kept order when the dogs were harnessed; and to him Kotuko gave a double allowance of meat as well as an extra crack of the whip.

"Ah!" said Kotuko, coiling up the lash, "I have a little one over the lamp that will make a great many howlings. *Sarpok!* Get in!"

He crawled back over the huddled dogs, dusted the dry snow from his furs with the whalebone beater that Amoraq kept by the door, tapped the skin-lined roof of the house to shake off any icicles that might have fallen from the dome of snow above, and curled up on the bench. The dogs in the passage snored and whined in their sleep, the boy-baby in Amoraq's deep fur hood kicked and choked and gurgled, and the mother of the newly named puppy lay at Kotuko's side, her eyes fixed on the bundle of sealskin, warm and safe above the broad yellow flame of the lamp.

And all this happened far away to the north, beyond Labrador, beyond Hudson's Strait, where the great tides heave the ice about, north of Melville Peninsula–north even of the narrow Fury and Hecla Straits–on the north shore of Baffin Land, where Bylot's Island stands above the ice of Lancaster Sound like a pudding-bowl wrong side up. North of Lancaster Sound there is little we know anything about, except North Devon and Ellesmere Land; but even there live a few scattered people, next door, as it were, to the very Pole.

Kadlu was an Inuit,–what you call an Esquimau,–and his tribe, some thirty persons all told, belonged to the Tununirmiut–"the country lying at the back of something." In the maps that desolate coast is written Navy Board Inlet, but the Inuit name is best, because the country lies at the very back of everything in the world. For nine months of the year there is only ice, snow, and gale after gale, with a cold that no one can realize who has never seen the thermometer even at zero. For six months of those nine it is dark; and that is what makes it so horrible. In the three months of the summer it only freezes every other day and every night, and then the snow begins to weep off on the southerly slopes, and a few ground-willows put out their woolly buds, a tiny stonecrop or so makes believe to blossom, beaches of fine gravel and rounded stones run down to the open sea, and polished boulders and streaked rocks lift up above the granulated snow. But all that is gone in a few weeks, and the wild winter locks down again on the land; while at sea the ice tears up and down the offing, jamming and ramming, and splitting and hitting, and pounding and grounding, till it all freezes together, ten feet thick, from the land outward to deep water.

In the winter Kadlu would follow the seal to the edge of this land-ice, and spear them as they came up to breathe at their blow-holes. The seal must have open water to live and catch fish in, and in the deep of winter the ice would sometimes run eighty miles without a break from the nearest shore. In the spring he and his people retreated from the floes to the rocky mainland, where they put up tents of skins, and snared the sea-birds, or speared the young seal basking on the beaches. Later, they would go south into Baffin Land after the reindeer, and to get their year's store of salmon from the hundreds of streams and lakes of the interior; coming back north in September or October for the musk-ox hunting and the regular winter sealery. This traveling was done with dog-sleighs, twenty and thirty miles a day, or sometimes down the coast in big skin "woman-boats," when the dogs and the babies lay among the feet of the rowers, and the women sang songs as they glided from cape to cape over the glassy, cold waters. All the luxuries that the Tununirmiut knew came from the south–driftwood for sleigh-runners, rod-iron for harpoon-tips, steel knives, tin kettles that cooked food much better than the old soap-stone affairs, flint and steel, and even matches, as well as colored ribbons for the women's hair, little cheap mirrors, and red cloth for the edging of deerskin dress-jackets. Kadlu traded the rich, creamy, twisted narwhal-horn and musk-ox teeth (these are just as valuable as pearls) to the Southern Inuit, and they, in turn, traded with the whalers and the missionary-posts of Exeter and Cumberland Sounds; and so the chain went on, till a kettle picked up by a ship's cook in the Bhendy Bazaar might end its days over a blubber-lamp somewhere on the cool side of the Arctic Circle.

Kadlu, being a good hunter, was rich in iron harpoons, snow-knives, bird-darts, and all the other things that make life easy up there in the great cold; and he was the head of this tribe, or, as they say, "the man who knows all about it by practice." This did not give him any authority, except now and then he could advise his friends to change their hunting-grounds; but Kotuko used it to domineer a little, in the lazy, fat Inuit fashion, over the other boys, when they came out at night to play ball in the moonlight, or to sing the Child's Song to the Aurora Borealis.

But at fourteen an Inuit feels himself a man, and Kotuko was tired of making snares for wild fowl and kit-foxes, and most tired of all of helping the women to chew seal- and deerskins (that supples them as nothing else can) the long day through, while the men were out hunting. He wanted to go into the *quaggi,* the Singing-House, when the hunters gathered there for their mysteries, and the *angekok,* the sorcerer, frightened them into the most delightful fits after the lamps were put out, and you could hear the Spirit of the Reindeer stamping on the roof; and when a spear was thrust out into the open black night it came back covered with hot blood. He wanted to throw his big boots into the net with the tired air of a head of a family, and to gamble with the hunters when they dropped in of an evening and played a sort of home-made roulette with a tin pot and a nail. There were hundreds of things that he wanted to do, but the grown men laughed at him and said, "Wait till you have been in the buckle, Kotuko. Hunting is not *all* catching."

Now that his father had named a puppy for him, things looked brighter. An Inuit does not waste a good dog on his son till the boy knows something of dog-driving; and Kotuko was more than sure that he knew more than everything.

If the puppy had not had an iron constitution he would have died from over-stuffing and over-handling. Kotuko made him a tiny harness with a trace to it, and hauled him all over the house floor, shouting: "Aua! Ja aua!" (Go to the right.) "Choiachoi! Ja choiachoi!" (Go to the left.) "Ohaha!" (Stop.) The puppy did not like it at all, but being fished for in this way was pure happiness beside being put to the sleigh for the first time. He just sat down on the snow, and played with the seal-hide trace that ran from his harness to the *pitu,* the big thong in the bows of the sleigh. Then the team started, and the puppy found the heavy ten-foot sleigh running up his back, and dragging him along the snow, while Kotuko laughed till the tears ran down his face. There followed days and days of the cruel whip that hisses like the wind over ice, and his companions all bit him because he did not know his work, and the harness chafed him, and he was not allowed to sleep with Kotuko any more, but had to take the coldest place in the passage. It was a sad time for the puppy.

The boy learned, too, as fast as the dog; though a dog-sleigh is a heart-breaking thing to manage. Each beast is harnessed, the weakest nearest to the driver, by his own separate trace, which runs under his left fore-leg to the main thong, where it is fastened by a sort of button and loop which can be slipped by a turn of the wrist, thus freeing one dog at a time. This is very necessary, because young dogs often get the trace between their hind legs, where it cuts to the bone. And they one and all *will* go visiting their friends as they run, jumping in and out among the traces. Then they fight, and the result is more mixed than a wet fishing-line next morning. A great deal of trouble can be avoided by scientific use of the whip. Every Inuit boy prides himself as being a master of the long lash; but it is easy to flick at a mark on the ground, and difficult to lean forward and catch a shirking dog just behind the shoulders when the sleigh is going at full speed. If you call one dog's name for "visiting," and accidentally lash another, the two will fight it out at once, and stop all the others. Again, if you travel with a companion and begin to talk, or by yourself and sing, the dogs will halt, turn round, and sit down to hear what you have to say. Kotuko was run away from once or twice through forgetting to block the sleigh when he stopped; and he broke many lashings, and ruined a few thongs, before he could be trusted with a full team of eight and the light sleigh. Then he felt himself a person of consequence, and on smooth, black ice, with a bold heart and a quick elbow, he smoked along over the levels as fast as a pack in full cry. He would go ten miles to the seal-holes, and when he was on the hunting-grounds he would twitch a trace loose from the *pitu,* and free the big black leader, who was the cleverest dog in the team. As soon as the dog had scented a breathing-hole Kotuko would reverse the sleigh, driving a couple of sawed-off antlers, that stuck up like perambulator-handles from the back-rest, deep into the snow, so that the team could not get away. Then he would crawl forward inch by inch, and wait till the seal came up to breathe. Then he would stab down swiftly with his spear and running-line, and presently would haul his seal up to the lip of the ice, while the black leader came up and helped to pull the carcass across the ice to the sleigh. That was the time when the harnessed dogs yelled and foamed with excitement, and Kotuko laid the long lash like a red-hot bar across all their faces, till the carcass froze stiff. Going home was the heavy work. The loaded sleigh had to be humored among the rough ice, and the dogs sat down and looked hungrily at the seal instead of pulling. At last they would strike the well-worn sleigh-road to the village, and toodle-kiyi along the ringing ice, heads down and tails up, while Kotuko struck up the "Angutivaun tai-na tau-na-ne taina" (The Song of the Returning Hunter), and voices hailed him from house to house under all that dim, star-litten sky.

When Kotuko the dog came to his full growth he enjoyed himself too. He fought his way up the team steadily, fight after fight, till one fine evening, over their food, he tackled the big, black leader (Kotuko the boy saw fair play), and made second dog of him, as they say. So he was promoted to the long thong of the leading dog, running five feet in advance of all the others: it was his bounden duty to stop all fighting, in harness or out of it, and he wore a collar of copper wire, very thick and heavy. On special occasions he was fed with cooked food inside the house, and sometimes was allowed to sleep on the bench with Kotuko. He was a good seal-dog, and would keep a musk-ox at bay by running round him and snapping at his heels. He would even–and this for a sleigh-dog is the last proof of bravery–he would even stand up to the gaunt Arctic wolf, whom all dogs of the North, as a rule, fear beyond anything that walks the snow. He and his master–they did not count the team of ordinary dogs as company–hunted together, day after day and night after night, fur-wrapped boy and savage, long-haired, narrow-eyed, white-fanged, yellow brute. All an Inuit has to do is to get food and skins for himself and his family. The women-folk make the skins into clothing, and occasionally help in trapping small game; but the bulk of the food–and they eat enormously–must be found by the men. If the supply fails there is no one up there to buy or beg or borrow from. The people must die.

An Inuit does not think of these chances till he is forced to. Kadlu, Kotuko, Amoraq, and the boy-baby who kicked about in Amoraq's fur hood and chewed pieces of blubber all day, were as happy together as any family in the world. They came of a very gentle race–an Inuit seldom loses his temper, and almost never strikes a child–who did not know exactly what telling a real lie meant, still less how to steal. They were content to spear their living out of the heart of the bitter, hopeless cold; to smile oily smiles, and tell queer ghost and fairy tales of evenings, and eat till they could eat no more, and sing the endless woman's song, "Amna aya, aya amna, ah! ah!" through the long, lamp-lighted days as they mended their clothes and their hunting-gear.

But one terrible winter everything betrayed them. The Tununirmiut returned from the yearly salmon-fishing, and made their houses on the early ice to the north of Bylot's Island, ready to go after the seal as soon as the sea froze. But it was an early and savage autumn. All through September there were continuous gales that broke up the smooth seal-ice when it was only four or five feet thick, and forced it inland, and piled a great barrier, some twenty miles broad, of lumped and ragged and needly ice, over which it was impossible to draw the dog-sleighs. The edge of the floe off which the seal were used to fish in winter lay, perhaps, twenty miles beyond this barrier, and out of reach of the Tununirmiut. Even so, they might have managed to scrape through the winter on their stock of frozen salmon and stored blubber, and what the traps gave them, but in December one of their hunters came across a *tupik* (a skin-tent) of three women and a girl nearly dead, whose men had come down from the far North and been crushed in their little skin hunting-boats while they were out after the long-horned narwhal. Kadlu, of course, could only distribute the women among the huts of the winter village, for no Inuit dare refuse a meal to a stranger. He never knows when his own turn may come to beg. Amoraq took the girl, who was about fourteen, into her own house as a sort of servant. From the cut of her sharp-pointed hood, and the long diamond pattern of her white deerskin leggings, they supposed she came from Ellesmere Land. She had never seen tin cooking-pots or wooden-shod sleighs before; but Kotuko the boy and Kotuko the dog were rather fond of her.

Then all the foxes went south, and even the wolverine, that growling, blunt-headed little thief of the snow, did not take the trouble to follow the line of empty traps that Kotuko set. The tribe lost a couple of their best hunters, who were badly crippled in a fight with a musk-ox, and this threw more work on the others. Kotuko went out, day after day, with a light hunting-sleigh and six or seven of the strongest dogs, looking till his eyes ached for some patch of clear ice where a seal might perhaps have scratched a breathing-hole. Kotuko the dog ranged far and wide, and in the dead stillness of the ice-fields Kotuko the boy could hear his half-choked whine of excitement, above a seal-hole three miles away, as plainly as though he were at his elbow. When the dog found a hole the boy would build himself a little, low snow wall to keep off the worst of the bitter wind, and there he would wait ten, twelve, twenty hours for the seal to come up to breathe, his eyes glued to the tiny mark he had made above the hole to guide the downward thrust of his harpoon, a little sealskin mat under his feet, and his legs tied together in the *tutareang* (the buckle that the old hunters had talked about). This helps to keep a man's legs from twitching as he waits and waits and waits for the quick-eared seal to rise. Though there is no excitement in it, you can easily believe that the sitting still in the buckle with the thermometer perhaps forty degrees below zero is the hardest work an Inuit knows. When a seal was caught Kotuko the dog would bound forward, his trace trailing behind him, and help to pull the body to the sleigh, where the tired and hungry dogs lay sullenly under the lee of the broken ice.

A seal did not go very far, for each mouth in the little village had a right to be filled, and neither bone, hide, nor sinew was wasted. The dogs' meat was taken for human use, and Amoraq fed the team with pieces of old summer skin-tents raked out from under the sleeping-bench, and they howled and howled again, and waked to howl hungrily. One could tell by the soap-stone lamps in the huts that famine was near. In good seasons, when blubber was plentiful, the light in the boat-shaped lamps would be two feet high—cheerful, oily, and yellow. Now it was a bare six inches: Amoraq carefully pricked down the moss wick when an unwatched flame brightened for a moment, and the eyes of all the family followed her hand. The horror of famine up there in the great cold is not so much dying, as dying in the dark. All the Inuit dread the dark that presses on them without a break for six months in each year; and when the lamps are low in the houses the minds of people begin to be shaken and confused.

But worse was to come.

The underfed dogs snapped and growled in the passages, glaring at the cold stars, and snuffing into the bitter wind, night after night. When they stopped howling the silence fell down again as solid and as heavy as a snowdrift against a door, and men could hear the beating of their blood in the thin passages of the ear, and the thumping of their own hearts, that sounded as loud as the noise of sorcerers' drums beaten across the snow. One night Kotuko the dog, who had been unusually sullen in harness, leaped up and pushed his head against Kotuko's knee. Kotuko patted him, but the dog still pushed blindly forward, fawning. Then Kadlu waked, and gripped the heavy wolf-like head, and stared into the glassy eyes. The dog whimpered and shivered between Kadlu's knees. The hair rose about his neck, and he growled as though a stranger were at the door; then he barked joyously, and rolled on the ground, and bit at Kotuko's boot like a puppy.

"What is it?" said Kotuko; for he was beginning to be afraid.

"The sickness," Kadlu answered. "It is the dog-sickness." Kotuko the dog lifted his nose, and howled and howled again.

"I have not seen this before. What will he do?" said Kotuko.

Kadlu shrugged one shoulder a little, and crossed the hut for his short stabbing-harpoon. The big dog looked at him, howled again, and slunk away down the passage, while the other dogs drew aside right and left to give him ample room. When he was out on the snow he barked furiously, as though on the trail of a musk-ox, and, barking and leaping and frisking, passed out of sight. This was not hydrophobia, but simple, plain madness. The cold and the hunger, and, above all, the dark, had turned his head; and when the terrible dog-sickness once shows itself in a team, it spreads like wildfire. Next hunting-day another dog sickened, and was killed then and there by Kotuko as he bit and struggled among the traces. Then the black second dog, who had been the leader in the old days, suddenly gave tongue on an imaginary reindeer-track, and when they slipped him from the *pitu* he flew at the throat of an ice-cliff, and ran away as his leader had done, his harness on his back. After that no one would take the dogs out again. They needed them for something else, and the dogs knew it; and though they were tied down and fed by hand, their eyes were full of despair and fear. To make things worse, the old women began to tell ghost-tales, and to say that they had met the spirits of the dead hunters lost that autumn, who prophesied all sorts of horrible things.

Kotuko grieved more for the loss of his dog than anything else; for, though an Inuit eats enormously, he also knows how to starve. But the hunger, the darkness, the cold, and the exposure told on his strength, and he began to hear voices inside his head, and to see people who were not there, out of the tail of his eye. One night—he had unbuckled himself after ten hours' waiting above a "blind" seal-hole, and was staggering back to the village faint and dizzy—he halted to lean his back against a boulder which happened to be supported like a rocking-stone on a single jutting point of ice. His weight disturbed the balance of the thing, it rolled over ponderously, and as Kotuko sprang aside to avoid it, slid after him, squeaking and hissing on the ice slope.

That was enough for Kotuko. He had been brought up to believe that every rock and boulder had its owner (its *innua),* who was generally a one-eyed kind of a Woman-Thing called a *tornaq,* and that when a *tornaq* meant to help a man she rolled after him inside her stone house, and asked him whether he would take her for a guardian spirit. (In summer thaws the ice-propped rocks and boulders roll and slip all over the face of the land, so you can easily see how the idea of live stones arose.) Kotuko heard the blood beating in his ears as he had heard it all day, and he thought that was the *tornaq* of the stone speaking to him. Before he reached home he was quite certain that he had held a long conversation with her, and as all his people believed that this was quite possible, no one contradicted him.

"She said to me, 'I jump down, I jump down from my place on the snow,'" cried Kotuko, with hollow eyes, leaning forward in the half-lighted hut. "She said, 'I will be a guide.' She says, 'I will guide you to the good seal-holes.' To-morrow I go out, and the *tornaq* will guide me."

Then the *angekok,* the village sorcerer, came in, and Kotuko told him the tale a second time. It lost nothing in the telling.

"Follow the *tornait* [the spirits of the stones], and they will bring us food again," said the *angekok.*

Now the girl from the North had been lying near the lamp, eating very little and saying less for days past; but when Amoraq and Kadlu next morning packed and lashed a little hand-sleigh for Kotuko, and loaded it with his hunting-gear and as much blubber and frozen seal-meat as they could spare, she took the pulling-rope, and stepped out boldly at the boy's side.

"Your house is my house," she said, as the little bone-shod sleigh squeaked and bumped behind them in the awful Arctic night.

"My house is your house," said Kotuko; "but *I* think that we shall both go to Sedna together."

Now Sedna is the Mistress of the Under-world, and the Inuit believe that every one who dies must spend a year in her horrible country before going to Quadliparmiut, the Happy Place, where it never freezes and the fat reindeer trot up when you call.

Through the village people were shouting: "The *tornait* have spoken to Kotuko. They will show him open ice. He will bring us the seal again!" Their voices were soon swallowed up by the cold, empty dark, and Kotuko and the girl shouldered close together as they strained on the pulling-rope or humored the sleigh through the broken ice in the direction of the Polar Sea. Kotuko insisted that the *tornaq* of the stone had told him to go north, and north they went under Tuktuqdjung the Reindeer—those stars that we call the Great Bear.

No European could have made five miles a day over the ice-rubbish and the sharp-edged drifts; but those two knew exactly the turn of the wrist that coaxes a sleigh round a hummock, the jerk that neatly lifts it out of an ice-crack, and the exact strength that goes to the few quiet strokes of the spear-head that make a path possible when everything looks hopeless.

The girl said nothing, but bowed her head, and the long wolverine-fur fringe of her ermine hood blew across her broad, dark face. The sky above them was an intense velvety-black, changing to bands of Indian red on the horizon, where the great stars burned like street lamps. From time to time a greenish wave of the Northern Lights would roll across the hollow of the high heavens, flick like a flag, and disappear; or a meteor would crackle from darkness to darkness, trailing a shower of sparks behind. Then they could see the ridged and furrowed surface of the floe tipped and laced with strange colors—red, copper, and bluish; but in the ordinary starlight everything turned to one frost-bitten gray. The floe, as you remember, had been battered and tormented by the autumn gales till it was one frozen earthquake. There were gullies and ravines, and holes like gravel-pits, cut in ice; lumps and scattered pieces frozen down to the original floor of the floe; blotches of old black ice that had been thrust under the floe in some gale and heaved up again; roundish boulders of ice; saw-like edges of ice carved by the snow that flies before the wind; and sunken pits where thirty or forty acres lay below the level of the rest of the field. From a little distance you might have taken the lumps for seal or walrus, overturned sleighs or men on a hunting expedition, or even the great Ten-legged White Spirit-Bear himself; but in spite of these fantastic shapes, all on the very edge of starting into life, there was neither sound nor the least faint echo of sound. And through this silence and through this waste, where the sudden lights flapped and went out again, the sleigh and the two that pulled it crawled like things in a nightmare—a nightmare of the end of the world at the end of the world.

When they were tired Kotuko would make what the hunters call a "half-house," a very small snow hut, into which they would huddle with the traveling-lamp, and try to thaw out the frozen seal-meat. When they had slept the march began again—thirty miles a day to get ten miles northward. The girl was always very silent, but Kotuko muttered to himself and broke out into songs he had learned in the Singing-House—summer songs, and reindeer and salmon songs—all horribly out of place at that season. He would declare that he heard the *tornaq* growling to him, and would run wildly up a hummock, tossing his arms and speaking in loud, threatening tones. To tell the truth, Kotuko was very nearly crazy for the time being; but the girl was sure that he was being guided by his guardian spirit, and that everything would come right. She was not surprised, therefore, when at the end of the fourth march Kotuko, whose eyes were burning like fire-balls in his head, told her that his *tornaq* was following them across the snow in the shape of a two-headed dog. The girl looked where Kotuko pointed, and something seemed to slip into a ravine. It was certainly not human, but everybody knew that the *tornait* preferred to appear in the shape of bear and seal, and such like.

It might have been the Ten-legged White Spirit-Bear himself, or it might have been anything, for Kotuko and the girl were so starved that their eyes were untrustworthy. They had trapped nothing, and seen no trace of game since they had left the village; their food would not hold out for another week, and there was a gale coming. A Polar storm can blow for ten days without a break, and all that while it is certain death to be abroad. Kotuko laid up a snow-house large enough to take in the hand-sleigh (never be separated from your meat), and while he was shaping the last irregular block of ice that makes the key-stone of the roof, he saw a Thing looking at him from a little cliff of ice half a mile away. The air was hazy, and the Thing seemed to be forty feet long and ten feet high, with twenty feet of tail and a shape that quivered all along the outlines. The girl saw it too, but instead of crying aloud with terror, said quietly, "That is Quiquern. What comes after?"

"He will speak to me," said Kotuko; but the snow-knife trembled in his hand as he spoke, because however much a man may believe that he is a friend of strange and ugly spirits, he seldom likes to be taken quite at his word. Quiquern, too, is the phantom of a gigantic toothless dog without any hair, who is supposed to live in the far North, and to wander about the country just before things are going to happen. They may be pleasant or unpleasant things, but not even the sorcerers care to speak about Quiquern. He makes the dogs go mad. Like the Spirit-Bear he has several extra pairs of legs,—six or eight,—and this Thing jumping up and down in the haze had more legs than any real dog needed. Kotuko and the girl huddled into their hut quickly. Of course if Quiquern had wanted them, he could have torn it to pieces above their heads, but the sense of a foot-thick snow wall between themselves and the wicked dark was great comfort. The gale broke with a shriek of wind like the shriek of a train, and for three days and three nights it held, never varying one point, and never lulling even for a minute. They fed the stone lamp between their knees, and nibbled at the half-warm seal-meat, and watched the black soot gather on the roof for seventy-two long hours. The girl counted up the food in the sleigh; there was not more than two days' supply, and Kotuko looked over the iron heads and the deer-sinew fastenings of his harpoon and his seal-lance and his bird-dart. There was nothing else to do.

"We shall go to Sedna soon—very soon," the girl whispered. "In three days we shall lie down and go. Will your *tornaq* do nothing? Sing her an *angekok's* song to make her come here."

He began to sing in the high-pitched howl of the magic songs, and the gale went down slowly. In the middle of his song the girl started, laid her mittened hand and then her head to the ice floor of the hut. Kotuko followed her example, and the two kneeled, staring into each other's eyes, and listening with every nerve. He ripped a thin sliver of whalebone from the rim of a bird-snare that lay on the sleigh, and, after straightening, set it upright in a little hole in the ice, firming it down with his mitten. It was almost as delicately adjusted as a compass-needle, and now instead of listening they watched. The thin rod quivered a little—the least little jar in the world; then it vibrated steadily for a few seconds, came to rest, and vibrated again, this time nodding to another point of the compass.

"Too soon!" said Kotuko. "Some big floe has broken far away outside."

The girl pointed at the rod, and shook her head. "It is the big breaking," she said. "Listen to the ground-ice. It knocks."

When they kneeled this time they heard the most curious muffled grunts and knockings, apparently under their feet. Sometimes it sounded as though a blind puppy were squeaking above the lamp; then as if a stone were being ground on hard ice; and again, like muffled blows on a drum: but all dragged out and made small, as though they traveled through a little horn a weary distance away.

"We shall not go to Sedna lying down," said Kotuko. "It is the breaking. The *tornaq* has cheated us. We shall die."

All this may sound absurd enough, but the two were face to face with a very real danger. The three days' gale had driven the deep water of Baffin's Bay southerly, and piled it on to the edge of the far-reaching land-ice that stretches from Bylot's Island to the west. Also, the strong current which sets east out of Lancaster Sound carried with it mile upon mile of what they call pack-ice—rough ice that has not frozen into fields; and this pack was bombarding the floe at the same time that the swell and heave of the storm-worked sea was weakening and undermining it. What Kotuko and the girl had been listening to were the faint echoes of that fight thirty or forty miles away, and the little telltale rod quivered to the shock of it.

Now, as the Inuit say, when the ice once wakes after its long winter sleep, there is no knowing what may happen, for solid floe-ice changes shape almost as quickly as a cloud. The gale was evidently a spring gale sent out of time, and anything was possible.

Yet the two were happier in their minds than before. If the floe broke up there would be no more waiting and suffering. Spirits, goblins, and witch-people were moving about on the racking ice, and they might find themselves stepping into Sedna's country side by side with all sorts of wild Things, the flush of excitement still on them. When they left the hut after the gale, the noise on the horizon was steadily growing, and the tough ice moaned and buzzed all round them.

"It is still waiting," said Kotuko.

On the top of a hummock sat or crouched the eight-legged Thing that they had seen three days before—and it howled horribly.

"Let us follow," said the girl. "It may know some way that does not lead to

Sedna"; but she reeled from weakness as she took the pulling-rope. The Thing moved off slowly and clumsily across the ridges, heading always toward the westward and the land, and they followed, while the growling thunder at the edge of the floe rolled nearer and nearer. The floe's lip was split and cracked in every direction for three or four miles inland, and great pans of ten-foot-thick ice, from a few yards to twenty acres square, were jolting and ducking and surging into one another, and into the yet unbroken floe, as the heavy swell took and shook and spouted between them. This battering-ram ice was, so to speak, the first army that the sea was flinging against the floe. The incessant crash and jar of these cakes almost drowned the ripping sound of sheets of pack-ice driven bodily under the floe as cards are hastily pushed under a table-cloth. Where the water was shallow these sheets would be piled one atop of the other till the bottom-most touched mud fifty feet down, and the discolored sea banked behind the muddy ice till the increasing pressure drove all forward again. In addition to the floe and the pack-ice, the gale and the currents were bringing down true bergs, sailing mountains of ice, snapped off from the Greenland side of the water or the north shore of Melville Bay. They pounded in solemnly, the waves breaking white round them, and advanced on the floe like an old-time fleet under full sail. A berg that seemed ready to carry the world before it would ground helplessly in deep water, reel over, and wallow in a lather of foam and mud and flying frozen spray, while a much smaller and lower one would rip and ride into the flat floe, flinging tons of ice on either side, and cutting a track half a mile long before it was stopped. Some fell like swords, shearing a raw-edged canal; and others splintered into a shower of blocks, weighing scores of tons apiece, that whirled and skirled among the hummocks. Others, again, rose up bodily out of the water when they shoaled, twisted as though in pain, and fell solidly on their sides, while the sea threshed over their shoulders. This trampling and crowding and bending and buckling and arching of the ice into every possible shape was going on as far as the eye could reach all along the north line of the floe. From where Kotuko and the girl were the confusion looked no more than an uneasy, rippling, crawling movement under the horizon; but it came toward them each moment, and they could hear, far away to landward, a heavy booming, as it might have been the boom of artillery through a fog. That showed that the floe was being jammed home against the iron cliffs of Bylot's Island, the land to the southward behind them.

"This has never been before," said Kotuko, staring stupidly. "This is not the time. How can the floe break *now?*"

"Follow *that!*" the girl cried, pointing to the Thing, half limping, half running distractedly before them. They followed, tugging at the hand-sleigh, while nearer and nearer came the roaring march of the ice. At last the fields round them cracked and starred in every direction, and the cracks opened and snapped like the teeth of wolves. But where the Thing rested, on a mound of old and scattered ice-blocks some fifty feet high, there was no motion. Kotuko leaped forward wildly, dragging the girl after him, and crawled to the bottom of the mound. The talking of the ice grew louder and louder round them, but the mound stayed fast, and, as the girl looked at him, he threw his right elbow upward and outward, making the Inuit sign for land in the shape of an island. And land it was that the eight-legged, limping Thing had led them to—some granite-tipped, sand-beached islet off the coast, shod and sheathed and masked with ice so that no man could have told it from the floe, but at the bottom solid earth, and not shifting ice! The smashing and rebound of the floes as they grounded and splintered marked the borders of it, and a friendly shoal ran out to the northward, and turned aside the rush of the heaviest ice, exactly as a ploughshare turns over loam. There was danger, of course, that some heavily squeezed ice-field might shoot up the beach, and plane off the top of the islet bodily; but that did not trouble Kotuko and the girl when they made their snow-house and began to eat, and heard the ice hammer and skid along the beach. The Thing had disappeared, and Kotuko was talking excitedly about his power over spirits as he crouched round the lamp. In the middle of his wild sayings the girl began to laugh, and rock herself backward and forward.

Behind her shoulder, crawling into the hut crawl by crawl, there were two heads, one yellow and one black, that belonged to two of the most sorrowful and ashamed dogs that ever you saw. Kotuko the dog was one, and the black leader was the other. Both were now fat, well-looking, and quite restored to their proper minds, but coupled to each other in an extraordinary fashion. When the black leader ran off, you remember, his harness was still on him. He must have met Kotuko the dog, and played or fought with him, for his shoulder-loop had caught in the plaited copper wire of Kotuko's collar, and had drawn tight, so that neither could get at the trace to gnaw it apart, but each was fastened sidelong to his neighbor's neck. That, with the freedom of hunting on their own account, must have helped to cure their madness. They were very sober.

The girl pushed the two shamefaced creatures toward Kotuko, and, sobbing with laughter, cried, "That is Quiquern, who led us to safe ground. Look at his eight legs and double head!"

Kotuko cut them free, and they fell into his arms, yellow and black together, trying to explain how they had got their senses back again. Kotuko ran a hand down their ribs, which were round and well clothed. "They have found food," he said, with a grin. "I do not think we shall go to Sedna so soon. My *tornaq* sent these. The sickness has left them."

As soon as they had greeted Kotuko, these two, who had been forced to sleep and eat and hunt together for the past few weeks, flew at each other's throat, and there was a beautiful battle in the snow-house. "Empty dogs do not fight," Kotuko said. "They have found the seal. Let us sleep. We shall find food."

When they waked there was open water on the north beach of the island, and all the loosened ice had been driven landward. The first sound of the surf is one of the most delightful that the Inuit can hear, for it means that spring is on the road. Kotuko and the girl took hold of hands and smiled, for the clear, full roar of the surge among the ice reminded them of salmon and reindeer time and the smell of blossoming ground-willows. Even as they looked, the sea began to skim over between the floating cakes of ice, so intense was the cold; but on the horizon there was a vast red glare, and that was the light of the sunken sun. It was more like hearing him yawn in his sleep than seeing him rise, and the glare only lasted for a few minutes, but it marked the turn of the year. Nothing, they felt, could alter that.

Kotuko found the dogs fighting over a fresh-killed seal who was following the fish that a gale always disturbs. He was the first of some twenty or thirty seal that landed on the island in the course of the day, and till the sea froze hard there were hundreds of keen black heads rejoicing in the shallow free water and floating about with the floating ice.

It was good to eat seal-liver again; to fill the lamps recklessly with blubber, and watch the flame blaze three feet in the air; but as soon as the new sea-ice bore, Kotuko and the girl loaded the hand-sleigh, and made the two dogs pull as they had never pulled in their lives, for they feared what might have happened in their village. The weather was as pitiless as usual; but it is easier to draw a sleigh loaded with good food than to hunt starving. They left five-and-twenty seal carcasses buried in the ice of the beach, all ready for use, and hurried back to their people. The dogs showed them the way as soon as Kotuko told them what was expected, and though there was no sign of a landmark, in two days they were giving tongue outside Kadlu's house. Only three dogs answered them; the others had been eaten, and the houses were all dark. But when Kotuko shouted, "Ojo!" (boiled meat), weak voices replied, and when he called the muster of the village name by name, very distinctly, there were no gaps in it.

An hour later the lamps blazed in Kadlu's house; snow-water was heating; the pots were beginning to simmer, and the snow was dripping from the roof, as Amoraq made ready a meal for all the village, and the boy-baby in the hood chewed at a strip of rich nutty blubber, and the hunters slowly and methodically filled themselves to the very brim with seal-meat. Kotuko and the girl told their tale. The two dogs sat between them, and whenever their names came in, they cocked an ear apiece and looked most thoroughly ashamed of themselves. A dog who has once gone mad and recovered, the Inuit say, is safe against all further attacks.

"So the *tornaq* did not forget us," said Kotuko. "The storm blew, the ice broke, and the seal swam in behind the fish that were frightened by the storm. Now the new seal-holes are not two days' distant. Let the good hunters go to-morrow and bring back the seal I have speared—twenty-five seal buried in the ice. When we have eaten those we will all follow the seal on the floe."

"What do *you* do?" said the sorcerer in the same sort of voice as he used to Kadlu, richest of the Tununirmiut.

Kotuko looked at the girl from the North, and said quietly, "*We* build a house." He pointed to the northwest side of Kadlu's house, for that is the side on which the married son or daughter always lives.

The girl turned her hands palm upward, with a little despairing shake of her head. She was a foreigner, picked up starving, and could bring nothing to the housekeeping.

Amoraq jumped from the bench where she sat, and began to sweep things into the girl's lap—stone lamps, iron skin-scrapers, tin kettles, deerskins embroidered with musk-ox teeth, and real canvas-needles such as sailors use—the finest dowry that has ever been given on the far edge of the Arctic Circle, and the girl from the North bowed her head down to the very floor.

"Also these!" said Kotuko, laughing and signing to the dogs, who thrust their cold muzzles into the girl's face.

"Ah," said the *angekok,* with an important cough, as though he had been thinking it all over. "As soon as Kotuko left the village I went to the Singing-House and sang magic. I sang all the long nights, and called upon the Spirit of the Reindeer. *My* singing made the gale blow that broke the ice and drew the two dogs toward Kotuko when the ice would have crushed his bones. *My* song drew the seal in behind the broken ice. My body lay still in the *quaggi,* but my spirit ran about on the ice, and guided Kotuko and the dogs in all the things they did. I did it."

Everybody was full and sleepy, so no one contradicted; and the *angekok,* by virtue of his office, helped himself to yet another lump of boiled meat, and lay down to sleep with the others in the warm, well-lighted, oil-smelling home.

. . . . .

Now Kotuko, who drew very well in the Inuit fashion, scratched pictures of all these adventures on a long, flat piece of ivory with a hole at one end. When he and the girl went north to Ellesmere Land in the year of the Wonderful Open Winter, he left the picture-story with Kadlu, who lost it in the shingle when his dog-sleigh broke down one summer on the beach of Lake Netilling at Nikosiring, and there a Lake Inuit found it next spring and sold it to a man at Imigen who was interpreter on a Cumberland Sound whaler, and he sold it to Hans Olsen, who was afterward a quartermaster on board a big steamer that took tourists to the North Cape in Norway. When the tourist season was over, the steamer ran between London and Australia, stopping at Ceylon, and there Olsen sold the ivory to a Cingalese jeweler for two imitation sapphires. I found it under some rubbish in a house at Colombo, and have translated it from one end to the other.

"Angutivun Tina"

[This is a very free translation of the Song of the Returning Hunter, as the men used to sing it after seal-spearing. The Inuit always repeat things over and over again.]

Our gloves are stiff with the frozen blood
    Our furs with the drifted snow,
As we come in with the seal—the seal!
    In from the edge of the floe.

Au jana! Aua! Oha! Haq!
    And the yelping dog-teams go,
And the long whips crack, and the men come back,
    Back from the edge of the floe!

We tracked our seal to his secret place,
    We heard him scratch below,
We made our mark, and we watched beside,
    Out on the edge of the floe.

We raised our lance when he rose to breathe,
    We drove it downward—so!
And we played him thus, and we killed him thus
    Out on the edge of the floe.

Our gloves are glued with the frozen blood,
    Our eyes with the drifting snow;
But we come back to our wives again,
    Back from the edge of the floe!

Au jana! Aua! Oha! Haq!
    And the loaded dog-teams go,
And the wives can hear their men come back,
    Back from the edge of the floe!

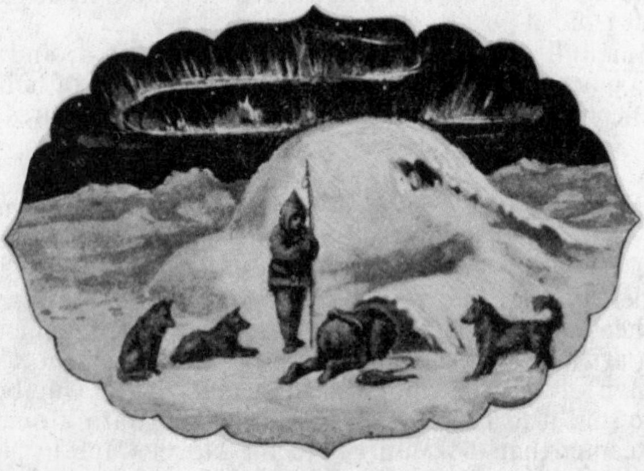

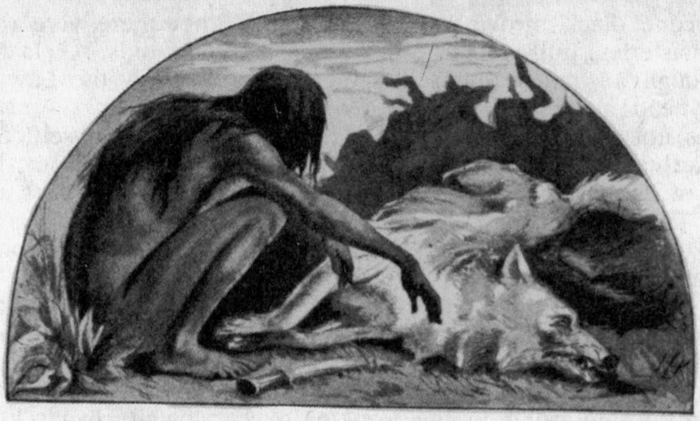

Red Dog

For our white and our excellent nights—for the nights of swift running,
Fair ranging, far-seeing, good hunting, sure cunning!
For the smells of the dawning, untainted, ere dew has departed!
For the rush through the mist, and the quarry blind-started!
For the cry of our mates when the sambhur has wheeled and is standing at bay,
For the risk and the riot of night!
For the sleep at the lair-mouth by day,
It is met, and we go to the fight.
Bay! O bay!

IT WAS AFTER the letting in of the Jungle that the pleasantest part of Mowgli's life began. He had the good conscience that comes from paying debts; all the Jungle was his friend, and just a little afraid of him. The things that he did and saw and heard when he was wandering from one people to another, with or without his four companions, would make many stories, each as long as this one. So you will never be told how he met the Mad Elephant of Mandla, who killed two-and-twenty bullocks drawing eleven carts of coined silver to the Government Treasury, and scattered the shiny rupees in the dust; how he fought Jacala, the Crocodile, all one long night in the Marshes of the North, and broke his skinning-knife on the brute's back-plates; how he found a new and longer knife round the neck of a man who had been killed by a wild boar, and how he tracked that boar and killed him as a fair price for the knife; how he was caught up once in the Great Famine, by the moving of the deer, and nearly crushed to death in the swaying hot herds; how he saved Hathi the Silent from being once more trapped in a pit with a stake at the bottom, and how, next day, he himself fell into a very cunning leopard-trap, and how Hathi broke the thick wooden bars to pieces above him; how he milked the wild buffaloes in the swamp, and how—

But we must tell one tale at a time. Father and Mother Wolf died, and Mowgli rolled a big boulder against the mouth of their cave, and cried the Death Song over them; Baloo grew very old and stiff, and even Bagheera, whose nerves were steel, and whose muscles were iron, was a shade slower on the kill than he had been. Akela turned from gray to milky white with pure age; his ribs stuck out, and he walked as though he had been made of wood, and Mowgli killed for him. But the young wolves, the children of the disbanded Seeonee Pack, throve and increased, and when there were about forty of them, masterless, full-voiced, clean-footed five-year-olds, Akela told them that they ought to gather themselves together and follow the Law, and run under one head, as befitted the Free People.

This was not a question in which Mowgli concerned himself, for, as he said, he had eaten sour fruit, and he knew the tree it hung from; but when Phao, son of Phaona (his father was the Gray Tracker in the days of Akela's headship), fought his way to the leadership of the Pack, according to Jungle Law, and the old calls and songs began to ring under the stars once more, Mowgli came to the Council Rock for memory's sake. When he chose to speak the Pack waited till he had finished, and he sat at Akela's side on the rock above Phao. Those were days of good hunting and good sleeping. No stranger cared to break into the jungles that belonged to Mowgli's people, as they called the Pack, and the young wolves grew fat and strong, and there were many cubs to bring to the Looking-over. Mowgli always attended a Looking-over, remembering the night when a black panther bought a naked brown baby into the Pack, and the long call, "Look, look well, O Wolves," made his heart flutter. Otherwise, he would be far away in the Jungle, with his four brothers, tasting, touching, seeing, and feeling new things.

One twilight when he was trotting leisurely across the ranges to give Akela the half of a buck that he had killed, while the Four jogged behind him, sparring a little, and tumbling one another over for joy of being alive, he heard a cry that had never been heard since the bad days of Shere Khan. It was what they call in the Jungle the *pheeal,* a hideous kind of shriek that the jackal gives when he is hunting behind a tiger, or when there is a big killing afoot. If you can imagine a mixture of hate, triumph, fear, and despair, with a kind of leer running through it, you will get some notion of the *pheeal* that rose and sank and wavered and quavered far away across the Waingunga. The Four stopped at once, bristling and growling. Mowgli's hand went to his knife, and he checked, the blood in his face, his eyebrows knotted.

"There is no Striped One dare kill here," he said.

"That is not the cry of the Forerunner," answered Gray Brother. "It is some great killing. Listen!"

It broke out again, half sobbing and half chuckling, just as though the jackal had soft human lips. Then Mowgli drew deep breath, and ran to the Council Rock, overtaking on his way hurrying wolves of the Pack. Phao and Akela were on the Rock together, and below them, every nerve strained, sat the others. The mothers and the cubs were cantering off to their lairs; for when the *pheeal* cries it is no time for weak things to be abroad.

They could hear nothing except the Waingunga rushing and gurgling in the dark, and the light evening winds among the tree-tops, till suddenly across the river a wolf called. It was no wolf of the Pack, for they were all at the Rock. The note changed to a long, despairing bay; and "Dhole!" it said, "Dhole! dhole! dhole!" They heard tired feet on the rocks, and a gaunt wolf, streaked with red on his flanks, his right fore-paw useless, and his jaws white with foam, flung himself into the circle and lay gasping at Mowgli's feet.

"Good hunting! Under whose Headship?" said Phao gravely.

"Good hunting! Won-tolla am I," was the answer. He meant that he was a solitary wolf, fending for himself, his mate, and his cubs in some lonely lair, as do many wolves in the south. Won-tolla means an Outlier–one who lies out from any Pack. Then he panted, and they could see his heart-beats shake him backward and forward.

"What moves?" said Phao, for that is the question all the Jungle asks after the *pheeal* cries.

"The dhole, the dhole of the Dekkan–Red Dog, the Killer! They came north from the south saying the Dekkan was empty and killing out by the way. When this moon was new there were four to me–my mate and three cubs. She would teach them to kill on the grass plains, hiding to drive the buck, as we do who are of the open. At midnight I heard them together, full tongue on the trail. At the dawn-wind I found them stiff in the grass–four, Free People, four when this moon was new. Then sought I my Blood-Right and found the dhole."

"How many?" said Mowgli quickly; the Pack growled deep in their throats.

"I do not know. Three of them will kill no more, but at the last they drove me like the buck; on my three legs they drove me. Look, Free People!"

He thrust out his mangled fore-foot, all dark with dried blood. There were cruel bites low down on his side, and his throat was torn and worried.

"Eat," said Akela, rising up from the meat Mowgli had brought him, and the Outlier flung himself on it.

"This shall be no loss," he said humbly, when he had taken off the first edge of his hunger. "Give me a little strength, Free People, and I also will kill. My lair is empty that was full when this moon was new, and the Blood Debt is not all paid."

Phao heard his teeth crack on a haunch-bone and grunted approvingly.

"We shall need those jaws," said he. "Were their cubs with the dhole?"

"Nay, nay. Red Hunters all: grown dogs of their Pack, heavy and strong, for all that they eat lizards in the Dekkan."

What Won-tolla had said meant that the dhole, the red hunting-dog of the Dekkan, was moving to kill, and the Pack knew well that even the tiger will surrender a new kill to the dhole. They drive straight through the Jungle, and what they meet they pull down and tear to pieces. Though they are not as big nor half as cunning as the wolf, they are very strong and very numerous. The dhole, for instance, do not begin to call themselves a pack till they are a hundred strong; whereas forty wolves make a very fair pack indeed. Mowgli's wanderings had taken him to the edge of the high grassy downs of the Dekkan, and he had seen the fearless dholes sleeping and playing and scratching themselves in the little hollows and tussocks that they use for lairs. He despised and hated them because they did not smell like the Free People, because they did not live in caves, and, above all, because they had hair between their toes while he and his friends were clean-footed. But he knew, for Hathi had told him, what a terrible thing a dhole hunting-pack was. Even Hathi moves aside from their line, and until they are killed, or till game is scarce, they will go forward.

Akela knew something of the dholes, too, for he said to Mowgli quietly, "It is better to die in a Full Pack than leaderless and alone. This is good hunting, and–my last. But, as men live, thou hast very many more nights and days, Little Brother. Go north and lie down, and if any live after the dhole has gone by he shall bring thee word of the fight."

"Ah," said Mowgli, quite gravely, "must I go to the marshes and catch little fish and sleep in a tree, or must I ask help of the Bandar-log and crack nuts, while the Pack fight below?"

"It is to the death," said Akela. "Thou hast never met the dhole–the Red Killer. Even the Striped One–"

"Aowa! Aowa!" said Mowgli pettingly. "I have killed one striped ape, and sure am I in my stomach that Shere Khan would have left his own mate for meat to the dhole if he had winded a pack across three ranges. Listen now: There was a wolf, my father, and there was a wolf, my mother, and there was an old gray wolf (not too wise: he is white now) was my father and my mother. Therefore I–"he raised his voice, "I say that when the dhole come, and if the dhole come, Mowgli and the Free People are of one skin for that hunting; and I say, by the Bull that bought me–by the Bull Bagheera paid for me in the old days which ye of the Pack do not remember–*I* say, that the Trees and the River may hear and hold fast if I forget; *I* say that this my knife shall be as a tooth to the Pack–and I do not think it is so blunt. This is

my Word which has gone from me."

"Thou dost not know the dhole, man with a wolf's tongue," said Won-tolla. "I look only to clear the Blood Debt against them ere they have me in many pieces. They move slowly, killing out as they go, but in two days a little strength will come back to me and I turn again for the Blood Debt. But for *ye,* Free People, my word is that ye go north and eat but little for a while till the dhole are gone. There is no meat in this hunting."

"Hear the Outlier!" said Mowgli with a laugh. "Free People, we must go north and dig lizards and rats from the bank, lest by any chance we meet the dhole. He must kill out our hunting-grounds, while we lie hid in the north till it please him to give us our own again. He is a dog–and the pup of a dog–red, yellow-bellied, lair-less, and haired between every toe! He counts his cubs six and eight at the litter, as though he were Chikai, the little leaping rat. Surely we must run away, Free People, and beg leave of the peoples of the north for the offal of dead cattle! Ye know the saying: 'North are the vermin; south are the lice. *We* are the Jungle.' Choose ye, O choose. It is good hunting! For the Pack–for the Full Pack–for the lair and the litter; for the in-kill and the out-kill; for the mate that drives the doe and the little, little cub within the cave; it is met!–it is met!–it is met!"

The Pack answered with one deep, crashing bark that sounded in the night like a big tree falling. "It is met!" they cried.

"Stay with these," said Mowgli to the Four. "We shall need every tooth. Phao and Akela must make ready the battle. I go to count the dogs."

"It is death!" Won-tolla cried, half rising. "What can such a hairless one do against the Red Dog? Even the Striped One, remember–"

"Thou art indeed an Outlier," Mowgli called back; "but we will speak when the dholes are dead. Good hunting all!"

He hurried off into the darkness, wild with excitement, hardly looking where he set foot, and the natural consequence was that he tripped full length over Kaa's great coils where the python lay watching a deer-path near the river.

"*Kssha!*" said Kaa angrily. "Is this jungle-work, to stamp and tramp and undo a night's hunting–when the game are moving so well, too?"

"The fault was mine," said Mowgli, picking himself up. "Indeed I was seeking thee, Flat-head, but each time we meet thou art longer and broader by the length of my arm. There is none like thee in the Jungle, wise, old, strong, and most beautiful Kaa."

"Now, whither does *this* trail lead?" Kaa's voice was gentler. "Not a moon since there was a Manling with a knife threw stones at my head, and called me bad little tree-cat names, because I lay asleep in the open."

"Ay, and turned every driven deer to all the winds, and Mowgli was hunting, and this same Flathead was too deaf to hear his whistle, and leave the deer-roads free," Mowgli answered composedly, sitting down among the painted coils.

"Now this same Manling comes with soft, tickling words to this same Flathead, telling him that he is wise and strong and beautiful, and this same old Flathead believes and makes a place, thus, for this same stone-throwing Manling, and–. Art thou at ease now? Could Bagheera give thee so good a resting-place?"

Kaa had, as usual, made a sort of soft, half-hammock of himself under Mowgli's weight. The boy reached out in the darkness, and gathered in the supple cable-like neck till Kaa's head rested on his shoulder, and then he told him all that had happened in the Jungle that night.

"Wise I may be," said Kaa at the end; "but deaf I surely am. Else I should have heard the *pheeal.* Small wonder the Eaters of Grass are uneasy. How many be the dhole?"

"I have not yet seen. I came hot-foot to thee. Thou art older than Hathi.

But oh, Kaa,"–here Mowgli wriggled with sheer joy,–"it will be good hunting. Few of us will see another moon."

"Dost *thou* strike in this? Remember thou art a Man; and remember what Pack cast thee out. Let the Wolf look to the Dog. Thou art a Man."

"Last year's nuts are this year's black earth," said Mowgli. "It is true that I am a Man, but it is in my stomach that this night I have said that I am a Wolf. I called the River and the Trees to remember. I am of the Free People, Kaa, till the dhole has gone by."

"Free People," Kaa grunted. "Free thieves! And thou hast tied thyself into the death-knot for the sake of the memory of the dead wolves? This is no good hunting."

"It is my Word which I have spoken. The Trees know, the River knows. Till the dhole have gone by my Word comes not back to me."

"*Ngssh!* This changes all trails. I had thought to take thee away with me to the northern marshes, but the Word–even the Word of a little, naked, hairless Manling–is the Word. Now I, Kaa, say–"

"Think well, Flathead, lest thou tie thyself into the death-knot also. I need no Word from thee, for well I know–"

"Be it so, then," said Kaa. "I will give no Word; but what is in thy stomach to do when the dhole come?"

"They must swim the Waingunga. I thought to meet them with my knife in the shallows, the Pack behind me; and so stabbing and thrusting we a little might turn them down-stream, or cool their throats."

"The dhole do not turn and their throats are hot," said Kaa. "There will be neither Manling nor Wolf-cub when that hunting is done, but only dry bones."

"*Alala!* If we die, we die. It will be most good hunting. But my stomach is young, and I have not seen many Rains. I am not wise nor strong. Hast thou a better plan, Kaa?"

"I have seen a hundred and a hundred Rains. Ere Hathi cast his milk-tushes my trail was big in the dust. By the First Egg I am older than many trees, and I have seen all that the Jungle has done."

"But *this* is new hunting," said Mowgli. "Never before have the dhole crossed our trail."

"What is has been. What will be is no more than a forgotten year striking backward. Be still while I count those my years."

For a long hour Mowgli lay back among the coils, while Kaa, his head motionless on the ground, thought of all that he had seen and known since the day he came from the egg. The light seemed to go out of his eyes and leave them like stale opals, and now and again he made little stiff passes with his head, right and left, as though he were hunting in his sleep. Mowgli dozed quietly, for he knew that there is nothing like sleep before hunting, and he was trained to take it at any hour of the day or night.

Then he felt Kaa's back grow bigger and broader below him as the huge python puffed himself out, hissing with the noise of a sword drawn from a steel scabbard.

"I have seen all the dead seasons," Kaa said at last, "and the great trees and the old elephants, and the rocks that were bare and sharp-pointed ere the moss grew. Art *thou* still alive, Manling?"

"It is only a little after moonset," said Mowgli. "I do not understand–"

"*Hssh!* I am again Kaa. I knew it was but a little time. Now we will go to the river, and I will show thee what is to be done against the dhole."

He turned, straight as an arrow, for the main stream of the Waingunga, plunging in a little above the pool that hid the Peace Rock, Mowgli at his side.

"Nay, do not swim. I go swiftly. My back, Little Brother!"

Mowgli tucked his left arm round Kaa's neck, dropped his right close to his body, and straightened his feet. Then Kaa breasted the current as he alone could, and the ripple of the checked water stood up in a frill round Mowgli's neck, and his feet were waved to and fro in the eddy under the python's lashing sides. A mile or two above the Peace Rock the Waingunga narrows between a gorge of marble rocks from eighty to a hundred feet high, and the current runs like a mill-race between and over all manner of ugly stones. But Mowgli did not trouble his head about the water; little water in the world could have given him a moment's fear. He was looking at the gorge on either side and sniffing uneasily, for there was a sweetish-sourish smell in the air, very like the smell of a big ant-hill on a hot day. Instinctively he lowered himself in the water, only raising his head to breathe from time to time, and Kaa came to anchor with a double twist of his tail round a sunken rock, holding Mowgli in the hollow of a coil, while the water raced on.

"This is the Place of Death," said the boy. "Why do we come here?"

"They sleep," said Kaa. "Hathi will not turn aside for the Striped One. Yet Hathi and the Striped One together turn aside for the dhole, and the dhole they say turn aside for nothing. And yet for whom do the Free People of the Rocks turn aside? Tell me, Master of the Jungle, who is the Master of the Jungle?"

"These," Mowgli whispered. "It is the Place of Death. Let us go."

"Nay, look well, for they are asleep. It is as it was when I was not the length of thy arm."

The split and weatherworn rocks of the gorge of the Waingunga had been used since the beginning of the Jungle by the Little People of the Rocks–the busy, furious, black wild bees of India; and, as Mowgli knew well, all trails turned off half a mile before they reached the gorge. For centuries the Little People had hived and swarmed from cleft to cleft, and swarmed again, staining the white marble with stale honey, and made their combs tall and deep in the dark of the inner caves, where neither man nor beast nor fire nor water had ever touched them. The length of the gorge on both sides was hung as it were with black shimmery velvet curtains, and Mowgli sank as he looked, for those were the clotted millions of the sleeping bees. There were other lumps and festoons and things like decayed tree-trunks studded on the face of the rock, the old combs of past years, or new cities built in the shadow of the windless gorge, and huge masses of spongy, rotten trash had rolled down and stuck among the trees and creepers that clung to the rock-face. As he listened he heard more than once the rustle and slide of a honey-loaded comb turning over or falling away somewhere in the dark galleries; then a booming of angry wings and the sullen drip, drip, drip, of the wasted honey, guttering along till it lipped over some ledge in the open air and sluggishly trickled down on the twigs. There was a tiny little beach, not five feet broad, on one side of the river, and that was piled high with the rubbish of uncounted years. There were dead bees, drones, sweepings, and stale combs, and wings of marauding moths that had strayed in after honey, all tumbled in smooth piles of the finest black dust. The mere sharp smell of it was enough to frighten anything that had no wings, and knew what the Little People were.

Kaa moved up-stream again till he came to a sandy bar at the head of the gorge.

"Here is this season's kill," said he. "Look!"

On the bank lay the skeletons of a couple of young deer and a buffalo. Mowgli could see that neither wolf nor jackal had touched the bones, which were laid out naturally.

"They came beyond the line; they did not know the Law," murmured Mowgli, "and the Little People killed them. Let us go ere they wake."

"They do not wake till the dawn," said Kaa. "Now I will tell thee. A hunted buck from the south, many, many Rains ago, came hither from the south, not knowing the Jungle, a Pack on his trail. Being made blind by fear, he leaped from above, the Pack running by sight, for they were hot and blind on the trail. The sun was high, and the Little People were many and very angry. Many too were those of the Pack who leaped into the Waingunga, but they were dead ere they took water. Those who did not leap died also in the rocks above. But the buck lived."

"How?"

"Because he came first, running for his life, leaping ere the Little People were aware, and was in the river when they gathered to kill. The Pack, following, was altogether lost under the weight of the Little People."

"The buck lived?" Mowgli repeated slowly.

"At least he did not die *then,* though none waited his coming down with a strong body to hold him safe against the water, as a certain old fat, deaf, yellow Flathead would wait for a Manling–yea, though there were all the dholes of the Dekkan on his trail. What is in thy stomach?" Kaa's head was close to Mowgli's ear; and it was a little time before the boy answered.

"It is to pull the very whiskers of Death, but–Kaa, thou art, indeed, the wisest of all the Jungle."

"So many have said. Look now, if the dhole follow thee–"

"As surely they will follow. Ho! ho! I have many little thorns under my tongue to prick into their hides."

"If they follow thee hot and blind, looking only at thy shoulders, those who do not die up above will take water either here or lower down, for the Little People will rise up and cover them. Now the Waingunga is hungry water, and they will have no Kaa to hold them, but will go down, such as live, to the shallows by the Seeonee lairs, and there thy Pack may meet them by the throat."

"Ahai! Eowawa! Better could not be till the Rains fall in the dry season. There is now only the little matter of the run and the leap. I will make me known to the dholes, so that they shall follow me very closely."

"Hast thou seen the rocks above thee? From the landward side?"

"Indeed, no. That I had forgotten."

"Go look. It is all rotten ground, cut and full of holes. One of thy clumsy feet set down without seeing would end the hunt. See, I leave thee here, and for thy sake only I will carry word to the Pack that they may know where to look for the dhole. For myself, I am not of one skin with *any* wolf."

When Kaa disliked an acquaintance he could be more unpleasant than any of the Jungle People, except perhaps Bagheera. He swam downstream and opposite the Rock he came on Phao and Akela listening to the night noises.

"*Hssh!* Dogs," he said cheerfully. "The dholes will come down-stream. If ye be not afraid ye can kill them in the shallows."

"When come they?" said Phao. "And where is my Man-cub?" said Akela.

"They come when they come," said Kaa. "Wait and see. As for *thy* Man-cub, from whom thou hast taken a Word and so laid him open to Death, *thy* Man-cub is with *me,* and if he be not already dead the fault is none of thine, bleached dog! Wait here for the dhole, and be glad that the Man-cub and I strike on thy side."

He flashed up-stream again, and moored himself in the middle of the gorge, looking upward at the line of the cliff. Presently he saw Mowgli's head move against the stars, and then there was a whizz in the air, the keen, clean *schloop* of a body falling feet first, and next minute the boy was at rest again in the loop of Kaa's body.

"It is no leap by night," said Mowgli quietly. "I have jumped twice as far for sport; but that is an evil place above–low bushes and gullies that go down very deep, all full of the Little People. I have put big stones one above the other by the side of three gullies. These I shall throw down with my feet in running, and the Little People will rise up behind me, very angry."

"That is Man's talk and Man's cunning," said Kaa. "Thou art wise, but the Little People are always angry."

"Nay, at twilight all wings near and far rest for a while. I will play with the dhole at twilight, for the dhole hunts best by day. He follows now Won-tolla's blood-trail."

"Chil does not leave a dead ox, nor the dhole the blood-trail," said Kaa.

"Then I will make him a new blood-trail, of his own blood, if I can, and give him dirt to eat. Thou wilt stay here, Kaa, till I come again with my dholes?"

"Ay, but what if they kill thee in the Jungle, or the Little People kill thee before thou canst leap down to the river?"

"When to-morrow comes we will kill for to-morrow," said Mowgli, quoting a Jungle saying; and again, "When I am dead it is time to sing the Death Song. Good hunting, Kaa!"

He loosed his arm from the python's neck and went down the gorge like a log in a freshet, paddling toward the far bank, where he found slack-water, and laughing aloud from sheer happiness. There was nothing Mowgli liked better than, as he himself said, "to pull the whiskers of Death," and make the Jungle know that he was their over-lord. He had often, with Baloo's help, robbed bees' nests in single trees, and he knew that the Little People hated the smell of wild garlic. So he gathered a small bundle of it, tied it up with a bark string, and then followed Won-tolla's blood-trail as it ran southerly from the lairs, for some five miles, looking at the trees with his head on one side, and chuckling as he looked.

"Mowgli the Frog have I been," said he to himself; "Mowgli the Wolf have I said that I am. Now Mowgli the Ape must I be before I am Mowgli the Buck. At the end I shall be Mowgli the Man. Ho!" and he slid his thumb along the eighteen-inch blade of his knife.

Won-tolla's trail, all rank with dark blood-spots, ran under a forest of thick trees that grew close together and stretched away northeastward, gradually growing thinner and thinner to within two miles of the Bee Rocks. From the last tree to the low scrub of the Bee Rocks was open country, where there was hardly cover enough to hide a wolf. Mowgli trotted along under the trees, judging distances between branch and branch, occasionally climbing up a trunk and taking a trial leap from one tree to another, till he came to the open ground, which he studied very carefully for an hour. Then he turned, picked up Won-tolla's trail where he had left it, settled himself in a tree with an outrunning branch some eight feet from the ground, and sat still, sharpening his knife on the sole of his foot and singing to himself.

A little before midday, when the sun was very warm, he heard the patter of feet and smelt the abominable smell of the dhole pack as they trotted pitilessly along Won-tolla's trail. Seen from above, the red dhole does not look half the size of a wolf, but Mowgli knew how strong his feet and jaws were. He watched the sharp bay head of the leader snuffing along the trail and gave him "Good hunting!"

The brute looked up, and his companions halted behind him, scores and scores of red dogs with low-hung tails, heavy shoulders, weak quarters, and bloody mouths. The dholes are a silent people as a rule, and they have no manners even in their own Jungle. Fully two hundred must have gathered below him, but he could see that the leaders sniffed hungrily on Won-tolla's trail, and tried to drag the Pack forward. That would never do, or they would be at the Lairs in broad daylight, and Mowgli intended to hold them under his tree till dusk.

"By whose leave do ye come here?" said Mowgli.

"All Jungles are our Jungle," was the reply, and the dhole that gave it bared his white teeth. Mowgli looked down with a smile, and imitated perfectly the sharp chitter-chatter of Chikai, the leaping rat of the Dekkan, meaning the dholes to understand that he considered them no better than Chikai. The Pack closed up round the tree-trunk and the leader bayed savagely, calling Mowgli a tree-ape. For all answer Mowgli stretched down one naked leg and wriggled his bare toes just above the leader's head. That was enough, and more than enough, to wake the Pack to stupid rage. Those who have hair between their toes do not care to be reminded of it. Mowgli caught his foot away as the leader leaped up, and said sweetly: "Dog, red dog! Go back to the Dekkan and eat lizards. Go to Chikai thy brother–dog, dog–red, red, dog! There is hair between every toe!" He twiddled his toes a second time.

"Come down ere we starve thee out, hairless ape!" yelled the Pack, and this was exactly what Mowgli wanted. He laid himself down along the branch, his cheek to the bark, his right arm free, and there he told the Pack what he thought and knew about them, their manners, their customs, their mates, and their puppies. There is no speech in the world so rancorous and so stinging as the language the Jungle People use to show scorn and contempt. When you come to think of it you will see how this must be so. As Mowgli told Kaa, he had many little thorns under his tongue, and slowly and deliberately he drove the dholes from silence to growls, from growls to yells, and from yells to hoarse slavery ravings. They tried to answer his taunts, but a cub might as well have tried to answer Kaa in a rage; and all the while Mowgli's right hand lay crooked at his side, ready for action, his feet locked round the branch. The big bay leader had leaped many times in the air, but Mowgli dared not risk a false blow. At last, made furious beyond his natural strength, he bounded up seven or eight feet clear of the ground. Then Mowgli's hand shot out like the head of a tree-snake, and gripped him by the scruff of his neck, and the branch shook with the jar as his weight fell back, almost wrenching Mowgli to the ground. But he never loosed his grasp, and inch by inch he hauled the beast, hanging like a drowned jackal, up on the branch. With his left hand he reached for his knife and cut off the red, bushy tail, flinging the dhole back to earth again. That was all he needed. The Pack would not go forward on Won-tolla's trail now till they had killed Mowgli or Mowgli had killed them. He saw them settle down in circles with a quiver of the haunches that meant they were going to stay, and so he climbed to a higher crotch, settled his back comfortably, and went to sleep.

After four or five hours he waked and counted the Pack. They were all there, silent, husky, and dry, with eyes of steel. The sun was beginning to sink. In half an hour the Little People of the Rocks would be ending their labors, and, as he knew, the dhole does not fight best in the twilight.

"I did not need such faithful watchers," he said politely, standing up on a branch, "but I will remember this. Ye be true dholes, but to my thinking over much of one kind. For that reason I do not give the big lizard-eater his tail again. Art thou not pleased, Red Dog?"

"I myself will tear out thy stomach!" yelled the leader, scratching at the foot of the tree.

"Nay, but consider, wise rat of the Dekkan. There will now be many litters of little tailless red dogs, yea, with raw red stumps that sting when the sand is hot. Go home, Red Dog, and cry that an ape has done this. Ye will not go? Come, then, with me, and I will make you very wise!"

He moved, Bandar-log fashion, into the next tree, and so on into the next and the next, the Pack following with lifted hungry heads. Now and then he would pretend to fall, and the Pack would tumble one over the other in their haste to be at the death. It was a curious sight–the boy with the knife that shone in the low sunlight as it shifted through the upper branches, and the silent Pack with their red coats all aflame, huddling and following below. When he came to the last tree he took the garlic and rubbed himself all over carefully, and the dholes yelled with scorn. "Ape with a wolf's tongue, dost thou think to cover thy scent?" they said. "We follow to the death."

"Take thy tail," said Mowgli, flinging it back along the course he had taken. The Pack instinctively rushed after it. "And follow now–to the death."

He had slipped down the tree-trunk, and headed like the wind in bare feet for the Bee Rocks, before the dholes saw what he would do.

They gave one deep howl, and settled down to the long, lobbing canter that can at the last run down anything that runs. Mowgli knew their pack-pace to be much slower than that of the wolves, or he would never have risked a two-mile run in full sight. They were sure that the boy was theirs at last, and he was sure that he held them to play with as he pleased. All his trouble was to keep them sufficiently hot behind him to prevent their turning off too soon. He ran cleanly, evenly, and springily; the tailless leader not five yards behind him; and the Pack tailing out over perhaps a quarter of a mile of ground, crazy and blind with the rage of slaughter. So he kept his distance by ear, reserving his last effort for the rush across the Bee Rocks.

The Little People had gone to sleep in the early twilight, for it was not the season of late-blossoming flowers; but as Mowgli's first footfalls rang hollow on the hollow ground he heard a sound as though all the earth were humming. Then he ran as he had never run in his life before, spurned aside one–two–three of the piles of stones into the dark, sweet-smelling gullies; heard a roar like the roar of the sea in a cave; saw with the tail of his eye the air grow dark behind him; saw the current of the Waingunga far below and a flat, diamond-shaped head in the water; leaped outward with all his strength, the tailless dhole snapping at his shoulder in mid-air, and dropped feet first to the safety of the river, breathless and triumphant. There was not a sting upon him, for the smell of the garlic had checked the Little People for just the few seconds that he was among them. When he rose Kaa's coils were steadying him and things were bounding over the edge of the cliff–great lumps, it seemed, of clustered bees falling like plummets; but before any lump touched water the bees flew upward and the body of a dhole whirled down-stream. Overhead they could hear furious short yells that were drowned in a roar like breakers–the roar of the wings of the Little People of the Rocks. Some of the dholes, too, had fallen into the gullies that communicated with the underground caves, and there choked and fought and snapped among the tumbled honeycombs, and at last, borne up even when they were dead on the heaving waves of bees beneath them, shot out of some hole in the river-face, to roll over on the black rubbish-heaps. There were dholes who had leaped short into the trees on the cliffs, and the bees blotted out their shapes; but the greater number of them, maddened by the stings, had flung themselves into the river; and, as Kaa said, the Waingunga was hungry water.

Kaa held Mowgli fast till the boy had recovered his breath.

"We may not stay here," he said. "The Little People are roused indeed. Come!"

Swimming low and diving as often as he could, Mowgli went down the river, knife in hand.

"Slowly, slowly," said Kaa. "One tooth does not kill a hundred unless it be a cobra's, and many of the dholes took water swiftly when they saw the Little People rise."

"The more work for my knife, then. *Phai!* How the Little People follow!" Mowgli sank again. The face of the water was blanketed with wild bees, buzzing sullenly and stinging all they found.

"Nothing was ever yet lost by silence," said Kaa–no sting could penetrate his scales–"and thou hast all the long night for the hunting. Hear them howl!"

Nearly half the pack had seen the trap their fellows rushed into, and turning sharp aside had flung themselves into the water where the gorge broke down in steep banks. Their cries of rage and their threats against the "tree-ape" who had brought them to their shame mixed with the yells and growls of those who had been punished by the Little People. To remain ashore was death, and every dhole knew it. Their pack was swept along the current, down to the deep eddies of the Peace Pool, but even there the angry Little People followed and forced them to the water again. Mowgli could hear the voice of the tailless leader bidding his people hold on and kill out every wolf in Seeonee. But he did not waste his time in listening.

"One kills in the dark behind us!" snapped a dhole. "Here is tainted water."

Mowgli had dived forward like an otter, twitched a struggling dhole under water before he could open his mouth, and dark rings rose as the body plopped up, turning on its side. The dholes tried to turn, but the current prevented them, and the Little People darted at their heads and ears, and they could hear the challenge of the Seeonee Pack growing louder and deeper in the gathering darkness. Again Mowgli dived, and again a dhole went under, and rose dead, and again the clamor broke out at the rear of the pack; some howling that it was best to go ashore, others calling on their leader to lead them back to the Dekkan, and others bidding Mowgli show himself and be killed.

"They come to the fight with two stomachs and several voices," said Kaa. "The rest is with thy brethren below yonder. The Little People go back to sleep. They have chased us far. Now I, too, turn back, for I am not of one skin with any wolf. Good hunting, Little Brother, and remember the dhole bites low."

A wolf came running along the bank on three legs, leaping up and down, laying his head sideways close to the ground, hunching his back, and breaking high into the air, as though he were playing with his cubs. It was Won-tolla, the Outlier, and he said never a word, but continued his horrible sport beside the dholes. They had been long in the water now, and were swimming wearily, their coats drenched and heavy, their bushy tails dragging like sponges, so tired and shaken that they, too, were silent, watching the pair of blazing eyes that moved abreast.

"This is no good hunting," said one, panting.

"Good hunting!" said Mowgli, as he rose boldly at the brute's side, and sent the long knife home behind the shoulder, pushing hard to avoid his dying snap.

"Art thou there, Man-cub?" said Won-tolla across the water.

"Ask of the dead, Outlier," Mowgli replied. "Have none come downstream? I have filled these dogs' mouths with dirt; I have tricked them in the broad daylight, and their leader lacks his tail, but here be some few for thee still. Whither shall I drive them?"

"I will wait," said Won-tolla. "The night is before me."

Nearer and nearer came the bay of the Seeonee wolves. "For the Pack, for the Full Pack it is met!" and a bend in the river drove the dholes forward among the sands and shoals opposite the Lairs.

Then they saw their mistake. They should have landed half a mile higher up, and rushed the wolves on dry ground. Now it was too late. The bank was lined with burning eyes, and except for the horrible *pheeal* that had never stopped since sundown, there was no sound in the Jungle. It seemed as though Won-tolla were fawning on them to come ashore; and "Turn and take hold!" said the leader of the dholes. The entire Pack flung themselves at the shore, threshing and squattering through the shoal water, till the face of the Waingunga was all white and torn, and the great ripples went from side to side, like bow-waves from a boat. Mowgli followed the rush, stabbing and slicing as the dholes, huddled together, rushed up the river-beach in one wave.

Then the long fight began, heaving and straining and splitting and scattering and narrowing and broadening along the red, wet sands, and over and between the tangled tree-roots, and through and among the brushes, and in and out of the grass clumps; for even now the dholes were two to one. But they met wolves fighting for all that made the Pack, and not only the short, high, deep-chested, white-tusked hunters of the Pack, but the anxious-eyed lahinis–the she-wolves of the lair, as the saying is–fighting for their litters, with here and there a yearling wolf, his first coat still half woolly, tugging and grappling by their sides. A wolf, you must know, flies at the throat or snaps at the flank, while a dhole, by preference, bites at the belly; so when the dholes were struggling out of the water and had to raise their heads, the odds were with the wolves. On dry land the wolves suffered; but in the water or ashore, Mowgli's knife came and went without ceasing. The Four had worried their way to his side. Gray Brother, crouched between the boy's knees, was protecting his stomach, while the others guarded his back and either side, or stood over him when the shock of a leaping, yelling dhole who had thrown himself full on the steady blade, bore him down. For the rest, it was one tangled confusion–a locked and swaying mob that moved from right to left and from left to right along the bank; and also ground round and round slowly on its own center. Here would be a heaving mound, like a water-blister in a whirlpool, which would break like a water-blister, and throw up four or five mangled dogs, each striving to get back to the center; here would be a single wolf borne down by two or three dholes, laboriously dragging them forward, and sinking the while; here a yearling cub would be held up by the pressure round him, though he had been killed early, while his mother, crazed with dumb rage, rolled over and over, snapping, and passing on; and in the middle of the thickest press, perhaps, one wolf and one dhole, forgetting everything else, would be manoeuvering for first hold till they were whirled away by a rush of furious fighters. Once Mowgli passed Akela, a dhole on either flank, and his all but toothless jaws closed over the loins of a third; and once he saw Phao, his teeth set in the throat of a dhole, tugging the unwilling beast forward till the yearlings could finish him. But the bulk of the fight was blind flurry and smother in the dark; hit, trip, and tumble, yelp, groan, and worry-worry-worry, round him and behind him and above him. As the night wore on, the quick, giddy-go-round motion increased. The dholes were cowed and afraid to attack the stronger wolves, but did not yet dare to run away. Mowgli felt that the end was coming soon, and contented himself with striking merely to cripple. The yearlings were growing bolder; there was time now and again to breathe, and pass a word to a friend, and the mere flicker of the knife would sometimes turn a dog aside.

"The meat is very near the bone," Gray Brother yelled. He was bleeding from a score of flesh-wounds.

"But the bone is yet to be cracked," said Mowgli. "*Eowawa! Thus* do we do in the Jungle!" The red blade ran like a flame along the side of a dhole whose hind-quarters were hidden by the weight of a clinging wolf.

"My kill!" snorted the wolf through his wrinkled nostrils. "Leave him to me."

"Is thy stomach still empty, Outlier?" said Mowgli. Won-tolla was fearfully punished, but his grip had paralyzed the dhole, who could not turn round and reach him.

"By the Bull that bought me," said Mowgli, with a bitter laugh, "it is the tailless one!" And indeed it was the big bay-colored leader.

"It is not wise to kill cubs and lahinis," Mowgli went on, philosophically, wiping the blood out of his eyes, "unless one has also killed the Outlier; and it is in my stomach that this Won-tolla kills thee."

A dhole leaped to his leader's aid; but before his teeth had found Won-tolla's flank, Mowgli's knife was in his throat, and Gray Brother took what was left.

"And thus do we do in the Jungle," said Mowgli.

Won-tolla said not a word, only his jaws were closing and closing on the backbone as his life ebbed. The dhole shuddered, his head dropped, and he lay still, and Won-tolla dropped above him.

"*Huh!* The Blood Debt is paid," said Mowgli. "Sing the song, Won-tolla."

"He hunts no more," said Gray Brother; "and Akela, too, is silent this long time."

"The bone is cracked!" thundered Phao, son of Phaona. "They go! Kill, kill out, O hunters of the Free People!"

Dhole after dhole was slinking away from those dark and bloody sands to the river, to the thick Jungle, up-stream or down-stream as he saw the road clear.

"The debt! The debt!" shouted Mowgli. "Pay the debt! They have slain the Lone Wolf! Let not a dog go!"

He was flying to the river, knife in hand, to check any dhole who dared to take water, when, from under a mound of nine dead, rose Akela's red head and fore-quarters, and Mowgli dropped on his knees beside the Lone Wolf.

"Said I not it would be my last fight?" Akela panted. "It is good hunting. And thou, Little Brother?"

"I live, having killed many."

"Even so. I die, and I would–I would die by thee, Little Brother."

Mowgli took the terrible scarred head on his knees, and put his arms round the torn neck.

"It is long since the old days of Shere Khan, and a Man-cub that rolled naked in the dust."

"Nay, nay, I am a wolf. I am of one skin with the Free People," Mowgli cried. "It is no will of mine that I am a man."

"Thou art a man, Little Brother, wolfling of my watching. Thou art a man, or else the Pack had fled before the dhole. My life I owe to thee, and to-day thou hast saved the Pack even as once I saved thee. Hast thou forgotten? All debts are paid now. Go to thine own people. I tell thee again, eye of my eye, this hunting is ended. Go to thine own people."

"I will never go. I will hunt alone in the Jungle. I have said it."

"After the summer come the Rains, and after the Rains comes the spring. Go back before thou art driven."

"Who will drive me?"

"Mowgli will drive Mowgli. Go back to thy people. Go to Man."

"When Mowgli drives Mowgli I will go," Mowgli answered.

"There is no more to say," said Akela. "Little Brother, canst thou raise me to my feet? I also was a leader of the Free People."

Very carefully and gently Mowgli lifted the bodies aside, and raised Akela to his feet, both arms round him, and the Lone Wolf drew a long breath, and began the Death Song that a leader of the Pack should sing when he dies. It gathered strength as he went on, lifting and lifting, and ringing far across the river, till it came to the last "Good hunting!" and Akela shook himself clear of Mowgli for an instant, and, leaping into the air, fell backward dead upon his last and most terrible kill.

Mowgli sat with the head on his knees, careless of anything else, while the remnant of the flying dholes were being overtaken and run down by the merciless lahinis. Little by little the cries died away, and the wolves returned limping, as their wounds stiffened, to take stock of the losses. Fifteen of the Pack, as well as half a dozen lahinis, lay dead by the river, and of the others not one was unmarked. And Mowgli sat through it all till the cold daybreak, when Phao's wet, red muzzle was dropped in his hand, and Mowgli drew back to show the gaunt body of Akela.

"Good hunting!" said Phao, as though Akela were still alive, and then over his bitten shoulder to the others: "Howl, dogs! A Wolf has died to-night!"

But of all the Pack of two hundred fighting dholes, whose boast was that all Jungles were their Jungle, and that no living thing could stand before them, not one returned to the Dekkan to carry that word.

Chil's Song

[This is the song that Chil sang as the kites dropped down one after another to the river-bed, when the great fight was finished. Chil is good friends with everybody, but he is a cold-blooded kind of creature at heart, because he knows that almost everybody in the Jungle comes to him in the long run.]

These were my companions going forth by night–
(For Chil! Look you, for Chil!)
Now come I to whistle them the ending of the fight.
(Chil! Vanguards of Chil!)
Word they gave me overhead of quarry newly slain,
Word I gave them underfoot of buck upon the plain.
Here's an end of every trail–they shall not speak again!

They that called the hunting-cry–they that followed fast–
(For Chil! Look you, for Chil!)
They that bade the sambhur wheel, and pinned him as he passed–
(Chil! Vanguards of Chil!)
They that lagged behind the scent–they that ran before,
They that shunned the level horn–they that overbore,
Here's an end of every trail–they shall not follow more.

These were my companions. Pity 't was they died!
(For Chil! Look you, for Chil!)
Now come I to comfort them that knew them in their pride.
(Chil! Vanguards of Chil!)
Tattered flank and sunken eye, open mouth and red,
Locked and lank and lone they lie, the dead upon their dead.
Here's an end of every trail–and here my hosts are fed!

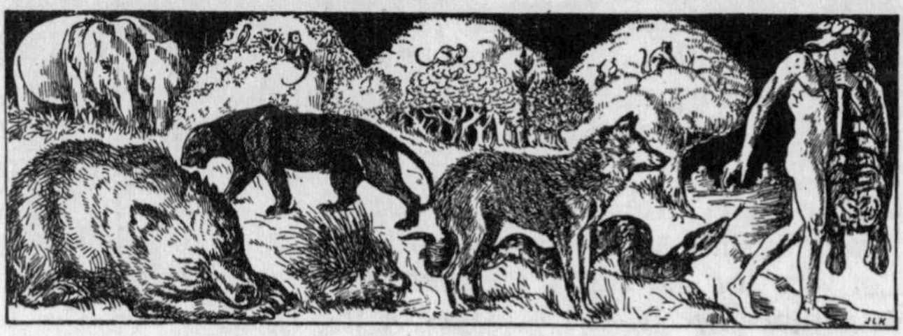

The Spring Running

Man goes to Man! Cry the challenge through the Jungle!
He that was our Brother goes away.
Hear, now, and judge, O ye People of the Jungle,–
Answer, who shall turn him–who shall stay?

Man goes to Man! He is weeping in the Jungle:
He that was our Brother sorrows sore!
Man goes to Man! (Oh, we loved him in the Jungle!)
To the Man-Trail where we may not follow more.

THE SECOND YEAR after the great fight with Red Dog and the death of Akela, Mowgli must have been nearly seventeen years old. He looked older, for hard exercise, the best of good eating, and baths whenever he felt in the least hot or dusty, had given him strength and growth far beyond his age. He could swing by one hand from a top branch for half an hour at a time, when he had occasion to look along the tree-roads. He could stop a young buck in mid-gallop and throw him sideways by the head. He could even jerk over the big, blue wild boars that lived in the Marshes of the North. The Jungle People who used to fear him for his wits feared him now for his strength, and when he moved quietly on his own affairs the mere whisper of his coming cleared the wood-paths. And yet the look in his eyes was always gentle. Even when he fought, his eyes never blazed as Bagheera's did. They only grew more and more interested and excited; and that was one of the things that Bagheera himself did not understand.

He asked Mowgli about it, and the boy laughed and said: "When I miss the kill I am angry. When I must go empty for two days I am very angry. Do not my eyes talk then?"

"The mouth is angry," said Bagheera, "but the eyes say nothing. Hunting, eating, or swimming, it is all one–like a stone in wet or dry weather." Mowgli looked at him lazily from under his long eyelashes, and, as usual, the panther's head dropped. Bagheera knew his master.

They were lying out far up the side of a hill overlooking the Waingunga, and the morning mist hung below them in bands of white and green. As the sun rose it changed into bubbling seas of red gold, churned off, and let the low rays stripe the dried grass on which Mowgli and Bagheera were resting. It was the end of the cold weather, the leaves and the trees looked worn and faded, and there was a dry, ticking rustle everywhere when the wind blew. A little leaf tap-tap-tapped furiously against a twig, as a single leaf caught in a current will. It roused Bagheera, for he snuffed the morning air with a deep, hollow cough, threw himself on his back, and struck with his fore-paws at the nodding leaf above.

"The year turns," he said. "The Jungle goes forward. The Time of New

Talk is near. That leaf knows. It is very good."

"The grass is dry," Mowgli answered, pulling up a tuft. "Even Eye-of-the-Spring [that is a little trumpet-shaped, waxy red flower that runs in and out among the grasses]–even Eye-of-the-Spring is shut, and . . . Bagheera, *is* it well for the Black Panther so to lie on his back and beat with his paws in the air, as though he were a tree-cat?"

"Aowh?" said Bagheera. He seemed to be thinking of other things.

"I say, *is* it well for the Black Panther so to mouth and cough, and howl and roll? Remember, we be the Masters of the Jungle, thou and I."

"Indeed, yes: I hear, Man-cub." Bagheera rolled over hurriedly and sat up, the dust on his ragged, black flanks. (He was just casting his winter coat.) "We be surely the Masters of the Jungle! Who is so strong as Mowgli? Who so wise?" There was a curious drawl in the voice that made Mowgli turn to see whether by any chance the Black Panther were making fun of him, for the Jungle is full of words that sound like one thing, but mean another. "I said we be beyond question the Masters of the Jungle," Bagheera repeated. "Have I done wrong? I did not know that the Man-cub no longer lay upon the ground. Does he fly, then?"

Mowgli sat with his elbows on his knees, looking out across the valley at the daylight. Somewhere down in the woods below a bird was trying over in a husky, reedy voice the first few notes of his spring song. It was no more than a shadow of the liquid, tumbling call he would be pouring later, but Bagheera heard it.

"I said the Time of New Talk is near," growled the panther, switching his tail.

"I hear," Mowgli answered. "Bagheera, why dost thou shake all over? The sun is warm."

"That is Ferao, the scarlet woodpecker," said Bagheera. "*He* has not forgotten. Now I, too, must remember my song," and he began purring and crooning to himself, harking back dissatisfied again and again.

"There is no game afoot," said Mowgli.

"Little Brother, are *both* thine ears stopped? That is no killing-word, but my song that I make ready against the need."

"I had forgotten. I shall know when the Time of New Talk is here, because then thou and the others all run away and leave me alone." Mowgli spoke rather savagely.

"But, indeed, Little Brother," Bagheera began, "we do not always–"

"I say ye do," said Mowgli, shooting out his forefinger angrily. "Ye *do* run away, and I, who am the Master of the Jungle, must needs walk alone. How was it last season, when I would gather sugar-cane from the fields of a Man-Pack? I sent a runner–I sent thee!–to Hathi, bidding him to come upon such a night and pluck the sweet grass for me with his trunk."

"He came only two nights later," said Bagheera, cowering a little; "and of that long, sweet grass that pleased thee so he gathered more than any Man-cub could eat in all the nights of the Rains. That was no fault of mine."

"He did not come upon the night when I sent him the word. No, he was trumpeting and running and roaring through the valleys in the moonlight. His trail was like the trail of three elephants, for he would not hide among the trees. He danced in the moonlight before the houses of the Man-Pack. I saw him, and yet he would not come to me; and *I* am the Master of the Jungle!"

"It was the Time of New Talk," said the panther, always very humble. "Perhaps, Little Brother, thou didst not that time call him by a Master-word? Listen to Ferao, and be glad!"

Mowgli's bad temper seemed to have boiled itself away. He lay back with his head on his arms, his eyes shut. "I do not know–nor do I care," he said sleepily. "Let us sleep, Bagheera. My stomach is heavy in me. Make me a rest for my head."

The panther lay down again with a sigh, because he could hear Ferao practicing and repracticing his song against the Springtime of New Talk, as they say.

In an Indian Jungle the seasons slide one into the other almost without division. There seem to be only two—the wet and the dry; but if you look closely below the torrents of rain and the clouds of char and dust you will find all four going round in their regular ring. Spring is the most wonderful, because he has not to cover a clean, bare field with new leaves and flowers, but to drive before her and to put away the hanging-on, over-surviving raffle of half-green things which the gentle winter has suffered to live, and to make the partly dressed stale earth feel new and young once more. And this she does so well that there is no spring in the world like the Jungle spring.

There is one day when all things are tired, and the very smells, as they drift on the heavy air, are old and used. One cannot explain this, but it feels so. Then there is another day—to the eye nothing whatever has changed—when all the smells are new and delightful, and the whiskers of the Jungle People quiver to their roots, and the winter hair comes away from their sides in long, draggled locks. Then, perhaps, a little rain falls, and all the trees and the bushes and the bamboos and the mosses and the juicy-leaved plants wake with a noise of growing that you can almost hear, and under this noise runs, day and night, a deep hum. *That* is the noise of the spring—a vibrating boom which is neither bees, nor falling water, nor the wind in tree-tops, but the purring of the warm, happy world.

Up to this year Mowgli had always delighted in the turn of the seasons. It was he who generally saw the first Eye-of-the-Spring deep down among the grasses, and the first bank of spring clouds which are like nothing else in the Jungle. His voice could be heard in all sorts of wet, star-lighted, blossoming places, helping the big frogs through their choruses, or mocking the little upside-down owls that hoot through the white nights. Like all his people, spring was the season he chose for his flittings—moving, for the mere joy of rushing through the warm air, thirty, forty, or fifty miles between twilight and the morning star, and coming back panting and laughing and wreathed with strange flowers. The Four did not follow him on these wild ringings of the Jungle, but went off to sing songs with other wolves. The Jungle People are very busy in the spring, and Mowgli could hear them grunting and screaming and whistling according to their kind. Their voices then are different from their voices at other times of the year, and that is one of the reasons why spring in the Jungle is called the Time of New Talk.

But that spring, as he told Bagheera, his stomach was changed in him. Ever since the bamboo shoots turned spotty-brown he had been looking forward to the morning when the smells should change. But when the morning came, and Mor the Peacock, blazing in bronze and blue and gold, cried it aloud all along the misty woods, and Mowgli opened his mouth to send on the cry, the words choked between his teeth, and a feeling came over him that began at his toes and ended in his hair—a feeling of pure unhappiness, so that he looked himself over to be sure that he had not trod on a thorn. Mor cried the new smells, the other birds took it over, and from the rocks by the Waingunga he heard Bagheera's hoarse scream—something between the scream of an eagle and the neighing of a horse. There was a yelling and scattering of *bandar-log* in the new-budding branches above, and there stood Mowgli, his chest, filled to answer Mor, sinking in little gasps as the breath was driven out of it by this unhappiness.

He stared all round him, but he could see no more than the mocking *bandar-log* scudding through the trees, and Mor, his tail spread in full splendor, dancing on the slopes below.

"The smells have changed," screamed Mor. "Good hunting, Little Brother! Where is thy answer?"

"Little Brother, good hunting!" whistled Chil the Kite and his mate, swooping down together. The two baffed under Mowgli's nose so close that a pinch of downy white feathers brushed away.

A light spring rain–elephant-rain they call it–drove across the Jungle in a belt half a mile wide, left the new leaves wet and nodding behind, and died out in a double rainbow and a light roll of thunder. The spring hum broke out for a minute, and was silent, but all the Jungle Folk seemed to be giving tongue at once. All except Mowgli.

"I have eaten good food," he said to himself. "I have drunk good water. Nor does my throat burn and grow small, as it did when I bit the blue-spotted root that Oo the Turtle said was clean food. But my stomach is heavy, and I have given very bad talk to Bagheera and others, people of the Jungle and my people. Now, too, I am hot and now I am cold, and now I am neither hot nor cold, but angry with that which I cannot see. Huhu! It is time to make a running! To-night I will cross the ranges; yes, I will make a spring running to the Marshes of the North, and back again. I have hunted too easily too long. The Four shall come with me, for they grow as fat as white grubs."

He called, but never one of the Four answered. They were far beyond earshot, singing over the spring songs–the Moon and Sambhur Songs–with the wolves of the Pack; for in the springtime the Jungle People make very little difference between the day and the night. He gave the sharp, barking note, but his only answer was the mocking *maiou* of the little spotted tree-cat winding in and out among the branches for early birds' nests. At this he shook all over with rage, and half drew his knife. Then he became very haughty, though there was no one to see him, and stalked severely down the hillside, chin up and eyebrows down. But never a single one of his people asked him a question, for they were all too busy with their own affairs.

"Yes," said Mowgli to himself, though in his heart he knew that he had no reason. "Let the Red Dhole come from the Dekkan, or the Red Flower dance among the bamboos, and all the Jungle runs whining to Mowgli, calling him great elephant-names. But now, because Eye-of-the-Spring is red, and Mor, forsooth, must show his naked legs in some spring dance, the Jungle goes mad as Tabaqui. . . . By the Bull that bought me! am I the Master of the Jungle, or am I not? Be silent! What do ye here?"

A couple of young wolves of the Pack were cantering down a path, looking for open ground in which to fight. (You will remember that the Law of the Jungle forbids fighting where the Pack can see.) Their neck-bristles were as stiff as wire, and they bayed furiously, crouching for the first grapple. Mowgli leaped forward, caught one outstretched throat in either hand, expecting to fling the creatures backward as he had often done in games or Pack hunts. But he had never before interfered with a spring fight. The two leaped forward and dashed him aside, and without word to waste rolled over and over close locked.

Mowgli was on his feet almost before he fell, his knife and his white teeth were bared, and at that minute he would have killed both for no reason but that they were fighting when he wished them to be quiet, although every wolf has full right under the Law to fight. He danced round them with lowered shoulders and quivering hand, ready to send in a double blow when the first flurry of the scuffle should be over; but while he waited the strength seemed to ebb from his body, the knife-point lowered, and he sheathed the knife and watched.

"I have surely eaten poison," he sighed at last. "Since I broke up the Council with the Red Flower–since I killed Shere Khan–none of the Pack could fling me aside. And these be only tail-wolves in the Pack, little hunters! My strength is gone from me, and presently I shall die. Oh, Mowgli, why dost thou not kill them both?"

The fight went on till one wolf ran away, and Mowgli was left alone on the torn and bloody ground, looking now at his knife, and now at his legs and arms, while the feeling of unhappiness he had never known before covered him as water covers a log.

He killed early that evening and eat but little, so as to be in good fettle for his spring running, and he eat alone because all the Jungle People were away singing or fighting. It was a perfect white night, as they call it. All green things seemed to have made a month's growth since the morning. The branch that was yellow-leaved the day before dripped sap when Mowgli broke it. The mosses curled deep and warm over his feet, the young grass had no cutting edges, and all the voices of the Jungle boomed like one deep harp-string touched by the moon—the Moon of New Talk, who splashed her light full on rock and pool. slipped it between trunk and creeper, and sifted it through a million leaves. Forgetting his unhappiness, Mowgli sang aloud with pure delight as he settled into his stride. It was more like flying than anything else, for he had chosen the long downward slope that leads to the Northern Marshes through the heart of the main Jungle, where the springy ground deadened the fall of his feet. A man-taught man would have picked his way with many stumbles through the cheating moonlight, but Mowgli's muscles, trained by years of experience, bore him up as though he were a feather. When a rotten log or a hidden stone turned under his foot he saved himself, never checking his pace, without effort and without thought. When he tired of ground-going he threw up his hands monkey-fashion to the nearest creeper, and seemed to float rather than to climb up into the thin branches, whence he would follow a tree-road till his mood changed, and he shot downward in a long, leafy curve to the levels again. There were still, hot hollows surrounded by wet rocks where he could hardly breathe for the heavy scents of the night flowers and the bloom along the creeper-buds; dark avenues where the moonlight lay in belts as regular as checkered marbles in a church aisle; thickets where the wet young growth stood breast-high about him and threw its arms round his waist; and hilltops crowned with broken rock, where he leaped from stone to stone above the lairs of the frightened little foxes. He would hear, very faint and far off, the *chug-drug* of a boar sharpening his tusks on a bole; and would come across the great gray brute all alone, scribing and rending the bark of a tall tree, his mouth dripping with foam, and his eyes blazing like fire. Or he would turn aside to the sound of clashing horns and hissing grunts, and dash past a couple of furious sambhur, staggering to and fro with lowered heads, striped with blood that showed black in the moonlight. Or at some rushing ford he would hear Jacala the Crocodile bellowing like a bull, or disturb a twined knot of the Poison People, but before they could strike he would be away and across the glistening shingle, deep in the Jungle again.

So he ran, sometimes shouting, sometimes singing to himself, the happiest thing in all the Jungle that night, till the smell of the flowers warned him that he was near the marshes, and those lay far beyond his furthest hunting-grounds.

Here, again, a man-trained man would have sunk overhead in three strides, but Mowgli's feet had eyes in them, and they passed him from tussock to tussock and clump to quaking clump without asking help from the eyes in his head. He ran out to the middle of the swamp, disturbing the duck as he ran, and sat down on a moss-coated tree-trunk lapped in the black water. The marsh was awake all round him, for in the spring the Bird-People sleep very lightly, and companies of them were coming or going the night through. But no one took any notice of Mowgli sitting among the tall reeds humming songs without words, and looking at the soles of his hard brown feet in case of neglected thorns. All his unhappiness seemed to have been left behind in his own jungle, and he was just beginning a full-throat song when it came back again—ten times worse than before.

This time Mowgli was frightened. "It is here also!" he said half aloud. "It has followed me," and he looked over his shoulder to see whether the It were not standing behind him. "There is no one here." The night noises of the marsh went on, but never a bird or beast spoke to him, and the new feeling of misery grew.

"I have surely eaten poison," he said in an awe-stricken voice. "It must be that carelessly I have eaten poison, and my strength is going from me. I was afraid—and yet it was not *I* that was afraid—Mowgli was afraid when the two wolves fought. Akela, or even Phao, would have silenced them; yet Mowgli was afraid. That is true sign I have eaten poison. . . . But what do they care in the Jungle? They sing and howl and fight, and run in companies under the moon, and I—*Hai-mai!*—I am dying in the marshes, of that poison which I have eaten." He was so sorry for himself that he nearly wept. "And after," he went on, "they will find me lying in the black water. Nay, I will go back to my own Jungle, and I will die upon the Council Rock, and Bagheera, whom I love, if he is not screaming in the valley—Bagheera, perhaps, may watch by what is left for a little, lest Chil use me as he used Akela."

A large, warm tear splashed down on his knee, and, miserable as he was, Mowgli felt happy that he was so miserable, if you can understand that upside-down sort of happiness. "As Chil the Kite used Akela," he repeated, "on the night I saved the Pack from Red Dog." He was quiet for a little, thinking of the last words of the Lone Wolf, which you, of course, remember. "Now Akela said to me many foolish things before he died, for when we die our stomachs change. He said . . . None the less, I *am* of the Jungle!"

In his excitement, as he remembered the fight on Waingunga bank, he shouted the last words aloud, and a wild buffalo-cow among the reeds sprang to her knees, snorting, "Man!"

"Uhh!" said Mysa the Wild Buffalo (Mowgli could hear him turn in his wallow), "*that* is no man. It is only the hairless wolf of the Seeonee Pack. On such nights runs he to and fro."

"Uhh!" said the cow, dropping her head again to graze, "I thought it was Man."

"I say no. Oh, Mowgli, is it danger?" lowed Mysa.

"Oh, Mowgli, is it danger?" the boy called back mockingly. "That is all Mysa thinks for: Is it danger? But for Mowgli, who goes to and fro in the Jungle by night, watching, what do ye care?"

"How loud he cries!" said the cow.

"Thus do they cry," Mysa answered contemptuously, "who, having torn up the grass, know not how to eat it."

"For less than this," Mowgli groaned to himself—"for less than this even last Rains I had pricked Mysa out of his wallow, and ridden him through the swamp on a rush halter." He stretched a hand to break one of the feathery reeds, but drew it back with a sigh. Mysa went on steadily chewing the cud, and the long grass ripped where the cow grazed. "I will not die *here,*" he said angrily. "Mysa, who is of one blood with Jacala and the pig, would see me. Let us go beyond the swamp, and see what comes. Never have I run such a spring running—hot and cold together. Up, Mowgli!"

He could not resist the temptation of stealing across the reeds to Mysa and pricking him with the point of his knife. The great dripping bull broke out of his wallow like a shell exploding, while Mowgli laughed till he sat down.

"Say now that the hairless wolf of the Seeonee Pack once herded thee, Mysa," he called.

"Wolf! *Thou?*" the bull snorted, stamping in the mud. "All the Jungle knows thou wast a herder of tame cattle—such a man's brat as shouts in the dust by the crops yonder. *Thou* of the Jungle! What hunter would have crawled like a snake among the leeches, and for a muddy jest—a jackal's jest—have shamed me before my cow? Come to firm ground, and I will—I will . . ." Mysa frothed at the mouth, for Mysa has nearly the worst temper of any one in the Jungle.

Mowgli watched him puff and blow with eyes that never changed. When he could make himself heard through the spattering mud, he said: "What Man-Pack lair here by the marshes, Mysa? This is new jungle to me."

"Go north, then," roared the angry bull, for Mowgli had pricked him rather sharply. "It was a naked cowherd's jest. Go and tell them at the village at the foot of the marsh."

"The Man-Pack do not love jungle-tales, nor do I think, Mysa, that a scratch more or less on thy hide is any matter for a council. But I will go and look at this village. Yes, I will go. Softly now. It is not every night that the Master of the Jungle comes to herd thee."

He stepped out to the shivering ground on the edge of the marsh, well knowing that Mysa would never charge over it, and laughed, as he ran, to think of the bull's anger.

"My strength is not altogether gone," he said. "It may be that the poison is not to the bone. There is a star sitting low yonder." He looked at it between his half-shut hands. "By the Bull that bought me, it is the Red Flower—the Red Flower that I lay beside before—before I came even to the first Seeonee Pack! Now that I have seen, I will finish the running."

The marsh ended in a broad plain where a light twinkled. It was a long time since Mowgli had concerned himself with the doings of men, but this night the glimmer of the Red Flower drew him forward.

"I will look," said he, "as I did in the old days, and I will see how far the Man-Pack has changed."

Forgetting that he was no longer in his own jungle, where he could do what he pleased, he trod carelessly through the dew-loaded grasses till he came to the hut where the light stood. Three or four yelping dogs gave tongue, for he was on the outskirts of a village.

"Ho!" said Mowgli, sitting down noiselessly, after sending back a deep wolf-growl that silenced the curs. "What comes will come. Mowgli, what hast thou to do any more with the lairs of the Man-Pack?" He rubbed his mouth, remembering where a stone had struck it years ago when the other Man-Pack had cast him out.

The door of the hut opened, and a woman stood peering out into the darkness. A child cried, and the woman said over her shoulder, "Sleep. It was but a jackal that waked the dogs. In a little time morning comes."

Mowgli in the grass began to shake as though he had fever. He knew that voice well, but to make sure he cried softly, surprised to find how man's talk came back, "Messua! O Messua!"

"Who calls?" said the woman, a quiver in her voice.

"Hast thou forgotten?" said Mowgli. His throat was dry as he spoke.

"If it be *thou,* what name did I give thee? Say!" She had half shut the door, and her hand was clutching at her breast.

"Nathoo! Ohé Nathoo!" said Mowgli, for, as you remember, that was the name Messua gave him when he first came to the Man-Pack.

"Come, my son," she called, and Mowgli stepped into the light, and looked full at Messua, the woman who had been good to him, and whose life he had saved from the Man-Pack so long before. She was older, and her hair was gray, but her eyes and her voice had not changed. Woman-like, she expected to find Mowgli where she had left him, and her eyes traveled upward in a puzzled way from his chest to his head, that touched the top of the door.

"My son," she stammered; and then, sinking to his feet: "But it is no longer my son. It is a Godling of the Woods! Ahai!"

As he stood in the red light of the oil-lamp, strong, tall, and beautiful, his long black hair sweeping over his shoulders, the knife swinging at his neck, and his head crowned with a wreath of white jasmine, he might easily have been mistaken for some wild god of a jungle legend. The child half asleep on a cot sprang up and shrieked aloud with terror. Messua turned to soothe him, while Mowgli stood still, looking in at the water-jars and the cooking-pots, the grain-bin, and all the other human belongings that he found himself remembering so well.

"What wilt thou eat or drink?" Messua murmured. "This is all thine. We owe our lives to thee. But art thou him I called Nathoo, or a Godling, indeed?"

"I am Nathoo," said Mowgli, "I am very far from my own place. I saw this light, and came hither. I did not know thou wast here."

"After we came to Kanhiwara," Messua said timidly, "the English would have helped us against those villagers that sought to burn us. Rememberest thou?"

"Indeed, I have not forgotten."

"But when the English Law was made ready, we went to the village of those evil people, and it was no more to be found."

"That also I remember," said Mowgli, with a quiver of his nostril.

"My man, therefore, took service in the fields, and at last—for, indeed, he was a strong man—we held a little land here. It is not so rich as the old village, but we do not need much—we two."

"Where is he—the man that dug in the dirt when he was afraid on that night?"

"He is dead—a year."

"And he?" Mowgli pointed to the child.

"My son that was born two Rains ago. If thou art a Godling, give him the Favor of the Jungle, that he may be safe among thy—thy people, as we were safe on that night."

She lifted up the child, who, forgetting his fright, reached out to play with the knife that hung on Mowgli's chest, and Mowgli put the little fingers aside very carefully.

"And if thou art Nathoo whom the tigers carried away," Messua went on, choking, "he is then thy younger brother. Give him an elder brother's blessing."

"*Hai-mai!* What do I know of the thing called a blessing? I am neither a Godling nor his brother, and—O mother, mother, my heart is heavy in me." He shivered as he set down the child.

"Like enough," said Messua, bustling among the cooking-pots. "This comes of running about the marshes by night. Beyond question, the fever has soaked thee to the marrow." Mowgli smiled a little at the idea of anything in the Jungle hurting him. "I will make a fire, and thou shalt drink warm milk. Put away the jasmine wreath: the smell is heavy in so small a place."

Mowgli sat down, muttering, with his face in his hands. All manner of strange feelings that he had never felt before were running over him, exactly as though he had been poisoned, and he felt dizzy and a little sick. He drank the warm milk in long gulps, Messua patting him on the shoulder from time to time, not quite sure whether he were her son Nathoo of the long ago days, or some wonderful Jungle being, but glad to feel that he was at least flesh and blood.

"Son," she said at last,—her eyes were full of pride,—"have any told thee that thou art beautiful beyond all men?"

"Hah?" said Mowgli, for naturally he had never heard anything of the kind. Messua laughed softly and happily. The look in his face was enough for her.

"I am the first, then? It is right, though it comes seldom, that a mother should tell her son these good things. Thou art very beautiful. Never have I looked upon such a man."

Mowgli twisted his head and tried to see over his own hard shoulder, and Messua laughed again so long that Mowgli, not knowing why, was forced to laugh with her, and the child ran from one to the other, laughing too.

"Nay, thou must not mock thy brother," said Messua, catching him to her breast. "When thou art one half as fair we will marry thee to the youngest daughter of a king, and thou shalt ride great elephants."

Mowgli could not understand one word in three of the talk here; the warm milk was taking effect on him after his long run, so he curled up and in a minute was deep asleep, and Messua put the hair back from his eyes, threw a cloth over him, and was happy. Jungle-fashion, he slept out the rest of that night and all the next day; for his instincts, which never wholly slept, warned him there was nothing to fear. He waked at last with a bound that shook the hut, for the cloth over his face made him dream of traps; and there he stood, his hand on his knife, the sleep all heavy in his rolling eyes, ready for any fight.

Messua laughed, and set the evening meal before him. There were only a few coarse cakes baked over the smoky fire, some rice, and a lump of sour preserved tamarinds–just enough to go on with till he could get to his evening kill. The smell of the dew in the marshes made him hungry and restless. He wanted to finish his spring running, but the child insisted on sitting in his arms, and Messua would have it that his long, blue-black hair must be combed out. So she sang, as she combed, foolish little baby-songs, now calling Mowgli her son, and now begging him to give some of his jungle power to the child. The hut door was closed, but Mowgli heard a sound he knew well, and saw Messua's jaw drop with horror as a great gray paw came under the bottom of the door, and Gray Brother outside whined a muffled and penitent whine of anxiety and fear.

"Out and wait! Ye would not come when I called," said Mowgli in jungle-talk, without turning his head, and the great gray paw disappeared.

"Do not–do not bring thy–thy servants with thee," said Messua. "I–we have always lived at peace with the Jungle."

"It is peace," said Mowgli, rising. "Think of that night on the road to Kanhiwara. There were scores of such folk before thee and behind thee. But I see that even in springtime the Jungle People do not always forget. Mother, I go."

Messua drew aside humbly–he was indeed a wood-god, she thought; but as his hand was on the door the mother in her made her throw her arms round Mowgli's neck again and again.

"Come back!" she whispered. "Son or no son, come back, for I love thee–Look, he too grieves."

The child was crying because the man with the shiny knife was going away.

"Come back again," Messua repeated. "By night or by day this door is never shut to thee."

Mowgli's throat worked as though the cords in it were being pulled, and his voice seemed to be dragged from it as he answered, "I will surely come back."

"And now," he said, as he put by the head of the fawning wolf on the threshold, "I have a little cry against thee, Gray Brother. Why came ye not all four when I called so long ago?"

"So long ago? It was but last night. I–we–were singing in the Jungle the new songs, for this is the Time of New Talk. Rememberest thou?"

"Truly, truly."

"And as soon as the songs were sung," Gray Brother went on earnestly, "I followed thy trail. I ran from all the others and followed hot-foot. But, O

Little Brother, what hast *thou* done, eating and sleeping with the Man-Pack?"

"If ye had come when I called, this had never been," said Mowgli, running much faster.

"And now what is to be?" said Gray Brother.

Mowgli was just going to answer when a girl in a white cloth came down some path that led from the outskirts of the village. Gray Brother dropped out of sight at once, and Mowgli backed noiselessly into a field of high-springing crops. He could almost have touched her with his hand when the warm, green stalks closed before his face and he disappeared like a ghost. The girl screamed, for she thought she had seen a spirit, and then she gave a deep sigh. Mowgli parted the stalks with his hands and watched her till she was out of sight.

"And now I do not know," he said, sighing in his turn. "*Why* did ye not come when I called?"

"We follow thee—we follow thee," Gray Brother mumbled, licking at Mowgli's heel. "We follow thee always, except in the Time of the New Talk."

"And would ye follow me to the Man-Pack?" Mowgli whispered.

"Did I not follow thee on the night our old Pack cast thee out? Who waked thee lying among the crops?"

"Ay, but again?"

"Have I not followed thee to-night?"

"Ay, but again and again, and it may be again, Gray Brother?"

Gray Brother was silent. When he spoke he growled to himself, "The Black One spoke truth."

"And he said?"

"Man goes to Man at the last. Raksha, our mother, said—"

"So also said Akela on the night of Red Dog," Mowgli muttered.

"So also says Kaa, who is wiser than us all."

"What dost thou say, Gray Brother?"

"They cast thee out once, with bad talk. They cut thy mouth with stones. They sent Buldeo to slay thee. They would have thrown thee into the Red Flower. Thou, and not I, hast said that they are evil and senseless. Thou, and not I—I follow my own people—didst let in the Jungle upon them. Thou, and not I, didst make song against them more bitter even than our song against Red Dog."

"I ask thee what *thou* sayest?"

They were talking as they ran. Gray Brother cantered on a while without replying, and then he said,—between bound and bound as it were,—"Man-cub—Master of the Jungle—Son of Raksha, Lair-brother to me—though I forget for a little while in the spring, thy trail is my trail, thy lair is my lair, thy kill is my kill, and thy death-fight is my death-fight. I speak for the Three. But what wilt thou say to the Jungle?"

"That is well thought. Between the sight and the kill it is not good to wait. Go before and cry them all to the Council Rock, and I will tell them what is in my stomach. But they may not come—in the Time of New Talk they may forget me."

"Hast thou, then, forgotten nothing?" snapped Gray Brother over his shoulder, as he laid himself down to gallop, and Mowgli followed, thinking.

At any other season the news would have called all the Jungle together with bristling necks, but now they were busy hunting and fighting and killing and singing. From one to another Gray Brother ran, crying, "The Master of the Jungle goes back to Man! Come to the Council Rock." And the happy, eager People only answered, "He will return in the summer heats. The Rains will drive him to lair. Run and sing with us, Gray Brother."

"But the Master of the Jungle goes back to Man," Gray Brother would repeat.

"Eee—Yoawa? Is the Time of New Talk any less sweet for that?" they would reply. So when Mowgli, heavy-hearted, came up through the well-remembered rocks to the place where he had been brought into the Council, he found only the Four, Baloo, who was nearly blind with age, and the heavy, cold-blooded Kaa coiled around Akela's empty seat.

"Thy trail ends here, then, Manling?" said Kaa, as Mowgli threw himself down, his face in his hands. "Cry thy cry." We be of one blood, thou and I—man and snake together."

"Why did I not die under Red Dog?" the boy moaned. "My strength is gone from me, and it is not any poison. By night and by day I hear a double step upon my trail. When I turn my head it is as though one had hidden himself from me that instant. I go to look behind the trees, and he is not there. I call and none cry again; but it is as though one listened and kept back the answer. I lie down, but I do not rest. I run the spring running, but I am not made still. I bathe, but I am not made cool. The kill sickens me, but I have no heart to fight except I kill. The Red Flower is in my body, my bones are water—and—I know not what I know."

"What need of talk?" said Baloo slowly, turning his head to where Mowgli lay. "Akela by the river said it, that Mowgli should drive Mowgli back to the Man-Pack. I said it. But who listens now to Baloo? Bagheera—where is Bagheera this night?—he knows also. It is the Law."

"When we met at Cold Lairs, Manling, I knew it," said Kaa, turning a little in his mighty coils. "Man goes to Man at the last, though the Jungle does not cast him out."

The Four looked at one another and at Mowgli, puzzled but obedient.

"The Jungle does not cast me out, then?" Mowgli stammered.

Gray Brother and the Three growled furiously, beginning, "So long as we live none shall dare—" But Baloo checked them.

"I taught thee the Law. It is for me to speak," he said; "and, though I cannot now see the rocks before me, I see far. Little Frog, take thine own trail; make thy lair with thine own blood and pack and people; but when there is need of foot or tooth or eye, or a word carried swiftly by night, remember, Master of the Jungle, the Jungle is thine at call."

"The Middle Jungle is thine also," said Kaa. "I speak for no small people."

"*Hai-mai,* my brothers," cried Mowgli, throwing up his arms with a sob. "I know not what I know! I would not go; but I am drawn by both feet. How shall I leave these nights?"

"Nay, look up, Little Brother," Baloo repeated. "There is no shame in this hunting. When the honey is eaten we leave the empty hive."

"Having cast the skin," said Kaa, "we may not creep into it afresh. It is the Law."

"Listen, dearest of all to me," said Baloo. "There is neither word nor will here to hold thee back. Look up! Who may question the Master of the Jungle? I saw thee playing among the white pebbles yonder when thou wast a little frog; and Bagheera, that bought thee for the price of a young bull newly killed, saw thee also. Of that Looking Over we two only remain; for Raksha, thy lair-mother, is dead with thy lair-father; the old Wolf Pack is long since dead; thou knowest whither Shere Khan went, and Akela died among the dholes, where, but for thy wisdom and strength, the second Seeonee Pack would also have died. There remains nothing but old bones. It is no longer the Man-cub that asks leave of his Pack, but the Master of the Jungle that changes his trail. Who shall question Man in his ways?"

"But Bagheera and the Bull that bought me," said Mowgli. "I would not—"

His words were cut short by a roar and a crash in the thicket below, and Bagheera, light, strong, and terrible as always, stood before him.

"*Therefore,*" he said, stretching out a dripping right paw, "I did not come. It was a long hunt, but he lies dead in the bushes now—a bull in his second year—the Bull that frees thee, Little Brother. All debts are paid now. For the rest, my word is Baloo's word." He licked Mowgli's foot. "Remember, Bagheera loved thee," he cried and bounded away. At the foot of the hill he cried again long and loud, "Good hunting on a new trail, Master of the Jungle! Remember, Bagheera loved thee."

"Thou hast heard," said Baloo. "There is no more. Go now; but first come to me. O wise Little Frog, come to me!"

"It is hard to cast the skin," said Kaa as Mowgli sobbed and sobbed, with his head on the blind bear's side and his arms round his neck, while Baloo tried feebly to lick his feet.

"The stars are thin," said Gray Brother, snuffing at the dawn-wind. "Where shall we lair to-day? for, from now, we follow new trails."

And this is the last of the Mowgli stories.

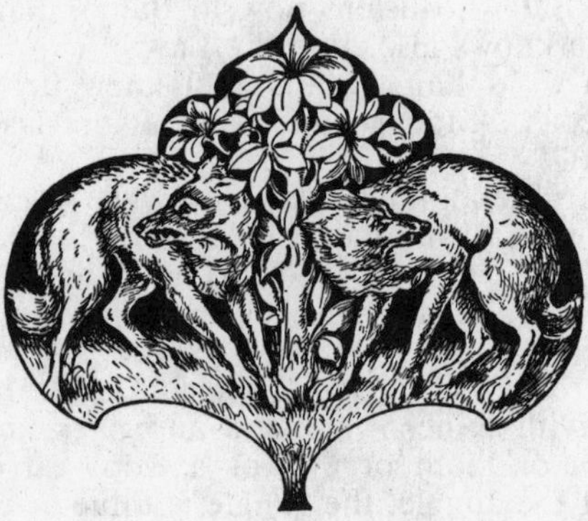

The Outsong

This is the song that Mowgli heard behind him in the Jungle till he came to Messua's door again:

Baloo—

For the sake of him who showed
One wise Frog the Jungle-Road,
Keep the Law the Man-Pack make–
For thy blind old Baloo's sake!
Clean or tainted, hot or stale,
Hold it as it were the Trail,
Through the day and through the night,
Questing neither left nor right.
For the sake of him who loves
Thee beyond all else that moves,
When thy Pack would make thee pain,
Say: "Tabaqui sings again."
When thy Pack would work thee ill,
Say: "Shere Khan is yet to kill."
When the knife is drawn to slay,
Keep the Law and go thy way.
(Root and honey, palm and spathe,
Guard a cub from harm and scathe!)
Wood and Water, Wind and Tree,
Jungle-Favor go with thee!

Kaa—

Anger is the egg of Fear–
Only lidless eyes are clear.
Cobra-poison none may leech;
Even so with Cobra-speech.
Open talk shall call to thee
Strength, whose mate is Courtesy.
Send no lunge beyond thy length;
Lend no rotten bough thy strength.
Gauge thy gape with buck or goat,
Lest thine eye should choke thy throat.
After gorging, wouldst thou sleep,
Look the den is hid and deep,
Lest a wrong, by thee forgot,
Draw thy killer to the spot.
East and West and North and South,
Wash thy hide and close thy mouth.
(Pit and rift and blue pool-brim,
Middle Jungle follow him!)
Wood and Water, Wind and Tree,
Jungle-Favor go with thee!

Bagheera—

In the cage my life began;
Well I know the worth of Man.
By the Broken Lock that freed—
Man-cub, 'ware the Man-cub's breed!
Scenting-dew or starlight pale,
Choose no tangled tree-cat trail.
Pack or council, hunt or den,
Cry no truce with Jackal-Men.
Feed them silence when they say:
"Come with us an easy way."
Feed them silence when they seek
Help of thine to hurt the weak.
Make no *bandar's* boast of skill;
Hold thy peace above the kill.
Let nor call nor song nor sign
Turn thee from thy hunting-line.
(Morning mist or twilight clear,
Serve him, Wardens of the Deer!)
Wood and Water, Wind and Tree,
Jungle-Favor go with thee!

The Three—

On the trail that thou must tread
To the thresholds of our dread,
Where the Flower blossoms red;
Through the nights when thou shalt lie
Prisoned from our Mother-sky,
Hearing us, thy loves, go by;
In the dawns, when thou shalt wake
To the toil thou canst not break,
Heartsick for the Jungle's sake:
Wood and Water, Wind and Tree,
Wisdom, Strength, and Courtesy,
Jungle-Favor go with thee!

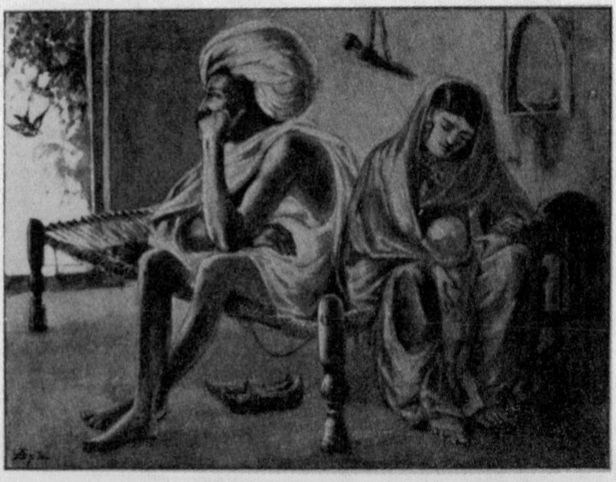

Just So Stories for Little Children

CONTENTS

How the Whale Got His Throat

In the sea, once upon a time, O my Best Beloved, there was a whale, and he ate fishes. He ate the starfish and the garfish, and the crab and the dab, and the plaice and the dace, and the skate and his mate, and the mackereel and the pickereel, and the really truly twirly-whirly eel. All the fishes he could find in all the sea he ate with his mouth—so! Till at last there was only one small fish left in all the sea, and he was a small 'Stute Fish, and he swam a little behind the Whale's right ear, so as to be out of harm's way. Then the Whale stood up on his tail and said, "I'm hungry." And the small 'Stute Fish said in a small 'stute voice, "Noble and generous Cetacean, have you ever tasted Man?"

"No," said the Whale. "What is it like?"

"Nice," said the small 'Stute Fish. "Nice but nubbly."

"Then fetch me some," said the Whale, and he made the sea froth up with his tail.

"One at a time is enough," said the 'Stute Fish. "If you swim to latitude Fifty North, longitude Forty West (that is Magic), you will find, sitting *on* a raft, *in* the middle of the sea, with nothing on but a pair of blue canvas breeches, a pair of suspenders (you must *not* forget the suspenders, Best Beloved), and a jack-knife, one shipwrecked Mariner, who, it is only fair to tell you, is a man of infinite-resource-and-sagacity."

So the Whale swam and swam to latitude Fifty North, longitude Forty West, as fast as he could swim, and *on* a raft, *in* the middle of the sea, *with* nothing to wear except a pair of blue canvas breeches, a pair of suspenders (you must particularly remember the suspenders, Best Beloved), *and* a jack-knife, he found one single, solitary shipwrecked Mariner, trailing his toes in the water. (He had his Mummy's leave to paddle, or else he would never have done it, because he was a man of infinite-resource-and-sagacity.)

Then the Whale opened his mouth back and back and back till it nearly touched his tail, and he swallowed the shipwrecked Mariner, and the raft he was sitting on, and his blue canvas breeches, and the suspenders (which you *must* not forget), *and* the jack-knife—He swallowed them all down into his warm, dark, inside cupboards, and then he smacked his lips—so, and turned round three times on his tail.

But as soon as the Mariner, who was a man of infinite-resource-and-sagacity, found himself truly inside the Whale's warm, dark, inside cupboards, he stumped and he jumped and he thumped and he bumped, and he pranced and he danced, and he banged and he clanged, and he hit and he bit, and he leaped and he creeped, and he prowled and he howled, and he hopped and he dropped, and he cried and he sighed, and he crawled and he bawled, and he stepped and he lepped, and he danced hornpipes where he

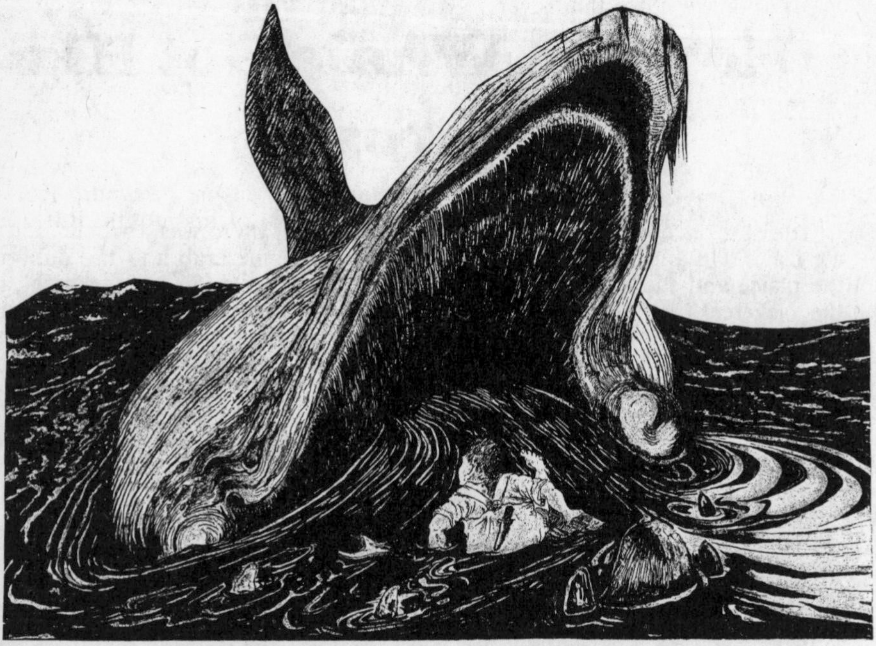

THIS IS THE PICTURE OF THE WHALE SWALLOWING THE MARINER WITH his infinite-resource-and-sagacity, and the raft and the jack-knife *and* his suspenders, which you must *not* forget. The buttony-things are the Mariner's suspenders, and you can see the knife close by them. He is sitting on the raft, but it has tilted up sideways, so you don't see much of it. The whity thing by the Mariner's left hand is a piece of wood that he was trying to row the raft with when the Whale came along. The piece of wood is called the jaws-of-a-gaff. The Mariner left it outside when he went in. The Whale's name was Smiler, and the Mariner was called Mr. Henry Albert Bivvens, A.B. The little 'Stute Fish is hiding under the Whale's tummy, or else I would have drawn him. The reason that the sea looks so ooshy-skooshy is because the Whale is sucking it all into his mouth so as to suck in Mr. Henry Albert Bivvens and the raft and the jack-knife and the suspenders. You must never forget the suspenders.

shouldn't, and the Whale felt most unhappy indeed. *(Have* you forgotten the suspenders?)

So he said to the 'Stute Fish, "This man is very nubbly, and besides he is making me hiccough. What shall I do?"

"Tell him to come out," said the 'Stute Fish.

So the Whale called down his own throat to the shipwrecked Mariner, "Come out and behave yourself. I've got the hiccoughs."

"Nay, nay!" said the Mariner. "Not so, but far otherwise. Take me to my natal-shore and the white-cliffs-of-Albion, and I'll think about it." And he began to dance more than ever.

"You had better take him home," said the 'Stute Fish to the Whale. "I ought to have warned you that he is a man of infinite-resource-and-sagacity."

So the Whale swam and swam and swam, with both flippers and his tail, as hard as he could for the hiccoughs; and at last he saw the Mariner's natal-shore and the white-cliffs-of-Albion, and he rushed half-way up the beach, and opened his mouth wide and wide and wide, and said, "Change here for Winchester, Ashuelot, Nashua, Keene, and stations on the *Fitch*burg Road"; and just as he said "Fitch" the Mariner walked out of his mouth. But while the Whale had been swimming, the Mariner, who was indeed a person of infinite-resource-and-sagacity, had taken his jack-knife and cut up the raft into a little square grating all running criss-cross, and he had tied it firm with his suspenders *(now* you know why you were not to forget the suspenders!), and he dragged that grating good and tight into the Whale's throat, and there it stuck! Then he recited the following *Sloka,* which, as you have not heard it, I will now proceed to relate—

By means of a grating
I have stopped your ating.

For the Mariner he was also an Hi-ber-ni-an. And he stepped out on the shingle, and went home to his Mother, who had given him leave to trail his toes in the water; and he married and lived happily ever afterward. So did the Whale. But from that day on, the grating in his throat, which he could neither cough up nor swallow down, prevented him eating anything except very, very small fish; and that is the reason why whales nowadays never eat men or boys or little girls.

The small 'Stute Fish went and hid himself in the mud under the Door-sills of the Equator. He was afraid that the Whale might be angry with him.

The Sailor took the jack-knife home. He was wearing the blue canvas breeches when he walked out on the shingle. The suspenders were left behind, you see, to tie the grating with; and that is the end of *that* tale.

When the cabin port-holes are dark and green
Because of the seas outside;
When the ship goes *wop* (with a wiggle between)
And the steward falls into the soup-tureen,
And the trunks begin to slide;
When Nursey lies on the floor in a heap,
And Mummy tells you to let her sleep,
And you aren't waked or washed or dressed,
Why, then you will know (if you haven't guessed)
You're "Fifty North and Forty West!"

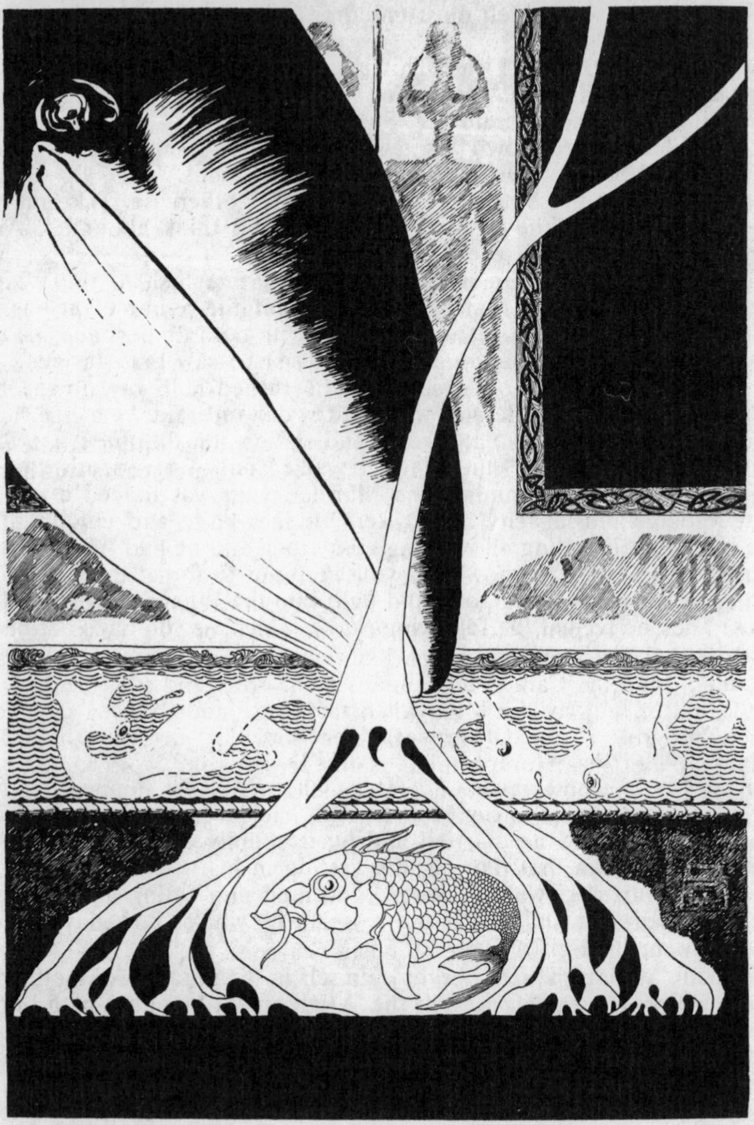

Here is the Whale looking for the little 'Stute Fish, who is hiding under the Door-sills of the Equator. The little 'Stute Fish's name was Pingle. He is hiding among the roots of the big seaweed that grows in front of the Doors of the Equator. I have drawn the Doors of the Equator. They are shut. They are always kept shut, because a door ought always to be kept shut. The ropy-thing right across is the Equator itself; and the things that look like rocks are the two giants Moar and Koar, that keep the Equator in order. They drew the shadow-pictures on the Doors of the Equator, and they carved all those twisty fishes under the Doors. The beaky-fish are called beaked Dolphins, and the other fish with the queer heads are called Hammer-headed Sharks. The Whale never found the little 'Stute Fish till he got over his temper, and then they became good friends again.

How the Camel Got His Hump

Now this is the next tale, and it tells how the Camel got his big hump.

In the beginning of years, when the world was so new-and-all, and the Animals were just beginning to work for Man, there was a Camel, and he lived in the middle of a Howling Desert because he did not want to work; and besides, he was a Howler himself. So he ate sticks and thorns and tamarisks and milkweed and prickles, most 'scruciating idle; and when anybody spoke to him he said "Humph!" Just "Humph!" and no more.

Presently the Horse came to him on Monday morning, with a saddle on his back and a bit in his mouth, and said, "Camel, O Camel, come out and trot like the rest of us."

"Humph!" said the Camel; and the Horse went away and told the Man.

Presently the Dog came to him, with a stick in his mouth, and said, "Camel, O Camel, come and fetch and carry like the rest of us."

"Humph!" said the Camel; and the Dog went away and told the Man.

Presently the Ox came to him, with the yoke on his neck, and said, "Camel, O Camel, come and plough like the rest of us."

"Humph!" said the Camel; and the Ox went away and told the Man.

At the end of the day the Man called the Horse and the Dog and the Ox together, and said, "Three, O Three, I'm very sorry for you (with the world so new-and-all); but that Humph-thing in the Desert can't work, or he would have been here by now, so I am going to leave him alone, and you must work double-time to make up for it."

That made the Three very angry (with the world so new-and-all), and they held a palaver, and an *indaba,* and a *punchayet,* and a pow-wow on the edge of the Desert; and the Camel came chewing milkweed *most* 'scruciating idle, and laughed at them. Then he said "Humph!" and went away again.

Presently there came along the Djinn in charge of All Deserts, rolling in a cloud of dust (Djinns always travel that way because it is Magic), and he stopped to palaver and pow-wow with the Three.

"Djinn of All Deserts," said the Horse, "*is* it right for any one to be idle, with the world so new-and-all?"

"Certainly not," said the Djinn.

"Well," said the Horse, "there's a thing in the middle of your Howling Desert (and he's a Howler himself) with a long neck and long legs, and he hasn't done a stroke of work since Monday morning. He won't trot."

"Whew!" said the Djinn, whistling, "that's my Camel, for all the gold in Arabia! What does he say about it?"

"He says 'Humph!' " said the Dog; "and he won't fetch and carry."

"Does he say anything else?"

"Only 'Humph!'; and he won't plough," said the Ox.

"Very good," said the Djinn. "I'll humph him if you will kindly wait a minute."

The Djinn rolled himself up in his dust-cloak, and took a bearing across the desert, and found the Camel most 'scruciatingly idle, looking at his own reflection in a pool of water.

"My long and bubbling friend," said the Djinn, "what's this I hear of your doing no work, with the world so new-and-all?"

"Humph!" said the Camel.

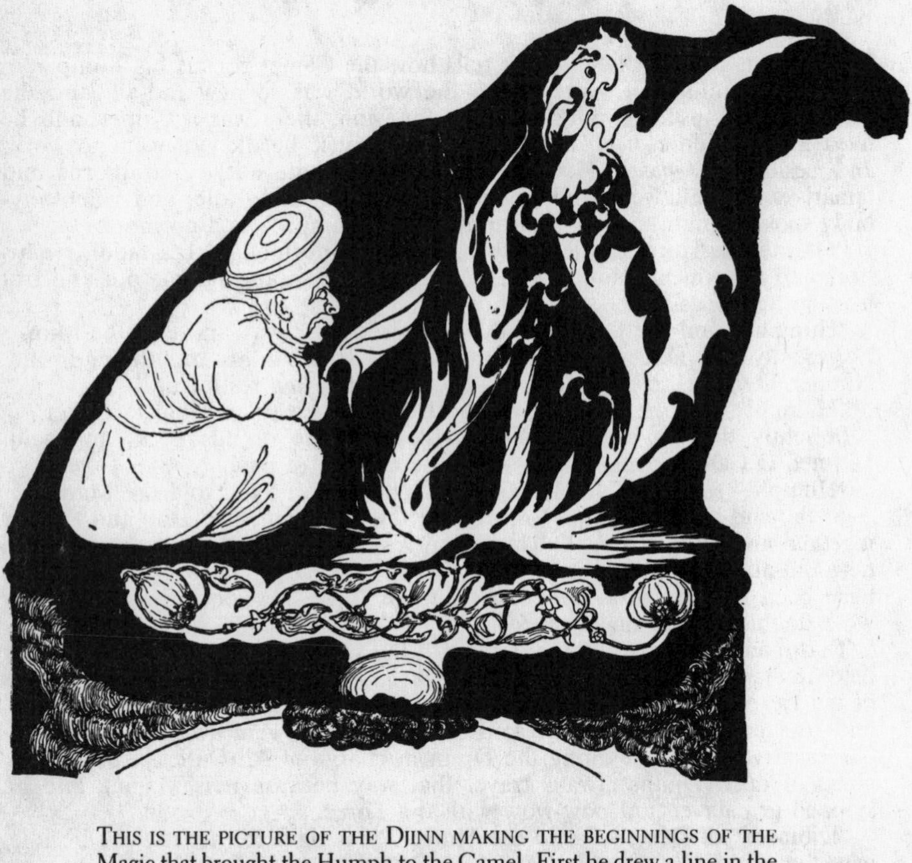

THIS IS THE PICTURE OF THE DJINN MAKING THE BEGINNINGS OF THE Magic that brought the Humph to the Camel. First he drew a line in the air with his finger, and it became solid; and then he made a cloud, and then he made an egg—you can see them at the bottom of the picture—and then there was a magic pumpkin that turned into a big white flame. Then the Djinn took his magic fan and fanned that flame till the flame turned into a Magic by itself. It was a good Magic and a very kind Magic really, though it had to give the Camel a Humph because the Camel was lazy. The Djinn in charge of All Deserts was one of the nicest of the Djinns, so he would never do anything really unkind.

The Djinn sat down, with his chin in his hand, and began to think a Great Magic, while the Camel looked at his own reflection in the pool of water.

"You've given the Three extra work ever since Monday morning, all on account of your 'scruciating idleness," said the Djinn; and he went on thinking Magics, with his chin in his hand.

"Humph!" said the Camel.

"I shouldn't say that again if I were you," said the Djinn; "you might say it once too often. Bubbles, I want you to work."

And the Camel said "Humph!" again; but no sooner had he said it than he saw his back, that he was so proud of, puffing up and puffing up into a great big lolloping humph.

"Do you see that?" said the Djinn. "That's your very own humph that you've brought upon your very own self by not working. To-day is Thursday, and you've done no work since Monday, when the work began. Now you are going to work."

"How can I," said the Camel, "with this humph on my back?"

"That's made a-purpose," said the Djinn, "all because you missed those three days. You will be able to work now for three days without eating, because you can live on your humph; and don't you ever say I never did anything for you. Come out of the Desert and go to the Three, and behave. Humph yourself!"

And the Camel humphed himself, humph and all, and went away to join the Three. And from that day to this the Camel always wears a humph (we call it "hump" now, not to hurt his feelings); but he has never yet caught up with the three days that he missed at the beginning of the world, and he has never yet learned how to behave.

The Camel's hump is an ugly lump
    Which well you may see at the Zoo;
But uglier yet is the hump we get
    From having too little to do.

Kiddies and grown-ups too-oo-oo,
If we haven't enough to do-oo-oo,
        We get the hump–
        Cameelious hump–
The hump that is black and blue!

We climb out of bed with a frouzly head
    And a snarly-yarly voice.
We shiver and scowl and we grunt and we growl
    At our bath and our boots and our toys;

And there ought to be a corner for me
(And I know there is one for you)
        When we get the hump–
        Cameelious hump–
The hump that is black and blue!

The cure for this ill is not to sit still,
    Or frowst with a book by the fire;
But to take a large hoe and a shovel also,
    And dig till you gently perspire;

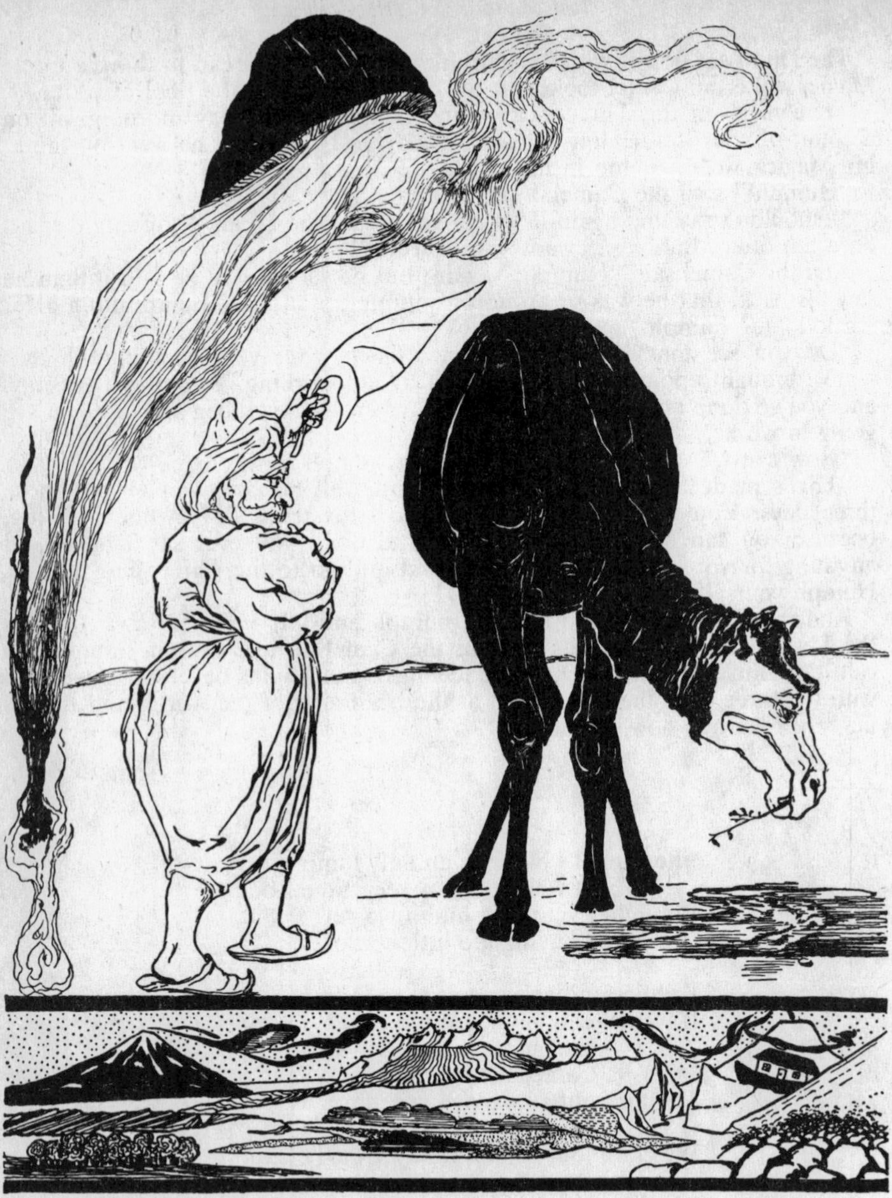

Here is the picture of the Djinn in charge of All Deserts guiding the Magic with his magic fan. The Camel is eating a twig of acacia, and he has just finished saying "humph" once too often (the Djinn told him he would), and so the Humph is coming. The long towelly-thing growing out of the thing like an onion is the Magic, and you can see the Humph on its shoulder. The Humph fits on the flat part of the Camel's back. The Camel is too busy looking at his own beautiful self in the pool of water to know what is going to happen to him.

Underneath the truly picture is a picture of the World-so-new-and-all. There are two smoky volcanoes in it, some other mountains and some stones and a lake and a black island and a twisty river and a lot of other things, as well as a Noah's Ark. I couldn't draw all the deserts that the Djinn was in charge of, so I only drew one, but it is a most deserty desert.

And then you will find that the sun and the wind,
And the Djinn of the Garden too,
Have lifted the hump—
The horrible hump—
The hump that is black and blue!

I get it as well as you-oo-oo—
If I haven't enough to do-oo-oo!
We all get hump—
Cameelious hump—
Kiddles and grown-ups too!

How the Rhinoceros Got His Skin

ONCE UPON A time, on an uninhabited island on the shores of the Red Sea, there lived a Parsee from whose hat the rays of the sun were reflected in more-than-oriental splendor. And the Parsee lived by the Red Sea with nothing but his hat and his knife and a cooking-stove of the kind that you must particularly never touch. And one day he took flour and water and currants and plums and sugar and things, and made himself one cake which was two feet across and three feet thick. It was indeed a Superior Comestible *(that's* Magic), and he put it on the stove because *he* was allowed to cook on that stove, and he baked it and he baked it till it was all done brown and smelt most sentimental. But just as he was going to eat it there came down to the beach from the Altogether Uninhabited Interior one Rhinoceros with a horn on his nose, two piggy eyes, and few manners. In those days the Rhinoceros's skin fitted him quite tight. There were no wrinkles in it anywhere. He looked exactly like a Noah's Ark Rhinoceros, but of course much bigger. All the same, he had no manners then, and he has no manners now, and he never will have any manners. He said, "How!" and the Parsee left that cake and climbed to the top of a palm-tree with nothing on but his hat, from which the rays of the sun were always reflected in more-than-oriental splendor. And the Rhinoceros upset the oil-stove with his nose, and the cake rolled on the sand, and he spiked that cake on the horn of his nose, and he ate it, and he went away, waving his tail, to the desolate and Exclusively Uninhabited Interior which abuts on the islands of Mazanderan, Socotra, and the Promontories of the Larger Equinox. Then the Parsee came down from his palm-tree and put the stove on its legs and recited the following *Sloka,* which, as you have not heard, I will proceed to relate:—

Them that takes cakes
Which the Parsee-man bakes
Makes dreadful mistakes.

And there was a great deal more in that than you would think.

Because, five weeks later, there was a heat-wave in the Red Sea, and everybody took off all the clothes they had. The Parsee took off his hat; but the Rhinoceros took off his skin and carried it over his shoulder as he came down to the beach to bathe. In those days it buttoned underneath with three

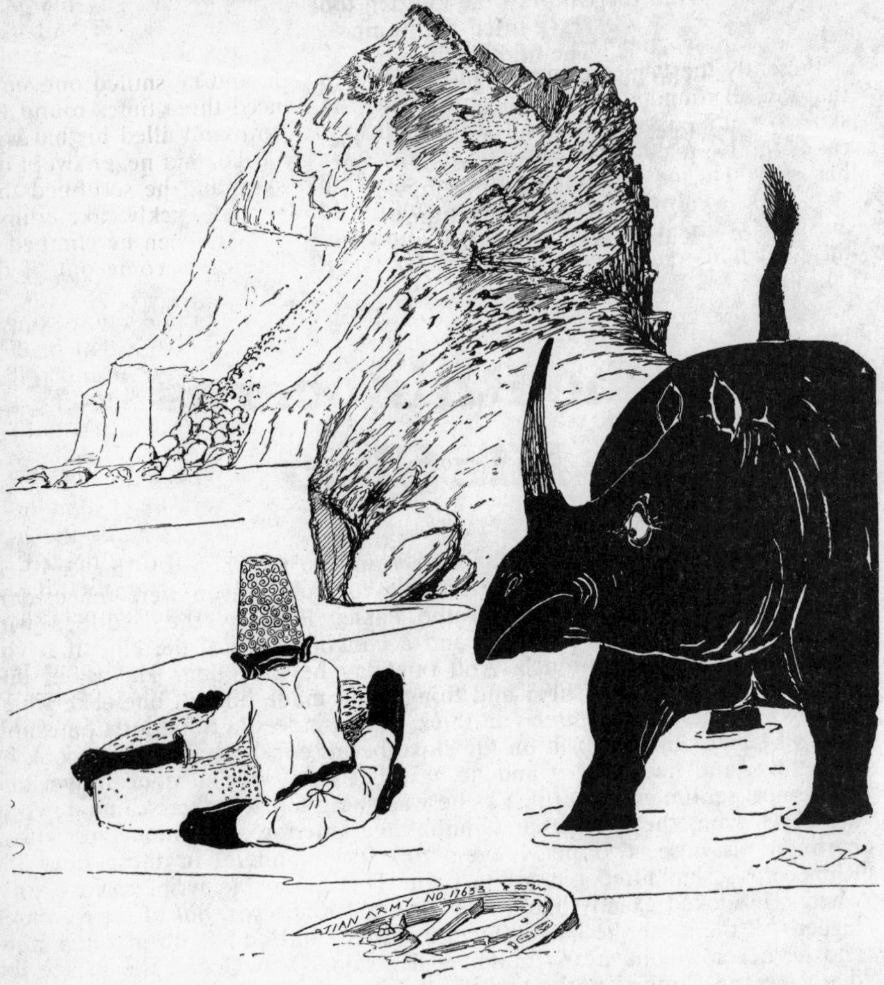

THIS IS THE PICTURE OF THE PARSEE BEGINNING TO EAT HIS CAKE ON THE Uninhabited Island in the Red Sea on a very hot day; and of the Rhinoceros coming down from the Altogether Uninhabited Interior, which, as you can truthfully see, is all rocky. The Rhinoceros's skin is quite smooth, and the three buttons that button it up are underneath, so you can't see them. The squiggly things on the Parsee's hat are the rays of the sun reflected in more-than-oriental splendour, because if I had drawn real rays they would have filled up all the picture. The cake has currants in it; and the wheel-thing lying on the sand in front belonged to one of Pharaoh's chariots when he tried to cross the Red Sea. The Parsee found it, and kept it to play with. The Parsee's name was Pestonjee Bomonjee, and the Rhinoceros was called Strorks, because he breathed through his mouth instead of his nose. I wouldn't ask anything about the cooking-stove if *I* were you.

buttons and looked like a waterproof. He said nothing whatever about the Parsee's cake, because he had eaten it all; and he never had any manners, then, since, or henceforward. He waddled straight into the water and blew bubbles through his nose, leaving his skin on the beach.

Presently the Parsee came by and found the skin, and he smiled one smile that ran all round his face two times. Then he danced three times round the skin and rubbed his hands. Then he went to his camp and filled his hat with cake-crumbs, for the Parsee never ate anything but cake, and never swept out his camp. He took that skin, and he shook that skin, and he scrubbed that skin, and he rubbed that skin just as full of old, dry, stale, tickly cake-crumbs and some burned currants as ever it could *possibly* hold. Then he climbed to the top of his palm-tree and waited for the Rhinoceros to come out of the water and put it on.

And the Rhinoceros did. He buttoned it up with the three buttons, and it tickled like cake-crumbs in bed. Then he wanted to scratch, but that made it worse; and then he lay down on the sands and rolled and rolled and rolled, and every time he rolled the cake-crumbs tickled him worse and worse and worse. Then he ran to the palm-tree and rubbed and rubbed and rubbed himself against it. He rubbed so much and so hard that he rubbed his skin into a great fold over his shoulders, and another fold underneath, where the buttons used to be (but he rubbed the buttons off), and he rubbed some more folds over his legs. And it spoiled his temper, but it didn't make the least difference to the cake-crumbs. They were inside his skin and they tickled. So he went home, very angry indeed and horribly scratchy; and from that day to this every rhinoceros has great folds in his skin and a very bad temper, all on account of the cake-crumbs inside.

But the Parsee came down from his palm-tree, wearing his hat, from which the rays of the sun were reflected in more-than-oriental splendor, packed up his cooking-stove, and went away in the direction of Orotavo, Amygdala, the Upland Meadows of Anantarivo, and the Marshes of Sonaput.

This Uninhabited Island
  Is off Cape Gardafui,
By the Beaches of Socotra
  And the Pink Arabian Sea:
But it's hot—too hot from Suez
  For the likes of you and me
    Ever to go
    In a P. and O.
  And call on the Cake-Parsee!

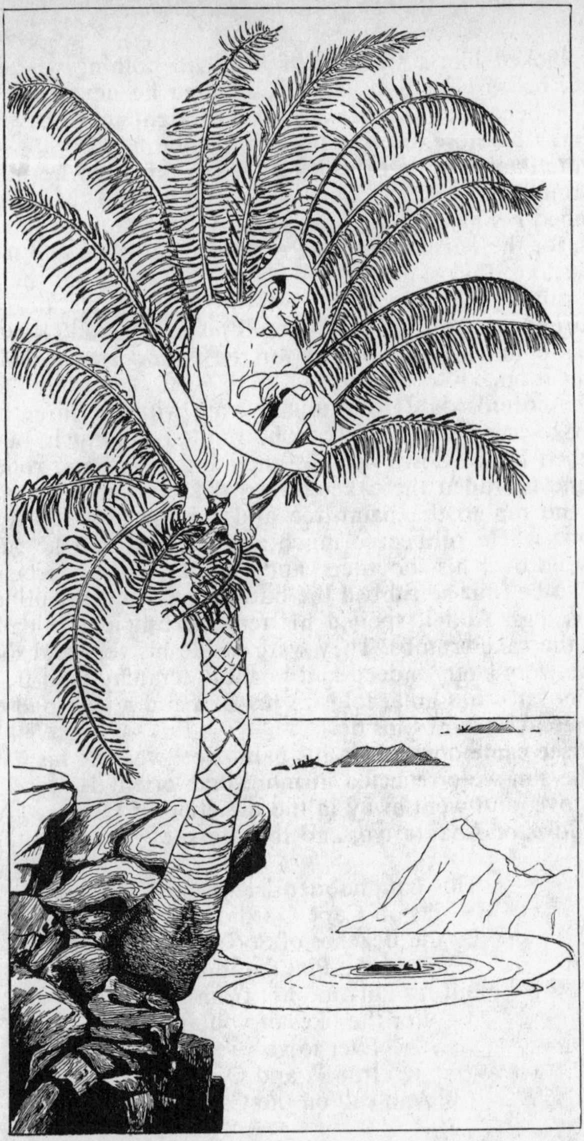

THIS IS THE PARSEE PESTONJEE BOMONJEE SITTING IN HIS PALM-TREE and watching the Rhinoceros Strorks bathing near the beach of the Altogether Uninhabited Island after Strorks had taken off his skin. The Parsee has rubbed the cake-crumbs into the skin, and he is smiling to think how they will tickle Strorks when Strorks puts it on again. The skin is just under the rocks below the palm-tree in a cool place; that is why you can't see it. The Parsee is wearing a new more-than-oriental-splendour hat of the sort that Parsees wear; and he has a knife in his hand to cut his name on palm-trees. The black things on the islands out at sea are bits of ships that got wrecked going down the Red Sea; but all the passengers were saved and went home.

The black thing in the water close to the shore is not a wreck at all. It is Strorks the Rhinoceros bathing without his skin. He was just as black underneath his skin as he was outside. I wouldn't ask anything about the cooking-stove if *I* were you.

How the Leopard Got His Spots

IN THE DAYS when everybody started fair, Best Beloved, the Leopard lived in a place called the High Veldt. 'Member it wasn't the Low Veldt, or the Bush Veldt, or the Sour Veldt, but the 'sclusively bare, hot, shiny High Veldt, where there was sand and sandy-colored rock and 'sclusively tufts of sandy-yellowish grass. The Giraffe and the Zebra and the Eland and the Koodoo and the Hartebeest lived there; and they were 'sclusively sandy-yellow-brownish all over; but the Leopard, he was the 'sclusivest sandiest-yellowest-brownest of them all—a grayish-yellowish catty-shaped kind of beast, and he matched the 'sclusively yellowish-grayish-brownish color of the High Veldt to one hair. This was very bad for the Giraffe and the Zebra and the rest of them; for he would lie down by a 'sclusively yellowish-grayish-brownish stone or clump of grass, and when the Giraffe or the Zebra or the Eland or the Koodoo or the Bush-Buck or the Bonte-Buck came by he would surprise them out of their jumpsome lives. He would indeed! And, also, there was an Ethiopian with bows and arrows (a 'sclusively grayish-brownish-yellowish man he was then), who lived on the High Veldt with the Leopard; and the two used to hunt together—the Ethiopian with his bows and arrows, and the Leopard 'sclusively with his teeth and claws—till the Giraffe and the Eland and the Koodoo and the Quagga and all the rest of them didn't know which way to jump, Best Beloved. They didn't indeed!

After a long time—things lived for ever so long in those days—they learned to avoid anything that looked like a Leopard or an Ethiopian; and bit by bit—the Giraffe began it, because his legs were the longest—they went away from the High Veldt. They scuttled for days and days and days till they came to a great forest, 'sclusively full of trees and bushes and stripy, speckly, patchy-blatchy shadows, and there they hid: and after another long time, what with standing half in the shade and half out of it, and what with the slippery-slidy shadows of the trees falling on them, the Giraffe grew blotchy, and the Zebra grew stripy, and the Eland and the Koodoo grew darker, with little wavy gray lines on their backs like bark on a tree trunk; and so, though you could hear them and smell them, you could very seldom see them, and then only when you knew precisely where to look. They had a beautiful time in the 'sclusively speckly-spickly shadows of the forest, while the Leopard and the Ethiopian ran about over the 'sclusively grayish-yellowish-reddish High Veldt outside, wondering where all their breakfasts and their dinners and their teas had gone. At last they were so hungry that they ate rats and beetles and rock-rabbits, the Leopard and the Ethiopian, and then they had the Big Tummy-ache, both together; and then they met Baviaan—the dog-headed, barking Baboon, who is Quite the Wisest Animal in All South Africa.

Said Leopard to Baviaan (and it was a very hot day), "Where has all the game gone?"

And Baviaan winked. *He* knew.

Said the Ethiopian to Baviaan, "Can you tell me the present habitat of the aboriginal Fauna?" (That meant just the same thing, but the Ethiopian always used long words. He was a grown-up.)

And Baviaan winked. *He* knew.

Then said Baviaan, "The game has gone into other spots; and my advice to you, Leopard, is to go into other spots as soon as you can."

And the Ethiopian said, "That is all very fine, but I wish to know whither the aboriginal Fauna has migrated."

Then said Baviaan, "The aboriginal Fauna has joined the aboriginal Flora because it was high time for a change; and my advice to you, Ethiopian, is to change as soon as you can."

That puzzled the Leopard and the Ethiopian, but they set off to look for the aboriginal Flora, and presently, after ever so many days, they saw a great, high, tall forest full of tree trunks all 'sclusively speckled and sprottled and spottled, dotted and splashed and slashed and hatched and cross-hatched with shadows. (Say that quickly aloud, and you will see how *very* shadowy the forest must have been.)

"What is this," said the Leopard, "that is so 'sclusively dark, and yet so full of little pieces of light?"

"I don't know," said the Ethiopian, "but it ought to be the aboriginal Flora. I can smell Giraffe, and I can hear Giraffe, but I can't see Giraffe."

"That's curious," said the Leopard. "I suppose it is because we have just come in out of the sunshine. I can smell Zebra, and I can hear Zebra, but I can't see Zebra."

"Wait a bit," said the Ethiopian. "It's a long time since we've hunted 'em. Perhaps we've forgotten what they were like."

"Fiddle!" said the Leopard. "I remember them perfectly on the High Veldt, especially their marrow-bones. Giraffe is about seventeen feet high, of a 'sclusively fulvous golden-yellow from head to heel; and Zebra is about four and a half feet high, of a 'sclusively gray-fawn color from head to heel."

"Umm," said the Ethiopian, looking into the speckly-spickly shadows of the aboriginal Flora-forest. "Then they ought to show up in this dark place like ripe bananas in a smoke-house."

But they didn't. The Leopard and the Ethiopian hunted all day; and though they could smell them and hear them, they never saw one of them.

"For goodness' sake," said the Leopard at tea-time, "let us wait till it gets dark. This daylight hunting is a perfect scandal."

So they waited till dark, and then the Leopard heard something breathing sniffily in the starlight that fell all stripy through the branches, and he jumped at the noise, and it smelt like Zebra, and it felt like Zebra, and when he knocked it down it kicked like Zebra, but he couldn't see it. So he said, "Be quiet, O you person without any form. I am going to sit on your head till morning, because there is something about you that I don't understand."

Presently he heard a grunt and a crash and a scramble, and the Ethiopian called out, "I've caught a thing that I can't see. It smells like Giraffe, and it kicks like Giraffe, but it hasn't any form."

"Don't you trust it," said the Leopard. "Sit on its head till the morning—same as me. They haven't any form—any of 'em."

So they sat down on them hard till bright morning-time, and then Leopard said, "What have you at your end of the table, Brother?"

The Ethiopian scratched his head and said, "It ought to be 'sclusively a rich fulvous orange-tawny from head to heel, and it ought to be Giraffe; but it is covered all over with chestnut blotches. What have you at *your* end of the table, Brother?"

And the Leopard scratched his head and said, "It ought to be 'sclusively a delicate grayish-fawn, and it ought to be Zebra; but it is covered all over with black and purple stripes. What in the world have you been doing to yourself, Zebra? Don't you know that if you were on the High Veldt I could see you ten miles off? You haven't any form."

"Yes," said the Zebra, "but this isn't the High Veldt. Can't you see?"

"I can now," said the Leopard. "But I couldn't all yesterday. How is it done?"

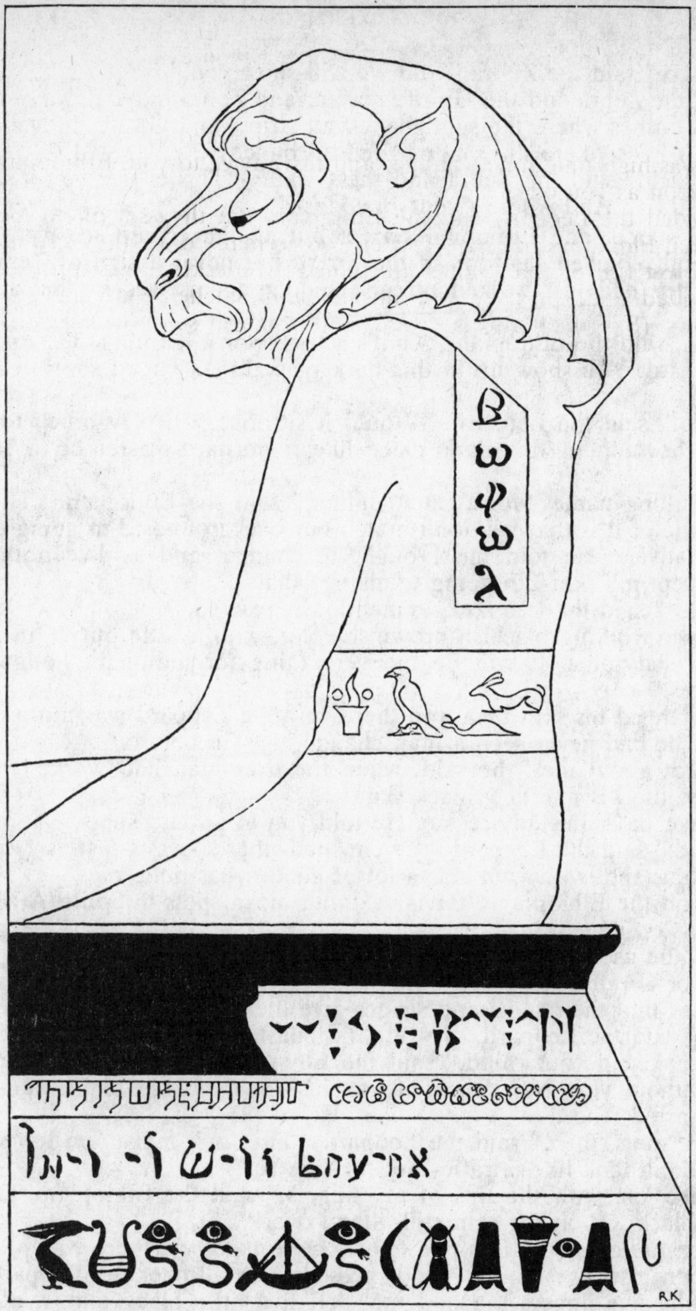

THIS IS WISE BAVIAAN, THE DOG-HEADED BABOON, WHO IS QUITE THE Wisest Animal in All South Africa. I have drawn him from a statue that I made up out of my own head, and I have written his name on his belt and on his shoulder and on the thing he is sitting on. I have written it in what is not called Coptic and Hieroglyphic and Cuneiformic and Bengalic and Burmic and Hebric, all because he is so wise. He is not beautiful, but he is very wise; and I should like to paint him with paint-box colours, but I am not allowed. The umbrella-ish thing about his head is his Conventional Mane.

"Let us up," said the Zebra, "and we will show you."

They let the Zebra and the Giraffe get up; and Zebra moved away to some little thorn-bushes where the sunlight fell all stripy, and Giraffe moved off to some tallish trees where the shadows fell all blotchy.

"Now watch," said the Zebra and the Giraffe. "This is the way it's done. One–two–three! And where's your breakfast?"

Leopard stared, and Ethiopian stared, but all they could see were stripy shadows and blotched shadows in the forest, but never a sign of Zebra and Giraffe. They had just walked off and hidden themselves in the shadowy forest.

"Hi! Hi!" said the Ethiopian. "That's a trick worth learning. Take a lesson by it, Leopard. You show up in this dark place like a bar of soap in a coal-scuttle."

"Ho! Ho!" said the Leopard. "Would it surprise you very much to know that you show up in this dark place like a mustard-plaster on a sack of coals?"

"Well, calling names won't catch dinner," said the Ethiopian. "The long and the little of it is that we don't match our backgrounds. I'm going to take Baviaan's advice. He told me I ought to change; and as I've nothing to change except my skin I'm going to change that."

"What to?" said the Leopard, tremendously excited.

"To a nice working blackish-brownish color, with a little purple in it, and touches of slaty-blue. It will be the very thing for hiding in hollows and behind trees."

So he changed his skin then and there, and the Leopard was more excited than ever; he had never seen a man change his skin before.

"But what about me?" he said, when the Ethiopian had worked his last little finger into his fine new black skin.

"You take Baviaan's advice too. He told you to go into spots."

"So I did," said the Leopard. "I went into other spots as fast as I could. I went into this spot with you, and a lot of good it has done me."

"Oh," said the Ethiopian, "Baviaan didn't mean spots in South Africa. He meant spots on your skin."

"What's the use of that?" said the Leopard.

"Think of Giraffe," said the Ethiopian. "Or if you prefer stripes, think of Zebra. They find their spots and stripes give them per-fect satisfaction."

"Umm," said the Leopard. "I wouldn't look like Zebra–not for ever so."

"Well, make up your mind," said the Ethiopian, "because I'd hate to go hunting without you, but I must if you insist on looking like a sun-flower against a tarred fence."

"I'll take spots, then," said the Leopard; "but don't make 'em too vulgar-big. I wouldn't look like Giraffe–not for ever so."

"I'll make 'em with the tips of my fingers," said the Ethiopian. "There's plenty of black left on my skin still. Stand over!"

Then the Ethiopian put his five fingers close together (there was plenty of black left on his new skin still) and pressed them all over the Leopard, and wherever the five fingers touched they left five little black marks, all close together. You can see them on any Leopard's skin you like, Best Beloved. Sometimes the fingers slipped and the marks got a little blurred; but if you look closely at any Leopard now you will see that there are always five spots–off five fat black fingertips.

"Now you *are* a beauty!" said the Ethiopian. "You can lie out on the bare ground and look like a heap of pebbles. You can lie out on the naked rocks and look like a piece of pudding-stone. You can lie out on a leafy branch and look like sunshine sifting through the leaves; and you can lie right across the center of a path and look like nothing in particular. Think of that and purr!"

"But if I'm all this," said the Leopard, "why didn't you go spotty too?"

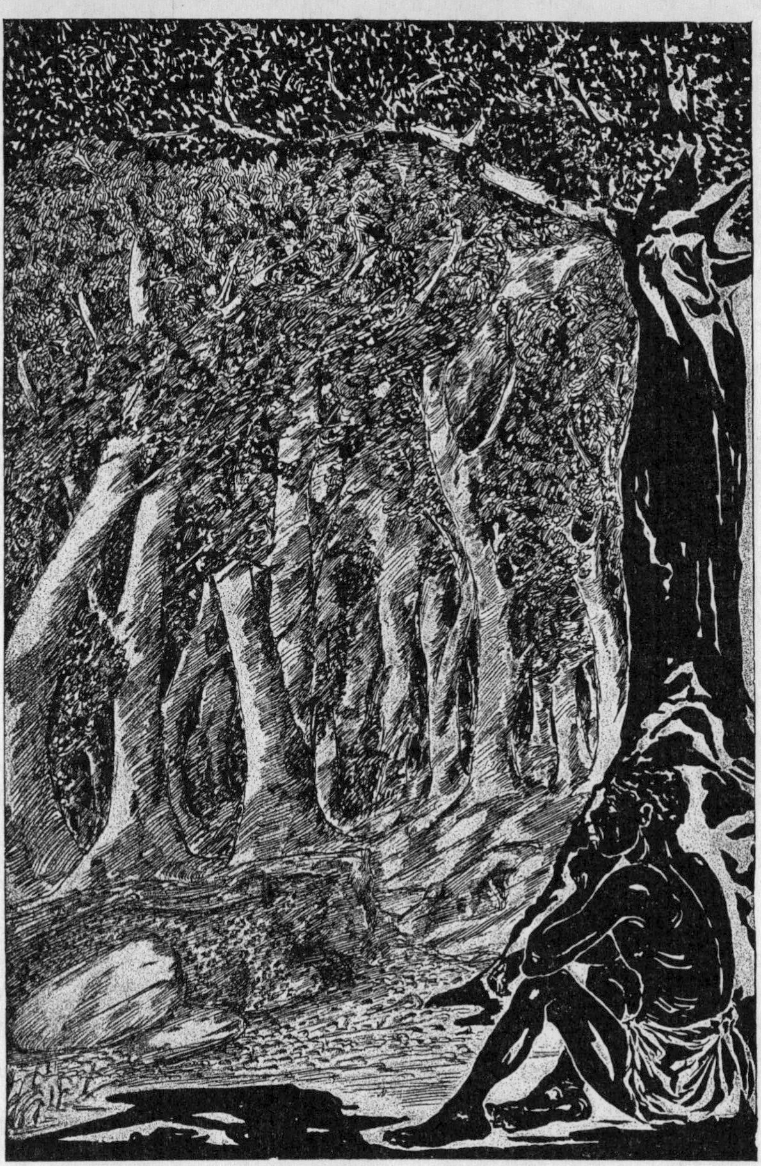

THIS IS THE PICTURE OF THE LEOPARD AND THE ETHIOPIAN AFTER THEY had taken Wise Baviaan's advice and the Leopard had gone into other spots and the Ethiopian had changed his skin. The Ethiopian was really a negro, and so his name was Sambo. The Leopard was called Spots, and he has been called Spots ever since. They are out hunting in the spickly-speckly forest, and they are looking for Mr. One-Two-Three-Where's-your-Breakfast. If you look a little you will see Mr. One-Two-Three not far away. The Ethiopian has hidden behind a splotchy-blotchy tree because it matches his skin, and the Leopard is lying beside a spickly-speckly bank of stones because it matches his spots. Mr. One-Two-Three-Where's-your-Breakfast is standing up eating leaves from a tall tree. This is really a puzzle-picture like "Find-the-Cat."

"Oh, plain black's best for a nigger," said the Ethiopian. "Now come along and we'll see if we can't get even with Mr. One-Two-Three-Where's-your-Breakfast!"

So they went away and lived happily ever afterward, Best Beloved. That is all.

Oh, now and then you will hear grown-ups say, "Can the Ethiopian change his skin or the Leopard his spots?" I don't think even grown-ups would keep on saying such a silly thing if the Leopard and the Ethiopian hadn't done it once—do you? But they will never do it again, Best Beloved. They are quite contented as they are.

I am the Most Wise Baviaan, saying in most wise tones,
"Let us melt into the landscape—just us two by our lones."
People have come—in a carriage—calling. But Mummy is there. . . .
Yes, I can go if you take me—Nurse says *she* don't care.
Let's go up to the pig-sties and sit on the farmyard rails!
Let's say things to the bunnies, and watch 'em skitter their tails!
Let's—oh, *anything,* daddy, so long as it's you and me,
And going truly exploring, and not being in till tea!
Here's your boots (I've brought 'em), and here's your cap and stick,
And here's your pipe and tobacco. Oh, come along out of it—quick!

The Elephant's Child

IN THE HIGH and Far-Off Times the Elephant, O Best Beloved, had no trunk. He had only a blackish, bulgy nose, as big as a boot, that he could wriggle about from side to side; but he couldn't pick up things with it. But there was one Elephant—a new Elephant—an Elephant's Child—who was full of 'satiable curtiosity, and that means he asked ever so many questions. *And* he lived in Africa, and he filled all Africa with his 'satiable curtiosities. He asked his tall aunt, the Ostrich, why her tail-feathers grew just so, and his tall aunt the Ostrich spanked him with her hard, hard claw. He asked his tall uncle, the Giraffe, what made his skin spotty, and his tall uncle, the Giraffe, spanked him with his hard, hard hoof. And still he was full of 'satiable curtiosity! He asked his broad aunt, the Hippopotamus, why her eyes were red, and his broad aunt, the Hippopotamus, spanked him with her broad, broad hoof; and he asked his hairy uncle, the Baboon, why melons tasted just so, and his hairy uncle, the Baboon, spanked him with his hairy, hairy paw. And *still* he was full of 'satiable curtiosity! He asked questions about everything that he saw, or heard, or felt, or smelt, or touched, and all his uncles and his aunts spanked him. And still he was full of 'satiable curtiosity!

One fine morning in the middle of the Precession of the Equinoxes this 'satiable Elephant's Child asked a new fine question that he had never asked before. He asked, "What does the Crocodile have for dinner?" Then everybody said, "Hush!" in a loud and dretful tone, and they spanked him immediately and directly, without stopping, for a long time.

By and by, when that was finished, he came upon Kolokolo Bird sitting in the middle of a wait-a-bit thorn-bush, and he said, "My father has spanked me, and my mother has spanked me; all my aunts and uncles have spanked me for my 'satiable curtiosity; and *still* I want to know what the Crocodile has for dinner!"

Then Kolokolo Bird said, with a mournful cry, "Go to the banks of the great gray-green, greasy Limpopo River, all set about with fever-trees, and find out."

That very next morning, when there was nothing left of the Equinoxes, because the Precession had preceded according to precedent, this 'satiable Elephant's Child took a hundred pounds of bananas (the little short red kind), and a hundred pounds of sugar-cane (the long purple kind), and seventeen melons (the greeny-crackly kind), and said to all his dear families, "Good-bye. I am going to the great gray-green, greasy Limpopo River, all set about with fever-trees, to find out what the Crocodile has for dinner." And they all spanked him once more for luck, though he asked them most politely to stop.

Then he went away, a little warm, but not at all astonished, eating melons, and throwing the rind about, because he could not pick it up.

He went from Graham's Town to Kimberley, and from Kimberley to Khama's Country, and from Khama's Country he went east by north, eating melons all the time, till at last he came to the banks of the great gray-green, greasy Limpopo River, all set about with fever-trees, precisely as Kolokolo Bird had said.

Now you must know and understand, O Best Beloved, that till that very week, and day, and hour, and minute, this 'satiable Elephant's Child had never seen a Crocodile, and did not know what one was like. It was all his 'satiable curtiosity.

The first thing that he found was a Bi-Colored-Python-Rock-Snake curled round a rock.

" 'Scuse me," said the Elephant's Child most politely, "but have you seen such a thing as a Crocodile in these promiscuous parts?"

"*Have* I seen a Crocodile?" said the Bi-Colored-Python-Rock-Snake, in a voice of dretful scorn. "What will you ask me next?"

" 'Scuse me," said the Elephant's Child, "but could you kindly tell me what he has for dinner?"

Then the Bi-Colored-Python-Rock-Snake uncoiled himself very quickly from the rock, and spanked the Elephant's Child with his scalesome, flail-some tail.

"That is odd," said the Elephant's Child, "because my father and my mother, and my uncle and my aunt, not to mention my other aunt, the Hippopotamus, and my other uncle, the Baboon, have all spanked me for my 'satiable curtiosity—and I suppose this is the same thing."

So he said good-bye very politely to the Bi-Colored-Python-Rock-Snake, and helped to coil him up on the rock again, and went on, a little warm, but not at all astonished, eating melons, and throwing the rind about, because he could not pick it up, till he trod on what he thought was a log of wood at the very edge of the great gray-green, greasy Limpopo River, all set about with fever-trees.

But it was really the Crocodile, O Best Beloved, and the Crocodile winked one eye—like this!

" 'Scuse me," said the Elephant's Child most politely, "but do you happen to have seen a Crocodile in these promiscuous parts?"

Then the Crocodile winked the other eye, and lifted half his tail out of the mud; and the Elephant's Child stepped back most politely, because he did not wish to be spanked again.

"Come hither, Little One," said the Crocodile. "Why do you ask such things?"

" 'Scuse me," said the Elephant's Child most politely, "but my father has spanked me, my mother has spanked me, not to mention my tall aunt, the Ostrich, and my tall uncle, the Giraffe, who can kick ever so hard, as well as my broad aunt, the Hippopotamus, and my hairy uncle, the Baboon, *and*

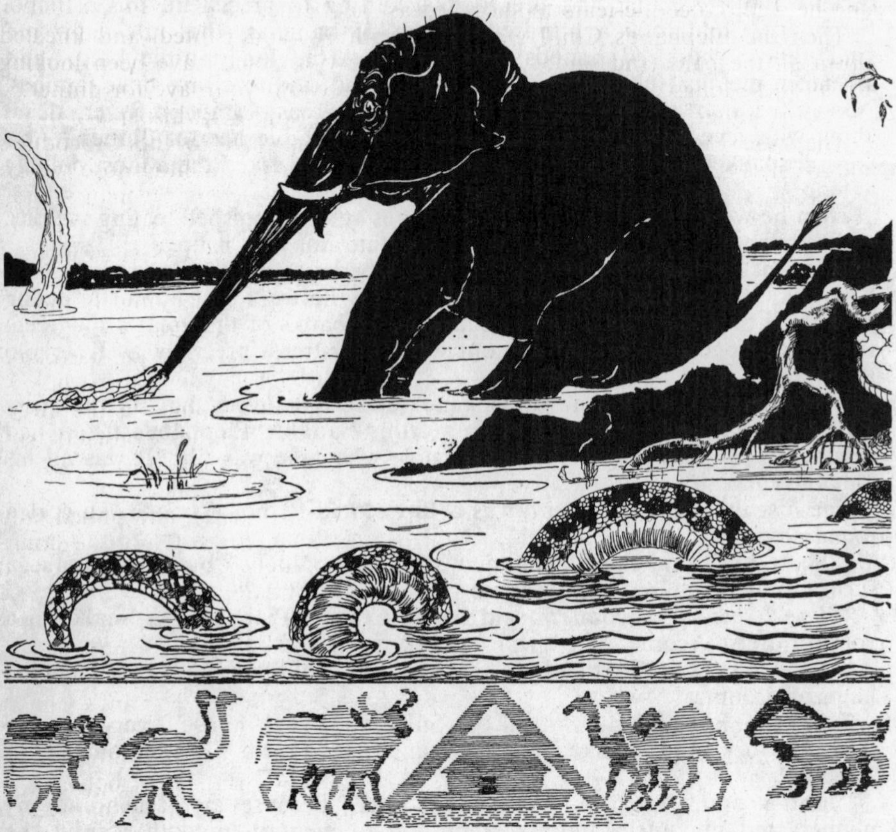

THIS IS THE ELEPHANT'S CHILD HAVING HIS NOSE PULLED BY THE Crocodile. He is much surprised and astonished and hurt, and he is talking through his nose and saying, "Led go! You are hurtig be!" He is pulling very hard, and so is the Crocodile; but the Bi-Coloured-Python-Rock-Snake is hurrying through the water to help the Elephant's Child. All that black stuff is the banks of the great grey-green, greasy Limpopo River (but I am not allowed to paint these pictures), and the bottly-tree with the twisty roots and the eight leaves is one of the fever trees that grow there.

Underneath the truly picture are shadows of African animals walking into an African ark. There are two lions, two ostriches, two oxen, two camels, two sheep, and two other things that look like rats, but I think they are rock-rabbits. They don't mean anything. I put them in because I thought they looked pretty. They would look very fine if I were allowed to paint them.

including the Bi-Colored-Python-Rock-Snake, with the scalesome, flailsome tail, just up the bank, who spanks harder than any of them; and *so,* if it's quite all the same to you, I don't want to be spanked any more."

"Come hither, Little One," said the Crocodile, "for I am the Crocodile," and he wept crocodile-tears to show it was quite true.

Then the Elephant's Child grew all breathless, and panted, and kneeled down on the bank and said, "You are the very person I have been looking for all these longs days. Will you please tell me what you have for dinner?"

"Come hither, Little One," said the Crocodile, "and I'll whisper."

Then the Elephant's Child put his head down close to the Crocodile's musky, tusky mouth, and the Crocodile caught him by his little nose, which up to that very week, day, hour, and minute, had been no bigger than a boot, though much more useful.

"I think," said the Crocodile—and he said it between his teeth, like this—"I think to-day I will begin with Elephant's Child!"

At this, O Best Beloved, the Elephant's Child was much annoyed, and he said, speaking through his nose, like this, "Led go! You are hurtig be!"

Then the Bi-Colored-Python-Rock-Snake scuffled down from the bank and said, "My young friend, if you do not now, immediately and instantly, pull as hard as ever you can, it is my opinion that your acquaintance in the large-pattern leather ulster" (and by this he meant the Crocodile) "will jerk you into yonder limpid stream before you can say Jack Robinson."

This is the way Bi-Colored-Python-Rock-Snakes always talk.

Then the Elephant's Child sat back on his little haunches, and pulled, and pulled, and pulled, and his nose began to stretch. And the Crocodile floundered into the water, making it all creamy with great sweeps of his tail, and *he* pulled, and pulled, and pulled.

And the Elephant's Child's nose kept on stretching; and the Elephant's Child spread all his little four legs and pulled, and pulled, and pulled, and his nose kept on stretching; and the Crocodile threshed his tail like an oar, and *he* pulled, and pulled, and pulled, and at each pull the Elephant's Child's nose grew longer and longer—and it hurt him hijjus!

Then the Elephant's Child felt his legs slipping, and he said through his nose, which was now nearly five feet long, "This is too butch for be!"

Then the Bi-Colored-Python-Rock-Snake came down from the bank, and knotted himself in a double-clove-hitch round the Elephant's Child's hind-legs, and said, "Rash and inexperienced traveller, we will now seriously devote ourselves to a little high tension, because if we do not, it is my impression that yonder self-propelling man-of-war with the armour-plated upper deck" (and by this, O Best Beloved, he meant the Crocodile) "will permanently vitiate your future career."

That is the way all Bi-Colored-Python-Rock-Snakes always talk.

So he pulled, and the Elephant's Child pulled, and the Crocodile pulled; but the Elephant's Child and the Bi-Colored-Python-Rock-Snake pulled hardest; and at last the Crocodile let go of the Elephant's Child's nose with a plop that you could hear all up and down the Limpopo.

Then the Elephant's Child sat down most hard and sudden; but first he was careful to say "Thank you" to the Bi-Colored-Python-Rock-Snake; and next he was kind to his poor pulled nose, and wrapped it all up in cool banana leaves, and hung it in the great gray-green, greasy Limpopo to cool.

"What are you doing that for?" said the Bi-Colored-Python-Rock-Snake.

"'Scuse me," said the Elephant's Child, "but my nose is badly out of shape, and I am waiting for it to shrink."

"Then you will have to wait a long time," said the Bi-Colored-Python-Rock-Snake. "Some people do not know what is good for them."

The Elephant's Child sat there for three days waiting for his nose to shrink. But it never grew any shorter, and, besides, it made him squint. For, O Best

Beloved, you will see and understand that the Crocodile had pulled it out into a really truly trunk same as all Elephants have to-day.

At the end of the third day a fly came and stung him on the shoulder, and before he knew what he was doing he lifted up his trunk and hit that fly dead with the end of it.

" 'Vantage number one!" said the Bi-Colored-Python-Rock-Snake. "You couldn't have done that with a mere-smear nose. Try and eat a little now."

Before he thought what he was doing the Elephant's Child put out his trunk and plucked a large bundle of grass, dusted it clean against his fore-legs, and stuffed it into his own mouth.

" 'Vantage number two!" said the Bi-Colored-Python-Rock-Snake. "You couldn't have done that with a mere-smear nose. Don't you think the sun is very hot here?"

"It is," said the Elephant's Child, and before he thought what he was doing he schlooped up a schloop of mud from the banks of the great gray-green, greasy Limpopo, and slapped it on his head, where it made a cool schloopy-sloshy mud-cap all trickly behind his ears.

" 'Vantage number three!" said the Bi-Colored-Python-Rock-Snake. "You couldn't have done that with a mere-smear nose. Now how do you feel about being spanked again?"

" 'Scuse me," said the Elephant's Child, "but I should not like it at all."

"How would you like to spank somebody?" said the Bi-Colored-Python-Rock-Snake.

"I should like it very much indeed," said the Elephant's Child.

"Well," said the Bi-Colored-Python-Rock-Snake, "you will find that new nose of yours very useful to spank people with."

"Thank you," said the Elephant's Child, "I'll remember that; and now I think I'll go home to all my dear families and try."

So the Elephant's Child went home across Africa frisking and whisking his trunk. When he wanted fruit to eat he pulled fruit down from a tree, instead of waiting for it to fall as he used to do. When he wanted grass he plucked grass up from the ground, instead of going on his knees as he used to do. When the flies bit him he broke off the branch of a tree and used it as a fly-whisk; and he made himself a new, cool, slushy-squshy mud-cap whenever the sun was hot. When he felt lonely walking through Africa he sang to himself down his trunk, and the noise was louder than several brass bands. He went especially out of his way to find a broad Hippopotamus (she was no relation of his), and he spanked her very hard, to make sure that the Bi-Colored-Python-Rock-Snake had spoken the truth about his new trunk. The rest of the time he picked up the melon rinds that he had dropped on his way to the Limpopo–for he was a Tidy Pachyderm.

One dark evening he came back to all his dear families, and he coiled up his trunk and said, "How do you do?" They were very glad to see him, and immediately said, "Come here and be spanked for your 'satiable curtiosity."

"Pooh," said the Elephant's Child. "I don't think you peoples know anything about spanking; but *I* do, and I'll show you."

Then he uncurled his trunk and knocked two of his dear brothers head over heels.

"O Bananas!" said they, "where did you learn that trick, and what have you done to your nose?"

"I got a new one from the Crocodile on the banks of the great gray-green, greasy Limpopo River," said the Elephant's Child. "I asked him what he had for dinner, and he gave me this to keep."

"It looks very ugly," said his hairy uncle, the Baboon.

"It does," said the Elephant's Child. "But it's very useful," and he picked up his hairy uncle, the Baboon, by one hairy leg, and hove him into a hornet's nest.

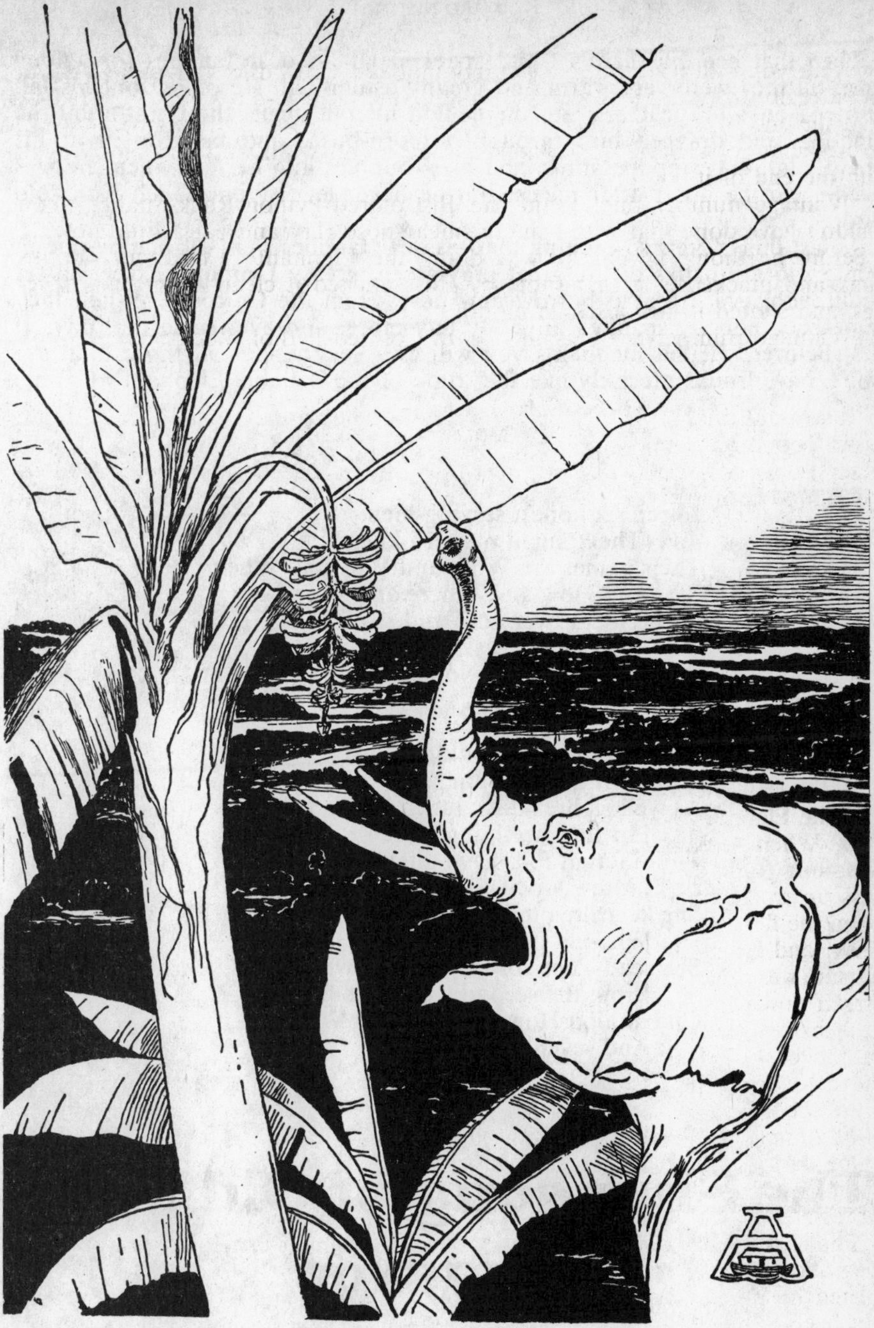

This is just a picture of the Elephant's Child going to pull bananas off a banana-tree after he had got his fine new long trunk. I don't think it is a very nice picture; but I couldn't make it any better, because elephants and bananas are hard to draw. The streaky things behind the Elephant's Child mean squoggy marshy country somewhere in Africa. The Elephant's Child made most of his mud-cakes out of the mud that he found there. I think it would look better if you painted the banana-tree green and the Elephant's Child red.

Then that bad Elephant's Child spanked all his dear families for a long time, till they were very warm and greatly astonished. He pulled out his tall Ostrich aunt's tail-feathers; and he caught his tall uncle, the Giraffe, by the hind-leg, and dragged him through a thorn-bush; and he shouted at his broad aunt, the Hippopotamus, and blew bubbles into her ear when she was sleeping in the water after meals; but he never let any one touch Kolokolo Bird.

At last things grew so exciting that his dear families went off one by one in a hurry to the banks of the great gray-green, greasy Limpopo River, all set about with fever-trees, to borrow new noses from the Crocodile. When they came back nobody spanked anybody any more; and ever since that day, O Best Beloved, all the Elephants you will ever see, besides all those that you won't, have trunks precisely like the trunk of the 'satiable Elephant's Child.

I keep six honest serving-men
(They taught me all I knew);
Their names are What and Why and When
And How and Where and Who.
I send them over land and sea,
I send them east and west;
But after they have worked for me,
I give them all a rest.

I let them rest from nine till five,
For I am busy then,
As well as breakfast, lunch, and tea,
For they are hungry men:
But different folk have different views;
I know a person small–
She keeps ten million serving-men,
Who get no rest at all!
She sends 'em abroad on her own affairs,
From the second she opens her eyes–
One million Hows, two million Wheres,
And seven million Whys!

The Sing-song of Old Man Kangaroo

NOT ALWAYS WAS the Kangaroo as now we do behold him, but a Different Animal with four short legs. He was gray and he was woolly, and his pride was inordinate: he danced on an outcrop in the middle of Australia, and he went to the Little God Nqa.

He went to Nqa at six before breakfast, saying, "Make me different from all other animals by five this afternoon."

Up jumped Nqa from his seat on the sand-flat and shouted, "Go away!"

He was gray and he was woolly, and his pride was inordinate: he danced on a rock-ledge in the middle of Australia, and he went to the Middle God Nquing.

He went to Nquing at eight before breakfast, saying, "Make me different from all other animals; make me, also, wonderfully popular by five this afternoon."

Up jumped Nquing from his burrow in the spinifex and shouted, "Go away!"

He was gray and he was woolly, and his pride was inordinate: he danced on a sandbank in the middle of Australia, and he went to the Big God Nqong.

He went to Nqong at ten before dinner-time saying, "Make me different from all other animals; make me popular and wonderfully run after by five this afternoon."

Up jumped Nqong from his bath in the salt-pan and shouted, "Yes, I will!"

Nqong called Dingo–Yellow-Dog Dingo–always hungry, dusty in the sunshine, and showed him Kangaroo. Nqong said, "Dingo! Wake up, Dingo! Do you see that gentleman dancing on an ashpit? He wants to be popular and very truly run after. Dingo, make him so!"

Up jumped Dingo–Yellow-Dog Dingo–and said, "What, *that* cat-rabbit?"

Off rang Dingo–Yellow-Dog Dingo–always hungry, grinning like a coal-scuttle,–ran after Kangaroo.

Off went the proud Kangaroo on his four little legs like a bunny.

This, O Beloved of mine, ends the first part of the tale!

He ran through the desert; he ran through the mountains; he ran through the salt-pans; he ran through the reed-beds; he ran through the blue gums; he ran through the spinifex; he ran till his front legs ached.

He had to!

Still ran Dingo–Yellow-Dog Dingo–always hungry, grinning like a rat-trap, never getting nearer, never getting farther,–ran after Kangaroo.

He had to!

Still ran Kangaroo–Old Man Kangaroo. He ran through the ti-trees; he ran through the mulga; he ran through the long grass; he ran through the short grass; he ran through the Tropics of Capricorn and Cancer; he ran till his hind legs ached.

He had to!

Still ran Dingo–Yellow-Dog Dingo–hungrier and hungrier, grinning like a horse-collar, never getting nearer, never getting farther; and they came to the Wollgong River.

Now, there wasn't any bridge, and there wasn't any ferry-boat, and Kangaroo didn't know how to get over; so he stood on his legs and hopped.

He had to!

He hopped through the Flinders; he hopped through the Cinders; he hopped through the deserts in the middle of Australia. He hopped like a Kangaroo.

First he hopped one yard; then he hopped three yards; then he hopped five yards; his legs growing stronger; his legs growing longer. He hadn't any time for rest or refreshment, and he wanted them very much.

Still ran Dingo–Yellow-Dog Dingo–very much bewildered, very much hungry, and wondering what in the world or out of it made Old Man Kangaroo hop.

For he hopped like a cricket; like a pea in a saucepan; or a new rubber ball on a nursery floor.

He had to!

He tucked up his front legs; he hopped on his hind legs; he stuck out his tail for a balance-weight behind him; and he hopped through the Darling Downs.

He had to!

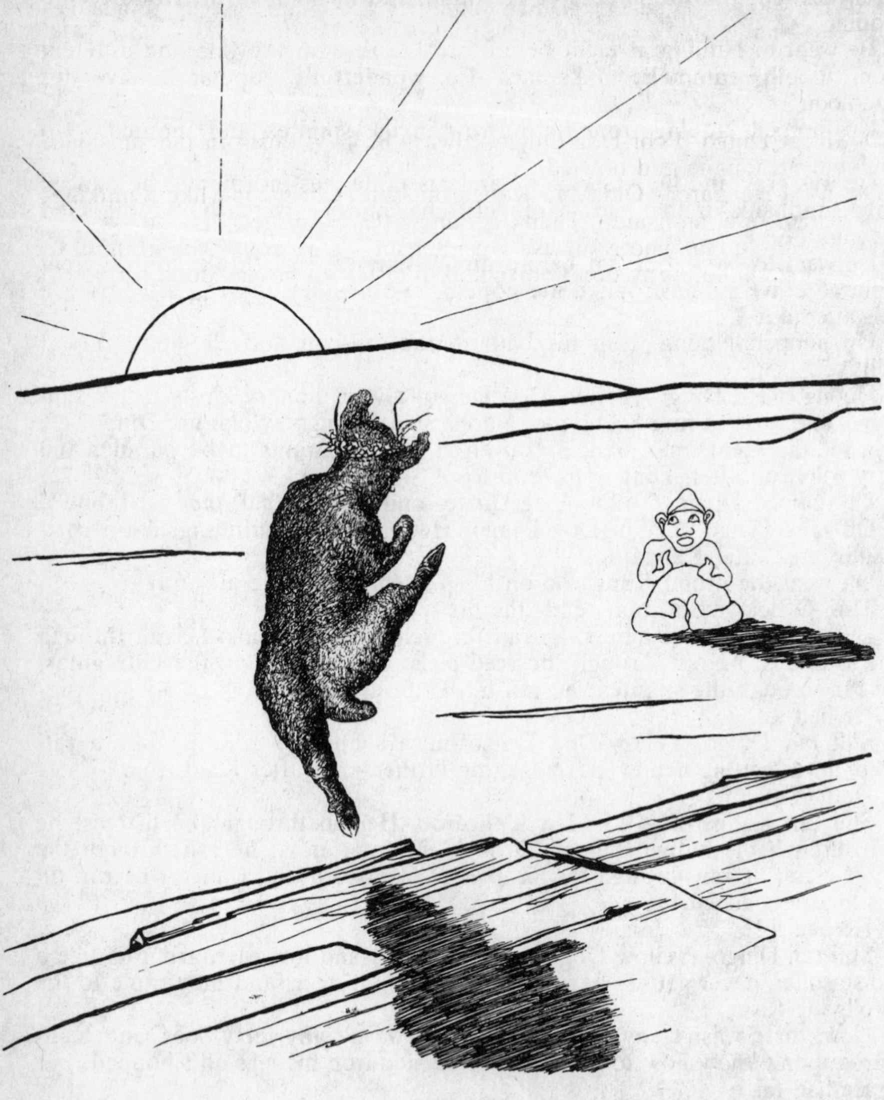

This is a picture of Old Man Kangaroo when he was the Different Animal with four short legs. I have drawn him grey and woolly, and you can see that he is very proud because he has a wreath of flowers in his hair. He is dancing on an outcrop (that means a ledge of rock) in the middle of Australia at six o'clock before breakfast. You can see that it is six o'clock, because the sun is just getting up. The thing with the ears and the open mouth is Little God Nqa. Nqa is very much surprised, because he has never seen a Kangaroo dance like that before. Little God Nqa is just saying, "Go away," but the Kangaroo is so busy dancing that he has not heard him yet.

The Kangaroo hasn't any real name except Boomer. He lost it because he was so proud.

Still ran Dingo—Tired-Dog Dingo—hungrier and hungrier, very much bewildered, and wondering when in the world or out of it would Old Man Kangaroo stop.

Then came Nqong from his bath in the salt-pans, and said, "It's five o'clock."

Down sat Dingo—Poor-Dog Dingo—always hungry, dusty in the sunshine; hung out his tongue and howled.

Down sat Kangaroo—Old Man Kangaroo—stuck out his tail like a milking-stool behind him, and said, "Thank goodness *that's* finished!"

Then said Nqong, who is always a gentleman, "Why aren't you grateful to Yellow-Dog Dingo? Why don't you thank him for all he has done for you?"

Then said Kangaroo—Tired Old Kangaroo—"He's chased me out of the homes of my childhood; he's chased me out of my regular meal-times; he's altered my shape so I'll never get it back; and he's played Old Scratch with my legs."

Then said Nqong, "Perhaps I'm mistaken, but didn't you ask me to make you different from all other animals, as well as to make you very truly sought after? And now it is five o'clock."

"Yes," said Kangaroo. "I wish that I hadn't. I thought you would do it by charms and incantations, but this is a practical joke."

"Joke!" said Nqong, from his bath in the blue gums. "Say that again and I'll whistle up Dingo and run your hind legs off."

"No," said the Kangaroo. "I must apologize. Legs are legs, and you needn't alter 'em so far as I am concerned. I only meant to explain to Your Lordliness that I've had nothing to eat since morning, and I'm very empty indeed."

"Yes," said Dingo—Yellow-Dog Dingo,—"I am just in the same situation. I've made him different from all other animals; but what may I have for my tea?"

Then said Nqong from his bath in the salt-pan, "Come and ask me about it to-morrow, because I'm going to wash."

So they were left in the middle of Australia, Old Man Kangaroo and Yellow-Dog Dingo, and each said, "That's *your* fault."

This is the mouth-filling song
Of the race that was run by a Boomer,
Run in a single burst—only event of its kind—
Started by Big God Nqong from Warrigaborrigarooma,
Old Man Kangaroo first: Yellow-Dog Dingo behind.

Kangaroo bounded away,
His back-legs working like pistons—
Bounded from morning till dark,
Twenty-five feet to a bound.
Yellow-Dog Dingo lay
Like a yellow cloud in the distance—
Much too busy to bark.
My! but they covered the ground!

Nobody knows where they went,
Or followed the track that they flew in,
For that Continent
Hadn't been given a name.
They ran thirty degrees,
From Torres Straits to the Leeuwin
(Look at the Atlas, please),
And they ran back as they came.

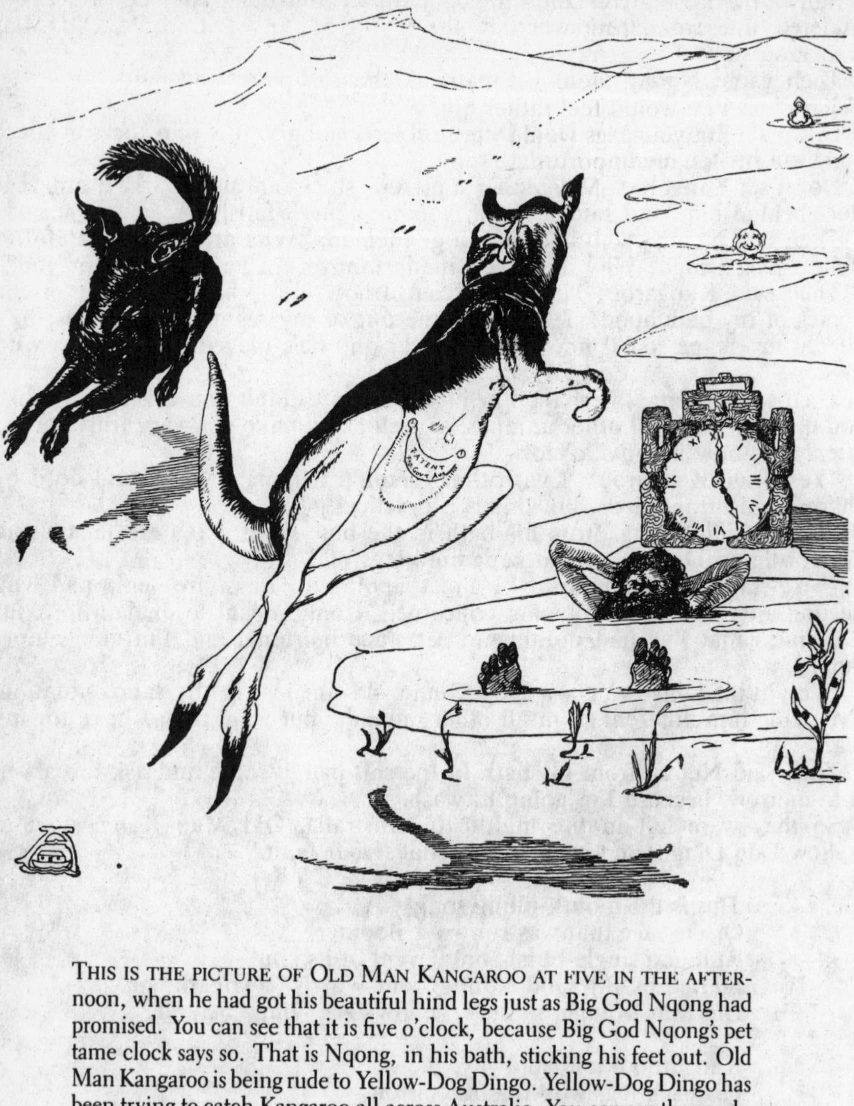

THIS IS THE PICTURE OF OLD MAN KANGAROO AT FIVE IN THE AFTERNOON, when he had got his beautiful hind legs just as Big God Nqong had promised. You can see that it is five o'clock, because Big God Nqong's pet tame clock says so. That is Nqong, in his bath, sticking his feet out. Old Man Kangaroo is being rude to Yellow-Dog Dingo. Yellow-Dog Dingo has been trying to catch Kangaroo all across Australia. You can see the marks of Kangaroo's big new feet running ever so far back over the bare hills. Yellow-Dog Dingo is drawn black, because I am not allowed to paint these pictures with real colours out of the paint-box; and besides, Yellow-Dog Dingo got dreadfully black and dusty after running through the Flinders and the Cinders.

I don't know the names of the flowers growing round Nqong's bath. The two little squatty things out in the desert are the other two gods that Old Man Kangaroo spoke to early in the morning. That thing with the letters on it is Old Man Kangaroo's pouch. He had to have a pouch just as he had to have legs.

S'posing you could trot
From Adelaide to the Pacific,
For an afternoon's run–
Half what these gentlemen did–
You would feel rather hot,
But your legs would develop terrific–
Yes, my importunate son,
You'd be a Marvellous Kid!

The Beginning of the Armadilloes

THIS, O BEST Beloved, is another story of the High and Far-Off Times. In the very middle of those times was a Stickly-Prickly Hedgehog, and he lived on the banks of the turbid Amazon, eating shelly snails and things. And he had a friend, a Slow-Solid Tortoise, who lived on the banks of the turbid Amazon, eating green lettuces and things. And so *that* was all right, Best Beloved. Do you see?

But also, and at the same time, in those High and Far-Off Times, there was a Painted Jaguar, and he lived on the banks of the turbid Amazon too; and he ate everything that he could catch. When he could not catch deer or monkeys he would eat frogs and beetles; and when he could not catch frogs and beetles he went to his Mother Jaguar, and she told him how to eat hedgehogs and tortoises.

She said to him ever so many times, graciously waving her tail, "My son, when you find a Hedgehog you must drop him into the water and then he will uncoil, and when you catch a Tortoise you must scoop him out of his shell with your paw." And so that was all right, Best Beloved.

One beautiful night on the banks of the turbid Amazon, Painted Jaguar found Stickly-Prickly Hedgehog and Slow-Solid Tortoise sitting under the trunk of a fallen tree. They could not run away, and so Stickly-Prickly curled himself up into a ball, because he was a Hedgehog, and Slow-Solid Tortoise drew in his head and feet into his shell as far as they would go, because he was a Tortoise; and so *that* was all right, Best Beloved. Do you see?

"Now attend to me," said Painted Jaguar, "because this is very important. My mother said that when I meet a Hedgehog I am to drop him into the water and then he will uncoil, and when I meet a Tortoise I am to scoop him out of his shell with my paw. Now which of you is Hedgehog and which is Tortoise? because, to save my spots, I can't tell."

"Are you sure of what your Mummy told you?" said Stickly-Prickly Hedgehog. "Are you quite sure? Perhaps she said that when you uncoil a Tortoise you must shell him out of the water with a scoop, and when you paw a Hedgehog you must drop him on the shell."

"Are you sure of what your Mummy told you?" said Slow-and-Solid Tortoise. "Are you quite sure? Perhaps she said that when you water a Hedgehog you must drop him into your paw, and when you meet a Tortoise you must shell him till he uncoils."

"I don't think it was at all like that," said Painted Jaguar, but he felt a little puzzled; "but, please, say it again more distinctly."

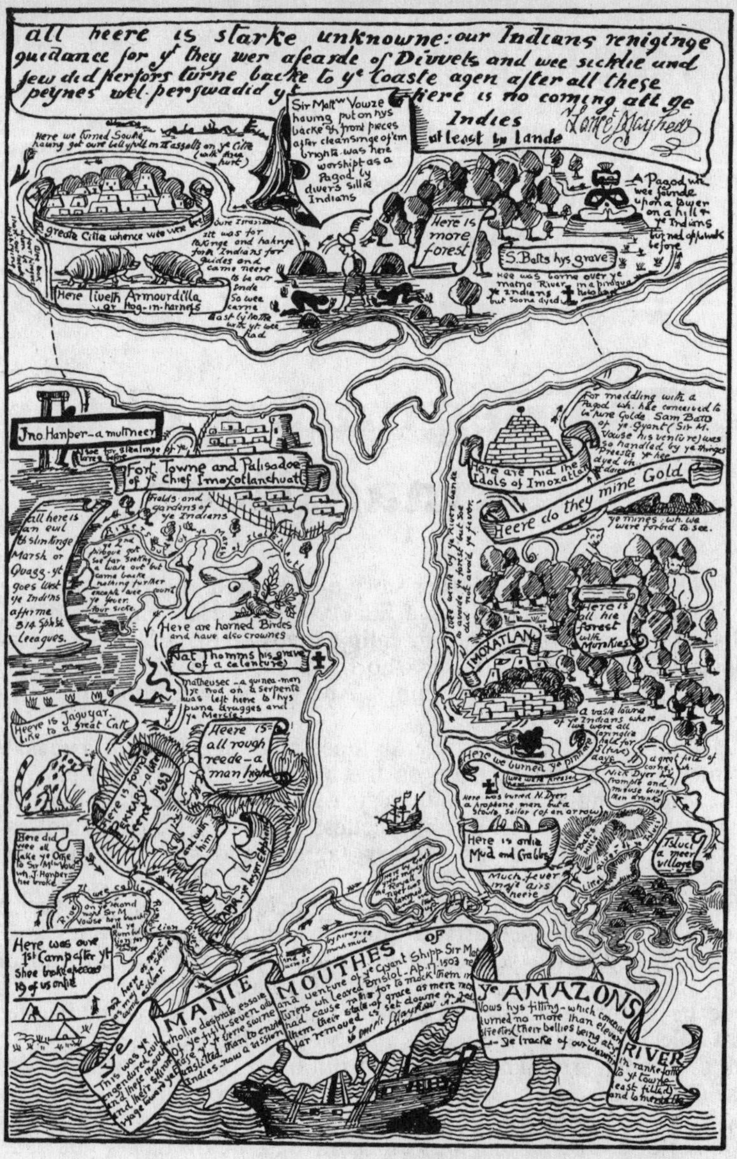

THIS IS AN INCITING MAP OF THE TURBID AMAZON DONE IN RED AND Black. It hasn't anything to do with the story except that there are two Armadilloes in it—up by the top. The inciting part are the adventures that happened to the men who went along the road marked in red. I meant to draw Armadilloes when I began the map, and I meant to draw manatees and spider-tailed monkeys and big snakes and lots of Jaguars, but it was more inciting to do the map and the venturesome adventures in red. You begin at the bottom left-hand corner and follow the little arrows all about, and then you come quite round again to where the adventuresome people went home in a ship called the *Royal Tiger*. This is a most adventuresome picture, and all the adventures are told about in writing, so you can be quite sure which is an adventure and which is a tree or a boat.

"When you scoop water with your paw you uncoil it with a Hedgehog," said Stickly-Prickly. "Remember that, because it's important."

"But," said the Tortoise, "when you paw your meat you drop it into a Tortoise with a scoop. Why can't you understand?"

"You are making my spots ache," said Painted Jaguar; "and besides, I didn't want your advice at all. I only wanted to know which of you is Hedgehog and which is Tortoise."

"I shan't tell you," said Stickly-Prickly. "But you can scoop me out of my shell if you like."

"Aha!" said Painted Jaguar. "Now I know you're Tortoise. You thought I wouldn't! Now I will." Painted Jaguar darted out his paddy-paw just as Stickly-Prickly curled himself up, and of course Jaguar's paddy-paw was just filled with prickles. Worse than that, he knocked Stickly-Prickly away and away into the woods and the bushes, where it was too dark to find him. Then he put his paddy-paw into his mouth, and of course the prickles hurt him worse than ever. As soon as he could speak he said, "Now I know he isn't Tortoise at all. But"—and then he scratched his head with his un-prickly paw—"how do I know that this other is Tortoise?"

"But I *am* Tortoise," said Slow-and-Solid. "Your mother was quite right. She said that you were to scoop me out of my shell with your paw. Begin."

"You didn't say she said that a minute ago," said Painted Jaguar, sucking the prickles out of his paddy-paw. "You said she said something quite different."

"Well, suppose you say that I said that she said something quite different, I don't see that it makes any difference; because if she said what you said I said she said, it's just the same as if I said what she said she said. On the other hand, if you think she said that you were to uncoil me with a scoop, instead of pawing me into drops with a shell, I can't help that, can I?"

"But you said you wanted to be scooped out of your shell with my paw," said Painted Jaguar.

"If you'll think again you'll find that I didn't say anything of the kind. I said that your mother said that you were to scoop me out of my shell," said Slow-and-Solid.

"What will happen if I do?" said the Jaguar most sniffily and most cautious.

"I don't know, because I've never been scooped out of my shell before; but I tell you truly, if you want to see me swim away you've only got to drop me into the water."

"I don't believe it," said Painted Jaguar. "You've mixed up all the things my mother told me to do with the things that you asked me whether I was sure that she didn't say, till I don't know whether I'm on my head or my painted tail; and now you come and tell me something I *can* understand, and it makes me more mixy than before. My mother told me that I was to drop one of you two into the water, and as you seem so anxious to be dropped I think you don't want to be dropped. So jump into the turbid Amazon and be quick about it."

"I warn you that your Mummy won't be pleased. Don't tell her I didn't tell you," said Slow-and-Solid.

"If you say another word about what my mother said—" the Jaguar answered, but he had not finished the sentence before Slow-and-Solid quietly dived into the turbid Amazon, swam under water for a long way, and came out on the bank where Stickly-Prickly was waiting for him.

"That was a very narrow escape," said Stickly-Prickly. "I don't like Painted Jaguar. What did you tell him that you were?"

"I told him truthfully that I was a truthful Tortoise, but he wouldn't believe it, and he made me jump into the river to see if I was, and I was, and he is surprised. Now he's gone to tell his Mummy. Listen to him!"

They could hear Painted Jaguar roaring up and down among the trees and the bushes by the side of the turbid Amazon, till his Mummy came.

"Son, son!" said his mother ever so many times, graciously waving her tail, "what have you been doing that you shouldn't have done?"

"I tried to scoop something that said it wanted to be scooped out of its shell with my paw, and my paw is full of per-ickles," said Painted Jaguar.

"Son, son!" said his mother ever so many times, graciously waving her tail, "by the prickles in your paddy-paw I see that that must have been a Hedgehog. You should have dropped him into the water."

"I did that to the other thing; and he said he was a Tortoise, and I didn't believe him, and it was quite true, and he has dived under the turbid Amazon, and he won't come up again, and I haven't anything at all to eat, and I think we had better find lodgings somewhere else. They are too clever on the turbid Amazon for poor me!"

"Son, son!" said his mother ever so many times, graciously waving her tail, "now attend to me and remember what I say. A Hedgehog curls himself up into a ball and his prickles stick out every which way at once. By this you may know the Hedgehog."

"I don't like this old lady one little bit," said Stickly-Prickly, under the shadow of a large leaf. "I wonder what else she knows?"

"A Tortoise can't curl himself up," Mother Jaguar went on, ever so many times, graciously waving her tail. "He only draws his head and legs into his shell. By this you may know the Tortoise."

"I don't like this old lady at all—at all," said Slow-and-Solid Tortoise. "Even Painted Jaguar can't forget those directions. It's a great pity that you can't swim, Stickly-Prickly."

"Don't talk to me," said Stickly-Prickly. "Just think how much better it would be if you could curl up. This *is* a mess! Listen to Painted Jaguar."

Painted Jaguar was sitting on the banks of the turbid Amazon sucking prickles out of his paws and saying to himself—

"Can't curl, but can swim—
Slow-Solid, that's him!
Curls up, but can't swim—
Stickly-Prickly, that's him!"

"He'll never forget that this month of Sundays," said Stickly-Prickly. "Hold up my chin, Slow-and-Solid. I'm going to try to learn to swim. It may be useful."

"Excellent!" said Slow-and-Solid; and he held up Stickly-Prickly's chin, while Stickly-Prickly kicked in the waters of the turbid Amazon.

"You'll make a fine swimmer yet," said Slow-and-Solid. "Now, if you can unlace my backplates a little, I'll see what I can do towards curling up. It may be useful."

Stickly-Prickly helped to unlace Tortoise's back-plates, so that by twisting and straining Slow-and-Solid actually managed to curl up a tiddy wee bit.

"Excellent!" said Stickly-Prickly; "but I shouldn't do any more just now. It's making you black in the face. Kindly lead me into the water once again and I'll practice that side-stroke which you say is so easy." And so Stickly-Prickly practiced, and Slow-and-Solid swam alongside.

"Excellent!" said Slow-and-Solid. "A little more practice will make you a regular whale. Now, if I may trouble you to unlace my back and front plates two holes more, I'll try that fascinating bend that you say is so easy. Won't Painted Jaguar be surprised!"

"Excellent!" said Stickly-Prickly, all wet from the turbid Amazon. "I declare, I shouldn't know you from one of my own family. Two holes, I think, you said? A little more expression, please, and don't grunt quite so much, or

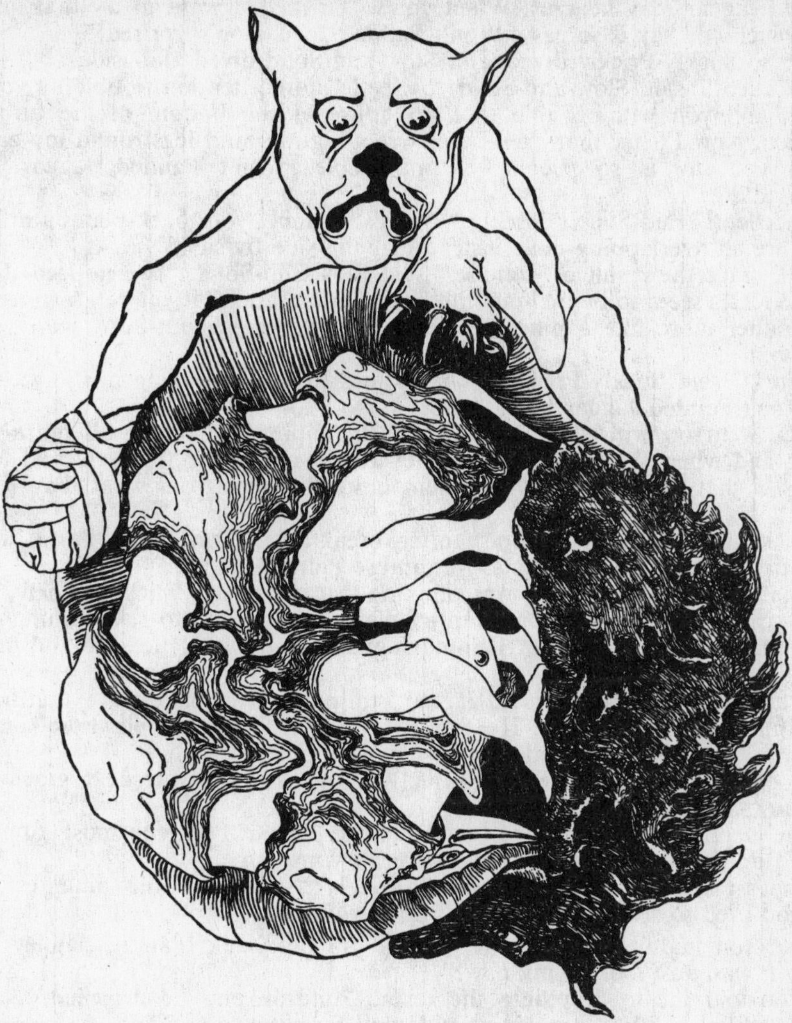

THIS IS A PICTURE OF THE WHOLE STORY OF THE JAGUAR AND THE Hedgehog and the Tortoise *and* the Armadillo all in a heap. It looks rather the same any way you turn it. The Tortoise is in the middle, learning how to bend, and that is why the shelly plates on his back are so spread apart. He is standing on the Hedgehog, who is waiting to learn how to swim. The Hedgehog is a Japanesy Hedgehog, because I couldn't find our own Hedgehogs in the garden when I wanted to draw them. (It was daytime, and they had gone to bed under the dahlias.) Speckly Jaguar is looking over the edge, with his paddy-paw carefully tied up by his mother, because he pricked himself scooping the Hedgehog. He is much surprised to see what the Tortoise is doing, and his paw is hurting him. The snouty thing with the little eye that Speckly Jaguar is trying to climb over is the Armadillo that the Tortoise and the Hedgehog are going to turn into when they have finished bending and swimming. It is all a magic picture, and that is one of the reasons why I haven't drawn the Jaguar's whiskers. The other reason was that he was so young that his whiskers had not grown. The Jaguar's pet name with his Mummy was Doffles.

Painted Jaguar may hear us. When you've finished, I want to try that long dive which you say is so easy. Won't Painted Jaguar be surprised!"

And so Stickly-Prickly dived, and Slow-and-Solid dived alongside.

"Excellent!" said Slow-and-Solid. "A leetle more attention to holding your breath and you will be able to keep house at the bottom of the turbid Amazon. Now I'll try that exercise of wrapping my hind legs round my ears which you say is so peculiarly comfortable. Won't Painted Jaguar be surprised!"

"Excellent!" said Stickly-Prickly. "But it's straining your back-plates a little. They are all overlapping now, instead of lying side by side."

"Oh, that's the result of exercise," said Slow-and-Solid. "I've noticed that your prickles seem to be melting into one another, and that you're growing to look rather more like a pine-cone, and less like a chestnut-burr, than you used to."

"Am I?" said Stickly-Prickly. "That comes from my soaking in the water. Oh, won't Painted Jaguar be surprised!"

They went on with their exercises, each helping the other, till morning came; and when the sun was high they rested and dried themselves. Then they saw that they were both of them quite different from what they had been.

"Stickly-Prickly," said Tortoise after breakfast, "I am not what I was yesterday; but I think that I may yet amuse Painted Jaguar."

"That was the very thing I was thinking just now," said Stickly-Prickly. "I think scales are a tremendous improvement on prickles–to say nothing of being able to swim. Oh, *won't* Painted Jaguar be surprised! Let's go and find him."

By and by they found Painted Jaguar, still nursing his paddy-paw that had been hurt the night before. He was so astonished that he fell three times backward over his own painted tail without stopping.

"Good morning!" said Stickly-Prickly. "And how is your dear gracious Mummy this morning?"

"She is quite well, thank you," said Painted Jaguar; "but you must forgive me if I do not at this precise moment recall your name."

"That's unkind of you," said Stickly-Prickly, "seeing that this time yesterday you tried to scoop me out of my shell with your paw."

"But you hadn't any shell. It was all prickles," said Painted Jaguar. "I know it was. Just look at my paw!"

"You told me to drop into the turbid Amazon and be drowned," said Slow-and-Solid. "Why are you so rude and forgetful to-day?"

"Don't you remember what your mother told you?" said Stickly-Prickly,–

"Can't curl, but can swim–
Stickly-Prickly, that's him!
Curls up, but can't swim–
Slow-Solid, that's him!"

Then they both curled themselves up and rolled round and round Painted Jaguar till his eyes turned truly cart-wheels in his head.

Then he went to fetch his mother.

"Mother," he said, "there are two new animals in the woods to-day, and the one that you said couldn't swim, swims, and the one that you said couldn't curl up, curls; and they've gone shares in their prickles, I think, because both of them are scaly all over, instead of one being smooth and the other very prickly; and, besides that, they are rolling round and round in circles, and I don't feel comfy."

"Son, son!" said Mother Jaguar ever so many times, graciously waving her tail, "a Hedgehog is a Hedgehog, and can't be anything but a Hedgehog; and a Tortoise is a Tortoise, and can never be anything else."

"But it isn't a Hedgehog, and it isn't a Tortoise. It's a little bit of both, and I don't know its proper name."

"Nonsense!" said Mother Jaguar. "Everything has its proper name. I should call it 'Armadillo' till I found out the real one. And I should leave it alone."

So Painted Jaguar did as he was told, especially about leaving them alone; but the curious thing is that from that day to this, O Best Beloved, no one on the banks of the turbid Amazon has ever called Stickly-Prickly and Slow-Solid anything except Armadillo. There are Hedgehogs and Tortoises in other places, of course (there are some in my garden); but the real old and clever kind, with their scales lying lippety-lappety one over the other, like pine-cone scales, that lived on the banks of the turbid Amazon in the High and Far-Off Days, are always called Armadillos, because they were so clever.

So *that's* all right, Best Beloved. Do you see?

I've never sailed the Amazon,
I've never reached Brazil;
But the *Don* and *Magdalena*,
They can go there when they will!

Yes, weekly from Southampton,
Great steamers, white and gold,
Go rolling down to Rio
(Roll down–roll down to Rio!).
And I'd like to roll to Rio
Some day before I'm old!

I've never seen a Jaguar,
Nor yet an Armadill–
O dilloing in his armour,
And I s'pose I never will,

Unless I go to Rio
These wonders to behold–
Roll down–roll down to Rio–
Roll really down to Rio!
Oh, I'd love to roll to Rio
Some day before I'm old!

How the First Letter Was Written

ONCE UPON A most early time was a Neolithic man. He was not a Jute or an Angle, or even a Dravidian, which he might well have been, Best Beloved, but never mind why. He was a Primitive, and he lived cavily in a Cave, and he wore very few clothes, and he couldn't read and he couldn't write and he didn't want to, and except when he was hungry he was quite happy. His name was Tegumai Bopsulai, and that means, "Man-who-does-not-put-his-foot-forward-in-a-hurry"; but we, O Best Beloved, will call him Tegumai, for short. And his wife's name was Teshumai Tewindrow, and that means, "Lady-who-asks-a-very-many-questions"; but we, O Best Beloved, will call her Teshumai, for short. And his little girl-daughter's name was Taffimai Metallumai, and that means, "Small-person-without-any-manners-who-ought-to-be-spanked"; but I'm going to call her Taffy. And she was Tegumai Bopsulai's Best Beloved and her own Mummy's Best Beloved, and she was not spanked half as much as was good for her; and they were all three very happy. As soon as Taffy could run about she went everywhere with her Daddy Tegumai, and sometimes they would not come home to the Cave till they were hungry, and then Teshumai Tewindrow would say, "Where in the world have you two been to, to get so shocking dirty? Really, my Tegumai, you're no better than my Taffy."

Now attend and listen!

One day Tegumai Bopsulai went down through the beaver-swamp to the Wagai river to spear carp-fish for dinner, and Taffy went too. Tegumai's spear was made of wood with shark's teeth at the end, and before he had caught any fish at all he accidentally broke it clean across by jabbing it down too hard on the bottom of the river. They were miles and miles from home (of course they had their lunch with them in a little bag), and Tegumai had forgotten to bring any extra spears.

"Here's a pretty kettle of fish!" said Tegumai. "It will take me half the day to mend this."

"There's your big black spear at home," said Taffy. "Let me run back to the Cave and ask Mummy to give it me."

"It's too far for your little fat legs," said Tegumai. "Besides, you might fall into the beaver-swamp and be drowned. We must make the best of a bad job." He sat down and took out a little leather mendy-bag, full of reindeer-sinews and strips of leather, and lumps of bee's-wax and resin, and began to mend the spear. Taffy sat down too, with her toes in the water and her chin in her hand, and thought very hard. Then she said–

"I say, Daddy, it's an awful nuisance that you and I don't know how to write, isn't it? If we did we could send a message for the new spear."

"Taffy," said Tegumai, "how often have I told you not to use slang? 'Awful' isn't a pretty word,–but it *would* be a convenience, now you mention it, if we could write home."

Just then a Stranger-man came along the river, but he belonged to a far tribe, the Tewaras, and he did not understand one word of Tegumai's language. He stood on the bank and smiled at Taffy, because he had a little girl-daughter of his own at home. Tegumai drew a hank of deer-sinews from his mendy-bag and began to mend his spear.

"Come here," said Taffy. "Do you know where my Mummy lives?" And the Stranger-man said "Um!"–being, as you know, a Tewara.

"Silly!" said Taffy, and she stamped her foot, because she saw a shoal of very big carp going up the river just when her Daddy couldn't use his spear.

"Don't bother grown-ups," said Tegumai, so busy with his spear-mending that he did not turn round.

"I aren't," said Taffy. "I only want him to do what I want him to do, and he won't understand."

"Then don't bother me," said Tegumai, and he went on pulling and straining at the deer-sinews with his mouth full of loose ends. The Stranger-man–a genuine Tewara he was–sat down on the grass, and Taffy showed him what her Daddy was doing. The Stranger-man thought, "This is a very wonderful child. She stamps her foot at me and she makes faces. She must be the daughter of that noble Chief who is so great that he won't take any notice of me." So he smiled more politely than ever.

"Now," said Taffy, "I want you to go to my Mummy, because your legs are longer than mine, and you won't fall into the beaver-swamp, and ask for Daddy's other spear—the one with the black handle that hangs over our fireplace."

The Stranger-man *(and* he was a Tewara) thought, "This is a very, very wonderful child. She waves her arms and she shouts at me, but I don't understand a word of what she says. But if I don't do what she wants, I greatly fear that that haughty Chief, Man-who-turns-his-back-on-callers, will be angry." He got up and twisted a big flat piece of bark off a birch-tree and gave it to Taffy. He did this, Best Beloved, to show that his heart was as white as the birch-bark and that he meant no harm; but Taffy didn't quite understand.

"Oh!" said she. "Now I see! You want my Mummy's living address? Of course I can't write, but I can draw pictures if I've anything sharp to scratch with. Please lend me the shark's tooth off your necklace."

The Stranger-man (and *he* was a Tewara) didn't say anything, so Taffy put up her little hand and pulled at the beautiful bead and seed and shark-tooth necklace round his neck.

The Stranger-man (and he *was* a Tewara) thought, "This is a very, very, very wonderful child. The shark's tooth on my necklace is a magic shark's tooth, and I was always told that if anybody touched it without my leave they would immediately swell up or burst, and that important Chief, Man-who-attends-strictly-to-his-business, who has not yet taken any notice of me at all, doesn't seem to be afraid that she will swell up or burst. I had better be more polite."

So he gave Taffy the shark's tooth, and she lay down flat on her tummy with her legs in the air, like some people on the drawing-room floor when they want to draw pictures, and she said, "Now I'll draw you some beautiful pictures! You can look over my shoulder, but you mustn't joggle. First I'll draw Daddy fishing. It isn't very like him; but Mummy will know, because I've drawn his spear all broken. Well, now I'll draw the other spear that he wants, the black-handled spear. It looks as if it was sticking in Daddy's back, but that's because the shark's tooth slipped and this piece of bark isn't big enough. That's the spear I want you to fetch; so I'll draw a picture of me myself 'splaining to you. My hair doesn't stand up like I've drawn, but it's easier to draw that way. Now I'll draw you. *I* think you're very nice really, but I can't make you pretty in the picture, so you mustn't be 'fended. Are you 'fended?"

The Stranger-man (and he was *a* Tewara) smiled. He thought, "There must be a big battle going to be fought somewhere, and this extraordinary child, who takes my magic shark's tooth but who does not swell up or burst, is telling me to call all the great Chief's tribe to help him. He *is* a great Chief, or he would have noticed me."

"Look," said Taffy, drawing very hard and rather scratchily, "now I've drawn you, and I've put the spear that Daddy wants into your hand, just to remind you that you're to bring it. Now I'll show you how to find my Mummy's living-address. You go along till you come to two trees (those are trees), and then you go over a hill (that's a hill), and then you come into a beaver-swamp all full of beavers. I haven't put in all the beavers, because I can't draw beavers, but I've drawn their heads, and that's all you'll see of them when you cross the swamp. Mind you don't fall in! Then our Cave is just beyond the beaver-swamp. It isn't as high as the hills really, but I can't draw things very small. That's my Mummy outside. She is beautiful. She is the most beautifullest Mummy there ever was, but she won't be 'fended when she sees I've drawn her so plain. She'll be pleased of me because I can draw. Now, in case you forget, I've drawn the spear that Daddy wants *outside* our Cave. It's *inside* really, but you show the picture to my Mummy and she'll give it you. I've made her holding up her hands, because I know she'll be so pleased to see you. Isn't it a beautiful picture? And do you quite understand, or shall I 'splain again?"

The Stranger-man (and he was a *Tewara)* looked at the picture and nodded very hard. He said to himself, "If I do not fetch this great Chief's tribe to help him, he will be slain by his enemies who are coming up on all sides with spears. Now I see why the great Chief pretended not to notice me! He feared that his enemies were hiding in the bushes and would see him deliver a message to me. Therefore he turned his back, and let the wise and wonderful child draw the terrible picture showing me his difficulties. I will away and get help for him from his tribe." He did not even ask Taffy the road, but raced off into the bushes like the wind, with the birch-bark in his hand, and Taffy sat down most pleased.

Now this is the picture that Taffy had drawn for him!

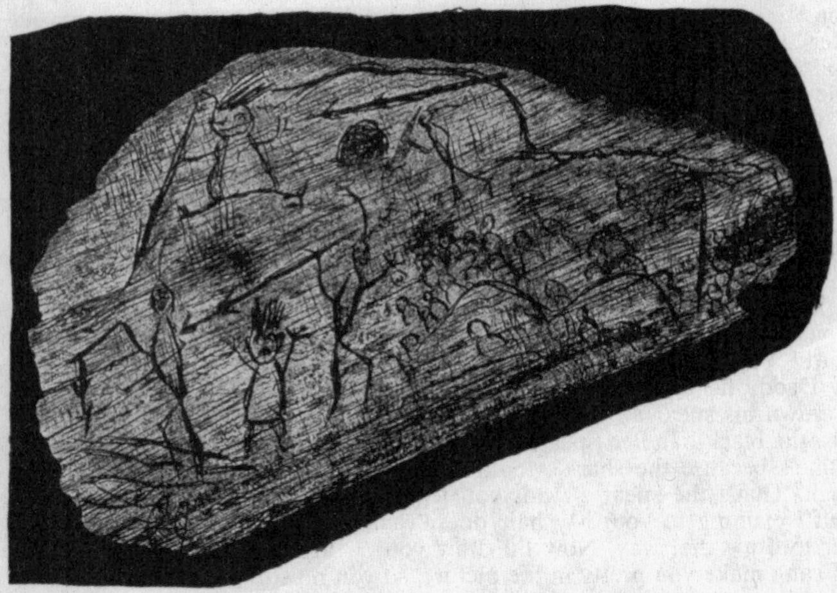

"What have you been doing, Taffy?" said Tegumai. He had mended his spear and was carefully waving it to and fro.

"It's a little berangement of my own, Daddy dear," said Taffy. "If you won't ask me questions, you'll know all about it in a little time, and you'll be surprised. You don't know how surprised you'll be, Daddy! Promise you'll be surprised."

"Very well," said Tegumai, and went on fishing.

The Stranger-man—did you know he was a Tewara?—hurried away with the picture and ran for some miles, till quite by accident he found Teshumai Tewindrow at the door of her Cave, talking to some other Neolithic ladies who had come in to a Primitive lunch. Taffy was very like Teshumai, specially about the upper part of the face and the eyes, so the Stranger-man—always a pure Tewara—smiled politely and handed Teshumai the birch-bark. He had run hard, so that he panted, and his legs were scratched with brambles, but he still tried to be polite.

As soon as Teshumai saw the picture she screamed like anything and flew at the Stranger-man. The other Neolithic ladies at once knocked him down and sat on him in a long line of six, while Teshumai pulled his hair. "It's as plain as the nose on this Stranger-man's face," she said. "He has stuck my

Tegumai all full of spears, and frightened poor Taffy so that her hair stands all on end; and not content with that, he brings me a horrid picture of how it was done. Look!" She showed the picture to all the Neolithic ladies sitting patiently on the Stranger-man. "Here is my Tegumai with his arm broken; here is a spear sticking into his back; here is a man with a spear ready to throw; here is another man throwing a spear from a Cave, and here are a whole pack of people" (they were Taffy's beavers really, but they did look rather like people) "coming up behind Tegumai. Isn't it shocking!"

"Most shocking!" said the Neolithic ladies, and they filled the Stranger-man's hair with mud (at which he was surprised), and they beat upon the Reverberating Tribal Drums, and called together all the chiefs of the Tribe of Tegumai, with their Hetmans and Dolmans, all Neguses, Woons, and Akhoonds of the organization, in addition to the Warlocks, Angekoks, Juju-men, Bonzes, and the rest, who decided that before they chopped the Stranger-man's head off he should instantly lead them down to the river and show them where he had hidden poor Taffy.

By this time the Stranger-man (in spite of being a Tewara) was really annoyed. They had filled his hair quite solid with mud; they had rolled him up and down on knobby pebbles; they had sat upon him in a long line of six; they had thumped him and bumped him till he could hardly breathe; and though he did not understand their language, he was almost sure that the names the Neolithic ladies called him were not ladylike. However, he said nothing till all the Tribe of Tegumai were assembled, and then he led them back to the bank of the Wagai river, and there they found Taffy making daisy-chains, and Tegumai carefully spearing small carp with his mended spear.

"Well, you *have* been quick!" said Taffy. "But why did you bring so many people? Daddy dear, this is my surprise. *Are* you surprised, Daddy?"

"Very," said Tegumai; "but it has ruined all my fishing for the day. Why, the whole dear, kind, nice, clean, quiet Tribe is here, Taffy."

And so they were. First of all walked Teshumai Tewindrow and the Neolithic ladies, tightly holding on to the Stranger-man, whose hair was full of mud (although he was a Tewara). Behind them came the Head Chief, the Vice-Chief, the Deputy and Assistant Chiefs (all armed to the upper teeth), the Hetmans and Heads of Hundreds, Platoffs with their Platoons, and Dolmans with their Detachments; Woons, Neguses, and Akhoonds ranking in the rear (still armed to the teeth). Behind them was the Tribe in hierarchical order, from owners of four caves (one for each season), a private reindeer-run, and two salmon-leaps, to feudal and prognathous Villeins, semi-entitled to half a bearskin of winter nights, seven yards from the fire, and adscript serfs, holding the reversion of a scraped marrow-bone under heriot (Aren't those beautiful words, Best Beloved?). They were all there, prancing and shouting, and they frightened every fish for twenty miles, and Tegumai thanked them in a fluid Neolithic oration.

Then Teshumai Tewindrow ran down and kissed and hugged Taffy very much indeed; but the Head Chief of the Tribe of Tegumai took Tegumai by the top-knot feathers and shook him severely.

"Explain! Explain! Explain!" cried all the Tribe of Tegumai.

"Goodness' sakes alive!" said Tegumai. "Let go of my top-knot. Can't a man break his carp-spear without the whole countryside descending on him? You're a very interfering people."

"I don't believe you've brought my Daddy's black-handled spear after all," said Taffy. "And what *are* you doing to my nice Stranger-man?"

They were thumping him by twos and threes and tens till his eyes turned round and round. He could only gasp and point at Taffy.

"Where are the bad people who speared you, my darling?" said Teshumai Tewindrow.

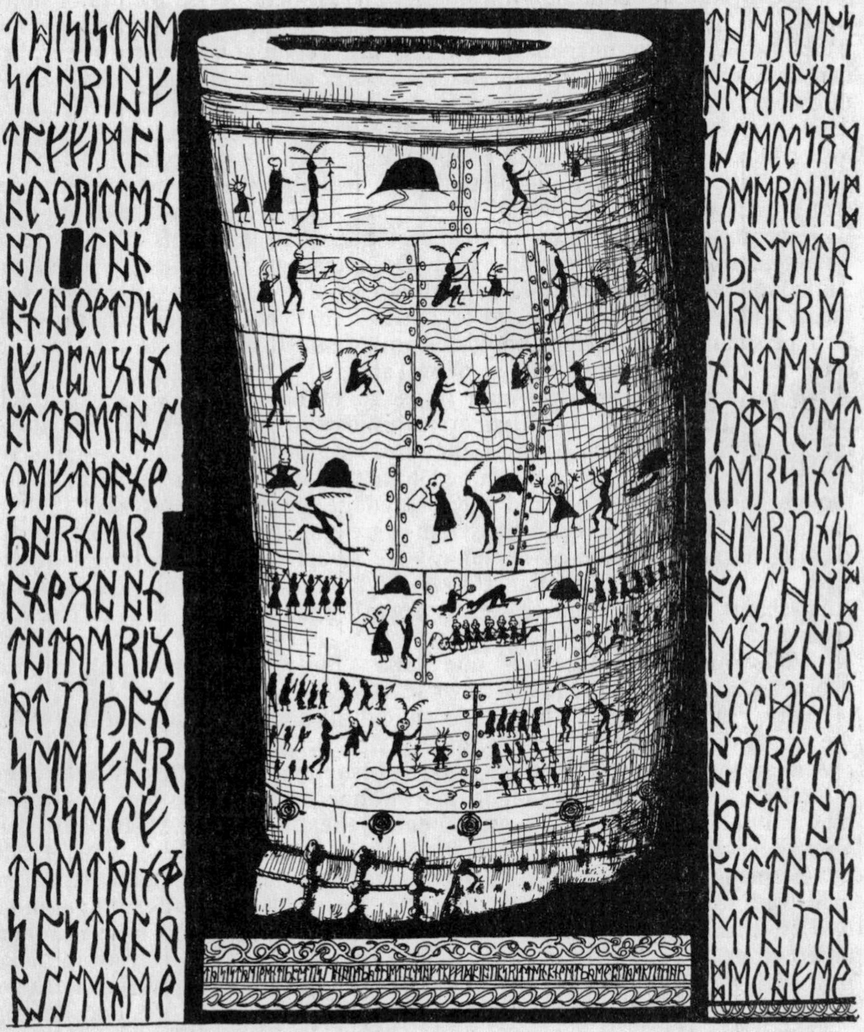

This is the story of Taffimai Metallumai carved on an old tusk a very long time ago by the Ancient Peoples. If you read my story, or have it read to you, you can see how it is all told out on the tusk. The tusk was part of an old tribal trumpet that belonged to the Tribe of Tegumai. The pictures were scratched on it with a nail or something, and then the scratches were filled up with black wax, but all the dividing lines and the five little rounds at the bottom were filled with red wax. When it was new there was a sort of network of beads and shells and precious stones at one end of it; but now that has been broken and lost—all except the little bit that you see. The letters round the tusk are magic—Runic magic,—and if you can read them you will find out something rather new. The tusk is of ivory—very yellow and scratched. It is two feet long and two feet round, and weighs eleven pounds nine ounces.

"There weren't any," said Tegumai. "My only visitor this morning was the poor fellow that you are trying to choke. Aren't you well, or are you ill, O Tribe of Tegumai?"

"He came with a horrible picture," said the Head Chief,—"a picture that showed you were full of spears."

"Er—um—P'raps I'd better 'splain that I gave him that picture," said Taffy, but she did not feel quite comfy.

"You!" said the Tribe of Tegumai all together. "Small-person-with-no-manners-who-ought-to-be-spanked! You?"

"Taffy dear, I'm afraid we're in for a little trouble," said her Daddy, and put his arm round her, so she didn't care.

"Explain! Explain! Explain!" said the Head Chief of the Tribe of Tegumai, and he hopped on one foot.

"I wanted the Stranger-man to fetch Daddy's spear, so I drawded it," said Taffy. "There wasn't lots of spears. There was only one spear. I drawded it three times to make sure. I couldn't help it looking as if it stuck into Daddy's head—there wasn't room on the birch-bark; and those things that Mummy called bad people are my beavers. I drawded them to show him the way through the swamp; and I drawded Mummy at the mouth of the Cave looking pleased because he is a nice Stranger-man, and *I* think you are just the stupidest people in the world," said Taffy. "He is a very nice man. Why have you filled his hair with mud? Wash him!"

Nobody said anything at all for a long time, till the Head Chief laughed; then the Stranger-man (who was at least a Tewara) laughed; then Tegumai laughed till he fell down flat on the bank; then all the Tribe laughed more and worse and louder. The only people who did not laugh were Teshumai Tewindrow and all the Neolithic ladies. They were very polite to all their husbands, and said "idiot!" ever so often.

Then the Head Chief of the Tribe of Tegumai cried and said and sang, "O Small-person-without-any-manners-who-ought-to-be-spanked, you've hit upon a great invention!"

"I didn't intend to; I only wanted Daddy's black-handled spear," said Taffy.

"Never mind. It *is* a great invention, and some day men will call it writing. At present it is only pictures, and, as we have seen to-day, pictures are not always properly understood. But a time will come, O Babe of Tegumai, when we shall make letters—all twenty-six of 'em,—and when we shall be able to read as well as to write, and then we shall always say exactly what we mean without any mistakes. Let the Neolithic ladies wash the mud out of the stranger's hair!"

"I shall be glad of that," said Taffy, "because, after all, though you've brought every single other spear in the Tribe of Tegumai, you've forgotten my Daddy's black-handled spear."

Then the Head Chief cried and said and sang, "Taffy dear, the next time you write a picture-letter, you'd better send a man who can talk our language with it, to explain what it means. I don't mind it myself, because I am a Head Chief, but it's very bad for the rest of the Tribe of Tegumai, and, as you can see, it surprises the stranger."

Then they adopted the Stranger-man (a genuine Tewara of Tewar) into the Tribe of Tegumai, because he was a gentleman and did not make a fuss about the mud that the Neolithic ladies had put into his hair. But from that day to this (and I suppose it is all Taffy's fault), very few little girls have ever liked learning to read or write. Most of them prefer to draw pictures and play about with their Daddies—just like Taffy.

There runs a road by Merrow Down–
    A grassy track to-day it is–
An hour out of Guildford town,
    Above the river Wey it is.

Here, when they heard the horse-bells ring,
    The ancient Britons dressed and rode
To watch the dark Phoenicians bring
    Their goods along the Western Road.

And here, or hereabouts, they met
    To hold their racial talks and such–
To barter beads for Whitby jet,
    And tin for gay shell torques and such.

But long and long before that time
    (When bison used to roam on it)
Did Taffy and her Daddy climb
    That down, and had their home on it.

Then beavers built in Broadstonebrook
    And made a swamp where Bramley stands;
And bears from Shere would come and look
    For Taffimai where Shamley stands.

The Wey, that Taffy called Wagai,
    Was more than six times bigger then;
And all the Tribe of Tegumai
    They cut a noble figure then!

How the Alphabet Was Made

THE WEEK AFTER Taffimai Metallumai (we will still call her Taffy, Best Beloved) made that little mistake about her Daddy's spear and the Stranger-man and the picture-letter and all, she went carp-fishing again with her Daddy. Her Mummy wanted her to stay at home and help hang up hides to dry on the big drying-poles outside their Neolithic Cave, but Taffy slipped away down to her Daddy quite early, and they fished. Presently she began to giggle, and her Daddy said, "Don't be silly, child."

"But wasn't it inciting!" said Taffy. "Don't you remember how the Head Chief puffed out his cheeks, and how funny the nice Stranger-man looked with the mud in his hair?"

"Well do I," said Tegumai. "I had to pay two deerskins–soft ones with fringes–to the Stranger-man for the things we did to him."

"*We* didn't do anything," said Taffy. "It was Mummy and the other Neolithic ladies–and the mud."

"We won't talk about that," said her Daddy. "Let's have lunch."

Taffy took a marrow-bone and sat mousy-quiet for ten whole minutes, while her Daddy scratched on pieces of birch-bark with a shark's tooth. Then she said, "Daddy, I've thinked of a secret surprise. You make a noise–any sort of noise."

"Ah!" said Tegumai. "Will that do to begin with?"

"Yes," said Taffy. "You look just like a carp-fish with its mouth open. Say it again, please."

"Ah! ah! ah!" said her Daddy. "Don't be rude, my daughter."

"I'm not meaning rude, really and truly," said Taffy. "It's part of my secret-surprise-think. *Do* say *ah,* Daddy, and keep your mouth open at the end, and lend me that tooth. I'm going to draw a carp-fish's mouth wide-open."

"What for?" said her Daddy.

"Don't you see?" said Taffy, scratching away on the bark. "That will be our little secret s'prise. When I draw a carp-fish with his mouth open in the smoke at the back of our Cave–if Mummy doesn't mind–it will remind you of that ah-noise. Then we can play that it was me jumped out of the dark and s'prised you with that noise–same as I did in the beaver-swamp last winter."

"Really?" said her Daddy, in the voice that grown-ups use when they are truly attending. "Go on, Taffy."

"Oh bother!" she said. "I can't draw all of a carp-fish, but I can draw something that means a carp-fish's mouth. Don't you know how they stand on their heads rooting in the mud? Well, here's a pretence carp-fish (we can play that the rest of him is drawn). Here's just his mouth, and that means *ah.*" And she drew this. (1.)

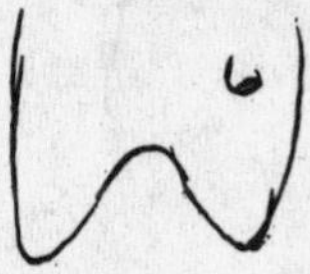

1.

"That's not bad," said Tegumai, and scratched on his own piece of bark for himself; "but you've forgotten the feeler that hangs across his mouth."

"But I can't draw, Daddy."

"You needn't draw anything of him except just the opening of his mouth and the feeler across. Then we'll know he's a carp-fish, 'cause the perches and trouts haven't got feelers. Look here, Taffy." And he drew this. (2.)

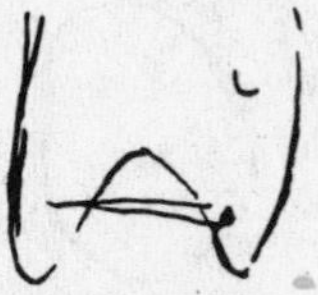

2.

"Now I'll copy it," said Taffy. "Will you understand *this* when you see it?" And she drew this. (3.)

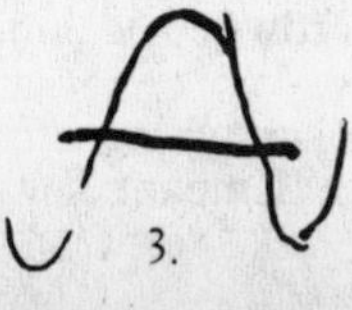

3.

"Perfectly," said her Daddy. "And I'll be quite as s'prised when I see it anywhere, as if you had jumped out from behind a tree and said 'Ah!' "

"Now, make another noise," said Taffy, very proud.

"Yah!" said her Daddy, very loud.

"H'm," said Taffy. "That's a mixy noise. The end part is *ah*-carp-fish-mouth; but what can we do about the front part? *Yer-yer-yer* and *ah! Ya!*"

"It's very like the carp-fish-mouth noise. Let's draw another bit of the carp-fish and join 'em," said her Daddy. *He* was quite incited too.

"No. If they're joined, I'll forget. Draw it separate. Draw his tail. If he's standing on his head the tail will come first. 'Sides, I think I can draw tails easiest," said Taffy.

"A good notion," said Tegumai. "Here's a carp-fish tail for the *yer*-noise." And he drew this. (4.)

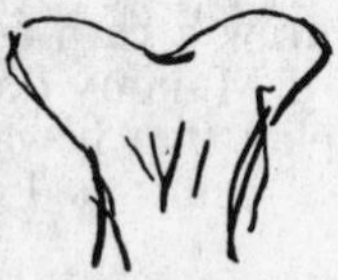

4.

"I'll try now," said Taffy. " 'Member I can't draw like you, Daddy. Will it do if I just draw the split part of the tail, and a sticky-down line for where it joins?" And she drew this. (5.)

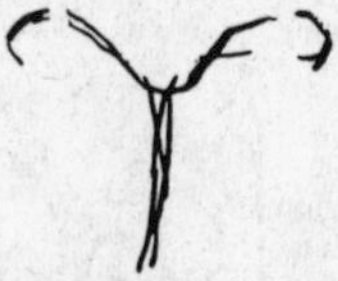

5.

Her Daddy nodded, and his eyes were shiny bright with 'citement.

"That's beautiful," she said. "Now, make another noise, Daddy."

"Oh!" said her Daddy, very loud.

"That's quite easy," said Taffy. "You make your mouth all round like an egg or a stone. So an egg or a stone will do for that."

"You can't always find eggs or stones. We'll have to scratch a round something like one." And he drew this. (6.)

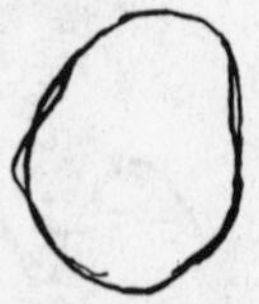

6.

"My gracious!" said Taffy, "what a lot of noise-pictures we've made,–carp-mouth, carp-tail, and egg! Now, make another noise, Daddy."

"Ssh!" said her Daddy, and frowned to himself, but Taffy was too incited to notice.

"That's quite easy," she said, scratching on the bark.

"Eh, what?" said her Daddy. "I meant I was thinking, and didn't want to be disturbed."

"It's a noise, just the same. It's the noise a snake makes, Daddy, when it is thinking and doesn't want to be disturbed. Let's make the *ssh*-noise a snake. Will this do?" And she drew this. (7.)

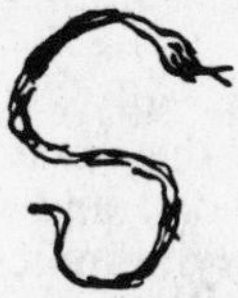

7.

"There," she said. "That's another s'prise-secret. When you draw a hissy-snake by the door of your little back-cave where you mend the spears, I'll know you're thinking hard; and I'll come in most mousy-quiet. And if you draw it on a tree by the river when you're fishing, I'll know you want me to walk most *most* mousy-quiet, so as not to shake the banks."

"Perfectly true," said Tegumai. "And there's more in this game than you think. Taffy, dear, I've a notion that your Daddy's daughter has hit upon the finest thing that there ever was since the Tribe of Tegumai took to using shark's teeth instead of flints for their spear-heads. I believe we've found out *the* big secret of the world."

"Why?" said Taffy, and her eyes shone too with incitement.

"I'll show," said her Daddy. "What's water in the Tegumai language?"

"*Ya,* of course, and it means river too—like Wagai-*ya*—the Wagai river."

"What is bad water that gives you fever if you drink it—black water—swamp-water?"

"*Yo,* of course."

"Now look," said her Daddy. "S'pose you saw this scratched by the side of a pool in the beaver-swamp?" And he drew this. (8.)

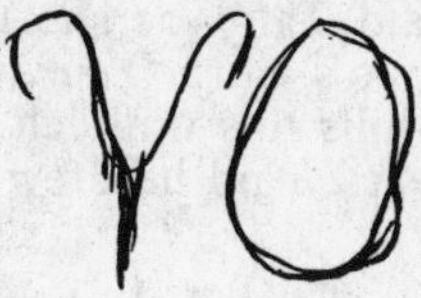

8.

"Carp-tail and round egg. Two noises mixed! *Yo,* bad water," said Taffy. " 'Course I wouldn't drink that water because I'd know you said it was bad."

"But I needn't be near the water at all. I might be miles away, hunting, and still—"

"And *still* it would be just the same as if you stood there and said, 'G'way, Taffy, or you'll get fever.' All that in a carp-fish-tail and a round egg! O Daddy, we must tell Mummy, quick!" and Taffy danced all round him.

"Not yet," said Tegumai; "not till we've gone a little further. Let's see. *Yo* is bad water, but *so* is food cooked on the fire, isn't it?" And he drew this. (9.)

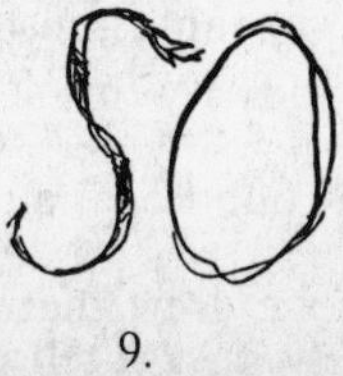

9.

"Yes. Snake and egg," said Taffy. "So that means dinner's ready. If you saw that scratched on a tree you'd know it was time to come to the Cave. So'd I."

"My Winkie!" said Tegumai. "That's true too. But wait a minute. I see a difficulty. *So* means 'come and have dinner,' but *sho* means the drying-poles where we hang our hides."

"Horrid old drying-poles!" said Taffy. "I hate helping to hang heavy, hot, hairy hides on them. If you drew the snake and egg, and I thought it meant dinner, and I came in from the wood and found that it meant I was to help Mummy hang the hides on the drying-poles, what *would* I do?"

"You'd be cross. So'd Mummy. We must make a new picture for *sho.* We must draw a spotty snake that hisses *sh-sh,* and we'll play that the plain snake only hisses *ssss.*"

"I couldn't be sure how to put in the spots," said Taffy. "And p'raps if *you* were in a hurry you might leave them out, and I'd think it was *so* when it was *sho,* and then Mummy would catch me just the same. *No!* I think we'd better draw a picture of the horrid high drying-poles their very selves, and make *quite* sure. I'll put 'em in just after the hissy-snake. Look!" And she drew this. (10.)

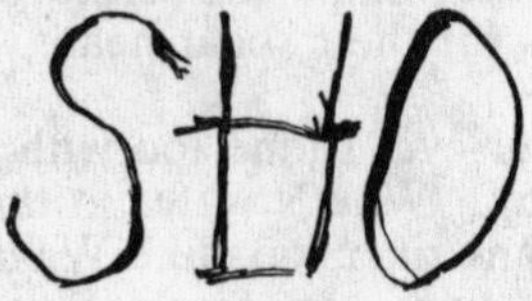

10.

"P'raps that's safest. It's very like our drying-poles, anyhow," said her Daddy, laughing. "Now I'll make a new noise with a snake and drying-pole sound in it. I'll say *shi.* That's Tegumai for spear, Taffy." And he laughed.

"Don't make fun of me," said Taffy, as she thought of her picture-letter and the mud in the Stranger-man's hair. "*You* draw it, Daddy."

"We won't have beavers or hills this time, eh?" said her Daddy. "I'll just draw a straight line for my spear." And he drew this. (11.)

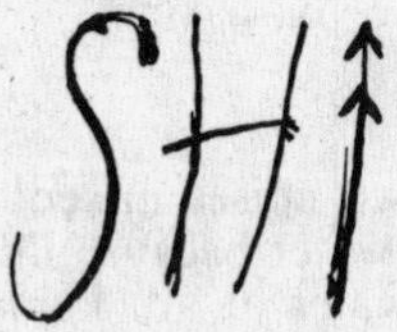

11.

"Even Mummy couldn't mistake that for me being killed."

"*Please* don't, Daddy. It makes me uncomfy. Do some more noises. We're getting on beautifully."

"Er-hm!" said Tegumai, looking up. "We'll say *shu.* That means sky."

Taffy drew the snake and the drying-pole. Then she stopped. "We must make a new picture for that end sound, mustn't we?"

"*Shu-shu-u-u-u!*" said her Daddy. "Why, it's just like the round-egg-sound made thin."

"Then s'pose we draw a thin round egg, and pretend it's a frog that hasn't eaten anything for years."

"N-no," said her Daddy. "If we drew that in a hurry we might mistake it for the round egg itself. *Shu-shu-shu! I'll* tell you what we'll do. We'll open a little hole at the end of the round egg to show how the O-noise runs out all thin, *ooo-oo-oo* Like this." And he drew this. (12.)

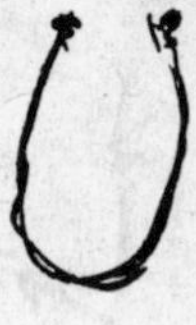

12.

"Oh, that's lovely! Much better than a thin frog. Go on," said Taffy, using her shark's tooth.

Her Daddy went on drawing, and his hand shook with incitement. He went on till he had drawn this. (13.)

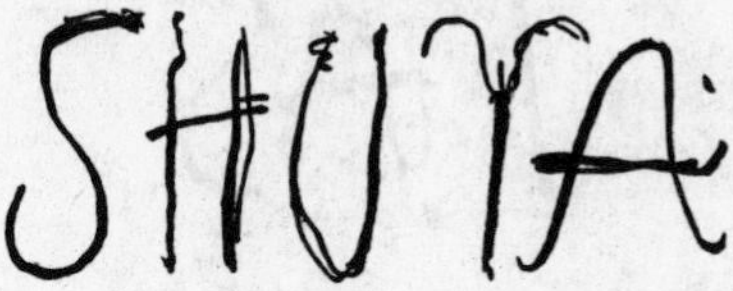

13.

"Don't look up, Taffy," he said. "Try if you can make out what that means in the Tegumai language. If you can, we've found the Secret."

"Snake—pole—broken-egg—carp-tail and carp-mouth," said Taffy. *"Shu-ya.* Sky-water (rain)." Just then a drop fell on her hand, for the day had clouded over. "Why, Daddy, it's raining. Was *that* what you meant to tell me?"

"Of course," said her Daddy. "And I told it you without saying a word, didn't I?"

"Well, I *think* I would have known it in a minute, but that raindrop made me quite sure. I'll always remember now. *Shu-ya* means rain, or 'it is going to rain.' Why, Daddy!" She got up and danced round him. "S'pose you went out before I was awake, and drawed *shu-ya* in the smoke on the wall, I'd know it was going to rain and I'd take my beaver-skin hood. Wouldn't Mummy be surprised!"

Tegumai got up and danced. (Daddies didn't mind doing those things in those days.) "More than that! More than that!" he said. "S'pose I wanted to tell you it wasn't going to rain much and you must come down to the river, what would we draw? Say the words in Tegumai-talk first."

"Shu-ya-las, ya maru. (Sky-water ending. River come to.) *What* a lot of new sounds! *I* don't see how we can draw them."

"But I do—but I do!" said Tegumai. "Just attend a minute, Taffy, and we won't do any more to-day. We've got *shu-ya* all right, haven't we? but this *las* is a teaser. *La-la-la!"* and he waved his shark-tooth.

"There's the hissy-snake at the end and the carp-mouth before the snake—*as-as-as.* We only want *la-la,"* said Taffy.

"I know it, but we have to make *la-la.* And we're the first people in all the world who've ever tried to do it, Taffimai!"

"Well," said Taffy, yawning, for she was rather tired. *"Las* means breaking or finishing as well as ending, doesn't it?"

"So it does," said Tegumai. *"Yo-las* means that there's no water in the tank for Mummy to cook with—just when I'm going hunting, too."

"And *shi-las* means that your spear is broken. If I'd only thought of *that* instead of drawing silly beaver-pictures for the Stranger!"

"*La! La! La!*" said Tegumai, waving his stick and frowning. "Oh bother!"

"I could have drawn *shi* quite easily," Taffy went on. "Then I'd have drawn your spear all broken—this way!" And she drew. (14.)

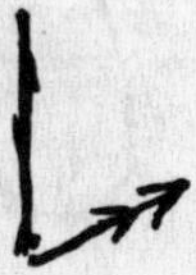

14.

"The very thing," said Tegumai. "That's *la* all over. It isn't like any of the other marks, either." And he drew this. (15.)

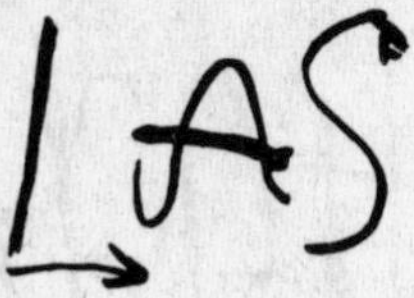

15.

"Now for *ya.* Oh, we've done that before. Now for *maru. Mum-mum-mum. Mum* shuts one's mouth up, doesn't it? We'll draw a shut mouth like this." And he drew. (16.)

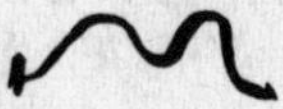

16.

"Then the carp-mouth open. That makes *Ma-ma-ma!* But what about this *rrrrr*-thing, Taffy?"

"It sounds all rough and edgy, like your shark-tooth saw when you're cutting out a plank for the canoe," said Taffy.

"You mean all sharp at the edges, like this?" said Tegumai. And he drew. (17.)

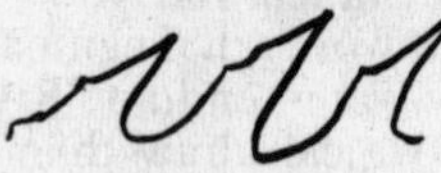

17.

" 'Xactly," said Taffy. "But we don't want all those teeth: only put two."

"I'll only put in one," said Tegumai. "If this game of ours is going to be what I think it will, the easier we make our sound-pictures the better for everybody." And he drew. (18.)

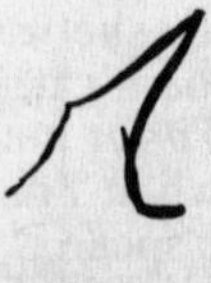

18.

"*Now* we've got it," said Tegumai, standing on one leg. "I'll draw 'em all in a string like fish."

"Hadn't we better put a little bit of stick or something between each word, so's they won't rub up against each other and jostle, same as if they were carps?"

"Oh, I'll leave a space for that," said her Daddy. And very incitedly he drew them all without stopping, on a big new bit of birch-bark. (19.)

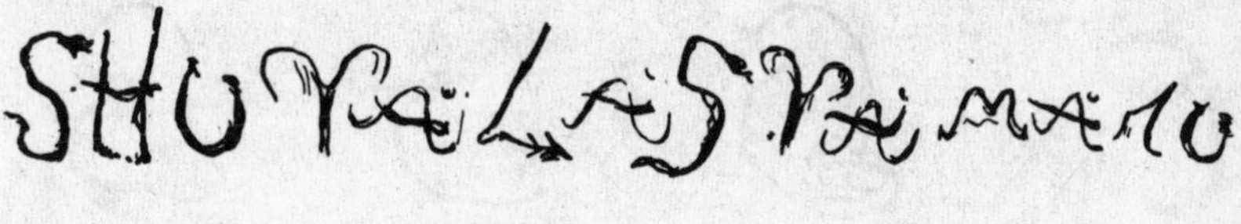

19.

"Shu-ya-las ya-maru," said Taffy, reading it out sound by sound.

"That's enough for to-day," said Tegumai. "Besides, you're getting tired, Taffy. Never mind, dear. We'll finish it all to-morrow, and then we'll be remembered for years and years after the biggest trees you can see are all chopped up for firewood."

So they went home, and all that evening Tegumai sat on one side of the fire and Taffy on the other, drawing *ya's* and *yo's* and *shu's* and *shi's* in the smoke on the wall and giggling together till her Mummy said, "Really, Tegumai, you're worse than my Taffy."

"Please don't mind," said Taffy. "It's only our secret-s'prise, Mummy dear, and we'll tell you all about it the very minute it's done; but *please* don't ask me what it is now, or else I'll have to tell."

So her Mummy most carefully didn't; and bright and early next morning Tegumai went down to the river to think about new sound-pictures, and when Taffy got up she saw *Ya-las* (water is ending or running out) chalked on the side of the big stone water-tank, outside the Cave.

"Um," said Taffy. "These picture-sounds are rather a bother! Daddy's just as good as come here himself and told me to get more water for Mummy to cook with." She went to the spring at the back of the house and filled the tank from a bark bucket, and then she ran down to the river and pulled her Daddy's left ear—the one that belonged to her to pull when she was good.

"Now come along and we'll draw all the left-over sound-pictures," said her Daddy, and they had a most inciting day of it, and a beautiful lunch in the middle, and two games of romps. When they came to T, Taffy said that as her name, and her Daddy's, and her Mummy's all began with that sound, they should draw a sort of family group of themselves holding hands. That was all very well to draw once or twice; but when it came to drawing it six or seven times, Taffy and Tegumai drew it scratchier and scratchier, till at last the T-sound was only a thin long Tegumai with his arms out to hold Taffy and Teshumai. You can see from these three pictures partly how it happened. (20, 21, 22.)

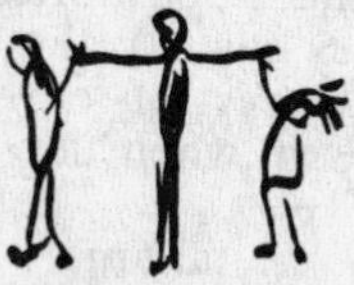

20.

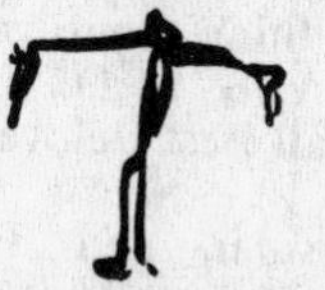

21.

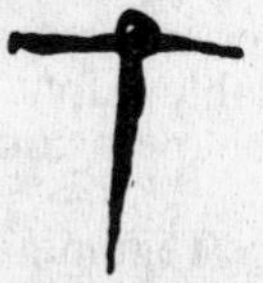

22.

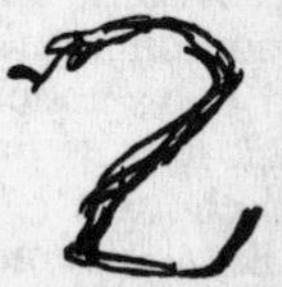

23.

Many of the other pictures were much too beautiful to begin with, especially before lunch; but as they were drawn over and over again on birch-bark, they became plainer and easier, till at last even Tegumai said he could find no fault with them. They turned the hissy-snake the other way round for the Z-sound, to show it was hissing backwards in a soft and gentle way (23); and they just made a twiddle for E, because it came into the pictures so often (24); and they drew pictures of the sacred Beaver of the Tegumais for the B-sound (25, 26, 27, 28); and because it was a nasty, nosy noise, they just drew

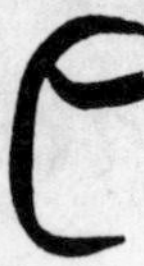

24.

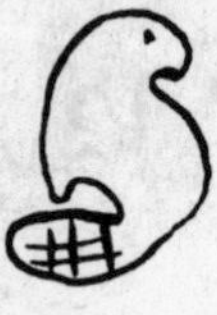

25.

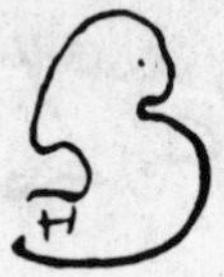

26.

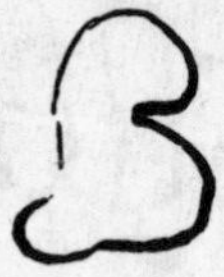

27.

noses for the N-sound, till they were tired (29); and they drew a picture of the big lake-pike's mouth for the greedy Ga-sound (30); and they drew the

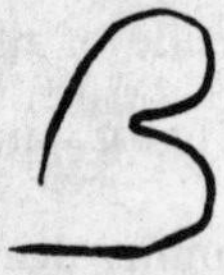

28.

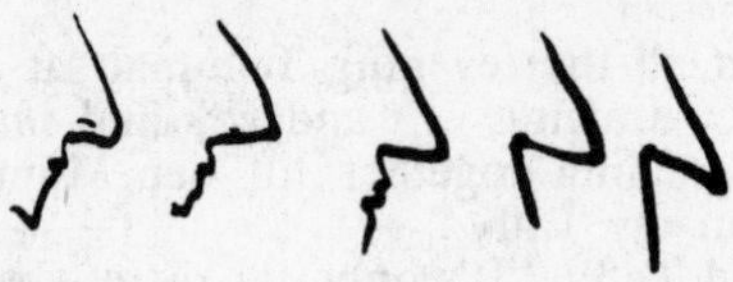

29.

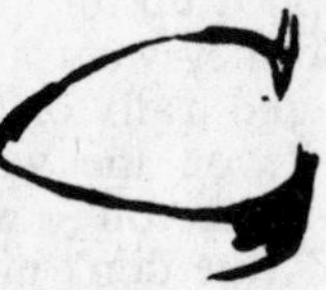

30.

pike's mouth again with a spear behind it for the scratchy, hurty Ka-sound (31); and they drew pictures of a little bit of the winding Wagai river for the nice windy-windy Wa-sound (32, 33); and so on and so forth and so follow-

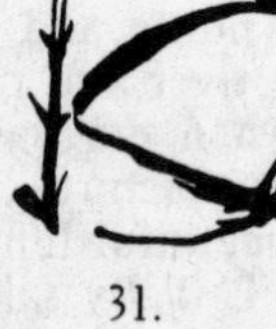

31.

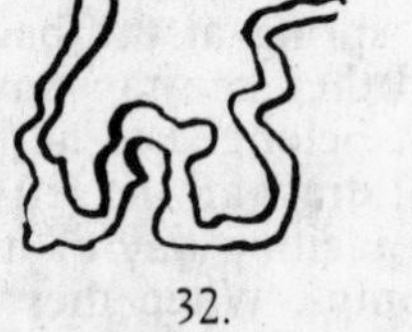

32.

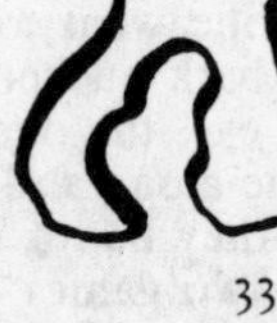

33.

ing till they had done and drawn all the sound-pictures that they wanted, and there was the Alphabet, all complete.

And after thousands and thousands and thousands of years, and after Hieroglyphics, and Demotics, and Nilotics, and Cryptics, and Cufics, and Runics, and Dorics, and Ionics, and all sorts of other ricks and tricks (because the Woons, and the Neguses, and the Akhoonds, and the Repositories of Tradition would never leave a good thing alone when they saw it), the fine old easy, understandable Alphabet—A, B, C, D, E, and the rest of 'em—got back into its proper shape again for all Best Beloveds to learn when they are old enough.

But *I* remember Tegumai Bopsulai, and Taffimai Metallumai and Teshumai Tewindrow, her dear Mummy, and all the days gone by. And it was so—just so—a long time ago—on the banks of the big Wagai!

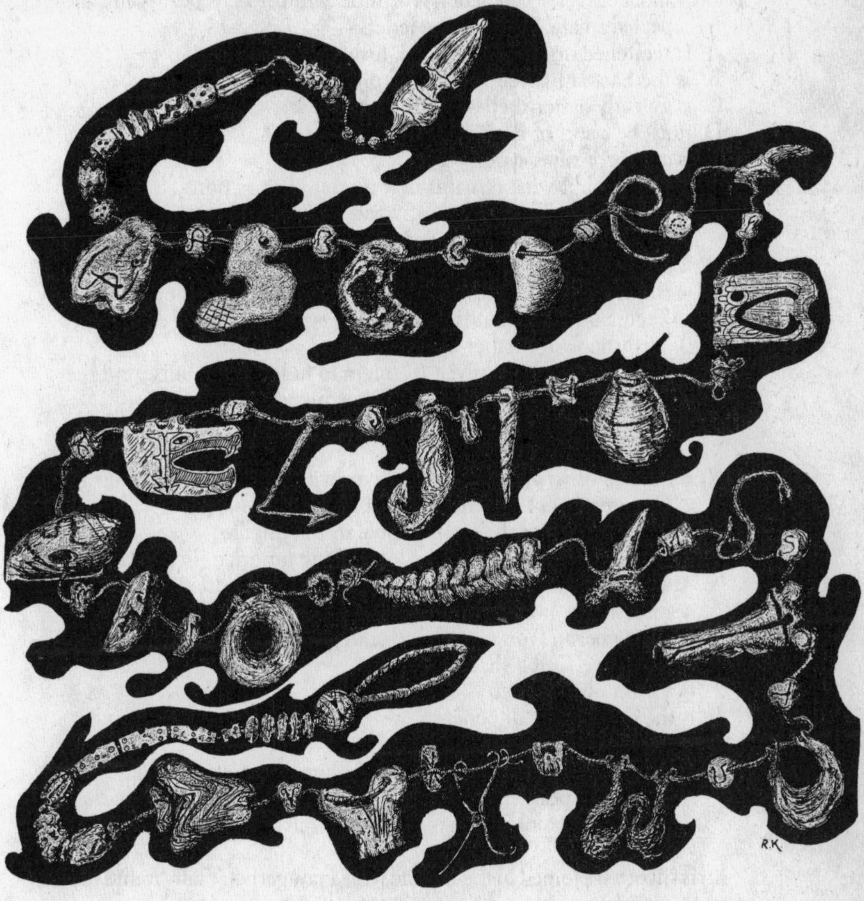

One of the first things that Tegumai Bopsulai did after Taffy and he had made the Alphabet was to make a magic Alphabet-necklace of all the letters, so that it could be put in the Temple of Tegumai and kept for ever and ever. All the Tribe of Tegumai brought their most precious beads and beautiful things, and Taffy and Tegumai spent five whole years getting the necklace in order. This is a picture of the magic Alphabet-necklace. The string was made of the finest and strongest reindeer-sinew, bound round with thin copper wire.

Beginning at the top, the first bead is an old silver one that belonged to the Head Priest of the Tribe of Tegumai; then come three black mussel-pearls; next is a clay bead (blue and grey); next a nubbly gold bead sent as a present by a tribe who got it from Africa (but it must have been Indian really); the next is a long flat-sided glass bead from Africa (the Tribe of Tegumai took it in a fight); then come two clay beads (white and green), with dots on one, and dots and bands on the other; next are three rather chipped amber beads; then three clay beads (red and white), two with dots, and the big one in the middle with a toothed pattern. Then the letters begin, and between each letter is a little whitish clay bead with the letter repeated small. Here are the letters:—

A is scratched on a tooth—an elk-tush, I think.
B is the Sacred Beaver of Tegumai on a bit of old ivory.
C is a pearly oyster-shell—inside front.
D must be a sort of mussel-shell—outside front.
E is a twist of silver wire.
F is broken, but what remains of it is a bit of stag's horn.
G is painted black on a piece of wood. (The bead after G is a small shell, and not a clay bead. I don't know why they did that.)
H is a kind of big brown cowrie-shell.
I is the inside part of a long shell ground down by hand. (It took Tegumai three months to grind it down.)
J is a fish-hook in mother-of-pearl.
L is the broken spear in silver. (K ought to follow J, of course; but the necklace was broken once and they mended it wrong.)
K is a thin slice of bone scratched and rubbed in black.
M is on a pale grey shell.
N is a piece of what is called porphyry with a nose scratched on it. (Tegumai spent five months polishing this stone.)
O is a piece of oyster-shell with a hole in the middle.
P and Q are missing. They were lost, a long time ago, in a great war, and the tribe mended the necklace with the dried rattles of a rattlesnake, but no one ever found P and Q. That is how the saying began 'You must mind your P's and Q's.'
R is, of course, just a shark's tooth.
S is a little silver snake.
T is the end of a small bone, polished brown and shiny.
U is another piece of oyster-shell.
W is a twisty piece of mother-of-pearl that they found inside a big mother-of-pearl shell, and sawed off with a wire dipped in sand and water. It took Taffy a month and a half to polish it and drill the holes.
X is silver wire joined in the middle with a raw garnet. (Taffy found the garnet.)
Y is the carp's tail in ivory.
Z is a bell-shaped piece of agate marked with Z-shaped stripes. They made the Z-snake out of one of the stripes by picking out the soft stone and rubbing in red sand and bee's-wax. Just in the mouth of the bell you see the clay bead repeating the Z-letter.

These are all the letters.

The next bed is a small round greeny lump of copper ore; the next is a lump of rough turquoise; the next is a rough gold nugget (what they call water-gold); the next is a melon-shaped clay bead (white with green spots). Then come four flat ivory pieces, with dots on them rather like dominoes; then come three stone beads, very badly worn; then two soft iron beads with rust-holes at the edges (they must have been magic, because they look very common); and last is a very very old African bead, like glass—blue, red, white, black, and yellow. Then comes the loop to slip over the big silver button at the other end, and that is all.

I have copied the necklace very carefully. It weighs one pound seven and a half ounces. The black squiggle behind is only put in to make the beads and things look better.

Of all the Tribe of Tegumai
Who cut that figure, none remain,–
On Merrow Down the cuckoos cry–
The silence and the sun remain.

But as the faithful years return
And hearts unwounded sing again,
Comes Taffy dancing through the fern
To lead the Surrey spring again.

Her brows are bound with bracken-fronds,
And golden elf-locks fly above;
Her eyes are bright as diamonds
And bluer than the skies above.

In mocassins and deer-skin cloak,
Unfearing, free and fair she flits,
And lights her little damp-wood smoke
To show her Daddy where she flits.

For far–oh, very far behind,
So far she cannot call to him,
Comes Tegumai alone to find
The daughter that was all to him.

The Crab That Played with the Sea

BEFORE THE HIGH and Far-Off Times, O my Best Beloved, came the Time of the Very Beginnings; and that was in the days when the Eldest Magician was getting Things ready. First he got the Earth ready; then he got the Sea ready; and then he told all the Animals that they could come out and play. And the Animals said, "O Eldest Magician, what shall we play at?" and he said, "I will show you." He took the Elephant–All-the-Elephant-there-was–and said, "Play at being an Elephant," and All-the-Elephant-there-was played. He took the Beaver–All-the-Beaver-there-was–and said, "Play at being a Beaver," and All-the-Beaver-there-was played. He took the Cow–All-the-Cow-there-was–and said, "Play at being a Cow," and –All-the-Cow-there-was played. He took the Turtle–All-the-Turtle-there-was–and said, "Play at being a Turtle," and All-the-Turtle-there-was played. One by one he took all the beasts and birds and fishes and told them what to play at.

But towards evening, when people and things grow restless and tired, there came up the Man (With his own little girl-daughter?)–Yes, with his own best-beloved little girl-daughter sitting upon his shoulder, and he said, "What is this play, Eldest Magician?" And the Eldest Magician said, "Ho, Son of Adam, this is the play of the Very Beginning; but you are too wise for this play." And the Man saluted and said, "Yes, I am too wise for this play; but see that you make all the Animals obedient to me."

Now, while the two were talking together, Pau Amma the Crab, who was next in the game, scuttled off sideways and stepped into the sea, saying to himself, "I will play my play alone in the deep waters, and I will never be obedient to this son of Adam." Nobody saw him go away except the little girl-daughter where she leaned on the Man's shoulder. And the play went on till there were no more Animals left without orders; and the Eldest Magician wiped the fine dust off his hands and walked about the world to see how the Animals were playing.

He went North, Best Beloved, and he found All-the-Elephant-there-was digging with his tusks and stamping with his feet in the nice new clean earth that had been made ready for him.

"Kun?" said All-the-Elephant-there-was, meaning, "Is this right?"

"Payah kun," said the Eldest Magician, meaning, "That is quite right"; and he breathed upon the great rocks and lumps of earth that All-the-Elephant-there-was had thrown up, and they became the great Himalayan Mountains, and you can look them out on the map.

He went East, and he found All-the-Cow-there-was feeding in the field that had been made ready for her, and she licked her tongue round a whole forest at a time, and swallowed it and sat down to chew her cud.

"Kun?" said All-the-Cow-there-was.

"Payah kun," said the Eldest Magician; and he breathed upon the bare patch where she had eaten, and upon the place where she had sat down, and one became the great Indian Desert, and the other became the Desert of Sahara, and you can look them out on the map.

He went West, and he found All-the-Beaver-there-was making a beaver-dam across the mouths of broad rivers that had been got ready for him.

"Kun?" said All-the-Beaver-there-was.

"Payah kun," said the Eldest Magician; and he breathed upon the fallen trees and the still water, and they became the Everglades in Florida, and you may look them out on the map.

Then he went South and found All-the-Turtle-there-was scratching with his flippers in the sand that had been got ready for him, and the sand and the rocks whirled through the air and fell far off into the sea.

"Kun?" said All-the-Turtle-there-was.

"Payah kun," said the Eldest Magician; and he breathed upon the sand and the rocks, where they had fallen in the sea, and they became the most beautiful islands of Borneo, Celebes, Sumatra, Java, and the rest of the Malay Archipelago, and you can look *them* out on the map!

By and by the Eldest Magician met the Man on the banks of the Perak River, and said, "Ho! Son of Adam, are all the Animals obedient to you?"

"Yes," said the Man.

"Is all the Earth obedient to you?"

"Yes," said the Man.

"Is all the Sea obedient to you?"

"No," said the Man. "Once a day and once a night the Sea runs up the Perak River and drives the sweet-water back into the forest, so that my house is made wet; once a day and once a night it runs down the river and draws all the water after it, so that there is nothing left but mud, and my canoe is upset. Is that the play you told it to play?"

"No," said the Eldest Magician. "That is a new and a bad play."

"Look!" said the Man, and as he spoke the great Sea came up the mouth of the Perak River, driving the river backwards till it overflowed all the dark forests for miles and miles, and flooded the Man's house.

"This is wrong. Launch your canoe and we will find out who is playing with the Sea," said the Eldest Magician. They stepped into the canoe; the little girl-daughter came with them; and the Man took his *kris*—a curving, wavy dagger with a blade like a flame,—and they pushed out on the Perak River. Then the Sea began to run back and back, and the canoe was sucked out of the mouth of the Perak River, past Selangor, past Malacca, past

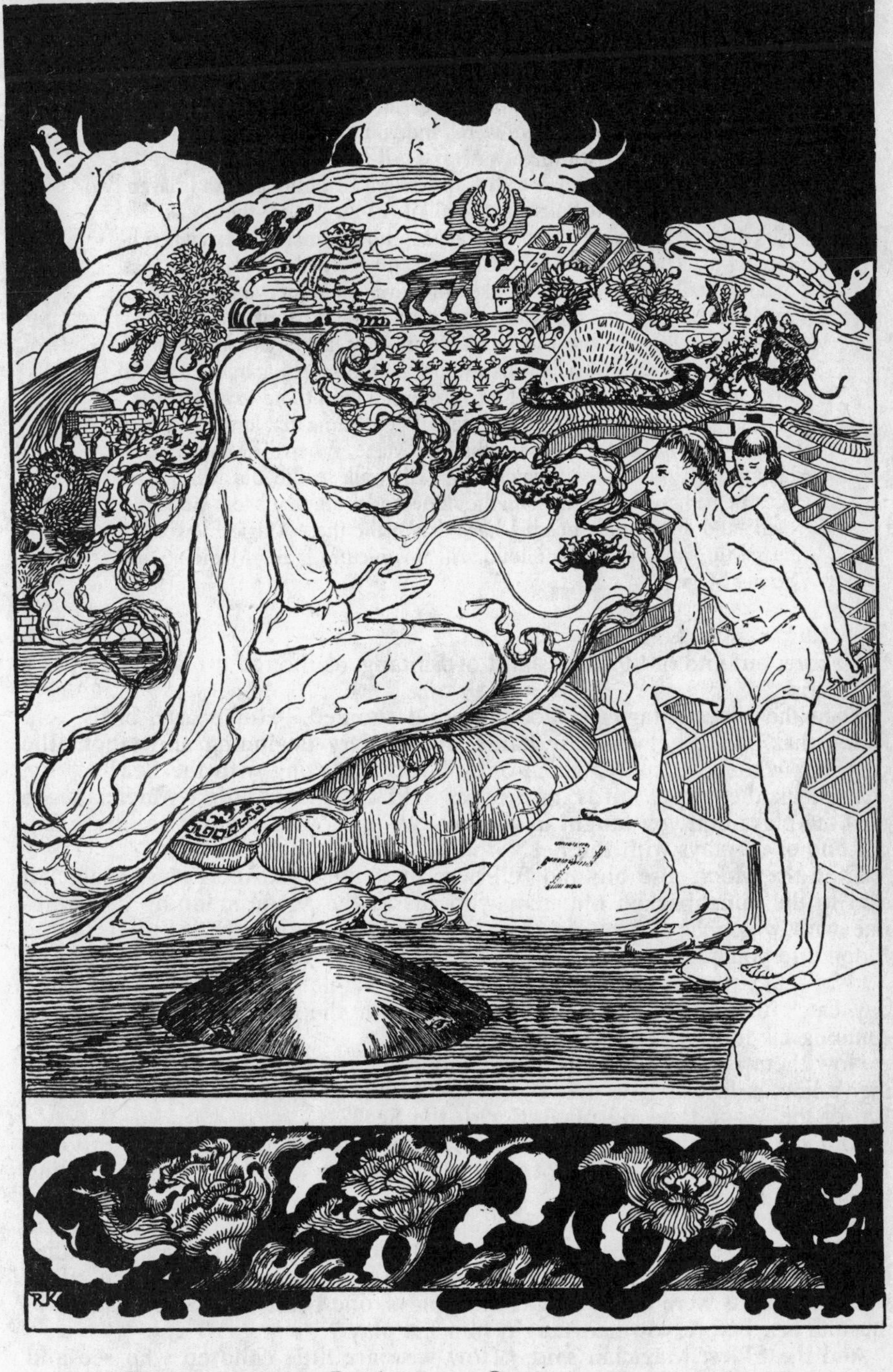

THIS IS A PICTURE OF PAU AMMA THE CRAB RUNNING AWAY WHILE THE Eldest Magician was talking to the Man and his Little Girl Daughter. The Eldest Magician is sitting on his magic throne, wrapped up in his Magic Cloud. The three flowers in front of him are the three Magic Flowers. On the top of the hill you can see All-the-Elephant-there-was, and All-the-

Cow-there-was, and All-the-Turtle-there-was going off to play as the Eldest Magician told them. The Cow has a hump, because she was All-the-Cow-there-was; so she had to have all there was for all the cows that were made afterwards. Under the hill there are Animals who have been taught the game they were to play. You can see All-the-Tiger-there-was smiling at All-the-Bones-there-were, and you can see All-the-Elk-there-was, and All-the-Parrot-there-was, and All-the-Bunnies-there-were on the hill. The other Animals are on the other side of the hill, so I haven't drawn them. The little house up the hill is All-the-House-there-was. The Eldest Magician made it to show the Man how to make houses when he wanted to. The Snake round that Spiky hill is All-the-snake-there-was, and he is talking to All-the-Monkey-there-was, and the Monkey is being rude to the Snake, and the Snake is being rude to the Monkey. The Man is very busy talking to the Eldest Magician. The Little Girl Daughter is looking at Pau Amma as he runs away. That humpy thing in the water in front is Pau Amma. He wasn't a common Crab in those days. He was a King Crab. That is why he looks different. The thing that looks like bricks that the Man is standing in, is the Big Miz-Maze. When the Man has done talking with the Eldest Magician he will walk in the Big Miz-Maze, because he has to. The mark on the stone under the Man's foot is a magic mark; and down underneath I have drawn the three Magic Flowers all mixed up with the Magic Cloud. All this picture is Big Medicine and Strong Magic.

Singapore, out and out to the Island of Bintang, as though it had been pulled by a string.

Then the Eldest Magician stood up and shouted, "Ho! beasts, birds, and fishes, that I took between my hands at the Very Beginning and taught the play that you should play, which one of you is playing with the Sea?"

Then all the beasts, birds, and fishes said together, "Eldest Magician, we play the plays that you taught us to play—we and our children's children. But not one of us plays with the Sea."

Then the Moon rose big and full over the water, and the Eldest Magician said to the hunchbacked old man who sits in the Moon spinning a fishing-line with which he hopes one day to catch the world, "Ho! Fisher of the Moon, are you playing with the Sea?"

"No," said the Fisherman, "I am spinning a line with which I shall some day catch the world; but I do not play with the Sea." And he went on spinning his line.

Now there is also a Rat up in the Moon who always bites the old Fisherman's line as fast as it is made, and the Eldest Magician said to him, "Ho! Rat of the Moon, are *you* playing with the Sea?"

And the Rat said, "I am too busy biting through the line that this old Fisherman is spinning. I do not play with the Sea." And he went on biting the line.

Then the little girl-daughter put up her little soft brown arms with the beautiful white shell bracelets and said, "O Eldest Magician! when my father here talked to you at the Very Beginning, and I leaned upon his shoulder while the beasts were being taught their plays, one beast went away naughtily into the Sea before you had taught him his play."

And the Eldest Magician said, "How wise are little children who see and are silent! What was that beast like?"

And the little girl-daughter said, "He was round and he was flat; and his eyes grew upon stalks; and he walked sideways like this; and he was covered with strong armor upon his back."

And the Eldest Magician said, "How wise are little children who speak truth! Now I know where Pau Amma went. Give me the paddle!"

So he took the paddle; but there was no need to paddle, for the water flowed steadily past all the islands till they came to the place called Pusat Tasek–the Heart of the Sea–where the great hollow is that leads down to the heart of the world, and in that hollow grows the Wonderful Tree, Pauh Janggi, that bears the magic twin-nuts. Then the Eldest Magician slid his arm up to the shoulder through the deep warm water, and under the roots of the Wonderful Tree he touched the broad back of Pau Amma the Crab. And Pau Amma settled down at the touch, and all the Sea rose up as water rises in a basin when you put your hand into it.

"Ah!" said the Eldest Magician. "Now I know who has been playing with the Sea"; and he called out, "What are you doing, Pau Amma?"

And Pau Amma, deep down below, answered, "Once a day and once a night I go out to look for my food. Once a day and once a night I return. Leave me alone."

Then the Eldest Magician said, "Listen, Pau Amma. When you go out from your cave the waters of the Sea pour down into Pusat Tasek, and all the beaches of all the islands are left bare, and the little fish die, and Raja Moyang Kaban, the King of the Elephants, his legs are made muddy. When you come back and sit in Pusat Tasek, the waters of the Sea rise, and half the little islands are drowned, and the Man's house is flooded, and Raja Abdullah, the King of the Crocodiles, his mouth is filled with the salt water."

Then Pau Amma, deep down below, laughed and said, "I did not know I was so important. Henceforward I will go out seven times a day, and the waters shall never be still."

And the Eldest Magician said, "I cannot make you play the play you were meant to play, Pau Amma, because you escaped me at the Very Beginning; but if you are not afraid, come up and we will talk about it."

"I am not afraid," said Pau Amma, and he rose to the top of the sea in the moonlight. There was nobody in the world so big as Pau Amma–for he was the King Crab of all Crabs. Not a common Crab, but a King Crab. One side of his great shell touched the beach at Sarawak; the other touched the beach at Pahang; and he was taller than the smoke of three volcanoes! As he rose up through the branches of the Wonderful Tree he tore off one of the great twin-fruits–the magic, double-kernelled nuts that make people young,–and the little girl-daughter saw it bobbing alongside the canoe, and pulled it in and began to pick out the soft eyes of it with her little golden scissors.

"Now," said the Magician, "make a Magic, Pau Amma, to show that you are really important."

Pau Amma rolled his eyes and waved his legs, but he could only stir up the Sea, because, though he was a King Crab, he was nothing more than a Crab, and the Eldest Magician laughed.

"You are not so important after all, Pau Amma," he said. "Now, let *me* try," and he made a Magic with his left hand–with just the little finger of his left hand–and–lo and behold, Best Beloved, Pau Amma's hard, blue-green-black shell fell off him as a husk falls off a cocoa-nut, and Pau Amma was left all soft–soft as the little crabs that you sometimes find on the beach, Best Beloved.

"Indeed, you are very important," said the Eldest Magician. "Shall I ask the Man here to cut you with his *kris?* Shall I send for Raja Moyang Kaban, the King of the Elephants, to pierce you with his tusks? or shall I call Raja Abdullah, the King of the Crocodiles, to bite you?"

And Pau Amma said, "I am ashamed! Give me back my hard shell and let me go back to Pusat Tasek, and I will only stir out once a day and once a night to get my food."

And the Eldest Magician said, "No, Pau Amma, I will *not* give you back your shell, for you will grow bigger and prouder and stronger, and perhaps you will forget your promise, and you will play with the Sea once more."

Then Pau Amma said, "What shall I do? I am so big that I can only hide in Pusat Tasek, and if I go anywhere else, all soft as I am now, the sharks and the dogfish will eat me. And if I go to Pusat Tasek, all soft as I am now, though I may be safe, I can never stir out to get my food, and so I shall die." Then he waved his legs and lamented.

"Listen, Pau Amma," said the Eldest Magician. "I cannot make you play the play you were meant to play, because you escaped me at the Very Beginning; but if you choose, I can make every stone and every hole and every bunch of weed in all the seas a safe Pusat Tasek for you and your children for always."

Then Pau Amma said, "That is good, but I do not choose yet. Look! there is that Man who talked to you at the Very Beginning. If he had not taken up your attention I should not have grown tired of waiting and run away, and all this would never have happened. What will *he* do for me?"

And the Man said, "If you choose, I will make a Magic, so that both the deep water and the dry ground will be a home for you and your children—so that you shall be able to hide both on the land and in the sea."

And Pau Amma said, "I do not choose yet. Look! there is that girl who saw me running away at the Very Beginning. If she had spoken then, the Eldest Magician would have called me back, and all this would never have happened. What will *she* do for me?"

And the little girl-daughter said, "This is a good nut that I am eating. If you choose, I will make a Magic and I will give you this pair of scissors, very sharp and strong, so that you and your children can eat cocoa-nuts like this all day long when you come up from the Sea to the land; or you can dig a Pusat Tasek for yourself with the scissors that belong to you when there is no stone or hole near by; and when the earth is too hard, by the help of these same scissors you can run up a tree."

And Pau Amma said, "I do not choose yet, for, all soft as I am, these gifts would not help me. Give me back my shell, O Eldest Magician, and then I will play your play."

And the Eldest Magician said, "I will give it back, Pau Amma, for eleven months of the year; but on the twelfth month of every year it shall grow soft again, to remind you and all your children that I can make magics, and to keep you humble, Pau Amma; for I see that if you can run both under the water and on land, you will grow too bold; and if you can climb trees and crack nuts and dig holes with your scissors, you will grow too greedy, Pau Amma."

Then Pau Amma thought a little and said, "I have made my choice. I will take all the gifts."

Then the Eldest Magician made a Magic with the right hand, with all five fingers of his right hand, and lo and behold, Best Beloved, Pau Amma grew smaller and smaller and smaller, till at last there was only a little green crab swimming in the water alongside the canoe, crying in a very small voice, "Give me the scissors!"

And the girl-daughter picked him up on the palm of her little brown hand, and sat him in the bottom of the canoe and gave him her scissors, and he waved them in his little arms, and opened them and shut them and snapped them, and said, "I can eat nuts. I can crack shells. I can dig holes. I can climb trees. I can breathe in the dry air, and I can find a safe Pusat Tasek under every stone. I did not know I was so important. *Kun?*" (Is this right?)

"Payah kun," said the Eldest Magician, and he laughed and gave him his blessing; and little Pau Amma scuttled over the side of the canoe into the water; and he was so tiny that he could have hidden under the shadow of a dry leaf on land or of a dead shell at the bottom of the sea.

"Was that well done?" said the Eldest Magician.

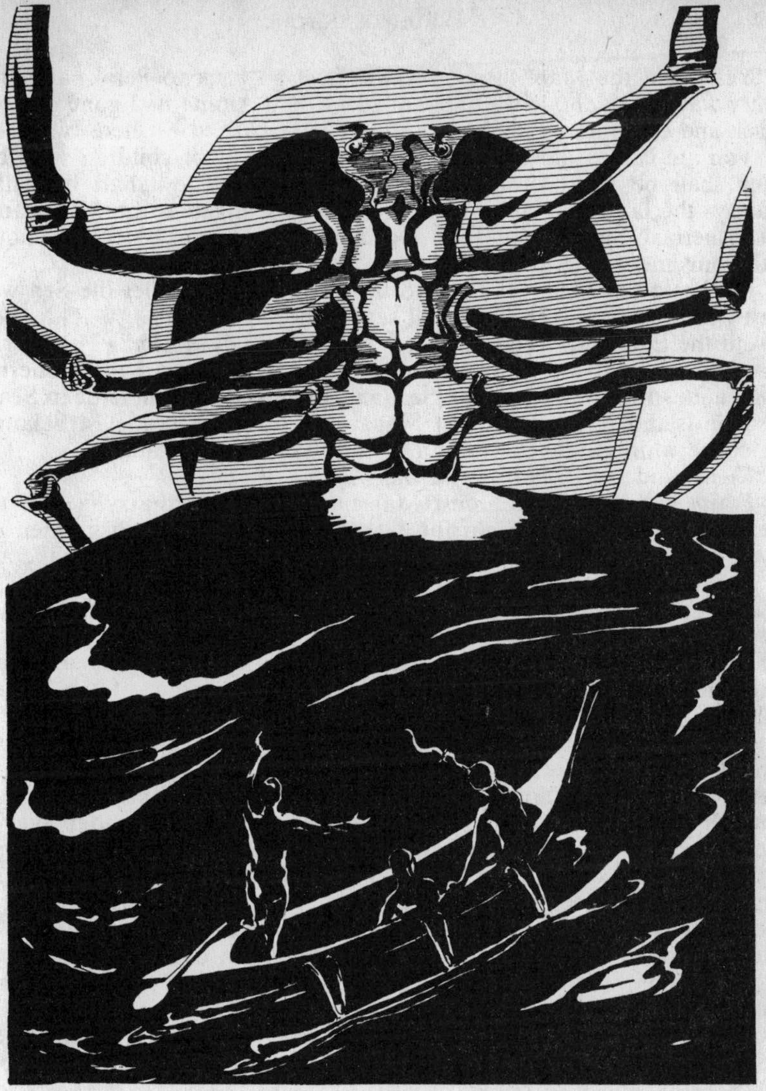

THIS IS THE PICTURE OF PAU AMMA THE CRAB RISING OUT OF THE SEA AS tall as the smoke of three volcanoes. I haven't drawn the three volcanoes, because Pau Amma was so big. Pau Amma is trying to make a Magic, but he is only a silly old King Crab, and so he can't do anything. You can see he is all legs and claws and empty hollow shell. The canoe is the canoe that the Man and the Girl Daughter and the Eldest Magician sailed from the Perak River in. The Sea is all black and bobbly, because Pau Amma has just risen up out of Pusat Tasek. Pusat Tasek is underneath, so I haven't drawn it. The Man is waving his curvy *kris*-knife at Pau Amma. The Little Girl Daughter is sitting quietly in the middle of the canoe. She knows she is quite safe with her Daddy. The Eldest Magician is standing up at the other end of the canoe beginning to make a Magic. He has left his magic throne on the beach, and he has taken off his clothes so as not to get wet, and he has left the Magic Cloud behind too, so as not to tip the boat over. The thing that looks like another little canoe outside the real canoe is called an outrigger. It is a piece of wood tied to sticks, and it prevents the canoe from being tipped over. The canoe is made out of one piece of wood, and there is a paddle at one end of it.

"Yes," said the Man. "But now we must go back to Perak, and that is a weary way to paddle. If we had waited till Pau Amma had gone out of Pusat Tasek and come home, the water would have carried us there by itself."

"You are lazy," said the Eldest Magician. "So your children shall be lazy. They shall be the laziest people in the world. They shall be called the Malazy–the lazy people"; and he held up his finger to the Moon and said, "O Fisherman, here is this Man too lazy to row home. Pull his canoe home with your line, Fisherman."

"No," said the Man. "If I am to be lazy all my days, let the Sea work for me twice a day for ever. That will save paddling."

And the Eldest Magician laughed and said, *"Payah kun"* (That is right).

And the Rat of the Moon stopped biting the line; and the Fisherman let his line down till it touched the Sea, and he pulled the whole deep Sea along, past the Island of Bintang, past Singapore, past Malacca, past Selangor, till the canoe whirled into the mouth of the Perak River again.

"Kun?" said the Fisherman of the Moon.

"Payah kun," said the Eldest Magician. "See now that you pull the Sea twice a day and twice a night for ever, so that the Malazy fishermen may be saved paddling. But be careful not to do it too hard, or I shall make a Magic on you as I did to Pau Amma."

Then they all went up the Perak River and went to bed, Best Beloved.

Now listen and attend!

From that day to this the Moon has always pulled the Sea up and down and made what we call the tides. Sometimes the Fisher of the Sea pulls a little too hard, and then we get spring-tides; and sometimes he pulls a little too softly, and then we get what are called neap-tides; but nearly always he is careful, because of the Eldest Magician.

And Pau Amma? You can see when you go to the beach, how all Pau Amma's babies make little Pusat Taseks for themselves under every stone and bunch of weed on the sands; you can see them waving their little scissors; and in some parts of the world they truly live on the dry land and run up the palm-trees and eat cocoa-nuts, exactly as the girl-daughter promised. But once a year all Pau Ammas must shake off their hard armor and be soft–to remind them of what the Eldest Magician could do. And so it isn't fair to kill or hunt Pau Amma's babies just because old Pau Amma was stupidly rude a very long time ago.

Oh yes! And Pau Amma's babies hate being taken out of their little Pusat Taseks and brought home in pickle-bottles. That is why they nip you with their scissors, and it serves you right!

China-going P. and O.'s
Pass Pau Amma's playground close,
And his Pusat Tasek lies
Near the track of most B.I.'s.
N.Y.K. and N.D.L.
Know Pau Amma's home as well
As the Fisher of the Sea knows
"Bens," M.M.'s, and Rubattinos.
But (and this is rather queer)
A.T.L.'s can *not* come here;
O. and O. and D.O.A.
Must go round another way.
Orient, Anchor, Bibby, Hall,
Never go that way at all.
U.C.S. would have a fit
If it found itself on it.
And if "Beavers" took their cargoes

To Penang instead of Lagos,
Or a fat Shaw-Savill bore
Passengers to Singapore,
Or a White Star were to try a
Little trip to Sourabaya,
Or a B.S.A. went on
Past Natal to Cheribon,
Then great Mr. Lloyds would come
With a wire and drag them home!

You'll know what my riddle means
When you've eaten mangosteens.

Or if you can't wait till then, ask them to let you have the outside page of the *Times;* turn over to page 2, where it is marked "Shipping" on the top left hand; then take the Atlas (and that is the finest picture-book in the world) and see how the names of the places that the steamers go to fit into the names of the places on the map. Any steamer-kiddy ought to be able to do that; but if you can't read, ask some one to show it you.

The Cat That Walked by Himself

HEAR AND ATTEND and listen; for this befell and behappened and became and was, O my Best Beloved, when the Tame animals were wild. The Dog was wild, and the Horse was wild, and the Cow was wild, and the Sheep was wild, and the Pig was wild—as wild as wild could be—and they walked in the Wet Wild Woods by their wild lones. But the wildest of all the wild animals was the Cat. He walked by himself, and all places were alike to him.

Of course the Man was wild too. He was dreadfully wild. He didn't even begin to be tame till he met the Woman, and she told him that she did not like living in his wild ways. She picked out a nice dry Cave, instead of a heap of wet leaves, to lie down in; and she strewed clean sand on the floor; and she lit a nice fire of wood at the back of the Cave; and she hung a dried wild-horse skin, tail-down, across the opening of the Cave; and she said, "Wipe your feet, dear, when you come in, and now we'll keep house."

That night, Best Beloved, they ate wild sheep roasted on the hot stones, and flavored with wild garlic and wild pepper; and wild duck stuffed with wild rice and wild fenugreek and wild coriander; and marrow-bones of wild oxen; and wild cherries, and wild grenadillas. Then the Man went to sleep in front of the fire ever so happy; but the Woman sat up, combing her hair. She took the bone of the shoulder of mutton—the big flat blade-bone—and she looked at the wonderful marks on it, and she threw more wood on the fire, and she made a Magic. She made the First Singing Magic in the world.

Out in the Wet Wild Woods all the wild animals gathered together where they could see the light of the fire a long way off, and they wondered what it meant.

Then Wild Horse stamped with his wild foot and said, "O my Friends and

O my Enemies, why have the Man and the Woman made that great light in that great Cave, and what harm will it do us?"

Wild Dog lifted up his wild nose and smelled the smell of the roast mutton, and said, "I will go up and see and look, and say; for I think it is good. Cat, come with me."

"Nenni!" said the Cat. "I am the Cat who walks by himself, and all places are alike to me. I will not come."

"Then we can never be friends again," said Wild Dog, and he trotted off to the Cave. But when he had gone a little way the Cat said to himself, "All places are alike to me. Why should I not go too and see and look and come away at my own liking?" So he slipped after Wild Dog softly, very softly, and hid himself where he could hear everything.

When Wild Dog reached the mouth of the Cave he lifted up the dried horse-skin with his nose and sniffed the beautiful smell of the roast mutton, and the Woman, looking at the blade-bone, heard him, and laughed, and said, "Here comes the first. Wild Thing out of the Wild Woods, what do you want?"

Wild Dog said, "O my Enemy and Wife of my Enemy, what is this that smells so good in the Wild Woods?"

Then the Woman picked up a roasted mutton-bone and threw it to Wild Dog, and said, "Wild Thing out of the Wild Woods, taste and try." Wild Dog gnawed the bone, and it was more delicious than anything he had ever tasted, and he said, "O my Enemy and Wife of my Enemy, give me another."

The Woman said, "Wild Thing out of the Wild Woods, help my Man to hunt through the day and guard this Cave at night, and I will give you as many roast bones as you need."

"Ah!" said the Cat, listening. "This is a very wise Woman, but she is not so wise as I am."

Wild Dog crawled into the Cave and laid his head on the Woman's lap, and said, "O my Friend and Wife of my Friend, I will help your Man to hunt through the day, and at night I will guard your Cave."

"Ah!" said the Cat, listening. "That is a very foolish Dog." And he went back through the Wet Wild Woods waving his wild tail, and walking by his wild lone. But he never told anybody.

When the Man waked up he said, "What is Wild Dog doing here?" And the Woman said, "His name is not Wild Dog any more, but the First Friend, because he will be our friend for always and always and always. Take him with you when you go hunting."

Next night the Woman cut great green armfuls of fresh grass from the water-meadows, and dried it before the fire, so that it smelt like new-mown hay, and she sat at the mouth of the Cave and plaited a halter out of horse-hide, and she looked at the shoulder-of-mutton bone—at the big broad blade-bone—and she made a Magic. She made the Second Singing Magic in the world.

Out in the Wild Woods all the wild animals wondered what had happened to Wild Dog, and at last Wild Horse stamped with his foot and said, "I will go and see and say why Wild Dog has not returned. Cat, come with me."

"Nenni!" said the Cat. "I am the Cat who walks by himself, and all places are alike to me. I will not come." But all the same he followed Wild Horse softly, very softly, and hid himself where he could hear everything.

When the Woman heard Wild Horse tripping and stumbling on his long mane, she laughed and said, "Here comes the second. Wild Thing out of the Wild Woods, what do you want?"

Wild Horse said, "O my Enemy and Wife of my Enemy, where is Wild Dog?"

The Woman laughed, and picked up the blade-bone and looked at it, and said, "Wild Thing out of the Wild Woods, you did not come here for Wild

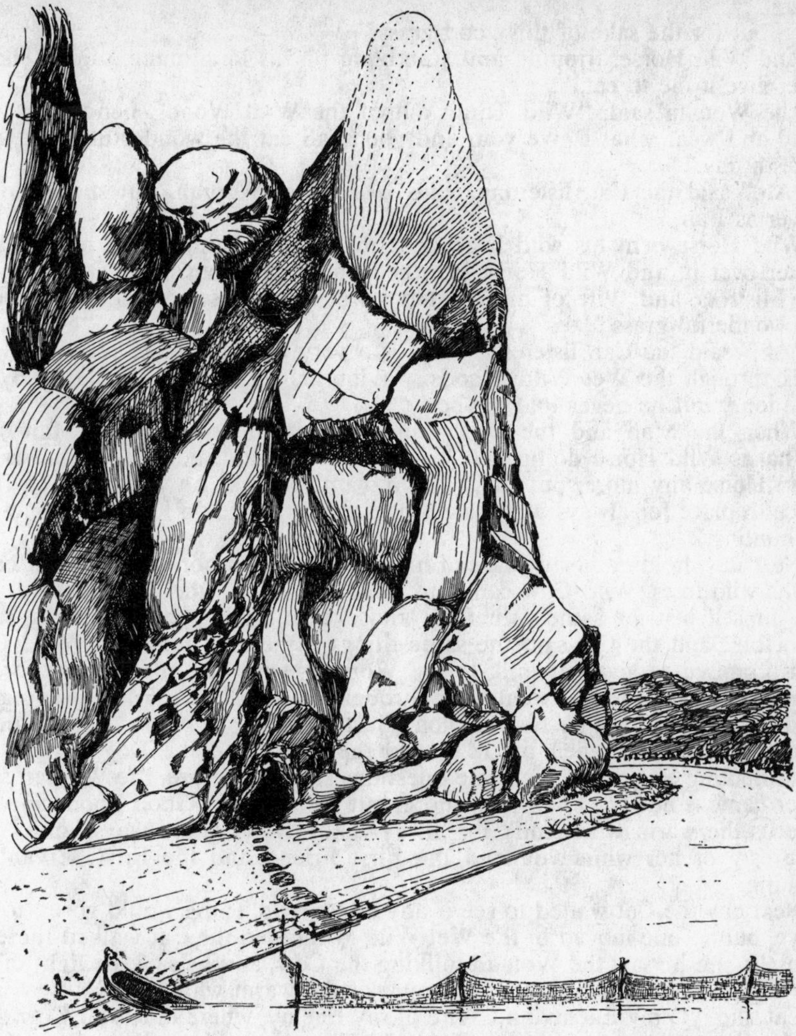

THIS IS THE PICTURE OF THE CAVE WHERE THE MAN AND THE WOMAN lived first of all. It was really a very nice Cave, and much warmer than it looks. The Man had a canoe. It is on the edge of the river, being soaked in water to make it swell up. The tattery-looking thing across the river is the Man's salmon-net to catch salmon with. There are nice clean stones leading up from the river to the mouth of the Cave, so that the Man and the Woman could go down for water without getting sand between their toes. The things like black-beetles far down the beach are really trunks of dead trees that floated down the river from the Wet Wild Woods on the other bank. The Man and the Woman used to drag them out and dry them and cut them up for firewood. I haven't drawn the horsehide curtain at the mouth of the Cave, because the Woman has just taken it down to be cleaned. All those little smudges on the sand between the Cave and the river are the marks of the Woman's feet and the Man's feet.

The Man and the Woman are both inside the Cave eating their dinner. They went to another cosier Cave when the Baby came, because the Baby used to crawl down to the river and fall in, and the Dog had to pull him out.

Dog, but for the sake of this good grass."

And Wild Horse, tripping and stumbling on his long mane, said, "That is true; give it me to eat."

The Woman said, "Wild Thing out of the Wild Woods, bend your wild head and wear what I give you, and you shall eat the wonderful grass three times a day."

"Ah," said the Cat, listening, "this is a clever Woman, but she is not so clever as I am."

Wild Horse bent his wild head, and the Woman slipped the plaited hide halter over it, and Wild Horse breathed on the Woman's feet and said, "O my Mistress, and Wife of my Master, I will be your servant for the sake of the wonderful grass."

"Ah," said the Cat, listening, "that is a very foolish Horse." And he went back through the Wet Wild Woods, waving his wild tail and walking by his wild lone. But he never told anybody.

When the Man and the Dog came back from hunting, the Man said, "What is Wild Horse doing here?" And the Woman said, "His name is not Wild Horse any more, but the First Servant, because he will carry us from place to place for always and always and always. Ride on his back when you go hunting."

Next day, holding her wild head high that her wild horns should not catch in the wild trees, Wild Cow came up to the Cave, and the Cat followed, and hid himself just the same as before; and everything happened just the same as before; and the Cat said the same things as before; and when Wild Cow had promised to give her milk to the Woman every day in exchange for the wonderful grass, the Cat went back through the Wet Wild Woods waving his wild tail and walking by his wild lone, just the same as before. But he never told anybody. And when the Man and the Horse and the Dog came home from hunting and asked the same questions same as before, the Woman said, "Her name is not Wild Cow any more, but the Giver of Good Food. She will give us the warm white milk for always and always and always, and I will take care of her while you and the First Friend and the First Servant go hunting."

Next day the Cat waited to see if any other Wild Thing would go up to the Cave, but no one moved in the Wet Wild Woods, so the Cat walked there by himself; and he saw the Woman milking the Cow, and he saw the light of the fire in the Cave, and he smelt the smell of the warm white milk.

Cat said, "O my Enemy and Wife of my Enemy, where did Wild Cow go?"

The Woman laughed and said, "Wild Thing out of the Wild Woods, go back to the Woods again, for I have braided up my hair, and I have put away the magic blade-bone, and we have no more need of either friends or servants in our Cave."

Cat said, "I am not a friend, and I am not a servant. I am the Cat who walks by himself, and I wish to come into your Cave."

Woman said, "Then why did you not come with First Friend on the first night?"

Cat grew very angry and said, "Has Wild Dog told tales of me?"

Then the Woman laughed and said, "You are the Cat who walks by himself, and all places are alike to you. You are neither a friend nor a servant. You have said it yourself. Go away and walk by yourself in all places alike."

Then Cat pretended to be sorry and said, "Must I never come into the Cave? Must I never sit by the warm fire? Must I never drink the warm white milk? You are very wise and very beautiful. You should not be cruel even to a Cat."

Woman said, "I knew I was wise, but I did not know I was beautiful. So I will make a bargain with you. If ever I say one word in your praise, you may come into the Cave."

"And if you say two words in my praise?" said the Cat.

"I never shall," said the Woman, "but if I say two words in your praise, you may sit by the fire in the Cave."

"And if you say three words?" said the Cat.

"I never shall," said the Woman, "but if I say three words in your praise, you may drink the warm white milk three times a day for always and always and always."

Then the Cat arched his back and said, "Now let the Curtain at the mouth of the Cave, and the Fire at the back of the Cave, and the Milk-pots that stand beside the Fire, remember what my Enemy and the Wife of my Enemy has said." And he went away through the Wet Wild Woods waving his wild tail and walking by his wild lone.

That night when the Man and the Horse and the Dog came home from hunting, the Woman did not tell them of the bargain that she had made with the Cat, because she was afraid that they might not like it.

Cat went far and far away and hid himself in the Wet Wild Woods by his wild lone for a long time till the Woman forgot all about him. Only the Bat—the little upside-down Bat—that hung inside the Cave knew where Cat hid; and every evening Bat would fly to Cat with news of what was happening.

One evening Bat said, "There is a Baby in the Cave. He is new and pink and fat and small, and the Woman is very fond of him."

"Ah," said the Cat, listening, "but what is the Baby fond of?"

"He is fond of things that are soft and tickle," said the Bat. "He is fond of warm things to hold in his arms when he goes to sleep. He is fond of being played with. He is fond of all those things."

"Ah," said the Cat, listening, "then my time has come."

Next night Cat walked through the Wet Wild Woods and hid very near the Cave till morning-time, and Man and Dog and Horse went hunting. The Woman was busy cooking that morning, and the Baby cried and interrupted. So she carried him outside the Cave and gave him a handful of pebbles to play with. But still the Baby cried.

Then the Cat put out his paddy paw and patted the Baby on the cheek, and it cooed; and the Cat rubbed against its fat knees and tickled it under its fat chin with his tail. And the Baby laughed; and the Woman heard him and smiled.

Then the Bat—the little upside-down Bat—that hung in the mouth of the Cave said, "O my Hostess and Wife of my Host and Mother of my Host's Son, a Wild Thing from the Wild Woods is most beautifully playing with your Baby."

"A blessing on that Wild Thing whoever he may be," said the Woman, straightening her back, "for I was a busy woman this morning and he has done me a service."

That very minute and second, Best Beloved, the dried horse-skin Curtain that was stretched tail-down at the mouth of the Cave fell down—*woosh!*—because it remembered the bargain she had made with the Cat; and when the Woman went to pick it up—lo and behold!—the Cat was sitting quite comfy inside the Cave.

"O my Enemy and Wife of my Enemy and Mother of my Enemy," said the Cat, "it is I: for you have spoken a word in my praise, and now I can sit within the Cave for always and always and always. But still I am the Cat who walks by himself, and all places are alike to me."

The Woman was very angry, and shut her lips tight and took up her spinning-wheel and began to spin.

But the Baby cried because the Cat had gone away, and the Woman could not hush it, for it struggled and kicked and grew black in the face.

"O my Enemy and Wife of my Enemy and Mother of my Enemy," said the Cat, "take a strand of the thread that you are spinning and tie it to your spinning-whorl and drag it along the floor, and I will show you a Magic that shall make your Baby laugh as loudly as he is now crying."

"I will do so," said the Woman, "because I am at my wits' end; but I will not thank you for it."

She tied the thread to the little clay spindle-whorl and drew it across the floor, and the Cat ran after it and patted it with his paws and rolled head over heels, and tossed it backward over his shoulder and chased it between his hind-legs and pretended to lose it, and pounced down upon it again, till the Baby laughed as loudly as it had been crying, and scrambled after the Cat and frolicked all over the Cave till it grew tired and settled down to sleep with the Cat in its arms.

"Now," said Cat, "I will sing the Baby a song that shall keep him asleep for an hour." And he began to purr, loud and low, low and loud, till the Baby fell fast asleep. The Woman smiled as she looked down upon the two of them, and said, "That was wonderfully done. No question but you are very clever, O Cat."

That very minute and second, Best Beloved, the smoke of the Fire at the back of the Cave came down in clouds from the roof–*puff!*–because it remembered the bargain she had made with the Cat; and when it had cleared away–lo and behold!–the Cat was sitting quite comfy close to the fire.

"O my Enemy and Wife of my Enemy and Mother of my Enemy," said the Cat, "it is I: for you have spoken a second word in my praise, and now I can sit by the warm fire at the back of the Cave for always and always and always. But still I am the Cat who walks by himself, and all places are alike to me."

Then the Woman was very very angry, and let down her hair and put more wood on the fire and brought out the broad blade-bone of the shoulder of mutton and began to make a Magic that should prevent her from saying a third word in praise of the Cat. It was not a Singing Magic, Best Beloved, it was a Still Magic; and by and by the Cave grew so still that a little wee-wee mouse crept out of a corner and ran across the floor.

"O my Enemy and Wife of my Enemy and Mother of my Enemy," said the Cat, "is that little mouse part of your Magic?"

"Ouh! Chee! No indeed!" said the Woman, and she dropped the blade-bone and jumped upon the footstool in front of the fire and braided up her hair very quick for fear that the mouse should run up it.

"Ah," said the Cat, watching, "then the mouse will do me no harm if I eat it?"

"No," said the Woman, braiding up her hair, "eat it quickly and I will ever be grateful to you."

Cat made one jump and caught the little mouse, and the Woman said, "A hundred thanks. Even the First Friend is not quick enough to catch little mice as you have done. You must be very wise."

That very moment and second, O Best Beloved, the Milk-pot that stood by the fire cracked in two pieces–*ffft!*–because it remembered the bargain she had made with the Cat; and when the Woman jumped down from the footstool–lo and behold!–the Cat was lapping up the warm white milk that lay in one of the broken pieces.

"O my Enemy and Wife of my Enemy and Mother of my Enemy," said the Cat, "it is I: for you have spoken three words in my praise, and now I can drink the warm white milk three times a day for always and always and always. But *still* I am the Cat who walks by himself, and all places are alike to me."

Then the Woman laughed and set the Cat a bowl of the warm white milk and said, "O Cat, you are as clever as a man, but remember that your bargain was not made with the Man or the Dog, and I do not know what they will do when they come home."

"What is that to me?" said the Cat. "If I have my place in the Cave by the

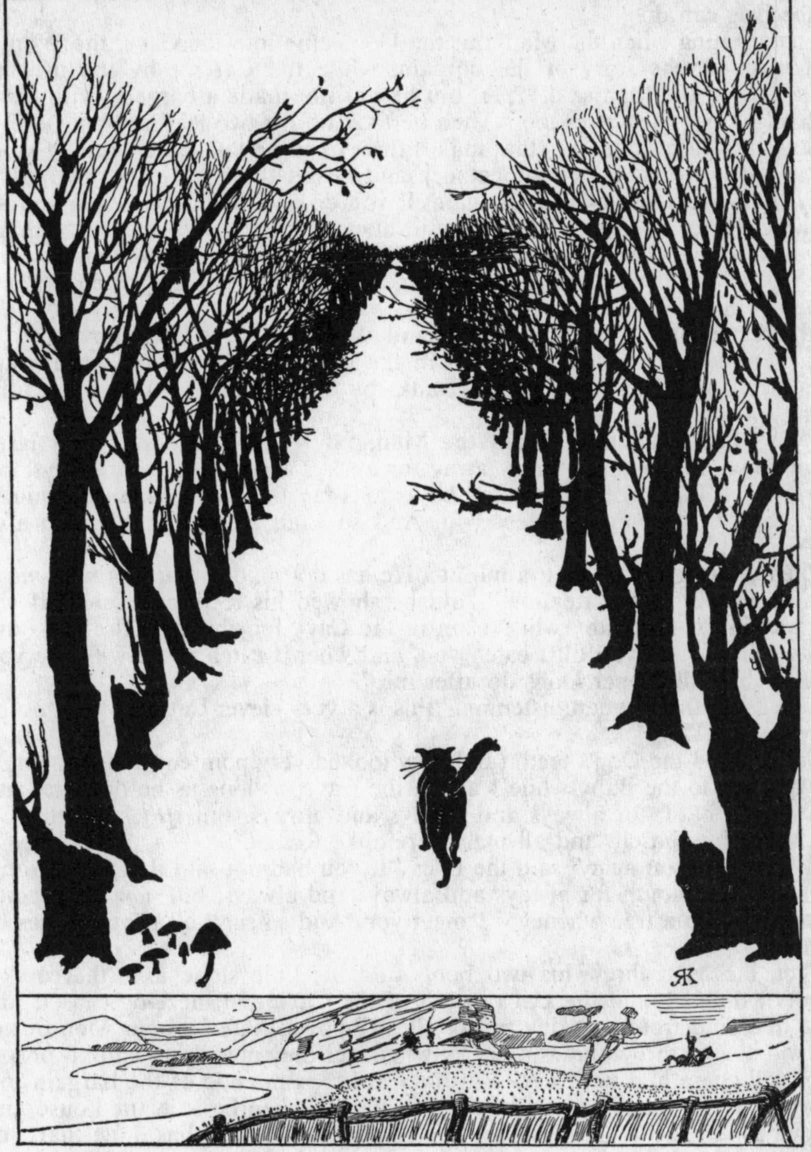

THIS IS THE PICTURE OF THE CAT THAT WALKED BY HIMSELF, WALKING by his wild lone through the Wet Wild Woods and waving his wild tail. There is nothing else in the picture except some toadstools. They had to grow there because the woods were so wet. The lumpy thing on the low branch isn't a bird. It is moss that grew there because the Wild Woods were so wet.

Underneath the truly picture is a picture of the cosy Cave that the Man and the Woman went to after the Baby came. It was their summer Cave, and they planted wheat in front of it. The Man is riding on the Horse to find the Cow and bring her back to the Cave to be milked. He is holding up his hand to call the Dog, who has swum across to the other side of the river, looking for rabbits.

fire and my warm white milk three times a day I do not care what the Man or the Dog can do."

That evening when the Man and the Dog came into the Cave, the Woman told them all the story of the bargain, while the Cat sat by the fire and smiled. Then the Man said, "Yes, but he has not made a bargain, with *me* or with all proper Men after me." Then he took off his two leather boots and he took up his little stone axe (that makes three) and he fetched a piece of wood and a hatchet (that is five altogether), and he set them out in a row and he said, "Now we will make *our* bargain. If you do not catch mice when you are in the Cave for always and always and always, I will throw these five things at you whenever I see you, and so shall all proper Men do after me."

"Ah," said the Woman, listening, "this is a very clever Cat, but he is not so clever as my Man."

The Cat counted the five things (and they looked very knobby) and he said, "I will catch mice when I am in the Cave for always and always and always; but *still* I am the Cat who walks by himself, and all places are alike to me."

"Not when I am near," said the Man. "If you had not said that last I would have put all these things away for always and always and always; but now I am going to throw my two boots and my little stone axe (that makes three) at you whenever I meet you. And so shall all proper Men do after me!"

Then the Dog said, "Wait a minute. He has not made a bargain with *me* or with all proper Dogs after me." And he showed his teeth and said, "If you are not kind to the Baby while I am in the Cave for always and always and always, I will hunt you till I catch you, and when I catch you I will bite you. And so shall all proper Dogs do after me."

"Ah," said the Woman, listening, "this is a very clever Cat, but he is not so clever as the Dog."

Cat counted the Dog's teeth (and they looked very pointed) and he said, "I will be kind to the Baby while I am in the Cave, as long as he does not pull my tail too hard, for always and always and always. But *still* I am the Cat that walks by himself, and all places are alike to me!"

"Not when I am near," said the Dog. "If you had not said that last I would have shut my mouth for always and always and always; but *now* I am going to hunt you up a tree whenever I meet you. And so shall all proper Dogs do after me."

Then the Man threw his two boots and his little stone axe (that makes three) at the Cat, and the Cat ran out of the Cave and the Dog chased him up a tree; and from that day to this, Best Beloved, three proper Men out of five will always throw things at a Cat whenever they meet him, and all proper Dogs will chase him up a tree. But the Cat keeps his side of the bargain too. He will kill mice, and he will be kind to Babies when he is in the house, just as long as they do not pull his tail too hard. But when he has done that, and between times, and when the moon gets up and night comes, he is the Cat that walks by himself, and all places are alike to him. Then he goes out to the Wet Wild Woods or up the Wet Wild Trees or on the Wet Wild Roofs, waving his wild tail and walking by his wild lone.

Pussy can sit by the fire and sing,
    Pussy can climb a tree,
Or play with a silly old cork and string
    To 'muse herself, not me.
But I like *Binkie* my dog, because
    He knows how to behave;
So, *Binkie's* the same as the First Friend was,
    And I am the Man in the Cave.

Pussy will play man-Friday till
    It's time to wet her paw
And make her walk on the window-sill
    (For the footprint Crusoe saw);
Then she fluffles her tail and mews,
    And scratches and won't attend.
But *Binkie* will play whatever I choose,
    And he is my true First Friend.

Pussy will rub my knees with her head
    Pretending she loves me hard;
But the very minute I go to my bed
    Pussy runs out in the yard,
And there she stays till the morning-light;
    So I know it is only pretend;
But *Binkie,* he snores at my feet all night,
    And he is my Firstest Friend!

The Butterfly That Stamped

THIS, O MY Best Beloved, is a story—a new and a wonderful story—a story quite different from the other stories—a story about The Most Wise Sovereign Suleiman-bin-Daoud—Solomon the Son of David.

There are three hundred and fifty-five stories about Suleiman-bin-Daoud; but this is not one of them. It is not the story of the Lapwing who found the Water; or the Hoopoe who shaded Suleiman-bin-Daoud from the heat. It is not the story of the Glass Pavement, or the Ruby with the Crooked Hole, or the Gold Bars of Balkis. It is the story of the Butterfly that Stamped.

Now attend all over again and listen!

Suleiman-bin-Daoud was wise. He understood what the beasts said, what the birds said, what the fishes said, and what the insects said. He understood what the rocks said deep under the earth when they bowed in towards each other and groaned; and he understood what the trees said when they rustled in the middle of the morning. He understood everything, from the bishop on the bench to the hyssop on the wall; and Balkis, his Head Queen, the Most Beautiful Queen Balkis, was nearly as wise as he was.

Suleiman-bin-Daoud was strong. Upon the third finger of his right hand he wore a ring. When he turned it once, Afrits and Djinns came out of the earth to do whatever he told them. When he turned it twice, Fairies came down from the sky to do whatever he told them; and when he turned it three times, the very great angel Azrael of the Sword came dressed as a water-carrier, and told him the news of the three worlds,—Above—Below—and Here.

And yet Suleiman-bin-Daoud was not proud. He very seldom showed off, and when he did he was sorry for it. Once he tried to feed all the animals in all the world in one day, but when the food was ready an Animal came out of the deep sea and ate it up in three mouthfuls. Suleiman-bin-Daoud was very surprised and said, "O Animal, who are you?" And the Animal said, "O King, live for ever! I am the smallest of thirty thousand brothers, and our home is at the bottom of the sea. We heard that you were going to feed all the animals in all the world, and my brothers sent me to ask when dinner would be ready." Suleiman-bin-Daoud was more surprised than ever and said, "O Animal, you have eaten all the dinner that I made ready for all the animals in the world." And the Animal said, "O King, live for ever, but do you really call *that* a dinner? Where I come from we each eat twice as much as that between meals." Then Suleiman-bin-Daoud fell flat on his face and said, "O Animal! I gave that dinner to show what a great and rich king I was, and not because I really wanted to be kind to the animals. Now I am ashamed, and it serves me right." Suleiman-bin-Daoud was a really truly wise man, Best Beloved. After that he never forgot that it was silly to show off; and now the real story part of my story begins.

He married ever so many wives. He married nine hundred and ninety-nine wives, besides the Most Beautiful Balkis; and they all lived in a great golden palace in the middle of a lovely garden with fountains. He didn't really want nine hundred and ninety-nine wives, but in those days everybody married ever so many wives, and of course the King had to marry ever so many more just to show that he was the King.

Some of the wives were nice, but some were simply horrid, and the horrid ones quarrelled with the nice ones and made them horrid too, and then they would all quarrel with Suleiman-bin-Daoud, and that was horrid for him. But Balkis the Most Beautiful never quarrelled with Suleiman-bin-Daoud. She loved him too much. She sat in her rooms in the Golden Palace, or walked in the Palace garden, and was truly sorry for him.

Of course if he had chosen to turn his ring on his finger and call up the Djinns and the Afrits they would have magicked all those nine hundred and ninety-nine quarrelsome wives into white mules of the desert or greyhounds or pomegranate seeds; but Suleiman-bin-Daoud thought that that would be showing off. So, when they quarrelled too much, he only walked by himself in one part of the beautiful Palace gardens and wished he had never been born.

One day, when they had quarrelled for three weeks—all nine hundred and ninety-nine wives together—Suleiman-bin-Daoud went out for peace and quiet as usual; and among the orange-trees he met Balkis the Most Beautiful, very sorrowful because Suleiman-bin-Daoud was so worried. And she said to him, "O my Lord and Light of my Eyes, turn the ring upon your finger and show these Queens of Egypt and Mesopotamia and Persia and China that you are the great and terrible King." But Suleiman-bin-Daoud shook his head and said, "O my Lady and Delight of my Life, remember the Animal that came out of the sea and made me ashamed before all the animals in all the world because I showed off. Now, if I showed off before these Queens of Persia and Egypt and Abyssinia and China, merely because they worry me, I might be made even more ashamed than I have been."

And Balkis the Most Beautiful said, "O my Lord and Treasure of my Soul, what will you do?"

And Suleiman-bin-Daoud said, "O my Lady and Content of my Heart, I shall continue to endure my fate at the hands of these nine hundred and ninety-nine Queens who vex me with their continual quarrelling."

So he went on between the lilies and the loquats and the roses and the cannas and the heavy-scented ginger-plants that grew in the garden, till he came to the great camphor-tree that was called the Camphor Tree of Suleiman-bin-Daoud. But Balkis hid among the tall irises and the spotted bamboos and the red lilies behind the camphor-tree, so as to be near her own true love, Suleiman-bin-Daoud.

Presently two Butterflies flew under the tree, quarrelling.

Suleiman-bin-Daoud heard one say to the other, "I wonder at your presumption in talking like this to me. Don't you know that if I stamped with

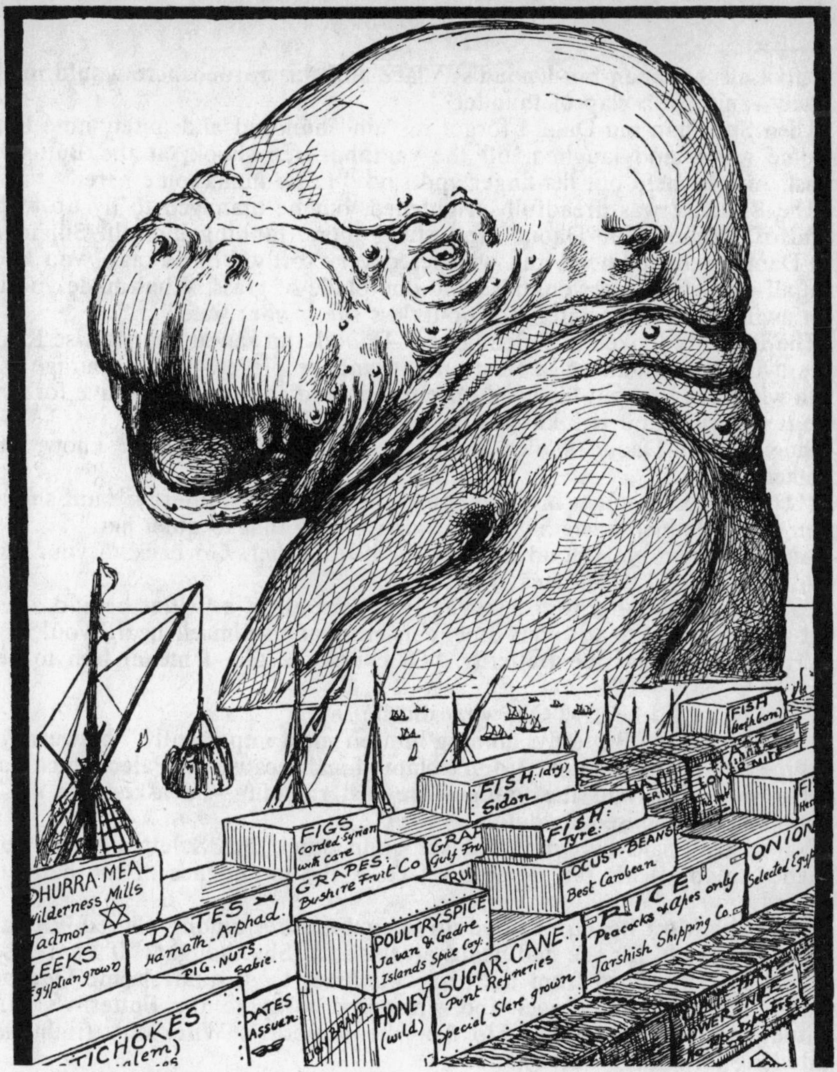

THIS IS THE PICTURE OF THE ANIMAL THAT CAME OUT OF THE SEA AND ate up all the food that Suleiman-bin-Daoud had made ready for all the animals in all the world. He was really quite a nice Animal, and his Mummy was very fond of him and of his twenty-nine thousand nine hundred and ninety-nine other brothers that lived at the bottom of the sea. You know that he was the smallest of them all, and so his name was Small Porgies. He ate up all those boxes and packets and bales and things that had been got ready for all the animals, without ever once taking off the lids or untying the strings, and it did not hurt him at all. The sticky-up masts behind the boxes of food belong to Suleiman-bin-Daoud's ships. They were busy bringing more food when Small Porgies came ashore. He did not eat the ships. They stopped unloading the foods and instantly sailed away to sea till Small Porgies had quite finished eating. You can see some of the ships beginning to sail away by Small Porgies' shoulder. I have not drawn Suleiman-bin-Daoud, but he is just outside the picture, very much astonished. The bundle hanging from the mast of the ship in the corner is really a package of wet dates for parrots to eat. I don't know the names of the ships. That is all there is in that picture.

my foot all Suleiman-bin-Daoud's Palace and this garden here would immediately vanish in a clap of thunder?"

Then Suleiman-bin-Daoud forgot his nine hundred and ninety-nine bothersome wives, and laughed, till the camphor-tree shook, at the Butterfly's boast. And he held out his finger and said, "Little man, come here."

The Butterfly was dreadfully frightened, but he managed to fly up to the hand of Suleiman-bin-Daoud, and clung there, fanning himself. Suleiman-bin-Daoud bent his head and whispered very softly, "Little man, you know that all your stamping wouldn't bend one blade of grass. What made you tell that awful fib to your wife?—for doubtless she is your wife."

The Butterfly looked at Suleiman-bin-Daoud and saw the most wise King's eyes twinkle like stars on a frosty night, and he picked up his courage with both wings, and he put his head on one side and said, "O King, live for ever. She *is* my wife; and you know what wives are like."

Suleiman-bin-Daoud smiled in his beard and said, "Yes, *I* know, little brother."

"One must keep them in order somehow," said the Butterfly, "and she has been quarrelling with me all the morning. I said that to quiet her."

And Suleiman-bin-Daoud said, "May it quiet her. Go back to your wife, little brother, and let me hear what you say."

Back flew the Butterfly to his wife, who was all of a twitter behind a leaf, and she said, "He heard you! Suleiman-bin-Daoud himself heard you!"

"Heard me!" said the Butterfly. "Of course he did. I meant him to hear me."

"And what did he say? Oh, what did he say?"

"Well," said the Butterfly, fanning himself most importantly, "between you and me, my dear—of course I don't blame him, because his Palace must have cost a great deal and the oranges are just ripening,—he asked me not to stamp, and I promised I wouldn't."

"Gracious!" said his wife, and sat quite quiet; but Suleiman-bin-Daoud laughed till the tears ran down his face at the impudence of the bad little Butterfly.

Balkis the Most Beautiful stood up behind the tree among the red lilies and smiled to herself, for she had heard all this talk. She thought, "If I am wise I can yet save my Lord from the persecutions of these quarrelsome Queens," and she held out her finger and whispered softly to the Butterfly's Wife, "Little woman, come here." Up flew the Butterfly's Wife, very frightened, and clung to Balkis's white hand.

Balkis bent her beautiful head down and whispered, "Little woman, do you believe what your husband has just said?"

The Butterfly's Wife looked at Balkis, and saw the Most Beautiful Queen's eyes shining like deep pools with starlight on them, and she picked up her courage with both wings and said, "O Queen, be lovely for ever. *You* know what men-folk are like."

And the Queen Balkis, the Wise Balkis of Sheba, put her hand to her lips to hide a smile and said, "Little sister, *I* know."

"They get angry," said the Butterfly's Wife, fanning herself quickly, "over nothing at all, but we must humor them, O Queen. They never mean half they say. If it pleases my husband to believe that I believe he can make Suleiman-bin-Daoud's Palace disappear by stamping his foot, I'm sure *I* don't care. He'll forget all about it to-morrow."

"Little sister," said Balkis, "you are quite right; but next time he begins to boast, take him at his word. Ask him to stamp, and see what will happen. *We* know what men-folk are like, don't we? He'll be very much ashamed."

Away flew the Butterfly's Wife to her husband, and in five minutes they were quarrelling worse than ever.

"Remember!" said the Butterfly. "Remember what I can do if I stamp my foot."

"I don't believe you one little bit," said the Butterfly's Wife. "I should very much like to see it done. Suppose you stamp now."

"I promised Suleiman-bin-Daoud that I wouldn't," said the Butterfly, "and I don't want to break my promise."

"It wouldn't matter if you did," said his wife. "You couldn't bend a blade of grass with your stamping. I dare you to do it," she said. "Stamp! Stamp! Stamp!"

Suleiman-bin-Daoud, sitting under the camphor-tree, heard every word of this, and he laughed as he had never laughed in his life before. He forgot all about his Queens; he forgot about the Animal that came out of the sea; he forgot about showing off. He just laughed with joy, and Balkis, on the other side of the tree, smiled because her own true love was so joyful.

Presently the Butterfly, very hot and puffy, came whirling back under the shadow of the camphor-tree and said to Suleiman, "She wants me to stamp! She wants to see what will happen, O Suleiman-bin-Daoud! You know I can't do it, and now she'll never believe a word I say. She'll laugh at me to the end of my days!"

"No, little brother," said Suleiman-bin-Daoud, "she will never laugh at you again," and he turned the ring on his finger—just for the little Butterfly's sake, not for the sake of showing off,—and, lo and behold, four huge Djinns came out of the earth!

"Slaves," said Suleiman-bin-Daoud, "when this gentleman on my finger" (that was where the impudent Butterfly was sitting) "stamps his left front forefoot you will make my Palace and these gardens disappear in a clap of thunder. When he stamps again you will bring them back carefully."

"Now, little brother," he said, "go back to your wife and stamp all you've a mind to."

Away flew the Butterfly to his wife, who was crying, "I dare you to do it! I dare you to do it! Stamp! Stamp now! Stamp!" Balkis saw the four vast Djinns stoop down to the four corners of the gardens with the Palace in the middle, and she clapped her hands softly and said, "At last Suleiman-bin-Daoud will do for the sake of a Butterfly what he ought to have done long ago for his own sake, and the quarrelsome Queens will be frightened!"

Then the Butterfly stamped. The Djinns jerked the Palace and the gardens a thousand miles into the air: there was a most awful thunder-clap, and everything grew inky-black. The Butterfly's Wife fluttered about in the dark, crying, "Oh, I'll be good! I'm so sorry I spoke! Only bring the gardens back, my dear darling husband, and I'll never contradict again."

The Butterfly was nearly as frightened as his wife, and Suleiman-bin-Daoud laughed so much that it was several minutes before he found breath enough to whisper to the Butterfly, "Stamp again, little brother. Give me back my Palace, most great magician."

"Yes, give him back his Palace," said the Butterfly's Wife, still flying about in the dark like a moth. "Give him back his Palace, and don't let's have any more horrid magic."

"Well, my dear," said the Butterfly as bravely as he could, "you see what your nagging has led to. Of course it doesn't make any difference to *me*—I'm used to this kind of thing—but as a favor to you and to Suleiman-bin-Daoud I don't mind putting things right."

So he stamped once more, and that instant the Djinns let down the Palace and the gardens, without even a bump. The sun shone on the dark-green orange-leaves; the fountains played among the pink Egyptian lilies; the birds went on singing; and the Butterfly's Wife lay on her side under the camphor-tree waggling her wings and panting, "Oh, I'll be good! I'll be good!"

Suleiman-bin-Daoud could hardly speak for laughing. He leaned back all weak and hiccoughy, and shook his finger at the Butterfly and said, "O great wizard, what is the sense of returning to me my Palace if at the same time you slay me with mirth!"

Then came a terrible noise, for all the nine hundred and ninety-nine Queens ran out of the Palace shrieking and shouting and calling for their babies. They hurried down the great marble steps below the fountain, one hundred abreast, and the Most Wise Balkis went statelily forward to meet them and said, "What is your trouble, O Queens?"

They stood on the marble steps one hundred abreast and shouted, "*What* is our trouble? We were living peacefully in our golden Palace, as is our custom, when upon a sudden the Palace disappeared, and we were left sitting in a thick and noisome darkness; and it thundered, and Djinns and Afrits moved about in the darkness! *That* is our trouble, O Head Queen, and we are most extremely troubled on account of that trouble, for it was a troublesome trouble, unlike any trouble we have known."

Then Balkis the Most Beautiful Queen–Suleiman-bin-Daoud's Very Best Beloved–Queen that was of Sheba and Sabie and the Rivers of the Gold of the South–from the Desert of Zinn to the Towers of Zimbabwe–Balkis, almost as wise as the Most Wise Suleiman-bin-Daoud himself, said, "It is nothing, O Queens! A Butterfly has made complaint against his wife because she quarrelled with him, and it has pleased our Lord Suleiman-bin-Daoud to teach her a lesson in low-speaking and humbleness, for that is counted a virtue among the wives of the butterflies."

Then up and spoke an Egyptian Queen–the daughter of a Pharaoh–and she said, "Our Palace cannot be plucked up by the roots like a leek for the sake of a little insect. No! Suleiman-bin-Daoud must be dead, and what we heard and saw was the earth thundering and darkening at the news."

Then Balkis beckoned that bold Queen without looking at her, and said to her and to the others, "Come and see."

They came down the marble steps, one hundred abreast, and beneath his camphor-tree, still weak with laughing, they saw the Most Wise King Suleiman-bin-Daoud rocking back and forth with a Butterfly on either hand, and they heard him say, "O wife of my brother in the air, remember after this to please your husband in all things, lest he be provoked to stamp his foot yet again; for he has said that he is used to this Magic, and he is most eminently a great magician–one who steals away the very Palace of Suleiman-bin-Daoud himself. Go in peace, little folk!" And he kissed them on the wings, and they flew away.

Then all the Queens except Balkis–the Most Beautiful and Splendid Balkis, who stood apart smiling–fell flat on their faces, for they said, "If these things are done when a Butterfly is displeased with his wife, what shall be done to us who have vexed our King with our loud-speaking and open quarrelling through many days?"

Then they put their veils over their heads, and they put their hands over their mouths, and they tiptoed back to the Palace most mousy-quiet.

Then Balkis–the Most Beautiful and Excellent Balkis–went forward through the red lilies into the shade of the camphor-tree and laid her hand upon Suleiman-bin-Daoud's shoulder and said, "O my Lord and Treasure of my Soul, rejoice, for we have taught the Queens of Egypt and Ethiopia and Abyssinia and Persia and India and China with a great and a memorable teaching."

And Suleiman-bin-Daoud, still looking after the Butterflies where they played in the sunlight, said, "O my Lady and Jewel of my Felicity, when did this happen? For I have been jesting with a Butterfly ever since I came into the garden." And he told Balkis what he had done.

Balkis–the Tender and Most Lovely Balkis–said, "O my Lord and Regent of my Existence, I hid behind the camphor-tree and saw it all. It was I who told the Butterfly's Wife to ask the Butterfly to stamp, because I hoped that for the sake of the jest my Lord would make some great Magic and that the Queens would see it and be frightened." And she told him what the Queens

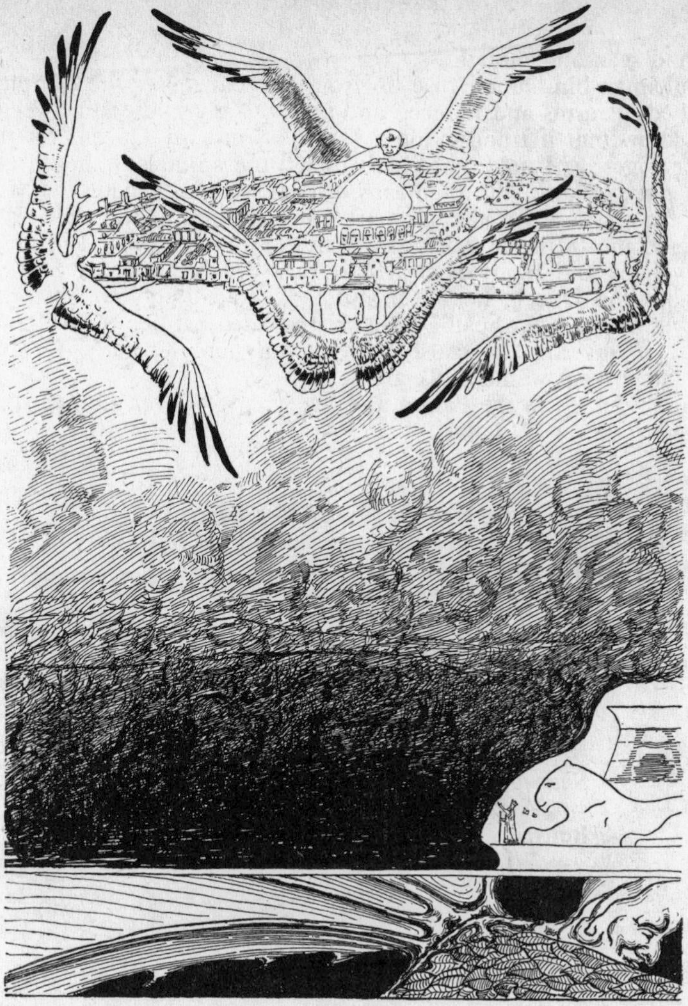

THIS IS THE PICTURE OF THE FOUR GULL-WINGED DJINNS LIFTING UP Suleiman-bin-Daoud's Palace the very minute after the Butterfly had stamped. The Palace and the gardens and everything came up in one piece like a board, and they left a big hole in the ground all full of dust and smoke. If you look in the corner, close to the thing that looks like a lion, you will see Suleiman-bin-Daoud with his magic stick and the two Butterflies behind him. The thing that looks like a lion is really a lion carved in stone, and the thing that looks like a milk-can is really a piece of a temple or a house or something. Suleiman-bin-Daoud stood there so as to be out of the way of the dust and the smoke when the Djinns lifted up the Palace. I don't know the Djinns' names. They were servants of Suleiman-bin-Daoud's magic ring, and they changed about every day. They were just common gull-winged Djinns.

The thing at the bottom is a picture of a very friendly Djinn called Akraig. He used to feed the little fishes in the sea three times a day, and his wings were made of pure copper. I put him in to show you what a nice Djinn is like. He did not help to lift the Palace. He was busy feeding little fishes in the Arabian Sea when it happened.

had said and seen and thought.

Then Suleiman-bin-Daoud rose up from his seat under the camphor-tree, and stretched his arms and rejoiced and said, "O my Lady and Sweetener of my Days, know that if I had made a Magic against my Queens for the sake of pride or anger, as I made that feast for all the animals, I should certainly have been put to shame. But by means of your wisdom I made the Magic for the sake of a jest and for the sake of a little Butterfly, and–behold–it has also delivered me from the vexations of my vexatious wives! Tell me, therefore, O my Lady and Heart of my Heart, how did you come to be so wise?"

And Balkis the Queen, beautiful and tall, looked up into Suleiman-bin-Daoud's eyes and put her head a little on one side, just like the Butterfly, and said, "First, O my Lord, because I loved you; and secondly, O my Lord, because I know what women-folk are."

Then they went up to the Palace and lived happily ever afterwards.

But wasn't it clever of Balkis?

There was never a Queen like Balkis,
    From here to the wide world's end;
But Balkis talked to a butterfly
    As you would talk to a friend.

There was never a King like Solomon,
    Not since the world began;
But Solomon talked to a butterfly
    As a man would talk to a man.

She was Queen of Sabaea–
    And *he* was Asia's Lord–
But they both of 'em talked to butterflies
    When they took their walks abroad!

Puck of Pook's Hill

CONTENTS

Weland's Sword

Puck's Song

See you the dimpled track that runs,
All hollow through the wheat?
O that was where they hauled the guns
That smote King Philip's fleet.

See you our little mill that clacks,
So busy by the brook?
She has ground her corn and paid her tax
Ever since Domesday Book.

See you our stilly woods of oak,
And the dread ditch beside?
O that was where the Saxons broke,
On the day that Harold died.

See you the windy levels spread
About the gates of Rye?
O that was where the Northmen fled,
When Alfred's ships came by.

See you our pastures wide and lone,
Where the red oxen browse?
O there was a City thronged and known,
Ere London boasted a house.

And see you, after rain, the trace
Of mound and ditch and wall?
O that was a Legion's camping-place,
When Caesar sailed from Gaul.

And see you marks that show and fade,
Like shadows on the Downs?
O they are the lines the Flint Men made,
To guard their wondrous towns.

Trackway and Camp and City lost,
Salt Marsh where now is corn;

Old Wars, old Peace, old Arts that cease,
And so was England born!

She is not any common Earth,
Water or wood or air,
But Merlin's Isle of Gramarye,
Where you and I will fare.

THE CHILDREN WERE at the Theatre, acting to Three Cows as much as they could remember of *Midsummer Night's Dream.* Their father had made them a small play out of the big Shakespeare one, and they had rehearsed it with him and with their mother till they could say it by heart. They began where Nick Bottom the weaver comes out of the bushes with a donkey's head on his shoulder, and finds Titania, Queen of the Fairies, asleep. Then they skipped to the part where Bottom asks three little fairies to scratch his head and bring him honey, and they ended where he falls asleep in Titania's arms. Dan was Puck and Nick Bottom, as well as all three Fairies. He wore a pointy-eared cloth cap for Puck, and a paper donkey's head out of a Christmas cracker—but it tore if you were not careful—for Bottom. Una was Titania, with a wreath of columbines and a foxglove wand.

The Theatre lay in a meadow called the Long Slip. A little mill-stream, carrying water to a mill two or three fields away, bent round one corner of it, and in the middle of the bend lay a large old fairy Ring of darkened grass, which was their stage. The mill-stream banks, overgrown with willow, hazel, and guelder rose made convenient places to wait in till your turn came; and a grown-up who had seen it said that Shakespeare himself could not have imagined a more suitable setting for his play. They were not, of course, allowed to act on Midsummer Night itself, but they went down after tea on Midsummer Eve, when the shadows were growing, and they took their supper—hard-boiled eggs, Bath Oliver biscuits, and salt in an envelope—with them. Three Cows had been milked and were grazing steadily with a tearing noise that one could hear all down the meadow; and the noise of the mill at work sounded like bare feet running on hard ground. A cuckoo sat on a gatepost singing his broken June tune, "cuckoo-cuk," while a busy kingfisher crossed from the mill-stream to the brook which ran on the other side of the meadow. Everything else was a sort of thick, sleepy stillness smelling of meadow-sweet and dry grass.

Their play went beautifully. Dan remembered all his parts—Puck, Bottom, and the three Fairies—and Una never forgot a word of Titania—not even the difficult piece where she tells the Fairies how to feed Bottom with "apricocks, ripe figs, and dewberries," and all the lines end in "ies." They were both so pleased that they acted it three times over from beginning to end before they sat down in the unthistly center of the Ring to eat eggs and Bath Olivers. This was when they heard a whistle among the alders on the bank, and they jumped.

The bushes parted. In the very spot where Dan had stood as Puck they saw a small, brown, broad-shouldered, pointy-eared person with a snub nose, slanting blue eyes, and a grin that ran right across his freckled face. He shaded his forehead as though he were watching Quince, Snout, Bottom, and the others rehearsing *Pyramis and Thisbe,* and, in a voice as deep as Three Cows asking to be milked, he began:

"What hempen homespuns have we swaggering here,
So near the cradle of our fairy Queen?"

He stopped, hollowed one hand round his ear, and, with a wicked twinkle in his eye, went on:

> "What a play toward? I'll be auditor,
> An actor too, perhaps, if I see cause."

The children looked and gasped. The small thing—he was no taller than Dan's shoulder—stepped quietly into the Ring.

"I'm rather out of practice," said he; "but that's the way my part ought to be played."

Still the children stared at him—from his dark blue cap, like a big columbine flower, to his bare, hairy feet. At last he laughed.

"Please don't look like that. It isn't *my* fault. What else could you expect?" he said.

"We didn't expect any one," Dan answered, slowly. "This is our field."

"Is it?" said their visitor, sitting down. "Then what on Human Earth made you act *Midsummer Night's Dream* three times over, *on* Midsummer Eve, *in* the middle of a Ring, and under—right *under* one of my oldest hills in Old England? Pook's Hill—Puck's Hill—Puck's Hill—Pook's Hill! It's as plain as the nose on my face."

He pointed to the bare, fern-covered slope of Pook's Hill that runs up from the far side of the mill-stream to a dark wood. Beyond that wood the ground rises and rises for five hundred feet, till at last you climb out on the bare top of Beacon Hill, to look over the Pevensey Levels and the Channel and half the naked South Downs.

"By Oak, Ash, and Thorn!" he cried, still laughing. "If this had happened a few hundred years ago you'd have had all the People of the Hills out like bees in June!"

"We didn't know it was wrong," said Dan.

"Wrong!" The little fellow shook with laughter. "Indeed, it isn't wrong. You've done something that Kings and Knights and Scholars in old days would have given their crowns and spurs and books to find out. If Merlin himself had helped you, you couldn't have managed better! You've broken the Hills—you've broken the Hills! It hasn't happened in a thousand years."

"We—we didn't mean to," said Una.

"Of course you didn't! That's just why you did it. Unluckily the Hills are empty now, and all the People of the Hills are gone. I'm the only one left. I'm Puck, the oldest Old Thing in England, very much at your service if—if you care to have anything to do with me. If you don't, of course you've only to say so, and I'll go."

He looked at the children and the children looked at him for quite half a minute. His eyes did not twinkle any more. They were very kind, and there was the beginning of a good smile on his lips.

Una put out her hand. "Don't go," she said. "We like you."

"Have a Bath Oliver," said Dan, and he passed over the squashy envelope with the eggs.

"By Oak, Ash, and Thorn!" cried Puck, taking off his blue cap, "I like you too. Sprinkle a little salt on the biscuit, Dan, and I'll eat it with you. That'll show you the sort of person I am. Some of us"—he went on, with his mouth full—"couldn't abide Salt, or Horseshoes over a door, or Mountain-ash berries, or Running Water, or Cold Iron, or the sound of Church Bells. But I'm Puck!"

"We always said, Dan and I," Una stammered, "that if it ever happened we'd know exactly what to do; but—but now it seems all different somehow."

"She means meeting a fairy," said Dan. "*I* never believed in 'em—not after I was six, anyhow."

"I did," said Una. "At least, I sort of half believed till we learned 'Farewell

Rewards.' Do you know 'Farewell Rewards and Fairies'?"

"Do you mean this?" said Puck. He threw his big head back and began at the second line:–

"Good housewives now may say,
For now foul sluts in dairies
Do fare as well as they;
For though they sweep their hearths no less

("Join in, Una!")

Than maids were wont to do,
Yet who of late for cleanliness,
Finds sixpence in her shoe?"

The echoes flapped all along the flat meadow.

"Of course I know it," he said.

"And then there's the verse about the Rings," said Dan. "When I was little it always made me feel unhappy in my inside."

" 'Witness those rings and roundelays,' do you mean?" boomed Puck, with a voice like a great church organ.

"Of theirs which yet remain,
Were footed in Queen Mary's days
On many a grassy plain.
But since of late Elizabeth,
And later James came in,
Are never seen on any heath
As when the time hath been.

"It's some time since I heard that sung, but there's no good beating about the bush: it's true. The People of the Hills have all left. I saw them come into Old England and I saw them go. Giants, trolls, kelpies, brownies, goblins, imps; wood, tree, mound, and water spirits; heath-people, hill-watchers, treasure-guards, good people, little people, pishogues, leprechauns, night-riders, pixies, nixies, gnomes and the rest–gone, all gone! I came into England with Oak, Ash, and Thorn, and when Oak, Ash, and Thorn are gone I shall go too."

Dan looked round the meadow–at Una's oak by the lower gate, at the line of ash trees that overhang Otter Pool where the mill-stream spills over when the mill does not need it, and at the gnarled old white-thorn where Three Cows scratched their necks.

"It's all right," he said; and added, "I'm planting a lot of acorns this autumn too."

"Then aren't you most awfully old?" said Una.

"Not old–fairly long-lived, as folk say hereabouts. Let me see–my friends used to set my dish of cream for me o' nights when Stonehenge was new. Yes, before the Flint Men made the Dewpound under Chanctonbury Ring."

Una clasped her hands, cried "Oh!" and nodded her head.

"She's thought a plan," Dan explained. "She always does like that when she thinks a plan."

"I was thinking–suppose we saved some of our porridge and put it in the attic for you. They'd notice if we left it in the nursery."

"Schoolroom," said Dan, quickly, and Una flushed, because they had made a solemn treaty that summer not to call the schoolroom the nursery any more.

"Bless your heart o' gold!" said Puck. "You'll make a fine considering wench some market-day. I really don't want you to put out a bowl for me;

but if I ever need a bite, be sure I'll tell you."

He stretched himself at length on the dry grass, and the children stretched out beside him, their bare legs waving happily in the air. They felt they could not be afraid of him any more than of their particular friend old Hobden, the hedger. He did not bother them with grown-up questions, or laugh at the donkey's head, but lay and smiled to himself in the most sensible way.

"Have you a knife on you?" he said at last.

Dan handed over his big one-bladed outdoor knife, and Puck began to carve out a piece of turf from the center of the Ring.

"What's that for–Magic?" said Una, as he pressed up the square of chocolate loam that cut like so much cheese.

"One of my little Magics," he answered, and cut another. "You see, I can't let you into the Hills because the People of the Hills have gone; but if you care to take seizin from me, I may be able to show you something out of the common here on Human Earth. You certainly deserve it."

"What's taking seizin?" said Dan, cautiously.

"It's an old custom the people had when they bought and sold land. They used to cut out a clod and hand it over to the buyer, and you weren't lawfully seized of your land–it didn't really belong to you–till the other fellow had actually given you a piece of it–like this." He held out the turves.

"But it's our own meadow," said Dan, drawing back. "Are you going to magic it away?"

Puck laughed. "I know it's your meadow, but there's a great deal more in it than you or your father ever guessed. Try!"

He turned his eyes on Una.

"I'll do it," she said. Dan followed her example at once.

"Now are you two lawfully seized and possessed of all Old England," began Puck, in a sing-song voice. "By Right of Oak, Ash, and Thorn are you free to come and go and look and know where I shall show or best you please. You shall see What you shall see and you shall hear What you shall hear, though It shall have happened three thousand year; and you shall know neither Doubt nor Fear. Fast! Hold fast all I give you."

The children shut their eyes, but nothing happened.

"Well?" said Una, disappointedly opening them. "I thought there would be dragons."

"Though It shall have happened three thousand year," said Puck, and counted on his fingers. "No; I'm afraid there were no dragons three thousand years ago."

"But there hasn't happened anything at all," said Dan.

"Wait awhile," said Puck. "You don't grow an oak in a year–and Old England's older than twenty oaks. Let's sit down again and think. *I* can do that for a century at a time."

"Ah, but you are a fairy," said Dan.

"Have you ever heard me use that word yet?" said Puck, quickly.

"No. You talk about 'the People of the Hills,' but you never say 'fairies,' " said Una. "I was wondering at that. Don't you like it?"

"How would you like to be called 'mortal' or 'human being' all the time?" said Puck; "or 'son of Adam' or 'daughter of Eve'?"

"I shouldn't like it at all," said Dan. "That's how the Djinns and Afrits talk in the *Arabian Nights.*"

"And that's how *I* feel about saying–that word that I don't say. Besides, what you call *them* are made-up things the People of the Hills have never heard of–little buzzflies with butterfly wings and gauze petticoats, and shiny stars in their hair, and a wand like a schoolteacher's cane for punishing bad boys and rewarding good ones. *I* know 'em!"

"We don't mean that sort," said Dan. "We hate 'em too."

"Exactly," said Puck. "Can you wonder that the People of the Hills don't care to be confused with that painty-winged, wand-waving, sugar-and-shake-your-head set of impostors? Butterfly wings, indeed! I've seen Sir Huon and a troop of his people setting off from Tintagel Castle for Hy-Brasil in the teeth of a sou'-westerly gale, with the spray flying all over the castle, and the Horses of the Hill wild with fright. Out they'd go in a lull, screaming like gulls, and back they'd be driven five good miles inland before they could come head to wind again. Butterfly-wings! It was Magic–Magic as black as Merlin could make it, and the whole sea was green fire and white foam with singing mermaids in it. And the Horses of the Hill picked their way from one wave to another by the lightning flashes! *That* was how it was in the old days!"

"Splendid," said Dan, but Una shuddered.

"I'm glad they're gone, then; but what made the People of the Hills go away?" Una asked.

"Different things. I'll tell you one of them some day–the thing that made the biggest fit of any," said Puck. "But they didn't all flit at once. They dropped off, one by one, through the centuries. Most of them were foreigners who couldn't stand our climate. *They* flitted early."

"How early?" said Dan.

"A couple of thousand years or more. The fact is they began as Gods. The Phoenicians brought some over when they came to buy tin; and the Gauls, and the Jutes, and the Danes, and the Frisians, and the Angles brought more when they landed. They were always landing in those days, or being driven back to their ships, and they always brought their Gods with them. England is a bad country for Gods. Now, *I* began as I mean to go on. A bowl of porridge, a dish of milk, and a little quiet fun with the country folk in the lanes was enough for me then, as it is now. I belong here, you see, and I have been mixed up with people all my days. But most of the others insisted on being Gods, and having temples, and altars, and priests, and sacrifices of their own."

"People burned in wicker baskets?" said Dan. "Like Miss Blake tells us about?"

"All sorts of sacrifices," said Puck. "If it wasn't men, it was horses, or cattle, or pigs, or metheglin–that's a sticky, sweet sort of beer. *I* never liked it. They were a stiff-necked, extravagant set of idols, the Old Things. But what was the result? Men don't like being sacrificed at the best of times; they don't even like sacrificing their farm-horses. After a while men simply left the Old Things alone, and the roofs of their temples fell in, and the Old Things had to scuttle out and pick up a living as they could. Some of them took to hanging about trees, and hiding in graves and groaning o' nights. If they groaned loud enough and long enough they might frighten a poor countryman into sacrificing a hen, or leaving a pound of butter for them. I remember one Goddess called Belisama. She became a common wet water-spirit somewhere in Lancashire. And there were hundreds of other friends of mine. First they were Gods. Then they were People of the Hills, and then they flitted to other places because they couldn't get on with the English for one reason or another. There was only one Old Thing, I remember, who honestly worked for his living after he came down in the world. He was called Weland, and he was a smith to some Gods. I've forgotten their names, but he used to make them swords and spears. I think he claimed kin with Thor of the Scandinavians."

"*Heroes of Asgard* Thor?" said Una. She had been reading the book.

"Perhaps," answered Puck. "None the less, when bad times came, he didn't beg or steal. He worked; and I was lucky enough to be able to do him a good turn."

"Tell us about it," said Dan. "I think I like hearing of Old Things."

They rearranged themselves comfortably, each chewing a grass stem. Puck propped himself on one strong arm and went on:

"Let's think! I met Weland first on a November afternoon in a sleet storm, on Pevensey Level——"

"Pevensey? Over the hill, you mean?" Dan pointed south.

"Yes; but it was all marsh in those days, right up to Horsebridge and Hydeneye. I was on Beacon Hill–they called it Brunanburgh then–when I saw the pale flame that burning thatch makes, and I went down to look. Some pirates–I think they must have been Peofn's men–were burning a village on the Levels, and Weland's image–a big, black wooden thing with amber beads round its neck–lay in the bows of a black thirty-two-oar galley that they had just beached. Bitter cold it was! There were icicles hanging from her deck, and the oars were glazed over with ice, and there was ice on Weland's lips. When he saw me he began a long chant in his own tongue, telling me how he was going to rule England, and how I should smell the smoke of his altars from Lincolnshire to the Isle of Wight. *I* didn't care! I'd seen too many Gods charging into Old England to be upset about it. I let him sing himself out while his men were burning the village, and then I said (I don't know what put it into my head), 'Smith of the Gods,' I said, 'the time comes when I shall meet you plying your trade for hire by the wayside.' "

"What did Weland say?" said Una. "Was he angry?"

"He called me names and rolled his eyes, and I went away to wake up the people inland. But the pirates conquered the country, and for centuries Weland was a most important God. He had temples everywhere–from Lincolnshire to the Isle of Wight, as he said–and his sacrifices were simply scandalous. To do him justice, he preferred horses to men; but men *or* horses, I knew that presently he'd have to come down in the world–like the other Old Things. I gave him lots of time–I gave him about a thousand years–and at the end of 'em I went into one of his temples near Andover to see how he prospered. There was his altar, and there was his image, and there were his priests, and there were the congregation, and everybody seemed quite happy, except Weland and the priests. In the old days the congregation were unhappy until the priests had chosen their sacrifices; and so would *you* have been. When the service began a priest rushed out, dragged a man up to the altar, pretended to hit him on the head with a little gilt axe, and the man fell down and pretended to die. Then everybody shouted: 'A sacrifice to Weland! A sacrifice to Weland!' "

"And the man wasn't really dead?" said Una.

"Not a bit. All as much pretense as a dolls' tea-party. Then they brought out a splendid white horse, and the priest cut some hair from its mane and tail and burned it on the altar, shouting, 'A sacrifice!' That counted the same as if a man and a horse had been killed. I saw poor Weland's face through the smoke, and I couldn't help laughing. He looked so disgusted and so hungry, and all he had to satisfy himself was a horrid smell of burning hair. Just a dolls' tea-party!

"I judged it better not to say anything then ('twouldn't have been fair), and the next time I came to Andover, a few hundred years later, Weland and his temple were gone, and there was a Christian bishop in a Church there. None of the People of the Hills could tell me anything about him, and I supposed that he had left England." Puck turned; lay on the other elbow, and thought for a long time.

"Let's see," he said at last. "It must have been some few years later–a year or two before the Conquest, I think–that I came back to Pook's Hill here, and one evening I heard old Hobden talking about Weland's Ford."

"If you mean old Hobden the hedger, he's only seventy-two. He told me so himself," said Dan. "He's a intimate friend of ours."

"You're quite right," Puck replied. "I meant old Hobden's ninth great-grandfather. He was a free man and burned charcoal hereabouts. I've known the family, father and son, so long that I get confused sometimes. Hob of the Dene was my Hobden's name, and he lived at the Forge cottage. Of course, I pricked up my ears when I heard Weland mentioned, and I scuttled through the woods to the Ford just beyond Bog Wood yonder." He jerked his head westward, where the valley narrows between wooded hills and steep hop-fields.

"Why, that's Willingford Bridge," said Una. "We go there for walks often. There's a kingfisher there."

"It was Weland's Ford then, dear. A road led down to it from the Beacon on the top of the hill–a shocking bad road it was–and all the hillside was thick, thick oak-forest, with deer in it. There was no trace of Weland, but presently I saw a fat old farmer riding down from the Beacon under the greenwood tree. His horse had cast a shoe in the clay, and when he came to the Ford he dismounted, took a penny out of his purse, laid it on a stone, tied the old horse to an oak, and called out: 'Smith, Smith, here is work for you!' Then he sat down and went to sleep. You can imagine how *I* felt when I saw a white-bearded, bent old blacksmith in a leather apron creep out from behind the oak and begin to shoe the horse. It was Weland himself. I was so astonished that I jumped out and said: 'What on Human Earth are you doing here, Weland?' "

"Poor Weland!" sighed Una.

"He pushed the long hair back from his forehead (he didn't recognize me at first). Then he said: '*You* ought to know. You foretold it, Old Thing. I'm shoeing horses for hire. I'm not even Weland now,' he said. 'They call me Wayland-Smith.' "

"Poor chap!" said Dan. "What did you say?"

"What could I say? He looked up, with the horse's foot on his lap, and he said, smiling, 'I remember the time when I wouldn't have accepted this old bag of bones as a sacrifice, and now I'm glad enough to shoe him for a penny.'

" 'Isn't there any way for you to get back to Valhalla, or wherever you come from?' I said.

" 'I'm afraid not,' he said, rasping away at the hoof. He had a wonderful touch with horses. The old beast was whinnying on his shoulder. 'You may remember that I was not a gentle God in my Day and my Time and my Power. I shall never be released till some human being truly wishes me well.'

" 'Surely,' said I, 'the farmer can't do less than that. You're shoeing the horse all round for him.'

" 'Yes,' said he, 'and my nails will hold a shoe from one full moon to the next. But farmers and Weald Clay,' said he, 'are both uncommon cold and sour.'

"Wouldn't you believe it, that when that farmer woke and found his horse shod he rode away without one word of thanks? I was so angry that I wheeled his horse right round and walked him back three miles to the Beacon just to teach the old sinner politeness."

"Were you invisible?" said Una. Puck nodded, gravely.

"The Beacon was always laid in those days ready to light, in case the French landed at Pevensey; and I walked the horse about and about it that lee-long summer night. The farmer thought he was bewitched–well, he *was,* of course–and began to pray and shout. *I* didn't care! I was as good a Christian as he any fair-day in the County, and about four o'clock in the morning a young novice came along from the monastery that used to stand on the top of Beacon hill."

"What's a novice?" said Dan.

"It really means a man who is beginning to be a monk, but in those days people sent their sons to a monastery just the same as a school. This young fellow had been to a monastery in France for a few months every year, and he was finishing his studies in the monastery close to his home here. Hugh was his name, and he had got up to go fishing hereabouts. His people owned all this valley. Hugh heard the farmer shouting, and asked him what in the world he meant. The old man spun him a wonderful tale about fairies and goblins and witches; and I *know* he hadn't seen a thing except rabbits and red deer all that night. (The People of the Hills are like otters–they don't show except when they choose.) But the novice wasn't a fool. He looked down at the horse's feet, and saw the new shoes fastened as only Weland knew how to fasten 'em. (Weland had a way of turning down the nails that folks called the Smith's Clinch.)

" 'H'm!' said the novice. 'Where did you get your horse shod?'

"The farmer wouldn't tell him at first, because the priests never liked their people to have any dealings with the Old Things. At last he confessed that the Smith had done it. 'What did you pay him?' said the novice. 'Penny,' said the farmer, very sulkily. 'That's less than a Christian would have charged,' said the novice. 'I hope you threw a "Thank you" into the bargain.' 'No,' said the farmer; 'Wayland-Smith's a heathen.' 'Heathen or no heathen,' said the novice, 'you took his help, and where you get help there you must give thanks.' 'What?' said the farmer–he was in a furious temper because I was walking the old horse in circles all this time–'What, you young jackanapes?' said he. 'Then by your reasoning I ought to say "Thank you" to Satan if he helped me?' 'Don't roll about up there splitting reasons with me,' said the novice. 'Come back to the Ford and thank the Smith, or you'll be sorry.'

"Back the farmer had to go! I led the horse, though no one saw me, and the novice walked beside us, his gown swishing through the shiny dew and his fishing-rod across his shoulders spearwise. When we reached the Ford again–it was five o'clock and misty still under the oaks–the farmer simply wouldn't say 'Thank you.' He said he'd tell the Abbot that the novice wanted him to worship heathen gods. Then Hugh the novice lost his temper. He just cried, 'Out!' put his arm under the farmer's fat leg, and heaved him from his saddle on to the turf, and before he could rise he caught him by the back of the neck and shook him like a rat till the farmer growled, 'Thank you, Wayland-Smith.' "

"Did Weland see all this?" said Dan.

"Oh, yes, and he shouted his old war-cry when the farmer thudded on to the ground. He was delighted. Then the novice turned to the oak and said, 'Ho! Smith of the Gods, I am ashamed of this rude farmer; but for all you have done in kindness and charity to him and to others of our people, I thank you and wish you well.' Then he picked up his fishing-rod–it looked more like a tall spear than ever–and tramped off down your valley."

"And what did poor Weland do?" said Una.

"He laughed and cried with joy, because he had been released at last, and could go away. But he was an honest Old Thing. He had worked for his living and he paid his debts before he left. 'I shall give that novice a gift,' said Weland. 'A gift that shall do him good the wide world over, and Old England after him. Blow up my fire, Old Thing, while I get the iron for my last task.' Then he made a sword–a dark gray, wavy-lined sword–and I blew the fire while he hammered. By Oak, Ash, and Thorn, I tell you, Weland was a Smith of the Gods! He cooled that sword in running water twice, and the third time he cooled it in the evening dew, and he laid it out in the moonlight and said Runes (that's charms) over it, and he carved Runes of Prophecy on the blade. 'Old Thing,' he said to me, wiping his forehead, 'this is the best blade that Weland ever made. Even the user will never know how good it is. Come to the monastery.'

"We went to the dormitory where the monks slept. We saw the novice fast asleep in his cot, and Weland put the sword into his hand, and I remember the young fellow gripped it in his sleep. Then Weland strode as far as he dared into the Chapel and threw down all his shoeing-tools–his hammer, and pincers, and rasps–to show that he had done with them for ever. It sounded like suits of armor falling, and the sleepy monks ran in, for they thought the monastery had been attacked by the French. The novice came first of all, waving his new sword and shouting Saxon battle-cries. When they saw the shoeing-tools they were very bewildered, till the novice asked leave to speak, and told what he had done to the farmer, and what he had said to Wayland-Smith, and how, though the dormitory light was burning, he had found the wonderful rune-carved sword in his cot.

"The Abbot shook his head at first, and then he laughed and said to the novice: 'Son Hugh, it needed no sign from a heathen God to show me that you will never be a monk. Take your sword, and keep your sword, and go with your sword, and be as gentle as you are strong and courteous. We will hang up the Smith's tools before the Altar,' he said, 'because, whatever the Smith of the Gods may have been in the old days, we know that he worked honestly for his living and made gifts to Mother Church.' Then they went to bed again, all except the novice, and he sat up in the garth playing with his sword. Then Weland said to me by the stables: 'Farewell, Old Thing; you had the right of it. You saw me come to England, and you see me go. Farewell!'

"With that he strode down the hill to the corner of the Great Woods—Woods Corner, you call it now—to the very place where he had first landed—and I heard him moving through the thickets toward Horsebridge for a little, and then he was gone. That was how it happened. I saw it."

Both children drew a long breath.

"But what happened to Hugh the novice?" said Una.

"And the sword?" said Dan.

Puck looked down the meadow that lay all quiet and cool in the shadow of Pook's Hill. A corncrake jarred in a hay-field nearby, and the small trouts of the brook began to jump. A big white moth flew unsteadily from the alders and flapped round the children's heads, and the least little haze of water-mist rose from the brook.

"Do you really want to know?" Puck said.

"We do," cried the children. "Awfully!"

"Very good. I promised you that you shall see What you shall see, and you shall hear What you shall hear, though It shall have happened three thousand year; but just now it seems to me that, unless you go back to the house, people will be looking for you. I'll walk with you as far as the gate."

"Will you be here when we come again?" they asked.

"Surely, sure-ly," said Puck. "I've been here some time already. One minute first, please."

He gave them each three leaves—one of Oak, one of Ash, and one of Thorn.

"Bite these," said he. "Otherwise you might be talking at home of what you've seen and heard, and—if I know human beings—they'd send for the doctor. Bite!"

They bit hard, and found themselves walking side by side to the lower gate. Their father was leaning over it.

"And how did your play go?" he asked.

"Oh, splendidly," said Dan. "Only afterwards, I think, we went to sleep. It was very hot and quiet. Don't you remember, Una?"

Una shook her head and said nothing.

"I see," said her father.

> Late—late in the evening Kilmeny came home,
> For Kilmeny had been she could not tell where,
> And Kilmeny had seen what she could not declare.

But why are you chewing leaves at your time of life, daughter? For fun?"

"No. It was for something, but I can't azactly remember," said Una.

And neither of them could till—

A Tree Song

Of all the trees that grow so fair,
Old England to adorn,
Greater are none beneath the Sun,
Than Oak, and Ash, and Thorn.
Sing Oak, and Ash, and Thorn, good Sirs
(All of a Midsummer morn)!
Surely we sing no little thing,
In Oak, and Ash, and Thorn!

Oak of the Clay lived many a day,
Or ever Aeneas began;
Ash of the Loam was a lady at home,
When Brut was an outlaw man;
Thorn of the Down saw New Troy Town
(From which was London born);
Witness hereby the ancientry
Of Oak, and Ash, and Thorn!

Yew that is old in churchyard mould,
He breedeth a mighty bow;
Alder for shoes do wise men choose,
And beech for cups also.
But when ye have killed, and your bowl is spilled
And your shoes are clean outworn,
Back ye must speed for all that ye need,
To Oak, and Ash, and Thorn!

Ellum she hateth mankind, and waiteth
Till every gust be laid,
To drop a limb on the head of him,
That anyway trusts her shade
But whether a lad be sober or sad,
Or mellow with ale from the horn,
He will take no wrong when he lieth along
'Neath Oak, and Ash, and Thorn!

Oh, do not tell the Priest our plight,
Or he would call it a sin;
But—we have been out in the woods all night
A-conjuring Summer in!
And we bring you news by word of mouth—
Good news for cattle and corn—
Now is the Sun come up from the South,
With Oak, and Ash, and Thorn!

Sing Oak, and Ash, and Thorn, good Sirs
(All of a Midsummer morn)!
England shall bide till Judgment Tide,
By Oak, and Ash and Thorn!

Young Men at the Manor

THEY WERE FISHING, a few days later, in the bed of the brook that for centuries had cut deep into the soft valley soil. The trees closing overhead made long tunnels through which the sunshine worked in blobs and patches. Down in the tunnels were bars of sand and gravel, old roots and trunks covered with moss or painted red by the irony water; foxgloves growing lean and pale towards the light; clumps of fern and thirsty shy flowers who could not live away from moisture and shade. In the pools you could see the wave thrown up by the trouts as they charged hither and yon, and the pools were joined to each other—except in flood time, when all was one brown rush—by sheets of thin broken water that poured themselves chuckling round the darkness of the next bend.

This was one of the children's most secret hunting-grounds, and their particular friend, old Hobden the hedger, had shown them how to use it. Except for the click of a rod hitting a low willow, or a switch and tussle among the young ash-leaves as a line hung up for the minute, nobody in the hot pasture could have guessed what game was going on among the trouts below the banks.

"We's got half-a-dozen," said Dan, after a warm, wet hour. "I vote we go up to Stone Bay and try Long Pool."

Una nodded—most of her talk was by nods—and they crept from the gloom of the tunnels towards the tiny weir that turns the brook into the mill-stream. Here the banks are low and bare, and the glare of the afternoon sun on the Long Pool below the weir makes your eyes ache.

When they were in the open they nearly fell down with astonishment. A huge gray horse, whose tail-hairs crinkled the glassy water, was drinking in the pool, and the ripples about his muzzle flashed like melted gold. On his back sat an old, white-haired man dressed in a loose glimmery gown of chain-mail. He was bareheaded, and a nut-shaped iron helmet hung at his saddle-bow. His reins were of red leather five or six inches deep, scalloped at the edges, and his high padded saddle with its red girths was held fore and aft by a red leather breastband and crupper.

"Look!" said Una, as though Dan were not staring his very eyes out. "It's like the picture in your room—'Sir Isumbras at the Ford.' "

The rider turned towards them, and his thin, long face was just as sweet and gentle as that of the knight who carries the children in that picture.

"They should be here now, Sir Richard," said Puck's deep voice among the willow-herb.

"They are here," the knight said, and he smiled at Dan with the string of trouts in his hand. "There seems no great change in boys since mine fished this water."

"If your horse has drunk, we shall be more at ease in the Ring," said Puck; and he nodded to the children as though he had never magicked away their memories the week before.

The great horse turned and hoisted himself into the pasture with a kick and a scramble that tore the clods down rattling.

"Your pardon!" said Sir Richard to Dan. "When these lands were mine, I never loved that mounted men should cross the brook except by the paved ford. But my Swallow here was thirsty, and I wished to meet you."

"We're very glad you've come, sir," said Dan. "It doesn't matter in the least about the banks."

He trotted across the pasture on the sword-side of the mighty horse, and it was a mighty iron-handled sword that swung from Sir Richard's belt. Una walked behind with Puck. She remembered everything now.

"I'm sorry about the Leaves," he said, "but it would never have done if you had gone home and told, would it?"

"I s'pose not," Una answered. "But you said that all the fair–People of the Hills had left England."

"So they have; but I told you that you should come and go and look and know, didn't I? The knight isn't a fairy. He's Sir Richard Dalyngridge, a very old friend of mine. He came over with William the Conqueror, and he wants to see you particularly."

"What for?" said Una.

"On account of your great wisdom and learning," Puck replied, without a twinkle.

"Us?" said Una. "Why, I don't know my Nine Times–not to say it dodging; and Dan makes the most *awful* mess of fractions. He can't mean *us!*"

"Una!" Dan called back. "Sir Richard says he is going to tell what happened to Weland's sword. He's got it. Isn't it splendid?"

"Nay–nay," said Sir Richard, dismounting as they reached the Ring, in the bend of the mill-stream bank. "It is you that must tell me, for I hear the youngest child in our England to-day is as wise as our wisest clerk." He slipped the bit out of Swallow's mouth, dropped the ruby-red reins over his head, and the wise horse moved off to graze.

Sir Richard (they noticed he limped a little) unslung his great sword.

"That's it," Dan whispered to Una.

"This is the sword that Brother Hugh had from Wayland-Smith," Sir Richard said. "Once he gave it to me, but I would not take it; but at the last it became mine after such a fight as never christened man fought. See!" He half drew it from its sheath and turned it before them. On either side just below the handle, where the Runic letters shivered as though they were alive, were two deep gouges in the dull, deadly steel. "Now, what Thing made those?" said he. "I know not, but you, perhaps, can say."

"Tell them all the tale, Sir Richard," said Puck. "It concerns their land somewhat."

"Yes, from the very beginning," Una pleaded, for the knight's good face and the smile on it more than ever reminded her of "Sir Isumbras at the Ford."

They settled down to listen, Sir Richard bare-headed to the sunshine, dandling the sword in both hands, while the gray horse cropped outside the Ring, and the helmet on the saddle-bow clinged softly each time he jerked his head.

"From the beginning, then," Sir Richard said, "since it concerns your land, I will tell the tale. When our Duke came out of Normandy to take his England, great knights (have ye heard?) came and strove hard to serve the Duke, because he promised them lands here, and small knights followed the great ones. My folk in Normandy were poor; but a great knight, Engerrard of the Eagle–Engenulf De Aquila–who was kin to my father, followed the Earl of Mortain, who followed William the Duke, and I followed De Aquila. Yes, with thirty men-at-arms out of my father's house and a new sword, I set out to conquer England three days after I was made knight. I did not then know that England would conquer me. We went up to Santlache with the rest–a very great host of us."

"Does that mean the Battle of Hastings–Ten Sixty-Six?" Una whispered, and Puck nodded, so as not to interrupt.

"At Santlache, over the hill yonder"–he pointed south-eastward towards

Fairlight–"we found Harold's men. We fought. At the day's end they ran. My men went with De Aquila's to chase and plunder, and in that chase Engerrard of the Eagle was slain, and his son Gilbert took his banner and his men forward. This I did not know till after, for Swallow here was cut in the flank, so I stayed to wash the wound at a brook by a thorn. There a single Saxon cried out to me in French, and we fought together. I should have known his voice, but we fought together. For a long time neither had any advantage, till by pure ill-fortune his foot slipped and his sword flew from his hand. Now I had but newly been made knight, and wished, above all, to be courteous and fameworthy, so I forebore to strike and bade him get his sword again. 'A plague on my sword,' said he. 'It has lost me my first fight. You have spared my life. Take my sword.' He held it out to me, but as I stretched my hand the sword groaned like a stricken man, and I leaped back crying, 'Sorcery!'

[The children looked at the sword as though it might speak again.]

"Suddenly a clump of Saxons ran out upon me and, seeing a Norman alone, would have killed me, but my Saxon cried out that I was his prisoner, and beat them off. Thus, see you, he saved my life. He put me on my horse and led me through the woods ten long miles to this valley."

"To here, d'you mean?" said Una.

"To this very valley. We came in by the Lower Ford under the King's Hill yonder"–he pointed eastward where the valley widens.

"And was that Saxon Hugh the novice?" Dan asked.

"Yes, and more than that. He had been for three years at the monastery at Bec by Rouen, where"–Sir Richard chuckled–"the Abbot Herluin would not suffer me to remain."

"Why wouldn't he?" said Dan.

"Because I rode my horse into the refectory, when the scholars were at meat, to show the Saxon boys we Normans were not afraid of an abbot. It was that very Saxon Hugh tempted me to do it, and we had not met since that day. I thought I knew his voice even inside my helmet, and, for all that our Lords fought, we each rejoiced we had not slain the other. He walked by my side, and he told me how a Heathen God, as he believed, had given him his sword, but he said he had never heard it sing before. I remember I warned him to beware of sorcery and quick enchantments." Sir Richard smiled to himself. "I was very young–very young!

"When we came to his house here we had almost forgotten that we had been at blows. It was near midnight, and the Great Hall was full of men and women waiting news. There I first saw his sister, the Lady Aelueva, of whom he had spoken to us in France. She cried out fiercely at me, and would have had me hanged in that hour, but her brother said that I had spared his life–he said not how he saved mine from his Saxons–and that our Duke had won the day; and even while they wrangled over my poor body, of a sudden he fell down in a swoon from his wounds.

" 'This is *thy* fault,' said the Lady Aelueva to me, and she kneeled above him and called for wine and cloths.

" 'If I had known,' I answered, 'he should have ridden and I walked. But he set me on my horse; he made no complaint; he walked beside me and spoke merrily throughout. I pray I have done him no harm.'

" 'Thou hast need to pray,' she said, catching up her underlip. 'If he dies, thou shalt hang!'

"They bore off Hugh to his chamber; but three tall men of the house bound me and set me under the beam of the Great Hall with a rope round my neck. The end of the rope they flung over the beam, and they sat them down by the fire to wait word whether Hugh lived or died. They cracked nuts with their knife-hilts the while."

"And how did you feel?" said Dan.

"Very weary; but I did heartily pray for my schoolmate Hugh his health. About noon I heard horses in the valley, and the three men loosed my ropes and fled out, and De Aquila's men rode up. Gilbert de Aquila came with them, for it was his boast that, like his father, he forgot no man that served him. He was little, like his father, but terrible, with a nose like an eagle's nose and yellow eyes like an eagle. He rode tall war-horses–roans, which he bred himself–and he could never abide to be helped into the saddle. He saw the rope hanging from the beam and laughed, and his men laughed, for I was too stiff to rise.

" 'This is poor entertainment for a Norman knight," he said, "but, such as it is, let us be grateful. Show me, boy, to whom thou owest most, and we will pay them out of hand.' "

"What did he mean? To kill 'em?" said Dan.

"Assuredly. But I looked at the Lady Aelueva where she stood among her maids, and her brother beside her. De Aquila's men had driven them all into the Great Hall."

"Was she pretty?" said Una.

"In all my life I had never seen woman fit to strew rushes before my Lady Aelueva," the knight replied, quite simply and quietly. "As I looked at her I thought I might save her and her house by a jest.

" 'Seeing that I came somewhat hastily and without warning,' said I to De Aquila, 'I have no fault to find with the courtesy that these Saxons have shown me.' But my voice shook. It is–it was not good to jest with that little man.

"All were silent awhile, till De Aquila laughed. 'Look, men–a miracle!' said he. 'The fight is scarce sped, my father is not yet buried, and here we find our youngest knight already set down in his Manor, while his Saxons–ye can see it in their fat faces–have paid him homage and service! By the Saints,' he said, rubbing his nose, 'I never thought England would be so easy won! Surely I can do no less than give the lad what he has taken. This Manor shall be thine, boy,' he said, 'till I come again, or till thou art slain. Now, mount, men, and ride. We follow our Duke into Kent to make him King of England.'

"He drew me with him to the door while they brought his horse–a lean roan, taller than my Swallow here, but not so well girthed.

" 'Hark to me,' he said, fretting with his great war-gloves. 'I have given thee this Manor, which is a Saxon hornets' nest, and I think thou wilt be slain in a month–as my father was slain. Yet if thou canst keep the roof on the hall, the thatch on the barn, and the plough in the furrow till I come back, thou shalt hold the Manor from me; for the Duke has promised our Earl Mortain all the lands by Pevensey, and Mortain will give me of them what he would have given my father. God knows if thou or I shall live till England is won; but remember, boy, that here and now fighting is foolishness and'–he reached for the reins–'craft and cunning is all.'

" 'Alas, I have no cunning,' said I.

" 'Not yet,' said he, hopping abroad, foot in stirrup, and poking his horse in the belly with his toe. 'Not yet, but I think thou hast a good teacher. Farewell! Hold the Manor and live. Lose the Manor and hang,' he said, and spurred out, his shield-straps squeaking behind him.

"So, children, here was I, little more than a boy, and Santlache fight not two days old, left alone with my thirty men-at-arms, in a land I knew not, among a people whose tongue I could not speak, to hold down the land which I had taken from them."

"And that was here at home?" said Una.

"Yes, here. See! From the Upper Ford, Weland's Ford, to the Lower Ford, by the Belle Allée, west and east it ran half a league. From the Beacon of Brunanburgh behind us here, south and north it ran a full league–and all the woods were full of broken men from Santlache, Saxon thieves, Norman plunderers, robbers, and deerstealers. A hornets' nest indeed!

"When De Aquila had gone, Hugh would have thanked me for saving their lives; but Lady Aelueva said that I had done it only for the sake of receiving the Manor.

" 'How could I know that De Aquila would give it me?' I said. 'If I had told him I had spent my night in your halter he would have burned the place twice over by now.'

" 'If any man had put *my* neck in a rope,' she said, 'I would have seen his house burned thrice over before *I* would have made terms.'

" 'But it was a woman,' I said; and I laughed and she wept and said that I mocked her in her captivity.

" 'Lady,' said I, 'there is no captive in this valley except one, and he is not a Saxon.'

"At this she cried that I was a Norman thief, who came with false, sweet words, having intended from the first to turn her out in the fields to beg her bread. Into the fields! She had never seen the face of war!

"I was angry, and answered, 'This much at least I can disprove, for I swear'—and on my sword-hilt I swore it in that place—'I swear I will never set foot in the Great Hall till the Lady Aelueva herself shall summons me there.'

"She went away, saying nothing, and I walked out, and Hugh limped after me, whistling dolorously (that is a custom of the English), and we came upon the three Saxons that had bound me. They were now bound by my men-at-arms, and behind them stood some fifty stark and sullen churls of the House and the Manor, waiting to see what should fall. We heard De Aquila's trumpets blow thin through the woods Kentward.

" 'Shall we hang these?' said my men.

" 'Then my churls will fight,' said Hugh, beneath his breath; but I bade him ask the three what mercy they hoped for.

" 'None,' said they all. 'She bade us hang thee if our master died. And we would have hanged thee. There is no more to it.'

"As I stood doubting a woman ran down from the oak wood above the King's Hill yonder, and cried out that some Normans were driving off the swine there.

" 'Norman or Saxon,' said I, 'we must beat them back, or they will rob us every day. Out at them with any arms ye have!' So I loosed those three carles and we ran together, my men-at-arms and the Saxons with bills and bows which they had hidden in the thatch of their huts, and Hugh led them. Half-way up the King's Hill we found a false fellow from Picardy—a sutler that sold wine in the Duke's camp—with a dead knight's shield on his arm, a stolen horse under him, and some ten or twelve wastrels at his tail, all cutting and slashing at the pigs. We beat them off, and saved our pork. One hundred and seventy pigs we saved in that great battle." Sir Richard laughed.

"That, then, was our first work together, and I bade Hugh tell his folk that so would I deal with any man, knight or churl, Norman or Saxon, who stole as much as one egg from our valley. Said he to me, riding home: 'Thou hast gone far to conquer England this evening.' I answered: 'England must be thine and mine, then. Help me, Hugh, to deal aright with this people. Make them to know that if they slay me De Aquila will surely send to slay them, and he will put a worse man in my place.' 'That may well be true,' said he, and gave me his hand. 'Better the devil we know than the devil we know not, till we can pack you Normans home.' And so, too, said his Saxons; and they laughed as we drove the pigs downhill. But I think some of them, even then, began not to hate me."

"I like Brother Hugh," said Una, softly.

"Beyond question he was the most perfect, courteous, valiant, tender, and wise knight that ever drew breath," said Richard, caressing the sword. "He hung up his sword—this sword—on the wall of the Great Hall, because he said it was fairly mine, and never he took it down till De Aquila returned, as I shall presently show. For three months his men and mine guarded the valley, till all robbers and nightwalkers learned there was nothing to get from us save hard tack and a hanging. Side by side we fought against all who came—thrice a week sometimes we fought—against thieves and landless knights looking formanors. Then we were in some peace, and I made shift by Hugh's help to govern the valley—for all this valley of yours was my Manor—as a knight should. I kept the roof on the hall and the thatch on the barn, but . . . The English are a bold people. His Saxons would laugh and jest with Hugh, and Hugh with them, and—this was marvellous to me—if even the meanest of them said that such and such a thing was the Custom of the Manor, then straightway would Hugh and such old men of the Manor as might be near forsake everything else to debate the matter—I have seen them stop the mill with the corn half ground—and if the custom or usage were proven to be as it was said, why, that was the end of it, even though it were flat against Hugh, his wish and command. Wonderful!"

"Aye," said Puck, breaking in for the first time. "The Custom of Old England was here before your Norman knights came, and it outlasted them, though they fought against it cruel."

"Not I," said Richard. "I let the Saxons go their stubborn way, but when my own men-at-arms, Normans not six months in England, stood up and told me what was the custom of the country, *then* I was angry. Ah, good days! Ah, wonderful people! And I loved them all."

The knight lifted his arms as though he would hug the whole dear valley, and Swallow, hearing the chink of his chain-mail, looked up and whinnied softly.

"At last," he went on, "after a year of striving and contriving and some little driving, De Aquila came to the valley, alone and without warning. I saw him first at the Lower Ford, with a swine-herd's brat on his saddle-bow.

" 'There is no need for thee to give any account of thy stewardship,' said he. 'I have it all from the child here.' And he told me how the young thing had stopped his tall horse at the Ford, by waving of a branch, and crying that the way was barred. 'And if one bold, bare babe be enough to guard the Ford in these days, thou hast done well,' said he, and puffed and wiped his head.

He pinched the child's cheek, and looked at our cattle in the flat by the brook.

" 'Both fat,' said he, rubbing his nose. 'This is craft and cunning such as I love. What did I tell thee when I rode away, boy?'

" 'Hold the Manor or hang,' said I. I had never forgotten it.

" 'True. And thou hast held.' He clambered from his saddle and with sword's point cut out a turf from the bank and gave it me where I kneeled."

Dan looked at Una, and Una looked at Dan.

"That's seizin," said Puck, in a whisper.

" 'Now thou art lawfully seized of the Manor, Sir Richard,' said he—'twas the first time he ever called me that—'thou and thy heirs for ever. This must serve till the King's clerks write out thy title on a parchment. England is all ours—if we can hold it.'

" 'What service shall I pay?' I asked, and I remember I was proud beyond words.

" 'Knight's fee, boy, knight's fee!' said he, hopping round his horse on one foot. (Have I said he was little, and could not endure to be helped to his saddle?) 'Six mounted men or twelve archers thou shalt send me whenever I call for them, and—where got you that corn?' said he, for it was near harvest, and our corn stood well. 'I have never seen such bright straw. Send me three bags of the same seed yearly, and furthermore, in memory of our last meeting—with the rope round thy neck—entertain me and my men for two days of each year in the Great Hall of thy Manor.'

" 'Alas!' said I, 'then my Manor is already forfeit. I am under vow not to enter the Great Hall.' And I told him what I had sworn to the Lady Aelueva."

"And hadn't you ever been into the house since?" said Una.

"Never," Sir Richard answered smiling. "I had made me a little hut of wood up the hill, and there I did justice and slept. . . . De Aquila wheeled aside, and his shield shook on his back. 'No matter, boy,' said he. 'I will remit the homage for a year.' "

"He meant Sir Richard needn't give him dinner there the first year," Puck explained.

"De Aquila stayed with me in the hut and Hugh, who could read and write and cast accounts, showed him the roll of the Manor, in which were written all the names of our fields and men, and he asked a thousand questions touching the land, the timber, the grazing, the mill, and the fish-ponds, and the worth of every man in the valley. But never he named the Lady Aelueva's name, nor went he near the Great Hall. By night he drank with us in the hut. Yes, he sat on the straw like an eagle ruffled in her feathers, his yellow eyes rolling above the cup, and he pounced in his talk like an eagle, swooping from one thing to another, but always binding fast. Yes; he would lie still awhile, and then rustle in the straw, and speak sometimes as though he were King William himself, and anon he would speak in parables and tales, and if at once we saw not his meaning he would yerk us in the ribs with his scabbarded sword.

" 'Look you, boys,' said he, 'I am born out of my due time. Five hundred years ago I would have made all England such an England as neither Dane, Saxon, nor Norman should have conquered. Five hundred years hence I should have been such a councillor to Kings, as the world hath never dreamed of. 'Tis all here,' said he, tapping his big head, 'but it hath no play in this black age. Now Hugh here is a better man than thou art, Richard.' He had made his voice harsh and croaking, like a raven's.

" 'Truth,' said I. 'But for Hugh, his help and patience and long-suffering, I could never have kept the Manor.'

" 'Nor thy life either,' said De Aquila. 'Hugh has saved thee not once, but a hundred times. Be still, Hugh!' he said. 'Dost thou know, Richard, why Hugh slept, and why he still sleeps, among thy Norman men-at-arms?'

" 'To be near me,' said I, for I thought this was truth.

" 'Fool!' said De Aquila. 'It is because his Saxons have begged him to rise against thee, and to sweep every Norman out of the valley. No matter how I know. It is truth. Therefore Hugh hath made himself an hostage for thy life, well knowing that if any harm befell thee from his Saxons thy Normans would slay him without remedy. And this his Saxons know. It is true, Hugh?'

" 'In some sort,' said Hugh, shamefacedly; 'at least, it was true half a year ago. My Saxons would not harm Richard now. I think they know him; but I judged it best to make sure.'

"Look, children, what that man had done—and I had never guessed it! Night after night had he lain down among my men-at-arms, knowing that if one Saxon had lifted knife against me his life would have answered for mine.

" 'Yes,' said De Aquila. 'And he is a swordless man.' He pointed to Hugh's belt, for Hugh had put away his sword—did I tell you?—the day after it flew from his hand at Santlache. He carried only the short knife and the long-bow. 'Swordless and landless art thou, Hugh; and they call thee kin to Earl Godwin.' (Hugh was indeed of Godwin's blood.) 'The Manor that was thine was given to this boy and to his children for ever. Sit up and beg, for he can turn thee out like a dog, Hugh!'

"Hugh said nothing, but I heard his teeth grind, and I bade De Aquila, my own overlord, hold his peace, or I would stuff his words down his throat.

Then De Aquila laughed till the tears ran down his face.

" 'I warned the King,' said he, 'what would come of giving England to us Norman thieves. Here art thou, Richard, less than two days confirmed in thy Manor, and already thou hast risen against thy overlord. What shall do to him, *Sir* Hugh?'

" 'I am a swordless man,' said Hugh. 'Do not jest with me,' and he laid his head on his knees and groaned.

" 'The greater fool thou,' said De Aquila, and all his voice changed; 'for I have given thee the Manor of Dallington up the hill this half-hour since,' and he yerked at Hugh with his scabbard across the straw.

" 'To me?' said Hugh. 'I am a Saxon, and, except that I love Richard here, I have not sworn fealty to any Norman.'

" 'In God's good time, which because of my sins I shall not live to see, there will be neither Saxon nor Norman in England,' said De Aquila. 'If I know men, thou art more faithful unsworn than a score of Normans I could name. Take Dallington, and join Sir Richard to fight me to-morrow, if it please thee!'

" 'Nay,' said Hugh. 'I am no child. Where I take a gift, there I render service'; and he put his hands between De Aquila's, and swore to be faithful, and, as I remember, I kissed him, and De Aquila kissed us both.

"We sat afterwards outside the hut while the sun rose, and De Aquila marked our churls going to their work in the fields, and talked of holy things, and how we should govern our Manors in time to come, and of hunting and of horse-breeding, and of the King's wisdom and unwisdom; for he spoke to us as though we were in all sorts now his brothers. Anon a churl stole up to me–he was one of the three I had not hanged a year ago–and he bellowed–which is the Saxon for whispering–that the Lady Aelueva would speak to me at the Great House. She walked abroad daily in the Manor, and it was her custom to send me word whither she went, that I might set an archer or two behind and in front to guard her. Very often I myself lay up in the woods and watched on her also.

"I went swiftly, and as I passed the great door it opened from within, and there stood my Lady Aelueva, and she said to me: 'Sir Richard, will it please you enter the Great Hall?' Then she wept, but we were alone."

The knight was silent for a long time, his face turned across the valley, smiling.

"Oh, well done!" said Una, and clapped her hands very softly. "She was sorry, and she said so."

"Aye, she was sorry, and she said so," said Sir Richard, coming back with a little start. "Very soon–but *he* said it was two full hours later–De Aquila rode to the door, with his shield new scoured (Hugh had cleansed it), and demanded entertainment, and called me a false knight, that would starve his overlord to death. Then Hugh cried out that no man should work in the valley that day, and our Saxons blew horns, and set about feasting and drinking, and running of races, and dancing and singing; and De Aquila climbed upon a horse-block and spoke to them in what he swore was good Saxon, but no man understood it. At night we feasted in the Great Hall, and when the harpers and the singers were gone we four sat late at the high table. As I remember, it was a warm night with a full moon, and De Aquila bade Hugh take down his sword from the wall again, for the honor of the Manor of Dallington, and Hugh took it gladly enough. Dust lay on the hilt, for I saw him blow it off.

"She and I sat talking a little apart, and at first we thought the harpers had come back, for the Great Hall was filled with a rushing noise of music. De Aquila leaped up; but there was only the moonlight fretty on the floor.

" 'Hearken!' said Hugh. 'It is my sword,' and as he belted it on the music ceased.

" 'Over Gods, forbid that I should ever belt blade like that,' said De

Aquila. 'What does it foretell?'

" 'The Gods that made it may know. Last time it spoke was at Hastings, when I lost all my lands. Belike it sings now that I have new lands and am a man again,' said Hugh.

"He loosed the blade a little and drove it back happily into the sheath, and the sword answered him low and crooningly, as—as a woman would speak to a man, her head on his shoulder.

"Now that was the second time in all my life I heard this Sword sing.' . . .

"Look!" said Una. "There's mother coming down the Long Slip. What will she say to Sir Richard? She can't help seeing him."

"And Puck can't magic us this time," said Dan.

"Are you sure?" said Puck; and he leaned forward and whispered to Sir Richard, who, smiling, bowed his head.

"But what befell the sword and my brother Hugh I will tell on another time," said he, rising. "Ohé, Swallow!"

The great horse cantered up from the far end of the meadow, close to mother.

They heard mother say: "Children, Gleason's old horse has broken into the meadow again. Where did he get through?"

"Just below Stone Bay," said Dan. "He tore down simple flobs of the bank! We noticed it just now. And we've caught no end of fish. We've been at it all the afternoon."

And they honestly believed that they had. They never noticed the Oak, Ash, and Thorn leaves that Puck had slyly thrown into their laps.

Sir Richard's Song

I followed my Duke ere I was a lover,
To take from England fief and fee;
But now this game is the other way over–
But now England hath taken me!

I had my horse, my shield and banner,
And a boy's heart, so whole and free;
But now I sing in another manner–
But now England hath taken me!

As for my Father in his tower,
Asking news of my ship at sea;
He will remember his own hour–
Tell him England hath taken me!

As for my Mother in her bower,
That rules my Father so cunningly;
She will remember a maiden's power–
Tell her England hath taken me!

As for my Brother in Rouen city,
A nimble and naughty page is he;
But he will come to suffer and pity–
Tell him England hath taken me!

As for my little Sister waiting
In the pleasant orchards of Normandie;
Tell her youth is the time for mating–
Tell her England hath taken me!

As for my Comrades in camp and highway,
That lift their eyebrows scornfully;
Tell them their way is not my way–
Tell them England hath taken me!

Kings and Princes and Barons famed,
Knights and Captains in your degree;
Hear me a little before I am blamed–
Seeing England hath taken me!

Howso great man's strength be reckoned,
There are two things he cannot flee;
Love is the first, and Death is the second–
And love, in England, hath taken me!

The Knights of the Joyous Venture

Harp Song of the Dane Women

What is a woman that you forsake her,
And the hearth-fire and the home-acre,
To go with the old gray Widow-maker?

She has no house to lay a guest in—
But one chill bed for all to rest in,
That the pale suns and the stray bergs nest in.

She has no strong white arms to fold you,
But the ten-times-fingering weed to hold you
Bound on the rocks where the tide has rolled you.

Yet, when the signs of summer thicken,
And the ice breaks, and the birch-buds quicken,
Yearly you turn from our side, and sicken—

Sicken again for the shouts and the slaughters,
You steal away to the lapping waters,
And look at your ship in her winter quarters.

You forget our mirth, and talk at the tables,
The kine in the shed and the horse in the stables—
To pitch her sides and go over her cables!

Then you drive out where the storm-clouds swallow:
And the sound of your oar-blades falling hollow,
Is all we have left through the months to follow!

Ah, what is Woman that you forsake her,
And the hearth-fire and the home-acre,
To go with the old gray Widow-maker?

It was too hot to run about in the open, so Dan asked their friend, old Hobden, to take their own dinghy from the pond and put her on the brook at the bottom of the garden. Her painted name was the *Daisy,* but for exploring expeditions she was the *Golden Hind* or the *Long Serpent,* or some such suitable name. Dan hiked and howked with a boat-hook (the brook was too narrow for sculls), and Una punted with a piece of hop-pole. When they came to a very shallow place (the *Golden Hind* drew quite three inches of water) they disembarked and scuffled her over the gravel by her tow-rope, and when they reached the over-grown banks beyond the garden they pulled themselves up stream by the low branches.

That day they intended to discover the North Cape like "Othere, the old sea-captain," in the book of verses which Una had brought with her; but on account of the heat they changed it to a voyage up the Amazon and the sources of the Nile. Even on the shaded water the air was hot and heavy with drowsy scents, while outside, through breaks in the trees, the sunshine burned the pasture like fire. The kingfisher was asleep on his watching-branch, and the blackbirds scarcely took the trouble to dive into the next bush. Dragon-flies wheeling and clashing were the only things at work, except the moor-hens and a big Red Admiral who flapped down out of the sunshine for a drink.

When they reached Otter Pool the *Golden Hind* grounded comfortably on a shallow, and they lay beneath a roof of close green, watching the water trickle over the flood-gates down the mossy brick chute from the mill-stream to the brook. A big trout—the children knew him well—rolled head and shoulders at some fly that sailed round the bend, while once in just so often the brook rose a fraction of an inch against all the wet pebbles, and they watched the slow draw and shiver of a breath of air through the tree-tops. Then the little voices of the slipping water began again.

"It's like the shadows talking, isn't it?" said Una. She had given up trying to read. Dan lay over the bows, trailing his hands in the current. They heard feet on the gravel-bar that runs half across the pool and saw Sir Richard Dalyngridge standing over them.

"Was yours a dangerous voyage?" he asked, smiling.

"She bumped a lot, sir," said Dan. "There's hardly any water this summer."

"Ah, the brook was deeper and wider when my children played at Danish pirates. Are you pirate-folk?"

"Oh, no. We gave up being pirates years ago," explained Una. "We're nearly always explorers now. Sailing round the world, you know."

"Round?" said Sir Richard. He sat him in the comfortable crotch of the old ash-root on the bank. "How can it be round?"

"Wasn't it in your books?" Dan suggested. He had been doing geography at his last lesson.

"I can neither write nor read," he replied. "Canst *thou* read, child?"

"Yes," said Dan, "barring the very long words."

"Wonderful! Read to me, that I may hear for myself."

Dan flushed, but opened the book and began—gabbling a little—at "The Discoverer of the North Cape."

"Othere, the old sea captain,
Who dwelt in Helgoland,
To Alfred, lover of truth,
Brought a snow-white walrus tooth,
That he held in his right hand."

"But—but—this I know! This is an old song! This I have heard sung! This is a miracle," Sir Richard interrupted. "Nay, do not stop!" He leaned forward, and the shadows of the leaves slipped and slid upon his chain-mail.

"I ploughed the land with horses,
But my heart was ill at ease,
For the old sea-faring men
Came to me now and then
With their Sagas of the Seas."

His hand fell on the hilt of the great sword. "This is truth," he cried, "for so did it happen to me," and he beat time delightedly to the tramp of verse after verse.

" 'And now the land,' said Othere,
'Bent southward suddenly,
And I followed the curving shore,
And ever southward bore
Into a nameless sea.' "

"A nameless sea!" he repeated. "So did I–so did Hugh and I."

"Where did you go? Tell us," said Una.

"Wait. Let me hear all first." So Dan read to the poem's very end.

"Good," said the knight. "That is Othere's tale–even as I have heard the men in the Dane ships sing it. Not in those same valiant words, but something like to them."

"Have you ever explored North?" Dan shut the book.

"Nay. My venture was South. Farther South than any man has fared, Hugh and I went down with Witta and his heathen." He jerked the tall sword forward, and leaned on it with both hands; but his eyes looked long past them.

"I thought you always lived here," said Una, timidly.

"Yes while my Lady Aelueva lived. But she died. She died. Then, my eldest son being a man, I asked De Aquila's leave that he should hold the Manor while I went on some journey or pilgrimage–to forget. De Aquila, whom the Second William had made Warden of Pevensey in Earl Mortain's place, was very old then, but still he rode his tall, roan horses, and in the saddle he looked like a little white falcon. When Hugh, at Dallington over yonder, heard what I did, he sent for my second son, whom being unmarried he had ever looked upon as his own child, and, by De Aquila's leave, gave him the Manor of Dallington to hold till he should return. Then Hugh came with me."

"When did this happen?" said Dan.

"That I can answer to the very day, for as we rode with De Aquila by Pevensey–have I said that he was Lord of Pevensey and of the Honor of the Eagle?–to the Bordeaux ship that fetched him his wines yearly out of France, a Marsh man ran to us crying that he had seen a great black goat which bore on his back the body of the King, and that the goat had spoken to him. On that same day Red William our King, the Conqueror's son, died of a secret arrow while he hunted in a forest. 'This is a cross matter,' said De Aquila, 'to meet on the threshold of a journey. If Red William be dead I may have to fight for my lands. Wait a little.'

"My Lady being dead, I cared nothing for signs and omens, nor Hugh either. We took that wine-ship to go to Bordeaux; but the wind failed while we were yet in sight of Pevensey; a thick mist hid us, and we drifted with the tide along the cliffs to the west. Our company was, for the most part, merchants returning to France, and we were laden with wool and there were three couple of tall hunting-dogs chained to the rail. Their master was a knight of Artois. His name I never learned, but his shield bore gold pieces on a red ground, and he limped much as I do, from a wound which he had got in his youth at Mantes siege. He served the Duke of Burgundy against the Moors in Spain, and was returning to that war with his dogs. He sang us strange Moorish songs that first night, and half persuaded us to go with him. I was on pilgrimage to forget–which is what no pilgrimage brings. I think I would have gone, but . . .

"Look you how the life and fortune of man changes! Towards morning a Dane ship, rowing silently, struck against us in the mist, and while we rolled hither and yon Hugh, leaning over the rail, fell outboard. I leaped after him, and we two tumbled aboard the Dane, and were caught and bound ere we could rise. Our own ship was swallowed up in the mist. I judge the Knight of the Gold Pieces muzzled his dogs with his cloak, lest they should give tongue and betray the merchants, for I heard their baying suddenly stop.

"We lay bound among the benches till morning, when the Danes dragged us to the high deck by the steering-place, and their captain–Witta, he was called–turned us over with his foot. Bracelets of gold from elbow to armpit he wore, and his red hair was long as a woman's, and came down in plaited locks on his shoulder. He was stout, with bowed legs and long arms. He spoiled us of all we had, but when he laid hand on Hugh's sword and saw the runes on the blade hastily he thrust it back. Yet his covetousness overcame him and he tried again and again, and the third time the Sword sang loud and angrily, so that the rowers leaned on their oars to listen. Here they all spoke together, screaming like gulls, and a Yellow Man, such as I have never seen, came to the high deck and cut our bonds. He was yellow–not from sickness, but by nature. Yellow as honey, and his eyes stood endwise in his head."

"How do you mean?" said Una, her chin on her hand.

"Thus," said Sir Richard. He put a finger to the corner of each eye, and pushed it up till his eyes narrowed to slits.

"Why, you look just like a Chinaman!" cried Dan. "Was the man a Chinaman?"

"I know not what that may be. Witta had found him half dead among ice on the shores of Muscovy. *We* thought he was a devil. He crawled before us and brought food in a silver dish which these sea-wolves had robbed from some rich abbey, and Witta with his own hands gave us wine. He spoke a little in French, a little in South Saxon, and much in the Northman's tongue. We asked him to set us ashore, promising to pay him better ransom than he would get price if he sold us to the Moors–as once befell a knight of my acquaintance sailing from Flushing.

" 'Not by my father Guthrum's head,' said he. 'The Gods sent ye into my ship for a luck-offering.'

"At this I quaked, for I knew it was still the Dane's custom to sacrifice captives to their gods for fair weather.

" 'A plague on thy four long bones!' said Hugh. 'What profit canst thou make of poor old pilgrims that can neither work nor fight?'

" 'Gods forbid I should fight against thee, poor Pilgrim with the Singing Sword,' said he. 'Come with us and be poor no more. Thy teeth are far apart, which is a sure sign thou wilt travel and grow rich.'

" 'What if we will not come?' said Hugh.

" 'Swim to England or France,' said Witta. 'We are midway between the two. Unless ye choose to drown yourselves no hair of your head will be harmed here aboard. We think ye bring us luck, and I myself know the runes on that Sword are good.' He turned and bade them hoist sail.

"Hereafter all made way for us as we walked about the ship, and the ship was full of wonders."

"What was she like?" said Dan.

"Long, low, and narrow, bearing one mast with a red sail, and rowed by fifteen oars a side," the knight answered. "At her bows was a deck under which men might lie, and at her stern another shut off by a painted door from the rowers' benches. Here Hugh and I slept, with Witta and the Yellow Man, upon tapestries as soft as wool. I remember"–he laughed to himself–"when first we entered there a loud voice cried, 'Out swords! Out swords! Kill, kill!'"Seeing us start Witta laughed, and showed us it was but a great-beaked gray bird with a red tail. He sat her on his shoulder, and she called for bread and wine hoarsely, and prayed him to kiss her. Yet she was no more than a silly bird. But—ye knew this?" He looked at their smiling faces.

"We weren't laughing at you," said Una. "That must have been a parrot. It's just what Pollies do."

"So we learned later. But here is another marvel. The Yellow Man, whose name was Kitai, had with him a brown box. In the box was a blue bowl with red marks upon the rim, and within the bowl, hanging from a fine thread, was a piece of iron no thicker than that grass stem, and as long, maybe, as my spur, but straight. In this iron, said Witta, abode an Evil Spirit which Kitai the Yellow Man, had brought by Art Magic out of his own country that lay three years' journey southward. The Evil Spirit strove day and night to return to his country, and therefore, look you, the iron needle pointed continually to the South."

"South?" said Dan, suddenly, and put his hand into his pocket.

"With my own eyes I saw it. Every day and all day long, though the ship rolled, though the sun and the moon and the stars were hid, this blind Spirit in the iron knew whither it would go, and strained to the South. Witta called it the Wise Iron, because it showed him his way across the unknowable seas." Again Sir Richard looked keenly at the children. "How think ye? Was it sorcery?"

"Was it anything like this?" Dan fished out his old brass pocket-compass, that generally lived with his knife and key-ring. "The glass has got cracked, but the needle waggles all right, sir."

The knight drew a long breath of wonder. "Yes, yes. The Wise Iron shook and swung in just this fashion. Now it is still. Now it points to the South."

"North," said Dan.

"Nay, South! There is the South," said Sir Richard. Then they both laughed, for naturally when one end of a straight compass-needle points to the North, the other must point to the South.

"Té," said Sir Richard, clicking his tongue. "There can be no sorcery if a child carries it. Wherefore does it point South—or North?"

"Father says that nobody knows," said Una.

Sir Richard looked relieved. "Then it may still be magic. It was magic to *us*. And so we voyaged. When the wind served we hoisted sail, and lay all up along the windward rail, our shields on our backs to break the spray. When it failed, they rowed with long oars; the Yellow Man sat by the Wise Iron, and Witta steered. At first I feared the great white-flowering waves, but as I saw how wisely Witta led his ship among them I grew bolder. Hugh liked it well from the first. My skill is not upon the water; and rocks, and whirlpools such as we saw by the West Isles of France, where an oar caught on a rock and broke, are much against my stomach. We sailed South across a stormy sea, where by moonlight, between clouds, we saw a Flanders ship roll clean over and sink. Again, though Hugh labored with Witta all night, I lay under the deck with the Talking Bird, and cared not whether I lived or died. There is a sickness of the sea which, for three days, is pure death! When we next saw land Witta said it was Spain, and we stood out to sea. That coast was full of ships busy in the Duke's war against the Moors, and we feared to be hanged by the Duke's men or sold into slavery by the Moors. So we put into a small harbor which Witta knew. At night men came down with loaded mules, and Witta exchanged amber out of the North against little wedges of iron and packets of beads in earthen pots. The pots he put under the decks, and the wedges of iron he laid on the bottom of the ship after he had cast out the stones and shingle which till then had been our ballast. Wine, too, he bought for lumps of sweet-smelling gray amber—a little morsel no bigger than a thumbnail purchased a cask of wine. But I speak like a merchant."

"No, no! Tell us what you had to eat," cried Dan.

"Meat dried in the sun, and dried fish and ground beans, Witta took in; and corded frails of a certain sweet, soft fruit, which the Moors use, which is like paste of figs, but with thin, long stones. Aha! Dates is the name.

" 'Now,' said Witta, when the ship was loaded, 'I counsel you strangers, to pray to your gods, for from here on our road is No Man's road.' He and his men killed a black goat for sacrifice on the bows; and the Yellow Man brought out a small, smiling image of dull-green grass and burned incense before it. Hugh and I commended ourselves to God, and Saint Bartholomew, and Our Lady of the Assumption, who was specially dear to my Lady. We were not young, but I think no shame to say, when as we drove out of that secret harbor at sunrise over a still sea, we two rejoiced and sang as did the knights of old when they followed our great Duke to England. Yet was our leader an heathen pirate; all our proud fleet but one galley perilously overloaded; for guidance we leaned on a pagan sorcerer; and our port was beyond the world's end. Witta told us that his father Guthrum had once in his life rowed along the shores of Africa to a land where naked men sold gold for iron and beads. There had he bought much gold, and no few elephants' teeth, and thither by help of the Wise Iron would Witta go. Witta feared nothing—except to be poor.

" 'My father told me,' said Witta, 'that a great Shoal runs three days' sail out from that land, and south of the shoal lies a Forest which grows in the sea. South and east of the Forest my father came to a place where the men hid gold in their hair; but all that country, he said, was full of Devils who lived in trees, and tore folk limb from limb. How think ye?'

" 'Gold or no gold,' said Hugh, fingering his sword, 'it is a joyous venture. Have at these devils of thine, Witta!'

" 'Venture!' said Witta, sourly. 'I am only a poor sea-thief. I do not set my life adrift on a plank for joy, or the venture. Once I beach ship again at Stavanger, and feel the wife's arms round my neck, I'll seek no more ventures. A ship is heavier care than a wife or cattle.'

"He leaped down among the rowers, chiding them for their little strength and their great stomachs. Yet Witta was a wolf in fight, and a very fox in cunning.

"We were driven South by a storm, and for three days and three nights he took the stern-oar and threddled the longship through the sea. When it rose beyond measure he brake a pot of whale's oil upon the water, which wonderfully smoothed it, and in that anointed patch he turned her head to the wind and threw out oars at the end of a rope, to make, he said, an anchor at which we lay rolling sorely, but dry. This craft his father Guthrum had shown him. He knew, too, all the Leech-Book of Bald, who was a wise doctor, and he knew the Ship-Book of Hlaf the Woman, who robbed Egypt. He knew all the care of a ship.

"After the storm we saw a mountain whose top was covered with snow and pierced the clouds. The grasses under this mountain, boiled and eaten, are a good cure for soreness of the gums and swelled ankles. We lay there eight days, till men in skins threw stones at us. When the heat increased Witta spread a cloth on bent sticks above the rowers, for the wind failed between the Island of the Mountain and the shore of Africa, which is east of it. That shore is sandy, and we rowed along it within three bowshots. Here we saw whales, and fish in the shape of shields, but longer than our ship. Some slept, some opened their mouths at us, and some danced on the hot waters. The water was hot to the hand, and the sky was hidden by hot, gray mists, out of which blew a fine dust that whitened our hair and beards of a morning. Here, too, were fish that flew in the air like birds. They would fall on the laps of the rowers, and when we went ashore we would roast and eat them."

The knight paused to see if the children doubted him, but they only nodded and said, "Go on."

"The yellow land lay on our left, the gray sea on our right. Knight though I was, I pulled my oar amongst the rowers. I caught seawood and dried it, and stuffed it between the pots of beads lest they should break. Knighthood is for the land. At sea, look you, a man is but a spurless rider on a bridleless horse. I learned to make strong knots in ropes—yes, and to join two ropes end to end, so that even Witta could scarcely see where they had been married. But Hugh had tenfold more sea-cunning than I. Witta gave him charge of the rowers of the left side. Thorkild of Borkum, a man with a broken nose, that wore a Norman steel cap, had the rowers of the right, and each side rowed and sang against the other. They saw that no man was idle. Truly, as Hugh said, and Witta would laugh at him, a ship is all more care than a Manor.

"How? Thus. There was water to fetch from the shore when we could find it, as well as wild fruit and grasses, and sand for scrubbing of the decks and benches to keep them sweet. Also we hauled the ship out on low islands and emptied all her gear, even to the iron wedges, and burned off the weed, that had grown on her, with torches of rush, and smoked below the decks with rushes dampened in salt water, as Hlaf the Woman orders in her Ship-Book. Once when we were thus stripped, and the ship lay propped on her keel, the bird cried, 'Out swords!' as though she saw an enemy. Witta vowed he would wring her neck."

"Poor Polly! Did he?" said Una.

"Nay. She was the ship's bird. She could call all the rowers by name. . . . Those were good days—for a wifeless man—with Witta and his heathen—beyond the world's end. . . . After many weeks we came on the Great Shoal which stretched, as Witta's father had said, far out to sea. We skirted it till we were giddy with the sight and dizzy with the sound of bars and breakers; and when we reached land again we found a naked black people dwelling among woods, who for one wedge of iron loaded us with fruits and grasses and eggs. Witta scratched his head at them in sign he would buy gold. They had no gold, but they understood the sign (all the gold-traders hide their gold in their thick hair), for they pointed along the coast. They beat, too, on their chests with their clenched hands, and that, if we had known it, was an evil sign."

"What did it mean?" said Dan.

"Patience. Ye shall hear. We followed the coast eastward sixteen days (counting time by sword-cuts on the helm-rail) till we came to the Forest in the Sea. Trees grew out of mud, arched upon lean and high roots, and many muddy water-ways ran allwhither into darkness under the trees. Here we lost the sun. We followed the winding channels between the trees, and where we could not row we laid hold of the crusted roots and hauled ourselves along. The water was foul, and great glittering flies tormented us. Morning and evening a blue mist covered the mud, which bred fevers. Four of our rowers sickened, and were bound to their benches, lest they should leap overboard and be eaten by the monsters of the mud. The Yellow Man lay sick beside the Wise Iron, rolling his head and talking in his own tongue. Only the Bird throve. She sat on Witta's shoulder and screamed in that noisome, silent darkness. Yes; I think it was the silence we feared."

He paused to listen to the comfortable home noises of the brook.

"When we had lost count of time among those black gullies and swashes, we heard, as it were, a drum beat far off, and following it we broke into a broad, brown river by a hut in a clearing among fields of pumpkins. We thanked God to see the sun again. The people of the village gave the good welcome, and Witta scratched his head at them (for gold), and showed them our iron and beads. They ran to the bank—we were still in the ship—and pointed to our swords and bows, for always when near shore we lay armed. Soon they fetched store of gold in bars and in dust from their huts, and some great blackened elephant teeth. These they piled on the bank, as though to tempt us, and made signs of dealing blows in battle, and pointed up to the tree tops, and to the forest behind. Their captain or chief sorcerer then beat on his chest with his fists, and gnashed his teeth.

"Said Thorkild of Borkum: 'Do they mean we must fight for all this gear?' and he half drew his sword.

" 'Nay,' said Hugh. 'I think they ask us to league against some enemy.'

" 'I like this not,' said Witta, of a sudden. 'Back into midstream.'

"So we did, and sat still all, watching the black folk and the gold they piled on the bank. Again we heard drums beat in the forest, and the people fled to their huts, leaving the gold unguarded.

"Then Hugh, at the bows, pointed without speech, and we saw a great Devil come out of the forest. He shaded his brows with his hand, and moistened his pink tongue between his lips—thus."

"A Devil!" said Dan, delightfully horrified.

"Yea. Taller than a man; covered with reddish hair. When he had well regarded our ship, he beat on his chest with his fists till it sounded like rolling drums, and came to the bank swinging all his body between his long arms, and gnashed his teeth at us. Hugh loosed arrow, and pierced him through the throat. He fell roaring, and three other Devils ran out of the forest and hauled him into a tall tree out of sight. Anon they cast down the blood-stained arrow, and lamented together among the leaves. Witta saw the gold on the bank; he was loath to leave it. 'Sirs,' said he (no man had spoken till then), 'yonder is that we have come so far and so painfully to find, laid out to our very hand. Let us row in while these Devils bewail themselves, and at least bear off what we may.'

"Bold as a wolf, cunning as a fox was Witta! He set four archers on the foredeck to shoot the Devils if they should leap from the tree, which was close to the bank. He manned ten oars a side, and bade them watch his hand to row in or back out, and so coaxed he them toward the bank. But none would set foot ashore, though the gold was within ten paces. No man is hasty to his hanging. They whimpered at their oars like beaten hounds, and Witta bit his fingers for rage.

"Said Hugh of a sudden, 'Hark!' At first we thought it was the buzzing of the glittering flies on the water, but it grew loud and fierce, so that all men heard."

"What?" said Dan and Una.

"It was the sword." Sir Richard patted the smooth hilt. "It sang as a Dane sings before battle. 'I go,' said Hugh, and he leaped from the bows and fell among the gold. I was afraid to my four bones' marrow, but for shame's sake I followed, and Thorkild of Borkum leaped after me. None other came. 'Blame me not,' cried Witta behind us, 'I must abide by my ship.' We three had no time to blame or praise. We stooped to the gold and threw it back over our shoulders, one hand on our swords and one eye on the tree, which nigh overhung us.

"I know not how the Devils leaped down, or how the fight began. I heard Hugh cry: 'Out! out!' as though he were at Santlache again; I saw Thorkild's steel cap smitten off his head by a great hairy hand, and I felt an arrow from the ship whistle past my ear. They say that till Witta took his sword to the rowers he could not bring his ship in shore; and each one of the four archers said afterwards that he alone had pierced the Devil that fought me. I do not know. I went to it in my mail-shirt, which saved my skin. With long-sword and belt-dagger I fought for the life against a Devil whose very feet were hands, and who whirled me back and forth like a dead branch. He had me by the waist, my arms to my side, when an arrow from the ship pierced him between the shoulders, and he loosened grip. I passed my sword twice through him, and he crutched himself away between his long arms, coughing and moaning. Next, as I remember, I saw Thorkild of Borkum bare-headed and smiling, leaping up and down before a Devil that leaped and gnashed his teeth. Then Hugh passed, his sword shifted to his left hand, and I wondered why I had not known that Hugh was a left-handed man; and thereafter I remembered nothing till I felt spray on my face, and we were in sunshine on the open sea. That was twenty days after."

"What had happened? Did Hugh die?" the children asked.

"Never was such a fight fought by christened man," said Sir Richard. "An arrow from the ship had saved me from my Devil, and Thorkild of Borkum had given back before his Devil, till the bowmen on the ship could shoot it all full of arrows from near by; but Hugh's Devil was cunning, and had kept behind trees, where no arrow could reach. Body to body there, by stark strength of sword and hand, had Hugh slain him, and, dying, the Thing had clenched his teeth on the sword. Judge what teeth they were!"

Sir Richard turned the sword again that the children might see the two great chiselled gouges on either side of the blade.

"Those same teeth met in Hugh's right arm and side," Sir Richard went on. "I? Oh, I had no more than a broken foot and a fever. Thorkild's ear was bitten, but Hugh's arm and side clean withered away. I saw him where he lay along, sucking a fruit in his left hand. His flesh was wasted off his bones, his hair was patched with white, and his hand was blue-veined like a woman's. He put his left hand round my neck and whispered, 'Take my sword. It has been thine since Hastings, O, my brother, but I can never hold hilt again.' We lay there on the high deck talking of Santlache and, I think, of every day since Santlache, and it came so that we both wept. I was weak, and he little more than a shadow.

" 'Nay–nay,' said Witta, at the helm-rail. 'Gold is a good right arm to any man. Look–look at the gold!' He bade Thorkild to show us the gold and the elephants' teeth, as though we had been children. He had brought away all the gold on the bank, and twice as much more, that the people of the village gave him for slaying the Devils. They worshipped us as gods, Thorkild told me: it was one of their old women healed up Hugh's poor arm."

"How much gold did you get?" asked Dan.

"How can I say? Where we came out with wedges of iron under the rowers' feet we returned with wedges of gold hidden beneath planks. There was dust of gold in packages where we slept; and along the side and crosswise under the benches we lashed the blackened elephants' teeth.

" 'I had sooner have my right arm,' said Hugh, when he had seen all.

" 'Ahai! That was my fault,' said Witta. 'I should have taken ransom and landed you in France when first you came aboard, ten months ago.'

" 'It is over-late now,' said Hugh, laughing.

"Witta plucked at his long shoulder-lock. 'But think!' said he. 'If I had let ye go–which I swear I would never have done, for I love ye more than brothers–if I had let ye go, by now ye might have been horribly slain by some mere Moor in the Duke of Burgundy's war, or ye might have been murdered by land-thieves, or ye might have died of the plague at an inn. Think of this and do not blame me overmuch, Hugh. See! I will only take a half of the gold.'

" 'I blame thee not at all, Witta,' said Hugh. 'It was a joyous venture, and we thirty-five here have done what never men have done. If I live till England, I will build me a stout keep over Dallington out of my share.'

" 'I will buy cattle and amber and warm red cloth for the wife,' said Witta, 'and I will hold all the land at the head of Stavanger Fiord. Many will fight for me now. But first we must turn North, and with this honest treasure aboard I pray we meet no pirate ships.'

"We did not laugh. We were careful. We were afraid lest we should lose one grain of our gold for which we had fought Devils.

" 'Where is the Sorcerer?' said I, for Witta was looking at the Wise Iron in the box, and I could not see the Yellow Man.

" 'He has gone to his own country,' said he. 'He rose up in the night while we were beating out of that forest in the mud, and said that he could see it behind the trees. He leaped out on to the mud, and did not answer when we called; so we called no more. He left the Wise Iron, which is all that I care for–and see, the Spirit still points to the South!'

"We were troubled for fear that the Wise Iron should fail us now that its Yellow Man had gone, and when we saw the Spirit still served us we grew afraid of too strong winds, and of shoals, and of careless leaping fish, and of all the people on all the shores where we landed."

"Why?" said Dan.

"Because of the gold–because of our gold. Gold changes men altogether. Thorkild of Borkum did not change. He laughed at Witta for his fears, and at us for our counselling Witta to furl sail when the ship pitched at all.

" 'Better be drowned out of hand,' said Thorkild of Borkum, 'than go tied to a deck-load of yellow dust.'

"He was a landless man, and had been slave to some King in the East. He would have beaten out the gold into deep bands to put round the oars, and round the prow.

"Yet, though he vexed himself for the gold, Witta waited upon Hugh like a woman, lending him his shoulder when the ship rolled, and tying of ropes from side to side that Hugh might hold by them. But for Hugh, he said–and so did all his men–they would never have won the gold. I remember Witta made a little, thin gold ring for our Bird to swing in. Three months we rowed and sailed and went ashore for fruits or to clean the ship. When we saw wild horsemen, riding among sand-dunes, flourishing spears we knew we were on the Moors' coast, and stood over north to Spain; and a strong south-west wind bore us in ten days to a coast of high red rocks, where we heard a hunting-horn blow among the yellow gorse and knew it was England.

" 'Now find ye Pevensey yourselves,' said Witta. 'I love not these narrow ship-filled seas.'

"He set the dried, salted head of the Devil, which Hugh had killed, high on our prow, and all boats fled from us. Yet, for our gold's sake, we were more afraid than they. We crept along the coast by night till we came to the chalk cliffs, and so east to Pevensey. Witta would not come ashore with us, though Hugh promised him wine at Dallington enough to swim in. He was on fire to see his wife, and ran into the Marsh after sunset, and there he left us and our share of gold, and backed out on the same tide. He made no promise; he swore no oath; he looked for no thanks; but to Hugh, an armless man, and to me, an old cripple whom he could have flung into the sea, he passed over wedge upon wedge, packet upon packet of gold and dust of gold, and only ceased when we would take no more. As he stooped from the rail to bid us farewell he stripped off his right-arm bracelets and put them all on Hugh's left, and he kissed Hugh on the cheek. I think when Thorkild of Borkum bade the rowers give way we were near weeping. It is true that Witta was an heathen and a pirate; true it is he held us by force many months in his ship, but I loved that bow-legged, blue-eyed man for his great boldness, his cunning, his skill, and, beyond all, for his simplicity."

"Did he get home all right?" said Dan.

"I never knew. We saw him hoist sail under the moon-track and stand away. I have prayed that he found his wife and the children."

"And what did you do?"

"We waited on the Marsh till the day. Then I sat by the gold, all tied in an old sail, while Hugh went to Pevensey, and De Aquila sent us horses."

Sir Richard crossed hands on his sword-hilt, and stared down stream through the soft warm shadows.

"A whole shipload of gold!" said Una, looking at the little *Golden Hind.* "But I'm glad I didn't see the Devils."

"I don't believe they were Devils," Dan whispered back.

"Eh?" said Sir Richard. "Witta's father warned him they were unquestionable Devils. One must believe one's father, and not one's children. What were my Devils, then?"

Dan flushed all over. "I—I only thought," he stammered; "I've got a book called *The Gorilla Hunters*—it's a continuation of *Coral Island*, sir—and it says there that the gorillas (they're big monkeys, you know) were always chewing iron up."

"Not always," said Una. "Only twice." They had been reading *The Gorilla Hunters* in the orchard.

"Well, anyhow, they always drummed on their chests, like Sir Richard's did, before they went for people. And they built houses in trees, too."

"Ha!" Sir Richard opened his eyes. "Houses like flat nests did our Devils make, where their imps lay and looked at us. I did not see them (I was sick after the fight), but Witta told me and, lo, ye know it also? Wonderful! Were our Devils only nest-building apes? Is there no sorcery left in the world?"

"I don't know," answered Dan, uncomfortably. "I've seen a man take rabbits out of a hat, and he told us we could see how he did it, if we watched hard. And we did."

"But we didn't," said Una sighing. "Oh! there's Puck!"

The little fellow, brown and smiling, peered between two stems of an ash, nodded, and slid down the bank into the cool beside them.

"No sorcery, Sir Richard?" he laughed, and blew on a full dandelion head he had picked.

"They tell me that Witta's Wise Iron was a toy. The boy carries such an Iron with him. They tell me our Devils were apes, called gorillas!" said Sir Richard, indignantly.

"That is the sorcery of books," said Puck. "I warned thee they were wise children. All people can be wise by reading of books."

"But are the books true?" Sir Richard frowned. "I like not all this reading and writing."

"Ye-es," said Puck, holding the naked dandelion head at arm's length. "But if we hang all fellows who write falsely, why did De Aquila not begin with Gilbert, the Clerk? *He* was false enough."

"Poor false Gilbert. Yet in his fashion, he was bold," said Sir Richard.

"What did he do?" said Dan.

"He wrote," said Sir Richard. "Is the tale meet for children, think you?" He looked at Puck; but, "Tell us! Tell us!" cried Dan and Una together.

Thorkild's Song

There is no wind along these seas,
Out oars for Stavanger!
Forward all for Stavanger!
So we must wake the white-ash breeze.
Let fall for Stavanger!
A long pull for Stavanger!

Oh, hear the benches creak and strain!
(A long pull for Stavanger!)
She thinks she smells the Northland rain!
(A long pull for Stavanger!)

She thinks she smells the Northland snow
And she's as glad as we to go!

She thinks she smells the Northland rime,
And the dear dark nights of winter-time.

Her very bolts are sick for shore,
And we—we want it ten times more!

Hoe—all you Gods that love brave men,
Send us a three-reef gale again!

Send us a gale, and watch us come,
With close-cropped canvas slashing home.

But—*there's no wind in all these seas,*
A long pull for Stavanger!
So we must wake the white-ash breeze,
A long pull for Stavanger!

Old Men at Pevensey

"It has nought to do with apes or devils," Sir Richard went on, in an undertone. "It concerns De Aquila, than whom there was never bolder nor craftier, nor more hardy knight born. And, remember, he was an old, old man at that time."

"When?" said Dan.

"When we came back from sailing with Witta."

"What did you do with your gold?" said Dan.

"Have patience. Link by link is chain-mail made. I will tell all in its place. We bore the gold to Pevensey on horseback—three loads of it—and then up to the north chamber, above the Great Hall of Pevensey Castle, where De Aquila lay in winter. He sat on his bed like a little white falcon, turning his head swiftly from one to the other, as we told our tale. Jehan the Crab, an old sour man-at-arms, guarded the stairway, but De Aquila bade him wait at the stair-foot, and let down both leather curtains over the door. It was Jehan whom De Aquila had sent to us with the horses, and only Jehan had loaded the gold. When our story was told, De Aquila gave us the news of England, for we were as men waked from a year-long sleep. The Red King was dead—slain (ye remember?) the day we set sail—and Henry, his younger brother, had made himself King of England over the head of Robert of Normandy. This was the very thing that the Red King had done to Robert when our Great William died. Then Robert of Normandy, mad, as De Aquila said, at twice missing of this kingdom, had sent an army against England, which army had been well beaten back to their ships at Portsmouth. A little earlier, and Witta's ship would have rowed through them.

" 'And now,' said De Aquila, 'half the great Barons of the north and west are out against the King between Salisbury and Shrewsbury; and half the other half wait to see which way the game shall go. They say Henry is overly English for their stomachs, because he hath married an English wife and she hath coaxed him to give back their old laws to our Saxons. (Better ride a horse on the bit he knows, *I* say.) But that is only a cloak to their falsehood.' He cracked his finger on the table where the wine was spilt, and thus he spoke:—

" 'William crammed us Norman barons full of good English acres after Santlache. *I* had my share too,' he said, and clapped Hugh on the shoulder; 'but I warned him—I warned him before Odo rebelled—that he should have bidden the Barons give up their lands and lordships in Normandy if they would be English lords. Now they are all but princes both in England and Normandy—trencher-fed hounds, with a foot in one trough and both eyes on the other! Robert of Normandy has sent them word that if they do not fight for him in England he will sack and harry out their lands in Normandy. Therefore Clare has risen, Fitz Osborn has risen, Montgomery has risen—whom our First William made an English earl. Even D'Arcy is out with his men, whose father I remember a little hedge-sparrow knight nearby Caen. If Henry wins, the Barons can still flee to Normandy, where Robert will welcome them. If Henry loses, Robert, he says, will give them more lands in England. Oh, a pest—a pest on Normandy, for she will be our England's curse this many a long year!'

" 'Amen,' said Hugh. 'But will the war come our ways, think you?'

" 'Not from the North,' said De Aquila. 'But the sea is always open. If the Barons gain the upper hand Robert will send another army into England for sure; and this time I think he will land here—where his father, the Conqueror, landed. Ye have brought your pigs to a pretty market! Half England alight, and gold enough on the ground"—he stamped on the bars beneath the table—"to set every sword in Christendom fighting."

" 'What is to do?' said Hugh. 'I have no keep at Dallington; and if we buried it, whom could we trust?'

" 'Me,' said De Aquila. 'Pevensey walls are strong. No man but Jehan, who is my dog, knows what is between them.' He drew a curtain by the shot-window and showed us the shaft of a well in the thickness of the wall.

" 'I made it for a drinking-well,' he said, 'but we found salt water, and it rises and falls with the tide. Hark!' We heard the water whistle and blow at the bottom. 'Will it serve?' said he.

" 'Needs must,' said Hugh. 'Our lives are in thy hands.' So we lowered all the gold down except one small chest of it by De Aquila's bed, which we kept as much for his delight in its weight and color as for any our needs.

"In the morning, ere we rode to our Manors, he said: 'I do not say farewell; because ye will return and bide here. Not for love nor for sorrow, but to be with the gold. Have a care,' he said, laughing, 'lest I use it to make myself Pope. Trust me not, but return!' "

Sir Richard paused and smiled sadly.

"In seven days, then, we returned from our Manors—from the Manors which had been ours."

"And were the children quite well?" said Una.

"My sons were young. Land and governance belong by right to young men." Sir Richard was talking to himself. "It would have broken their hearts if we had taken back our Manors. They made us great welcome, but we could see—Hugh and I could see—that our day was done. I was a cripple and he a one-armed man. No!" He shook his head. "And therefore"—he raised his voice—"we rode back to Pevensey."

"I'm sorry," said Una, for the knight seemed very sorrowful.

"Little maid, it all passed long ago. They were young; we were old. We let them rule the Manors. 'Aha!' cried De Aquila from his shot-window, when we dismounted. 'Back again to earth, old foxes?' but when we were in his chamber above the hall he puts his arms about us and says, 'Welcome, ghosts! Welcome, poor ghosts!' . . . Thus it fell out that we were rich beyond belief, and lonely. And lonely!"

"What did you do?" said Dan.

"We watched for Robert of Normandy," said the knight. "De Aquila was like Witta. He suffered no idleness. In fair weather we would ride along between Bexlei on the one side, to Cuckmere on the other—sometimes with hawk, sometimes with hound (there are stout hares both on the Marsh and the Downland), but always with an eye to the sea, for fear of fleets from Normandy. In foul weather he would walk on the top of his tower, frowning against the rain—peering here and pointing there. It always vexed him to think how Witta's ship had come and gone without his knowledge. When the wind ceased and ships anchored, to the wharf's edge he would go and, leaning on his sword among the stinking fish, would call to the mariners for their news from France. His other eye he kept landward for word of Henry's war against the Barons.

"Many brought him news—jongleurs, harpers, pedlars, sutlers, priests, and the like; and, though he was secret enough in small things, yet, if their news misliked him, then, regarding neither time nor place nor people, would he curse our King Henry for a fool or a babe. I have heard him cry aloud by the fishing-boats: 'If I were King of England I would do thus and thus'; and when I rode out to see that the warning-beacons were laid and dry, he hath often called to me from the shot-window: 'Look to it, Richard! Do not copy our blind King, but see with thine own eyes and feel with thine own hands.' I do not think he knew any sort of fear. And so we lived at Pevensey, in the little chamber above the Hall.

"One foul night came word that a messenger of the King waited below. We were chilled after a long riding in the fog towards Bexlei, which is an easy place for ships to land. De Aquila sent word the man might either eat with us or wait till we had fed. Anon Jehan, at the stair-head, cried that he had called for horse, and was gone. 'Pest on him!' said De Aquila. 'I have more to do than to shiver in the Great Hall for every gadling the King sends. Left he no word?'

" 'None,' said Jehan, 'except'—he had been with De Aquila at Santlache—"except he said that if an old dog could not learn new tricks it was time to sweep out the kennel.'

" 'Oho!' said De Aquila, rubbing his nose, 'to whom did he say that?'

" 'To his beard, chiefly, but some to his horse's flank as he was girthing up. I followed him out,' said Jehan the Crab.

" 'What was his shield-mark?'

" 'Gold horseshoes on black,' said the Crab.

" 'That is one of Fulke's men,' said De Aquila."

Puck broke in very gently, "Gold horseshoes on black is *not* the Fulkes' shield. The Fulkes' arms are—"

The knight waved one hand statelily.

"Thou knowest the evil man's true name," he replied, "but I have chosen to call him Fulke because I promised him I would not tell the story of his wickedness so that any man might guess it. I have changed *all* the names in my tale. His children's children may be still alive."

"True—true," said Puck, smiling softly. "It is knightly to keep faith—even after a thousand years."

Sir Richard bowed a little and went on:—

" 'Gold horseshoes on black?' said De Aquila. 'I had heard Fulke had joined the Barons, but if this is true our King must be of the upper hand. No matter, all Fulkes are faithful. Still, I would not have sent the man away empty.'

" 'He fed,' said Jehan. 'Gilbert the Clerk fetched him meat and wine from the kitchens. He ate at Gilbert's table.'

"This Gilbert was a clerk from Battle Abbey, who kept the accounts of the Manor of Pevensey. He was tall and pale-colored, and carried those new-fashioned beads for counting of prayers. They were large brown nuts or seeds, and hanging from his girdle with his penner and inkhorn they clashed when he walked. His place was in the great fireplace. There was his table of accounts, and there he lay o' nights. He feared the hounds in the Hall that came nosing after bones or to sleep on the warm ashes, and would slash at them with his beads—like a woman. When De Aquila sat in Hall to do justice, take fines, or grant lands, Gilbert would so write it in the Manor-roll. But it was none of his work to feed our guests, or to let them depart without his lord's knowledge.

"Said De Aquila, after Jehan was gone down the stair: 'Hugh, hast thou ever told my Gilbert thou canst read Latin hand-of-write?'

" 'No,' said Hugh. 'He is no friend to me, or to Odo my hound either.' 'No matter,' said De Aquila. 'Let him never know thou canst tell one letter from its fellow, and'—here he jerked us in the ribs with his scabbard—'watch him both of ye. There be devils in Africa, as I have heard, but by the Saints there be greater devils in Pevensey!' And that was all he would say.

"It chanced, some small while afterwards, a Norman man-at-arms would wed a Saxon wench of the Manor, and Gilbert (we had watched him well since De Aquila spoke) doubted whether her folk were free or slave. Since De Aquila would give them a field of good land, if she were free, the matter came up at the justice in Great Hall before De Aquila. First the wench's father spoke; then her mother; then all together, till the hall rang and the hounds bayed. De Aquila held up his hands. 'Write her free,' he called to Gilbert by the fireplace. 'A' God's Name write her free, before she deafens me! Yes, yes,' he said to the wench that was on her knees at him; 'thou art Cerdic's sister, and own cousin to the Lady of Mercia, if thou wilt be silent. In fifty years there will be neither Norman nor Saxon, but all English,' said he, 'and *these* are the men that do our work!' He clapped the man-at-arms, that was Jehan's nephew, on the shoulder, and kissed the wench, and fretted with his feet among the rushes to show it was finished. (The Great Hall is always bitter cold.) I stood at his side; Hugh was behind Gilbert in the fireplace making to play with wise rough Odo. He signed to De Aquila, who bade Gilbert measure the new field for the new couple. Out then runs our Gilbert between man and maid, his beads clashing at his waist, and the Hall being empty, we three sit by the fire.

"Said Hugh, leaning down to the hearthstones, 'I saw this stone move under Gilbert's foot when Odo snuffed at it. Look!' De Aquila digged in the ashes with his sword; the stone tilted; beneath it lay a parchment folden, and the writing atop was: 'Words spoken against the King by our Lord of Pevensey–the second part.'

"Here was set out (Hugh read it us whispering) every jest De Aquila had made to us touching the King; every time he had called out to me from the shot-window, and every time he had said what he would do if he were King of England. Yes, day by day had his daily speech, which he never stinted, been set down by Gilbert, tricked out and twisted from its true meaning, yet withal so cunningly that none could deny who knew him that De Aquila had in some sort spoken those words. Ye see?"

Dan and Una nodded.

"Yes," said Una, gravely. "It isn't what you say so much. It's what you mean when you say it. Like calling Dan a beast in fun. Only grown-ups don't always understand."

" 'He hath done this day by day before our very face?' said De Aquila.

" 'Nay, hour by hour,' said Hugh. 'When De Aquila spoke even now, in the hall, of Saxons and Normans, I saw Gilbert write on a parchment, which he kept beside the Manor-roll, that De Aquila said soon there would be no Normans left in England if his men-at-arms did their work aright.'

" 'Bones of the Saints!' said De Aquila. 'What avail is honor or a sword against a pen? Where did Gilbert hide that writing? He shall eat it.'

" 'In his breast when he ran out,' said Hugh. 'Which made me look to see where he kept his finished stuff. When Odo scratched at this stone here, I saw his face change. So I was sure.'

" 'He is bold,' said De Aquila. 'Do him justice. In his own fashion, my Gilbert is bold.'

" 'Overbold,' said Hugh. 'Hearken here,' and he read: 'Upon the feast of St. Agatha, our Lord of Pevensey, lying in his upper chamber, being clothed in his second fur gown reversed with rabbit–'

" 'Pest on him! He is not my tire-woman!' said De Aquila, and Hugh and I laughed.

" 'Reversed with rabbit, seeing a fog over the marshes, did wake Sir Richard Dalyngridge, his drunken cup-mate' (here they laughed at me) 'and said, "Peer out, old fox, for God is on the Duke of Normandy's side." '

" 'So did I. It was a black fog. Robert could have landed ten thousand men, and we none the wiser. Does he tell how we were out all day riding the marsh, and how I near perished in a quicksand, and coughed like a sick ewe for ten days after?' cried De Aquila.

" 'No,' said Hugh. 'But here is the prayer of Gilbert himself to his master Fulke.'

" 'Ah,' said De Aquila. 'Well I knew it was Fulke. What is the price of my blood?'

" 'Gilbert prayeth that when our Lord of Pevensey is stripped of his lands on this evidence which Gilbert hath, with fear and pains, collected–'

" 'Fear and pains is a true word,' said De Aquila, and sucked in his cheeks. 'But how excellent a weapon is a pen! I must learn it.'

" 'He prays that Fulke will advance him from his present service to that honor in the Church which Fulke promised him. And lest Fulke should forget, he has written below, "To be Sacristan of Battle." '

"At this De Aquila whistled. 'A man who can plot against one lord can plot against another. When I am stripped of my lands Fulke will whip off my Gilbert's foolish head. None the less Battle needs a new Sacristan. They tell me the Abbot Henry keeps no sort of rule there.'

" 'Let the Abbot wait,' said Hugh. 'It is our heads and our lands that are in danger. This parchment is the second part of the tale. The first has gone to Fulke, and so to the King, who will hold us traitors.'

" 'Assuredly,' said De Aquila. 'Fulke's man took the first part that evening when Gilbert fed him, and our King is so beset by his brother and his Barons (small blame, too!) that he is mad with mistrust. Fulke has his ear, and pours poison into it. Presently the King gives him my land and yours. This is old,' and he leaned back and yawned.

" 'And thou wilt surrender Pevensey without word or blow?' said Hugh. 'We Saxons will fight your King then. I will go warn my nephew at Dallington. Give me a horse!'

" 'Give thee a toy and a rattle,' said De Aquila. 'Put back the parchment, and rake over the ashes. If Fulke is given my Pevensey which is England's gate, what will he do with it? He is Norman at heart, and his heart is in Normandy, where he can kill peasants at his pleasure. He will open England's gate to our sleepy Robert, as Odo and Mortain tried to do, and then there will be another landing and another Santlache. Therefore I cannot give up Pevensey.'

" 'Good,' said we two.

" 'Ah, but wait! If my King be made, on Gilbert's evidence, to mistrust me, he will send his men against me here, and, while we fight, England's gate is left unguarded. Who will be the first to come through thereby? Even Robert of Normandy. Therefore I cannot fight my King.' He nursed his sword–thus.

" 'This is saying and unsaying like a Norman,' said Hugh. 'What of our Manors?'

" 'I do not think for myself,' said De Aquila, 'nor for our King, nor for your lands. I think for England, for whom neither King nor Baron thinks. I am not Norman, Sir Richard, nor Saxon, Sir Hugh. English am I.'

" 'Saxon, Norman, or English,' said Hugh, 'our lives are thine, however the game goes. When do we hang Gilbert?'

" 'Never,' said De Aquila. 'Who knows he may yet be Sacristan of Battle, for, to do him justice, he is good writer. Dead men make dumb witnesses. Wait.'

" 'But the King may give Pevensey to Fulke. And our Manors go with it,' said I. 'Shall we tell our sons?'

" 'No. The King will not wake up a hornet's nest in the South till he has smoked out the bees in the North. He may hold me a traitor; but at least he sees I am not fighting against him, and every day that I lie still is so much gain to him while he fights the barons. If he were wise he would wait till that war were over before he made new enemies. But I think Fulke will play upon him to send for me, and if I do not obey the summons that will, to Henry's mind, be proof of my treason. But mere talk, such as Gilbert sends, is no proof nowadays. We Barons follow the Church, and, like Anselm, we speak what we please. Let us go about our day's dealings, and say naught to Gilbert.'

" 'Then we do nothing?' said Hugh.

" 'We wait,' said De Aquila. 'I am old, but still I find that the most grievous work I know.'

"And so we found it, but in the end De Aquila was right.

"A little later in the year, armed men rode over the hill, the Golden Horseshoes flying behind the King's banner. Said De Aquila, at the window of our chamber: 'How did I tell you? Here comes Fulke himself to spy out his new lands which our King hath promised him if he can bring proof of my treason.'

" 'How dost thou know?' said Hugh.

" 'Because that is what I would do if I were Fulke, but *I* should have brought more men. My roan horse to your old shoes,' said he, 'Fulke brings me the King's Summons to leave Pevensey and join the war.' He sucked in his cheeks and drummed on the edge of the shaft, where the water sounded all hollow.

" 'Shall we go?' said I.

" 'Go! At this time of year? Stark madness,' said he. 'Take *me* from Pevensey to fisk and flyte through fern and forest, and in three days Robert's keels would be lying on Pevensey mud with ten thousand men! Who would stop them—Fulke?'

"The horns blew without, and anon Fulke cried the King's Summons at the great door that De Aquila with all men and horse should join the King's camp at Salisbury.

" 'How did I tell you?' said De Aquila. 'There are twenty Barons 'twixt here and Salisbury could give King Henry good land-service, but he has been worked upon by Fulke to send south and call me—*me!*—off the Gate of England, when his enemies stand about to batter it in. See that Fulke's men lie in the big south barn,' said he. 'Give them drink, and when Fulke has eaten we will drink in my chamber. The Great Hall is too cold for old bones.'

"As soon as he was off-horse Fulke went to the chapel with Gilbert to give thanks for his safe coming, and when he had eaten—he was a fat man, and rolled his eyes greedily at our good roast Sussex wheatears—we led him to the little upper chamber, whither Gilbert had already gone with the Manor-roll. I remember when Fulke heard the tide blow and whistle in the shaft he leaped back, and his long down-turned stirrup-shoes caught in the rushes and he stumbled, so that Jehan behind him found it easy to knock his head against the wall."

"Did you know it was going to happen?" said Dan.

"Assuredly," said Sir Richard, with a sweet smile. "I put my foot on his sword and plucked away his dagger, but he knew not whether it was day or night for a while. He lay rolling his eyes and bubbling with his mouth, and Jehan roped him like a calf. He was cased all in that new-fangled armor which we call lizard-mail. Not rings like my hauberk here"—Sir Richard tapped his chest—"but little pieces of dagger-proof steel overlapping on stout leather. We stripped it off (no need to spoil good harness by wetting it), and in the neck-piece De Aquila found the same folden piece of parchment which we had put back under the hearthstone.

"At this Gilbert would have run out. I laid my hand on his shoulder. It sufficed. He fell to trembling and praying on his beads.

" 'Gilbert,' said De Aquila, 'here be more notable sayings and doings of our Lord of Pevensey for thee to write down. Take penner and inkhorn, Gilbert. We cannot all be Sacristans of Battle.'

"Said Fulke from the floor, 'Ye have bound a King's messenger. Pevensey shall burn for this!'

" 'Maybe. I have seen it besieged once,' said De Aquila, 'but heart up,

Fulke. I promise thee that thou shalt be hanged in the middle of the flames at the end of that siege, if I have to share my last loaf with thee; and that is more than Odo would have done when we starved out him and Mortain.'

"Then Fulke sat up and looked long and cunningly at De Aquila.

" 'By the Saints,' said he, 'why didst thou not say thou wast on the Duke's side at the first?'

" 'Am I?' said De Aquila.

"Fulke laughed and said, 'No man who serves King Henry dare do this much to his messenger. When didst thou come over to the Duke? Let me up and we can smooth it out together.' And he smiled and becked and winked.

" 'Yes, we will smooth it out,' said De Aquila. He nodded to me, and Jehan and I heaved up Fulke—he was a heavy man—and lowered him into the shaft by a rope, not so as to stand on our gold, but dangling by his shoulders a little above. It was turn of ebb, and the water came to his knees. He said nothing, but shivered somewhat.

"Then Jehan of a sudden beat down Gilbert's wrist with his sheathed dagger, 'Stop!' he said. 'He swallows his beads.'

" 'Poison, belike,' said De Aquila. 'It is good for men who know too much. I have carried it these thirty years. Give me!'

"Then Gilbert wept and howled. De Aquila ran the beads through his fingers. The last one—I have said they were large nuts—opened in two halves on a pin, and there was a small folded parchment within. On it was written: *'The Old Dog goes to Salisbury to be beaten. I have his Kennel. Come quickly.'*

" 'This is worse than poison,' said De Aquila, very softly, and sucked in his cheeks. Then Gilbert grovelled in the rushes, and told us all he knew. The letter, as we guessed, was from Fulke to the Duke (and not the first that had passed between them); Fulke had given it to Gilbert in the chapel, and Gilbert thought to have taken it by morning to a certain fishing-boat at the wharf, which trafficked between Pevensey and the French shore. Gilbert was a false fellow, but he found time between his quakings and shakings to swear that the master of the boat knew nothing of the matter.

" 'He hath called me shaved head,' said Gilbert, 'and he hath thrown haddock-guts at me; but for all that, he is no traitor.'

" 'I will have no clerk of mine mishandled or miscalled,' said De Aquila. 'That seaman shall be whipped at his own mast. Write me first a letter, and thou shalt bear it, with the order for the whipping, to-morrow to the boat.'

" 'At this Gilbert would have kissed De Aquila's hand—he had not hoped to live until the morning—and when he trembled less he wrote a letter as from Fulke to the Duke saying that the Kennel, which signified Pevensey, was shut, and that the old Dog (which was De Aquila) sat outside it, and, moreover, that all had been betrayed.

" 'Write to any man that all is betrayed,' said De Aquila, 'and even the Pope himself would sleep uneasily. Eh, Jehan? If one told thee all was betrayed, what wouldst thou do?'

" 'I would run away,' said Jehan. 'It might be true.'

" 'Well said,' quoth De Aquila. 'Write, Gilbert, that Montgomery, the great Earl, hath made his peace with the King, and that little D'Arcy, whom I hate, hath been hanged by the heels. We will give Robert full measure to chew upon. Write also that Fulke himself is sick to death of a dropsy.'

" 'Nay?' cried Fulke, hanging in the well-shaft. 'Drown me out of hand, but do not make a jest of me.'

" 'Jest? I?' said De Aquila. 'I am but fighting for life and lands with a pen, as thou hast shown me, Fulke.'

"Then Fulke groaned, for he was cold, and, 'Let me confess,' said he.

" 'Now, this is right neighborly,' said De Aquila, leaning over the shaft. 'Thou hast read my sayings and doings—or at least the first part of them—and thou art minded to repay me with thy own doings and sayings. Take penner and inkhorn, Gilbert. Here is work that will not irk thee.'

" 'Let my men go without hurt, and I will confess my treason against the King,' said Fulke.

" 'Now, why has he grown so tender of his men of a sudden?' said Hugh to me; for Fulke had no name for mercy to his men. Plunder he gave them, but pity, none.

" 'Té! Té!' said De Aquila. 'Thy treason was all confessed long ago by Gilbert. It would be enough to hang Montgomery himself.'

" 'Nay; but spare my men,' said Fulke; and we heard him splash like a fish in a pond, for the tide was rising.

" 'All in good time,' said De Aquila. 'The night is young; the wine is old; and we need only the merry tale. Begin the story of thy life since when thou wast a lad at Tours. Tell it nimbly!'

" 'Ye shame me to my soul,' said Fulke.

" 'Then I have done what neither King nor Duke could do,' said De Aquila. 'But begin, and forget nothing.'

" 'Send thy man away,' said Fulke.

" 'That much I can,' said De Aquila. 'But, remember, I am like the Danes' King; I cannot turn the tide.'

" 'How long will it rise?' said Fulke, and splashed anew.

" 'For three hours,' said De Aquila. 'Time to tell all thy good deeds. Begin, and Gilbert–I have heard thou art somewhat careless–do not twist his words from their true meaning.'

"So–fear of death in the dark being upon him–Fulke began; and Gilbert, not knowing what his fate might be, wrote it word by word. I have heard many tales, but never heard I aught to match the tale of Fulke, his black life, as Fulke told it hollowly, hanging in the shaft."

"Was it bad?" said Dan, awestruck.

"Beyond belief," Sir Richard answered. "None the less, there was that in it which forced even Gilbert to laugh. We three laughed till we ached. At one place his teeth so chattered that we could not well hear, and we reached him down a cup of wine. Then he warmed to it, and smoothly set out all his shifts, malices, and treacheries, his extreme boldnesses (he was desperate bold); his retreats, shufflings, and counterfeitings (he was also inconceivably a coward); his lack of gear and honor; his despair at their loss; his remedies, and well-colored contrivances. Yes, he waved the filthy rags of his life before us, as though they had been some proud banner. When he ceased, we saw by torches that the tide stood at the corners of his mouth, and he breathed strongly through his nose.

"We had him out, and rubbed him; we wrapped him in a cloak, and gave him wine, and we leaned and looked upon him the while he drank. He was shivering, but shameless.

"Of a sudden we heard Jehan at the stairway wake, but a boy pushed past him, and stood before us, the hall rushes in his hair, all slubbered with sleep. 'My father! My father! I dreamed of treachery,' he cried, and babbled thickly.

" 'There is no treachery here,' said Fulke. 'Go,' and the boy turned, even then not fully awake, and Jehan led him by the hand to the Great Hall.

" 'Thy only son!' said De Aquila, 'Why didst thou bring the child here?'

" 'He is my heir. I dared not trust him to my brother,' said Fulke, and now he was ashamed. De Aquila said nothing, but sat weighing a wine cup in his two hands–thus, Anon, Fulke touched him on the knee.

" 'Let the boy escape to Normandy,' said he, 'and do with me at thy pleasure. Yea, hang me to-morrow, with my letter to Robert round my neck, but let the boy go.'

" 'Be still,' said De Aquila. 'I think for England.'

"So we waited what our Lord of Pevensey should devise; and the sweat ran down Fulke's forehead.

"At last said De Aquila: 'I am too old to judge, or to trust any man. I do not covet thy lands, as thou hast coveted mine; and whether thou art any better or any worse than any other black Angevin thief, it is for thy King to find out. Therefore, go back to thy King, Fulke.'

" 'And thou wilt say nothing of what has passed?' said Fulke.

" 'Why should I? Thy son will stay with me. If the King calls me again to leave Pevensey, which I must guard against England's enemies; if the King sends his men against me for a traitor; or if I hear that the King in his bed thinks any evil of me or my two knights, thy son will be hanged from out this window, Fulke.' "

"But it hadn't anything to do with his son," cried Una, startled.

"How could we have hanged Fulke?" said Sir Richard. "We needed him to make our peace with the King. He would have betrayed half England for the boy's sake. Of that we were sure."

"I don't understand," said Una. "But I think it was simply awful."

"So did not Fulke. He was well pleased."

"What? Because his son was going to be killed?'

"Nay. Because De Aquila had shown him how he might save the boy's life and his own lands and honors. 'I will do it,' he said. 'I swear I will do it. I will tell the King thou art no traitor, but the most excellent, valiant, and perfect of us all. Yes, I will save thee.'

"De Aquila looked still into the bottom of the cup, rolling the wine-dregs to and fro.

" 'Ay,' he said. 'If I had a son, I would, I think, save him. But do not by any means tell me how thou wilt go about it.'

" 'Nay, nay,' said Fulke, nodding his bald head wisely. 'That is my secret. But rest at ease, De Aquila, no hair of thy head nor rood of thy land shall be forfeited,' and he smiled like one planning great good deeds.

" 'And henceforward,' said De Aquila, 'I counsel thee to serve one master–not two.'

" 'What?' said Fulke. 'Can I work no more honest trading between the two sides these troublous times?'

" 'Serve Robert or the King–England or Normandy,' said De Aquila. 'I care not which it is, but make thy choice here and now.'

" 'The King, then,' said Fulke, 'for I see he is better served than Robert. Shall I swear it?'

" 'No need,' said De Aquila, and he laid his hand on the parchments which Gilbert had written. 'It shall be some part of my Gilbert's penance to copy out the savory tale of thy life, till we have made ten, twenty, an hundred, maybe, copies. How many cattle, think you, would the Bishop of Tours give for that tale? Or thy brother? Or the Monks of Blois? Minstrels will turn it into songs which thy own Saxon serfs shall sing behind their plough-stilts, and men-at-arms riding through thy Norman towns. From here to Rome, Fulke, men will make very merry over that tale, and how Fulke told it, hanging in a well, like a drowned puppy. This shall be thy punishment, if ever I find thee double-dealing with thy King any more. Meantime, the parchments stay here with thy son. Him I will return to thee when thou hast made my peace with the King. The parchments never.'

"Fulke hid his face and groaned.

" 'Bones of the Saints!' said De Aquila, laughing. 'The pen cuts deep. I could never have fetched that grunt out of thee with any sword.'

" 'But so long as I do not anger thee, my tale will be secret?' said Fulke.

" 'Just so long. Does that comfort thee, Fulke?' said De Aquila.

" 'What other comfort have ye left me?' he said, and of a sudden he wept hopelessly like a child, dropping his face on his knees."

"Poor Fulke," said Una.

"I pitied him also," said Sir Richard.

" 'After the spur, corn,' said De Aquila, and he threw Fulke three wedges of gold that he had taken from our little chest by the bedplace.

" 'If I had known this,' said Fulke, catching his breath, 'I would never have lifted hand against Pevensey. Only lack of this yellow stuff has made me so unlucky in my dealings.'

"It was dawn then, and they stirred in the Great Hall below. We sent down Fulke's mail to be scoured, and when he rode away at noon under his own and the King's banner very splendid and stately did he show. He smoothed his long beard, and called his son to his stirrup and kissed him. De Aquila rode with him as far as the New Mill landward. We thought the night had been all a dream."

"But did he make it right with the King?" Dan asked. "About your not being traitors, I mean?"

Sir Richard smiled. "The King sent no second summons to Pevensey, nor did he ask why De Aquila had not obeyed the first. Yes, that was Fulke's work. I know not how he did it, but it was well and swiftly done."

"Then you didn't do anything to his son?" said Una.

"The boy? Oh, he was an imp. He turned the keep doors out of dortoirs while we had him. He sang foul songs, learned in the Barons' camps—poor fool; he set the hounds fighting in hall; he lit the rushes to drive out, as he said, the fleas; he drew his dagger on Jehan, who threw him down the stairway for it; and he rode his horse through crops and among sheep. But when we had beaten him, and showed him wolf and deer, he followed us old men like a young, eager hound, and called us 'uncle.' His father came the summer's end to take him away, but the boy had no lust to go, because of the otter-hunting, and he stayed on till the fox-hunting. I gave him a bittern's claw to bring him good luck at shooting. An imp, if ever there was!"

"And what happened to Gilbert?" said Dan.

"Not even a whipping. De Aquila said he would sooner a clerk, however false, that knew the Manor-roll than a fool, however true, that must be taught his work afresh. Moreover, after that night I think Gilbert loved as much as he feared De Aquila. At least he would not leave us—not even when Vivian, the King's Clerk, would have made him Sacristan of Battle Abbey. A false fellow, but, in his fashion, bold."

"Did Robert ever land in Pevensey after all?" Dan went on.

"We guarded the coast too well while Henry was fighting his Barons; and three or four years later, when England had peace, Henry crossed to Normandy and showed his brother some work at Tenchebrai that cured Robert of fighting. Many of Henry's men sailed from Pevensey to that war. Fulke came, I remember, and we all four lay in the little chamber once again, and drank together. De Aquila was right. One should not judge men. Fulke was merry. Yes, always merry—with a catch in his breath."

"And what did you do afterwards?" said Una.

"We talked together of times past. That is all men can do when they grow old, little maid."

The bell for tea rang faintly across the meadows. Dan lay in the bows of the *Golden Hind;* Una in the stern, the book of verses open in her lap, was reading from "The Slave's Dream":—

> "Again in the mist and shadow of sleep
> He saw his native land."

"I don't know when you began that," said Dan, sleepily.

On the middle thwart of the boat, beside Una's sun-bonnet, lay an Oak leaf, an Ash leaf, and a Thorn leaf, that must have dropped down from the trees above; and the brook giggled as though it had just seen some joke.

The Runes on Weland's Sword

A Smith makes me
To betray my Man
In my first fight.

To gather Gold
At the world's end
I am sent.

The Gold I gather
Comes into England
Out of deep Water.

Like a shining Fish
Then it descends
Into deep Water.

It is not given
For goods or gear.
But for The Thing

The Gold I gather
A King covets
For an ill use.

The Gold I gather
Is drawn up
Out of deep Water.

Like a shining Fish
Then it descends
Into deep Water.

It is not given
For goods or gear
But for The Thing.

A Centurion of the Thirtieth

Cities and Thrones and Powers,
Stand in Time's eye,
Almost as long as flowers,
Which daily die:
But, as new buds put forth,
To glad new men,
Out of the spent and unconsidered Earth,
The Cities rise again.

This season's Daffodil,
She never hears,
What change, what chance, what chill,
Cut down last year's;
But with bold countenance,
And knowledge small,
Esteems her seven days' continuance
To be perpetual.

So Time that is o'er-kind,
To all that be,
Ordains us e'en as blind,
As bold as she:
That in our very death,
And burial sure,
Shadow to shadow, well-persuaded, saith,
"See how our works endure"

DAN HAD COME to grief over his Latin, and was kept in; so Una went alone to Far Wood. Dan's big catapult and the lead bullets that Hobden had made for him were hidden in an old hollow beech-stub on the west of the wood. They had named the place out of the verse in *Lays of Ancient Rome.*

From lordly Volaterrae,
Where scowls the far-famed hold,
Piled by the hands of giants
For Godlike Kings of old.

They were the "Godlike Kings," and when old Hobden piled some comfortable brushwood between the big wooden knees of Volaterrae, they called him "Hands of Giants."

Una slipped through their private gap in the fence, and sat still a while, scowling as scowlily and lordlily as she knew how; for "Volaterrae" is an important watch-tower that juts out of Far Wood just as Far Wood juts out of the hillside. Pook's Hill lay below her, and all the turns of the brook as it wanders from out of the Willingford Woods, between hop-gardens, to old

Hobden's cottage at the Forge. The Sou'-West wind (there is always a wind by "Volaterrae") blew from the bare ridge where Cherry Clack Windmill stands.

Now wind prowling through woods sounds like exciting things going to happen, and that is why on "blowy days" you stand up in Volaterrae and shout bits of the *Lays* to suit its noises.

Una took Dan's catapult from its secret place, and made ready to meet Lars Porsena's army stealing through the wind-whitened aspens by the brook. A gust boomed up the valley, and Una chanted sorrowfully:

"Verbenna down to Ostia
Hath wasted all the plain;
Astur hath stormed Janiculum
And the stout guards are slain."

But the wind, not charging fair to the wood, started aside and shook a single oak in Gleason's pasture. Here it made itself all small and crouched among the grasses, waving the tips of them as a cat waves the tip of her tail before she springs.

"Now welcome–welcome Sextus," sang Una, loading the catapult–

"Now welcome to thy home,
Why dost thou turn and run away?
Here lies the rod of Rome."

She fired into the face of the lull, to wake up the cowardly wind, and heard a grunt from behind a thorn in the pasture.

"Oh, my Winkie!" she said aloud, and that was something she had picked up from Dan. "I believe I've tickled up a Gleason cow."

"You little painted beast!" a voice cried. "I'll teach you to sling your masters!"

She looked down most cautiously, and saw a young man covered with hoopy bronze armor all glowing among the late broom. But what Una admired beyond all was his great bronze helmet with its red horse-tail that flicked in the wind. She could hear the long hairs rasp on his shimmery shoulder-plates.

"What does the Faun mean," he said, half aloud to himself, "by telling me the Painted People have changed?" He caught sight of Una's yellow head. "Have you seen a painted lead-slinger?" he called.

"No-o," said Una. "But if you've seen a bullet——"

"Seen?" cried the man. "It passed within a hair's breadth of my ear."

"Well, that was me. I'm most awfully sorry."

"Didn't the Faun tell you I was coming?" He smiled.

"Not if you mean Puck. I thought you were a Gleason cow. I–I didn't know you were a–a–– What are you?"

He laughed outright, showing a set of splendid teeth. His face and eyes were dark, and his eyebrows met above his big nose in one bushy black bar.

"They call me Parnesius. I have been an officer of the Seventh Cohort of the Thirtieth Legion–the Ulpia Victrix. Did you sling that bullet?"

"I did. I was using Dan's catapult," said Una.

"Catapults!" said he. "I ought to know something about them. Show me!"

He leaped the rough fence with a rattle of spear, shield, and armor, and hoisted himself into "Volaterrae" as quickly as a shadow.

"A sling on a forked stick. *I* understand!" he cried, and pulled at the elastic. "But what wonderful beast yields this stretching leather?"

"It's laccy–elastic. You put the bullet into that loop, and then you pull hard."

The man pulled, and hit himself square on his thumb-nail.

"Each to his own weapon," he said, gravely, handing it back. "I am better with the bigger machine, little maiden. But it's a pretty toy. A wolf would laugh at it. Aren't you afraid of wolves?"

"There aren't any," said Una.

"Never believe it! A wolf is like a Winged Hat. He comes when he isn't expected. Don't they hunt wolves here?"

"We don't hunt," said Una, remembering what she had heard from grown-ups. "We preserve–pheasants. Do you know them?"

"I ought to," said the young man, smiling again, and he imitated the cry of the cock-pheasant so perfectly that a bird answered out of the wood.

"What a big painted clucking fool is a pheasant," he said. "Just like some Romans!"

"But you're a Roman yourself, aren't you?" said Una.

"Ye-es and no. I'm one of a good few thousands who have never seen Rome except in a picture. My people have lived at Vectis for generations. Vectis! That island West yonder that you can see from so far in clear weather."

"Do you mean the Isle of Wight? It lifts up just before rain, and we see it from the Downs."

"Very likely. Our Villa's on the South edge of the Island, by the Broken Cliffs. Most of it is three hundred years old, but the cow-stables, where our first ancestor lived, must be a hundred years older. Oh, quite that, because the founder of our family had his land given him by Agricola at the Settlement. It's not a bad little place for its size. In spring-time violets grow down to the very beach. I've gathered sea-weeds for myself and violets for my Mother many a time with our old nurse."

"Was your nurse a–a Romaness too?"

"No, a Numidian. Gods be good to her! A dear, fat, brown thing with a tongue like a cowbell. She was a free woman. By the way, are you free, maiden?"

"Oh, quite," said Una. "At least, till tea-time; and in summer our governess doesn't say much if we're late."

The young man laughed again–a proper understanding laugh.

"I see," said he. "That accounts for your being in the wood. *We* hid among the cliffs."

"Did *you* have a governess, then?"

"Did we not? A Greek, too. She had a way of clutching her dress when she hunted us among the gorze-bushes that made us laugh. Then she'd say she'd get us whipped. She never did, though, bless her! Aglaia was a thorough sportswoman, for all her learning."

"But what lessons did you do–when–when you were little!"

"Ancient history, the Classics, arithmetic, and so on," he answered. "My sister and I were thickheads, but my two brothers (I'm the middle one) liked those things, and, of course, Mother was clever enough for any six. She was nearly as tall as I am, and she looked like the new statue on the Western Road–the Demeter of the Baskets, you know. And funny! Roma Dea! How Mother could make us laugh!"

"What at?"

"Little jokes and sayings that every family has. Don't you know?"

"I know *we* have, but I didn't know other people had them too," said Una. "Tell me about your family, please."

"Good families are very much alike. Mother would sit spinning of evenings while Aglaia read in her corner, and Father did accounts, and we four romped about the passages. When our noise grew too loud the Pater would say, 'Less tumult! Less tumult! Have you never heard of a Father's right over his children? He can slay them, my loves–slay them dead, and the Gods highly approve of the action!' Then Mother would prim up her dear mouth over the wheel and answer: 'H'm! I'm afraid there can't be much of the

Roman Father about you!' Then the Pater would roll up his accounts, and say, 'I'll show you!' and then–then, he'd be worse than any of us!"

"Fathers can–if they like," said Una, her eyes dancing.

"Didn't I say all good families are very much the same?"

"What did you do in summer?" said Una. "Play about like us?"

"Yes, and we visited our friends. There are no wolves in Vectis. We had many friends, and as many ponies as we wished."

"It must have been lovely," said Una. "I hope it lasted for ever."

"Not quite, little maid. When I was about sixteen or seventeen, the Father felt gouty, and we all went to the Waters."

"What waters?"

"At Aquae Solis. Every one goes there. You ought to get your Father to take you some day."

"But where? I don't know," said Una.

The young man looked astonished for a moment. "Aquae Solis," he repeated. "The best baths in Britain. Just as good, I'm told, as Rome. All the old gluttons sit in its hot water, and talk scandal and politics. And the Generals come through the streets with their guards behind them; and the magistrates come in their chairs with their stiff guards behind them; and you meet fortune-tellers, and goldsmiths, and merchants, and philosophers, and feather-sellers, and ultra-Roman Britons, and ultra-British Romans, and tame tribesmen pretending to be civilized, and Jew lecturers, and–oh, everybody interesting. We young people, of course, took no interest in politics. We had not the gout: there were many of our age like us. We did not find life sad.

"But while we were enjoying ourselves without thinking, my sister met the son of a magistrate in the West–and a year afterwards she was married to him. My young brother, who was always interested in plants and roots, met the First Doctor of a Legion from the City of the Legions, and he decided that he would be an Army doctor. I do not think it is a profession for a well-born man, but then–I'm not my brother. He went to Rome to study medicine, and now he's First Doctor of a Legion in Egypt–at Antinoe, I think, but I have not heard from him for some time.

"My eldest brother came across a Greek philosopher, and told my Father that he intended to settle down on the estate as a farmer and a philosopher. You see"–the young man's eyes twinkled–"his philosopher was a long-haired one!"

"I thought philosophers were bald," said Una.

"Not all. She was very pretty. I don't blame him. Nothing could have suited me better than my eldest brother's doing this, for I was only too keen to join the Army. I had always feared I should have to stay at home and look after the estate while my brother took *this.*"

He rapped on his great glistening shield that never seemed to be in his way.

"So we were well contented–we young people–and we rode back to Clausentum along the Wood Road very quietly. But when we reached home, Aglaia, our governess, saw what had come to us. I remember her at the door, the torch over her head, watching us climb the cliff-path from the boat. 'Aie! Aie!' she said. 'Children you went away. Men and a woman you return!' Then she kissed Mother, and Mother wept. Thus our visit to the Waters settled our fates for each of us, Maiden."

He rose to his feet and listened, leaning on the shield-rim.

"I think that's Dan–my brother," said Una.

"Yes; and the Faun is with him," he replied, as Dan with Puck stumbled through the copse.

"We should have come sooner," Puck called, "but the beauties of your native tongue, O Parnesius, have enthralled this young citizen."

Parnesius looked bewildered, even when Una explained.

"Dan said the plural of 'dominus' was 'dominoes,' and when Miss Blake said it wasn't he said he supposed it was 'backgammon,' and so he had to write it out twice–for cheek, you know."

Dan had climbed into Volaterrae, hot and panting.

"I've run nearly all the way," he gasped, "and then Puck met me. How do you do, Sir?"

"I am in good health," Parnesius answered. "See! I have tried to bend the bow of Ulysses, but––" He held up his thumb.

"I'm sorry. You must have pulled off too soon," said Dan. "Puck said you were telling Una a story."

"Continue, O Parnesius," said Puck, who had perched himself on a dead branch above them. "I will be chorus. Has he puzzled you much, Una?"

"Not a bit, except–I didn't know where Ak–Ak something was," she answered.

"Oh, Aquae Solis. That's Bath, where the buns come from. Let the hero tell his own tale."

Parnesius pretended to thrust his spear at Puck's legs, but Puck reached down, caught at the horse-tail plume, and pulled off the tall helmet.

"Thanks, jester," said Parnesius, shaking his curly dark head. "That is cooler. Now hang it up for me. . . .

"I was telling your sister how I joined the Army," he said to Dan.

"Did you have to pass an Exam?" Dan asked, eagerly.

"No. I went to my Father, and said I should like to enter the Dacian Horse (I had seen some at Aquae Solis); but he said I had better begin service in a regular Legion from Rome. Now, like many of our youngsters, I was not too fond of anything Roman. The Roman-born officers and magistrates looked down on us British-born as though we were barbarians. I told my Father so.

" 'I know they do,' he said; 'but remember, after all, we are the people of the Old Stock, and our duty is to the Empire.'

" 'To which Empire?' I asked. 'We split the Eagle before I was born.'

" 'What thieves' talk is that?' said my Father. He hated slang.

" 'Well, Sir,' I said, 'we've one Emperor in Rome, and I don't know how many Emperors the outlying Provinces have set up from time to time. Which am I to follow?'

" 'Gratian,' said he. 'At least he's a sportsman.'

" 'He's all that,' I said. 'Hasn't he turned himself into a raw-beef-eating Scythian?'

" 'Where did you hear of it?' said the Pater.

" 'At Aquae Solis,' I said. It was perfectly true. This precious Emperor Gratian of ours had a bodyguard of fur-cloaked Scythians, and he was so crazy about them that he dressed like them. In Rome of all places in the world! It was as bad as if my own Father had painted himself blue!

" 'No matter for the clothes,' said the Pater. 'They are only the fringe of the trouble. It began before your time or mine. Rome has forsaken her Gods, and must be punished. The great war with the Painted People broke out in the very year the temples of our Gods were destroyed. We beat the Painted People in the very year our temples were rebuilt. Go back further still.' . . . He went back to the time of Diocletian; and to listen to him you would have thought Eternal Rome herself was on the edge of destruction, just because a few people had become a little large-minded.

"*I* knew nothing about it. Aglaia never taught us the history of our own country. She was so full of her ancient Greeks.

" 'There is no hope for Rome,' said the Pater, at last. 'She has forsaken her Gods, but if the Gods forgive *us* here, we may save Britain. To do that, we must keep the Painted People back. Therefore, I tell you, Parnesius, as a Father, that if your heart is set on service, your place is among men on the Wall–and not with women among the cities.' "

"What Wall?" asked Dan and Una at once.

"Father meant the one we call Hadrian's Wall. I'll tell you about it later. It was built long ago, across North Britain, to keep out the Painted People—Picts you call them. Father had fought in the great Pict War that lasted more than twenty years, and he knew what fighting meant. Theodosius, one of our great Generals, had chased the little beasts back far into the North before I was born: down at Vectis, of course, we never troubled our heads about them. But when my Father spoke as he did, I kissed his hand, and waited for orders. We British-born Romans know what is due to our parents."

"If I kissed my Father's hand, he'd laugh," said Dan.

"Customs change; but if you do not obey your father, the Gods remember it. You may be quite sure of *that.*

"After our talk, seeing I was in earnest, the Pater sent me over to Clausentum to learn my foot-drill in a barrack full of foreign Auxiliaries—as unwashed and unshaved a mob of mixed barbarians as ever scrubbed a breastplate. It was your stick in your stomachs and your shield in their faces to push them into any sort of formation. When I had learned my work the Instructor gave me a handful—and they were a handful!—of Gauls and Iberians to polish up till they were sent to their stations up-country. I did my best, and one night a villa in the suburbs caught fire, and I had my handful out and at work before any of the other troops. I noticed a quiet-looking man on the lawn, leaning on a stick. He watched us passing buckets from the pond, and at last he said to me: 'Who are you?'

" 'A probationer, waiting for a cohort,' I answered. *I* didn't know who he was from Deucalion!

" 'Born in Britain?' he said.

" 'Yes, if you were born in Spain,' I said, for he neighed his words like an Iberian mule.

" 'And what might you call yourself when you are at home?' he said laughing.

" 'That depends,' I answered; 'sometimes one thing and sometimes another. But now I'm busy.'

"He said no more till we had saved the family gods (they were respectable householders), and then he grunted across the laurels: 'Listen, young sometimes-one-thing-and-sometimes-another. In future call yourself Centurion of the Seventh Cohort of the Thirtieth, the Ulpia Victrix. That will help me to remember you. Your Father and a few other people call me Maximus.'

"He tossed me the polished stick he was leaning on, and went away. You might have knocked me down with it!"

"Who was he?" said Dan.

"Maximus himself, our great General! *The* General of Britain who had been Theodosius's right hand in the Pict War! Not only had he given me my Centurion's stick direct, but three steps in a good Legion as well! A new man generally begins in the Tenth Cohort of his Legion, and works up."

"And were you pleased?" said Una.

"Very. I thought Maximus had chosen me for my good looks and fine style in marching, but, when I went home, the Pater told me he had served under Maximus in the great Pict War, and had asked him to promote me."

"A child you were!" said Puck, from above.

"I was," said Parnesius. "Don't begrudge it me, Faun. Afterwards—the Gods know I put aside the games!" And Puck nodded, brown chin on brown hand, his big eyes still.

"The night before I left we sacrificed to our ancestors—the usual little Home Sacrifice—but I never prayed so earnestly to all the Good Shades, and then I went with my Father by boat to Regnum, and across the chalk eastwards to Anderida yonder."

"Regnum? Anderida?" The children turned their faces to Puck.

"Regnum's Chichester," he said, pointing towards Cherry Clack, and—he threw his arm South behind him—"Anderida's Pevensey."

"Pevensey again!" said Dan. "Where Weland landed?"

"Weland and a few others," said Puck. "Pevensey isn't young–even compared to me!"

"The head-quarters of the Thirtieth lay at Anderida in summer, but my own Cohort, the Seventh, was on the Wall up North. Maximus was inspecting Auxiliaries–the Abulci, I think–at Anderida, and we stayed with him, for he and my Father were very old friends. I was only there ten days when I was ordered to go up with thirty men to my Cohort." He laughed merrily. "A man never forgets his first march. I was happier than any Emperor when I led my handful through the North Gate of the Camp, and we saluted the guard and the Altar of Victory there."

"How? How?" said Dan and Una.

Parnesius smiled, and stood up, flashing in his armor.

"So!" said he; and he moved slowly through the beautiful movements of the Roman Salute, that ends with a hollow clang of the shield coming into its place between the shoulders.

"Hai!" said Puck. "That sets one thinking!"

"We went out fully armed," said Parnesius, sitting down; "but as soon as the road entered the Great Forest, my men expected the pack-horses to hang their shields on. 'No!' I said; 'you can dress like women in Anderida, but while you're with me you will carry your own weapons and armor.'

" 'But it's hot,' said one of them, 'and we haven't a doctor. Suppose we get sunstroke, or a fever?'

" 'Then die,' I said, 'and a good riddance to Rome! Up shield–up spears, and tighten your foot-wear!'

" 'Don't think yourself Emperor of Britain already,' a fellow shouted. I knocked him over with the butt of my spear, and explained to these Roman-born Romans that, if there were any further trouble, we should go on with one man short. And, by the Light of the Sun, I meant it too! My raw Gauls at Clausentum had never treated me so.

"Then, quietly as a cloud, Maximus rode out of the fern (my Father behind him), and reined up across the road. He wore the Purple, as though he were already Emperor; his leggings were of white buckskin laced with gold.

"My men dropped like–like partridges.

"He said nothing for some time, only looked, with his eyes puckered. Then he crooked his forefinger, and my men walked–crawled, I mean–to one side.

" 'Stand in the sun, children,' he said, and they formed up on the hard road.

" 'What would you have done?' he said to me, 'If I had not been here?'

" 'I should have killed that man,' I answered.

" 'Kill him now,' he said. 'He will not move a limb.'

" 'No,' I said. 'You've taken my men out of my command. I should only be your butcher if I killed him now.' Do you see what I meant?" Parnesius turned to Dan.

"Yes," said Dan. "It wouldn't have been fair, somehow."

"That was what I thought," said Parnesius. But Maximus frowned. 'You'll never be an Emperor,' he said. 'Not even a General will you be.'

"I was silent, but my Father seemed pleased.

" 'I came here to see the last of you,' he said.

" 'You have seen it,' said Maximus. 'I shall never need your son any more. He will live and he will die an officer of a Legion–and he might have been Prefect of one of my Provinces. Now eat and drink with us,' he said. 'Your men will wait till you have finished.'

"My miserable thirty stood like wine-skins glistening in the hot sun, and Maximus led us to where his people had set a meal. Himself he mixed the wine.

" 'A year from now,' he said, 'you will remember that you have sat with the Emperor of Britain—and Gaul.'

" 'Yes,' said the Pater, 'you can drive two mules—Gaul and Britain.'

" 'Five years hence you will remember that you have drunk'—he passed me the cup and there was blue borage in it—'with the Emperor of Rome!'

" 'No; you can't drive three mules; they will tear you in pieces,' said my Father.

" 'And you on the Wall, among the heather, will weep because your notion of justice was more to you than the favor of the Emperor of Rome.'

"I sat quite still. One does not answer a General who wears the Purple.

" 'I am not angry with you,' he went on; 'I owe too much to your Father—'

" 'You owe me nothing but advice that you never took,' said the Pater.

" '—to be unjust to any of your family. Indeed, I say you will make a good officer, but, so far as I am concerned, on the Wall you will live, and on the Wall you will die,' said Maximus.

" 'Very like,' said my Father. 'But we shall have the Picts *and* their friends breaking through before long. You cannot move all troops out of Britain to make you Emperor, and expect the North to sit quiet.'

" 'I follow my destiny,' said Maximus.

" 'Follow it, then,' said my Father pulling up a fern root; 'and die as Theodosius died.'

" 'Ah!' said Maximus. 'My old General was killed because he served the Empire too well. *I* may be killed, but not for that reason,' and he smiled a little pale gray smile that made my blood run cold.

" 'Then I had better follow my destiny,' I said, 'and take my men to the Wall.'

"He looked at me a long time, and bowed his head slanting like a Spaniard. 'Follow it, boy,' he said. That was all. I was only too glad to get away, though I had many messages for home. I found my men standing as they had been put—they had not even shifted their feet in the dust,—and off I marched, still feeling that terrific smile like an east wind up my back. I never halted them till sunset, and"—he turned about and looked at Pook's Hill below him—"then I halted yonder." He pointed to the broken, bracken-covered shoulder of the Forge Hill behind old Hobden's cottage.

"There? Why, that's only the old Forge—where they made iron once," said Dan.

"Very good stuff it was too," said Parnesius, calmly. "We mended three shoulder-straps here and had a spear-head riveted. The forge was rented from the Government by a one-eyed smith from Carthage. I remember we called him Cylops. He sold me a beaver-skin rug for my sister's room."

"But it couldn't have been here," Dan insisted.

"But it was! From the Altar of Victory at Anderida to the First Forge in the Forest here is twelve miles seven hundred paces. It is all in the Road Book. A man doesn't forget his first march. I think I could tell you every station between this and——" He leaned forward, but his eye was caught by the setting sun.

It had come down to the top of Cherry Clack Hill, and the light poured in between the tree trunks so that you could see red and gold and black deep into the heart of Far Wood; and Parnesius in his armor shone as though he had been afire.

"Wait," he said, lifting a hand, and the sunlight jinked on his glass bracelet. "Wait! I pray to Mithras!"

He rose and stretched his arms westward, with deep, splendid-sound words.

Then Puck began to sing too, in a voice like bells tolling, and as he sang he slipped from "Volaterrae" to the ground, and beckoned the children to follow. They obeyed; it seemed as though the voices were pushing them along; and through the goldy-brown light on the beech leaves they walked, while Puck between them chanted something like this:—

Cur mundus militat sub vana gloria
Cujus prosperitas est transitoria?
Tam cito labitur ejus potentia
Quam vasa figuli quae sunt fragilia.

They found themselves at the little locked gates of the wood.

Quo Caesar abiit celsus imperio?
Vel Dives splendidus totus in prandio?
Dic ubi Tullius——

Still singing, he took Dan's hand and wheeled him round to face Una as she came out of the gate. It shut behind her, at the same time as Puck threw the memory-magicking Oak, Ash, and Thorn leaves over their heads.

"Well, you *are* jolly late," said Una. "Couldn't you get away before?"

"I did," said Dan. "I got away in lots of time, but—but I didn't know it was so late. Where've you been?"

"In Volaterrae—waiting for you."

"Sorry," said Dan. "It was all that beastly Latin."

A British-Roman Song

(A. D. 406)

My father's father saw it not,
And I, belike, shall never come,
To look on that so-holy spot—
The very Rome—

Crowned by all Time, all Art, all Might,
The equal work of Gods and Man—
City beneath whose oldest height
The Race began,—

Soon to send forth again a brood
Unshakeable, we pray, that clings,
To Rome's thrice-hammered hardihood—
In arduous things.

Strong heart with triple armor bound,
Beat strongly, for thy life-blood runs
Age after Age, the Empire round—
In us thy Sons,

Who, distant from the Seven Hills,
Loving and serving much, require
Thee, Thee to guard 'gainst home-born ills,
The Imperial Fire!

On the Great Wall

When I left Rome for Lalage's sake
    By the Legions' Road to Rimini,
She vowed her heart was mine to take
    With me and my shield to Rimini–
    (Till the Eagles flew from Rimini!)
        And I've tramped Britain and I've tramped Gaul
        And the Pontic shore where the snow-flakes fall
    As white as the neck of Lalage–
    As cold as the heart of Lalage!
        And I've lost Britain and I've lost Gaul

(the voice seemed very cheerful about it),

        And I've lost Rome, and worst of all,
            I've lost Lalage!

THEY WERE STANDING by the gate to Far Wood when they heard this song. Without a word they hurried to their private gap and wriggled through the hedge almost atop of a jay that was feeding from Puck's hand.

"Gently!" said Puck. "What are you looking for?"

"Parnesius, of course," Dan answered. "We've only just remembered yesterday. It isn't fair."

Puck chuckled as he rose. "I'm sorry, but children who spend the afternoon with me and a Roman Centurion need a little settling dose of Magic before they go to tea with their governess. Ohé, Parnesius!" he called.

"Here, Faun!" came the answer from "Volaterrae." They could see the shimmer of bronze armor in the beech crotch, and the friendly flash of the great shield uplifted.

"I have driven out the Britons," Parnesius laughed like a boy. "I occupy their high forts. But Rome is merciful! You may come up." And up they three all scrambled.

"What was the song you were singing just now?" said Una, as soon as she had settled herself.

"That? Oh, *Rimini.* It's one of the tunes that are always being born somewhere in the Empire. They run like a pestilence for six months or a year, till another one pleases the Legions, and then they march to *that.*"

"Tell them about the marching, Parnesius. Few people nowadays walk from end to end of this country," said Puck.

"The greater their loss. I know nothing better than the Long March when your feet are hardened. You begin after the mists have risen, and you end, perhaps, an hour after sundown."

"And what do you have to eat?" Dan asked, promptly.

"Fat bacon, beans, and bread, and whatever wine happens to be in the rest-houses. But soldiers are born grumblers. Their very first day out, my men complained of our water-ground British corn. They said it wasn't so filling as the rough stuff that is ground in the Roman ox-mills. However, they had to fetch and eat it."

"Fetch it? Where from?" said Una.

"From that newly-invented water-mill below the Forge."

"That's Forge Mill–*our* Mill!" Una looked at Puck.

"Yes; yours," Puck put in. "How old did you think it was?"

"I don't know. Didn't Sir Richard Dalyngridge talk about it?"

"He did, and it was old in his day," Puck answered. "Hundreds of years old."

"It was new in mine," said Parnesius. "My men looked at the flour in their helmets as though it had been a nest of adders. They did it to try my patience. But I—addressed them, and we became friends. To tell the truth, they taught me the Roman Step. You see, I'd only served with quick-marching Auxiliaries. A Legion's pace is altogether different. It is a long, slow stride, that never varies from sunrise to sunset. 'Rome's Race—Rome's Pace,' as the proverb says. Twenty-four miles in eight hours, neither more nor less. Head and spear up, shield on your back, cuirass-collar open one hand's breadth—and that's how you take the Eagles through Britain."

"And did you meet any adventures?" said Dan.

"There are no adventures South the Wall," said Parnesius. "The worst thing that happened me was having to appear before a magistrate up North, where a wandering philosopher had jeered at the Eagles. I was able to show that the old man had deliberately blocked our road, and the magistrate told him, out of his own Book, I believe, that, whatever his God might be, he should pay proper respect to Caesar."

"What did you do?" said Dan.

"Went on. Why should *I* care for such things, my business being to reach my station? It took me twenty days.

"Of course, the farther North you go the emptier are the roads. At last you fetch clear of the forests and climb bare hills, where wolves howl in the ruins of our cities that have been. No more pretty girls; no more jolly magistrates who knew your Father when he was young, and invite you to stay with them; no news at the temples and way-stations except bad news of wild beasts. There's where you meet hunters, and trappers for the Circuses, prodding along chained bears and muzzled wolves. Your pony shies at them, and your men laugh.

"The houses change from gardened villas to shut forts with watch-towers of gray stone, and great stone-walled sheepfolds, guarded by armed Britons of the North Shore. In the naked hills beyond the naked houses, where the shadows of the clouds play like cavalry charging, you see puffs of black smoke from the mines. The hard road goes on and on—and the wind sings through your helmet-plume—past altars to Legions and Generals forgotten, and broken statues of Gods and Heroes, and thousands of graves where the mountain foxes and hares peep at you. Red-hot in summer, freezing in winter, is that big, purple heather country of broken stone.

"Just when you think you are at the world's end, you see a smoke from East to West as far as the eye can turn, and then, under it, also as far as the eye can stretch, houses and temples, shops and theaters, barracks, and granaries, trickling along like dice behind—always behind—one long, low, rising and falling, and hiding and showing line of towers. And that is the Wall!"

"Ah!" said the children taking breath.

"You may well," said Parnesius. "Old men who have followed the Eagles since boyhood say nothing in the Empire is more wonderful than first sight of the Wall!"

"Is it just *a* Wall? Like the one round the kitchen-garden?" said Dan.

"No, no! It is *the* Wall. Along the top are towers with guard-houses, small towers, between. Even on the narrowest part of it three men with shields can walk abreast from guard-house to guard-house. A little curtain wall, no higher than a man's neck, runs along the top of the thick wall, so that from a distance you see the helmets of the sentries sliding back and forth like beads. Thirty feet high is the Wall, and on the Picts' side, the North, is a ditch, strewn with blades of old swords and spear-heads set in wood, and tyres of wheels joined by chains. The Little People come there to steal iron for their arrow-heads.

"But the Wall itself is not more wonderful than the town behind it. Long ago there were great ramparts and ditches on the South side, and no one was allowed to build there. Now the ramparts are partly pulled down and built over, from end to end of the Wall; making a thin town eighty miles long. Think of it! One roaring, rioting, cockfighting, wolf-baiting, horse-racing town, from Ituna on the West to Segedunum on the cold eastern beach! On one side heather, woods and ruins where Picts hide, and on the other, a vast town–long like a snake, and wicked like a snake. Yes, a snake basking beside a warm wall!

"My Cohort, I was told, lay at Hunno, where the Great North Road runs through the Wall into the Province of Valentia." Parnesius laughed scornfully. "The Province of Valentia! We followed the road, therefore, into Hunno town, and stood astonished. The place was a fair–a fair of peoples from every corner of the Empire. Some were racing horses: some sat in wine-shops: some watched dogs baiting bears, and many gathered in a ditch to see cocks fight. A boy not much older than myself, but I could see he was an Officer, reined up before me and asked what I wanted.

" 'My station,' I said, and showed him my shield." Parnesius held up his broad shield with its three X's like letters on a beer-cask.

" 'Lucky omen!' said he. 'Your Cohort's the next tower to us, but they're all at the cock-fight. This is a happy place. Come and wet the Eagles.' He meant to offer me a drink.

" 'When I've handed over my men,' I said. I felt angry and ashamed.

" 'Oh, you'll soon outgrow that sort of nonsense,' he answered. 'But don't let me interfere with your hopes. Go on to the Statue of Roma Dea. You can't miss it. The main road into Valentia!' and he laughed and rode off. I could see the Statue not a quarter of a mile away, and there I went. At some time or other the Great North Road ran under it into Valentia; but the far end had been blocked up because of the Picts, and on the plaster a man had scratched, 'Finish!' It was like marching into a cave. We grounded spears together, my little thirty, and it echoed in the barrel of the arch, but none came. There was a door at one side painted with our number. We prowled in, and I found a cook asleep, and ordered him to give us food. Then I climbed to the top of the Wall, and looked out over the Pict country, and I–thought," said Parnesius. "The bricked-up arch with 'Finish!' on the plaster was what shook me, for I was not much more than a boy."

"What a shame!" said Una. "But did you feel happy after you'd had a good——" Dan stopped her with a nudge.

"Happy?" said Parnesius. "When the men of the Cohort I was to command came back unhelmeted from the cock-fight, their birds under their arms, and asked me who I was? No, I was not happy; but I made my new Cohort unhappy too. . . . I wrote my Mother I was happy, but, oh, my friends"–he stretched arms over bare knees–"I would not wish my worst enemy to suffer as I suffered through my first months on the Wall. Remember this: among the officers was scarcely one, except myself (and I thought I had lost the favor of Maximus, my General), scarcely one who had not done something of wrong or folly. Either he had killed a man, or taken money, or insulted the magistrates, or blasphemed the Gods, and so had been sent to the Wall as a hiding-place from shame or fear. And the men were as the officers. Remember, also, that the Wall was manned by every breed and race in the Empire. No two towers spoke the same tongue, or worshipped the same Gods. In one thing only we were all equal. No matter what arms we had used before we came to the Wall, *on* the Wall we were all archers, like the Scythians. The Pict cannot run away from the arrow, or crawl under it. He is a bowman himself. *He* knows!"

"I suppose you were fighting Picts all the time," said Dan.

"Picts seldom fight. I never saw a fighting Pict for half a year. The tame Picts told us they had all gone North."

"What is a tame Pict?" said Dan.

"A Pict–there were many such–who speaks a few words of our tongue, and slips across the Wall to sell ponies and wolf-hounds. Without a horse and a dog, *and* a friend, man would perish. The Gods gave me all three, and there is no gift like friendship. Remember this"–Parnesius turned to Dan–"when you become a young man. For your fate will turn on the first true friend you make."

"He means," said Puck, grinning, "that if you try to make yourself a decent chap when you're young, you'll make rather decent friends when you grow up. If you're a beast, you'll have beastly friends. Listen to the Pious Parnesius on Friendship!"

"I am not pious," Parnesius answered, "but I know what goodness means; and my friend, though he was without hope, was ten thousand times better than I. Stop laughing, Faun!"

"Oh Youth Eternal and All-believing," cried Puck, as he rocked on the branch above. "Tell them about your Pertinax."

"He was that friend the Gods sent me–the boy who spoke to me when I first came. Little older than myself, commanding the Augusta Victoria Cohort on the tower next to us and the Numidians. In virtue he was far my superior."

"Then why was he on the Wall?" Una asked, quickly. "They'd all done something bad. You said so yourself."

"He was the nephew, his Father had died, of a great rich man in Gaul who was not always kind to his Mother. When Pertinax grew up, he discovered this, and so his uncle shipped him off, by trickery and force, to the Wall. We came to know each other at a ceremony in our Temple–in the dark. It was the Bull Killing," Parnesius explained to Puck.

"*I* see," said Puck, and turned to the children. "That's something you wouldn't quite understand. Parnesius means he met Pertinax in church."

"Yes–in the Cave we first met, and we were both raised to the Degree of Gryphons together." Parnesius lifted his hand towards his neck for an instant. "He had been on the Wall two years, and knew the Picts well. He taught me first how to take Heather."

"What's that?" said Dan.

"Going out hunting in the Pict country with a tame Pict. You are quite safe so long as you are his guest, and wear a sprig of heather where it can be seen. If you went alone you would surely be killed, if you were not smothered first in the bogs. Only the Picts know their way about those black and hidden bogs. Old Allo, the one-eyed, withered little Pict from whom we bought our ponies, was our special friend. At first we went only to escape from the terrible town, and to talk together about our homes. Then he showed us how to hunt wolves and those great red deer with horns like Jewish candlesticks. The Roman-born officers rather looked down on us for doing this, but we preferred the heather to their amusements. Believe me," Parnesius turned again to Dan, "a boy is safe from all things that really harm when he is astride a pony or after a deer. Do you remember, O Faun," he turned to Puck, "the little altar I built to the Sylvan Pan by the pine-forest beyond the brook?"

"Which? The stone one with the line from Xenophon?" said Puck, in quite a new voice.

"No. What do *I* know of Xenophon? That was Pertinax–after he had shot his first mountain-hare with an arrow–by chance! Mine I made of round pebbles in memory of my first bear. It took me one happy day to build." Parnesius faced the children quickly.

"And that was how we lived on the Wall for two years–a little scuffling with the Picts, and a great deal of hunting with old Allo in the Pict country. He called us his children sometimes, and we were fond of him and his barbarians, though we never let them paint us Pict fashion. The marks endure till you die."

"How's it done?" said Dan. "Anything like tattooing?"

"They prick the skin till the blood runs, and rub in colored juices. Allo was painted blue, green, and red from his forehead to his ankles. He said it was part of his religion. He told us about his religion (Pertinax was always interested in such things), and as we came to know him well, he told us what was happening in Britain behind the Wall. Many things took place behind us in those days. And, by the Light of the Sun," said Parnesius, earnestly, "there was not much that those little people did not know! He told me when Maximus crossed over to Gaul, after he had made himself Emperor of Britain, and what troops and emigrants he had taken with him. *We* did not get the news on the Wall till fifteen days later. He told me what troops Maximus was taking out of Britain every month to help him to conquer Gaul; and I always found the numbers as he said. Wonderful! And I tell another strange thing!"

He jointed his hands across his knees, and leaned his head on the curve of the shield behind him.

"Late in the summer, when the first frosts begin and the Picts kill their bees, we three rode out after wolf with some new hounds. Rutilianus, our General, had given us ten days' leave, and we had pushed beyond the Second Wall—beyond the Province of Valentia—into the higher hills, where there are not even any of Rome's old ruins. We killed a she-wolf before noon, and while Allo was skinning her he looked up and said to me, 'When you are Captain of the Wall, my child, you won't be able to do this any more!'

"I might as well have been made Prefect of Lower Gaul, so I laughed and said, 'Wait till I am Captain.' 'No don't, wait,' said Allo. 'Take my advice and go home—both of you.' 'We have no homes,' said Pertinax. 'You know that as well as we do. We're finished men—thumbs down against both of us. Only men without hope would risk their necks on your ponies.' The old man laughed one of those short Pict laughs—like a fox barking on a frosty night. 'I'm fond of you two,' he said. 'Besides, I've taught you what little you know about hunting. Take my advice and go home.'

" 'We can't,' I said. 'I'm out of favor with my General, for one thing; and for another, Pertinax has an uncle.'

" 'I don't know about his uncle,' said Allo, 'but the trouble with you, Parnesius, is that your General thinks well of you.'

" 'Roma Dea!' said Pertinax, sitting up. 'What can you guess what Maximus thinks, you old horse-coper?'

"Just then (you know how near the brutes creep when one is eating?) a great dog-wolf jumped out behind us, and away our rested hounds tore after him, with us at their tails. He ran us far out of any country we'd ever heard of, straight as an arrow till sunset, towards the sunset. We came at last to long capes stretching into winding waters, and on a gray beach below us we saw ships drawn up. Forty-seven we counted—not Roman galleys but the raven-winged ships from the North where Rome does not rule. Men moved in the ships, and the sun flashed on their helmets—winged helmets of the red-haired men from the North where Rome does not rule. We watched, and we counted, and we wondered; for though we had heard rumors concerning these Winged Hats, as the Picts called them, never before had we looked upon them.

" 'Come away! Come away!' said Allo. 'My Heather won't protect you here. We shall all be killed!' His legs trembled like his voice. Back we went—back across the heather under the moon, till it was nearly morning, and our poor beasts stumbled on some ruins.

"When we woke, very stiff and cold, Allo was mixing the meal and water. One does not light fires in the Pict country except near a village. The little men are always signalling to each other with smokes, and a strange smoke brings them out buzzing like bees. They can sting, too!

" 'What we saw last night was a trading-station,' said Allo. 'Nothing but a trading-station.'

" 'I do not like lies on an empty stomach,' said Pertinax. 'I suppose' (he had eyes like an eagle's), 'I suppose *that* is a trading-station also?' He pointed to a smoke far off on a hill-top, ascending in what we call the Pict's Call:—Puff—double-puff: double-puff—puff! They make it by raising and dropping a wet hide on a fire.

" 'No,' said Allo, pushing the platter back into the bag. 'That is for you and me. Your fate is fixed. Come.'

"We came. When one takes Heather, one must obey one's Pict—but that wretched smoke was twenty miles distant, well over on the east coast, and the day was as hot as a bath.

" 'Whatever happens,' said Allo, while our ponies grunted along, 'I want you to remember me.'

" 'I shall not forget,' said Pertinax. 'You have cheated me out of my breakfast.'

" 'What is a handful of crushed oats to a Roman?' he said. Then he laughed his laugh that was not a laugh. 'What would *you* do if *you* were a handful of oats being crushed between the upper and lower stones of a mill?'

" 'I'm Pertinax, not a riddle-guesser,' said Pertinax.

" 'You're a fool,' said Allo. 'Your Gods and my Gods are threatened by strange Gods, and all you can do is to laugh.'

" 'Threatened men live long,' I said.

" 'I pray the Gods that may be true,' he said. 'But I ask you again not to forget me.'

"We climbed the last hot hill and looked out on the eastern sea, three or four miles off. There was a small sailing-galley of the North Gaul pattern at anchor, her landing-plank down and her sail half up; and below us, alone in a hollow, holding his pony, sat Maximus, Emperor of Britain! He was dressed like a hunter, and he leaned on his little stick; but I knew that back as far as I could see it, and I told Pertinax.

" 'You're madder than Allo!' he said. 'It must be the sun!'

"Maximus never stirred till we stood before him. Then he looked me up and down, and said: 'Hungry again? It seems to be my destiny to feed you whenever we meet. I have food here. Allo shall cook it.'

" 'No,' said Allo. 'A Prince in his own land does not wait on wandering Emperors. I feed my two children without asking your leave.' He began to blow up the ashes.

" 'I was wrong,' said Pertinax. 'We are all mad. Speak up, O Madman called Emperor!'

"Maximus smiled his terrible tight-lipped smile, but two years on the Wall do not make a man afraid of mere looks. So I was not afraid.

" 'I meant you, Parnesius, to live and die an Officer of the Wall,' said Maximus. 'But it seems from these,' he fumbled in his breast, 'you can think as well as draw.' He pulled out a roll of letters I had written to my people, full of drawings of Picts, and bears and men I had met on the Wall. Mother and my sister always liked my pictures.

"He handed me one that I had called 'Maximus's Soldiers.' It showed a row of fat wine-skins, and our old Doctor of the Hunno hospital snuffing at them. Each time that Maximus had taken troops out of Britain to help him to conquer Gaul, he used to send the garrisons more wine—to keep them quiet, I suppose. On the Wall, we always called a wine-skin a 'Maximus.' Oh, yes; and I had drawn them in Imperial helmets!

" 'Not long since,' he went on, 'men's names were sent up to Caesar for smaller jokes than this.'

" 'True, Caesar,' said Pertinax; 'but you forget that was before I, your friend's friend, became such a good spear-thrower.'

"He did not actually point his hunting spear at Maximus, but balanced it on his palm–so!

"'I was speaking of time past,' said Maximus, never fluttering an eyelid. 'Nowadays one is only too pleased to find boys who can think for themselves, *and* their friends.' He nodded at Pertinax. 'Your Father lent me the letters, Parnesius, so you run no risk from me.'

"'None whatever,' said Pertinax, and rubbed the spear-point on his sleeve.

"'I have been forced to reduce the garrisons in Britain, because I need troops in Gaul. Now I come to take troops from the Wall itself,' said he.

"'I wish you joy of us,' said Pertinax. 'We're the last sweepings of the Empire–the men without hope. Myself, I'd sooner trust condemned criminals.'

"'You think so?' he said, quite seriously. 'But it will only be till I win Gaul. One must always risk one's life, or one's soul, or one's peace–or some little thing.'

"Allo passed round the fire with the sizzling deer's meat. He served us two first.

"'Ah!' said Maximus, waiting his turn. 'I perceive you are in your own country. Well, you deserve it. They tell me you have quite a following among the Picts, Parnesius.'

"'I have hunted with them,' I said. 'Maybe I have a few friends among the Heather.'

"'He is the only armored man of you all who understands us,' said Allo, and he began a long speech about our virtues, and how we had saved one of his grandchildren from a wolf the year before."

"Had you?" said Una.

"Yes; but that was neither here nor there. The little green man orated like a–like Cicero. He made us out to be magnificent fellows. Maximus never took his eyes off our faces.

"'Enough,' he said. 'I have heard Allo on you. I wish to hear you on the Picts.'

"I told him as much as I knew, and Pertinax helped me out. There is never harm in a Pict if you but take the trouble to find out what he wants. Their real grievance against us came from our burning their heather. The whole garrison of the Wall moved out twice a year, and solemnly burned the heather for ten miles North. Rutilianus, our General, called it clearing the country. The Picts, of course, scampered away, and all we did was to destroy their bee-bloom in the summer, and ruin their sheep-food in the spring.

"'True, quite true,' said Allo. 'How can we make our holy heather-wine, if you burn our bee-pasture?'

"We talked long, Maximus asking keen questions that showed he knew much and had thought more about the Picts. He said presently to me: 'If I gave you the old Province of Valentia to govern, could you keep the Picts contented till I won Gaul? Stand away, so that you do not see Allo's face; and speak your own thoughts.'

"'No,' I said. 'You cannot re-make that Province. The Picts have been free too long.'

"'Leave them their village councils, and let them furnish their own soldiers,' he said. 'You, I am sure, would hold the reins very lightly.'

"'Even then, no,' I said. 'At least not now. They have been too oppressed by us to trust anything with a Roman name for years and years.'

"I heard old Allo behind me mutter: 'Good child!'

"'Then what do you recommend,' said Maximus, 'to keep the North quiet till I win Gaul?'

"'Leave the Picts alone,' I said. 'Stop the heather-burning at once, and–they are improvident little animals–send them a shipload or two of corn now and then.'

"'Their own men must distribute it–not some cheating Greek accountant,' said Pertinax.

" 'Yes, and allow them to come to our hospitals when they are sick,' I said.

" 'Surely they would die first,' said Maximus.

" 'Not if Parnesius brought them in,' said Allo. 'I could show you twenty wolf-bitten, bear-clawed Picts within twenty miles of here. But Parnesius must stay with them in Hospital, else they would go mad with fear.'

" '*I* see,' said Maximus. 'Like everything else in the world, it is one man's work. You, I think, are that one man.'

" 'Pertinax and I are one,' I said.

" 'As you please, so long as you work. Now, Allo, you know that I mean your people no harm. Leave us to talk together,' said Maximus.

" 'No need!' said Allo. 'I am the corn between the upper and lower millstones. I must know what the lower millstone means to do. These boys have spoken the truth as far as they know it. I, a Prince, will tell you the rest. I am troubled about the Men of the North.' He squatted like a hare in the heather, and looked over his shoulder.

" 'I also,' said Maximus, 'or I should not be here.'

" 'Listen,' said Allo. 'Long and long ago the Winged Hats'–he meant the Northmen–'came to our beaches and said, "Rome falls! Push her down!" We fought you. You sent men. We were beaten. After that we said to the Winged Hats, "You are liars! Make our men alive that Rome killed, and we will believe you." They went away ashamed. Now they come back bold, and they tell the old tale, which we begin to believe–that Rome falls!'

" 'Give me three years' peace on the Wall,' cried Maximus, 'and I will show you and all the ravens how they lie!'

" 'Ah, I wish it too! I wish to save what is left of the corn from the millstones. But you shoot us Picts when we come to borrow a little iron from the Iron Ditch; you burn our heather, which is all our crop; you trouble us with your great catapults. Then you hide behind the Wall, and scorch us with Greek fire. How can I keep my young men from listening to the Winged Hats–in winter especially, when we are hungry? My young men will say, "Rome can neither fight nor rule. She is taking her men out of Britain. The Winged Hats will help us to push down the Wall. Let us show them the secret roads across the bogs." Do *I* want that? No!' He spat like an adder. '*I* would keep the secrets of my people though I were burned alive. My two children here have spoken truth. Leave us Picts alone. Comfort us, and cherish us, and feed us from far off–with the hand behind your back. Parnesius understands us. Let *him* have rule on the Wall, and I will hold my young men quiet for'–he ticked it off on his fingers–'one year easily: the next year not so easily: the third year, perhaps! See, I give you three years. If then you do not show us that Rome is strong in men and terrible in arms, the Winged Hats, I tell you, will sweep down the Wall from either sea till they meet in the middle, and you will go. *I* shall not grieve over that, but well I know tribe never helps tribe except for one price. We Picts will go too. The Winged Hats will grind us to this!' He tossed a handful of dust in the air.

" 'Oh, Roma Dea!' said Maximus, half aloud. 'It is always one man's work–always and everywhere!'

" 'And one man's life,' said Allo. 'You are Emperor, but not a God. You may die.'

" 'I have thought of that, too,' said he. 'Very good. If this wind holds, I shall be at the East end of the Wall by morning. Tomorrow, then, I shall see you two when I inspect; and I will make you Captains of the Wall for this work.'

" 'One instant, Caesar,' said Pertinax. 'All men have their price. I am not bought yet.'

" 'Do *you* also begin to bargain so early?' said Maximus. 'Well?'

" 'Give me justice against my uncle Icenus, the Duumvir of Divio in Gaul,' he said.

" 'Only a life? I thought it would be money or an office. Certainly you shall have him. Write his name on these tablets–on the red side; the other is for the living!' And Maximus held out his tablets.

" 'He is of no use to me dead,' said Pertinax. 'My mother is a widow. I am far off. I am not sure he pays her all her dowry.'

" 'No matter. My arm is reasonably long. We will look through your uncle's accounts in due time. Now, farewell till to-morrow, O Captains of the Wall!'

"We saw him grow small across the heather as he walked to the galley. There were Picts, scores, each side of him, hidden behind stones. He never looked left or right. He sailed away Southerly, full spread before the evening breeze, and when we had watched him out to sea, we were silent. We understood Earth bred few men like to this man.

"Presently Allo brought the ponies and held them for us to mount–a thing he had never done before.

" 'Wait awhile,' said Pertinax, and he made a little altar of cut turf, and strewed heather-bloom atop, and laid upon it a letter from a girl in Gaul.

" 'What do you do, O my friend?' I said.

" 'I sacrifice to my dead youth,' he answered, and, when the flames had consumed the letter, he ground them out with his heel. Then we rode back to that Wall of which we were to be Captains."

Parnesius stopped. The children sat still, not even asking if that were all the tale. Puck beckoned, and pointed the way out of the wood. "Sorry," he whispered, "but you must go now."

"We haven't made him angry, have we?" said Una. "He looks so far off, and–and–thinky."

"Bless your heart, no. Wait till to-morrow. It won't be long. Remember, you've been playing *'Lays of Ancient Rome.'* "

And as soon as they had scrambled through their gap, where Oak, Ash and Thorn grow, that was all they remembered.

A Song to Mithras

Mithras, God of the Morning, our trumpets waken the Wall!
Rome is above the Nations, but Thou art over all!'
Now as the names are answered and the guards are marched away,
Mithras, also a soldier, give us strength for the day!

Mithras, God of the Noontide, the heather swims in the heat,
Our helmets scorch our foreheads; our sandals burn our feet!
Now in the ungirt hour; now ere we blink and drowse,
Mithras, also a soldier, keep us true to our vows!

Mithras, God of the Sunset, low on the Western main,
Thou descending immortal, immortal to rise again!
Now when the watch is ended, now when the wine is drawn,
Mithras, also a soldier, keep us pure till the dawn!

Mithras, God of the Midnight, here where the great bull lies,
Look on thy children in darkness. Oh take our sacrifice!
Many roads Thou hast fashioned: all of them lead to the Light,
Mithras, also a soldier, teach us to die aright!

The Winged Hats

THE NEXT DAY happened to be what they called a Wild Afternoon. Father and Mother went out to pay calls; Miss Blake went for a ride on her bicycle, and they were left all alone till eight o'clock.

When they had seen their dear parents and their dear preceptress politely off the premises they got a cabbage-leaf full of raspberries from the gardener, and a Wild Tea from Ellen. They ate the raspberries to prevent their squashing, and they meant to divide the cabbage-leaf with Three Cows down at the Theatre, but they came across a dead hedgehog which they simply *had* to bury, and the leaf was too useful to waste.

Then they went on to the Forge and found old Hobden the hedger at home with his son the Bee Boy who is not quite right in his head, but who can pick up swarms of bees in his naked hands; and the Bee Boy told them the rhyme about the slow-worm:–

"If I had eyes *as* I could see,
No mortal man would trouble me."

They all had tea together by the hives, and Hobden said the loaf-cake which Ellen had given them was almost as good as what his wife used to make, and he showed them how to set a wire at the right height for hares. They knew about rabbits already.

Then they climbed up Long Ditch into the lower end of Far Wood. This is sadder and darker than the "Volaterrae" end because of an old marlpit full of black water, where weepy, hairy moss hangs round the stumps of the willows and alders. But the birds come to perch on the dead branches, and Hobden says that the bitter willow-water is a sort of medicine for sick animals.

They sat down on a felled oak-trunk in the shadows of the beech undergrowth, and were looping the wires Hobden had given them, when they saw Parnesius.

"How quietly you came!" said Una, moving up to make room. "Where's Puck?"

"The Faun and I have disputed whether it is better that I should tell you all my tale, or leave it untold," he replied.

"I only said that if he told it as it happened you wouldn't understand it," said Puck, jumping up like a squirrel from behind the log.

"I don't understand all of it," said Una, "but I like hearing about the little Picts."

"What *I* can't understand," said Dan, "is how Maximus knew all about the Picts when he was over in Gaul."

"He who makes himself Emperor anywhere must know everything, everywhere," said Parnesius. "We had this much from Maximus' mouth after the Games."

"Games? What games?" said Dan.

Parnesius stretched his arm out stiffly, thumb pointed to the ground. "Gladiators! *That* sort of game," he said. "There were two days' Games in his honor when he landed all unexpected at Segedunum on the East end of the Wall. Yes, the day after we had met him we held two days' games; but I think the greatest risk was run, not by the poor wretches on the sand, but by Maximus. In the old days the Legions kept silence before their Emperor. So did not we! You could hear the solid roar run West along the Wall as his chair was carried rocking through the crowds. The garrison beat round him—clamoring, clowning, asking for pay, for change of quarters, for anything that came into their wild heads. That chair was like a little boat among waves, dipping and falling, but always rising again after one had shut the eyes." Parnesius shivered.

"Were they angry with him?" said Dan.

"No more angry than wolves in a cage when their trainer walks among them. If he had turned his back an instant, or for an instant had ceased to hold their eyes, there would have been another Emperor made on the Wall that hour. Was it not so, Faun?"

"So it was. So it always will be," said Puck.

"Late in the evening his messenger came for us, and we followed to the Temple of Victory, where he lodged with Rutilianus, the General of the Wall. I had hardly seen the General before, but he always gave me leave when I wished to take Heather. He was a great glutton, and kept five Asian cooks, and he came of a family that believed in oracles. We could smell his good dinner when we entered, but the tables were empty. He lay snorting on a couch. Maximus sat apart among long rolls of accounts. Then the doors were shut.

" 'These are your men,' said Maximus to the General, who propped his eye-corners open with his gouty fingers, and stared at us like a fish.

" 'I shall know them again, Caesar,' said Rutilianus.

" 'Very good,' said Maximus. 'Now hear! You are not to move man or shield on the Wall except as these boys shall tell you. You will do nothing, except eat, without their permission. They are the head and arms. You are the belly!'

" 'As Caesar pleases,' the old man grunted. 'If my pay and profits are not cut, you may make my Ancestors' Oracle my master. Rome has been! Rome has been!' Then he turned on his side to sleep.

" 'He has it,' said Maximus. 'We will get to what *I* need.'

"He unrolled full copies of the number of men and supplies on the Wall—down to the sick that very day in Hunno Hospital. Oh, but I groaned when his pen marked off detachment after detachment of our best—of our least worthless men! He took two towers of our Scythians, two of our North British auxiliaries, two Numidian cohorts, the Dacians all, and half the Belgians. It was like an eagle pecking a carcass.

" 'And now, how many catapults have you?' He turned up a new list, but Pertinax laid his open hand there.

" 'No, Caesar,' said he. 'Do not tempt the Gods too far. Take men, or engines, but not both; else we refuse.' "

"Engines?" said Una.

"The catapults of the Wall—huge things forty feet high to the head—firing nets of raw stone or forged bolts. Nothing can stand against them. He left us our catapults at last, but he took a Caesar's half of our men without pity. We were a shell when he rolled up the lists!

" 'Hail, Caesar! We, about to die, salute you!' said Pertinax, laughing. 'If any enemy even leans against the Wall now, it will tumble.'

" 'Give me the three years Allo spoke of,' he answered, 'and you shall have twenty thousand men of your own choosing up here. But now it is a gamble—a game played against the Gods, and the stakes are Britain, Gaul, and perhaps, Rome. You play on my side?'

" 'We will play, Caesar,' I said for I had never met a man like this man.

" 'Good. To-morrow,' said he, I proclaim you Captains of the Wall before the troops.'

"So we went into the moonlight, where they were cleaning the ground after the Games. We saw great Roma Dea atop of the Wall, the frost on her helmet, and her spear pointed towards the North Star. We saw the twinkle of night-fires all along the guard-towers, and the line of the black catapults growing smaller and smaller in the distance. All these things we knew till we were weary; but that night they seemed very strange to us, because the next day we knew we were to be their masters.

"The men took the news well; but when Maximus went away with half our strength, and we had to spread ourselves into the emptied towers, and the townspeople complained that trade would be ruined, and the Autumn gales blew–it was dark days for us two. Here Pertinax was more than my right hand. Being born and bred among the great country-houses in Gaul, he knew the proper words to address to all–from Roman-born Centurions to those dogs of the Third–the Libyans. And he spoke to each as though that man were as high-minded as himself. Now *I* saw so strongly what things were needed to be done, that I forgot things are only accomplished by means of men. That was a mistake.

"I feared nothing from the Picts, at least for that year, but Allo warned me that the Winged Hats would soon come in from the sea at each end of the Wall to prove to the Picts how weak we were. So I made ready in haste, and none too soon. I shifted our best men to the ends of the Wall, and set up screened catapults by the beach. The Winged Hats would drive in before the snow-squalls–ten or twenty boats at a time–on Segedunum or Ituna, according as the wind blew.

"Now a ship coming in to land men must furl her sail. If you wait till you see her men gather up the sail's foot, your catapults can jerk a net of loose stones (bolts only cut through the cloth) into the bag of it. Then she turns over, and the sea makes everything clean again. A few men may come ashore, but very few. . . . It was not hard work, except the waiting on the beach in blowing sand and snow. And that was how we dealt with the Winged Hats that winter.

"Early in the Spring, when the East winds blow like skinning-knives, they gathered again off the East end with many ships. Allo told me they would never rest till they had taken a tower in open fight. Certainly they fought in the open. We dealt with them thoroughly through a long day: and when all was finished, one man dived clear of the wreckage of his ship, and swam towards shore. I waited, and a wave tumbled him at my feet.

"As I stooped, I saw he wore such a medal as I wear." Parnesius raised his hand to his neck. "Therefore, when he could speak, I addressed him a certain Question which can only be answered in a certain manner. He answered with the necessary Word–the Word that belongs to the Degree of Gryphons in the science of Mithras my God. I put my shield over him till he could stand up. You see I am not short, but he was a head taller than I. He said: 'What now?' I said: 'At your pleasure, my brother, to stay or go.'

"He looked out across the surf. There remained one ship unhurt, beyond range of our catapults. I checked the catapults and he waved her in. She came as a hound comes to a master. When she was yet a hundred paces from the beach, he flung back his hair, and swam out. They hauled him in, and went away. I knew that those who worship Mithras are many and of all races, so I did not think much more upon the matter.

"A month later I saw Allo with his horses–by the Temple of Pan, O Faun!–and he gave me a great necklace of gold studded with coral.

"At first I thought it was a bribe from some tradesman in the town–meant for old Rutilianus. 'Nay,' said Allo. 'This is a gift from Amal, that Winged Hat whom you saved on the beach. He says you are a Man.'

" 'He is a Man, too. Tell him I can wear his gift,' I answered.

" 'Oh, Amal is a young fool; but, speaking as sensible men, your Emperor is doing such great things in Gaul that the Winged Hats are anxious to be his friends, or, better still, the friends of his servants. They think you and Pertinax could lead them to victories.' Allo looked at me like a one-eyed raven.

" 'Allo,' I said, 'you are the corn between the two millstones. Be content if they grind evenly, and don't thrust your hand between them.'

" 'I?' said Allo. 'I hate Rome and the Winged Hats equally; but if the Winged Hats thought that some day you and Pertinax might join them against Maximus, they would leave you in peace while you considered. Time is what we need—you and I and Maximus. Let me carry a pleasant message back to the Winged Hats—something for them to make a council over. We barbarians are all alike. We sit up half the night to discuss anything a Roman says. Eh?'

" 'We have no men. We must fight with words,' said Pertinax. 'Leave it to Allo and me.'

"So Allo carried word back to the Winged Hats that we would not fight them if they did not fight us; and they (I think they were a little tired of losing men in the sea) agreed to a sort of truce. I believe Allo, who being a horse-dealer loved lies, also told them we might some day rise against Maximus as Maximus had risen against Rome.

"Indeed, they permitted the corn-ships which I sent to the Picts to pass North that season without harm. Therefore the Picts were well fed that winter, and since they were in some sort my children, I was glad of it. We had only two thousand men on the Wall, and I wrote many times to Maximus and begged—prayed—him to send me only one cohort of my old North British troops. He could not spare them. He needed them to win more victories in Gaul.

"Then came news that he had defeated and slain the Emperor Gratian, and thinking he must now be secure, I wrote again for men. He answered: 'You will learn that I have at last settled accounts with the pup Gratian. There was no need that he should have died, but he became confused and lost his head, which is a bad thing to befall any Emperor. Tell your Father I am content to drive two mules only; for unless my old General's son thinks himself destined to destroy me, I shall rest Emperor of Gaul and Britain, and then you, my two children, will presently get all the men you need. Just now I can spare none.' "

"What did he mean by his General's son?" said Dan.

"He meant Theodosius Emperor of Rome, who was the son of Theodosius the General under whom Maximus had fought in the old Pict War. The two men never loved each other, and when Gratian made the younger Theodosius Emperor of the East (at least, so I've heard), Maximus carried on the war to the second generation. It was his fate, and it was his fall. But Theodosius the Emperor is a good man. As I know." Parnesius was silent for a moment and then continued.

"I wrote back to Maximus that, though we had peace on the Wall, I should be happier with a few more men and some new catapults. He answered: 'You must live a little longer under the shadow of my victories, till I can see what young Theodosius intends. He may welcome me as a brother-Emperor, or he may be preparing an army. In either case I cannot spare men just now.' "

"But he was always saying that," cried Una.

"It was true. He did not make excuses; but thanks, as he said, to the news of his victories, we had no trouble on the Wall for a long, long time. The Picts grew fat as their own sheep among the heather, and as many of my men as lived were well exercised in their weapons. Yes, the Wall looked strong. For myself, I knew how weak we were. I knew that if even a false rumor of any defeat to Maximus broke loose among the Winged Hats, they might come down in earnest, and then—the Wall must go! For the Picts I never cared, but in those years I learned something of the strength of the Winged Hats. They increased their strength every day, but I could not increase my men. Maximus had emptied Britain behind us, and I felt myself to be a man with a rotten stick standing before a broken fence to turn bulls.

"Thus, my friends, we lived on the Wall, waiting–waiting–waiting for the men that Maximus never sent.

"Presently he wrote that he was preparing an army against Theodosius. He wrote–and Pertinax read it over my shoulder in our quarters: *'Tell your Father that my destiny orders me to drive three mules or be torn in pieces by them. I hope within a year to finish with Theodosius, son of Theodosius, once and for all. Then you shall have Britain to rule, and Pertinax, if he chooses, Gaul. To-day I wish strongly you were with me to beat my Auxiliaries into shape. Do not, I pray you, believe any rumor of my sickness. I have a little evil in my old body which I shall cure by riding swiftly into Rome.'*

"Said Pertinax: 'It is finished with Maximus! He writes as a man without hope. I, a man without hope, can see this. What does he add at the bottom of the roll? *"Tell Pertinax I have met his late Uncle, the Duumvir of Divio, and that he accounted to me quite truthfully for all his Mother's monies. I have sent her with a fitting escort, for she is the mother of a hero, to Nicoea, where the climate is warm."*

" 'That is proof!' said Pertinax. 'Nicaea is not far by sea from Rome. A woman there could take ship and fly to Rome in time of war. Yes, Maximus foresees his death, and is fulfilling his promises one by one. But I am glad my Uncle met him.' "

" 'You think blackly to-day?' I asked.

" 'I will think truth. The Gods weary of the play we have played against them. Theodosius will destroy Maximus. It is finished!'

" 'Will you write him that?' I said.

" 'See what I shall write,' he answered, and he took pen and wrote a letter cheerful as the light of day, tender as a woman's and full of jests. Even I, reading over his shoulder, took comfort from it till–I saw his face!

" 'And now,' he said, sealing it, 'we be two dead men, my brother. Let us go to the Temple.'

"We prayed awhile to Mithras, where we had many times prayed before. After that we lived day by day among evil rumors till winter came again.

"It happened one morning that we rode to the East Shore, and found on the beach a fair-haired man, half frozen, bound to some broken planks. Turning him over, we saw by his belt-buckle that he was a Goth of an Eastern Legion. Suddenly he opened his eyes and cried loudly: 'He is dead! The letters were with me, but the Winged Hats sunk the ship.' So saying, he died between our hands.

"We asked not who was dead. We knew! We raced before the driving snow to Hunno, thinking perhaps Allo might be there. We found him already at our stables, and he saw by our faces what we had heard.

" 'It was in a tent by the Sea,' he stammered. 'He was beheaded by Theodosius. He sent a letter to you, written while he waited to be slain. The Winged Hats met the ship and took it. The news is running through the heather like fire. Blame me not! I cannot hold back my young men any more.'

" 'I would we could say as much for our men,' said Pertinax, laughing. 'But, Gods be praised, they cannot run away.'

" 'What do you do?' said Allo. 'I bring an order–a message–from the Winged Hats that you join them with your men, and march South to plunder Britain.'

" 'It grieves me,' said Pertinax, 'but we are stationed here to stop that thing.'

" 'If I carry back such an answer they will kill me,' said Allo. 'I always promised the Winged Hats that you would rise when Maximus fell. I–I did not think he could fall.'

" 'Alas! my poor barbarian,' said Pertinax, still laughing. 'Well, you have sold us too many good ponies to be thrown back to your friends. We will make you a prisoner, although you are an ambassador.'

" 'Yes, that will be best,' said Allo, holding out a halter. We bound him lightly, for he was an old man.

" 'Presently the Winged Hats may come to look for you, and that will give us more time. See how the habit of playing for time sticks to a man!' said Pertinax, as he tied the rope.

" 'No,' I said. 'Time may help. If Maximus wrote us letters while he was a prisoner, Theodosius must have sent the ship that brought it. If he can send ships, he can send men.'

" 'How will that profit us?' said Pertinax. 'We serve Maximus, not Theodosius. Even if by some miracle of the Gods Theodosius down South sent and saved the Wall, we could not expect more than the death Maximus died.'

" 'It concerns us to defend the Wall, no matter what Emperor dies, or makes die,' I said.

" 'That is worthy of your brother the philosopher,' said Pertinax. 'Myself I am without hope, so I do not say solemn and stupid things! Rouse the Wall!'

"We armed the Wall from end to end; we told the officers that there was a rumor of Maximus's death which might bring down the Winged Hats, but we were sure, even if it were true, that Theodosius, for the sake of Britain, would send us help. Therefore, we must stand fast. . . . My friends, it is above all things strange to see how men bear ill news! Often the strongest till then become the weakest, while the weakest, as it were, reach up and steal strength from the Gods. So it was with us. Yet my Pertinax by his jests and his courtesy and his labors had put heart and training into our poor numbers during the past years–more than I should have thought possible. Even our Libyan Cohort–the Thirds–stood up in their padded cuirasses and did not whimper.

"In three days came seven chiefs and elders of the Winged Hats. Among them was that tall young man, Amal, whom I had met on the beach, and he smiled when he saw my necklace. We made them welcome, for they were ambassadors. We showed them Allo, alive but bound. They thought we had killed him, and I saw it would not have vexed them if we had. Allo saw it too, and it vexed him. Then in our quarters at Hunno we came to Council.

"They said that Rome was falling, and that we must join them. They offered me all South Britain to govern after they had taken a tribute out of it.

"I answered, 'Patience. This Wall is not weighed off like plunder. Give me proof that my General is dead.'

" 'Nay,' said one elder, 'prove to us that he lives'; and another said, cunningly, 'What will you give us if we read you his last words?'

" 'We are not merchants to bargain,' cried Amal. 'Moreover, I owe this man my life. He shall have his proof.' He threw across to me a letter (well I knew the seal) from Maximus.

" 'We took this out of the ship we sunk,' he cried. 'I cannot read, but I know one sign, at least, which makes me believe.' He showed me a dark stain on the outer roll that my heavy heart perceived was the valiant blood of Maximus.

" 'Read!' said Amal. 'Read, and then let us hear whose servants you are!'

"Said Pertinax, very softly, after he had looked through it: 'I will read it all. Listen, barbarians!' He read from that which I have carried next my heart ever since."

Parnesius drew from his neck a folded and spotted piece of parchment, and began in a hushed voice:–

" '*To Parnesius and Pertinax, the not unworthy Captains of the Wall, from*

Maximus, once Emperor of Gaul and Britain, now prisoner waiting death by the sea in the camp of Theodosius–Greeting and Good-bye!'

" 'Enough,' said young Amal; 'there is your proof! You must join us now!'

"Pertinax looked long and silently at him, till that fair man blushed like a girl. Then read Pertinax:–

" *'I have joyfully done much evil in my life to those who have wished me evil, but if ever I did any evil to you two I repent, and I ask your forgiveness. The three mules which I strove to drive have torn me in pieces as your Father prophesied. The naked swords wait at the tent door to give me the death I gave to Gratian. Therefore I, your General and your Emperor, send you free and honorable dismissal from my service, which you entered, not for money or office, but, as it makes me warm to believe, because you loved me!'*

" 'By the Light of the Sun,' Amal broke in. 'This was in some sort a Man! We may have been mistaken in his servants!'

"And Pertinax read on: *'You gave me the time for which I asked. If I have failed to use it, do not lament. We have gambled very splendidly against the Gods, but they hold weighted dice, and I must pay the forfeit. Remember, I have been; but Rome is; and Rome will be! Tell Pertinax his Mother is in safety at Nicaea, and her monies are in charge of the Prefect at Antipolis. Make my remembrances to your Father and to your Mother, whose friendship was great gain to me. Give also to my little Picts and to the Winged Hats such messages as their thick heads can understand. I would have sent you three Legions this very day if all had gone aright. Do not forget me. We have worked together. Farewell! Farewell! Farewell!'*

"Now, that was my Emperor's last letter. (The children heard the parchment crackle as Parnesius returned it to its place.)

" 'I was mistaken,' said Amal. 'The servants of such a man will sell nothing except over the sword. I am glad of it.' He held out his hand to me.

" 'But Maximus has given you your dismissal,' said an elder. 'You are certainly free to serve–or to rule–whom you please. Join–do not follow–join us!'

" 'We thank you,' said Pertinax. 'But Maximus tells us to give you such messages as–pardon me, but I use his words–your thick heads can understand.' He pointed through the door to the foot of a catapult wound up.

" 'We understand,' said an elder. 'The Wall must be won at a price?'

" 'It grieves me,' said Pertinax, laughing, 'but so it must be won,' and he gave them of our best Southern wine.

"They drank, and wiped their yellow beards in silence till they rose to go.

"Said Amal, stretching himself (for they were barbarians), 'We be a goodly company; I wonder what the ravens and the dogfish will make of some of us before this snow melts.'

" 'Think rather what Theodosius may send,' I answered; and though they laughed, I saw that my chance shot troubled them.

"Only old Allo lingered behind a little.

" 'You see,' he said, winking and blinking, 'I am no more than their dog. When I have shown their men the secret short ways across our bogs, they will kick me like one.'

" 'Then I should not be in haste to show them those ways,' said Pertinax, 'till I were sure that Rome could not save the Wall.'

" 'You think so? Woe is me!' said the old man. 'I only wanted peace for my people,' and he went out stumbling through the snow behind the tall Winged Hats.

"In this fashion then, slowly, a day at a time, which is very bad for doubting troops, the War came upon us. At first the Winged Hats swept in from the sea as they had done before, and there we met them as before–with the catapults; and they sickened of it. Yet for a long time they would not trust their duck-legs on land, and I think when it came to revealing the secrets of the tribe, the little Picts were afraid or ashamed to show them all the roads across the heather. I had this from a Pict prisoner. They were as much our spies as our enemies, for the Winged Hats oppressed them, and took their winter stores. Ah, foolish Little People!

"Then the Winged Hats began to roll us up from each end of the Wall. I sent runners Southward to see what the news might be in Britain; but the wolves were very bold that winter among the deserted stations where the troops had once been, and none came back. We had trouble too with the forage for the ponies along the Wall. I kept ten, and so did Pertinax.We lived and slept in the saddle riding east or west, and we ate our worn-out ponies. The people of the town also made us some trouble till I gathered them all in one quarter behind Hunno. We broke down the Wall on either side of it to make as it were a citadel. Our men fought better in close order.

"By the end of the second month we were deep in the War as a man is deep in a snowdrift or in a dream. I think we fought in our sleep. At least I know I have gone on the Wall and come off again, remembering nothing between, though my throat was harsh with giving orders, and my sword, I could see, had been used.

"The Winged Hats fought like wolves–all in a pack. Where they had suffered most there they charged in most hotly. This was hard for the defender, but it held them from sweeping on into Britain.

"In those days Pertinax and I wrote on the plaster of the bricked archway into Valentia the names of the towers, and the days on which they fell one by one. We wished for some record.

"And the fighting? The fight was always hottest to left and right of the great Statue of Roma Dea, near to Rutilianus' house. By the light of the Sun, that old fat man, whom we had not considered at all, grew young again among the trumpets! I remember he said his sword was an oracle! 'Let us consult the Oracle,' he would say, and put the handle against his ear, and shake his head wisely. 'And *this* day is allowed Rutilianus to live,' he would say, and, tucking up his cloak, he would puff and pant and fight well. Oh, there were jests in plenty on the Wall to take the place of food!

"We endured for two months and seventeen days–always being pressed from three sides into a smaller space. Several times Allo sent in word that help was at hand. We did not believe it, but it cheered our men.

"The end came not with shoutings of joy, but, like the rest, as in a dream. The Winged Hats suddenly left us in peace for one night, and the next day; which is too long for spent men. We slept at first lightly, expecting to be roused, and then like logs, each where he lay. May you never need such sleep! When I waked our towers were full of strange armed men, who watched us snoring. I roused Pertinax, and we leaped up together.

" 'What?' said a young man in clean armor. 'Do you fight against Theodosius? Look!'

"North we looked over the red snow. No Winged Hats were there. South we looked over the white snow, and behold there were the Eagles of two strong Legions encamped. East and west we saw flame and fighting, but by Hunno all was still.

" 'Trouble no more,' said the young man. 'Rome's arm is long. Where are the Captains of the Wall?'

"We said we were those men.

" 'But you are old and gray-haired,' he cried. 'Maximus said that they were boys.'

" 'Yes that was true some years ago,' said Pertinax. 'What is our fate to be, you fine and well-fed child?'

" 'I am called Ambrosius, a secretary of the Emperor,' he answered. 'Show me a certain letter which Maximus wrote from a tent at Aquileia, and perhaps I will believe.'

"I took it from my breast, and when he had read it he saluted us, saying: 'Your fate is in your own hands. If you choose to serve Theodosius, he will give you a Legion. If it suits you to go to your homes, we will give you a Triumph.'

" 'I would like better a bath, wine, food, razors, soaps, oils, and scents,' said Pertinax, laughing.

" 'Oh, I see you are a boy,' said Ambrosius. 'And you?' turning to me.

" 'We bear no ill-will against Theodosius, but in War——' I began.

" 'In War it is as it is in Love,' said Pertinax. 'Whether she be good or bad, one gives one's best once, to one only. That given, there remains no second worth giving or taking.'

" 'That is true,' said Ambrosius. 'I was with Maximus before he died. He warned Theodosius that you would never serve him, and frankly I say I am sorry for my Emperor.'

" 'He has Rome to console him,' said Pertinax. 'I ask you of your kindness to let us go to our homes and get this smell out of our nostrils.'

"None the less they gave us a Triumph!"

"It was well earned," said Puck, throwing some leaves into the still water of the marlpit. The black, oily circles spread dizzily as the children watched them.

"I want to know, oh, ever so many things," said Dan. "What happened to old Allo? Did the Winged Hats ever come back? And what did Amal do?"

"And what happened to the fat old General with the five cooks?" said Una. "And what did your Mother say when you came home?" . . .

"She'd say you're settin' too long over this old pit, so late as 'tis already," said old Hobden's voice behind them. "Hst!" he whispered.

He stood still, for not twenty paces away a magnificent dog-fox sat on his haunches and looked at the children as though he were an old friend of theirs.

"Oh, Mus' Reynolds, Mus' Reynolds!" said Hobden, under his breath. "If I knowed all was inside your head, I'd know something wuth knowin'. Mus' Dan an' Miss Una, come along o' me while I lock up my liddle hen-house."

A Pict Song

Rome never looks where she treads,
Always her heavy hooves fall,
On our stomachs, our hearts or our heads;
And Rome never heeds when we bawl.
Her sentries pass on—that is all,
And we gather behind them in hordes,
And plot to reconquer the Wall,
With only our tongues for our swords.

We are the Little Folk—we!
Too little to love or to hate.
Leave us alone and you'll see
How we can drag down the Great!
We are the worm in the wood!
We are the rot at the root!
We are the germ in the blood!
We are the thorn in the foot!

Mistletoe killing an oak—
Rats gnawing cables in two—
Moths making holes in a cloak—
How they must love what they do!
Yes,—and we Little Folk too,
We are as busy as they—
Working our works out of view—
Watch, and you'll see it some day!

No indeed! We are not strong,
But we know Peoples that are.
Yes, and we'll guide them along,
To smash and destroy you in War!
We shall be slaves just the same?
Yes, we have always been slaves;
But you—you will die of the shame,
And then we shall dance on your graves!

We are the Little Folk, we! etc.

Hal o' the Draft

Prophets have honor all over the Earth,
Except in the village where they were born;
Where such as knew them boys from birth,
Nature-ally hold 'em in scorn.

When Prophets are naughty and young and vain,
They make a won'erful grievance of it;
(You can see by their writings how they complain,
But O, 'tis won'erful good for the Prophet!

There's nothing Nineveh Town can give,
(Nor being swallowed by whales between),
Makes up for the place where a man's folk live,
That don't care nothing what he has been.
He might ha' been that, or he might ha' been this,
But they love and they hate him for what he is!

A RAINY AFTERNOON drove Dan and Una over to play pirates in the Little Mill. If you don't mind rats on the rafters and oats in your shoes, the mill-attic, with its trap-doors and inscriptions on beams about floods and sweet-hearts, is a splendid place. It is lighted by a foot-square window, called Duck Window, that looks across to Little Lindens Farm, and the spot where Jack Cade was killed.

When they had climbed the attic ladder (they called it the "mainmast tree" out of the ballad of Sir Andrew Barton, and Dan "swarved it with might and main," as the ballad says) they saw a man sitting on Duck window-sill. He was dressed in a plum colored doublet and tight plum-colored hose, and he drew busily in a red-edged book.

"Sit ye! Sit ye!" Puck cried from a rafter overhead. "See what it is to be beautiful! Sir Harry Dawe—pardon, Hal—says I am the very image of a head for a gargoyle."

The man laughed and raised his dark velvet cap to the children, and his grizzled hair bristled out in a stormy fringe. He was old—forty at least—but his eyes were young, with funny little wrinkles all round them. A satchel of embroidered leather hung from his broad belt, which looked interesting.

"May we see?" said Una, coming forward.

"Surely—sure-ly!" he said, moving up on the window-seat, and returned to his work with a silver-pointed pencil. Puck sat as though the grin were fixed for ever on his broad face, while they watched the quick, certain fingers that copied it. Presently the man took a reed pen from his satchel, and trimmed it with a little ivory knife, carved in the semblance of a fish.

"Oh, what a beauty!" cried Dan.

" 'Ware fingers! That blade is perilous sharp. I made it myself of the best Low Country cross-bow steel. And so, too, this fish. When his back-fin travels to his tail—so—he swallows up the blade, even as the whale swallowed Gaffer Jonah. . . . Yes, and that's my ink-horn. I made the four silver saints round it. Press Barnabas's head. It opens, and then—" He dipped the trimmed pen, and with careful boldness began to put in the essential lines of Puck's rugged face, that had been but faintly revealed by the silver-point.

The children gasped, for it fairly leaped from the page.

As he worked, and the rain fell on the tiles, he talked—now clearly, now muttering, now breaking off to frown or smile at his work. He told them he was born at Little Lindens Farms, and his father used to beat him for drawing things instead of doing things, till an old priest called Father Roger, who drew illuminated letters in rich people's books, coaxed the parents to let him take the boy as a sort of painter's apprentice. Then he went with Father Roger to Oxford, where he cleaned plates and carried cloaks and shoes for the scholars of a College called Merton.

"Didn't you hate that?" said Dan after a great many other questions.

"I never thought on't. Half Oxford was building new colleges or beautifying the old, and she had called to her aid the master-craftsmen of all Christendie—kings in their trade and honored of Kings. I knew them. I worked for them: that was enough. No wonder——" He stopped and laughed.

"You became a great man," said Puck.

"They said so, Robin. Even Bramante said so."

"Why? What did you do?" Dan asked.

The artist looked at him queerly. "Things in stone and such, up and down England. You would not have heard of 'em. To come nearer home, I re-builded this little St. Bartholomew's church of ours. It cost me more trouble and sorrow than aught I've touched in my life. But 'twas a sound lesson."

"Um," said Dan. "We had lessons this morning."

"I'll not afflict ye, lad," said Hal, while Puck roared. "Only 'tis strange to think how that little church was re-built, re-roofed, and made glorious, thanks to some few godly Sussex iron-masters, a Bristol sailor lad, a proud ass called Hal o' the Draft because, d'you see, he was always drawing and drafting; and"—he dragged the words slowly—*"and* a Scotch pirate."

"Pirate?" said Dan. He wriggled like a hooked fish.

"Even that Andrew Barton you were singing of on the stair just now." He dipped again in the ink-well, and held his breath over a sweeping line, as though he had forgotten everything else.

"Pirates don't build churches, do they?" said Dan. "Or *do* they?"

"They help mightily," Hal laughed. "But you were at your lessons this morn, Jack Scholar?"

"Oh, pirates aren't lessons. It was only Bruce and his silly old spider," said Una. "Why did Sir Andrew Barton help you?"

"I question if he ever knew it," said Hal, twinkling. "Robin, how a-mischief's name am I to tell these innocents what comes of sinful pride?"

"Oh, we know all about *that,*" said Una pertly. "If you get too beany—that's cheeky—you get sat upon, of course."

Hal considered a moment, pen in air, and Puck said some long words.

"Aha! That was my case too," he cried. "Beany—you say—but certainly I did not conduct myself well. I was proud of—of such things as porches—a Galilee porch at Lincoln for choice—proud of one Torrigiano's arm on my shoulder, proud of my knighthood when I made the gilt scroll-work for *The Sovereign*—our King's ship. But Father Roger sitting in Merton Library, he did not forget me. At the top of my pride, when I and no other should have builded the porch at Lincoln, he laid it on me with a terrible forefinger to go back to my Sussex clays and re-build, at my own charges, my own church, where we Dawes have been buried for six generations. 'Out! Son of my Art!' said he. 'Fight the Devil at home ere you call yourself a man and a craftsman.' And I quaked, and I went. . . . How's yon, Robin?" He flourished the finished sketch before Puck.

"Me! Me past peradventure," said Puck, smirking like a man at a mirror. "Ah, see! The rain has took off! I hate housen in daylight."

"Whoop! Holiday!" cried Hal, leaping up. "Who's for my Little Lindens? We can talk there."

They tumbled downstairs, and turned past the dripping willows by the sunny mill dam.

"Body o' me," said Hal, staring at the hop-garden, where the hops were just ready to blossom. "What are these vines? No, not vines, and they twine the wrong way to beans." He began to draw in his ready book.

"Hops. New since your day," said Puck. "They're an herb of Mars, and their flowers dried flavor ale. We say:–

" 'Turkeys, Heresy, Hops, and Beer
Came into England all in one year.' "

"Heresy I know. I've seen Hops–God be praised for their beauty! What is your Turkis?"

The children laughed. They knew the Lindens turkeys, and as soon as they reached Lindens' orchard on the hill the flock charged at them.

Out came Hal's book at once. "Hoity-toity!" he cried. "Here's Pride in purple feathers! Here's wrathy contempt and the Pomps of the Flesh! How d'you call *them?"*

"Turkeys! Turkeys!" the children shouted, as the old gobbler raved and flamed against Hal's plum-colored hose.

"Save Your Magnificence!" he said. "I've drafted two good new things to-day." And he doffed his cap to the bubbling bird.

Then they walked through the grass to the knoll where Little Lindens stands. The old farm-house, weather-tiled to the ground, took almost the color of a blood-ruby in the afternoon light. The pigeons pecked at the mortar in the chimney-stacks; the bees that had lived under the tiles since it was built filled the hot August air with their booming; and the smell of the box-tree by the dairy-window mixed with the smell of earth after rain, bread after baking, and a tickle of wood-smoke.

The farmer's wife came to the door, baby on arm, shaded her brows against the sun, stooped to pluck a sprig of rosemary, and turned down the orchard. The old spaniel in his barrel barked once or twice to show he was in charge of the empty house. Puck clicked back the garden-gate.

"D'you marvel that I love it?" said Hal, in a whisper. "What can town folk know of the nature of housen–or land?"

They perched themselves arow on the old hacked oak bench in Lindens' garden, looking across the valley of the brook at the fern-covered dimples and hollows of the Forge behind Hobden's cottage. The old man was cutting a faggot in his garden by the hives. It was quite a second after his chopper fell that the chump of the blow reached their lazy ears.

"Eh–yeh!" said Hal. "I mind when where that old gaffer stands was Nether Forge–Master John Collins's foundry. Many a night has his big trip-hammer shook me in my bed here. *Boom-bitty! Boom-bitty!* If the wind was east, I could hear Master Tom Collins's forge at Stockens answering his brother, *Boom-oop! Boom-oop!* and midway between, Sir John Pelham's sledge-hammers at Brightling would strike in like a pack o'scholars, and *'Hic-haec-hoc'* they'd say, *'Hic-haec-hoc,'* till I fell asleep. Yes. The valley was as full o' forges and fineries as a May shaw o' cuckoos. All gone to grass now!"

"What did they make?" said Dan.

"Guns for the King's ships–and for others. Serpentines and cannon mostly. When the guns were cast, down would come the King's Officers, and take our plough-oxen to haul them to the coast. Look! Here's one of the first and finest craftsmen of the Sea!"

He fluttered back a page of his book, and showed them a young man's head. Underneath was written: "Sebastianus."

"He came down with a King's Order on Master John Collins for twenty serpentines (wicked little cannon they be!) to furnish a venture of ships. I drafted him thus sitting by our fire telling Mother of the new lands he'd find the far side the world. And he found them, too! There's a nose to cleave through unknown seas! Cabot was his name—a Bristol lad—half a foreigner. I set a heap by him. He helped me to my church-building."

"I thought that was Sir Andrew Barton," said Dan.

"Ay, but foundations before roofs," Hal answered. "Sebastian first put me in the way of it. I had come down here, not to serve God as a craftsman should, but to show my people how great a craftsman I was. They cared not, and it served me right, one split straw for my craft or my greatness. What a murrain call had I, they said, to mell with old St. Barnabas's? Ruinous the church had been since the Black Death, and ruinous she should remain; and I could hang myself in my new scaffold-ropes! Gentle and simple, high and low—the Hayes, the Fowles, the Fanners, the Collinses—they were all in a tale against me. Only Sir John Pelham up yonder to Brightling bade me heart-up and go on. Yet how could I? Did I ask Master Collins for his timber-tug to haul beams? The oxen had gone to Lewes after lime. Did he promise me a set of iron cramps or ties for the roof? They never came to hand, or else they were spaulty or cracked. So with everything. Nothing said, but naught done except I stood by them, and then done amiss. I thought the countryside was fair bewitched."

"It was sure-ly," said Puck, knees under chin. "Did you ever suspect any one?"

"Not till Sebastian came for his guns, and John Collins played him the same dog's tricks as he'd played me with my ironwork. Week in, week out, two of three serpentines would be flawed in the casting, and only fit, they said, to be remelted. Then John Collins would shake his head, and vow he could pass no cannon for the King's service that were not perfect. Saints! How Sebastian stormed! *I* know, for we sat on this bench sharing our sorrows inter-common.

"When Sebastian had fumed away six weeks at Lindens and gotten just six serpentines, Dirk Brenzett, Master of the *Cygnet* hoy, sends me word that the block of stone he was fetching me from France for our new font he'd hove overboard to lighten his ship, chased by Andrew Barton up to Rye Port."

"Ah! The pirate!" said Dan.

"Yes. And while I am tearing my hair over this, Ticehurst Will, my best mason, comes to me shaking, and vowing that the Devil, horned, tailed, and chained, has run out on him from the church-tower, and the men would work there no more. So I took 'em off the foundations, which we were strengthening, and went into the Bell Tavern for a cup of ale. Says Master John Collins: 'Have it your own way, lad; but if I was you, I'd take the sinnification o' the sign, and leave old Barnabas's Church alone!' And they all wagged their sinful heads, and agreed. Less afraid of the Devil than of me—as I saw later.

"When I brought my sweet news to Lindens, Sebastian was limewashing the kitchen-beams for Mother. He loved her like a son.

" 'Cheer up, lad,' he says. 'God's where He was. Only you and I chance to be pure pute asses! We've been tricked, Hal, and more shame to me, a sailor, that I did not guess it before! You must leave your belfry alone, forsooth, because the Devil is adrift there; and I cannot get my serpentines because John Collins cannot cast them aright. Meantime Andrew Barton hawks off the Port of Rye. And why? To take those very serpentines which poor Cabot must whistle for; the said serpentines, I'll wager my share of new Continents, being now hid away in St. Barnabas church tower. Clear as the Irish coast at noonday!'

" 'They'd sure never dare to do it,' I said; 'and for another thing, selling cannon to the King's enemies is black treason—hanging and fine.'

"'It is sure large profit. Men'll dare any gallows for that. I have been a trader myself,' says he. 'We must be upsides with 'em for the honor of Bristol.'

"Then he hatched a plot, sitting on the lime-wash bucket. We gave out to ride o' Tuesday to London and made a show of making farewells of our friends–especially of Master John Collins. But at Wadhurst Woods we turned; rode by night to the watermeadows; hid our horses in a willow-tot at the foot of the glebe, and stole a-tiptoe up hill to Barnabas's church again. A thick mist, and a moon coming through.

"I had no sooner locked the tower-door behind us than over goes Sebastian full length in the dark.

"'Pest!' he says. 'Step high and feel low, Hal. I've stumbled over guns before.'

"I groped, and one by one–the tower was pitchy dark–I counted the lither barrels of twenty serpentines laid out on pease-straw. No conceal at all!

"'There's two demi-cannon my end,' says Sebastian, slapping metal. 'They'll be for Andrew Barton's lower deck. Honest–honest John Collins! So this is his warehouse, his arsenal, his armory! Now, see you why your pokings and pryings have raised the Devil in Sussex? You've hindered John's lawful trade for months,' and he laughed where he lay.

"A clay-cold tower is no fireside at midnight, so we climbed the belfry stairs, and there Sebastian tips over a cow-hide with its horns and tail.

"'Aha! Your Devil has left his doublet! Does it become me, Hal?' He draws it on and capers in the slits of window-moonlight–won'erful devilish-like. Then he sits on the stair, rapping with his tail on a board, and his back-aspect was dreader than his front; and a howlet lit in, and screeched at the horns of him.

"'If you'd keep out the Devil, shut the door,' he whispered. 'And that's another false proverb, Hal, for I can hear your tower-door opening.'

"'I locked it. Who a-plague has another key, then?' I said.

"'All the congregation, to judge by their feet,' he says, and peers into the blackness. 'Still! Still, Hal! Hear 'em grunt! That's more o' my serpentines, I'll be bound. One–two–three–four they bear in! Faith, Andrew equips himself like an admiral! Twenty-four serpentines in all!'

"As if it had been an echo, we heard John Collins's voice come up all hollow: 'Twenty-four serpentines and two demi-cannon. That's the full tally for Sir Andrew Barton.'

"'Courtesy costs naught,' whispers Sebastian. 'Shall I drop my dagger on his head?'

"'They go over to Rye o' Thursday in the woolwains, hid under the wool packs. Dirk Brenzett meets them at Udimore, as before," says John.

"'Lord! What a worn, handsmooth trade it is!' says Sebastian. 'I lay we are the sole two babes in the village that have not our lawful share in the venture.'

"There was a full score folk below, talking like all Robertsbridge Market. We counted them by voice.

"Master John Collins pipes: 'The guns for the French carrack must lie here next month. Will, when does your young fool (me, so please you!) come back from Lunnon?'

"'No odds,' I heard Ticehurst Will answer, 'Lay 'em just where you've a mind, Mus' Collins. We're all too afraid o' the Devil to mell with the tower now.' And the long knave laughed.

"'Ah! 'tis easy enow for you to raise the Devil, Will,' says another–Ralph Hobden from the Forge.

"'Aaa-men!' roars Sebastian, and ere I could hold him, he leaps down the stairs–won'erful devilish-like–howling no bounds. He had scarce time to lay out for the nearest than they ran. Saints, how they ran! We heard them pound on the door of the Bell Tavern, and then we ran too.

" 'What's next?' says Sebastian, looping up his cow-tail as he leaped the briars. 'I've broke honest John's face.'

" 'Ride to Sir John Pelham's,' I said. 'He is the only one that ever stood by me.'

"We rode to Brightling, and past Sir John's lodges, where the keepers would have shot at us for deer-stealers, and we had Sir John down into his Justice's chair, and when we had told him our tale and showed him the cow-hide which Sebastian wore still girt about him, he laughed till the tears ran.

" 'Wel-a-well!' he says. 'I'll see justice done before daylight. What's your complaint? Master Collins is my old friend.'

" 'He's none of mine,' I cried. 'When I think how he and his likes have baulked and dozened and cozened me at every turn over the church'—and I choked at the thought.

" 'Ah, but ye see now they needed it for another use,' says he, smoothly.

" 'So they did my serpentines,' Sebastian cries. 'I should be half across the Western Ocean by this if my guns had been ready. But they're sold to a Scotch pirate by your old friend.'

" 'Where's your proof?' says Sir Joh, stroking his beard.

" 'I broke my shins over them not an hour since, and I heard John give order where they were to be taken,' says Sebastian.

" 'Words! Words only,' says Sir John. 'Master Collins is somewhat of a liar at best.'

"He carried it so gravely, that for the moment, I thought he was dipped in this secret traffick too, and that there was not an honest ironmaster in Sussex.

" 'Name o' Reason!' says Sebastian, and raps with his cow-tail on the table, 'Whose guns are they, then?'

" 'Yours, manifestly,' says Sir John. 'You come with the King's Order for 'em, and Master Collins casts them in his foundry. If he chooses to bring them up from Nether Forge and lay 'em out in the church tower, why they are e'en so much the nearer to the main road and you are saved a day's hauling. What a coil to make of a mere act of neighborly kindness, lad!'

" 'I fear I have requited him very scurvily,' says Sebastian, looking at his knuckles. 'But what of the demi-cannon? I could do with 'em well, but *they* are not in the King's Order.'

" 'Kindness–loving-kindness,' says Sir John. 'Questionless, in his zeal for the King and his love for you, John adds those two cannon as a gift. 'Tis plain as this coming daylight, ye stockfish!'

" 'So it is,' says Sebastian. 'Oh, Sir John, Sir John, why did you never use the sea? You are lost ashore.' And he looked on him with great love.

" 'I do my best in my station.' Sir John strokes his beard again and rolls forth his deep drumming Justice's voice thus:–'But–suffer me!–you two lads, on some midnight frolic into which I probe not, roystering around the taverns, surprise Master Collins at his'–he thinks a moment–'at his good deeds done by stealth. Ye surprise him, I say, cruelly.'

" 'Truth, Sir John. If you had seen him run!' says Sebastian.

" 'On this you ride breakneck to me with a tale of pirates, and wool-wains, and cow-hides, which, though it hath moved my mirth as a man, offendeth my reason as a magistrate. So I will e'en accompany you back to the tower with, perhaps, some few of my own people, and three to four wagons, and I'll be your warrant that Master John Collins will freely give you your guns and your demi-cannon, Master Sebastian.' He breaks into his proper voice–'I warned the old tod and his neighbors long ago that they'd come to trouble with their side-sellings and bye-dealings; but we cannot have half Sussex hanged for a little gun-running. Are ye content, lads?'

" 'I'd commit any treason for two demi-cannon,' said Sebastian, and rubs his hands.

" 'Ye have just compounded with rank treason-felony for the same bribe,' says Sir John. 'Wherefore to horse, and get the guns.' "

"But Master Collins meant the guns for Sir Andrew Barton all along, didn't he?" said Dan.

"Questionless, that he did," said Hal. "But he lost them. We poured into the village on the red edge of dawn, Sir John horsed, in half-armor, his pennon flying; behind him thirty stout Brightling knaves, five abreast; behind them four wool-wains, and behind them four trumpets to triumph over the jest, blowing: *Our King went forth to Normandie.* When we halted and rolled the ringing guns out of the tower, 'twas for all the world like Friar Roger's picture of the French siege in the Queen's Missal-book."

"And what did we—I mean, what did our village do?" said Dan.

"Oh! Bore it nobly—nobly," cried Hal. "Though they had tricked me, I was proud of us. They came out of their housen, looked at that little army as though it had been a post, and went their shut-mouthed way. Never a sign! Never a word! They'd ha' perished sooner than let Brightling overcrow us. Even that villain, Ticehurst Will, coming out of the Bell for his morning ale, he all but ran under Sir John's horse.

" 'Ware, Sirrah Devil!' cries Sir John, reining back.

" 'Oh!' says Will. 'Market day, is it! And all the bullocks from Brightling here?'

"I spared him his belting for that—the brazen knave!

"But John Collins was our masterpiece! He happened along-street (his jaw tied up where Sebastian had clouted him) when we were trundling the first demi-cannon through the lych-gate.

" 'I reckon you'll find her middlin' heavy,' he says. 'If you've a mind to pay, I'll loan ye my timber-tug. She won't lie easy on ary wool-wain.'

"That was the one time I ever saw Sebastian taken flat aback. He opened and shut his mouth, fishy-like.

" 'No offense,' says Master John. 'You've got her reasonable good cheap. I thought ye might not grudge me a groat if I help move her.' Ah, he was a masterpiece! They say that morning's work cost our John two hundred pounds, and he never winked an eyelid, not even when he saw the guns all carted off to Lewes."

"Neither then nor later?" said Puck.

"Once. 'Twas after he gave St. Barnabas the new chime of bells. (Oh, there was nothing the Collinses, or the Hayes, or the Fowles, or the Fanners would not do for the church then! 'Ask and have' was their song.) We had rung 'em in, and he was in the tower with Black Nick Fowle, that gave us our rood-screen. The old man pinches the bell-rope one hand and scratches his neck with t'other. 'Sooner she was pulling yon clapper than my neck,' he says. That was all! That was Sussex—seely Sussex for everlastin'!"

"And what happened after?" said Una.

"I went back into England," said Hal slowly. "I'd had my lesson against pride. But they tell me I left St. Barnabas's a jewel—justabout a jewel! Wel-a-well! 'Twas done for and among my own people, and—Father Roger was right—I never knew such trouble or such triumph since. That's the nature o' things. A dear—dear land." He dropped his chin on his chest.

"There's your Father at the Forge. What's he talking to old Hobden about?" said Puck, opening his hand with three leaves in it.

Dan looked towards the cottage.

"Oh, I know. It's that old oak lying across the brook. Pater always wants it grubbed."

In the still valley they could hear old Hobden's deep tones.

"Have it as you've a mind to," he was saying. "But the vivers of her roots they hold the bank together. If you grub her out, the bank she'll all come tearin' down, an' next floods the brook'll swarve up. But have it *as* you've a mind. The mistuss she sets a heap by the ferns on her trunk."

"Oh! I'll think it over," said the Pater.

Una laughed a little bubbling chuckle.

"What Devil's in *that* belfry?" said Hal, with a lazy laugh. "That should be Hobden by his voice."

"Why, the oak is the regular bridge for all the rabbits between the Three Acre and our meadow. The best place for wires on the farm, Hobden says. He's got two there now," Una answered. "*He* won't ever let it be grubbed!"

"Ah, Sussex! Silly Sussex for everlastin'," murmured Hal; and the next moment their Father's voice calling across to Little Lindens broke the spell as St. Barnabas's clock struck five.

Smugglers' Song

If you wake at midnight, and hear a horse's feet,
Don't go drawing back the blind, or looking in the street,
Them that asks no questions isn't told a lie.
Watch the wall, my darling, while the Gentlemen go by!

Five and twenty ponies
Trotting through the dark;
Brandy for the Parson,
'Baccy for the Clerk
Laces for a lady, letters for a spy,

And watch the wall, my darling, while the Gentlemen go by!

Running round the woodlump if you chance to find
Little barrels, roped and tarred, all full of brandy-wine;
Don't you shout to come and look, nor take 'em for your play;
Put the brishwood back again,—and they'll be gone next day!

If you see the stableyard setting open wide;
If you see a tired horse lying down inside;
If your mother mends a coat cut about and tore;
If the lining's wet and warm—don't you ask no more!

If you meet King George's men, dressed in blue and red,
You be careful what you say, and mindful what is said.
If they call you "pretty maid," and chuck you 'neath the chin,
Don't you tell where no one is, nor yet where no one's been!

Knocks and footsteps round the house—whistles after dark—
You've no call for running out till the house-dogs bark.
Trusty's *here, and* Pincher's *here, and see how dumb they lie—*
They *don't fret to follow when the Gentlemen go by!*

If you do as you've been told, likely there's a chance,
You'll be give a dainty doll, all the way from France,
With a cap of Valenciennes, and a velvet hood—
A present from the Gentlemen, along o' being good!

Five and twenty ponies,
Trotting through the Park—
Brandy for the Parson,
'Baccy for the Clerk.

Them that asks no questions isn't told a lie.
Watch the wall, my darling, while the Gentlemen go by!

"Dymchurch Flit"

The Bee Boy's Song

Bees! Bees! Hark to the Bees!
"Hide from your neighbors as much as you please,
But all that has happened to *us* you must tell!
Or else we will give you no honey to sell."

A maiden in her glory,
Upon her wedding-day,
Must tell her Bees the story,
Or else they'll fly away.
Fly away–die away–
Dwindle down and leave you!
But if you don't deceive your Bees,
Your Bees will not deceive you!–

Marriage, birth or buryin',
News across the seas,
All you're sad or merry in,
You must tell the Bees.
Tell 'em coming in an' out,
Where the Fanners fan,
'Cause the Bees are justabout
As curious as a man!

Don't you wait where trees are,
When the lightnings play;
Nor don't you hate where Bees are,
Or else they'll pine away.
Pine away–dwine away–
Anything to leave you!
But if you never grieve your Bees,
Your Bees'll never grieve you.

JUST AT DUSK, a soft September rain began to fall on the hop-pickers. The mothers wheeled the bouncing perambulators out of the gardens; bins were put away, and tally-books made up. The young couples strolled home, two to each umbrella, and the single men walked behind them laughing. Dan and Una, who had been picking after their lessons, marched off to roast potatoes at the oast-house, where old Hobden, with Blue-eyed Bess, his lurcher-dog, lived all the month through, drying the hops.

They settled themselves, as usual, on the sack-strewn cot in front of the fires, and, when Hobden drew up the shutter, stared, as usual, at the flameless bed of coals spouting its heat up the dark well of the old-fashioned roundel. Slowly he cracked off a few fresh pieces of coal, packed them, with fingers that never flinched, exactly where they would do most good; slowly he reached behind him till Dan tilted the potatoes into his iron scoop of a hand;

carefully he arranged them round the fire, and then stood for a moment, black against the glare. As he closed the shutter, the oast-house seemed dark before the day's end, and he lit the candle in the lanthorn. The children liked all these things because they knew them so well.

The Bee Boy, Hobden's son, who is not quite right in his head, though he can do anything with bees, slipped in like a shadow. They only guessed it when Bess's stump-tail wagged against them.

A big voice began singing outside in the drizzle:–

"Old Mother Laidinwool had nigh twelve months been dead,
She heard the hops were doing well, and then popped up her head."

"There can't be two people made to holler like that!" cried old Hobden, wheeling round.

"For, says she, 'The boys I've picked with when I was young and fair,
They're bound to be at hoppin', and I'm—' "

A man showed at the doorway.

"Well, well! They do say hoppin'll draw the very deadest; and now I belieft 'em. You, Tom? Tom Shoesmith!" Hobden lowered his lanthorn.

"You're a hem of a time makin' your mind to it, Ralph!" The stranger strode in–three full inches taller than Hobden, a gray-whiskered, brown-faced giant with clear blue eyes. They shook hands, and the children could hear the hard palms rasp together.

"You ain't lost none o' your grip," said Hobden. "Was it thirty or forty year back you broke my head at Peasmarsh Fair?"

"Only thirty, an' no odds 'tween us regardin' heads, neither. You had it back at me with a hop-pole. How did we get home that night? Swimmin'?"

"Same way the pheasant come into Gubbs's pocket–by a little luck an' a deal o' conjurin." Old Hobden laughed in his deep chest.

"I see you've not forgot your way about the woods. D'ye do any o' *this* still?" The stranger pretended to look along a gun.

Hobden answered with a quick movement of the hand as though he were pegging down a rabbit-wire.

"No. *That's* all that's left me now. Age she must as Age she can. An' what's your news since all these years?"

"Oh, I've bin to Plymouth, I've bin to Dover–
I've bin ramblin', boys, the wide world over,"

the man answered cheerily. "I reckon I know as much of Old England as most." He turned towards the children and winked boldly.

"I lay they told you a sight o' lies, then I've been into England fur as Wiltsheer once. I was cheated proper over a pair of hedging-gloves," said Hobden.

"There's fancy-talkin' everywhere. *You've* cleaved to your own parts pretty middlin' close, Ralph."

"Can't shift an old tree 'thout it dyin'," Hobden chuckled. "An' I be no more anxious to die than you look to be to help me with my hops to-night."

The great man leaned against the brick-work of the roundel, and swung his arms abroad. "Hire me!" was all he said, and they stumped upstairs laughing.

The children heard their shovels rasp on the cloth where the yellow hops lie drying above the fires, and all the oast-house filled with the sweet, sleepy smell as they were turned.

"Who is it?" Una whispered to the Bee Boy.

"Dunno, no more'n you–if *you* dunno," said he, and smiled.

The voices on the drying-floor talked and chuckled together, and the heavy footsteps went back and forth. Presently a hop-pocket dropped through the press-hole overhead, and stiffened and fattened as they shovelled it full. "Clank!" went the press, and rammed the loose stuff into tight cake.

"Gently!" they heard Hobden cry. "You'll bust her crop if you lay on so. You be as careless as Gleason's bull, Tom. Come an' sit by the fires. She'll do now."

They came down, and as Hobden opened the shutter to see if the potatoes were done Tom Shoesmith said to the children, "Put a plenty salt on 'em. That'll show you the sort o' man *I* be." Again he winked, and again the Bee Boy laughed and Una stared at Dan.

"*I* know what sort o' man you be," old Hobden grunted, groping for the potatoes round the fire.

"Do ye?" Tom went on behind his back. "Some of us can't abide Horseshoes, or Church Bells, or Running Water; an', talkin' o' runnin' water"–he turned to Hobden, who was backing out of the roundel–"d'you mind the great floods at Robertsbridge, when the miller's man was drowned in the street?"

"Middlin' well." Old Hobden let himself down on the coals by the fire door. "I was courtin' my woman on the Marsh that year. Carter to Mus' Plum I was–gettin' ten shillin's week. Mine was a Marsh woman."

"Won'erful odd-gates place–Romney Marsh," said Tom Shoesmith. "I've heard say the world's divided like into Europe, Ashy, Afriky, Ameriky, Australy, an' Romney Marsh."

"The Marsh folk think so," said Hobden. "I had a hem o' trouble to get my woman to leave it."

"Where did she come out of? I've forgot, Ralph."

Dymchurch under the Wall," Hobden answered, a potato in his hand.

"Then she'd be a Pett–or a Whitgift, would she?"

"Whitgift." Hobden broke open the potato and ate it with the curious neatness of men who make most of their meals in the blowy open. "She growed to be quite reasonable-like after livin' in the Weald awhile, but our first twenty year or two she was odd-fashioned, no bounds. And she was a won'erful hand with bees." He cut away a little piece of potato and threw it out to the door.

"Ah! I've heard say the Whitgifts could see further through a millstone than most," said Shoesmith. "Did she, now?"

"She was honest-innocent of any nigromancin'," said Hobden. "Only she'd read signs and sinnifications out o' birds flyin', stars fallin', bees hivin', and such. An' she'd lie awake–listenin' for calls, she said."

"That don't prove naught," said Tom. "All Marsh folk has been smugglers since time everlastin'. 'Twould be in her blood to listen out o' nights."

"Nature-ally,' old Hobden replied, smiling. "I mind when there was smugglin' a sight nearer us than the Marsh be. But that wasn't my woman's trouble. 'Twas a passel o' no-sense talk," he dropped his voice, "about Pharisees."

"Yes. I've heard Marsh men beleft in 'em." Tom looked straight at the wide-eyed children beside Bess.

"Pharisees," cried Una. "Fairies? Oh, I see!"

"People o' the Hills," said the Bee Boy, throwing half of his potato towards the door.

"There you be!" said Hobden, pointing at him. "My boy, he has her eyes and her outgate senses. That's what *she* called 'em!"

"And what did you think of it all?"

"Um–um," Hobden rumbled. "A man that uses fields an' shaws after dark as much as I've done, he don't go out of his road excep' for keepers."

"But settin' that aside?" said Tom, coaxingly. "I saw ye throw the Good

Piece out-at doors just now. Do ye believe or–*do* ye?"

"There was a great black eye to that tater," said Hobden, indignantly.

"My liddle eye didn't see un, then. It looked as if you meant it for–for Any One that might need it. But settin' that aside. D'ye believe or–*do* ye?"

"I ain't sayin' nothin', because I've heard naught, an' I've seen naught. But if you was to say there was more things after dark in the shaws than men, or fur, or feather, or fin, I dunno as I'd go farabout to call you a liar. Now turn again, Tom. What's your say?"

"I'm like you. I say nothin'. But I'll tell you a tale, an' you can fit it *as* how you please."

"Passel o' no-sense stuff," growled Hobden, but he filled his pipe.

"The Marsh men they call it Dymchurch Flit," Tom went on slowly. "Hap you've heard it?"

"My woman she've told it me scores o' times. Dunno as I didn't end by belieft in' it–sometimes."

Hobden crossed over as he spoke, and sucked with his pipe at the yellow lanthorn-flame. Tom rested one great elbow on one great knee, where he sat among the coal.

"Have you ever bin in the Marsh?" he said to Dan.

"Only as far as Rye, once," Dan answered.

"Ah, that's but the edge. Back behind of her there's steeples settin' beside churches, an' wise women settin' beside their doors, an' the sea settin' above the land, an' ducks herdin' wild in the diks" (he meant ditches). "The Marsh is justabout riddled with diks an' sluices, an' tide-gates an' water-lets. You can hear em' bubblin' an' grummelin' when the tide works in em', an' then you hear the sea rangin' left and right-handed all up along the Wall. You've seen how flat she is–the Marsh? You'd think nothin' easier than to walk eend-on acrost her? Ah, but the diks an' the water-lets, they twists the roads about as ravelly as witch-yarn on the spindles. So ye get all turned round in broad daylight."

"That's because they've dreened the waters into the diks,' said Hobden. "When I courted my woman the rushes was green–Eh me! the rushes was green–an' the Bailiff o' the Marshes, he rode up and down as free as the fog."

"Who was he?" said Dan.

"Why, the Marsh fever an' ague. He've clapped me on the shouder once or twice till I shook proper. But now the dreenin' off of the waters have done away with the fevers; so they make a joke, like, that the Bailiff o' the Marshes broke his neck in a dik. A won'erful place for bees an' ducks 'tis too."

"An' old!" Tom went on. "Flesh an' Blood have been there since Time Everlastin' Beyond. Well, now, speakin' among themselves, the Marshmen say that from Time Everlastin' beyond the Pharisees favored the Marsh above the rest of Old England. I lay the Marshmen ought to know. They've been out after dark, father an' son, smugglin' some one thing or t'other, since ever wool grew to sheep's backs. They say there was always a middlin' few Pharisees to be seen on the Marsh. Impident as rabbits, they was. They'd dance on the nakid roads in the nakid daytime; they'd flash their liddle green lights along the diks, comin' an' goin', like honest smugglers. Yes, an' times they'd lock the church doors against parson an' clerk of Sundays!"

"That 'ud be smugglers layin' in the lace or the brandy till they could run it out o' the Marsh. I've told my woman so," said Hobden.

"I'll lay she didn't beleft it, then–not if she was a Whitgift. A won'erful choice place for Pharisees, the Marsh, by all accounts, till Queen Bess's father he come in with his Reformatories."

"Would that be a Act o' Parliament like?" Hobden asked.

"Sure-ly! 'Can't do nothing in Old England without Act, Warrant, an' Summons. He got his Act allowed him, an', they say, Queen Bess's father he used the parish churches something shameful. Justabout tore the gizzards out of I dunnamany. Some folk in England they held with 'en; but some they saw it different, an' it eended in 'em takin' sides an' burnin' each other no bounds, accordin' which side was top, time bein'. That tarrified the Pharisees: for Goodwill among Flesh an' Blood is meat an' drink to 'em, an' ill-will is poison."

"Same as bees," said the Bee Boy. "Bees won't stay by a house where there's hating."

"True," said Tom. "This Reformations tarrified the Pharisees same as the reaper goin' round a last stand o' wheat tarrifies rabbits. They packed into the Marsh from all parts, and they says, 'Fair or foul, we must flit out o' this, for Merry England's done with, an' we're reckoned among the Images.' "

"Did they *all* see it that way?" said Hobden.

"All but one that was called Robin—if you've heard of him. What are you laughing at?" Tom turned to Dan. "The Pharisees's trouble didn't tech Robin, because he'd cleaved middlin' close to people like. No more he never meant to go out of Old England—not he; so he was sent messagin' for help among Flesh an' Blood. But Flesh an' Blood must always think of their own concerns, an' Robin couldn't get *through* at 'em, ye see. They thought it was tide-echoes off the Marsh."

"What did you—what did the fai—Pharisees want?" Una asked.

"A boat to be sure. Their liddle wings could no more cross Channel than so many tired butterflies. A boat an' a crew they desired to sail 'em over to France, where yet awhile folks hadn't tore down the Images. They couldn't abide cruel Canterbury Bells ringin' to Bulverhithe for more pore men an' women to be burnded, nor the King's proud messenger ridin' through the land givin' orders to tear down the Images. They couldn't abide it no shape. Nor yet they couldn't get their boat an' crew to flit by without Leave an' Good-will from Flesh an' Blood; an' Flesh an' Blood came an' went about its own business the while the Marsh was swarvin' up, an' swarvin' up with Pharisees from all England over, striving all means to get *through* at Flesh an' Blood to tell 'en their sore need. . . . I don't know as you've ever heard say Pharisees are like chickens?"

"My woman used to say that too," said Hobden, folding his brown arms.

"They be. You run too many chickens together, an' the ground sickens like, an' you get a squat, an' your chickens die. 'Same way, you crowd Pharisees all in one place—*they* don't die, but Flesh an' Blood walkin' among 'em is apt to sick up an' pine off. *They* don't mean it, an' Flesh an' Blood don't know it, but that's the truth—as I've heard. The Pharisees through bein' all stenched up an' frighted, an' tryin' to come *through* with their supplications, they nature-ally changed the thin airs and humours in Flesh an' Blood. It lay on the Marsh like thunder. Men saw their churches ablaze with the wildfire in the windows after dark; they saw their cattle scatterin' and no man scarin'; their sheep flockin' and no man drivin'; their horses latherin' an' no man leadin'; they saw the liddle low green lights more than ever in the dik-sides; they heard the liddle feet patterin' more than ever round the houses; an' night an' day, day an' night, 'twas all as though they were bein' creeped up on, and hinted at by some One or Other that couldn't rightly shape their trouble. Oh, I lay they sweated! Man an' maid, woman an' child, their Nature done 'em no service all the weeks while the Marsh was swarvin' up with Pharisees. But they was Flesh an' Blood, an' Marsh men before all. They reckoned the signs sinnified trouble for the Marsh. Or that the sea 'ud rear up against Dymchurch Wall an' they'd be drownded like Old Winchelsea; or that the Plague was comin'. So they looked for the meanin' in the sea or in the clouds—far an' high up. They never thought to look near an' knee-high, where they could see naught.

"Now there was a poor widow at Dymchurch under the Wall, which, lacking man or property, she had the more time for feeling; and she come to feel there was a Trouble outside her doorstep bigger an' heavier than aught she'd ever carried over it. She had two sons–one born blind, and t'other struck dumb through fallin' off the Wall when he was liddle. They was men grown, but not wage-earnin' Questions."

"What sort of questions?" said Dan.

"Like where lost things might be found, an' what to put about a crooked baby's neck, an' how to join parted sweethearts. She felt the Trouble on the Marsh same as eels feel thunder. She was a wise woman."

"My woman was won'erful weather-tender, too," said Hobden. "I've seen her brish sparks like off an anvil out of her hair in thunderstorms. But she never laid out to answer Questions."

"This woman was a Seeker like, an' Seekers they sometimes find. One night, while she lay abed, hot an' aching, there come a Dream an tapped at her window, and 'Widow Whitgift,' it said, 'Widow Whitgift!'

"First, by the wings an' the whistling, she thought it was peewits, but last she arose an' dressed herself, an' opened her door to the Marsh, an' she felt the Trouble an' the Groaning all about her, strong as fever an' ague, an' she calls: 'What is it? Oh, what is it?'

"Then 'twas all like the frogs in the diks peeping: then 'twas all like the reeds in the diks clipclapping; an' then the great Tidewave rummelled along the Wall, an' she couldn't hear proper.

"Three times she called, an' three times the Tide-wave did her down. But she catched the quiet between, an' she cries out, 'What is the Trouble on the Marsh that's been lying down with my heart an' arising with my body this month gone?' She felt a liddle hand lay hold on her gown-hem, an' she stooped to the pull o' that liddle hand."

Tom Shoesmith spread his huge fist before the fire and smiled at it.

" 'Will the sea drown the Marsh?' she says. She was a Marsh-woman first an' foremost.

" 'No,' says the liddle voice. 'Sleep sound for all o' that.'

" 'Is the Plague comin' to the Marsh?' she says. Them was all the ills she knowed.

" 'No. Sleep sound for all o' that,' says Robin.

"She turned about, half mindful to go in, but the liddle voices grieved that shrill an' sorrowful she turns back, an' she cries 'If it is not a Trouble of Flesh an' Blood, what can I do?'

"The Pharisees cried out upon her from all round to fetch them a boat to sail to France, an' come back no more.

" 'There's a boat on the Wall,' she says, 'but I can't push it down to the sea, nor sail it when 'tis there.'

" 'Lend us your sons,' says all the Pharisees. 'Give 'em Leave an' Good-will to sail it for us, Mother–O Mother!'

" 'One's dumb, an' t'other's blind,' she says. 'But all the dearer me for that; and you'll lose them in the big sea.' The voices justabout pierced through her. An' there was children's voices too. She stood out all she could, but she couldn't rightly stand against *that.* So she says: 'If you can draw my sons for your job, i'll not hinder 'em. You can't ask no more of a Mother.'

"She saw them liddle green lights dance an' cross till she was dizzy; she heard them liddle feet patterin' by the thousand; she heard cruel Canterbury Bells ringing to Bulverhithe, an' she heard the great Tide-wave ranging along the Wall. That was while the Pharisees was workin' a Dream to wake her two sons asleep: an' while she bit on her fingers she saw them two she'd bore come out an' pass her with never a word. She followed 'em, cryin' pitiful, to the old boat on the Wall, an' that they took an' runned down to the Sea.

"When they'd stepped mast an' sail the blind son speaks up: 'Mother, we're waitin' your Leave an' Good-will to take Them over.' "

Tom Shoesmith threw back his head and half shut his eyes.

"Eh, me!" he said. "She was a fine, valiant woman, the Widow Whitgift. She stood twistin' the ends of her long hair over her fingers, an' she shook like a poplar, makin' up her mind. The Pharisees all about they hushed their children from cryin' an' they waited dumb-still. She was all their dependence. 'Thout her Leave an' Goodwill they could not pass; for she was the Mother. So she shook like a asp-tree makin' up her mind. 'Last she drives the word past her teeth, an' 'Go!' she says. 'Go with my Leave an' Goodwill.'

"Then I saw–then, they say, she had to brace back same as if she was wadin' in tidewater; for the Pharisees justabout flowed past her–down the beach to the boat, *I* dunnamany of 'em–with their wives an' children an' valooables, all escapin' out of cruel Old England. Silver you could hear clinkin', an' liddle bundles hove down dunt on the bottom-boards, an' passels o' liddle swords an' shield's raklin', an' liddle fingers an' toes scratchin' on the boatside to board her when the two sons pushed her off. That boat she sunk lower an' lower, but all the Widow could see in it was her boys movin' hampered-like to get at the tackle. Up sail they did, an' away they went, deep as a Rye barge, away into the off-shore mistes, an' the Widow Whitgift she sat down and eased her grief till mornin' light."

"I never heard she was *all* alone," said Hobden.

I remember now. The one called Robin he stayed with her, they tell. She was all too grievious to listen to his promises."

"Ah! She should ha' made her bargain beforehand. I allus told my woman so!" Hobden cried.

"No. She loaned her sons for a pure loveloan, bein' as she sensed the Trouble on the Marshes. an' was simple good-willing to ease it." Tom laughed softly. "She done that. Yes, she done that! From Hithe to Bulverthithe, fretty man an' petty maid, ailin' woman an' wailin' child, they took the advantage of the change in the thin airs just about *as* soon as the Pharisees flitted. Folks come out fresh an' shining all over the Marsh like snails after wet. An' that while the Widow Whitgift sat grievin' on the Wall. She might have beleft us–she might have trusted her sons would be sent back! She fussed, no bounds, when their boat come in after three days."

"And, of course, the sons were both quite cured?" said Una.

"No-o. That would have been out o' Nature. She got 'em back *as* she sent 'em. The blind man he hadn't seen naught of anything, an' the dumb man nature-ally, he couldn't say aught of what he'd seen. I reckon that was why the Pharisees pitched on 'em for the ferrying job."

"But what did you–what did Robin, promise the Widow?" said Dan.

"What *did* he promise, now?" Tom pretended to think. "Wasn't your woman a Whitgift, Ralph? Didn't she say?"

"She told me a passel o' no-sense stuff when he was born." Hobden pointed at his son. "There was always to be one of 'em that could see further into a millstone that most."

"Me! That's me!" said the Bee Boy so suddenly that they all laughed.

"I've got it now!" cried Tom, slapping his knee. "So long as Whitgift blood lasted, Robin promised there would allers be one o' her stock that–that no Trouble 'ud lie on, no Maid 'ud sigh on, no Night could frighten, no Fright could harm, no Harm could make sin, an' no Woman could make a fool."

"Well, ain't that just me?" said the Bee Boy, where he sat in the silver square of the great September moon that was staring into the oast-house door.

"They was the exact words she told me when we first found he wasn't like others. But it beats me how you know 'em," said Hobden.

"Aha! There's more under my hat besides hair!" Tom laughed and stretched himself. "When I've seen these two young folk home, we'll make a night of old days, Ralph, with passin' old tales–eh? An' where might you live?" he said, gravely, to Dan. "An' do you think your Pa 'ud give me a drink for takin' you there, Missy?"

They giggled so at this that they had to run out. Tom picked them both up, set one on each broad shoulder, and tramped across the ferny pasture where the cows puffed milky puffs at them in the moonlight.

"Oh, Puck! Puck! I guessed you right from when you talked about the salt. How could you ever do it?" Una cried, swinging along delighted.

"Do what?" he said, and climbed the stile by the pollard oak.

"Pretend to be Tom Shoesmith," said Dan, and they ducked to avoid the two little ashes that grow by the bridge over the brook. Tom was almost running.

"Yes. That's my name, Mus' Dan," he said, hurrying over the silent shining lawn, where a rabbit sat by the big white-thorn near the croquet ground. "Here you be." He strode into the old kitchen yard, and slid them down as Ellen came to ask questions.

"I'm helping in Mus' Spray's oast-house," he said to her. "No, I'm no foreigner. I knowed this country 'fore your Mother was born; an'—yes it's dry work oasting, Miss. Thank you."

Ellen went to get a jug, and the children went in—magicked once more by Oak, Ash, and Thorn!

A Three-Part Song

I'm just in love with all these three,
The Weald and the Marsh and the Down countrie
Nor I don't know which I love the most,
The Weald or the Marsh or the white chalk coast!

I've buried my heart in a ferny hill,
Twix' a liddle low Shaw an' a great high Gill.
Oh hop-vine yaller and woodsmoke blue,
I reckon you'll keep her middling true!

I've loosed my mind for to out and run,
On a Marsh that was old when Kings begun;
Oh Romney Level and Brenzett reeds,
I reckon you know what my mind needs!

I've given my soul to the Southdown grass,
And sheep-bells tinkled where you pass.
Oh Firle an' Ditchling an' sails at sea,
I reckon you'll keep my soul or me!

The Treasure and the Law

Song of the Fifth River

When first by Eden Tree,
The Four Great Rivers ran,
To each was appointed a Man
Her Prince and Ruler to be.

But after this was ordained,
(The ancient legends tell),
There came dark Israel,
For whom no River remained.

Then He That is Wholly Just,
Said to him: "Fling on the ground
A handful of yellow dust,
And a Fifth Great River shall run,
Mightier than these Four,
In secret the Earth around;
And Her secret evermore,
Shall be shown to thee and thy Race."

So it was said and done.
And, deep in the veins of Earth,
And, fed by a thousand springs
That comfort the market-place,
Or sap the power of Kings,
The Fifth Great River had birth,
Even as it was foretold—
The Secret River of Gold!

And Israel laid down
His sceptre and his crown,
To brood on that River bank,
Where the waters flashed and sank,
And burrowed in earth and fell,
And bided a season below;
For reason that none might know.
Save only Israel.

He is Lord of the Last—
The Fifth, most wonderful, Flood.
He hears her thunder past
And Her Song is in his blood.
He can foresay: "She will fall,"
For he knows which fountain dries,
Behind which desert belt

A thousand leagues to the South.
He can foresay: "She will rise."
He knows what for snows melt;
Along what mountain wall
A thousand leagues to the North.
He snuffs the coming drouth
As he snuffs the coming rain,
He knows what each will bring forth
And turns it to his gain.

A Prince without a Sword,
A Ruler without a Throne;
Israel follows his quest:–
In every land a guest.
Of many lands the lord.
In no land King is he.
But the Fifth Great River keeps
The secret of her deeps
For Israel alone,
As it was ordered to be.

NOW IT WAS the third week in November, and the woods rang with the noise of pheasant-shooting. No one hunted that steep, cramped country except the village beagles, who, as often as not, escaped from their kennels and made a day of their own. Dan and Una found a couple of them towling round the kitchen-garden after the laundry cat. The little brutes were only too pleased to go rabbiting, so the children ran them all along the brook pastures and into Little Lindens farm-yard, where the old sow vanquished them–and up to the quarry-hole, where they started a fox. He headed for Far Wood, and there they frightened out all the pheasants who were sheltering from a big beat across the valley. Then the cruel guns began again, and they grabbed the beagles lest they should stray and get hurt.

"I wouldn't be a pheasant–in November–for a lot," Dan panted, as he caught *Folly* by the neck. "Why did you laugh that horrid way?"

"I didn't," said Una, sitting on *Flora,* the fat lady-dog. "Oh, look! The silly birds are going back to their own woods instead of ours, where they would be safe."

"Safe till it pleased you to kill them." An old man, so tall he was almost a giant, stepped from behind the clump of hollies by "Volaterrae." The children jumped, and the dogs dropped like setters. He wore a sweeping gown of dark thick stuff, lined and edged with yellowish fur, and he bowed a bent-down bow that made them feel both proud and ashamed. Then he looked at them steadily, and they stared back without doubt or fear.

"You are not afraid?" he said, running his hands through his splendid gray beard. "Not afraid that those men yonder"–he jerked his head towards the incessant pop-pop of the guns from the lower woods–"will do you hurt?"

"We-ell"–Dan liked to be accurate, especially when he was shy–"old Hobd–a friend of mine told me that one of the beaters got peppered last week–hit in the leg, I mean. You see, Mr. Meyer *will* fire at rabbits. But he gave Waxy Garnett a quid–sovereign, I mean–and Waxy told Hobden he'd have stood both barrels for half the money."

"He doesn't understand," Una cried, watching the pale, troubled face. "Oh, I wish—"

She had scarcely said it when Puck rustled out of the hollies and spoke to the man quickly in foreign words. Puck wore a long cloak too–the afternoon was just frosting down–and it changed his appearance altogether.

"Nay, nay!" he said at last. "You did not understand the boy. A freeman was a little hurt, by pure mischance, at the hunting."

"I know that mischance! What did his Lord do? Laugh and ride over him?" the old man sneered.

"It was one of your own people did the hurt, Kadmiel." Puck's eyes twinkled maliciously. "So he gave the freeman a piece of gold, and no more was said."

"A Jew drew blood from a Christian and no more was said?" Kadmiel cried. "Never! When did they torture him?"

"No man may be bound, or fined, or slain till he has been judged by his peers," Puck insisted. "There is but one Law in Old England for Jew or Christian—the Law that was signed at Runnymede."

"Why, that's Magna Charta!" Dan whispered. It was one of the few history dates that he could remember. Kadmiel turned on him with a sweep and a whirr of his spicy-scented gown.

"Dost *thou* know of that, babe?" he cried, and lifted his hands in wonder.

"Yes," said Dan, firmly.

"Magna Charta was signed by John,
That Henry the Third put his heel upon.

And old Hobden says that if it hadn't been for her (he calls everything 'her,' you know), the keepers would have him clapped in Lewes Gaol all the year round."

Again Puck translated to Kadmiel in the strange, solemn-sounding language, and at last Kadmiel laughed.

"Out of the mouths of babes do we learn," said he. "But tell me now, and I will not call you a babe but a Rabbi, *why* did the King sign the roll of the New Law at Runnymede? For he was a King."

Dan looked sideways at his sister. It was her turn.

"Because he jolly well had to," said Una, softly. "The Barons made him."

"Nay," Kadmiel answered, shaking his head. "You Christians always forget that gold does more than the sword. Our good King signed because he could not borrow more money from us bad Jews," He curved his shoulders as he spoke. "A King without gold is a snake with a broken back, and"—his nose sneered up and his eyebrows frowned down—it is a good deed to break a snake's back. That was my work," he cried, triumphantly, to Puck. "Spirit of Earth, bear witness that that was *my* work!" He shot up to his full towering height, and his words rang like a trumpet. He had a voice that changed its tone almost as an opal changes color—sometimes deep and thundery, sometimes thin and waily, but always it made you listen.

"Many people can bear witness to that," Puck answered. "Tell these babes how it was done. Remember, Master, they do not know Doubt or Fear."

"So I saw in their faces when we met," said Kadmiel. "Yet surely, surely they are taught to spit upon Jews?"

"Are they?" said Dan, much interested. "Where at?"

Puck fell back a pace, laughing. Kadmiel is thinking of King John's reign," he explained. "His people were badly treated then."

"Oh, we know *that,*" they answered, and (it was very rude of them, but they could not help it) they stared straight at Kadmiel's mouth to see if his teeth were all there. It stuck in their lesson-memory that King John used to pull out Jews' teeth to make them lend him money.

Kadmiel understood the look and smiled bitterly.

"No. Your King never drew my teeth: I think, perhaps, I drew his. Listen! I was not born among Christians, but among Moors—in Spain—in a little white town under the mountains. Yes, the Moors are cruel, but at least their learned men dare to think. It was prophesied of me at my birth that I should be a Lawgiver to a People of a strange speech and a hard language. We Jews are always looking for the Prince and the Lawgiver to come. Why not? My people in the town (we were very few) set me apart as a child of the prophecy–the Chosen of the Chosen. We Jews dream so many dreams. You would never guess it to see us slink about the rubbish-heaps in our quarter; but at the day's end–doors shut, candles lit–aha! *then* we become the Chosen again."

He paced back and forth through the wood as he talked. The rattle of the shot-guns never ceased, and the dogs whimpered a little and lay flat on the leaves.

"I was a Prince. Yes! Think of a little Prince who had never known rough words in his own house handed over to shouting, bearded Rabbis, who pulled his ears and filliped his nose, all that he might learn–learn–learn to be King when his time came. Hé! Such a little Prince it was! One eye he kept on the stone-throwing Moorish boys, and the other it roved about the streets looking for his Kingdom. Yes, and he learned to cry softly when he was hunted up and down those streets. He learned to do all things without noise. He played beneath his father's table when the Great Candle was lit, and he listened as children listen to the talk of his father's friends above the table. They came across the mountains, from out of all the world; for my Prince's father was their councillor. They came from behind the armies of Sala-ud-Din: from Rome: from Venice: from England. They stole down our alley, they tapped secretly at our door, they took off their rags, they arrayed themselves, and they talked to my father at the wine. All over the world the heathen fought each other. They brought news of these wars, and while he played beneath the table, my Prince heard these meanly-dressed ones decide between themselves how, and when, and for how long King should draw sword against King, and People rise up against People. Why not? There can be no war without gold, and we Jews know how the earth's gold moves with the seasons, and the crops, and the winds; circling and looping and rising and sinking away like a river–a wonderful underground river. How should the foolish Kings know *that* while they fight and steal and kill?"

The children's faces showed that they knew nothing at all as, with open eyes, they trotted and turned beside the long-striding old man. He twitched his gown over his shoulders, and a square plate of gold, studded with jewels, gleamed for an instant through the fur, like a star through flying snow.

"No matter," he said. "But, credit me, my Prince saw peace or war decided not once, but many times, by the fall of a coin spun between a Jew from Bury and a Jewess from Alexandria, in his father's house, when the Great Candle was lit. Such power had we Jews among the Gentiles. Ah, my little Prince! Do you wonder that he learned quickly? Why not?" He muttered to himself and went on:–

"My trade was that of a physician. When I had learned it in Spain I went to the East to find my Kingdom. Why not? A Jew is as free as a sparrow–or a dog. He goes where he is hunted. In the East I found libraries where men dared to think–schools of medicine where they dared to learn. I was diligent in my business. Therefore I stood before Kings. I have been a brother to Princes and a companion to beggars, and I have walked between the living and the dead. There was no profit in it. I did not find my Kingdom. So, in the tenth year of my travels, when I had reached the Uttermost Eastern Sea, I returned to my father's house. God had wonderfully preserved my people. None had been slain, none even wounded, and only a few scourged. I became once more a son in my father's house. Again the Great Candle was lit; again the meanly-apparelled ones tapped on our door after dusk; and again I heard them weigh out peace and war, as they weighed out the gold on the table. But I was not rich–not very rich. Therefore, when those that had power and knowledge and wealth talked together, I sat in the shadow. Why not?

"Yet all my wanderings had shown me one sure thing, which is, that a King without money is like a spear without a head. He cannot do much harm. I said, therefore, to Elias of Bury, a great one among our people: 'Why do our people lend any more to the Kings that oppress us?' 'Because,' said Elias, 'if we refuse they stir up their people against us, and the People are tenfold more cruel than Kings. If thou doubtest, come with me to Bury in England and live as I live.'

"I saw my mother's face across the candle-flame, and I said, 'I will come with thee to Bury. Maybe my Kingdom shall be there.'

"So I sailed with Elias to the darkness and the cruelty of Bury in England, where there are no learned men. How can a man be wise if he hate? At Bury I kept his accounts for Elias, and I saw men kill Jews there by the tower. No–none laid hands on Elias. He lent money to the King, and the King's favour was about him. A King will not take the life so long as there is any gold. This King–yes, John–oppressed his people bitterly because they would not give him money. Yet his land was a good land. If he had only given it rest he might have cropped it as a Christian crops his beard. But even *that* little he did not know; for God had deprived him of all understanding, and had multiplied pestilence, and famine, and despair upon the people. Therefore his people turned against us Jews, who are all people's dogs. Why not? Lastly the Barons and the people rose together against the King because of his cruelties. Nay–nay–the Barons did not love the people, but they saw that if the King eat up and destroyed the common people, he would presently destroy the Barons. They joined then, as cats and pigs will join to slay a snake. I kept the accounts, and I watched all these things, for I remembered the Prophecy.

"A great gathering of Barons (to most of whom we had lent money) came to Bury, and there, after much talk and a thousand runnings-about, they made a roll of the New Laws that they would force on the King. If he swore to keep those Laws, they would allow him a little money. That was the King's God–Money–to waste. They showed us the roll of the New Laws. Why not? We had lent them money. We knew all their counsels–we Jews shivering behind our doors in Bury." He threw out his hands suddenly. "We did not seek to be paid *all* in money. We sought Power–Power–Power! That is *our* God in our captivity. Power to use!

"I said to Elias: 'These New Laws are good. Lend no more money to the King: so long as he has money he will lie and slay the people.'

" 'Nay,' said Elias. 'I know this people. They are madly cruel. Better one King than a thousand butchers. I have lent a little money to the Barons, or they would torture us, but my most I will lend to the King. He hath promised me a place near him at Court, where my wife and I shall be safe.'

" 'But if the King be made to keep these New Laws,' I said, 'the land will have peace, and our trade will grow. If we lend he will fight again.'

" 'Who made thee a Lawgiver in England?' said Elias. 'I know this people. Let the dogs tear one another! I will lend the King ten thousand pieces of gold, and he can fight the Barons at his pleasure.'

" 'There are not two thousand pieces of gold in all England this summer,' I said, for I kept the accounts, and I knew how the earth's gold moved–that wonderful underground river! Elias barred home the windows, and, his hands about his mouth, he told me how, when he was trading with small wares in a French ship, he had come to the Castle of Pevensey."

"Oh!" said Dan. "Pevensey again!" and looked at Una, who nodded and skipped.

"There, after they had scattered his pack up and down the Great Hall, some young knights carried him to an upper room, and dropped him into a well in a wall, that rose and fell with the tide. They called him Joseph, and threw torches at his wet head. Why not?"

"Why, of course," cried Dan. "Didn't you know it was——" Puck held up his hand to stop him, and Kadmiel, who never noticed, went on.

"When the tide dropped he thought he stood on old armor, but feeling with his toes, he raked up bar on bar of soft gold. Some wicked treasure of the old days put away, and the secret cut off by the sword. I have heard the like before."

"So have we," Una whispered. "But it wasn't wicked a bit."

"Elias took a morsel of the stuff with him, and thrice yearly he would return to Pevensey as a chapman, selling at no price or profit, till they suffered him to sleep in the empty room, where he would plumb and grope, and steal away a few bars. The great store of it still remained, and by long brooding he had come to look on it as his own. Yet when we thought how we should lift and convey it, we saw no way. This was before the Word of the Lord had come to me. A walled fortress possessed by Normans; in the midst a forty-foot tide-well out of which to remove secretly many horse-loads of gold! Hopeless! So Elias wept. Adah, his wife, wept too. She had hoped to stand beside the Queen's Christian tiring-maids at Court, when the King should give them that place at Court which he had promised. Why not? She was born in England–an odious woman.

"The present evil to us was that Elias, out of his strong folly, had, as it were, promised the King that he would arm him with more gold. Wherefore the King in his camp stopped his ears against the Barons and the people. Wherefore men died daily. Adah so desired her place at Court, she besought Elias to tell the king where the treasure lay, that the King might take it by force, and–they would trust in his gratitude. Why not? This Elias refused to do, for he looked on the gold as he own. They quarrelled, and they wept at the evening meal, and late in the night came one Langton–a priest, almost learned–to borrow more money for the Barons. Elias and Adah went to their chamber."

Kadmiel laughed scornfully in his beard. The shots across the valley stopped as the shooting-party changed their ground for the last beat.

"So it was I, not Elias," he went on, quietly, "that made terms with Langton touching the fortieth of the New Laws."

"What terms?" said Puck, quickly. "The Fortieth of the Great Charter say: 'To none will we sell, refuse, or deny right or justice.'"

"True, but the Barons had written first: *To no free man.* It cost me two hundred broad pieces of gold to change those narrow words. Langton, the priest, understood. 'Jew though thou art,' said he, 'the change is just, and if ever Christian and Jew come to be equal in England thy people may thank thee.' Then he went out stealthily, as men do who deal with Israel by night. I think he spent my gift upon his altar. Why not? I have spoken with Langton. He was such a man as I might have been if–if we Jews had been a people. But yet, in many things, a child.

"I heard Elias and Adah abovestairs quarrel, and, knowing the woman was the stronger, I saw that Elias would tell the King of the gold and that the King would continue in his stubbornness. Therefore I saw that the gold must be put away from the reach of any man. Of a sudden, the Word of the Lord came to me saying, 'The Morning is come, O thou that dwellest in the land.'"

Kadmiel halted, all black against the pale green sky beyond the wood–a huge robed figure, like the Moses in the picture-Bible.

"I rose. I went out, and as I shut the door on that House of Foolishness, the woman looked from the window and whispered, 'I have prevailed on my husband to tell the King!' I answered, 'There is no need. The Lord is with me.'

"In that hour the Lord gave me full understanding of all that I must do; and His Hand covered me in my ways. First I went to London, to a physician of our people, who sold me certain drugs that I needed. You shall see why. Thence I went swiftly to Pevensey. Men fought all around me, for there were neither rulers nor judges in the abominable land. Yet when I walked by them they cried out that I was one Ahasuerus, a Jew, condemned, as they believe, to live for ever, and they fled from me everyways. Thus the Lord saved me for my work, and at Pevensey I bought me a little boat and moored it on the mud beneath the Marsh-gate of the Castle. That also God showed me."

He was as calm as though he were speaking of some stranger, and his voice filled the little bare wood with rolling music.

"I cast"–his hand went to his breast, and again the strange jewel gleamed–"I cast the drugs which I had prepared into the common well of the Castle. Nay, I did no harm. The more we physicians know, the less do we do. Only the fool says: 'I dare.' I caused a blotched and itching rash to break out upon their skins, but I knew it would fade in fifteen days. I did not stretch out my hand again their life. They in the Cstle thought it was the Plague, and they ran forth, taking with them their very dogs.

"A Christian physician, seeing that I was a Jew and a stranger, vowed that I had brought the sickness from London. This is the one time I have ever heard a Christian leech speak truth of any disease. Thereupon the people beat me, but a merciful woman said; 'Do not kill him now. Push him into our Castle with his plague, and if, as he says, it will abate on the fifteenth day, we can kill him then.' Why not? They drove me across the drawbridge of the Castle, and fled back to their booths. Thus I came to be alone with the treasure."

"But did you know this was all going to happen just right?" said Una.

"My Prophecy was that I should be a Lawgiver to a People of a strange land and a hard speech. I knew I should not die. I washed my cuts. I found the tide-well in the wall, and from Sabbath to Sabbath I dove and dug there in that empty, Christian-smelling fortress. Hé! I spoiled the Egyptians! Hé! If they had only known! I drew up many good loads of gold, which I loaded by night into my boat. There had been gold-dust too, but that had been washed away by the tides."

"Didn't you ever wonder who had put it there?" said Dan, stealing a glance at Puck's calm, dark face under the hood of his gown. Puck shook his head and pursed his lips.

"Often; for the gold was new to me," Kadmiel replied. "I know the Golds. I can judge them in the dark; but this was heavier and redder than any we deal in. Perhaps it was the very gold of Parvaim. Eh, why not? It went to my heart to heave it on to the mud, but I saw well that if the evil thing remained, or if even the hope of finding it remained, the King would not sign the New Laws, and the land would perish."

"Oh, Marvel!" said Puck, beneath his breath, rustling in the dead leaves.

"When the boat was loaded I washed my hands seven times, and pared beneath my nails, for I would not keep one grain. I went out by the little gate where the Castle's refuse is thrown. I dared not hoist sail lest men should see me; but the Lord commanded the tide to bear me carefully, and I was far from land before the morning."

"Weren't you afraid?" said Una.

"Why ? There were no Christians in the boat. At sunrise I made my prayer, and cast the gold–all–all that gold into the deep sea! A King's ransom–no, the ransom of a People! When I had loosed hold of the last bars, the Lord commanded the tide to return me to a haven at the mouth of a river, and thence I walked across a wilderness to Lewes, where I have brethren. They opened the door to me, and they say–I had not eaten for two days–they say that I fell across the threshold, crying, 'I have sunk an army with horsemen in the sea!' "

"But you hadn't," said Una. "Oh, yes! I see! You meant that King John might have spent it on that?"

"Even so," said Kadmiel.

The firing broke out again close behind them. The pheasants poured over the top of a belt of tall firs. They could see young Mr. Meyer, in his new yellow gaiters, very busy and excited at the end of the line, and they could hear the thud of the falling birds.

"But what did Elias of Bury do?" Puck demanded. "He had promised money to the King."

Kadmiel smiled grimly. "I sent him word from London that the Lord was on my side. When he heard that the Plague had broken out in Pevensey, and that a Jew had been thrust into the Castle to cure it, he understood my word was true. He and Adah hurried to Lewes and asked me for an accounting. He still looked on the gold as his own. I told them where I had laid it, and I gave them full leave to pick it up. . . . Eh, well! The curses of a fool and the dust of a journey are two things no wise man can escape. . . . But I pitied Elias! The King was wroth at him because he could not lend; the Barons were wroth at him because they heard that he would have lent to the King; and Adah was wroth at him because she was an odious woman. They took ship from Lewes to Spain. That was wise!"

"And you? Did you see the signing of the Law at Runnymede?" said Puck, as Kadmiel laughed noiselessly.

"Nay. Who am I to meddle with things too high for me? I returned to Bury, and lent money on the autumn crops. Why not?"

There was a crackle overhead. A cockpheasant that had sheered aside after being hit spattered down almost on top of them, driving up the dry leaves like a shell. *Flora* and *Folly* threw themselves at it; the children rushed forward, and when they had beaten them off and smoothed down the plumage Kadmiel had disappeared.

"Well," said Puck, calmly, "what did you think of it? Weland gave the Sword. The Sword gave the Treasure, and the Treasure gave the Law. It's as natural as an oak growing."

"I don't understand. Didn't he know it was Sir Richard's old treasure?" said Dan. "And why did Sir Richard and Brother Hugh leave it lying about? And–and—"

"Never mind," said Una, politely. "He'll let us come and go, and look, and know another time. Won't you, Puck?"

"Another time maybe," Puck answered. "Brr! It's cold–and late. I'll race you towards home!"

They hurried down into the sheltered valley. The sun had almost sunk behind Cherry Clack, the trodden ground by the cattle-gates was freezing at the edges, and the new-waked north wind blew the night on them from over the hills. They picked up their feet and flew across the browned pastures, and when they halted, panting in the steam of their own breath, the dead leaves whirled up behind them. There was Oak and Ash and Thorn enough in that year-end shower to magic away a thousand memories.

So they trotted to the brook at the bottom of the lawn, wondering why *Flora* and *Folly* had missed the quarry-hole fox.

Old Hobden was just finishing some hedge-work. They saw his white smock glimmer in the twilight where he faggoted the rubbish.

"Winter, he's come, I rackon, Mus' Dan," he called. "Hard times now till Heffle Cuckoo Fair. Yes, we'll all be glad to see the Old Woman let the Cuckoo out o' the basket for to start lawful Spring in England." They heard a crash, and a stamp and a splash of water as though a heavy old cow were crossing almost under their noses.

Hobden ran forward angrily to the ford.

"Gleason's bull again, playin' Robin all over the Farm! Oh, look, Mus' Dan–his great footmark as big as a trencher. No bounds to his impidence! He might count himself to be a man–or Somebody."

A voice the other side of the brook boomed:

I marvel who his cloak would turn
When Puck had led him round
Or where those walking fires would burne—"

Then the children went in singing "Farewell Rewards and Fairies" at the tops of their voices. They had forgotten that they had not even said good-night to Puck.

The Children's Song

Land of our Birth, we pledge to thee
Our love and toil in the years to be,
When we are grown and take our place,
As men and women with our race.

Father in Heaven who lovest all,
Oh help Thy children when they call;
That they may build from age to age,
And undefiled heritage!

Teach us to bear the yoke in youth,
With steadfastness and careful truth;
That, in our time, Thy Grace may give
The Truth whereby the Nations live.

Teach us to rule ourselves alway,
Controlled and cleanly night and day;
That we may bring, if need arise,
No maimed or worthless sacrifice.

Teach us to look in all our ends,
On Thee for judge, and not our friends;
That we, with Thee, may walk uncowed
By fear or favor of the crowd.

Teach us the Strength that cannot seek,
By deed or thought, to hurt the weak;
That, under Thee, we may possess
Man's strength to comfort man's distress.

Teach us Delight in simple things,
And Mirth that has no bitter springs;
Forgiveness free of evil done,
And Love to all men 'neath the sun!

Land of our Birth, our Faith our Pride,
For whose dear sake our fathers died;
O Motherland, we pledge to thee,
Head, heart, and hand through the years to be!

Captains Courageous

Chapter One

THE WEATHER DOOR of the smoking-room had been left open to the North Atlantic fog, as the big liner rolled and lifted, whistling to warn the fishing-fleet.

"That Cheyne boy's the biggest nuisance aboard," said a man in a frieze overcoat, shutting the door with a bang. "He isn't wanted here. He's too fresh."

A white-haired German reached for a sandwich, and grunted between bites: "I know der breed. Ameriga is full of dot kind. I dell you you should imbort ropes' ends free under your dariff."

"Pshaw! There isn't any real harm to him. He's more to be pitied than anything," a man from New York drawled, as he lay at full length along the cushions under the wet skylight. "They've dragged him around from hotel to hotel ever since he was a kid. I was talking to his mother this morning. She's a lovely lady, but she don't pretend to manage him. He's going to Europe to finish his education."

"Education isn't begun yet." This was a Philadelphian, curled up in a corner. "That boy gets two hundred a month pocket-money, he told me. He isn't sixteen either."

"Railroads, his father, aind't it?" said the German.

"Yep. That and mines and lumber and shipping. Built one place at San Diego, the old man has; another at Los Angeles; owns half a dozen railroads, half the lumber on the Pacific slope, and lets his wife spend the money," the Philadelphian went on lazily. "The West don't suit her, she says. She just tracks around with the boy and her nerves, trying to find out what'll amuse *him,* I guess. Florida, Adirondacks, Lakewood, Hot Springs, New York, and round again. He isn't much more than a second-hand hotel clerk now. When he's finished in Europe he'll be a holy terror."

"What's the matter with the old man attending to him personally?" said a voice from the frieze ulster.

"Old man's piling up the rocks. 'Don't want to be disturbed, I guess. He'll find out his error a few years from now. 'Pity, because there's a heap of good in the boy if you could get at it."

"Mit a rope's end; mit a rope's end!" growled the German.

Once more the door banged, and a slight, slim-built boy perhaps fifteen years old, a half-smoked cigarette hanging from one corner of his mouth, leaned in over the high footway. His pasty yellow complexion did not show well on a person of his years, and his look was a mixture of irresolution, bravado, and very cheap smartness. He was dressed in a cherry-colored blazer, knickerbockers, red stockings, and bicycle shoes, with a red flannel cap at the back of the head. After whistling between his teeth, as he eyed the company, he said in a loud, high voice: "Say, it's thick outside. You can hear the fish-boats squawking all around us. Say, wouldn't it be great if we ran down one?"

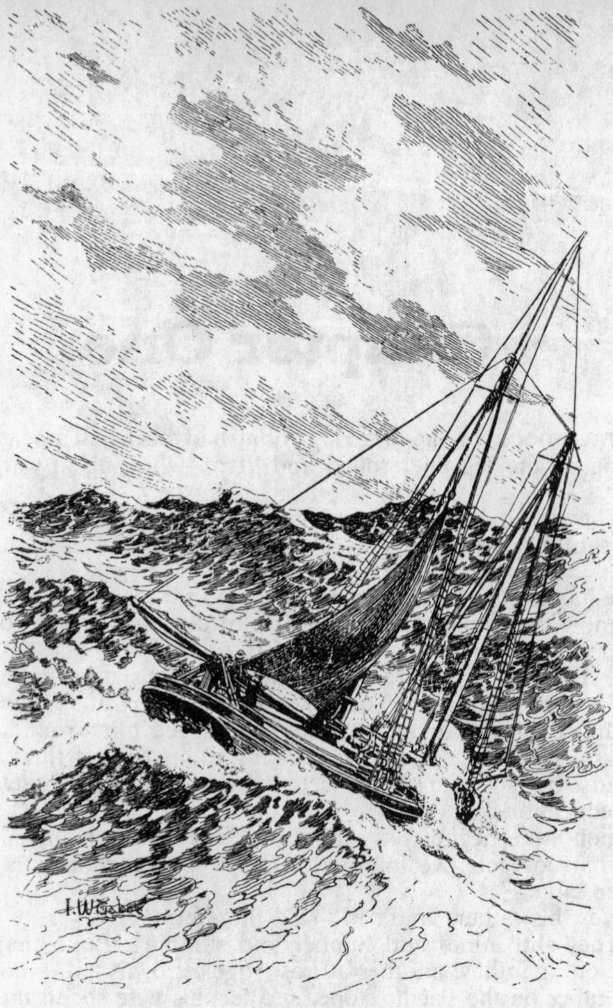

“IT WAS THICK WEATHER OUTSIDE, WITH A RISING WIND . . . .
THE NOSING BOWS SLAPPED AND SCUFFLED WITH THE SEAS.”

“Shut the door, Harvey,” said the New Yorker. “Shut the door and stay outside. You’re not wanted here.”

“Who’ll stop me?” he answered, deliberately. “Did *you* pay for my passage, Mister Martin? ’Guess I’ve as good right here as the next man.”

He picked up some dice from a checkerboard and began throwing, right hand against left.

“Say, gen’elmen, this is deader’n mud. Can’t we make a game of poker between us?”

There was no answer, and he puffed his cigarette, swung his legs, and drummed on the table with rather dirty fingers. Then he pulled out a roll of bills as if to count them.

“How’s your mama this afternoon?” a man said. “I didn’t see her at lunch.”

“In her state-room, I guess. She’s ’most always sick on the ocean. I’m going to give the stewardess fifteen dollars for looking after her. I don’t go down more ’n I can avoid. It makes me feel mysterious to pass that butler’s-pantry place. Say, this is the first time I’ve been on the ocean.”

"Oh, don't apologize, Harvey.

"Who's apologizing? This is the first time I've crossed the ocean, gen'elmen, and, except the first day, I haven't been sick one little bit, *No,* sir!" He brought down his fist with a triumphant bang, wetted his finger, and went on counting the bills.

"Oh, you're a high-grade machine, with the writing in plain sight," the Philadelphian yawned. "You'll blossom into a credit to your country if you don't take care."

"I know it. I'm an American—first, last, and all the time. I'll show 'em that when I strike Europe. Pff! My cig's out. I can't smoke the truck the steward sells. Any gen'elman got a real Turkish cig on him?"

The chief engineer entered for a moment, red, smiling, and wet. "Say, Mac," cried Harvey cheerfully, "how are we hitting it?"

"Vara much in the ordinary way," was the grave reply. "The young are as polite as ever to their elders, an' their elders are e'en tryin' to appreciate it."

A low chuckle came from a corner. The German opened his cigar-case and handed a shiny black cigar to Harvey.

"Dot is der broper apparatus to smoke, my young friendt," he said. "You vill dry it? Yes? Den you vill be efer so happy."

Harvey lit the unlovely thing with a flourish: he felt that he was getting on in grownup society.

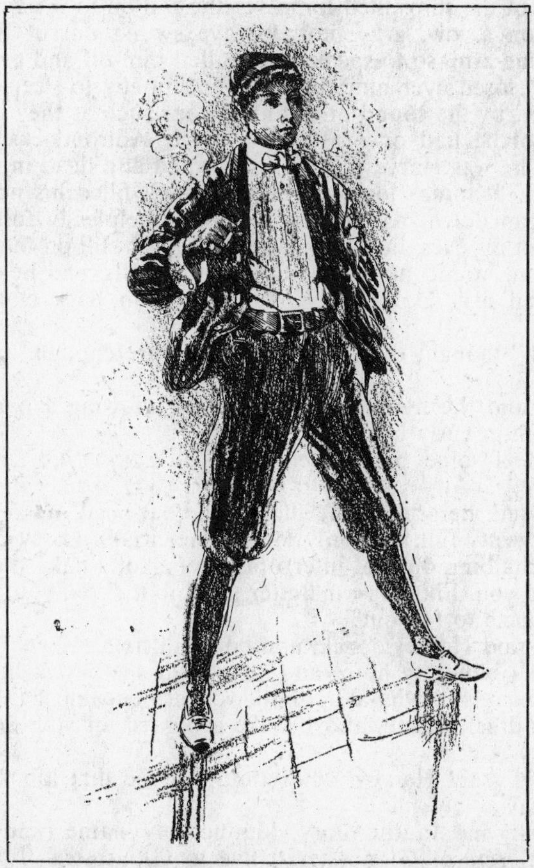

HARVEY.

"It would take more 'n this to keel me over," he said, ignorant that he was lighting that terrible article, a Wheeling "stogie."

"Dot we shall bresently see," said the German. "Where are we now, Mr. Mactonal'? "

"Just there or thereabouts, Mr. Schaefer," said the engineer. "We'll be on the Grand Bank to-night; but in a general way o' speakin', we're all among the fishing-fleet now. We've shaved three dories an' near skelped the boom off a Frenchman since noon, an' that's close sailin', ye may say."

"You like my cigar, eh?" the German asked, for Harvey's eyes were full of tears.

"Fine, full flavour," he answered through shut teeth. "Guess we've slowed down a little, haven't we? I'll skip out and see what the log says."

"I might if I vhas you," said the German.

Harvey staggered over the wet decks to the nearest rail. He was very unhappy; but he saw the deck-steward lashing chairs together, and, since he had boasted before the man that he was never seasick, his pride made him go aft to the second-saloon deck at the stern, which was finished in a turtle-back. The deck was deserted, and he crawled to the extreme end of it, near the flag-pole. There he doubled up in limp agony, for the Wheeling "stogie" joined with the surge and jar of the screw to sieve out his soul. His head swelled; sparks of fire danced before his eyes; his body seemed to lose weight, while his heels wavered in the breeze. He was fainting from seasickness, and a roll of the ship tilted him over the rail on to the smooth lip of the turtle-back. Then a low, gray mother-wave swung out of the fog, tucked Harvey under one arm, so to speak, and pulled him off and away to leeward; the great green closed over him, and he went quietly to sleep.

He was roused by the sound of a dinner-horn such as they used to blow at a summer-school he had once attended in the Adirondacks. Slowly he remembered that he was Harvey Cheyne, drowned and dead in mid-ocean, but was too weak to fit things together. A new smell filled his nostrils; wet and clammy chills ran down his back, and he was helplessly full of salt water. When he opened his eyes, he perceived that he was still on the top of the sea, for it was running round him in silver-coloured hills, and he was lying on a pile of half-dead fish, looking at a broad human back clothed in a blue jersey.

"It's no good," thought the boy. "I'm dead, sure enough, and this thing is in charge."

He groaned, and the figure turned its head, showing a pair of little gold rings half hidden in curly black hair.

"Aha! You feel some pretty well now?" it said. "Lie still so: we trim better."

With a swift jerk he sculled the flickering boat-head on to a foamless sea that lifted her twenty full feet, only to slide her into a glassy pit beyond. But this mountain-climbing did not interrupt blue-jersey's talk. "Fine good job, *I* say, that I catch you. Eh, wha-at? Better good job, *I* say, your boat not catch me. How you come to fall out?"

"I was sick," said Harvey; "sick, and couldn't help it."

"Just in time I blow my horn, and your boat she yaw a little. Then I see you come all down. Eh, wha-at? I think you are cut into baits by the screw, but you dreeft–dreeft to me, and I make a big fish of you. So you shall not die this time."

"Where am I?" said Harvey, who could not see that life was particularly safe where he lay.

"You are with me in the dory–Manuel my name, and I come from schooner *We're Here* of Gloucester. I live to Gloucester. By-and-by we get supper. Eh, wha-at?"

He seemed to have two pairs of hands and a head of cast-iron, for, not

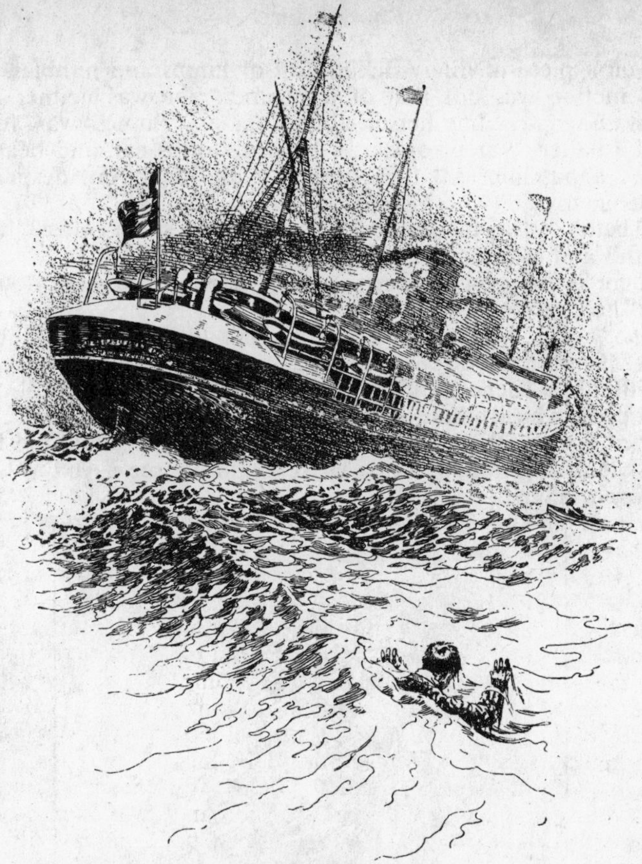

"THEN A LOW, GREY MOTHER-WAVE SWUNG OUT OF THE FOG,
TUCKED HARVEY UNDER ONE ARM, SO TO SPEAK,
AND PULLED HIM OFF AND AWAY TO LEEWARD."

content with blowing through a big conch-shell, he must needs stand up to it, swaying with the sway of the flat-bottomed dory, and send a grinding, thuttering shriek through the fog. How long this entertainment lasted, Harvey could not remember, for he lay back terrified at the sight of the smoking swells. He fancied he heard a gun and a horn and shouting. Something bigger than the dory, but quite as lively, loomed alongside. Several voices talked at once; he was dropped into a dark, heaving hole, where men in oilskins gave him a hot drink and took off his clothes, and he fell asleep.

When he waked he listened for the first breakfast-bell on the steamer, wondering why his state-room had grown so small. Turning, he looked into a narrow, triangular cave, lit by a lamp hung against a huge square beam. A three-cornered table within arm's reach ran from the angle of the bows to the foremast. At the after end, behind a well-used Plymouth stove, sat a boy about his own age, with a flat red face and a pair of twinkling gray eyes. He was dressed in a blue jersey and high rubber boots. Several pairs of the same sort of foot-wear, an old cap, and some worn-out woollen socks lay on the floor, and black and yellow oilskins swayed to and fro beside the bunks. The place was packed as full of smells as a bale is of cotton. The oilskins had a peculiarly thick flavor of their own which made a sort of background to the smells of fried fish, burnt grease, paint, pepper, and stale tobacco; but these, again, were all hooped together by one encircling smell of ship and salt water. Harvey saw with disgust that there were no sheets on his bed-place. He was lying on a piece of dingy ticking full of lumps and nubbles. Then, too, the boat's motion was not that of a steamer. She was neither sliding nor rolling, but rather wriggling herself about in a silly, aimless way, like a colt at the end of a halter. Water-noises ran by close to his ear, and beams creaked and whined about him. All these things made him grunt despairingly and think of his mother.

"Feelin' better?" said the boy, with a grin. "Hev some coffee?" He brought a tin cup full and sweetened it with molasses.

"Isn't there milk?" said Harvey, looking around the dark double tier of bunks as if he expected to find a cow there.

"Well, no," said the boy. "Ner there ain't likely to be till 'baout mid-September. 'Tain't bad coffee. I made it."

Harvey drank in silence, and the boy handed him a plate full of pieces of crisp fried pork, which he ate ravenously.

"I've dried your clothes. Guess they've shrunk some," said the boy. "They ain't our style much–none of 'em. Twist round an' see if you're hurt any."

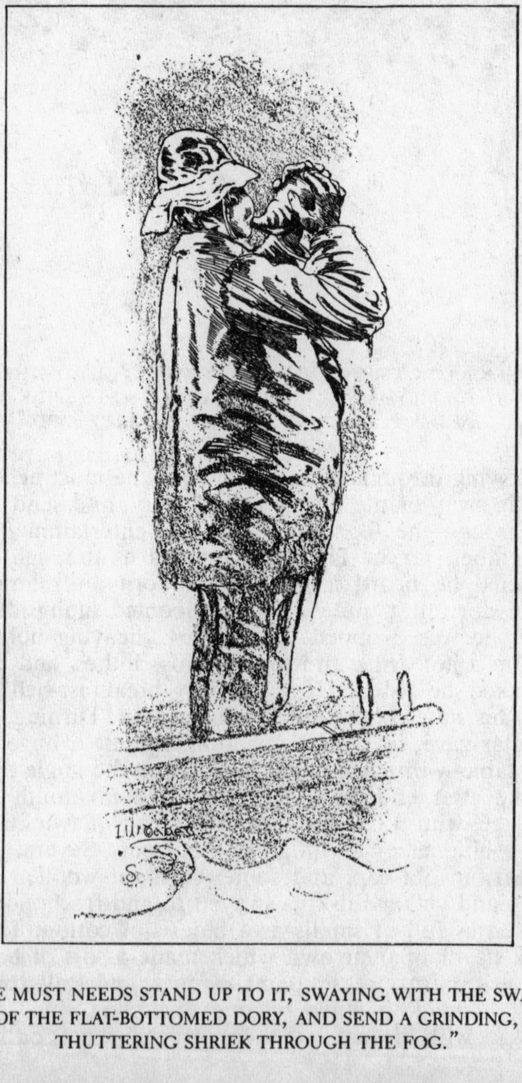

"HE MUST NEEDS STAND UP TO IT, SWAYING WITH THE SWAY OF THE FLAT-BOTTOMED DORY, AND SEND A GRINDING, THUTTERING SHRIEK THROUGH THE FOG."

Harvey stretched himself in every direction, but could not report any injuries.

"That's good," the boy said heartily. "Fix yerself an' go on deck. Dad wants to see you. I'm his son,—Dan, they call me,—an' I'm cook's helper an' everything else aboard that's too dirty for the men. There ain't no boy here 'cep' me sence Otto went overboard—an' he was only a Dutchy, an' twenty year old at that. How d'you come to fall off in a dead flat ca'am?"

" 'Twasn't a calm," said Harvey, sulkily. "It was a gale, and I was seasick. Guess I must have rolled over the rail."

"There was a little common swell yes'day an' last night," said the boy. "But ef thet's your notion of a gale—" He whistled. "You'll know more 'fore you're through. Hurry! Dad's waitin'."

Like many other unfortunate young people, Harvey had never in all his life received a direct order—never, at least, without long, and sometimes tearful, explanations of the advantages of obedience and the reasons for the request. Mrs. Cheyne lived in fear of breaking his spirit, which, perhaps, was the reason that she herself walked on the edge of nervous prostration. He could not see why he should be expected to hurry for any man's pleasure, and said so. "Your dad can come down here if he's so anxious to talk to me. I want him to take me to New York right away. I'll pay him."

Dan opened his eyes as the size and beauty of this joke dawned on him. "Say, Dad!" he shouted up the foc'sle hatch, "he says you kin slip down an' see him ef you're anxious that way. 'Hear, Dad?"

The answer came back in the deepest voice Harvey had ever heard from a human chest: "Quit foolin', Dan, and send him to me."

Dan sniggered, and threw Harvey his warped bicycle shoes. There was something in the tones on the deck that made the boy dissemble his extreme rage and console himself with the thought of gradually unfolding the tale of his own and his father's wealth on the voyage home. This rescue would certainly make him a hero among his friends for life. He hoisted himself on deck up a perpendicular ladder, and stumbled aft, over a score of obstructions, to where a small, thick-set, clean-shaven man with gray eyebrows sat on a step that led up to the quarterdeck. The swell had passed in the night, leaving a long, oily sea, dotted round the horizon with the sails of a dozen fishing-boats. Between them lay little black specks, showing where the dories were out fishing. The schooner, with a triangular riding-sail on the mainmast, played easily at anchor, and except for the man by the cabin-roof—"house" they call it—she was deserted.

"Mornin'—Good afternoon, I should say. You've nigh slep' the clock round, young feller," was the greeting.

"Mornin'," said Harvey. He did not like being called "young feller"; and, as one rescued from drowning, expected sympathy. His mother suffered agonies whenever he got his feet wet; but this mariner did not seem excited.

"Naow let's hear all about it. It's quite providential, first an' last, fer all concerned. What might be your name? Where from (we mistrust it's Noo York), an' where baound (we mistrust it's Europe)?"

Harvey gave his name, the name of the steamer, and a short history of the accident, winding up with a demand to be taken back immediately to New York, where his father would pay anything any one chose to name.

"H'm," said the shaven man, quite unmoved by the end of Harvey's speech. "I can't say we think special of any man, or boy even, that falls overboard from that kind o' packet in a flat ca'am. Least of all when his excuse is that he's seasick."

"Excuse!" cried Harvey. "D'you suppose I'd fall overboard into your dirty little boat for fun?"

"Not knowin' what your notions o' fun may be, I can't rightly say, young feller. But if I was *you,* I wouldn't call the boat which, under Providence, was

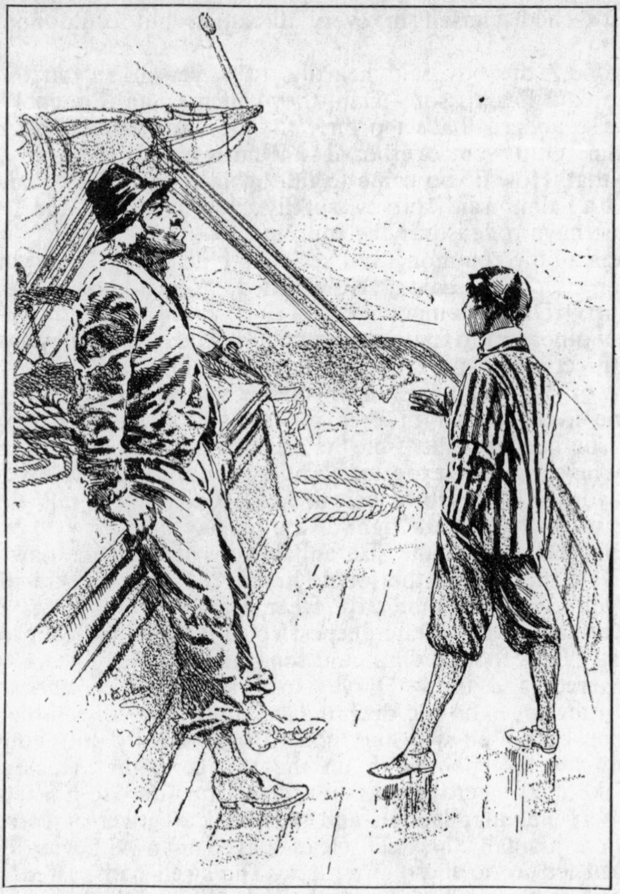

"'EXCUSE!' CRIED HARVEY. 'D' YOU SUPPOSE I'D FALL OVERBOARD INTO YOUR DIRTY LITTLE BOAT FOR FUN?'"

the means o' savin' ye, names. In the first place, it's blame irreligious. In the second, it's annoyin' to my feelin's—an' I'm Disko Troop o' the *We're Here* o' Gloucester, which you don't seem rightly to know."

"I don't know and I don't care," said Harvey. "I'm grateful enough for being saved and all that, of course! but I want you to understand that the sooner you take me back to New York the better it'll pay you."

"Meanin'—haow?" Troop raised one shaggy eyebrow over a suspiciously mild blue eye.

"Dollars and cents," said Harvey, delighted to think that he was making an impression. "Cold dollars and cents." He thrust a hand in his pocket, and threw out his stomach a little, which was his way of being grand. "You've done the best day's work you ever did in your life when you pulled me in. I'm all the son Harvey Cheyne has."

"He's bin favored," said Disko, dryly.

"And if you don't know who Harvey Cheyne is, you don't know much—that's all. Now turn her around and let's hurry."

Harvey had a notion that the greater part of America was filled with people discussing and envying his father's dollars.

"Mebbe I do, an' mebbe I don't. Take a reef in your stummick, young feller. It's full o' *my* vittles."

Harvey heard a chuckle from Dan, who was pretending to be busy by the stump-foremast, and blood rushed to his face. "We'll pay for that too," he said. "When do you suppose we shall get to New York?"

"I don't use Noo York any. Ner Boston. We may see Eastern Point about September; an' your pa—I'm real sorry I hain't heerd tell of him—may give me ten dollars efter all your talk. Then o' course he mayn't."

"Ten dollars! Why, see here, I—" Harvey dived into his pocket for the wad of bills. All he brought up was a soggy packet of cigarettes.

"Not lawful currency, an' bad for the lungs. Heave 'em overboard, young feller, and try agin."

"It's been stolen!" cried Harvey, hotly.

"You'll hev to wait till you see your pa to reward me, then?"

"A hundred and thirty-four dollars—all stolen," said Harvey, hunting wildly through his pockets. "Give them back."

A curious change flitted across old Troop's hard face. "What might *you* have been doin' at your time o' life with one hundred an' thirty-four dollars, young feller?"

"It was part of my pocket-money—for a month." This Harvey thought would be a knock-down blow, and it was—indirectly.

"Oh! One hundred and thirty-four dollars is only part of his pocket-money—for one month only! You don't remember hittin' anything when you fell over, do you? Crack agin a stanchion, le's say. Old man Hasken o' the *East Wind*"—Troop seemed to be talking to himself—"he tripped on a hatch an' butted the mainmast with his head—hardish. 'Baout three weeks afterwards, old man Hasken he would hev it that the *East Wind* was a commerce-destroyin' man-o'-war, an' so he declared war on Sable Island because it was Bridish, an' the shoals run aout too far. They sewed him up in a bed-bag, his head an' feet appearin', fer the rest o' the trip, an' now he's to home in Essex playin' with little rag dolls."

Harvey choked with rage, but Troop went on consolingly: "We're sorry fer you. We're very sorry fer you—an' so young. We won't say no more about the money, I guess."

"'Course you won't. You stole it."

"Suit yourself. We stole it ef it's any comfort to you. Naow, abaout goin' back. Allowin' we could do it, which we can't, you ain't in no fit state to go back to your home, an' *we've* jest come on to the Banks, workin' fer our bread. *We* don't see the ha'af of a hundred dollars a month, let alone pocket-money; an' with good luck we'll be ashore again somewheres abaout the first weeks o' September.

"But—but it's May now, and I can't stay here doin' nothing just because you want to fish. I *can't*, I tell you!"

"Right an' jest; *an'* right. No one asks you to do nothin'. There's a heap as you *can* do, for Otto he went overboard on Le Have. I mistrust he lost his grip in a gale we f'und there. Anyways, he never come back to deny it. *You've* turned up, plain plumb providential for all concerned. I mistrust, though, there's ruther few things you kin do. Ain't thet so?"

"I can make it lively for you and your crowd when we get ashore," said Harvey, with a vicious nod, murmuring vague threats about "piracy," at which Troop almost—not quite—smiled.

"Excep' talk. I'd forgot that. You ain't asked to talk more'n you've a mind to aboard the *We're Here*. Keep your eyes open, an' help Dan to do ez he's bid, an' sechlike, an' I'll give you—you ain't wuth it, but I'll give—ten an' a ha'af a month; say thirty-five at the end o' the trip. A little work will ease up your head, and you kin tell us all abaout your dad an' your ma an' your money afterwards."

"She's on the steamer," said Harvey, his eyes filling with tears. "Take me to New York at once."

"Poor woman—poor woman! When she has you back she'll forgit it all, though. There's eight of us on the *We're Here,* an' ef we went back naow—it's more'n a thousand mile—we'd lose the season. The men they wouldn't hev it, allowin' I was agreeable."

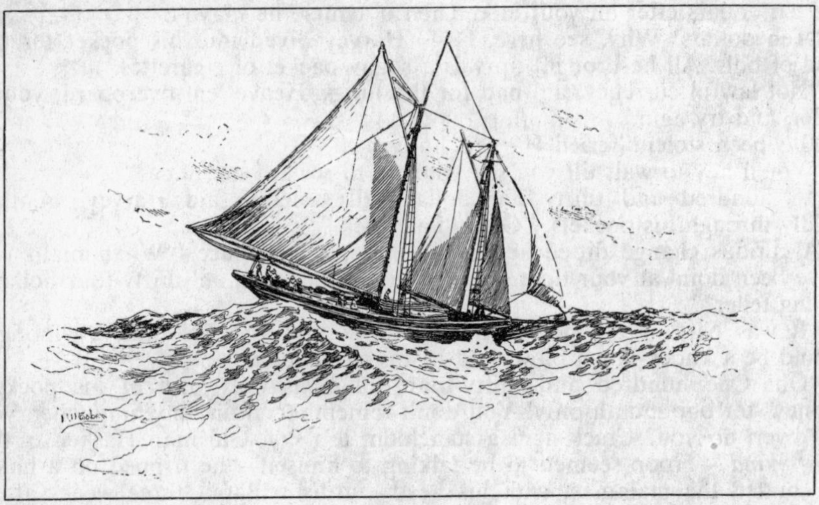

THE "WE'RE HERE."

"But my father would make it all right."

"He'd try. I don't doubt he'd try," said Troop; "but a whole season's catch is eight men's bread; an' you'll be better in your health when you see him in the fall. Go forward an' help Dan. It's ten an' a ha'af a month, ez I said, an' o' course, all f'und, same ez the rest o' us."

"Do you mean I'm to clean pots and pans and things?" said Harvey.

"An' other things. You've no call to shout, young feller."

"I won't! My father will give you enough to buy this dirty little fish-kettle"—Harvey stamped on the deck—"ten times over, if you take me to New York safe; and—and—you're in a hundred and thirty by me, anyhow."

"Ha-ow?" said Troop, the iron face darkening.

"How? You know how, well enough. On top of all that, you want me to do menial work"—Harvey was very proud of that adjective—"till the Fall. I tell you I will *not.* You hear?"

Troop regarded the top of the mainmast with deep interest for a while, as Harvey harangued fiercely all around him.

"Hsh!" he said at last. "I'm figurin' out my responsibilities in my own mind. It's a matter o' jedgment."

Dan stole up and plucked Harvey by the elbow. "Don't go to tamperin' with Dad any more," he pleaded. "You've called him a thief two or three times over, an' he don't take that from any livin' bein'."

"I won't!" Harvey almost shrieked, disregarding the advice, and still Troop meditated.

"Seems kinder unneighbourly," he said at last, his eye traveling down to Harvey. "I don't blame you, not a mite, young feller, nor you won't blame *me* when the bile's out o' your systim. Be sure you sense what I say? Ten an' a ha'af fer second boy on the schooner—an' all found—fer to teach you *an'* fer the sake o' your health. Yes or no?"

"No!" said Harvey. "Take me back to New York or I'll see you——"

He did not exactly remember what followed. He was lying in the scuppers, holding on to a nose that bled while Troop looked down on him serenely.

"Dan," he said to his son, "I was sot agin this young feller when I first saw him on account o' hasty jedgments. Never you be led astray by hasty jedgments, Dan. Naow I'm sorry for him, because he's clear distracted in his upper works. He ain't responsible fer the names he's give me, nor fer his other statements–nor fer jumpin' overboard, which I'm abaout ha'af convinced he did. You be gentle with him, Dan, 'r I'll give you twice what I've give him. Them hemmeridges clears the head. Let him sluice it off!"

Troop went down solemnly into the cabin, where he and the older men bunked, leaving Dan to comfort the luckless heir to thirty millions.

Chapter Two

"I WARNED YE," said Dan, as the drops fell thick and fast on the dark, oiled planking. "Dad ain't noways hasty, but you fair earned it. Pshaw! there's no sense takin' on so." Harvey's shoulders were rising and falling in spasms of dry sobbing. "I know the feelin'. First time Dad laid me out was the last–and that was my first trip. Makes ye feel sickish an' lonesome. *I* know."

"It does," moaned Harvey. "That man's either crazy or drunk, and–and I can't do anything."

"Don't say that to Dad," whispered Dan. "He's set agin all liquor, an'–well, he told me *you* was the madman. What in creation made you call him a thief? He's my dad."

Harvey sat up, mopped his nose, and told the story of the missing wad of bills. "I'm not crazy," he wound up. "Only–your father has never seen more than a five-dollar bill at a time, and *my* father could buy up this boat once a week and never miss it."

"You don't know what the *We're Here's* worth. Your dad must hev a pile o' money. How did he git it? Dad sez loonies can't shake out a straight yarn. Go ahead."

"In gold mines and things, West."

"I've read o' that kind o' business. Out West, too? Does he go around with a pistol on a trick-pony, same ez the circus? They call that the Wild West, and I've heard that their spurs an' bridles was solid silver."

"You *are* a chump!" said Harvey, amused in spite of himself. "My father hasn't any use for ponies. When he wants to ride he takes his car."

"Haow? Lobster-car?"

"No. His own private car, of course. You've seen a private car some time in your life?"

"Slatin Beeman he hez one," said Dan, cautiously. "I saw her at the Union Depot in Boston, with three niggers hoggin' her run." (Dan meant cleaning the windows.) "But Slatin Beeman he owns 'baout every railroad on Long Island, they say, an' they say he's bought 'baout ha'af Noo Hampshire an' run a line fence around her, an' filled her up with lions an' tigers an' bears an' buffalo an' crocodiles an' such all. Slatin Beeman he's a millionaire. I've seen *his* car. Yes?"

"Well, my father's what they call a multi-millionaire, and he has two private cars. One's named for me, the Harvey, and one for my mother, the Constance."

"Hold on," said Dan. "Dad don't ever let me swear, but I guess *you can*. 'Fore we go ahead, I want you to say hope you may die if you're lyin'."

"Of course," said Harvey.

"Thet ain't 'nuff. Say, 'Hope I may die if I ain't speakin' truth.' "

"Hope I may die right here," said Harvey, "if every word I've spoken isn't the cold truth."

"Hundred an' thirty-four dollars an' all?" said Dan. "I heard ye talkin' to Dad, an' I ha'af looked you'd be swallered up, same's Jonah."

Harvey protested himself red in the face. Dan was a shrewd young person along his own lines, and ten minutes' questioning convinced him that Harvey was not lying–much. Besides, he had bound himself by the most terrible oath known to boyhood, and yet he sat, alive, with a red-ended nose, in the scuppers, recounting marvels upon marvels.

"Gosh!" said Dan at last from the very bottom of his soul when Harvey had completed an inventory of the car named in his honor. Then a grin of mischievous delight overspread his broad face. "I believe you, Harvey, Dad's made a mistake fer once in his life."

"He has, sure," said Harvey, who was meditating an early revenge.

"He'll be mad clear through. Dad jest hates to be mistook in his jedgments." Dan lay back and slapped his thigh. "Oh, Harvey, don't you spile the catch by lettin' on."

"I don't want to be knocked down again. I'll get even with him, though."

"Never heard any man ever got even with Dad. But he'd knock ye down again sure. The more he was mistook the more he'd do it. But gold mines *and* pistols—"

"I never said a word about pistols," Harvey cut in, for he was on his oath.

"That's so; no more you did. Two private cars, then, one named fer you an' one fer her; an' two hundred dollars a month pocket-money, all knocked into the scuppers fer not workin' fer ten an' a ha'af a month! It's the top haul o' the season." He exploded with noiseless chuckles.

"Then I was right?" said Harvey, who thought he had found a sympathizer.

"You was wrong; the wrongest kind o' wrong! You take right hold an' pitch in 'longside o' me, or you'll catch it, an' I'll catch it fer backin' you up. Dad always gives me double helps 'cause I'm his son, an' he hates favorin' folk. Guess you're kinder mad at Dad. I've been that way time an' again. But Dad's a mighty jest man; all the Fleet says so."

"Looks like justice, this, don't it?" Harvey pointed to his outraged nose.

"Thet's nothin'. Lets the shore blood outer you. Dad did it for yer health. Say, though, I can't have dealin's with a man that thinks me or Dad or any one on the *We're Here's* a thief. We ain't any common wharf-end crowd by any manner o' means. We're fishermen, an' we've shipped together for six years an' more. Don't you make any mistake on *that!* I told ye Dad don't let me swear. He calls 'em vain oaths, and pounds me; but ef I could say what you said 'baout your pap an' his fixin's, I'd say that 'baout your dollars. I dunno what was in your pockets when I dried your kit fer I didn't look to see; but I'd say, using the very same words ez you used just now, neither me nor Dad–an' we was the only two that teched you after you was brought aboard–knows anythin' 'baout the money. Thet's *my* say. Naow?"

The blood letting had certainly cleared Harvey's brain, and maybe the loneliness of the sea had something to do with it. "That's all right," he said. Then he looked down confusedly. "Seems to me that for a fellow just saved from drowning I haven't been over and above grateful, Dan."

"Well, you was shook up and silly," said Dan. "Anyway there was only Dad an' me aboard to see it. The cook he don't count."

"I might have thought about losing the bills that way," Harvey said, half to himself, "instead of calling everybody in sight a thief. Where's your father?"

"In the cabin. What d' you want o' him again?"

"You'll see," said Harvey, and he stepped, rather groggily, for his head was still singing, to the cabin steps where the little ship's clock hung in plain sight of the wheel. Troop, in the chocolate-and-yellow painted cabin, was busy with a note-book and an enormous black pencil which he sucked hard from time to time.

"I haven't acted quite right," said Harvey, surprised at his own meekness.

"What's wrong naow?" said the skipper. "Walked into Dan, hev ye?"

"No; it's about you."

"I'm here to listen."

"Well, I—I'm here to take things back," said Harvey very quickly. "When a man's saved from drowning—" he gulped.

"Ey? You'll make a man yet ef you go on this way."

"He oughtn't begin by calling people names."

"Jest an' right—right an' jest," said Troop, with the ghost of a dry smile.

"So I'm here to say I'm sorry." Another gulp.

Troop heaved himself slowly off the locker he was sitting on and held out an eleven-inch hand. "I mistrusted 'twould do you sights o' good; an' this shows I weren't mistook in my jedgments." A smothered chuckle on deck caught his ear. "I am very seldom mistook in my jedgments." The eleven-inch hand closed on Harvey's, numbing it to the elbow. "We'll put a little more gristle to that 'fore we've done with you, young feller; an' I don't think any worse of ye fer anythin' thet's gone by. You wasn't fairly responsible. Go right abaout your business an' you won't take no hurt."

"You're white," said Dan, as Harvey regained the deck, flushed to the tips of his ears.

"I don't feel it," said he.

"I didn't mean that way. I heard what Dad said. When Dad allows he don't think the worse of any man, Dad's give himself away. He hates to be mistook in his jedgments too. Ho! ho! Onct Dad *has* a jedgment, he'd sooner dip his colors to the British than change it. I'm glad it's settled right eend up. Dad's right when he says he can't take you back. It's all the livin' we make here—fishin'. The men'll be back like sharks after a dead whale in ha'af an hour."

"What for?" said Harvey.

"Supper, o' course. Don't your stummick tell you? You've a heap to learn."

"Guess I have," said Harvey, dolefully, looking at the tangle of ropes and blocks overhead.

"She's a daisy," said Dan, enthusiastically, misunderstanding the look. "Wait till our mainsail's bent, an' she walks home with all her salt wet. There's some work first, though." He pointed down into the darkness of the open main-hatch between the two masts.

"What's that for? It's all empty," said Harvey.

"You an' me an' a few more hev got to fill it," said Dan. "That's where the fish goes."

"Alive?" said Harvey.

"Well, no. They're so's to be ruther dead—an' flat—an' salt. There's a hundred hogshead o' salt in the bins, an' we hain't more'n covered our dunnage to now."

"Where are the fish, though?"

"In the sea they say, in the boats we pray," said Dan, quoting a fisherman's proverb. "You come in last night with 'baout forty of 'em."

He pointed to a sort of wooden pen just in front of the quarter-deck.

"You an' me we'll sluice that out when they're through. 'Send we'll hev full pens to-night! I've seen her down ha'af a foot with fish waitin' to clean, an' we stood to the tables till he was splittin' ourselves instid o' them, we was so sleepy. Yes, they're comin' in naow." Dan looked over the low bulwarks at half a dozen dories rowing towards them over the shining, silky sea.

"I've never seen the sea from so low down," said Harvey. "It's fine."

The low sun made the water all purple and pinkish, with golden lights on the barrels of the long swells, and blue and green mackerel shades in the hollows. Each schooner in sight seemed to be pulling her dories towards her by invisible strings, and the little black figures in the tiny boats pulled like clockwork toys.

"They've struck on good," said Dan, between his half-shut eyes. "Manuel hain't room fer another fish. Low ez a lily-pad in still water, ain't he?"

"Which is Manuel? I don't see how you can tell 'em 'way off, as you do."

"Last boat to the south'ard. He f'und you last night," said Dan, pointing. "Manuel rows Portugoosey; ye can't mistake him. East o' him–*he's* a heap better'n he rows–is Pennsylvania. Loaded with saleratus, by the looks of him. East o' him–see how pretty they string out all along–with the humpy shoulders, is Long Jack. He's a Galway man inhabitin' South Boston, where they all live mostly, an' mostly them Galway men are good in a boat. North, away yonder–you'll hear him tune up in a minute–is Tom Platt. Man-o'war's man he was on the old *Ohio*–first of our navy, he says, to go araound the Horn. He never talks of much else, 'cept when he sings, but he has fair fishin' luck. There! What did I tell you?"

A melodious bellow stole across the water from the northern dory. Harvey heard something about somebody's hands and feet being cold, and then:

"Bring forth the chart, the doleful chart,
See where them mountings meet!
The clouds are thick around their heads,
The mists around their feet."

"Full boat," said Dan, with a chuckle. "If he give us 'O Captain' it's toppin' too!"

The bellow continued:

"And naow to thee, O Capting,
Most earnestly I pray,
That they shall never bury me
In church or cloister gray."

"Double game for Tom Platt. He'll tell you all about the old *Ohio* tomorrow. 'See that blue dory behind him? He's my uncle,–Dad's own brother,–an' ef there's any bad luck loose on the Banks she'll fetch up agin Uncle Salters, sure. Look how tender he's rowin'. I'll lay my wage and share he's the only man stung up to-day–an' he's stung up good."

"What'll sting him?" said Harvey, getting interested.

"Strawberries, mostly. Pumpkins, sometimes, an' sometimes lemons an' cucumbers. Yes, he's stung up from his elbows down. That man's luck's perfectly paralyzin'. Naow we'll take a-holt o' the tackles an' hist 'em in. Is it true what you told me jest now, that you never done a hand's turn o' work in all your born life? Must feel kinder awful, don't it?"

"I'm going to try to work, anyway," Harvey replied stoutly. "Only it's all dead new."

"Lay a-holt o' that tackle, then. Behind ye!"

Harvey grabbed at a rope and long iron hook dangling from one of the stays of the mainmast, while Dan pulled down another that ran from something he called a "topping-lift," as Manuel drew alongside in his loaded dory. The Portuguese smiled a brilliant smile that Harvey learned to know well later, and with a short-handled fork began to throw fish into the pen on deck. "Two hundred and thirty-one," he shouted.

"Give him the hook," said Dan, and Harvey ran it into Manuel's hands. He slipped it through a loop of rope at the dory's bow, caught Dan's tackle, hooked it to the stern-becket, and clambered into the schooner.

"Pull!" shouted Dan, and Harvey pulled, astonished to find how easily the dory rose.

"Hold on, she don't nest in the cross-trees!" Dan laughed; and Harvey held on, for the boat lay in the air above his head.

"Lower away," Dan shouted, and as Harvey lowered, Dan swayed the light boat with one hand till it landed softly just behind the mainmast. "They don't weigh nothin' empty. Thet was right smart fer a passenger. There's more trick to it in a sea-way."

"Ah ha!" said Manuel, holding out a brown hand. "You are some pretty well now? This time last night the fish they fish for you. Now you fish for fish. Eh, wha-at?"

"I'm—I'm ever so grateful," Harvey stammered, and his unfortunate hand stole to his pocket once more, but he remembered that he had no money to offer. When he knew Manuel better the mere thought of the mistake he might have made would cover him with hot, uneasy blushes in his bunk.

"There is no to be thankful for to *me!*" said Manuel. "How shall I leave you dreeft, dreeft all around the Banks? Now you are a fisherman—eh, wha-at? Ouh! Auh!" He bent backward and forward stiffly from the hips to get the kinks out of himself.

"I have not cleaned boat to-day. Too busy. They struck on queek. Danny, my son, clean for me."

Harvey moved forward at once. Here was something he could do for the man who had saved his life.

Dan threw him a swab, and he leaned over the dory, mopping up the slime clumsily, but with great good-will. "Hike out the foot-boards; they slide in them grooves," said Dan. "Swab 'em an' lay 'em down. Never let a foot-board jam. Ye may want her bad some day. Here's Long Jack."

A stream of glittering fish flew into the pen from a dory alongside.

"Manuel, you take the tackle. I'll fix the tables. Harvey, clear Manuel's boat. Long Jack's nestin' on the top of her."

Harvey looked up from his swabbing at the bottom of another dory just above his head.

"Jest like the Injian puzzle-boxes, ain't they?" said Dan, as the one boat dropped into the other.

"Takes to ut like a duck to water," said Long Jack, a grizzly-chinned, long-lipped Galway man, bending to and fro exactly as Manuel had done. Disko in the cabin growled up the hatchway, and they could hear him suck his pencil.

"Wan hunder an' forty-nine an' a half—bad luck to ye, Discobolus!" said Long Jack. "I'm murderin' meself to fill your pockuts. Slate ut for a bad catch. The Portugee has bate me."

Whack came another dory alongside, and more fish shot into the pen.

"Two hundred and three. Let's look at the passenger!" The speaker was even larger than the Galway man, and his face was made curious by a purple cut running slantways from his left eye to the right corner of his mouth.

Not knowing what else to do, Harvey swabbed each dory as it came down, pulled out the foot-boards, and laid them in the bottom of the boat.

"He's caught on good," said the scarred man, who was Tom Platt, watching him critically. "There are two ways o' doin' everything. One's fisher-fashion—any end first an' a slippery hitch over all—an' the other's——"

"What we did on the old *Ohio!*" Dan interrupted, brushing into the knot of men with a long board on legs. "Get out o' here, Tom Platt, an' leave me fix the tables."

He jammed one end of the board into two nicks in the bulwarks, kicked out the leg, and ducked just in time to avoid a swinging blow from the man-o'-war's man.

"An' they did that on the *Ohio,* too, Danny. See?" said Tom Platt, laughing.

"Guess they was swivel-eyed, then, fer it didn't git home, and I know who'll find his boots on the main-truck ef he don't leave us alone. Haul ahead! I'm busy, can't ye see?"

"Danny, ye lie on the cable an' sleep all day," said Long Jack. "You're the hoight av impidence, an' I'm persuaded ye'll corrupt our supercargo in a week."

"His name's Harvey," said Dan, waving two strangely shaped knives, "an' he'll be worth five of any Sou' Boston clam-digger 'fore long." He laid the knives tastefully on the table, cocked his head on one side, and admired the effect.

"I think it's forty-two," said a small voice overside, and there was a roar of laughter as another voice answered, "Then my luck's turned fer onct, 'caze I'm forty-five, though I be stung outer all shape."

"Forty-two *or* forty-five. I've lost count," the small voice said.

"It's Penn an' Uncle Salters caountin' catch. This beats the circus any day," said Dan. "Jest look at 'em!"

"Come in–come in!" roared Long Jack. "It's wet out yondher, children."

"Forty-two, ye said." This was Uncle Salters.

"I'll count again, then," the voice replied meekly.

The two dories swung together and bunted into the schooner's side.

"Patience o' Jerusalem!" snapped Uncle Salters, backing water with a splash. "What possest a farmer like you to set foot in a boat beats me. You've nigh stove me all up."

"I am sorry, Mr. Salters. I came to sea on account of nervous dyspepsia. You advised me, I think."

"You an' your nervis dyspepsy be drowned in the Whale-hole," roared Uncle Salters, a fat and tubby little man. "You're comin' down on me agin. *Did* ye say forty-two or forty-five?"

"I've forgotten, Mr. Salters. Let's count."

"Don't see as it *could* be forty-five. *I'm* forty-five," said Uncle Salters. "You count keerful, Penn."

Disko Troop came out of the cabin. "Salters, you pitch your fish in naow at once," he said in the tone of authority.

"Don't spile the catch, Dad," Dan murmured. "Them two are on'y jest beginnin'."

"Mother av delight! He's forkin' them wan by wan," howled Long Jack, as Uncle Salters got to work laboriously; the little man in the other dory counting a line of notches on the gunwale.

"That was last week's catch," he said, looking up plaintively, his forefinger where he had left off.

Manuel nudged Dan, who darted to the after-tackle, and, leaning far overside, slipped the hook into the sternrope as Manuel made her fast forward. The others pulled gallantly and swung the boat in–man, fish, and all.

"One, two, four–nine," said Tom Platt, counting with a practiced eye. "Forty-seven. Penn, you're it!" Dan let the after-tackle run, and slid him out of the stern on to the deck amid a torrent of his own fish.

"Hold on!" roared Uncle Salters, bobbing by the waist. "Hold on, I'm a bit mixed in my caount."

He had no time to protest, but was hove inboard and treated like "Pennsylvania."

"Forty-one," said Tom Platt. "Beat by a farmer, Salters. An' you sech a sailor, too!"

" 'Tweren't fair caount," said he, stumbling out of the pen; "an' I'm stung up all to pieces."

His thick hands were puffy and mottled purply white.

"Some folks will find strawberry-bottom," said Dan, addressing the newly risen moon, "ef they hev to dive fer it, seems to me."

"An' others," said Uncle Salters, "eats the fat o' the land in sloth, an' mocks their own blood-kin."

"Seat ye! Seat ye!" a voice Harvey had not heard called from the foc'sle. Disko Troop, Tom Platt, Long Jack, and Salters went forward on the word. Little Penn bent above his square deep-sea reel and the tangled cod-lines; Manuel lay down full length on the deck, and Dan dropped into the hold, where Harvey heard him banging casks with a hammer.

"Salt," he said, returning. "Soon as we're through supper we git to dressing-down. You'll pitch to Dad. Tom Platt an' Dad they stow together, an' you'll hear 'em arguin'. We're second ha'af, you an' me an' Manuel an' Penn—the youth an' beauty o' the boat."

"What's the good of that?" said Harvey. "I'm hungry."

"They'll be through in a minute. Snff! She smells good to-night. Dad ships a good cook ef he *do* suffer with his brother. It's a full catch to-day, ain't it?" He pointed at the pens piled high with cod. "What water did ye hev, Manuel?"

"Twenty-fife father," said the Portuguese, sleepily. "They strike on good an' queek. Some day I show you, Harvey."

The moon was beginning to walk on the still sea before the elder men came aft. The cook had no need to cry "second half." Dan and Manuel were down the hatch and at table ere Tom Platt, last and most deliberate of the elders, had finished wiping his mouth with the back of his hand. Harvey followed Penn, and sat down before a tin pan of cod's tongues and sounds, mixed with scraps of pork and fried potato, a loaf of hot bread, and some black and powerful coffee. Hungry as they were, they waited while "Pennsylvania" solemnly asked a blessing. Then they stoked in silence till Dan drew a breath over his tin cup and demanded of Harvey how he felt.

" 'Most full, but there's just room for another piece."

The cook was a huge, jet-black negro, and, unlike all the negroes Harvey had met, did not talk, contenting himself with smiles and dumb-show invitations to eat more.

"See, Harvey," said Dan, rapping with his fork on the table, "it's jest as I said. The young an' handsome men—like me an' Pennsy an' you an' Manuel—we're second ha'af, an' we eats when the first ha'af are through. They're the old fish; an' they're mean an' humpy, an' their stummicks has to be humored; so they come first, which they don't deserve. Ain't that so, doctor?"

The cook nodded.

"Can't he talk?" said Harvey in a whisper.

" 'Nough to get along. Not much o' anything we know. His natural tongue's kinder curious. Comes from the innards of Cape Breton, he does, where the farmers speak homemade Scotch. Cape Breton's full o' niggers whose folk run in there durin' aour war, an' they talk like farmers—all huffy-chuffy."

"That is not Scotch," said "Pennsylvania." "That is Gaelic. So I read in a book."

"Penn reads a heap. Most of what he says is so—'cep' when it comes to a caount o' fish—eh?"

"Does your father just let them *say* how many they've caught without checking them?" said Harvey.

"Why, yes. Where's the sense of a man lyin' fer a few old cod?"

"Was a man once lied for his catch," Manuel put in. "Lied every day. Fife, ten, twenty-fife more fish than come he say there was."

"Where was that?" said Dan. "None o' aour folk."

"Frenchman of Anguille."

"Ah! Them West Shore Frenchmen don't caount anyway. Stands to reason they can't caount. Ef you run acrost any of their soft hooks, Harvey, you'll know why," said Dan, with an awful contempt.

"Always more and never less,
Every time we come to dress,"

Long Jack roared down the hatch, and the "second ha'af" scrambled up at once.

The shadow of the masts and rigging, with the never-furled riding-sail, rolled to and fro on the heaving deck in the moonlight; and the pile of fish by the stern shone like a dump of fluid silver. In the hold there were tramplings and rumblings where Disko Troop and Tom Platt moved among the salt-bins. Dan passed Harvey a pitchfork, and led him to the inboard end of the rough table, where Uncle Salters was drumming impatiently with a knife-haft. A tub of salt water lay at his feet.

"You pitch to Dan an' Tom Platt down the hatch, an' take keer Uncle Salters don't cut yer eye out," said Dan, swinging himself into the hold. "I'll pass salt below."

Penn and Manuel stood knee deep among cod in the pen, flourishing drawn knives. Long Jack, a basket at his feet and mittens on his hands, faced Uncle Salters at the table, and Harvey stared at the pitchfork and the tub.

"Hi!" shouted Manuel, stooping to the fish, and bringing one up with a finger under its gill and a finger in its eyes. He laid it on the edge of the pen; the knife-blade glimmered with a sound of tearing, and the fish, slit from throat to vent, with a nick on either side of the neck, dropped at Long Jack's feet.

"Hi!" said Long Jack, with a scoop of his mittened hand. The cod's liver dropped in the basket. Another wrench and scoop sent the head and offal flying, and the empty fish slid across to Uncle Salters, who snorted fiercely. There was another sound of tearing, the backbone flew over the bulwarks, and the fish, headless, gutted, and open, splashed in the tub, sending the salt water into Harvey's astonished mouth. After the first yell, the men were silent. The cod moved along as though they were alive, and long ere Harvey had ceased wondering at the miraculous dexterity of it all, his tub was full.

"Pitch!" grunted Uncle Salters, without turning his head, and Harvey pitched the fish by twos and threes down the hatch.

"Hi! Pitch 'em bunchy," shouted Dan. "Don't scatter! Uncle Salters is the best splitter in the fleet. Watch him mind his book!"

Indeed, it looked a little as though the round uncle were cutting magazine pages against time. Manuel's body, cramped over from the hips, stayed like a statue; but his long arms grabbed the fish without ceasing. Little Penn toiled valiantly, but it was easy to see he was weak. Once or twice Manuel found time to help him without breaking the chain of supplies, and once Manuel howled because he had caught his finger in a Frenchman's hook. These hooks are made of soft metal, to be rebent after use; but the cod very often get away with them and are hooked again elsewhere; and that is one of the many reasons why the Gloucester boats despise the Frenchmen.

Down below, the rasping sound of rough salt rubbed on rough flesh sounded like the whirring of a grindstone—a steady undertune to the "click-nick" of knives in the pen; the wrench and shloop of torn heads, dropped liver, and flying offal; the "caraaah" of Uncle Salters's knife scooping away backbones; and the flap of wet, open bodies falling into the tub.

At the end of an hour Harvey would have given the world to rest; for fresh, wet cod weigh more than you would think, and his back ached with the steady pitching. But he felt for the first time in his life that he was one of the working gang of men, took pride in the thought, and held on sullenly.

"Knife oh!" shouted Uncle Salters at last. Penn doubled up, gasping among the fish, Manuel bowed back and forth to supple himself, and Long Jack leaned over the bulwarks. The cook appeared, noiseless as a black shadow, collected a mass of backbones and heads, and retreated.

"Blood-ends for breakfast an' head-chowder," said Long Jack, smacking his lips.

"Knife oh!" repeated Uncle Salters, waving the flat, curved splitter's weapon.

"Look by your foot, Harve," cried Dan below.

Harvey saw half a dozen knives stuck in a cleat in the hatch combing. He dealt these around, taking over the dulled ones.

"Water!" said Disko Troop.

"Scuttle-butt's for'ard an' the dipper's alongside. Hurry, Harve," said Dan.

He was back in a minute with a big dipperful of stale brown water which tasted like nectar, and loosed the jaws of Disko and Tom Platt.

"These are cod," said Disko. "They ain't Damarskus figs, Tom Platt, nor yet silver bars. I've told you that ever single time since we've sailed together."

"A matter o' seven seasons," returned Tom Platt coolly. "Good stowin's good stowin' all the same, an' there's a right an' a wrong way o' stowin' ballast even. If you'd ever seen four hundred ton o' iron set into the—"

"Hi!" With a yell from Manuel the work began again, and never stopped till the pen was empty. The instant the last fish was down, Disko Troop rolled aft to the cabin with his brother; Manuel and Long Jack went forward; Tom Platt only waited long enough to slide home the hatch ere he too disappeared. In half a minute Harvey heard deep snores in the cabin, and he was staring blankly at Dan and Penn.

"I did a little better that time, Danny," said Penn, whose eyelids were heavy with sleep. "But I think it is my duty to help clean."

"'Wouldn't hev your conscience fer a thousand quintal," said Dan. "Turn in, Penn. You've no call to do boy's work. Draw a bucket, Harvey. Oh, Penn, dump these in the gurry-butt 'fore you sleep. Kin you keep awake that long?"

Penn took up the heavy basket of fish-livers, emptied them into a cask with a hinged top lashed by the foc'sle; then he too dropped out of sight in the cabin.

"Boys clean up after dressin' down an' first watch in ca'am weather is boy's watch on the *We're Here.*" Dan sluiced the pen energetically, unshipped the table, set it up to dry in the moonlight, ran the red knife-blades through a wad of oakum, and began to sharpen them on a tiny grindstone, as Harvey threw offal and backbones overboard under his direction.

At the first splash a silvery-white ghost rose bolt upright from the oily water and sighed a weird whistling sigh. Harvey started back with a shout, but Dan only laughed. "Grampus," said he. "Beggin' fer fish-heads. They up-eend thet way when they're hungry. Breath on him like the doleful tombs, hain't he?" A horrible stench of decayed fish filled the air as the pillar of white sank, and the water bubbled oilily. "Hain't ye never seen a grampus up-eend before? You'll see 'em by hundreds 'fore ye're through. Say, it's good to hev a boy aboard again. Otto was too old, an' a Dutchy at that. Him an' me we fought consid'ble. 'Wouldn't ha' keered fer that ef he'd hed a Christian tongue in his head. Sleepy?"

"Dead sleepy," said Harvey, nodding forward.

"Mustn't sleep on watch. Rouse up an' see ef our anchor-light's bright an' shinin'. You're on watch now, Harve."

"Pshaw! What's to hurt us? 'Bright's day. Sn—orrr!"

"Jest when things happen, Dad says. Fine weather's good sleepin', an' 'fore you know, mebbe, you're cut in two by a liner, an' seventeen brass-bound officers, all gen'elmen, lift their hand to it that your lights was aout an' there was a thick fog. Harve, I've kinder took to you, but ef you nod onct more I'll lay into you with a rope's end."

The moon, who sees many strange things on the Banks, looked down on a slim youth in knickerbockers and a red jersey, staggering around the cluttered decks of a seventy-ton schooner, while behind him, waving a knotted rope, walked, after the manner of an executioner, a boy who yawned and nodded between the blows he dealt.

The lashed wheel groaned and kicked softly, the riding-sail slatted a little in the shifts of the light wind, the windlass creaked, and the miserable procession continued. Harvey expostulated, threatened, whimpered, and at last wept outright, while Dan, the words clotting on his tongue, spoke of the beauty of watchfulness and slashed away with the rope's end, punishing the dories as often as he hit Harvey. At last the clock in the cabin struck ten, and upon the tenth stroke little Penn crept on deck. He found two boys in two tumbled heaps side by side on the main hatch, so deeply asleep that he actually rolled them to their berths.

Chapter Three

IT WAS THE forty-fathom slumber that clears the soul and eye and heart, and sends you to breakfast ravening. They emptied a big tin dish of juicy fragments of fish–the blood-ends the cook had collected overnight. They cleaned up the plates and pans of the elder mess, who were out fishing, sliced pork for the midday meal, swabbed down the foc'sle, filled the lamps, drew coal and water for the cook, and investigated the fore-hold, where the boat's stores were stacked. It was another perfect day–soft, mild, and clear; and Harvey breathed to the very bottom of his lungs.

More schooners had crept up in the night, and the long blue seas were full of sails and dories. Far away on the horizon, the smoke of some liner, her hull invisible, smudged the blue, and to eastward a big ship's top-gallant sails, just lifting, made a square nick in it. Disko Troop was smoking by the roof of the cabin–one eye on the craft around, and the other on the little fly at the mainmast-head.

"When Dad kerflummoxes that way," said Dan in a whisper, "he's doin' some high-line thinkin' fer all hands. I'll lay my wage an' share we'll make berth soon. Dad he knows the cod, an' the Fleet they know Dad knows. 'See 'em comin' up one by one, lookin' fer nothin' in particular, o' course, but scrowgin' on us all the time? There's the *Prince Leboo;* she's a Chat-ham boat. She's crep' up sence last night. An' see that big one with a patch in her foresail an' a new jib? She's the *Carrie Pitman* from West Chat-ham. She won't keep her canvas long onless her luck's changed since last season. She don't do much 'cep' drift. There ain't an anchor made 'll hold her. . . . When the smoke puffs up in little rings like that, Dad's studyin' the fish. Ef we speak to him now, he'll git mad. Las' time I did, he jest took an' hove a boot at me."

Disko Troop stared forward, the pipe between his teeth, with eyes that saw nothing. As his son said, he was studying the fish–pitting his knowledge and experience on the Banks against the roving cod in his own sea. He accepted the presence of the inquisitive schooners on the horizon as a compliment to his powers. But now that it was paid, he wished to draw away and make his berth alone, till it was time to go up to the Virgin and fish in the streets of that roaring town upon the waters. So Disko Troop thought of recent weather, and gales, currents, food-supplies, and other domestic arrangements, from the point of view of a twenty-pound cod; was, in fact, for an hour a cod himself, and looked remarkably like one. Then he removed the pipe from his teeth.

"Dad," said Dan, "we've done our chores. Can't we go overside a piece? It's good catchin' weather."

"Not in that cherry-coloured rig ner them ha'af baked brown shoes. Give him suthin' fit to wear."

"Dad's pleased–that settles it," said Dan, delightedly, dragging Harvey into the cabin, while Troop pitched a key down the steps. "Dad keeps my spare rig where he kin overhaul it, 'cause Ma sez I'm keerless." He rummaged through a locker, and in less than three minutes Harvey was adorned with fisherman's rubber boots that came half up his thigh, a heavy blue jersey well darned at the elbows, a pair of nippers, and a sou'wester.

"Naow ye look somethin' like," said Dan. "Hurry!"

"Keep nigh an' handy," said Troop "an' don't go visitin' raound the Fleet. If any one asks you what I'm cal'latin' to do, speak the truth–fer ye don't know."

A little red dory, labelled *Hattie S.,* lay astern of the schooner. Dan hauled in the painter, and dropped lightly on to the bottom boards, while Harvey tumbled clumsily after.

"That's no way o' gettin' into a boat," said Dan. "Ef there was any sea you'd go to the bottom, sure. You got to learn to meet her."

Dan fitted the thole-pins, took the forward thwart and watched Harvey's work. The boy had rowed, in a lady-like fashion, on the Adirondack ponds; but there is a difference between squeaking pins and well-balanced rullocks–light sculls and stubby, eight-foot sea-oars. They stuck in the gentle swells, and Harvey grunted.

"Short! Row short!" said Dan. "Ef you cramp your oar in any kind o' sea you're liable to turn her over. Ain't she a daisy? Mine, too."

The little dory was specklessly clean. In her bows lay a tiny anchor, two jugs of water, and some seventy fathoms of thin, brown dory-roding. A tin dinner-horn rested in cleats just under Harvey's right hand, beside an ugly-looking maul, a short gaff, and a shorter wooden stick. A couple of lines, with very heavy leads and double cod-hooks, all neatly coiled on square reels, were stuck in their place by the gunwale.

"Where's the sail and mast?" said Harvey, for his hands were beginning to blister.

Dan chuckled. "Ye don't sail fishin'-dories much. Ye pull; but ye needn't pull so hard. Don't you wish you owned her?"

"Well, I guess my father might give me one or two if I asked 'em," Harvey replied. He had been too busy to think much of his family till then.

"That's so. I forgot your dad's a millionaire. You don't act millionary any, naow. But a dory an' craft an' gear"–Dan spoke as though she were a whaleboat–"costs a heap. Think your dad 'u'd give you one fer–fer a pet like?"

"Shouldn't wonder. It would be 'most the only thing I haven't stuck him for yet."

" 'Must be an expensive kinder kid to home. Don't slitheroo thet way, Harve. Short's the trick, because no sea's ever dead still, an' the swells 'll——"

Crack! The loom of the oar kicked Harvey under the chin and knocked him backwards.

"That was what I was goin' to say. I hed to learn too, but *I* wasn't more than eight years old when I got my schoolin'."

Harvey regained his seat with aching jaws and a frown.

"No good gettin' mad at things, Dad says. It's our own fault ef we can't handle 'em, he says. Let's try here. Manuel'll give us the water."

The "Portugee" was rocking fully a mile away, but when Dan up-ended an oar he waved his left arm three times.

"Thirty fathom," said Dan, stringing a salt clam on to the hook. "Over with the doughboys. Bait same's I do, Harvey, an' don't snarl your reel."

Dan's line was out long before Harvey had mastered the mystery of baiting and heaving out the leads. The dory drifted along easily. It was not worth while to anchor till they were sure of good ground.

"Here we come!" Dan shouted, and a shower of spray rattled on Harvey's shoulders as a big cod flapped and kicked alongside. "Muckle, Harvey, muckle! Under your hand! Quick!"

Evidently "muckle" could not be the dinner-horn, so Harvey passed over the maul, and Dan scientifically stunned the fish before he pulled it inboard, and wrenched out the hook with the short wooden stick he called a "gob-stick." Then Harvey felt a tug, and pulled up zealously.

"Why, these are strawberries!" he shouted. "Look!"

The hook had fouled among a bunch of strawberries, red on one side and white on the other–perfect reproductions of the land fruit, except that there were no leaves, and the stem was all pipy and slimy.

"Don't tech 'em. Slat 'em off. Don't—"

The warning came too late. Harvey had picked them from the hook, and was admiring them.

"Ouch!" he cried, for his fingers throbbed as though he had grasped many nettles.

"Naow ye know what strawberry-bottom means. Nothin' 'cep' fish should be teched with the naked fingers, Dad says. Slat 'em off agin the gunnel, an' bait up, Harve. Lookin' won't help any. It's all in the wages."

Harvey smiled at the thought of his ten and a half dollars a month, and wondered what his mother would say if she could see him hanging over the edge of a fishing-dory in mid-ocean. She suffered agonies whenever he went out on Saranac Lake; and, by the way, Harvey remembered distinctly that he used to laugh at her anxieties. Suddenly the line flashed through his hand, stinging even through the "nippers," the woolen circlets supposed to protect it.

"He's a logy. Give him room accordin' to his strength," cried Dan. "I'll help ye."

"No, you won't," Harvey snapped, as he hung on to the line. "It's my first fish. Is–is it a whale?"

"Halibut, mebbe." Dan peered down into the water alongside, and flourished the big "muckle," ready for all chances. Something white and oval flickered and fluttered through the green. "I'll lay my wage an' share he's over a hundred. Are you so everlastin' anxious to land him alone?"

Harvey's knuckles were raw and bleeding where they had been banged against the gunwale; his face was purple-blue between excitement and exertion; he dripped with sweat, and was half-blinded from staring at the circling sunlit ripples about the swiftly moving line. The boys were tired long ere the halibut, who took charge of them and the dory for the next twenty minutes. But the big flat fish was gaffed and hauled in at last.

"Beginner's luck," said Dan, wiping his forehead. "He's all of a hundred."

Harvey looked at the huge gray-and-mottled creature with unspeakable pride. He had seen halibut many times on marble slabs ashore, but it had never occurred to him to ask how they came inland. Now he knew; and every inch of his body ached with fatigue.

"Ef Dad was along," said Dan, hauling up, "he'd read the signs plain's print. The fish are runnin' smaller an' smaller, an' you've took 'baout as logy a halibut's we're apt to find this trip. Yesterday's catch–did ye notice it?–was all big fish an' no halibut. Dad he'd read them signs right off. Dad says everythin' on the Banks is signs, an' can be read wrong er right. Dad's deeper'n the Whale-hole."

Even as he spoke some one fired a pistol on the *We're Here,* and a potato-basket was run up in the fore-rigging.

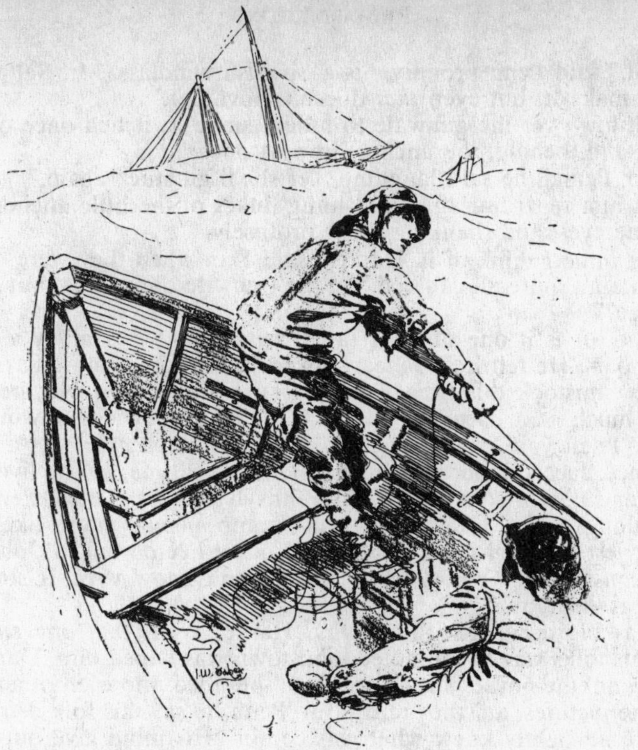

"'I'LL LAY MY WAGE AN' SHARE HE'S OVER A HUNDRED.'"

"What did I say, naow? That's the call fer the whole crowd. Dad's onter something, er he'd never break fishin' this time o' day. Reel up, Harve, an' we'll pull back."

They were to windward of the schooner, just ready to flirt the dory over the still sea, when sounds of woe half a mile off led them to Penn, who was careering around a fixed point for all the world like a gigantic water-bug. The little man backed away and came down again with enormous energy, but at the end of each maneuver his dory swung round and snubbed herself on her rope.

"We'll heve to help him, else he'll root an' seed here," said Dan.

"What's the matter?" said Harvey. This was a new world, where he could not lay down the law to his elders, but had to ask questions humbly. And the sea was horribly big and unexcited.

"Anchor's fouled. Penn's always losing 'em. Lost two this trip a'ready—on sandy bottom too—an' Dad says next one he loses, sure's fishin', he'll give him the kelleg. That 'u'd break Penn's heart."

"What's a 'kelleg'?" said Harvey, who had a vague idea it might be some kind of marine torture, like keel-hauling in the storybooks.

"Big stone instid of an anchor. You kin see a kelleg ridin' in the bows fur's you can see a dory, an' all the Fleet knows what it means. They'd guy him dreadful. Penn couldn't stand that no more'n a dog with a dipper to his tail. He's so everlastin' sensitive. Hello, Penn! Stuck again? Don't try any more o' your patents. Come up on her, and keep your rodin' straight up an' down."

"It doesn't move," said the little man, panting. "It doesn't move at all, and instead I tried everything."

"What's all this hurrah's-nest for'ard?" said Dan, pointing to a wild tangle of spare oars and dory-roding, all matted together by the hand of inexperience.

"Oh, that," said Penn proudly, "is a Spanish windlass. Mr. Salters showed me how to make it; but even *that* doesn't move her."

Dan bent low over the gunwale to hide a smile, twitched once or twice on the roding, and, behold, the anchor drew at once.

"Haul up, Penn," he said laughing, "er she'll git stuck again."

They left him regarding the weed-hung flukes of the little anchor with big, pathetic blue eyes, and thanking them profusely.

"Oh, say, while I think of it, Harve," said Dan when they were out of ear-shot, "Penn ain't quite all caulked. He ain't nowise dangerous, but his mind's give out. See?"

"Is that so, or is it one of your father's judgments?" Harvey asked as he bent to his oars. He felt he was learning to handle them more easily.

"Dad ain't mistook this time, Penn's a sure 'nuff loony. No, he ain't thet exactly, so much ez a harmless ijjit. It was this way (you're rowin' quite so, Harve), an' I tell you 'cause it's right you orter know. He was a Moravian preacher once. Jacob Boller wuz his name, Dad told me, an' he lived with his wife an' four children somewhere out Pennsylvania way. Well, Penn he took his folks along to a Moravian meetin'–camp-meetin' most like–an' they stayed over jest one night in Johnstown. You've heered talk o' Johnstown?"

Harvey considered. "Yes, I have. But I don't know why. It sticks in my head same as Ashtabula."

"Both was big accidents–thet's why, Harve. Well, that one single night Penn and his folks was to the hotel Johnstown was wiped out. 'Dam bust an' flooded her, an' the houses struck adrift an' bumped into each other an' sunk. I've seen the pictures, an' they're dretful. Penn he saw his folk drowned all'n a heap 'fore he rightly knew what was comin'. His mind give out from that on. He mistrusted somethin' hed happened up to Johnstown, but for the poor life of him he couldn't remember what, an' he jest drifted around smilin' an' wonderin'. He didn't know what he was, nor yit what he hed bin, an' thet way he run agin Uncle Salters, who was visitin' 'n Allegheny City. Ha'af my mother's folks they live scattered inside o' Pennsylvania, an' Uncle Salters he visits araound winters. Uncle Salters he kinder adopted Penn, well knowin' what his trouble wuz; an' he brought him East, an' he give him work on his farm."

"Why, I heard him calling Penn a farmer last night when the boats bumped. Is your Uncle Salters a farmer?"

"Farmer!" shouted Dan. "There ain't water enough 'tween here an' Hatt'rus to wash the furrer-mold off'n *his* boots. He's jest everlastin' farmer. Why, Harve, I've seen thet man hitch up a bucket, long towards sundown, an' set twiddlin' the spigot to the scuttle-butt same's ef 'twas a cow's bag. He's thet much farmer. Well, Penn an' he they ran the farm–up Exeter way 'twuz. Uncle Salters he sold it this spring to a jay from Boston as wanted to build a summer-house, an' he got a heap for it. Well, them two loonies scratched along till, one day, Penn's church he'd belonged to–the Moravians–found out where he wuz drifted an' layin', an' wrote to Uncle Salters. 'Never heerd what they said exactly; but Uncle Salters was mad. He's a 'piscopolian mostly–but he jest let 'em hev it both sides o' the bow, 's if he was a Baptist; an' sez he warn't goin' to give up Penn to any blame Moravian connection in Pennsylvania or anywheres else. Then he come to Dad, towin' Penn,–thet was two trips back,–an' sez he an' Penn must fish a trip fer their health. 'Guess he thought the Moravians wouldn't hunt the Banks fer Jacob Boller. Dad was agreeable, fer Uncle Salters he'd been fishin' off an' on fer thirty years, when he warn't inventin' patent manures, an' he took quarter-share in the *We're Here;* an' the trip done Penn so much good, Dad made a habit o' takin' him. Some day, Dad sez, he'll remember his wife an' kids *an'* Johnstown, an' then, like as not, he'll die, Dad sez. Don't ye talk about

Johnstown ner such things to Penn, 'r Uncle Salters he'll heave ye overboard."

"Poor Penn!" murmured Harvey. "I shouldn't ever have thought Uncle Salters cared for him by the look of 'em together."

"I like Penn, though; we all do," said Dan. "We ought to ha' give him a tow, but I wanted to tell ye first."

They were close to the schooner now, the other boats a little behind them.

"You needn't heave in the dories till after dinner," said Troop from the deck. "We'll dress down right off. Fix table, boys!"

"Deeper'n the Whale-deep," said Dan, with a wink, as he set the gear for dressing down. "Look at them boats that hev edged up sence mornin'. They're all waitin' on Dad. See 'em, Harve?"

"They are all alike to me." And indeed to a landsman, the nodding schooners around seemed run from the same mold.

"They ain't, though. That yaller, dirty packet with her bowsprit steeved that way, she's the *Hope of Prague.* Nick Brady's her skipper, the meanest man on the Banks. We'll tell him so when we strike the Main Ledge. 'Way off yonder's the *Day's Eye.* The two Jeraulds own her. She's from Harwich; fastish, too, an' hez good luck; but Dad he'd find fish in a graveyard. Them other three, side along, they're the *Margie Smith, Rose,* and *Edith S. Walen,* all from home. 'Guess we'll see the *Abbie M. Deering* to-morrer, Dad, won't we? They're all slippin' over from the shaol o' 'Queereau."

"You won't see many boats to-morrow, Danny." When Troop called his son Danny, it was a sign that the old man was pleased. "Boys, we're too crowded," he went on, addressing the crew as they clambered inboard. "We'll leave 'em to bait big an' catch small." He looked at the catch in the pen, and it was curious to see how little and level the fish ran. Save for Harvey's halibut, there was nothing over fifteen pounds on deck.

"I'm waitin' on the weather," he added.

"Ye'll have to make it yourself, Disko, for there's no sign *I* can see," said Long Jack, sweeping the clear horizon.

And yet, half an hour later, as they were dressing down, the Bank fog dropped on them, "between fish and fish," as they say. It drove steadily and in wreaths, curling and smoking along the colorless water. The men stopped dressing-down without a word. Long Jack and Uncle Salters slipped the windlass brakes into their sockets, and began to heave up the anchor; the windlass jarring as the wet hempen cable strained on the barrel. Manuel and Tom Platt gave a hand at the last. The anchor came up with a sob, and the riding-sail bellied as Troop steadied her at the wheel. "Up jib and foresail," said he.

"Slip 'em in the smother," shouted Long Jack, making fast the jib-sheet, while the others raised the clacking, rattling rings of the foresail; and the fore-boom creaked as the *We're Here* looked up into the wind and dived off into blank, whirling white.

"There's wind behind this fog," said Troop.

It was wonderful beyond words to Harvey; and the most wonderful part was that he heard no orders except an occasional grunt from Troop, ending with, "That's good, my son!"

" 'Never seen anchor weighed before?" said Tom Platt, to Harvey gaping at the damp canvas of the foresail.

"No. Where are we going?"

"Fish and make berth, as you'll find out 'fore you've been a week aboard. It's all new to you, but we never know what may come to us. Now, take me—Tom Platt—*I'd* never ha' thought—"

"It's better than fourteen dollars a month an' a bullet in your belly," said Troop, from the wheel. "Ease your jumbo a grind."

"Dollars an' cents better," returned the man-o'-war's man, doing something to a big jib with a wooden spar tied to it. "But we didn't think o' that when we manned the windlass-brakes on the *Miss Jim Buck,*[1] outside Beaufort Harbor, with Fort Macon heavin' hot shot at our stern, an' a livin' gale atop of all. Where was you then, Disko?"

"Jest here, or hereabouts," Disko replied, "earnin' my bread on the deep waters, an' dodgin' Reb privateers. Sorry I can't accommodate you with red-hot shot, Tom Platt; but I guess we'll come about all right on wind 'fore we see Eastern Point."

There was an incessant slapping and chatter at the bows now, varied by a solid thud and a little spout of spray that clattered down on the foc'sle. The rigging dripped clammy drops, and the men lounged along the lee of the house—all save Uncle Salters, who sat stiffly on the main-hatch nursing his stung hands.

" 'Guess she'd carry stays'l," said Disko, rolling one eye at his brother.

" 'Guess she wouldn't to any sorter profit. What's the sense o' wastin' canvas?" the farmer-sailor replied.

The wheel twitched almost imperceptibly in Disko's hands. A few seconds later a hissing wave-top slashed diagonally across the boat, smote Uncle Salters between the shoulders, and drenched him from head to foot. He rose sputtering, and went forward only to catch another.

"See Dad chase him all around the deck," said Dan. "Uncle Salters he thinks his quarter share's our canvas. Dad's put this duckin' act up on him two trips runnin'. Hi! That found him where he feeds." Uncle Salters had taken refuse by the foremast, but a wave slapped him over the knees. Disko's face was as blank as the circle of the wheel.

"Guess she'd lie easier under stays'l, Salters," said Disko, as though he had seen nothing.

"Set your old kite, then," roared the victim through a cloud of spray; "only don't lay it to me if anything happens. Penn, you go below right off an' git your coffee. You ought to hev more sense than to bum araound on deck this weather."

"Now they'll swill coffee an' play checkers till the cows come home," said Dan, as Uncle Salters hustled Penn into the fore-cabin. " 'Looks to me like's if we'd all be doin' so fer a spell. There's nothin' in creation deader-limpsey-idler'n a Banker when she ain't on fish."

"I'm glad ye spoke, Danny," cried Long Jack, who had been casting round in search of amusement. "I'd clean forgot we'd a passenger under that T-wharf hat. There's no idleness for thim that don't know their ropes. Pass him along, Tom Platt, an' we'll larn him."

" 'Tain't my trick this time," grinned Dan. "You've got to go it alone. Dad learned *me* with a rope's end."

For an hour Long Jack walked his prey up and down, teaching, as he said, "things at the sea that ivry man must know, blind, dhrunk, or asleep." There is not much gear to a seventy-ton schooner with a stump-foremast, but Long Jack had a gift of expression. When he wished to draw Harvey's attention to the peak-halyards, he dug his knuckles into the back of the boy's neck and kept him at gaze for half a minute. He emphasized the difference between fore and aft generally by rubbing Harvey's nose along a few feet of the boom, and the lead of each rope was fixed in Harvey's mind by the end of the rope itself.

The lesson would have been easier had the deck been at all free; but there appeared to be a place on it for everything and anything except a man. Forward lay the windlass and its tackle, with the chain and hemp cables, all very unpleasant to trip over; the foc'sle stovepipe, and the gurry-butts by the foc'sle hatch to hold the fish-livers. Aft of these the foreboom and booby of

[1] The *Gemsbok,* U.S.N.?

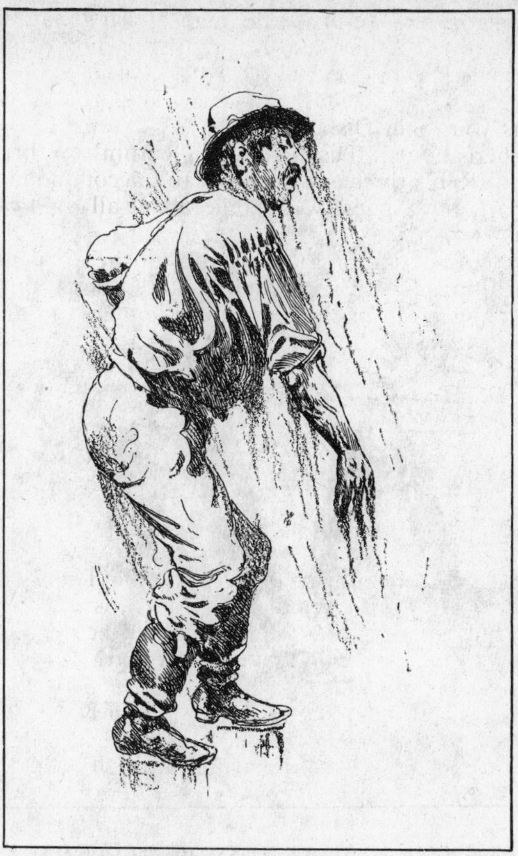

"A FEW SECONDS LATER A HISSING WAVE-TOP . . .
SMOTE UNCLE SALTERS BETWEEN THE SHOULDERS,
AND DRENCHED HIM FROM HEAD TO FOOT."

the main-hatch took all the space that was not needed for the pumps and dressing-pens. Then came the nests of dories lashed to ring-bolts by the quarter-deck; the house, with tubs and oddments lashed all around it; and, last, the sixty-foot main boom in its crutch, splitting things length-wise, to duck and dodge under every time.

Tom Platt, of course, could not keep his oar out of the business, but ranged alongside with enormous and unnecessary descriptions of sails and spars on the old *Ohio*.

"Niver mind fwhat he says; attind to me, Innocince. Tom Platt, this bally-hoo's not the *Ohio,* an' you're mixing the bhoy bad."

"He'll be ruined for life, beginnin' on a fore-an'-after this way," Tom Platt pleaded. "Give him a chance to know a few leadin' principles. Sailin's an art, Harvey, as I'd show you if I had ye in the fore-top o' the—"

"I know ut. Ye'd talk him dead an' cowld. Silince, Tom Platt! Now, after all I've said, how'd you reef the foresail, Harve? Take your time answerin'."

"Haul that in," said Harvey, pointing to leeward.

"Fwhat? The North Atlantuc?"

"No, the boom. Then run that rope you showed me back there—"

"That's no way," Tom Platt burst in.

"Quiet! He's larnin', an' has not the names good yet. Go on, Harve."

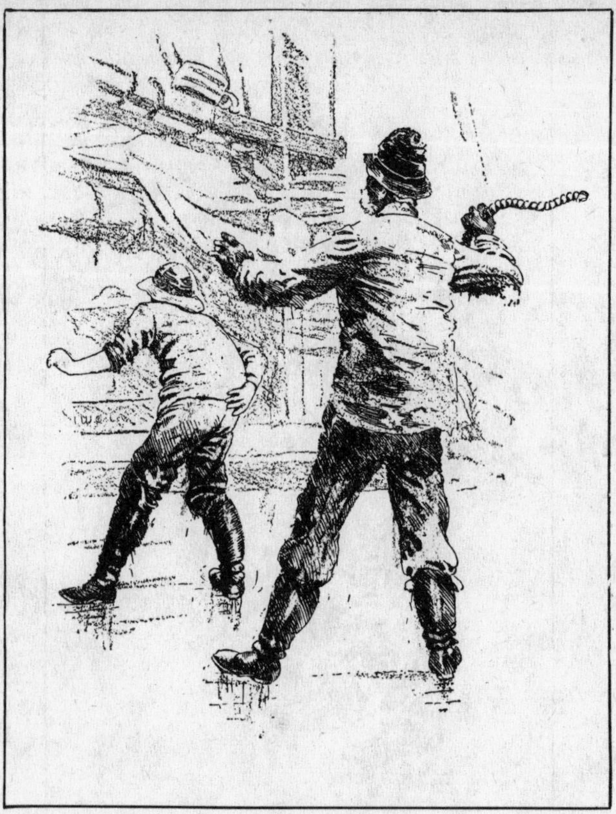

"FOR AN HOUR LONG JACK WALKED HIS PREY UP AND DOWN,
TEACHING, AS HE SAID,
'THINGS IVRY MAN MUST KNOW, BLIND, DHRUNK, OR ASLEEP.'"

"Oh, it's the reef-pennant. I'd hook the tackle on to the reef-pennant, and then let down——"

"Lower the sail, child! Lower!" said Tom Platt, in a professional agony.

"Lower the throat and peak halyards," Harvey went on. Those names stuck in his head.

"Lay your hand on thim," said Long Jack.

Harvey obeyed. "Lower till that rope-loop–on the after-leach–kris–no, it's cringle–till the cringle was down on the boom. Then I'd tie her up the way you said, and then I'd hoist up the peak and throat halyards again."

"You've forgot to pass the tack-earing, but wid time and help ye'll larn. There's good and just reason for ivry rope aboard, or else 'twould be overboard. D'ye follow me? 'Tis dollars an' cents I'm puttin' into your pocket, ye skinny little supercargo, so that fwhin ye've filled out ye can ship from Boston to Cuba an' tell them Long Jack larned you. Now I'll chase ye around a piece, callin' the ropes, an' you'll lay your hand on thim as I call."

He began, and Harvey, who was feeling rather tired, walked slowly to the rope named. A rope's end licked round his ribs, and nearly knocked the breath out of him.

"When you own a boat," said Tom Platt, with severe eyes, "you can walk. Till then, take all orders at the run. Once more–to make sure!"

Harvey was in a glow with the exercise, and this last cut warmed him thoroughly. Now he was a singularly smart boy, the son of a very clever man and a very sensitive woman, with a fine resolute temper that systematic spoiling had nearly turned to mulish obstinacy. He looked at the other men, and saw that even Dan did not smile. It was evidently all in the day's work, though it hurt abominably; so he swallowed the hint with a gulp and a gasp and a grin. The same smartness that led him to take such advantage of his mother made him very sure that no one on the boat, except, maybe, Penn, would stand the least nonsense. One learns a great deal from a mere tone. Long Jack called over half a dozen ropes, and Harvey danced over the deck like an eel at ebb-tide, one eye on Tom Platt.

"Ver' good. Ver' good don," said Manuel. "After supper I show you a little schooner I make, with all her ropes. So we shall learn."

"Fust-class fer–a passenger," said Dan. "Dad he's jest allowed you'll be wuth your salt maybe 'fore you're draowned. Thet's a heap fer Dad. I'll learn you more our next watch together."

"Taller!" grunted Disko, peering through the fog as it smoked over the bows. There was nothing to be seen ten feet beyond the surging jib-boom, while alongside rolled the endless procession of solemn, pale waves whispering and lipping one to the other.

"Now I'll learn you something Long Jack can't," shouted Tom Platt, as from a locker by the stern he produced a battered deep-sea lead hollowed at one end, smeared the hollow from a saucer full of mutton tallow, and went forward. "I'll learn you how to fly the Blue Pigeon. Shooo!"

Disko did something to the wheel that checked the schooner's way, while Manuel, with Harvey to help (and a proud boy was Harvey), let down the jib in a lump on the boom. The lead sung a deep droning song as Tom Platt whirled it round and round.

"Go ahead, man," said Long Jack, impatiently. "We're not drawin' twenty-five fut off Fire Island in a fog. There's no trick to ut."

"Don't be jealous, Galway." The released lead plopped into the sea far ahead as the schooner surged slowly forward.

"Soundin' *is* a trick, though," said Dan, "when your dipsey lead's all the eye you're like to hev for a week. What d'you make it, Dad?"

Disko's face relaxed. His skill and honour were involved in the march he had stolen on the rest of the Fleet, and he had his reputation as a master artist who knew the Banks blindfold. "Sixty, mebbe–ef I'm any judge," he replied, with a glance at the tiny compass in the window of the house.

"Sixty," sung out Tom Platt, hauling in great wet coils.

The schooner gathered way once more. "Heave!" said Disko, after a quarter of an hour.

"What d'you make it?" Dan whispered, and he looked at Harvey proudly. But Harvey was too proud of his own performances to be impressed just then.

"Fifty," said the father. "I mistrust we're right over the nick o' Green Bank on old Sixty-Fifty."

"Fifty!" roared Tom Platt. They could scarcely see him through the fog. "She's bust within a yard–like the shells at Fort Macon."

"Bait up, Harve," said Dan, diving for a line on the reel.

The schooner seemed to be straying promiscuously through the smother, her headsail banging wildly. The men waited and looked at the boys who began fishing.

"Heugh!" Dan's lines twitched on the scored and scarred rail. "Now haow in thunder did Dad know? Help us here, Harve. It's a big un. Poke-hooked, too." They hauled together, and landed a goggle-eyed twenty-pound cod. He had taken the bait right into his stomach.

"Why, he's all covered with little crabs," cried Harvey, turning him over.

"By the great hook-block, they're lousy already," said Long Jack. "Disko, ye kape your spare eyes under the keel."

Splash went the anchor, and they all heaved over the lines, each man taking his own place at the bulwarks.

"Are they good to eat?" Harvey panted, as he lugged in another crab-covered cod.

"Sure. When they're lousy it's a sign they've all been herdin' together by the thousand, and when they take the bait that way they're hungry. Never mind how the bait sets. They'll bite on the bare hook."

"Say, this is great!" Harvey cried, as the fish came in gasping and splashing—nearly all poke-hooked, as Dan had said. "Why can't we always fish from the boat instead of from the dories?"

"Allus can, till we begin to dress down. Efter thet, the heads and offals 'u'd scare the fish to Fundy. Boatfishin' ain't reckoned progressive, though, unless ye know as much as dad knows. Guess we'll run aout aour trawl to-night. Harder on the back, this, than frum the dory, ain't it?"

It was rather back-breaking work, for in a dory the weight of a cod is water-borne till the last minute, and you are, so to speak, abreast of him; but the few feet of a schooner's freeboard make so much extra dead-hauling, and stooping over the bulwarks cramps the stomach. But it was wild and furious sport so long as it lasted; and a big pile lay aboard when the fish ceased biting.

"Where's Penn and Uncle Salters?" Harvey asked, slapping the slime off his oilskins, and reeling up the line in careful imitation of the others.

"Git 's coffee and see."

Under the yellow glare of the lamp on the pawl-post, the foc'sle table down and opened, utterly unconscious of fish or weather, sat the two men, a checker-board between them, Uncle Salters snarling at Penn's every move.

"What's the matter naow?" said the former, as Harvey, one hand in the leather loop at the head of the ladder, hung shouting to the cook.

"Big fish and lousy—heaps and heaps," Harvey replied, quoting Long Jack. "How's the game?"

Little Penn's jaw dropped. " 'Tweren't none o' his fault," snapped Uncle Salters. "Penn's deef."

"Checkers, weren't it?" said Dan, as Harvey staggered aft with the steaming coffee in a tin pail. "That lets us out o' cleanin' up to-night. Dad's a jest man. They'll have to do it."

"An' two young fellers I know'll bait up a tub or so o' trawl, while they're cleanin'," said Disko, lashing the wheel to his taste.

"Um! Guess I'd ruther clean up, Dad."

"Don't doubt it. Ye wun't, though. Dress daown! Dress daown! Penn'll pitch while you two bait up."

"Why in thunder didn't them blame boys tell us you'd struck on?" said Uncle Salters, shuffling to his place at the table. "This knife's gum-blunt, Dan."

"Ef stickin' out cable don't wake ye, guess you'd better hire a boy o' your own," said Dan, muddling about in the dusk over the tubs full of trawl-line lashed to windward of the house. "Oh, Harve, don't ye want to slip down an' git 's bait?"

"Bait ez we are," said Disko. "I mistrust shag-fishin' will pay better, ez things go."

That meant the boys would bait with selected offal of the cod as the fish were cleaned—an improvement on paddling bare-handed in the little bait-barrels below. The tubs were full of neatly coiled line carrying a big hook each few feet; and the testing and baiting of every single hook, with the stowage of the baited line so that it should run clear when shot from the dory, was a scientific business. Dan managed it in the dark, without looking, while Harvey caught his fingers on the barbs and bewailed his fate. But the hooks flew through Dan's fingers like tatting on an old maid's lap. "I helped bait up trawl ashore 'fore I could well walk," he said. "But it's a putterin' job all the same. Oh, Dad!" This shouted towards the hatch, where Disko and Tom Platt were salting. "How many skates you reckon we'll need?"

" 'Baout three. Hurry!"

"There's three hundred fathom to each tub," Dan explained; "more'n enough to lay out to-night. Ouch! 'Slipped up there, I did." He stuck his finger in his mouth. "I tell you, Harve, there ain't money in Gloucester 'u'd hire me to ship on a reg'lar trawler. It may be progressive, but, barrin' that, it's the putterin'est, slimjammest business top of earth."

"I don't know what this is, if 'tisn't regular trawling," said Harvey sulkily. "My fingers are all cut to frazzles."

"Pshaw! This is just one o' Dad's blame experiments. He don't trawl 'less there's mighty good reason fer it. Dad knows. Thet's why he's baitin' ez he is. We'll hev her saggin' full when we take her up er we won't see a fin."

Penn and Uncle Salters cleaned up as Disko had ordained, but the boys profited little. No sooner were the tubs furnished than Tom Platt and Long Jack, who had been exploring the inside of a dory with a lantern, snatched them away, loaded up the tubs and some small, painted trawl-buoys, and hove the boat overboard into what Harvey regarded as an exceedingly rough sea. "They'll be drowned. Why, the dory's loaded like a freight-car," he cried.

"We'll be back," said Long Jack, "an' in case you'll not be lookin' for us, we'll lay into you both if the trawl's snarled."

The dory surged up on the crest of a wave, and just when it seemed impossible that she could avoid smashing against the schooner's side, slid over the ridge, and was swallowed up in the damp dusk.

"Take ahold here, an' keep ringin' steady," said Dan, passing Harvey the lanyard of a bell that hung just behind the windlass.

Harvey rang lustily, for he felt two lives depended on him. But Disko in the cabin, scrawling in the log-book, did not look like a murderer, and when he went to supper he even smiled dryly at the anxious Harvey.

"*This* ain't no weather," said Dan. "Why, you an' me could set thet trawl! They've only gone out jest far 'nough so's not to foul our cable. They don't need no bell reelly."

"Clang! clang! clang!" Harvey kept it up, varied with occasional rub-a-dubs, for another half-hour. There was a bellow and a bump alongside. Manuel and Dan raced to the hooks of the dory-tackle; Long Jack and Tom Platt arrived on deck together, it seemed, one half the North Atlantic at their backs, and the dory followed them in the air, landing with a clatter.

"Nary snarl," said Tom Platt as he dripped "Danny, you'll do yet."

"The pleasure av your comp'ny to the banquit," said Long Jack, squelching the water from his boots as he capered like an elephant and stuck an oil-skinned arm into Harvey's face. "We do be condescending to honour the second half wid our presence." And off they all four rolled to supper, where Harvey stuffed himself to the brim on fish-chowder and fried pies, and fell fast asleep just as Manuel produced from a locker a lovely two-foot model of the *Lucy Holmes,* his first boat, and was going to show Harvey the ropes. Harvey never even twiddled his fingers as Penn pushed him into his bunk.

"It must be a sad thing–a very sad thing," said Penn, watching the boy's face, "for his mother and his father, who think he is dead. To lose a child–to lose a man-child!"

"Git out o' this, Penn," said Dan. "Go aft and finish your game with Uncle Salters. Tell Dad I'll stand Harve's watch ef he don't keer. He's played aout."

"Ver' good boy," said Manuel, slipping out of his boots and disappearing into the black shadows of the lower bunk. "Expec' he make good man, Danny. I no see he is any so mad as your parpa he says. Eh, wha-at?"

Dan chuckled, but the chuckle ended in a snore.

It was thick weather outside, with a rising wind, and the elder men stretched their watches. The hour struck clear in the cabin; the nosing bows slapped and scuffed with the seas; the foc'sle stove-pipe hissed and sputtered as the spray caught it; and the boys slept on, while Disko, Long Jack, Tom Platt, and Uncle Salters, each in turn, stumped aft to look at the wheel, forward to see that the anchor held, or to veer out a little more cable against chafing, with a glance at the dim anchor-light between each round.

Chapter Four

HARVEY WAKED TO find the "first half" at breakfast, the foc'sle door drawn to a crack, and every square inch of the schooner singing its own tune. The black bulk of the cook balanced behind the tiny galley over the glare of the stove, and the pots and pans in the pierced wooden board before it jarred and racketed to each plunge. Up and up the foc'sle climbed, yearning and surging and quivering, and then, with a clear, sickle-like swoop, came down into the seas. He could hear the flaring bows cut and squelch, and there was a pause ere the divided waters came down on the deck above, like a volley of buckshot. Followed the woolly sound of the cable in the hawse-hole; and a grunt and squeal of the windlass; a yaw, a punt, and a kick, and the *We're Here* gathered herself together to repeat the motions.

"Now, ashore," he heard Long Jack saying, "ye've chores, an' ye must do thim in any weather. Here we're well clear of the fleet, an' we've no chores– an' that's a blessin'. Good night, all." He passed like a big snake from the table to his bunk, and began to smoke. Tom Platt followed his example; Uncle Salters, with Penn, fought his way up the ladder to stand his watch, and the cook set for the "second half."

It came out of its bunks as the others had entered theirs, with a shake and a yawn. It ate till it could eat no more; and then Manuel filled his pipe with some terrible tobacco, crotched himself between the pawl-post and a forward bunk, cocked his feet up on the table, and smiled tender and indolent smiles at the smoke. Dan lay at length in his bunk, wrestling with a gaudy, gilt-stopped accordion, whose tunes went up and down with the pitching of the *We're Here*. The cook, his shoulders against the locker where he kept the fried pies (Dan was fond of fried pies), peeled potatoes, with one eye on the stove in event of too much water finding its way down the pipe; and the general smell and smother were past all description.

Harvey considered affairs, wondered that he was not deathly sick, and crawled into his bunk again, as the softest and safest place, while Dan struck up, "I don't want to play in your yard," as accurately as the wild jerks allowed.

"How long is this for?" Harvey asked of Manuel.

"Till she get a little quiet, and we can row to trawl. Perhaps to-night. Perhaps two days more. You do not like? Eh, wha-at?"

"I should have been crazy sick a week ago, but it doesn't seem to upset me now–much."

"That is because we make you fisherman, these days. If I was you, when I come to Gloucester I would give two, three big candles for my good luck."

"Give who?"

"To be sure–the Virgin of our Church on the Hill. She is very good to fishermen all the time. That is why so few of us Portugee men ever are drowned."

"You're a Roman Catholic, then?"

"I am a Madeira man. I am not a Porto Pico boy. Shall I be Baptist, then? Eh, wha-at? I always give candles—two, three more when I come to Gloucester. The good Virgin she never forgets me, Manuel."

"I don't sense it that way," Tom Platt put in from his bunk, his scarred face lit up by the glare of a match as he sucked at his pipe. "It stands to reason the sea's the sea; and you'll get jest about what's goin', candles or kerosene, fer that matter."

" 'Tis a mighty good thing," said Long Jack, "to have a frind at coort, though. I'm o' Manuel's way o' thinkin'. About ten years back I was crew to a Sou' Boston market-boat. We was off Minot's Ledge wid a northeaster, butt first, atop of us, thicker'n burgoo. The ould man was dhrunk, his chin waggin' on the tiller, an' I sez to myself, 'If iver I stick my boat-huk into T-wharf again, I'll show the saints fwhat manner o' craft they saved me out av.' Now, I'm here, as ye can well see, an' the model of the dhirty ould *Kathleen,* that took me a month to make, I gave ut to the priest, an' he hung ut up forninst the altar. There's more sense in givin' a model that's by way o' bein' a work av art than any candle. Ye can buy candles at store, but a model shows the good saints ye've tuk trouble an' are grateful."

"D'you believe that, Irish?" said Tom Platt, turning on his elbow.

"Would I do ut if I did not, Ohio?"

"Wa-al, Enoch Fuller he made a model o' the old *Ohio*, and she's to Calem museum now. Mighty pretty model, too, but I guess Enoch he never done it fer no sacrifice; an' the way I take it is—"

There were the makings of an hour-long discussion of the kind that fishermen love, where the talk runs in shouting circles and no one proves anything at the end, had not Dan struck up this cheerful rhyme:

"Up jumped the mackerel with his stripèd back.
Reef in the mainsail, and haul on the tack;
For it's windy weather—"

Here Long Jack joined in:

And it's blowy weather;
When the winds begin to blow, pipe all hands together!"

Dan went on, with a cautious look at Tom Platt, holding the accordion low in the bunk:

"Up jumped the cod with his chuckle-head,
Went to the main-chains to heave at the lead;
For it's windy weather," etc.

Tom Platt seemed to be hunting for something. Dan crouched lower, but sang louder:

"Up jumped the flounder that swims to the ground.
Chuckle-head! Chuckle-head! Mind where ye sound!"

Tom Platt's huge rubber boot whirled across the foc'sle and caught Dan's uplifted arm. There was war between the man and the boy ever since Dan had discovered that the mere whistling of that tune would make him angry as he heaved the lead.

"Thought I'd fetch yer," said Dan, returning the gift with precision. "Ef you don't like my music, git out your fiddle. I ain't goin' to lie here all day an' listen to you an' Long Jack arguin' 'baout candles. Fiddle, Tom Platt; or

I'll learn Harve here the tune!"

Tom Platt leaned down to a locker and brought up an old white fiddle. Manuel's eye glistened, and from somewhere behind the pawl-post he drew out a tiny, guitar-like thing with wire strings, which he called a *machette*.

" 'Tis a concert," said Long Jack, beaming through the smoke. "A reg'lar Boston concert."

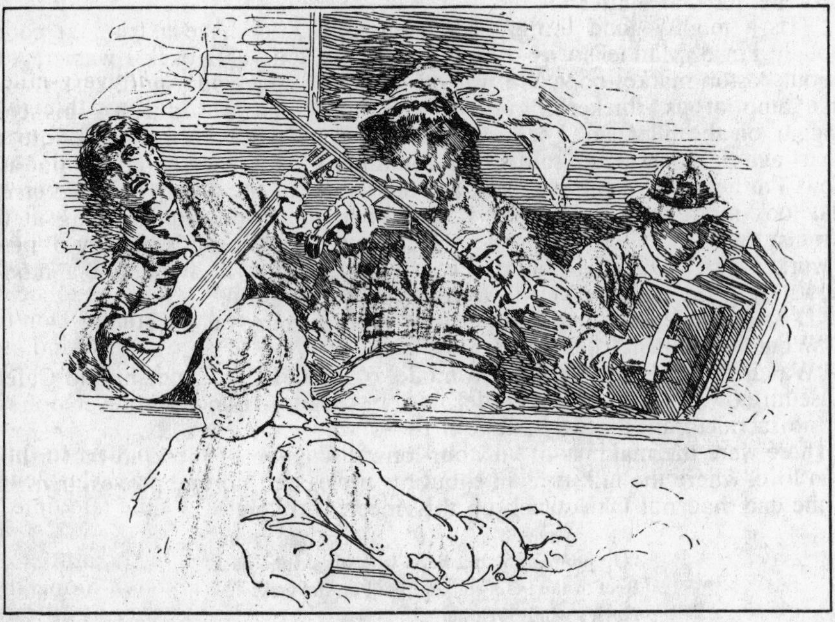

"'T IS A CONCERT,' SAID LONG JACK, BEAMING THROUGH THE SMOKE. 'A REG'LAR BOSTON CONCERT.'"

There was a burst of spray as the hatch opened, and Disko, in yellow oilskins, descended.

"Ye're just in time, Disko. Fwhat's she doin' outside?"

"Jest this!" He dropped on to the lockers with the push and heave of the *We're Here*.

"We're singin' to kape our breakfasts down. Ye'll lead, av course, Disko," said Long Jack.

"Guess there ain't more'n 'baout two old songs I know, an' ye've heerd them both."

His excuses were cut short by Tom Platt launching into a most dolorous tune, like unto the moaning of winds and the creaking of masts. With his eyes fixed on the beams above, Disko began this ancient, ancient ditty, Tom Platt flourishing all round him to make the tune and words fit a little:

"There is a crack packet—crack packet o' fame,
She hails from Noo York, an' the *Dreadnought*'s her name.
You may talk o' your fliers—Swallow-tail and Black Ball—
But the *Dreadnought*'s the packet that can beat them all.

"Now the *Dreadnought* she lies in the River Mersey,
Because of the tug-boat to take her to sea;
But when she's off soundings you shortly will know

(Chorus.)
She's the Liverpool packet–O Lord, let her go!

"Now the *Dreadnought* she's howlin' crost the Banks o' Newfoundland,
Where the water's all shallow and the bottom's all sand.
Sez all the little fishes that swim to and fro:

(Chorus.)
'She's the Liverpool packet–O Lord, let her go!' "

There were scores of verses, for he worked the *Dreadnought* every mile of the way between Liverpool and New York as conscientiously as though he were on her deck, and the accordion pumped and the fiddle squeaked beside him. Tom Platt followed with something about "the rough and tough McGinn, who would pilot the vessel in." Then they called on Harvey, who felt very flattered, to contribute to the entertainment; but all that he could remember were some pieces of "Skipper Ireson's Ride" that he had been taught at the camp-school in the Adirondacks. It seemed that they might be appropriate to the time and place, but he had no more than mentioned the title when Disko brought down one foot with a bang, and cried, "Don't go on, young feller. That's a mistaken jedgment–one o' the worst kind, too, becaze it's catchin' to the ear."

"I orter ha' warned you," said Dan. "Thet allus fetches Dad."

"What's wrong?" said Harvey, surprised and a little angry.

"All you're goin' to say," said Disko. "All dead wrong from start to finish, an' Whittier he's to blame. I have no special call to right any Marblehead man, but 'tweren't no fault o' Ireson's. My father he told me the tale time an' again, an' this is the way 'twuz."

"For the wan hundredth time," put in Long Jack under his breath.

"Ben Ireson he was skipper o' the *Betty,* young feller, comin' home frum the Banks–that was before the war of 1812, but jestice is jestice at all times. They f'und the *Active* o' Portland, an' Gibbons o' that town he was her skipper; they f'und her leakin' off Cape Cod Light. There was a terr'ble gale on, an' they was gettin' the *Betty* home's fast as they could craowd her. Well, Ireson he said there warn't any sense to reskin' a boat in that sea; the men they wouldn't hev it; and he laid it before them to stay by the *Active* till the sea run daown a piece. They wouldn't hev that either, hangin' araound the Cape in any sech weather, leak or no leak. They jest up stays'l an' quit, nat'rally takin' Ireson with 'em. Folks to Marblehead was mad at him not runnin' the risk, and becaze nex' day, when the sea was ca'am (they never stopped to think o' *that*), some of the *Active's* folks was took off by a Truro man. They come into Marblehead with their own tale to tell, sayin' how Ireson had shamed his town, an' so forth an' so on; an' Ireson's men they was scared, seein' public feelin' agin' 'em, an' they went back on Ireson, an' swore he was respons'ble for the hull act. 'Tweren't the women neither that tarred and feathered him–Marblehead women don't act that way–'twas a passel o' men an' boys, an' they carted him araound town in an old dory till the bottom fell aout, and Ireson he told 'em they'd be sorry for it some day. Well, the facts come aout later, same's they usually do, too late to be any ways useful to an honest man; an' Whittier he come along an' picked up the slack eend of a lyin' tale, an' tarred and feathered Ben Ireson all over onct more after he was dead. 'Twas the only time Whittier ever slipped up, an' 'tweren't fair. I whaled Dan good when he brought that piece back from school. *You* don't know no better, o' course; but I've give you the facts, hereafter an' evermore to be remembered. Ben Ireson weren't no sech kind o' man as Whittier makes aout; my father he knew him well, before an' after that business, an' you beware o' hasty jedgments, young feller. Next!"

Harvey had never heard Disko talk so long, and collapsed with burning cheeks; but, as Dan said promptly, a boy could only learn what he was taught at school, and life was too short to keep track of every lie along the coast.

Then Manuel touched the jangling, jarring little *machette* to a queer tune, and sang something in Portuguese about *"Nina, innocente!"* ending with a full-handed sweep that brought the song up with a jerk. Then Disko obliged with his second song, to an old-fashioned creaky tune, and all joined in the chorus. This is one stanza:

"Now Aprile is over and melted the snow,
And outer Noo Bedford we shortly must tow;
Yes, out o' Noo Bedford we shortly must clear,
We're the whalers that never see wheat in the ear."

Here the fiddle went very softly for a while by itself, and then:

"Wheat-in-the-ear, my true-love's posy blowin';
Wheat-in-the-ear, we're goin' off to sea;
Wheat-in-the-ear, I left you fit for sowin';
When I come back a loaf o' bread you'll be!"

That made Harvey almost weep, though he could not tell why. But it was much worse when the cook dropped the potatoes and held out his hands for the fiddle. Still leaning against the locker door, he struck into a tune that was like something very bad but sure to happen whatever you did. After a little he sang, in an unknown tongue, his big chin down on the fiddle-tail, his white eyeballs glaring in the lamp-light. Harvey swung out of his bunk to hear better; and amid the straining of the timbers and the wash of the waters the tune crooned and moaned on, like lee surf in a blind fog, till it ended with a wail.

"Jiminy Christmas! Thet gives me the blue creevles," said Dan. "What in thunder is it?"

"The song of Fin McCoul," said the cook, "when he wass going to Norway." His English was not thick, but all clear-cut, as though it came from a phonograph.

"Faith, I've been to Norway, but I didn't make that unwholesim noise. 'Tis like some of the old songs, though," said Long Jack, sighing.

"Don't let's hev another 'thout somethin' between," said Dan; and the accordion struck up a rattling, catchy tune that ended:

"It's six an' twenty Sundays sence las' we saw the land,
With fifteen hunder quintal,
An' fifteen hunder quintal,
'Teen hunder toppin' quintal,
'Twix' old 'Queereau an' Grand!"

"Hold on!" roared Tom Platt. "D'ye want to nail the trip, Dan? That's Jonah sure, 'less you sing it after all our salt's wet."

"No, 'tain't. Is it, Dad? Not unless you sing the very las' verse. You can't learn *me* anything on Jonahs!"

"What's that?" said Harvey. "What's a Jonah?"

"A Jonah's anything that spoils the luck. Sometimes it's a man–sometimes it's a boy–or a bucket. I've known a splittin'-knife Jonah two trips till we was on to her," said Tom Platt. "There's all sorts o' Jonahs. Jim Bourke was one till he was drowned on Georges. I'd never ship with Jim Bourke, not if I was starvin'. There wuz a green dory on the *Ezra Flood.* Thet was a Jonah, too, the worst sort o' Jonah. Drowned four men, she did, an' used to shine fiery o' nights in the nest."

"And you believe that?" said Harvey, remembering what Tom Platt had said about candles and models. "Haven't we all got to take what's served?"

A mutter of dissent ran round the bunks. "Outboard, yes; inboard, things can happen," said Disko. "Don't you go makin' a mock of Jonahs, young feller."

"Well, Harve ain't no Jonah. Day after we catched him," Dan cut in, "we had a toppin' good catch."

The cook threw up his head and laughed suddenly–a queer, thin laugh. He was a most disconcerting nigger.

"Murder!" said Long Jack. "Don't do that again, doctor. We ain't used to ut."

"What's wrong?" said Dan. "Ain't he our mascot, and didn't they strike on good after we'd struck him?"

"Oh! yess," said the cook. "I know that, but the catch iss not finish yet."

"He ain't goin' to do us any harm," said Dan, hotly. "Where are ye hintin' an' edgin' to? *He's* all right."

"No harm. No. But one day he will be your master, Danny."

"That all?" said Dan, placidly. "He wun't–not by a jugful."

"Master!" said the cook, pointing to Harvey. "Man!" and he pointed to Dan.

"That's news. Haow soon?" said Dan, with a laugh.

"In some years, and I shall see it. Master and man–man and master."

"Haow in thunder d'ye work that out?" said Tom Platt.

"In my head, where I can see."

"How?" This from all the others at once.

"I do not know, but so it will be." He dropped his head, and went on peeling the potatoes, and not another word could they get out of him.

"Well," said Dan, "a heap o' thing'll hev to come abaout 'fore Harve's any master o' mine; but I'm glad the doctor ain't choosen to mark him for a Jonah. Now, I mistrust Uncle Salters fer the Jonerest Jonah in the Fleet regardin' his own special luck. Dunno ef it's spreadin' same's smallpox. He ought to be on the *Carrie Pitman.* That boat's her own Jonah, sure–crews an' gear made no differ to her driftin'. Jiminy Christmas! She'll etch loose in a flat ca'am."

"We're well clear o' the Fleet, anyway," said Disko. "*Carrie Pitman* an' all." There was a rapping on the deck.

"Uncle Salters has catched his luck," said Dan as his father departed.

"It's blown clear," Disko cried, and all the foc'sle tumbled up for a bit of fresh air. The fog had gone, but a sullen sea ran in great rollers behind it. The *We're Here* slid, as it were, into long, sunk avenues and ditches which felt quite sheltered and homelike if they would only stay still; but they changed without rest or mercy, and flung up the schooner to crown one peak of a thousand gray hills, while the wind hooted through her rigging as she zigzagged down the slopes. Far away a sea would burst into a sheet of foam, and the others would follow suit as at a signal, till Harvey's eyes swam with the vision of interlacing whites and grays. Four or five Mother Carey's chickens stormed round in circles, shrieking as they swept past the bows. A rain-squall or two strayed aimlessly over the hopeless waste, ran down wind and back again, and melted away.

"Seems to me I saw somethin' flicker jest naow over yonder," said Uncle Salters, pointing to the northeast.

"Can't be any of the fleet," said Disko, peering under his eyebrows, a hand on the foc'sle gangway as the solid bows hatcheted into the troughs. "Sea's oilin' over dretful fast. Danny, don't you want to skip a piece an' see how aour trawl-buoy lays?"

Danny, in his big boots, trotted rather than climbed up the main rigging (this consumed Harvey with envy), hitched himself around the reeling cross-trees, and let his eye rove till it caught the tiny black buoy-flag on the shoulder of a mile-away swell.

"She's all right," he hailed. "Sail O! Dead to the no'th'ard, comin' down like smoke! Schooner she be, too."

They waited yet another half-hour, the sky clearing in patches, with a flicker of sickly sun from time to time that made patches of olive-green water. Then a stump-foremast lifted, ducked, and disappeared, to be followed on the next wave by a high stern with old-fashioned wooden snail's-horn davits. The snails were redtanned.

"Frenchmen!" shouted Dan. "No, 'tain't neither. Daad!"

"That's no French," said Disko. "Salters, your blame luck holds tighter'n a screw in a keg-head."

"I've eyes. It's Uncle Abishai."

"You can't nowise tell fer sure."

"The head-king of all Jonahs," groaned Tom Platt. "Oh, Salters, Salters, why wasn't you abed an' asleep?"

"How could I tell?" said poor Salters, as the schooner swung up.

She might have been the very *Flying Dutchman,* so foul, draggled, and unkempt was every rope and stick aboard. Her old-style quarterdeck was some four or five feet high, and her rigging flew knotted and tangled like weed at a wharf-end. She was running before the wind–yawing frightfully–her staysail let down to act as a sort of extra foresail,–"scandalized," they call it,–and her foreboom guyed out over the side. Her bowsprit cocked up like an old-fashioned frigate's; her jib-boom had been fished and spliced and nailed and clamped beyond further repair; and as she hove herself forward, and sat down on her broad tail, she looked for all the world like a blouzy, frouzy, bad old woman sneering at a decent girl.

"That's Abishai," said Salters. "Full o' gin an' Judique men, an' the judgments o' Providence layin' fer him an' never takin' good holt. He's run in to bait, Miquelon way."

"He'll run her under," said Long Jack. "That's no rig fer this weather."

"Not he, 'r he'd'a done it long ago," Disko replied. "Looks 's if he cal'lated to run *us* under. Ain't she daown by the head more 'n natural, Tom Platt?"

"Ef it's his style o' loadin' her she ain't safe," said the sailor slowly. "Ef she's spewed her oakum he'd better git to his pumps mighty quick."

The creature threshed up, wore round with a clatter and rattle, and lay head to wind within ear-shot.

A gray-beard wagged over the bulwark, and a thick voice yelled something Harvey could not understand. But Disko's face darkened. "He'd resk every stick he hez to carry bad news. Says we're in fer a shift o' wind. He's in fer worse. Abishai! Abi-*shai!*" He waved his arm up and down with the gesture of a man at the pumps, and pointed forward. The crew mocked him and laughed.

"Jounce ye, an' strip ye an' trip ye!" yelled Uncle Abishai. "A livin' gale–a livin' gale. Yah! Cast up fer your last trip, all your Gloucester haddocks. *You* won't see Gloucester no more, no more!"

"Crazy full–as usual," said Tom Platt. "Wish he hadn't spied us, though."

She drifted out of hearing while the gray-head yelled something about a dance at the Bay of Bulls and a dead man in the foc'sle. Harvey shuddered. He had seen the sloven tilled decks and the savage-eyed crew.

"An' that's a fine little floatin' hell fer her draught," said Long Jack. "I wondher what mischief he's been at ashore."

"He's a trawler," Dan explained to Harvey, "an he runs in fer bait all along the coast. Oh, no, not home, he don't go. He deals along the south an' east shore up yonder." He nodded in the direction of the pitiless Newfoundland beaches. "Dad won't never take me ashore there. They're a mighty tough crowd—an' Abishai's the toughest. You saw his boat? Well, she's nigh seventy year old, they say; the last o' the old Marblehead heeltappers. They don't make them quarterdecks any more. Abishai don't use Marblehead, though. He ain't wanted there. He jes' drif's araound, in debt, trawlin' an' cussin' like you've heard. Bin a Jonah fer years an' years, he hez. 'Gits liquor frum the Feecamp boats fer makin' spells an' selling winds an' such truck. Crazy, I guess."

" 'Twon't be any use underrunnin' the trawl to-night," said Tom Platt, with quiet despair. "He come alongside special to cuss us. I'd give my wage an' share to see him at the gangway o' the old *Ohio* 'fore we quit floggin'. Jest abaout six dozen, an' Sam Mocatta layin' 'em on criss-cross!"

The dishevelled "heel-tapper" danced drunkenly down wind, and all eyes followed her. Suddenly the cook cried in his phonograph voice: "It wass his own death made him speak so! He iss fey—fey, I tell you! Look!" She sailed into a patch of watery sunshine three or four miles distant. The patch dulled and faded out, and even as the light passed so did the schooner. She dropped into a hollow and—was not.

"Run under, by the Great Hook-Block!" shouted Disko, jumping aft. "Drunk or sober, we've got to help 'em. Heave short and break her out! Smart!"

Harvey was thrown on the deck by the shock that followed the setting of the jib and foresail, for they hove short on the cable, and to save time, jerked the anchor bodily from the bottom, heaving in as they moved away. This is a bit of brute force seldom resorted to except in matters of life and death, and the little *We're Here* complained like a human. They ran down to where Abishai's craft had vanished; found two or three trawl-tubs, a gin-bottle, and a stove-in dory, but nothing more. "Let 'em go," said Disko, though no one had hinted at picking them up. "I wouldn't hev a match that belonged to Abishai aboard. Guess she run clear under. Must ha' been spewin' her

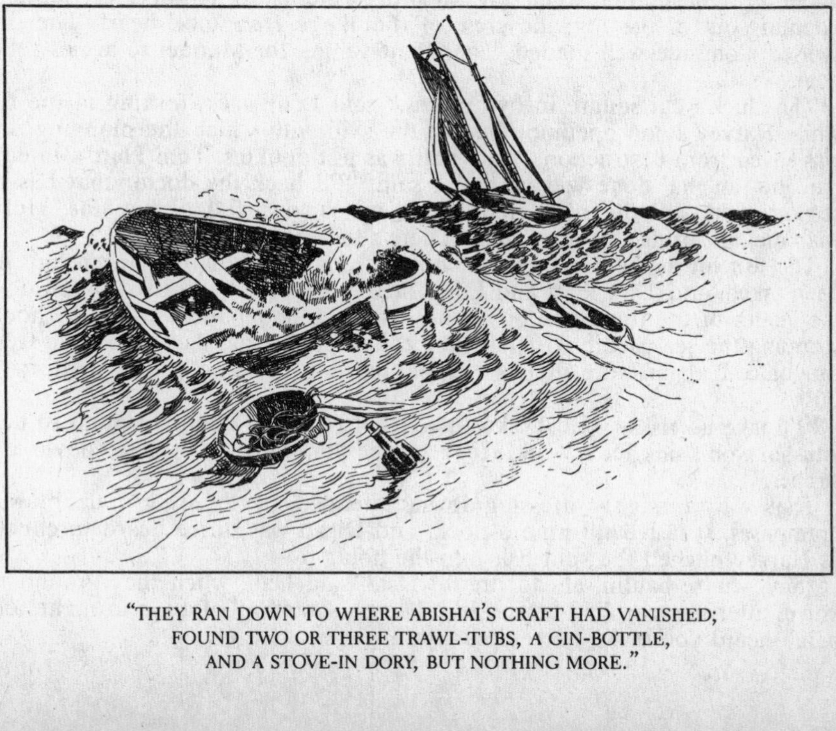

"THEY RAN DOWN TO WHERE ABISHAI'S CRAFT HAD VANISHED; FOUND TWO OR THREE TRAWL-TUBS, A GIN-BOTTLE, AND A STOVE-IN DORY, BUT NOTHING MORE."

oakum fer a week, an' they never thought to pump her. That's one more boat gone along o' leavin' port all hands drunk."

"Glory be!" said Long Jack. "We'd ha' been obliged to help 'em if they was top o' water."

" 'Thinkin' o' that myself," said Tom Platt.

"Fey! Fey!" said the cook, rolling his eyes. "He haas taken his own luck with him."

"Ver' good thing, I think, to tell the Fleet when we see. Eh, wha-at?" said Manuel. "If you runna that way before the wind, and she work open her seams–" He threw out his hands with an indescribable gesture, while Penn sat down on the house and sobbed at the sheer horror and pity of it all. Harvey could not realize that he had seen death on the open waters, but he felt very sick.

Then Dan went up the cross-trees, and Disko steered them back to within sight of their own trawl-buoys just before the fog blanketed the sea once again.

"We go mighty quick hereabouts when we do go," was all he said to Harvey. "You think on that fer a spell, young feller. That was liquor."

After dinner it was calm enough to fish from the decks,–Penn and Uncle Salters were very zealous this time,–and the catch was large and large fish.

"Abishai has shorely took his luck with him," said Salters. "The wind hain't backed ner riz ner nothin'. How abaout the trawl? I despise superstition, anyway."

Tom Platt insisted that they had much better haul the thing and make a new berth. But the cook said: "The luck is in two pieces. You will find it so when you look. *I* know." This so tickled Long Jack that he overbore Tom Platt and the two went out together.

Underrunning a trawl means pulling it in on one side of the dory, picking off the fish, rebaiting the hooks, and passing them back to the sea again–something like pinning and unpinning linen on a wash-line. It is a lengthy business and rather dangerous, for the long, sagging line may twitch a boat under in a flash. But when they heard, "And naow to thee, O Capting," booming out of the fog, the crew of the *We're Here* took heart. The dory swirled alongside well loaded, Tom Platt yelling for Manuel to act as relief-boat.

"The luck's cut square in two pieces," said Long Jack, forking in the fish, while Harvey stood openmouthed at the skill with which the plunging dory was saved from destruction. "One half was jest punkins. Tom Platt wanted to haul her an' ha' done wid ut; but I said, "I'll back the doctor that has the second sight, an' the other half come up sagging full o' big uns. Hurry, Man'nle, an' bring's a tub o' bait. There's luck afloat to-night."

The fish bit at the newly baited hooks from which their brethren had just been taken, and Tom Platt and Long Jack moved methodically up and down the length of the trawl, the boat's nose surging under the wet line of hooks, stripping the sea-cucumbers that they called pumpkins, slatting off the fresh-caught cod against the gunwale, rebaiting, and loading Manuel's dory till dusk.

"I'll take no risks," said Disko then–"not with him floatin' around so near. Abishai won't sink fer a week. Heave in the dories an' we'll dress daown after supper."

That was a mighty dressing-down, attended by three or four blowing grampuses. It lasted till nine o'clock, and Disko was thrice heard to chuckle as Harvey pitched the split fish into the hold.

"Say, you're haulin' ahead dretful fast," said Dan, when they ground the knives after the men had turned in. "There's somethin' of a sea to-night, an' I hain't heard you make no remarks on it."

"Too busy," Harvey replied, testing a blade's edge. "Come to think of it, she *is* a high-kicker."

The little schooner was gambolling all around her anchor among the silver-tipped waves. Backing with a start of affected surprise at the sight of the strained cable, she pounced on it like a kitten, while the spray of her descent burst through the hawse-holes with the report of a gun. Shaking her head, she would say: "Well, I'm sorry I can't stay any longer with you. I'm going North," and would sidle off, halting suddenly with a dramatic rattle of her rigging. "As I was just going to observe," she would begin, as gravely as a drunken man addressing a lamp-post. The rest of the sentence (she acted her words in dumb-show, of course) was lost in a fit of the fidgets, when she behaved like a puppy chewing a string, a clumsy woman in a side-saddle, a hen with her head cut off, or a cow stung by a hornet, exactly as the whims of the sea took her.

"See her sayin' her piece. She's Patrick Henry naow," said Dan.

She swung sideways on a roller, and gesticulated with her jib-boom from port to starboard.

"But–ez–fer me, give me liberty–er give me–death!"

Wop! She sat down in the moon-path on the water, courtesying with a flourish of pride impressive enough had not the wheel-gear sniggered mockingly in its box.

Harvey laughed aloud. "Why, it's just as if she was alive," he said.

"She's as stiddy as a haouse an' as dry as a herrin'," said Dan enthusiastically, as he was slung across the deck in a batter of spray. "Fends 'em off an' fends 'em off, an' 'Don't ye come anigh me,' she sez. Look at her–jest look at her! Sakes! You should see one o' them toothpicks histin' up her anchor on her spike outer fifteen-fathom water."

"What's a toothpick, Dan?"

"Them new haddockers an' herrin'-boats. Fine's a yacht forward, with yacht sterns to 'em, an' spike bowsprits, an' a haouse that 'u'd take our hold. I've heard that Burgess himself he made the models fer three or four of 'em. Dad's sot agin 'em on account o' their pitchin' an' joltin', but there's heaps o' money in 'em. Dad can find fish, but he ain't no ways progressive–he don't go with the march o' the times. They're chock-full o' labor-savin' jigs an' sech all. 'Ever seed the *Elector* o' Gloucester? She's a daisy, ef she is a toothpick."

"What do they cost, Dan?"

"Hills o' dollars. Fifteen thousand, p'haps; more, mebbe. There's gold-leaf an' everything you kin think of." Then to himself, half under his breath, "Guess I'd call her *Hattie S.*, too."

Chapter Five

THAT WAS THE first of many talks with Dan, who told Harvey why he would transfer his dory's name to the imaginary Burgess-modelled haddocker. Harvey heard a good deal about the real Hattie at Gloucester; saw a lock of her hair–which Dan, finding fair words of no avail, had "hooked" as she sat in front of him at school that winter–and a photograph. Hattie was about fourteen years old, with an awful contempt for boys, and had been trampling on Dan's heart through the winter. All this was revealed under oath of solemn secrecy on moonlit decks, in the dead dark, or in choking fog; the whining wheel behind them, the climbing deck before, and without, the unresting, clamorous sea. Once, of course, as the boys came to know each other, there was a fight, which raged from bow to stern till Penn came up and separated them, but promised not to tell Disko, who thought fighting on watch rather worse than sleeping. Harvey was no match for Dan physically, but it says a great deal for his new training that he took his defeat and did not try to get even with his conqueror by underhand methods.

That was after he had been cured of a string of boils between his elbows and wrists, where the wet jersey and oilskins cut into the flesh. The salt water stung them unpleasantly, but when they were ripe Dan treated them with Disko's razor, and assured Harvey that now he was a "blooded Banker"; the affliction of gurry-sores being the mark of the caste that claimed him.

Since he was a boy and very busy, he did not bother his head with too much thinking. He was exceedingly sorry for his mother, and often longed to see her and above all to tell her of this wonderful new life, and how brilliantly he was acquitting himself in it. Otherwise he preferred not to wonder too much how she was bearing the shock of his supposed death. But one day, as he stood on the foc'sle ladder, guying the cook, who had accused him and Dan of hooking fried pies, it occurred to him that this was a vast improvement on being snubbed by strangers in the smoking-room of a hired liner.

He was a recognized part of the scheme of things on the *We're Here;* had his place at the table and among the bunks; and could hold his own in the long talks on stormy days, when the others were always ready to listen to what they called his "fairy-tales" of his life ashore. It did not take him more than two days and a quarter to feel that if he spoke of his own life–it seemed very far away–no one except Dan (and even Dan's belief was sorely tried) credited him. So he invented a friend, a boy he had heard of, who drove a miniature four-pony drag in Toledo, Ohio, and ordered five suits of clothes at a time and led things called "germans" at parties where the oldest girl was not quite fifteen, but all the presents were solid silver. Salters protested that this kind of yarn was desperately wicked, if not indeed positively blasphemous, but he listened as greedily as the others; and their criticisms at the end gave Harvey entirely new notions on "germans," clothes, cigarettes with gold-leaf tips, rings, watches, scent, small dinner-parties, champagne, card-playing, and hotel accommodation. Little by little he changed his tone when speaking of his "friend," whom Long Jack had christened "the Crazy Kid," "the Gilt-edged Baby," "the Suckin' Vanderpoop," and other pet names; and with his sea-booted feet cocked up on the table would even invent histories about silk pajamas and specially imported neckwear, to the "friend's" discredit. Harvey was a very adaptable person, with a keen eye and ear for every face and tone about him.

Before long he knew where Disko kept the old green-crusted quadrant that they called the "hog-yoke"–under the bed-bag in his bunk. When he took the sun, and with the help of "The Old Farmer's" almanac found the latitude, Harvey would jump down into the cabin and scratch the reckoning and date with a nail on the rust of the stove-pipe. Now, the chief engineer of the liner could have done no more, and no engineer of thirty years' service could have assumed one half of the ancient-mariner air with which Harvey, first careful to spit over the side, made public the schooner's position for that day, and then and not till then relieved Disko of the quadrant. There is an etiquette in all these things.

The said "hog-yoke," an Eldridge chart, the farming almanac, Blunt's "Coast Pilot," and Bowditch's "Navigator" were all the weapons Disko needed to guide him, except the deep-sea lead that was his spare eye. Harvey nearly slew Penn with it when Tom Platt taught him first how to "fly the blue pigeon"; and, though his strength was not equal to continuous sounding in any sort of a sea, for calm weather with a seven-pound lead on shoal water

Disko used him freely. As Dan said: " 'Tain't soundin's dad wants. It's samples. Grease her up good, Harve." Harvey would tallow the cup at the end, and carefully bring the sand, shell, sludge, or whatever it might be, to Disko, who fingered and smelt it and gave judgment. As has been said, when Disko thought of cod he thought as a cod; and by some long-tested mixture of instinct and experience, moved the *We're Here* from berth to berth, always with the fish, as a blindfolded chess-player moves on the unseen board.

But Disko's board was the Grand Bank–a triangle two hundred and fifty miles on each side–a waste of wallowing sea, cloaked with dank fog, vexed with gales, harried with drifting ice, scored by the tracks of the reckless liners, and dotted with the sails of the fishing-fleet.

For days they worked in fog–Harvey at the bell–till, grown familiar with the thick airs, he went out with Tom Platt, his heart rather in his mouth. But the fog would not lift, and the fish were biting, and no one can stay helplessly afraid for six hours at a time. Harvey devoted himself to his lines and the gaff or gob-stick as Tom Platt called for them; and they rowed back to the schooner guided by the bell and Tom's instinct; Manuel's conch sounding thin and faint beside them. But it was an unearthly experience, and, for the first time in a month, Harvey dreamed of the shifting, smoking floors of water round the dory, the lines that strayed away into nothing, and the air above that melted on the sea below ten feet from his straining eyes. A few days later he was out with Manuel on what should have been forty-fathom bottom, but the whole length of the roding ran out, and still the anchor found nothing, and Harvey grew mortally afraid, for that his last touch with earth was lost. "Whale-hole," said Manuel, hauling in. "That is good joke on Disko. Come!" and he rowed to the schooner to find Tom Platt and the others jeering at the skipper because, for once, he had led them to the edge of the barren Whale-deep, the blank hole of the Grand Bank. They made another berth through the fog, and that time the hair of Harvey's head stood up when he went out in Manuel's dory. A whiteness moved in the whiteness of the fog with a breath like the breath of the grave, and there was a roaring, a plunging, and spouting. It was his first introduction to the dread summer berg of the Banks, and he cowered in the bottom of the boat while Manuel laughed. There were days, though, clear and soft and warm, when it seemed a sin to do anything but loaf over the hand-lines and spank the drifting "sun-scalds" with an oar; and there were days of light airs, when Harvey was taught how to steer the schooner from one berth to another.

It thrilled through him when he first felt the keel answer to his hand on the spokes and slide over the long hollows as the foresail scythed back and forth against the blue sky. That was magnificent, in spite of Disko saying that it would break a snake's back to follow his wake. But, as usual, pride ran before a fall. They were sailing on the wind with the staysail–an old one, luckily–set, and Harvey jammed her right into it to show Dan how completely he had mastered the art. The foresail went over with a bang, and the foregaff stabbed and ripped through the staysail, which was, of course, prevented from going over by the mainstay. They lowered the wreck in awful silence, and Harvey spent his leisure hours for the next few days under Tom Platt's lee, learning to use a needle and palm. Dan hooted with joy, for, as he said, he had made the very same blunder himself in his early days.

Boylike, Harvey imitated all the men by turns, till he had combined Disko's peculiar stoop at the wheel, Long Jack's swinging overhand when the lines were hauled, Manuel's round-shouldered but effective stroke in a dory, and Tom Platt's generous *Ohio* stride along the deck.

" 'Tis beautiful to see how he takes to ut," said Long Jack, when Harvey was looking out by the windlass one thick noon. "I'll lay my wage an' share 'tis more'n half play-actin' to him, an' he consates himself he's a bowld mariner. Watch his little bit av a back now!"

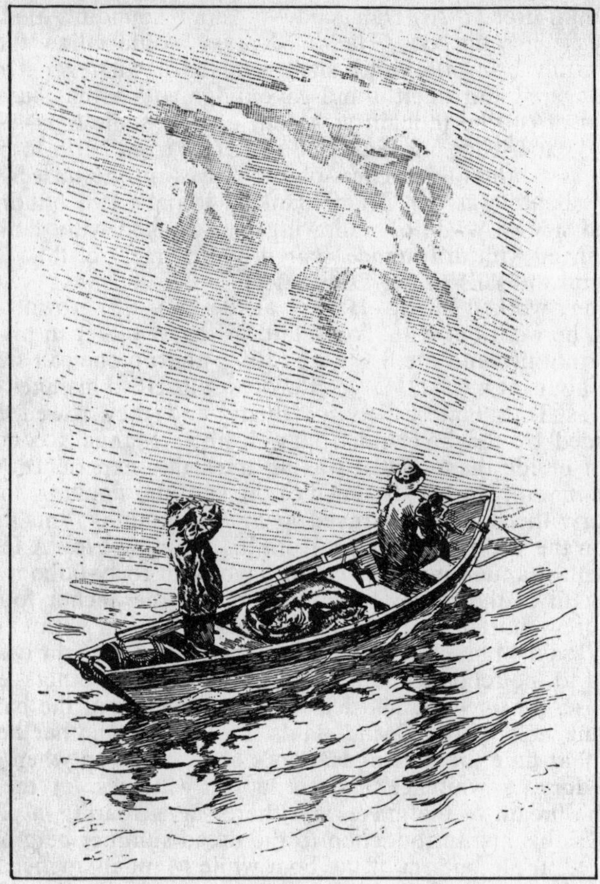

"A WHITENESS MOVED IN THE WHITENESS OF THE FOG . . . IT WAS HIS FIRST INTRODUCTION TO THE DREAD SUMMER BERG OF THE BANK."

"That's the way we all begin," said Tom Platt. "The boys they make believe all the time till they've cheated 'emselves into bein' men, an' so till they die—pretendin' an' pretendin'. *I* done it on the old *Ohio,* I know. Stood my first watch—harbor-watch—feelin' finer'n Farragut. Dan's full o' the same kind o' notions. See 'em now, actin' to be genewine moss-backs—every hair a rope-yarn an' blood Stockholm tar." He spoke down the cabin stairs. "Guess you're mistook in your judgments fer once, Disko. What in Rome made ye tell us all here the kid was crazy?"

"He wuz," Disko replied. "Crazy ez a loon when he come aboard; but I'll say he's sobered up consid'ble sence. I cured him."

"He yarns good," said Tom Platt. "T'other night he told us abaout a kid of his own size steerin' a cunnin' little rig an' four ponies up an' down Toledo, Ohio, I think 'twas, an' givin' suppers to a crowd o' sim'lar kids. Cur'us kind o' fairy-tale, but blame interestin'. He knows scores of 'em."

"Guess he strikes 'em outen his own head," Disko called from the cabin, where he was busy with the logbook. "Stands to reason that sort is all made up. It don't take in no one but Dan, an' he laughs at it. I've heard him, behind my back."

"Y'ever hear what Sim'on Peter Ca'houn said when they whacked up a match 'twix' his sister Hitty an' Lorin' Jerauld, an' the boys put up that joke on him down to Georges?" drawled Uncle Salters, who was dripping peaceably under the lee of the starboard dory-nest.

Tom Platt puffed at his pipe in scornful silence: he was a Cape Cod man, and had not known that tale more than twenty years. Uncle Salters went on with a rasping chuckle:

"Sim'on Peter Ca'houn he said, an' he was jest right, about Lorin', 'Ha'af on the taown,' he said, 'an' t'other ha'af blame fool; an' they told me she's married a 'ich man.' Sim'on Peter Ca'houn he hedn't no roof to his mouth, an' talked that way."

"He didn't talk any Pennsylvania Dutch," Tom Platt replied. "You'd better leave a Cape man to tell that tale. The Ca'houns was gypsies frum 'way back."

"Wal, I don't profess to be any elocutionist," Salters said. "I'm comin' to the moral o' things. That's jest abaout what our Harve be! Ha'af on the taown, an' t'other ha'af blame fool; an' there's some'll believe he's a rich man. Yah!"

"Did ye ever think how sweet 'twould be to sail wid a full crew o' Salterses?" said Long Jack. "Ha'af in the furrer an' other ha'af in the muck-heap, as Ca'houn did *not* say, an' makes out he's a fisherman!"

A little laugh went round at Salters's expense.

Disko held his tongue, and wrought over the log-book that he kept in a hatchet-faced, square hand; this was the kind of thing that ran on, page after soiled page:

"July 17. *This day thick fog and few fish. Made berth to northward. So ends this day.*

"July 18. *This day comes in with thick fog. Caught a few fish.*

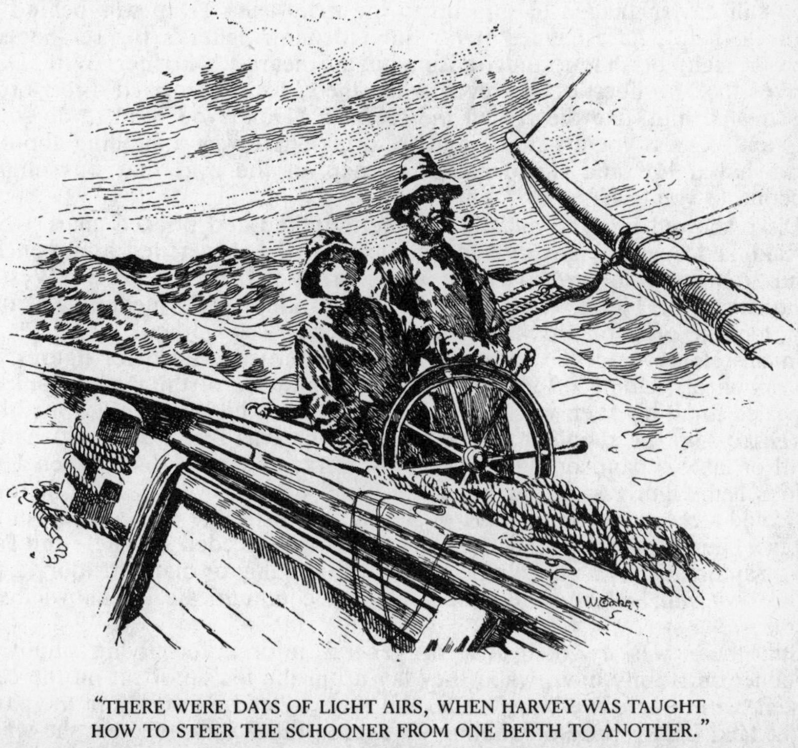

"THERE WERE DAYS OF LIGHT AIRS, WHEN HARVEY WAS TAUGHT HOW TO STEER THE SCHOONER FROM ONE BERTH TO ANOTHER."

"July 19. This day comes in with light breeze from N. E. and fine weather. Made a berth to eastward. Caught plenty fish.

"July 20. *This, the Sabbath, comes in with fog and light winds. So ends this day. Total fish caught this week,* 3,478."

They never worked on Sundays, but shaved, and washed themselves if it were fine, and Pennsylvania sang hymns. Once or twice he suggested that, if it was not an impertinence, he thought he could preach a little. Uncle Salters nearly jumped down his throat at the mere notion, reminding him that he was not a preacher and mustn't think of such things. "We'd hev him rememberin' Johnstown next," Salters explained, "an' what would happen then?" so they compromised on his reading aloud from a book called "Josephus." It was an old leather-bound volume, smelling of a hundred voyages, very solid and very like the Bible, but enlivened with accounts of battles and sieges; and they read it nearly from cover to cover. Otherwise Penn was a silent little body. He would not utter a word for three days on end sometimes, though he played checkers, listened to the songs, and laughed at the stories. When they tried to stir him up, he would answer: "I don't wish to seem unneighbourly, but it is because I have nothing to say. My head feels quite empty. I've almost forgotten my name." He would turn to Uncle Salters with an expectant smile.

"Why, Pennsylvania *Pratt,"* Salters would shout. "You'll fergit *me* next!"

"No–never," Penn would say, shutting his lips firmly. "Pennsylvania Pratt, of course," he would repeat over and over. Sometimes it was Uncle Salters who forgot, and told him he was Haskins or Rich or McVitty; but Penn was equally content–till next time.

He was always very tender with Harvey, whom he pitied both as a lost child and as a lunatic; and when Salters saw that Penn liked the boy, he relaxed, too. Salters was not an amiable person (he esteemed it his business to keep the boys in order); and the first time Harvey, in fear and trembling, on a still day, managed to shin up to the main-truck (Dan was behind him ready to help), he esteemed it *his* duty to hang Salters's big sea-boots up there–a sight of shame and derision to the nearest schooner. With Disko, Harvey took no liberties; not even when the old man dropped direct orders, and treated him, like the rest of the crew, to "Don't you want to do so and so?" and "Guess you'd better," and so forth. There was something about the clean-shaven lips and the puckered corners of the eyes that was mightily sobering to young blood.

Disko showed him the meaning of the thumbed and pricked chart, which, he said, laid over any government publication whatsoever; led him, pencil in hand, from berth to berth over the whole string of banks–Le Have, Western, Banquereau, St. Pierre, Green, and Grand–talking "cod" meantime. Taught him, too, the principle on which the "hog-yoke" was worked.

In this Harvey excelled Dan, for he had inherited a head for figures, and the notion of stealing information from one glimpse of the sullen Bank sun appealed to all his keen wits. For other sea-matters his age handicapped him. As Disko said, he should have begun when he was ten. Dan could bait up trawl or lay his hand on any rope in the dark; and at a pinch, when Uncle Salters had a gurry-score on his palm, could dress down by sense of touch. He could steer in anything short of half a gale from the feel of the wind on his face, humoring the *We're Here* just when she needed it. These things he did as automatically as he skipped about the rigging, or made his dory a part of his own will and body. But he could not communicate his knowledge to Harvey.

Still there was a good deal of general information flying about the schooner on stormy days, when they lay up in the foc'sle or sat on the cabin lockers, while spare eye-bolts, leads, and rings rolled and rattled in the pauses of the talk. Disko spoke of whaling voyages in the Fifties; of great she-whales slain beside their young; of death agonies on the black tossing seas, and blood that spurted forty feet in the air; of boats smashed to splinters; of patent rockets that went off wrong-end-first and bombarded the trembling crews; of cuttin-in and boiling-down, and that terrible "nip" of '71, when twelve hundred men were made homeless on the ice in three days—wonderful tales, all true. But more wonderful still were his stories of the cod, and how they argued and reasoned on their private businesses deep down below the keel.

Long Jack's tastes ran more to the supernatural. He held them silent with ghastly stories of the "Yo-hoes" on Monomoy Beach, that mock and terrify lonely clamdiggers; of sand-walkers and dune-haunters who were never properly buried; of hidden treasure on Fire Island guarded by the spirits of Kidd's men; of ships that sailed in the fog straight over Truro township; of that harbor in Maine where no one but a stranger will lie at anchor twice in a certain place because of a dead crew who row alongside at midnight with the anchor in the bow of their old-fashioned boat, whistling—not calling, but whistling—for the soul of the man who broke their rest.

Harvey had a notion that the east coast of his native land, from Mount Desert south, was populated chiefly by people who took their horses there in the summer and entertained in country-houses with hardwood floors and Vantine portières. He laughed at the ghost-tales,—not as much as he would have done a month before,—but ended by sitting still and shuddering.

Tom Platt dealt with his interminable trip round the Horn on the old *Ohio* in flogging days, with a navy more extinct than the dodo—the navy that passed away in the great war. He told them how red-hot shot are dropped into a cannon, a wad of wet clay between them and the cartridge; how they sizzle and reek when they strike wood, and how the little ship-boys of the *Miss Jim Buck* hove water over them and shouted to the fort to try again. And he told tales of blockade—long weeks of swaying at anchor, varied only by the departure and return of steamers that had used up their coal (there was no chance for the sailing-ships); of gales and cold—cold that kept two hundred men, night and day, pounding and chopping at the ice on cable, blocks, and rigging, when the galley was as red-hot as the fort's shot, and men drank cocoa by the bucket. Tom Platt had no use for steam. His service closed when that thing was comparatively new. He admitted that it was a specious invention in time of peace, but looked hopefully for the day when sails should come back again on ten-thousand-ton frigates with hundred-and-ninety-foot booms.

Manuel's talk was slow and gentle—all about pretty girls in Madeira washing clothes in the dry beds of streams, by moonlight, under waving bananas; legends of saints, and tales of queer dances or fights away in the cold Newfoundland baiting-ports. Salters was mainly agricultural; for, though he read "Josephus" and expounded it, his mission in life was to prove the value of green manures, and specially of clover, against every form of phosphate whatsoever. He grew libellous about phosphates; he dragged greasy "Orange Judd" books from his bunk and intoned them, wagging his finger at Harvey, to whom it was all Greek. Little Penn was so genuinely pained when Harvey made fun of Salters's lectures that the boy gave it up, and suffered in polite silence. That was very good for Harvey.

The cook naturally did not join in these conversations. As a rule, he spoke only when it was absolutely necessary; but at times a queer gift of speech descended on him, and he held forth, half in Gaelic, half in broken English, an hour at a time. He was especially communicative with the boys, and he never withdrew his prophecy that one day Harvey would be Dan's master, and that he would see it. He told them of mail-carrying in the winter up Cape Breton way, of the dog-train that goes to Coudray, and of the ram-steamer *Arctic,* that breaks the ice between the mainland and Prince Edward

Island. Then he told them stories that his mother had told him, of life far to the southward, where water never froze; and he said that when he died his soul would go to lie down on a warm white beach of sand with palm-trees waving above. That seemed to the boys a very odd idea for a man who had never seen a palm in his life. Then, too, regularly at each meal, he would ask Harvey, and Harvey alone, whether the cooking was to his taste; and this always made the "second half" laugh. Yet they had a great respect for the cook's judgment, and in their hearts considered Harvey something of a mascot by consequence.

And while Harvey was taking in knowledge of new things at each pore and hard health with every gulp of the good air, the *We're Here* went her ways and did her business on the Bank, and the silvery-gray kenches of well-pressed fish mounted higher and higher in the hold. No one day's work was out of common, but the average days were many and close together.

Naturally, a man of Disko's reputation was closely watched—"scrowged upon," Dan called it—by his neighbors, but he had a very pretty knack of giving them the slip through the curdling, glidy fog-banks. Disko avoided company for two reasons. He wished to make his own experiments, in the first place; and in the second, he objected to the mixed gatherings of a fleet of all nations. The bulk of them were mainly Gloucester boats, with a scattering from Provincetown, Harwich, Chatham, and some of the Maine ports, but the crews drew from goodness knows where. Risk breeds recklessness, and when greed is added there are fine chances for every kind of accident in the crowded fleet, which, like a mob of sheep, is huddled round some unrecognized leader. "Let the two Jeraulds lead 'em," said Disko. "We're bound to lay among 'em for a spell on the Eastern Shoals; though ef luck holds, we won't hev to lay long. Where we are naow, Harve, ain't considered noways good graound."

"Ain't it?" said Harvey, who was drawing water (he had learned just how to wiggle the bucket), after an unusually long dressing-down. "Shouldn't mind striking some poor ground for a change, then."

"All the graound I want to see—don't want to strike her—is Eastern Point," said Dan. "Say, Dad, it looks 's if we wouldn't hev to lay more'n two weeks on the Shoals. You'll meet all the comp'ny you want then, Harve. That's the time we begin to work. No reg'lar meals fer no one then. 'Mug-up when ye're hungry, an' sleep when ye can't keep awake. Good job you wasn't picked up a month later than you was, or we'd never ha' had you dressed in shape fer the Old Virgin."

Harvey understood from the Eldridge chart that the Old Virgin and a nest of curiously named shoals were the turning-point of the cruise, and that with good luck they would wet the balance of their salt there. But seeing the size of the Virgin (it was one tiny dot), he wondered how even Disko with the hog-yoke and the lead could find her. He learned later that Disko was entirely equal to that and any other business and could even help others. A big four-by-five blackboard hung in the cabin, and Harvey never understood the need of it till, after some blinding thick days, they heard the unmelodious tooting of a foot-power fog-horn—a machine whose note is as that of a consumptive elephant.

They were making a short berth, towing the anchor under their foot to save trouble. "Square-rigger bellowin' fer his latitude," said Long Jack. The dripping red headsails of a bark glided out of the fog, and the *We're Here* rang her bell thrice, using sea shorthand.

The larger boat backed her topsail with shrieks and shoutings.

"Frenchman," said Uncle Salters, scornfully. "Miquelon boat from St. Malo." The farmer had a weatherly sea-eye. "I'm 'most outer 'baccy, too, Disko."

"Same here," said Tom Platt. "Hi! *Backez vous—backez vous! Standez awayez,* you butt-ended *mucho-bono!* Where you from—St. Malo, eh?"

"Ah, ha! *Mucho bono! Oui! oui! Clos Poulet—St. Malo! St. Pierre et Miquelon,"* cried the other crowd, waving woollen caps and laughing. Then all together, *"Bord! Bord!"*

"Bring up the board, Danny. Beats me how them Frenchmen fetch anywheres, exceptin' America's fairish broadly. Forty-six forty-nine's good enough fer them; an' I guess it's about right, too."

Dan chalked the figures on the board, and they hung it in the main-rigging to a chorus of *mercis* from the bark.

"Seems kinder unneighbourly to let 'em swedge off like this," Salters suggested, feeling in his pockets.

"Hev ye learned French then sence last trip?" said Disko. "*I* don't want no more stone-ballast hove at us 'long o' you callin' Miquelon boats 'footy cochins,' same's you did off Le Have."

"Harmon Rush he said that was the way to rise 'em. Plain United States is good enough fer me. We're all dretful short on tearakker. Young feller, don't *you* speak French?"

"Oh, yes," said Harvey valiantly; and he bawled: "Hi! Say! *Arrêtez vous! Attendez! Nous sommes venant pour tabac."*

"Ah, *tabac, tabac!"* they cried, and laughed again.

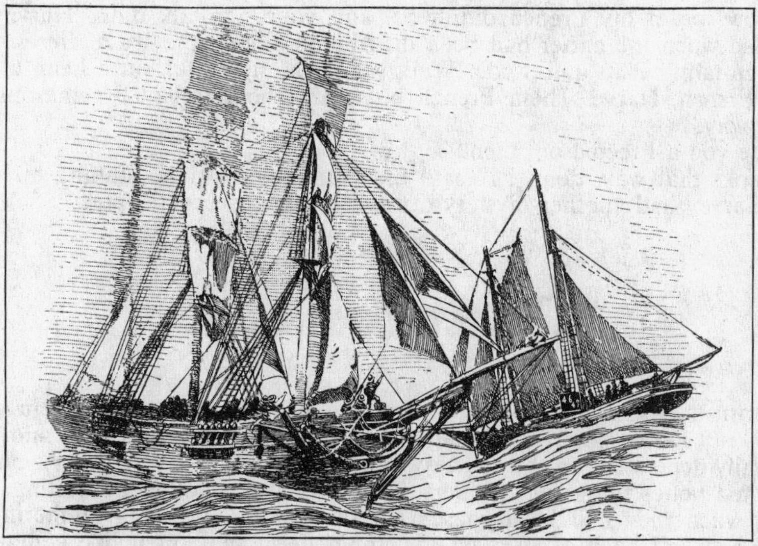

"'HI! SAY! ARRÊTEZ VOUS! ATTENDEZ! NOUS SOMMES VENANT POUR TABAC.' 'AH, TABAC, TABAC!'"

"That hit 'em. Let's heave a dory over, anyway," said Tom Platt. "I don't exactly hold no certificates on French, but I know another lingo that goes, I guess. Come on, Harve, an' interpret."

The raffle and confusion when he and Harvey were hauled up the bark's black side was indescribable. Her cabin was all stuck round with glaring colored prints of the Virgin—the Virgin of Newfoundland, they called her. Harvey found his French of no recognized Bank brand, and his conversation was limited to nods and grins. But Tom Platt waved his arms and got along swimmingly. The captain gave him a drink of unspeakable gin, and the opera-comique crew, with their hairy throats, red caps, and long knives, greeted him as a brother. Then the trade began. They had tobacco, plenty of it–American, that had never paid duty to France. They wanted chocolate and crackers. Harvey rowed back to arrange with the cook and Disko, who owned the stores, and on his return the cocoa-tins and cracker-bags were counted out by the Frenchman's wheel. It looked like a piratical division of loot; but Tom Platt came out of it roped with black pigtail and stuffed with cakes of chewing and smoking tobacco. Then those jovial mariners swung off into the mist, and the last Harvey heard was a gay chorus:

"Par derrière chez ma tante,
Il y a un bois joli,
Et le rossignol y chante
Et le jour et la nuit . . .

Que donneriez vous, belle,
Qui l'amènerait ici?
Je donnerai Québec,
Sorel et Saint Denis."

"How was it my French didn't go, and your sign-talk did?" Harvey demanded when the barter had been distributed among the *We're Heres.*

"Sign-talk!" Platt guffawed. "Well, yes, 'twas sign-talk, but a heap older'n your French, Harve. Them French boats are chock-full o' Freemasons, an' that's why."

"Are you a Freemason, then?"

"Looks that way, don't it?" said the man-o'-war's man, stuffing his pipe; and Harvey had another mystery of the deep sea to brood upon.

Chapter Six

THE THING THAT struck him most was the exceedingly casual way in which some craft loafed about the broad Atlantic. Fishing-boats, as Dan said, were naturally dependent on the courtesy and wisdom of their neighbours; but one expected better things of steamers. That was after another interesting interview, when they had been chased for three miles by a big lumbering old cattle-boat, all boarded over on the upper deck, that smelt like a thousand cattle-pens. A very excited officer yelled at them through a speaking-trumpet, and she lay and lollopped helplessly on the water while Disko ran the *We're Here* under her lee and gave the skipper a piece of his mind. "Where might ye be–eh? Ye don't deserve to be anywheres. You barn-yard tramps go hoggin' the road on the high seas with no blame consideration fer your neighbours, an' your eyes in your coffee-cups instid o' in your silly heads."

At this the skipper danced on the bridge and said something about Disko's own eyes. "We haven't had an observation for three days. D'you suppose we can run her blind?" he shouted.

"Wa-al, *I* can," Disko retorted. "What's come to your lead? Et it? Can't ye smell bottom, or are them cattle too rank?"

"What d' ye feed 'em?" said Uncle Salters with intense seriousness, for the smell of the pens woke all the farmer in him. "They say they fall off dretful on a v'yage. Dunno as it's any o' my business, but I've a kind o' notion that oil-cake broke small an' sprinkled—"

"Thunder!" said a cattle-man in a red jersey as he looked over the side. "What asylum did they let His Whiskers out of?"

"Young feller," Salters began, standing up in the fore-rigging, "let me tell *yeou* 'fore we go any further that I've—"

The officer on the bridge took off his cap with immense politeness. "Excuse me," he said, "but I've asked for my reckoning. If the agricultural person with the hair will kindly shut his head, the sea-green barnacle with the wall-eye may per-haps condescend to enlighten us."

"Now you've made a show o' me, Salters," said Disko, angrily. He could not stand up to that particular sort of talk, and snapped out the latitude and longitude without more lectures.

"Well, that's a boat-load of lunatics, sure," said the skipper, as he rang up the engine-room and tossed a bundle of newspapers into the schooner.

"Of *all* the blamed fools, next to you, Salters, him an' his crowd are about the likeliest I've ever seen," said Disko as the *We're Here* slid away. "I was jest givin' him my jedgment on lullsikin' round these waters like a lost child, an' you must cut in with your fool farmin'. Can't ye never keep things sep'rate?"

Harvey, Dan, and the others stood back, winking one to the other and full of joy; but Disko and Salters wrangled seriously till evening, Salters arguing that a cattle-boat was practically a barn on blue water, and Disko insisting that, even if this were the case, decency and fisher-pride demanded that he should have kept "things sep'rate." Long Jack stood it in silence for a time,—an angry skipper makes an unhappy crew,—and then he spoke across the table after supper:

"Fwhat's the good o' bodderin' fwhat they'll say?" said he.

"They'll tell that tale agin us fer years—that's all," said Disko. "Oil-cake sprinkled!"

"With salt, o' course," said Salters, impenitent, reading the farming reports from a week-old New York paper.

"It's plumb mortifyin' to all my feelin's," the skipper went on.

"Can't see ut that way," said Long Jack, the peacemaker. "Look at here, Disko! Is there another packet afloat this day in this weather cud ha' met a tramp an', over an' above givin' her her reckonin',—over an' above that, I say,—cud ha' discoorsed wid her quite intelligent on the management av steers an' such at sea? Forgit ut! Av coorse they will not. 'Twas the most compenjus conversation that iver accrued. Double game an' twice runnin'—all to us." Dan kicked Harvey under the table, and Harvey choked in his cup.

"Well," said Salters, who felt that his honor had been somewhat plastered, "I *said* I didn't know as 'twuz any business o' mine, 'fore I spoke."

"An' right there," said Tom Platt, experienced in discipline and etiquette—"right there, I take it, Disko, you should ha' asked him to stop ef the conversation wuz likely, in your jedgment, to be anyways—what it shouldn't."

" 'Dunno but that's so," said Disko, who saw his way to an honorable retreat from a fit of the dignities.

"Why, o' course it was so," said Salters, "you bein' skipper here; an' I'd cheerful hev stopped on a hint—not from any leadin' *or* conviction, but fer the sake o' bearin' an example to these two blame boys of aours."

"Didn't I tell you, Harve, 'twould come araound to us 'fore we'd done? Always those blame boys. But I wouldn't have missed the show fer a half-share in a halibutter," Dan whispered.

"Still, things should ha' been kep' sep'rate," said Disko, and the light of new argument lit in Salters's eye as he crumbled cut plug into his pipe.

"There's a power av vartue in keepin' things sep'rate," said Long Jack, intent on stilling the storm. "That's fwhat Steyning of Steyning and Hare's f'und when he sent Counahan fer skipper on the *Marilla D. Kuhn,* instid o'

Cap. Newton that was took with inflam'try rheumatism an' couldn't go, Counahan the Navigator we called him."

"Nick Counahan he never went aboard fer a night 'thout a pond o' rum somewheres in the manifest," said Tom Platt, playing up to the lead. "He used to bum araound the c'mission houses to Boston lookin' fer the Lord to make him captain of a tow-boat on his merits. Sam Coy, up to Atlantic Avenoo, give him his board free fer a year or more on account of his stories. Counahan the Navigator! Tck! Tck! Dead these fifteen year, ain't he?"

"Seventeen, I guess. He died the year the *Caspar McVeagh* was built; but he could niver keep things sep'rate. Steyning tuk him fer the reason the thief tuk the hot stove—bekaze there was nothin' else that season. The men was all to the Banks, and Counahan he whacked up an iverlastin' hard crowd fer crew. Rum! Ye cud ha' floated the *Marilla,* insurance an' all, in fwhat they stowed aboard her. They lef' Boston Harbor for the great Grand Bank wid a roarin' nor'wester behind 'em an' all hands full to the bung. An' the hivens looked after thim, for divil a watch did they set, an' divil a rope did they lay hand to, till they'd seen the bottom av a fifteen-gallon cask o' bug-juice. That was about wan week, so far as Counahan remembered. (If I cud only tell the tale as he told ut!) All that whoile the wind blew like ould glory, an' the *Marilla*—'twas summer, and they'd give her a foretopmast—struck her gait and kept ut. Then Counahan tuk the hog-yoke an' thrembled over it for a whoile, an' made out, betwix' that an' the chart an' the singin' in his head, that they was to the south'ard o' Sable Island, gettin' along glorious, but speakin' nothin'. Then they broached another keg, an' quit speculatin' about anythin' fer another spell. The *Marilla* she lay down whin she dropped Boston Light, and she never lufted her lee-rail up to that time—hustlin' on one an' the same slant. But they saw no weed, nor gulls, nor schooners; an' prisintly they observed they'd bin out a matter o' fourteen days and they mistrusted the Bank has suspinded payment. So they sounded, an' got sixty fathom. 'That's me,' sez Counahan. 'That's me iv'ry time! I've run her slat on the Bank fer you, an' when we get thirty fathom we'll turn in like little men. Counahan is the b'y,' sez he. 'Counahan the Navigator!'

"Nex' cast they got ninety. Sez Counahan: 'Either the lead-line's tuk to stretchin' or else the Bank's sunk.'

"They hauled ut up, bein' just about in that state when ut seemed right an' reasonable, and sat down on the deck countin' the knots, an' gettin' her snarled up hijjus. The *Marilla* she'd struck her gait, an' she hild ut, an' prisintly along came a tramp, an' Counahan spoke her.

" 'Hev ye seen any fishin'-boats now?" sez he, quite casual.

" 'There's lashin's av them off the Irish coast,' sez the tramp.

" 'Aah! go shake yerself,' sez Counahan. 'Fwhat have I to do wid the Irish coast?"

" 'Then fwhat are ye doin' here?' sez the tramp.

" 'Sufferin' Christianity!' sez Counahan (he always said that whin his pumps sucked an' he was not feelin' good)—'Sufferin' Christianity!' he sez, 'where am I at?'

" 'Thirty-five mile west-sou'west o' Cape Clear,' sez the tramp, 'if that's any consolation to you.'

"Counahan fetched wan jump, four feet sivin inches, measured by the cook.

" 'Consolation!' sez he, bould as brass. 'D'ye take me fer a dialect? Thirty-five mile from Cape Clear, an' fourteen days from Boston Light. Sufferin' Christianity, 'tis a record, an' by the same token I've a mother to Skibbereen!' Think av ut! The gall av um! But ye see he could niver keep things sep'rate.

"The crew was mostly Cork an' Kerry men, barrin' one Marylander that wanted to go back, but they called him a mutineer, an' they ran the ould *Marilla* into Skibbereen, an' they had an illigant time visitin' around with frinds on the ould sod fer a week. Thin they wint back, an' it cost 'em two an' thirty days to beat to the Banks again. 'Twas gettin' on towards fall, and grub was low, so Counahan ran her back to Boston, wid no more bones to ut."

"And what did the firm say?" Harvey demanded.

"Fwhat could they? The fish was on the Banks, an' Counahan was at T-wharf talkin' av his record trip east! They tuk their satisfaction out av that, an' ut all came av not keepin' the crew and the rum sep'rate in the first place; an' confusin' Skibbereen wid 'Queereau, in the second. Counahan the Navigator, rest his sowl! He was an imprompju citizen!"

"Once I was in the *Lucy Holmes,*" said Manuel, in his gentle voice. "They not want any of her feesh in Gloucester. Eh, wha-at? Give us no price. So we go across the water, and think to sell to some Fayal man. Then it blow fresh, and we cannot see well. Eh, wha-at? Then it blow some more fresh, and we go down below and drive very fast–no one know where. By and by we see a land, and it get some hot. Then come two, three nigger in a brick. Eh, wha-at? We ask where we are, and they say–now, what you all think?"

"Grand Canary," said Disko, after a moment. Manuel shook his head, smiling.

"Blanco," said Tom Platt.

"No. Worse than that. We was below Bezagos, and the brick she was from Liberia! So we sell our feesh *there!* Not bad, so? Eh, wha-at?"

"Can a schooner like this go right across to Africa?" said Harvey.

"Go around the Horn ef there's anything worth goin' fer, and the grub holds aout," said Disko. "My father he run his packet, an' she was a kind o' pinkey, abaout fifty ton, I guess,–the *Rupert,*–he run her over to Greenland's icy mountains the year ha'af our fleet was tryin' after cod there. An' what's more, he took my mother along with him,–to show her haow the money was earned, I presoom,–an' they was all iced up, an' I was born at Disko. Don't remember nothin' abaout it, o' course. We come back when the ice eased in the spring, but they named me fer the place. Kinder mean trick to put up on a baby, but we're all baound to make mistakes in aour lives."

"Sure! Sure!" said Salters, wagging his head. "All baound to make mistakes, an' I tell you two boys here thet after you've made a mistake–ye don't make fewer'n a hundred a day–the next best thing's to own up to it like men."

Long Jack winked one tremendous wink that embraced all hands except Disko and Salters, and the incident was closed.

Then they made berth after berth to the northward, the dories out almost every day, running along the east edge of the Grand Bank in thirty- to forty-fathom water, and fishing steadily.

It was here Harvey first met the squid, who is one of the best cod-baits, but uncertain in his moods. They were waked out of their bunks one black night by yells of "Squid O!" from Salters, and for an hour and a half every soul aboard hung over his squid-jig–a piece of lead painted red and armed at the lower end with a circle of pins bent backward like half-opened umbrella ribs. The squid–for some unknown reason–likes, and wraps himself round, this thing, and is hauled up ere he can escape from the pins. But as he leaves his home he squirts first water and next ink into his captor's face; and it was curious to see the men weaving their heads from side to side to dodge the shot. They were as black as sweeps when the flurry ended; but a pile of fresh squid lay on the deck, and the large cod thinks very well of a little shiny piece of squid tentacle at the tip of a clam-baited hook. Next day they caught many fish, and met the *Carrie Pitman,* to whom they shouted their luck, and she wanted to trade–seven cod for one fair-sized squid; but Disko would not agree at the price, and the *Carrie* dropped sullenly to leeward and anchored half a mile away, in the hope of striking on to some for herself.

Disko said nothing till after supper, when he sent Dan and Manuel out to buoy the *We're Here's* cable and announced his intention of turning in with the broadaxe. Dan naturally repeated these remarks to the dory from the

Carrie, who wanted to know why they were buoying their cable, since they were not on rocky bottom.

"Dad sez he wouldn't trust a ferryboat within five mile o' you," Dan howled cheerfully.

"Why don't he git out, then? Who's hinderin'?" said the other.

" 'Cause you've jest the same ez lee-bowed him, an' he don't take that from any boat, not to speak o' sech a driftin' gurry-butt as you be."

"She ain't driftin' any this trip," said the man angrily, for the *Carrie Pitman* had an unsavory reputation for breaking her ground-tackle.

"Then haow d'you make berths?" said Dan. "It's her best p'int o' sailin'. An' ef she's quit driftin', what in thunder are you doin' with a new jib-boom?" That shot went home.

"Hey, you Portugoosy organ-grinder, take your monkey back to Gloucester. Go back to school, Dan Troop," was the answer.

"O-ver-alls! O-ver-alls!" yelled Dan, who knew that one of the *Carrie's* crew had worked in an overall factory the winter before.

"Shrimp! Gloucester shrimp! Git out, you Novy!"

To call a Gloucester man a Nova Scotian is not well received. Dan answered in kind.

"Novy yourself, ye Scrabble-towners! ye Chatham wreckers! Git aout with your brick in your stockin'!" And the forces separated, but Chatham had the worst of it.

"I knew haow 'twould be," said Disko. "She's drawed the wind raound already. Some one oughter put a *dee*sist on thet packet. She'll snore till midnight, an' jest when we're gettin' our sleep she'll strike adrift. Good job we ain't crowded with craft hereaways. But I ain't goin' to up anchor fer Chatham. She may hold."

The wind, which had hauled round, rose at sundown and blew steadily. There was not enough sea, though, to disturb even a dory's tackle, but the *Carrie Pitman* was a law unto herself. At the end of the boys' watch they heard the *crack-crack-crack* of a huge muzzle-loading revolver aboard her.

"Glory, glory, hallelujah!" sung Dan. "Here she comes, Dad; butt-end first, walkin' in her sleep same's she done on 'Queereau."

Had she been any other boat Disko would have taken his chances, but now he cut the cable as the *Carrie Pitman,* with all the North Atlantic to play in, lurched down directly upon them. The *We're Here,* under jib and riding-sail, gave her no more room than was absolutely necessary,–Disko did not wish to spend a week hunting for his cable,–but scuttled up into the wind as the *Carrie* passed within easy hail, a silent and angry boat, at the mercy of a raking broadside of Bank chaff.

"Good evenin'," said Disko, raising his head-gear, "an' haow does your garden grow?"

"Go to Ohio an' hire a mule," said Uncle Salters. "We don't want no farmers here."

"Will I lend you my dory-anchor?" cried Long Jack.

"Unship your rudder an' stick it in the mud," said Tom Platt.

"Say!" Dan's voice rose shrill and high, as he stood on the wheel-box. "Sa-ay! Is there a strike in the o-ver-all factory; or hev they hired girls, ye Shackamaxons?"

"Veer out the tiller-lines," cried Harvey, "and nail 'em to the bottom." That was a salt-flavored jest he had been put up to by Tom Platt. Manuel leaned over the stern and yelled: "Johanna Morgan play the organ! Ahaaaa!" He flourished his broad thumb with a gesture of unspeakable contempt and derision, while little Penn covered himself with glory by piping up: "Gee a little! Hssh! Come here. Haw!"

They rode on their chain for the rest of the night, a short, snappy, uneasy motion, as Harvey found, and wasted half the forenoon recovering the cable.

But the boys agreed the trouble was cheap at the price of triumph and glory, and they thought with grief over all the beautiful things that they might have said to the discomfited *Carrie.*

Chapter Seven

NEXT DAY THEY fell in with more sails, all circling slowly from the east northerly towards the west. But just when they expected to make the shoals by the Virgin the fog shut down, and they anchored, surrounded by the tinklings of invisible bells. There was not much fishing, but occasionally dory met dory in the fog and exchanged news.

That night, a little before dawn, Dan and Harvey, who had been sleeping most of the day, tumbled out to "hook" fried pies. There was no reason why they should not have taken them openly; but they tasted better so, and it made the cook angry. The heat and smell below drove them on deck with their plunder, and they found Disko at the bell, which he handed over to Harvey.

"Keep her goin'," said he. "I mistrust I hear somethin'. Ef it's anything, I'm best where I am so's to get at things."

It was a forlorn little jingle; the thick air seemed to pinch it off, and in the pauses Harvey heard the muffled shriek of a liner's siren, and he knew enough of the Banks to know what that meant. It came to him, with horrible distinctness, how a boy in a cherry-colored jersey—he despised fancy blazers now with all a fisherman's contempt—how an ignorant, rowdy boy had once said it would be "great" if a steamer ran down a fishing-boat. That boy had a stateroom with a hot and cold bath, and spent ten minutes each morning picking over a gilt-edged bill of fare. And that same boy—no, his very much older brother—was up at four of the dim dawn in streaming, crackling oilskins, hammering, literally for the dear life, on a bell smaller than the steward's breakfast-bell, while somewhere close at hand a thirty-foot steel stem was storming along at twenty miles an hour! The bitterest thought of all was that there were folks asleep in dry, upholstered cabins who would never learn that they had massacred a boat before breakfast. So Harvey rang the bell.

"Yes, they slow daown one turn o' their blame propeller," said Dan, applying himself to Manuel's conch, "fer to keep inside the law, an' that's consolin' when we're all at the bottom. Hark to her! She's a humper!"

"*Aoooo—whoooo—whupp!*" went the siren. "*Wingle—tingle—tink,*" went the bell. "*Graaa—ouch!*" went the conch, while sea and sky were all milled up in milky fog. Then Harvey felt that he was near a moving body, and found himself looking up and up at the wet edge of a cliff-like bow, leaping, it seemed, directly over the schooner. A jaunty little feather of water curled in front of it, and as it lifted it showed a long ladder of Roman numerals—XV., XVI., XVII., XVIII., and so forth—on a salmon-colored gleaming side. It tilted forward and downward with a heart-stilling "Ssssooo"; the ladder disappeared; a line of brass-rimmed portholes flashed past; a jet of steam puffed in Harvey's helplessly uplifted hands; a spout of hot water roared along the rail of the *We're Here,* and the little schooner staggered and shook in a rush of screw-torn water, as a liner's stern vanished in the fog. Harvey got ready to faint or be sick, or both, when he heard a crack like a trunk thrown on a sidewalk, and, all small in his ear, a far-away telephone voice drawling: "Heave to! You've sunk us!"

"Is it us?" he gasped.

"No! Boat out yonder. Ring! We're goin' to look," said Dan, running out a dory.

In half a minute all except Harvey, Penn, and the cook were overside and away. Presently a schooner's stump-foremast, snapped clean across, drifted past the bows. Then an empty green dory came by, knocking on the *We're Here's* side, as though she wished to be taken in. Then followed something, face down, in a blue jersey, but–it was not the whole of a man. Penn changed color and caught his breath with a click. Harvey pounded despairingly at the bell, for he feared they might be sunk at any minute, and he jumped at Dan's hail as the crew came back.

"The *Jennie Cushman,*" said Dan, hysterically, "cut clean in half–graound up an' trompled on at that! Not a quarter of a mile away. Dad's got the old man. There ain't any one else, and–there was his son, too. Oh, Harve, Harve, I can't stand it! I've seen——" He dropped his head on his arms and sobbed while the others dragged a gray-headed man aboard.

"What did you pick me up for?" the stranger groaned. "Disko, what did you pick me up for?"

Disko dropped a heavy hand on his shoulder, for the man's eyes were wild and his lips trembled as he stared at the silent crew. Then up and spoke Pennsylvania Pratt, who was also Haskins or Rich or McVitty when Uncle Salters forgot; and his face was changed on him from the face of a fool to the countenance of an old, wise man, and he said in a strong voice: "The Lord gave, and the Lord hath taken away; blessed be the name of the Lord! I was–I am a minister of the Gospel. Leave him to me."

"Oh, you be, be you?" said the man. "Then pray my son back to me! Pray back a nine-thousand-dollar boat an' a thousand quintal of fish. If you'd left me alone my widow could ha' gone on to the Provident an' worked fer her board, an' never known–an' never known. Now I'll hev to tell her."

"There ain't nothin' to say," said Disko. "Better lie down a piece, Jason Olley."

When a man has lost his only son, his summer's work, and his means of livelihood, in thirty counted seconds, it is hard to give consolation.

"All Gloucester men, wasn't they?" said Tom Platt, fiddling helplessly with a dory-becket.

"Oh, *that* don't make no odds," said Jason, wringing the wet from his beard. "I'll be rowin' summer boarders araound East Gloucester this fall." He rolled heavily to the rail, singing:

> "Happy birds that sing and fly
> Round thine altars, O Most High!"

"Come with me. Come below!" said Penn, as though he had a right to give orders. Their eyes met and fought for a quarter of a minute.

"I dunno who you be, but I'll come," said Jason submissively. "Mebbe I'll get back some o' the–some o' the–nine thousand dollars." Penn led him into the cabin and slid the door behind.

"That ain't Penn," cried Uncle Salters. "It's Jacob Boller, an'–he's remembered Johnstown! I never seed such eyes in any livin' man's head. What's to do naow? What'll I do naow?"

They could hear Penn's voice and Jason's together. Then Penn's went on alone, and Salters slipped off his hat, for Penn was praying. Presently the little man came up the steps, huge drops of sweat on his face, and looked at the crew. Dan was still sobbing by the wheel.

"He don't know us," Salters groaned. "It's all to do over again, checkers and everything–an' what'll he say to *me?*"

Penn spoke; they could hear that it was to strangers. "I have prayed," said he. "Our people believe in prayer. I have prayed for the life of this man's son. Mine were drowned before my eyes–she and my eldest and–the others. Shall a man be more wise than his Maker? I prayed never for their lives, but I have prayed for this man's son, and he will surely be sent him."

Salters looked pleadingly at Penn to see if he remembered.

"How long have I been mad?" Penn asked suddenly. His mouth was twitching.

"Pshaw, Penn! You weren't never mad," Salters began. "Only a little distracted like."

"I saw the houses strike the bridge before the fires broke out. I do not remember any more. How long ago is that?"

"I can't stand it! I can't stand it!" cried Dan, and Harvey whimpered in sympathy.

"About five year," said Disko, in a shaking voice.

"Then I have been a charge on some one for every day of that time. Who was the man?"

Disko pointed to Salters.

"Ye hain't–ye hain't!" cried the sea-farmer, twisting his hands together. "Ye've more'n earned your keep twice-told; an' there's money owin' you, Penn, besides ha'af o' my quarter-share in the boat, which is yours fer value received."

"You are good men. I can see that in your faces. But—"

"Mother av Mercy," whispered Long Jack, "an' he's been wid us all these trips! He's clean bewitched."

A schooner's bell struck up alongside, and a voice hailed through the fog: "O Disko! 'Heard abaout the *Jennie Cushman?*"

"They have found his son," cried Penn. "Stand you still and see the salvation of the Lord!"

"Got Jason aboard here," Disko answered, but his voice quavered. "There–warn't any one else?"

"We've f'und one, though. 'Run acrost him snarled up in a mess o' lumber thet might ha' bin a foc'sle. His head's cut some."

"Who is he?"

The *We're Here's* heart-beats answered one another.

"Guess it's young Olley," the voice drawled.

Penn raised his hands and said something in German. Harvey could have sworn that a bright sun was shining upon his lifted face; but the drawl went on: "Sa-ay! You fellers guyed us consid'rable t'other night."

"We don't feel like guyin' any now," said Disko.

"I know it; but to tell the honest truth we was kinder–kinder driftin' when we run agin young Olley."

It was the irrepressible *Carrie Pitman,* and a roar of unsteady laughter went up from the deck of the *We're Here.*

"Hedn't you 'baout's well send the old man aboard? We're runnin' in fer more bait an' graound-tackle. Guess you won't want him, anyway, an' this blame windlass work makes us short-handed. We'll take care of him. He married my woman's aunt."

"I'll give you anything in the boat," said Troop.

"Don't want nothin', 'less, mebbe, an anchor that'll hold. Say! Young Olley's gittin' kinder baulky an' excited. Send the old man along."

Penn waked him from his stupor of despair, and Tom Platt rowed him over. He went away without a word of thanks, not knowing what was to come; and the fog closed over all.

"And now," said Penn, drawing a deep breath as though about to preach. "And now"–the erect body sank like a sword driven home into the scabbard; the light faded from the overbright eyes; the voice returned to its usual pitiful little titter–"and now," said Pennsylvania Pratt, "do you think it's too early for a little game of checkers, Mr. Salters?"

"The very thing–the very thing I was goin' to say myself," cried Salters promptly. "It beats all, Penn, how ye git on to what's in a man's mind."

The little fellow blushed and meekly followed Salters forward.

"Up anchor! Hurry! Let's quit these crazy waters," shouted Disko, and never was he more swiftly obeyed.

"Now what in creation d'ye suppose is the meanin' o' that all?" said Long Jack, when they were working through the fog once more, damp, dripping, and bewildered.

"The way I sense it," said Disko, at the wheel, "is this: The *Jennie Cushman* business comin' on an empty stummick——"

"He–we saw one of them go by," sobbed Harvey.

"An' *that,* o' course, kinder hove him outer water, julluk runnin' a craft ashore; hove him right aout, I take it, to rememberin' Johnstown an' Jacob Boller an' such-like reminiscences. Well, consolin' Jason there held him up a piece, same's shorin' up a boat. Then, bein' weak, them props slipped an' slipped, an' he slided down the ways, an' now he's water-borne agin. That's haow *I* sense it."

They decided that Disko was entirely correct.

" 'Twould ha' bruk Salters all up," said Long Jack, "if Penn had stayed Jacob Bollerin'. Did ye see his face when Penn asked who he'd been charged on all these years? How is ut, Salters?"

"Asleep–dead asleep. Turned in like a child," Salters replied, tiptoeing aft. "There won't be no grub till he wakes, natural. Did ye ever see sech a gift in prayer? He everlastin'ly hiked young Olley outer the ocean. Thet's my belief. Jason was tur-ble praoud of his boy, an' I mistrusted all along 'twas a jedgment on worshippin' vain idols."

"There's others jes as sot," said Disko.

"That's dif'runt," Salters retorted quickly. "Penn's not all caulked, an' I ain't only but doin' my duty by him."

They waited, those hungry men, three hours, till Penn reappeared with a smooth face and a blank mind. He said he believed that he had been dreaming. Then he wanted to know why they were so silent, and they could not tell him.

Disko worked all hands mercilessly for the next three or four days; and when they could not go out, turned them into the hold to stack the ship's stores into smaller compass, to make more room for the fish. The packed mass ran from the cabin partition to the sliding door behind the foc'sle stove; and Disko showed how there is great art in stowing cargo so as to bring a schooner to her best draft. The crew were thus kept lively till they recovered their spirits; and Harvey was tickled with a rope's end by Long Jack for being, as the Galway man said, "sorrowful as a sick cat over fwhat couldn't be helped." He did a great deal of thinking in those weary days, and told Dan what he thought, and Dan agreed with him–even to the extent of asking for fried pies instead of hooking them.

But a week later the two nearly upset the *Hattie S.* in a wild attempt to stab a shark with an old bayonet tied to a stick. The grim brute rubbed alongside the dory begging for small fish, and between the three of them it was a mercy they all got off alive.

At last, after playing blindman's-buff in the fog, there came a morning when Disko shouted down the foc'sle: "Hurry, boys! We're in taown!"

Chapter Eight

To THE END of his days, Harvey will never forget that sight. The sun was just clear of the horizon they had not seen for nearly a week, and his low red light struck into the riding-sails of three fleets of anchored schooners—one to the north, one to the westward, and one to the south. There must have been nearly a hundred of them, of every possible make and build, with, far away, a square-rigged Frenchman, all bowing and courtesying one to the other. From every boat dories were dropping away like bees from a crowded hive, and the clamour of voices, the rattling of ropes and blocks, and the splash of the oars carried for miles across the heaving water. The sails turned all colors, black, pearly-gray, and white, as the sun mounted; and more boats swung up through the mists to the southward.

The dories gathered in clusters, separated, reformed, and broke again, all heading one way; while men hailed and whistled and cat-called and sang, and the water was speckled with rubbish thrown overboard.

"It's a town," said Harvey. "Disko was right. It *is* a town!"

"I've seen smaller," said Disko. "There's about a thousand men here; an' yonder's the Virgin." He pointed to a vacant space of greenish sea, where there were no dories.

The *We're Here* skirted round the northern squadron, Disko waving his hand to friend after friend, and anchored as neatly as a racing yacht at the end of the season. The Bank fleet pass good seamanship in silence; but a bungler is jeered all along the line.

"Jest in time fer the caplin," cried the *Mary Chilton.*

" 'Salt 'most wet?" asked the *King Philip.*

"Hey, Tom Platt! Come t' supper to-night?" said the *Henry Clay;* and so questions and answers flew back and forth. Men had met one another before, dory-fishing in the fog, and there is no place for gossip like the Bank fleet. They all seemed to know about Harvey's rescue, and asked if he were worth his salt yet. The young bloods jested with Dan, who had a lively tongue of his own, and inquired after their health by the town-nicknames they least liked. Manuel's countrymen jabbered at him in their own language; and even the silent cook was seen riding the jib-boom and shouting Gaelic to a friend as black as himself. After they had buoyed the cable—all around the Virgin is rocky bottom, and carelessness means chafed ground-tackle and danger from drifting—after they had buoyed the cable, their dories went forth to join the mob of boats anchored about a mile away. The schooners rocked and dipped at a safe distance, like mother ducks watching their brood, while the dories behaved like mannerless ducklings.

As they drove into the confusion, boat banging boat, Harvey's ears tingled at the comments on his rowing. Every dialect from Labrador to Long Island, with Portuguese, Neapolitan, Lingua Franca, French, and Gaelic, with songs and shoutings and new oaths, rattled round him, and he seemed to be the butt of it all. For the first time in his life he felt shy—perhaps that came from living so long with only the *We're Heres*—among the scores of wild faces that rose and fell with the reeling small craft. A gentle, breathing swell, three furlongs from trough to barrel, would quietly shoulder up a string of variously painted dories. They hung for an instant, a wonderful frieze against the sky-line, and their men pointed and hailed. Next moment the open mouths, waving arms, and bare chests disappeared, while on another swell came up an entirely new line of characters like paper figures in a toy theatre. So

Harvey stared. "Watch out!" said Dan, flourishing a dip-net. "When I tell you dip, you dip. The caplin'll school any time from naow on. Where'll we lay, Tom Platt?"

Pushing, shoving, and hauling, greeting old friends here and warning old enemies there, Commodore Tom Platt led his little fleet well to leeward of the general crowd, and immediately three or four men began to haul on their anchors with intent to lee-bow the *We're Heres.* But a yell of laughter went up as a dory shot from her station with exceeding speed, its occupant pulling madly on the roding.

"Give her slack!" roared twenty voices. "Let him shake it out."

"What's the matter?" said Harvey, as the boat flashed away to the southward. "He's anchored, isn't he?"

"Anchored, sure enough, but his ground-tackle's kinder shifty," said Dan, laughing. "Whale's fouled it. . . . Dip, Harve! Here they come!"

The sea round them clouded and darkened, and then frizzed up in showers of tiny silver fish, and over a space of five or six acres the cod began to leap like trout in May; while behind the cod three or four broad gray-backs broke the water into boils.

Then everybody shouted and tried to haul up his anchor to get among the school, and fouled his neighbor's line and said what was in his heart, and dipped furiously with his dip-net, and shrieked cautions and advice to his companions, while the deep fizzed like freshly opened soda-water, and cod, men, and whales together flung in upon the luckless bait. Harvey was nearly knocked overboard by the handle of Dan's net. But in all the wild tumult he noticed, and never forgot, the wicked, set little eye–something like a circus elephant's eye–of a whale that drove along almost level with the water, and, so he said, winked at him. Three boats found their rodings fouled by these reckless mid-sea hunters, and were towed half a mile ere their horses shook the line free.

Then the caplin moved off, and five minutes later there was no sound except the splash of the sinkers overside, the flapping of the cod, and the whack of the muckles as the men stunned them. It was wonderful fishing. Harvey could see the glimmering cod below, swimming slowly in droves, biting as steadily as they swam. Bank law strictly forbids more than one hook on one line when the dories are on the Virgin or the Eastern Shoals; but so close lay the boats that even single hooks snarled, and Harvey found himself in hot argument with a gentle, hairy Newfoundlander on one side and a howling Portuguese on the other.

Worse than any tangle of fishing-lines was the confusion of the dory-rodings below water. Each man had anchored where it seemed good to him, drifting and rowing round his fixed point. As the fish struck on less quickly, each man wanted to haul up and get to better ground; but every third man found himself intimately connected with some four or five neighbours. To cut another's roding is crime unspeakable on the Banks; yet it was done, and done without detection, three or four times that day. Tom Platt caught a Maine man in the black act and knocked him over the gunwale with an oar, and Manuel served a fellow-countryman in the same way. But Harvey's anchor-line was cut, and so was Penn's, and they were turned into relief-boats to carry fish to the *We're Here* as the dories filled. The caplin schooled once more at twilight, when the mad clamor was repeated; and at dusk they rowed back to dress down by the light of kerosene-lamps on the edge of the pen.

It was a huge pile, and they went to sleep while they were dressing. Next day several boats fished right above the cap of the Virgin; and Harvey, with them, looked down on the very weed of that lonely rock, which rises to within twenty feet of the surface. The cod were there in legions, marshing solemnly over the leathery kelp. When they bit, they bit all together; and so when they stopped. There was a slack time at noon, and the dories began to

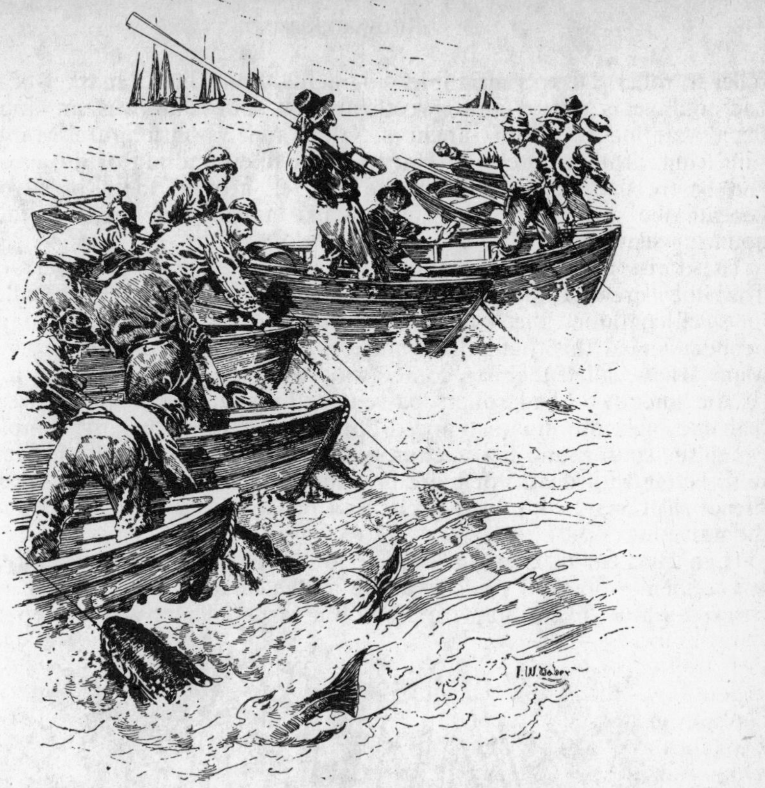

"IT WAS WONDERFUL FISHING. HARVEY COULD SEE THE GLIMMERING COD BELOW, ... BITING AS STEADILY AS THEY SWAM.... BUT SO CLOSE LAY THE BOATS THAT EVEN SINGLE HOOKS SNARLED."

search for amusement. It was Dan who sighted the *Hope of Prague* just coming up, and as her boats joined the company they were greeted with the question: "Who's the meanest man in the Fleet?"

Three hundred voices answered cheerily: "Nick Bra-ady." It sounded like an organ chant.

"Who stole the lamp-wicks?" That was Dan's contribution.

"Nick Bra-ady," sang the boats.

"Who biled the salt bait fer soup?" This was an unknown backbiter a quarter of a mile away.

Again the joyful chorus. Now, Brady was not especially mean, but he had that reputation, and the Fleet made the most of it. Then they discovered a man from a Truro boat who, six years before, had been convicted of using a tackle with five or six hooks—a "scrowger," they call it—on the Shoals. Naturally, he had been christened "Scrowger Jim"; and though he had hidden himself on the Georges ever since, he found his honors waiting for him full blown. They took it up in a sort of firecracker chorus: "Jim! O Jim! Jim! *O* Jim! Sssscrowger Jim!" That pleased everybody. And when a poetical Beverly man—he had been making it up all day, and talked about it for weeks—sang, "The *Carrie Pitman's* anchor doesn't hold her for a cent" the dories felt that they were indeed fortunate. Then they had to ask that Beverly man how he was off for beans, because even poets must not have things all their own way. Every schooner and nearly every man got it in turn. Was there a careless or dirty cook anywhere? The dories sang about him and his food. Was a schooner badly found? The Fleet was told at full length. Had a man hooked tobacco from a messmate? He was named in meeting; the name tossed from roller to roller. Disko's infallible judgments, Long Jack's market-boat that he had sold years ago, Dan's sweetheart (oh, but Dan was an angry boy!), Penn's bad luck with dory-anchors, Salters's views on manure, Manuel's little slips from virtue ashore, and Harvey's ladylike handling of the oar—all were laid before the public; and as the fog fell around them in silvery sheets beneath the sun, the voices sounded like a bench of invisible judges pronouncing sentence.

The dories roved and fished and squabbled till a swell underran the sea. Then they drew more apart to save their sides, and some one called that if the swell continued the Virgin would break. A reckless Galway man with his nephew denied this, hauled up anchor, and rowed over the very rock itself. Many voices called them to come away, while others dared them to hold on. As the smooth-backed rollers passed to the southward, they hove the dory high and high into the mist, and dropped her in ugly, sucking, dimpled water, where she spun round her anchor, within a foot or two of the hidden rock. It was playing with death for mere bravado; and the boats looked on in uneasy silence till Long Jack rowed up behind his countrymen and quietly cut their roding.

"Can't ye hear ut knockin'?" he cried. "Pull for you miserable lives! Pull!"

The men swore and tried to argue as the boat drifted; but the next swell checked a little, like a man tripping on a carpet. There was a deep sob and a

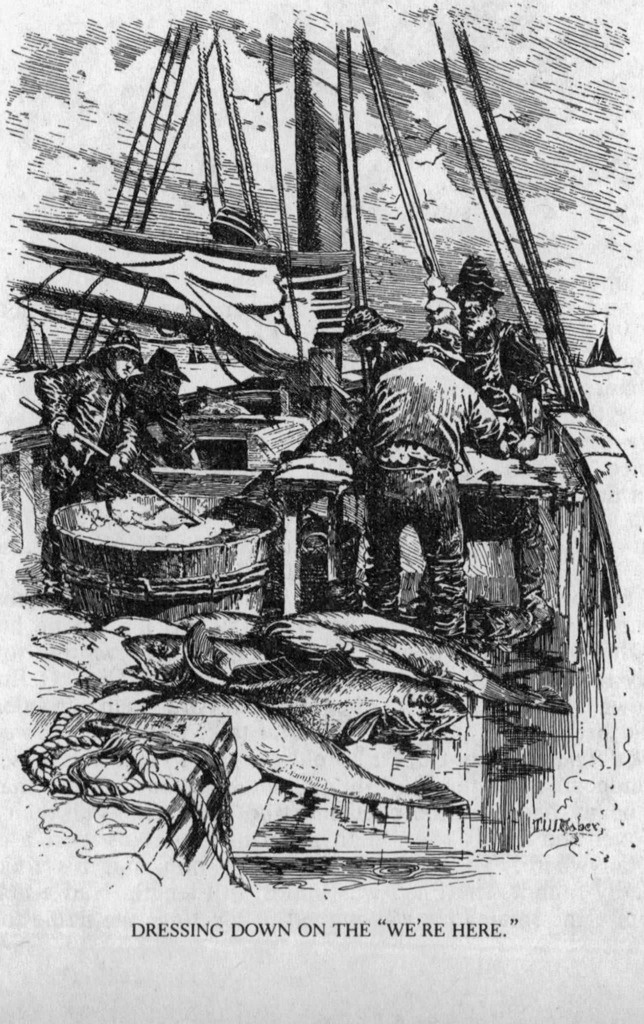

DRESSING DOWN ON THE "WE'RE HERE."

gathering roar, and the Virgin flung up a couple of acres of foaming water, white, furious, and ghastly over the shoal sea. Then all the boats greatly applauded Long Jack, and the Galway men held their tongue.

"Ain't it elegant?" said Dan, bobbing like a young seal at home. "She'll break about once every ha'af hour now, 'les the swell piles up good. What's her reg'lar time when she's at work, Tom Platt?"

"Once ivry fifteen minutes, to the tick. Harve, you've seen the greatest thing on the Banks; an' but for Long Jack you'd seen some dead men too."

There came a sound of merriment where the fog lay thicker and the schooners were ringing their bells. A big bark nosed cautiously out of the mist, and was received with shouts and cries of, "Come along, darlin'," from the Irishry.

"Another Frenchman?" said Harvey.

"Hain't you eyes? She's a Baltimore boat; goin' in fear an' tremblin'," said Dan. "We'll guy the very sticks out of her. Guess its the fust time her skipper ever met up with the Fleet this way."

She was a black, buxom, eight-hundred-ton craft. Her mainsail was looped up, and her topsail flapped undecidedly in what little wind was moving. Now a bark is feminine beyond all other daughters of the sea, and this tall, hesitating creature, with her white and gilt figurehead, looked just like a bewildered woman half lifting her skirts to cross a muddy street under the jeers of bad little boys. That was very much her situation. She knew she was somewhere in the neighborhood of the Virgin, had caught the roar of it, and was, therefore, asking her way. This is a small part of what she heard from the dancing dories:

"The Virgin? Fwhat are you talkin' of? This is Le Have on a Sunday mornin'. Go home an' sober up."

"Go home, ye tarrapin! Go home an' tell 'em we're comin'."

Half a dozen voices together, in a most tuneful chorus, as her stern went down with a roll and a bubble into the troughs: "Thay-aah–she–strikes!"

"Hard up! Hard up fer your life! You're on top of her now."

"Daown! Hard daown! Let go everything!"

"All hands to the pumps!"

"Daown jib an' pole her!"

Here the skipper lost his temper and said things. Instantly fishing was suspended to answer him, and he heard many curious facts about his boat and her next port of call. They asked him if he were insured; and whence he had stolen his anchor, because, they said, it belonged to the *Carrie Pitman;* they called his boat a mud-scow, and accused him of dumping garbage to frighten the fish; they offered to tow him and charge it to his wife; and one audacious youth slipped up almost under the counter, smacked it with his open palm, and yelled: "Gid up, Buck!"

The cook emptied a pan of ashes on him, and he replied with cod-heads. The bark's crew fired small coal from the galley, and the dories threatened to come aboard and "razee" her. They would have warned her at once had she been in real peril; but, seeing her well clear of the Virgin, they made the most of their chances. The fun was spoilt when the rock spoke again, a half-mile to windward, and the tormented bark set everything that would draw and went her ways; but the dories felt that the honours lay with them.

All that night the Virgin roared hoarsely; and next morning, over an angry, white-headed sea, Harvey saw the Fleet with flickering masts waiting for a lead. Not a dory was hove out till ten o'clock, when the two Jeraulds of the *Day's Eye,* imagining a lull which did not exist, set the example. In a minute half the boats were out and bobbing in the cockly swells, but Troop kept the *We're Heres* at work dressing down. He saw no sense in "dares"; and as the storm grew that evening they had the pleasure of receiving wet strangers only too glad to make any refuge in the gale. The boys stood by the dory-tackles with lanterns, the men ready to haul, one eye cocked for the sweeping wave that would make them drop everything and hold on for dear life. Out of the dark would come a yell of "Dory, dory!" They would hook up and haul in a drenched man and a half-sunk boat, till their decks were littered down with nests of dories and the bunks were full. Five times in their watch did Harvey, with Dan, jump at the foregaff where it lay lashed on the boom, and cling with arms, legs, and teeth to rope and spar and sodden canvas as a big wave filled the decks. One dory was smashed to pieces, and the sea pitched the man head first on to the decks, cutting his forehead open; and about dawn, when the racing seas glimmered white all along their cold edges, another man, blue and ghastly, crawled in with a broken hand, asking news of his brother. Seven extra mouths sat down to breakfast: A Swede; a Chatham skipper; a boy from Hancock, Maine; one Duxbury, and three Provincetown men.

There was a general sorting out among the Fleet next day; and though no one said anything, all ate with better appetites when boat after boat reported full crews aboard. Only a couple of Portuguese and an old man from Gloucester were drowned, but many were cut or bruised; and two schooners had parted their tackle and been blown to the southward, three days' sail. A man died on a Frenchman–it was the same bark that had traded tobacco with the *We're Heres.* She slipped away quite quietly one wet, white morning, moved to a patch of deep water, her sails all hanging anyhow, and Harvey saw the funeral through Disko's spy-glass. It was only an oblong bundle slid overside. They did not seem to have any form of service, but in the night, at anchor, Harvey heard them across the star-powdered black water, singing something that sounded like a hymn. It went to a very slow tune.

"La brigantine
Qui va tourner,
Roule et s'incline
Pour m'entrainer.
Oh, Vierge Marie,
Pour moi priez Dieu!
Adieu, patrie;
Québec, adieu!"

Tom Platt visited her, because, he said, the dead man was his brother as a Freemason. It came out that a wave had doubled the poor fellow over the heel of the bowsprit and broken his back. The news spread like a flash, for, contrary to general custom, the Frenchman held an auction of the dead man's kit,–he had no friends at St. Malo or Miquelon,–and everything was spread out on the top of the house, from his red knitted cap to the leather belt with the sheath-knife at the back. Dan and Harvey were out on twenty-fathom water in the *Hattie S.,* and naturally rowed over to join the crowd. It was a long pull, and they stayed some little time while Dan bought the knife, which had a curious brass handle. When they dropped overside and pushed off into a drizzle of rain and a lop of sea, it occurred to them that they might get into trouble for neglecting the lines.

"Guess 'twon't hurt us any to be warmed up," said Dan, shivering under his oilskins, and they rowed on into the heart of a white fog, which, as usual, dropped on them without warning.

"There's too much blame tide hereabouts to trust to your instinks," he said. "Heave over the anchor, Harve, and we'll fish a piece till the thing lifts. Bend on your biggest lead. Three pound ain't any too much in this water. See how she's tightened on her rodin' already."

There was quite a little bubble at the bows, where some irresponsible Bank current held the dory full stretch on her rope; but they could not see a boat's length in any direction. Harvey turned up his collar and bunched himself over his reel with the air of a wearied navigator. Fog had no special terrors for him now. They fished a while in silence, and found the cod struck on well. Then Dan drew the sheath-knife and tested the edge of it on the gunwale.

"That's a daisy," said Harvey. "How did you get it so cheap?"

"On account o' their blame Cath'lic superstitions," said Dan, jabbing with the bright blade. "They don't fancy takin' iron from off a dead man, so to speak. 'See them Arichat Frenchmen step back when I bid?"

"But an auction ain't taking anythink off a dead man. It's business."

"*We* know it ain't, but there's no goin' in the teeth o' superstition. That's one o' the advantages o' livin' in a progressive country." And Dan began whistling:

"Oh, Double Thatcher, how are you?
Now Eastern Point comes inter view.
The girls an' boys we soon shall see,
At anchor off Cape Ann!"

"Why didn't that Eastport man bid, then? He bought his boots. Ain't Maine progressive?"

"Maine? Pshaw! They don't know enough, or they hain't got money enough, to paint their haouses in Maine. I've seen 'em. The Eastport man he told me that the knife had been used—so the French captain told him—used up on the French coast last year."

"Cut a man? Heave's the muckle." Harvey hauled in his fish, rebaited, and threw over.

"Killed him! Course, when I heard *that* I was keener'n ever to get it."

"Christmas! I didn't know it," said Harvey, turning round. "I'll give you a dollar for it when I—get my wages. Say, I'll give you two dollars."

"Honest? D'you like it as much as all that?" said Dan, flushing. "Well, to tell the truth, I kinder got it for you—to give; but I didn't let on till I saw how you'd take it. It's yours and welcome, Harve, because we're dory-mates, and so on and so forth, an' so followin'. Catch a-holt!"

He held it out, belt and all.

"But look at here. Dan, I don't see—"

"Take it. 'Tain't no use to me. I wish you to hev it."

The temptation was irresistible. "Dan, you're a white man," said Harvey. "I'll keep it as long as I live."

"That's good hearin'," said Dan, with a pleasant laugh; and then, anxious to change the subject: " 'Look's if your line was fast to somethin'."

"Fouled, I guess," said Harve, tugging. Before he pulled up he fastened the belt round him, and with deep delight heard the tip of the sheath click on the thwart. "Concern the thing!" he cried. "She acts as though she were on strawberry-bottom. It's all sand here, ain't it?"

Dan reached over and gave a judgmatic tweak. "Holibut'll act that way 'f he's sulky. Thet's no strawberry-bottom. Yank her once or twice. She gives, sure. Guess we'd better haul up an' make certain."

They pulled together, making fast at each turn on the cleats, and the hidden weight rose sluggishly.

"Prize, oh! Haul!" shouted Dan, but the shout ended in a shrill, double shriek of horror, for out of the sea came—the body of the dead Frenchman buried two days before! The hook had caught him under the right armpit, and he swayed, erect and horrible, head and shoulders above water. His arms were tied to his side, and—he had no face. The boys fell over each other in a heap at the bottom of the dory, and there they lay while the thing bobbed alongside, held on the shortened line.

"The tide—the tide brought him!" said Harvey with quivering lips, as he fumbled at the clasp of the belt.

"Oh, Lord! Oh, Harve!" groaned Dan, "be quick. He's come for it. Let him have it. Take it off."

"I don't want it! *I* don't want it!" cried Harvey. "I can't find the bu-buckle."

"Quick, Harve! He's on your line!"

Harvey sat up to unfasten the belt, facing the head that had no face under its streaming hair. "He's fast still," he whispered to Dan, who slipped out his knife and cut the line, as Harvey flung the belt far overside. The body shot down with a plop, and Dan cautiously rose to his knees, whiter than the fog.

"He come for it. He come for it. I've seen a stale one hauled up on a trawl and I didn't much care, but *he* come to us special."

"I wish—I wish I hadn't taken the knife. Then he'd have come on *your* line."

"Dunno as thet would ha' made any differ. We're both scared out o' ten years' growth. Oh, Harve, did ye see his head?"

"Did I? I'll never forget it. But look at here, Dan; it couldn't have been *meant.* It was only the tide."

"Tide! He come for it, Harve. Why, they sunk him six miles to south'ard o' the Fleet, an' we're two miles from where she's lyin' now. They told me he was weighted with a fathom an' a half o' chain-cable."

" 'Wonder what he did with the knife—up on the French coast?"

"Something bad. 'Guess he's bound to take it with him to the Judgment, an' so— What are you doin' with the fish?"

"Heaving 'em overboard," said Harvey.

"What for? *We* sha'n't eat 'em."

"I don't care. I had to look at his face while I was takin' the belt off. You can keep your catch if you like. I've no use for mine."

Dan said nothing, but threw his fish over again.

"Guess it's best to be on the safe side," he murmured at last. "I'd give a month's pay if this fog 'u'd lift. Things go abaout in a fog that ye don't see in clear weather—yo-hoes an' hollerers and such like. I'm sorter relieved he come the way he did instid o' walkin'. He might ha' walked."

"Do-on't, Dan! We're right on top of him now. 'Wish I was safe aboard, bein' pounded by Uncle Salters."

"They'll be lookin' fer us in a little. Gimme the tooter." Dan took the tin dinner-horn, but paused before he blew.

"Go on," said Harvey. "I don't want to stay here all night."

"Question is, haow *he'd* take it. There was a man frum down the coast told me once he was in a schooner where they darsen't ever blow a horn to the dories, becaze the skipper—not the man he was with, but a captain that had run her five years before—he'd drowned a boy alongside in a drunk fit; an' ever after, that boy he'd row alongside too and shout, 'Dory! dory!' with the rest."

"Dory! dory!" a muffled voice cried through the fog. They cowered again, and the horn dropped from Dan's hand.

"Hold on!" cried Harvey; "it's the cook."

"Dunno what made me think o' thet fool tale, either," said Dan. "It's the doctor, sure enough."

"Dan! Danny! Oooh, Dan! Harve! Harvey! Oooh, Haarveee!"

"We're here," sung both boys together. They heard oars, but could see nothing till the cook, shining and dripping, rowed into them.

"What iss happened?" said he. "You will be beaten at home."

"Thet's what we want. Thet's what we're sufferin' for," said Dan. "Anything homey's good enough fer us. We've had kinder depressin' company." As the cook passed them a line, Dan told him the tale.

"Yess! He come for hiss knife," was all he said at the end.

Never had the little rocking *We're Here* looked so deliciously home-like as when the cook, born and bred in fogs, rowed them back to her. There was a warm glow of light from the cabin and a satisfying smell of food forward, and it was heavenly to hear Disko and the others, all quite alive and solid, leaning over the rail and promising them a first-class pounding. But the cook was a black master of strategy. He did not get the dories aboard till he had given the more striking points of the tale, explaining as he backed and bumped round the counter how Harvey was the mascot to destroy any possible bad luck. So the boys came overside as rather uncanny heroes, and every one asked them questions instead of pounding them for making trouble. Little Penn delivered quite a speech on the folly of superstitions; but public opinion was against him and in favor of Long Jack, who told the most excruciating ghost-stories, till nearly midnight. Under that influence no one except Salters and Penn said anything about "idolatry," when the cook put a lighted candle, a cake of flour and water, and a pinch of salt on a shingle, and floated them out astern to keep the Frenchman quiet in case he was still restless. Dan lit the candle because he had bought the belt, and the cook grunted and muttered charms as long as he could see the ducking point of flame.

Said Harvey to Dan, as they turned in after watch: "How about progress and Catholic superstitions?"

"Huh! I guess I'm as enlightened and progressive as the next man, but when it comes to a dead St. Malo deck-hand scarin' a couple o' pore boys stiff fer the sake of a thirty-cent knife, why, then, the cook can take hold fer all o' me. I mistrust furriners, livin' or dead."

Next morning all, except the cook, were rather ashamed of the ceremonies, and went to work double tides, speaking gruffly to one another.

The *We're Here* was racing neck and neck for her last few loads against the *Parry Norman;* and so close was the struggle that the Fleet took side and betted tobacco. All hands worked at the lines or dressing-down till they fell asleep where they stood—beginning before dawn and ending when it was too dark to see. They even used the cook as pitcher, and turned Harvey into the hold to pass salt, while Dan helped to dress down. Luckily a *Parry Norman* man sprained his ankle falling down the foc'sle, and the *We're Heres* gained. Harvey could not see how one more fish could be crammed into her, but Disko and Tom Platt stowed and stowed, and planked the mass down with big stones from the ballast, and there was always "jest another day's work." Disko did not tell them when all the salt was wetted. He rolled to the lazarette aft the cabin and began hauling out the big mainsail. This was at ten in the morning. The riding-sail was down and the main- and topsail were up by noon, and dories came alongside with letters for home, envying their good fortune. At last she cleared decks, hoisted her flag,—as is the right of the first boat off the Banks,—up-anchored, and began to move. Disko pretended that he wished to accommodate folk who had not sent in their mail, and so worked her gracefully in and out among the schooners. In reality, that was his little triumphant procession, and for the fifth year running it showed what kind of mariner he was. Dan's accordion and Tom Platt's fiddle supplied the music of the magic verse you must not sing till all the salt is wet:

"Hih! Yih! Yoho! Send your letters raound!
All our salt is wetted, an' the anchor's off the graound!
Bend, oh, bend your mains'l, we're back to Yankeeland—
With fifteen hunder' quintal,
An' fifteen hunder' quintal,
'Teen hunder' toppin' quintal,
'Twix' old 'Queereau an' Grand."

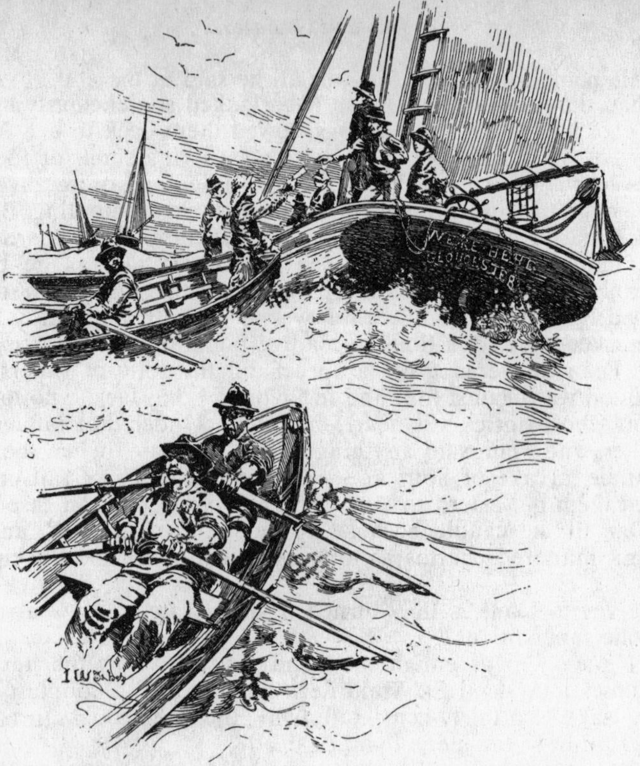

"DORIES CAME ALONGSIDE WITH LETTERS FOR HOME."

The last letters pitched on deck wrapped round pieces of coal, and the Gloucester men shouted messages to their wives and womenfolks and owners, while the *We're Here* finished the musical ride through the Fleet, her head-sails quivering like a man's hand when he raises it to say good-by.

Harvey very soon discovered that the *We're Here,* with her riding-sail, strolling from berth to berth, and the *We're Here* headed west by south under home canvas, were two very different boats. There was a bite and kick to the wheel even in "boy's" weather; he could feel the dead weight in the hold flung forward mightily across the surges, and the streaming line of bubbles overside made his eyes dizzy.

Disko kept them busy fiddling with the sails; and when those were flattened like a racing yacht's, Dan had to wait on the big topsail, which was put over by hand every time she went about. In spare moments they pumped, for the packed fish dripped brine, which does not improve a cargo. But since there was no fishing, Harvey had time to look at the sea from another point of view. The low-sided schooner was naturally on most intimate terms with her surroundings. They saw little of the horizon save when she topped a swell; and usually she was elbowing, fidgeting, and coaxing her steadfast way through gray, gray-blue, or black hollows laced across and across with streaks of shivering foam; or rubbing herself caressingly along the flank of some bigger water-hill. It was as if she said: "You wouldn't hurt me, surely? I'm only the little *We're Here.*" Then she would slide away chuckling softly to herself till she was brought up by some fresh obstacle. The dullest of folk cannot see this kind of thing hour after hour through long days without noticing it; and Harvey, being anything but dull, began to comprehend and enjoy the dry chorus of wave-tops turning over with a sound of incessant tearing; the hurry of the winds working across open spaces and herding the purple-blue cloud-shadows; the splendid upheaval of the red sunrise; the folding and packing away of the morning mists, wall after wall withdrawn across the white floors; the salty glare and blaze of noon; the kiss of rain falling over thousands of dead, flat square miles; the chilly blackening of everything at the day's end; and the million wrinkles of the sea under the moonlight, when the jib-boom solemnly poked at the low stars, and Harvey went down to get a doughnut from the cook.

But the best fun was when the boys were put on the wheel together, Tom Platt within hail, and she cuddled her lee-rail down to the crashing blue, and kept a little home-made rainbow arching unbroken over her windlass. Then the jaws of the booms whined against the masts, and the sheets creaked, and the sails filled with roaring; and when she slid into a hollow she trampled like a woman tripped in her own silk dress, and came out, her jib wet half-way up, yearning and peering for the tall twin-lights of Thatcher's Island.

The left the cold gray of the Bank sea, saw the lumberships making for Quebec by the Straits of St. Lawrence, with the Jersey salt-brigs from Spain and Sicily; found a friendly northeaster off Artimon Bank that drove them within view of the East light of Sable Island,—a sight Disko did not linger over,—and stayed with them past Western and Le Have, to the northern fringe of George's. From there they picked up the deeper water, and let her go merrily.

"Hattie's pulling on the string," Dan confided to Harvey. "Hattie an' Ma. Next Sunday you'll be hirin' a boy to throw water on the windows to make ye go to sleep. 'Guess you'll keep with us till your folks come. Do you know the best of gettin' ashore again?"

"Hot bath?" said Harvey. His eyebrows were all white with dried spray.

"That's good, but a night-shirt's better. I've been dreamin' o' night-shirts ever since we bent our mainsail. Ye can wiggle your toes then. Ma'll hev a new one fer me, all washed soft. It's home, Harve. It's home! Ye can sense it in the air. We're runnin' into the aidge of a hot wave now, an' I can smell the bayberries. Wonder if we'll get in fer supper. Port a trifle."

The hesitating sails flapped and lurched in the close air as the deep smoothed out, blue and oily, round them. When they whistled for a wind only the rain came in spiky rods, bubbling and drumming, and behind the rain the thunder and the lightning of mid-August. They lay on the deck with bare feet and arms, telling one another what they would order at their first meal ashore; for now the land was in plain sight. A Gloucester swordfish-boat drifted alongside, a man in the little pulpit on the bowsprit flourished his harpoon, his bare head plastered down with the wet. "And all's well!" he sang cheerily, as though he were watch on a big liner. "Wouverman's waiting fer you, Disko. What's the news o' the Fleet?"

Disko shouted it and passed on, while the wild summer storm pounded overhead and the lightning flickered along the capes from four different quarters at once. It gave the low circle of hills round Gloucester Harbor, Ten Pound Island, the fish-sheds, with the broken line of house-roofs, and each spar and buoy on the water, in blinding photographs that came and went a dozen times to the minute as the *We're Here* crawled in on half-flood, and the whistling-buoy moaned and mourned behind her. Then the storm died out in long, separated, vicious dags of blue-white flame, followed by a single roar like the roar of a mortar-battery, and the shaken air tingled under the stars as it got back to silence.

"The flag, the flag!" said Disko, suddenly, pointing upward.

"What is ut?" said Long Jack.

"Otto! Ha'af mast. They can see us frum shore now."

"I'd clean forgot. He's no folk to Gloucester, has he?"

"Girl he was goin' to be married to this fall."

"Mary pity her!" said Long Jack, and lowered the little flag half-mast for the sake of Otto, swept overboard in a gale off Le Have three months before.

Disko wiped the wet from his eyes and led the *We're Here* to Wouverman's wharf, giving his orders in whispers, while she swung round moored tugs and night-watchmen hailed her from the ends of inky-black piers. Over and above the darkness and the mystery of the procession, Harvey could feel the land close round him once more, with all its thousands of people asleep, and the smell of earth after rain, and the familiar noise of a switching-engine coughing to herself in a freight-yard; and all those things made his heart beat and his throat dry up as he stood by the foresheet. They heard the anchor-watch snoring on a lighthouse-tug, nosed into a pocket of darkness where a lantern glimmered on either side; somebody waked with a grunt, threw them a rope, and they made fast to a silent wharf flanked with great iron-roofed sheds full of warm emptiness, and lay there without a sound.

Then Harvey sat down by the wheel, and sobbed and sobbed as though his heart would break, and a tall woman who had been sitting on a weigh-scale dropped down into the schooner and kissed Dan once on the cheek; for she was his mother, and she had seen the *We're Here* by the lightning flashes. She took no notice of Harvey till he had recovered himself a little and Disko had told her his story. Then they went to Disko's house together as the dawn was breaking; and until the telegraph office was open and he could wire his folk, Harvey Cheyne was perhaps the loneliest boy in all America. But the curious thing was that Disko and Dan seemed to think none the worse of him for crying.

Wouverman was not ready for Disko's prices till Disko, sure that the *We're Here* was at least a week ahead of any other Gloucester boat, had given him a few days to swallow them; so all hands played about the streets, and Long Jack stopped the Rocky Neck trolley, on principle, as he said, till the conductor let him ride free. But Dan went about with his freckled nose in the air, bung-full of mystery and most haughty to his family.

"Dan, I'll hev to lay inter you ef you act this way," said Troop, pensively. "Sence we've come ashore this time you've bin a heap too fresh."

"I'd lay into him naow ef he was mine," said Uncle Salters, sourly. He and Penn boarded with the Troops.

"Oho!" said Dan, shuffling with the accordion round the backyard, ready to leap the fence if the enemy advanced. "Dan, you're welcome to your own judgment, but remember I've warned ye. Your own flesh an' blood ha' warned ye! 'Tain't any o' *my* fault ef you're mistook, but I'll be on deck to watch ye. An' ez fer *yeou*, Uncle Salters, Pharaoh's chief butler ain't in it 'longside o' you! You watch aout an' wait. You'll be plowed under like your own blamed clover; but me–Dan Troop–I'll flourish like a green bay-tree because *I* warn't stuck on my own opinion."

Disko was smoking in all his shore dignity and a pair of beautiful carpet-slippers. "You're gettin' ez crazy as poor Harve. You two go around gigglin' an squinchin' an' kickin' each other under the table till there's no peace in the house," said he.

"There's goin' to be a heap less–fer some folks," Dan replied. "You wait an' see."

He and Harvey went out on the trolley to East Gloucester, where they tramped through the bayberry bushes to the lighthouse, and lay down on the big red boulders and laughed themselves hungry. Harvey had shown Dan a telegram, and the two swore to keep silence till the shell burst.

"Harve's folk?" said Dan, with an unruffled face after supper. "Well, I guess they don't amount to much of anything, or we'd ha' heard from 'em by naow. His pop keeps a kind o' store out West. Maybe he'll give you's much as five dollars, Dad."

"What did I tell ye?" said Salters. "Don't sputter over your vittles, Dan."

Chapter Nine

WHATEVER HIS PRIVATE sorrows may be, a multimillionaire, like any other workingman, should keep abreast of his business. Harvey Cheyne, senior, had gone East late in June to meet a woman broken down, half mad, who dreamed day and night of her son drowning in the gray seas. He had surrounded her with doctors, trained nurses, massage-women, and even faith-cure companions, but they were useless. Mrs. Cheyne lay still and moaned, or talked of her boy by the hour together to any one who would listen. Hope she had none, and who could offer it? All she needed was assurance that drowning did not hurt; and her husband watched to guard lest she should make the experiment. Of his own sorrow he spoke little–hardly realized the depth of it till he caught himself asking the calendar on his writing-desk, "What's the use of going on?"

There had always lain a pleasant notion at the back of his head that, some day, when he had rounded off everything and the boy had left college, he would take his son to his heart and lead him into his possessions. Then that boy, he argued, as busy fathers do, would instantly become his companion, partner, and ally, and there would follow splendid years of great works carried out together–the old head backing the young fire. Now his boy was dead–lost at sea, as it might have been a Swede sailor from one of Cheyne's big teaships; the wife dying, or worse; he himself was trodden down by platoons of women and doctors and maids and attendants; worried almost beyond endurance by the shift and change of her poor restless whims; hopeless, with no heart to meet his many enemies.

He had taken the wife to his raw new palace in San Diego, where she and her people occupied a wing of great price, and Cheyne, in a veranda-room, between a secretary and a typewriter, who was also a telegraphist, toiled along wearily from day to day. There was a war of rates among four Western railroads in which he was supposed to be interested; a devastating strike had developed in his lumber camps in Oregon, and the Legislature of the State of California, which has no love for its makers, was preparing open war against him.

Ordinarily he would have accepted battle ere it was offered, and have waged a pleasant and unscrupulous campaign. But now he sat limply, his soft black hat pushed forward on to his nose, his big body shrunk inside his loose clothes, staring at his boots or the Chinese junks in the bay, and assenting absently to the secretary's questions as he opened the Saturday mail.

Cheyne was wondering how much it would cost to drop everything and pull out. He carried huge insurances, could buy himself royal annuities, and between one of his places in Colorado and a little society (that would do the wife good), say in Washington and the South Carolina islands, a man might forget plans that had come to nothing. On the other hand . . .

The click of the typewriter stopped; the girl was looking at the secretary, who had turned white.

He passed Cheyne a telegram repeated from San Francisco:

Picked up by fishing schooner We're Here having fallen off boat great times on Banks fishing all well waiting Gloucester Mass care Disko Troop for money or orders wire what shall do and how is Mama Harvey N. Cheyne.

The father let it fall, laid his head down on the roller-top of the shut desk.

and breathed heavily. The secretary ran for Mrs. Cheyne's doctor who found Cheyne pacing to and fro.

"What—what d' you think of it? Is it possible? Is there any meaning to it? I can't quite make it out," he cried.

"I can," said the doctor. "I lose seven thousand a year—that's all." He thought of the struggling New York practice he had dropped at Cheyne's imperious bidding, and returned the telegram with a sigh.

"You mean you'd tell her? 'May be a fraud?"

"What's the motive?" said the doctor, coolly. "Detection's too certain. It's the boy sure enough."

Enter a French maid, impudently, as an indispensable one who is kept on only by large wages.

"Mrs. Cheyne she say you must come at once. She think you are seek."

The master of thirty millions bowed his head meekly and followed Suzanne; and a thin, high voice on the upper landing of the great white-wood square staircase cried: "What is it? What has happened?"

No doors could keep out the shriek that rang through the echoing house a moment later, when her husband blurted out the news.

"And that's all right," said the doctor, serenely, to the typewriter. "About the only medical statement in novels with any truth to it is that joy don't kill, Miss Kinzey."

"I know it; but we've a heap to do first." Miss Kinzey was from Milwaukee, somewhat direct of speech; and as her fancy leaned towards the secretary, she divined there was work in hand. He was looking earnestly at the vast roller-map of America on the wall.

"Milsom, we're going right across. Private car—straight through—Boston. Fix the connections," shouted Cheyne down the staircase.

"I thought so."

The secretary turned to the typewriter, and their eyes met (out of that was born a story—nothing to do with this story). She looked inquiringly, doubtful of his resources. He signed to her to move to the Morse as a general brings brigades into action. Then he swept his hand musician-wise through his hair, regarded the ceiling, and set to work, while Miss Kinzey's white fingers called up the Continent of America.

"*K. H. Wade, Los Angeles*— The 'Constance' is at Los Angeles, isn't she, Miss Kinzey?"

"Yep." Miss Kinzey nodded between clicks as the secretary looked at his watch.

"Ready? *Send 'Constance,' private car, here, and arrange for special to leave here Sunday in time to connect with New York Limited at Sixteenth Street, Chicago, Tuesday next.*"

Click—click—click! "Couldn't you better that?"

"Not on those grades. That gives 'em sixty hours from here to Chicago. They won't gain anything by taking a special east of that. Ready? *Also arrange with Lake Shore and Michigan Southern to take 'Constance' on New York Central and Hudson River Buffalo to Albany, and B. and A. the same Albany to Boston. Indispensable I should reach Boston Wednesday evening. Be sure nothing prevents. Have also wired Canniff, Toucey, and Barnes.*—Sign, Cheyne."

Miss Kinzey nodded, and the secretary went on.

"Now then. Canniff, Toucey, and Barnes, of course. Ready? *Canniff, Chicago. Please take my private car 'Constance' from Santa Fé at Sixteenth Street next Tuesday p. m. on N. Y. Limited through to Buffalo and deliver N. Y. C. for Albany.*—Ever bin to N' York, Miss Kinzey? We'll go some day.—Ready? *Take car Buffalo to Albany on Limited Tuesday p. m.* That's for Toucey."

"Haven't bin to Noo York, but I know *that!*" with a toss of the head.

"Beg pardon. Now, Boston and Albany, Barnes, same instructions from

Albany through to Boston. Leave three-five P. M. (you neen't wire that); arrive nine-five P. M. Wednesday. That covers everything Wade will do, but it pays to shake up the managers."

"It's great," said Miss Kinzey, with a look of admiration. This was the kind of man she understood and appreciated.

" 'Tisn't bad," said Milsom, modestly. "Now, any one but me would have lost thirty hours and spent a week working out the run, instead of handing him over to the Santa Fé straight through to Chicago."

"But see here, about that Noo York Limited. Chauncey Depew himself couldn't hitch his car to *her,"* Miss Kinzey suggested, recovering herself.

"Yes, but this isn't Chauncey. It's Cheyne–lightning. It goes."

"Even so. Guess we'd better wire the boy. You've forgotten that, anyhow."

"I'll ask."

When he returned with the father's message bidding Harvey meet them in Boston at an appointed hour, he found Miss Kinzey laughing over the keys. Then Milsom laughed too, for the frantic clicks from Los Angeles ran: *"We want to know why–why–why? General uneasiness developed and spreading."*

Ten minutes later Chicago appealed to Miss Kinzey in these words: *"If crime of century is maturing please warn friends in time. We are all getting to cover here."*

This was capped by a message from Topeka (and wherein Topeka was concerned even Milsom could not guess): *"Don't shoot, Colonel. We'll come down."*

Cheyne smiled grimly at the consternation of his enemies when the telegrams were laid before him. "They think we're on the warpath. Tell 'em we don't feel like fighting just now, Milsom. Tell 'em what we're going for. I guess you and Miss Kinzey had better come along, though it isn't likely I shall do any business on the road. Tell 'em the truth–for once."

So the truth was told. Miss Kinzey clicked in the sentiment while the secretary added the memorable quotation, "Let us have peace," and in board rooms two thousand miles away the representatives of sixty-three million dollars' worth of variously manipulated railroad interests breathed more freely. Cheyne was flying to meet the only son, so miraculously restored to him. The bear was seeking his cub, not the bulls. Hard men who had their knives drawn to fight for their financial lives put away the weapons and wished him God-speed, while half a dozen panic-smitten tin-pot roads perked up their heads and spoke of the wonderful things they would have done had not Cheyne buried the hatchet.

It was a busy week-end among the wires; for now that their anxiety was removed, men and cities hastened to accommodate. Los Angeles called to San Diego and Barstow that the Southern California engineers might know and be ready in their lonely roundhouses; Barstow passed the word to the Atlantic and Pacific; and Albuquerque flung it the whole length of the Atchinson, Topeka, and Santa Fé management, even into Chicago. An engine, combination-car with crew, and the great and gilded "Constance" private car were to be "expedited" over those two thousand three hundred and fifty miles. The train would take precedence of one hundred and seventy-seven others meeting and passing; despatchers and crews of every one of those said trains must be notified. Sixteen locomotives, sixteen engineers, and sixteen firemen would be needed–each and every one the best available. Two and one half minutes would be allowed for changing engines, three for watering, and two for coaling. "Warn the men, and arrange tanks and chutes accordingly; for Harvey Cheyne is in a hurry, a hurry–a hurry," sang the wires. "Forty miles an hour will be expected, and division superintendents will accompany this special over their respective divisions. From San Diego to Sixteenth Street, Chicago, let the magic carpet be laid down. Hurry! Oh, hurry!"

"It will be hot," said Cheyne, as they rolled out of San Diego in the dawn of Sunday. "We're going to hurry, Mama, just as fast as ever we can; but I really don't think there's any good of your putting on your bonnet and gloves yet. You'd much better lie down and take your medicine. I'd play you a game of dominoes, but it's Sunday."

"I'll be good. Oh, I *will* be good. Only–taking off my bonnet makes me feel as if we'd never get there."

"Try to sleep a little, Mama, and we'll be in Chicago before you know."

"But it's Boston, Father. Tell them to hurry."

The six-foot drivers were hammering their way to San Bernardino and the Mohave wastes, but this was no grade for speed. That would come later. The heat of the desert followed the heat of the hills as they turned east to the Needles and the Colorado River. The car cracked in the utter drouth and glare, and they put crushed ice to Mrs. Cheyne's neck, and toiled up the long, long grades, past Ash Fork, towards Flagstaff, where the forests and quarries are, under the dry, remote skies. The needle of the speed-indicator flicked and wagged to and fro; the cinders rattled on the roof, and a whirl of dust sucked after the whirling wheels. The crew of the combination sat on their bunks, panting in their shirtsleeves, and Cheyne found himself among them shouting old, old stories of the railroad that every trainman knows, above the roar of the car. He told them about his son, and how the sea had given up its dead, and they nodded and spat and rejoiced with him; asked after "her, back there," and whether she could stand it if the engineer "let her out a piece," and Cheyne thought she could. Accordingly, the great fire-horse was "let-out" from Flagstaff to Winslow, till a division superintendent protested.

But Mrs. Cheyne, in the boudoir stateroom, where the French maid, sallow-white with fear, clung to the silver door-handle, only moaned a little and begged her husband to bid them "hurry." And so they dropped the dry sands

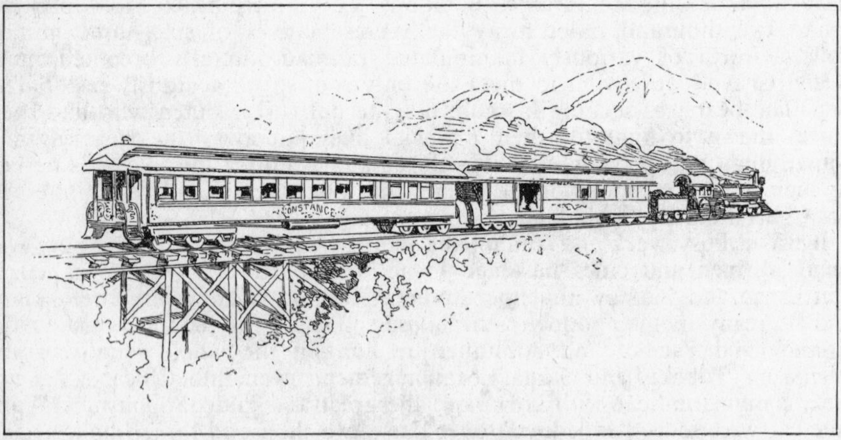

THE "CONSTANCE."

and moon-struck rocks of Arizona behind them, and grilled on till the crash of the couplings and the wheeze of the brake-hose told them they were at Coolidge by the Continental Divide.

Three bold and experienced men–cool, confident, and dry when they began; white, quivering, and wet when they finished their trick at those terrible wheels–swung her over the great lift from Albuquerque to Glorietta and beyond Springer, up and up to the Raton Tunnel on the State line, whence they dropped rocking into La Junta, had sight of the Arkansaw, and tore down the long slope to Dodge City, where Cheyne took comfort once again from setting his watch an hour ahead.

There was very little talk in the car. The secretary and typewriter sat together on the stamped Spanish-leather cushions by the plate-glass observation-window at the rear end, watching the surge and ripple of the ties crowded back behind them, and, it is believed, making notes of the scenery. Cheyne moved nervously between his own extravagant gorgeousness and the naked necessity of the combination, an unlit cigar in his teeth, till the pitying crews forgot that he was their tribal enemy, and did their best to entertain him.

At night the bunched electrics lit up that distressful palace of all the luxuries, and they fared sumptuously, swinging on through the emptiness of abject desolation. Now they heard the swish of a water-tank, and the guttural voice of a Chinaman, the click-clink of hammers that tested the Krupp steel wheels, and the oath of a tramp chased off the rear-platform; now the solid crash of coal shot into the tender; and now a beating back of noises as they flew past a waiting train. Now they looked out into great abysses, a trestle purring beneath their tread, or up to rocks that barred out half the stars. Now scaur and ravine changed and rolled back to jagged mountains on the horizon's edge, and now broke into hills lower and lower, till at last came the true plains.

At Dodge City an unknown hand threw in a copy of a Kansas paper containing some sort of an interview with Harvey, who had evidently fallen in with an enterprising reporter, telegraphed on from Boston. The joyful journalese revealed that it was beyond question their boy, and it soothed Mrs. Cheyne for a while. Her one word "hurry" was conveyed by the crews to the engineers at Nickerson, Topeka, and Marceline, where the grades are easy, and they brushed the Continent behind them. Towns and villages were close together now, and a man could feel here that he moved among people.

"I can't see the dial, and my eyes ache so. What are we doing?"

"The very best we can, Mama. There's no sense in getting in before the Limited. We'd only have to wait."

"I don't care. I want to feel we're moving. Sit down and tell me the miles."

Cheyne sat down and read the dial for her (there were some miles which stand for records to this day), but the seventy-foot car never changed its long steamer-like roll, moving through the heat with the hum of a giant bee. Yet the speed was not enough for Mrs. Cheyne; and the heat, the remorseless August heat, was making her giddy; the clock-hands would not move, and when, oh, when would they be in Chicago?

It is not true that, as they changed engines at Fort Madison, Cheyne passed over to the Amalgamated Brotherhood of Locomotive Engineers an endowment sufficient to enable them to fight him and his fellows on equal terms for evermore. He paid his obligations to engineers and firemen as he believed they deserved, and only his bank knows what he gave the crews who had sympathized with him. It is on record that the last crew took entire charge of switching operations at Sixteenth Street, because "she" was in a doze at last, and Heaven was to help any one who bumped her.

Now the highly paid specialist who conveys the Lake Shore and Michigan Southern Limited from Chicago to Elkhart is something of an autocrat, and he does not approve of being told how to back up to a car. None the less he handled the "Constance" as if she might have been a load of dynamite, and when the crew rebuked him, they did it in whispers and dumb show.

"Pshaw!" said the Atchinson, Topeka, and Santa Fé men, discussing life later, "we weren't runnin' for a record. Harvey Cheyne's wife, she were sick back, an' we didn't want to jounce her. 'Come to think of it, our runnin' time from San Diego to Chicago was 57.54. You can tell that to them Eastern way-trains. When we're tryin' for a record, we'll let you know."

To the Western man (though this would not please either city) Chicago and Boston are cheek by jowl, and some railroads encourage the delusion. The Limited whirled the "Constance" into Buffalo and the arms of the New York Central and Hudson River (illustrious magnates with white whiskers and gold charms on their watch-chains boarded her here to talk a little business to Cheyne), who slid her gracefully into Albany, where the Boston and Albany completed the run from tide-water to tide-water–total time, eighty-seven hours and thirty-five minutes, or three days, fifteen hours and one half. Harvey was waiting for them.

After violent emotion most people and all boys demand food. They feasted the returned prodigal behind drawn curtains, cut off in their great happiness, while the trains roared in and out around them. Harvey ate, drank, and enlarged on his adventures all in one breath, and when he had a hand free his mother fondled it. His voice was thickened with living in the open, salt air; his palms were rough and hard, his wrists dotted with marks of gurry-sores; and a fine full flavor of codfish hung round rubber boots and blue jersey.

The father, well used to judging men, looked at him keenly. He did not know what enduring harm the boy might have taken. Indeed, he caught himself thinking that he knew very little whatever of his son; but he distinctly remembered an unsatisfied, dough-faced youth who took delight in "calling down the old man," and reducing his mother to tears–such a person as adds to the gaiety of public rooms and hotel piazzas, where the ingenuous young of the wealthy play with or revile the bell-boys. But this well set-up fisher-youth did not wriggle, looked at him with eyes steady, clear, and unflinching, and spoke in a tone distinctly, even startlingly, respectful. There was that in his voice, too, which seemed to promise that the change might be permanent, and that the new Harvey had come to stay.

"Some one's been coercing him," thought Cheyne. "Now Constance would never have allowed that. Don't see as Europe could have done it any better."

"But why didn't you tell this man, Troop, who you were?" the mother repeated, when Harvey had expanded his story at least twice.

"Disko Troop, dear. The best man that ever walked a deck. I don't care who the next is."

"Why didn't you tell him to put you ashore? You know Papa would have made it up to him ten times over."

"I know it; but he thought I was crazy. I'm afraid I called him a thief because I couldn't find the bills in my pocket."

"A sailor found them by the flagstaff that–that night," sobbed Mrs. Cheyne.

"That explains it, then. I don't blame Troop any. I just said I wouldn't work–on a Banker, too–and of course he hit me on the nose, and oh! I bled like a stuck hog."

"My poor darling! They must have abused you horribly."

"Dunno quite. Well, after that, I saw a light."

Cheyne slapped his leg and chuckled. This was going to be a boy after his own hungry heart. He had never seen precisely that twinkle in Harvey's eye before.

"And the old man gave me ten and a half a month; he's paid me half now; and I took hold with Dan and pitched right in. I can't do a man's work yet. But I can handle a dory 'most as well as Dan, and I don't get rattled in a fog–much; and I can take my trick in light winds–that's steering, dear–and I can 'most bait up a trawl, and I know my ropes, of course; and I can pitch fish till the cows come home, and I'm great on old Josephus, and I'll show you how I can clear coffee with a piece of fish-skin, and–I think I'll have another cup, please. Say, you've no notion what a heap of work there is in ten and a half a month!"

"I began with eight and a half, my son," said Cheyne.

" 'That so? You never told me, sir."

"You never asked, Harve. I'll tell you about it some day, if you care to listen. Try a stuffed olive."

"Troop says *the* most interesting thing in the world is to find out how the next man gets his vittles. It's great to have a trimmed-up meal again. We were well fed, though. But mug on the Banks. Disko fed us first-class. He's a great man. And Dan–that's his son–Dan's *my* partner. And there's Uncle Salters and his manures, an' he reads Josephus. He's sure I'm crazy yet. And there's poor little Penn, and he *is* crazy. You mustn't talk to him about Johnstown, because— And, oh, you *must* know Tom Platt and Long Jack and Manuel. Manuel saved my life. I'm sorry he's a Portuguee. He can't talk much, but he's an everlasting musician. He found me struck adrift and drifting, and hauled me in."

"I wonder your nervous system isn't completely wrecked," said Mrs. Cheyne.

"What for, Mama? I worked like a horse and I ate like a hog and I slept like a dead man."

That was too much for Mrs. Cheyne, who began to think of her visions of a corpse rocking on the salty seas. She went to her stateroom, and Harvey curled up beside his father, explaining his indebtedness.

"You can depend upon me to do everything I can for the crowd, Harve. They seem to be good men on your showing."

"Best in the Fleet, sir. Ask at Gloucester," said Harvey. "But Disko believes still he's cured me of being crazy. Dan's the only one I've let on to about you, and our private cars and all the rest of it, and I'm not *quite* sure Dan believes. I want to paralyze 'em to'morrow. Say, can't they run the 'Constance' over to Gloucester? Mama don't look fit to be moved, anyway, and we're bound to finish cleaning out by to-morrow. Wouverman takes our fish. You see, we're the first off the Banks this season, and it's four twenty-five a quintal. We held out till he paid it. They want it quick."

"You mean you'll have to work to-morrow, then?"

"I told Troop I would. I'm on the scales. I've brought the tallies with me." He looked at the greasy notebook with an air of importance that made his father choke. "There isn't but three–no–two ninety-four or five quintal more by my reckoning."

"Hire a substitute," suggested Cheyne, to see what Harvey would say.

"Can't, sir. I'm tally-man for the schooner. Troop says I've a better head for figures than Dan. Troop's a mighty just man."

"Well, suppose I don't move the 'Constance' to-night, how'll you fix it?"

Harvey looked at the clock, which marked twenty past eleven.

"Then I'll sleep here till three and catch the four o'clock freight. They let us men from the Fleet ride free as a rule."

"That's a notion. But I think we can get the 'Constance' around about as soon as your men's freight. Better go to bed now."

Harvey spread himself on the sofa, kicked off his boots, and was asleep before his father could shade the electrics. Cheyne sat watching the young face under the shadow of the arm thrown over the forehead, and among many things that occurred to him was the notion that he might perhaps have been neglectful as a father.

"One never knows when one's taking one's biggest risks," he said. "It might have been worse than drowning; but I don't think it has–I don't think it has. If it hasn't, I haven't enough to pay Troop, that's all; and I don't think it has."

Morning brought a fresh sea breeze through the windows, the "Constance" was side-tracked among freight-cars at Gloucester, and Harvey had gone to his business.

"Then he'll fall overboard again and be drowned," the mother said bitterly.

"We'll go and look, ready to throw him a rope in case. You've never seen him working for his bread," said the father.

"What nonsense! As if any one expected—"

"Well, the man that hired him did. He's about right, too."

They went down between the stores full of fishermen's oilskins to Wouverman's wharf where the *We're Here* rode high, her Bank flag still flying, all hands busy as beavers in the glorious morning light. Disko stood by the main hatch superintending Manuel, Penn, and Uncle Salters at the tackle. Dan was swinging the loaded baskets inboard as Long Jack and Tom Platt filled them, and Harvey, with a notebook, represented the skipper's interests before the clerk of the scales on the salt-sprinkled wharf-edge.

"Ready!" cried the voices below. "Haul!" cried Disko. "Hi!" said Manuel. "Here!" said Dan, swinging the basket. Then they heard Harvey's voice, clear and fresh, checking the weights.

The last of the fish had been whipped out, and Harvey leaped from the string-piece six feet to a ratline, as the shortest way to hand Disko the tally, shouting, "Two ninety-seven, and an empty hold!"

"What's the total, Harve?" said Disko.

"Eight sixty-five. Three thousand six hundred and seventy-six dollars *and* a quarter. 'Wish I'd share as well as wage."

"Well, I won't go so far as to say you heven't deserved it, Harve. Don't you want to slip up to Wouverman's office and take him our tallies?"

"Who's that boy?" said Cheyne to Dan, well used to all manner of questions from those idle imbeciles called summer boarders.

"Well, he's kind o' supercargo," was the answer. "We picked him up struck adrift on the Banks. Fell overboard from a liner, he sez. He was a passenger. He's by way o' bein' a fisherman now."

"Is he worth his keep?"

"Ye-ep. Dad, this man wants to know ef Harve's worth his keep. Say, would you like to go aboard? We'll fix up a ladder for her."

"I should very much, indeed. 'Twon't hurt you, Mama, and you'll be able to see for yourself."

The woman who could not lift her head a week ago scrambled down the ladder, and stood aghast amid the mess and tangle aft.

"Be you anyways interested in Harve?" said Disko.

"Well, ye-es."

"He's a good boy, an' ketches right hold jest as he's bid. You've heard haow we found him? He was sufferin' from nervous prostration, I guess, 'r else his head had hit somethin', when we hauled him aboard. He's all over that naow. Yes, this is the cabin. 'Tain't anyways in order, but you're quite welcome to look araound. Those are his figures on the stove-pipe, where we keep the reckonin' mostly."

"Did he sleep here?" said Mrs. Cheyne, sitting on a yellow locker and surveying the disorderly bunks.

"No. He berthed forward, madam, an' only fer him an' my boy hookin' fried pies an' muggin' up when they ought to ha' been asleep, I dunno as I've any special fault to find with him."

"There weren't nothin' wrong with Harve," said Uncle Salters, descending the steps. "He hung my boots on the main-truck, and he ain't over an' above respectful to such as knows more'n he do, specially about farmin'; but he were mostly misled by Dan."

Dan in the meantime, profiting by dark hints from Harvey early that morning, was executing a war-dance on deck. "Tom, Tom!" he whispered down the hatch. "His folks has come, an' Dad hain't caught on yet, an' they're pow-wowin' in the cabin. She's a daisy, an' he's all Harve claimed he was, by the looks of him."

"Howly Smoke!" said Long Jack, climbing out covered with salt and fish-skin. "D'ye belave his tale av the kid an' the little four-horse rig was thrue?"

"I knew it all along," said Dan. "Come an' see Dad mistook in his judgments."

They came delightedly, just in time to hear Cheyne say: "I'm glad he has a good character, because—he's my son."

Disko's jaw fell,—Long Jack always vowed that he heard the click of it,—and he stared alternately at the man and the woman.

"I got his telegram in San Diego four days ago, and we came over."

"In a private car?" said Dan. "He said ye might."

"In a private car, of course."

Dan looked at his father with a hurricane of irreverent winks.

"There was a tale he told us av drivin' four little ponies in a rig av his own," said Long Jack. "Was that thrue now?"

"Very likely," said Cheyne. "Was it, Mama?"

"He had a little drag when we were in Toledo, I think," said the mother.

Long Jack whistled. "Oh, Disko!" said he, and that was all.

"I wuz—I am mistook in my jedgments—worse'n the men o' Marblehead," said Disko, as though the words were being windlassed out of him. "I don't mind ownin' to you, Mr. Cheyne, as I mistrusted the boy to be crazy. He talked kinder odd about money."

"So he told me."

"Did he tell ye anything else? 'Cause I pounded him once." This with a somewhat anxious glance at Mrs. Cheyne.

"Oh, yes," Cheyne replied. "I should say it probably did him more good than anything else in the world."

"I jedged 'twuz necessary, er I wouldn't ha' done it. I don't want you to think we abuse our boys any on this packet."

"I don't think you do, Mr. Troop."

Mrs. Cheyne had been looking at the faces—Disko's ivory-yellow, hairless, iron countenance; Uncle Salters's, with its rim of agricultural hair; Penn's bewildered simplicity; Manuel's quiet smile; Long Jack's grin of delight, and Tom Platt's scar. Rough, by her standards, they certainly were; but she had a mother's wits in her eyes, and she rose with out-stretched hands.

"Oh, tell me, which is who?" said she, half sobbing. "I want to thank you and bless you—all of you."

"Faith, that pays me a hunder time," said Long Jack.

Disko introduced them all in due form. The captain of an old-time China-man could have done no better, and Mrs. Cheyne babbled incoherently. She nearly threw herself into Manuel's arms when she understood that he had first found Harvey.

"But how *shall* I leave him dreeft?" said poor Manuel. "What do you yourself if you find him so? Eh, wha-at? We are in one good boy, and I am *ever* so pleased he come to be your son."

"And he told me Dan was his partner!" she cried. Dan was already sufficiently pink, but he turned a rich crimson when Mrs. Cheyne kissed him on both cheeks before the assembly. Then they led her forward to show her the foc'sle, at which she wept again, and must needs go down to see Harvey's identical bunk, and there she found the nigger cook cleaning up the stove, and he nodded as though she were some one he had expected to meet for years. They tried, two at a time, to explain the boat's daily life to her, and she sat by the pawl-post, her gloved hands on the greasy table, laughing with trembling lips and crying with dancing eyes.

"And who's ever to use the *We're Here* after this?" said Long Jack to Tom Platt. "I feel as if she'd made a cathedral av ut all."

"Cathedral!" sneered Tom Platt. "Oh, ef it had bin even the Fish C'mmission boat instid of this bally-hoo o' blazes. Ef we only hed some decency an' order an' side-boys when she goes over! She'll have to climb that ladder like a hen, an' we—we ought to be mannin' the yards!"

"Then Harvey was *not* mad," said Penn, slowly, to Cheyne.

"No, indeed—thank God," the big millionaire replied, stooping down tenderly.

"It must be terrible to be mad. Except to lose your child, I do not know anything more terrible. But your child has come back? Let us thank God for that."

"Hello!" cried Harvey, looking down upon them benignly from the wharf.

"I wuz mistook, Harve. I wuz mistook," said Disko, swiftly, holding up a hand. "I wuz mistook in my jedgments. Ye needn't rub in any more."

"Guess I'll take care o' that," said Dan, under his breath.

"You'll be goin' off naow, won't ye?"

"Well, not without the balance of my wages, 'less you want to have the *We're Here* attached."

"Thet's so; I'd clean forgot"; and he counted out the remaining dollars. "You done all you contracted to do, Harve; and you done it 'bout's well as ef you'd been brought up——" Here Disko brought himself up. He did not quite see where the sentence was going to end.

"Outside of a private car?" suggested Dan, wickedly.

"Come on, and I'll show her to you," said Harvey.

Cheyne stayed to talk with Disko, but the others made a procession to the depot, with Mrs. Cheyne at the head. The French maid shrieked at the invasion; and Harvey laid the glories of the "Constance" before them without a word. They took them in in equal silence—stamped leather, silver door-handles and rails, cut velvet, plate-glass, nickel, bronze, hammered iron, and the rare woods of the continent inlaid.

"I told you," said Harvey; "I told you." This was his crowning revenge, and a most ample one.

Mrs. Cheyne decreed a meal, and that nothing might be lacking to the tale Long Jack told afterwards in his boarding-house, she waited on them herself. Men who are accustomed to eat at tiny tables in howling gales have curiously neat and finished manners; but Mrs. Cheyne, who did not know this, was surprised. She longed to have Manuel for a butler; so silently and easily did he comport himself among the frail glassware and dainty silver. Tom Platt remembered the great days on the *Ohio* and the manners of foreign potentates who dined with the officers; and Long Jack, being Irish, supplied the small talk till all were at their ease.

In the *We're Here's* cabin the fathers took stock of each other behind their cigars. Cheyne knew well enough when he dealt with a man to whom he could not offer money; equally well he knew that no money could pay for what Disko had done. He kept his own counsel and waited for an opening.

"I hevn't done anything *to* your boy or *fer* your boy excep' make him work a piece an' learn him how to handle the hog-yoke," said Disko. "He has twice my boy's head for figgers."

"By the way," Cheyne answered casually, "what d'you calculate to make of your boy?"

Disko removed his cigar and waved it comprehensively round the cabin. "Dan's jest plain boy, an' he don't allow me to do any of his thinkin'. He'll hev this able little packet when I'm laid by. He ain't noways anxious to quit the business. I know that."

"Mmm! 'Ever been West, Mr. Troop?"

" 'Bin's fer ez Noo York once in a boat. I've no use for railroads. No more hez Dan. Salt water's good enough fer the Troops. I've been 'most everywhere—in the nat'ral way, o' course."

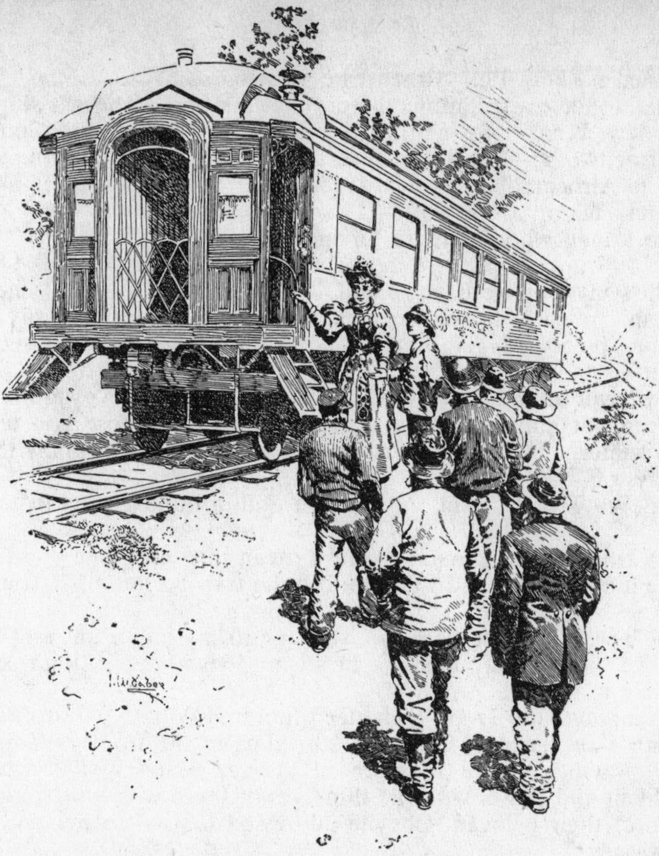

MRS. CHEYNE INTRODUCES THE CREW OF THE "WE'RE HERE" TO THE "CONSTANCE."

"I can give him all the salt water he's likely to need–till he's a skipper."

"Haow's that? I thought you wuz a kinder railroad king. Harve told me so when–I was mistook in my jedgments."

"We're all apt to be mistaken. I fancied perhaps you might know I own a line of tea-clippers–San Francisco to Yokohama–six of 'em–iron-built, about seventeen hundred and eighty tons apiece."

"Blame that boy! He never told. I'd ha' listened to *that,* instid o' his truck abaout railroads an' pony-carriages."

"He didn't know."

" 'Little thing like that slipped his mind, I guess."

"No, I only capt–took hold of the 'Blue M.' freighters–Morgan and McQuade's old line–this summer."

Disko collapsed where he sat, beside the stove.

"Great Caesar Almighty! I mistrust I've been fooled from one end to the other. Why, Phil Airheart he went from this very town six year back–no, seven–an' he's mate on the *San José* now–twenty-six days was her time out. His sister she's livin' here yet, an' she reads his letters to my woman. An' *you* own the 'Blue M.' freighters?"

Cheyne nodded.

"If I'd known that I'd ha' jerked the *We're Here* back to port all standin', on the word."

"Perhaps that wouldn't have been so good for Harvey."

"Ef I'd only known! Ef he'd only *said* about the cussed Line, I'd ha' understood! I'll never stand on my own jedgments again–never. They're well-founded packets. Phil Airheart he says so."

"I'm glad to have a recommend from that quarter. Airheart's skipper of the *San José* now. What I was getting at is to know whether you'd lend me Dan for a year or two, and we'll see if we can't make a mate of him. Would you trust him to Airheart?"

"It's a resk taking a raw boy—"

"I know a man who did more for me."

"That's diff'runt. Look at here naow, I ain't recommendin' Dan special because he's my own flesh an' blood. *I* know Bank ways ain't clipper ways, but he hain't much to learn. Steer he can–no boy better, ef I say it–an' the rest's in our blood an' get; but I could wish he warn't so cussed weak on navigation."

"Airheart will attend to that. He'll ship as boy for a voyage or two, and then we can put him in the way of doing better. Suppose you take him in hand this winter, and I'll send for him early in the spring. I know the Pacific's a long ways off—"

"Pshaw! We Troops, livin' an' dead, are all around the earth an' the seas thereof."

"But I want you to understand–and I mean this–any time you think you'd like to see him, tell me, and I'll attend to the transportation. 'Twon't cost you a cent."

"Ef you'll walk a piece with me, we'll go to my house an' talk this to my woman. I've bin so crazy mistook in all my jedgments, it don't seem to me this was like to be real."

They went over to Troop's eighteen-hundred-dollar, blue-trimmed white house, with a retired dory full of nasturtiums in the front yard and a shuttered parlor which was a museum of oversea plunder. There sat a large woman, silent and grave, with the dim eyes of those who look long to sea for the return of their beloved. Cheyne addressed himself to her, and she gave consent wearily.

"We lose one hundred a year from Gloucester only, Mr. Cheyne," she said–"one hundred boys an' men; and I've come so's to hate the sea as if 'twuz alive an' listenin'. God never made it fer humans to anchor on. These packets o' yours they go straight out, I take it, and straight home again?"

"As straight as the winds let 'em, and I give a bonus for record passages. Tea don't improve by being at sea."

"When he wuz little he used to play at keeping store, an' I had hopes he might follow that up. But soon's he could paddle a dory I knew that were goin' to be denied me."

"They're square-riggers, Mother; iron-built an' well found. Remember what Phil's sister reads you when she gits his letters."

"I've never known as Phil told lies, but he's too venturesome (like most of 'em that use the sea). Ef Dan sees fit, Mr. Cheyne, he can go–fer all o' me."

"She jest despises the ocean," Disko explained, "an' I–I dunno haow to act polite, I guess, er I'd thank you better."

"My father–my own eldest brother–two nephews–an' my second sister's man," she said, dropping her head on her hand. "Would *you* care fer any one that took all those?"

Cheyne was relieved when Dan turned up and accepted with more delight than he was able to put into words. Indeed, the offer meant a plain and sure road to all desirable things; but Dan thought most of commanding watch on broad decks, and looking into far-away harbours.

Mrs. Cheyne had spoken privately to the unaccountable Manuel in the matter of Harvey's rescue. He seemed to have no desire for money. Pressed hard, he said that he would take five dollars, because he wanted to buy something for a girl. Otherwise–"How shall I take money when I make so easy my eats and smokes? You *will* giva some if I like or no? Eh, wha-at?

Then you shall giva me money, but not that way. You shall giva all you can think." He introduced her to a snuffy Portuguese priest with a list of semi-destitute widows as long as his cassock. As a strict Unitarian, Mrs. Cheyne could not sympathize with the creed, but she ended by respecting the brown, voluble little man.

Manuel, faithful son of the Church, appropriated all the blessings showered on her for her charity. "That letta me out," said he. "I have now ver' good absolutions for six months"; and he strolled forth to get a handkerchief for the girl of the hour and to break the hearts of all the others.

Salters went West for a season with Penn, and left no address behind. He had a dread that these millionary people, with wasteful private cars, might take undue interest in his companion. It was better to visit inland relatives till the coast was clear. "Never you be adopted by rich folk, Penn," he said in the cars, "or I'll take 'n' break this checker-board over your head. Ef you forgit your name agin—which is Pratt—you remember you belong with Salters Troop, an' set down right where you are till I come fer you. Don't go taggin' araound after them whose eyes bung out with fatness, accordin' to Scripcher."

Chapter Ten

BUT IT WAS otherwise with the *We're Here's* silent cook, for he came up, his kit in a handkerchief, and boarded the "Constance." Pay was no particular object, and he did not in the least care where he slept. His business, as revealed to him in dreams, was to follow Harvey for the rest of his days. They tried argument and, at last, persuasion; but there is a difference between one Cape Breton and two Alabama negroes, and the matter was referred to Cheyne by the cook and porter. The millionaire only laughed. He presumed Harvey might need a body-servant some day or other, and was sure that one volunteer was worth five hirelings. Let the man stay, therefore; even though he called himself MacDonald and swore in Gaelic. The car could go back to Boston, where, if he were still of the same mind, they would take him West.

With the "Constance," which in his heart of hearts he loathed, departed the last remnant of Cheyne's millionairedom, and he gave himself up to an energetic idleness. This Gloucester was a new town in a new land, and he purposed to "take it in," as of old he had taken in all the cities from Snohomish to San Diego of that world whence he hailed. They made money along the crooked street which was half wharf and half ship's store: as a leading professional he wished to learn how the noble game was played. Men said that four out of every five fish-balls served at New England's Sunday breakfast came from Gloucester, and overwhelmed him with figures in proof—statistics of boats, gear, wharf-frontage, capital invested, salting, packing, factories, insurance, wages, repairs, and profits. He talked with the owners of the large fleets whose skippers were little more than hired men, and whose crews were almost all Swedes or Portuguese. Then he conferred with Disko, one of the few who owned their craft, and compared notes in his vast head. He coiled himself away on chain-cables in marine junk-shops, asking questions with cheerful, unslaked Western curiosity, till all the water-front wanted to know "what in thunder that man was after, anyhow." He prowled into the Mutual Insurance rooms, and demanded explanations of the mysterious remarks chalked up on the blackboard day by day; and that brought down upon him secretaries of every Fisherman's Widow and Orphan Aid Society within the city limits. They begged shamelessly, each man anxious to beat the other institution's record, and Cheyne tugged at his beard and handed them all over to Mrs. Cheyne.

She was resting in a boarding-house near Eastern Point–a strange establishment, managed, apparently, by the boarders, where the table-cloths were red-and-white-checkered and the population, who seemed to have known one another intimately for years, rose up at midnight to make Welsh rarebits if it felt hungry. On the second morning of her stay Mrs. Cheyne put away her diamond solitaires before she came down to breakfast.

"They're most delightful people," she confided to her husband; "so friendly and simple, too, though they are all Boston, nearly."

"That isn't simpleness, Mama," he said, looking across the boulders behind the apple-trees where the hammocks were slung. "It's the other thing, that we–that I haven't got."

"It can't be," said Mrs. Cheyne quietly. "There isn't a woman here owns a dress that cost a hundred dollars. Why, we——"

"I know it, dear. We have–of course we have. I guess it's only the style they wear East. Are you having a good time?"

"I don't see very much of Harvey; he's always with you; but I ain't near as nervous as I was."

"*I* haven't had such a good time since Willie died. I never rightly understood that I had a son before this. Harve's got to be a great boy. 'Anything I can fetch for you, dear? 'Cushion under your head? Well, we'll go down to the wharf again and look around."

Harvey was his father's shadow in those days, and the two strolled along side by side, Cheyne using the grades as an excuse for laying his hand on the boy's square shoulder. It was then that Harvey noticed and admired what had never struck him before–his father's curious power of getting at the heart of new matters as learned from men in the street.

"How d'you make 'em tell you everything without opening your head?" demanded the son, as they came out of a rigger's loft.

"I've dealt with quite a few men in my time, Harve, and one sizes 'em up somehow, I guess. I know something about myself, too." Then, after a pause, as they sat down on a wharf-edge: "Men can 'most always tell when a man has handled things for himself, and then they treat him as one of themselves."

"Same as they treat me down at Wouverman's wharf. I'm one of the crowd now. Disko has told every one I've earned my pay." Harvey spread out his hands and rubbed the palms together. "They're all soft again," he said dolefully.

"Keep 'em that way for the next few years, while you're getting your education. You can harden 'em up after."

"Ye-es, I suppose so," was the reply, in no delighted voice.

"It rests with you, Harve. You can take cover behind your mama, of course, and put her on to fussing about your nerves and your high-strungness and all that kind of poppycock."

"Have I ever done that?" said Harvey, uneasily.

His father turned where he sat and thrust out a long hand. "*You* know as well as I do that I can't make anything of you if you don't act straight by me. I can handle you alone if you'll stay alone, but I don't pretend to manage both you *and* Mama. Life's too short, anyway."

"Don't make me out much of a fellow, does it?"

"I guess it was my fault a good deal; but if you want the truth, you haven't been much of anything up to date. Now, have you?"

"Umm! Disko thinks . . . Say, what d'you reckon it's cost you to raise me from the start–first, last and all over?"

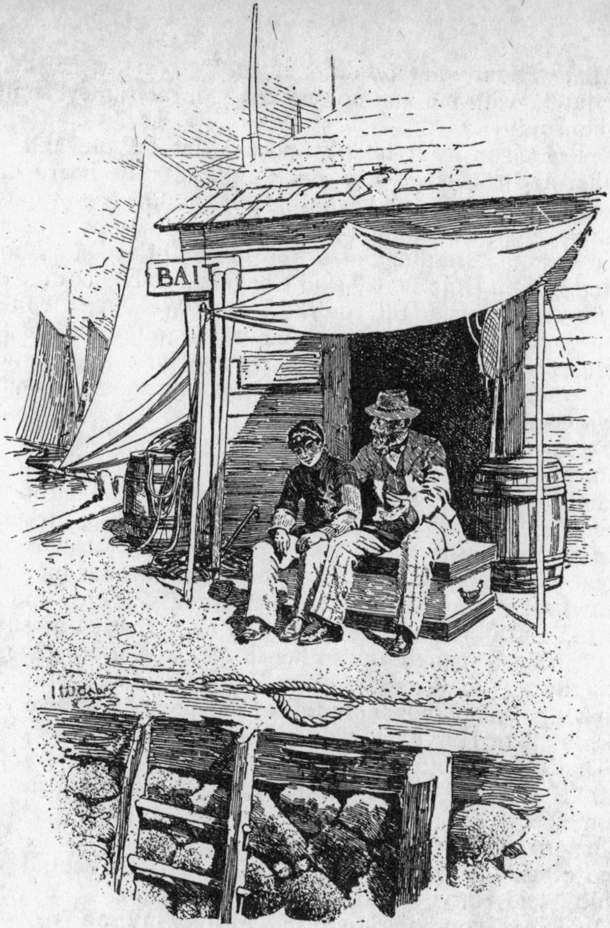

"HIS FATHER TURNED WHERE HE SAT AND THRUST OUT
A LONG HAND. '*YOU* KNOW AS WELL AS I DO
THAT I CAN'T MAKE ANYTHING OF YOU
IF YOU DON'T ACT STRAIGHT BY ME.'"

Cheyne smiled. "I've never kept track, but I should estimate, in dollars and cents, nearer fifty than forty thousand; maybe sixty. The young generation comes high. It has to have things, and it tires of 'em, and—the old man foots the bill."

Harvey whistled, but at heart he was rather pleased to think that his upbringing had cost so much. "And all that's sunk capital, isn't it?"

"Invested, Harve. Invested, I hope."

"Making it only thirty thousand, the thirty I've earned is about ten cents on the hundred. That's a mighty poor catch." Harvey wagged his head solemnly.

Cheyne laughed till he nearly fell off the pile into the water.

"Disko has got a heap more than that out of Dan since he was ten; and Dan's at school half the year, too."

"Oh, that's what you're after, is it?"

"No. I'm not after anything. I'm not stuck on myself any just now—that's all. . . . I ought to be kicked."

"I can't do it, old man; or I would, I presume, if I'd been made that way."

"Then I'd have remembered it to the last day I lived—and *never* forgiven you," said Harvey, his chin on his doubled fists.

"Exactly. That's about what *I'd* do. You see?"

"I see. The fault's with me and no one else. All the samey, something's got to be done about it."

Cheyne drew a cigar from his vest-pocket, bit off the end, and fell to smoking. Father and son were very much alike; for the beard hid Cheyne's mouth, and Harvey had his father's slightly aquiline nose, close-set black eyes, and narrow, high cheek-bones. With a touch of brown paint he would have made up very picturesquely as a Red Indian of the story-books.

"Now you can go on from here," said Cheyne, slowly, "costing me between six or eight thousand a year till you're a voter. Well, we'll call you a man then. You can go right on from *that,* living on me to the tune of forty or fifty thousand, besides what your mother will give you, with a valet and a yacht or a fancy-ranch where you can pretend to raise trotting-stock and play cards with your own crowd."

"Like Lorry Tuck?" Harvey put in.

"Yep; or the two De Vitré boys or old man McQuade's son. California's full of 'em, and here's an Eastern sample while we're talking."

A shiny black steam-yacht, with mahogany deck-house, nickel-plated binnacles, and pink-and-white-striped awnings puffed up the harbor, flying the burgee of some New York club. Two young men in what they conceived to be sea costumes were playing cards by the saloon skylight; and a couple of women with red and blue parasols looked on and laughed noisily.

"Shouldn't care to be caught out in her in any sort of a breeze. No beam," said Harvey, critically, as the yacht slowed to pick up her mooring-buoy.

"They're having what stands them for a good time. I can give you that, and twice as much as that, Harve. How'd you like it?"

"Caesar! That's no way to get a dinghy overside," said Harvey, still intent on the yacht. "If I couldn't slip a tackle better than that I'd stay ashore. . . . What if I don't?"

"Stay ashore—or what?"

"Yacht and ranch and live on 'the old man,' and—get behind Mama where there's trouble," said Harvey, with a twinkle in his eye.

"Why, in that case, you come right in with me, my son."

"Ten dollars a month?" Another twinkle.

"Not a cent more until you're worth it, and you won't begin to touch that for a few years."

"I'd sooner begin sweeping out the office—isn't that how the big bugs start?—and touch something now than—"

"I know it; we all feel that way. But I guess we can hire any sweeping we need. I made the same mistake myself of starting in too soon."

"Thirty million dollars' worth o' mistake, wasn't it? I'd risk it for that."

"I lost some; and I gained some. I'll tell you."

Cheyne pulled his beard and smiled as he looked over the still water, and spoke away from Harvey, who presently began to be aware that his father was telling the story of his life. He talked in a low, even voice, without gesture and without expression; and it was a history for which a dozen leading journals would cheerfully have paid many dollars—the story of forty years that was at the same time the story of the New West, whose story is yet to be written.

It began with a kinless boy turned loose in Texas, and went on fantastically through a hundred changes and chops of life, the scenes shifting from State after Western State, from cities that sprang up in a month and in a season utterly withered away, to wild ventures in wilder camps that are now laborious, paved municipalities. It covered the building of three railroads and the deliberate wreck of a fourth. It told of steamers, townships, forests, and mines, and the men of every nation under heaven, manning, creating, hewing, and digging these. It touched on chances of gigantic wealth flung before eyes that could not see, or missed by the merest accident of time and travel; and through the mad shift of things, sometimes on horseback, more often afoot, now rich, now poor, in and out, and back and forth, deck-hand, train-hand, contractor, boarding-house keeper, journalist, engineer, drummer, real-estate agent, politician, dead-beat, rum-seller, mine-owner, speculator, cattle-man, or tramp, moved Harvey Cheyne, alert and quiet, seeking his own ends, and, so he said, the glory and advancement of his country.

He told of the faith that never deserted him even when he hung on the ragged edge of despair—the faith that comes of knowing men and things. He enlarged, as though he were talking to himself, on his very great courage and resource at all times. The thing was so evident in the man's mind that he never even changed his tone. He described how he had bested his enemies, or forgiven them, exactly as they had bested or forgiven him in those careless days; how he had entreated, cajoled, and bullied towns, companies, and syndicates, all for their enduring good; crawled round, through, or under mountains and ravines, dragging a string and hoop-iron railroad after him, and in the end, how he had sat still while promiscuous communities tore the last fragments of his character to shreds.

The tale held Harvey almost breathless, his head a little cocked to one side, his eyes fixed on his father's face, as the twilight deepened and the red cigar-end lit up the furrowed cheeks and heavy eyebrows. It seemed to him like watching a locomotive storming across country in the dark—a mile between each glare of the open fire-door: but this locomotive could talk, and the words shook and stirred the boy to the core of his soul. At last Cheyne pitched away the cigar-butt, and the two sat in the dark over the lapping water.

"I've never told that to any one before," said the father.

Harvey gasped. "It's just the greatest thing that ever was!" said he.

"That's what I *got.* Now I'm coming to what I didn't get. It won't sound much of anything to you, but I don't wish you to be as old as I am before you find out. I can handle men, of course, and I'm no fool along my own lines, but—but—I can't compete with the man who has been *taught!* I've picked up as I went along, and I guess it sticks out all over me."

"I've never seen it," said the son, indignantly.

"You will, though, Harve. You will—just as soon as you're through college. Don't I know it? Don't I know the look on men's faces when they think me a—a 'mucker,' as they call it out here? I can break them to little pieces—yes—but I can't get back at 'em to hurt 'em where they live. I don't say they're 'way 'way up, but I feel I'm 'way, 'way, 'way off, somehow. Now *you've* got your chance. You've got to soak up all the learning that's around, and you'll live with a crowd that are doing the same thing. They'll be doing it for a few thousand dollars a year at most; but remember *you'll* be doing it for millions. You'll learn law enough to look after your own property when I'm out o' the light, and you'll have to be solid with the best men in the market (they are useful later); and above all, you'll have to stow away the plain, common, sit-down-with-your-chin-on-your-elbows book-learning. Nothing pays like that, Harve, and it's bound to pay more and more each year in our country—in business *and* in politics. You'll see."

"There's no sugar in my end of the deal," said Harvey. "Four years at college! 'Wish I'd chosen the valet and the yacht!"

"Never mind, my son," Cheyne insisted. "You're investing your capital where it'll bring in the best returns; and I guess you won't find our property shrunk any when you're ready to take hold. Think it over, and let me know in the morning. Hurry! We'll be late for supper!"

As this was a business talk, there was no need for Harvey to tell his mother about it; and Cheyne naturally took the same point of view. But Mrs. Cheyne saw and feared, and was a little jealous. Her boy, who rode rough-shod over her, was gone, and in his stead reigned a keen-faced youth, abnormally silent, who addressed most of his conversation to his father. She understood it was business, and therefore a matter beyond her premises. If she had any doubts, they were resolved when Cheyne went to Boston and brought back a new diamond marquise ring.

"What have you two been doing now?" she said, with a weak little smile, as she turned it in the light.

"Talking–just talking, Mama; there's nothing mean about Harvey."

There was not. The boy had made a treaty on his own account. Railroads, he explained gravely, interested him as little as lumber, real estate, or mining. What his soul yearned after was control of his father's newly-purchased sailing-ship. If that could be promised him within what he conceived to be a reasonable time, he, for his part, guaranteed diligence and sobriety at college for four or five years. In vacation he was to be allowed full access to all details connected with the line–he had not asked more than two thousand questions about it,–from his father's most private papers in the safe to the tug in San Francisco harbour.

"It's a deal," said Cheyne at the last. "You'll alter your mind twenty times before you leave college, o' course; but if you take hold of it in proper shape, and if you don't tie it up before you're twenty-three, I'll make the thing over to you. How's that, Harve?"

"Nope; never pays to split up a going concern. There's too much competition in the world anyway, and Disko says 'blood-kin *hev* to stick together.' His crowd never go back on him. That's one reason, he says, why they make such big fares. Say, the *We're Here* goes off to the Georges on Monday. They don't stay long ashore, do they?"

"Well, we ought to be going, too, I guess. I've left my business hung up at loose ends between two oceans, and it's time to connect again. I just hate to do it, though; haven't had a holiday like this for twenty years."

"We *can't* go without seeing Disko off," said Harvey; "and Monday's Memorial Day. Let's stay over that, anyway."

"What is this memorial business? They were talking about it at the boarding-house," said Cheyne weakly. He, too, was not anxious to spoil the golden days.

"Well, as far as I can make out, *this* business is a sort of song-and-dance act, whacked up for the summer boarders. Disko don't think much of it, he says, because they take up a collection for the widows and orphans. Disko's independent. Haven't you noticed that?"

"Well–yes. A little. In spots. Is it a town show, then?"

"The summer convention is. They read out the names of the fellows drowned or gone astray since last time, and they make speeches, and recite, and all. Then, Disko says, the secretaries of the Aid Societies go into the back yard and fight over the catch. The real show, he says, is in the spring. The ministers all take a hand then, and there aren't any summer boarders around."

"I see," said Cheyne, with the brilliant and perfect comprehension of one born into and bred up to city pride. "We'll stay over for Memorial Day, and get off in the afternoon."

"Guess I'll go down to Disko's and make him bring his crowd up before they sail. I'll have to stand with them, of course."

"Oh, that's it, is it," said Cheyne. "I'm only a poor summer boarder, and you're–"

"A Banker–full-blooded Banker," Harvey called back as he boarded a trolley, and Cheyne went on with his blissful dreams for the future.

Disko had no use for public functions where appeals were made for charity, but Harvey pleaded that the glory of the day would be lost, so far as he was concerned, if the *We're Heres* absented themselves. Then Disko made conditions. He had heard—it was astonishing how all the world knew all the world's business along the water-front—he had heard that a "Philadelphia actress-woman" was going to take part in the exercises; and he mistrusted that she would deliver "Skipper Ireson's Ride." Personally, he had as little use for actresses as for summer boarders; but justice was justice, and though he himself (here Dan giggled) had once slipped up on a matter of judgment, this thing must not be. So Harvey came back to East Gloucester, and spent half a day explaining to an amused actress with a royal reputation on two seaboards the inwardness of the mistake she contemplated; and she admitted that it was justice, even as Disko had said.

Cheyne knew by old experience what would happen; but anything of the nature of a public palaver as meat and drink to the man's soul. He saw the trolleys hurrying west, in the hot, hazy morning, full of women in light summer dresses, and white-faced straw-hatted men fresh from Boston desks; the stack of bicycles outside the post-office; the come-and-go of busy officials, greeting one another; the slow flick and swash of bunting in the heavy air; and the important man with a hose sluicing the brick sidewalk.

"Mother," he said suddenly, "don't you remember—after Seattle was burned out—and they got her going again?"

Mrs. Cheyne nodded, and looked critically down the crooked street. Like her husband, she understood these gatherings, all the West over, and compared them one against another. The fishermen began to mingle with the crowd about the town-hall doors—blue-jowled Portuguese, their women bareheaded or shawled for the most part; clear-eyed Nova Scotians, and men of the Maritime Provinces; French, Italians, Swedes, and Danes, with outside crews of coasting schooners; and everywhere women in black, who saluted one another with gloomy pride, for this was their day of great days. And there were ministers of many creeds,—pastors of great, gilt-edged congregations, at the seaside for a rest, with shepherds of the regular work,—from the priests of the Church on the Hill to bush-bearded ex-sailor Lutherans, hail-fellow with the men of a score of boats. There were owners of lines of schooners, large contributors to the societies, and small men, their few craft pawned to the mastheads, with bankers and marine-insurance agents, captains of tugs and water-boats, riggers, fitters, lumpers, salters, boat-builders, and coopers, and all the mixed population of the water-front.

They drifted along the line of seats made gay with the dresses of the summer boarders, and one of the town officials patrolled and perspired till he shone all over with pure civic pride. Cheyne had met him for five minutes a few days before, and between the two there was entire understanding.

"Well, Mr. Cheyne, and what d'you think of our city?—Yes, madam, you can sit anywhere you please.—You have this kind of thing out West, I presume?"

"Yes, but we aren't as old as you."

"That's so, of course. You ought to have been at the exercises when we celebrated our two hundred and fiftieth birthday. I tell you, Mr. Cheyne, the old city did herself credit."

"So I heard. It pays, too. What's the matter with the town that it don't have a first-class hotel, though?"

"—Right over there to the left, Pedro. Heaps o' room for you and your crowd.—Why, that's what *I* tell 'em all the time, Mr. Cheyne. There's big money in it, but I presume that don't affect you any. What we want is——"

A heavy hand fell on his broadcloth shoulder, and the flushed skipper of a Portland coal-and-ice coaster spun him half round. "What in thunder do you fellows mean by clappin' the law on the town when all decent men are at sea this way? Heh? Town's dry as a bone, an' smells a sight worse sence I quit. 'Might ha' left us one saloon for soft drinks, anyway."

"Don't seem to have hindered your nourishment this morning, Carsen. I'll go into the politics of it later. Sit down by the door and think over your arguments till I come back."

"What good is arguments to me? In Miquelon champagne's eighteen dollars a case and—" The skipper lurched into his seat as an organ-prelude silenced him.

"Our new organ," said the official proudly to Cheyne. "'Cost us four thousand dollars, too. We'll have to get back to high-license next year to pay for it. I wasn't going to let the ministers have all the religion at their convention. Those are some of our orphans standing up to sing. My wife taught 'em. See you again later, Mr. Cheyne. I'm wanted on the platform."

High, clear, and true, children's voices bore down the last noise of those settling into their places.

"O all ye Works of the Lord, bless ye the Lord: praise him and magnify him for ever!"

The women throughout the hall leaned forward to look as the reiterated cadences filled the air. Mrs. Cheyne, with some others, began to breathe short; she had hardly imagined there were so many widows in the world; and instinctively searched for Harvey. He had found the *We're Heres* at the back of the audience, and was standing, as by right, between Dan and Disko. Uncle Salters, returned the night before with Penn, from Pamlico Sound, received him suspiciously.

"Hain't your folk gone yet?" he grunted. "What are you doin' here, young feller?"

"O ye Seas and Floods, bless ye the Lord: praise him, and magnify him for ever!"

"Hain't he good right?" said Dan. "He's bin there, same as the rest of us."

"Not in them clothes," Salters snarled.

"Shut your head, Salters," said Disko. "Your bile's gone back on you. Stay right where ye are, Harve."

Then up and spoke the orator of the occasion, another pillar of the municipality, bidding the world welcome to Gloucester, and incidentally pointing out wherein Gloucester excelled the rest of the world. Then he turned to the sea-wealth of the city, and spoke of the price that must be paid for the yearly harvest. They would hear later the names of their lost dead–one hundred and seventeen of them. (The widows stared a little, and looked at one another here.) Gloucester could not boast any overwhelming mills or factories. Her sons worked for such wage as the sea gave; and they all knew that neither Georges nor the Banks were cow-pastures. The utmost that folk ashore could accomplish was to help the widows and the orphans, and after a few general remarks he took this opportunity of thanking, in the name of the city, those who had so public-spiritedly consented to participate in the excercises of the occasion.

"I jest despise the beggin' pieces in it," growled Disko. "It don't give folk a fair notion of us."

"Ef folk won't be fore-handed an' put by when they've the chance," returned Salters, "it stands in the nature o' things they *hev* to be 'shamed. You take warnin' by that, young feller. Riches endureth but for a season, ef you scatter them around on lugsuries—"

"But to lose everything, everything," said Penn. "What can you do *then?* Once I"–the watery blue eyes stared up and down as if looking for something to steady them–"once I read–in a book, I think–of a boat where every one was run down–except some one–and he said to me—"

"Shucks!" said Salters, cutting in. "You read a little less an' take more int'rust in your vittles, and you'll come nearer earnin' your keep, Penn."

Harvey, jammed among the fishermen, felt a creepy, crawly, tingling thrill that began in the back of his neck and ended at his boots. He was cold, too, though it was a stifling day.

" 'That the actress from Philadelphia?" said Disko Troop, scowling at the platform. "You've fixed it about old man Ireson, hain't ye, Harve? Ye know why naow."

It was not "Ireson's Ride" that the woman delivered, but some sort of poem about a fishing-port called Brixham and a fleet of trawlers beating in against storm by night, while the women made a guiding fire at the head of the quay with everything they could lay hands on.

"They took the grandma's blanket,
Who shivered and bade them go;
They took the baby's cradle,
Who could not say them no."

"Whew!" said Dan, peering over Long Jack's shoulder. "That's great! Must ha' bin expensive, though."

"Ground-hog case," said the Galway man. "Badly lighted port, Danny."

"And knew not all the while
If they were lighting a bonfire
Or only a funeral pile."

The wonderful voice took hold of people by their heartstrings; and when she told how the drenched crews were flung ashore, living and dead, and they carried the bodies to the glare of the fires, asking: "Child, is this your father?" or "Wife, is this your man?" you could hear hard breathing all over the benches.

"And when the boats of Brixham
Go out to face the gales,
Think of the love that travels
Like light upon their sails!"

There was very little applause when she finished. The women were looking for their handkerchiefs, and many of the men stared at the ceiling with shiny eyes.

"H'm," said Salters; "that 'u'd cost ye a dollar to hear at any theatre—maybe two. Some folk, I presoom, can afford it. 'Seems downright waste to me. . . . Naow, how in Jerusalem did Cap. Bart Edwardes strike adrift here?"

"No keepin' him under," said an Eastport man behind. "He's a poet, an' he's baound to say his piece. 'Comes from daown aour way, too."

He did not say that Captain B. Edwardes had striven for five consecutive years to be allowed to recite a piece of his own composition on Gloucester Memorial Day. An amused and exhausted committee had at last given him his desire. The simplicity and utter happiness of the old man, as he stood up in his very best Sunday clothes, won the audience ere he opened his mouth. They sat unmurmuring through seven-and-thirty hatchet-made verses describing at fullest length the loss of the schooner *Joan Hasken* off the Georges in the gale of 1867, and when he came to an end they shouted with one kindly throat.

A far-sighted Boston reporter slid away for a full copy of the epic and an interview with the author; so that earth had nothing more to offer Captain Bart Edwardes, ex-whaler, shipwright, master-fisherman, and poet, in the seventy-third year of his age.

"Naow, I call that sensible," said the Eastport man. "I've bin over that graound with his writin', jest as he read it, in my two hands, and I can testify that he's got it all in."

"If Dan here couldn't do better'n that with one hand before breakfast, he ought to be switched," said Salters, upholding the honor of Massachusetts on general principles. "Now but what I'm free to own he's considerable litt'ery–fer Maine. Still—"

"Guess Uncle Salters's goin' to die this trip. Fust compliment he's ever paid me," Dan sniggered. "What's wrong with you, Harve? You act all quiet and you look greenish. Feelin' sick?"

"Don't know what's the matter with me," Harvey replied. " 'Seems if my insides were too big for my outsides. I'm all crowded up and shivery."

"Dispepsy? Pshaw–too bad. We'll wait for the readin', an' then we'll quit, an' catch the tide."

The widows–they were nearly all of that season's making–braced themselves rigidly like people going to be shot in cold blood, for they knew what was coming. The summer-boarder girls in pink and blue shirt-waists stopped tittering over Captain Edwardes's wonderful poem, and looked back to see why all was silent. The fishermen pressed forward as that town official who had talked to Cheyne bobbed up on the platform and began to read the year's list of losses, dividing them into months. Last September's casualties were mostly single men and strangers, but his voice rang very loud in the stillness of the hall.

"September 9th.–Schooner *Florrie Anderson* lost, with all aboard, off the Georges.

"Reuben Pitman, master, 50, single, Main Street, City.

"Emil Olsen, 19, single, 329 Hammond Street, City. Denmark.

"Oscar Standberg, single, 25, Sweden.

"Carl Stanberg, single, 29, Main Street. City.

"Petro, supposed Madeira, single, Keene's boarding-house. City.

"Joseph Welsh, alias Joseph Wright, 30, St. John's, Newfoundland."

"No–Augusty, Maine," a voice cried from the body of the hall.

"He shipped from St. John's," said the reader, looking to see.

"I know it. He belongs in Augusty. My nevvy."

The reader made a pencilled correction on the margin of the list, and resumed.

"Same schooner, Charlie Ritchie, Liverpool, Nova Scotia, 33, single.

"Albert May, 267 Rogers Street, City, 27, single.

"September 27th.–Orvin Dollard, 30, married, drowned in dory off Eastern Point."

That shot went home, for one of the widows flinched where she sat, clasping and unclasping her hands. Mrs. Cheyne, who had been listening with wide-opened eyes, threw up her head and choked. Dan's mother, a few seats to the right, saw and heard and quickly moved to her side. The reading went on. By the time they reached the January and February wrecks the shots were falling thick and fast, and the widows drew breath between their teeth.

"February 14th.–Schooner *Harry Randolph* dismasted on the way home from Newfoundland; Asa Musie, married, 32, Main Street, City, lost overboard.

"February 23d.–Schooner *Gilbert Hope;* went astray in dory, Robert Beavon, 29, married, native of Pubnico, Nova Scotia."

But his wife was in the hall. They heard a low cry, as though a little animal had been hit. It was stifled at once, and a girl staggered out of the hall. She had been hoping against hope for months, because some who have gone adrift in dories have been miraculously pickd up by deep-sea sailing-ships. Now she had her certainty, and Harvey could see the policeman on the sidewalk hailing a hack for her. "It's fifty cents to the depot"–the driver began, but the policemen held up his hand–"but I'm goin' there anyway. Jump right in. Look at here, Alf; you don't pull me next time my lamps ain't lit. See?"

The side-door closed on the patch of bright sunshine, and Harvey's eyes turned again to the reader and his endless list.

"April 19th–Schooner *Mamie Douglas* lost on the Banks with all hands.
"Edward Canton, 43, master, married, City.
"D. Hawkins, alias Williams, 34, married, Shelbourne, Nova Scotia.
"G. W. Clay, colored, 28, married, City."

And so on, and so on. Great lumps were rising in Harvey's throat, and his stomach reminded him of the day when he fell from the liner.

"May 10th.–Schooner *We're Here* [the blood tingled all over him]. Otto Svendson, 20, single, City, lost overboard."

Once more a low, tearing cry from somewhere at the back of the hall.

"She shouldn't ha' come. She shouldn't ha' come," said Long Jack, with a cluck of pity.

"Don't scrowge, Harve," grunted Dan. Harvey heard that much, but the rest was all darkness spotted with fiery wheels. Disko leaned forward and spoke to his wife, where she sat with one arm round Mrs. Cheyne, and the other holding down the snatching, catching, ringed hands.

"Lean your head daown–right daown!" she whispered. "It'll go off in a minute."

"I ca-an't! I do-don't! Oh, let me—" Mrs. Cheyne did not at all know what she said.

"You must," Mrs. Troop repeated. "Your boy's jest fainted dead away. They do that some when they're gettin' their growth. 'Wish to tend to him? We can git aout this side. Quite quiet. You come right along with me. Psha', my dear, we're both women, I guess. We must tend to aour men-folk. Come!"

The *We're Heres* promptly went through the crowd as a body-guard, and it was a very white and shaken Harvey that they propped up on a bench in an anteroom.

"Favors his ma," was Mrs. Troop's only comment, as the mother bent over her boy.

"How d'you suppose he could ever stand it?" she cried indignantly to Cheyne, who had said nothing at all. "It was horrible–horrible! We shouldn't have come. It's wrong and wicked! It–it isn't right! Why–why couldn't they put these things in the papers, where they belong? Are you better, darling?"

That made Harvey very properly ashamed. "Oh, I'm all right, I guess," he said, struggling to his feet, with a broken giggle. "Must ha' been something I ate for breakfast."

"Coffee, perhaps," said Cheyne, whose face was all in hard lines, as though it had been cut out of bronze. "We won't go back again."

"Guess 'twould be 'baout's well to git daown to the wharf," said Disko. "It's close in along with them Dagoes, an' the fresh air will fresh Mrs. Cheyne up."

Harvey announced that he never felt better in his life; but it was not till he saw the *We're Here,* fresh from the lumper's hands, at Wouverman's wharf, that he lost his all-overish feelings in a queer mixture of pride and sorrowfulness. Other people–summer boarders and such-like–played about in cat-boats or looked at the sea from pier-heads; but he understood things from the inside—more things than he could begin to think about. None the less, he could have sat down and howled because the little schooner was going off. Mrs. Cheyne simply cried and cried every step of the way and said most extraordinary things to Mrs. Troop, who "babied" her till Dan, who had not been "babied" since he was six, whistled aloud.

And so the old crowd—Harvey felt like the most ancient of mariners—dropped into the old schooner among the battered dories, while Harvey slipped the stern-fast from the pier-head, and they slid her along the wharf-side with their hands. Every one wanted to say so much that no one said anything in particular. Harvey bade Dan take care of Uncle Salters's sea-boots and Penn's dory-anchor, and Long Jack entreated Harvey to remember his lessons in seamanship; but the jokes fell flat in the presence of the two women, and it is hard to be funny with green harbor-water widening between good friends.

"Up jib and fores'l!" shouted Disko, getting to the wheel, as the wind took her. " 'See you later, Harve. Dunno but I come near thinkin' a heap o' you an' your folks."

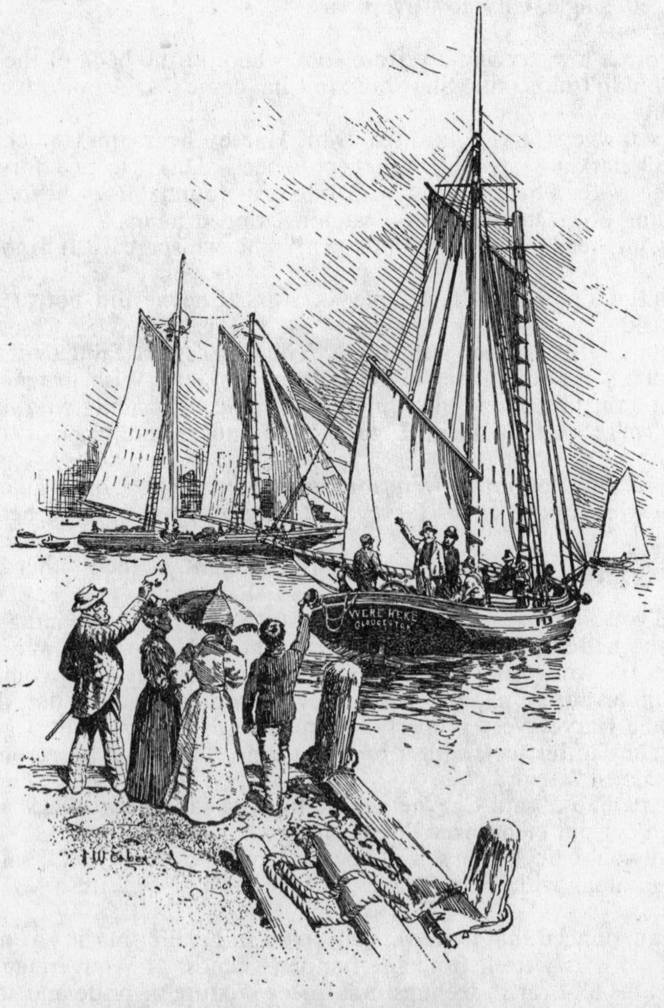

BIDDING FAREWELL TO THE "WE'RE HERE."

Then she glided beyond ear-shot, and they sat down to watch her up the harbor. And still Mrs. Cheyne wept.

"Pshaw, my dear," said Mrs. Troop: "we're both women, I guess. Like's not it'll ease your heart to hev your cry aout. God He knows it never done me a mite o' good, but then He knows I've had something to cry fer!"

Now it was a few years later, and upon the other edge of America, that a young man came through the clammy sea fog up a windy street which is flanked with most expensive houses built of wood to imitate stone. To him, as he was standing by a hammered iron gate, entered on horseback—and the horse would have been cheap at a thousand dollars—another young man. And this is what they said:

"Hello, Dan!"

"Hello, Harve!"

"What's the best with you?"

"Well, I'm so's to be that kind o' animal called second mate this trip. Ain't you most through with that triple-invoiced college of yours?"

"Getting that way. I tell you, the Leland Stanford Junior, isn't a circumstance to the old *We're Here;* but I'm coming into the business for keeps next fall."

"Meanin' aour packets?"

"Nothing else. You just wait till I get my knife into you, Dan. I'm going to make the old line lie down and cry when I take hold."

"I'll resk it," said Dan, with a brotherly grin, as Harvey dismounted and asked whether he were coming in.

"That's what I took the cable fer; but, say, is the doctor anywheres araound? I'll drown that crazy nigger some day, his one cussed joke an' all."

There was a low, triumphant chuckle, as the ex-cook of the *We're Here* came out of the fog to take the horse's bridle. He allowed no one but himself to attend to any of Harvey's wants.

"Thick as the Banks, ain't it, doctor?" said Dan, propitiatingly.

But the coal-black Celt with the second-sight did not see fit to reply till he had tapped Dan on the shoulder, and for the twentieth time croaked the old, old prophecy in his ear.

"Master—man. Man—master," said he. "You remember, Dan Troop, what I said? On the *We're Here?*"

"Well, I won't go as far as to deny that it do look like it as things stand at present," said Dan. "She was a noble packet, and one way an' another I owe her a heap—her and Dad."

"Me too," quoth Harvey Cheyne.

Stalky & Co.

TO
CORMELL PRICE

Headmaster, United Services College
Westward Ho! Bideford, North Devon
1874–1894

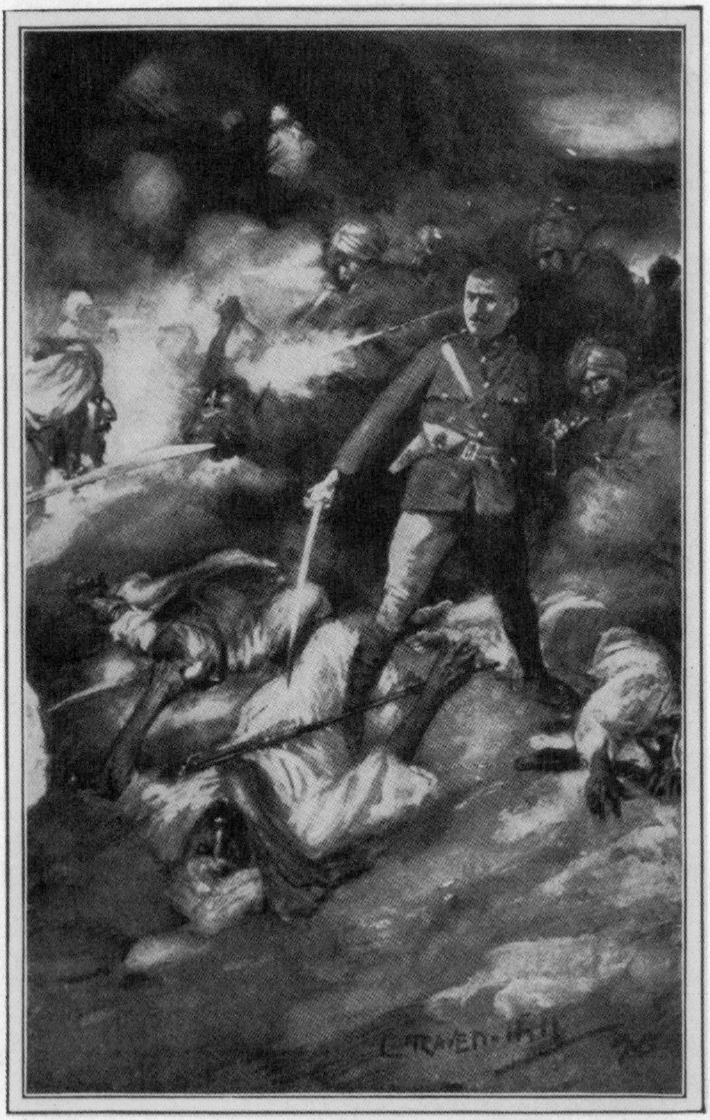

"'THERE WAS A BIT OF SCRIMMAGE.'"

"Let us now praise famous men"–
Men of little showing–
For their work continueth,
And their work continueth,
Greater than their knowing.

Western wind and open surge
Tore us from our mothers;
Flung us on a naked shore
(Twelve bleak houses by the shore!
Seven summers by the shore!)
'Mid two hundred brothers.

There we met with famous men
Set in office o'er us.
And they beat on us with rods–
Faithfully with many rods–
Daily beat us on with rods–
For the love they bore us!

Out of Egypt unto Troy–
Over Himalaya–
Far and sure our bands have gone–
Hy–Brasil or Babylon,
Islands of the Southern Run,
And cities of Cathaia!

And we all praise famous men–
Ancients of the College;
For they taught us common sense–
Tried to teach us common sense–
Truth and God's Own Common Sense
Which is more than knowledge!

Each degree of Latitude
Strung about Creation
Seeth one (or more) of us,
(Of one muster all of us–
Of one master all of us–)
Keen in his vocation.

This we learned from famous men
Knowing not its uses
When they showed in daily work
Man must finish off his work–
Right or wrong, his daily work–
And without excuses.

Servants of the staff and chain,
   Mine and fuse and grapnel–
Some before the face of Kings,
Stand before the face of Kings;
Bearing gifts to divers Kings–
   Gifts of Case and Shrapnel.

This we learned from famous men
   Teaching in our borders.
Who declared it was best,
Safest, easiest and best–
Expeditious, wise and best–
   To obey your orders.

Some beneath the further stars
   Bear the greater burden.
Set to serve the lands they rule,
(Save he serve no man may rule)
Serve and love the lands they rule;
   Seeking praise nor guerdon.

This we learned from famous men
   Knowing not we learned it.
Only, as the years went by–
Lonely, as the years went by–
Far from help as years went by
   Plainer we discerned it.

Wherefore praise we famous men
   From whose bays we borrow–
They that put aside Today–
All the joys of their Today–
And with toil of their Today
   Bought for us Tomorrow!

Bless and praise we famous men–
   Men of little showing!
For their work continueth
And their work continueth
Broad and deep continueth
   Great beyond their knowing!

"In Ambush"

IN SUMMER ALL right-minded boys built huts in the furze-hill behind the College—little lairs whittled out of the heart of the prickly bushes, full of stumps, odd root-ends, and spikes, but, since they were strictly forbidden, palaces of delight. And for the fifth summer in succession, Stalky, McTurk, and Beetle (this was before they reached the dignity of a study) had built like beavers a place of retreat and meditation, where they smoked.

Now, there was nothing in their characters as known to Mr. Prout, their house-master, at all commanding respect; nor did Foxy, the subtle red-haired school Sergeant, trust them. His business was to wear tennis-shoes, carry binoculars, and swoop hawklike upon evil boys. Had he taken the field alone, that hut would have been raided, for Foxy knew the manners of his quarry; but Providence moved Mr. Prout, whose school-name, derived from the size of his feet, was Hoofer, to investigate on his own account; and it was the cautious Stalky who found the track of his pugs on the very floor of their lair one peaceful afternoon when Stalky would fain have forgotten Prout and his works in a volume of Surtees and a new briarwood pipe. Crusoe, at sight of the footprint, did not act more swiftly than Stalky. He removed the pipes, swept up all loose match-ends, and departed to warn Beetle and McTurk.

But it was characteristic of the boy that he did not approach his allies till he had met and conferred with little Hartopp, President of the Natural History Society, an institution which Stalky held in contempt. Hartopp was more than surprised when the boy meekly, as he knew how, begged to propose himself, Beetle, and McTurk as candidates; confessed to a long-smothered interest in first-flowerings, early butterflies, and new arrivals, and volunteered, if Mr. Hartopp saw fit, to enter on the new life at once. Being a master, Hartopp was suspicious; but he was also an enthusiast, and his gentle little soul had been galled by chance-heard remarks from the three, and specially Beetle. So he was gracious to that repentant sinner, and entered the three names in his book.

Then, and not till then, did Stalky seek Beetle and McTurk in their house form-room. They were stowing away books for a quiet afternoon in the furze, which they called the "wuzzy."

"All up," said Stalky, serenely. "I spotted Heffy's fairy feet round our hut after dinner. 'Blessing they're so big."

"Con-found! Did you hide our pipes?" said Beetle.

"Oh, no. Left 'em in the middle of the hut, of course. What a blind ass you are, Beetle! D'you think nobody thinks but yourself? Well, we can't use the hut any more. Hoofer will be watchin' it."

" 'Bother! Likewise blow!' " said McTurk thoughtfully, unpacking the volumes with which his chest was cased. The boys carried their libraries between their belt and their collar. "Nice job! This means we're under suspicion for the rest of the term."

"Why? All that Heffy has found is *a* hut. He and Foxy will watch it. It's nothing to do with us; only we mustn't be seen that way for a bit."

"Yes, and where else are we to go?" said Beetle. "You chose that place, too–an'–an' I wanted to read this afternoon."

Stalky sat on a desk drumming his heels on the form.

"You're a despondin' brute, Beetle. Sometimes I think I shall have to drop you altogether. Did you ever know your Uncle Stalky forget you yet? *His rebus infectis*–after I'd seen Heffy's man-tracks marchin' round our hut, I found little Hartopp–*destricto ense*–wavin' a butterfly-net. I conciliated Hartopp. 'Told him that you'd read papers to the Bug-hunters if he'd let you join, Beetle. 'Told him you liked butterflies, Turkey. Anyhow, I soothed the Hartoffles, and we're Bug-hunters now."

"What's the good of that?" said Beetle.

"Oh, Turkey, kick him!"

In the interests of science bounds were largely relaxed for the members of the Natural History Society. They could wander, if they kept clear of all houses, practically where they chose; Mr. Hartopp holding himself responsible for their good conduct.

Beetle began to see this as McTurk began the kicking.

"I'm an ass, Stalky!" he said, guarding the afflicted part. "*Pax,* Turkey. I'm an ass."

"Don't stop, Turkey. Isn't your Uncle Stalky a great man?"

"Great man," said Beetle.

"All the same bug-huntin's a filthy business," said McTurk. "How the deuce does one begin?"

"This way," said Stalky, turning to some fags' lockers behind him. "Fags are dabs at Natural History. Here's young Braybrooke's botany-case." He flung out a tangle of decayed roots and adjusted the slide. " 'Gives one no end of a professional air, I think. Here's Clay Minor's geological hammer. Beetle can carry that. Turkey, you'd better covet a butterfly-net from somewhere."

"I'm blowed if I do," said McTurk, simply, with immense feeling. "Beetle, give me the hammer."

"All right. *I*'m not proud. Chuck us down that net on top of the lockers, Stalky."

"That's all right. It's a collapsible jamboree, too. Beastly luxurious dogs these fags are. Built like a fishin'-rod. 'Pon my sainted Sam, but we look the complete Bug-hunters! Now, listen to your Uncle Stalky! We're goin' along the cliffs after butterflies. Very few chaps come there. We're goin' to leg it, too. You'd better leave your book behind."

"Not much!" said Beetle, firmly. "I'm not goin' to be done out of my fun for a lot of filthy butterflies."

"Then you'll sweat horrid. You'd better carry my Jorrocks. 'Twon't make you any hotter."

They all sweated; for Stalky led them at a smart trot west away along the cliffs under the furze-hills, crossing combe after gorzy combe. They took no heed to flying rabbits or fluttering fritillaries, and all that Turkey said of geology was utterly unquotable.

"Are we going to Clovelly?" he puffed at last, and they flung themselves down on the short, springy turf between the drone of the sea below and the light summer wind among the inland trees. They were looking into a combe half full of old, high furze in gay bloom that ran up to a fringe of brambles and a dense wood of mixed timber and hollies. It was as though one-half the combe were filled with golden fire to the cliff's edge. The side nearest to them was open grass, and fairly bristled with notice-boards.

"Fee-rocious old cove, this," said Stalky, reading the nearest. " '*Prosecuted with the utmost rigour of the law. G. M. Dabney, Col., J. P.,'* an' all the rest of it. 'Don't seem to me that any chap in his senses would trespass here, does it?"

"You've got to prove damage 'fore you can prosecute for anything! 'Can't prosecute for trespass," said McTurk, whose father held many acres in Ireland. "That's all rot!"

"Glad of that, 'cause this looks like what we wanted. Not straight across, Beetle, you blind lunatic! Anyone could spot us half a mile off. This way; and furl up your beastly butterfly-net."

Beetle disconnected the ring, thrust the net into a pocket, shut up the handle to a two-foot stave, and slid the cane-ring round his waist. Stalky led inland to the wood, which was, perhaps, a quarter of a mile from the sea, and reached the fringe of the brambles.

"*Now* we can get straight down through the furze, and never show up at all," said the tactician. "Beetle, go ahead and explore. Snf! Snf! Beastly stink of fox somewhere!"

On all fours, save when he clung to his spectacles, Beetle wormed into the gorse, and presently announced between grunts of pain that he had found a very fair fox-track. This was well for Beetle, since Stalky pinched him *a tergo.* Down that tunnel they crawled. It was evidently a highway for the inhabitants of the combe; and, to their inexpressible joy, ended, at the very edge of the cliff, in a few square feet of dry turf walled and roofed with impenetrable gorse.

"By gum! There isn't a single thing to do except lie down," said Stalky, returning a knife to his pocket. "Look here!"

He parted the tough stems before him, and it was as a window opened on a far view of Lundy, and the deep sea sluggishly nosing the pebbles a couple of hundred feet below. They could hear young jackdaws squawking on the ledges, the hiss and jabber of a nest of hawks somewhere out of sight; and, with great deliberation, Stalky spat on to the back of a young rabbit sunning himself far down where only a cliff-rabbit could have found foot-hold. Great gray and black gulls screamed against the jackdaws; the heavy-scented acres of bloom round them were alive with low-nesting birds, singing or silent as the shadow of the wheeling hawks passed and returned; and on the naked turf across the combe rabbits thumped and frolicked.

"Whew! What a place! Talk of natural history; this is it," said Stalky, filling himself a pipe. "Isn't it scrumptious? Good old sea!" He spat again approvingly, and was silent.

McTurk and Beetle had taken out their books and were lying on their stomachs, chin in hand. The sea snored and gurgled; the birds, scattered for the moment by these new animals, returned to their businesses, and the boys read on in the rich, warm, sleepy silence.

"Hullo, here's a keeper," said Stalky, shutting "Handley Cross" cautiously, and peering through the jungle. A man with a gun appeared on the sky-line to the east. "Confound him, he's going to sit down."

"He'd swear we were poachin', too," said Beetle. "What's the good of pheasants' eggs? They're always addled, too."

"Might as well get up to the wood, *I* think," said Stalky. "We don't want G. M. Dabney, Col., J.P., to be bothered about us so soon. Up the wuzzy and keep quiet! He may have followed us, you know."

Beetle was already far up the tunnel. They heard him gasp indescribably: there was the crash of a heavy body leaping through the furze.

"Aie! yeou little red rascal. I see yeou!" The keeper threw the gun to his shoulder, and fired both barrels in their direction. The pellets dusted the dry stems round them as a big fox plunged between Stalky's legs, and ran over the cliff-edge.

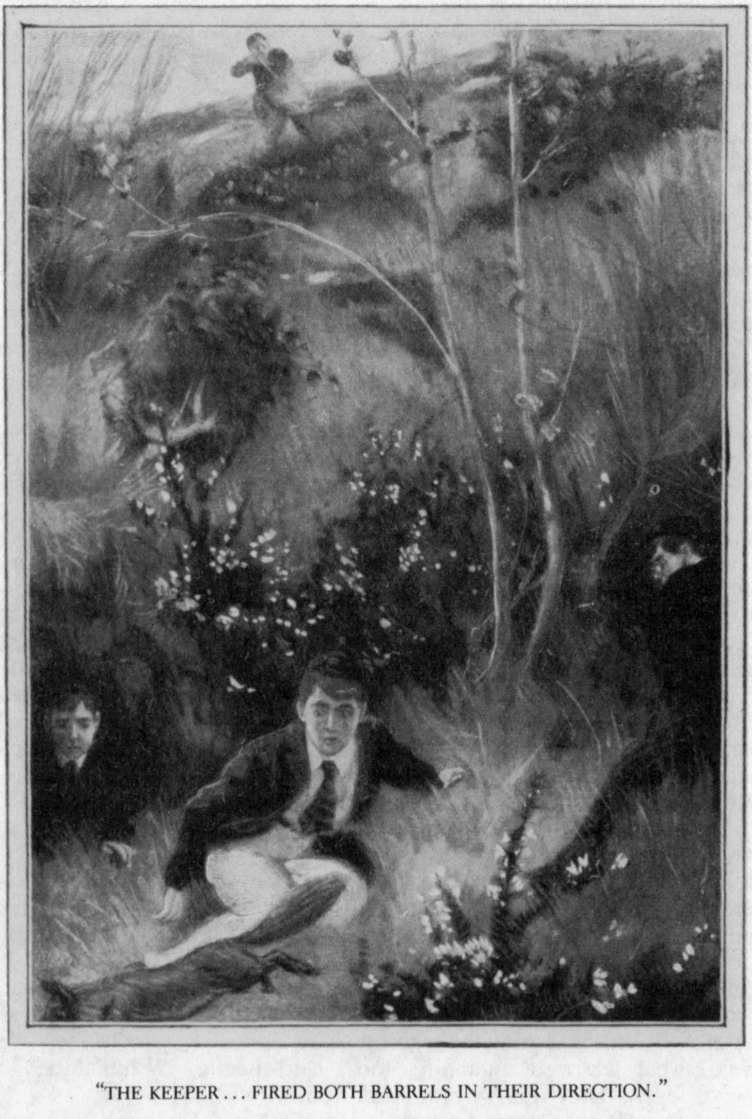

"THE KEEPER . . . FIRED BOTH BARRELS IN THEIR DIRECTION."

They said nothing till they reached the wood, torn, dishevelled, hot, but unseen.

"Narrow squeak," said Stalky. "I'll swear some of the pellets went through my hair."

"Did you see him?" said Beetle. "I almost put my hand on him. Wasn't he a wopper! Didn't he stink! Hullo, Turkey, what's the matter? Are you hit?"

McTurk's lean face had turned pearly white; his mouth, generally half open, was tight shut, and his eyes blazed. They had never seen him like this save once in a sad time of civil war.

"Do you know that that was just as bad as murder?" he said, in a grating voice, as he brushed prickles from his head.

"Well, he didn't hit us," said Stalky. "I think it was rather a lark. Here, where are you going?"

"I'm going up to the house, if there is one," said McTurk, pushing through the hollies. "I am going to tell this Colonel Dabney."

"Are you crazy? He'll swear it served us jolly well right. He'll report us. It'll be a public lickin'. Oh, Turkey, don't be an ass! Think of us!"

"You fool!" said McTurk, turning savagely. "D'you suppose I'm thinkin' of *us?* It's the keeper."

"He's cracked,' said Beetle, miserably, as they followed. Indeed, this was a new Turkey–a haughty, angular, nose-lifted Turkey–whom they accompanied through a shrubbery on to a lawn, where a white-whiskered old gentleman with a cleek was alternately putting and blaspheming vigorously.

"Are you Colonel Dabney?" McTurk began in this new creaking voice of his.

"I–I am, and–" his eyes traveled up and down the boy–"who–what the devil d'you want? Ye've been disturbing my pheasants. Don't attempt to deny it. Ye needn't laugh at it." (McTurk's not too lovely features had twisted themselves into a horrible sneer at the word pheasant.) "You've been birds'-nesting. You needn't hide your hat. I can see that you belong to the College. Don't attempt to deny it. Ye do! Your name and number at once, sir. Ye want to speak to me–Eh? You saw my notice-boards? Must have. Don't attempt to deny it. Ye did! Damnable, oh damnable!"

He choked with emotion. McTurk's heel tapped the lawn and he stuttered a little–two sure signs that he was losing his temper. But why should he, the offender, be angry?

"Lo-look here, sir. Do–do you shoot foxes? Because, if you don't, your keeper does. We've seen him! I do-don't care what you call us–but it's an awful thing. It's the ruin of good feelin' among neighbors. A ma-man ought to say once and for all how he stands about preservin'. It's worse than murder, because there's no legal remedy." McTurk was quoting confusedly from his father, while the old gentleman made noises in his throat.

"Do you know who I am?" he gurgled at last; Stalky and Beetle quaking.

"No, sorr, nor do I care if ye belonged to the Castle itself. Answer me now, as one gentleman to another. Do ye shoot foxes or do ye not?"

And four years before Stalky and Beetle had carefully kicked McTurk out of his Irish dialect! Assuredly he had gone mad or taken a sunstroke, and as assuredly he would be slain–once by the old gentleman and once by the Head. A public licking for the three was the least they could expect. Yet–if their eyes and ears were to be trusted–the old gentleman had collapsed. It might be a lull before the storm, but–

"I do not." He was still gurgling.

"Then you must sack your keeper. He's not fit to live in the same county with a God-fearin' fox. An' a vixen, too–at this time o' year!"

"Did ye come up on purpose to tell me this?"

"Of course I did, ye silly man," with a stamp of the foot. "Would you not have done as much for me if you'd seen that thing happen on my land, now?"

Forgotten–forgotten was the College and the decency due to elders! McTurk was treading again the barren purple mountains of the rainy West coast, where in his holidays he was viceroy of four thousand naked acres, only son of a three-hundred-year-old house, lord of a crazy fishing-boat, and the idol of his father's shiftless tenantry. It was the landed man speaking to his equal–deep calling to deep–and the old gentleman acknowledged the cry.

"I apologize," said he. "I apologize unreservedly–to you, and to the Old Country. Now, will you be good enough to tell me your story?"

"We were in your combe," McTurk began, and he told his tale alternately as a schoolboy and, when the iniquity of the thing overcame him, as an indignant squire; concluding: "So you see he must be in the habit of it. I–we–one never wants to accuse a neighbor's man; but I took the liberty in this case–"

"I see. Quite so. For a reason ye had. Infamous–oh, infamous!" The two had fallen into step beside each other on the lawn, and Colonel Dabney was talking as one man to another. "This comes of promoting a fisherman–a fisherman–from his lobster-pots. It's enough to ruin the reputation of an archangel. Don't attempt to deny it. It is! Your father has brought you up well. He has. I'd much like the pleasure of his acquaintance. Very much, indeed. And these young gentlemen? English they are. Don't attempt to deny it. They came up with you, too? Extraordinary! Extraordinary, now! In the present state of education I shouldn't have thought any three boys would be well enough grounded. . . . But out of the mouths of—No–no! Not that by any odds. Don't attempt to deny it. Ye're not! Sherry always catches me under the liver, but–beer, now? Eh? What d'you say to beer, and something to eat? It's long since I was a boy–abominable nuisances; but exceptions prove the rule. And a vixen, too!"

They were fed on the terrace by a gray-haired housekeeper. Stalky and Beetle merely ate, but McTurk with bright eyes continued a free and lofty discourse; and ever the old gentleman treated him as a brother.

"My dear man, of *course* ye can come again. Did I not say exceptions prove the rule? The lower combe? Man, dear, anywhere ye please, so long as you do not disturb my pheasants. The two are not incompatible. Don't attempt to deny it. They're not! I'll never allow another gun, though. Come and go as ye please. I'll not see you, and ye needn't see me. Ye've been well brought up. Another glass of beer, now? I tell you a fisherman he was and a fisherman he shall be to-night again. He shall! Wish I could drown him. I'll convoy you to the Lodge. My people are not precisely–ah–broke to boy, but they'll know *you* again."

He dismissed them with many compliments by the high Lodge-gate in the split-oak park palings and they stood still; even Stalky, who had played second, not to say a dumb, fiddle, regarding McTurk as one from another world. The two glasses of strong home-brewed had brought a melancholy upon the boy, for, slowly strolling with his hands in his pockets, he crooned:–"Oh, Paddy dear, and did ye hear the news that's goin' round?"

Under other circumstances Stalky and Beetle would have fallen upon him, for that song was barred utterly–anathema–the sin of witchcraft. But seeing what he had wrought, they danced round him in silence, waiting till it pleased him to touch earth.

The tea-bell rang when they were still half a mile from College. McTurk shivered and came out of dreams. The glory of his holiday estate had left him. He was a Colleger of the College, speaking English once more.

"Turkey, it was immense!" said Stalky, generously. "I didn't know you had it in you. You've got us a hut for the rest of the term, where we simply *can't* be collared. Fids! Fids! Oh, Fids! I gloat! Hear me gloat!"

They spun wildly on their heels, jodeling after the accepted manner of a "gloat," which is not unremotely allied to the primitive man's song of triumph, and dropped down the hill by the path from the gasometer just in time to meet their house-master, who had spent the afternoon watching their abandoned hut in the "wuzzy."

Unluckily, all Mr. Prout's imagination leaned to the darker side of life, and he looked on those young-eyed cherubims most sourly. Boys that he understood attended house-matches and could be accounted for at any moment. But he had heard McTurk openly deride cricket—even house-matches; Beetle's views on the honor of the house he knew were incendiary; and he could never tell when the soft and smiling Stalky was laughing at him. Consequently—since human nature is what it is—those boys had been doing wrong somewhere. He hoped it was nothing very serious, but . . .

"Ti-ra-la-la-i-tu! I gloat! Hear me!" Stalky, still on his heels, whirled like a dancing dervish to the dining-hall.

"Ti-ra-la-la-i-tu! I gloat! Hear me!" Beetle spun behind him with outstretched arms.

"Ti-ra-la-la-i-tu! I gloat! Hear me!" McTurk's voice cracked.

Now was there or was there not a distinct flavor of beer as they shot past Mr. Prout?

He was unlucky in that his conscience as a housemaster impelled him to consult his associates. Had he taken his pipe and his troubles to little Hartopp's rooms he would, perhaps, have been saved confusion, for Hartopp believed in boys, and knew something about them. His fate led him to King, a fellow house-master, no friend of his, but a zealous hater of Stalky & Co.

"Ah-haa!" said King, rubbing his hands when the tale was told. "Curious! Now *my* house never dream of doing these things."

"But you see I've no proof, exactly."

"Proof? With the egregious Beetle! As if one wanted it! I suppose it is not impossible for the Sergeant to supply it? Foxy is considered at least a match for any evasive boy in my house. Of course they were smoking and drinking somewhere. That type of boy always does. They think it manly."

"But they've no following in the school, and they are distinctly—er—brutal to their juniors," said Prout, who had from a distance seen Beetle return, with interest, his butterfly-net to a tearful fag.

"Ah! They consider themselves superior to ordinary delights. Self-sufficient little animals! There's something in McTurk's Hibernian sneer that would make *me* a little annoyed. And they are so careful to avoid all overt acts, too. It's sheer calculated insolence. I am strongly opposed, as you know, to interfering with another man's house; but they need a lesson, Prout. They need a sharp lesson, if only to bring down their overweening self-conceit. Were I you, I should devote myself for a week to their little performances. Boys of that order—and I may flatter myself, but I think I know boys—don't join the Bug-hunters for love. Tell the Sergeant to keep his eye open; and, of course, in my peregrinations I may casually keep mine open, too."

"Ti-ra-la-la-i-tu! I gloat! Hear me!" far down the corridor.

"Disgusting!" said King. "Where do they pick up these obscene noises? One sharp lesson is what they want."

The boys did not concern themselves with lessons for the next few days. They had all Colonel Dabney's estate to play with, and they explored it with the stealth of Red Indians and the accuracy of burglars. They could enter either by the Lodge-gates on the upper road—they were careful to ingratiate themselves with the Lodge-keeper and his wife—drop down into the combe, and return along the cliffs; or they could begin at the combe, and climb up into the road.

They were careful not to cross the Colonel's path—he had served his turn, and they would not outwear their welcome—nor did they show up on the sky-line when they could move in cover. The shelter of the gorze by the cliff-edge was their chosen retreat. Beetle christened it the Pleasant Isle of Aves, for the peace and the shelter of it; and here, the pipes and tobacco once cachéd in a convenient ledge an arm's length down the cliff, their position was legally unassailable.

For, observe, Colonel Dabney had not invited them to enter his house. Therefore, they did not need to ask specific leave to go visiting; and school rules were strict on that point. He had merely thrown open his grounds to them; and, since they were lawful Bug-hunters, their extended bounds ran up to his notice-boards in the combe and his Lodge-gates on the hill.

They were amazed at their own virtue.

"And even if it wasn't," said Stalky, flat on his back, staring into the blue. "Even suppose we were miles out of bounds, no one could get at us through this wuzzy, unless he knew the tunnel. Isn't this better than lyin' up just behind the Coll.—in a blue funk every time we had a smoke? Isn't your Uncle Stalky—?"

"No," said Beetle—he was stretched at the edge of the cliff spitting thoughtfully. "We've got to thank Turkey for this. Turkey is the Great Man. Turkey, dear, you're distressing Heffles."

"Gloomy old ass!" said McTurk, deep in a book.

"They've got us under suspicion," said Stalky. "Hoophats *is* so suspicious somehow; and Foxy always makes every stalk he does a sort of—sort of—"

"Scalp," said Beetle. "Foxy's a giddy Chingangook."

"Poor Foxy," said Stalky. "He's goin' to catch us one of these days. 'Said to me in the Gym last night, 'I've got my eye on you, Mister Corkran. I'm only warning you for your good.' Then I said: 'Well, you jolly well take it off again, or you'll get into trouble. I'm only warnin' you for your good.' Foxy was wrath."

"Yes, but it's only fair sport for Foxy," said Beetle. "It's Hefflelinga that has the evil mind. 'Shouldn't wonder if he thought we got tight."

"I never got squiffy but once—that was in the holidays," said Stalky, reflectively; "an' it made me horrid sick. 'Pon my sacred Sam, though, it's enough to drive a man to drink, havin' an animal like Hoof for house-master."

"If we attended the matches an' yelled, 'Well hit, sir,' an' stood on one leg an' grinned every time Heffy said, 'So ho, my sons. Is it thus?' an' said, 'Yes, sir,' an' 'No, sir,' an' 'O, sir,' an' 'Please, sir,' like a lot o' filthy fa-ags, Heffy 'ud think no end of us," said McTurk with a sneer.

"Too late to begin that."

"It's all right. The Hefflelinga means well. *But* he is an ass. *And* we show him that we think he's an ass. An' *so* Heffy don't love us. 'Told me last night after prayers that he was *in loco parentis,*" Beetle grunted.

"The deuce he did!" cried Stalky. "That means he's maturin' something unusual dam' mean. Last time he told me that he gave me three hundred lines for dancin' the cachuca in Number Ten dormitory. *Loco parentis,* by gum! But what's the odds as long as you're 'appy? *We're* all right."

They were, and their very rightness puzzled Prout, King, and the Sergeant. Boys with bad consciences show it. They slink out past the Fives Court in haste, and smile nervously when questioned. They return, disordered, in bare time to save a call-over. They nod and wink and giggle one to the other, scattering at the approach of a master. But Stalky and his allies had long outlived these manifestations of youth. They strolled forth unconcernedly, and returned in excellent shape after a light refreshment of strawberries and cream at the Lodge.

The Lodge-keeper had been promoted to keeper, *vice* the murderous fisherman, and his wife made much of the boys. The man, too, gave them a squirrel, which they presented to the Natural History Society; thereby checkmating little Hartopp, who wished to know what they were doing for Science. Foxy faithfully worked some deep Devon lanes behind a lonely cross-roads inn; and it was curious that Prout and King, members of Common-room seldom friendly, walked together in the same direction—that is to say northeast. Now, the Pleasant Isle of Aves lay due southwest.

"They're deep—day-vilish deep," said Stalky. "Why are they drawin' those covers?"

"Me," said Beetle sweetly. "I asked Foxy if he had ever tasted the beer there. That was enough for Foxy, and it cheered him up a little. He and Heffy were sniffin' round our old hut so long I thought they'd like a change."

"Well, it can't last forever," said Stalky. "Heffy's bankin' up like a thundercloud, an' King goes rubbin' his beastly hands, an' grinnin' like a hyena. It's shockin' demoralizin' for King. He'll burst some day."

That day came a little sooner than they expected—came when the Sergeant, whose duty it was to collect defaulters, did not attend an afternoon callover.

"Tired of pubs, eh? He's gone up to the top of the hill with his binoculars to spot us," said Stalky. "Wonder he didn't think of that before. Did you see old Heffy cock his eye at us when we answered our names? Heffy's in it, too. *Ti-ra-la-la-i-tu!* I gloat! Hear me! Come on!"

"Aves?" said Beetle.

"Of course, but I'm not smokin' *aujourd hui. Parce que je* jolly well *pense* that we'll be *suivi.* We'll go along the cliffs, slow, an' give Foxy lots of time to parallel us up above."

They strolled towards the swimming-baths, and presently overtook King.

"Oh, don't let *me* interrupt you," he said. "Engaged in scientific pursuits, of course? I trust you will enjoy yourselves, my young friends."

"You see!" said Stalky, when they were out of ear-shot. "He *can't* keep a secret. He's followin' to cut off our line of retreat. He'll wait at the baths till Heffy comes along. They've tried every blessed place except along the cliffs, and now they think they've bottled us. No need to hurry."

They walked leisurely over the combes till they reached the line of notice-boards.

"Listen a shake. Foxy's up wind comin' down hill like beans. When you hear him move in the bushes, go straight across to Aves. They want to catch us *flagrante delicto.*"

They dived into the gorse at right angles to the tunnel, openly crossing the grass, and lay still in Aves.

"What did I tell you?" Stalky carefully put away the pipes and tobacco. The Sergeant, out of breath, was leaning against the fence, raking the furze with his binoculars, but he might as well have tried to see through a sand-bag. Anon, Prout and King appeared behind him. They conferred.

"Aha! Foxy don't like the notice-boards, and he don't like the prickles either. Now we'll cut up the tunnel and go to the Lodge. Hullo! They've sent Foxy into cover."

The Sergeant was waist-deep in crackling, swaying furze, his ears filled with the noise of his own progress. The boys reached the shelter of the wood and looked down through a belt of hollies.

"Hellish noise!" said Stalky, critically. " 'Don't think Colonel Dabney will like it. I move we go into the Lodge and get something to eat. We might as well see the fun out."

Suddenly the keeper passed them at a trot.

"Who'm they to combe-bottom for Lard's sake? Master'll be crazy," he said.

"Poachers simly," Stalky replied in the broad Devon that was the boy's *langue de guerre.*

"I'll poach 'em to raights!" He dropped into the funnel-like combe, which presently began to fill with noises, notably King's voice crying: "Go on, Sergeant! Leave him alone, you, sir.. He is executing *my* orders."

"Who'm yeou to give arders here, gingy whiskers? Yeou come up to the master. Come out o' that wuzzy! [This is to the Sergeant.] Yiss, I reckon us knows the boys yeou'm after. They've tu long ears an' vuzzy bellies, an' you nippies they in yeour pockets when they'm dead. Come on up to master! He'll boy yeou all you'm a mind to. Yeou other folk bide your side fence."

"Explain to the proprietor. You can explain, Sergeant," shouted King. Evidently the Sergeant had surrendered to the major force.

Beetle lay at full length on the turf behind the Lodge, literally biting the earth in spasms of joy.

Stalky kicked him upright. There was nothing of levity about Stalky or McTurk save a stray muscle twitching on the cheek.

They tapped at the Lodge door, where they were always weclome.

"Come yeou right in an' set down, my little dearrs," said the woman. "They'll niver touch my man. He'll poach 'em to rights. Iss fai! Fresh berries an' cream. Us Dartymoor folk niver forgit their friends. But them Bidevor poachers, they've no hem to their garments. Sugar? My man he've digged a badger for yeou, my dearrs. 'Tis in the linhay in a box."

"Us'll take un with us when we'm finished here. I reckon yeou'm busy. We'll bide here an'–'tis washin' day with yeou, simply," said Stalky. "We'm no company to make all vitty for. Never yeou mind us. Yiss. There's plenty cream."

The woman withdrew, wiping her pink hands on her apron, and left them in the parlor. There was a scuffle of feet on the gravel outside the heavily-leaded diamond panes, and then the voice of Colonel Dabney, something clearer than a bugle.

"Ye can read? You've eyes in your head? Don't attempt to deny it. Ye have!"

Beetle snatched a crochet-work antimacassar from the shiny horsehair sofa, stuffed it into his mouth, and rolled out of sight.

"You saw my notice-boards. Your duty? Curse your impudence, sir. Your duty was to keep off my grounds. Talk of duty to *me!* Why–why–why, ye misbegotten poacher, ye'll be teaching me my A B C next! Roarin' like a bull in the bushes down there! Boys? Boys? Boys? Keep your boys at home, then! *I'm* not responsible for your boys! But I don't believe it–I don't believe a word of it. Ye've a furtive look in your eye–a furtive, sneakin', poachin' look in your eye, that 'ud ruin the reputation of an archangel! Don't attempt to deny it! Ye have! A sergeant? More shame to you, then, an' the worst bargain Her Majesty ever made! A sergeant, to run about the country poachin'–on your pension! Damnable! Oh, damnable! But I'll be considerate. I'll be merciful. By gad, I'll be the very essence o' humanity! Did ye, or did ye not, see my notice-boards? Don't attempt to deny it! Ye did. Silence, Sergeant!"

Twenty-one years in the army had left their mark on Foxy. He obeyed.

"Now. March!"

The high Lodge gate shut with a clang. "My duty! A sergeant to tell me my duty!" puffed Colonel Dabney. "Good Lard! more sergeants!"

"It's King! It's King!" gulped Stalky, his head on the horsehair pillow. McTurk was eating the rag-carpet before the speckless hearth, and the sofa heaved to the emotions of Beetle. Through the thick glass the figures without showed blue, distorted, and menacing.

"I–I protest against this outrage." King had evidently been running up hill. "The man was entirely within his duty. Let–let me give you my card."

"He's in flannels!" Stalky buried his head again.

"Unfortunately–*most* unfortunately–I have not one with me, but my name is King, sir, a housemaster of the College, and you will find me prepared—fully prepared—to answer for this man's action. We've seen three—"

"*Did* ye see my notice-boards?"

"I admit we did; but under the circumstances—"

"I stand in *loco parentis.*" Prout's deep voice was added to the discussion. They could hear him pant.

"F'what?" Colonel Dabney was growing more and more Irish.

"I'm responsible for the boys under my charge."

"Ye are, are ye? Then all I can say is that ye set them a very bad example—a dam' bad example, if I may say so. I do not own your boys. I've not seen your boys, an' I tell you that if there was a boy grinnin' in every bush on the place, *still* ye've no shadow of a right here, comin' up from the combe that way, an' frightenin' everything in it. Don't attempt to deny it. Ye did. Ye should have come to the Lodge an' seen me like Christians, instead of chasin' your dam' boys through the length and breadth of my covers. In *loco parentis* ye are? Well, I've not forgotten my Latin either, an' I'll say to you: *'Quis custodiet ipsos custodes.'* If the masters trespass, how can we blame the boys?"

"But if I could speak to you privately," said Prout.

"I'll have nothing private with you! Ye can be as private as ye please on the other side o' that gate an'—I wish ye a very good afternoon."

A second time the gate clanged. They waited till Colonel Dabney had returned to the house, and fell into one another's arms, crowing for breath.

"Oh, my Soul! Oh, my King! Oh, my Heffy! Oh, my Foxy! Zeal, all zeal, Mr. Simple." Stalky wiped his eyes. "Oh! Oh! Oh!—'I *did* boil the exciseman!' We must get out of this or we'll be late for tea."

"Ge—ge—get the badger and make little Hartopp happy. Ma—ma—make 'em all happy," sobbed McTurk, groping for the door and kicking the prostrate Beetle before him.

They found the beast in an evil-smelling box, left two half-crowns for payment, and staggered home. Only the badger grunted most marvelous like Colonel Dabney, and they dropped him twice or thrice with shrieks of helpless laughter. They were but imperfectly recovered when Foxy met them by the Fives Court with word that they were to go up to their dormitory and wait till sent for.

"Well, take this box to Mr. Hartopp's rooms, then. We've done something for the Natural History Society, at any rate," said Beetle.

"'Fraid that won't save you, young gen'elmen," Foxy answered, in an awful voice. He was sorely ruffled in his mind.

"All sereno, Foxibus." Stalky had reached the extreme stage of hiccups. "We—we'll never desert you, Foxy. Hounds choppin' foxes in cover is more a proof of vice, ain't it? . . . No, you're right. I'm—I'm not quite well."

"They've gone a bit too far this time," Foxy thought to himself. "Very far gone, *I'd* say, excep' there was no smell of liquor. An' yet it isn't like 'em—somehow. King and Prout they 'ad their dressin'-down same as me. That's one comfort."

"Now, we must pull up," said Stalky, rising from the bed on which he had thrown himself. "We're injured innocence—as usual. *We* don't know what we've been sent up here for, do we?"

"No explanation. Deprived of tea. Public disgrace before the house," said McTurk, whose eyes were running over. "It's dam' serious."

"Well, hold on, till King loses his temper," said Beetle. "He's a libelous old rip, an' he'll be in a ravin' paddy-wack. Prout's too beastly cautious. Keep your eye on King, and, if he gives us a chance, appeal to the Head. That always makes 'em sick."

They were summoned to their house-master's study, King and Foxy supporting Prout, and Foxy had three canes under his arm. King leered triumphantly, for there were tears, undried tears of mirth, on the boys' cheeks. Then the examination began.

Yes, they had walked along the cliffs. Yes, they had entered Colonel Dabney's grounds. Yes, they had seen the notice-boards (at this point Beetle sputtered hysterically). For what purpose had they entered Colonel Dabney's grounds? "Well, sir, there was a badger."

Here King, who loathed the Natural History Society because he did not like Hartopp, could no longer be restrained. He begged them not to add mendacity to open insolence. But the badger was in Mr. Hartopp's rooms, sir. The Sergeant had kindly taken it up for them. That disposed of the badger, and the temporary check brought King's temper to boiling-point. They could hear his foot on the floor while Prout prepared his lumbering inquiries. They had settled into their stride now. Their eyes ceased to sparkle; their faces were blank; their hands hung beside them without a twitch. They were learning, at the expense of a fellow-countryman, the lesson of their race, which is to put away all emotion and entrap the alien at the proper time.

So far good. King was importing himself more freely into the trial, being vengeful where Prout was grieved. They knew the penalties of trespassing? With a fine show of irresolution, Stalky admitted that he had gathered some information vaguely bearing on this head, but he thought—The sentence was dragged out to the uttermost: Stalky did not wish to play his trump with such an opponent. Mr. King desired no buts, nor was he interested in Stalky's evasions. They, on the other hand, might be interested in his poor views. Boys who crept–who sneaked–who lurked–out of bounds, even the generous bounds of the Natural History Society, which they had falsely joined as a cloak for their misdeeds–their vices–their villainies–their immoralities—

"He'll break cover in a minute," said Stalky to himself. "Then we'll run into him before he gets away."

Such boys, scabrous boys, moral lepers–the current of his words was carrying King off his feet–evil-speakers, liars, slow-bellies–yea, incipient drunkards . . .

He was merely working up to a peroration, and the boys knew it; but McTurk cut through the frothing sentence, the others echoing:

"I appeal to the Head, sir."

"I appeal to the Head, sir."

"I appeal to the Head, sir."

It was their unquestioned right. Drunkenness meant expulsion after a public flogging. They had been accused of it. The case was the Head's, and the Head's alone.

"Thou hast appealed unto Caesar: unto Caesar shalt thou go." They had heard that sentence once or twice before in their careers. "None the less," said King, uneasily, "you would be better advised to abide by our decision, my young friends."

"Are we allowed to associate with the rest of the school till we see the Head, sir?" said McTurk to his house-master, disregarding King. This at once lifted the situation to its loftiest plane. Moreover, it meant no work, for moral leprosy was strictly quarantined, and the Head never executed judgment till twenty-four cold hours later.

"Well–er–if you persist in your defiant attitude," said King, with a loving look at the canes under Foxy's arm. "There is no alternative."

Ten minutes later the news was over the whole school. Stalky and Co. had fallen at last–fallen by drink. They had been drinking. They had returned blind-drunk from a hut. They were even now lying hopelessly intoxicated on the dormitory floor. A few bold spirits crept up to look, and received boots about the head from the criminals.

"We've got him–got him on the Caudine Toasting-fork!" said Stalky, after those hints were taken. "King'll have to prove his charges up to the giddy hilt."

"Too much ticklee, him bust," Beetle quoted from a book of his reading. "Didn't I say he'd go pop if we lat un bide?"

"No prep., either, O ye incipient drunkards," said McTurk, "and it's trig night, too. Hullo! Here's our dear friend Foxy. More tortures, Foxibus?"

"I've brought you something to eat, young gentlemen," said the Sergeant from behind a crowded tray. Their wars had ever been waged without malice, and a suspicion floated in Foxy's mind that boys who allowed themselves to be tracked so easily might, perhaps, hold something in reserve. Foxy had served through the Mutiny, when early and accurate information was worth much.

"I–I noticed you 'adn't 'ad anything to eat, an' I spoke to Gumbly, an' he said you wasn't exactly cut off from supplies. So I brought up this. It's your potted 'am tin, ain't it, Mr. Corkran?"

"Why, Foxibus, you're a brick," said Stalky. "I didn't think you had this much–what's the word, Beetle?"

"Bowels," Beetle replied, promptly. "Thank you, Sergeant. That's young Carter's potted ham, though."

"There was a C on it. I thought it was Mr. Corkran's. This is a very serious business, young gentlemen. That's what it is. I didn't know, perhaps, but there might be something on your side which you hadn't said to Mr. King or Mr. Prout, maybe."

"There is. Heaps, Foxibus." This from Stalky through a full mouth.

"Then you see, if that was the case, it seemed to me I might represent it, quiet so to say, to the 'Ead when he asks me about it. I've got to take 'im the charges to-night, an'–it looks bad on the face of it."

" 'Trocious bad, Foxy. Twenty-seven cuts in the Gym before all the school, and public expulsion. 'Wine is a mocker, strong drink is ragin',' " quoth Beetle.

"It's nothin' to make fun of, young gentlemen. I 'ave to go to the 'Ead with the charges. An'–an' you mayn't be aware, per'aps, that I was followin' you this afternoon; havin' my suspicions."

"Did ye see the notice-boards?" croaked McTurk, in the very brogue of Colonel Dabney.

"Ye've eyes in your head. Don't attempt to deny it. Ye did!" said Beetle.

"A sergeant! To run about poachin' on your pension! Damnable, O damnable!" said Stalky, without pity.

"Good Lord!" said the Sergeant, sitting heavily upon a bed. "Where–where the devil *was* you? I might ha' known it was a do–somewhere."

"Oh, you clever maniac!" Stalky resumed. "We mayn't be aware you were followin' us this afternoon, mayn't we? 'Thought you were stalkin' us, eh? Why, we led you bung into it, of course. Colonel Dabney–don't you think he's a nice man, Foxy?–Colonel Dabney's our pet particular friend. We've been goin' there for weeks and weeks. He invited us. You and your duty! Curse your duty, sir! Your duty was to keep off his covers."

"You'll never be able to hold up your head again, Foxy. The fags 'll hoot at you," said Beetle. "Think of your giddy prestige!"

The Sergeant was thinking–hard.

"Look 'ere, young gentlemen," he said, earnestly. "You aren't surely ever goin' to tell, are you? Wasn't Mr. Prout and Mr. King in–in it too?"

"Foxibusculus, they *was*. They was–singular horrid. Caught it worse than you. We heard every word of it. You got off easy, considerin'. If I'd been Dabney I swear I'd ha' quodded you. I think I'll suggest it to him to-morrow."

"An' it's all goin' up to the 'Ead. Oh, Good Lord!"

"Every giddy word of it, my Chingangook," said Beetle, dancing. "Why shouldn't it? *We've* done nothing wrong. *We* ain't poachers. *We* didn't cut about blastin' the characters of poor, innocent boys–saying they were drunk."

"That I didn't," said Foxy. "I–I only said that you be'aved uncommon odd when you come back with that badger. Mr. King may have taken the wrong hint from that."

" 'Course he did; an' he'll jolly well shove all the blame on you when he finds out he's wrong. We know King, if you don't. I'm ashamed of you. You ain't fit to be a sergeant," said McTurk.

"Not with three thorough-goin' young devils like you, I ain't. I've been had. I've been ambuscaded. Horse, foot, an' guns, I've been had, an'–an' there'll be no holdin' the junior forms after this. M'rover, the 'Ead will send me with a note to Colonel Dabney to ask if what you say about bein' invited was true."

"Then you'd better go in by the Lodge-gates this time, instead of chasin' your dam' boys–oh, that was the Epistle to King–so it was. We-el, Foxy?" Stalky put his chin on his hands and regarded the victim with deep delight.

"Ti-ra-la-la-i-tu! I gloat! Hear me!" said McTurk. "Foxy brought us tea when we were moral lepers. Foxy has a heart. Foxy has been in the Army, too."

"I wish I'd ha' had you in my company, young gentlemen," said the Sergeant from the depths of his heart; "I'd ha' given you something."

"Silence at drum-head court-martial," McTurk went on. "I'm advocate for the prisoner; and, besides, this is much too good to tell all the other brutes in the Coll. They'd *never* understand. They play cricket, and say: 'Yes, sir,' and 'O, sir,' and 'No, sir.' "

"Never mind that. Go ahead," said Stalky.

"Well, Foxy's a good little chap when he does not esteem himself so as to be clever."

" 'Take not out your 'ounds on a werry windy day,' " Stalky struck in. *"I* don't care if you let him off."

"Nor me," said Beetle. "Heffy is my only joy–Heffy and King."

"I 'ad to do it," said the Sergeant, plaintively.

"Right, O! Led away by bad companions in the execution of his duty or–or words to that effect. You're dismissed with a reprimand, Foxy. *We* won't tell about *you.* I swear we won't," McTurk concluded. "Bad for the discipline of the school. Horrid bad."

"Well," said the Sergeant, gathering up the tea-things, "knowin' what I know o' the young dev–gentlemen of the College, I'm very glad to 'ear it. But what am I to tell the 'Ead?"

"Anything you jolly well please, Foxy. *We* aren't the criminals."

To say that the Head was annoyed when the Sergeant appeared after dinner with the day's crime-sheet would be putting it mildly.

"Corkran, McTurk, and Co., I see. Bounds as usual. Hullo! What the deuce is this? Suspicion of drinking. Whose charge?"

"Mr. King's, sir. I caught 'em out of bounds, sir; at least that was 'ow it looked. But there's a lot be'ind, sir." The Sergeant was evidently troubled.

"Go on," said the Head. "Let us have your version."

He and the Sergeant had dealt with one another for some seven years; and the Head knew that Mr. King's statements depended very largely on Mr. King's temper.

"I thought they were out of bounds along the cliffs. But it come out they wasn't, sir. I saw them go into Colonel Dabney's woods, and–Mr. King and Mr. Prout come along–and–the fact was, sir, we was mistook for poachers by

Colonel Dabney's people–Mr. King and Mr. Prout and me. There were some words, sir, on both sides. The young gentlemen slipped 'ome somehow, and they seemed 'ighly humorous, sir. Mr. King was mistook by Colonel Dabney himself–Colonel Dabney bein' strict. Then they preferred to come straight to you, sir, on account of what–what Mr. King may 'ave said about their 'abits afterwards in Mr. Prout's study. I only said they was 'ighly humorous, laughin' an' gigglin', an' a bit above 'emselves. They've since told me, sir, in a humorous way, that they was invited by Colonel Dabney to go into 'is woods."

"I see. They didn't tell their house-master that, of course."

"They took up Mr. King on appeal just as soon as he spoke about their–'abits. Put in the appeal at once, sir, an' asked to be sent to the dormitory waitin' for you. I've since gathered, sir, in their humorous way, sir, that some'ow or other they've 'eard about every word Colonel Dabney said to Mr. King and Mr. Prout when he mistook 'em for poachers. I–I might ha' known when they led me on so that they 'eld the inner line of communications. It's–it's a plain do, sir, if you ask *me;* an' they're gloatin' over it in the dormitory."

The Head saw–saw even to the uttermost farthing–and his mouth twitched a little under his mustache.

"Send them to me at once, Sergeant. This case needn't wait over."

"Good evening," said he when the three appeared under escort. "I want your undivided attention for a few minutes. You've known me for five years, and I've known you for–twenty-five. I think we understand one another perfectly. I am now going to pay you a tremendous compliment (the brown one, please, Sergeant. Thanks. You needn't wait). I'm going to execute you without rhyme, Beetle, or reason. I know you went to Colonel Dabney's covers because you were invited. I'm not even going to send the Sergeant with a note to ask if your statement is true; because I am convinced that on this occasion you have adhered strictly to the truth. I know, too, that you were not drinking. (You can take off that virtuous expression, McTurk, or I shall begin to fear you don't understand me.) There is not a flaw in any of your characters. And that is why I am going to perpetrate a howling injustice. Your reputations have been injured, haven't they? You have been disgraced before the house, haven't you? You have a peculiarly keen regard for the honor of your house, haven't you? Well, *now* I am going to lick you."

Six apiece was their portion upon that word.

"And this I think"–the Head replaced the cane, and flung the written charge into the wastepaper basket–"covers the situation. When you find a variation from the normal–this will be useful to you in later life–always meet him in an abnormal way. And that reminds me. There are a pile of paper-backs on that shelf. You can borrow them if you put them back. I don't think they'll take any harm from being read in the open. They smell of tobacco rather. You will go to prep. this evening as usual. Good-night," said that amazing man.

"Good-night, and thank you, sir."

"I swear I'll pray for the Head to-night," said Beetle. "Those last two cuts were just flicks on my collar. There's a 'Monte Cristo' in that lower shelf. I saw it. Bags I, next time we go to Aves!"

"Dearr man!" said McTurk. "No gating. No impots. No beastly questions. All settled. Hullo! what's King goin' in to him for–King and Prout?"

Whatever the nature of that interview, it did not improve either King's or Prout's ruffled plumes, for, when they came out of the Head's house, six eyes noted that the one was red and blue with emotion as to his nose, and that the other was sweating profusely. That sight compensated them amply for the Imperial Jaw with which they were favored by the two. It seems–and who so astonished as they?—that they had held back material facts; that they were guilty both of *suppressio veri* and *suggestio falsi* (well-known gods against whom they often offended); further, that they were malignant in their dispositions, untrustworthy in their characters, pernicious and revolutionary in their influences, abandoned to the devils of wilfulness, pride, and a most intolerable conceit. Ninthly, and lastly, they were to have a care and to be very careful.

They were careful, as only boys can be when there is a hurt to be inflicted. They waited through one suffocating week till Prout and King were their royal selves again; waited till there was a house-match—their own house, too—in which Prout was taking part; waited, further, till he had buckled on his pads in the pavilion and stood ready to go forth. King was scoring at the window, and the three sat on a bench without.

Said Stalky to Beetle: "I say, Beetle, *quis custodiet ipsos custodes?*"

"Don't ask me," said Beetle. "I'll have nothin' private with you. Ye can be as private as ye please the other end of the bench; and I wish ye a very good afternoon."

McTurk yawned.

"Well, ye should ha' come up to the lodge like Christians instead o' chasin' your—a-hem—boys through the length an' breadth of my covers. *I* think these house-matches are all rot. Let's go over to Colonel Dabney's an' see if he's collared any more poachers."

That afternoon there was joy in Aves.

Slaves of the Lamp

Part I.

THE MUSIC-ROOM on the top floor of Number Five was filled with the "Aladdin" company at rehearsal. Dickson Quartus, commonly known as Dick Four, was Aladdin, stage-manager, ballet-master, half the orchestra, and largely librettist, for the "book" had been rewritten and filled with local allusions. The pantomime was to be given next week, in the down-stairs study occupied by Aladdin, Abanazar, and the Emperor of China. The Slave of the Lamp, with the Princess Badroulbadour and the Widow Twankay, owned Number Five study across the same landing, so that the company could be easily assembled. The floor shook to the stamp-and-go of the ballet, while Aladdin, in pink cotton tights, a blue and tinsel jacket, and a plumed hat, banged alternately on the piano and his banjo. He was the moving spirit of the game, as befitted a senior who had passed his Army Preliminary and hoped to enter Sandhurst next spring.

Aladdin came to his own at last, Abanazar lay poisoned on the floor, the Widow Twankay danced her dance, and the company decided it would "come all right on the night."

"What about the last song, though?" said the Emperor, a tallish, fair-headed boy with a ghost of a mustache, at which he pulled manfully. "We need a rousing old tune."

" 'John Peel'? 'Drink, Puppy, Drink'?" suggested Abanazar, smoothing his baggy lilac pajamas. "Pussy" Abanazar never looked more than one-half awake, but he owned a soft, slow smile which well suited the part of the Wicked Uncle.

"Stale," said Aladdin. "Might as well have 'Grandfather's Clock.' What's that thing you were humming at prep. last night, Stalky?"

Stalky, The Slave of the Lamp, in black tights and doublet, a black silk half-mask on his forehead, whistled lazily where he lay on the top of the piano. It was a catchy music-hall tune.

Dick Four cocked his head critically, and squinted down a large red nose. "Once more, and I can pick it up," he said, strumming. "Sing the words."

"Arrah, Patsy, mind the baby! Arrah, Patsy, mind the child!
Wrap him in an overcoat, he's surely going wild!
Arrah, Patsy, mind the baby! just you mind the child awhile!
He'll kick and bite and cry all night! Arrah, Patsy, mind the child!"

"Rippin'! Oh, rippin'!" said Dick Four. "Only we shan't have any piano on the night. We must work it with the banjoes–play an' dance at the same time. You try, Tertius."

The Emperor pushed aside his pea-green sleeves of state, and followed Dick Four on a heavy nickel-plated banjo.

"Yes, but I'm dead all this time. Bung in the middle of the stage, too," said Abanazar.

"Oh, that's Beetle's biznai," said Dick Four. "Vamp it up, Beetle. Don't keep us waiting all night. You've got to get Pussy out of the light somehow, and bring us all in dancin' at the end."

"All right. You two play it again," said Beetle, who, in a gray skirt and a wig of chestnut sausage-curls, set slantwise above a pair of spectacles mended with an old boot-lace, represented the Widow Twankay. He waved one leg in time to the hammered refrain, and the banjoes grew louder.

"Um! Ah! Er–'Aladdin now has won his wife,' " he sang, and Dick Four repeated it.

" 'Your Emperor is appeased.' " Tertius flung out his chest as he delivered his line.

"Now jump up, Pussy! Say, 'I think I'd better come to life!' Then we all take hands and come forward: 'We hope you've all been pleased.' *Twiggez-vous?"*

"Nous twiggons. Good enough. What's the chorus for the final ballet? It's four kicks and a turn," said Dick Four.

"Oh! Er!

John Short will ring the curtain down.
And ring the prompter's bell;
We hope you know before you go
That we all wish you well."

"Rippin'! Rippin'! Now for the Widow's scene with the Princess. Hurry up, Turkey."

McTurk, in a violet silk skirt and a coquettish blue turban, slouched forward as one thoroughly ashamed of himself. The Slave of the Lamp climbed down from the piano, and dispassionately kicked him. "Play up, Turkey," he said; "this is serious." But there fell on the door the knock of authority. It happened to be King, in gown and mortar-board, enjoying a Saturday evening prowl before dinner.

"Locked doors! Locked doors!" he snapped with a scowl. "What's the meaning of this; and what, may I ask, is the intention of this–this epicene attire?"

"Pantomime, sir. The Head gave us leave," said Abanazar, as the only member of the Sixth concerned. Dick Four stood firm in the confidence born of well-fitting tights, but Beetle strove to efface himself behind the piano. A gray princess-skirt borrowed from a day-boy's mother and a spotted cotton bodice unsystematically padded with imposition-paper make one ridiculous. And in other regards Beetle had a bad conscience.

"As usual!" sneered King. "Futile foolery just when your careers, such as they may be, are hanging in the balance. I see! Ah, I see! The old gang of criminals–allied forces of disorder–Corkran"–the Slave of the Lamp smiled politely–"McTurk"–the Irishman scowled–"and, of course, the unspeakable Beetle, our friend Gigadibs." Abanazar, the Emperor, and Aladdin had more or less of characters, and King passed them over. "Come forth, my inky buffoon, from behind yonder instrument of music! You supply, I presume, the doggerel for this entertainment. Esteem yourself to be, as it were, a poet?"

"He's found one of 'em," thought Beetle, noting the flush on King's cheek-bone.

"I have just had the pleasure of reading an effusion of yours to my address, I believe–an effusion intended to rhyme. So–so you despise me, Master Gigadibs, do you? I am quite aware–you need not explain–that it was ostensibly *not* intended for my edification. I read it with laughter–yes, with laughter. These paper pellets of inky boys–still a boy we are, Master Gigadibs–do not disturb my equanimity."

"Wonder which it was," thought Beetle. He had launched many lampoons on an appreciative public ever since he discovered that it was possible to convey reproof in rhyme.

In sign of his unruffled calm, King proceeded to tear Beetle, whom he called Gigadibs, slowly asunder. From his untied shoestring to his mended spectacles (the life of a poet at a big school is hard) he held him up to the derision of his associates–with the usual result. His wild flowers of speech–King had an unpleasant tongue–restored him to good humor at the last. He drew a lurid picture of Beetle's latter end as a scurrilous pamphleteer dying in an attic, scattered a few compliments over McTurk and Corkran, and, reminding Beetle that he must come up for judgment when called upon, went to Common-room, where he triumphed anew over his victims.

"And the worst of it," he explained in a loud voice over his soup, "is that I waste such gems of sarcasm on their thick heads. It's miles above them, I'm certain."

"We-ell," said the school chaplain slowly, "I don't know what Corkran's appreciation of your style may be, but young McTurk reads Ruskin for his amusement."

"Nonsense! He does it to show off. I mistrust the dark Celt."

"He does nothing of the kind. I went into their study the other night, unofficially, and McTurk was gluing up the back of four odd numbers of 'Fors Clavigera.' "

"I don't know anything about their private lives," said a mathematical master hotly, "but I've learned by bitter experience that Number Five study are best left alone. They are utterly soulless young devils." He blushed as the others laughed.

But in the music-room there were wrath and bad language. Only Stalky, Slave of the Lamp, lay on the piano unmoved.

"That little swine Manders minor must have shown him your stuff. He's always suckin' up to King. Go and kill him," he drawled. "Which one was it, Beetle?"

"Dunno," said Beetle, struggling out of the skirt. "There was one about his hunting for popularity with the small boys, and the other one was one about him in hell, tellin' the Devil he was a Balliol man. I swear both of 'em rhymed all right. By gum! P'raps Manders minor showed him both! *I'll* correct his caesuras for him."

He disappeared down two flights of stairs, flushed a small pink and white boy in a form-room next door to King's study, which, again, was immediately below his own, and chased him up the corridor into a form-room sacred to the revels of the Lower Third. Thence he came back, greatly disordered, to find McTurk, Stalky, and the others of the company, in his study enjoying an unlimited "brew"—coffee, cocoa, buns, new bread hot and steaming, sardine, sausage, ham-and-tongue paste, pilchards, three jams, and at least as many pounds of Devonshire cream.

"My Hat!" said he, throwing himself upon the banquet. "Who stumped up for this, Stalky?" It was within a month of term end, and blank starvation had reigned in the studies for weeks.

"You," said Stalky, serenely.

"Confound you! You haven't been popping my Sunday bags, then?"

"Keep your hair on. It's only your watch."

"Watch! I lost it—weeks ago. Out on the Burrows, when we tried to shoot the old ram—the day our pistol burst."

"It dropped out of your pocket (you're so beastly careless, Beetle), and McTurk and I kept it for you. I've been wearing it for a week, and you never noticed. Took it into Bideford after dinner to-day. Got thirteen and seven-pence. Here's the ticket."

"Well, that's pretty average cool," said Abanazar behind a slab of cream and jam, as Beetle, reassured upon the safety of his Sunday trousers, showed not even surprise, much less resentment. Indeed, it was McTurk who grew angry, saying:

"You gave him the ticket, Stalky? You *pawned* it? You unmitigated beast! Why, last month you and Beetle sold mine! 'Never got a sniff of any ticket."

"Ah, that was because you locked your trunk, and we wasted half the afternoon hammering it open. We might have pawned it if you'd behaved like a Christian, Turkey."

"My Aunt!" said Abanazar, "you chaps *are* communists. Vote of thanks to Beetle, though."

"That's beastly unfair," said Stalky, "when I took all the trouble to pawn it. Beetle never knew he had a watch. Oh, I say, Rabbits-Eggs gave me a lift into Bideford this afternoon."

Rabbits-Eggs was the local carrier—an outcrop of the early Devonian formation. It was Stalky who had invented his unlovely name. "He was pretty average drunk, or he wouldn't have done it. Rabbits-Eggs is a little shy of me, somehow. But I swore it was *pax* between us, and gave him a bob. He stopped at two pubs on the way in, so he'll be howling drunk to-night. Oh, don't begin reading, Beetle; there's a council of war on. What the deuce is the matter with your collar?"

"'Chivied Manders minor into the Lower Third box-room. 'Had all his beastly little friends on top of me," said Beetle from behind a jar of pilchards and a book.

"You ass! Any fool could have told you where Manders would bunk to," said McTurk.

"I didn't think," said Beetle, meekly, scooping out pilchards with a spoon.

"Course you didn't. You never do." McTurk adjusted Beetle's collar with a savage tug. "Don't drop oil all over my 'Fors,' or I'll scrag you!"

"Shut up, you—you Irish Biddy! 'Tisn't your beastly 'Fors.' It's one of mine."

The book was a fat, brown-backed volume of the later Sixties, which King had once thrown at Beetle's head that Beetle might see whence the name Gigadibs came. Beetle had quietly annexed the book, and had seen–several things. The quarter-comprehended verses lived and ate with him, as the bedropped pages showed. He removed himself from all that world, drifting at large with wondrous Men and Women, till McTurk hammered the pilchard spoon on his head and he snarled.

"Beetle! You're oppressed and insulted and bullied by King. Don't you feel it?"

"Let me alone! I can write some more poetry about him if I am, I suppose."

"Mad! Quite mad!" said Stalky to the visitors, as one exhibiting strange beasts. "Beetle reads an ass called Brownin', and McTurk reads an ass called Ruskin; and—"

"Ruskin isn't an ass," said McTurk. "He's almost as good as the Opium Eater. He says 'we're children of noble races trained by surrounding art.' That means *me,* and the way I decorated the study when you two badgers would have stuck up brackets and Christmas cards. Child of a noble race, trained by surrounding art, stop reading, or I'll shove a pilchard down your neck!"

"It's two to one," said Stalky, warningly, and Beetle closed the book, in obedience to the law under which he and his companions had lived for six checkered years.

The visitors looked on delighted. Number Five study had a reputation for more variegated insanity than the rest of the school put together; and so far as its code allowed friendship with outsiders it was polite and open-hearted to its neighbors on the same landing.

"What rot do you want now?" said Beetle.

"King! War!" said McTurk, jerking his head toward the wall, where hung a small wooden West-African war-drum, a gift to McTurk from a naval uncle.

"Then we shall be turned out of the study again," said Beetle, who loved his flesh-pots. "Mason turned us out for–just warbling on it." Mason was the mathematical master who had testified in Common-room.

"Warbling?–O Lord!" said Abanazar. "We couldn't hear ourselves speak in our study when you played the infernal thing. What's the good of getting turned out of your study, anyhow?"

"We lived in the form-rooms for a week, too." said Beetle, tragically. "And it was beastly cold."

"Ye-es, but Mason's rooms were filled with rats every day we were out. It took him a week to draw the inference," said McTurk. "He loathes rats. 'Minute he let us go back the rats stopped. Mason's a little shy of us now, but there was no evidence."

"Jolly well there wasn't," said Stalky, "when I got out on the roof and dropped the beastly things down his chimney. But, look here–question is, are our characters good enough just now to stand a study row?"

"Never mind mine," said Beetle. "King swears I haven't any."

"I'm not thinking of you," Stalky returned scornfully. "You aren't going up for the Army, you old bat. I don't want to be expelled–and the Head's getting rather shy of us, too."

"Rot!" said McTurk. "The Head never expels except for beastliness or stealing. But I forgot; you and Stalky *are* thieves–regular burglars."

The visitors gasped, but Stalky interpreted the parable with large grins.

"Well, you know, that little beast Manders minor saw Beetle and me hammerin' McTurk's trunk open in the dormitory when we took his watch last month. Of course Manders sneaked to Mason, and Mason solemnly took it up as a case of theft, to get even with us about the rats."

"That just put Mason into our giddy hands," said McTurk, blandly. "We were nice to him, 'cause he was a new master and wanted to win the confidence of the boys. 'Pity he draws inferences, though. Stalky went to his study and pretended to blub, and told Mason he'd lead a new life if Mason would let him off this time, but Mason wouldn't. 'Said it was his duty to report him to the Head."

"Vindictive swine!" said Beetle. "It was all those rats! Then *I* blubbed, too, and Stalky confessed that he'd been a thief in regular practice for six years, ever since he came to the school; and that I'd taught him—*à la* Fagin. Mason turned white with joy. He thought he had us on toast."

"Gorgeous! Gorgeous!" said Dick Four. "We never heard of this."

" 'Course not. Mason kept it jolly quiet. He wrote down all our statements on impot-paper. There wasn't anything he wouldn't believe," said Stalky.

"And handed it all up to the Head, *with* an extempore prayer. It took about forty pages," said Beetle. "I helped him a lot."

"And then, you crazy idiots?" said Abanazar.

"Oh, we were sent for; and Stalky asked to have the 'depositions' read out, and the Head knocked him spinning into a waste-paper basket. Then he gave us eight cuts apiece—welters—for—for—takin' unheard-of liberties with a new master. I saw his shoulders shaking when we went out. Do you know," said Beetle, pensively, "that Mason can't look at us now in second lesson without blushing? We three stare at him sometimes till he regularly trickles. He's an awfully sensitive beast."

"He read 'Eric, or Little by Little,' " said McTurk; "so we gave him 'St. Winifred's, *or* the World of School.' They spent all their spare time stealing at St. Winifred's, when they weren't praying or getting drunk at pubs. Well, that was only a week ago, and the Head's a little bit shy of us. He called it constructive deviltry. Stalky invented it all."

"Not the least good having a row with a master unless you can make an ass of him," said Stalky, extended at ease on the hearth-rug. "If Mason didn't know Number Five—well, he's learnt, that's all. Now, my dearly beloved 'earers"—Stalky curled his legs under him and addressed the company—"we've got that strong, perseverin' man King on our hands. He went miles out of his way to provoke a conflict." (Here Stalky snapped down the black silk domino and assumed the air of a judge.) "He has oppressed Beetle, McTurk, and me, *privatim et seriatim,* one by one, as he could catch us. But *now* he has insulted Number Five up in the music-room, and in the presence of these—these ossifers of the Ninety-third, wot look like hairdressers. Binjimin, we must make him cry 'Capivi!' "

Stalky's reading did *not* include Browning or Ruskin.

"And, besides," said McTurk, "he's a Philistine, a basket-hanger. He wears a tartan tie. Ruskin says that any man who wears a tartan tie will, without doubt, be damned everlastingly."

"Bravo, McTurk," said Tertius; "I thought he was only a beast."

"He's that, too, of course, but he's worse. He has a china basket with blue ribbons and a pink kitten on it, hung up in his window to grow musk in. You know when I got all that old oak carvin' out of Bideford Church, when they were restoring it (Ruskin says that any man who'll restore a church is an unmitigated sweep), and stuck it up here with glue? Well, King came in and wanted to know whether we'd done it with a fret-saw! Yah! He is the King of basket-hangers!"

Down went McTurk's inky thumb over an imaginary arena full of bleeding Kings. "*Placetne,* child of a generous race!" he cried to Beetle.

"Well," began Beetle, doubtfully, "he comes from Balliol, but I'm going to give the beast a chance. You see I can always make him hop with some more poetry. He can't report me to the Head, because it makes him ridiculous.

(Stalky's quite right.) But he shall have his chance."

Beetle opened the book on the table, ran his finger down a page, and began at random:

"Or who in Moscow toward the Czar
With the demurest of footfalls,
Over the Kremlin's pavement white
With serpentine and syenite,
Steps with five other generals—"

"That's no good. Try another," said Stalky.

"Hold on a shake; I know what's coming." McTurk was reading over Beetle's shoulder.

"That simultaneously take snuff,
For each to have pretext enough
And kerchiefwise unfold his sash,
Which–softness' self–is yet the stuff

(Gummy! What a sentence!)

To hold fast where a steel chain snaps
And leave the grand white neck no gash.

(Full stop.)"

" 'Don't understand a word of it," said Stalky.

"More fool you! Construe," said McTurk. "Those six bargees scragged the Czar, and left no evidence. *Actum est* with King."

"He gave me that book, too," said Beetle, licking his lips:

"There's a great text in Galatians,
Once you trip on it entails
Twenty-nine distinct damnations,
One sure if another fails."

Then irrelevantly:

"Setebos! Setebos! and Setebos!
Thinketh he lived in the cold of the moon."

"He's just come in from dinner," said Dick Four, looking through the window. "Manders minor is with him."

" 'Safest place for Manders minor just now," said Beetle.

"Then you chaps had better clear out," said Stalky politely to the visitors. " 'Tisn't fair to mix you up in a study row. Besides, we can't afford to have evidence."

"Are you going to begin at once?" said Aladdin.

"Immediately, if not sooner," said Stalky, and turned out the gas. "Strong, perseverin' man–King. Make him cry 'Capivi.' G'way, Binjimin."

The company retreated to their own neat and spacious study with expectant souls.

"When Stalky blows out his nostrils like a horse," said Aladdin to the Emperor of China, "he's on the war-path. 'Wonder what King will get."

"Beans," said the Emperor. "Number Five generally pays in full."

"Wonder if I ought to take any notice of it officially," said Abanazar, who had just remembered he was a prefect.

"It's none of your business, Pussy. Besides, if you did, we'd have them hostile to *us;* and we shouldn't be able to do any work," said Aladdin. "They've begun already."

Now that West-Africa war-drum had been made to signal across estuaries and deltas. Number Five was forbidden to wake the engine within earshot of the school. But a deep, devastating drone filled the passages as McTurk and Beetle scientifically rubbed its top. Anon it changed to the blare of trumpets—of savage pursuing trumpets. Then, as McTurk slapped one side, smooth with the blood of ancient sacrifice, the roar broke into short coughing howls such as the wounded gorilla throws in his native forest. These were followed by the wrath of King—three steps at a time, up the staircase, with a dry whir of the gown. Aladdin and company, listening, squeaked with excitement as the door crashed open. King stumbled into the darkness, and cursed those performers by the gods of Balliol and quiet repose.

"Turned out for a week," said Aladdin, holding the study door on the crack. "Key to be brought down to his study in five minutes. 'Brutes! Barbarians! Savages! Children!' He's rather agitated. 'Arrah, Patsy, mind the baby,'" he sang in a whisper as he clung to the door-knob, dancing a noiseless war-dance.

King went down-stairs again, and Beetle and McTurk lit the gas to confer with Stalky. But Stalky had vanished.

"Looks like no end of a mess," said Beetle, collecting his books and mathematical instrument case. "A week in the form-rooms isn't any advantage to us."

"Yes, but don't you see that Stalky isn't here, you owl!" said McTurk. "Take down the key, and look sorrowful. King'll only jaw you for half an hour. I'm going to read in the lower form-room."

"But it's always me," mourned Beetle.

"Wait till we see," said McTurk, hopefully. "I don't know any more than you do what Stalky means, but it's something. Go down and draw King's fire. You're used to it."

No sooner had the key turned in the door than the lid of the coal-box, which was also the window-seat, lifted cautiously. It had been a tight fit, even for the lithe Stalky, his head between his knees, and his stomach under his right ear. From a drawer in the table he took a well-worn catapult, a handful of buckshot, and a duplicate key of the study; noiselessly he raised the window and kneeled by it, his face turned to the road, the wind-sloped trees, the dark levels of the Burrows, and the white line of breakers falling nine-deep along the Pebble-ridge. Far down the steep-banked Devonshire lane he heard the husky hoot of the carrier's horn. There was a ghost of melody in it, as it might have been the wind in a gin-bottle essaying to sing, "It's a way we have in the Army."

Stalky smiled a tight-lipped smile, and at extreme range opened fire: the old horse half wheeled in the shafts.

"Where he gwaine tu?" hiccoughed Rabbits-Eggs. Another buckshot tore through the rotten canvas tilt with a vicious zipp.

"Habet!" murmured Stalky, as Rabbits-Eggs swore into the patient night, protesting that he saw the "dommed colleger" who was assaulting him.

. . . .

"And so," King was saying in a high head voice to Beetle, whom he had kept to play with before Manders minor, well knowing that it hurts a Fifth-form boy to be held up to a fag's derision, "and so, Master Beetle, in spite of all our verses, which we are so proud of, when we presume to come into direct conflict with even so humble a representative of authority as myself, for instance, we are turned out of our studies, are we not?"

"Yes, sir," said Beetle, with a sheepish grin on his lips and murder in his heart. Hope had nearly left him, but he clung to a well-established faith that never was Stalky so dangerous as when he was invisible.

"You are *not* required to criticise, thank you. Turned out of our studies, we are, just as if we were no better than little Manders minor. Only inky schoolboys we are, and must be treated as such."

Beetle pricked up his ears, for Rabbits-Eggs was swearing savagely on the road, and some of the language entered at the upper sash. King believed in ventilation. He strode to the window, gowned and majestic, very visible in the gaslight.

"I zee 'un! I zee 'un!" roared Rabbits-Eggs, now that he had found a visible foe—another shot from the darkness above. "Yiss, yeou, yeou long-nosed, fower-eyed, gingy-whiskered beggar! Yeu'm tu old for such goin's on. Aie! Poultice yeour nose, I tall 'ee! Poultice yeour long nose!"

Beetle's heart leaped up within him. Somewhere, somehow, he knew, Stalky moved behind these manifestations. There were hope and the prospect of revenge. He would embody the suggestion about the nose in deathless verse. King threw up the window, and sternly rebuked Rabbits-Eggs. But the carrier was beyond fear or fawning. He had descended from the cart, and was stooping by the roadside.

It all fell swiftly as a dream. Manders minor raised his hand to his head with a cry, as a jagged flint cannoned on to some rich tree-calf bindings in the bookshelf. Another quoited along the writing-table. Beetle made zealous feint to stop it, and in that endeavor overturned a student's lamp, which dripped, *via* King's papers and some choice books, greasily on to a Persian rug. There was much broken glass on the window-seat; the china basket—McTurk's aversion—cracked to flinders, had dropped her musk plant and its earth over the red rep cushions; Manders minor was bleeding profusely from a cut on the cheek-bone; and King, using strange words, every one of which Beetle treasured, ran forth to find the school-sergeant, that Rabbits-Eggs might be instantly cast into jail.

"Poor chap!" said Beetle, with a false, feigned sympathy. "Let it bleed a little. That'll prevent apoplexy," and he held the blind head skilfully over the table, and the papers on the table, as he guided the howling Manders to the door.

Then did Beetle, alone with the wreckage, return good for evil. How, in that office, a complete set of "Gibbon" was scarred all along the back as by a flint; how so much black and copying ink came to be mingled with Manders's gore on the table-cloth; why the big gum-bottle, unstoppered, had rolled semicircularly across the floor; and in what manner the white china door-knob grew to be painted with more of Manders's young blood, were matters which Beetle did not explain when the rabid King returned to find him standing politely over the reeking hearth-rug.

"You never told me to go, sir," he said, with the air of Casabianca, and King consigned him to the outer darkness.

But it was to a boot-cupboard under the staircase on the ground floor that he hastened, to loose the mirth that was destroying him. He had not drawn breath for a first whoop of triumph when two hands choked him dumb.

"Go to the dormitory and get me my things. Bring 'em to Number Five lavatory. I'm still in tights," hissed Stalky, sitting on his head. "Don't run. Walk."

But Beetle staggered into the form-room next door, and delegated his duty to the yet unenlightened McTurk, with an hysterical précis of the campaign thus far. So it was McTurk, of the wooden visage, who brought the clothes from the dormitory while Beetle panted on a form. Then the three buried themselves in Number Five lavatory, turned on all the taps, filled the place with steam, and dropped weeping into the baths, where they pieced out the war.

"Moi! Je! Ich! Ego!" gasped Stalky. "I waited till I couldn't hear myself think, while you played the drum! Hid in the coal-locker–and tweaked Rabbits-Eggs–and Rabbits-Eggs rocked King. Wasn't it beautiful? Did you hear the glass?"

"Why, he–he–he," shrieked McTurk, one trembling finger pointed at Beetle.

"Why, I–I–I was through it all," Beetle howled; "in his study, being jawed."

"Oh, my soul!" said Stalky with a yell, disappearing under water.

"The–the glass was nothing. Manders minor's head's cut open. La–la–lamp upset all over the rug. Blood on the books and papers. The gum! The gum! The ink! The ink! The ink! Oh, Lord!"

Then Stalky leaped out, all pink as he was, and shook Beetle into some sort of coherence; but his tale prostrated them afresh.

"I bunked for the boot-cupboard the second I heard King go down-stairs. Beetle tumbled in on top of me. The spare key's hid behind the loose board. There isn't a shadow of evidence," said Stalky. They were all chanting together.

"And he turned us out himself–himself–him-*self!"* This from McTurk. "He can't begin to suspect us. Oh, Stalky, it's the loveliest thing we've ever done."

"Gum! Gum! Dollops of gum!" shouted Beetle, his spectacles gleaming through a sea of lather. "Ink and blood all mixed. I held the little beast's head all over the Latin proses for Monday. Golly, how the oil stunk! And Rabbits-Eggs told King to poultice his nose! Did you hit Rabbits-Eggs, Stalky?"

"Did I jolly well not? Tweaked him all over. Did you hear him curse? Oh, I shall be sick in a minute if I don't stop."

But dressing was a slow process, because McTurk was obliged to dance when he heard that the musk basket was broken, and, moreover, Beetle retailed all King's language with emendations and purple insets.

"Shockin'! " said Stalky, collapsing in a helpless welter of half-hitched trousers. "So dam' bad, too, for innocent boys like us! Wonder what they'd say at 'St. Winifred's, *or* the World of School.' By gum! That reminds me we owe the Lower Third one for assaultin' Beetle when he chivied Manders minor. Come on! It's an alibi, Samivel; and, besides, if we let 'em off they'll be worse next time."

The Lower Third had set a guard upon their form-room for the space of a full hour, which to a boy is a lifetime. Now they were busy with their Saturday evening businesses–cooking sparrows over the gas with rusty nibs; brewing unholy drinks in gallipots; skinning moles with pocket-knives; attending to paper trays full of silkworms, or discussing the iniquities of their elders with a freedom, fluency, and point that would have amazed their parents. The blow fell without warning. Stalky upset a form crowded with small boys among their own cooking utensils, McTurk raided the untidy lockers as a terrier digs at a rabbit-hole, while Beetle poured ink upon such heads as he could not appeal to with a Smith's Classical Dictionary. Three brisk minutes accounted for many silkworms, pet larvae, French exercises, school caps, half-prepared bones and skulls, and a dozen pots of home-made sloe jam. It was a great wreckage, and the form-room looked as though three conflicting tempests had smitten it.

"Phew!" said Stalky, drawing breath outside the door (amid groans of "Oh, you beastly ca-ads! You think yourselves awful funny," and so forth). *"That's* all right. Never let the sun go down upon your wrath. Rummy little devils, fags. Got no notion o' combinin'. "

"Six of 'em sat on my head when I went in after Manders minor," said Beetle. "I warned 'em what they'd get, though."

"Everybody paid in full–beautiful feelin'," said McTurk, absently, as they strolled along the corridor. "Don't think we'd better say much about King, though, do you, Stalky?"

"Not *much.* Our line is injured innocence, of course–same as when the Sergeant reported us on suspicion of smoking in the bunkers. If I hadn't thought of buyin' the pepper and spillin' it all over our clothes, he'd have smelt us. King was gha-astly facetious about that. 'Called us bird-stuffers in form for a week."

"Ah, King hates the Natural History Society because little Hartopp is president. Mustn't do anything in the Coll. without glorifyin' King," said McTurk. "But he must be a putrid ass, you know, to suppose at our time o' life we'd go out and stuff birds like fags."

"Poor old King!" said Beetle. "He's awf'ly unpopular in Common-room, and they'll chaff his head off about Rabbits-Eggs. Golly! How lovely! How beautiful! How holy! But you should have seen his face when the first rock came in! *And* the earth from the basket!"

So they were all stricken helpless for five minutes.

They repaired at last to Abanazar's study, and were received reverently.

"What's the matter?" said Stalky, quick to realize new atmospheres.

"You know jolly well," said Abanazar. "You'll be expelled if you get caught. King is a gibbering maniac."

"Who? Which? What? Expelled for how? We only played the war-drum. We've got turned out for that already."

"Do you chaps mean to say you didn't make Rabbits-Eggs drunk and bribe him to rock King's rooms?"

"Bribe him? No, that I'll swear we didn't," said Stalky, with a relieved heart, for he loved not to tell lies. "What a low mind you've got, Pussy! We've been down having a bath. Did Rabbits-Eggs rock King? Strong, per-severin' man King? Shockin'!"

"Awf'ly. King's frothing at the mouth. There's bell for prayers. Come on."

"Wait a sec," said Stalky, continuing the conversation in a loud and cheerful voice, as they descended the stairs. "What did Rabbits-Eggs rock King for?"

"I know," said Beetle, as they passed King's open door. "I was in his study."

"Hush, you ass!" hissed the Emperor of China. "Oh, he's gone down to prayers," said Beetle, watching the shadow of the house-master on the wall. "Rabbits-Eggs was only a bit drunk, swearin' at his horse, and King jawed him through the window, and then, of course, he rocked King."

"Do you mean to say," said Stalky, "that King began it?"

King was behind them, and every well-weighed word went up the staircase like an arrow. "I can only swear," said Beetle, "that King cursed like a bargee. Simply disgustin'. I'm goin' to write to my father about it."

"Better report it to Mason," suggested Stalky. "He knows our tender con-sciences. Hold on a shake. I've got to tie my bootlace."

The other study hurried forward. They did not wish to be dragged into stage asides of this nature. So it was left to McTurk to sum up the situation beneath the guns of the enemy.

"You see," said the Irishman, hanging on the banister, "he begins by bullying little chaps; then he bullies the big chaps; then he bullies some one who isn't connected with the College, and then he catches it. Serves him jolly well right. . . . I beg your pardon, sir. I didn't see you were coming down the staircase."

The black gown tore past like a thunder-storm, and in its wake, three abreast, arms linked, the Aladdin company rolled up the big corridor to prayers, singing with most innocent intention:

> "Arrah, Patsy, mind the baby! Arrah, Patsy, mind the child!
> Wrap him up in an overcoat, he's surely goin' wild!
> Arrah, Patsy, mind the baby; just ye mind the child awhile!
> He'll kick an' bite an' cry all night! Arrah, Patsy, mind the child!"

An Unsavory Interlude

It was a maiden aunt of Stalky who sent him both books, with the inscription, "To dearest Artie, on his sixteenth birthday;" it was McTurk who ordered their hypothecation; and it was Beetle, returned from Bideford, who flung them on the window-sill of Number Five study with news that Bastable would advance but ninepence on the two; "Eric; or, Little by Little," being almost as great a drug as "St. Winifred's." "An' I don't think much of your aunt. We're nearly out of cartridges, too—Artie, dear."

Whereupon Stalky rose up to grapple with him, but McTurk sat on Stalky's head, calling him a "pure-minded boy" till peace was declared. As they were grievously in arrears with a Latin prose, as it was a blazing July afternoon, and as they ought to have been at a house cricket-match, they began to renew their acquaintance, intimate and unholy, with the volumes.

"Here we are!" said McTurk. " 'Corporal punishment produced on Eric the worst effects. He burned *not* with remorse or regret'—make a note o' that, Beetle—'but with shame and violent indignation. He glared'—oh, naughty Eric! Let's get to where he goes in for drink."

"Hold on half a shake. Here's another sample. 'The Sixth,' he says, 'is the palladium of all public schools.' But this lot"—Stalky rapped the gilded book—"can't prevent fellows drinkin' and stealin', an' lettin' fags out of window at night, an'—an' doin' what they please. Golly, what we've missed—not goin' to St. Winifred's! . . ."

"I'm sorry to see any boys of my house taking so little interest in their matches."

Mr. Prout could move very silently if he pleased, though that is no merit in a boy's eyes. He had flung open the study-door without knocking—another sin—and looked at them suspiciously. "Very sorry, indeed, I am to see you frowsting in your studies."

"We've been out ever since dinner, sir," said McTurk wearily. One house-match is just like another, and their "ploy" of that week happened to be rabbit-shooting with saloon-pistols.

"I can't see a ball when it's coming, sir," said Beetle. "I've had my gig-lamps smashed at the Nets till I got excused. I wasn't any good even as a fag, then, sir."

"Tuck is probably your form. Tuck and brewing. Why can't you three take any interest in the honor of your house?"

They had heard that phrase till they were wearied. The "honor of the house" was Prout's weak point, and they knew well how to flick him on the raw.

"If you order us to go down, sir, of course we'll go," said Stalky, with maddening politeness. But Prout knew better than that. He had tried the experiment once at a big match, when the three, self-isolated, stood to attention for half an hour in full view of all the visitors, to whom fags, subsidized for that end, pointed them out as victims of Prout's tyranny. And Prout was a sensitive man.

In the infinitely petty confederacies of the Common-room, King and Macrea, fellow house-masters, had borne it in upon him that by games, and games alone, was salvation wrought. Boys neglected were boys lost. They must be disciplined. Left to himself, Prout would have made a sympathetic house-master; but he was never so left, and with the devilish insight of youth, the boys knew to whom they were indebted for his zeal.

"Must we go down, sir?" said McTurk.

"I don't want to order you to do what a right-thinking boy should do gladly. I'm sorry." And he lurched out with some hazy impression that he had sown good seed on poor ground.

"Now what does he suppose is the use of that?" said Beetle.

"Oh, he's cracked. King jaws him in Common-room about not keepin' us up to the mark, an' Macrea burbles about 'dithcipline,' an' old Heffy sits between 'em sweatin' big drops. I heard Oke (the Common-room butler) talking to Richards (Prout's house-servant) about it down in the basement the other day when I went down to bag some bread," said Stalky.

"What did Oke say?" demanded McTurk, throwing "Eric" into a corner.

"Oh, he said, 'They make more nise nor a nest full o' jackdaws, an' half of it like we'd no ears to our heads that waited on 'em. They talks over old Prout–what he've done an' left undone about his boys. An' how their boys be fine boys, an' his'n be dom bad.' Well, Oke talked like that, you know, and Richards got awf'ly wrathy. He has a down on King for something or other. Wonder why?"

"Why, King talks about Prout in form-room–makes allusions, an' all that–only half the chaps are such asses they can't see what he's drivin' at. And d'you remember what he said about the 'Casual House' last Tuesday? He meant us. They say he says perfectly beastly things to his own house, making fun of Prout's," said Beetle.

"Well, we didn't come here to mix up in their rows," McTurk said wrathfully. "Who'll bathe after call-over? King's takin' it in the cricket-field. Come on." Turkey seized his straw and led the way.

They reached the sun-blistered pavilion over against the gray Pebbleridge just before roll-call, and, asking no questions, gathered from King's voice and manner that his house was on the road to victory.

"Ah, ha!" said he, turning to show the light of his countenance. "Here we have the ornaments of the Casual House at last. You consider cricket beneath you, I believe"–the crowd, flannelled, sniggered–"and from what I have seen this afternoon, I fancy many others of your house hold the same view. And may I ask what you purpose to do with your noble selves till tea-time?"

"Going down to bathe, sir," said Stalky.

"And whence this sudden zeal for cleanliness? There is nothing about you that particularly suggests it. Indeed, so far as I remember–I may be at fault–but a short time ago——"

"Five years, sir," said Beetle hotly.

King scowled. "*One* of you was that thing called a water-funk. Yes, a water-funk. So now you wish to wash? It is well. Cleanliness never injured a boy or–a house. We will proceed to business," and he addressed himself to the call-over board.

"What the deuce did you say anything to him for, Beetle?" said McTurk angrily, as they strolled towards the big, open sea-baths.

" 'Twasn't fair—remindin' one of bein' a water-funk. My first term, too. Heaps of chaps are—when they can't swim."

"Yes, you ass; but he saw he'd fetched you. You ought never to answer King."

"But it wasn't fair, Stalky."

"My Hat! You've been here six years, and you expect fairness. Well, you *are* a dithering idiot."

A knot of King's boys, also bound for the baths, hailed them, beseeching them to wash—for the honor of their house.

"That's what comes of King's jawin' and messin'. Those young animals wouldn't have thought of it unless he'd put it into their heads. Now they'll be funny about it for weeks," said Stalky. "Don't take any notice."

The boys came nearer, shouting an opprobrious word. At last they moved to windward, ostentatiously holding their noses.

"That's pretty," said Beetle. "They'll be sayin' our house stinks next."

When they returned from the baths, damp-headed, languid, at peace with the world, Beetle's forecast came only too true. They were met in the corridor by a fag—a common, Lower-Second fag—who at arm's length handed them a carefully wrapped piece of soap "with the compliments of King's house."

"Hold on," said Stalky, checking immediate attack. "Who put you up to this, Nixon? Rattray and White? (Those were two leaders in King's house.) Thank you. There's no answer."

"Oh, it's too sickening to have this kind o' rot shoved on to a chap. What's the sense of it? What's the fun of it?" said McTurk.

"It will go on to the end of the term, though," Beetle wagged his head sorrowfully. He had worn many jests threadbare on his own account.

In a few days it became an established legend of the school that Prout's house did not wash and were therefore noisome. Mr. King was pleased to smile succulently in form when one of his boys drew aside from Beetle with certain gestures.

"There seems to be some disability attaching to you, my Beetle, or else why should Burton major withdraw, so to speak, the hem of his garments? I confess I am still in the dark. Will some one be good enough to enlighten me?"

Naturally, he was enlightened by half the form.

"Extraordinary! Most extraordinary! However, each house has its traditions, with which I would not for the world interfere. *We* have a prejudice in favor of washing. Go on, Beetle—from *'jugurtha tamen'*—and, if you can, avoid the more flagrant forms of guessing."

Prout's house was furious because Macrea's and Hartopp's houses joined King's to insult them. They called a house-meeting after dinner—an excited and angry meeting of all save the prefects, whose dignity, though they sympathized, did not allow them to attend. They read ungrammatical resolutions, and made speeches beginning, "Gentlemen, we have met on this occasion," and ending with, "It's a beastly shame," precisely as houses have done since time and schools began.

Number Five study attended, with its usual air of bland patronage. At last McTurk, of the lanthorn jaws, delivered himself:

"You jabber and jaw and burble, and that's about all you can do. What's the good of it? King's house'll only gloat because they've drawn you, and King will gloat, too. Besides, that resolution of Orrin's is chock-full of bad grammar, and King'll gloat over *that.*"

"I thought you an' Beetle would put it right, an'—an' we'd post in the corridor," said the composer meekly.

"Par si je le connai. I'm not goin' to meddle with the biznai," said Beetle. "It's a gloat for King's house. Turkey's quite right."

"Well, won't Stalky, then?"

But Stalky puffed out his cheeks and squinted down his nose in the style of Panurge, and all he said was, "Oh, you abject burblers!"

"You're three beastly scabs!" was the instant retort of the democracy, and they went out amid execrations.

"This is piffling," said McTurk. "Let's get our sallies, and go and shoot bunnies."

Three saloon-pistols, with a supply of bulleted breech-caps, were stored in Stalky's trunk, and this trunk was in their dormitory, and their dormitory was a three-bed attic one, opening out of a ten-bed establishment, which, in turn, communicated with the great range of dormitories that ran practically from one end of the College to the other. Macrea's house lay next to Prout's, King's next to Macrea's, and Hartopp's beyond that again. Carefully locked doors divided house from house, but each house, in its internal arrangements–the College had originally been a terrace of twelve large houses–was a replica of the next; one straight roof covering all.

They found Stalky's bed drawn out from the wall to the left of the dormer window, and the latter end of Richards protruding from a two-foot-square cupboard in the wall.

"What's all this? I've never noticed it before. What are you tryin' to do, Fatty?"

"Fillin' basins, Muster Corkran." Richards's voice was hollow and muffled. "They've been savin' me trouble. Yiss."

" 'Looks like it," said McTurk. "Hi! You'll stick if you don't care."

Richards backed puffing.

"I can't rache un. Yiss, 'tess a turncock, Muster McTurk. They've took an' runned all the watter-pipes a storey higher in the houses–runned 'em all along under the 'ang of the heaves, like. Runned 'em in last holidays. *I* can't rache the turncock."

"Let me try," said Stalky, diving into the aperture.

"Slip 'ee to the left, then, Muster Corkran. Slip 'ee to the left, an' feel in the dark."

To the left Stalky wriggled, and saw a long line of lead pipe disappearing up a triangular tunnel, whose roof was the rafters and boarding of the college roof, whose floor was sharp-edged joists, and whose side was the rough studding of the lath and plaster wall under the dormer.

"Rummy show. How far does it go?"

"Right along, Muster Cockran–right along from end to end. Her runs under the 'ang of the heaves. Have 'ee rached the stopcock yet? Mr. King got un put in to save us carryin' watter from downstairs to fill the basins. No place for a lusty man like old Richards. I'm tu thickabout to go ferritin'. Thank 'ee, Muster Corkran."

The water squirted through the tap just inside the cupboard, and, having filled the basins, the grateful Richards waddled away.

The boys sat round-eyed on their beds considering the possibilities of this trove. Two floors below them they could hear the hum of the angry house; for nothing is so still as a dormitory in mid-afternoon of a midsummer term.

"It has been papered over till now." McTurk examined the little door. "If we'd only known before!"

"I vote we go down and explore. No one will come up this time o' day. We needn't keep *cavé.*"

They crawled in, Stalky leading, drew the door behind them, and on all fours embarked on a dark and dirty road full of plaster, odd shavings, and all the raffle that builders leave in the waste room of a house. The passage was perhaps three feet wide, and, except for the struggling light round the edges of the cupboards (there was one to each dormer), almost pitchy dark.

"Here's Macrea's house," said Stalky, his eye at the crack of the third cupboard. "I can see Barnes's name on his trunk. Don't make such a row, Beetle! We can get right to the end of the Coll. Come on! . . . We're in King's house now–I can see a bit of Rattray's trunk. How these beastly boards hurt one's knees!" They heard his nails scraping on plaster.

"That's the ceiling below. Look out! If we smashed that the plaster 'ud fall down in the lower dormitory," said Beetle.

"Let's," whispered McTurk.

"An' be collared first thing? Not much. Why, I can shove my hand ever so far up between these boards."

Stalky thrust an arm to the elbow between the joists.

"No good stayin' here. I vote we go back and talk it over. It's a crummy place. 'Must say I'm grateful to King for his water-works."

They crawled out, brushed one another clean, slid the saloon-pistols down a trouser-leg, and hurried forth to a deep and solitary Devonshire lane in whose flanks a boy might sometimes slay a young rabbit. They threw themselves down under the rank elder bushes, and began to think aloud.

"You know," said Stalky at last, sighting at a distant sparrow, "we could hide our sallies in there like anything."

"Huh!" Beetle snorted, choked, and gurgled. He had been silent since they left the dormitory. "Did you ever read a book called 'The History of a House' or something? I got it out of the library the other day. A French woman wrote it–Violet somebody. But it's translated, you know; and it's very interestin'. Tells you how a house is built."

"Well, if you're in a sweat to find out *that,* you can go down to the new cottages they're building for the coastguard."

"My Hat! I will." He felt in his pockets. "Give me tuppence, some one."

"Rot! Stay here, and don't mess about in the sun."

"Gi' me tuppence."

"I say, Beetle, you aren't stuffy about anything, are you?" said McTurk, handing over the coppers. His tone was serious, for though Stalky often, and McTurk occasionally, maneuvered on his own account, Beetle had never been known to do so in all the history of the confederacy.

"No, I'm not. I'm thinking."

"Well, we'll come, too," said Stalky, with a general's suspicion of his aides.

"Don't want you."

"Oh, leave him alone. He's been taken worse with a poem," said McTurk. "He'll go burbling down to the Pebbleridge and spit it all up in the study when he comes back."

"Then why did he want the tuppence, Turkey? He's gettin' too beastly independent. Hi! There's a bunny. No, it ain't. It's a cat, by Jove! You plug first."

Twenty minutes later a boy with a straw hat at the back of his head, and his hands in his pockets, was staring at workmen as they moved about a half-finished cottage. He produced some ferocious tobacco, and was passed from the forecourt into the interior, where he asked many questions.

"Well, let's have your beastly epic," said Turkey, as they burst into the study, to find Beetle deep in Viollet-le-Duc and some drawings. "We've had no end of a lark."

"Epic? What epic? I've been down to the coastguard."

"No epic? Then we will slay you, O Beetle," said Stalky, moving to the attack. "You've got something up your sleeve. *I* know, when you talk in that tone!"

"Your Uncle Beetle"–with an attempt to imitate Stalky's war-voice–"is a great man."

"Oh, no; he jolly well isn't anything of the kind. You deceive yourself,

Beetle. Scrag him, Turkey!"

"A great man," Beetle gurgled from the floor. "*You* are futile–look out for my tie!–futile burblers. I am the Great Man. I gloat. Ouch! Hear me!"

"Beetle, de-ah"–Stalky dropped unreservedly on Beetle's chest–"we love you, an' you're a poet. If I ever said you were a doggaroo, I apologize; but you know as well as we do that you can't do anything by yourself without mucking it."

"I've got a notion."

"And you'll spoil the whole show if you don't tell your Uncle Stalky. Cough it up, ducky, and we'll see what we can do. Notion, you fat impostor–I knew you had a notion when you went away! Turkey said it was a poem."

"I've found out how houses are built. Le' me get up. The floor-joists of one room are the ceiling-joists of the room below."

"Don't be so filthy technical."

"Well, the man told me. The floor is laid on top of those joists–those boards on edge that we crawled over–but the floor stops at a partition. Well, if you get behind a partition, same as you did in the attic, don't you see that you can shove anything you please under the floor between the floor-boards and the lath and plaster of the ceiling below? Look here. I've drawn it."

He produced a rude sketch, sufficient to enlighten the allies. There is no part of the modern school curriculum that deals with architecture, and none of them had yet reflected whether floors and ceilings were hollow or solid. Outside his own immediate interests the boy is as ignorant as the savage he so admires; but he has also the savage's resource.

"I see," said Stalky. "I shoved my hand there. An' then?"

"An' then . . . They've been calling us stinkers, you know. We might shove somethin' under–sulphur, or something that stunk pretty bad–an' stink 'em out. I know it can be done somehow." Beetle's eyes turned to Stalky handling the diagrams.

"Stinks?" said Stalky interrogatively. Then his face grew luminous with delight. "By gum! I've got it. Horrid stinks! Turkey!" He leaped at the Irishman. "This afternoon–just after Beetle went away! *She's* the very thing!"

"Come to my arms, my beamish boy," caroled McTurk, and they fell into each other's arms dancing. "Oh, frabjous day! Calloo, callay! She will! She will!"

"Hold on," said Beetle. "I don't understand."

"Dearr man! It shall, though. Oh, Artie, my pure-souled youth, let us tell our darling Reggie about Pestiferous Stinkadores."

"Not until after call-over. Come on!"

"I say," said Orrin, stiffly, as they fell into their places along the walls of the gymnasium. "The house are goin' to hold another meeting."

"Hold away, then." Stalky's mind was elsewhere.

"It's about you three this time."

"All right, give 'em my love . . . *Here, sir,*" and he tore down the corridor.

Gamboling like kids at play, with bounds and sidestarts, with caperings and curvetings, they led the almost bursting Beetle to the rabbit-lane, and from under a pile of stones drew forth the new-slain corpse of a cat. Then did Beetle see the inner meaning of what had gone before, and lifted up his voice in thanksgiving for that the world held warriors so wise as Stalky and McTurk.

"Well-nourished old lady, ain't she?" said Stalky. "How long d'you suppose it'll take her to get a bit whiff in a confined space?"

"Bit whiff! What a coarse brute you are!" said McTurk. "Can't a poor pussy-cat get under King's dormitory floor to die without your pursuin' her with your foul innuendoes?"

"What did she die under the floor for?" said Beetle, looking to the future.

"Oh, they won't worry about *that* when they find her," said Stalky.

"A cat may look at a king." McTurk rolled down the bank at his own jest. "Pussy, you don't know how useful you're goin' to be to three pure-souled, high-minded boys."

"They'll have to take up the floor for her, same as they did in Number Nine when the rat croaked. Big medicine–heap big medicine! Phew! Oh, Lord, I wish I could stop laughin', " said Beetle.

"Stinks! Hi, stinks! Clammy ones!" McTurk gasped as he regained his place. "And"–the exquisite humor of it brought them sliding down together in a tangle–"it's all for the honor of the house, too!"

"An' they're holdin' another meetin'–on us," Stalky panted, his knees in the ditch and his face in the long grass. "Well, let's get the bullet out of her and hurry up. The sooner she's bedded out the better."

Between them they did some grisly work with a penknife; between them (ask not who buttoned her to his bosom) they took up the corpse and hastened back, Stalky arranging their plan of action at the full trot.

The afternoon sun, lying in broad patches on the bed-rugs, saw three boys and an umbrella disappear into a dormitory wall. In five minutes they emerged, brushed themselves all over, washed their hands, combed their hair, and descended.

"Are you sure you shoved her far enough under?" said McTurk suddenly.

"Hang it, man, I shoved her the full length of my arm and Beetle's brolly. That must be about six feet. She's bung in the middle of King's big upper ten-bedder. Eligible central situation, *I* call it. She'll stink out his chaps, and Hartopp's and Macrea's, when she really begins to fume. I swear your Uncle Stalky is a great man. Do you realize what a great man he is, Beetle?"

"Well, I had the notion first, hadn't I–? Only–"

"You couldn't do it without your Uncle Stalky, could you?"

"They've been calling us stinkers for a week now," said McTurk. "Oh, *won't* they catch it!"

"Stinker! Yah! Stink-ah!" rang down the corridor.

"And she's there," said Stalky, a hand on either boy's shoulder. "She–is–there, gettin' ready to surprise 'em. Presently she'll begin to whisper to 'em in their dreams. Then she'll whiff. Golly, how she'll whiff! Oblige me by thinkin' of it for two minutes."

They went to their study in more or less of silence. There they began to laugh–laugh as only boys can. They laughed with their foreheads on the tables, or on the floor; laughed at length, curled over the backs of chairs or clinging to a book-shelf; laughed themselves limp.

And in the middle of it Orrin entered on behalf of the house.

"Don't mind us, Orrin; sit down. You don't know how we respect and admire you. There's something about your pure, high young forehead, full of the dreams of innocent boyhood, that's no end fetchin'. It is, indeed."

"The house sent me to give you this." He laid a folded sheet of paper on the table and retired with an awful front.

"It's the resolution! Oh, read it, some one. I'm too silly-sick with laughin' to see," said Beetle.

Stalky jerked it open with a precautionary sniff.

"Phew! Phew! Listen. *'The house notices with pain and contempt the attitude of indiference'*–how many f's in indifference, Beetle?"

"Two for choice."

"Only one here–*'adopted by the occupants of Number Five study in relation to the insults offered to Mr. Prout's house at the recent meeting in Number Twelve form-room, and the house hereby pass a vote of censure on the said study.'* That's all."

"And she bled all down my shirt, too!" said Beetle.

"An' I'm catty all over," said McTurk, "though I washed twice."

"An' I nearly broke Beetle's brolly plantin' her where she would blossom!"

The situation was beyond speech, but not laughter. There was some attempt that night to demonstrate against the three in their dormitory; so they came forth.

"You see," Beetle began suavely as he loosened his braces, "the trouble with you is that you're a set of unthinkin' asses. You've no more brains than spiders. We've told you that heaps of times, haven't we?"

"We'll give all three of you a dormitory lickin'. You always jaw at us as if you were prefects," cried one.

"Oh, no, you won't," said Stalky, "because you know that if you did you'd get the worst of it sooner or later. *We* aren't in any hurry. *We* can afford to wait for our little revenges. You've made howlin' asses of yourselves, and just as soon as King gets hold of your precious resolutions to-morrow you'll find that out. If you aren't sick an' sorry by to-morrow night, I'll–I'll eat my hat."

But or ever the dinner-bell rang the next day Prout's were sadly aware of their error. King received stray members of that house with an exaggerated attitude of fear. Did they purpose to cause him to be dismissed from the College by unanimous resolution? What were their views concerning the government of the school, that he might hasten to give effect to them? He would not offend them for worlds; but he feared–he sadly feared–that his own house, who did not pass resolutions (but washed), might somewhat deride.

King was a happy man, and his house, basking in the favor of his smile, made that afternoon a long penance to the misled Prouts. And Prout himself, with a dull and lowering visage, tried to think out the rights and wrongs of it all, only plunging deeper into bewilderment. Why should his house be called "Stinkers"? Truly, it was a small thing, but he had been trained to believe that there is no smoke without fire. He approached King in Common-room with a sense of injustice, but King was pleased to be full of airy persiflage that tide, and brilliantly danced dialectical rings round Prout.

"Now," said Stalky at bedtime, making pilgrimage through the dormitories before the prefects came up, "*now* what have you got to say for yourselves? Foster, Carton, Finch, Longbridge, Marlin, Brett! I heard you chaps catchin' it from King–he made hay of you–an' all you could do was to wriggle an' grin an' say, 'Yes, sir,' an' 'No, sir,' an' 'O, sir,' an' 'Please, sir'! You an' your resolution! Urh!"

"Oh, shut up, Stalky."

"Not a bit of it. You're a gaudy lot of resolutionists, you are! You've made a sweet mess of it. Perhaps you'll have the decency to leave us alone next time."

Here the house grew angry, and in many voices pointed out how this blunder would never have come to pass if Number Five study had helped them from the first.

"But you chaps are so beastly conceited, an'–an' you swaggered into the meetin' as if we were a lot of idiots," growled Orrin of the resolution.

"That's precisely what you *are!* That's what we've been tryin' to hammer into your thick heads all this time," said Stalky. "Never mind, we'll forgive you. Cheer up. You can't help bein' asses, you know," and, the enemy's flank deftly turned, Stalky hopped into bed.

That night was the first of sorrow among the jubilant King's. By some accident of under-floor drafts the cat did not vex the dormitory beneath which she lay, but the next one to the right; stealing on the air rather as a pale-blue sensation than as any poignant offense. But the mere adumbration of an odor is enough for the sensitive nose and clean tongue of youth. Decency demands that we draw several carbolized sheets over what the dormitory said to Mr. King and what Mr. King replied. He was genuinely proud of his house and fastidious in all that concerned their well-being. He came; he sniffed; he said things. Next morning a boy in that dormitory confided to his bosom friend, a fag of Macrea's, that there was trouble in their midst which King would fain keep secret.

But Macrea's boy had also a bosom friend in Prout's, a shock-headed fag of malignant disposition, who, when he had wormed out the secret, told—told it in a high-pitched treble that rang along the corridor like a bat's squeak.

"An'—an' they've been calling us 'stinkers' all this week. Why, Harland minor says they simply can't sleep in his dormitory for the stink. Come on!"

"With one shout and with one cry" Prout's juniors hurled themselves into the war, and through the interval between first and second lesson some fifty twelve-year-olds were embroiled on the gravel outside King's windows to a tune whose *leit-motif* was the word "stinker."

"Hark to the minute-gun at sea!" said Stalky. They were in their study collecting books for second lesson—Latin, with King. "I thought his azure brow was a bit cloudy at prayers. 'She is comin', sister Mary. She is—' "

"If they make such a row now, what *will* they do when she really begins to look up an' take notice?"

"Well, no vulgar repartee, Beetle. All we want is to keep out of this row like gentlemen."

" 'Tis but a little faded flower.' Where's my Horace? Look here, I don't understand what she means by stinkin' out Rattray's dormitory first. We holed in under White's didn't we?" asked McTurk, with a wrinkled brow.

"Skittish little thing. She's rompin' about all over the place, I suppose."

"My Aunt! King'll be a cheerful customer at second lesson. I haven't prepared my Horace one little bit, either," said Beetle. "Come on!"

They were outside the form-room door now. It was within five minutes of the bell, and King might arrive at any moment.

Turkey elbowed into a cohort of scuffling fags, cut out Thornton tertius (he that had been Harland's bosom friend), and bade him tell his tale.

It was a simple one, interrupted by tears. Many of King's house had already battered him for libel.

"Oh, it's nothing," McTurk cried. "He says that King's house stinks. That's all."

"Stale!" Stalky shouted. "We knew that years ago, only we didn't choose to run about shoutin' 'stinker.' We've got some manners, if they haven't. Catch a fag, Turkey, and make sure of it."

Turkey's long arm closed on a hurried and anxious ornament of the Lower Second.

"Oh, McTurk, please let me go. I don't stink—I swear I don't!"

"Guilty conscience!" cried Beetle. "Who said you did?"

"What d'you make of it?" Stalky punted the small boy into Beetle's arms.

"Snf! Snf! He does, though. I think it's leprosy—or thrush. P'raps it's both. Take it away."

"Indeed, Master Beetle"—King generally came to the house-door for a minute or two as the bell rang—"we are vastly indebted to you for your diagnosis, which seems to reflect almost as much credit on the natural unwholesomeness of your mind as it does upon your pitiful ignorance of the diseases of which you discourse so glibly. We will, however, test your knowledge in other directions."

That was a merry lesson, but, in his haste to scarify Beetle, King clean neglected to give him an imposition, and since at the same time he supplied him with many priceless adjectives for later use, Beetle was well content, and applied himself most seriously throughout third lesson (algebra with little Hartopp) to composing a poem entitled "The Lazar-House."

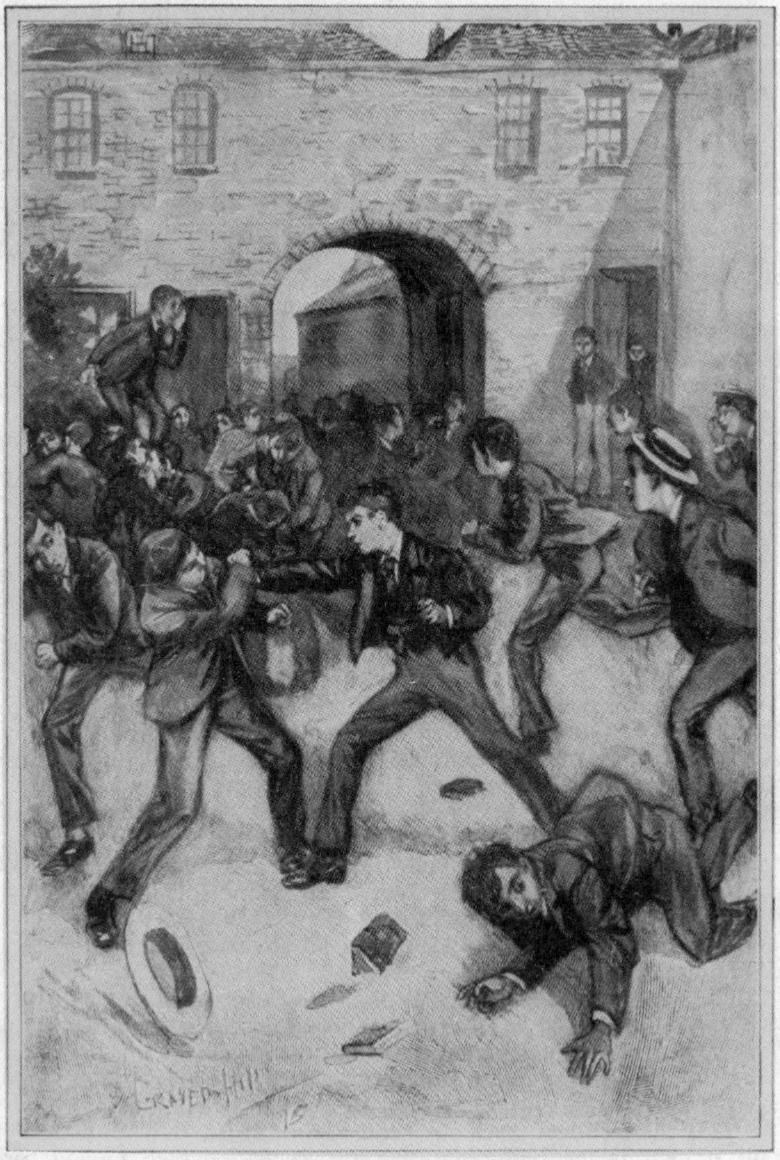

"PROUST'S JUNIORS HURLED THEMSELVES INTO THE WAR."

After dinner King took his house to bathe in the sea off the Pebbleridge. It was an old promise; but he wished he could have evaded it, for all Prout's lined up by the Fives Court and cheered with intention. In his absence not less than half the school invaded the infected dormitory to draw their own conclusions. The cat had gained in the last twelve hours, but a battlefield of the fifth day could not have been so flamboyant as the spies reported.

"My word, she *is* doin' herself proud," said Stalky. "Did you ever smell anything like it? Ah, an' she isn't under White's dormitory at all yet."

"But she will be. Give her time," said Beetle. "She'll twine like a giddy honeysuckle. What howlin' Lazarites they are! No house is justified in makin' itself a stench in the nostrils of decent——"

"High-minded, pure-souled boys. *Do* you burn with remorse and regret?" said McTurk, as they hastened to meet the house coming up from the sea. King had deserted it, so speech was unfettered. Round its front played a crowd of skirmishers–all houses mixed–flying, reforming, shrieking insults. On its tortured flanks marched the Hoplites, seniors hurling jests one after another–simple and primitive jests of the Stone Age. To these the three added themselves, dispassionately, with an air of aloofness, almost sadly.

"And they look all right, too," said Stalky. "It can't be Rattray, can it? Rattray?"

No answer.

"Rattray, dear? He seems stuffy about something or other. Look here, old man, *we* don't bear any malice about your sending that soap to us last week, do we? Be cheerful, Rat. You can live this down all right. I dare say it's only a few fags. Your house is so beastly slack, though."

"You aren't going back to the house, are you?" said McTurk. The victims desired nothing better. "You've simply no conception of the reek up there. Of course, frowzin' as you do, you wouldn't notice it; but, after this nice wash and the clean, fresh air, even *you'd* be upset. 'Much better camp on the Burrows. We'll get you some straw. Shall we?" The house hurried in to the tune of "John Brown's body," sung by loving schoolmates, and barricaded themselves in their form-room. Straightway Stalky chalked a large cross, with "Lord, have mercy upon us," on the door, and left King to find it.

The wind shifted that night and wafted a carrion-reek into Macrea's dormitories; so that boys in nightgowns pounded on the locked door between the houses, entreating King's to wash. Number Five study went to second lesson with not more than half a pound of camphor apiece in their clothing; and King, too wary to ask for explanations, gibbered a while and hurled them forth. So Beetle finished yet another poem at peace in the study.

"They're usin' carbolic now. Malpas told me," said Stalky. "King thinks it's the drains."

"She'll need a lot o' carbolic," said McTurk. "No harm tryin', I suppose. It keeps King out of mischief."

"I swear I thought he was goin' to kill me when I sniffed just now. He didn't mind Burton major sniffin' at me the other day, though. He never stopped Alexander howlin' 'Stinker!' into our form-room before–before we doctored 'em. He just grinned," said Stalky. "What was he frothing over you for, Beetle?"

"Aha! That was my subtle jape. I had him on toast. You know he always jaws about the learned Lipsius."

" 'Who at the age of four'–*that* chap?" said McTurk.

"Yes. Whenever he hears I've written a poem. Well, just as I was sittin' down, I whispered, 'How is our learned Lepsius?' to Burton major. Old Butt grinned like an owl. *He* didn't know what I was drivin' at; but King jolly well did. That was really why he hove us out. Ain't you grateful? Now shut up. I'm goin' to write the 'Ballad of the Learned Lipsius.' "

"Keep clear of anything coarse, then," said Stalky. "I shouldn't like to be coarse on this happy occasion."

"Not for wo-orlds. What rhymes to 'stenches,' some one?"

In Common-room at lunch King discoursed acridly to Prout of boys with prurient minds, who perverted their few and baleful talents to sap discipline and corrupt their equals, to deal in foul imagery and destroy reverence.

"But you didn't seem to consider this when your house called us–ah–stinkers. If you hadn't assured me that you never interfere with another man's house, I should almost believe that it was a few casual remarks of yours that started all this nonsense."

Prout had endured much, for King always took his temper to meals.

"You spoke to Beetle yourself, didn't you? Something about not bathing, and being a water-funk?" the school chaplain put in. "I was scoring in the pavilion that day."

"I may have–jestingly. I really don't pretend to remember every remark I let fall among small boys; and full well I know the Beetle has no feelings to be hurt."

"May be; but he, or they–it comes to the same thing–have the fiend's own knack of discovering a man's weak place. I confess I rather go out of my way to conciliate Number Five study. It may be soft, but so far, I believe, I am the only man here whom they haven't maddened by their–well–attentions."

"That is all beside the point. I flatter myself I can deal with them alone as occasion arises. But if they feel themselves morally supported by those who should wield an absolute and open-handed justice, then I say that my lot is indeed a hard one. Of all things I detest, I admit that anything verging on disloyalty among ourselves is the first."

The Common-room looked at one another out of the corners of their eyes, and Prout blushed.

"I deny it absolutely," he said. "Er–in fact, I own that I personally object to all three of them. It is not fair, therefore, to—"

"How long do you propose to allow it?" said King.

"But surely," said Macrea, deserting his usual ally, "the blame, if there be any, rests with you, King. You can't hold them responsible for the–you prefer the good old Anglo-Saxon, I believe–stink in your house. My boys are complaining of it now."

"What can you expect? You know what boys are. Naturally they take advantage of what to them is a heaven-sent opportunity," said little Hartopp. "What *is* the trouble in your dormitories, King?"

Mr. King explained that as he had made it the one rule of nis life never to interfere with another man's house, so he expected not to be too patently interfered with. They might be interested to learn–here the chaplain heaved a weary sigh–that he had taken all steps that, in his poor judgment, would meet the needs of the case. Nay, further, he had himself expended, with no thought of reimbursement, sums, the amount of which he would not specify, on disinfectants. This he had done because he knew by bitter–by most bitter–experience that the management of the college was slack, dilatory, and inefficient. He might even add, almost as slack as the administration of certain houses which now thought fit to sit in judgment on his actions. With a short summary of his scholastic career, and a précis of his qualifications, including his degrees, he withdrew, slamming the door.

"Heigho!" said the chaplain. "Ours is a dwarfing life–a belittling life, my brethren. God help all schoolmasters! They need it."

"I don't like the boys, I own"–Prout dug viciously with his fork into the table-cloth–"and I don't pretend to be a strong man, as you know. But I confess I can't see any reason why I should take steps against Stalky and the others because King happens to be annoyed by–by—"

"Falling into the pit he has digged," said little Hartopp. "Certainly not, Prout. No one accuses *you* of setting one house against another through sheer idleness."

"A belittling life—a belittling life." The chaplain rose. "I go to correct French exercises. By dinner King will have scored off some unlucky child of thirteen; he will repeat to us every word of his brilliant repartees, and all will be well."

"But about those three. Are they so prurient-minded?"

"Nonsense," said little Hartopp. "If you thought for a minute, Prout, you would see that the 'precocious flow of fetid imagery' that King complains of, is borrowed wholesale from King. *He* 'nursed the pinion that impelled the steel.' Naturally he does not approve. Come into the smoking-room for a minute. It isn't fair to listen to boys; but they should be now rubbing it into King's house outside. Little things please little minds."

The dingy den off the Common-room was never used for anything except gowns. Its windows were ground glass; one could not see out of it, but one could hear almost every word on the gravel outside. A light and wary footstep came up from Number Five.

"Rattray!" in a subdued voice—Rattray's study fronted that way. "D'you know if Mr. King's anywhere about? I've got a——" McTurk discreetly left the end of the sentence open.

"No. He's gone out," said Rattray unguardedly.

"Ah! The learned Lipsius is airing himself, is he? His Royal Highness has gone to fumigate." McTurk climbed on the railings, where he held forth like the never-wearied rook.

"Now in all the Coll. there was no stink like the stink of King's house, for it stank vehemently and none knew what to make of it. Save King. And he washed the fags *privatim et seriatim.* In the fishpools of Hesbon washed he them, with an apron about his loins."

"Shut up, you mad Irishman!" There was the sound of a golf-ball spurting up gravel.

"It's no good getting wrathy, Rattray. We've come to jape with you. Come on, Beetle. They're all at home. You can wind 'em."

"Where's the Pomposo Stinkadore? 'Tisn't safe for a pure-souled, high-minded boy to be seen round his house these days. Gone out, has he? Never mind. I'll do the best I can, Rattray. I'm *in loco parentis* just now."

("One for you, Prout," whispered Macrea, for this was Mr. Prout's pet phrase.)

"I have a few words to impart to you, my young friend. We will discourse together a while."

Here the listening Prout sputtered: Beetle, in a strained voice, had chosen a favorite gambit of King's.

"I repeat, Master Rattray, we will confer, and the matter of our discourse shall not be stinks, for that is a loathsome and obscene word. We will, with your good leave—granted, I trust, Master Rattray, granted, I trust—study this—this scabrous upheaval of latent demoralization. What impresses me most is not so much the blatant indecency with which you swagger abroad under your load of putrescence" (you must imagine this discourse punctuated with golf-balls, but old Rattray was ever a bad shot) "as the cynical immorality with which you revel in your abhorrent aromas. Far be it from me to interfere with another's house——"

("Good Lord!" said Prout, "but this *is* King."

"Line for line, letter for letter; listen," said little Hartopp.)

"But to say that you stink, as certain lewd fellows of the baser sort aver, is to say nothing—less than nothing. In the absence of your beloved house-master, for whom no one has a higher regard than myself, I will, if you will allow me, explain the grossness–the unparallelled enormity–the appalling fetor of the stenches (I believe in the good old Anglo-Saxon word), stenches, sir, with which you have seen fit to infect your house. . . . Oh, bother! I've forgotten the rest, but it was very beautiful. Aren't you grateful to us for laborin' with you this way, Rattray? Lots of chaps 'ud never have taken the trouble, but we're grateful, Rattray."

"Yes, we're horrid grateful," grunted McTurk. "We don't forget that soap. *We*'re polite. Why ain't you polite, Rat?"

"Hallo!" Stalky cantered up, his cap over one eye. "Exhortin' the Whiffers, eh? I'm afraid they're too far gone to repent. Rattray! White! Perowne! Malpas! No answer. This is distressin'. This is truly distressin'. Bring out your dead, you glandered lepers!"

"You think yourself funny, don't you?" said Rattray, stung from his dignity by this last. "It's only a rat or something under the floor. We're going to have it up to-morrow."

"Don't try to shuffle it off on a poor dumb animal, and dead, too. I loathe prevarication. 'Pon my soul, Rattray—"

"Hold on. The Hartoffles never said ' 'Pon my soul' in all his little life," said Beetle critically.

("Ah!" said Prout to little Hartopp.)

"Upon my word, sir, upon my word, sir, I expected better things of you, Rattray. Why can you not own up to your misdeeds like a man? Have *I* ever shown any lack of confidence in *you?*"

("It's not brutality," murmured little Hartopp, as though answering a question no one had asked. "It's boy; only boy.")

"And this was the house," Stalky changed from a pecking, fluttering voice to tragic earnestness. "This was the–the–open cesspit that dared to call us 'stinkers.' And now–and now, it tries to shelter itself behind a dead rat. You annoy me, Rattray. You disgust me! You irritate me unspeakably! Thank Heaven, I am a man of equable temper—"

("This is to your address, Macrea," said Prout.

"I fear so, I fear so.")

"Or I should scarcely be able to contain myself before your mocking visage."

"*Cavé!*" in an undertone. Beetle had spied King sailing down the corridor.

"And what may you be doing here, my little friends?" the house-master began. "I had a fleeting notion–correct me if I am wrong" (the listeners with one accord choked)–"that if I found you outside my house I should visit you with dire pains and penalties."

"We were just goin' for a walk, sir," said Beetle.

"And you stopped to speak to Rattray *en route?*"

"Yes, sir. We've been throwing golf-balls," said Rattray, coming out of the study.

("Old Rat is more of a diplomat than I thought. So far he is strictly within the truth," said little Hartopp. "Observe the ethics of it, Prout.")

"Oh, you were sporting with them, were you? I must say I do not envy you your choice of associates. I fancied they might have been engaged in some of the prurient discourse with which they have been so disgustingly free of late. I should strongly advise you to direct your steps most carefully in the future. Pick up those golf-balls." He passed on.

. . . .

Next day Richards, who had been a carpenter in the Navy, and to whom odd jobs were confided, was ordered to take up a dormitory floor; for Mr. King held that something must have died there.

"We need not neglect all our work for a trumpery incident of this nature;

though I am quite aware that little things please little minds. Yes, I have decreed the boards to be taken up after lunch under Richards's auspices. I have no doubt it will be vastly interesting to a certain type of so-called intellect; but any boy of my house or another's found on the dormitory stairs will *ipso facto* render himself liable to three hundred lines."

The boys did not collect on the stairs, but most of them waited outside King's. Richards had been bound to cry the news from the attic window, and, if possible, to exhibit the corpse.

"'Tis a cat, a dead cat!" Richards's face showed purple at the window. He had been in the chamber of death and on his knees for some time.

"Cat be blowed!" cried McTurk. "It's a dead fag left over from last term. Three cheers for King's dead fag!"

They cheered lustily.

"Show it, show it! Let's have a squint at it!" yelled the juniors. "Give her to the Bug-hunters." (This was the Natural History Society.) "The cat looked at the King–and died of it! Hoosh! Yai! Yaow! Maiow! Ftzz!" were some of the cries that followed.

Again Richards appeared.

"She've been"–he checked himself suddenly–"dead a long taime."

The school roared.

"Well, come on out for a walk," said Stalky in a well-chosen pause. "It's all very disgustin', and I do hope the Lazar-house won't do it again."

"Do what?" a King's boy cried furiously.

"Kill a poor innocent cat every time you want to get off washing. It's awfully hard to distinguish between you as it is. I prefer the cat, I must say. She isn't quite so whiff. What are you goin' to do, Beetle?"

"Je vais gloater. Je vais gloater tout le blessed afternoon. *Jamais j'ai gloaté comme je gloaterai aujourd'hui. Nous bunkerons aux* bunkers."

And it seemed good to them so to do.

. . . .

Down in the basement, where the gas flickers and the boots stand in racks, Richards, amid his blacking-brushes, held forth to Oke of the Common-room, Gumbly of the dining-halls, and fair Lena of the laundry.

"Yiss. Her were in a shockin' staate an' condition. Her nigh made me sick, I tal 'ee. But I rowted un out, and I rowted un out, an' I made all shipshape, though her smelt like to bilges."

"Her died mousin', I rackon, poor thing," said Lena.

"Then her moused different to any made cat o' God's world, Lena. I up with the top-board, an' she were lying on her back, an' I turned un ovver with the brume-handle, an' 'twas her back was all covered with the plaster from 'twixt the lathin'. Yiss, I tal'ee. An' under her head there lay, like, so's to say, a little pillow o' plaster druv up in front of her by raison of her slidin' along on her back. No cat niver went mousin' on her back, Lena. Some one had shoved her along right underneath, so far as they could shove un. Cats don't make theyselves pillows for to die on. Shoved along, she were, when she was settin' for to be cold, laike."

"Oh, yeou'm too clever to live, Fatty. Yeou go get wed an' taught some sense," said Lena, the affianced of Gumbly.

"Larned a little 'fore iver some maidens was born. Sarved in the Queen's Navy, I have, where yeou'm taught to use your eyes. Yeou go 'tend your own business, Lena."

"Do 'ee mean what you'm been tellin' us?" said Oke.

"Ask me no questions, I'll give 'ee no lies. Bullet-hole clane thru from side to side, an' tu heart-ribs broke like withies. I seed un when I turned un ovver. They'm clever, oh, they'm clever, but they'm not too clever for old Richards!

'Twas on the born tip o' my tongue to tell, tu, but . . . he said us niver washed, he did. Let his dom boys call us 'stinkers,' he did. Sarve un dom well raight, I say!"

Richards spat on a fresh boot and fell to his work, chuckling.

The Impressionists

THEY HAD DROPPED into the chaplain's study for a Saturday night smoke—all four house-masters—and the three briars and the one cigar reeking in amity proved the Rev. John Gillett's good generalship. Since the discovery of the cat, King had been too ready to see affront where none was meant, and the Reverend John, buffer-state and general confidant, had worked for a week to bring about a good understanding. He was fat, clean-shaven, except for a big mustache, of an imperturbable good temper, and, those who loved him least said, a guileful Jesuit. He smiled benignantly upon his handiwork—four sorely tried men talking without very much malice.

"Now remember," he said, when the conversation turned that way, "I impute nothing. But every time that any one has taken direct steps against Number Five study, the issue has been more or less humiliating to the taker."

"I can't admit that. I pulverize the egregious Beetle daily for his soul's good; and the others with him," said King.

"Well, take your own case, King, and go back a couple of years. Do you remember when Prout and you were on their track—for hutting and trespass, wasn't it? Have you forgotten Colonel Dabney?"

The others laughed. King did not care to be reminded of his career as a poacher.

"That was one instance. Again, when you had rooms below them—I always said that that was entering the lion's den—you turned them out."

"For making disgusting noises. Surely, Gillett, you don't excuse—"

"All I say is that you turned them out. That same evening your study was wrecked."

"By Rabbits-Eggs—most beastly drunk—from the road," said King. "What has that—?"

The Reverend John went on.

"Lastly, they conceive that aspersions are cast upon their personal cleanliness—a most delicate matter with all boys. Ve-ry good. Observe how, in each case, the punishment fits the crime. A week after your house calls them 'stinkers,' King, your house is, not to put too fine a point on it, stunk out by a dead cat who chooses to die in the one spot where she can annoy you most. Again the long arm of coincidence! *Summa.* You accuse them of trespass. Through some absurd chain of circumstances—they may or may not be at the other end of it—you and Prout are made to appear as trespassers. You evict them. For a time your study is made untenable. I have drawn the parallel in the last case. Well?"

"She was under the center of White's dormitory," said King. "There are double floor-boards there to deaden noise. No boy, even in my own house, could possibly have pried up the boards without leaving some trace—and Rabbits-Eggs was phenomenally drunk that other night."

"They are singularly favored by fortune. That is all I ever said. Personally,

I like them immensely, and I believe I have a little of their confidence. I confess I like being called 'Padre.' They are at peace with me; consequently I am not treated to bogus confessions of theft."

"You mean Mason's case?" said Prout heavily. "That always struck me as peculiarly scandalous. I thought the Head should have taken up the matter more thoroughly. Mason may be misguided, but at least he is thoroughly sincere and means well."

"I confess I cannot agree with you, Prout," said the Reverend John. "He jumped at some silly tale of theft on their part; accepted another boy's evidence without, so far as I can see, any inquiry; and–frankly, I think he deserved all he got."

"They deliberately outraged Mason's best feelings," said Prout. "A word to me on their part would have saved the whole thing. But they preferred to lure him on; to play on his ignorance of their characters——"

"That may be," said King, "but I don't like Mason. I dislike him for the very reason that Prout advances to his credit. He means well."

"Our criminal tradition is not theft–among ourselves, at least," said little Hartopp.

"For the head of a house that raided seven head of cattle from the innocent pot-wallopers of Northam, isn't that rather a sweeping statement?" said Macrea.

"Precisely so," said Hartopp, unabashed. "That, with gate-lifting, and a little poaching and hawk-hunting on the cliffs, is our salvation."

"It does us far more harm as a school–" Prout began.

"Than any hushed-up scandal could? Quite so. Our reputation among the farmers is most unsavory. But I would much sooner deal with any amount of ingenious crime of that nature than–some other offenses."

"They may be all right, but they are unboylike, abnormal, and, in my opinion, unsound," Prout insisted. "The moral effect of their performances must pave the way for greater harm. It makes me doubtful how to deal with them. I might separate them."

"You might, of course; but they have gone up the school together for six years. *I* shouldn't care to do it," said Macrea.

"They use the editorial 'we,'" said King, irrelevantly. "It annoys me. 'Where's your prose, Corkran?' 'Well, sir, we haven't quite done it yet.' 'We'll bring it in a minute,' and so on. And the same with the others."

"There's great virtue in that 'we,'" said little Hartopp. "You know I take them for trig. McTurk may have some conception of the meaning of it; but Beetle is as the brutes that perish about sines and cosines. He copies serenely from Stalky, who positively rejoices in mathematics."

"Why don't you stop it?" said Prout.

"It rights itself at the exams. Then Beetle shows up blank sheets, and trusts to his 'English' to save him from a fall. I fancy he spends most of his time with me in writing verse."

"I wish to Heaven he would transfer a little of his energy in that direction to Elegiacs." King jerked himself upright. "He is, with the single exception of Stalky, the very vilest manufacturer of 'barbarous hexameters' that I have ever dealt with."

"The work is combined in that study" said the chaplain. "Stalky does the mathematics, McTurk the Latin, and Beetle attends to their English and French. At least, when he was in the sick-house last month——"

"Malingering," Prout interjected.

"Quite possibly. I found a very distinct falling off in their 'Roman d'un Jeune Homme Pauvre' translations."

"I think it is profoundly immoral," said Prout. "I've always been opposed to the study system."

"It would be hard to find any study where the boys don't help each other; but in Number Five the thing has probably been reduced to a system," said little Hartopp. "They have a system in most things."

"They confess as much," said the Reverend John. "I've seen McTurk being hounded up the stairs to elegise the 'Elegy in a Churchyard,' while Beetle and Stalky went to punt-about."

"It amounts to systematic cribbing," said Prout, his voice growing deeper and deeper.

"No such thing," little Hartopp returned. "You can't teach a cow the violin."

"In intention it is cribbing."

"But we spoke under the seal of the confessional, didn't we?" said the Reverend John.

"You say you've heard them arranging their work in this way, Gillett," Prout persisted.

"Good Heavens! Don't make *me* Queen's evidence, my dear fellow. Hartopp is equally incriminated. If they ever found out that I had sneaked, our relations would suffer–and I value them."

"I think your attitude in this matter is weak," said Prout, looking round for support. "It would be really better to break up the study–for a while–wouldn't it?"

"Oh, break it up by all means," said Macrea. "We shall see then if Gillett's theory holds water."

"Be wise, Prout. Leave them alone, or calamity will overtake you; and what is much more important, they will be annoyed with me. I am too fat, alas! to be worried by bad boys. Where are you going?"

"Nonsense! They would not dare–but I am going to think this out," said Prout. "It needs thought. In intention they cribbed, and I must think out my duty."

"He's perfectly capable of putting the boys on their honor. It's *I* that am a fool." The Reverend John looked round remorsefully. "Never again will I forget that a master is not a man. Mark my words," said the Reverend John. "There will be trouble."

. . . .

But by the yellow Tiber
Was tumult and affright.

Out of the blue sky (they were still rejoicing over the cat war) Mr. Prout had dropped into Number Five, read them a lecture on the enormity of cribbing, and bidden them return to the form-rooms on Monday. They had raged, solo and chorus, all through the peaceful Sabbath, for their sin was more or less the daily practice of all the studies.

"What's the good of cursing?" said Stalky at last. "We're all in the same boat. We've got to go back and consort with the house. A locker in the form-room, and a seat at prep. in Number Twelve." (He looked regretfully round the cozy study which McTurk, their leader in matters of Art, had decorated with a dado, a stencil, and cretonne hangings.)

"Yes! Heffy lurchin' into the form-rooms like a frowzy old retriever, to see if we aren't up to something. You know he never leaves his house alone, these days," said McTurk. "Oh, it will be giddy!"

"Why aren't you down watchin' cricket? I like a robust, healthy boy. You mustn't frowst in a form-room. Why don't you take an interest in your house? Yah!" quoted Beetle.

"Yes, why don't we? Let's! We'll take an interest in the house. We'll take no end of interest in the house! He hasn't had us in the form-rooms for a year. We've learned a lot since then. Oh, we'll make it a be-autiful house before we've done! 'Member that chap in 'Eric' or 'St. Winifred's'—Belial somebody? I'm goin' to be Belial," said Stalky, with an ensnaring grin.

"Right O," said Beetle, "and I'll be Mammon. I'll lend money at usury—that's what they do at all schools accordin' to the B. O. P. Penny a week on a shillin'. That'll startle Heffy's weak intellect. You can be Lucifer, Turkey."

"What have I got to do?" McTurk also smiled.

"Head conspiracies—and cabals—and boycotts. Go in for that 'stealthy intrigue' that Heffy is always talkin' about. Come on!"

The house received them on their fall with the mixture of jest and sympathy always extended to boys turned out of their study. The known aloofness of the three made them more interesting.

"Quite like old times, ain't it?" Stalky selected a locker and flung in his books. "We've come to sport with you, my young friends, for a while, because our beloved house-master has hove us out of our diggin's."

" 'Serve you jolly well right," said Orrin, "you cribbers!"

"This will never do," said Stalky. "We can't maintain our giddy prestige, Orrin, de-ah, if you make these remarks."

They wrapped themselves lovingly ahout the boy, thrust him to the opened window, and drew down the sash to the nape of his neck. With an equal swiftness they tied his thumbs together behind his back with a piece of twine, and then, because he kicked furiously, removed his shoes.

There Mr. Prout happened to find him a few minutes later, guillotined and helpless, surrounded by a convulsed crowd who would not assist.

Stalky, in an upper form-room, had gathered himself allies against vengeance. Orrin presently tore up at the head of a boarding party, and the form-room grew one fog of dust through which boys wrestled, stamped, shouted, and yelled. A desk was carried away in the tumult, a knot of warriors reeled into and split a door-panel, a window was broken, and a gas-jet fell. Under cover of the confusion the three escaped to the corridor, whence they called in and sent up passers-by to the fray.

"Rescue, Kings! Kings! Kings! Number Twelve form-room! Rescue, Prouts—Prouts! Rescue, Macreas! Rescue, Hartopps!"

The juniors hurried out like bees aswarm, asking no questions, clattered up the staircase, and added themselves to the embroilment.

"Not bad for the first evening's work," said Stalky, rearranging his collar. "I fancy Prout'll be somewhat annoyed. We'd better establish an *alibi.*" So they sat on Mr. King's railings till prep.

"You see," quoth Stalky, as they strolled up to prep. with the ignoble herd, "if you get the houses well mixed up an' scufflin', it's even bettin' that some ass will start a real row. Hullo, Orrin, you look rather metagrobolized."

"It was all your fault, you beast! You started it. We've got two hundred lines apiece, and Heffy's lookin' for you. Just see what that swine Malpas did to my eye!"

"I like your saying *we* started it. Who called us cribbers? Can't your infant mind connect cause and effect yet? Some day you'll find out that it don't pay to jest with Number Five."

"Where's that shillin' you owe me?" said Beetle suddenly.

Stalky could not see Prout behind him, but returned the lead without a quaver.

"I only owed you ninepence, you old usurer."

"You've forgotten the interest," said McTurk. "A halfpenny a week per bob is Beetle's charge. You must be beastly rich, Beetle."

"Well, Beetle lent me sixpence." Stalky came to a full stop and made as to work it out on his fingers. "Sixpence on the nineteenth, didn't he?"

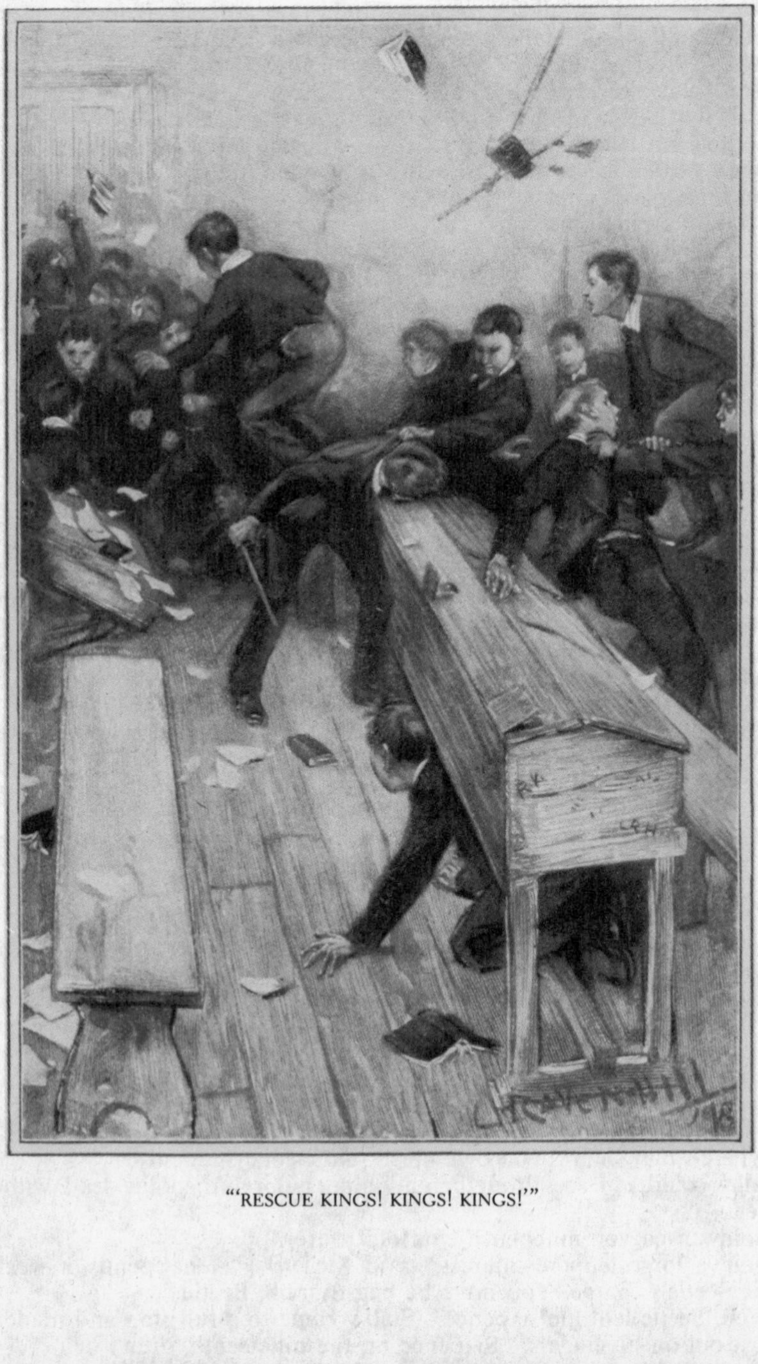

"'RESCUE KINGS! KINGS! KINGS!'"

"Yes; but you've forgotten you paid no interest on the other bob–the one I lent you before."

"But you took my watch as security." The game was developing itself almost automatically.

"Never mind. Pay me my interest, or I'll charge you interest on interest. Remember, I've got your note-of-hand!" shouted Beetle.

"You are a cold-blooded Jew," Stalky groaned.

"Hush!" said McTurk very loudly indeed, and started as Prout came upon them.

"I didn't see you in that disgraceful affair in the form-room just now," said he.

"What, sir? We're just come up from Mr. King's," said Stalky. "Please, sir, what am I to do about prep.? They've broken the desk you told me to sit at, and the form's just swimming with ink."

"Find another seat–find another seat. D'you expect me to dry-nurse you? I wish to know whether you are in the habit of advancing money to your associates, Beetle?"

"No, sir; not as a general rule, sir."

"It is a most reprehensible habit. I thought that my house, at least, would be free from it. Even with my opinion of you, I hardly thought it was one of your vices."

"There's no harm in lending money, sir, is there?"

"I am not going to bandy words with you on your notions of morality. How much have you lent Corkran?"

"I–I don't quite know," said Beetle. It is difficult to improvise a going concern on the spur of the minute.

"You seemed certain enough just now."

"I think it's two and fourpence," said McTurk, with a glance of cold scorn at Beetle.

In the hopelessly involved finances of the study there was just that sum to which both McTurk and Beetle laid claim, as their share in the pledging of Stalky's second-best Sunday trousers. But Stalky had maintained for two terms that the money was his "commission" for effecting the pawn; and had, of course, spent it on a study "brew."

"Understand this, then. You are not to continue your operations as a money-lender. Two and fourpence, you said, Corkran?"

Stalky had said nothing, and continued so to do.

"Your influence for evil is quite strong enough without buying a hold over your companions." He felt in his pockets, and (oh joy!) produced a florin and fourpence. "Bring me what you call Corkran's note-of-hand, and be thankful that I do not carry the matter any further. The money is stopped from your pocket-money, Corkran. The receipt to my study, at once."

Little they cared! Two and fourpence in a lump is worth six weekly sixpences any hungry day of the week.

"But what the dooce *is* a note-of-hand?" said Beetle. "I only read about it in a book."

"Now you've jolly well got to make one," said Stalky.

"Yes–but our ink don't turn black till next day. S'pose he'll spot that?"

"Not him. He's too worried," said McTurk. "Sign your name on a bit of import-paper, Stalky, and write, 'I O U two and fourpence.' Aren't you grateful to me for getting that out of Prout? Stalky'd never have paid. . . . Why, you ass!"

Mechanically Beetle had handed over the money to Stalky as treasurer of the study. The custom of years is not lightly broken.

In return for the document, Prout expounded to Beetle the enormity of money-lending, which, like everything except compulsory cricket, corrupted houses and destroyed good feeling among boys, made youth cold and calculating, and opened the door to all evil. Finally, did Beetle know of any other cases? If so, it was his duty as proof of repentance to let his house-master know. No names need be mentioned.

Beetle did not know—at least, he was not quite sure, sir. How could he give evidence against his friends? The house might, of course—here he feigned an anguished delicacy—be full of it. He was not in a position to say. He had not met with any open competition in his trade; but if Mr. Prout considered it was a matter that affected the honor of the house (Mr. Prout did consider it precisely that), perhaps the house-prefects would be better . . .

He spun it out till half-way through prep.

"And," said the amateur Shylock, returning to the form-room and dropping at Stalky's side, "if he don't think the house is putrid with it, I'm several Dutchmen—that's all. . . . I've been to Mr. Prout's study, sir." This to the prep.-master. "He said I could sit where I liked, sir. . . . Oh, he is just tricklin' with emotion. . . . Yes, sir, I'm only askin' Corkran to let me have a dip in his ink."

After prayers, on the road to the dormitories, Harrison and Craye, senior house-prefects, zealous in their office, waylaid them with great anger.

"What have you been doing to Heffy this time, Beetle? He's been jawing us all the evening."

"What has His Serene Transparency been vexin' you for?" said McTurk.

"About Beetle lendin' money to Stalky," began Harrison; "and then Beetle went and told him that there was any amount of money-lendin' in the house."

"No, you don't," said Beetle, sitting on a bootbasket. "That's just what I didn't tell him. I spoke the giddy truth. He asked me if there was much of it in the house; and I said I didn't know."

"He thinks you're a set of filthy Shylocks," said McTurk. "It's just as well for you he don't think you're burglars. You know he never gets a notion out of his conscientious old head."

"Well-meanin' man. Did it all for the best." Stalky curled gracefully round the stair-rail. "Head in a drain-pipe. Full confession in the left boot. Bad for the honor of the house—very."

"Shut up," said Harrison. "You chaps always behave as if you were jawin' us when we come to jaw you."

"You're a lot too cheeky," said Craye.

"I don't quite see where the cheek comes in, except on your part, in interferin' with a private matter between me an' Beetle after it has been settled by Prout." Stalky winked cheerfully at the others.

"That's the worst of clever little swots," said McTurk, addressing the gas. "They get made prefects before they have any tact, and then they annoy chaps who could really help 'em to look after the honor of the house."

"We won't trouble you to do that!" said Craye hotly.

"Then what are you badgerin' us for?" said Beetle. "On your own showing, you've been so beastly slack, looking after the house, that Prout believes it's a nest of money-lenders. I've told him that I've lent money to Stalky, and no one else. I don't know whether he believes me, but that finishes my case. The rest is *your* business."

"Now we find out," Stalky's voice rose, "that there is apparently an organized conspiracy throughout the house. For aught we know, the fags may be lendin' and borrowin' far beyond their means. *We* aren't responsible for it. We're only the rank and file."

"Are you surprised we don't wish to associate with the house?" said McTurk, with dignity. "We've kept ourselves to ourselves in our study till we were turned out, and now we find ourselves let in for—for this sort of thing. It's simply disgraceful."

"Then you hector and bullyrag us on the stairs," said Stalky, "about matters that are your business entirely. You know we aren't prefects."

"You threatened us with a prefect's lickin' just now," said Beetle, boldly inventing as he saw the bewilderment in the faces of the enemy.

"And if you expect you'll gain anything from us by your way of approachin' us, you're jolly well mistaken. That's all. Good-night."

They clattered up-stairs, injured virtue on every inch of their backs.

"But–but what the dickens have *we* done?" said Harrison, amazedly, to Craye.

"I don't know. Only–it always happens that way when one has anything to do with them. They're so beastly plausible."

And Mr. Prout called the good boys into his study anew, and succeeded in sinking both his and their innocent minds ten fathoms deeper in blindfolded bedazement. He spoke of steps and measures, of tone and loyalty in the house and to the house, and urged them to take up the matter tactfully.

So they demanded of Beetle whether he had any connection with any other establishment. Beetle promptly went to his house-master, and wished to know by what right Harrison and Craye had reopened a matter already settled between him and his house-master. In injured innocence no boy excelled Beetle.

Then it occurred to Prout that he might have been unfair to the culprit, who had not striven to deny or palliate his offense. He sent for Harrison and Craye, reprehending them very gently for the tone they had adopted to a repentant sinner, and when they returned to their study, they used the language of despair. They then made headlong inquisition through the house, driving the fags to the edge of hysterics, and unearthing, with tremendous pomp and parade, the natural and inevitable system of small loans that prevails among small boys.

"You see, Harrison, Thornton minor lent me a penny last Saturday, because I was fined for breaking the window; and I spent it at Keyte's. I didn't know there was any harm in it. And Wray major borrowed twopence from me when my uncle sent me a post-office order–I cashed it at Keyte's–for five bob; but he'll pay me back before the holidays. We didn't know there was anything wrong in it."

They waded through hours of this kind of thing, but found no usury, or anything approaching to Beetle's gorgeous scale of interest. The seniors–for the school had no tradition of deference to prefects outside compulsory games–told them succinctly to go about their business. They would not give evidence on any terms. Harrison was one idiot, and Craye was another; but the greatest of all, they said, was their house-master.

When a house is thoroughly upset, however good its conscience, it breaks into knots and coteries–small gatherings in the twilight, box-room committees, and groups in the corridor. And when from group to group, with an immense affectation of secrecy, three wicked boys steal, crying *"Cavé"* when there is no need of caution, and whispering "Don't tell!" on the heels of trumpery confidences that instant invented, a very fine air of plot and intrigue can be woven round such a house.

At the end of a few days, it dawned on Prout that he moved in an atmosphere of perpetual ambush. Mysteries hedged him on all sides, warnings ran before his heavy feet, and countersigns were muttered behind his attentive back. McTurk and Stalky invented many absurd and idle phrases–catch-words that swept through the house as fire through stubble. It was a rare jest, and the only practical outcome of the Usury Commission, that one boy should say to a friend, with awful gravity, "Do you think there's much of it going on in the house?" The other would reply, "Well, one can't be too careful, you know." The effect on a house-master of humane conscience and good intent may be imagined. Again, a man who has sincerely devoted himself to gaining the esteem of his charges does not like to hear himself described, even at a distance, as "Popularity Prout" by a dark and scowling Celt with a fluent tongue. A rumor that stories–unusual stories–are told in the form-rooms, between the lights, by a boy who does not command his confidence, agitates such a man; and even elaborate and tender politeness–for the courtesy wise-grown men offer to a bewildered child was the courtesy that Stalky wrapped round Prout–restores not his peace of mind.

"The tone of the house seems changed–changed for the worse," said Prout to Harrison and Craye. "Have you noticed it? I don't for an instant impute—"

He never imputed anything; but, on the other hand, he never did anything else, and, with the best intentions in the world, he had reduced the house-prefects to a state as nearly bordering on nervous irritation as healthy boys can know. Worst of all, they began at times to wonder whether Stalky & Co. had not some truth in their often-repeated assertions that Prout was a gloomy ass.

"As you know, I am not the kind of man who puts himself out for every little thing he hears. *I* believe in letting the house work out their own salvation–with a light guiding hand on the reins, of course. But there is a perceptible lack of reverence–a lower tone in matters that touch the honor of the house, a sort of hardness."

Oh, Prout he is a nobleman, a nobleman, a nobleman!
Our Heffy is a nobleman–
He does an awful lot,
Because his popularity–
Oh, pop-u-pop-u-larity–
His giddy popularity
Would suffer did he not!

The study door stood ajar; and the song, borne by twenty clear voices, came faint from a form-room. The fags rather liked the tune; the words were Beetle's.

"That's a thing no sensible man objects to," said Prout with a lop-sided smile; "but you know straws show which way the wind blows. Can you trace it to any direct influence? I am speaking to you now as heads of the house."

"There isn't the least doubt of it," said Harrison angrily. "I know what you mean, sir. It all began when Number Five study came to the form-rooms. There's no use blinkin' it, Craye. You know that, too."

"They make things rather difficult for us, sometimes," said Craye. "It's more their manner than anything else, that Harrison means."

"Do they hamper you in the discharge of your duties, then?"

"Well, no, sir. They only look on and grin–and turn up their noses generally."

"Ah," said Prout sympathetically.

"I think, sir," said Craye, plunging into the business boldly, "it would be a great deal better if they were sent back to their study–better for the house. They are rather old to be knocking about the form-rooms."

"They are younger than Orrin, or Flint, and a dozen others that I can think of."

"Yes, sir; but that's different, somehow. They're rather influential. They have a knack of upsettin' things in a quiet way that one can't take hold of. At least, if one does—"

"And you think they would be better in their own study again?"

Emphatically Harrison and Craye were of that opinion. As Harrison said to Craye, afterwards, "They've weakened our authority. They're too big to lick;

they've made an exhibition of us over this usury business, and we're a laughing-stock to the rest of the school. I'm going up (for Sandhurst, understood) next term. They've managed to knock me out of half my work already with their—their lunacy. If they go back to their study we may have a little peace."

"Hullo, Harrison." McTurk ambled round the corner, with a roving eye on all possible horizons. "Bearin' up, old man? That's right. Live it down! Live it down!"

"What d'you mean?"

"You look a little pensive," said McTurk. "Exhaustin' job superintendin' the honor of the house, ain't it? By the way, how are you off for mares'-nests?"

"Look here," said Harrison, hoping for instant reward. "We've recommended Prout to let you go back to your study."

"The dooce you have! And who under the sun are *you* to interfere between us and our house-master? Upon my Sam, you two try us very hard—you do, indeed. Of course we don't know how far you abuse your position to prejudice us with Mr. Prout; but when you deliberately stop me to tell me you've been makin' arrangements behind our back—in secret—with Prout—I—I don't know really what we ought to do."

"That's beastly unfair!" cried Craye.

"It is." McTurk had adopted a ghastly solemnity that sat well on his long, lean face. "Hang it all! A prefect's one thing and an usher's another; but you seem to combine 'em. You recommend this—you recommend that! *You* say how and when we go back to our study!"

"But—but—we thought you'd like it, Turkey. We did, indeed. You know you'll be ever so much more comfortable there." Harrison's voice was almost tearful.

McTurk turned away as though to hide his emotions.

"They're broke!" He hunted up Stalky and Beetle in a box-room. "They're sick! They've been beggin' Heffy to let us go back to Number Five. Poor devils! Poor little devils!"

"It's the olive branch," was Stalky's comment. "It's the giddy white flag, by gum! Come to think of it, we *have* metagrobolized 'em."

Just after tea that day, Mr. Prout sent for them to say that if they chose to ruin their future by neglecting their work, it was entirely their own affair. He wished them, however, to understand that their presence in the form-rooms could not be tolerated one hour longer. He personally did not care to think of the time he must spend in eliminating the traces of their evil influences. How far Beetle had pandered to the baser side of youthful imagination he would ascertain later; and Beetle might be sure that if Mr. Prout came across any soul-corrupting consequences——

"Consequences of what, sir?" said Beetle, genuinely bewildered this time; and McTurk quietly kicked him on the ankle for being "fetched" by Prout.

Beetle, the house-master continued, knew very well what was intended. Evil and brief had been their careers under his eye; and as one standing *in loco parentis* to their yet uncontaminated associates, he was bound to take his precautions. The return of the study key closed the sermon.

"But what was the baser-side-of-imagination business?" said Beetle on the stairs.

"I never knew such an ass as you are for justifyin' yourself," said McTurk. "I hope I jolly well skinned your ankle. Why do you let yourself be drawn by everybody?"

"Draws be blowed! I must have tickled him up in some way I didn't know about. If I'd had a notion of that before, of course I could have rubbed it in better. It's too late now. What a pity! 'Baser side.' What *was* he drivin' at?"

"Never mind," said Stalky. "I knew we could make it a happy little house. I said so, remember–but I swear I didn't think we'd do it so soon."

. . . .

"No," said Prout most firmly in Common-room. "I maintain that Gillett is wrong. True, I let them return to their study."

"With your known views on cribbing, too?" purred little Hartopp. "What an immoral compromise!"

"One moment," said the Reverend John. "I–we–all of us have exercised an absolutely heart-breaking discretion for the last ten days. Now we want to know. Confess–have you known a happy minute since—"

"As regards my house, I have not," said Prout. "But you are entirely wrong in your estimate of those boys. In justice to the others–in self-defence—"

"Ha! I said it would come to that," murmured the Reverend John.

"—I was forced to send them back. Their moral influence was unspeakable–simply unspeakable."

And bit by bit he told his tale, beginning with Beetle's usury, and ending with the house-prefects' appeal.

"Beetle in the *rôle* of Shylock is new to me," said King, with twitching lips. "I heard rumors of it—"

"Before?" said Prout.

"No, after you had dealt with them; but I was careful not to inquire. I never interfere with—"

"I myself," said Hartopp, "would cheerfully give him five shillings if he could work out one simple sum in compound interest without three gross errors."

"Why–why–why!" Mason, the mathematical master, stuttered, a fierce joy on his face, "you've been had–precisely the same as me!"

"And so you held an inquiry?" Little Hartopp's voice drowned Mason's ere Prout caught the import of the sentence.

"The boy himself hinted at the existence of a good deal of it in the house," said Prout.

"He is past master in that line," said the chaplain. "But, as regards the honor of the house—"

"They lowered it in a week. I have striven to build it up for years. My own house-prefects–and boys do not willingly complain of each other–besought me to get rid of them. You say you have their confidence, Gillett: they may tell you another tale. As far as I am concerned, they may go to the devil in their own way. I'm sick and tired of them," said Prout bitterly.

But it was the Reverend John, with a smiling countenance, who went to the devil just after Number Five had cleared away a very pleasant little brew (it cost them two and fourpence) and was settling down to prep.

"Come in, Padre, come in," said Stalky, thrusting forward the best chair. "We've only met you official-like these last ten days."

"You were under sentence," said the Reverend John. "I do not consort with malefactors."

"Ah, but we're restored again," said McTurk. "Mr. Prout has relented."

"Without a stain on our characters," said Beetle. "It was a painful episode, Padre, most painful."

"Now, consider for a while, and perpend, *mes enfants.* It is about your characters that I've called to-night. In the language of the schools, what the dooce *have* you been up to in Mr. Prout's house? It isn't anything to laugh over. He says that you so lowered the tone of the house he had to pack you back to your studies. Is that true?"

"Every word of it, Padre."

"Don't be flippant, Turkey. Listen to me. I've told you very often that no boys in the school have a greater influence for good or evil than you have. You know I don't talk about ethics and moral codes, because I don't believe that the young of the human animal realizes what they mean for some years to come. All the same, I don't want to think you've been perverting the juniors. Don't interrupt, Beetle. Listen to me! Mr. Prout has a notion that you have been corrupting your associates somehow or other."

"Mr. Prout has so many notions, Padre," said Beetle wearily. "Which one is this?"

"Well, he tells me that he heard you telling a story in the twilight in the form-room, in a whisper. And Orrin said, just as he opened the door, 'Shut up, Beetle; it's too beastly.' Now then?"

"You remember Mrs. Oliphant's 'Beleaguered City' that you lent me last term?" said Beetle.

The Padre nodded.

"I got the notion out of that. Only, instead of a city, I made it the Coll. in a fog–besieged by ghosts of dead boys, who hauled chaps out of their beds in the dormitory. All the names are quite real. You tell it in a whisper, you know–with the names. Orrin didn't like it one little bit. None of 'em have ever let me finish it. It gets just awful at the end part."

"But why in the world didn't you explain to Mr. Prout, instead of leaving him under the impression——?"

"Padre Sahib," said McTurk, "it isn't the least good explainin' to Mr. Prout. If he hasn't one impression, he's bound to have another."

"He'd do it with the best o' motives. He's *in loco parentis*," purred Stalky.

"You young demons!" the Reverend John replied. "And am I to understand that the–the usury business was another of your house-master's impressions?"

"Well–we helped a little in that," said Stalky. "I did owe Beetle two and fourpence–at least, Beetle says I did, but I never intended to pay him. Then we started a bit of an argument on the stairs, and–and Mr. Prout dropped into it accidental. That was how it was, Padre. He paid me cash down like a giddy Dook (stopped it out of my pocket-money just the same), and Beetle gave him my note-of-hand all correct. I don't know what happened after that."

"I was too truthful," said Beetle. "I always am. You see, he was under an impression, Padre, and I suppose I ought to have corrected that impression; but of course I couldn't be *quite* certain that his house wasn't given over to money-lendin', could I? I thought the house-prefects might know more about it than I did. They ought to. They're giddy palladiums of public schools."

"They did, too–by the time they'd finished," said McTurk. "As nice a pair of conscientious, well-meanin', upright, pure-souled boys as you'd ever want to meet, Padre. They turned the house upside down–Harrison and Craye–with the best motives in the world."

"They said so. 'They said it very loud and clear. They went and shouted in our ear,' " said Stalky.

"My own private impression is that all three of you will infallibly be hanged," said the Reverend John.

"Why, *we* didn't do anything," McTurk replied. "It was all Mr. Prout. Did you ever read a book about Japanese wrestlers? My uncle–he's in the Navy–gave me a beauty once."

"Don't try to change the subject, Turkey."

"I'm not, sir. I'm givin' an illustration–same as a sermon. These wrestler-chaps have got some sort of trick that lets the other chap do all the work. Then they give a little wriggle, and he upsets himself. It's called *shibbuwichee* or *tokonoma,* or somethin'. Mr. Prout's a *shibbuwicher.* It isn't our fault."

"Did you suppose we went round corruptin' the minds of the fags?" said

Beetle. "They haven't any, to begin with; and if they had, they're corrupted long ago. I've been a fag, Padre."

"Well, I fancied I knew the normal range of your iniquities; but if you take so much trouble to pile up circumstantial evidence against yourselves, you can't blame any one if—"

"We don't blame any one, Padre. We haven't said a word against Mr. Prout, have we?" Stalky looked at the others. "We love him. He hasn't a notion how we love him."

"H'm! You dissemble your love very well. Have you ever thought who got you turned out of your study in the first place?"

"It was Mr. Prout turned us out," said Stalky, with significance.

"Well, I was that man. I didn't mean it; but some words of mine, I'm afraid, gave Mr. Prout the impression—"

Number Five laughed aloud.

"You see it's just the same thing with you, Padre," said McTurk. "He *is* quick to get an impression, ain't he? But you mustn't think we don't love him, 'cause we do. There isn't an ounce of vice about him."

A double knock fell on the door.

"The Head to see Number Five study in his study at once," said the voice of Foxy, the school sergeant.

"Whew!" said the Reverend John. "It seems to me that there is a great deal of trouble coming for some people."

"My word! Mr. Prout's gone and told the Head," said Stalky. "He's a moral double-ender. Not fair, luggin' the Head into a house-row."

"I should recommend a copy-book on a–h'm–safe and certain part," said the Reverend John disinterestedly.

"Huh! He licks across the shoulders, an' it would slam like a beastly barn-door," said Beetle. "Good night, Padre. We're in for it."

Once more they stood in the presence of the Head–Belial, Mammon, and Lucifer. But they had to deal with a man more subtle than them all. Mr. Prout had talked to him, heavily and sadly, for half an hour; and the Head had seen all that was hidden from the house-master.

"You've been bothering Mr. Prout," he said pensively. "House-masters aren't here to be bothered by boys more than is necessary. I don't like being bothered by these things. You are bothering *me*. That is a very serious offense. You see it?"

"Yes, sir."

"Well, now, I purpose to bother you, on personal and private grounds, because you have broken into my time. You are much too big to lick, so I suppose I shall have to mark my displeasure in some other way. Say, a thousand lines apiece, a week's gating, and a few things of that kind. Much too big to lick, aren't you?"

"Oh, no, sir," said Stalky cheerfully; for a week's gating in the summer term is serious.

"Ve-ry good. Then we will do what we can. I wish you wouldn't bother me."

It was a fair, sustained, equable stroke, with a little draw to it, but what they felt most was his unfairness in stopping to talk between executions. Thus:

"Among the–lower classes this would lay me open to a charge of–assault. You should be more grateful for your–privileges than you are. There is a limit–one finds it by experience, Beetle–beyond which it is never safe to pursue private vendettas, because–don't move–sooner or later one comes–into collision with the–higher authority, who has studied the animal. *Et ego*–McTurk, please–*in Arcadia vixi.* There's a certain flagrant injustice about this that ought to appeal to–your temperament. And that's all! You will tell your house-master that you have been formally caned by me."

"My word!" said McTurk, wriggling his shoulder-blades all down the corridor. "That was business! The Prooshan Bates has an infernal straight eye."

"Wasn't it wily of me to ask for the lickin'," said Stalky, "instead of those impots?"

"Rot! We were in for it from the first. *I* knew the cock of his old eye," said Beetle. "I was within an inch of blubbing."

"Well, I didn't exactly smile," Stalky confessed.

"Let's go down to the lavatory and have a look at the damage. One of us can hold the glass and t'others can squint."

They proceeded on these lines for some ten minutes. The wales were very red and very level. There was not a penny to choose between any of them for thoroughness, efficiency, and a certain clarity of outline that stamps the work of the artist.

"What are you doing down there?" Mr. Prout was at the head of the lavatory stairs, attracted by the noise of splashing.

"We've only been caned by the Head, sir, and we're washing off the blood. The Head said we were to tell you. We were coming to report ourselves in a minute, sir. *(Sotto voce.)* That's a score for Heffy!"

"Well, he deserves to score something, poor devil," said McTurk, putting on his shirt. "We've sweated a stone and a half off him since we began."

"But look here, why aren't we wrathy with the Head? He said it was a flagrant injustice. So it is!" said Beetle.

"Dear man," said McTurk, and vouchsafed no further answer.

It was Stalky who laughed till he had to hold on by the edge of a basin.

"You *are* a funny ass! What's that for?" said Beetle.

"I'm–I'm thinking of the flagrant injustice of it!"

The Moral Reformers

THERE WAS NO disguising the defeat. The victory was to Prout, but they grudged it not. If he had broken the rules of the game by calling in the Head, they had had a good run for their money.

The Reverend John sought the earliest opportunity of talking things over. Members of a bachelor Common-room, of a school where masters' studies are designedly dotted among studies and form-rooms, can, if they choose, see a great deal of their charges. Number Five had spent some cautious years in testing the Reverend John. He was emphatically a gentleman. He knocked at a study door before entering; he comported himself as a visitor and not a strayed lictor; he never prosed, and he never carried over into official life the confidences of idle hours. Prout was ever an unmitigated nuisance; King came solely as an avenger of blood; even little Hartopp, talking natural history, seldom forgot his office; but the Reverend John was a guest desired and beloved by Number Five.

Behold him, then, in their only arm-chair, a bent briar between his teeth, chin down in three folds on his clerical collar, and blowing like an amiable whale, while Number Five discoursed of life as it appeared to them, and specially of that last interview with the Head–in the matter of usury.

"One licking once a week would do you an immense amount of good," he said, twinkling and shaking all over; "and, as you say, you were entirely in the right."

"Ra-ather, Padre! We could have proved it if he'd let us talk," said Stalky; "but he didn't. The Head's a downy bird."

"He understands you perfectly. Ho! ho! Well, you worked hard enough for it."

"But he's awfully fair. He doesn't lick a chap in the morning an' preach at him in the afternoon," said Beetle.

"He can't; he ain't in Orders, thank goodness," said McTurk. Number Five held the very strongest views on clerical head-masters, and were ever ready to meet their pastor in argument.

"Almost all other schools have clerical Heads," said the Reverend John gently.

"It isn't fair on the chaps," Stalky replied. "Makes 'em sulky. Of course it's different with *you,* sir. You belong to the school–same as we do. I mean ordinary clergymen."

"Well, I am a most ordinary clergyman; and Mr. Hartopp's in Orders, too."

"Ye–es but he took 'em after he came to the Coll. We saw him go up for his exam. That's all right," said Beetle. "But just think if the Head went and got ordained!"

"What would happen, Beetle?"

"Oh, the Coll. 'ud go to pieces in a year, sir. There's no doubt o' that."

"How d'you know?" The Reverend John was smiling.

"We've been here nearly six years now. There are precious few things about the Coll. we don't know," Stalky replied. "Why, even you came the term after I did, sir. I remember your asking our names in form your first lesson. Mr. King, Mr. Prout, and the Head, of course, are the only masters senior to us–in that way."

"Yes, we've changed a good deal–in Common-room."

"Huh!" said Beetle with a grunt. "They came here, an' they went away to get married. Jolly good riddance, too!"

"Doesn't our Beetle hold with matrimony?"

"No, Padre; don't make fun of me. I've met chaps in the holidays who've got married house-masters. It's perfectly awful! They have babies and teething and measles and all that sort of thing right bung *in* the school; and the masters' wives give tea-parties–tea-parties, Padre!–and ask the chaps to breakfast."

"That don't matter so much," said Stalky. "But the house-masters let their houses alone, and they leave everything to the prefects. Why, in one school, a chap told me, there were big baize doors and a passage about a mile long between the house and the master's house. They could do just what they pleased."

"Satan rebuking sin with a vengeance."

"Oh, larks are right enough; but you know what we mean, Padre. After a bit it gets worse an' worse. Then there's a big bust-up and a row that gets into the papers, and a lot of chaps are expelled, you know."

"Always the wrong un's; don't forget that. Have a cup of cocoa, Padre?" said McTurk with the kettle.

"No, thanks; I'm smoking. Always the wrong 'uns? Pro-ceed, my Stalky."

"And then"–Stalky warmed to the work–"everybody says, 'Who'd ha' thought it? Shockin' boys! Wicked little kids!' It all comes of havin' married house-masters, *I* think."

"A Daniel come to judgment."

"But it does," McTurk interrupted. "I've met chaps in the holidays, an' they've told me the same thing. It looks awfully pretty for one's people to see—a nice separate house with a nice lady in charge, an' all that. But it isn't. It takes the house-masters off their work, and it gives the prefects a heap too much power, an'—an'—it rots up everything. You see, it isn't as if we were just an ordinary school. We take crammers' rejections as well as good little boys like Stalky. We've got to do that to make our name, of course, and we get 'em into Sandhurst somehow or other, don't we?"

"True, O Turk. Like a book thou talkest, Turkey."

"And so we want rather different masters, don't you think so, to other places? We aren't like the rest of the schools."

"It leads to all sorts of bullyin', too, a chap told me," said Beetle.

"Well, you *do* need most of a single man's time, I must say." The Reverend John considered his hosts critically. "But do you never feel that the world—the Common-room—is too much with you sometimes?"

"Not exactly—in summer, anyhow." Stalky's eye roved contentedly to the window. "Our bounds are pretty big, too, and they leave us to ourselves a good deal."

"For example, here am I sitting in your study, very much in your way, eh?"

"Indeed you aren't, Padre. Sit down. Don't go, sir. You know we're glad whenever you come."

There was no doubting the sincerity of the voices. The Reverend John flushed a little with pleasure and refilled his briar.

"And we generally know where the Common-room are,' said Beetle triumphantly. "Didn't you come through our lower dormitories last night after ten, sir?"

"I went to smoke a pipe with your house-master. No, I didn't give him any impressions. I took a short cut through your dormitories."

"I sniffed a whiff of 'baccy, this mornin'. Yours is stronger than Mr. Prout's. *I* knew," said Beetle, wagging his head.

"Good heavens!" said the Reverend John absently. It was some years before Beetle perceived that this was rather a tribute to innocence than observation. The long, light, blindless dormitories, devoid of inner doors, were crossed at all hours of the night by masters visiting one another; for bachelors sit up later than married folk. Beetle had never dreamed that there might be a purpose in this steady policing.

"Talking about bullying," the Reverend John resumed, "you all caught it pretty hot when you were fags, didn't you?"

"Well, we must have been rather awful little beasts," said Beetle, looking serenely over the gulf between eleven and sixteen. "My Hat, what bullies they were then—Fairburn, 'Gobby' Maunsell, and all that gang!"

" 'Member when 'Gobby' called us the Three Blind Mice, and we had to get up on the lockers and sing while he buzzed inkpots at us?" said Stalky. "They *were* bullies if you like!"

"But there isn't any of it now," said McTurk soothingly.

"That's where you make a mistake. We're all inclined to say that everything is all right as long as we aren't ourselves hurt. I sometimes wonder if it is extinct—bullying."

"Fags bully each other horrid; but the upper forms are supposed to be swottin' for exams. They've got something else to think about," said Beetle.

"Why? What do you think?" Stalky was watching the chaplain's face.

"I have my doubts." Then, explosively, "On my word, for three moderately intelligent boys you aren't very observant. I suppose you were too busy making things warm for your house-master to see what lay under your noses when you were in the form-rooms last week?"

"What, sir? I—I swear we didn't see anything," said Beetle.

"Then I'd advise you to look. When a little chap is whimpering in a corner and wears his clothes like rags, and never does any work, and is notoriously the dirtiest little 'corridor-caution' in the Coll., something's wrong somewhere."

"That's Clewer," said McTurk under his breath.

"Yes, Clewer. He comes to me for his French. It's his first term, and he's almost as complete a wreck as you were, Beetle. He's not naturally clever, but he has been hammered till he's nearly an idiot."

"Oh, no. They sham silly to get off more lickings," said Beetle. "*I* know that."

"I've never actually seen him knocked about," said the Reverend John.

"The genuine article don't do that in public," said Beetle. "Fairburn never touched me when any one was looking on."

"You needn't swagger about it, Beetle," said McTurk. "We all caught it in our time."

"But I got it worse than any one," said Beetle. "If you want an authority on bullyin', Padre, come to me. Corkscrews–brush-drill–keys–head-knucklin'–arm-twistin'–rockin'–Ag Ags–and all the rest of it."

"Yes. I do want you as an authority, or rather I want you as an authority to stop it–all of you."

"What about Abana and Pharpar, Padre–Harrison and Craye? They are Mr. Prout's pets," said McTurk a little bitterly. "*We* aren't even sub-prefects."

"I've considered that, but on the other hand, since most bullying is mere thoughtlessness——"

"Not one little bit of it, Padre," said McTurk. "Bullies like bullyin'. They mean it. They think it up in lesson and practise it in the quarters."

"Never mind. If the thing goes up to the prefects it may make another house-row. You've have one already. Don't laugh. Listen to me. I ask you–my own Tenth Legion–to take the thing up quietly. I want little Clewer made to look fairly clean and decent——"

"Blowed if *I* wash him!" whispered Stalky.

"Decent and self-respecting. As for the other boy, whoever he is, you can use your influence"–a purely secular light flickered in the chaplain's eye–"in any way you please to–to dissuade him. That's all. I'll leave it to you. Good-night, *mes enfants.*"

. . . .

"Well, what are we goin' to do?" Number Five stared at each other.

"Young Clewer would give his eyes for a place to be quiet in. *I* know that," said Beetle. "If we made him a study-fag, eh?"

"No!" said McTurk firmly. "He's a dirty little brute, and he'd mess up everything. Besides, we ain't goin' to have any beastly Erickin'. D'you want to walk about with your arm round his neck?"

"He'd clean out the jam-pots, anyhow; an' the burnt-porridge saucepan–it's filthy now."

"Not good enough," said Stalky, bringing up both heels with a crash on the table. "If we find the merry jester who's been bullyin' him an' make him happy, that'll be all right. Why didn't we spot him when we were in the form-rooms, though?"

"Maybe a lot of fags have made a dead set at Clewer. They do that sometimes."

"Then we'll have to kick the whole of the lower school in our house–on spec. Come on," said McTurk.

"Keep your hair on! We mustn't make a fuss about the biznai. Whoever it is he's kept quiet or we'd have seen him," said Stalky. "We'll walk round and sniff about till we're sure."

They drew the house form-rooms, accounting for every junior and senior against whom they had suspicions; investigated, at Beetle's suggestion, the lavatories and box-rooms, but without result. Everybody seemed to be present save Clewer.

"Rum!" said Stalky, pausing outside a study door. "Golly!"

A thin piping mixed with tears came muffled through the panels.

"As beautiful Kitty one morning was tripping——"

"Louder, you young devil, or I'll buzz a book at you!"

"With a pitcher of milk– Oh, Campbell, *please* don't! *To the fair of——"*

A book crashed on something soft, and squeals arose.

"Well, I never thought it was a study-chap, anyhow. That accounts for our not spotting him," said Beetle. "Sefton and Campbell are rather hefty chaps to tackle. Besides, one can't go into their study like a form-room."

"What swine!" McTurk listened. "Where's the fun of it? I suppose Clewer's faggin' for them."

"They aren't prefects. That's one good job," said Stalky, with his war-grin. "Sefton and Campbell! Um! Campbell and Sefton! Ah! One of 'em's a crammer's pup."

The two were precocious hairy youths between seventeen and eighteen, sent to the school in despair by parents who hoped that six months' steady cram might, perhaps, jockey them into Sandhurst. Nominally they were in Mr. Prout's house; actually they were under the Head's eye; and since he was very careful never to promote strange new boys to prefectships, they considered they had a grievance against the school. Sefton had spent three months with a London crammer, and the tale of his adventures there lost nothing in the telling. Campbell, who had a fine taste in clothes and a fluent vocabulary, followed his lead in looking down loftily on the rest of the world. This was only their second term, and the school, used to what it profanely called "crammers' pups," had treated them with rather galling reserve. But their whiskers–Sefton owned a real razor–and their mustaches were beyond question impressive.

"Shall we go in an' dissuade 'em?" McTurk asked. "I've never had much to do with 'em, but I'll bet my hat Campbell's a funk."

"No-o! That's *oratio directa,"* said Stalky, shaking his head. "I like *oratio obliqua.* 'Sides, where'd our moral influence be then? Think o' that!"

"Rot! What are you goin' to do?" Beetle turned into Lower Number Nine form-room, next door to the study.

"Me?" The lights of war flickered over Stalky's face. "Oh, I want to jape with 'em. Shut up a bit!"

He drove his hands into his pockets and stared out of window at the sea, whistling between his teeth. Then a foot tapped the floor; one shoulder lifted; he wheeled, and began the short quick double-shuffle–the war-dance of Stalky in meditation. Thrice he crossed the empty form-room, with compressed lips and expanded nostrils, swaying to the quick-step. Then he halted before the dumb Beetle and softly knuckled his head, Beetle bowing to the strokes. McTurk nursed one knee and rocked to and fro. They could hear Clewer howling as though his heart would break.

"Beetle is the sacrifice," Stalky said at last. "I'm sorry for you, Beetle. 'Member Galton's 'Art of Travel' [one of the forms had been studying that pleasant work] an' the kid whose bleatin' excited the tiger?"

"Oh, curse!" said Beetle uneasily. It was not his first season as a sacrifice. "Can't you get on without me?"

" 'Fraid not, Beetle, dear. You've got to be bullied by Turkey an' me. The more you howl, o' course, the better it'll be. Turkey, go an' covet a stump and a box-rope from somewhere. We'll tie him up for a kill–*à la* Galton. 'Member when 'Molly' Fairburn made us cock-fight with our shoes off, an' tied up our knees?"

"But that hurt like sin."

"Course it did. What a clever chap you are, Beetle! Turkey'll knock you all over the place. 'Member we've had a big row all round, an' I've trapped you into doin' this. Lend us your wipe."

Beetle was trussed for cock-fighting; but, in addition to the transverse stump between elbow and knee, his knees were bound with a box-rope. In this posture, at a push from Stalky he rolled over sideways, covering himself with dust.

"Ruffle his hair, Turkey. Now you get down, too. 'The bleatin' of the kid excites the tiger.' You two are in such a sweatin' wax with me that you only curse. 'Member that. I'll tickle you up with a stump. You'll have to blub, Beetle."

"Right O! I'll work up to it in half a shake," said Beetle.

"Now begin–and remember the bleatin' o' the kid."

"Shut up, you brutes! Let me up! You're nearly cut my knees off. Oh, you *are* beastly cads! *Do* shut up. 'Tisn't a joke!" Beetle's protest was, in tone, a work of art.

"Give it to him, Turkey! Kick him! Roll him over! Kill him! Don't funk, Beetle, you brute. Kick him again, Turkey.

"He's not blubbin' really. Roll up, Beetle, or I'll kick you into the fender," roared McTurk.

They made a hideous noise among them, and the bait allured their quarry.

"Hello! What's the giddy jest?" Sefton and Campbell entered to find Beetle on his side, his head against the fender, weeping copiously, while McTurk prodded him in the back with his toes.

"It's only Beetle," Stalky explained. "He's shammin' hurt. I can't get Turkey to go for him properly."

Sefton promptly kicked both boys, and his face lighted. "All right, I'll attend to 'em. Get up an' cock-fight, you two. Give me the stump. I'll tickle 'em. Here's a giddy jest! Come on, Campbell. Let's cook 'em."

Then McTurk turned on Stalky and called him very evil names.

"You said you were goin' to cock-fight too, Stalky. Come on!"

"More ass you for believin' me, then!" shrieked Stalky.

"Have you chaps had a row?" said Campbell.

"Row?" said Stalky. "Huh! I'm only educatin' them. D'you know anythin' about cock-fighting, Seffy?"

"Do I know? Why, at Maclagan's, where I was crammin' in town, we used to cock-fight in his drawing-room, and little Maclagan daren't say anything. But we were just the same as men there, of course. Do I know? *I'll* show you."

"Can't I get up?" moaned Beetle, as Stalky sat on his shoulder.

"Don't jaw, you fat piffler. You're going to fight Seffy."

"He'll slay me!"

"Oh, lug 'em into our study," said Campbell. "It's nice an' quiet in there. I'll cock-fight Turkey. This is an improvement on young Clewer."

"Right O! I move it's shoes-off for them an' shoes-on for us," said Sefton joyously, and the two were flung down on the study floor. Stalky rolled them behind an arm-chair.

"Now I'll tie you two up an' direct the bull-fight. Golly, what wrists you have, Seffy. They're too thick for a wipe; got a box-rope?" said he.

"Lots in the corner," Sefton replied. "Hurry up! Stop blubbin', you brute, Beetle. We're goin' to have a giddy campaign. Losers have to sing for the winners–sing odes in honor of the conqueror. You call yourself a beastly poet, don't you, Beetle? I'll poet you." He wriggled into position by Campbell's side.

Swiftly and scientifically the stumps were thrust through the natural crooks,

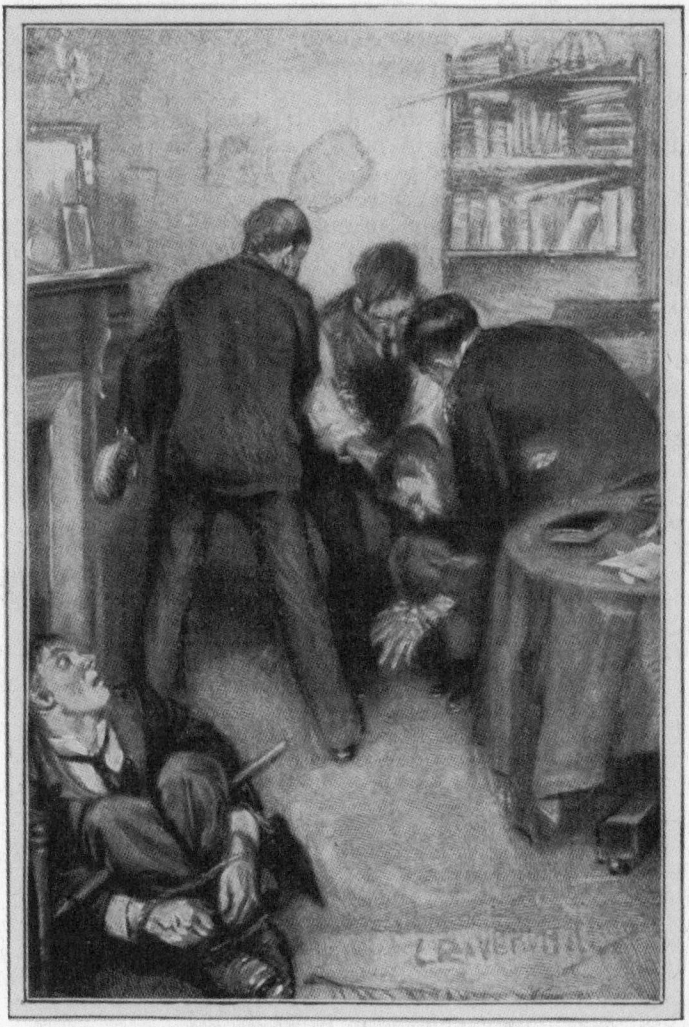

"THE BLEATIN' OF THE KID EXCITES THE TIGER."

and the wrists tied with well-stretched box-ropes to an accompaniment of insults from McTurk, bound, betrayed, and voluble behind the chair.

Stalky set away Campbell and Sefton, and strode over to his allies, locking the door on the way.

"And that's all right," said he in a changed voice.

"What the devil—?" Sefton began. Beetle's false tears had ceased; McTurk, smiling, was on his feet. Together they bound the knees and ankles of the enemy even more straitly.

Stalky took the arm-chair and contemplated the scene with his blandest smile. A man trussed for cock-fighting is, perhaps, the most helpless thing in the world.

" 'The bleatin' of the kid excites the tiger.' Oh, you frabjous asses!" He lay back and laughed till he could no more. The victims took in the situation but slowly.

"We'll give you the finest lickin' you ever had in your young lives when we get up!" thundered Sefton from the floor. "You'll laugh the other side of your mouth before you've done. What the deuce d'you mean by this?"

"You'll see in two shakes," said McTurk. "Don't swear like that. What we want to know is, why you two hulkin' swine have been bullyin' Clewer?"

"It's none of your business."

"What did you bully Clewer for?" The question was repeated with maddening iteration by each in turn. They knew their work.

"Because we jolly well chose!" was the answer at last. "Let's get up." Even then they could not realize the game.

"Well, now we're goin' to bully you because we jolly well choose. We're goin' to be just as fair to you as you were to Clewer. He couldn't do anything against you. You can't do anything to us. Odd, isn't it?"

"Can't we? You wait an' see."

"Ah," said Beetle reflectively, "that shows you've never been properly jested with. A public lickin' ain't in it with a gentle jape. Bet a bob you'll weep an' promise anything."

"Look here, young Beetle, we'll half kill you when we get up. I'll promise you that, at any rate."

"You're going to be half killed first, though. Did you give Clewer Head-knuckles?"

"Did you give Clewer Head-knuckles?" McTurk echoed. At the twentieth repetition–no boy can stand the torture of one unvarying query, which is the essence of bullying–came confession.

"We did, confound you!"

"Then you'll be knuckled;" and knuckled they were, according to ancient experience. Head-knuckling is no trifle; "Molly" Fairburn of the old days could not have done better.

"Did you give Clewer Brush-drill?"

This time the question was answered sooner, and Brush-drill was dealt out for the space of five minutes by Stalky's watch. They could not even writhe in their bonds. No brush is employed in Brush-drill.

"Did you give Clewer the Key?"

"No; we didn't. I swear we didn't!" from Campbell, rolling in agony.

"Then we'll give it to you, so you can see what it would be like if you had."

The torture of the Key–which has no key at all–hurts excessively. They endured several minutes of it, and their language necessitated the gag.

"Did you give Clewer Corkscrews?"

"Yes. Oh, curse your silly souls! Let us alone, you cads."

They were corkscrewed, and the torture of the Corkscrew–this has nothing to do with corkscrews–is keener than the torture of the Key.

The method and silence of the attacks was breaking their nerves. Between each new torture came the pitiless, dazing rain of questions, and when they did not answer to the point, Isabella-colored handkerchiefs were thrust into their mouths.

"Now are those all the things you did to Clewer? Take out the gag, Turkey, and let 'em answer."

"Yes, I swear that was all. Oh, you're killing us, Stalky!" cried Campbell.

"Pre-cisely what Clewer said to you. I heard him. Now we're goin' to show you what real bullyin' is. What I don't like about you, Sefton, is, you come to the Coll. with your stick-up collars an' patent-leather boots, an' you think you can teach us something about bullying. *Do* you think you can teach us anything about bullying? Take out the gag and let him answer."

"No!"—ferociously.

"He says no. Rock him to sleep. Campbell can watch."

It needs three boys and two boxing-gloves to rock a boy to sleep. Again the operation has nothing to do with its name. Sefton was "rocked" till his eyes set in his head and he gasped and crowed for breath, sick and dizzy.

"My Aunt!" said Campbell, appalled, from his corner, and turned white.

"Put him away," said Stalky. "Bring on Campbell. Now this *is* bullyin'. Oh, I forgot! I say, Campbell, what did you bully Clewer for? Take out his gag and let him answer."

"I—I don't know. Oh, let me off! I swear I'll make it *pax*. Don't 'rock' me!"

" 'The bleatin' of the kid excites the tiger.' He says he don't know. Set him up, Beetle. Give me the glove an' put in the gag."

In silence Campbell was "rocked" sixty-four times.

"I believe I'm goin' to die!" he gasped.

"He says he is goin' to die. Put him away. Now, Sefton! Oh, I forgot! Sefton, what did you bully Clewer for?"

The answer is unprintable; but it brought not the faintest flush to Stalky's downy cheek.

"Make him an Ag Ag, Turkey!"

And an Ag Ag was he made, forthwith. The hard-bought experience of nearly eighteen years was at his disposal, but he did not seem to appreciate it.

"He says we are sweeps. Put him away! Now, Campbell! Oh, I forgot! I say, Campbell, what did you bully Clewer for?"

Then came the tears—scalding tears; appeals for mercy and abject promises of peace. Let them cease the tortures and Campbell would never lift hand against them. The questions began again—to an accompaniment of small persuasions.

"You seem hurt, Campbell. Are you hurt?"

"Yes. Awfully!"

"He says he is hurt. Are you broke?"

"Yes, yes! I swear I am. Oh, stop!"

"He says he is broke. Are you humble?"

"Yes!"

"He says he is humble. Are you devilish humble?"

"Yes!"

"He says he is devilish humble. Will you bully Clewer any more?"

"No. No—ooh!"

"He says he won't bully Clewer. Or any one else?"

"No. I swear I won't."

"Or any one else. What about that lickin' you and Sefton were goin' to give us?"

"I won't! I won't! I swear I won't!"

"He says he won't lick us. Do you esteem yourself to know anything about bullyin'? "

"No, I don't!"

"He says he doesn't know anything about bullyin'. Haven't we taught you a lot?"

"Yes–yes!"

"He says we've taught him a lot. Aren't you grateful?"

"Yes!"

"He says he is grateful. Put him away. Oh, I forgot! I say, Campbell, what did you bully Clewer for?"

He wept anew; his nerves being raw. "Because I was a bully. I suppose that's what you want me to say?"

"He says he is a bully. Right he is. Put him in the corner. No more japes for Campbell. Now, Sefton!"

"You devils! You young devils!" This and much more as Sefton was punted across the carpet by skilful knees.

" 'The bleatin' of the kid excites the tiger.' We're goin' to make you beautiful. Where does he keep his shaving things? [Campbell told.] Beetle, get some water. Turkey, make the lather. We're goin' to shave you, Seffy, so you'd better lie jolly still, or you'll get cut. I've never shaved any one before."

"Don't! Oh, don't! Please don't!"

"Gettin' polite, eh? I'm only goin' to take off one ducky little whisker—"

"I'll–I'll make it *pax,* if you don't. I swear I'll let you off your lickin' when I get up!"

"*And* half that mustache we're so proud of. He says he'll let us off our lickin'. Isn't he kind?"

McTurk laughed into the nickel-plated shaving-cup, and settled Sefton's head between Stalky's viselike knees.

"Hold on a shake," said Beetle, "you can't shave long hairs. You've got to cut that mustache short first, an' then scrope him."

"Well, I'm not goin' to hunt about for scissors. Won't a match do? Chuck us the match-box. He *is* a hog, you know; we might as well singe him. Lie still!"

He lit a vesta, but checked his hand. "I only want to take off half, though."

"That's all right." Beetle waved the brush. "I'll lather up to the middle–see? and you can burn off the rest."

The thin-haired first mustache of youth fluffed off in flame to the lather-line in the centre of the lip, and Stalky rubbed away the burnt stumpage with his thumb. It was not a very gentle shave, but it abundantly accomplished its purpose.

"Now the whisker on the other side. Turn him over!" Between match and razor this, too, was removed. "Give him his shaving-glass. Take the gag out. I want to hear what he'll say."

But there were no words. Sefton gazed at the lop-sided wreck in horror and despair. Two fat tears rolled down his cheek.

"Oh, I forgot! I say, Sefton, what did you bully Clewer for?"

"Leave me alone! Oh, you infernal bullies, leave me alone! Haven't I had enough?"

"He says we must leave him alone," said McTurk.

"He says we are bullies, an' we haven't even begun yet," said Beetle. "You're ungrateful, Seffy. Golly! You *do* look an atrocity and a half!"

"He says he has had enough," said Stalky. "He errs!"

"Well, to work, to work!" chanted McTurk, waving a stump. "Come on, my giddy Narcissus. Don't fall in love with your reflection!"

"Oh, let him off," said Campbell from his corner; "he's blubbing, too."

Sefton cried like a twelve-year-old with pain, shame, wounded vanity, and utter helplessness.

"You'll make it *pax,* Sefton, won't you? You can't stand up to those young devils—"

"Don't be rude, Campbell, de-ah," said McTurk, "or you'll catch it again!"

"You *are* devils, you know," said Campbell.

"What? for a little bullyin'–same as you've been givin' Clewer! How long have you been jestin' with him?" said Stalky. "All this term?"

"We didn't always knock him about, though!"

"You did when you could catch him," said Beetle, cross-legged on the floor, dropping a stump from time to time across Sefton's instep. "Don't I know it!"

"I–perhaps we did."

"And you went out of your way to catch him? Don't I know it! Because he was an awful little beast, eh? Don't I know it! Now, you see, *you*'re awful beasts, and you're gettin' what he got–for bein' a beast. Just because we choose."

"We never really bullied him–like you've done us."

"Yah!" said Beetle. "They never really bully–'Molly' Fairburn didn't. Only knock 'em about a little bit. That's what they say. Only kick their souls out of 'em, and they go and blub in the box-rooms. Shove their heads into the ulsters an' blub. Write home three times a day–yes, you brute, I've done that–askin' to be taken away. You're never been bullied properly, Campbell. I'm sorry you made *pax.*"

"I'm not!" said Campbell, who was a humorist in a way. "Look out, you're slaying Sefton!"

In his excitement Beetle had used the stump unreflectively, and Sefton was now shouting for mercy.

"An' you!" he cried, wheeling where he sat. "You're never been bullied, either. Where were you before you came here?"

"I–I had a tutor."

"Yah! You would. You never blubbed in your life. But you're blubbin' now, by gum. Aren't you blubbin'?"

"Can't you see, you blind beast?" Sefton fell over sideways, tear-tracks furrowing the dried lather. Crack came the cricket-stump on the curved latter-end of him.

"Blind, am I," said Beetle, "and a beast? Shut up, Stalky. I'm goin' to jape a bit with our friend, *à la* 'Molly' Fairburn. *I* think I can see. Can't I see, Sefton!"

"The point is well taken," said McTurk, watching the stump at work. "You'd better say that he sees, Seffy."

"You do–you can! I swear you do!" yelled Sefton, for strong arguments were coercing him.

"Aren't my eyes lovely?" The stump rose and fell steadily throughout this catechism.

"Yes."

"A gentle hazel, aren't they?"

"Yes–oh, yes!"

"What a liar you are! They're sky-blue. Ain't they sky-blue?"

"Yes–oh, yes!"

"You don't know your mind from one minute to another. You must learn–you must learn."

"What a bait you're in!" said Stalky. "Keep your hair on, Beetle."

"I've had it done to me," said Beetle. "Now–about my being a beast."

"*Pax*–oh, *pax!*" cried Sefton; "make it *pax*. I'll give up! Let me off! I'm broke! I can't stand it!"

"Ugh! Just when we were gettin' our hand in!" grunted McTurk. "They didn't let Clewer off, I'll swear."

"Confess–apologize–quick!" said Stalky.

From the floor Sefton made unconditional surrender, more abjectly even than Campbell. He would never touch any one again. He would go softly all the days of his life.

"We're got to take it, I suppose?" said Stalky. "All right, Sefton. You're broke? Very good. Shut up, Beetle! But before we let you up, you an' Campbell will kindly oblige us with 'Kitty of Coleraine'–*à la* Clewer."

"That's not fair," said Campbell; "we've surrendered."

"'Course you have. Now you're goin' to do what we tell you–same as Clewer would. If you hadn't surrendered you'd ha' been really bullied. Havin' surrendered–do you follow, Seffy?–you sing odes in honor of the conquerors. Hurry up!"

They dropped into chairs luxuriously. Campbell and Sefton looked at each other, and, neither taking comfort from that view, struck up "Kitty of Coleraine."

"Vile bad," said Stalky, as the miserable wailing ended. "If you hadn't surrendered it would have been our painful duty to buzz books at you for singin' out o' tune. Now then."

He freed them from their bonds, but for several minutes they could not rise. Campbell was first on his feet, smiling uneasily. Sefton staggered to the table, buried his head in his arms, and shook with sobs. There was no shadow of fight in either–only amazement, distress, and shame.

"Ca–can't he shave clean before tea, please?" said Campbell. "It's ten minutes to bell."

Stalky shook his head. He meant to escort the half-shaved one to the meal.

McTurk yawned in his chair and Beetle mopped his face. They were all dripping with excitement and exertion.

"If I knew anything about it, I swear I'd give you a moral lecture," said Stalky severely.

"Don't jaw; they're surrendered," said McTurk. "This moral suasion biznai takes it out of a chap."

"Don't you see how gentle we've been? We might have called Clewer in to look at you," said Stalky. "'The bleatin' of the tiger excites the kid.' But we didn't. We've only got to tell a few chaps in Coll. about this and you'd be hooted all over the shop. Your life wouldn't be worth havin'. But we aren't goin' to do that, either. We're strictly moral suasers, Campbell; so, unless you or Seffy split about this, no one will."

"I swear you're a brick," said Campbell. "I suppose I was rather a brute to Clewer."

"It looked like it," said Stalky. "But I don't think Seffy need come into hall with cock-eye whiskers. Horrid bad for the fags if they saw him. He can shave. Ain't you grateful, Sefton?"

The head did not lift. Sefton was deeply asleep.

"That's rummy," said McTurk, as a snore mixed with a sob. "'Cheek, *I* think; or else he's shammin'."

"No, 'tisn't," said Beetle. "When 'Molly' Fairburn had attended to me for an hour or so I used to go bung off to sleep on a form sometimes. Poor devil! But he called me a beastly poet, though."

"Well, come on." Stalky lowered his voice. "Good-by, Campbell. 'Member, if you don't talk, nobody will."

There should have been a war-dance, but that all three were so utterly tired that they almost went to sleep above the tea-cups in their study, and slept till prep.

. . . .

"A most extraordinary letter. Are *all* parents incurably mad? What do you make of it?" said the Head, handing a closely written eight pages to the Reverend John.

"'The only son of his mother, and she a widow.' That is the least reasonable sort." The chaplain read with pursed lips.

"If half those charges are true he should be in the sick-house; whereas he

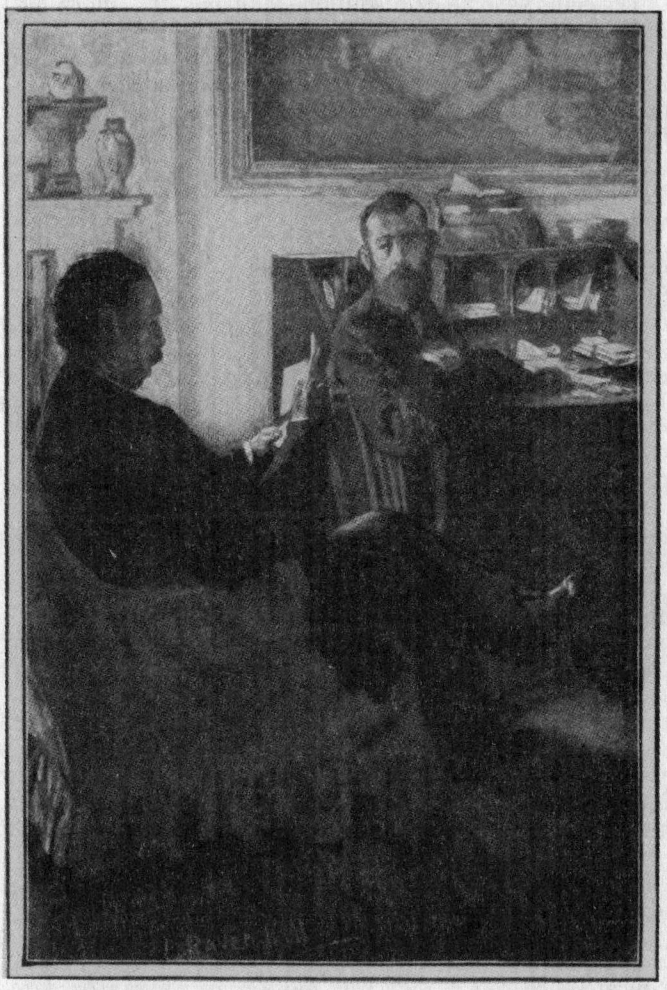

"'ARE ALL PARENTS INCURABLY MAD?'"

is disgustingly well. Certainly he has shaved. I noticed that."

"Under compulsion, as his mother points out. How delicious! How salutary!"

"You haven't to answer her. It isn't often I don't know what has happened in the school; but this is beyond me."

"If you asked me I should say seek not to propitiate. When one is forced to take crammers' pups—"

"He was perfectly well at extra-tuition—with me—this morning," said the Head, absently. "Unusually well behaved, too."

"—they either educate the school, or the school, as in this case, educates them. I prefer our own methods," the chaplain concluded.

"You think it was that?" A lift of the Head's eyebrow.

"I'm sure of it! And nothing excuses his trying to give the College a bad name."

"That's the line I mean to take with him," the Head answered.

The Augurs winked.

. . . .

A few days later the Reverend John called on Number Five. "Why haven't we seen you before, Padre?" said they.

"I've been watching times and seasons and events and men—and boys," he replied. "I am pleased with my Tenth Legion. I make them my compliments. Clewer was throwing ink-balls in form this morning, instead of doing his work. He is now doing fifty lines for—unheard-of audacity."

"You can't blame us, sir," said Beetle. "You told us to remove the—er—pressure. That's the worst of a fag."

"I've known boys five years his senior throw ink-balls, Beetle. To such an one have I given two hundred lines—not so long ago. And now I come to think of it, were those lines ever shown up?"

"Were they, Turkey?" said Beetle unblushingly.

"Don't you think Clewer looks a little cleaner, Padre?" Stalky interrupted.

"We're no end of moral reformers," said McTurk.

"It was all Stalky, but it was a lark," said Beetle.

"I have noticed the moral reform in several quarters. Didn't I tell you you had more influence than any boys in the Coll. if you cared to use it?"

"It's a trifle exhaustin' to use frequent—our kind of moral suasion. Besides, you see, it only makes Clewer cheeky."

"I wasn't thinking of Clewer; I was thinking of—the other people, Stalky."

"Oh, we didn't bother much about the other people," said McTurk. "Did we?"

"But *I* did—from the beginning."

"Then you knew, sir?"

A downward puff of smoke.

"Boys educate each other, they say, more than we can or dare. If I had used one half of the moral suasion you may or may not have employed—"

"With the best motives in the world. Don't forget our pious motives, Padre," said McTurk.

"—I suppose I should be now languishing in Bideford jail, shouldn't I? Well, to quote the Head, in a little business which we have agreed to forget, that strikes me as flagrant injustice. . . . What are you laughing at, you young sinners? Isn't it true? I will not stay to be shouted at. What I looked into this den of iniquity for was to find out if any one cared to come down for a bathe off the Ridge. But I see you won't."

"Won't we, though! Half a shake, Padre Sahib, till we get our towels, and *nous sommes avec vous!*"

A Little Prep

THE EASTER TERM was but a month old when Stettson major, a day-boy, contracted diphtheria, and the Head was very angry. He decreed a new and narrower set of bounds—the infection had been traced to an outlying farm-house—urged the prefects severely to lick all trespassers, and promised extra attentions from his own hand. There were no words bad enough for Stettson major, quarantined at his mother's house, who had lowered the school-average of health. This he said in the gymnasium after prayers. Then he wrote some two hundred letters to as many anxious parents and guardians, and bade the school carry on. The trouble did not spread, but, one night, a dog-cart drove to the Head's door, and in the morning the Head had gone, leaving all things in charge of Mr. King, senior house-master. The Head often ran up to town, where the school devoutly believed he bribed officials for early proofs of the Army Examination papers; but this absence was unusually prolonged.

"Downy old bird!" said Stalky to the allies, one wet afternoon, in the study. "He must have gone on a bend an' been locked up, under a false name."

"What for?" Beetle entered joyously into the libel.

"Forty shillin's or a month for hackin' the chucker-out of the Pavvy on the shins. Bates always has a spree when he goes to town. Wish he was back, though. I'm about sick o' King's 'whips an' scorpions' an' lectures on public-school spirit—yah!—and scholarship!"

" 'Crass an' materialized brutality of the middle-classes—readin' solely for marks. Not a scholar in the whole school,' " McTurk quoted, pensively boring holes in the mantel-piece with a hot poker.

"That's rather a sickly way of spending an afternoon. Stinks, too. "Let's come out an' smoke. Here's a treat." Stalky held up a long Indian cheroot. " 'Bagged it from my pater last holidays. I'm a bit shy of it, though; it's heftier than a pipe. We'll smoke it palaver-fashion. Hand it round, eh? Let's lie up behind the old harrow on the Monkey-farm Road."

"Out of bounds. Bounds beastly strict these days, too. Besides, we shall cat." Beetle sniffed the cheroot critically. "It's a regular Pomposo Stinkadore."

"You can; I shan't. What d'you say, Turkey?"

"Oh, may's well, I s'pose."

"Chuck on your cap, then. It's two to one. Beetle, out you come!"

They say a group of boys by the notice-board in the corridor; little Foxy, the school sergeant, among them.

"More bounds, I expect," said Stalky. "Hullo, Foxibus, who are you in mournin' for?" There was a broad band crape round Foxy's arm.

"He was in my old regiment," said Foxy, jerking his head towards the notices, where a newspaper cutting was thumb-tacked between call-over lists.

"By gum!" quoth Stalky, uncovering as he read. "It's old Duncan—Fat-Sow Duncan—killed on duty at something or other Kotal. *'Rallyin' his men with conspicuous gallantry.'* He would, of course. *'The body was recovered.'* That's all right. They cut 'em up sometimes, don't they, Foxy?"

"Horrid," said the sergeant briefly.

"Poor old Fat-Sow! I was a fag when he left. How many does that make to us, Foxy?"

"Mr. Duncan, he is the ninth. He come here when he was no bigger than little Grey tertius. My old regiment, too. Yiss, nine to us, Mr. Corkran, up to date."

The boys went out into the wet, walking swiftly.

"Wonder how it feels—to be shot and all that," said Stalky, as they splashed down a lane. "Where did it happen, Beetle?"

"Oh, out in India somewhere. We're always rowin' there. But look here, Stalky, what *is* the good o' sittin' under a hedge an' cattin'? It's be-eastly cold. It's be-eastly wet, and we'll be collared as sure as a gun."

"Shut up! Did you ever know your Uncle Stalky get you into a mess yet?" Like many other leaders, Stalky did not dwell on past defeats.

They pushed through a dripping hedge, landed among water-logged clods, and sat down on a rust-coated harrow. The cheroot burned with sputterings of saltpetre. They smoked it gingerly, each passing to the other between closed forefinger and thumb.

"Good job we hadn't one apiece, ain't it?" said Stalky, shivering through set teeth. To prove his words he immediately laid all before them, and they followed his example. . . .

"I told you," moaned Beetle, sweating clammy drops. "Oh, Stalky, you *are* a fool!"

"Je cat, tu cat, il cat. Nous cattons!" McTurk handed up his contribution and lay hopelessly on the cold iron.

"Something's wrong with the beastly thing. I say, Beetle, have you been droppin' ink on it?"

But Beetle was in no case to answer. Limp and empty, they sprawled across the harrow, the rust marking their ulsters in red squares and the abandoned cheroot-end reeking under their very cold noses. Then—they had heard nothing—the Head himself stood before them—the Head who should have been in town bribing examiners—the Head fantastically attired in old tweeds and a deer-stalker!

"Ah," he said, fingering his mustache. "Very good. I might have guessed who it was. You will go back to the College and give my compliments to Mr. King and ask him to give you an extra-special licking. You will then do me five hundred lines. I shall be back to-morrow. Five hundred lines by five o'clock to-morrow. You are also gated for a week. This is not exactly the time for breaking bounds. *Extra*-special, please."

He disappeared over the hedge as lightly as he had come. There was a murmur of women's voices in the deep lane.

"Oh, you Prooshan brute!" said McTurk as the voices died away. "Stalky, it's all your silly fault."

"Kill him! Kill him!" gasped Beetle.

"I ca-an't. I'm going to cat again . . . I don't mind that, but King'll gloat over us horrid. Extra-special, ooh!"

Stalky made no answer—not even a soft one. They went to College and received that for which they had been sent. King enjoyed himself most thoroughly, for by virtue of their seniority the boys were exempt from his hand, save under special order. Luckily, he was no expert in the gentle art.

" 'Strange, how desire doth outrun performance,' " said Beetle irreverently, quoting from some Shakespeare play that they were cramming that term. They regained their study and settled down to the imposition.

"You're quite right, Beetle." Stalky spoke in silky and propitiating tones. "Now, if the Head had sent us up to a prefect, we'd have got something to remember!"

"Look here," McTurk began with cold venom, "we aren't goin' to row you about this business, because it's too bad for a row; but we want you to understand you're jolly well excommunicated, Stalky. You're a plain ass."

"How was I to know that the Head 'ud collar us? What was he doin' in those ghastly clothes, too?"

"Don't try to raise a side-issue," Beetle grunted severely.

"Well, it was all Stettson major's fault. If he hadn't gone an' got diphtheria 'twouldn't have happened. But don't you think it rather rummy–the Head droppin' on us that way?"

"Shut up! You're dead!" said Beetle. "We've chopped your spurs off your beastly heels. We've cocked your shield upside down and–and I don't think you ought to be allowed to brew for a month."

"Oh, stop jawin' at me. I want—"

"Stop? Why–why, we're gated for a week." McTurk almost howled as the agony of the situation overcame him. "A lickin' from King, five hundred lines, *and* a gatin'. D'you expect us to kiss you, Stalky, you beast?"

"Drop rottin' for a minute. I want to find out about the Head bein' where he was."

"Well, you have. You found him quite well and fit. Found him makin' love to Stettson major's mother. That was her in the lane–I heard her. And *so* we were ordered a lickin' before a day-boy's mother. Bony old widow, too," said McTurk. "Anything else you'd like to find out?"

"I don't care. I swear I'll get even with him some day," Stalky growled.

"Looks like it," said McTurk. "Extra-special, week's gatin' and five hundred . . . and now you're goin' to row about it! Help scrag him, Beetle!" Stalky had thrown his Virgil at them.

The Head returned next day without explanation, to find the lines waiting for him and the school a little relaxed under Mr. King's viceroyalty. Mr. King had been talking at and round and over the boy's heads, in a lofty and promiscuous style, of public-school spirit and the traditions of ancient seats; for he always improved an occasion. Beyond waking in two hundred and fifty young hearts a lively hatred of all other foundations, he accomplished little–so little, indeed, that when, two days after the Head's return, he chanced to come across Stalky & Co., gated but ever resourceful, playing marbles in the corridor, he said that he was not surprised–not in the least surprised. That was what he had expected from persons of their *morale.*

"But there isn't any rule against marbles, sir. Very interestin' game," said Beetle, his knees white with chalk and dust. Then he received two hundred lines for insolence, besides an order to go to the nearest prefect for judgment and slaughter.

This is what happened behind the closed doors of Flint's study, and Flint was then Head of the Games:–

"Oh, I say, Flint. King has sent me to you for playin' marbles in the corridor an' shoutin' 'alley tor' an' 'knuckle down.' "

"What does he suppose I have to do with that?" was the answer.

"Dunno. Well?" Beetle grinned wickedly. "What am I to tell him? He's rather wrathy about it."

"If the Head chooses to put a notice in the corridor forbiddin' marbles, I can do something; but I can't move on a house-master's report. He knows that as well as I do."

The sense of this oracle Beetle conveyed, all unsweetened, to King, who hastened to interview Flint.

Now Flint had been seven and a half years at the College, counting six months with a London crammer, from whose roof he had returned, home-sick, to the Head for the final Army polish. There were four or five other seniors who had gone through much the same mill, not to mention boys, rejected by other establishments on account of a certain overwhelmingness, whom the Head had wrought into very fair shape. It was not a Sixth to be handled without gloves, as King found.

"Am I to understand it is your intention to allow board-school games under your study windows, Flint? If so, I can only say—" He said much, and Flint listened politely.

"Well, sir, if the Head sees fit to call a prefects' meeting we are bound to take the matter up. But the tradition of the school is that the prefects can't move in any matter affecting the whole school without the Head's direct order."

Much more was then delivered, both sides a little losing their temper.

After tea, at an informal gathering of prefects in his study, Flint related the adventure.

"He's been playin' for this for a week, and now he's got it. You know as well as I do that if he hadn't been gassing at us the way he has, that young devil Beetle wouldn't have dreamed of marbles."

"We know that," said Perowne, "but that isn't the question. On Flint's showin' King has called the prefects names enough to justify a first-class row. Crammers' rejections, ill-regulated hobble-de-hoys, wasn't it? Now it's impossible for prefects—"

"Rot," said Flint. "King's the best classical cram we've got; and 'tisn't fair to bother the Head with a row. He's up to his eyes with extra-tu. and Army work as it is. Besides, as I told King, we *aren't* a public school. We're a limited liability company payin' four per cent. My father's a shareholder, too."

"What's that got to do with it?" said Venner, a red-headed boy of nineteen.

"Well, seems to me that we should be interferin' with ourselves. We've got to get into the Army or—get out, haven't we? King's hired by the Council to teach us. All the rest's flumdiddle. Can't you see?"

It might have been because he felt the air was a little thunderous that the Head took his after-dinner cheroot to Flint's study; but he so often began an evening in a prefect's room that nobody suspected when he drifted in pensively, after the knocks that etiquette demanded.

"Prefects' meeting?" A cock of one wise eyebrow.

"Not exactly, sir; we're just talking things over. Won't you take the easy chair?"

"Thanks. Luxurious infants, you are." He dropped into Flint's big half-couch and puffed for a while in silence. "Well, since you're all here, I may confess that I'm the mute with the bowstring."

The young faces grew serious. The phrase meant that certain of their number would be withdrawn from all further games for extra-tuition. It might also mean future success at Sandhurst; but it was present ruin for the First Fifteen.

"Yes, I've come for my pound of flesh. I ought to have had you out before the Exeter match; but it's our sacred duty to beat Exeter."

"Isn't the Old Boys' match sacred, too, sir?" said Perowne. The Old Boys' match was the event of the Easter term.

"We'll hope they aren't in training. Now for the list. First I want Flint. It's the Euclid that does it. You must work deductions with me. Perowne, extra mechanical drawing. Dawson goes to Mr. King for extra Latin, and Venner to me for German. Have I damaged the First Fifteen much?" He smiled sweetly.

"Ruined it, I'm afraid, sir," said Flint. "Can't you let us off till the end of the term?"

"Impossible. It will be a tight squeeze for Sandhurst this year."

"And all to be cut up by those vile Afghans, too," said Dawson. "Wouldn't think there'd be so much competition, would you?"

"Oh, that reminds me. Crandall is coming down with the Old Boys–I've asked twenty of them, but we shan't get more than a weak team. I don't know whether he'll be much use, though. He was rather knocked about, recovering poor old Duncan's body."

"Crandall major–the Gunner?" Perowne asked.

"No, the minor–'Toffee' Crandall–in a native infantry regiment. He was almost before your time, Perowne."

"The papers didn't say anything about him. We read about Fat-Sow, of course. What's Crandall done, sir?"

"I've brought over an Indian paper that his mother sent me. It was rather a–hefty, I think you say–piece of work. Shall I read it?"

The Head knew how to read. When he had finished the quarter-column of close type everybody thanked him politely.

"Good for the old Coll.!" said Perowne. "Pity he wasn't in time to save Fat-Sow though. That's nine to us, isn't it, in the last three years?"

"Yes . . . And I took old Duncan off all games for extra-tu. five years ago this term," said the Head. "By the way, who do you hand over the Games to, Flint?"

"Haven't thought yet. Who'd you recommend, sir?"

"No thank you. I've heard it casually hinted behind my back that the Prooshan Bates is a downy bird, but he isn't going to make himself responsible for a new Head of the Games. Settle it among yourselves. Good-night."

"And that's the man," said Flint, when the door shut, "that you want to bother with a dame's school row."

"I was only pullin' your fat leg," Perowne returned, hastily. "You're so easy to draw, Flint."

"Well, never mind that. The Head's knocked the First Fifteen to bits, and we've got to pick up the pieces, or the Old Boys will have a walk-over. Let's promote all the Second Fifteen and make Big Side play up. There's heaps of talent somewhere that we can polish up between now and the match."

The case was represented so urgently to the school that even Stalky and McTurk, who affected to despise football, played one Big-Side game seriously. They were forthwith promoted ere their ardor had time to cool, and the dignity of their Caps demanded that they should keep some show of virtue. The match-team was worked at least four days out of seven, and the school saw hope ahead.

With the last week of the term the Old Boys began to arrive, and their welcome was nicely proportioned to their worth. Gentlemen cadets from Sandhurst and Woolwich, who had only left a year ago, but who carried enormous side, were greeted with a cheerful "Hullo! What's the Shop like?" from those who had shared their studies. Militia subalterns had more consideration, but it was understood they were not precisely of the true metal. Recreants who, failing for the Army, had gone into business or banks were received for old sake's sake, but in no way made too much of. But when the real subalterns, officers and gentlemen full-blown–who had been to the ends of the earth and back again and so carried no side–came on the scene strolling about with the Head, the school divided right and left in admiring silence. And when one laid hands on Flint, even upon the Head of the Games, crying, "Good Heavens! What do you mean by growing in this way? You were a beastly little fag when I left," visible haloes encircled Flint. They would walk to and fro in the corridor with the little red school-sergeant, telling news of old regiments; they would burst into form-rooms sniffing the well-remembered smells of ink and whitewash; they would find nephews and cousins in the lower forms and present them with enormous wealth; or they would invade the gymnasium and make Foxy show off the new stock on the bars.

Chiefly, though, they talked with the Head, who was father-confessor and agent-general to them all; for what they shouted in their unthinking youth, they proved in their thoughtless manhood—to wit, that the Prooshan Bates was "a downy bird." Young blood who had stumbled into an entanglement with a pastry-cook's daughter at Plymouth; experience who had come into a small legacy but mistrusted lawyers; ambition halting at cross-roads, anxious to take the one that would lead him farthest; extravagance pursued by the money-lender; arrogance in the thick of a regimental row—each carried his trouble to the Head; and Chiron showed him, in language quite unfit for little boys, a quiet and safe way round, out, or under. So they overflowed his house, smoked his cigars, and drank his health as they had drunk it all the earth over when two or three of the old school had foregathered.

"Don't stop smoking for a minute," said the Head. "The more you're out of training the better for us. I've demoralized the First Fifteen with extra-tu."

"Ah, but we're a scratch lot. Have you told 'em we shall need a substitute even if Crandall can play?" said a Lieutenant of Engineers with a D.S.O. to his credit.

"He wrote me he'd play, so he can't have been much hurt. He's coming down to-morrow morning."

"Crandall minor that was, and brought off poor Duncan's body?" The Head nodded. "Where are you going to put him? We've turned you out of house and home already, Head Sahib." This was a Squadron Commander of Bengal Lancers, home on leave.

"I'm afraid he'll have to go up to his old dormitory. You know old boys can claim that privilege. Yes, I think leetle Crandall minor must bed down there once more."

"Bates Sahib"—a Gunner flung a heavy arm round the Head's neck—"you've got something up your sleeve. Confess! I know that twinkle."

"Can't you see, you cuckoo?" a Submarine Miner interrupted. "Crandall goes up to the dormitory as an object-lesson, for moral effect and so forth. Isn't that true, Head Sahib?"

"It is. You know too much, Purvis. I licked you for that in '79."

"You did, sir, and it's my private belief you chalked the cane."

"N-no. But I've a very straight eye. Perhaps that misled you."

That opened the flood-gates of fresh memories, and they all told tales out of school.

When Crandall minor that was—Lieutenant T. Crandall of an ordinary Indian regiment—arrived from Exeter on the morning of the match, he was cheered along the whole front of the College, for the prefects had repeated the sense of that which the Head had read them in Flint's study. When Prout's house understood that he would claim his Old Boy's right to a bed for one night, Beetle ran into King's house next door and executed a public "gloat" up and down the enemy's big form-room, departing in a haze of ink-pots.

"What d'you take any notice of these rotters for?" said Stalky, playing substitute for the Old Boys, magnificent in black jersey, white knickers, and black stockings. "I talked to *him* up in the dormitory when he was changin'. Pulled his sweater down for him. He's cut about all over his arms—horrid purply ones. He's goin' to tell us about it to-night. I asked him to when I was lacin' his boots."

"Well, you *have* got cheek," said Beetle, enviously.

"Slipped out before I thought. But he wasn't a bit angry. He's no end of a chap. I swear I'm goin' to play up like beans. Tell Turkey!"

The technique of that match belongs to a bygone age. Scrimmages were tight and enduring; hacking was direct and to the purpose; and around the scrimmage stood the school, crying, "Put down your heads and shove!" Toward the end everybody lost all sense of decency, and mothers of day-boys too close to the touch-line heard language not included in the bills. No one was actually carried off the field, but both sides felt happier when time was called, and Beetle helped Stalky and McTurk into their overcoats. The two had met in the many-legged heart of things, and, as Stalky said, had "done each other proud." As they swaggered woodenly behind the teams—substitutes do not rank as equals of hairy men—they passed a pony-carriage near the wall, and a husky voice cried, "Well played. Oh, played indeed!" It was Stettson major, white-cheeked and hollow-eyed, who had fought his way to the ground under escort of an impatient coachman.

"Hullo, Stettson," said Stalky, checking. "Is it safe to come near you yet?"

"Oh, yes. I'm all right. They wouldn't let me out before, but I had to come to the match. Your mouth looks pretty plummy."

"Turkey trod on it accidental-done-a-purpose. Well, I'm glad you're better, because we owe you something. You and your membranes got us into a sweet mess, young man."

"I heard of that," said the boy, giggling. "The Head told me."

"Dooce he did! When?"

"Oh, come on up to Coll. My shin'll stiffen if we stay jawin' here."

"Shut up, Turkey. I want to find out about this. Well?"

"He was stayin' at our house all the time I was ill."

"What for? Neglectin' the Coll. that way? 'Thought he was in town."

"I was off my head, you know, and they said I kept on callin' for him."

"Cheek! You're only a day-boy."

"He came just the same, and he about saved my life. I was all bunged up one night—just goin' to croak, the doctor said—and they stuck a tube or somethin' in my throat, and the Head sucked out the stuff."

"Ugh! 'Shot if *I* would!"

"He ought to have got diphtheria himself, the doctor said. So he stayed on at our house instead of going back. I'd ha' croaked in another twenty minutes, the doctor says."

Here the coachman, being under orders, whipped up and nearly ran over the three.

"My Hat!" said Beetle. "That's pretty average heroic."

"Pretty average!" McTurk's knee in the small of his back cannoned him into Stalky, who punted him back. "You ought to be hung!"

"And the Head ought to get the V.C.," said Stalky. "Why, he might have been dead *and* buried by now. But he wasn't. But he didn't. Ho! ho! He just nipped through the hedge like a lusty old blackbird. Extra-special, five hundred lines, an' gated for a week—all sereno!"

"I've read o' somethin' like that in a book," said Beetle. "Gummy, what a chap! Just think of it!"

"I'm thinking," said McTurk; and he delivered a wild Irish yell that made the team turn around.

"Shut your fat mouth," said Stalky, dancing with impatience. "Leave it to your Uncle Stalky, and he'll have the Head on toast. If you say a word, Beetle, till I give you leave, I swear I'll slay you. *Habeo Capitem crinibus minimis.* I've got him by the short hairs! Now look as if nothing had happened."

There was no need of guile. The school was too busy cheering the drawn match. It hung round the lavatories regardless of muddy boots while the team washed. It cheered Crandall minor whenever it caught sight of him, and it cheered more wildly than ever after prayers, because the Old Boys in evening dress, openly twirling their mustaches, attended, and instead of standing with the masters, ranged themselves along the wall immediately before the prefects; and the Head called them over, too—majors, minors, and tertiuses, after their old names.

"Yes, it's all very fine," he said to his guests after dinner, "but the boys are getting a little out of hand. There will be trouble and sorrow later, I'm afraid. You'd better turn in early, Crandall. The dormitory will be sitting up for you. I don't know to what dizzy heights you may climb in your profession, but I do know you'll never get such absolute adoration as you're getting now."

"Confound the adoration. I want to finish my cigar, sir."

"It's all pure gold. Go where glory waits, Crandall–minor."

The setting of that apotheosis was a ten-bed attic dormitory, communicating through doorless openings with three others. The gas flickered over the raw pine washstands. There was an incessant whistling of drafts, and outside the naked windows the sea beat on the Pebbleridge.

"Same old bed–same old mattress, I believe," said Crandall, yawning. "Same old everything. Oh, but I'm lame! I'd no notion you chaps could play like this." He caressed a battered shin. "You've given us all something to remember you by."

It needed a few minutes to put them at their ease; and, in some way they could not understand, they were more easy when Crandall turned round and said his prayers–a ceremony he had neglected for some years.

"Oh, I *am* sorry. I've forgotten to put out the gas."

"Please don't bother," said the prefect of the dormitory. "Worthington does that."

A nightgowned twelve-year-old, who had been waiting to show off, leaped from his bed to the bracket and back again, by way of a washstand.

"How d'you manage when he's asleep?" said Crandall, chuckling.

"Shove a cold cleek down his neck."

"It was a wet sponge when *I* was junior in the dormitory. . . . Hullo! What's happening?"

The darkness had filled with whispers, the sound of trailing rugs, bare feet on bare boards, protests, giggles, and threats such as:

"Be quiet, you ass! . . . *Squattez-vous* on the floor, then! . . . I swear you aren't going to sit on *my* bed! . . . Mind the tooth-glass," etc.

"Sta–Corkran said," the prefect began, his tone showing his sense of Stalky's insolence, "that perhaps you'd tell us about that business with Duncan's body."

"Yes–yes–yes," ran the keen whispers. "Tell us."

"There's nothing to tell. What on earth are you chaps hoppin' about in the cold for?"

"Never mind us," said the voices. "Tell about Fat-Sow."

So Crandall turned on his pillow and spoke to the generation he could not see.

"Well, about three months ago he was commanding a treasure-guard–a cart full of rupees to pay troops with–five thousand rupees in silver. He was comin' to a place called Fort Pearson, near Kalabagh."

"I was born there," squeaked a small fag. "It was called after my uncle."

"Shut up–you and your uncle! Never mind *him,* Crandall."

"Well, ne'er mind. The Afridis found out that this treasure was on the move, and they ambushed the whole show a couple of miles before he got to the fort, and cut up the escort. Duncan was wounded, and the escort hooked it. There weren't more than twenty Sepoys all told, and there were any amount of Afridis. As things turned out, I was in charge at Fort Pearson. Fact was, I'd heard the firing and was just going to see about it, when Duncan's men came up. So we all turned back together. They told me something about an officer, but I couldn't get the hang of things till I saw a chap under the wheels of the cart out in the open, propped up on one arm, blazing away with a revolver. You see, the escort had abandoned the cart, and the Afridis–they're an awfully suspicious gang–thought the retreat was a trap–sort of draw, you know–and the cart was the bait. So they had left poor old Duncan alone. 'Minute they spotted how few *we* were, it was a race

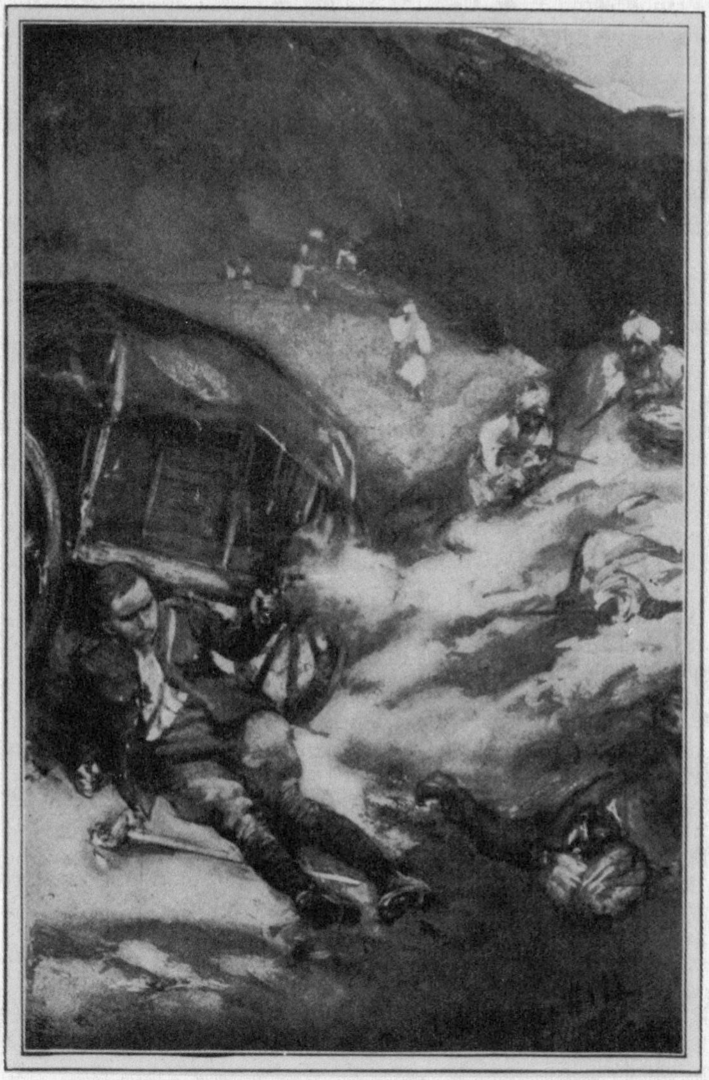

"'PROPPED UP ON ONE ARM, BLAZING AWAY WITH A REVOLVER.'"

across the flat who should reach old Duncan first. We ran, and they ran, and we won, and after a little hackin' about they pulled off. I never knew it was one of us till I was right on top of him. There are heaps of Duncans in the service, and of course the name didn't remind me. He wasn't changed at all hardly. He'd been shot through the lungs, poor old man, and he was pretty thirsty. I gave him a drink and sat down beside him, and—funny thing, too—he said, 'Hullo, Toffee!' and I said, 'Hullo, Fat-Sow! hope you aren't hurt,' or something of the kind. But he died in a minute or two—never lifted his head off my knees. . . . I say, you chaps out there will get your death of cold. Better go to bed."

"All right. In a minute. But your cuts—your cuts. How did you get wounded?"

"That was when we were taking the body back to the Fort. They came on again, and there was a bit of a scrimmage."

"Did you kill any one?"

"Yes. Shouldn't wonder. Good-night."

"Good-night. Thank you, Crandall. Thanks awf'ly, Crandall. Good-night."

The unseen crowds withdrew. His own dormitory rustled into bed and lay silent for a while.

"I say, Crandall"—Stalky's voice was tuned to a wholly foreign reverence.

"Well, what?"

"Suppose a chap found another chap croaking with diphtheria—all bunged up with it—and they stuck a tube in his throat and the chap sucked the stuff out, what would you say?"

"Um," said Crandall, reflectively. "I've only heard of one case, and that was a doctor. He did it for a woman."

"Oh, this wasn't a woman. It was just a boy."

"Makes it all the finer, then. It's about the bravest thing a man can do. Why?"

"Oh, I heard of a chap doin' it. That's all."

"Then he's a brave man."

"Would *you* funk it?"

"Ra-ather. Anybody would. Fancy dying of diphtheria in cold blood."

"Well—ah! Er! Look here!" The sentence ended in a grunt, for Stalky had leaped out of bed and with McTurk was sitting on the head of Beetle, who would have sprung the mine there and then.

Next day, which was the last of the term and given up to a few wholly unimportant examinations, began with wrath and war. Mr. King had discovered that nearly all his house—it lay, as you know, next door but one to Prout's in the long range of buildings—had unlocked the doors between the dormitories and had gone in to listen to a story told by Crandall. He went to the Head, clamorous, injured, appealing; for he never approved of allowing so-called young men of the world to contaminate the morals of boyhood. Very good, said the Head. He would attend to it.

"Well, I'm awf'ly sorry," said Crandall guiltily. "I don't think I told 'em anything they oughtn't to hear. Don't let them get into trouble on my account."

"Tck!" the Head answered, with the ghost of a wink. "It isn't the boys that make trouble; it's the masters. However, Prout and King don't approve of dormitory gatherings on this scale, and one must back up the house-masters. Moreover, it's hopeless to punish two houses only, so late in the term. We must be fair and include everybody. Let's see. They have a holiday task for the Easters, which, of course, none of them will ever look at. We will give the whole school, except prefects and study-boys, regular prep. to-night; and the Common-room will have to supply a master to take it. We must be fair to all."

"Prep. on the last night of the term. Whew!" said Crandall, thinking of his own wild youth. "I fancy there will be larks."

The school, frolicking among packed trunks, whooping down the corridor, and "gloating" in form-rooms, received the news with amazement and rage. No school in the world did prep. on the last night of the term. This thing was monstrous, tyrannical, subversive of law, religion, and morality. They would go into the form-rooms, and they would take their degraded holiday task with them, but—here they smiled and speculated what manner of man the Common-room would send up against them. The lot fell on Mason, credulous and enthusiastic, who loved youth. No other master was anxious to take that "prep.," for the school lacked the steadying influence of tradition; and men accustomed to the ordered routine of ancient foundations found it occasionally insubordinate. The four long form-rooms, in which all below the rank of study-boys worked, received him with thunders of applause. Ere he had coughed twice they favored him with a metrical summary of the marriage-laws of Great Britain, as recorded by the High Priest of the Israelites and commented on by the leader of the host. The lower forms reminded him that it was the last day, and that therefore he must "take it all in play." When he dashed off to rebuke them, the Lower Fourth and Upper Third began with one accord to be sick, loudly and realistically. Mr. Mason tried, of all vain things under heaven, to argue with them, and a bold soul at a back desk bade him "take fifty lines for not 'olding up 'is 'and before speaking." As one who prided himself upon the precision of his English this cut Mason to the quick, and while he was trying to discover the offender, the Upper and Lower Second, three form-rooms away, turned out the gas and threw ink-pots. It was a pleasant and stimulating "prep." The study-boys and prefects heard the echoes of it far off, and the Common-room at dessert smiled.

Stalky waited, watch in hand, till half-past eight.

"If it goes on much longer the Head will come up," said he. "We'll tell the studies first, and then the form-rooms. Look sharp!"

He allowed no time for Beetle to be dramatic or McTurk to drawl. They poured into study after study, told their tale, and went again so soon as they saw they were understood, waiting for no comment; while the noise of that unholy "prep." grew and deepened. By the door of Flint's study they met Mason flying towards the corridor.

"He's gone to fetch the Head. Hurry up! Come on!"

They broke into Number Twelve form-room abreast and panting.

"The Head! The Head! The Head!" That call stilled the tumult for a minute, and Stalky, leaping to a desk, shouted, "He went and sucked the diphtheria stuff out of Stettson major's throat when we thought he was in town. Stop rotting, you asses! Stettson major would have croaked if the Head hadn't done it. The Head might have died himself. Crandall says it's the bravest thing any livin' man can do, and I"—his voice cracked—"the Head don't know we know!"

McTurk and Beetle, jumping from desk to desk, drove the news home among the junior forms. There was a pause, and then, Mason behind him, the Head entered. It was in the established order of things that no boy should speak or move under his eye. He expected the hush of awe. He was received with cheers—steady, ceaseless cheering. Being a wise man, he went away, and the forms were silent and a little frightened.

"It's all right," said Stalky. "He can't do much. 'Tisn't as if you'd pulled the desks up like we did when old Carleton took prep. once. Keep it up! Hear 'em cheering in the studies!" He rocketed out with a yell, to find Flint and the prefects lifting the roof off the corridor.

When the Head of a limited liability company, paying four per cent., is cheered on his saintly way to prayers, not only by four form-rooms of boys waiting punishment, but by his trusted prefects, he can either ask for an explanation or go his road with dignity, while the senior house-master glares like an excited cat and points out to a white and trembling mathematical master that certain methods–not his, thank God–usually produce certain results. Out of delicacy the Old Boys did not attend that call-over; and it was to the school drawn up in the gymnasium that the Head spoke icily.

"It is not often that I do not understand you; but I confess I do not to-night. Some of you, after your idiotic performances at prep., seem to think me a fit person to cheer. I am going to show you that I am not."

Crash–crash–crash–came the triple cheer that disproved it, and the Head glowered under the gas.

"That is enough. You will gain nothing. The little boys (the Lower School did not like that form of address) will do me three hundred lines apiece in the holidays. I shall take no further notice of them. The Upper School will do me one thousand lines apiece in the holidays, to be shown up the evening of the day they come back. And further——"

"Gummy, what a glutton!" Stalky whispered.

"For your behavior towards Mr. Mason I intend to lick the whole of the Upper School to-morrow when I give you your journey-money. This will include the three study-boys I found dancing on the form-room desks when I came up. Prefects will stay after call-over."

The school filed out in silence, but gathered in groups by the gymnasium door waiting what might befall.

"And now, Flint," said the Head, "will you be good enough to give me some explanation of your conduct?"

"Well, sir," said Flint desperately, "if you save a chap's life at the risk of your own when he's dyin' of diphtheria, and the Coll. finds it out, wha-what *can* you expect, sir?"

"Um, I see. Then that noise was not meant for–ah, cheek. I can connive at immorality, but I cannot stand impudence. However, it does not excuse their insolence to Mr. Mason. I'll forego the lines this once, remember; but the lickings hold good."

When this news was made public, the school, lost in wonder and admiration, gasped at the Head as he went to his house. Here was a man to be reverenced. On the rare occasions when he caned he did it very scientifically, and the execution of a hundred boys would be epic–immense.

"It's all right, Head Sahib. *We* know," said Crandall, as the Head slipped off his gown with a grunt in his smoking-room. "I found out just now from our substitute. He was gettin' my opinion of your performance last night in the dormitory. I didn't know then that it was you he was talkin' about. Crafty young animal. Freckled chap with eyes–Corkran, I think his name is."

"Oh, I know *him,* thank you," said the Head, and reflectively. "Ye-es, I should have included them even if I hadn't seen 'em."

"If the old Coll. weren't a little above themselves already, we'd chair you down the corridor," said the Engineer. "Oh, Bates, how could you? You might have caught it yourself, and where would we have been, then?"

"I always knew you were worth twenty of us any day. Now I'm sure of it," said the Squadron Commander, looking round for contradictions.

"He isn't fit to manage a school, though. Promise you'll never do it again, Bates Sahib. We–we can't go away comfy in our minds if you take these risks," said the Gunner.

"Bates Sahib, you aren't ever goin' to cane the whole Upper School, are you?" said Crandall.

"I can connive at immorality, as I said, but I can't stand impudence. Mason's lot is quite hard enough even when I back him. Besides, the men at the golf-club heard them singing 'Aaron and Moses.' I shall have complaints about that from the parents of day-boys. Decency must be preserved."

"We're coming to help," said all the guests.

. . . .

The Upper School were caned one after the other, their overcoats over their arms, the brakes waiting in the road below to take them to the station, their journey-money on the table. The Head began with Stalky, McTurk, and Beetle. He dealt faithfully by them.

"And here's your journey-money. Good-by, and pleasant holidays."

"Good-by. Thank you, sir. Good-by."

They shook hands.

"Desire don't outrun performance–*much*–this mornin'. We got the cream of it," said Stalky. "Now wait till a few chaps come out, and we'll really cheer him."

"Don't wait on our account, please," said Crandall, speaking for the Old Boys. "We're going to begin now."

It was very well so long as the cheering was confined to the corridor, but when it spread to the gymnasium, when the boys awaiting their turn cheered, the Head gave it up in despair, and the remnant flung themselves upon him to shake hands.

Then they seriously devoted themselves to cheering till the brakes were hustled off the premises in dumb-show.

"Didn't I say I'd get even with him?" said Stalky on the box-seat, as they swung into the narrow Northam street. "Now all together–takin' time from your Uncle Stalky:

"It's a way we have in the Army,
It's a way we have in the Navy,
It's a way we have at the Public Schools,
Which nobody can deny!"

The Flag of Their Country

IT WAS WINTER and bitter cold of mornings. Consequently Stalky and Beetle–McTurk being of the offensive type that makes ornate toilet under all circumstances–drowsed till the last moment before turning out to call-over in the gas-lit gymnasium. It followed that they were often late; and since every unpunctuality earned them a black mark, and since three black marks a week meant defaulters' drill, equally it followed that they spent hours under the Sergeant's hand. Foxy drilled the defaulters with all the pomp of his old parade-ground.

"Don't think it's any pleasure to me" (his introduction never varied). "I'd much sooner be smoking a quiet pipe in my own quarters–but I see we 'ave the Old Brigade on our 'ands this afternoon. If I only 'ad you regular, Muster Corkran," said he, dressing the line.

"You've had me for nearly six weeks, you old glutton. Number off from the right!"

"Not *quite* so previous, please. I'm taking this drill. Left, half–turn! Slow–march." Twenty-five sluggards, all old offenders, filed into the gymnasium.

"Quietly provide yourselves with the requisite dumb-bells; returnin' quietly to your place. Number off from the right, in *a* low voice. Odd numbers one pace to the front. Even numbers stand fast. Now, leanin' forward from the 'ips, takin' your time from me."

The dumb-bells rose and fell, clashed and were returned as one. The boys were experts at the weary game.

"Ve-ry good. I shall be sorry when any of you resume your 'abits of punctuality. Quietly return dumb-bells. We will now try some simple drill."

"Ugh! I know that simple drill."

"It would be 'ighly to your discredit if you did not, Muster Corkran. *At* the same time, it is not so easy as it looks."

"Bet you a bob, I can drill as well as you, Foxy."

"We'll see later. Now try to imagine you ain't defaulters at all, but an 'arf company on parade, me bein' your commandin' officer. There's no call to laugh. If you're lucky, most of you will 'ave to take drills 'arf your life. Do me a little credit. You've been at it long enough, goodness knows."

They were formed into fours, marched, wheeled, and countermarched, the spell of ordered motion strong on them. As Foxy said, they had been at it a long time.

The gymnasium door opened, revealing McTurk in charge of an old gentleman.

The Sergeant, leading a wheel, did not see. "Not so bad," he murmured. "Not 'arf so bad. The pivot-man of the wheel *honly* marks time, Muster Swayne. Now, Muster Corkran, you say you know the drill? Oblige me by takin' over the command and, reversin' my words step by step, relegate them to their previous formation."

"What's this? What's this?" cried the visitor authoritatively.

"A–a little drill, sir," stammered Foxy, saying nothing of first causes.

"Excellent–excellent. I only wish there were more of it," he chirruped. "Don't let me interrupt. You were just going to hand over to some one, weren't you?" He sat down, breathing frostily in the chill air.

"I shall muck it. I know I shall," whispered Stalky uneasily; and his discomfort was not lightened by a murmur from the rear rank that the old gentleman was General Collinson, a member of the College Board of Council.

"Eh–what?" said Foxy.

"Collinson, K.C.B.–He commanded the Pompadours–my father's old regiment," hissed Swayne major.

"Take your time," said the visitor. "*I* know how it feels. Your first drill–eh?"

"Yes, sir." He drew an unhappy breath. " 'Tention. Dress!" The echo of his own voice restored his confidence.

The wheel was faced about, flung back, broken into fours, and restored to line without a falter. The official hour of punishment was long passed, but no one thought of that. They were backing up Stalky–Stalky in deadly fear lest his voice should crack.

"He does you credit, Sergeant," was the visitor's comment. "A good drill–and good material to drill. Now, it's an extraordinary thing: I've been lunching with your head-master and he never told me you had a cadet-corps in the College."

"We 'aven't, sir. This is only a little drill," said the Sergeant.

"But aren't they keen on it?" said McTurk, speaking for the first time, with a twinkle in his deep-set eyes.

"Why aren't *you* in it, though, Willy?"

"Oh, I'm not punctual enough," said McTurk. "The Sergeant only takes the pick of us."

"Dismiss! Break off!" cried Foxy, fearing an explosion in the ranks. "I–I ought to have told you, sir, that——"

"But you should have a cadet-corps." The General pursued his own line of thought. "You *shall* have a cadet-corps, too, if my recommendation in Council is any use. I don't know when I've been so pleased. Boys animated by a spirit like yours should set an example to the whole school."

"They do," said McTurk.

"Bless my soul! Can it be so late? I've kept my fly waiting half an hour. Well, I must run away. Nothing like seeing things for one's self. Which end of the buildings does one get out at? Will you show me, Willy? Who was that boy who took the drill?"

"Corkran, I think his name is."

"You ought to know him. That's the kind of boy you should cultivate. Evidently an unusual sort. A wonderful sight. Five and twenty boys, who, I dare say, would much sooner be playing cricket–" (it was the depth of winter; but grown people, especially those who have lived long in foreign parts, make these little errors, and McTurk did not correct him)–"drilling for the sheer love of it. A shame to waste so much good stuff; but I think I can carry my point."

"An' who's your friend with the white whiskers?" demanded Stalky, on McTurk's return to the study.

"General Collinson. He comes over to shoot with my father sometimes. Rather a decent old bargee, too. He said I ought to cultivate your acquaintance, Stalky."

"Did he tip you?"

McTurk exhibited a blessed whole sovereign.

"Ah," said Stalky, annexing it, for he was treasurer. "We'll have a hefty brew. You'd pretty average cool cheek, Turkey, to jaw about our keenness an' punctuality."

"Didn't the old boy know we were defaulters?" said Beetle.

"Not him. He came down to lunch with the Head. I found him pokin' about the place on his own hook afterwards, an' I thought I'd show him the giddy drill. When I found he was so pleased, I wasn't goin' to damp his giddy ardor. He mightn't ha' given me the quid if I had."

"Wasn't old Foxy pleased? Did you see him get pink behind the ears?" said Beetle. "It was an awful score for him. Didn't we back him up beautifully? Let's go down to Keyte's and get some cocoa and sassingers."

They overtook Foxy, speeding down to retail the adventure to Keyte, who in his time had been Troop Sergeant-Major in a cavalry regiment, and now, a war-worn veteran, was local postmaster and confectioner.

"You owe us something," said Stalky, with meaning.

"I'm 'ighly grateful, Muster Corkran. I've 'ad to run against you pretty hard in the way o' business, now and then, but I *will* say that outside o' business–bounds an' smokin', an' such like–I don't wish to have a more trustworthy young gentleman to 'elp me out of a hole. The way you 'andled the drill was beautiful, though I say it. Now, if you come regular henceforward——"

"But he'll have to be late three times a week," said Beetle. "You can't expect a chap to do that–just to please you, Foxy."

"Ah, that's true. Still, if you could manage it–and you, Muster Beetle–it would give you a big start when the cadet-corps is formed. I expect the General will recommend it."

They raided Keyte's very much at their own sweet will, for the old man, who knew them well, was deep in talk with Foxy.

"I make what we've taken seven and six," Stalky called at last over the counter; "but you'd better count for yurself."

"No–no. I'd take your word any day, Muster Corkran.–In the Pompadours, was he, Sergeant? We lay with them once–at Umballa, I think it was."

"I don't know whether this ham-and-tongue tin is eighteen pence or one an' four."

"Say one an' fourpence, Muster Corkran. . . . Of course, Sergeant, if it was any use to give my time, I'd be pleased to do it, but I'm too old. I'd like to see a drill again."

"Oh, come on, Stalky," cried McTurk. "He isn't listenin' to you. Chuck over the money."

"I want the quid changed, you ass. Keyte! Private Keyte! Corporal Keyte! Terroop-Sergeant-Major Keyte, will you give me change for a quid?"

"Yes–yes, of course. Seven an' six." He stared abstractedly, pushed the silver over, and melted away into the darkness of the back room.

"Now those two'll jaw about the Mutiny till tea-time," said Beetle.

"Old Keyte was at Sobraon," said Stalky. "Hear him talk about that sometimes! Beats Foxy hollow."

. . . .

The Head's face, inscrutable as ever, was bent over a pile of letters.

"What do you think?" he said at last to the Reverend John Gillett.

"It's a good idea. There's no denying that–an estimable idea."

"We concede that much. Well?"

"I have my doubts about it–that's all. The more I know of boys the less do I profess myself capable of following their moods; but I own I shall be very much surprised if the scheme takes. It–it isn't the temper of the school. We prepare for the Army."

"My business–in *this* matter–is to carry out the wishes of the Council. They demand a volunteer cadet-corps. A volunteer cadet-corps will be furnished. I have suggested, however, that we need not embark upon the expense of uniforms till we are drilled. General Collinson is sending us fifty lethal weapons–cut-down Sniders, he calls them–all carefully plugged."

"Yes, that is necessary in a school that uses loaded saloon-pistols to the extent we do." The Reverend John smiled.

"Therefore there will be no outlay except the Sergeant's time."

"But if he fails you will be blamed."

"Oh, assuredly. I shall post a notice in the corridor this afternoon, and——"

"I shall watch the result."

. . . .

"Kindly keep your 'ands off the new arm-rack."

Foxy wrestled with a turbulent crowd in the gymnasium. "Nor it won't do even a condemned Snider any good to be continual snappin' the lock, Mr. Swayne.–Yiss, the uniforms will come later, when we're more proficient; at present we will confine ourselves to drill. I am 'ere for the purpose of takin' the names o' those willin' to join.–Put down that Snider, Muster Hogan!"

"What are you goin' to do, Beetle?" said a voice.

"I've had all the drill *I* want, thank you."

"What! After all you've learned? Come on. Don't be a scab! They'll make you corporal in a week," cried Stalky.

"I'm not goin' up for the Army." Beetle touched his spectacles.

"Hold on a shake, Foxy," said Hogan. "Where are you goin' to drill us?"

"Here–in the gym–till you are fit an' capable to be taken out on the road." The Sergeant threw a chest.

"For all the Northam cads to look at? Not good enough, Foxibus."

"Well, we won't make a point of it. You learn your drill first, an' later we'll see."

"Hullo," said Ansell of Macrea's, shouldering through the mob. "What's all this about a giddy cadet-corps?"

"It will save you a lot o' time at Sandhurst," the Sergeant replied promptly. "You'll be dismissed your drills early if you go up with a good groundin' before'and."

"Hm! 'Don't mind learnin' my drill, but I'm not goin' to ass about the country with a toy Snider. Perowne, what are you goin' to do? Hogan's joinin'."

"Don't know whether I've the time," said Perowne. "I've got no end of extra-tu as it is."

"Well, call this extra-tu," said Ansell. " 'Twon't take us long to mug up the drill."

"Oh, that's right enough, but what about marchin' in public?" said Hogan, not foreseeing that three years later he should die in the Burmese sunlight outside Minhla Fort.

"Afraid the uniform won't suit your creamy complexion?" McTurk asked with a villainous sneer.

"Shut up, Turkey. You aren't goin' up for the Army."

"No, but I'm goin' to send a substitute. Hi! Morrell an' Wake! You two fags by the arm-rack, you've got to volunteer."

Blushing deeply—they had been too shy to apply before—the youngsters sidled towards the Sergeant.

"But I don't want the little chaps—not at first," said the Sergeant disgustedly. "I want—I'd like some of the Old Brigade—the defaulters—to stiffen 'em a bit."

"Don't be ungrateful, Sergeant. They're nearly as big as you get 'em in the Army now." McTurk read the papers of those years and could be trusted for general information, which he used as he used his "tweaker." Yet he did not know that Wake minor would be a bimbashi of the Egyptian Army ere his thirtieth year.

Hogan, Swayne, Stalky, Perowne, and Ansell were deep in consultation by the vaulting-horse, Stalky as usual laying down the law. The Sergeant watched them uneasily, knowing that many waited on their lead.

"Foxy don't like my recruits," said McTurk, in a pained tone, to Beetle. "You get him some."

Nothing loath, Beetle pinioned two more fags—each no taller than a carbine.

"Here you are, Foxy. Here's food for powder. Strike for your hearths an' homes, you young brutes—an' be jolly quick about it."

"Still he isn't happy," said McTurk.

"For the way we have with our Army
Is the way we have with our Navy."

Here Beetle joined in. They had found the poem in an old volume of "Punch," and it seemed to cover the situation:

"An' both of 'em led to adversity,
Which nobody can deny!"

"You be quiet, young gentlemen. If you can't 'elp—don't 'inder." Foxy's eye was still on the council by the horse. Carter, White, and Tyrrell, all boys of influence, had joined it. The rest fingered the rifles irresolutely.

"Half a shake," cried Stalky. "Can't we turn out those rotters before we get to work?"

"Certainly," said Foxy. "Any one wishful to join will stay 'ere. Those who do not so intend will go out, quietly closin' the door be'ind 'em."

Half a dozen of the earnest-minded rushed at them, and they had just time to escape into the corridor.

"Well, why don't you join?" Beetle asked, resettling his collar.

"Why didn't you?"

"What's the good? We aren't goin' up for the Army. Besides, I know the drill–all except the manual, of course. 'Wonder what they're doin' inside?"

"Makin' a treaty with Foxy. Didn't you hear Stalky say: 'That's what we'll do–an' if he don't like it he can lump it'? They'll use Foxy for a cram. Can't you see, you idiot? They're goin' up for Sandhurst or the Shop in less than a year. They'll learn their drill an' then they'll drop it like a shot. D'you suppose chaps with their amount of extra-tu are takin' up volunteerin' for fun?"

"Well, I don't know. I thought of doin' a poem about it–rottin' 'em, you know–'The Ballad of the Dogshooters'–eh?"

"I don't think you can, because King'll be down on the corps like a cartload o' bricks. He hasn't been consulted. He's sniffin' round the notice-board now. Let's lure him." They strolled up carelessly towards the house-master–a most meek couple.

"How's this?" said King with a start of feigned surprise. "Methought you would be learning to fight for your country."

"I think the company's full, sir," said McTurk.

"It's a great pity," sighed Beetle.

"Forty valiant defenders, have we, then? How noble! What devotion! I presume that it is possible that a desire to evade their normal responsibilities may be at the bottom of this zeal. Doubtless they will be accorded special privileges, like the Choir and the Natural History Society–one must not say Bug-hunters."

"Oh, I suppose so, sir," said McTurk, cheerily. "The Head hasn't said anything about it yet, but he will, of course."

"Oh, sure to."

"It is just possible, my Beetle," King wheeled on the last speaker, "that the house-masters–a necessary but somewhat neglected factor in our humble scheme of existence–may have a word to say on the matter. Life, for the young at least, is not all weapons and munitions of war. Education is incidentally one of our aims."

"What a consistent pig he is," cooed McTurk, when they were out of earshot. "One always knows where to have him. Did you see how he rose to that draw about the Head and special privileges?"

"Confound him, he might have had the decency to have backed the scheme. I could do such a lovely ballad, rottin' it; and now I'll have to be a giddy enthusiast. It don't bar our pulling Stalky's leg in the study, does it?"

"Oh, no; but in the Coll. we must be pro-cadet-corps like anything. Can't you make up a giddy epigram, *à la* Catullus, about King objectin' to it?" Beetle was at this noble task when Stalky returned all hot from his first drill.

"Hullo, my ramrod-bunger!" began McTurk. "Where's your dead dog? Is it Defence or Defiance?"

"Defiance," said Stalky, and leaped on him at that word. "Look here, Turkey, you mustn't rot the corps. We've arranged it beautifully. Foxy swears he won't take us out into the open till we say we want to go."

"*Dis*-gustin' exhibition of immature infants apin' the idiosyncrasies of their elders. Snff!"

"Have you drawn King, Beetle?" Stlaky asked in a pause of the scuffle.

"Not exactly; but that's his genial style."

"Well, listen to your Uncle Stalky–who is a great man. Moreover and subsequently, Foxy's goin' to let us drill the corps in turn–*privatim et seriatim*–so that we'll all know how to handle a half company anyhow. *Ergo*, an' *propter hoc*, when we go to the Shop we shall be dismissed drill early; thus, my beloved 'earers, combinin' education with wholesome amusement."

"I knew you'd make a sort of extra-tu of it, you cold-blooded brute," said McTurk. "Don't you want to die for your giddy country?"

"Not if I can jolly well avoid it. So you mustn't rot the corps."

"We'd decided on that, years ago," said Beetle, scornfully. "King'll do the rottin'."

"Then you've got to rot King, my giddy poet. Make up a good catchy Limerick, and let the fags sing it."

"Look here, you stick to volunteerin', and don't jog the table."

"He won't have anything to take hold of," said Stalky, with dark significance.

They did not know what that meant till, a few days later, they proposed to watch the corps at drill. They found the gymnasium door locked and a fag on guard.

"This is sweet cheek," said McTurk, stooping.

"Mustn't look through the key-hole," said the sentry.

"I like that. Why, Wake, you little beast, I made you a volunteer."

"Can't help it. My orders are not to allow any one to look."

"S'pose we do?" said McTurk. "S'pose we jolly well slay you?"

"My orders are, I am to give the name of anybody who interfered with me on my post, to the corps, an' they'd deal with him after drill, accordin' to martial law."

"What a brute Stalky is!" said Beetle. They never doubted for a moment who had devised that scheme.

"You esteem yourself a giddy centurion, don't you?" said Beetle, listening to the crash and rattle of grounded arms within.

"My orders are, not to talk except to explain my orders–they'll lick me if I do."

McTurk looked at Beetle. The two shook their heads and turned away.

"I swear Stalky *is* a great man," said Beetle after a long pause. "One consolation is that this sort of secret-society biznai will drive King wild."

It troubled many more than King, but the members of the corps were muter than oysters. Foxy, being bound by no vow, carried his woes to Keyte.

"I never come across such nonsense in my life. They've tiled the lodge, inner and outer guard all complete, and then they get to work, keen as mustard."

"But what's it all for?" asked the ex-Troop Sergeant-Major.

"To learn their drill. You never saw anything like it. They begin after I've dismissed 'em–practisin' tricks; but out into the open they will *not* come–not for ever so. The 'ole thing is pre-posterous. If you're a cadet-corps, *I* say, be a cadet-corps, instead o' hidin' be'ind locked doors."

"And what do the authorities say about it?"

"That beats me again." The Sergeant spoke fretfully. "I go to the 'Ead an' 'e gives me no help. There's times when I think he's makin' fun o' me. I've never been a Volunteer-sergeant, thank God–but I've always had the consideration to pity 'em. I'm glad o' that."

"I'd like to see 'em," said Keyte. "From your statements, Sergeant, I can't get at what they're after."

"Don't ask me, Major! Ask that freckle-faced young Corkran. He's their generalissimo."

One does not refuse a warrior of Sobraon, or deny the only pastry-cook within bounds. So Keyte came, by invitation, leaning upon a stick, tremulous with old age, to sit in a corner and watch.

"They shape well. They shape uncommon well," he whispered between evolutions.

"Oh, *this* isn't what they're after. Wait till I dismiss 'em."

At the "break-off" the ranks stood fast. Perowne fell out, faced them, and, refreshing his memory by glimpses at a red-bound, metal-clasped book, drilled them for ten minutes. (This is that Perowne who was shot in Equatorial Africa by his own men.)

Ansell followed him, and Hogan followed Ansell. All three were implicitly obeyed.

Then Stalky laid aside his Snider, and, drawing a long breath, favored the company with a blast of withering invective.

" 'Old 'ard, Muster Corkran. That ain't in any drill," cried Foxy.

"All right, Sergeant. You never know what you may have to say to your men.—For pity's sake, try to stand up without leanin' against each other, you blear-eyed, herrin'-gutted gutter-snipes. It's no pleasure to me to comb you out. That ought to have been done before you came here, you—you militia broom-stealers."

"The old touch—the old touch. *We* know it," said Keyte, wiping his rheumy eyes. "But where did he pick it up?"

"From his father—or his uncle. Don't ask me! Half of 'em must have been born within earshot o' the barracks." (Foxy was not far wrong in his guess.) "I've heard more back-talk since this volunteerin' nonsense began than I've heard in a year in the service."

"There's a rear-rank man lookin' as though his belly were in the pawnshop. Yes, you, Private Ansell," and Stalky tongue-lashed the victim for three minutes, in gross and in detail.

"Hullo!" He returned to his normal tone. "First blood to me. You flushed, Ansell. You wriggled."

"Couldn't help flushing," was the answer. "Don't think I wriggled, though."

"Well, it's your turn now." Stalky resumed his place in the ranks.

"Lord, Lord! It's as good as a play," chuckled the attentive Keyte.

Ansell, too, had been blessed with relatives in the service, and slowly, in a lazy drawl—his style was more reflective than Stalky's—descended the abysmal depths of personality.

"Blood to me!" he shouted triumphantly. "You couldn't stand it, either." Stalky was a rich red, and his Snider shook visibly.

"I didn't think I would," he said, struggling for composure, "but after a bit I got in no end of a bait. Curious, ain't it?"

"Good for the temper," said the slow-moving Hogan, as they returned arms to the rack.

"Did you ever?" said Foxy, hopelessly, to Keyte.

"I don't know much about volunteers, but it's the rummiest show I ever saw. I can see what they're gettin' at, though. Lord! how often I've been told off an' dressed down in my day! They shape well—extremely well they shape."

"If I could get 'em out into the open, there's nothing I couldn't do with 'em, Major. Perhaps when the uniforms come down, they'll change their mind."

Indeed it was time that the corps made some concession to the curiosity of the school. Thrice had the guard been maltreated and thrice had the corps dealt out martial law to the offender. The school raged. What was the use, they asked, of a cadet-corps which none might see? Mr. King congratulated them on their invisible defenders, and they could not parry his thrusts. Foxy was growing sullen and restive. A few of the corps expressed openly doubts as to the wisdom of their course; and the question of uniforms loomed on the near horizon. If these were issued, they would be forced to wear them.

But, as so often happens in this life, the matter was suddenly settled from without.

The Head had duly informed the Council that their recommendation had been acted upon, and that, so far as he could learn, the boys were drilling.

He said nothing of the terms on which they drilled. Naturally, General Collinson was delighted and told his friends. One of his friends rejoiced in a friend, a Member of Parliament—a zealous, an intelligent, and, above all, a patriotic person, anxious to do the most good in the shortest possible time. But we cannot answer, alas! for the friends of our friends. If Collinson's friend had introduced him to the General, the latter would have taken his measure and saved much. But the friend merely spoke of his friend; and since no two people in the world see eye to eye, the picture conveyed to Collinson was inaccurate. Moreover, the man was an M.P., an impeccable Conservative, and the General had the English solider's lurking respect for any member of the Court of Last Appeal. He was going down into the West country, to spread light in somebody's benighted constituency. Wouldn't it be a good idea if, armed with the General's recommendation, he, taking the admirable and newly established cadet-corps for his text, spoke a few words—"Just talked to the boys a little—eh? You know the kind of thing that would be acceptable; and he'd be the very man to do it. The sort of talk that boys understand, you know."

"They didn't talk to 'em much in my time," said the General, suspiciously.

"Ah! but times change—with the spread of education and so on. The boys of to-day are the men of to-morrow. An impression in youth is likely to be permanent. And in these times, you know, with the country going to the dogs?"

"You're quite right." The island was then entering on five years of Mr. Gladstone's rule; and the General did not like what he had seen of it. He would certainly write to the Head, for it was beyond question that the boys of to-day made the men of to-morrow. That, if he might say so, was uncommonly well put.

In reply, the Head stated that he should be delighted to welcome Mr. Raymond Martin, M.P., of whom he had heard so much; to put him up for the night, and to allow him to address the school on any subject that he conceived would interest them. If Mr. Martin had not yet faced an audience of this particular class of British youth, the Head had no doubt that he would find it an interesting experience.

"And I don't think I am very far wrong in that last," he confided to the Reverend John. "Do you happen to know anything of one Raymond Martin?"

"I was at College with a man of that name," the chaplain replied. "He was without form and void, so far as I remember, but desperately earnest."

"He will address the Coll. on 'Patriotism' next Saturday."

"If there is one thing our boys detest more than another it is having their Saturday evenings broken into. Patriotism has no chance beside 'brewing.' "

"Nor art either. D'you remember our 'Evening with Shakespeare'?" The Head's eyes twinkled. "Or the humorous gentleman with the magic lantern?"

. . . .

"An' who the dooce is this Raymond Martin, M.P.?" demanded Beetle, when he read the notice of the lecture in the corridor. "Why do the brutes always turn up on a Saturday?"

"Ouh! Reomeo, Reomeo. Wherefore art thou Reomeo?" said McTurk over his shoulder, quoting the Shakespeare artiste of last term. "Well, he won't be as bad as *her*, I hope. Stalky, are you properly patriotic? Because if you ain't, this chap's goin' to make you."

"Hope he won't take up the whole of the evening. I suppose we've got to listen to him."

"Wouldn't miss him for the world," said McTurk. "A lot of chaps thought that Romeo-Romeo woman was a bore. *I* didn't. I liked her! 'Member when she began to hiccough in the middle of it? P'raps he'll hiccough. Whoever gets into the Gym first, bags seats for the other two."

. . . .

There was no nervousness, but a brisk and cheery affability about Mr. Raymond Martin, M.P., as he drove up, watched by many eyes, to the Head's house.

"Looks a bit of a bargee," was McTurk's comment. "Shouldn't be surprised if he was a Radical. He rowed the driver about the fare. I heard him."

"That was his giddy patriotism," Beetle explained.

After tea they joined the rush for seats, secured a private and invisible corner, and began to criticise. Every gas-jet was lit. On the little dais at the far end stood the Head's official desk, whence Mr. Martin would discourse, and a ring of chairs for the masters.

Entered then Foxy, with official port, and leaned something like a cloth rolled round a stick against the desk. No one in authority was yet present, so the school applauded, crying: "What's that, Foxy? What are you stealin' the gentleman's brolly for?–We don't birch here. We cane! Take away that bauble!–Number off from the right"–and so forth, till the entry of the Head and the masters ended all demonstrations.

"One good job–the Common-room hate this as much as we do. Watch King wrigglin' to get out of the draft."

"Where's the Raymondiferous Martin? Punctuality, my beloved 'earers, is the image o' war—"

"Shut up. Here's the giddy Dook. Golly, what a dewlap!" Mr. Martin, in evening dress, was undeniably throaty–a tall, generously designed, pink-and-white man. Still, Beetle need not have been coarse.

"Look at his back while he's talkin' to the Head. Vile bad form to turn your back on the audience! He's a Philistine–a Bopper–a Jebusite–an' a Hivite." McTurk leaned back and sniffed contemptuously.

In a few colorless words, the Head introduced the speaker and sat down amid applause. When Mr. Martin took the applause to himself, they naturally applauded more than ever. It was some time before he could begin. He had no knowledge of the school–its tradition or heritage. He did not know that the last census showed that eighty per cent. of the boys had been born abroad–in camp, cantonment, or upon the high seas; or that seventy-five per cent. were sons of officers in one or other of the services–Willoughbys, Paulets, De Castros, Maynes, Randalls, after their kind–looking to follow their fathers' profession. The Head might have told him this, and much more; but, after an hour-long dinner in his company, the Head decided to say nothing whatever. Mr. Raymond Martin seemed to know so much already.

He plunged into his speech with a long-drawn, rasping "Well, boys," that, though they were not conscious of it, set every young nerve ajar. He supposed they knew–hey?–what he had come down for? It was not often that he had an opportunity to talk to boys. He supposed that boys were very much the same kind of persons–some people thought them rather funny persons–as they had been in his youth.

"This man," said McTurk, with conviction, "is *the* Gadarene Swine."

But they must remember that they would not always be boys. They would grow up into men, because the boys of to-day made the men of tomorrow, and upon the men of to-morrow the fair fame of their glorious native land depended.

"If this goes on, my beloved 'earers, it will be my painful duty to rot this bargee." Stalky drew a long breath through his nose.

"Can't do that," said McTurk. "He ain't chargin' anything for his Romeo."

And so they ought to think of the duties and responsibilities of the life that was opening before them. Life was not all–he enumerated a few games, and, that nothing might be lacking to the sweep and impact of his fall, added "marbles." "Yes, life was not," he said, "all marbles."

There was one tense gasp–among the juniors almost a shriek–of quivering horror. He was a heathen–an outcast–beyond the extremest pale of toleration–self-damned before all men. Stalky bowed his head in his hands. McTurk, with a bright and cheerful eye, drank in every word, and Beetle nodded solemn approval.

Some of them, doubtless, expected in a few years to have the honor of a commission from the Queen, and to wear a sword. Now, he himself had had some experience of these duties, as a Major in a volunteer regiment, and he was glad to learn that they had established a volunteer corps in their midst. The establishment of such an establishment conduced to a proper and healthy spirit, which, if fostered, would be of great benefit to the land they loved and were so proud to belong to. Some of those now present expected, he had no doubt–some of them anxiously looked forward to leading their men against the bullets of England's foes; to confronting the stricken field in all the pride of their youthful manhood.

Now the reserve of a boy is tenfold deeper than the reserve of a maid, she being made for one end only by blind Nature, but man for several. With a large and healthy hand, he tore down these veils, and trampled them under the well-intentioned feet of eloquence. In a raucous voice, he cried aloud little matters, like the hope of Honor and the dream of Glory, that boys do not discuss even with their most intimate equals, cheerfully assuming that, till he spoke, they had never considered these possibilities. He pointed them to shining goals, with fingers which smudged out all radiance on all horizons. He profaned the most secret places of their souls with outcries and gesticulations. He bade them consider the deeds of their ancestors in such a fashion that they were flushed to their tingling ears. Some of them–the rending voice cut a frozen stillness–might have had relatives who perished in defence of their country. They thought, not a few of them, of an old sword in a passage, or above a breakfast-room table, seen and fingered by stealth since they could walk. He adjured them to emulate those illustrious examples; and they looked all ways in their extreme discomfort.

Their years forbade them even to shape their thoughts clearly to themselves. They felt savagely that they were being outraged by a fat man who considered marbles a game.

And so he worked towards his peroration–which, by the way, he used later with overwhelming success at a meeting of electors–while they sat, flushed and uneasy, in sour disgust. After many, many words, he reached for the cloth-wrapped stick and thrust one hand in his bosom. This–this was the concrete symbol of their land–worthy of all honor and reverence! Let no boy look on this flag who did not purpose to worthily add to its imperishable luster. He shook it before them–a large calico Union Jack, staring in all three colors, and waited for the thunder of applause that should crown his effort.

They looked in silence. They had certainly seen the thing before–down at the coastguard station, or through a telescope, half-mast high when a brig went ashore on Braunton Sands; above the roof of the Golf-club, and in Keyte's window, where a certain kind of striped sweetmeat bore it in paper on each box. But the College never displayed it; it was no part of the scheme of their lives; the Head had never alluded to it; their fathers had not declared it unto them. It was a matter shut up, sacred and apart. What, in the name of everything caddish, was he driving at, who waved that horror before their eyes? Happy thought! Perhaps he was drunk.

The Head saved the situation by rising swiftly to propose a vote of thanks, and at his first motion, the school clapped furiously, from a sense of relief.

"And I am sure," he concluded, the gaslight full on his face, "that you will all join me in a very hearty vote of thanks to Mr. Raymond Martin for the most enjoyable address he has given us."

To this day we shall never know the rights of the case. The Head vows that he did no such thing; or that, if he did, it must have been something in his eye; but those who were present are persuaded that he winked, once, openly and solemnly, after the word "enjoyable." Mr. Raymond Martin got his applause full tale. As he said, "Without vanity, I think my few words went to their hearts. I never knew boys could cheer like that."

He left as the prayer-bell rang, and the boys lined up against the wall. The flag lay still unrolled on the desk, Foxy regarding it with pride, for he had been touched to the quick by Mr. Martin's eloquence. The Head and the Common-room, standing back on the dais, could not see the glaring offence, but a prefect left the line, rolled it up swiftly, and as swiftly tossed it into a glove and foil locker.

Then, as though he had touched a spring, broke out the low murmur of content, changing to quick-volleyed hand-clapping.

They discussed the speech in the dormitories. There was not one dissentient voice. Mr. Raymond Martin, beyond question, was born in a gutter, and bred in a board-school, where they played marbles. He was further (I give the barest handful from great store) a Flopshus Cad, an Outrageous Stinker, a Jelly-bellied Flag-flapper (this was Stalky's contribution), and several other things which it is not seemly to put down.

The volunteer cadet-corps fell in next Monday, depressedly, with a face of shame. Even then, judicious silence might have turned the corner.

Said Foxy: "After a fine speech like what you 'eard night before last, you ought to take 'old of your drill with *re*-newed activity. I don't see how you can avoid comin' out an' marchin' in the open now."

"Can't we get out of it, then, Foxy?" Stalky's fine old silky tone should have warned him.

"No, not with his giving the flag so generously. He told me before he left this morning that there was no objection to the corps usin' it as their own. It's a handsome flag."

Stalky returned his rifle to the rack in dead silence, and fell out. His example was followed by Hogan and Ansell.

Perowne hesitated. "Look here, oughtn't we—?" he began.

"I'll get it out of the locker in a minute," said the Sergeant, his back turned. "Then we can—"

"Come on!" shouted Stalky. "What the devil are you waiting for? Dismiss! Break off."

"Why–what the–where the—?"

The rattle of Sniders, slammed into the rack, drowned his voice, as boy after boy fell out.

"I–I don't know that I shan't have to report this to the Head," he stammered.

"Report, then, and be damned to you," cried Stalky, white to the lips, and ran out.

. . . .

"Rummy thing!" said Beetle to McTurk. "I was in the study, doin' a simply lovely poem about the Jelly-Bellied Flag-Flapper, an' Stalky came in, an' I said 'Hullo!' an' he cursed me like a bargee, and then he began to blub like anything. Shoved his head on the table and howled. Hadn't we better do something?"

McTurk was troubled. "P'raps he's smashed himself up somehow."

They found him, with very bright eyes, whistling between his teeth.

"Did I take you in, Beetle? I thought I would. Wasn't it a good draw? Didn't you think I was blubbin'? Didn't I do it well? Oh, you fat old ass!" And he began to pull Beetle's ears and cheeks, in the fashion that was called "milking."

"I knew you were blubbin'," Beetle replied, composedly. "Why aren't you at drill?"

"Drill! What drill?"

"Don't try to be a clever fool. Drill in the Gym."

"'Cause there isn't any. The volunteer cadet-corps is broke up—disbanded—dead—putrid—corrupt—stinkin'. An' if you look at me like that, Beetle, I'll slay you too. . . . Oh, yes, an' I'm goin' to be reported to the Head for swearin'."

The Last Term

IT WAS WITHIN a few days of the holidays, the term-end examinations, and, more important still, the issue of the College paper which Beetle edited. He had been cajoled into that office by the blandishments of Stalky and McTurk and the extreme rigor of study law. Once installed, he discovered, as others have done before him, that his duty was to do the work while his friends criticized. Stalky christened it the "Swillingford Patriot," in pious memory of Sponge—and McTurk compared the output unfavorably with Ruskin and De Quincey. Only the Head took an interest in the publication, and his methods were peculiar. He gave Beetle the run of his brown-bound, tobacco-scented library; prohibiting nothing, recommending nothing. There Beetle found a fat arm-chair, a silver inkstand, and unlimited pens and paper. There were scores and scores of ancient dramatists; there were Hakluyt, his voyages; French translations of Muscovite authors called Pushkin and Lermontoff; little tales of a heady and bewildering nature, interspersed with unusual songs—Peacock was that writer's name; there was Borrow's "Lavengro"; an odd theme, purporting to be a translation of something, called a "Rubáiyát," which the Head said was a poem not yet come to its own; there were hundreds of volumes of verse—Crashaw; Dryden; Alexander Smith; L. E. L.; Lydia Sigourney; Fletcher and a purple island; Donne; Marlowe's "Faust"; and—this made McTurk (to whom Beetle conveyed it) sheer drunk for three days—Ossian; "The Earthly Paradise"; "Atalanta in Calydon"; and Rossetti—to name only a few. Then the Head, drifting in under pretense of playing censor to the paper, would read here a verse and here another of these poets, opening up avenues. And, slow breathing, with half-shut eyes above his cigar, would he speak of great men living, and journals, long dead, founded in their riotous youth; of years when all the planets were little new-lit stars trying to find their places in the uncaring void, and he, the Head, knew them as young men know one another. So the regular work went to the dogs, Beetle being full of other matters and meters, hoarded in secret and only told to McTurk of an afternoon, on the sands, walking high and disposedly round the wreck of the Armada galleon, shouting and declaiming against the long-ridged seas.

Thanks in large part to their house-master's experienced distrust, the three for three consecutive terms had been passed over for promotion to the rank of prefect–an office that went by merit, and carried with it the honor of the ground-ash, and liberty, under restrictions, to use it.

"*But*," said Stalky, "come to think of it, we've done more giddy jesting with the Sixth since we've been passed over than any one else in the last seven years."

He touched his neck proudly. It was encircled by the stiffest of stick-up collars, which custom decreed could be worn only by the Sixth. And the Sixth saw those collars and said no word. "Pussy," Abanazar, or Dick Four of a year ago would have seen them discarded in five minutes or . . . But the Sixth of that term was made up mostly of young but brilliantly clever boys, pets of the house-masters, too anxious for their dignity to care to come to open odds with the resourceful three. So they crammed their caps at the extreme back of their heads, instead of a trifle over one eye as the Fifth should, and rejoiced in patent-leather boots on week-days, and marvellous made-up ties on Sundays–no man rebuking. McTurk was going up for Cooper's Hill, and Stalky for Sandhurst, in the spring; and the Head had told them both that, unless they absolutely collapsed during the holidays, they were safe. As a trainer of colts, the Head seldom erred in an estimate of form.

He had taken Beetle aside that day and given him much good advice, not one word of which did Beetle remember when he dashed up to the study, white with excitement, and poured out the wondrous tale. It demanded a great belief.

"*You* begin on a hundred a year?" said McTurk unsympathetically. "Rot!"

"*And* my passage out! It's all settled. The Head says he's been breaking me in for this for ever so long, and I never knew–I never knew. One don't begin with writing straight off, y'know. Begin by filling in telegrams and cutting things out o' papers with scissors."

"Oh, Scissors! What an ungodly mess you'll make of it," said Stalky. "But, anyhow, this will be your last term, too. Seven years, my dearly beloved 'earers–though not prefects."

"Not half bad years, either," said McTurk. "I shall be sorry to leave the old Coll.; shan't you?"

They looked out over the sea creaming along the Pebbleridge in the clear winter light. "Wonder where we shall all be this time next year?" said Stalky absently.

"This time five years," said McTurk.

"Oh," said Beetle, "my leavin's between ourselves. The Head hasn't told any one. I know he hasn't, because Prout grunted at me to-day that if I were more reasonable–yah!–I might be a prefect next term. I suppose he's hard up for his prefects."

"Let's finish up with a row with the Sixth," suggested McTurk.

"Dirty little schoolboys!" said Stalky, who already saw himself a Sandhurst cadet. "What's the use?"

"Moral effect," quoth McTurk. "Leave an imperishable tradition, and all the rest of it."

"Better go into Bideford an' pay up our debts," said Stalky. "I've got three quid out of my father–*ad hoc.* Don't owe more than thirty bob, either. Cut along, Beetle, and ask the Head for leave. Say you want to correct the 'Swillingford Patriot.' "

"Well, I do," said Beetle. "It'll be my last issue, and I'd like it to look decent. I'll catch him before he goes to his lunch."

Ten minutes later they wheeled out in line, by grace released from five o'clock call-over, and all the afternoon lay before them. So also unluckily did King, who never passed without witticisms. But brigades of Kings could not have ruffled Beetle that day.

"Aha! Enjoying the study of light literature, my friends," said he, rubbing his hands. "Common mathematics are not for such soaring minds as yours, are they?"

("One hundred a year," thought Beetle, smiling into vacancy.)

"Our open incompetence takes refuge in the flowery paths of inaccurate fiction. But a day of reckoning approaches, Beetle mine. I myself have prepared a few trifling foolish questions in Latin prose which can hardly be evaded even by your practised acts of deception. Ye-es, Latin prose. I think, if I may say so—but we shall see when the papers are set—'Ulpian serves *your* need.' Aha! '*Elucescebat*, quoth our friend.' We shall see! We shall see!"

Still no sign from Beetle. He was on a steamer, his passage paid into the wide and wonderful world—a thousand leagues beyond Lundy Island.

King dropped him with a snarl.

"He doesn't know. He'll go on correctin' exercises an' jawin' an' showin' off before the little boys next term—and next." Beetle hurried after his companions up the steep path of the furze-clad hill behind the College.

They were throwing pebbles on the top of the gasometer, and the grimy gas-man in charge bade them desist. They watched him oil a turncock sunk in the ground between two furze-bushes.

"Cokey, what's that for?" said Stalky.

"To turn the gas on to the kitchens," said Cokey. "If so be I didn't turn her on, yeou young gen'lemen 'ud be larnin' your book by candlelight."

"Um!" said Stalky, and was silent for at least a minute.

"Hullo! Where are you chaps going?"

A bend of the lane brought them face to face with Tulke, senior prefect of King's house—a smallish, white-haired boy, of the type that must be promoted on account of its intellect, and ever afterwards appeals to the Head to support its authority when zeal has outrun discretion.

The three took no sort of notice. They were on lawful pass. Tulke repeated his question hotly, for he had suffered many slights from Number Five study, and fancied that he had at last caught them tripping.

"What the devil is that to you?" Stalky replied with his sweetest smile.

"Look here, I'm not goin'—I'm not goin' to be sworn at by the Fifth!" sputtered Tulke.

"Then cut along and call a prefects' meeting," said McTurk, knowing Tulke's weakness.

The prefect became inarticulate with rage.

"Mustn't yell at the Fifth that way," said Stalky. "It's vile bad form."

"Cough it up, ducky!" McTurk said calmly.

"I—I want to know what you chaps are doing out of bounds?" This with an important flourish of his ground-ash.

"Ah," said Stalky. "Now we're gettin' at it. Why didn't you ask that before?"

"Well, I ask it now. What are you doing?"

"We're admiring you, Tulke," said Stalky. "We think you're no end of a fine chap, don't we?"

"We do! We do!" A dog-cart with some girls in it swept round the corner, and Stalky promptly kneeled before Tulke in the attitude of prayer; so Tulke turned a color.

"I've reason to believe—" he began.

"Oyez! Oyez! Oyez!" shouted Beetle, after the manner of Bideford's town crier, "Tulke has reason to believe! Three cheers for Tulke!"

They were given. "It's all our giddy admiration," said Stalky. "You know how we love you, Tulke. We love you so much we think you ought to go home and die. You're too good to live, Tulke."

"Yes," said McTurk. "*Do* oblige us by dyin'. Think how lovely you'd look stuffed!"

Tulke swept up the road with an unpleasant glare in his eye.

"That means a prefects' meeting–sure pop," said Stalky. "Honor of the Sixth involved, and all the rest of it. Tulke'll write notes all this afternoon, and Carson will call us up after tea. They daren't overlook that."

"But you a bob he follows us!" said McTurk. "He's King's pet, and it's scalps to both of 'em if we're caught out. We must be virtuous."

"Then I move we go to Mother Yeo's for a last gorge. We owe her about ten bob, and Mary'll weep sore when she knows we're leaving," said Beetle.

"She gave me an awful wipe on the head last time–Mary," said Stalky.

"She does if you don't duck," said McTurk. "But she generally kisses one back. Let's try Mother Yeo."

They sought a little bottle-windowed half dairy, half restaurant, a dark-browed, two-hundred-year-old house, at the head of a narrow side street. They had patronized it from the days of their fagdom, and were very much friends at home.

"We've come to pay our debts, mother," said Stalky, sliding his arm round the fifty-six-inch waist of the mistress of the establishment. "To pay our debts and say good-by–and–and we're awf'ly hungry."

"Aie!" said Mother Yeo, "makkin' love to me! I'm shaamed of 'ee."

" 'Rackon us wouldn't du no such thing if Mary was here," said McTurk, lapsing into the broad North Devon that the boys used on their campaigns.

"Who'm takin' my name in vain?" The inner door opened, and Mary, fair-haired, blue-eyed, and apple-cheeked, entered with a bowl of cream in her hands. McTurk kissed her. Beetle followed suit, with exemplary calm. Both boys were promptly cuffed.

"Niver kiss the maid when 'e can kiss the mistress," said Stalky, shamelessly winking at Mother Yeo, as he investigated a shelf of jams.

"Glad to see one of 'ee don't want his head slapped no more?" said Mary invitingly, in that direction.

"Neu! Reckon I can get 'em give me," said Stalky, his back turned.

"Not by me–yeo little masterpiece!"

"Niver ask 'ee. There's maids to Northam. Yiss–an' Appledore." An unreproducible sniff, half contempt, half reminiscence, rounded the retort.

"Aie! Yeou won't niver come to no good end. Whutt be 'baout, smellin' the cream?"

"'Tees bad," said Stalky. "Zmell 'un."

Incautiously Mary did as she was bid.

"Bidevoor kiss."

"Niver amiss," said Stalky, taking it without injury.

"Yeou–yeou–yeou–" Mary began, bubbling with mirth.

"They'm better to Northam–more rich, laike–an' us gets them give back again," he said, while McTurk solemnly waltzed Mother Yeo out of breath, and Beetle told Mary the sad news, as they sat down to clotted cream, jam, and hot bread.

"Yiss. Yeou'll niver zee us no more, Mary. We'm goin' to be passons an' missioners."

"Steady the Buffs!" said McTurk, looking through the blind. "Tulke *has* followed us. He's comin' up the street now."

"They've niver put us out o' bounds," said Mother Yeo. "Bide yeou still, my little dearrs." She rolled into the inner room to make the score.

"Mary," said Stalky, suddenly, with tragic intensity. "Do 'ee lov' me, Mary?"

"Iss–fai! Talled 'ee zo since yeou was zo high!" the damsel replied.

"Zee 'un comin' up street, then?" Stalky pointed to the unconscious Tulke. "He've niver been kissed by no sort or manner o' maid in hees borned laife, Mary. Oh, 'tees shaamful!"

"Whutt's to do with me? 'Twill come to 'un in the way o' nature, I rackon."

She nodded her head sagaciously. "You niver want me to kiss un—sure-*ly?*"

"Give 'ee half-a-crown if 'ee will," said Stalky, exhibiting the coin.

Half-a-crown was much to Mary Yeo, and a jest was more; but——

"Yeu'm afraid," said McTurk, at the psychological moment.

"Aie!" Beetle echoed, knowing her weak point. "There's not a maid to Northam 'ud think twice. An' yeou such a fine maid, tu!"

McTurk planted one foot firmly against the inner door lest Mother Yeo should return inopportunely, for Mary's face was set. It was then that Tulke found his way blocked by a tall daughter of Devon—that county of easy kisses, the pleasantest under the sun. He dodged aside politely. She reflected a moment, and laid a vast hand upon his shoulder.

"Where be'ee gwaine tu, my dearr?" said she.

Over the handkerchief he had crammed into his mouth Stalky could see the boy turn scarlet.

"Gie I a kiss! Don't they larn 'ee manners to College?"

Tulke gasped and wheeled. Solemnly and conscientiously Mary kissed him twice, and the luckless prefect fled.

She stepped into the shop, her eyes full of simple wonder.

"Kissed 'un?" said Stalky, handing over the money.

"Iss, fai! But, oh, my little body, *he*'m no Colleger. 'Zeemed tu-minded to cry, laike."

"Well, we won't. You couldn't make us cry that way," said McTurk. "Try."

Whereupon Mary cuffed them all round.

As they went out with tingling ears, said Stalky generally, "Don't think there'll be much of a prefects' meeting."

"Won't there, just!" said Beetle. "Look here. If he kissed her—which is our tack—he is a cynically immoral hog, and his conduct is blatant indecency. *Confer orationes Regis furiosissimi,* when he collared me readin' 'Don Juan.' "

" 'Course he kissed her," said McTurk. "In the middle of the street. With his house-cap on!"

"Time, 3.57 P.M. Make a note o' that. What d'you mean, Beetle?" said Stalky.

"Well! He's a truthful little beast. He may say he was kissed."

"And then?"

"Why, then!" Beetle capered at the mere thought of it. "Don't you see? The corollary to the giddy proposition is that the Sixth can't protect 'emselves from outrages an' ravishin's. Want nursemaids to look after 'em! We've only got to whisper that to the Coll. Jam for the Sixth! Jam for us! Either way it's jammy!"

"By Gum!" said Salky. "Our last term's endin' well. Now you cut along an' finish up your old rag, and Turkey and me will help. We'll go in the back way. No need to bother Randall."

"Don't play the giddy garden-goat, then?" Beetle knew what help meant, though he was by no means averse to showing his importance before his allies. The little loft behind Randall's printing-office was his own territory, where he saw himself already controlling the "Times." Here, under the guidance of the inky apprentice, he had learned to find his way more or less circuitously about the case, and considered himself an expert compositor.

The school paper in its locked formes lay on a stone-topped table, a proof by the side; but not for worlds would Beetle have corrected from the mere proof. With a mallet and a pair of tweezers, he knocked out mysterious wedges of wood that released the forme, picked a letter here and inserted a letter there, reading as he went along and stopping much to chuckle over his own contributions.

"You won't show off like that," said McTurk, "when you've got to do it for your living. Upside down and backwards, isn't it? Let's see if I can read it."

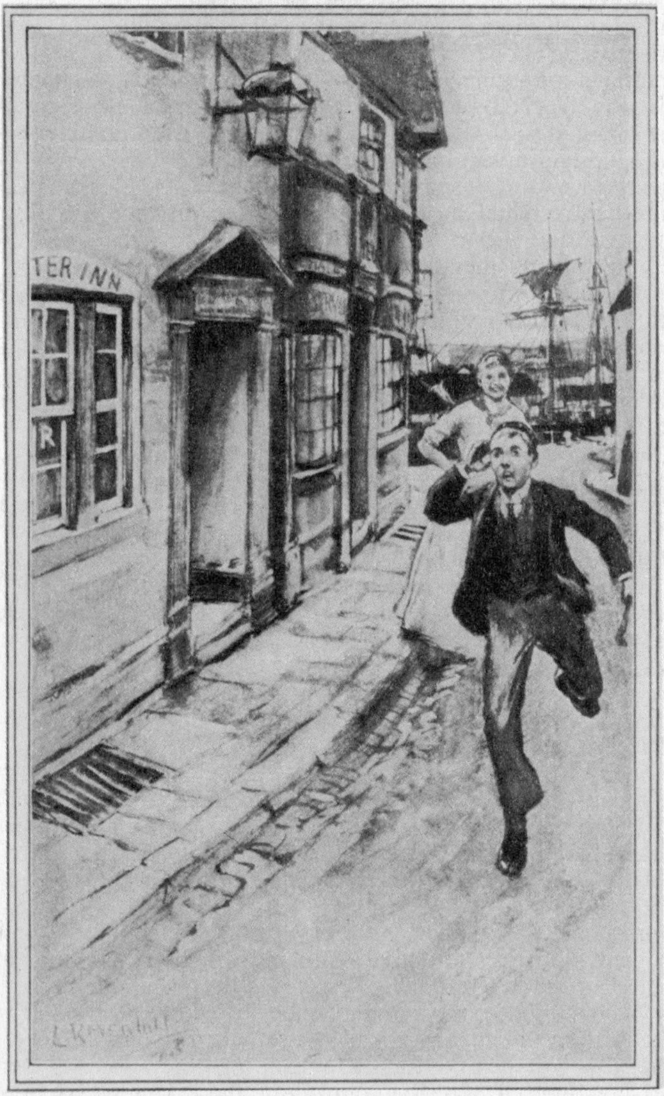

"THE LUCKLESS PREFECT FLED."

"Get out!" said Beetle. "Go and read those formes in the rack there, if you think you know so much."

"Formes in a rack! What's that? Don't be so beastly professional."

McTurk drew off with Stalky to prowl about the office. They left little unturned.

"Come here a shake, Beetle. What's this thing?" said Stalky, in a few minutes. "Looks familiar."

Said Beetle, after a glance: "It's King's Latin prose exam. paper. *In–In Verrem: actio prima.* What a lark!"

"Think o' the pure-souled, high-minded boys who'd give their eyes for a squint of it!" said McTurk.

"No, Willie dear," said Stalky; "that would be wrong and painful to our kind teachers. You wouldn't crib, Willie, would you?"

"Can't read the beastly stuff, anyhow," was the reply. "Besides, we're leavin' at the end o' the term, so it makes no difference to us."

" 'Member what the Considerate Bloomer did to Spraggon's account of the Puffin'ton Hounds? We must sugar Mr. King's milk for him," said Stalky, all lighted from within by a devilish joy. "Let's see what Beetle can do with those forceps he's so proud of."

"Don't see how you can make Latin prose much more cock-eye than it is, but we'll try," said Beetle, transposing an *aliud* and *Asiœ* from two sentences. "Let's see! We'll put that full-stop a little further on, and begin the sentence with the next capital. Hurrah! Here's three lines that can move up all in a lump."

" 'One of those scientific rests for which this eminent huntsman is so justly celebrated.' " Stalky knew the Puffington run by heart.

"Hold on! Here a *vol–voluntate quidnam* all by itself," said McTurk.

"I'll attend to her in a shake. *Quidnam* goes after *Dolabella.*"

"Good old Dolabella," murmured Stalky. "Don't break him. Vile prose Cicero wrote, didn't he? He ought to be grateful for—"

"Hullo!" said McTurk, over another forme. "What price a giddy ode? *Qui–quis*–oh, it's *Quis multa gracilis,* o' course."

"Bring it along. We've sugared the milk here," said Stalky, after a few minutes' zealous toil. "Never thrash your hounds unnecessarily."

"Quis munditiis? I swear that's not bad," began Beetle, plying the tweezers. "Don't that interrogation look pretty? *Heu quoties fidem!* That sounds as if the chap were anxious an' excited. *Cui flavam religas in rosa*–Whose flavor is relegated to a rose. *Mutatosque Deos flebit in antro.*"

"Mute gods weepin' in a cave," suggested Stalky. " 'Pon my Sam, Horace needs as much lookin' after as–Tulke."

They edited him faithfully till it was too dark to see.

. . . .

" 'Aha! *Elucescebat,* quoth our friend.' Ulpian serves my need, does it? If King can make anything out of *that,* I'm a blue-eyed squatteroo," said Beetle, as they slid out of the loft window into a back alley of old acquaintance and started on a three-mile trot to the College. But the revision of the classics had detained them too long. They halted, blown and breathless, in the furze at the back of the gasometer, the College lights twinkling below, ten minutes at least late for tea and lock-up.

"It's no good," puffed McTurk. "Bet a bob Foxy is waiting for defaulters under the lamp by the Fives Court. It's a nuisance, too, because the Head gave us long leave, and one doesn't like to break it."

" 'Let me now from the bonded ware'ouse of my knowledge,' " began Stalky.

"Oh, rot! Don't Jorrock. Can we make a run for it?" snapped McTurk.

"'Bishops' boots Mr. Radcliffe also condemned, an' spoke 'ighly in favor of tops cleaned with champagne an' abricot jam.' Where's the thing Cokey was twiddlin' this afternoon?"

They heard him groping in the wet, and presently beheld a great miracle. The lights of the Coastguard cottages near the sea went out; the brilliantly illuminated windows of the Golf-club disappeared, and were followed by the frontages of the two hotels. Scattered villas dulled, twinkled, and vanished. Last of all, the College lights died also. They were left in the pitchy darkness of a windy winter's night.

"'Blister my kidneys. It *is* a frost. The dahlias are dead!'" said Stalky. "Bunk!"

They squattered through the dripping gorse as the College hummed like an angry hive and the dining-rooms chorused, "Gas! gas! gas!" till they came to the edge of the sunk path that divided them from their study. Dropping that ha-ha like bullets, and rebounding like boys, they dashed to their study, in less than two minutes had changed into dry trousers and coat, and, ostentatiously slippered, joined the mob in the dining-hall, which resembled the storm-centre of a South American revolution.

"'Hellish dark and smells of cheese.'" Stalky elbowed his way into the press, howling lustily for gas. "Cokey must have gone for a walk. Foxy'll have to find him."

Prout, as the nearest house-master, was trying to restore order, for rude boys were flicking butter-pats across chaos, and McTurk had turned on the fags' tea-urn, so that many were parboiled and wept with unfeigned dolor. The Fourth and Upper Third broke into the school song, the *"Vive la Compagnie,"* to the accompaniment of drumming knife-handles; and the junior forms shrilled bat-like shrieks and raided one another's victuals. Two hundred and fifty boys in high condition, seeking for more light, are truly earnest inquirers.

When a most vile smell of gas told them that supplies had been renewed, Stalky, waistcoat unbuttoned, sat gorgedly over what might have been his fourth cup of tea. "And that's all right," he said. "Hullo! 'Ere's Pomponius Ego!"

It was Carson, the head of the school, a simple, straight-minded soul, and a pillar of the First Fifteen, who crossed over from the prefects' table and in a husky, official voice invited the three to attend in his study in half an hour.

"Prefects' meetin'! Prefects' meetin'!" hissed the tables, and they imitated barbarically the actions and effects of the ground-ash.

"How are we goin' to jest with 'em?" said Stalky, turning half-face to Beetle. "It's your play this time!"

"Look here," was the answer, "All I want you to do is not to laugh. I'm goin' to take charge o' young Tulke's immorality—*à la* King, and it's goin' to be serious. If you can't help laughin' don't look at me, or I'll go pop."

"I see. All right," said Stalky.

McTurk's lank frame stiffened in every muscle and his eyelids dropped half over his eyes. That last was a war-signal.

The eight or nine seniors, their faces very set and sober, were ranged in chairs round Carson's severely Philistine study. Tulke was not popular among them, and a few who had had experience of Stalky and Company doubted that he might, perhaps, have made an ass of himself. But the dignity of the Sixth was to be upheld. So Carson began hurriedly:

"Look here, you chaps, I've—we've sent for you to tell you you're a good deal too cheeky to the Sixth—have been for some time—and—and we've stood about as much as we're goin' to, and it seems you've been cursin' and swearin' at Tulke on the Bideford road this afternoon, and we're goin' to show you you can't do it. That's all."

"Well, that's awfully good of you," said Stalky, "but we happen to have a few rights of our own, too. You can't, just because you happen to be made prefects, haul up seniors and jaw 'em on spec., like a house-master. *We* aren't fags, Carson. This kind of thing may do for Davies Tertius, but it won't do for us."

"It's only old Prout's lunacy that we weren't prefects long ago. You know that," said McTurk. "You haven't any tact."

"Hold on," said Beetle. "A prefects' meetin' has to be reported to the Head. I want to know if the Head backs Tulke in this business?"

"Well–well, it isn't exactly a prefects' meeting," said Carson. "We only called you in to warn you."

"But all the prefects are here," Beetle insisted. "Where's the difference?"

"My Gum!" said Stalky. "Do you mean to say you've just called us in for a jaw–after comin' to us before the whole school at tea an' givin' 'em the impression it was a prefects' meeting? 'Pon my Sam, Carson, you'll get into trouble, you will."

"Hole-an'-corner business–hole-an'-corner business," said McTurk, wagging his head. "Beastly suspicious."

The Sixth looked at each other uneasily. Tulke had called three prefects' meeting in two terms, till the Head had informed the Sixth that they were expected to maintain discipline without the recurrent menace of his authority. Now, it seemed that they had made a blunder at the outset, but any right-minded boy would have sunk the legality and been properly impressed by the Court. Beetle's protest was distinct "cheek."

"Well, you chaps deserve a lickin'," cried one Naughten incautiously. Then was Beetle filled with a noble inspiration.

"For interferin' with Tulke's amours, eh?" Tulke turned a rich sloe color. "Oh, no, you don't!" Beetle went on. "You've had your innings. We've been sent up for cursing and swearing at you, and we're goin' to be let off with a warning! *Are* we? Now then, you're going to catch it."

"I–I–I–" Tulke began. "Don't let that young devil start jawing."

"If you've anything to say you must say it decently," said Carson.

"Decently? I will. Now look here. When we went into Bideford we met this ornament of the Sixth–is that decent enough?–hanging about on the road with a nasty look in his eye. We didn't know *then* why he was so anxious to stop us, *but* at five minutes to four, when we were in Yeo's shop, we saw Tulke *in* broad daylight, *with* his house-cap on, kissin' an' huggin' a woman *on* the pavement. Is that decent enough for you?"

"I didn't–I wasn't."

"We saw you!" said Beetle. "And now–I'll be decent, Carson–you sneak back with her kisses" (not for nothing had Beetle perused the later poets) "hot on your lips, and call prefects' meetings, which aren't prefects' meetings, to uphold the honor of the Sixth." A new and heaven-cleft path opened before him that instant. "And how do we know," he shouted–"how do we know how many of the Sixth are mixed up in this abominable affair?"

"Yes, that's what we want to know," said McTurk, with simple dignity.

"We meant to come to you about it quietly, Carson, but you *would* have the meeting," said Stalky sympathetically.

The Sixth were too taken aback to reply. So, carefully modelling his rhetoric on King, Beetle followed up the attack, surpassing and surprising himself.

"It–it isn't so much the cynical immorality of the biznai, as the blatant indecency of it, that's so awful. As far as we can see, it's impossible for us to go into Bideford without runnin' up against some prefect's unwholesome amours. There's nothing to snigger over, Naughten. *I* don't pretend to know much about these things–but it seems to me a chap must be pretty far dead in sin" (that was a quotation from the school chaplain) "when he takes to embracing his paramours" (that was Hakluyt) "before all the city" (a reminiscence of Milton). "He might at least have the decency–you're authorities on decency, I believe–to wait till dark. But he didn't. You didn't! Oh, Tulke. You–you incontinent little animal!"

"Here, shut up a minute. What's all this about, Tulke?" said Carson.

"I–look here. I'm awfully sorry. I never thought Beetle would take this line."

"Because–you've–no decency–you–thought–I hadn't," cried Beetle all in one breath.

"Tried to cover it all up with a conspiracy, did you?" said Stalky.

"Direct insult of all three of us," said McTurk. "A most filthy mind you have, Tulke."

"I'll shove you fellows outside the door if you go on like this," said Carson angrily.

"That proves it's a conspiracy," said Stalky, with the air of a virgin martyr.

"I–I was goin' along the street–I swear I was," cried Tulke, "and–and I'm awfully sorry about it–a woman came up and kissed me. I swear I didn't kiss her."

There was a pause, filled by Stalky's long, liquid whistle of contempt, amazement, and derision.

"On my honor," gulped the persecuted one. "Oh, do stop him jawing."

"Very good," McTurk interjected. "We are compelled, of course, to accept your statement."

"Confound it!" roared Naughten. "You aren't head-prefect here, McTurk."

"Oh, well," returned the Irishman, "you know Tulke better than we do. I am only speaking for ourselves. *We* accept Tulke's word. But all I can say is that if I'd been collared in a similarly disgustin' situation, and had offered the same explanation Tulke has, I–I wonder what you'd have said. However, it seems on Tulke's word of honor—"

"And Tulkus–beg pardon–*kiss,* of course–Tulkiss is an honorable man," put in Stalky.

"—that the Sixth can't protect 'emselves from bein' kissed when they go for a walk!" cried Beetle, taking up the running with a rush. "Sweet business, isn't it? Cheerful thing to tell the fags, ain't it? We aren't prefects, of course, but we aren't kissed very much. Don't think that sort of thing ever enters our heads; does it, Stalky?"

"Oh, no!" said Stalky, turning aside to hide his emotions. McTurk's face merely expressed lofty contempt and a little weariness.

"Well, you seem to know a lot about it," interposed a prefect.

"Can't help it–when you chaps shove it under our noses." Beetle dropped into a drawling parody of King's most biting colloquial style–the gentle rain after the thunder-storm. "Well, it's all very sufficiently vile and disgraceful, isn't it? I don't know who comes out of it worst: Tulke, who happens to have been caught; or the other fellows who haven't. And we–" here he wheeled fiercely on the other two–"we've got to stand up and be jawed by them because we've disturbed their intrigues."

"Hang it! I only wanted to give you a word of warning," said Carson, thereby handing himself bound to the enemy.

"Warn? You?" This with the air of one who finds loathsome gifts in his locker. "Carson, *would* you be good enough to tell us what conceivable thing there is that you are entitled to warn us about after this exposure? Warn? Oh, it's a little too much! Let's go somewhere where it's clean."

The door banged behind their outraged innocence.

"Oh, Beetle! Beetle! Beetle! Golden Beetle!" sobbed Stalky, hurling himself on Beetle's panting bosom as soon as they reached the study. "However did you do it?"

"Dear-r man!" said McTurk, embracing Beetle's head with both arms, while he swayed it to and fro on the neck, in time to this ancient burden–

"Pretty lips–sweeter than–cherry or plum,
Always look–jolly and–never look glum;
Seem to say–Come away. Kissy!–come, come!
Yummy-yum! Yummy-yum! Yummy-yum-yum!"

"Look out. You'll smash my gig-lamps," puffed Beetle, emerging. "Wasn't it glorious? Didn't I 'Eric' 'em splendidly? Did you spot my cribs from King? Oh, blow!" His countenance clouded. "There's one adjective I didn't use–obscene. Don't know how I forgot that. It's one of King's pet ones, too."

"Never mind. They'll be sendin' ambassadors round in half a shake to beg us not to tell the school. It's a deuced serious business for them," said McTurk. "Poor Sixth–poor old Sixth!"

"Immoral young rips," Stalky snorted. "What an example to pure-souled boys like you and me!"

And the Sixth in Carson's study sat aghast, glowering at Tulke, who was on the edge of tears.

"Well," said the head-prefect acidly. "You've made a pretty average ghastly mess of it, Tulke."

"Why–why didn't you lick that young devil Beetle before he began jawing?" Tulke wailed.

"I knew there'd be a row," said a prefect of Prout's house. "But you would insist on the meeting, Tulke."

"Yes, and a fat lot of good it's done us," said Naughten. "They come in here and jaw our heads off when we ought to be jawin' them. Beetle talks to us as if we were a lot of blackguards and–and all that. And when they've hung us up to dry, they go out and slam the door like a house-master. All your fault, Tulke."

"But I didn't kiss her."

"You ass! If you'd said you *had* and stuck to it, it would have been ten times better than what you did," Naughten retorted. "Now they'll tell the whole school–and Beetle'll make up a lot of beastly rhymes and nicknames."

"But, hang it, she kissed me!" Outside of his work, Tulke's mind moved slowly.

"I'm not thinking of you. I'm thinking of *us.* I'll go up to their study and see if I can make 'em keep quiet!"

"Tulke's awf'ly cut up about this business," Naughten began, ingratiatingly, when he found Beetle.

"Who's kissed him this time?"

"—and I've come to ask you chaps, and especially you, Beetle, not to let the thing be known all over the school. Of course, fellows as senior as you are can easily see why."

"Um!" said Beetle, with the cold reluctance of one who foresees an unpleasant public duty. "I suppose I must go and talk to the Sixth again."

"Not the least need, my dear chap, I assure you," said Naughten hastily. "I'll take any message you care to send."

But the chance of supplying the missing adjective was too tempting. So Naughten returned to that still undissolved meeting, Beetle, white, icy, and aloof, at his heels.

"There seems," he began, with laboriously crisp articulation, "there seems to be a certain amount of uneasiness among you as to the steps we may think fit to take in regard to this last revelation of the–ah–obscene. If it is any consolation to you to know that we have decided–for the honor of the school, you understand–to keep our mouths shut as to these–ah–obscenities, you–ah–have it."

He wheeled, his head among the stars, and strode statelily back to his study, where Stalky and McTurk lay side by side upon the table wiping their tearful eyes–too weak to move.

. . . .

The Latin prose paper was a success beyond their wildest dreams. Stalky and McTurk were, of course, out of all examinations (they did extra-tuition with the Head), but Beetle attended with zeal.

"This, I presume, is a par-ergon on your part," said King, as he dealt out the papers. "One final exhibition ere you are translated to loftier spheres? A last attack on the classics? It seems to confound you already."

Beetle studied the print with knit brows. "*I* can't make head or tail of it," he murmured. "What does it mean?"

"No, no!" said King, with scholastic coquetry. "We depend upon *you* to give us the meaning. This is an examination, Beetle mine, not a guessing-competition. You will find your associates have no difficulty in—"

Tulke left his place and laid the paper on the desk. King looked, read, and turned a ghastly green.

"Stalky's missing a heap," thought Beetle. "Wonder how King'll get out of it?"

"There seems," King began with a gulp, "a certain modicum of truth in our Beetle's remark. I am–er–inclined to believe that the worthy Randall must have dropped this in forme–if you know what that means. Beetle, you purport to be an editor. Perhaps you can enlighten the form as to formes."

"What, sir? Whose form? I don't see that there's any verb in this sentence at all, an'–an'–the Ode is all different, somehow."

"I was about to say, before you volunteered your criticism, that an accident must have befallen the paper in type, and that the printer reset it by the light of nature. No–" he held the thing at arm's length–"our Randall is not an authority on Cicero or Horace."

"Rather mean to shove it off on Randall," whispered Beetle to his neighbor. "King must ha' been as screwed as an owl when he wrote it out."

"But we can amend the error by dictating it."

"No, sir." The answer came pat from a dozen throats at once. "That cuts the time for the exam. Only two hours allowed, sir. 'Tisn't fair. It's a printed-paper exam. How're we goin' to be marked for it? It's all Randall's fault. It isn't *our* fault, anyhow. An exam.'s an exam.," etc., etc.

Naturally Mr. King considered this was an attempt to undermine his authority, and, instead of beginning dictation at once, delivered a lecture on the spirit in which examinations should be approached. As the storm subsided, Beetle fanned it afresh.

"Eh? What? What was that you were saying to MacLagan?"

"I only said I thought the papers ought to have been looked at before they were given out, sir."

"Hear, hear!" from a back bench.

Mr. King wished to know whether Beetle took it upon himself personally to conduct the traditions of the school. His zeal for knowledge ate up another fifteen minutes, during which the prefects showed unmistakable signs of boredom.

"Oh, it was a giddy time," said Beetle, afterwards, in dismantled Number Five. "He gibbered a bit, and I kept him on the gibber, and then he dictated about a half of Dolabella & Co."

"Good old Dolabella! Friend of mine. Yes?" said Stalky, pensively.

"Then we had to ask him how every other word was spelt, of course, and he gibbered a lot more. He cursed me and MacLagan (Mac played up like a trump) and Randall, and the 'materialized ignorance of the unscholarly middle classes,' 'lust for mere marks,' and all the rest. It was what you might call a final exhibition—a last attack—a giddy par-ergon."

"But o' course he was blind squiffy when he wrote the paper. I hope you explained *that?*" said Stalky.

"Oh, yes. I told Tulke so. I said an immoral prefect an' a drunken housemaster were legitimate inferences. Tulke nearly blubbed. He's awfully shy of us since Mary's time."

Tulke preserved that modesty till the last moment—till the journey-money had been paid, and the boys were filling the brakes that took them to the station. Then the three tenderly constrained him to wait a while.

"You see, Tulke, you may be a prefect," said Stalky, "but I've left the Coll. Do you see, Tulke, dear?"

"Yes, I see. Don't bear malice, Stalky."

"Stalky? Curse your impudence, you young cub," shouted Stalky, magnificent in top-hat, stiff collar, spats, and high-waisted, snuff-colored ulster. "I want you to understand that *I'm* Mister Corkran, an' you're a dirty little schoolboy."

"Besides bein' frabjously immoral," said McTurk. "Wonder you aren't ashamed to foist your company on pure-minded boys like us."

"Come on, Tulke," cried Naughten, from the prefects' brake.

"Yes, we're comin'. Shove up and make room, you Collegers. You've all got to be back next term, with your 'Yes, sir,' and 'Oh, sir,' an' 'No, sir,' an' 'Please, sir'; but before we say good-bye we're going to tell you a little story. Go on, Dickie" (this to the driver); "we're quite ready. Kick that hat-box under the seat, an' don't crowd your Uncle Stalky."

"As nice a lot of high-minded youngsters as you'd wish to see," said McTurk, gazing round with bland patronage. "A trifle immoral, but then—boys will be boys. It's no good tryin' to look stuffy, Carson. *Mister* Corkran will now oblige with the story of Tulke an' Mary Yeo!"

Slaves of the Lamp

Part II.

THAT VERY INFANT who told the story of the capture of Boh Na Ghee* to Eustace Cleaver, novelist, inherited an estateful baronetcy, with vast revenues, resigned the service, and became a landholder, while his mother stood guard over him to see that he married the right girl. But, new to his position, he presented the local volunteers with a full-sized magazine-rifle range, two miles long, across the heart of his estate, and the surrounding families, who lived in savage seclusion among woods full of pheasants, regarded him as an erring maniac. The noise of the firing disturbed their poultry, and Infant was cast out from the society of J.P.'s and decent men till such time as a daughter of the county might lure him back to right thinking. He took his revenge by filling the house with choice selections of old schoolmates home on leave—affable detrimentals, at whom the bicycle-riding maidens of the surrounding families were allowed to look from afar. I knew when a troop-ship was in port by the Infant's invitations. Sometimes he would produce old friends of

* *A Conference of the Powers:* "Many Inventions."

equal seniority; at others, young and blushing giants whom I had left small fags far down in the Lower Second; and to these Infant and the elders expounded the whole duty of man in the Army.

"I've had to cut the service," said the Infant; "but that's no reason why my vast stores of experience should be lost to posterity." He was just thirty, and in the same summer an imperious wire drew me to his baronial castle: "Got good haul; ex *Tamar.* Come along."

It was an unusually good haul, arranged with a single eye to my benefit. There was a baldish, broken-down captain of Native Infantry, shivering with ague behind an indomitable red nose—and they called him Captain Dickson. There was another captain, also of Native Infantry, with a fair mustache; his face was like white glass, and his hands were fragile, but he answered joyfully to the cry of Tertius. There was an enormously big and well-kept man, who had evidently not campaigned for years, clean-shaved, soft-voiced, and cat-like, but still Abanazar for all that he adorned the Indian Political Service; and there was a lean Irishman, his face tanned blue-black with the suns of the Telegraph Department. Luckily the baize doors of the bachelors' wing fitted tight, for we dressed promiscuously in the corridor or in each other's rooms, talking, calling, shouting; and anon waltzing by pairs to songs of Dick Four's own devising.

There were sixty years of mixed work to be sifted out between us, and since we met one another from time to time in the quick scene-shifting of India—a dinner, camp, or a race-meeting here; a dak-bungalow or railway station up country somewhere else—we had never quite lost touch. Infant sat on the banisters, hungrily and enviously drinking it in. He enjoyed his baronetcy, but his heart yearned for the old days.

It was a cheerful babel of matters personal, provincial, and imperial, pieces of old call-over lists, and new policies, cut short by the roar of a Burmese gong, and we went down not less than a quarter of a mile of stairs to meet Infant's mother, who had known us all in our school-days and greeted us as if those had ended a week ago. But it was fifteen years since, with tears of laughter, she had lent me a gray princess-skirt for amateur theatricals.

That was a dinner from the "Arabian Nights," served in an eighty-foot hall full of ancestors and pots of flowering roses, and, what was more impressive, heated by steam. When it was ended and the little mother had gone away—("You boys want to talk, so I shall say good-night now")—we gathered about an apple-wood fire, in a gigantic polished steel grate, under a mantelpiece ten feet high, and the Infant compassed us about with curious liqueurs and that kind of cigarette which serves best to introduce your own pipe.

"Oh, bliss!" grunted Dick Four from a sofa, where he had been packed with a rug over him. "First time I've been warm since I came home."

We were all nearly on top of the fire, except Infant, who had been long enough at Home to take exercise when he felt chilled. This is a grisly diversion, but much affected by the English of the Island.

"If you say a word about cold tubs and brisk walks," drawled McTurk, "I'll kill you, Infant. I've got a liver, too. 'Member when we used to think it a treat to turn out of our beds on a Sunday morning—thermometer fifty-seven degrees if it was summer—and bathe off the Pebbleridge? Ugh!"

" 'Thing I don't understand," said Tertius, "was the way we chaps used to go down into the lavatories, boil ourselves pink, and then come up with all our pores open into a young snow-storm or a black frost. Yet none of our chaps died, that I can remember."

"Talkin' of baths," said McTurk, with a chuckle, " 'member our bath in Number Five, Beetle, the night Rabbits-Eggs rocked King? What wouldn't I give to see old Stalky now! He is the only one of the two Studies not here."

"Stalky is the great man of his Century," said Dick Four.

"How d'you know?" I asked.

"How do I know?" said Dick Four, scornfully. "If you've ever been in a tight place with Stalky you wouldn't ask."

"I haven't seen him since the camp at Pindi in '87," I said. "He was goin' strong then–about seven feet high and four feet through."

"Adequate chap. Infernally adequate," said Tertius, pulling his mustache and staring into the fire.

"Got dam' near court-martialed and broke in Egypt in '84," the Infant volunteered. "I went out in the same trooper with him–as raw as he was. Only *I* showed it, and Stalky didn't."

"What was the trouble?" said McTurk, reaching forward absently to twitch my dress-tie into position.

"Oh, nothing. His colonel trusted him to take twenty Tommies out to wash, or groom camels, or something at the back of Suakin, and Stalky got embroiled with Fuzzies five miles in the interior. He conducted a masterly retreat and wiped up eight of 'em. He knew jolly well he'd no right to go out so far, so he took the initiative and pitched in a letter to his colonel, who was frothing at the mouth, complaining of the 'paucity of support accorded to him in his operations.' Gad, it might have been one fat brigadier slangin' another! Then he went into the Staff Corps."

"That–is–entirely–Stalky," said Abanazar from his arm-chair.

"You've come across him, too?" I said.

"Oh, yes," he replied in his softest tones. "I was at the tail of that–that epic. Don't you chaps know?"

We did not–Infant, McTurk, and I; and we called for information very politely.

" 'Twasn't anything," said Tertius. "We got into a mess up in the Khye-Kheen Hills a couple o' years ago, and Stalky pulled us through. That's all."

McTurk gazed at Tertius with all an Irishman's contempt for the tongue-tied Saxon.

"Heavens!" he said. "And it's you and your likes govern Ireland. Tertius, aren't you ashamed?"

"Well, I can't tell a yarn. I can chip in when the other fellow starts *bukhing.* Ask him." He pointed to Dick Four, whose nose gleamed scornfully over the rug.

"I knew you wouldn't," said Dick Four. "Give me a whiskey and soda. I've been drinking lemon-squash and ammoniated quinine while you chaps were bathin' in champagne, and my head's singin' like a top."

He wiped his ragged mustache above the drink; and, his teeth chattering in his head, began:

"You know the Khye-Kheen-Malôt expedition, when we scared the souls out of 'em with a field force they daren't fight against? Well, both tribes–there was a coalition against us–came in without firing a shot; and a lot of hairy villains, who had no more power over their men than I had, promised and vowed all sorts of things. On that very slender evidence, Pussy dear–"

"I was at Simla," said Abanazar, hastily.

"Never mind, you're tarred with the same brush. On the strength of those tuppenny-ha'penny treaties, your asses of Politicals reported the country as pacified, and the Government, being a fool, as usual, began road-makin'–dependin' on local supply for labor. 'Member *that,* Pussy? 'Rest of our chaps who'd had no look-in during the campaign didn't think there'd be any more of it, and were anxious to get back to India. But I'd been in two of these little rows before, and I had my suspicions. I engineered myself, *summo ingenio,* into command of a road-patrol–no shovellin', only marching up and down genteelly with a guard. They'd withdrawn all the troops they could, but I nucleused about forty Pathans, recruits chiefly, of my regiment, and sat tight at the base-camp while the road-parties went to work, as per Political survey."

"Had some rippin' sing-songs in camp, too," said Tertius.

"My pup"—thus did Dick Four refer to his subaltern—"was a pious little beast. He didn't like the sing-songs, and so he went down with pneumonia. I rootled round the camp, and found Tertius gassing about as a D.A.Q.M.G., which, God knows, he isn't cut out for. There were six or eight of the old Coll. at base-camp (we're always in force for a frontier row), but I'd heard of Tertius as a steady old hack, and I told him he had to shake off his D.A.Q.M.G. breeches and help *me*. Tertius volunteered like a shot, and we settled it with the authorities, and out we went—forty Pathans, Tertius, and me, looking up the road-parties. Macnamara's—'member old Mac, the Sapper, who played the fiddle so damnably at Umballa?—Mac's party was the last but one. The last was Stalky's. He was at the head of the road with some of his pet Sikhs. Mac said he believed he was all right."

"Stalky *is* a Sikh," said Tertius. "He takes his men to pray at the Durbar Sahib at Amritzar, regularly as clockwork, when he can."

"Don't interrupt, Tertius. It was about forty miles beyond Mac's before I found him; and my men pointed out gently, but firmly, that the country was risin'. What kind o' country, Beetle? Well, *I*'m no word-painter, thank goodness, but *you* might call it a hellish country! When we weren't up to our necks in snow, we were rolling down the khud. The well-disposed inhabitants, who were to supply labor for the road-making (don't forget that, Pussy dear), sat behind rocks and took pot-shots at us. 'Old, old story! We all legged it in search of Stalky. I had a feeling that he'd be in good cover, and about dusk we found him and his road-party, as snug as a bug in a rug, in an old Malôt stone fort, with a watch-tower at one corner. It overhung the road they had blasted out of the cliff fifty feet below; and under the road things went down pretty sheer, for five or six hundred feet, into a gorge about half a mile wide and two or three miles long. There were chaps on the other side of the gorge scientifically gettin' our range. So I hammered on the gate and nipped in, and tripped over Stalky in a greasy, bloody old poshteen, squatting on the ground, eating with his men. I'd only seen him for half a minute about three months before, but I might have met him yesterday. He waved his hand all sereno.

" 'Hullo, Aladdin! Hullo, Emperor!' he said. 'You're just in time for the performance.'

"I saw his Sikhs looked a bit battered. 'Where's your command? Where's your subaltern?' I said.

" 'Here—all there is of it,' said Stalky. 'If you want young Everett, he's dead, and his body's in the watch-tower. They rushed our road-party last week, and got him and seven men. We've been besieged for five days. I suppose they let you through to make sure of you. The whole country's up. 'Strikes me you've walked into a first-class trap.' He grinned, but neither Tertius nor I could see where the deuce the fun was. We hadn't any grub for our men, and Stalky had only four days' whack for his. That came of dependin' upon your asinine Politicals, Pussy dear, who told us that the inhabitants were friendly.

"To make us *quite* comfy, Stalky took us to the watch-tower to see poor Everett's body, lyin' in a foot o' drifted snow. It looked like a girl of fifteen—not a hair on the little fellow's face. He'd been shot through the temple, but the Malôts had left their mark on him. Stalky unbuttoned the tunic, and showed it to us—a rummy sickle-shaped cut on the chest. 'Member the snow all white on his eyebrows, Tertius? 'Member when Stalky moved the lamp and it looked as if he was alive?"

"Ye-es," said Tertius, with a shudder. " 'Member the beastly look on Stalky's face, though, with his nostrils all blown out, same as he used to look when he was bullyin' a fag? That was a lovely evening."

"We held a council of war up there over Everett's body. Stalky said the

Malôts and Khye-Kheens were up together; havin' sunk their blood feuds to settle us. The chaps we'd seen across the gorge were Khye-Kheens. It was about half a mile from them to us as a bullet flies, and they'd made a line of sungars under the brow of the hill to sleep in and starve us out. The Malôts, he said, were in front of us promiscuous. There wasn't good cover behind the fort, or they'd have been there, too. Stalky didn't mind the Malôts half as much as he did the Khye-Kheens. He said the Malôts were treacherous curs. What I couldn't understand was, why in the world the two gangs didn't join in and rush us. There must have been at least five hundred of 'em. Stalky said they didn't trust each other very well, because they were ancestral enemies when they were at home; and the only time they'd tried a rush he'd hove a couple of blasting-charges among 'em, and that had sickened 'em a bit.

"It was dark by the time we finished, and Stalky, always sereno, said: 'You command now. I don't suppose you mind my taking any action I may consider necessary to reprovision the fort?' I said, 'Of course not,' and then the lamp blew out. So Tertius and I had to climb down the tower steps (we didn't want to stay with Everett) and got back to our men. Stalky had gone off–to count the stores, I supposed. Anyhow, Tertius and I sat up in case of a rush (they were plugging at us pretty generally, you know), relieving each other till the mornin'.

"Mornin' came. No Stalky. Not a sign of him. I took counsel with his senior native officer–a grand, white-whiskered old chap–Rutton Singh, from Jullunder-way. He only grinned, and said it was all right. Stalky had been out of the fort twice before, somewhere or other, accordin' to him. He said Stalky 'ud come back unchipped, and gave me to understand that Stalky was an invulnerable *Guru* of sorts. All the same, I put the whole command on half rations, and set 'em to pickin' out loopholes.

"About noon there was no end of a snow-storm, and the enemy stopped firing. We replied gingerly, because we were awfully short of ammunition. Don't suppose we fired five shots an hour, but we generally got our man. Well, while I was talking with Rutton Singh I saw Stalky coming down from the watch-tower, rather puffy about the eyes, his poshteen coated with claret-colored ice.

" 'No trustin' these snow-storms,' he said. 'Nip out quick and snaffle what you can get. There's a certain amout of friction between the Khye-Kheens and the Malôts just now.'

"I turned Tertius out with twenty Pathans, and they bucked about in the snow for a bit till they came on to a sort of camp about eight hundred yards away, with only a few men in charge and half a dozen sheep by the fire. They finished off the men, and snaffled the sheep and as much grain as they could carry, and came back. No one fired a shot at 'em. There didn't seem to be anybody about, but the snow was falling pretty thick.

" 'That's good enough,' said Stalky when we got dinner ready and he was chewin' mutton-kababs off a cleanin' rod. 'There's no sense riskin' men. They're holding a pow-wow between the Khye-Kheens and the Malôts at the head of the gorge. I don't think these so-called coalitions are much good.'

"Do you know what that maniac had done? Tertius and I shook it out of him by instalments. There was an underground granary cellar-room below the watch-tower, and in blasting the road Stalky had blown a hole into one side of it. Being no one else *but* Stalky, he'd kept the hole open for his own ends; and laid poor Everett's body slap over the well of the stairs that led down to it from the watch-tower. He'd had to move and replace the corpse every time he used the passage. The Sikhs wouldn't go near the place, of course. Well, he'd got out of this hole, and dropped on to the road. Then, in the night *and* a howling snow-storm, he'd dropped over the edge of the khud, made his way down to the bottom of the gorge, forded the nullah, which was half frozen, climbed up on the other side along a track he'd discovered, and come out on the right flank of the Khye-Kheens. He had then–listen to this!–crossed over a ridge that paralleled their rear, walked half a mile behind that, and come out on the left of their line where the gorge gets shallow and where there was a regular track between the Malôt and the Khye-Kheen camps. That was about two in the morning, and, as it turned out, a man spotted him–a Khye-Kheen. So Stalky abolished him quietly, and left him–*with* the Malôt mark on his chest, same as Everett had.

" 'I was just as economical as I could be,' Stalky said to us. 'If he'd shouted I should have been slain. I'd never had to do that kind of thing but once before, and that was the first time I tried that path. It's perfectly practicable for infantry, you know.'

" 'What about your first man?' I said.

" 'Oh, that was the night after they killed Everett, and I went out lookin' for a line of retreat for my men. A man found me. I abolished him–*privatim*–scragged him. But on thinkin' it over it occurred to me that if I could find the body (I'd hove it down some rocks) I might decorate it with the Malôt mark and leave it to the Khye-Kheens to draw inferences. So I went out again the next night and did. The Khye-Kheens are shocked at the Malôts perpetratin' these two dastardly outrages after they'd sworn to sink all blood feuds. I lay up behind their sungars early this morning and watched 'em. They all went to confer about it at the head of the gorge. Awf'ly annoyed they are. Don't wonder.' You know the way Stalky drops out his words, one by one."

"My God!" said the Infant, explosively, as the full depth of the strategy dawned on him.

"Dear-r man!" said McTurk, purring, rapturously.

"Stalky stalked," said Tertius. "That's all there is to it."

"No, he didn't," said Dick Four. "Don't you remember how he insisted that he had only applied his luck? Don't you remember how Rutton Singh grabbed his boots and grovelled in the snow, and how our men shouted?"

"None of our Pathans believed that was luck," said Tertius. "They swore Stalky ought to have been born a Pathan, and–'member we nearly had a row in the fort when Rutton Singh said Stalky was a Pathan? God, how furious the old chap was with my Jemadar! But Stalky just waggled his finger and they shut up.

"Old Rutton Singh's sword was half out, though, and he swore he'd cremate every Khye-Kheen and Malôt he killed. That made the Jemadar pretty wild, because he didn't mind fighting against his own creed, but he wasn't going to crab a fellow Mussulman's chances of Paradise. Then Stalky jabbered Pushtu and Punjabi in alternate streaks. Where the deuce did he pick up his Pushtu from, Beetle?"

"Never mind his language, Dick," said I. "Give us the gist of it."

"I flatter myself I can address the wily Pathan on occasion, but, hang it all, I can't make puns in Pushtu, or top off my arguments with a smutty story, as he did. He played on those two old dogs o' war like a–like a concertina. Stalky said–and the other two backed up his knowledge of Oriental nature–that the Khye-Kheens and the Malôts between 'em would organize a combined attack on us that night, as a proof of good faith. They wouldn't drive it home, though, because neither side would trust the other on account, as Rutton Singh put it, of the little accidents. Stalky's notion was to crawl out at dusk with his Sikhs, manoeuvre 'em along this ungodly goat-track that he'd found, to the back of the Khye-Kheen position, and then lob in a few long shots at the Malôts when the attack was well on. 'That'll divert their minds and help to agitate 'em,' he said. 'Then you chaps can come out and sweep up the pieces, and we'll rendezvous at the head of the gorge. After that, I move we get back to Mac's camp and have something to eat.' "

"*You* were commandin'? " the Infant suggested.

"I was about three months senior to Stalky, and two months Tertius' senior," Dick Four replied. "*But* we were all from the same old Coll. I should say ours was the only little affair on record where some one wasn't jealous of some one else."

"*We* weren't," Tertius broke in, "but there was another row between Gul Sher Khan and Rutton Singh. Our Jemadar said—he was quite right—that no Sikh living could stalk worth a damn; and that Koran Sahib had better take out the Pathans, who understood that kind of mountain work. Rutton Singh said that Koran Sahib jolly well knew every Pathan was a born deserter, and every Sikh was a gentleman, even if he couldn't crawl on his belly. Stalky struck in with some woman's proverb or other, that had the effect of doublin' both men up with a grin. He said the Sikhs and the Pathans could settle their claims on the Khye-Kheens and Malôts later on, but he was going to take his Sikhs along for this mountain-climbing job, because Sikhs could shoot. They can, too. Give 'em a mule-load of ammunition apiece, and they're perfectly happy."

"And out he gat," said Dick Four. "As soon as it was dark, and he'd had a bit of a snooze, him and thirty Sikhs went down through the staircase in the tower, every mother's son of 'em salutin' little Everett where It stood propped up against the wall. The last I heard him say was, 'Kubbadar! tumbleinga!' * and they tumbleingaed over the black edge of nothing. Close upon 9 P.M. the combined attack developed; Khye-Kheens across the valley, and Malôts in front of us, pluggin' at long range and yellin' to each other to come along and cut our infidel throats. Then they skirmished up to the gate, and began the old game of calling our Pathans renegades, and invitin' 'em to join the holy war. One of our men, a young fellow from Dera Ismail, jumped on the wall to slang 'em back, and jumped down, blubbing like a child. He'd been hit smack in the middle of the hand. 'Never saw a man yet who could stand a hit in the hand without weepin' bitterly. It tickles up all the nerves. So Tertius took his rifle and smote the others on the head to keep them quiet at the loopholes. The dear children wanted to open the gate and go in at 'em generally, but that didn't suit our book.

"At last, near midnight, I heard the wop, wop, wop, of Stalky's Martinis across the valley, and some general cursing among the Malôts, whose main body was hid from us by a fold in the hillside. Stalky was brownin' 'em at a great rate, and very naturally they turned half right and began to blaze at their faithless allies, the Khye-Kheens—regular volley firin'. In less than ten minutes after Stalky opened the diversion they were going it hammer and tongs, both sides the valley. When we could see, the valley was rather a mixed-up affair. The Khye-Kheens had streamed out of their sungars above the gorge to chastise the Malôts, and Stalky—I was watching him through a glass—had slipped in behind 'em. Very good. The Khye-Kheens had to leg it along the hillside up to where the gorge got shallow and they could cross over to the Malôts, who were awfully cheered to see the Khye-Kheens taken in the rear.

"Then it occurred to me to comfort the Khye-Kheens. So I turned out the whole command, and we advanced *à la pas de charge,* doublin' up what, for the sake of argument, we'll call the Malôts' left flank. Even then, if they'd sunk their differences, they could have eaten us alive; but they'd been firin' at each other half the night, and they went on firin'. Queerest thing you ever saw in your born days! As soon as our men doubled up to the Malôts, they'd blaze at the Khye-Kheens more zealously than ever, to show they were on our side, run up the valley a few hundred yards, and halt to fire again. The moment Stalky saw our game he duplicated it his side the gorge; and, by Jove! the Khye-Kheens did just the same thing."

* "Look out; you'll fall!"

"Yes, but," said Tertius, "You've forgot him playin' 'Aarah, Patsy, mind the baby' on the bugle to hurry us up."

"Did he?" roared McTurk. Somehow we all began to sing it, and there was an interruption.

"Rather," said Tertius, when we were quiet. No one of the Aladdin company could forget that tune. "Yes, he played 'Patsy.' Go on, Dick."

"Finally," said Dick Four, "we drove both mobs into each other's arms on a bit of level ground at the head of the valley, and saw the whole crew whirl off, fightin' and stabbin' and swearin' in a blindin' snow-storm. They were a heavy, hairy lot, and we didn't follow 'em.

"Stalky had captured one prisoner—an old pensioned Sepoy of twenty-five years' service, who produced his discharge—an awf'ly sportin' old card. He had been tryin' to make his men rush us early in the day. He was sulky—angry with his own side for their cowardice, and Rutton Singh wanted to bayonet him—Sikhs don't understand fightin' against the Government after you've served it honestly—but Stalky rescued him, and froze on to him tight—with ulterior motives, I believe. When we got back to the fort, we buried young Everett—Stalky wouldn't hear of blowin' up the place—and bunked. We'd only lost ten men, all told."

"Only ten, out of seventy. How did you lose 'em?" I asked.

"Oh, there was a rush on the fort early in the night, and a few Malôts got over the gate. It was rather a tight thing for a minute or two, but the recruits took it beautifully. Lucky job we hadn't any badly wounded men to carry, because we had forty miles to Macnamara's camp. By Jove, how we legged it! Half way in, old Rutton Singh collapsed, so we slung him across four rifles and Stalky's overcoat; and Stalky, his prisoner, and a couple of Sikhs were his bearers. After that I went to sleep. You can, you know, on the march, when your legs get properly numbed. Mac swears we all marched into his camp snoring and dropped where we halted. His men lugged us into the tents like gram-bags. I remember wakin' up and seeing Stalky asleep with his head on old Rutton Singh's chest. *He* slept twenty-four hours. I only slept seventeen, but then I was coming down with dysentery."

"Coming down? What rot! He had it on him before we joined Stalky in the fort," said Tertius.

"Well, *you* needn't talk! You hove your sword at Macnamara and demanded a drumhead courtmartial every time you saw him. The only thing that soothed you was putting you under arrest every half hour. You were off your head for three days."

"Don't remember a word of it," said Tertius, placidly. "I remember my orderly giving me milk, though."

"How did Stalky come out?" McTurk demanded, puffing hard over his pipe.

"Stalky? Like a serene Brahmini bull. Poor old Mac was at his Royal Engineers' wits' end to know what to do. You see I was putrid with dysentery, Tertius was ravin', half the men had frost-bite, and Macnamara's orders were to break camp and come in before winter. So Stalky, who hadn't turned a hair, took half his supplies to save him the bother o' luggin' 'em back to the plains, and all the ammunition he could get at, and, *consilio et auxilio* Rutton Singhi, tramped back to his fort with all his Sikhs and his precious prisoners, *and* a lot of dissolute hangers-on that he and the prisoner had seduced into service. He had sixty men of sorts—and his brazen cheek. Mack nearly wept with joy when he went. You see there weren't any explicit orders to Stalky to come in before the passes were blocked; Mac is a great man for orders, and Stalky's a great man for orders—when they suit his book."

"He told me he was goin' to the Engadine," said Tertius. "Sat on my cot smokin' a cigarette, and makin' me laugh till I cried. Macnamara bundled the whole lot of us down to the plains next day. We were a walkin' hospital."

"Stalky told me that Macnamara was a simple godsend to him," said Dick Four. "I used to see him in Mac's tent listenin' to Mac playin' the fiddle, and, between the pieces, wheedlin' Mac out of picks and shovels and dynamite cartridges hand-over-fist. Well, that was the last we saw of Stalky. A week or so later the passes were shut with snow, and I didn't think Stalky wanted to be found particularly just then."

"He didn't," said the fair and fat Abanazar. "He didn't. Ho. ho!"

Dick Four threw up his thin, dry hand with the blue veins at the back of it. "Hold on a minute, Pussy; I'll let you in at the proper time. I went down to my regiment, and that spring, five months later, I got off with a couple of companies on detachment: nominally to look after some friends of ours across the border; actually, of course, to recruit. It was a bit unfortunate, because an ass of a young Naick carried a frivolous blood-feud he'd inherited from his aunt into those hills, and the local gentry wouldn't volunteer into my corps. Of course, the Naick had taken short leave to manage the business; that was all regular enough; *but* he'd stalked my pet orderly's uncle. It was an infernal shame, because I knew Harris of the Ghuznees would be covering that ground three months later, and he'd snaffle all the chaps I had my eyes on. Everybody was down on the Naick, because they felt he ought to have had the decency to postpone his–his disgustful amours till our companies were full strength.

"Still the beast had a certain amount of professional feeling left. He sent one of his aunt's clan by night to tell me that, if I'd take safeguard, he'd put me on to a batch of beauties. I nipped over the border like a shot, and about ten miles the other side, in a nullah, my rapparee-in-charge showed me about seventy men variously armed, but standing up like a Queen's company. Then one of 'em stepped out and lugged round an old bugle, just like–who's the man?–Bancroft, ain't it?–feeling for his eyeglass in a farce, and played 'Aarah, Patsy, mind the baby. Arrah, Patsy, mind'–that was as far as he could get.

That, also, was as far as Dick Four could get, because we had to sing the old song through twice, again and once more, and subsequently, in order to repeat it.

"He explained that if I knew the rest of the song he had a note for me from the man the song belonged to. Whereupon, my children, I finished that old tune on that bugle, and *this* is what I got. I knew you'd like to look at it. Don't grab." (We were all struggling for a sight of the well-known unformed handwriting.) "I'll read it aloud.

" 'FORT EVERETT, *February 19*.

" 'DEAR DICK, OR TERTIUS: The bearer of this is in charge of seventy-five recruits, all pukka devils, but desirous of leading new lives. They have been slightly polished, and after being boiled may shape well. I want you to give thirty of them to my adjutant, who, though God's own ass, will need men this spring. The rest you can keep. You will be interested to learn that I have extended my road to the end of the Malôt country. All headmen and priests concerned in last September's affair worked one month each, supplying road metal from their own houses. Everett's grave is covered by a forty-foot mound, which should serve well as a base for future triangulations. Rutton Singh sends his best salaams. I am making some treaties, and have given my prisoner–who also sends his salaams–local rank of Khan Bahadur.

" 'A. L. COCKRAN.'

"Well, that was all," said Dick Four, when the roaring, the shouting, the laughter, and, I think, the tears, had subsided. "I chaperoned the gang across the border as quick as I could. They were rather homesick, but they cheered up when they recognized some of my chaps, who had been in the Khye-Kheen row, and they made a rippin' good lot. It's rather more than three hundred miles from Fort Everett to where I picked 'em up. Now, Pussy, tell 'em the latter end o' Stalky as you saw it."

Abanazar laughed a little nervous, misleading, official laugh.

"Oh, it wasn't much. I was at Simla in the spring, when our Stalky, out of his snows, began corresponding direct with the Government."

"After the manner of a king," suggested Dick Four.

"My turn now, Dick. He'd done a whole lot of things he shouldn't have done, and constructively pledged the Government to all sorts of action."

"Pledged the State's ticker, eh?" said McTurk, with a nod to me.

"About that; but the embarrassin' part was that it was all so thunderin' convenient, so well reasoned, don't you know? Came in as pat as if he'd had access to all sorts of information–which he couldn't, of course."

"Pooh!" said Tertius, "I back Stalky against the Foreign Office any day."

"He'd done pretty nearly everything he could think of, except strikin' coins in his own image and superscription, all under cover of buildin' this infernal road and bein' blocked by the snow. His report was simply amazin'. Von Lennaert tore his hair over it at first, and then he gasped, 'Who the dooce is this unknown Warren Hastings? He must be slain. He must be slain officially! The Viceroy'll never stand it. It's unheard of. He must be slain by his Excellency in person. Order him up here and pitch in a stinger.' Well, I sent him no end of an official stinger, and I pitched in an unofficial telegram at the same time."

"You!" This with amazement from the Infant, for Abanazar resembled nothing so much as a fluffy Persian cat.

"Yes–me," said Abanazar. "'Twasn't much, but after what you've said, Dicky, it was rather a coincidence, because I wired:

"'Aladdin now has got his wife,
Your Emperor is appeased.
I think you'd better come to life:
We hope you've all been pleased.'

"Funny how that old song came up in my head. That was fairly non-committal and encouragin'. The only flaw was that his Emperor wasn't appeased by very long chalks. Stalky extricated himself from his mountain fastnesses and loafed up to Simla at his leisure, to be offered up on the horns of the altar."

"But," I began, "surely the Commander-in-Chief is the proper—"

"His Excellency had an idea that if he blew up one single junior captain–same as King used to blow us up–he was holdin' the reins of empire, and, of course, as long as he had that idea, Von Lennaert encouraged him. I'm not sure Von Lennaert didn't put that notion into his head."

"They've changed the breed, then, since my time," I said.

"P'r'aps. Stalky was sent up for his wiggin' like a bad little boy. I've reason to believe that His Excellency's hair stood on end. He walked into Stalky for one hour–Stalky at attention in the middle of the floor, and (so he vowed) Von Lennaert pretending to soothe down His Excellency's topknot in dumb show in the background. Stalky didn't dare to look up, or he'd have laughed.

"Now, wherefore was Stalky not broken publicly?" said the Infant, with a large and luminous leer.

"Ah, wherefore?" said Abanazar. "To give him a chance to retrieve his blasted career, and not to break his father's heart. Stalky hadn't a father, but that didn't matter. He behaved like a–like the Sanawar Orphan Asylum, and

His Excellency graciously spared him. Then he came round to my office and sat opposite me for ten minutes, puffing out his nostrils. Then he said, 'Pussy, if I thought that basket-hanger—' "

"Hah! He remembered *that,*" said McTurk.

" 'That two-anna basket-hanger governed India, I swear I'd become a naturalized Muscovite to-morrow. I'm a *femme incomprise.* This thing's broken my heart. It'll take six months' shootin'-leave in India to mend it. Do you think I can get it, Pussy?"

"He got it in about three minutes and a half, and seventeen days later he was back in the arms of Rutton Singh—horrid disgraced—with orders to hand over his command, etc., to Cathcart MacMonnie."

"Observe!" said Dick Four. "One colonel of the Political Department in charge of thirty Sikhs, on a hilltop. Observe, my children!"

"Naturally, Cathcart not being a fool, even if he *is* a Political, let Stalky do his shooting within fifteen miles of Fort Everett for the next six months, and I always understood they and Rutton Singh *and* the prisoner were as thick as thieves. Then Stalky loafed back to his regiment, I believe. I've never seen him since."

"I have, though," said McTurk, swelling with pride.

We all turned as one man.

"It was at the beginning of this hot weather. I was in camp in the Jullunder doab and stumbled slap on Stalky in a Sikh village; sitting on the one chair of state, with half the population grovellin' before him, a dozen Sikh babies on his knees, an old harridan clappin' him on the shoulder, and a garland o' flowers round his neck. Told me he was recruitin'. We dined together that night, but he never said a word of the business at the Fort. Told me, though, that if I wanted any supplies I'd better say I was Koran Sahib's *blai;* and I did, and the Sikhs wouldn't take my money."

"Ah! That must have been one of Rutton Singh's villages," said Dick Four; and we smoked for some time in silence.

"I say," said McTurk, casting back through the years, "did Stalky ever tell you *how* Rabbits-Eggs came to rock King that night?"

"No," said Dick Four.

Then McTurk told.

"I see," said Dick Four, nodding. "Practically he duplicated that trick over again. There's nobody like Stalky."

"That's just where you make the mistake," I said. "India's full of Stalkies—Cheltenham and Haileybury and Marlborough chaps—that we don't know anything about, and the surprises will begin when there is really a big row on."

"Who will be surprised?" said Dick Four.

"The other side. The gentlemen who go to the front in first-class carriages. Just imagine Stalky let loose on the south side of Europe with a sufficiency of Sikhs and a reasonable prospect of loot. Consider it quietly."

"There's something in that, but you're too much of an optimist, Beetle," said the Infant.

'Well, I've a right to be. Ain't I responsible for the whole thing? You needn't laugh. Who wrote 'Aladdin now has got his wife'—eh?"

"What's that got to do with it?" said Tertius.

"Everything," said I.

"Prove it," said the Infant.

And I have.

Kim

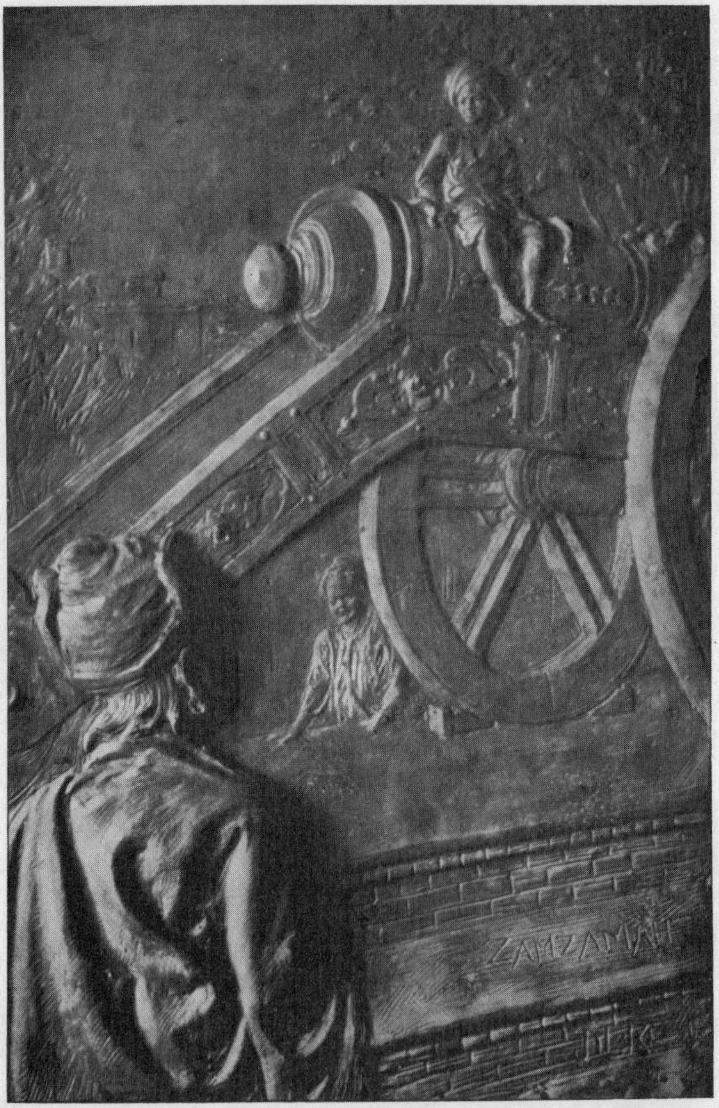

KIM.

Chapter One

Oh ye who tread the Narrow Way
By Tophet-flare to Judgment Day,
Be gentle when the heathen pray
To Buddha at Kamakura!

HE SAT, IN defiance of municipal orders, astride the gun Zam-Zammah on her brick platform opposite the old Ajaib-Gher—the Wonder House, as the natives called the Lahore Museum. Who hold Zam-Zammah, that "fire-breathing dragon," hold the Punjab; for the great green-bronze piece is always first of the conqueror's loot.

There was some justification for Kim,—he had kicked Lala Dinanath's boy off the trunnions,—since the English held the Punjab and Kim was English. Though he was burned black as any native; though he spoke the vernacular by preference, and his mother-tongue in a clipped, uncertain sing-song; though he consorted on terms of perfect equality with the small boys of the bazar; Kim was white—a poor white of the very poorest. The half-caste woman who looked after him (she smoked opium, and pretended to keep a second-hand furniture shop by the square where the cheap cabs wait) told the missionaries that she was Kim's mother's sister; but his mother had been nursemaid in a colonel's family and had married Kimball O'Hara, a young color-sergeant of the Mavericks, an Irish regiment. He afterwards took a post on the Sind, Punjab, and Delhi Railway, and his regiment went home without him. The wife died of cholera in Ferozepore, and O'Hara fell to drink and loafing up and down the line with the keen-eyed three-year-old baby. Societies and chaplains, anxious for the child, tried to catch him, but O'Hara drifted away, till he came across the woman who took opium and learned the taste from her, and died as poor whites die in India. His estate at death consisted of three papers—one he called his *ne varietur* because those words were written below his signature thereon, and another his "clearance-certificate." The third was Kim's birth-certificate. Those things, he was used to say, in his glorious opium hours, would yet make little Kimball a man. On no account was Kim to part with them, for they belonged to a great piece of magic—such magic as men practised over yonder behind the Museum, in the big blue and white Jadoo-Gher—the Magic House, as we name the Masonic Lodge. It would, he said, all come right some day, and Kim's horn would be exalted between pillars—monstrous pillars—of beauty and strength. The Colonel himself, riding on a horse, at the head of the finest regiment in the world, would attend to Kim,—little Kim that should have been better off than his father. Nine hundred first-class devils, whose god was a Red Bull on a green field, would attend to Kim, if they had not forgotten O'Hara—poor O'Hara that was gang-foreman on the Ferozepore line. Then he would weep bitterly in the broken rush chair on the verandah. So it came about after his death that the woman sewed parchment, paper, and birth-certificate into a leather amulet-case which she strung round Kim's neck.

"And some day," she said, confusedly remembering O'Hara's prophecies, "there will come for you a great Red Bull on a green field, and the Colonel riding on his horse, yes, and"—dropping into English—"nine hundred devils."

"Ah," said Kim, "I shall remember. A Red Bull and a Colonel on a horse will come, but first, my father said, come the two men making ready the ground for these matters. That is how, my father said, they always did; and it is always so when men work magic."

If the woman had sent Kim up to the local Jadoo-Gher with those papers, he would, of course, have been taken over by the Provincial Lodge and sent to the Masonic Orphanage in the Hills; but what she had heard of magic she distrusted. Kim, too, held views of his own. As he reached the years of indiscretion, he learned to avoid missionaries and white men of serious aspect who asked who he was, and what he did. For Kim did nothing with an immense success. True, he knew the wonderfull walled city of Lahore from the Delhi Gate to the outer Fort Ditch; was hand in glove with men who led lives stranger than anything Haroun al Raschid dreamed of; and he lived in a life wild as that of the Arabian Nights, but missionaries and secretaries of charitable societies could not see the beauty of it. His nickname through the wards was "Little Friend of all the World"; and very often, being lithe and inconspicuous, he executed commissions by night on the crowded house-tops for sleek and shiny young men of fashion. It was intrigue, of course,—he knew that much, as he had known all evil since he could speak,—but what he loved was the game for its own sake—the stealthy prowl through the dark gullies and lanes, the crawl up a water-pipe, the sights and sounds of the women's world on the flat roofs, and the head-long flight from housetop to housetop under cover of the hot dark. Then there were holy men, ash-smeared *faquirs* by their brick shrines under the trees at the riverside, with whom he was quite familiar—greeting them as they returned from begging-tours, and, when no one was by, eating from the same dish. The woman who looked after him insisted with tears that he should wear European clothes—trousers, a shirt, and a battered hat. Kim found it easier to slip into Hindu or Mahommedan garb when engaged on certain business. One of the young men of fashion—he who was found dead at the bottom of a well on the night of the earthquake—had once given him a complete suit of Hindu kit, the costume of a low-caste street boy, and Kim stored it in a secret place under some baulks in Nila Ram's timber-yard, beyond the Punjab High Court, where the fragrant deodar logs lie seasoning after they have driven down the Ravee. When there was business or frolic afoot, Kim would use his properties, returning at dawn to the verandah, all tired out from shouting at the heels of a marriage procession, or yelling at a Hindu festival. Sometimes there was food in the house, more often there was not, and Kim went out again to eat with his native friends.

As he drummed his heels against Zam-Zammah he turned now and again from his king-of-the-castle game with little Chota Lal and Abdullah the sweetmeat-seller's son, to make a rude remark to the native policeman on guard over rows of shoes at the Museum door. The big Punjabi grinned tolerantly: he knew Kim of old. So did the water-carrier, sluicing water on the dry road from his goat-skin bag. So did Jawahir Singh, the Museum carpenter, bent over new packing-cases. So did everybody in sight except the peasants from the country, hurrying up to the Wonder House to view the things that men made in their own province and elsewhere. The Museum was given up to Indian arts and manufactures, and anybody who sought wisdom could ask the curator to explain.

"Off! Off! Let me up!" cried Abdullah, climbing up Zam-Zammah's wheel.

"Thy father was a pastry-cook, Thy mother stole the *ghi,*" sang Kim. "All Mussalmans fell off Zam-Zammah long ago!"

"Let *me* up!" shrilled little Chota Lal in his gilt-embroidered cap. His father was worth perhaps half a million sterling, but India is the only democratic land in the world.

"The Hindus fell off Zam-Zammah too. The Mussalmans pushed them off. Thy father was a pastry-cook–"

He stopped; for there shuffled round the corner, from the roaring Motee Bazar, such a man as Kim, who thought he knew all castes, had never seen. He was nearly six feet high, dressed in fold upon fold of dingy stuff like horse-blanketing, and not one fold of it could Kim refer to any known trade or profession. At his belt hung a long open-work iron pencase and a wooden rosary such as holy men wear. On his head was a gigantic sort of tam-o-shanter. His face was yellow and wrinkled, like that of Fook Shing, the Chinese bootmaker in the bazar. His eyes turned up at the corners and looked like little slits of onyx.

"Who is that?" said Kim to his companions.

"Perhaps it is a man," said Abdullah, finger in mouth, staring.

"Without doubt," returned Kim; "but he is no man of India that *I* have ever seen."

"A priest, perhaps," said Chota Lal, spying the rosary. "See! He goes into the Wonder House!"

"Nay, nay," said the policeman, shaking his head. "I do not understand your talk." The constable spoke Punjabi. "Oh, The Friend of all the World, what does he say?"

"Send him hither," said Kim, dropping from Zam-Zammah, flourishing his bare heels. "He is a foreigner, and thou art a buffalo."

The man turned helplessly and drifted towards the boys. He was old, and his woollen gaberdine still reeked of the stinking artemisia of the mountain passes. "O Children, what is that big house?" he said in very fair Urdu.

"The Ajaib-Gher, the Wonder House!" Kim gave him no title–such as Lala or Mian. He could not divine the man's creed.

"Ah! The Wonder House! Can any enter?"

"It is written above the door–all can enter."

"Without payment?"

"I go in and out. *I* am no banker," laughed Kim.

"Alas! I am an old man. I did not know." Then, fingering his rosary, he half turned to the Museum.

"What is your caste? Where is your house? Have you come far?" Kim asked.

"I came by Kulu–from beyond the Kailas–but what know you? From the hills where"–he sighed–"the air and water are fresh and cool."

"Aha! Khitai (a Chinaman)," said Abdullah proudly. Fook Shing had once chased him out of his shop for spitting at the joss above the boots.

"Parhari (a hillman)," said Little Chota Lal.

"Ay, child–a hillman from hills thou'lt never see. Didst hear of Bhotiyal (Tibet)? I am no Khitai, but a Bhotiya (Tibetan), since you must know–a lama–or, say a *guru* in your tongue."

"A *guru* from Tibet," said Kim. "I have not seen such a man. They be Hindus in Tibet, then?"

"We be followers of the Middle Way, living in peace in our lamaseries, and I go to see the Four Holy Places before I die. Now do you, who are children, know as much as I do whom am old." He smiled benignantly on the boys.

"Hast thou eaten?"

He fumbled in his bosom and drew forth a worn wooden begging-bowl.

The boys nodded. All priests of their acquaintance begged.

"I do not wish to eat yet." He turned his head like an old tortoise in the sunlight. "Is it true that there are many images in the Wonder House of Lahore?" He repeated the last words as one making sure of an address.

"That is true," said Abdullah. "It is full of heathen *būts.* Thou also art an idolater."

"Never mind *him,*" said Kim. "That is the Government's house and there is no idolatry in it, but only a Sahib with a white beard. Come with me and I will show."

"Strange priests eat boys," whispered Chota Lal.

"And he is a stranger and a *būt-parast* (idolater)," said Abdullah, the Mohammedan.

Kim laughed. "He is new. Run to your mothers' laps, and be safe. Come!"

Kim clicked round the self-registering turnstile; the old man followed and halted amazed. In the entrance-hall stood the larger figures of the Greco-Buddhist sculptures done, savants know how long since, by forgotten workmen whose hands were feeling, and not unskilfully, for the mysteriously transmitted Grecian touch. There were hundreds of pieces, friezes of figures in relief, fragments of statues and slabs crowded with figures that had encrusted the brick walls of the Buddhist *stupas* and *viharas* of the North Country and now, dug up and labelled, made the pride of the Museum. In open-mouthed wonder the lama turned to this and that, and finally checked in rapt attention before a large alto-relief representing a coronation or apotheosis of the Lord Buddha. The Master was represented seated on a lotus the petals of which were so deeply undercut as to show almost detached. Round Him was an adoring hierarchy of kings, elders, and old-time Buddhas. Below were lotus-covered waters with fishes and waterbirds. Two butterfly-winged dewas held a wreath over His head; above them another pair supported an umbrella surmounted by the jewelled headdress of the Bodhisat.

"The Lord! The Lord! It is Sakya Muni himself," the lama half sobbed; and under his breath began the wonderful Buddhist invocation:—

"To Him the Way—the Law—Apart—
Whom Maya held beneath her heart.
Ananda's Lord—the Bodhisat."

"And He is here! The Most Excellent Law is here also. My pilgrimage is well begun. And what work! What work!"

"Yonder is the Sahib," said Kim, and dodged sideways among the cases of the arts and manufactures wing. A white-bearded Englishman was looking at the lama, who gravely turned and saluted him and after some fumbling drew forth a note-book and a scrap of paper.

"Yes, that is my name," smiling at the clumsy, childish print.

"One of us who had made pilgrimage to the Holy Places—he is now Abbot of the Lung-Cho Monastery—gave it me," stammered the lama. "He spoke of these." His lean hand moved tremulously round.

"Welcome, then, O lama from Tibet. Here be the images, and I am here"—he glanced at the lama's face—"to gather knowledge. Come to my office awhile." The old man was trembling with excitement.

The office was but a little wooden cubicle partitioned off from the sculpture-lined gallery. Kim laid himself down, his ear against a crack in the heat-split cedar door, and, following his instinct, stretched out to listen and watch.

Most of the talk was altogether above his head. The lama, haltingly at first, spoke to the curator of his own lamasery, the Such-zen, opposite the Painted Rocks, four months' march away. The curator brought out a huge book of photos and showed him that very place, perched on its crag, overlooking the gigantic valley of many-hued strata.

"Ay, ay!" The lama mounted a pair of horn-rimmed spectacles of Chinese work. "Here is the little door through which we bring wood before winter. And thou–the English know of these things? He who is now Abbott of Lung-Cho told me, but I did not believe. The Lord–the Excellent One–He has honor here too? And His life is known?"

"It is all carven upon the stones. Come and see, if thou art rested."

Out shuffled the lama to the main hall, and, the curator beside him, went through the collection with the reverence of a devotee and the appreciative instinct of a craftsman.

Incident by incident in the beautiful story he identified on the blurred stone, puzzled here and there by the unfamiliar Greek convention, but delighted as a child at each new trove. Where the sequence failed, as in the Annunciation, the curator supplied it from his mound of books–French and German, with photographs and reproductions.

Here was the devout Asita, the pendant of Simeon in the Christian story, holding the Holy Child on his knee while mother and father listened; and here were incidents in the legend of the cousin Devadatta. Here was the wicked woman who accused the Master of impurity, all confounded; here was the teaching in the Deer-park; the miracle that stunned the fire-worshippers; here was the Bodhisat in royal state as a prince; the miraculous birth; the death at Kusinagara, where the weak disciple fainted; while there were almost countless repetitions of the meditation under the Bodhi tree; and the adoration of the alms-bowl was everywhere. In a few minutes the curator saw that his guest was no mere bead-telling mendicant, but a scholar of parts. And they went at it all over again, the lama taking snuff, wiping his spectacles, and talking at railway speed in a bewildering mixture of Urdu and Tibetan. He had heard of the travels of the Chinese pilgrims, Fo-Hian and Hwen-Thiang, and was anxious to know if there was any translation of their record. He drew in his breath as he turned helplessly over the pages of Beal and Stanislas Julien. " 'Tis all here. A treasure locked." Then he composed himself reverently to listen to fragments, hastily rendered into Urdu. For the first time he heard of the labors of European scholars, who by the help of these and a hundred other documents have identified the Holy Places of Buddhism. Then he was shown a mighty map, spotted and traced with yellow. The brown finger followed the curator's pencil from point to point. Here was Kapilavastu, here the Middle Kingdom, and here Mahabodi, the Mecca of Buddhism; and here was Kusinagara, sad place of the Holy One's death. The old man bowed his head over the sheets in silence for a while, and the curator lit another pipe. Kim had fallen asleep. When he waked, the talk, still in spate, was more within his comprehension.

"And thus it was, O Fountain of Wisdom, that I decided to go to the Holy Places which His foot had trod–to the Birthplace, even to Kapila; then to Maha Bodhi, which is Buddh Gaya–to the Monastery–to the Deer-park–to the place of His death."

The lama lowered his voice. "And I come here alone. For five–seven–eighteen–forty years it was in my mind that the Old Law was not well followed; being overlaid, as thou knowest, with devildom, charms, and idolatry. Even as the child outside said but now. Ay, even as the child said, with *būt-parasti.*"

"So it comes with all faiths."

"Thinkest thou? The books of my lamasery I read, and they were dried pith; and the later ritual with which we of the Reformed Law have cumbered ourselves–that, too, had no worth to these old eyes. Even the followers of the Excellent One are at feud on feud with one another. It is an illusion. Ay, *maya,* illusion. But I have another desire"–the seamed yellow face drew within three inches of the curator, and the long forefinger nail tapped on the table. "Your scholars, by these books, have followed the Blessed Feet in all their wanderings; but there are things which they have not sought out. I know nothing,—nothing do I know,—but I go to free myself from the Wheel of Things by a broad and open road." He smiled with most simple triumph. "As a pilgrim to the Holy Places I acquire merit. But there is more. Listen to a true thing. When our gracious Lord, being as yet a youth, sought a mate, men said, in His father's court, that He was too tender for marriage. Thou knowest?"

The curator nodded; wondering what would come next.

"So they made the triple trial of strength against all comers. And at the test of the Bow, our Lord, first breaking that which they gave Him, called for such a bow as none might bend. Thou knowest?"

"It is written. I have read."

"And, overshooting all other marks, the arrow passed far and far beyond sight. At the last it fell; and, where it touched earth, there broke out a stream which presently became a River, whose nature, by our Lord's beneficence, and that merit He acquired ere He freed Himself, is that whoso bathes in it washes away all taint and speckle of sin."

"So it is written," said the curator sadly.

The lama drew a long breath. "Where is that River? Fountain of Wisdom, where fell the arrow?"

"Alas, my brother, I do not know," said the curator.

"Nay, if it please thee to forget—the one thing only that thou hast not told me. Surely thou must know? See, I am an old man! I ask with my head between thy feet, O Fountain of Wisdom. We *know* He drew the bow! We *know* the arrow fell! We *know* the stream gushed! Where, then, is the River? My dream told me to find it. So I came. I am here. But where is the River?"

"If I knew, think you I would not cry it aloud?"

"By it one attains freedom from the Wheel of Things," the lama went on, unheeding. "The River of the Arrow! Think again! Some little stream, maybe—dried in the heats? But the Holy One would never so cheat an old man."

"I do not know. I do not know."

The Lama brought his thousand-wrinkled face once more a handsbreadth from the Englishman's. "I see thou dost not know. Not being of the Law, the matter is hid from thee."

"Ay—hidden—hidden."

"We are both bound, thou and I, my brother. But I"—he rose with a sweep of the soft thick drapery—"I go to cut myself free. Come also!"

"I am bound," said the curator. "But whither goest thou?"

"First to Kashi (Benares): where else? There I shall meet one of the pure faith in a Jain temple of that city. He also is a Seeker in secret, and from him haply I may learn. Maybe he will go with me to Buddh Gaya. Thence north and west to Kapilavastu, and there will I seek for the River. Nay, I will seek everywhere as I go—for the place is not known where the arrow fell."

"And how wilt thou go? It is a far cry to Delhi, and farther to Benares."

"By road and the trains. From Pathânkot, having left the Hills, I came hither in a *te-rain*. It goes swiftly. At first I was amazed to see those tall poles by the side of the road snatching up and snatching up their threads,"—he illustrated the stoop and whirl of a telegraph-pole flashing past the train. "But later I was cramped and desired to walk, as I am used."

"And thou art sure of thy road?" said the curator.

"Oh, for that one but asks a question and pays money, and the appointed persons despatch all to the appointed place. That much I knew in my lamasery from sure report," said the lama proudly.

"And when dost thou go?" The curator smiled at the mixture of old-world piety and modern progress that is the note of India to-day.

"As soon as may be. I follow the places of His life till I come to the River of the Arrow. There is, moreover, a written paper of the hours of the trains that go south."

"And for food?" Lamas, as a rule, have good store of money somewhere about them, but the curator wished to make sure.

"For the journey, I take up the Master's begging-bowl. Yes. Even as He went so go I, forsaking the ease of my monastery. There was with me when I left the Hills a *chela* (disciple) who begged for me as the Rule demands, but halting in Kulu awhile a fever took him and he died. I have now no *chela,* but I will take the alms-bowl and thus enable the charitable to acquire merit." He nodded his head valiantly. Learned doctors of a lamasery do not beg, but the lama was an enthusiast in this quest.

"Be it so," said the curator, smiling. "Suffer me now to acquire merit. We be craftsmen together, thou and I. Here is a new book of white English paper: here be sharpened pencils two and three–thick and thin, all good for a scribe. Now lend me thy spectacles."

The curator looked through them. They were heavily scratched, but the power was almost exactly that of his own pair, which he slid into the lama's hand, saying: "Try these."

"A feather! A very feather upon the face!" The old man turned his head delightedly and wrinkled up his nose. "How scarcely do I feel them! How clearly do I see!"

"They be *bilaur*–crystal and will never scratch. May they help thee to thy River, for they are thine."

"I will take them and the pencils and the white note-book," said the lama, "as a sign of friendship between priest and priest–and now–" he fumbled at his belt, detached the open iron-work pencase, and laid it on the curator's table. "That is for a memory between thee and me–my pencase. It is something old–even as I am."

It was a piece of ancient design, Chinese, of an iron that is not smelted these days; and the collector's heart in the curator's bosom had gone out to it from the first. For no persuasion would the lama resume his gift.

"When I return, having found the River, I will bring thee a written picture of the Padma Samthora–such as I used to make on silk at the lamasery. Yes–and of the Wheel of Life," he chuckled, "for we be craftsman together, thou and I."

The curator would have detained him: they are few in the world who still have the secret of the conventional brush-pen Buddhist pictures which are, as it were, half written and half drawn. But the lama strode out, head high in air, and pausing an instant before the great statue of a Bodhisat in meditation, brushed through the turnstiles.

Kim followed like a shadow. What he had overheard excited him wildly. This man was entirely new to all his experience, and he meant to investigate further: precisely as he would have investigated a new building or a strange festival in Lahore city. The lama was his trove, and he purposed to take possession. Kim's mother had been Irish too.

The old man halted by Zam-Zammah and looked round till his eye fell on Kim. The inspiration of his pilgrimage had left him for awhile, and he felt old, forlorn, and very empty.

"Do not sit under that gun," said the policeman loftily.

"Huh! Owl!" was Kim's retort on the lama's behalf. "Sit under that gun if it please thee. When didst thou steal the milk-woman's slippers, Dunnoo?"

That was an utterly unfounded charge sprung on the spur of the moment, but it silenced Dunnoo, who knew that Kim's clear yell could call up legions of bad bazar boys if need arose.

"And whom didst thou worship within?" said Kim affably, squatting in the shade beside the lama.

"I worshipped none, child. I bowed before the Excellent Law."

Kim accepted this new god without emotion. He knew already a few score. "And what dost thou do?"

"I beg. I remember now it is long since I have eaten or drunk. What is the custom of charity in this town? In silence, as we do of Tibet, or speaking aloud?"

"Those who beg in silence starve in silence," said Kim, quoting a native proverb. The lama tried to rise, but sank back again, sighing for his disciple, dead in far-away Kulu. Kim watched–head to one side, considering and interested.

"Give me the bowl. I know the people of this city–all who are charitable. Give, and I will bring it back filled." Simply as a child the old man handed him the bowl.

"Rest thou. *I* know the people."

He trotted off to the open shop of a *kunjri,* a low-caste vegetable-seller, which lay opposite the belt-tramway line down the Motee Bazar. She knew Kim of old.

"Oho, hast thou turned *yogi* with thy begging-bowl?" she cried.

"Nay," said Kim proudly. "There is a new priest in the city–a man such as I have never seen."

"Old priest–young tiger," said the woman angrily. "I am tired of new priests! They settle on our wares like flies. Is the father of my son a well of charity to give to all who ask?"

"No," said Kim. "Thy man is rather *yagi* (bad-tempered) than *yogi* (a holy man). But this priest is new. The Sahib in the Wonder House has talked to him like a brother. O my mother, fill me this bowl. He waits."

"That bowl indeed! That cow-bellied basket! Thou hast as much grace as the holy bull of Shiv. He has taken the best of a basket of onions already, this morn; and forsooth, I must fill thy bowl. He comes here again."

The huge, mouse-colored Brahminee bull of the ward was shouldering his way through the many-colored crowd, a stolen plantain hanging out of his mouth. He headed straight for the shop, well knowing his privileges as a sacred beast, lowered his head, and puffed heavily along the line of baskets ere making his choice. Up flew Kim's hard little heel and caught him on his moist blue nose. He snorted indignantly, and walked away across the tram rails, his hump quivering with rage.

"See! I have saved more than the bowl will cost thrice over. Now, mother, a little rice and some dried fish atop–yes, and some vegetable curry."

A growl came out of the back of the shop, where a man lay. "He drove away the bull," said the woman in an undertone. "It is good to give to the poor." She took the bowl and returned it full of hot rice.

"But my *yogi* is not a cow," said Kim gravely, making a hole with his fingers in the top of the mound. "A little curry is good, and a fried cake, and a morsel of conserve would please him, I think."

"It is a hole as big as thy head," said the woman fretfully. But she filled it, none the less, with good, steaming vegetable curry, clapped a fried cake atop, and a morsel of clarified butter on the cake, dabbed a lump of sour tamarind conserve at the side; and Kim looked at the load lovingly.

"That is good. When I am in the bazar the bull shall not come to this house. He is a bold beggarman."

"And thou?" laughed the woman. "But speak well of bulls. Hast thou not told me that some day a Red Bull will come out of a field to help thee? Now hold all straight and ask for the holy man's blessing upon me. Perhaps, too, he knows a cure for my daughter's sore eyes. Ask him that also, O thou Little

Friend of all the World."

But Kim had danced off ere the end of the sentence, dodging pariah dogs and hungry acquaintances.

"Thus do we beg who know the way of it," said he proudly to the lama, who opened his eyes at the contents of the bowl. "Eat now and–I will eat with thee. Ohé *bhistie!*" he called to the water-carrier, sluicing the crotons by the Museum. "Give water here. We men are thirsty."

"We men!" said the *bhistie,* laughing. "Is one skinful enough for such a pair? Drink then, in the name of the Compassionate."

He loosed a thin stream into Kim's hands, who drank native fashion; but the lama must needs pull out a cup from his inexhaustible upper draperies and drink ceremonially. "*Pardesi* (a foreigner)," Kim explained, as the old man delivered in an unknown tongue what was evidently a blessing.

They ate together in great content, clearing the beggar's bowl. Then the lama took snuff from a portentous wooden snuff-gourd, fingered his rosary awhile, and so dropped into the easy sleep of age, as the shadow of Zam-Zammah grew long.

Kim loafed over to the nearest tobacco-seller, a rather lively young Mohammedan woman, and begged a rank cigar of the brand that they sell to students of the Punjab University who copy English customs. Then he smoked and thought, knees to chin, under the belly of the gun, and the outcome of his thoughts was a sudden and stealthy departure in the direction of Nila Ram's timber-yard.

The lama did not wake till the evening life of the city had begun with lamp-lighting and the return of white-robed clerks and subordinates from the Government offices. He stared dizzily in all directions, but none looked at him save a Hindu urchin in a dirty turban and Isabella-colored clothes. Suddenly he bowed his head on his knees and wailed.

"What is this?" said the boy, standing before him. "Hast thou been robbed?"

"It is my new *chela* (my disciple) that is gone away from me, and I know not where he is."

"And what like of man was thy disciple?"

"It was a boy who came to me in place of him who died, on account of the merit which I had gained when I bowed before the Law within there." He pointed towards the Museum. "He came upon me to show me a road which I had lost. He led me into the Wonder House, and by his talk emboldened to speak to the Keeper of the Images, so that I was cheered and made strong. And when I was faint with hunger he begged for me, as would a *chela* for his teacher. Suddenly was he sent. Suddenly has he gone away. It was in my mind to have taught him the Law upon the road to Benares."

Kim stood amazed at this, because he had overheard the talk in the Museum, and knew that the old man was speaking the truth, which is a thing a native seldom presents to a stranger.

"But I see now that he was but sent upon a purpose. By this I know that I shall find a certain River for which I seek."

"The River of the Arrow?" said Kim, with a superior smile.

"Is this yet another Sending?" cried the lama. "To none have I spoken of my search, save to the Priest of the Images. Who art thou?"

"Thy *chela,*" said Kim simply, sitting on his heels. "I have never seen any one like to thee in all this my life. I go with thee to Benares. And, too, I think that so old a man as thou, speaking truth to chance-met people at dusk, is in great need of a disciple."

"But the River–the River of the Arrow?"

"Oh, that I heard when thou wast speaking to the Englishman. I lay against the door."

The lama sighed. "I thought thou hadst been a guide permitted. Such things fall sometimes–but I am not worthy. Thou dost not, then, know the River?"

"Not I." Kim laughed uneasily. "I go to look for–for a bull–a Red Bull on a green field who shall help me." Boy-like, if an acquaintance had a scheme, Kim was quite ready with one of his own; and he had really thought for as much as twenty minutes at a time of his father's prophecy.

"To what, child?" said the lama.

"God knows, but so my father told me. I heard thy talk in the Wonder House of all those new strange places in the Hills, and if one so old and so little–so used to truth-telling–may go out for the small matter of a river, it seemed to me that I too must go a-traveling. If it is our fate to find those things we shall find them–thou, thy river; and I, my bull, and the strong Pillars and some other matters that I forget."

"It is not pillars but a Wheel from which I would be free," said the lama.

"That is all one. Perhaps they will make me a king," said Kim, serenely prepared for anything.

"I will teach thee other and better desires upon the road," the lama replied in the voice of authority. "Let us go to Benares."

"Not by night. Thieves are abroad. Wait till the day."

"But there is no place to sleep." The old man was used to the order of his monastery, and though he slept on the ground, as the Rule decrees, preferred a decency in these things.

"We shall get good lodging at the Kashmir Serai," said Kim, laughing at his perplexity. "I have a friend there. Come!"

The hot and crowded bazars blazed with light as they made their way through the press of all the races in Upper India, and the lama mooned through it like a man in a dream. It was his first experience of a large manufacturing city, and the crowded tram-car with its continually squealing brakes frightened him. Half pushed, half towed, he arrived at the high gate of the Kashmir Serai: that huge open square over against the railway station, surrounded with arched cloisters where the camel and horse caravans put up on their return from Central Asia. Here were all manner of Northern folk, tending tethered ponies and kneeling camels; loading and unloading bales and bundles; drawing water for the evening meal at the creaking well-windlasses; piling grass before the shrieking, wild-eyed stallions; cuffing the surly caravan dogs; paying off camel-drivers; taking on new grooms; swearing, shouting, arguing, and chaffering in the packed square. The cloisters, reached by three or four masonry steps, made a haven of refuge around this turbulent sea. Most of them were rented to traders, as we rent the arches of a viaduct; the space between pillar and pillar being bricked or boarded off into rooms, which were guarded by heavy wooden doors and cumbrous native padlocks. Locked doors showed that the owner was away, and a few rude–sometimes very rude–chalk or paint scratches told where he had gone. Thus: "Lutuf Ullah is gone to Kurdistan." Below, in coarse verse: "O Allah, who sufferest lice to kive on the coat of a Kabuli, why hast thou allowed this louse Lutuf to live so long?"

Kim, fending the lama between excited men and excited beasts, sidled along the cloisters to the far end, nearest the railway station, where Mahbub Ali, the horse-trader, lived when he came in from that mysterious land beyond the Passes of the North.

Kim had had many dealings with Mahbub in his little life,–especially between his tenth and his thirteenth year,–and the big burly Afghan, his beard dyed scarlet with lime (for he was elderly and did not wish his gray hairs to show), knew the boy's value as a gossip. Sometimes he would tell Kim to watch a man who had nothing whatever to do with horses: to follow him for one whole day and report every soul with whom he talked. Kim would deliver himself of his tale at evening, and Mahbub would listen without a word or gesture. It was intrigue of some kind, Kim knew; but its worth lay in saying nothing whatever to any one except Mahbub, who gave him beautiful meals all hot from the cookshop at the head of the serai, and once as much as eight annas in money.

"He is here," said Kim, hitting a bad-tempered camel on the nose. "Ohé, Mahbub Ali!" He halted at a dark arch and slipped behind the bewildered lama.

The horse-trader, his deep, embroidered Bokhariot belt unloosed, was lying on a pair of silk carpet saddle-bags, pulling lazily at an immense silver hookah. He turned his head very slightly at the cry; and seeing only the tall silent figure, chuckled in his deep chest.

"Allah! A lama! A Red Lama! It is far from Lahore to the Passes. What dost thou do here?"

The lama held out the begging-bowl mechanically.

"God's curse on all unbelievers!" said Mahbub. "I do not give to a lousy Tibetan; but ask my Baltis over yonder behind the camels. They may value your blessings. Oh, horse-boys, here is a countryman of yours. See if he be hungry."

A shaven, crouching Balti, who had come down with the horses, and who was nominally some sort of degraded Buddhist, fawned upon the priest, and in thick gutturals besought the Holy One to sit at the horse-boys' fire.

"Go!" said Kim, pushing him lightly, and the lama strode away, leaving Kim at the edge of the cloister.

"Go!" said Mahbub Ali, returning to his hookah. "Little Hindu, run away. God's curse on all unbelievers! Beg from those of my tail who are of thy faith."

"Maharaj," whined Kim, using the Hindu form of address, and thoroughly enjoying the situation, "my father is dead–my mother is dead–my stomach is empty."

"Beg from my men among the horses, I say. There must be some Hindus in my tail."

"Oh, Mahbub Ali, but am *I* a Hindu?" said Kim in English.

The trader gave no sign of astonishment, but looked under shaggy eyebrows.

"Little Friend of all the World," said he, "what is this?"

"Nothing. I am now that holy man's disciple; and we go a pilgrimage together–to Benares, he says. He is quite mad, and I am tired of Lahore city. I wish new air and water."

"But for whom dost thou work? Why come to me?" The voice was harsh with suspicion.

"To whom else should I come? I have no money. It is not good to go about without money. Thou wilt sell many horses to the officers. They are very fine horses, these new ones: I have seen them. Give me a rupee, Mahbub Ali, and when I come to my wealth I will give thee a bond and pay."

"Um," said Mahbub Ali, thinking swiftly. "Thou hast never before lied to me. Call that lama–stand back in the dark."

"Oh, our tales will agree," said Kim, laughing.

"We go to Benares," said the lama, as soon as he understood the drift of Mahbub Ali's questions. "The boy and I. I go to seek for a certain River."

"Maybe–but the boy?"

"He is my disciple. He was sent, I think, to guide me to that River. Sitting under a gun was I when he came suddenly. Such things have befallen the fortunate to whom guidance was allowed. But I remember now, he said he was of this world–a Hindu."

"And his name?"

"That I did not ask. Is he not my disciple?"

"His country–his race–his village? Mussalman–Sikh–Hindu–Jain–low caste or high?"

"Why should I ask? There is neither high nor low in the Middle Way. If he is my *chela*–does–will–can any one take him from me? for, look you, without him I shall not find my River." He wagged his head solemnly.

"None shall take him from thee. Go, sit among my Baltis," said Mahbub Ali, and the lama drifted off, soothed by the promise.

"Is he not quite mad?" said Kim, coming forward to the light again. "Why should I lie to thee, Hajji?"

Mahbub puffed his hookah in silence. Then he began, almost whispering: "Umballa is on the road to Benares–if indeed ye two go there."

"Tck! Tck! I tell thee he does not know how to lie–as we two know."

"And if thou wilt carry a message for me as far as Umballa, I will give thee money. It concerns a horse–a white stallion which I have sold to an officer upon the last time I returned from the Passes. But then–stand nearer and hold up hands as begging–the pedigree of the white stallion was not fully established, and that officer, who is now at Umballa, bade me make it clear." (Mahbub here described the horse and the appearance of the officer.) "So the message to that officer will be: 'The pedigree of the white stallion is fully established.' By this will he know that thou comest from me. He will then say: 'What proof hast thou?' and thou wilt answer: 'Mahbub Ali has given me the proof.' "

"And all for the sake of a white stallion," said Kim, with a giggle, his eyes aflame.

"That pedigree I will give thee now–in my own fashion–and some hard words as well." A shadow passed behind Kim, and a feeding camel. Mahbub Ali raised his voice.

"Allah! Art thou the only beggar in the city? Thy mother is dead. Thy father is dead. So is it with all of them. Well, well–" he turned as feeling on the floor beside him and tossed a flap of soft, greasy Mussalman bread to the boy. "Go and lie down among my horse-boys for to-night–thou and the lama. To-morrow I may give thee service."

Kim slunk away, his teeth in the bread, and, as he expected, he found a small wad of folded tissue-paper wrapped in oil-skin, with three silver rupees–enormous largesse. He smiled and thrust money and paper into his leather amulet-case. The lama, sumptuously fed by Mahbub's Baltis, was already asleep in a corner of one of the stalls. Kim lay down beside him and laughed. He knew he had rendered a service to Mahbub Ali, and not for one little minute did he believe the tale of the stallion's pedigree.

But Kim did not suspect that Mahbub Ali, known as one of the best horse-dealers in the Punjab, a wealthy and enterprising trader, whose caravans penetrated far and far into the Back of Beyond, was registered in one of the locked books of the Indian Survey Department as C.25.1B. Twice or thrice yearly C.25 would send in a little story, badly told but most interesting, and generally–it was checked by the statements of R.17 and M.4–quite true. It concerned all manner of out-of-the-way mountain principalities, explorers of nationalities other than English, and the gun-trade–was, in brief, a small portion of that vast mass of "information received" on which the Indian Government acts. But, recently, five confederated Kings, who had no business to confederate, had been informed by a kindly Northern Power that there was a leakage of news from their territories into British India. So those Kings' prime ministers were seriously annoyed and took steps, after the Oriental fashion. They suspected, among many others, the bullying, red-bearded horse-dealer whose caravans ploughed through their fastnesses belly deep in snow. At least, his caravan that season had been ambushed and shot at twice on the way down, when Mahbub's men accounted for three strange ruffians who might, or might not, have been hired for the job. Therefore Mahbub had avoided halting at the insalubrious city of Peshawur, and had come through without stop to Lahore, where, knowing his country-people, he anticipated curious developments.

And there was that on Mahbub Ali which he did not wish to keep an hour longer than was necessary–a wad of closely folded tissue-paper, wrapped in oil-skin–an impersonal, unaddressed statement, with five microscopic pin-holes in one corner, that most scandalously betrayed the five confederated Kings, the sympathetic Northern Power, a Hindu banker in Peshawur, a firm of gun-makers in Belgium, and an important, semi-independent Mohammedan ruler to the south. This last was R.17's work, which Mahbub had picked up beyond the Dora Pass and was carrying in for R.17, who, owing to circumstances over which he had no control, could not leave his post of observation. Dynamite was milky and innocuous beside that report of C.25; and even an Oriental, with an Oriental's views of the value of time, could see that the sooner it was in the proper hands the better. Mahbub had no particular desire to die by violence, because two or three family blood-feuds across the border hung unfinished on his hands, and when these scores were cleared he intended to settle down as a more or less virtuous citizen. He had never passed the serai gate since his arrival two days ago, but had been ostentatious in sending telegrams to Bombay, where he banked some of his money; to Delhi, where a sub-partner of his own clan was selling horses to the agent of a Rajputana state; and to Umballa, where an Englishman was excitedly demanding the pedigree of a white stallion. The public letter-writer, who knew English, composed excellent telegrams, such as:–*"Creighton, Laurel Bank, Umballa.–Horse is Arabian as already advised. Sorrowful delayed-pedigree which am translating."* And later to the same address: *"Much sorrowful delay. Will forward pedigree."* To his sub-partner at Delhi he wired: *"Lutuf Ullah.–Have wired two thousand rupees your credit Luchman Narain's bank."* This was entirely in the way of trade, but every one of those telegrams was discussed and re-discussed, by parties who conceived themselves to be interested, before they went over to the railway station in charge of a foolish Balti, who allowed all sorts of people to read them on the road.

When, in Mahbub's own picturesque language, he had muddied the wells of inquiry with the stick of precaution, Kim had dropped on him, sent from heaven; and, being as prompt as he was unscrupulous, Mahbub Ali, used to taking all sorts of gusty chances, pressed him into service on the spot.

A wandering lama with a low-caste boy-servant might attract a moment's interest as they wandered about India, the land of pilgrims; but no one would suspect them or, what was more to the point, rob.

He called for a new light-ball to his hookah, and considered the case. If the worst came to the worst, and the boy came to harm, the paper would incriminate nobody. And he would go up to Umballa leisurely and–at a certain risk of exciting fresh suspicion–repeat his tale by word of mouth to the people concerned.

But R.17's report was the kernel of the whole affair, and it would be distinctly inconvenient if that failed to come to hand. However, God was great, and Mahbub Ali felt he had done all he could for the time being. Kim was the one soul in the world who had never told him a lie. That would have been a fatal blot on Kim's character if Mahbub had not known that to others, for his own ends or Mahbub's business, Kim could lie like an Oriental.

Then Mahbub Ali rolled across the serai to the Gate of the Harpies who paint their eyes and trap the stranger, and was at some pains to call on the one girl who, he had reason to believe, was a particular friend of a smooth-faced Kashmiri pundit who had waylaid his simple Balti in the matter of the telegrams. It was an utterly foolish thing to do; because they fell to drinking perfumed brandy against the Law of the Prophet, and Mahbub grew wonderfully drunk, and the gates of his mouth were loosened, and he pursued the Flower of Delight with the feet of intoxication till he fell flat among the cushions, where the Flower of Delight, aided by a smooth-faced Kashmiri pundit, searched him from head to foot most thoroughly.

About the same hour Kim heard soft feet in Mahbub's deserted stall. The horse-trader, curiously enough, had left his door unlocked, and his men were busy celebrating their return to India with a whole sheep of Mahbub's bounty. A sleek young gentleman from Delhi, armed with a bunch of keys which the Flower had unshackled from the senseless one's belt, went through every single box, bundle, mat, and saddle-bag in Mahbub's possession even more systematically than the Flower and the pundit were searching the owner.

"And I think," said the Flower scornfully an hour later, one rounded elbow on the snoring carcase, "that he is no more than a pig of an Afghan horse-dealer, with no thought except women and horses. Moreover, he may have sent it away by now–if ever there were such a thing."

"Nay–in a matter touching Five Kings it would be next his black heart," said the pundit. "Was there nothing?"

The Delhi man laughed and resettled his turban as he entered. "I searched between the soles of his slippers as the Flower searched his clothes. This is not the man but another. I leave little unseen."

"They did not say he was the very man," said the pundit thoughtfully. "They said, 'Look if he be the man, since our councils are troubled.' "

"That North country is full of horse-dealers as an old coat of lice. There is Sikandar Khan, Nur Ali Beg, and Farrukh Shah–all heads of Kafilas–who deal there," said the Flower.

"They have not yet come in," said the pundit. "Thou must ensnare them later."

"Phew!" said the Flower with deep disgust, rolling Mahbub's head from her lap. "I earn my money. Farrukh Shah is a bear, Ali Beg a swashbuckler, and old Sikandar Khan–yaie! Go! I sleep now. This swine will not stir till dawn."

When Mahbub woke, the Flower talked to him severely on the sin of drunkenness. Asiatics do not wink when they have out-manoeuvred an enemy, but as Mahbub Ali cleared his throat, tightened his belt, and staggered forth under the early morning stars, he came very near to it.

"What a colt's trick," said he to himself. "As if every girl in Peshawur did not use it! But 'twas prettily done. Now God He knows how many more there be upon the road who have orders to test me–perhaps with the knife. So it stands that the boy must go to Umballa–and by rail–for the writing is something urgent. I abide here, following the Flower and drinking wine as an Afghan coper should."

He halted at the stall next but one to his own. His men lay there heavy with sleep. There was no sign of Kim or the lama.

"Up!" He stirred a sleeper. "Whither went those who lay here last even–the lama and the boy? Is aught missing?"

"Nay," grunted the man; "the old madman rose at second cockcrow, saying he would go to Benares, and the young one led him away."

"The curse of Allah on all unbelievers," said Mahbub heartily, and climbed into his own stall, growling in his beard.

But it was Kim who had wakened the lama–Kim with one eye laid against a knot-hole in the planking, who had seen the Delhi man's search through the boxes. This was no common thief that turned over letters, bills, and saddles–no mere burglar who ran a little knife sideways into the soles of

Mahbub's slippers, or picked the seams of the saddle-bags so deftly. At first Kim had been minded to give the alarm—the long-drawn *cho-or—choor!* (thief! thief!) that sets the serai ablaze of nights; but he looked more carefully, and, hand on amulet, drew his own conclusions.

"It must be the pedigree of that made-up horse-lie," said he, "the thing that I carry to Umballa. Better that we go now. Those who search bags with knives may presently search bellies with knives. Surely there is a woman behind this. Hai! Hai!" in a whisper to the light-sleeping old man. "Come. It is time—time to go to Benares."

The lama rose obediently, and they passed out of the serai like shadows.

Chapter Two

For whoso will, from Pride released,
Contemning neither man nor beast,
May hear the Soul of all the East
About him at Kamakura.

THEY ENTERED THE fort-like railway station, black in the end of night; the electrics sizzling over the goods-yard where they handle the heavy Northern grain traffic.

"This is the work of devils!" said the lama, recoiling from the hollow echoing darkness, the glimmer of rails between the masonry platforms, and the maze of girders above. He stood in a gigantic stone hall paved, it seemed, with the sheeted dead—third-class passengers who had taken their tickets overnight and were sleeping in the waiting-rooms. All hours of the twenty-four are alike to Orientals, and their passenger traffic is regulated accordingly.

"This is where the fire-carriages come. One stands behind that hole"—Kim pointed to the ticket-office—"who will give thee a paper to take thee to Umballa."

"But we go to Benares," he replied petulantly.

"All one. Benares then. Quick: she comes!"

"Take thou the purse."

The lama, not so well used to trains as he had pretended, started as the 3.25 A.M. south bound roared in. The sleepers sprung to life, and the station filled with clamour and shoutings, cries of water and sweetmeat vendors, shouts of native policemen, and shrill yells of women gathering up their baskets, their families, and their husbands.

"It is the train—only the *te-rain.* It will not come here. Wait!" Amazed at the lama's immense simplicity (he had handed him a small bag full of rupees), Kim asked and paid for a ticket to Umballa. A sleepy clerk grunted and flung out a ticket to the next station, just six miles distant.

"Nay," said Kim, scanning it with a grin. "This may serve for farmers, but I live in the city of Lahore. It was cleverly done, babu. Now give the ticket to Umballa."

The babu scowled and dealt the proper ticket.

"Now another to Amritzar," said Kim, who had no notion of spending Mahbub Ali's money on anything so crude as a paid ride to Umballa. "The price is so much. The small money in return is just so much. I know the ways of the *te-rain*. . . . Never did *yogi* need *chela* as thou dost," he went on merrily to the bewildered lama. "They would have flung thee out at Mian Mir but for me. This way! Come." He returned the money, keeping only one anna in each rupee of the price of the Umballa ticket as his commission–the immemorial commission of Asia.

The lama jibbed at the open door of a crowded third-class carriage. "Were it not better to walk?" said he weakly.

A burly Sikh artisan thrust forth his bearded head. "Is he afraid? Do not be afraid. I remember the time when I was afraid of the train. Enter! This thing is the work of the Government."

"I do not fear," said the lama. "Have ye room within for two?"

"There is no room even for a mouse," shrilled the wife of a well-to-do cultivator–a Hindu Jat from the rich Jullunder district. Our night trains are not as well looked after as the day ones, where the sexes are very strictly kept to separate carriages.

"Oh, mother of my son, we can make space," said the husband. "Pick up the child. It is a holy man, see'st thou?"

"And my lap full of seventy times seven bundles! Why not bid him sit on my knee, Shameless? But men are ever thus!" She looked round for approval. An Amritzar courtesan near the window sniffed behind her head-drapery.

"Enter! Enter!" cried a fat Hindu money-lender, his folded account-book in a cloth under his arm. With an oily smirk: "It is well to be kind to the poor."

"Ay, at seven per cent a month with a mortgage on the unborn calf," said a young Dogra soldier going south on leave; and they all laughed.

"Will it travel to Benares?" said the lama.

"Assuredly. Else why should we come? Enter, or we are left," cried Kim.

"See!" shrilled the Amritzar girl. "He has never entered a train. Oh, see!"

"Nay, help," said the cultivator, putting out a large brown hand and hauling him in. "Thus is it done, father."

"But–but–I sit on the floor. It is against the Rule to sit on a bench," said the lama. "Moreover, it cramps me."

"I say," began the money-lender, pursing his lips, "that there is not one rule of right living which these *te-rains* do not cause us to break. We sit, for example, side by side with all castes and peoples."

"Yea, and with most outrageously shameless ones," said the wife, scowling at the Amritzar girl making eyes at the young sepoy.

"I said we might have gone by cart along the road," said the husband, "and thus have saved some money."

"Yes–and spent twice over what we saved on food by the way. That was talked out ten thousand times."

"Ay, by ten thousand tongues," grunted he.

"The Gods help us poor women if we may not speak. Oho! He is of that sort which may not look at or reply to a woman." For the lama, constrained by his Rule, took not the faintest notice of her. "And his disciple is like him?"

"Nay, mother," said Kim most promptly. "Not when the woman is well-looking and above all charitable to the hungry."

"A beggar's answer," said the Sikh, laughing. "Thou hast brought it on thyself, sister!" Kim's hands were crooked in supplication.

"And whither goest thou?" said the woman, handing him the half of a cake from a greasy package.

"Even to Benares."

"Jugglers belike?" the young soldier suggested. "Have ye any tricks to pass the time? Why does not that yellow man answer?"

"Because," said Kim stoutly, "he is holy, and thinks upon matters hidden from thee."

"That may be well. We of the Loodhiana Sikhs," he rolled it out sonorously, "do not trouble our heads with doctrine. We fight."

"My sister's brother's son is *naik* (corporal) in that regiment," said the Sikh craftsman quietly. "There are also some Dogra companies there." The soldier glared, for a Dogra is of other caste than a Sikh, and the banker tittered.

"They are all one to me," said the Amritzar girl.

"That we believe," snorted the cultivator's wife malignantly.

"Nay, but all who serve the Sirkar with weapons in their hands are, as it were, one brotherhood. There is one brotherhood of the caste, but beyond that again"–she looked round timidly–"the bond of the *Pulton*–the Regiment–eh?"

"My brother is in a Jat regiment," said the cultivator. "Dogras be good men."

"Thy Sikhs at least were of that opinion," said the soldier, with a scowl at the placid old man in the corner. "*Thy* Sikhs thought so when our two companies came to help them at the Pirzai Kotal in the face of eight Afreedee standards on the ridge not three months gone."

He told the story of a Border action in which the Dogra companies of the Loodhiana Sikhs had acquitted themselves well. The Amritzar girl smiled; for she knew the tale was to win her approval.

"Alas!" said the cultivator's wife at the end. "So their villages were burnt and their little children made homeless?"

"They had marked our dead. They paid a great payment after we of the Sikhs had schooled them. So it was. Is this Amritzar?"

"Ay, and here they cut our tickets," said the banker, fumbling at his belt.

The lamps were paling in the dawn when the half-caste guard came round. Ticket-collecting is a slow business in the East, where people secret their tickets in all sorts of curious places. Kim produced his and was told to get out.

"But I go to Umballa," he protested. "I go with this holy man."

"Thou canst go to Jehannum for aught I care. This ticket is only to Amritzar. Out!"

Kim burst into a flood of tears, protesting that the lama was his father and his mother, that he was the prop of the lama's declining years, and that the lama would die without his care. All the carriage bade the guard be merciful,–the banker was specially eloquent here,–but the guard hauled Kim on to the platform. The lama blinked, he could not overtake the situation, and Kim lifted up his voice and wept outside the carriage window.

"I am very poor. My father is dead–my mother is dead. Oh, charitable ones, if I am left here, who shall tend that old man?"

"What–what is this?" the lama repeated. "He must go to Benares. He must come with me. He is my *chela*. If there is money to be paid–"

"Oh, be silent," whispered Kim; "are we Rajahs to throw away good silver when the world is so charitable?"

The Amritzar girl stepped out with her bundles, and it was on her that Kim kept his watchful eye. Ladies of that persuasion, he knew, were generous.

"A ticket–a little *tikkut* to Umballa–O Breaker of Hearts!" She laughed. "Hast thou no charity?"

"Does the holy man come from the North?"

"From far and far in the North he comes," cried Kim. "From among the Hills."

"There is snow among the pine-trees in the North–in the Hills there is snow. My mother was from Kulu. Get thee a ticket. Ask him for a blessing."

"Ten thousand blessings," shrilled Kim. "O Holy One, a woman has given us in charity so that I can come with thee–a woman with a golden heart. I run for the *tikkut.*"

The girl looked up at the lama, who had mechanically followed Kim to the platform. He bowed his head that he might not see her, and muttered in Tibetan as she passed on with the crowd.

"Light come–light go," said the cultivator's wife viciously.

"She has acquired merit," returned the lama. "Beyond doubt it was a nun."

"There be ten thousand such nuns in Amritzar alone. Return, old man, or the train may depart without thee," cried the banker.

"Not only was it sufficient for the ticket, but for a little food also," said Kim, leaping to his place. "Now eat, Holy One. Look. Day comes!"

Golden, rose, saffron, and pink, the morning mists smoked away across the flat green levels. All the rich Punjab lay out in the splendor of the keen sun. The lama flinched a little as the telegraph-posts swung by.

"Great is the speed of the train," said the banker, with a patronising grin. "We have gone farther since Lahore than thou couldst walk in two days: at even, we shall enter Umballa."

"And that is still far from Benares," said the lama wearily, mumbling over the cakes that Kim offered. They all unloosed their bundles and made their morning meal. Then the banker, the cultivator, and the soldier prepared their pipes and wrapped the compartment in choking, acrid smoke, spitting and coughing and enjoying themselves. The Sikh and the cultivator's wife chewed *pan;* the lama took snuff and told his beads, while Kim, cross-legged, smiled over the comfort of a full stomach.

"What rivers have ye by Benares?" said the lama of a sudden to the carriage at large.

"We have Gunga," returned the banker, when the little titter had subsided.

"What others?"

"What other than Gunga?"

"Nay, but in my mind was the thought of a certain River of healing."

"That is Gunga. Who bathes in her is made clean and goes to the Gods. Thrice have I made pilgrimage to Gunga." He looked round proudly.

"There was need," said the young sepoy drily, and the travellers' laugh turned against the banker.

"Clean–to return again to the Gods," the lama muttered. "And to go forth on the round of lives anew–still tied to the Wheel." He shook his head testily. "But maybe there is a mistake. Who, then, made Gunga in the beginning?"

"The Gods. Of what known faith art thou?" the banker said, appalled.

"I follow the Law–the Most Excellent Law. So it was the Gods that made Gunga. What like of Gods were they?"

The carriage looked at him in amazement. It was inconceivable that any one should be ignorant of Gunga.

"What–what is thy God?" said the money-lender at last.

"Hear!" said the lama, shifting the rosary to his hand. "Hear: for I speak of Him now! O people of Hind, listen!"

He began in Urdu the tale of the Lord Buddha, but, borne by his own thoughts, slid into Tibetan and long-droned texts from a Chinese book of the Buddha's life. The gentle, tolerant folk looked on reverently. All India is full of holy men stammering gospels in strange tongues; shaken and consumed in the fires of their own zeal; dreamers, babblers, and visionaries: as it has been from the beginning and will continue to the end.

"Um!" said the soldier of the Loodhiana Sikhs. "There was a Mohammedan regiment lay next to us at the Pirzai Kotal, and a priest of theirs,–he was, as I remember, a *naik,*–when the fit was on him, spake prophecies. But the mad all are in God's keeping. His officers overlooked much in that man."

The lama fell back on Urdu, remembering that he was in a strange land. "Hear the tale of the Arrow which our Lord loosed from the bow," he said.

This was much more to their taste, and they listened curiously while he told it. "Now, O people of Hind, I go to seek that River. Know ye aught that may guide me, for we be all men and women in evil case?"

"There is Gunga—and Gunga alone—who washes away sin," ran the murmur round the carriage.

"Though past question we have good Gods Jullunderway," said the cultivator's wife, looking out of window. "See how they have blessed the crops."

"To search every river in the Punjab is no small matter," said her husband. "For me, a stream that leaves good silt on my land suffices, and I thank Bhumia, the God of the Homestead." He shrugged one knotted, bronzed shoulder.

"Think you our Lord came so far north?" said the lama, turning to Kim.

"It may be," Kim replied soothingly, as he spat red *pan*-juice on the floor.

"The last of the Great Ones," said the Sikh with authority, "was Sikander Julkarn (Alexander the Great). He paved the streets of Jullunder and built a great tank near Umballa. That pavement holds to this day; and the tank is there also. I never heard of thy God."

"Let thy hair grow long and talk Punjabi," said the young soldier jestingly to Kim, quoting a Northern proverb. "That is all that makes a Sikh." But he did not say this very loud.

The lama sighed and shrunk into himself, a dingy, shapeless mass. In the pauses of their talk they could hear the low droning—"*Om mane pudme hum! Om mane pudme hum!*"—and the thick click of the wooden rosary beads.

"It irks me," he said at last. "The speed and the clatter irk me. Moreover, my *chela,* I think that maybe we have overpassed that River."

"Peace, peace," said Kim. "Was not the River near Benares? We are yet far from the place."

"But—if our Lord came north, it may be any one of these little ones that we have run across."

"I do not know."

"But thou wast sent to me—wast thou sent to me?—for the merit I had acquired over yonder at Such-zen. From beside the cannon didst thou come—bearing two faces—and two garbs."

"Peace. One must not speak of these things here," whispered Kim. "There was but one of me. Think again and thou wilt remember. A boy—a Hindu boy—by the great green cannon."

"But was there not also an Englishman with a white beard—holy among images—who himself made more sure my assurance of the River of the Arrow?"

"He—we—went to the Ajaib-Gher in Lahore to pray before the Gods there," Kim explained to the openly listening company. "And the Sahib of the Wonder House talked to him—yes, this is truth—as a brother. He is a very holy man, from far beyond the Hills. Rest thou. In time we come to Umballa."

"But my River—the River of my healing?"

"And then, if it please thee, we will go hunting for that River on foot. So that we miss nothing—not even a little rivulet in a field-side."

"But thou hast a Search of thine own?" The lama—very pleased that he remembered so well—sat bolt upright.

"Ay," said Kim, humouring him. The boy was entirely happy to be out chewing *pan* and seeing new people in the great good-tempered world.

"It was a bull—a Red Bull that shall come and help thee—and carry thee—whither? I have forgotten. A Red Bull on a green field, was it not?"

"Nay, it will carry me nowhere," said Kim. "It is but a tale I told thee."

"What is this?" The cultivator's wife leaned forward, her bracelets clinking on her arm. "Do ye both dream dreams? A Red Bull on a green field, that shall carry thee to the Heavens–or what? Was it a vision? Did one make a prophecy? *We* have a Red Bull in our village behind Jullunder city, and he grazes by choice in the very greenest of our fields!"

"Give a woman an old wife's tale and a weaver-bird a leaf and a thread, they will weave wonderful things," said the Sikh. "All holy men dream dreams, and by following holy men their disciples attain that power."

"A Red Bull on a green field, was it?" the lama repeated. "In a former life it may be thou hast acquired merit, and the Bull will come to reward thee."

"Nay–nay–it was but a tale one told to me–for a jest belike. But I will seek the Bull about Umballa, and thou canst look for thy River and rest from the clatter of the train."

"It may be that the Bull knows–that he is sent to guide us both," said the lama, hopefully as a child. Then to the company, indicating Kim: "This one was sent to me but yesterday. He is not, I think, of this world."

"Beggars a plenty have I met, and holy men to boot, but never such a *yogi* nor such a disciple," said the woman.

Her husband touched his forehead lightly with one finger and smiled. But the next time the lama would eat they took care to give him their best.

And at last–tired, sleepy, and dusty–they reached Umballa City Station.

"We abide here upon a lawsuit," said the cultivator's wife to Kim. "We lodge with my man's cousin's younger brother. There is room also in the courtyard for thy *yogi* and for thee. Will–will he give me a blessing?"

"O holy man! A woman with a heart of gold gives us lodging for the night. It is a kindly land, this land of the South. See how we have been helped since the dawn!"

The lama bowed his head in benediction.

"To fill my cousin's younger brother's house with wastrels–" the husband began, as he shouldered his heavy bamboo staff.

"Thy cousin's younger brother owes my father's cousin something yet on his daughter's marriage-feast," said the woman crisply. "Let him put their food to that account. The *yogi* will beg, I doubt not."

"Ay, I beg for him," said Kim, anxious only to get the lama under shelter for the night, that he might seek Mahbub Ali's Englishman and deliver himself of the white stallion's pedigree.

"Now," said he, when the lama had come to an anchor in the inner courtyard of a decent Hindu house behind the cantonments, "I go away for awhile–to–to buy us victual in the bazar. Do not stray abroad till I return."

"Thou wilt return? Thou wilt surely return?" The old man caught at his wrist. "And thou wilt return in this very same shape? Is it too late to look to-night for the River?"

"Too late and too dark. Be comforted. Think how far thou art on the road–an hundred *kos* from Lahore already."

"Yea–and farther from my monastery. Alas! It is a great and terrible world."

Kim stole out and away, as unremarkable a figure as ever carried his own and a few score thousand other folks' fate slung round his neck. Mahbub Ali's directions left him little doubt of the house in which his Englishman lived; and a groom, bringing a dog-cart home from the Club, made him quite sure. It remained only to identify his man, and Kim slipped through the garden hedge and hid in a clump of plumed grass close to the verandah. The house blazed with lights, and servants moved about tables dressed with flowers, glass, and silver. Presently forth came an Englishman, dressed in

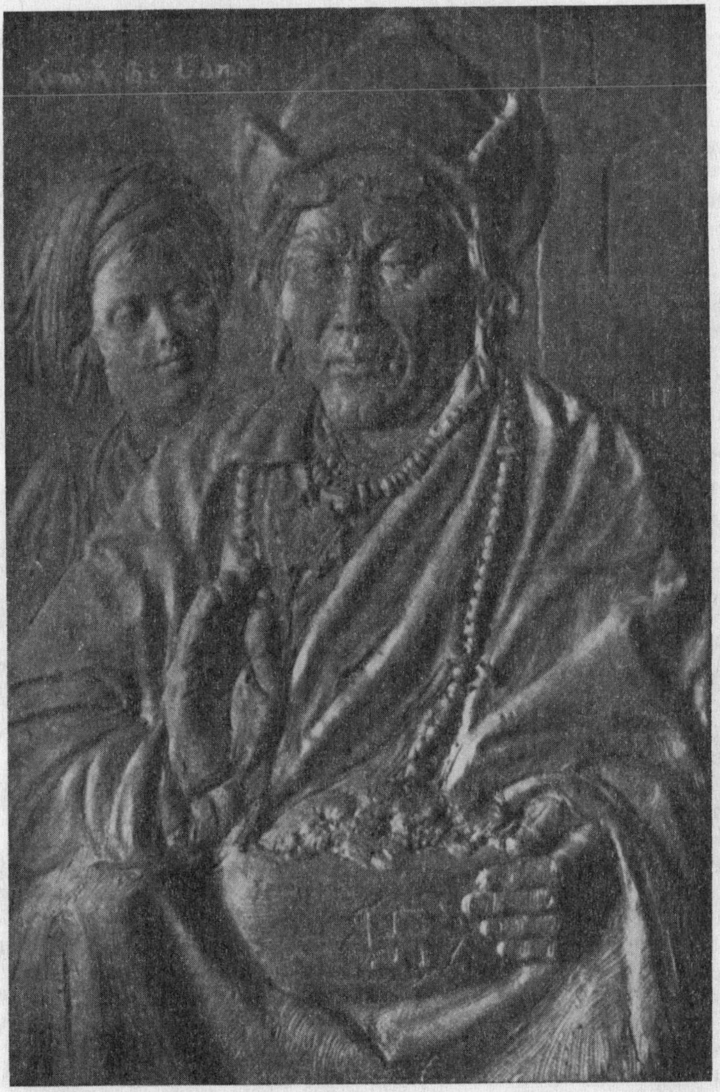

"'BEGGARS A PLENTY HAVE I MET, AND HOLY MEN TO BOOT, BUT NEVER SUCH A *YOGI* NOR SUCH A DISCIPLE.'"

black and white, humming a tune. It was too dark to see his face, so Kim, beggar-wise, tried an old experiment. "Protector of the Poor!"

The man backed towards the voice.

"Mahbub Ali says–"

"Hah! What says Mahbub Ali?" He made no attempt to look for the speaker, and that showed Kim that he knew.

"The pedigree of the white stallion is fully established."

"What proof is there?" The Englishman switched at the rose-hedge in the side of the drive.

"Mahbub Ali has given me this proof." Kim flipped the wad of folded paper into the air, and it fell on the path beside the man, who put his foot on it as a gardener came round the corner. When the servant passed he picked it up, dropped a rupee,–Kim could hear the clink,–and strode into the house, never turning round. Swiftly Kim took up the money; but, for all his training, he was Irish enough by birth to reckon silver the least part of any game. What he desired was the visible effect of action; so, instead of slinking away, he lay close in the grass and wormed nearer to the house.

He saw–Indian bungalows are open through and through–the Englishman return to a small dressing-room, in a corner of the verandah, that was half-office, littered with papers and desptach-boxes, and sit down to study Mahbub Ali's message. His face, by the full ray of the kerosene lamp, changed and darkened, and Kim, used as every beggar must be to watching countenances, took good note.

"Will! Will, dear!" called a woman's voice. "You ought to be in the drawing-room. They'll be here in a minute."

The man still read intently.

"Will!" said the voice, five minutes later. "*He's* come. I can hear the troopers in the drive."

The man dashed out bareheaded as a big landau with four native troopers behind it halted at the verandah, and a tall, black-haired man, erect as an arrow, swung out, preceded by a young officer who laughed pleasantly.

Flat on his belly lay Kim, almost touching the high wheels. His man and the black stranger exchanged two sentences.

"Certainly, sir," said the young officer promptly. "Everything waits while a horse is concerned."

"We shan't be more than twenty minutes," said Kim's man. "You can do the honors–keep 'em amused, and all that."

"Tell one of the troopers to wait," said the tall man, and they both passed into the dressing-room together as the landau rolled away. Kim saw their heads bent over Mahbub Ali's message, and heard the voices–one low and deferential, the other sharp and decisive.

"It isn't a question of weeks. It is a question of days–hours almost," said the elder. "I'd been expecting it for some time, but this"–he tapped Mahbub Ali's paper–"clenches it. Grogan's dining here to-night, isn't he?"

"Yes, sir, and Macklin too."

"Very good. I'll speak to them myself. The matter will be referred to the Council, of course, but this is a case where one is justified in assuming that we take action at once. Warn the Pindi and Peshawur brigades. It will disorganise all the summer reliefs, but we can't help that. This comes of not smashing them thoroughly the first time. Eight thousand should be enough."

"What about artillery, sir?"

"I must consult Macklin."

"Then it means war?"

"No. Punishment. When a man is bound by the action of his predecessor–"

"But C.25 may have lied."

"He bears out the other's information. Practically, they showed their hand six months back. But Devenish would have it there was a chance of peace. Of course they used it to make themselves stronger. Send off those telegrams at once,—the new code, not the old,—mine and Wharton's. I don't think we need keep the ladies waiting any longer. We can settle the rest over the cigars. I thought it was coming. It's punishment—not war."

"As the trooper cantered off, Kim crawled round to the back of the house, where, going on his Lahore experiences, he judged there would be food—and information. The kitchen was crowded with excited scullions, one of whom kicked him.

"Aie," said Kim, feigning tears. "I came only to wash dishes in return for a bellyful."

"All Umballa is on the same errand. Get hence. They go in now with the soup. Think you that we who serve Creighton Sahib need strange scullions to help us through a big dinner?"

"It is a very big dinner," said Kim, looking at the plates.

"Small wonder. The guest of honor is none other than the Jang-i-Lat Sahib (the Commander-in-Chief)."

"Ho!" said Kim, with the correct guttural note of wonder. He had learned what he wanted, and when the scullion turned he was gone.

"And all that trouble," said he to himself, thinking as usual in Hindustanee, "for a horse's pedigree! Mahbub Ali should have come to me to learn a little lying. Every time before that I have borne a message it concerned a woman. Now it is men. Better. The tall man said that they will loose a great army to punish some one—somewhere—the news goes to Pindi and Peshawur. There are also guns. Would I had crept nearer. It is big news!"

He returned to find the cultivator's cousin's younger brother discussing the family lawsuit in all its bearings with the cultivator and his wife and a few friends, while the lama dozed. After the evening meal some one passed him a water-pipe; and Kim felt very much of a man as he pulled at the smooth cocoanut-shell, his legs spread abroad in the moonlight, his tongue clicking in remarks from time to time. His hosts were most polite; for the cultivator's wife had told them of his vision of the Red Bull, and of his probable descent from another world. Moreover, the lama was a great and venerable curiosity. The family priest, an old, tolerant Sarsut Brahmin, dropped in later and naturally started a theological argument to impress the family. By creed, of course, they were all on their priest's side, but the lama was the guest and the novelty. His gentle kindliness, and his impressive Chinese quotations, that sounded like spells, delighted them hugely; and in this sympathetic, simple air, he expanded like the Bodhisat's own lotus, speaking of his life in the great hills of Such-zen, before, as he said, "I rose up to seek enlightenment."

Then it came out that in those worldy days he had been a master-hand at casting horoscopes and nativities; and the family priest led him on to describe his methods; each giving the planets names that the other could not understand, and pointing upwards as the big stars sailed across the dark. The children of the house tugged unrebuked at his rosary; and he clean forgot the Rule which forbids looking at women as he talked of enduring snows, landslips, blocked passes, the remote cliffs where men find sapphires and turquoise, and that wonderful upland road that leads at last into Great China itself.

"How thinkest thou of this one?" said the cultivator aside to the priest.

"A holy man—a holy man indeed. His Gods are not the Gods, but his feet are upon the Way," was the answer. "And his methods of nativities, though that is beyond thee, are wise and sure."

"Tell me," said Kim lazily, "whether I find my Red Bull on a green field, as was promised me."

"What knowledge has thou of thy birth-hour?" the priest asked, swelling with importance.

"Between first and second cockcrow of the first night in May."

"Of what year?"

"I do not know; but upon the hour that I cried first fell the great earthquake in Srinagur which is in Kashmir." This Kim had from the woman who took care of him, and she again from Kimball O'Hara. The earthquake had been felt in India, and for long stood a leading date in the Punjab.

"Ai!" said a woman excitedly. This seemed to make Kim's supernatural origin more certain. "Was not such an one's daughter born then–"

"And her mother bore her husband four sons in four years–all likely boys," cried the cultivator's wife, sitting outside the circle in the shadow.

"None reared in the knowledge," said the family priest, "forget how the planets stood in their Houses upon that night." He began to draw in the dust of the courtyard. "At least thou hast good claim to a half of the House of the Bull. How runs thy prophecy?"

"Upon a day," said Kim, delighted at the sensation he was creating, "I shall be made great by means of a Red Bull on a green field, but first there will enter two men making all things ready."

"Yes: thus ever at the opening of a vision. A thick darkness that clears slowly; anon one enters with a broom making ready the place. Then begins the Sight. Two men–thou sayest? Ay, ay. The Sun, leaving the House of the Bull, enters that of the Twins. Hence the two men of the prophecy. Let us now consider. Fetch me a twig, little one."

He knitted his brows, scratched, smoothed out, and scratched again in the dust mysterious signs–to the wonder of all save the lama, who, with fine instinct, forbore to interfere.

At the end of half an hour, he tossed the twig from him with a grunt.

"Hm. Thus say the stars. Within three days come the two men to make all things ready. After them follows the Bull; but the sign over against him is the sign of War and armed men."

"There was indeed a man of the Loodhiana Sikhs in the carriage from Lahore," said the cultivator's wife hopefully.

"Tck! Armed men–many hundreds. What concern hast thou with war?" said the priest to Kim. "Thine is a red and an angry sign of War to be loosed very soon."

"None–none," said the lama earnestly. "We seek only peace and our River."

Kim smiled, remembering what he had overheard in the dressing-room. Decidedly he was a favorite of the stars.

The priest brushed his foot over the rude horoscope. "More than this I cannot see. In three days comes the Bull to thee, boy."

"And my River, my River," pleaded the lama. "I had hoped his Bull would lead us both to the River."

"Alas, for that wondrous River, my brother," the priest replied. "Such things are not common."

Next morning, though they were pressed to stay, the lama insisted on departure. They gave Kim a large bundle of good food and nearly three annas in copper money for the needs of the road, and with many blessings watched the two go southward in the dawn.

"Pity it is that these and such as these could not be freed from the Wheel of Things," said the lama.

"Nay, then would only evil people be left on the earth, and who would give us meat and shelter?" quoth Kim, stepping merrily under his burden.

"Yonder is a small stream. Let us look," said the lama, and he led from the white road across the fields; walking into a very hornets'-nest of pariah dogs.

Chapter Three

Yea, voice of every Soul that clung
To Life that strove from rung to rung
When Devadatta's rule was young,
The warm wind brings Kamakura.

BEHIND THEM AN angry farmer brandished a bamboo pole. He was a market-gardener, Arain by caste, growing vegetables and flowers for Umballa city, and well Kim knew the breed.

"Such an one," said the lama, disregarding the dogs, "is impolite to strangers, intemperate of speech, and uncharitable. Be warned by his demeanour, my disciple."

"Ho, shameless beggars!" shouted the farmer. "Begone! Get hence!"

"We go," the lama returned, with quiet dignity. "We go from these unblessed fields."

"Ah," said Kim, sucking in his breath. "If the next crops fail, thou canst only blame thy own tongue."

The man shuffled uneasily in his slippers. "The land is full of beggars," he began, half apologetically.

"And by what sign didst thou know that we would beg from thee, O Mali?" said Kim tartly, using the name that a market-gardener least likes. "All we sought was to look at that river beyond the field there."

"River, forsooth!" the man snorted. "What city do ye hail from not to know a canal-cut? It runs as straight as an arrow, and I pay for the water as though it were molten silver. There is a branch of a river beyond. But if ye need water I can give that–and milk."

"Nay, we will go to the river," said the lama, striding out.

"Milk and a meal," the man stammered, as he looked at the strange tall figure. "I–I would not draw evil upon myself–or my crops; but beggars are so many in these hard days."

"Take notice," the lama turned to Kim. "He was led to speak harshly by the Red Mist of anger. That clearing from his eyes, he becomes courteous and of an affable heart. May his fields be blessed. Beware not to judge men too hastily, O farmer."

"I have met holy ones who would have cursed thee from hearthstone to byre," said Kim to the abashed man. "Is he not wise and holy? I am his disciple."

He cocked his nose in the air loftily and stepped across the narrow field-borders with great dignity.

"There is no pride," said the lama, after a pause, "there is no pride among such as follow the Middle Way."

"But thou hast said he was low caste and discourteous."

"Low caste I did not say, for how can that be which is not? Afterwards he amended his discourtesy, and I forgot the offence. Moreover, he is, as we are, bound upon the Wheel of Things; but he does not tread the way of deliverance." He halted at a little runlet among the fields, and considered the hoof-pitted bank.

"Now, how wilt thou know thy River?" said Kim, squatting in the shade of some tall sugar-cane.

"When I find it, an enlightenment will surely be given. This, I feel, is not the place. O littlest among the waters, if only thou couldst tell me where runs my River! But be thou blessed to make the fields bear!"

"Look! Look!" Kim sprang to his side and dragged him back. A yellow and brown streak glided from the purple rustling stems to the bank, stretched its neck to the water, drank, and lay still–a big cobra with fixed, lidless eyes.

"I have no stick–I have no stick," said Kim. "I will get me one and break his back."

"Why? He is upon the Wheel as we are–a life ascending or descending–very far from deliverance. Great evil must the soul have done that is cast into this shape."

"I hate all snakes," said Kim. No native training can quench the white man's horror of the Serpent.

"Let him live out his life." The coiled thing hissed and half opened its hood. "May thy release come soon, brother," the lama continued placidly. "Hast *thou* knowledge, by chance, of my River?"

"Never have I seen such a man as thou art," Kim whispered, overwhelmed. "Do the very snakes understand thy talk?"

"Who knows?" He passed within a foot of the cobra's poised head. It flattened itself among the dusty coils.

"Come thou!" he called over his shoulder.

"Not I," said Kim. "I go round."

"Come. He does no hurt."

Kim hesitated for a moment. The lama backed his order by some droned Chinese quotation which Kim took for a charm. He obeyed and bounded across the rivulet, and the snake, indeed, made no sign.

"Never have I seen such a man." Kim wiped the sweat from his forehead. "And now, whither go we?"

"That is for thee to say. I am old, and a stranger–far from my own place. But that the *rêl*-carriage fills my head with noises of devil-drums I would go in it to Benares now . . . yet by so going we may miss the River. Let us find another river."

Where the hard-worked soil gives three and even four crops a year–through patches of sugar-cane, tobacco, long white radishes, and nol-kol, all that day they strolled on, turning aside to every glimpse of water; rousing village dogs and sleeping villages at noonday; the lama replying to the vollied questions with an unswerving simplicity. They sought a River–a River of miraculous healing. Had any one knowledge of such a stream? Sometimes men laughed, but more often heard the story out to the end and offered them a place in the shade, a drink of milk, and a meal. The women were always kind, and the little children, as children are the world over, alternately shy and venturesome. Evening found them at rest under the village tree of a mud-walled, mud-roofed hamlet, talking to the headman as the cattle came in from the grazing-grounds and the women prepared the day's last meal. They had passed beyond the belt of market-gardens round hungry Umballa, and were among the mile-wide green of the staple crops.

He was a white-bearded and affable elder, used to entertaining strangers. He dragged out a string bedstead for the lama, set warm cooked food before him, prepared him a pipe, and, the evening ceremonies being finished in the village temple, sent for the village priest.

Kim told the older children tales of the size and beauty of Lahore, of railway travel, and such like city things, while the men talked, slowly as their cattle chew the cud.

"I cannot fathom it," said the headman at last to the priest. "How readest thou this talk?" The lama, his tale told, was silently telling his beads.

"He is a Seeker," the priest answered. "The land is full of such. Remember him who came only last month–the *faquir* with the tortoise?"

"Ay, but that man had right and reason, for Krishna Himself appeared in a vision promising him Paradise without the burning-pyre if he journeyed to Prayag. This man seeks no god who is within my knowledge."

"Peace, he is old: he comes from far off, and he is mad," the smooth-shaven priest replied. "Hear me." He turned to the lama. "Three *kos* (six miles) to the westward runs the great road to Calcutta."

"But I would go to Benares–to Benares."

"And to Benares also. It crosses all streams on this side of Hind. Now my word to thee, Holy One, is rest here till tomorrow. Then take the road" (it was the Grand Trunk Road he meant) "and test each stream that it over-passes; for, as I understand, the virtue of thy River lies neither in one pool nor place, but throughout its length. Then, if thy gods will, be assured that thou wilt come upon thy freedom."

"That is well said." The lama was much impressed by the plan. "We will begin to-morrow, and a blessing on thee for showing old feet such a near road." A deep, sing-song Chinese half-chant closed the sentence. Even the priest was impressed, and the headman feared an evil spell; but none could look at the lama's simple, eager face and doubt him long.

"Seest thou my *chela?*" he said, diving into his snuff-gourd with an important sniff. It was his duty to repay courtesy with courtesy.

"I see–and hear." The headman rolled his eye where Kim was chatting to a girl in blue as she laid crackling thorns on a fire.

"He also has a Search of his own. No river, but a Bull. Yea, a Red Bull on a green field will some day raise him to honor. He is, I think, not altogether of this world. He was sent of a sudden to aid me in this search, and his name is Friend of all the World."

The priest smiled. "Ho there, Friend of all the World," he cried across the sharp-smelling smoke, "what art thou?"

"This Holy One's disciple," said Kim.

"He says thou are a *būt (a spirit)."*

"Can būts eat?" said Kim, with a twinkle. "For I am hungry."

"It is no jest," cried the lama. "A certain astrologer of that city whose name I have forgotten–"

"That is no more than the city of Umballa, where we slept last night," Kim whispered to the priest.

"Ay, Umballa was it? He cast a horoscope and declared that my *chela* should find his desire within two days. But what said he of the meaning of the stars, Friend of all the World?"

Kim cleared his throat and looked around at the village graybeards.

"The meaning of my Star is War," he replied pompously.

Somebody laughed at the little tattered figure strutting on the brickwork plinth under the great tree. Where a native would have lain down, Kim's white blood set him upon his feet. "Ay, War," he answered.

"That is a sure prophecy," rumbled a deep voice. "For there is always war along the Border–as I know."

It was an old, withered man, who had served the Government in the days of the Mutiny as a native officer in a newly raised cavalry regiment. The Government had given him a good holding in the village, and though the demands of his sons, now gray-bearded officers on their own account, had impoverished him, he was still a person of consequence. English officials–Deputy Commissioners even–turned aside from the main road to visit him, and on those occasions he dressed himself in the uniform of ancient days, and stood up like a ramrod.

"But this shall be a great war–a war of eight thousand," Kim's voice shrilled across the quick-gathering crowd, astonishing himself.

"Redcoats or our own regiments?" the old man snapped, as though he were asking an equal. His tone made men respect Kim.

"Redcoats," said Kim at a venture. "Redcoats and guns."

"But–but the astrologer said no word of this," cried the lama, snuffing prodigiously in his excitement.

"But *I* know. The word has come to me, who am this Holy One's disciple. There will rise a war–a war of eight thousand redcoats. From Pindi and Peshawur they will be drawn. This is sure."

"The boy has heard bazar-talk," said the priest.

"But he was always by my side," said the lama. "How should he know? I did not know."

"He will make a clever juggler when the old man is dead," muttered the priest to the headman. "What new trick is this?"

"A sign. Give me a sign," thundered the old soldier suddenly. "If there were war my sons would have told me."

"When all is ready, thy sons, doubt not, will be told. But it is a long road from thy sons to the man in whose hands these things lie." Kim warmed to the game, for it reminded him of experiences in the letter-carrying line, when, for the sake of a few pice, he pretended to know more than he knew. But now he was playing for larger things–the sheer excitement and the sense of power. He drew a new breath and went on.

"Old man, give *me* a sign. Do underlings order the goings of eight thousand redcoats–with guns?"

"No." Still the old man answered as though Kim were an equal.

"Dost thou know who He is then that gives the order?"

"I have seen Him."

"To know again?"

"I have known Him since He was a lieutenant in the *topkhana* (the Artillery)."

"A tall man. A tall man with black hair, walking thus?" Kim took a few paces in a stiff, wooden style.

"Ay, But that any one may have seen." The crowd were breathless-still through all this talk.

"That is true," said Kim. "But I will say more. Look now. First the great man walks thus. Then He thinks thus. (Kim drew a forefinger over his forehead and downwards till it came to rest by the angle of the jaw.) Anon He twitches his fingers thus. Anon He thrusts his hat under his left armpit." Kim illustrated the motion and stood like a stork.

The old man groaned, inarticulate with amazement; and the crowd shivered. "So–so–so. But what does He when He is about to give an order?"

"He rubs the skin at the back of his neck–thus. Then falls one finger on the table and He makes a small sniffing noise through his nose. Then He speaks, saying: 'Loose such and such a regiment. Call out such guns.' "

The old man rose stiffly and saluted.

" 'For' "–Kim translated into the vernacular the clinching sentences he had heard in the dressing-room at Umballa–" 'For,' says He, 'we should have done this long ago. It is not war–it is a chastisement. Snff!' "

"Enough. I believe. I have seen Him thus in the smoke of battles. Seen and heard. It is He!"

"I saw no smoke"–Kim's voice shifted to the rapt sing-song of the wayside fortune-teller. "I saw this in darkness. First came a man to make things clear. Then came horsemen. Then came He, standing in a ring of light. The rest followed as I have said. Old man, have I spoken truth?"

"It is He. Past all doubt it is He."

The crowd drew a long, quavering breath, staring alternately at the old man, still at attention, and ragged Kim against the purple twilight.

"Said I not—said I not he was from the other world?" cried the lama proudly. "He is the Friend of all the World. He is the Friend of the Stars!"

"At least it does not concern us," a man cried. "O thou young soothsayer, if the gift abides with thee at all seasons, I have a red-spotted cow. She may be sister to thy Bull for aught I know—"

"Or I care," said Kim. "My Stars do not concern themselves with thy cattle."

"Nay, but she is very sick," a woman struck in. "My man is a buffalo, or he would have chosen his words better. Tell me if she recover?"

Had Kim been at all an ordinary boy, he would have carried on the play; but one does not know Lahore city, and least of all the *faquirs* by the Taksali Gate, for thirteen years without also knowing human nature.

The priest looked at him sideways, something bitterly—a dry and blighting smile.

"Is there no priest then in the village? I thought I had seen a great one even now," cried Kim.

"Ay—but—" the woman began.

"But thou and thy husband hoped to get the cow cured for a handful of thanks." The shot told: they were notoriously the closest-fisted couple in the village. "It is not well to cheat the temples. Give a young calf to thy own priest, and, unless thy gods are angry past recall, she will give milk within a month."

"A master-beggar art thou," purred the priest approvingly. "Not the cunning of forty years could have done better. Surely thou hast made the old man rich?"

"A little flour, a little butter, and a mouthful of cardamoms," Kim retorted, flushed with the praise, but still cautious—"does one grow rich on that? And, as thou canst see, he is mad. But it serves me while I learn the road at least."

He knew what the *faquirs* of the Taksali Gate were like when they talked among themselves, and copied the very inflection of their lewd disciples.

"Is his Search, then, truth or a cloak to other ends? It may be treasure."

"He is mad—many times mad. There is nothing else."

Here the old soldier hobbled up and asked if Kim would accept his hospitality for the night. The priest recommended him to do so, but insisted that the honor of entertaining the lama belonged to the temple—at which the lama smiled guilelessly. Kim glanced from one face to the other, and drew his own conclusions.

"Where is the money?" he whispered, beckoning the old man off in the darkness.

"In my bosom. Where else?"

"Give it me. Quietly and swiftly give it me."

"But why? Here is no ticket to buy."

"Am I thy *chela,* or am I not? Do I not safeguard thy old feet about the ways? Give me the money and at dawn I will return it." He slipped his hand above the lama's girdle and brought away the purse.

"Be it so—be it so." The old man nodded his head. "This is a great and terrible world. I never knew there were so many men alive in it."

Next morning the priest was in a very bad temper, but the lama was quite happy; and Kim had enjoyed a most interesting evening with the old man, who brought out his cavalry sabre and, balancing it on his dry knees, told tales of the Mutiny and young captains thirty years in their graves, till Kim dropped off to sleep.

"Certainly the air of this country is good," said the lama. "I sleep lightly, as do all old men; but last night I slept unwaking till broad day. Even now I am heavy."

"Drink a draught of hot milk," said Kim, who had carried not a few such remedies to opium-smokers of his acquaintance. "It is time to take the road again."

"The long road that overpasses all the rivers of Hind," said the lama gaily. "Let us go. But how thinkest thou, *chela,* to recompense these people, and especially the priest, for their great kindness? Truly they are *būt-parast,* but in other lives, maybe, they will receive enlightenment. A rupee to the temple? The thing within is no more than stone and red paint, but the heart of man we must acknowledge when and where it is good."

"Holy One, hast thou ever taken the road alone?" Kim looked up sharply, like the Indian crows so busy about the fields.

"Surely, child: from Kulu to Pathâkot–from Kulu, where my first *chela* died. When men were kind to us we made offerings, and all men were well-disposed throughout all the Hills."

"It is otherwise in Hind," said Kim drily. "Their gods are many-armed and malignant. Let them alone."

"I would set thee on thy road for a little, Friend of all the World–thou and thy yellow man." The old soldier ambled up the village street, all shadowy in the dawn, on a gaunt, scissor-hocked pony. "Last night broke up the fountains of remembrance in my so-dried heart, and it was as a blessing to me. Truly there is war abroad in the air. I smell it. See! I have brought my sword."

He sat long-legged on the little beast, with the big sword at his side,–hand dropped on the pommel,–staring fiercely over the flat lands towards the north. "Tell me again how He showed in thy vision. Come up and sit behind me. The beast will carry two."

"I am this Holy One's disciple," said Kim, as they cleared the village-gate. The villagers seemed almost sorry to be rid of them, but the priest's farewell was cold and distant. He had wasted some opium on a man who carried no money.

"That is well spoken. I am not much used to holy men, but respect is always good. There is no respect in these days–not even when a Commissioner Sahib comes to see me. But why should one whose Star leads him to war follow a holy man?"

"But he *is* a holy man," said Kim earnestly. "In truth, and in talk and in act, holy. He is not like the others. I have never seen such an one. We be not fortune-tellers, or jugglers, or beggars."

"Thou art not, that I can see; but I do not know that other. He marches well, though."

The first freshness of the day carried the lama forward with long, easy, camel-like strides. He was deep in meditation, mechanically clicking his rosary.

They followed the rutted and worn country road that wound across the flat between the great dark-green mango-groves, the line of the snow-capped Himalayas faint to the eastward. All India was at work in the fields, to the creaking of well-wheels, the shouting of ploughmen behind their cattle, and the clamor of the crows. Even the pony felt the good influence and almost broke into a trot as Kim laid a hand on the stirrup-leather.

"It repents me that I did not give a rupee to the shrine," said the lama on the last bead of his eighty-one.

The old soldier growled in his beard, so that the lama for the first time was aware of him.

"Seekest thou the River also?" said he, turning.

"The day is new," was the reply. "What need of a river save to water at before sundown? I come to show thee a short lane to the Big Road."

"That is a courtesy to be remembered, O man of good will; but why the sword?"

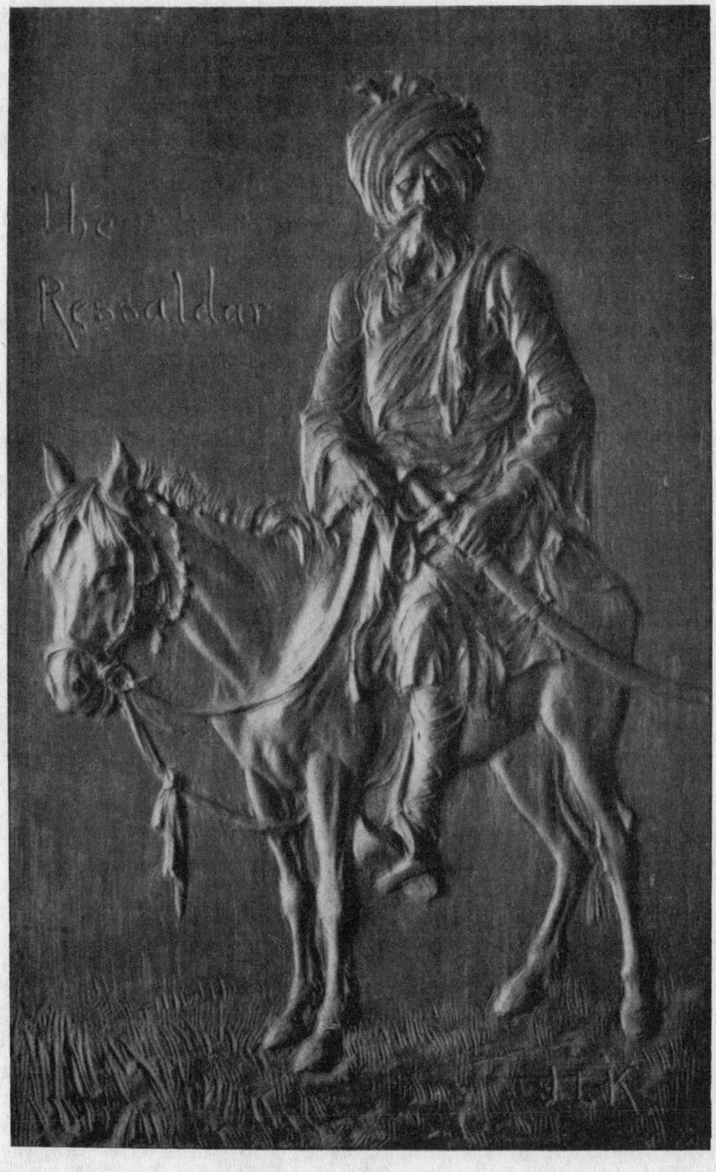

"HE SAT LONG-LEGGED ON THE LITTLE BEAST, WITH THE BIG SWORD AT HIS SIDE—HAND DROPPED ON THE POMMEL—STARING FIERCELY OVER THE FLAT LANDS . . ."

The old soldier looked as abashed as a child interrupted in his game of make-believe.

"The sword," he said, fumbling it. "Oh, that was a fancy of mine—an old man's fancy. Truly the police orders are that no man must bear weapons throughout Hind, but"—he cheered up and slapped the hilt—"all the constabeels here-about know me."

"It is not a good fancy," said the lama. "What profit to kill men?"

"Very little—as I know; but if evil men were not now and then slain it would not be a good world for weaponless dreamers. I do not speak without knowledge who have seen the land from Delhi south awash with blood."

"What madness was that, then?"

"The Gods, who sent it for a plague, alone know. A madness ate into all the Army, and they turned against their officers. That was the first evil, but not past remedy if they had then held their hands. But they chose to kill the Sahibs' wives and children. Then came the Sahibs from over the sea and called them to most strict account."

"Some such rumor, I believe, reached me once long ago. They called it the Black Year, as I remember."

"What manner of life hast thou led, not to know The Year? A rumor indeed! All earth knew, and trembled."

"Our earth never shook but once—upon the day that the Excellent One received Enlightenment."

"Umph! I saw Delhi shake at least; and Delhi is the navel of the world."

"So they turned against women and children? That was a bad deed, for which the punishment cannot be avoided."

"Many strove to do so, but with very small profit. I was then in a regiment of cavalry. It broke. Of six hundred and eighty sabres stood fast to their salt—how many think you? Three. Of whom I was one."

"The greater merit."

"Merit! We did not consider it merit in those days. My people, my friends, my brothers fell from me. They said: 'The time of the English is accomplished. Let each strike out a little holding for himself.' But I had talked with the men of Sobraon, of Chillianwallah, of Moodkee and Ferozeshan. I said: 'Abide a little and the wind turns. There is no blessing in this work.' In those days I rode seventy miles with an English mem'sahib and her babe on my saddle-bow. (Wow! That was a horse fit for a man!) I placed them in safety, and back came I to my officer—the one that was not killed of our five. 'Give me work,' said I, 'for I am an outcast among my own kin, and my cousin's blood is wet on my sabre.' 'Be content,' said he. 'There is great work forward. When this madness is over there is a recompense.' "

"Ay, there is a recompense when the madness is over, surely?" the lama muttered half to himself.

"They did not hang medals in those days on all who by accident had heard a gun fired. No! In nineteen pitched battles was I; in six-and-forty skirmishes of horse; and in small affairs without number. Nine wounds I bear; a medal and four clasps and the medal of an Order, for my captains, who are now generals, remembered me when the Kaiser-i-Hind had accomplished fifty years of her reign, and all the land rejoiced. They said: 'Give him the Order of Berittish India.' I carry it upon my neck now. I have also my *jaghir* (holding) from the hands of the State—a free gift to me and mine. The men of the old days—they are now Commissioners—come riding to me through the crops,—high upon horses so that all the village sees,—and we talk out the old skirmishes, one dead man's name leading to another."

"And after?" said the lama.

"Oh, afterwards they go away, but not before my village has seen."

"And at the last what wilt thou do?"

"At the last I shall die."

"And after?"

"Let the Gods order it. I have never pestered them with prayers: I do not think they will pester me. Look you, I have noticed in my long life that those who eternally break in upon Those Above with complaints and reports and bellowings and weepings are presently sent for in haste, as our colonel used to send for slack-jawed down-country men who talked too much. No, I have never wearied the Gods. They will remember this, and give me a quiet place where I can drive my lance in the shade, and wait to welcome my sons: I have no less than three—ressaldar-majors all—in the regiments."

"And they likewise, bound upon the Wheel, go forth from life to life—from despair to despair," said the lama below his breath, "hot, uneasy, snatching."

"Ay," the old soldier chuckled. "Three ressaldar-majors in three regiments. Gamblers a little, but so am I. They must be well-mounted; and one cannot take the horses as in the old days one took women. Well, well, my holding can pay for all. How thinkest thou? It is a well-watered strip, but my men cheat me. I do not know how to ask save at the lance's point. Ugh! I grow angry and I curse them, and they feign penitence, but behind my back I know they call me a toothless old ape."

"Hast thou never desired any other thing?"

"Yes—yes—a thousand times! A straight back and a close-clinging knee once more; a quick wrist and a keen eye; and the marrow that makes a man. Oh, the old days—the good days of my strength!"

"That strength is weakness."

"It has turned so; but fifty years since I could have proved it otherwise," the old soldier retorted, driving his stirrup-edge into the pony's lean flank.

"But I know a River of great healing."

"I have drank Gunga-water to the edge of dropsy. All she gave me was a flux, and no sort of strength."

"It is not Gunga. The River that I know washes from all taint of sin. Ascending the far bank one is assured of Freedom. I do not know thy life, but thy face is the face of the honorable and courteous. Thou hast clung to thy Way, rendering fidelity when it was hard to give, in that Black Year of which I now remember other tales. Enter now upon the Middle Way, which is the path to Freedom. Hear the Most Excellent Law, and do not follow dreams."

"Speak then, old man," the soldier smiled, half saluting. "We be all babblers at our age."

The lama squatted under the shade of a mango, whose shadow played checkerwise over his face; the soldier sat stiffly on the pony; and Kim, making sure that there were no snakes, lay down in the crotch of the twisted roots.

There was a drowsy buzz of small life in hot sunshine, a cooing of doves, and a sleepy drone of well-wheels across the fields. Slowly and impressively the lama began. At the end of ten minutes the old soldier slid from his pony, to hear better as he said, and sat with the reins round his wrist. The lama's voice faltered—the periods lengthened. Kim was busy watching a gray squirrel. When the little scolding bunch of fur, close pressed to the branch, disappeared, preacher and audience were fast asleep, the old officer's strong-cut head pillowed on his arm, the lama's thrown back against the tree bole, where it showed like yellow ivory. A naked child toddled up, stared, and, moved by some quick impulse of reverence, made a solemn little obeisance before the lama—only the child was so short and fat that it toppled over sideways, and Kim laughed at the sprawling, chubby legs. The child, scared and indignant, yelled aloud.

"Hai! Hai!" said the soldier, leaping to his feet. "What is it? What orders? . . . It is . . . a child! I dreamed it was an alarm. Little one—little one—do not cry. Have I slept? That was discourteous indeed!"

"I fear! I am afraid!" roared the child.

"What is it to fear? Two old men and a boy? How wilt thou ever make a soldier, Princeling?"

The lama had waked too, but, taking no direct notice of the child, clicked his rosary.

"What is that?" said the child, stopping a yell midway. "I have never seen such things. Give them me."

"Aha," said the lama, smiling, and trailing a loop of it on the grass:

"This is a handful of cardamoms,
This is a lump of *ghi:*
This is millet and chillies and rice,
A supper for thee and me!"

The child shrieked with joy, and snatched at the dark, glancing beads.

"Oho!" said the old soldier. "Whence had thou that song, despiser of this world?"

"I learned it in Pathânkot—sitting on a doorstep," said the lama shyly. "It is good to be kind to babes."

"As I remember, before the sleep came on us, thou hadst told me that marriage and bearing were darkeners of the true light, stumbling-blocks upon the way. Do children drop from heaven in thy country? Is it the Way to sing them songs?"

"No man is all perfect," said the lama gravely, re-coiling the rosary. "Run now to thy mother, little one."

"Hear him!" said the soldier to Kim. "He is ashamed for that he has made a child happy. There was a very good householder lost in thee, my brother. Hai, child!" He threw it a pice. "Sweetmeats are always sweet." And as the little figure capered away into the sunshine: "They grow up and become men. Holy One, I grieve that I slept in the midst of thy preaching. Forgive me."

"We be two old men," said the lama. "The fault is mine. I listened to thy talk of the world and its madness, and one fault led to the next."

"Hear him! What harm do thy Gods suffer from play with a babe? And that song was very well sung. Let us go on and I will sing thee the song of Nikal Seyn before Delhi—the old song."

And they fared out from the gloom of the mango tope, the old man's high, shrill voice ringing across the field, as wail by long-drawn wail he unfolded the story of Nikal Seyn (Nicholson)—the song that men sing in the Punjab to this day. Kim was delighted, and the lama listened with deep interest.

"Ahi! Nikal Seyn is dead—he died before Delhi! Lances of North take vengeance for Nikal Seyn." He quavered it out to the end, marking the trills with the flat of his sword on the pony's rump.

"And now we come to the Big Road," said he, after receiving the compliments of Kim; for the lama was markedly silent. "It is long since I have ridden this way, but thy boy's talk stirred me. See, Holy One—the Great Road which is the backbone of all Hind. For the most part it is shaded, as here, with four lines of trees; the middle road—all hard—takes the quick traffic. In the days before rail-carriages the Sahibs travelled up and down here in hundreds. Now there are only country-carts and such like. Left and right is the rougher road for the heavy carts—grain and cotton and timber, bhoosa, lime, and hides. A man goes in safety here—for at every few *kos* is a police-station. The police are thieves and extortioners (I myself would patrol it with cavalry—young recruits under a strong captain), but at least they do not suffer any rivals. All castes and kinds of men move here. Look! Brahmins and chumars, bankers and tinkers, barbers and bunnyas, pilgrims and potters–all the world going and coming. It is to me as a river from which I am withdrawn like a log after a flood."

And truly the Grand Trunk Road is a wonderful spectacle. It runs straight, bearing without crowding India's traffic for fifteen hundred miles–such a river of life as nowhere else exists in the world. They looked at the green-arched, shade-flecked length of it, the white breadth speckled with slow-pacing folk; and the two-roomed police-station opposite.

"Who bears arms against the law?" a constable called out laughingly, as he caught sight of the soldier's sword. "Are not the police enough to destroy evil-doers?"

"It was because of the police I bought it," was the answer. "Does all go well in Hind?"

"Ressaldar Sahib, all goes well."

"I am like an old tortoise, look you, who puts his head out from the bank and draws it in again. Ay, this is the road of Hindustan. All men come by this way. . . ."

"Son of a swine, is the soft part of the road meant for thee to scratch thy back upon? Father of all the daughters of shame and husband of ten thousand virtueless ones, thy mother was devoted to a devil, being led thereto by her mother; thy aunts have never had a nose for seven generations! Thy sister!–What owl's folly told thee to draw thy carts across the road? A broken wheel? Then take a broken head and put the two together at leisure!"

The voice and a venomous whip-cracking came out of a pillar of dust fifty yards away, where a cart had broken down. A thin, high Kattiwar mare, with eyes and nostrils aflame, rocketted out of the jam, snorting and wincing as her rider bent her across the road in chase of a shouting man. He was tall and gray-bearded, sitting the almost mad beast as a piece of her, and scientifically lashing his victim between plunges.

The old man's face lit with pride. "My child!" said he briefly, and strove to rein the pony's neck to a fitting arch.

"Am I to be beaten before the police?" cried the carter. "Justice! I will have Justice–"

"Am I to be blocked by a shouting ape who upsets ten thousand sacks under a young horse's nose? That is the way to ruin a mare."

"He speaks truth. He speaks truth. But she follows her man close," said the old man. The carter ran under the wheels of his cart and thence threatened all sorts of vengeance.

"They are strong men, thy sons," said the policeman serenely, picking his teeth.

The horseman delivered one last vicious cut with his whip and came on at a canter.

"My father!" He reined back ten yards and dismounted.

The old man was off his pony in an instant, and they embraced as do father and son in the East.

Chapter Four

Good Luck, she is never a lady,
But the cursedest quean alive.
Tricksy, wincing, and jady–
Kittle to lead or drive.
Greet her–she's hailing a stranger!
Meet her–she's busking to leave!
Let her alone for a shrew to the bone
And the hussy comes plucking your sleeve!
    Largesse! Largesse, O Fortune!
    Give or hold at your will.
    If I've no care for Fortune,
    Fortune must follow me still!

The Wishing Caps.

THEN, LOWERING THEIR voices, they spoke together. Kim came to rest under a tree, but the lama tugged impatiently at his elbow. "Let us go on. The River is not here."

"Hai mai! Have we not walked enough for a little? Our River will not run away. Patience, and he will give us a dole."

"That," said the old soldier suddenly, "is the Friend of the Stars. He brought me the news yesterday. Having seen the very man Himself, in a vision, giving orders for the war."

"Hm!" said his son, all deep in his broad chest. "He came by a bazar-rumor and made profit of it."

His father laughed. "At least he did not ride to me begging for a new charger and the gods know how many rupees. Are thy brothers' regiments also under orders?"

"I do not know. I took leave and came swiftly to thee in case–"

"In case they ran before thee to beg. O gamblers and spendthrifts all! But thou has never yet ridden in a charge. A good horse is needed there, truly. A good follower and a good pony also for the marching. Let us see–let us see." He thrummed on the pommel.

"This is no place to cast accounts in, my father. Let us go to thy house."

"At least pay the boy then: I have no pice with me, and he brought auspicious news. Ho! Friend of all the World, a war is toward as thou hast said."

"Nay, as I know, *the* war," returned Kim composedly.

"Eh?" said the lama, fingering his beads, all eager for the road.

"My master does not trouble the Stars for hire. We brought the news–bear witness, we brought the news, and now we go." Kim half-crooked his hand at his side.

The son tossed a silver coin through the sunlight, grumbling something about beggars and jugglers. It was a four-anna piece, and would feed them well for some days. The lama, seeing the flash of the metal, droned a blessing.

"Go thy way, Friend of all the World," piped the old soldier, wheeling his scrawny mount. "For once in all my days I have met a true prophet–who was not in the Army."

Father and son swung round together: the old man sitting as erect as the younger.

A Punjabi constable in yellow linen trousers slouched across the road. He had seen the money pass.

"Halt!" he cried in impressive English. "Know ye not that there is a *takkus* of two annas a head, which is four annas, on those who enter the road from this side-road? It is the order of the Sirkar, and the money is spent for the planting of trees and the beautification of the ways."

"And the bellies of the police," said Kim, skipping out of arm's reach. "Consider for awhile, man with a mud head. Think you we came from the nearest pond like the frog, thy father-in-law? Hast thou ever heard the name of thy brother?"

"And who was he? Leave the boy alone," cried a senior constable, immensely delighted, as he squatted down to smoke his pipe in the verandah.

"He took a label from a bottle of *belaitee-pani* (soda-water), and, affixing it to a bridge, collected taces for a month from those who passed, saying that it was the Sirkar's order. Then came an Englishman and broke his head. Ah, brother, I am a town-crow, not a village-crow!"

The policeman drew back abashed, and Kim hooted at him all down the road.

"Was there ever such a disciple as I?" he cried merrily to the lama. "All earth would have picked thy bones within ten mile of Lahore city if I had not guarded thee."

"I consider in my own mind whether thou art a spirit, sometimes, or sometimes an evil imp," said the lama, smiling slowly.

"I am thy *chela,*" Kim dropped into step at his side–that indescribable gait of the long-distance tramp all the world over.

"Now let us walk," muttered the lama, and to the click of his rosary they walked in silence mile upon mile. The lama, as usual, was deep in meditation, but Kim's bright eyes were open wide. This broad, smiling river of life, he considered, was a vast improvement on the cramped and crowded Lahore streets. There were new people and new sights at every stride–castes he knew and castes that were altogether out of his experience.

They met a troop of long-haired, strong-scented Sansis with baskets of lizards and other unclean food on their backs, the lean dogs sniffing at their heels. These people kept their own side of the road, moving at a quick, furtive jog-trot, and all other castes gave them ample room; for the Sansi is deep pollution. Behind them, walking wide and stiffly across the strong shadows, the memory of his leg-irons still on him, strode one newly released from the jail; his full stomach and shiny skin to prove that the Government fed its prisoners better than most honest men could feed themselves. Kim knew that walk well, and made broad jest of it as they passed. Then an Akali, a wild-eyed, wild-haired Sikh devotee in the blue-checked clothes of his faith, with polished-steel quoits glistening on the cone of his tall blue turban, stalked past, returning from a visit to one of the independent Sikh States, where he had been singing the ancient glories of the Khalsa to College-trained princelings in top-boots and white-cord breeches. Kim was careful not to irritate that man; for the Akali's temper is short and his arm quick. Here and there they met or were overtaken by the gaily dressed crowds of whole villages turning out to some local fair; the women, with their babes on their hips, walking behind the men, the older boys prancing on sticks of sugar-cane, dragging rude brass models of locomotives such as they sell for a halfpenny, or flashing the sun into the eyes of their betters from cheap toy mirrors. One could see at a glance what each had bought; and if there were any doubt it needed only to watch the wives comparing, brown arm against brown arm, the newly purchased dull glass bracelets that come from the North-West. These merry-makers stepped slowly, calling one to the other and stopping to haggle with sweetmeat-sellers, or to make a prayer before one of the wayside shrines–sometimes Hindu, sometimes Mussalman–which the low caste of both creeds share with beautiful impartiality. A solid line of blue, rising and falling like the back of a caterpillar in haste, would swing up through the quivering dust and trot past to a chorus of quick cackling. That was a gang of *changars*–the women who have taken all the embankments of all the Northern railways under their charge–a flat-footed, big-bosomed, strong-limbed, blue-petticoated clan of earth-carriers, hurrying north on news of a job, and wasting no time by the road. They belong to the caste whose men do not count, and they walked with squared elbows, swinging hips, and heads on high, as suits women who carry heavy weights. A little later a marriage procession would strike into the Grand Trunk with music and shoutings, and a smell of marigold and jasmine stronger even than the reek of the dust. One could see the bride's litter, a blur of red and tinsel, staggering through the haze, while the bridegroom's bewreathed pony turned aside to snatch a mouthful from a passing fodder-cart. Then Jim would join the Kentish-fire of good wishes and bad jokes, wishing the couple a hundred sons and no daughters, as the saying is. Still more interesting and more to be shouted over it was when a strolling juggler with some half-trained monkeys, or a panting, feeble bear, or a woman who tied goats' horns to her feet, and with these danced on a slack-rope, set the horses to shying and the women to shrill, long-drawn quavers of amazement.

The lama never raised his eyes. He did not note the money-lender on his goose-rumped pony, hastening along to collect the cruel interest; or the long-shouting, deep-voiced little mob–still in military formation–of native soldiers on leave, rejoicing to be rid of their breeches and puttees, and saying the most outrageous things to the most respectable women in sight. Even the seller of Ganges-water he did not see, and Kim expected that he would at least buy a bottle of that precious stuff. He looked steadily at the ground, and strode as steadily hour after hour, his soul busied elsewhere. But Kim was in the seventh heaven of joy. The Grand Trunk at this point was built on an embankment to guard against winter floods from the foothills, so that one walked, as it were, a little above the country, along a stately corridor, seeing all India spread out to left and right. It was beautiful to behold the many-yoked grain and cotton waggons crawling over the country roads: one could hear their axles, complaining a mile away, coming nearer, till with shouts and yells and bad words they climbed up the steep incline and plunged on to the hard main road, carter reviling carter. It was equally beautiful to watch the people, little clumps of red and blue and pink and white and saffron, turning aside to go to their own villages, dispersing and growing small by twos and threes across the level plain. Kim felt these things, though he could not give tongue to his feelings, and so contented himself with buying peeled sugar-cane and spitting the pith generously about his path. From time to time the lama took snuff, and at last Kim could endure the silence no longer.

"This is a good land–the land of the South!" said he. "The air is good; the water is good. Eh?"

"And they are all bound upon the Wheel," said the lama. "Bound from life after life. To none of these has the Way been shown." He shook himself back to this world.

"And now we have walked a weary way," said Kim. "Surely we shall soon come to a *parao* (a resting-place). Shall we stay there? Look, the sun is sloping."

"Who will receive us this evening?"

"That is all one. This country is full of good folk. Besides,"–he sunk his voice beneath a whisper,–"we have money."

The crowd thickened as they neared the resting-place which marked the end of their day's journey. A line of stalls selling very simple food and tobacco, a stack of firewood, a police-station, a well, a horse-trough, a few trees, and, under them, some trampled ground dotted with the black ashes of old fires, are all that mark a *parao* on the Grand Trunk; if you except the beggars and the crows–both hungry.

By this time the sun was driving broad golden spokes through the lower branches of the mango-trees; the parakeets and doves were coming home in their hundreds; the chattering, gray-backed Seven Sisters, talking over the day's adventures, walked back and forth in twos and threes almost under the feet of the travellers; and shufflings and scufflings in the branches showed that the bats were ready to go out on the night-picket. Swiftly the light gathered itself together, painted for an instant the faces and the cart-wheels and the bullocks' horns as red as blood. Then the night fell, changing the touch of the air, drawing a low, even haze, like a gossamer veil of blue, across the face of the country, and bringing out, keen and distinct, the smell of wood-smoke and cattle and the good scent of wheaten cakes cooked on ashes. The evening patrol hurried out of the police-station with important coughings and reiterated orders; and a live charcoal ball in the cup of a wayside carter's hookah glowed red while Kim's eye mechanically watched the last flicker of the sun on the brass tweezers.

The life of the *parao* was very like that of the Kashmir Serai on a small scale. Kim dived into the happy Asiatic disorder which, if you only allow time, will bring you everything that a simple man needs.

His wants were few, because, since the lama had no caste scruples, cooked food from the nearest staff would serve; but, for luxury's sake, Kim bought a handful of dung-cakes to build a fire. All about, coming and going round the little flames, men cried for oil, or grain, or sweetmeats, or tobacco, jostling one another while they waited their turn at the well; and under the men's voices you heard from halted, shuttered carts the high squeals and giggles of women whose faces should not be seen in public.

Nowadays, well-educated natives are of opinion that when their womenfolk travel–and they visit a good deal–it is better to take them quickly by rail in a properly screened compartment; and that custom is spreading. But there are always those of the old rock who hold by the use of their forefathers; and, above all, there are always the old women,–more conservative than the men,–who towards the end of their days go a pilgrimage. They, being withered and undesirable, do not, under certain circumstances, object to unveiling. After their long seclusion, during which they have always been in business touch with a thousand outside interests, they love the bustle and stir of the open road, the gatherings at the shrines, and the infinite possibilities of gossip with like-minded dowagers. Very often it suits a long-suffering family that a strong-tongued, iron-willed old lady should disport herself about India in this fashion; for certainly pilgrimage is grateful to the Gods. So all about India, in the most remote places, as in the most public, you find some knot of grizzled servitors in nominal charge of an old lady who is more or less curtained and hid away in a bullock-cart. Such men are staid and discreet, and when a European or a high-caste native is near will net their charge with most elaborate precautions; but in the ordinary haphazard chances of pilgrimage the precautions are not taken. The old lady is, after all, intensely human, and lives to look upon life.

Kim marked down a gaily ornamented *ruth* or family bullock-cart, with a broidered canopy of two domes, like a double-humped camel, which had just been drawn into the *parao*. Eight men made its retinue, and two of the eight were armed with rusty sabres–sure signs that they followed a person of distinction, for the common folk do not bear arms. An increasing cackle of complaints, orders, and jests, and what to a European would have been bad language, came from behind the curtains. Here was evidently a woman used to command.

Kim looked over the retinue critically. Half of them were thin-legged, gray-bearded Ooryas from down country. The other half were duffle-clad, felt-hatted hillmen of the North; and that mixture told its own tale, even if he had not overheard the incessant sparring between the two divisions. The old lady was going south on a visit–probably to a rich relative, most probably to a son-in-law, who had sent up an escort as a mark of respect. The hillmen would be of her own people–Kulu or Kangra folk. It was quite clear that she was not taking her daughter down to be wedded, or the curtains would have been laced home and the guard would have allowed no one near the car. A merry and a high-spirited dame, thought Kim, balancing the dung-cake in one hand, the cooked food in the other, and piloting the lama with a nudging shoulder. Something might be made out of the meeting. The lama would give him no help, but, as a conscientious *chela,* Kim was delighted to beg for two.

He built his fire as close to the cart as he dared, waiting for one of the escort to order him away. The lama dropped wearily to the ground, much as a heavy fruit-eating bat cowers, and returned to his rosary.

"Stand farther off, beggar!" The order was shouted in broken Hindustanee by one of the hillmen.

"Huh! It is only a *pahari* (a hillman)," said Kim over his shoulder. "Since when have the hill-asses owned all Hindustan?"

The retort was a swift and brilliant sketch of Kim's pedigree for three generations.

"Ah!" Kim's voice was sweeter than ever, as he broke the dung-cake into fit pieces. "In *my* country we call that the beginning of love-talk."

A harsh, thin cackle behind the curtains put the hillman on his mettle for a second shot.

"Not so bad–not so bad," said Kim with calm. "But have a care, my brother, lest we–*we,* I say–be minded to give a curse or so in return. And our curses have the knack of bitting home."

The Ooryas laughed; the hillman sprang forward threateningly; the lama suddenly raised his head, bringing his huge tam-o'shanter cap into the full light of Kim's new-started fire.

"What is it?" said he.

The man halted as though struck to stone. "I–I–am saved from a great sin," he stammered.

"The foreigner has found him a priest at last," whispered one of the Ooryas.

"Hai! Why is that beggar-brat not well beaten?" the old woman cried.

The hillman drew back to the cart and whispered something to the curtain. There was dead silence, then a muttering.

"This goes well," thought Kim, pretending neither to see nor hear.

"When–when–he has eaten"–the hillman fawned on Kim–"it–it is requested that the Holy One will do the honor to talk to one who would speak to him."

"After he has eaten he will sleep," Kim returned loftily. He could not quite see what new turn the game had taken, but stood resolute to profit by it. "Now, I will get him his food." The last sentence, spoken loudly, ended with a sigh as of faintness.

"I–I myself and the others of my people will look to that–if it is permitted."

"It is permitted," said Kim, more loftily than ever. "Holy One, these people will bring us food."

"The land is good. All the country of the South is good—a great and terrible world," mumbled the lama drowsily.

"Let him sleep," said Kim, "but look to it that we are well fed when he wakes. He is a very holy man."

Again one of the Ooryas said something contemptuously.

"He is not a *faquir.* He is not a down-country beggar," Kim went on severely, addressing the stars. "He is the most holy of holy men. He is above all castes. I am his *chela.*"

"Come here!" said the flat thin voice behind the curtain; and Kim came, conscious that eyes he could not see were staring at him. One skinny brown finger heavy with rings lay on the edge of the cart, and the talk went this way:

"Who is that one?"

"An exceeding holy one. He comes from far off. He comes from Tibet."

"Where in Tibet?"

"From behind the snows—from a very far place. He knows the stars; he makes horoscopes; he reads nativities. But he does not do this for money. He does it for kindness and great charity. I am his disciple. I am called also the Friend of the Stars."

"Thou art no hillman."

"Ask him. He will tell thee I was sent to him from the stars to show him an end to his pilgrimage."

"Humph! Consider, brat, that I am an old woman and not altogether a fool. Lamas I know and to these I give reverence, but thou art no more a lawful *chela* than this my finger is the pole of this waggon. Thou art a casteless Hindu—a bold and unblushing beggar, attached, belike, to the Holy One for the sake of gain."

"Do we not all work for gain?" Kim changed his tone promptly to match that altered voice. "I have heard"—this was a bow drawn at a venture—"I have heard—"

"What hast thou heard?" she snapped, rapping with the finger.

"Nothing that I well remember, but some talk in the bazars, which is doubtless a lie, that even Rajahs—small Hill Rajahs—"

"But none the less of good Rajput blood."

"Assuredly of good blood. That these even sell the more comely of their womenfolk for gain. Down south they sell them—to zemindars and such-all of Oudh."

If there be one thing in the world that the small Hill Rajahs deny it is just this charge; but it happens to be one thing that the bazars believe, when they discuss the mysterious slave-traffics of India. The old lady explained to Kim, in a tense, indignant whisper, precisely what manner and fashion of malignant liar he was. Had Kim hinted this when she was a girl, he would have been pommelled to death that same evening by an elephant. This was perfectly true.

"Ahai! I am only a beggar's brat, as the Eye of Beauty has said," he wailed in extravagant terror.

"Eye of Beauty, forsooth! Who am I that thou shouldst fling beggar-endearments to me?" And yet she laughed at the long-forgotten word. "Forty years ago that might have been said, and not without truth. Ay, thirty years ago. But it is the fault of this gadding up and down Hind that a king's widow must jostle all the scum of the land, and be made a mock by beggars."

"Great Queen," said Kim promptly, for he heard her shaking with indignation, "I am even what the Great Queen says I am; but none the less is my master holy. He has not yet heard the Great Queen's order that—"

"Order? I order a Holy One—a Teacher of the Law—to come and speak to a woman? Never!"

"Pity my stupidity. I thought it was given as an order—"

"It was not. It was a petition. Does this make all clear?"

A silver coin clicked on the edge of the cart. Kim took it and salaamed profoundly. The old lady recognised that, as the eyes and the ears of the lama, he was to be propitiated.

"I am but the Holy One's disciple. When he has eaten perhaps he will come."

"Oh, villain and shameless rogue!" The jewelled forefinger shook itself at him reprovingly; but he could hear the old lady's chuckle.

"Nay, what is it?" he said, dropping into his most caressing and confidential tone—the one, he well knew, that few could resist. "Is—is there any need of a son in thy family? Speak freely, for we priests—" That last was a direct plagiarism from a *faquir* by the Taksali Gate.

"We priests! Thou art not yet old enough to—" She checked the joke with another laugh. "Believe me, now and again, we women, O priest, think of other matters than sons. Moreover, my daughter has borne her man-child."

"Two arrows in the quiver are better than one; and three are better still." Kim quoted the proverb with a meditative cough, looking discreetly earthward.

"True—oh, true. But perhaps that will come. Certainly those down-country Brahmins are utterly useless. I sent gifts and monies and gifts again to them, and they prophesied."

"Ah," drawled Kim, with infinite contempt, "they prophesied!" A professional could have done no better.

"And it was not till I remembered my own Gods that my prayers were heard. I chose an auspicious hour, and—perhaps thy Holy One has heard of the Abbot of the Lung-Cho lamasery. It was to him I put the matter, and behold in the due time all came about as I desired. The Brahmin in the house of the father of my daughter's son has since said that it was through *his* prayers—which is a little error that I will explain to him when we reach our journey's end. And so afterwards I go to Buddh Gaya, to make *shraddha* for the father of my children."

"Thither go we."

"Doubly auspicious," chirruped the old lady. "A second son at least!"

"O Friend of all the World!" The lama had waked, and, simply as a child bewildered in a strange bed, called for Kim.

"I come! I come, Holy One!" He dashed to the fire, where he found the lama already surrounded by dishes of food, the hillmen visibly adoring him and the Southerners looking sourly. "Go back! Withdraw!" Kim cried. "Do we eat publicly like dogs?" They finished the meal in silence, each turned a little from the other, and Kim topped it with a native-made cigarette.

"Have I not said an hundred times that the South is a good land? Here is a virtuous and high-born widow of a Hill Rajah on pilgrimage, she says, to Buddh Gaya. She it is sends us those dishes; and when thou art well rested she would speak to thee."

"Is this also thy work?" The lama dipped deep into his snuff-gourd.

"Who else watched over thee since our wonderful journey began?" Kim's eyes danced in his head as he blew the rank smoke through his nostrils and stretched him on the dusty ground. "Have I failed to oversee thy comforts, Holy One?"

"A blessing on thee." The lama inclined his solemn head. "I have known many men in my so long life, and disciples not a few. But to none among men, if so be thou art woman-born, has my heart gone out as it has to thee—thoughtful, wise, and courteous, but something of a small imp."

"And I have never seen such a priest as thou." Kim considered the benevolent yellow face wrinkle by wrinkle. "It is less than three days since we took road together, and it is as though it were a hundred years."

"Perhaps in a former life it was permitted that I should have rendered thee some service. Maybe"–and he smiled–"I freed thee from a trap; or, having caught thee on a hook in the days when I was not enlightened, cast thee back into the river."

"Maybe," said Kim quietly. He had heard this sort of speculation again and again, from the mouths of many whom the English would not consider imaginative. "Now, as regards that woman in the bullock-cart, *I* think she needs a second son for her daughter."

"That is no part of the Way," sighed the lama. "But at least she is from the Hills. Ah, the Hills, and the snow of the Hills!"

He rose and stalked to the cart. Kim would have given his ears to come too, but the lama did not invite him; and the few words he caught were in an unknown tongue, for they spoke some common speech of the mountains. The woman seemed to ask questions which the lama turned over in his mind before answering. Now and again he heard the sing-song cadence of a Chinese quotation. It was a strange picture that Kim watched between drooped eyelids. The lama, very straight and erect, the deep folds of his yellow clothing slashed with black in the light of the *parao* fires precisely as a knotted tree-trunk is slashed with the shadow of the long sun, addressed a tinsel and lacquered *ruth* which burned like a many-colored jewel in the same uncertain light. The patterns on the gold-worked curtains ran up and down, melting and reforming as the folds shook and quivered to the night wind; and when the talk grew more earnest the jewelled forefinger snapped out little sparks of light between the embroideries. Behind the cart was a wall of uncertain darkness speckled with little flames and alive with half-caught forms and faces and shadows. The voices of early evening had settled down to one soothing hum whose deepest note was the steady chumping of the bullocks above their chopped straw, and whose highest was the tinkle of a Bengali dancing-girl's *sitar.* Most men had eaten and pulled deep at their gurgling, grunting hookahs, which in full blast sound like bull-frogs.

At last the lama returned. A hillman walked behind him with a wadded cotton-quilt and spread it carefully by the fire. "She deserves ten thousand grandchildren," thought Kim. "None the less, but for me, these gifts would not have come."

"A virtuous woman–and a wise one." The lama slackened off, joint by joint, like a slow camel. "The world is full of charity to those who follow the Way." He flung a fair half of the quilt over Kim.

"And what said she?" Kim rolled up in his share of it.

"She asked me many questions and propounded many problems–the most of which were idle tales which she had heard from devil-serving priests who pretend to follow the Way. Some I answered, and some I said were foolish. Many wear the Robe, but few keep the Way."

"True. That is true." Kim used the thoughtful, conciliatory tone of those who wish to draw confidences.

"But by her lights she is most right-minded. She desires greatly that we should go with her to Buddh Gaya; her road being ours, as I understand, for many days' journey to the southward."

"And?"

"Patience a little. To this I said that my Search came before all things. She had heard many foolish legends, but this great truth of my River she had never heard. Such are the priests of the lower hills! She knew the Abbot of Lung-Cho, but she did not know of my River–nor the tale of the Arrow."

"And?"

"I spoke therefore of the Search, and of the Way, and of matters that were profitable; she desiring only that I should accompany her and make prayer for a second son."

"Aha! 'We women' do *not* think of anything save children," said Kim sleepily.

"Now, since our roads run together for awhile, I do not see that we in any way depart from our Search if so be we accompany her–at least as far as–I have forgotten the name of the city."

"Ohé!" said Kim, turning and speaking in a sharp whisper to one of the Ooryas a few yards away. "Where is your master's house?"

"A little behind Saharunpore, among the fruit-gardens." He named the village.

"That was the place," said the lama. "So far, at least, we can go with her."

"Flies go to carrion," said the Oorya, in an abstracted voice.

"For the sick cow a crow; for the sick man a Brahmin." Kim breathed the proverb impersonally to the shadow-tops of the trees overhead.

The Oorya grunted and held his peace.

"So then we go with her, Holy One?"

"Is there any reason against? I can still step aside and try all the rivers that the road overpasses. She desires that I should come. She very greatly desires it."

Kim stifled a laugh in the quilt. When once that imperious old lady had recovered from her natural awe of a lama he thought it probable that she would be worth listening to.

He was nearly asleep when the lama suddenly quoted a proverb: "The husbands of the talkative have a great reward hereafter." Then Kim heard him snuff thrice, and dozed off, still laughing.

The diamond-bright dawn woke men and crows and bullocks together. Kim sat up and yawned, shook himself, and thrilled with delight. This was seeing the world in real truth; this was life as he would have it–bustling and shouting, the buckling of belts, and beating of bullocks and creaking of wheels, lighting of fires and cooking of food, and new sights at every turn of the approving eye. The morning mist swept off in a whorl of silver, the parrots shot away to some distant river in shrieking green hosts: all the well-wheels within earshot went to work. India was awake, and Kim was in the middle of it, more awake and more excited than any one, chewing on a twig that he would presently use as a tooth-brush; for he borrowed right- and left-handedly from all the customs of the country he knew and loved. There was no need to worry about food–no need to spend a cowrie at the crowded stalls. He was the disciple of a holy man annexed by a strong-willed old lady. All things would be prepared for them, and when they were respectfully invited so to do they would sit and eat. For the rest,–Kim giggled here as he cleaned his teeth,–his hostess would rather heighten the enjoyment of the road. He inspected her bullocks critically, as they came up grunting and blowing under the yokes. If they went too fast–it was not likely–there would be a pleasant seat for himself along the pole; the lama would sit beside the driver. The escort, of course, would walk. The old lady, equally of course, would talk a great deal, and by what he had heard that conversation would not lack salt. She was already ordering, haranguing, rebuking, and, it must be said, cursing her servants for delays.

"Get her her pipe. In the name of the Gods, get her her pipe and stop her ill'omened mouth," cried an Oorya, tying up his shapeless bundles of bedding. "She and the parrots are alike. They screech in the dawn."

"The lead-bullocks! Hai! Look to the lead-bullocks!" They were backing and wheeling as a grain-cart's axle caught them by the horns. "Son of an owl, where dost thou go?" This to the grinning carter.

"Ai! Yai! Yai! That within there is the Queen of Delhi going to pray for a son," the man called back over his high load. "Room for the Queen of Delhi and her prime minister the gray monkey climbing up his own sword!" Another cart loaded with bark for a down-country tannery followed close behind, and its driver added a few compliments as the *ruth*-bullocks backed and backed again.

From behind the shaking curtains came one volley of invective. It did not last long, but in kind and quality, in blistering appropriateness, it was beyond anything that even Kim had heard. He could see the carter's bare chest collapse with amazement, as the man salaamed reverently to the voice, leaped from the pole, and helped the escort haul their volcano on to the main road. Here the voice told him truthfully what sort of wife he had wedded, and what she was doing in his absence.

"Oh, *shabash!*" murmured Kim, unable to contain himself, as the man slunk away.

"Well done, indeed! It is a shame and a scandal that a poor woman may not go to make prayer to her gods except she be jostled and insulted by all the refuse of Hindustan–that she must eat *gâli* (abuse) as men eat *ghi.* But I have yet a wag left to my tongue–a word or two well spoken that serves the occasion. And *still* am I without my tobacco! Who is the one-eyed and luckless son of shame that has not yet prepared my pipe?"

It was hastily thrust in by a hillman, and a trickle of thick smoke from each corner of the curtains showed that peace was restored.

If Kim had walked proudly the day before, disciple of a holy man, to-day he paced with ten-fold pride in the train of a semi-royal procession, with a recognised place under the patronage of an old lady of charming manners and infinite resource. The escort, their heads tied up native fashion, fell in on either side the cart, shuffling enormous clouds of dust.

The lama and Kim walked a little to one side: Kim chewing his stick of sugar-cane, and making way for no one under the status of a priest. They could hear the old lady's tongue clack as steadily as a rice-husker. She bade the escort tell her what was going on on the road; and so soon as they were clear of the *parao* she flung back the curtains and peered out, her veil a third across her face. Her men did not eye her directly when she addressed them, and thus the proprieties were more or less observed.

A dark, sallowish District Superintendent of Police, faultlessly uniformed, an Englishman, trotted by on a tired horse, and, seeing from her retinue what manner of person she was, chaffed her. "O mother," he cried, "do they do this in the *zenanas?* Suppose an Englishman came by and saw that thou hadst no nose?"

"What?" she shrilled back. "Thy own mother has no nose? Why say so, then, on the open road?"

It was a fair counter. The Englishman threw up his hand with the gesture of a man hit at sword-play. She laughed and nodded. "Is this a face to tempt virtue aside?" She withdrew all her veil and stared at him.

It was by no means lovely, but as the man gathered up his reins he called it a Moon of Paradise, a Disturber of Integrity, and a few other fantastic epithets which doubled her up with mirth.

"That is a *nut-cut* (rogue)," she said. "All police-constables are *nut-cuts;* but the police-wallahs are the worst. Hai, my son, thou hast never learned all hat since thou camest from *Belait* (Europe). Who suckled thee?"

"A *pahreen*–a hillwoman of Dalhousie, my mother. Keep thy beauty under a shade–O Dispenser of Delights," and he was gone.

"These be the sort"–she took a fine judicial tone, and stuffed her mouth with *pan*–"These be the sort to oversee justice. They know the land and the customs of the land. The others, all new from Europe, suckled by white

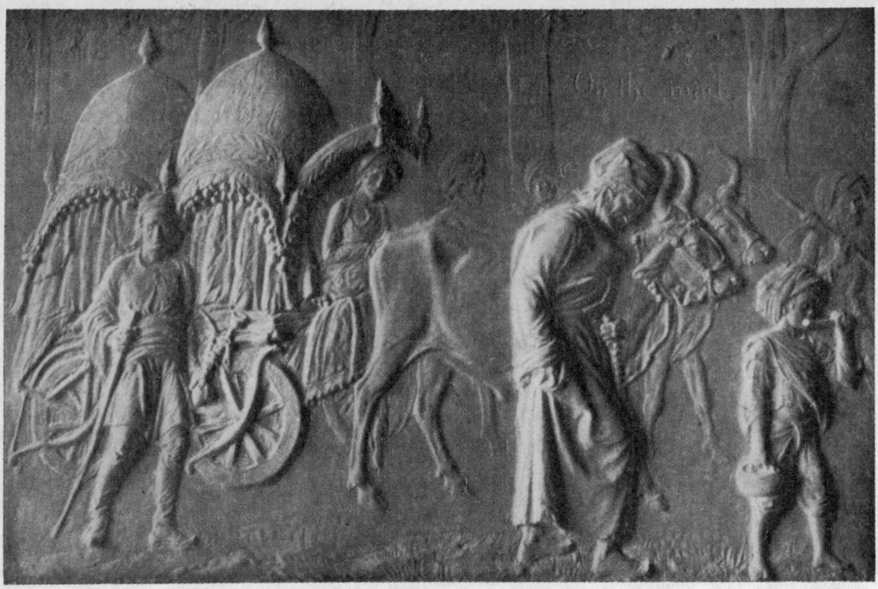

"THE LAMA AND KIM WALKED A LITTLE TO ONE SIDE;
KIM CHEWING HIS STICK OF SUGAR-CANE, AND MAKING WAY
FOR NO ONE UNDER THE STATUS OF A PRIEST."

women and learning our tongues from books, are worse than the pestilence. They do harm to Kings." Then she told a long, long tale to the world at large, of an ignorant young policeman who had disturbed some small Hill Rajah, a ninth cousin of her own, in the matter of a trivial land-case, winding up with a quotation from a work by no means devotional.

Then her mood changed, and she bade one of the escort ask whether the lama would walk alongside and discuss matters of religion. So Kim dropped back into the dust and returned to his sugar-cane. For an hour or more the lama's tam-o-shanter showed like a moon through the haze; and, from all he heard, Kim gathered that the old woman wept. One of the Ooryas half apologised for his rudeness overnight, saying that he had never known his mistress of so bland a temper, and he ascribed it to the presence of the strange priest. Personally, he believed in Brahmins, though, like all natives, he was acutely aware of their cunning and their greed. Still, when Brahmins but irritated with begging demands the mother of his master's wife, and when she sent them away so angry that they cursed the whole retinue (which was the real reason for the second off-side bullock going lame, and of the pole breaking the night before), he was prepared to accept any priest of any other denomination in or out of India. To this Kim assented with wise nods, and bade the Oorya observe that the lama took no money, and that the cost of his and Kim's food would be repaid a hundred times in the good luck that would attend the caravan henceforward. He also told stories of Lahore city, and sang a song or two which made the escort laugh. As a town-mouse well acquainted with the latest songs by the most fashionable composers,—they are women for the most part,—Kim had a distinct advantage over men from a little fruit-village behind Saharunpore, but he let that advantage be inferred.

At noon they turned aside to eat, and the meal was good, plentiful, and well-served on plates of clean leaves, in decency, out of drift of the dust. They gave the scraps to certain beggars, that all requirements might be fulfilled, and sat down to a long, luxurious smoke. The old lady had retreated behind her curtains, but mixed most freely in the talk, her servants arguing with and contradicting her as servants do throughout the East. She compared the cool and the pines of the Kangra and Kulu hills with the dust and the mangoes of the South; she told a tale of some old local Gods at the edge of her husband's territory; she roundly abused the tobacco which she was then smoking, reviled all Brahmins, and speculated without reserve on the coming of many grandsons.

Chapter Five

Here come I to my own again–
Fed, forgiven, and known again–
Claimed by bone of my bone again,
And sib to flesh of my flesh!
The fatted calf is dressed for me,
But the husks have greater zest for me . . .
I think my pigs will be best for me,
So I'm off to the styes afresh.

The Prodigal Son.

ONCE MORE THE lazy, string-tied, shuffling procession got under way, and she slept till they reached the next halting-stage. It was a very short march, and time lacked an hour to sundown, so Kim cast about for means of amusement.

"But why not sit and rest?" said one of the escort. "Only the devils and the English walk to and fro without reason."

"Never make friends with the Devil, a monkey, or a boy. No man knows what they will do next," said his fellow.

Kim turned a scornful back–he did not want to hear the old story how the Devil played with the boys and repented of it–and walked idly across country.

The lama strode after him. All that day, whenever they passed a stream, he had turned aside to look at it, but in no case had he received any warning that he had found his River. Insensibly too the comfort of speaking to some one in a reasonable tongue, and of being properly considered and respected as her spiritual adviser by a well-born woman, had weaned his thoughts a little from the Search. And further, he was prepared to spend serene years in his quest; having nothing of the white man's impatience, but a great faith.

"Where goest thou?" he called after Kim.

"No whither–it was a small march, and all this"–Kim waved his hands abroad–"is new to me."

"She is beyond question a wise and a discerning woman. But it is hard to meditate when–"

"All women are thus." Kim spoke as might have Solomon.

"Before the lamasery was a broad platform," the lama muttered, looping up the well-worn rosary, "of stone. On that I have left the marks of my feet–pacing to and fro with these."

He clicked the beads, and began the "*Om mane pudme hum*" of his devotion; grateful for the cool, the quiet, and the absence of dust.

One thing after another drew Kim's idle eye across the plain. There was no purpose in his wanderings, except that the build of the huts near by seemed new, and he wished to investigate.

They came out on a broad tract of grazing-ground, brown and purple in the afternoon light, with a heavy clump of mangoes in the centre. It struck Kim as curious that no shrine stood in so eligible a spot: the boy was observing as any priest for these things. Far across the plain walked side by side four men, made small by the distance. He looked intently under his curved palms and caught the sheen of brass.

"Soldiers. White soldiers!" said he. "Let us see."

"It is always soldiers when thou and I go out alone together. But I have never seen the white soldiers."

"They do no harm except when they are drunk. Keep behind this tree."

They stepped behind the thick trunks in the cool dark of the mango-tope. Two little figures halted; the other two came forward uncertainly. They were the advance-party of a regiment on the march, sent out, as usual, to mark the camp. They bore five-foot sticks with fluttering flags, and called to each other as they spread over the flat earth.

At last they entered the mango-grove, walking heavily.

"It's here or hereabouts–officers' tents under the trees, I take it, an' the rest of us can stay outside. Have they marked out for the baggage-waggons behind?"

They cried again to their comrades in the distance, and the rough answer came back faint and mellowed.

"Shove the flag in here, then," said one.

"What do they prepare?" said the lama, wonder-struck. "This is a great and terrible world. What is the device on the flag?"

A soldier thrust a stave within a few feet of them, grunted discontentedly, pulled it up again, conferred with his companion, who looked up and down the shaded case of greenery, and returned it.

Kim stared with all his eyes, his breath coming short and sharp between his teeth. The soldiers stamped off into the sunshine.

"O Holy One," he gasped, "my horoscope! The drawing in the dust by the priest at Umballa! Remember what he said. First come two–*ferashes*–to make all things ready–in a dark place, as it is always at the beginning of a vision."

"But this is not vision," said the lama. "It is the world's Illusion, and no more."

"And after them comes the Bull–the Red Bull on the green field. Look! It is he!"

He pointed to the flag that was snap-snapping in the evening breeze not ten feet away. It was no more than an ordinary camp marking-flag; but the regiment, always punctilious in matters of millinery, had charged it with the regimental device, the Red Bull, which is the crest of the Mavericks–the great Red Bull on a background of Irish green.

"I see, and now I remember," said the lama. "Certainly it is thy Bull. Certainly, also, the two men came to make all ready."

"They are soldiers–white soldiers. What said the priest? 'The sign over against the Bull is the sign of War and armed men.' Holy One, this thing touches my Search."

"True. It is true." The lama stared fixedly at the device that flamed like a ruby in the dusk. "The priest at Umballa said that thine was the sign of War."

"What is to do now?"

"Wait. Let us wait."

"Even now the darkness clears," said Kim. It was only natural that the descending sun should at last strike through the tree-trunks, across the grove, filling it with mealy gold light for a few minutes; but to Kim it was crown of the Umballa Brahmin's prophecy.

"Hark!" said the lama. "One beats a drum–far off!"

At first the sound, carrying diluted through the still air, resembled the beating of an artery in the head. Soon a sharpness was added.

"Ah! The music," Kim explained. He knew the sound of a regimental band, but it amazed the lama.

At the far end of the plain a heavy, dusty column crawled in sight. Then the wind brought the tune:–

We crave your condescension
To tell you what we know
Of marching in the Mulligan Guards
To Sligo Port below.

Here broke in the shrill-tongued fifes:–

We shouldered arms,
We marched–we marched away
From Phoenix Park
We marched to Dublin Bay.
The drums and the fifes,
Oh, sweetly they did play,
As we marched–marched–marched–with the
Mulligan Guards!

It was the band of the Mavericks playing the regiment to camp; for the men were route-marching with their baggage. The rippling column swung into the level–carts behind it–divided left and right, ran about like an ant-hill, and . . .

"But this is sorcery!" said the lama.

The plain dotted itself with tents that seemed to rise, all spread, from the carts. Another rush of men invaded the grove, pitched a huge tent in silence, ran up yet eight or nine more by the side of it, unearthed cooking-pots, pans, and bundles, which were taken possession of by a crowd of native servants; and behold the mango-tope turned into an orderly town as they watched!

"Let us go," said the lama, sinking back afraid, as the fires twinkled and white officers with jingling swords stalked into the mess-tent.

"Stand back in the shadow. No one can see beyond the light of a fire," said Kim, his eyes still on the flag. He had never before watched the routine of a seasoned regiment pitching camp in thirty minutes.

"Look! look! look!" clucked the lama. "Yonder comes a priest."

It was Bennett, the Church of England chaplain of the regiment, limping in dusty black. One of his flock had made some rude remarks about the chaplain's mettle; and to abash him Bennett had marched step by step with the men that day. The black dress, gold cross on the watch-chain, the hairless face, and the soft, black wideawake hat would have marked him as a holy man anywhere in all India. He dropped into a camp-chair by the door of the mess-tent and slid off his boots. Three or four officers gathered round him, laughing and joking over his exploit.

"The talk of white men is wholly lacking in dignity," said the lama, who judged only by tone. "But I have considered the countenance of that priest, and I think he is learned. Is it likely that he will understand our talk? I would talk to him of my Search."

"Never speak to a white man till he is fed," said Kim, quoting a well-known proverb. "They will eat now, and—and I do not think they are good to beg from. Let us go back to the resting-place. After we have eaten we will come again. It certainly was a Red Bull—*my* Red Bull."

They were both noticeably absent-minded when the old lady's retinue set their meal before them; so none broke their reserve, for it is not lucky to annoy guests.

"Now," said Kim, picking his teeth, "we will return to that place; but thou, O Holy One, must wait a little way off, because thy feet are heavier than mine and I am anxious to see more of that Red Bull."

"But how canst thou understand the talk? Walk slowly. The road is dark," the lama replied uneasily.

Kim put the question aside. "I marked a place near to the trees," said he, "where thou canst sit till I call. Nay," as the lama made some sort of protest, "remember this is *my* Search—the Search for my Red Bull. The sign in the Stars was not for thee. I know a little of the customs of white soldiers, and I always desire to see some new things."

"What dost thou not know of this world?" The lama squatted obediently in a little hollow of the ground not a hundred yards from the hump of the mango-trees dark against the star-powdered sky.

"Stay till I call." Kim flitted into the dusk. He knew that in all probability there would be sentries round the camp, and smiled to himself as he heard the thick boots of one. A boy who can dodge over the roofs of Lahore city on a moonlight night, using every little patch and corner of darkness to discomfit his pursuer, is not likely to be checked by a line of well-trained soldiers. He paid them the compliment of crawling between a couple, and, running and halting, crouching and dropping flat, worked his way towards the lighted mess-tent, where, close pressed behind the mango-tree, he waited till some chance word should give him a returnable lead.

The one thing now in his mind was further information as to the Red Bull. For aught he knew, and Kim's limitations were as curious and sudden as his expansions, the men, the nine hundred thorough devils of his father's prophecy, might pray to the beast after dark, as Hindus pray to the Holy Cow. That at least would be entirely right and logical, and the padre with the gold cross would be therefore the man to consult in the matter. On the other hand, remembering sober-faced padres whom he had avoided in Lahore city, the priest might be an inquisitive nuisance who would bid him learn. But had it not been proven at Umballa that his sign in the high heavens portended war and armed men? Was he not the Friend of the Stars as well as of all the world, crammed to the teeth with dreadful secrets? Lastly,—and firstly as the undercurrent of all his quick thoughts,—this adventure, though he did not know the English word, was a stupendous lark—a delightful continuation of his old flights across the housetops, as well as the fulfillment of sublime prophecy. He lay belly-flat and wriggled towards the mess-tent door, a hand on the amulet round his neck.

It was as he suspected. The Sahibs prayed to their God; for in the centre of the mess-table—its sole ornament when they were on the line of march—stood a golden bull fashioned from old-time loot of the Summer Palace at Pekin—a red-gold bull with lowered head, ramping upon a field of Irish green. To him the Sahibs held out their glasses and cried aloud confusedly.

Now the Reverend Arthur Bennett always left mess after that toast, and being rather tired by his march his movements were more abrupt than usual. Kim, with slightly raised head, was still staring at his totem on the table, when the chaplain stepped on his right shoulder-blade. Kim flinched under the leather, and, rolling sideways, brought down the chaplain, who, ever a man of action, caught him by the throat and nearly choked the life out of him. Kim then kicked him desperately in the stomach. Mr. Bennett gasped and doubled up but without relaxing his grip, rolled over again, and silently hauled Kim to his own tent. The Mavericks were incurable practical jokers; and it occurred to the Englishman that silence was best till he had made complete inquiry.

"Why, it's a boy!" he said, as he drew his prize under the light of the tent-pole lantern, then shaking him severely cried: "What were you doing? You're a thief. *Choor? Mallum?*" His Hindustanee was very limited, and the ruffled and disgusted Kim intended to keep to the character laid down for him. As he recovered his breath he was inventing a beautifully plausible tale of his relations to some mess-scullion, and at the same time keeping a keen eye on and a little under the chaplain's left arm-pit. The chance came; he ducked for the doorway, but a long arm shot out and clutched his neck, snapping the amulet string and closing on the amulet.

"Give it me. O give it me. Is it lost? Give me the papers."

The words were in English–the tinny, saw-cut English of the native-bred, and the chaplain jumped.

"A scapular," said he, opening his hand. "No, some sort of heathen charm. Why–why, do you speak English? Little boys who steal are beaten. You know that?"

"I do not–I did not steal." Kim danced in agony like a terrier at a lifted stick. "O give it me. It is my charm. Do not thieve it from me."

The chaplain took no heed, but, going to the tent door, called aloud. A fattish, clean-shaven man appeared.

"I want your advice, Father Victor," said Bennett. "I found this boy in the dark outside the mess-tent. Ordinarily, I should have chastised him and let him go, because I believe him to be a thief. But it seems he talks English, and he attaches some sort of value to a charm round his neck. I thought perhaps you might help me."

Between himself and the Roman Catholic chaplain of the Irish contingent lay, as Bennett believed, an unbridgeable gulf, but it was noticeable that whenever the Church of England dealt with a human problem she was very likely to call in the Church of Rome. Bennett's official abhorrence of the Scarlet Woman and all her ways was only equalled by his private respect for Father Victor.

"A thief talking English is it? Let's look at his charm. No, it is not a scapular, Bennett." He held out his hand.

"But have we any right to open it? A sound whipping–"

"I did *not* thieve," protested Kim. "You can hit me kicks all over my body. Now give me my charm and I will go away."

"Not quite so fast; we'll look first," said Father Victor, leisurely rolling out poor Kimball O'Hara's *ne varietur* parchment, his clearance-certificate, and Kim's baptismal certificate. On this last O'Hara–with some confused idea that he was doing wonders for his son–had scrawled scores of times: *"Look after the boy. Please look after the boy."*–signing his name and regimental number in full.

"Powers of Darkness below!" said Father Victor, passing all over to Mr. Bennett. "Do you know what these things are?"

"Yes," said Kim. "They are mine, and I want to go away."

"I do not quite understand," said Mr. Bennett. "He probably brought them on purpose. It may be a begging trick of some kind."

"I never saw a beggar less anxious to stay with his company, then. There's the makings of a gay mystery here. Ye believe in Providence, Bennett?"

"I hope so."

"Well, I believe in miracles, so it comes to the same thing. Powers of Darkness! Kimball O'Hara! And his son! But then he's a native, and I saw

Kimball married myself to Annie Shott. How long have you had these things, boy?"

"Ever since I was a little baby." Father Victor stepped forward quickly and opened the front of Kim's upper garment. "You see, Bennett, he's not very black. What's your name?"

"Kim."

"Or Kimball?"

"Perhaps. Will you let me go away?"

"What else?"

"They call me Kim Rishti ke. That is Kim of the Rishti."

"What is that–'Rishti'?"

"Eye-rishti–that was the regiment–my father's."

"Irish, oh I see."

"Yes. That was how my father told me. My father, he has lived."

"Has lived where?"

"Has lived. Of *course* he is dead–gone-out."

"Oh. That's your abrupt way of putting it, is it?"

Bennett interrupted. "It is possible I have done the boy an injustice. He is certainly white, though evidently neglected. I am sure I must have bruised him. I do not think spirits–"

"Get him a glass of sherry, then, and let him squat on the cot. Now, Kim" continued Father Victor, "no one is going to hurt you. Drink that down and tell us about yourself. The truth, if you've no objection."

Kim coughed a little as he put down the empty glass, and considered. This seemed a time for caution and fancy. Small boys who prowl about camps are generally turned out after a whipping. But he had received no stripes; the amulet was evidently working in his favour, and it looked as though the Umballa horoscope and the few words that he could remember of his father's maunderings fitted in most miraculously. Else why did the fat padre seem so impressed, and why the glass of hot yellow wine from the lean one?

"My father, he is dead in Lahore city since I was very little. The woman, she kept *kabarri* shop near where the hire-carriages are." Kim began with a plunge, not quite sure how far the truth would serve him.

"Your mother?"

"No"–with a gesture of disgust. "She went out when I was born. My father, he got these papers from the Jadoo-Gher–what do you call that?" (Bennett nodded) "because he was in–good-standing. What do you call that?" (again Bennett nodded). "My father told me that. He said too, and also the Brahmin who made the drawing in the dust at Umballa two days ago, *he* said, that I shall find a Red Bull on a green field and that the Bull shall help me."

"A phenomenal little liar," muttered Bennett.

"Powers of Darkness below, what a country!" murmured Father Victor. "Go on, Kim."

"I did *not* thieve. Besides, I am just now disciple of a very holy man. He is sitting outside. We saw two men come with flags, making the place ready. That is *always* so in a dream, or on account of a–a–prophecy. So I knew it was come true. I saw the Red Bull on the green field, and my father he said: 'Nine hundred *pukka* devils and the Colonel riding on a horse will look after you when you find the Red Bull!' I did not know what to do when I saw the Bull, but I went away and I came again when it was dark. I wanted to see the Bull again, and I saw the Bull again with the–the Sahibs praying to it. I think the Bull shall help me. The holy man said so too. He is sitting outside. Will you hurt him, if I call him a shout now? He is very holy. He can witness to all the things I say, and he knows I am not a thief."

" 'Officers praying to a bull!' What in the world do you make of that?"

said Bennett. " 'Disciple of a holy man!' Is the boy mad?"

"It's O'Hara's boy, sure enough. O'Hara's boy leagued with all the Powers of Darkness. It's very much what his father would have done—if he was drunk. We'd better invite the holy man. He may know something."

"He does not know anything," said Kim. "I will show you him if you come. He is my master. Then afterwards we can go."

"Power of Darkness!" was all that Father Victor could say, as Bennett marched off, with a firm hand on Kim's shoulder.

They found the lama where he had dropped.

"The Search is at an end for me," shouted Kim in the vernacular. "I have found the Bull, but God knows what comes next. They will not hurt you. Come to the fat priest's tent with this thin man and see the end. It is all new, and they cannot talk Hindi. They are only uncurried donkeys."

"Then it is not well to make a jest of their ignorance," the lama returned. "I am glad if thou art rejoiced, *chela.*"

Dignified and unsuspicious, he strode into the little tent, saluted the Churches as a Churchman, and sat down by the open charcoal brazier. The yellow lining of the tent reflected in the lamp-light made his face red-gold.

Bennett looked at him with the tripple-ringed uninterest of the creed that lumps nine-tenths of the world under the title of "heathen."

"And what was the end of the Search? What gift has the Red Bull brought?" The lama addressed himself to Kim.

"He says, 'What are you going to do?' " Bennett was staring uneasily at Father Victor, and Kim, for his own ends, took upon himself the office of interpreter.

"I do not see what concern this *faquir* has with the boy, who is probably his dupe or his confederate," Bennett began. "We cannot allow an English boy—Assuming that he is the son of a Mason, the sooner he goes to the Masonic Orphanage the better."

"Ah! That's your opinion as Secretary to the Regimental Lodge," said Father Victor; "but we might as well tell the old man what we are going to do. He doesn't look like a villain."

"My experience is that one can never fathom the Oriental mind. Now, Kimball, I will you to tell this man what I say—word for word."

Kim gathered the import of the next few sentences and began thus:

"Holy One, the thin fool who looks like a camel says that I am the son of a Sahib."

"But how?"

"Oh, it is true. I knew it since my birth, but *he* could only find it out by reading the amulet from my neck and reading all the papers. He thinks that once a Sahib is always a Sahib, and between the two of them they purpose to keep me in this regiment or to send me to a *madrissah* (a school). It has happened before. I have always avoided it. The fat fool is of one mind and the camel-like one of another. But that is no odds. I may spend one night here and perhaps the next. It has happened before. Then I will run away and return to thee."

"But tell them that thou art my *chela.* Tell them how thou didst come to me when I was faint and bewildered. Tell them of our Search, and they will surely let thee go now."

"I have already told them. They laugh, and they talk of the police."

"What are you saying?" asked Mr. Bennett.

"Oah. He only says that if you do not let me go it will stop him in his business—his ur-gent private af-fairs." This last was a reminiscence of some talk with a Eurasian clerk in the Canal Department, but it only drew a smile, which nettled him. "And if you *did* know what his business was you would not be in such a beastly hurry to interfere."

"What is it then?" said Father Victor, not without feeling, as he watched the lama's face.

"There is a River in this country which he wishes to find so verree much. It was put out by an Arrow which–" Kim tapped his foot impatiently as he translated in his own mind from the vernacular to his clumsy English. "Oah, it was made by our Lord God Buddha you know, and if you wash there you are washed away from all your sins and made as white as cotton-wool." (Kim had heard mission-talk in his time.) "I am his disciple, and we *must* find that River. It is so veree valuable to us."

"Say that again," said Bennett. Kim obeyed, with amplifications.

"But this is gross blasphemy," cried the Church of England.

"Tck! Tck!" said Father Victor sympathetically. "I'd give a good deal to be able to talk the vernacular. A river that washes away sin! And how long have you two been looking for it?"

"Oh, many days. Now we wish to go away and look for it again. It is not here, you see."

"I see," said Father Victor gravely. "But he can't go on in that old man's company. It would be different, Kim, if you were not a soldier's son. Tell him that the regiment will take care of you and make you as good a man as your–as good a man as can be. Tell him that if he believes in miracles he must believe that–"

"There is no need to play on his credulity," Bennett interrupted.

"I'm doing no such thing. He must believe that the boy's coming here–to his own regiment–in search of his Red Bull is in the nature of a miracle. Consider the chances against it, Bennett. This one boy in all India, and our regiment of all others on the line o' march for him to meet with! It's predestined on the face of it. Yes, tell him it's *Kismet. Kismet, mallum?* (Do you understand?)"

He turned towards the lama, to whom he might as well have talked of Mesopotamia.

"They say,"–the old man's eye lighted at Kim's speech,–"They say that the meaning of my horoscope is now accomplished, and that being led back–though as thou knowest I went out of curiosity–to these people and their Red Bull I must needs go to a *madrissah* and be turned into a Sahib. Now I make pretence of agreement, for at the worst it will be but a few meals eaten away from thee. Then I will slip away and follow down the road to Saharunpore. Therefore, Holy One, keep with that Kulu woman–on no account stray far from her car till I come again. Past question, my sign is of War and of armed men. See how they have given me wine to drink and set me upon a bed of honor! My father must have been some great person. So if they raise me to honor among them, good. If not, good again. However it goes, I will run back to thee when I am tired. But stay with the Rajputni, or I shall miss thy feet. . . . Oah yess," said the boy, "I have told him everything you tell me to say."

"And I cannot see any need why he should wait," said Bennett, feeling in his trouser-pocket. "We can investigate the details later–and I will give him a ru–"

"Give him time. Maybe he's fond of the lad," said Father Victor, half-arresting the clergyman's motion.

The lama dragged forth his rosary and pulled his huge hat-brim over his eyes.

"What can he want now?"

"He says"–Kim put up one hand. "He says: Be quiett. He wants to speak to me by himself. You see you do not know one little word of what he says, and I think if you talk he will perhaps give you very bad curses. When he takes those beads like that, you see he always wants to be quiett."

The two Englishmen sat overwhelmed, but there was a look in Bennett's eye that promised ill for Kim when he should be relaxed to the religious arm.

"A Sahib and the son of a Sahib–" The lama's voice was harsh with pain. "But no white man knows the land and the customs of the land as thou knowest. How comes it this is true?"

"What matter, Holy One: but remember it is only for a night or two. Remember, I can change swiftly. It will all be as it was when I first spoke to thee under Zam-Zammah the great gun–"

"As a boy in the dress of white men–when I first went to the Wonder House. And a second time thou wast a Hindu. What shall the third incarnation be?" He chuckled drearily. "Ah, *chela*, thou hast done a wrong to an old man because my heart went out to thee."

"And mine to thee. But how could I know that the Red Bull would bring me to this business?"

The lama covered his face afresh, and nervously rattled the rosary. Kim squatted beside him and laid hold upon a fold of his clothing.

"Now it is understood that the boy is a Sahib?" he went on in a muffled tone. "Such a Sahib as was he who kept the images in the Wonder House." The lama's experience of white men was limited. He seemed to be repeating a lesson. "So then it is not seemly that he should do other than as the Sahibs do. He must go back to his own people."

"For a day and a night and a day," Kim pleaded.

"No, ye don't!" Father Victor saw Kim edging towards the door, and interposed a strong leg.

"I do not understand the customs of white men. The Priest of the Images in the Wonder House in Lahore was more courteous than the thin one here. This boy will be taken from me. They will make a Sahib of my disciple? Woe to me, how shall I find my River? Have *they* no disciples? Ask."

"He says he is very sorry that he cannot find the River now any more. He says, Why have you no disciples, and stop bothering him. He wants to be washed of his sins."

Neither Bennett nor Father Victor found any answer ready.

Said Kim in English, distressed for the lama's agony: "I think if you will let me go now we will walk away quietly and not steal. We will look for that River like before I was caught. I wish I did not come here to find the Red Bull and all that sort of thing. I do not want it."

"It's the very best day's work you ever did for yourself, young man," said Bennett.

"Good heavens, I don't know how to console him," said Father Victor, watching the lama intently. "He can't take the boy away with him, and yet he's a good man–I'm sure he's a good man. Bennett, if you give him that rupee he'll curse you root and branch!"

They listened to each other's breathing–three–five full minutes. Then the lama raised his head, and looked forth across them into space and emptiness.

"And I am a follower of the Way," he said bitterly. "The sin is mine and the punishment is mine. I made believe to myself–for now I see it was but make-belief–that thou wast sent to me to aid in the Search. So my heart went out to thee for thy charity and thy courtesy and the wisdom of thy little years. But those who follow the Way must permit not the fire of any desire or attachment, for that is all illusion. As says . . ." He quoted an old, old Chinese text, backed it with another, and reinforced these with a third. "I stepped aside from the Way, my *chela*. It was no fault of thine. I delighted in the sight of life, the new people upon the roads, and in thy joy at seeing these things. I was pleased with thee who should have considered my Search and my Search alone. Now I am sorrowful because thou art taken away and my

River is far from me. It is the Law which I have broken!"

"Powers of Darkness below!" said Father Victor, who, wise in the confessional, heard the pain in every sentence.

"I see now that the sign of the Red Bull was a sign for me as well as for thee. All Desire is red—and evil. I will do penance and find my River alone."

"At least go back to the Kulu woman," said Kim, "otherwise thou wilt be lost upon the roads. She will feed thee till I run back to thee."

The lama waved a hand to show that the matter was finally settled in his mind.

"Now,"—his tone altered as he turned to Kim,—"what will they do with thee? At least I may, acquiring merit, wipe out past ill."

"Make me a Sahib—so they think. The day after tomorrow I return. Do not grieve."

"Of what sort? Such an one as this or that man?" He pointed to Father Victor. "Such an one as those I saw this evening—men wearing swords and stamping heavily?"

"Maybe."

"That is not well. These men follow desire and come to emptiness. Thou must not be of their sort."

"The Umballa priest said that my Star was War," Kim interjected. "I will ask these fools—but there is truly no need. I will run away this night, for all I wanted to see the new things."

Kim put two or three questions in English to Father Victor, translating the replies to the lama.

Then: "He says, 'You take him from me and you cannot say what you will make him.' He says, 'Tell me before I go, for it is not a small thing to make a child.' "

"You will be sent to a school. Later on, we shall see. Kimball, I suppose you'd like to be a soldier?"

"*Gorah-log* (white-folk). No-ah! No-ah!" Kim shook his head violently. There was nothing in his composition to which drill and routine appealed. "I will not be a soldier."

"You will be what you're told to be," said Bennett; "and you should be grateful that we're going to help you."

Kim smiled compassionately. If these men lay under the delusion that he would do anything that he did not fancy, so much the better.

Another long silence followed. Bennett fidgeted with impatience, and suggested calling a sentry to evict the *faquir*.

"Do they give or sell learning among the Sahibs? Ask them," said the lama, and Kim interpreted.

"They say that money is paid to the teacher—but that money the regiment will give. . . . What need? It is only for a night."

"And—the more money is paid the better learning is given?" The lama disregarded Kim's plans for an early fight. "It is no wrong to pay for learning; to help the ignorant to wisdom is always a merit." The rosary clicked furiously as an abacus. Then he faced his oppressors.

"Ask them for how much money do they give a wise and suitable teaching? and in what city is that teaching given?"

"Well," said Father Victor in English, when Kim had translated, "that depends. The regiment would pay for you all the time you are at the Military Orphanage; or you might go on the Punjab Masonic Orphanage's list (not that he or you 'ud understand what that means); but the best schooling a boy can get in India is, of course, at St. Xavier's in Partibus at Lucknow." This took some time to interpret, for Bennett wished to cut it short.

"He wants to know how much?" said Kim placidly.

"Two or three hundred rupees a year." Father Victor was long past any sense of amazement. Bennett, impatient, did not understand.

"He says: 'Write that name and the money upon a paper and give it him.' And he says you must write your name below, because he is going to write a letter in some days to you. He says you are a good man. He says the other man is a fool. He is going away."

The lama rose suddenly. "I follow my Search," he cried, and was gone.

"He'll run slap into the sentries," cried Father Victor, jumping up as the lama stalked out; "but I can't leave the boy." Kim made swift motion to follow, but checked himself. There was no sound of challenge outside. The lama had disappeared.

Kim settled himself composedly on the chaplain's cot. At least the lama had promised that he would stay with the Rajput woman from Kulu, and the rest was of the smallest importance. It pleased him that the two padres were so evidently excited. They talked long in undertones, Father Victor urging some scheme on Mr. Bennett, who seemed incredulous. All this was very new and fascinating, but Kim felt sleepy. They called men into the tent—one of them certainly was the Colonel, as his father had prophesied—and they asked him an infinity of questions, chiefly about the woman who looked after him, all of which Kim answered truthfully. They did not seem to think the woman a good guardian.

After all, this was the newest of his experiences. Sooner or later, if he chose, he could escape into great, gray, formless India, beyond tents and padres and colonels. Meantime, if the Sahibs were to be impressed, he would do his best to impress them. He too was a white man.

After much talk that he could not comprehend, they handed him over to a sergeant, who had strict instructions not to let him escape. The regiment would go on to Umballa, and Kim would be sent up, partly at the expense of the Lodge and in part by subscription, to a place called Sanawar.

"It's miraculous past all whooping, Colonel," said Father Victor, when he had talked without a break for ten minutes. "His Buddhist friend has levanted after taking my name and address. I can't quite make out whether he'll pay for the boy's education or whether he is preparing some sort of witchcraft on his own account." Then to Kim: "You'll live to be grateful to your friend the Red Bull yet. We'll make a man of you at Sanawar—even at the price o' making you a Protestant."

"Certainly—most certainly," said Bennett.

"But you will not go to Sanawar," said Kim.

"But we will go to Sanawar, little man. That's the order of the Commander-in-Chief, who's a trifle more important than O'Hara's son."

"You will not go to Sanawar. You will go to thee war."

There was a shout of laughter from the full tent.

"When you know your own regiment a trifle better you won't confuse the line of march with line of battle, Kim. We hope to go to 'thee war' sometime."

"Oah, I know all thatt." Kim drew his bow again at a venture. If they were not going to the war, at least they did not know what he knew of the talk in the verandah at Umballa.

"I know you are not at thee war now; but I tell *you* that as soon as you get to Umballa you will be sent to the war—the new war. It is a war of eight thousand men, besides the guns."

"That's explicit. D'you add prophecy to your other gifts? Take him along, Sergeant. Take up a suit for him from the Drums, an' take care he doesn't slip through your fingers. Who says the age of miracles is gone by? I think I'll go to bed. My poor mind's weakening."

At the far end of the camp, silent as a wild animal, an hour later sat Kim, newly washed all over, in a horrible stuff suit that rasped his arms and legs.

"A most amazin' young bird," said the sergeant. "He turns up in charge of a yellow-headed buck-Brahmin priest, with his father's lodge-certificates round his neck, talkin' God knows what all of a red bull. The buck-Brahmin evaporates without explanations, an' the bhoy sets cross-legged on the chaplain's bed prophesyin' bloody war to the men at large. Injia's a wild land for a God-fearin' man. I'll just tie his leg to the tent-pole in case he'll go through the roof. What did ye say about the war?"

"Eight thousand men, besides guns," said Kim. "Very soon you will see."

"You're a consolin' little imp. Lie down between the Drums an' go to bye-bye. Those two bhoys beside ye will watch your slumbers."

Chapter Six

Now I remember comrades–
    Old playmates on new seas–
Whenas we traded orpiment
    Among the savages.
Ten thousand leagues to southward,
    And thirty years removed–
They knew not noble Valdez,
    But me they knew and loved.
        Song of Diego Valdez.

Very early in the morning the white tents came down and disappeared as the Mavericks took a side-road to Umballa. It did not skirt the resting-place, and Kim, trudging beside a baggage-cart under fire of comments from soldiers' wives, was not so confident as overnight. He discovered that he was closely watched–Father Victor on the one side, and Mr. Bennett on the other.

In the forenoon the column checked. A camel-orderly handed the Colonel a letter. He read it, and spoke to a Major. Half a mile in the rear, Kim heard a hoarse and joyful clamour rolling down on him through the thick dust. Then some one beat him on the back, crying: "Tell us how ye knew, ye little limb of Satan? Father dear, see if ye can make him tell."

A pony ranged alongside, and he was hauled on to the priest's saddle-bow. "Now, my son, your prophecy of last night has come true. Our orders are to entrain at Umballa for the front to-morrow."

"What is that?" said Kim, for *front* and *entrain* were newish words to him.

"We are going to 'thee war,' as you called it."

"Of course you are going to thee war. I said last night."

"Ye did; but, Powers o' Darkness, how did ye know?"

Kim's eyes sparkled. He shut his lips, nodded his head, and looked unspeakable things. The chaplain moved on through the dust, and privates, sergeants, and subalterns called one another's attention to the boy. The Colonel, at the head of the column, stared at him curiously. "It was probably some bazar-rumor," he said; "but even then–" He referred to the paper in his hand. "Hang it all, the thing was only decided within the last forty-eight hours."

"Are there many more like you in India?" said Father Victor, "or are you by way o' being a *lusus naturoe?*"

"Now I have told you," said the boy, "will you let me go back to my old man? If he has not stayed with that woman from Kulu, I am afraid he will die."

"By what I saw of him he's as well able to take care of himself as you. No. Ye've brought us luck, an' we're goin' to make a man of you. I'll take ye back to your baggage-cart and ye'll come to me this evening."

For the rest of the day Kim found himself an object of distinguished consideration among a few hundred white men. The story of his appearance in camp, the discovery of his parentage, and his prophecy, had lost nothing in the telling. A big, shapeless white woman on a pile of bedding asked him mysteriously whether he thought her husband would come back from the war. Kim reflected gravely, and said that he would, and the woman gave him food. In many respects, this big procession that played music at intervals–this crowd that talked and laughed so easily–resembled a festival in Lahore city. So far, there was no sign of hard work, and he resolved to lend the spectacle his patronage. At evening there came out to meet them bands of music, and played the Mavericks into camp near Umballa railway station. That was an interesting night. Men of other regiments came to visit the Mavericks. The Mavericks went visiting on their own account. Their pickets hurried forth to bring them back, met pickets of strange regiments on the same duty; and, after a while, the bugles blew madly for more pickets with officers to control the tumult. The Mavericks had a reputation for liveliness to live up to. But they fell in on the platform next morning in perfect shape and condition; and Kim, left behind with the sick, women, and boys, found himself shouting farewells excitedly as the trains drew away. Life as a Sahib was amusing so far; but he touched it with a very cautious hand. Then they marched him back in charge of a drummer-boy to empty, lime-washed barracks, whose floors were covered with rubbish and string and paper, and whose ceilings gave back his lonely footfall. Native fashion, he curled himself up on a stripped cot and went to sleep. An angry man stumped down the verandah, woke him up, and said he was a schoolmaster. This was enough for Kim, and he retired into his shell. He could just puzzle out the various English Police notices in Lahore city, because they affected his comfort; and among the many guests of the woman who looked after him had been a queer German who painted scenery for the Parsee travelling theatre. He told Kim that he had been "on the barricades in Forty-eight," and therefore–at least that was how it struck Kim–he would teach the boy to write in return for food. Kim had been kicked as far as single letters, but did not think well of them.

"I do not know anything. Go away!" said Kim, scenting evil. Hereupon the man caught him by the ear, dragged him to a room in a far-off wing where a dozen drummer-boys were sitting on forms, and told him to be still if he could do nothing else. This he managed very successfully. The man explained something or other with white lines on a blackboard for at least half an hour, and Kim continued his interrupted nap. He much disapproved of the present aspect of affairs, for this was the very school and discipline he had spent two-thirds of his young life in avoiding. Suddenly a beautiful idea occurred to him, and he wondered that he had not thought of it before.

The man dismissed them, and first to spring through the verandah into the open sunshine was Kim.

" 'Ere you! 'Alt! Stop!" said a high voice at his heels. "I've got to look after you. My orders are not to let you out of my sight. Where are you goin'?"

It was the drummer-boy who had been hanging round him all the forenoon–a fat and freckled person of about fourteen, and Kim loathed him from the soles of his boots to his cap-ribbons.

"To the bazar–to get sweets–for you," said Kim, after thought.

"Well, the bazar's out o' bounds. If we go there we'll get a dressing-down. You come back."

"How near can we go?" Kim did not know what bounds meant, but he wished to be polite–for the present.

" 'Ow near? 'Ow far, you mean? We can go as far as that tree down the road."

"Then I will go there."

"All right. I ain't goin'. It's too 'ot. I can watch you from 'ere. It's no good your runnin' away. If you did, they'd spot you by your clothes. That's regimental stuff you're wearin'. There ain't a picket in Umballa wouldn't 'ead you back quicker than you started out."

This did not impress Kim as much as the knowledge that his raiment would tire him out if he tried to run. He slouched to the tree at the corner of a bare road leading towards the bazar, and eyed the natives passing. Most of them were barrack-servants of the lowest caste. Kim hailed a sweeper, who promptly retorted with a piece of unnecessary insolence, in the natural belief that the European boy could not follow. The low, quick answer undeceived him. Kim put his fettered soul into it, thankful for the late chance to abuse somebody in the tongue he knew best. "And now, go to the nearest letter-writer in the bazar and tell him to come here. I would write a letter."

"But–but what manner of white man's son art thou, to need a bazar letter-writer? Is there not a schoolmaster in the barracks?"

"Ay; and Hell is full of the same sort. Do my order, you–you Od! Thy mother was married under a basket! Servant of Lal Beg" (Kim knew the god of the sweepers), "run on my business or we will talk again."

The sweeper shuffled off in haste. "There is a white boy by the barracks waiting under a tree who is not a white boy," he stammered to the first bazar letter-writer he came across. "He needs thee."

"Will he pay?" said that spruce scribe, gathering up his desk and pens and sealing-wax all in order.

"I do not know. He is not like other boys. Go and see. It is well worth."

Kim danced with impatience when the slim young Kayeth hove in sight. As soon as his voice could carry he cursed him volubly.

"First I will take my pay," the letter-writer said. "Bad words have made the price higher. But who art thou, dressed in that fashion, to speak in this fashion?"

"Aha! That is in the letter which thou shalt write. Never was such a tale. But I am in no haste. Another write will serve me. Umballa city is as full of them as in Lahore."

"Four annas," said the writer, sitting down and spreading his cloth in the shade of a deserted barrack-wing.

Mechanically Kim squatted beside him,–squatted as only the natives can,–in spite of the abominable clinging trousers. The writer regarded him sideways.

"That is the price to ask of Sahibs," said Kim. "Now fix me a true one."

"An anna and a half. How do I know, having written the letter, that thou wilt not run away?"

"I must not go beyond this tree, and there is also the stamp to be considered."

"I get no commission on the price of the stamp. Once more, what manner of white boy art thou?"

"That shall be said in the letter, which is to Mahbub Ali, the horse-dealer in the Kashmir Serai, at Lahore. He is my friend."

"Wonder on wonder!" murmured the letter-writer, dipping a reed in the inkstand. "To be written in Hindi?"

"Assuredly. To Mahbub Ali then. Begin! *I have come down with the old man as far as Umballa in the train. At Umballa I carried the news of the bay mare's pedigree.*" After what he had seen in the garden, he was not going to write of white stallions.

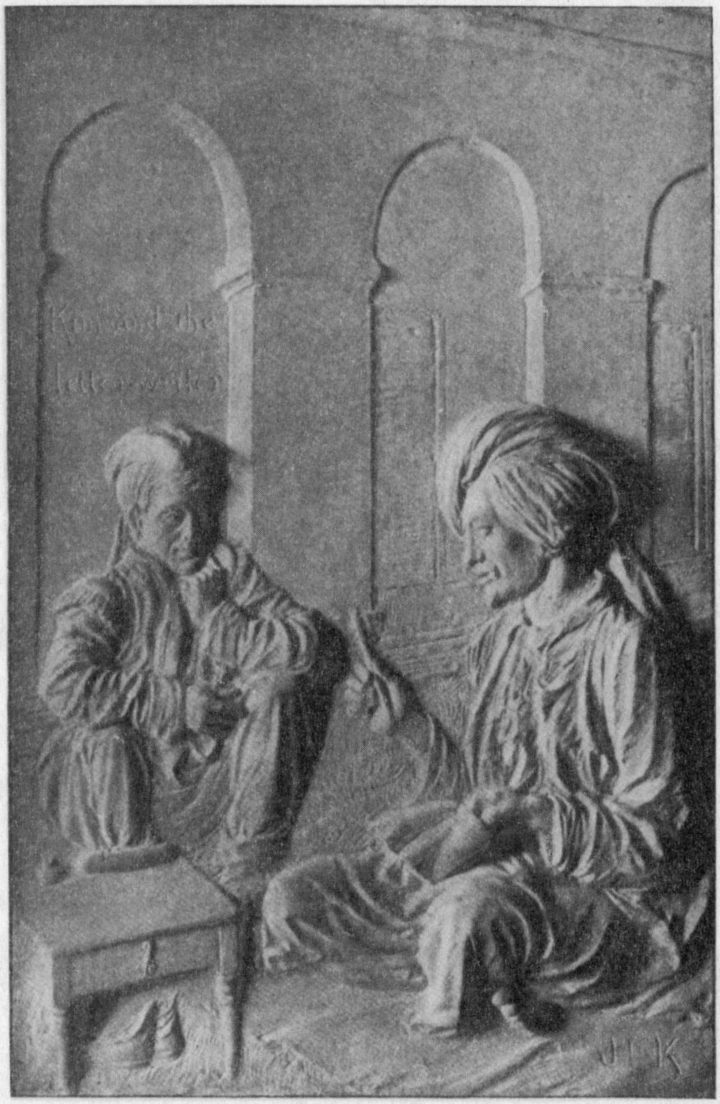

"FIRST I WILL TAKE MY PAY," THE LETTER-WRITER SAID.

"Slower a little. What has a bay mare to do? . . . Is it Mahbub Ali the great dealer?"

"Who else? I have been in his service. Take more ink. Again. *As the order was, so I did it. We then went on foot towards Benares, but on the third day we found a certain regiment.* Is that down?"

"Ay, *pulton,*" murmured the writer, all ears.

"*I went into their camp and was caught, and by means of the charm about my neck, which thou knowest, it was established that I was the son of some man in the regiment: according to the prophecy of the Red Bull, which thou knowest was common talk of our bazar.*" Kim waited for this shaft to sink into the letter-writer's heart, cleared his throat, and continued: "*A priest clothed me and gave me a new name. . . . One priest, however, was a fool. The clothes are very heavy, but I am a Sahib and my heart is heavy too. They send me to a school and beat me. I do not like the air and water here. Come then and help me, Mahbub Ali, or send me some money, for I have not sufficient to pay the writer who writes this.*"

" 'Who writes this.' It is my own fault that I was tricked. Thou art as clever as Husain Bux that forged the Treasury stamps at Nucklao. But what a tale! What a tale! Is it true by any chance?"

"It does not profit to tell lies to Mahbub Ali. It is better to help his friends by lending them a stamp. When the money comes I will repay."

The writer grunted doubtfully, but took a stamp out of his desk, sealed the letter, handed it over to Kim, and departed. Mahbub Ali's was a name of power in Umballa.

"That is the way to win a good account with the Gods," Kim shouted after him.

"Pay me twice over when the money comes," the man cried over his shoulder.

"What was you bukkin' to that nigger about?" said the drummer-boy when Kim returned to the verandah. "I was watchin' you."

"I was only talkin' to him."

"You talk the same as a nigger, don't you?"

"No-ah! No-ah! I onlee speak a little. What shall we do now?"

"The bugles 'ill go for dinner in 'arf a minute. My Gawd! I wish I'd gone up to the front with the regiment. It's awful doin' nothin' but school down 'ere. Don't you 'ate it?"

"Oah yess!"

"I'd run away if I knew where to go to, but, as the men say, in this bloomin' Injia you're only a prisoner at large. You can't desert without bein' took back at once. I'm fair sick of it."

"You have been in Be–England?"

"W'y, I only come out last troopin' season with my mother. I should think I 'ave been in England. What a ignorant little beggar you are. You was brought up in the gutter, wasn't you?"

"Oah yess. Tell me something about England. My father he came from there."

Though he would not say so, Kim of course disbelieved every word the drummer-boy spoke about the Liverpool suburb which was his England. It passed the heavy time till dinner–a most unappetising meal served to the boys and a few invalids in a corner of a barrack-room. But that he had written to Mahbub Ali, Kim would have been almost depressed. The indifference of native crowds he was used to; but this strong loneliness among white men preyed on him. He was grateful when, in the course of the afternoon, a big soldier took him over to Father Victor, who lived in another wing across another dusty parade-ground. The priest was reading an English letter written in purple ink. He looked at Kim more curiously than ever.

"An' how do you like it, my son, as far as you've gone? Not much, eh? It must be hard—very hard on a wild animal. Listen now. I've an amazin' epistle from your friend."

"Where is he? Is he well? Oah! If he knows to write me letters, it is all right."

"You're fond of him then?"

"*Of* course I am fond of him. He was fond of me."

"It seems so by the look of this. He can't write English, can he?"

"Oah no. Not that I know, but *of* course he found a letter-writer who can write English verree well, and so he wrote. I do hope you understand."

"That accounts for it. D'you know anything about his money affairs?" Kim's face showed that he did not.

"How can I tell?"

"That's what I'm askin'. Now listen if you can make head or tail o' this. We'll skip the first part. . . . It's written from Jagadhir road. . . . *'Sitting on wayside in grave meditation, trusting to be favored with your Honor's applause of present step, which recommend your Honor to execute for Almighty God's sake. Education is greatest blessing if of best sorts. Otherwise no earthly use.'* Faith, the old man's hit the bull's-eye that time! *'If your Honor condescending giving my boy best educations Xavier'* (I suppose that's St. Xavier in Partibus) *'in terms of our conversation dated in your tent 15th instant'* (a business-like touch there!) *'then Almighty God blessing your Honor's succeedings to third an' fourth generation and'*—now listen!—*'confide in your Honor's humble servant for adequate remuneration per hoondie per annum three hundred rupees a year to one expensive education St. Xavier, Lucknow, and allow small time to forward same per hoondie sent to any part of India as your Honor shall address yourself. This servant of your Honor has presently no place to lay crown of his head, but going to Benares by train on account of persecution of old woman talking so much and unanxious residing Saharunpore in any domestic capacity.'* Now what in the world does that mean?"

"She has asked him to be *puro*—her clergyman—at Saharunpore, *I* think. He would not do that on account of his River. She *did* talk."

"It's clear to you, is it? It beats me altogether. *'So going to Benares, where will find address and forward rupees for boy who is apple of eye, and for Almighty God's sake execute this education, and your petitioner as in duty bound shall ever awfully pray. Written by Sobrao Satai, Failed Entrance Allahabad University, for Venerable Teshoo Lama the priest of Such-zen looking for a River, address care of Tirthankers' Temple, Benares. P. M.—Please note boy is apple of eye, and rupees shall be sent per hoondie three hundred per annum. For God Almighty's sake.'* Now, is that ravin' lunacy or a business proposition? I ask you, because I'm fairly at my wits' end."

"He says he will give me three hundred rupees a year, so he will give me them."

"Oh, that's the way you look at it, is it?"

"*Of* course. If he says so!"

The priest whistled; then he addressed Kim as an equal.

"I don't believe it; but we'll see. You were goin' off to-day to the Military Orphanage at Sanawar, where the regiment would keep you till you were old enough to enlist. Ye'd be brought up to the Church of England. Bennett arranged for that. On the other hand, if ye go to St. Xavier's ye'll get a better education an'—an' can have the religion. D'ye see my dilemma?"

Kim saw nothing save a vision of the lama going south in a train with none to beg for him.

"Like most people, I'm going to temporise. If your friend sends the money from Benares—Powers of Darkness below, where's a street-beggar to raise three hundred rupees?—ye'll go down to Lucknow and I'll pay your fare, because I can't touch the subscription-money if I intend, as I do, to make ye a Catholic. If he doesn't, ye'll go to the Military Orphanage at the regiment's expense. I'll allow him three days' grace, though I don't believe it at all. Even then, if he fails in his payments later on . . . but it's beyond me. We can only walk one step at a time in this world, praise God. An' they sent Bennett to the front an' left me behind. He can't expect everything."

"Oah yess," said Kim vaguely.

The priest leaned forward. "I'd give a month's pay to find what's goin' on inside that little round head of yours."

"There is nothing," said Kim, and scratched it. He was wondering whether Mahbub Ali would send him as much as a whole rupee. Then he could pay the letter-writer and write letters to the lama at Benares. Perhaps Mahbub Ali would visit him next time he came south with horses. Surely he must know that Kim's delivery of the letter to the officer at Umballa had caused the great war which the men and boys had discussed so loudly over the barrack dinner-tables. But if Mahbub Ali did not know this, it would be very unsafe to tell him so. Mahbub Ali was hard upon boys who knew, or thought they knew, too much.

"Well, till I get further news"–Father Victor's voice interrupted the reverie–"ye can run along and play with the other boys. They'll teach ye something–but I don't think ye'll like it."

The day dragged to its weary end. When he wished to sleep he was instructed how to fold up his clothes and set out his boots; the other boys deriding. Bugles waked him in the dawn; the schoolmaster caught him after breakfast, thrust a page of meaningless characters under his nose, gave them senseless names, and whacked him without reason. Kim meditated poisoning him with opium borrowed from a barrack-sweeper, but reflected that, as they all ate at one table in public (this was peculiarly revolting to Kim, who preferred to turn his back on the world at meals), the stroke might be dangerous. Then he attempted running off to the village where the priest had tried to drug the lama–the village where the old soldier lived. But far-seeing sentries at every exit headed back the little scarlet figure. Trousers and jacket crippled body and mind alike, so he abandoned the project and fell back, Oriental fashion, on time and chance. Three days of torment passed in the big, echoing white rooms. He walked out of afternoons under escort of the drummer-boy, and all he heard from his companion were the few useless words which seemed to make two-thirds of the white man's abuse. Kim knew and despised them all long ago. The boy resented his silence and lack of interest by beating him, as was only natural. He did not care for any of the bazars which were in bounds. He styled all natives "niggers"; yet servants and sweepers called him abominable names to his face, and, misled by their deferential attitude, he never understood. This somewhat consoled Kim for the beatings.

On the morning of the fourth day a judgment overtook that drummer. They had gone out together towards Umballa race-course. He returned alone, weeping, with news that young O'Hara, to whom he had been doing nothing in particular, had hailed a scarlet-bearded nigger on horseback; that the nigger had then and there laid into him with a peculiarly adhesive quirt, picked up young O'Hara, and borne him off at full gallop. These tidings came to Father Victor, and he drew down his long upper lip. He was already sufficiently startled by a letter from the Temple of the Tirthankers at Benares, enclosing a native banker's note of hand for three hundred rupees, and an amazing prayer to "Almighty God." The lama would have been more annoyed than the priest had he known how the bazar letter-writter had translated his phrase "to acquire merit."

"Powers of Darkness below!" Father Victor fumbled with the note. "An' now he's off with another of his peep-o'-day friends. I don't know whether it will be a greater relief to me to get him back or to have him lost. He's beyond my comprehension. How the Divil—yes, he's the man I mean—can a street-beggar raise money to educate white boys?"

Three miles off, on Umballa race-course, Mahbub Ali, reining a gray Cabuli stallion with Kim in front of him, was saying:

"But, Little Friend of all the World, there is *my* honor and reputation to be considered. All the officer-sahibs in all the regiments, and all Umballa, know Mahbub Ali. Men saw me pick thee up and chastise that boy. We are seen now from far across this plain. How can I take thee away, or account for thy disappearing if I set thee down and let thee run off into the crops? They would put me in jail. Be patient. Once a Sahib, always a Sahib. When thou art a man—who knows—thou wilt be grateful to Mahbub Ali."

"Take me beyond their sentries where I can change this red. Give me money and I will go to Benares and be with my lama again. I do not want to be a Sahib, and remember I did deliver that message."

The stallion bounded wildly. Mahbub Ali had incautiously driven home the sharp-edged stirrup. (He was not the new sort of fluent horse-dealer who wears English boots and spurs.) Kim drew his own conclusions from that betrayal.

"That was a small matter. It lay on the straight road to Benares. I and the Sahib have by this time forgotten it. I send so many letters and messages to men who ask questions about horses, I cannot well remember one from the other. Was it some matter of a bay mare that Peters Sahib wished the pedigree of?"

Kim saw the trap at once. If he had said "bay mare" Mahbub would have known by his very readiness to fall in with the amendment that the boy suspected something. Kim replied therefore: "Bay mare. No. *I* do not forget my messages thus. It was a white stallion."

"Ay, so it was. A white Arab stallion. But thou didst write bay mare to me."

"Who cares to tell truth to a letter-writer?" Kim answered, feeling Mahbub's palm on his heart.

"Hi! Mahbub, you old villain, pull up!" cried a voice, and an Englishman raced alongside on a little polo-pony. "I've been chasing you half over the country. That Cabuli of yours can go. For sale, I suppose?"

"I have some young stuff coming on made by Heaven for the delicate and difficult polo-game. He has no equal. He—"

"Plays polo and waits at table. Yes. We know all that. What the deuce have you got there?"

"A boy," said Mahbub gravely. "He was being beaten by another boy. His father was once a white soldier in the big war. The boy was a child in Lahore city. He played with my horses when he was a babe. Now I think they will make him a soldier. He has been newly caught by his father's regiment that went up to the war last week. But I do not think he wants to be a soldier. I take him for a ride. Tell me where thy barracks are and I will set thee there."

"Let me go. I can find the barracks alone."

"And if thou runnest away who will say it is not my fault?"

"He'll run back to his dinner. Where has he to run to?" the Englishman asked.

"He was born in the land. He has friends. He goes where he chooses. He is a *chabuk sawai* (a sharp chap). It needs only to change his clothing, and in a twinkling he would be a low-caste Hindi boy."

"The deuce he would!" The Englishman looked critically at the boy as Mahbub headed towards the barracks. Kim ground his teeth. Mahbub was mocking him, as faithless Afghans will; for he went on:

"They will send him to a school and put heavy boots on his feet and swaddle him in these clothes. Then he will forget all he knows. Now which of the barracks is thine?"

Kim pointed—he could not speak—to Father Victor's wing, all staring white near by.

"Perhaps he will make a good soldier," said Mahbub reflectively. "He will make a good orderly at least. I sent him to deliver a message once from Lahore. A message concerning the pedigree of a white stallion."

Here was deadly insult on deadlier injury—and the Sahib to whom he had so craftily given that war-waking letter heard it all. Kim beheld Mahbub Ali frying in flame for his treachery, but for himself he saw one long gray vista of barracks, schools, and barracks again. He gazed imploringly at the clear-cut face in which there was no glimmer of recognition; but even at this extremity it never occurred to him to throw himself on the white man's mercy or to denounce the Afghan. And Mahbub stared deliberately at the Englishman, who stared as deliberately at Kim, quivering and tongue-tied.

"My horse is well trained," said the dealer. "Others would have kicked, Sahib."

"Ah," said the Englishman at last, rubbing his pony's damp withers with his whip-butt. "Who makes the boy a soldier?"

"He says the regiment that found him, and especially the padre-sahib of that regiment."

"There is the padre!" Kim choked as bareheaded Father Victor sailed down upon them from the verandah.

"Powers o' Darkness below, O'Hara! How many more mixed friends do you keep in Asia?" he cried, as Kim slid down and stood helplessly before him.

"Good morning, Padre," the Colonel said cheerily. "I know you by reputation well enough. Meant to have come over and called before this. I'm Creighton."

"Of the Ethnological Survey?" said Father Victor. The Colonel nodded. "Faith I'm glad to meet ye then; an' I owe you some thanks for bringing back the boy."

"No thanks to me, Padre. Besides, the boy wasn't going away. You don't know old Mahbub Ali"—the horse-dealer sat impassive in the sunlight. "You will when you have been in the station a month. He sells us all our crocks. That boy is rather a curiosity. Can you tell me anything about him?"

"Can I tell you?" puffed Father Victor. "You'll be the one man that could help me in my quandaries. Tell you! Powers o' Darkness, I'm bursting to tell some one who knows something o' the native!"

A groom came round the corner. Colonel Creighton raised his voice, speaking in Urdu. "Very good, Mahbub Ali, but what is the use of telling me all those stories about the pony? Not one pie more than three hundred and fifty rupees will I give."

"The Sahib is a little hot and angry after riding," the horse-dealer returned, with the leer of a privileged jester. "Presently he will see my horse's points more clearly. I will wait till he has finished his talk with the padre. I will wait under that tree."

"Confound you!" The Colonel laughed. "That comes of looking at one of Mahbub's horses. He's a regular old leech, Padre. Wait then, if thou hast so much time to spare, Mahbub. Now I'm at your service, Padre. Where is the boy? Oh, he's gone off to collogue with Mahbub. Queer sort of boy. Might I ask you to send my mare round under cover?" He dropped into a chair which commanded a clear view of Kim and Mahbub Ali in conference beneath the tree. The padre went indoors for cheroots.

Creighton heard Kim say bitterly: "Trust a Brahmin before a snake, and a snake before a harlot, and a harlot before an Afghan, Mahbub Ali."

"That is all one," the great red beard wagged solemnly. "Children should not see a carpet on the loom till the pattern is made plain. Believe me, Friend of all the World, I do thee great service. They will not make a soldier of thee."

"You crafty old sinner," thought Creighton. "But you're not far wrong. That boy mustn't be wasted if he is as advertised."

"Excuse me half a minute," cried the padre from within, "but I'm gettin' the documents of the case."

"If through me the favor of this bold and wise Colonel Sahib comes to thee, and thou art raised to honor, what thanks wilt thou give Mahbub Ali when thou art a man?"

"Nay, nay; I begged thee to let me take the road again, where I should have been safe; and thou hast sold me back to the English. What will they give thee for blood-money?"

"A cheerful young demon!" The Colonel bit his cigar, and turned politely to Father Victor.

"What are the letters that the fat priest is waving before the Colonel? Stand behind the stallion as though looking at my bridle!" said Mahbub Ali.

"A letter from my lama which he wrote from Jakadhir Road, saying that he will pay three hundred rupees by the year for my schooling."

"Oho! Is old Red Hat of that sort? At which school?"

"God knows. I think in Nucklao."

"Yes. There is a big school there for the sons of Sahibs–and half-Sahibs. I have seen it when I sell horses there. So the lama also loved the Friend of all the World?"

"Ay; and *he* did not tell lies, or return me to captivity."

"Small wonder the padre does not know how to unravel the thread. How fast he talks to the Colonel Sahib." Mahbub Ali chuckled. "By Allah!"–the keen eyes swept the verandah for an instant–"thy lama has sent what to me looks like a note of hand. I have had some small dealings in *hoondies.* The Colonel Sahib is looking at it."

"What good is all this to me?" said Kim wearily. "Thou wilt go away, and they will return me to those empty rooms where there is no good place to sleep and where the boys beat me."

"I do not think that. Have patience, child. All Pathans are not faithless–except in horse-flesh."

Five–ten–fifteen minutes passed, Father Victor talking energetically or asking questions which the Colonel answered. "Now I've told you everything that I know about the boy from beginnin' to end; and it's a blessed relief to me. Did ye ever hear the like?"

"At any rate, the old man has sent the money. Gobind Sahai's notes of hand are good from here to China," said the Colonel. "The more one knows about natives the less can one say what they will or won't do."

"That's consolin'–from the head of the Ethnological Survey. It's this mixture of Red Bulls and Rivers of Healing (poor heathen, God help him!) an' notes of hand and Masonic certificates. Are you a Mason, by any chance?"

"By Jove, I am, now I come to think of it. That's an additional reason," said the Colonel absently.

"I'm glad ye see a reason in it. But as I said, it's the mixture o' things that's beyond me. An' his prophesyin' to our Colonel sitting on my bed with his little shimmy torn open showing his white skin; an' the prophecy comin' true! They'll cure all that nonsense at St. Xavier's, eh?"

"Sprinkle him with holy water," the Colonel laughed.

"On my word, I fancy I ought to sometimes. But I'm hoping he'll be brought up as a good Catholic. All that troubles me is what'll happen if the old beggar man–"

"Lama, lama, my dear sir; and some of them are gentlemen in their own country."

"The lama, then, fails to pay next year. He's a fine business head to plan

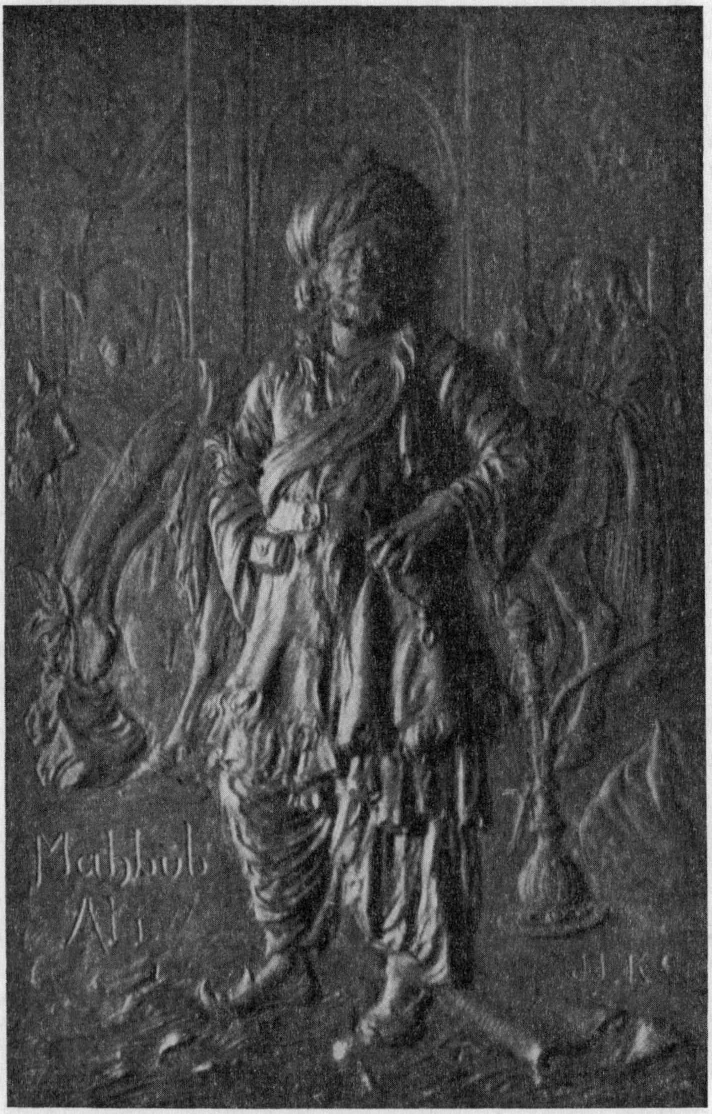

"'... PATHANS ARE NOT FAITHLESS—EXCEPT IN HORSE-FLESH.'"

on the spur of moment, but he's bound to die some day. An' takin' a heathen's money to give a child a Christian education–"

"But he said explicitly what he wanted. As soon as he knew the boy was a white he seems to have made his arrangements accordingly. I'd give a month's pay to hear how he explained it all at the Tirthankers' Temple at Benares. Look here, Padre, I don't pretend to know much about natives, but if he says he'll pay, he'll pay–dead or alive. I mean his heirs will assume the debt. My advice to you is, send the boy down to Lucknow. If your Anglican chaplain thinks you've stolen a march on him–"

"Bad luck to Bennett! He was sent to the front instead o' me. Doughty certified me medically unfit. I'll excommunicate Doughty if he comes back alive! Surely Bennett ought to be content with–"

"Glory, leaving you the religion. Quite so! As a matter of fact I don't think Bennett will mind. Put the blame on me. I–er–strongly recommend sending the boy to St. Xavier's. He can go down on pass as a soldier's orphan, so the railway fare will be saved. You can buy him an outfit from the regimental subscription. The Lodge will be saved the expense of his education, and that will put the Lodge in a good temper. It's perfectly easy. I've got to go down to Lucknow next week. I'll look after the boy on the way–give him in charge of my servants, and so on."

"You're a good man."

"Not in the least. Don't make that mistake. The lama has sent us money for a definite end. We can't very well return it. We shall have to do as he says. Well, that's settled, isn't it? Shall we say that, Tuesday next, you'll hand him over to me at the night train south? That's only three days. He can't do much harm in three days."

"It's a weight off my mind, but–this thing here?"–he waved the note of hand–"I don't know Gobind Sahai: or his bank, which may be a hole in a wall."

"*You've* never been a subaltern in debt. I'll cash it if you like, and send you the vouchers in proper order."

"But with all your own work too! It's askin'–"

"It's not the least trouble indeed. You see, as an ethnologist, the thing's very interesting to me. I'd like to make a note of it for some Government work that I'm doing. The transformation of a regimental badge like your Red Bull into a sort of fetish that the boy follows is very interesting."

"But I can't thank you enough."

"There's one thing you can do. All we Ethnological men are as jealous as jackdaws of one another's discoveries. They're of no interest to any one but ourselves, of course, but you know what book-collectors are like. Well, don't say a word, directly or indirectly, about the Asiatic side of the boy's character–his adventures and his prophecy, and so on. I'll worm them out of the boy later on and–you see?"

"I do. Ye'll make a wonderful account of it. Never a word will I say to any one till I see it in print."

"Thank you. That goes straight to an ethnologist's heart. Well, I must be getting back to my breakfast. Good Heavens! Old Mahbub here still?" He raised his voice, and the horse-dealer came out from under the shadow of the tree. "Well, what is it?"

"As regards that young horse," said Mahbub, "I say that when a colt is born to be a polo-pony, closely following the ball without teaching–when such a colt knows the game by divination–then I say it is a great wrong to break that colt to a heavy cart, Sahib!"

"So do I say also, Mahbub. The colt will be entered for polo only. (These fellows think of nothing in the world but horses, Padre.) I'll see you to-morrow, Mahbub, if you've anything likely for sale."

The dealer saluted, horseman fashion, with a sweep of the off hand. "Be patient a little, Friend of all the World," he whispered to the agonised Kim. "Thy fortune is made. In a little while thou goest to Nucklao, and–here is something to pay the letter-writer. I shall see thee again, I think, many times," and he cantered off down the road.

"Listen to me," said the Colonel from the verandah, speaking in the vernacular. "In three days thou wilt go with me to Lucknow, seeing and hearing new things all the while. Therefore sit still for three days and do not run away. Thou wilt go to school at Lucknow."

"Shall I meet my Holy One there?" Kim whimpered.

"At least Lucknow is nearer to Benares than Umballa. It may be thou wilt go under my protection. Mahbub Ali knows this, and he will be angry if thou returnest to the road now. Remember–much has been told me which I do not forget."

"I will wait," said Kim, "but the boys will beat me."

Then the bugles blew for dinner.

Chapter Seven

Unto whose use the pregnant suns are poised
With idiot moons and stars retracting stars?
Creep thou betweene–thy coming's all unnoised.
Heaven hath her high as earth her baser wars.
Heir to these tumults, this affright, that fraye
(By Adam's fathers' own sin bound alway);
Peer up, draw out thy horoscope and say
Which planet mends thy threadbare fate or mars!

SIR JOHN CHRISTIE

IN THE AFTERNOON the red-faced schoolmaster told Kim that he had been "struck off the strength," which conveyed no meaning to him till he was ordered to go away and play. Then he ran to the bazar, and found the young letter-writer to whom he owed a stamp.

"Now I pay," said Kim royally, "and now I need another letter to be written.

"Mahbub Ali is in Umballa," said the writer jauntily. He was, by virtue of his office, a bureau of general misinformation.

"This is not to Mahbub, but to a priest. Take thy pen and write quickly. *To Teshoo Lama, the holy one from Bhotiyal seeking for a River, who is now in the Temple of the Tirthankers at Benares.* Take more ink! *In three days I am to go down to Nucklao to the school at Nucklao. The name of the school is Xavier. I do not know where that school is, but it is at Nucklao.*"

"But I know Nucklao," the writer interrutped. "I know the school."

"Tell him where it is, and I give half an anna."

The reed pen scratched busily. "He cannot mistake." The man lifted his head. "Who watches us across the street?"

Kim looked up hurriedly and saw Colonel Creighton in tennis-flannels. "Oh, that is some Sahib who knows the fat priest in the barracks. He is beckoning me."

"What dost thou?" said the Colonel, when Kim trotted up.

"I–I am not running away. I send a letter to my Holy One at Benares. "

"I had not thought of that. Hast thou said that I take thee to Lucknow?"

"Nay, I have not. Read the letter, if there be a doubt."

"Then why hast thou left out my name in writing to that Holy One?" The Colonel smiled a queer smile. Kim took his courage in both hands.

"It was said once to me that it is inexpedient to write the names of strangers concerned in any matter, beause by the naming of names many good plans are brought to confusion."

"Thou hast been well taught," the Colonel replied, and Kim flushed. "I have left my cheroot-case in the padre's verandah. Bring it to my house this even."

"Where is the house?" said Kim. His quick wit told him that he was being tested in some fashion or another, and he stood on guard.

"Ask any one in the big bazar." The Colonel walked on.

"He has forgotten his cheroot-case," said Kim, returning. "I must bring it to him this evening. That is all my letter except, thrice over, *Come to me! Come to me! Come to me!* Now I will pay for a stamp and put it in the post." He rose to go, and as an after-thought asked: "Who is that angry-faced Sahib who lost the cheroot-case?"

"Oh, he is only Creighton Sahib–a very foolish Sahib, who is a Colonel Sahib without a regiment."

"What is his business?"

"God knows. He is always buying horses which he cannot ride, and asking riddles about the works of God–such as plants and stones and the customs of people. The dealers call him the father of fools, because he is so easily cheated about a horse. Mahbub Ali says he is madder than all other Sahibs."

"Oh!" said Kim, and departed. His training had given him some small knowledge of character, and he argued that fools are not given information which leads to calling out eight thousand men besides guns. The Commander-in-Chief of all India does not talk, as Kim had heard him talk, to fools. Nor would Mahbub Ali's tone have changed, as it did every time he mentioned the Colonel's name, if the Colonel had been a fool. Consequently–and this set Kim to skipping–there was a mystery somewhere, and Mahbub Ali probably spied for the Colonel much as Kim had spied for Mahbub. And, like the horse-dealer, the Colonel evidently respected people who did not show themselves to be too clever.

He rejoiced that he had not betrayed his knowledge of the Colonel's house; and when, on his return to barracks, he discovered that no cheroot-case had been left behind, he beamed with delight. Here was a man after his own heart–a tortuous and indirect person playing a hidden game. Well, if he could be a fool, so could Kim.

He showed nothing of his mind when Father Victor, for three long mornings, discoursed to him of an entirely new set of gods and godlings–notably of a goddess called Mary, who, he gathered, was one with Bibi Miriam of Mahbub Ali's theology. He betrayed no emotion when, after the lecture, Father Victor dragged him from shop to shop buying articles of outfit, nor when envious drummer-boys kicked him because he was going to a superior school did he complain, but awaited the play of circumstances with an interested soul. Father Victor, good man, took him to the station, put him into an empty second-class next to Colonel Creighton's first, and bade him farewell with genuine feeling.

"They'll make a man o' you, O'Hara, at St. Xavier's–a white man, an', I hope, a good man. They know all about your comin', an' the Colonel will see that ye're not lost or mislaid anywhere on the road. I've given you a notion of religious matters,–at least I hope so,–and you'll remember, when they ask you your religion, that you're a Cath'lic. Better say Roman Cath'lic, though

I'm not fond of the word."

Kim lit a rank cigarette–he had been careful to buy a stock in the bazar–and lay down to think. This solitary passage was very different from that joyful down-journey in the third-class with the lama. "Sahibs get little pleasure of travel," he reflected. *"Hai mai!* I go from one place to another as it might be a kick-ball. It is my *Kismet.* No man can escape his *Kismet.* But I am to pray to Bibi Miriam, and I am a Sahib"–he looked at his boots ruefully. "No; I am Kim. This is the great world, and I am only Kim. Who is Kim?" He considered his own identity, a thing he had never done before, till his head swam. He was one insignificant person in all this roaring whirl of India, going southward to he knew not what fate.

Presently the Colonel sent for him, and talked for a long time. So far as Kim could gather, he was to be diligent and enter the Survey of India as a chain-man. If he were very good, and passed the proper examinations, he would be earning thirty rupees a month at seventeen years old, and Colonel Creighton would see that he found suitable employment.

Kim pretended at first to understand perhaps one word in three of this talk. Then the Colonel, seeing his mistake, turned to fluent and picturesque Urdu, and Kim was contented. No man could be a fool who knew the language so intimately, who moved so gently and silently, and whose eyes were so different from the dull fat eyes of other Sahibs.

"Yes, and thou must learn how to make pictures of roads and mountains and rivers–to carry these pictures in thy eye till a suitable time comes to set them upon paper. Perhaps some day, when thou art a chain-man, I may say to thee when we are working together: 'Go across those hills and see what lies beyond.' Then one will say: 'There are bad people living in those hills who will slay the chain-man if he be seen to look like a Sahib.' What then?"

Kim thought. Would it be safe to return the Colonel's lead?

"I would tell what that other man had said."

"But if I answered: 'I will give thee a hundred rupees for knowledge of what is behind those hills–for a picture of a river and a little news of what the people say in the villages there'?"

"How can I tell? I am only a boy. Wait till I am a man." Then, seeing the Colonel's brow clouded, he went on: "But I think I should in a few days earn the hundred rupees."

"By what road?"

Kim shook his head resolutely. "If I said how I would earn them, another man might hear and forestall me. It is no good to sell knowledge for nothing."

"Tell now." The Colonel held up a rupee. Kim's hand half reached towards it, and dropped.

"Nay, Sahib; nay. I know the price that will be paid for the answer, but I do not know why the question is asked."

"Take it for a gift, then," said Creighton, tossing it over. "There is a good spirit in thee. Do not let it be blunted at St. Xavier's. There are many boys there who despise the black men."

"Their mothers were bazar-women," said Kim. He knew well there is no hatred like that of the half-caste for his brother-in-law.

"True; but thou art a Sahib and the son of a Sahib. Therefore, do not at any time be led to contemn the black men. I have known boys newly entered into the service of the Government who feigned not to understand the talk or the customs of black men. Their pay was cut for ignorance. There is no sin so great as ignorance. Remember this."

Several times in the course of the long twenty-four hours' run south did the Colonel send for Kim, always developing this latter text.

"We be all on one lead-rope, then," said Kim at last, "the Colonel, Mahbub Ali, and I—when I become a chain-man. He will use me as Mahbub Ali employed me, I think. That is good, if it allows me to return to the road again. This clothing grows no easier by wear."

When they came to the crowded Lucknow station there was no sign of the lama. He swallowed his disappointment, while the Colonel bundled him into a *ticca-garri* with his neat belongings and despatched him alone to St. Xavier's.

"I do not say farewell, because we shall meet again," he cried. "Again, and many times, if thou art one of good spirit. But thou art not yet tried."

"Not when I brought thee"—Kim actually dared to use the *tum* of equals—"a white stallion's pedigree that night?"

"Much is gained by forgetting, little brother," said the Colonel, with a look that pierced through Kim's shoulderblades as he scuttled into the carriage.

It took him nearly five minutes to recover. Then he sniffed the new air appreciatively. "A rich city," he said. "Richer than Lahore. How good the bazars must be. Coachman, drive me a little through the bazars here."

"My order is to take thee to the school." The driver used the "thou," which is rudeness when applied to a white man. In the clearest and most fluent vernacular Kim pointed out his error, climbed on to the box-seat, and, perfect understanding established, drove for a couple of hours up and down, estimating, comparing, and enjoying. There is no city—except Bombay, the queen of all—more beautiful in her garish style than Lucknow, whether you see her from the bridge over the river, or from the top of the Imambara looking down on the gilt umbrellas of the Chutter Munzil, and the trees in which the town is bedded. Kings have adorned her with fantastic buildings, endowed her with charities, crammed her with pensioners, and drenched her with blood. She is the center of all idleness, intrigue, and luxury, and shares with Delhi the claim to talk the only pure Urdu.

"A fair city—a beautiful city." The driver, as a Lucknow man, was pleased with the compliment, and told Kim many astounding things where an English guide would have talked of the Mutiny.

"Now we will go to the school," said Kim at last. The great old school of St. Xavier's in Partibus, block on block of low white buildings, stands in vast grounds over against the Gumti River, at some distance from the city.

"What like of folk are they within?" said Kim.

"Young Sahibs—all devils; but to speak truth, and I drive many of them to and fro from the railway station, I have never seen one that had in him the making of a more perfect devil than thou—this young Sahib whom I am now driving."

Naturally, for he was never trained to consider them in any way improper, Kim had passed the time of day with one or two frivolous ladies at upper windows in a certain street, and naturally, in the exchange of compliments, had acquitted himself well. He was about to acknowledge the driver's last insolence, when his eye—it was growing dusk—caught a figure sitting by one of the white plaster gate-pillers in the long sweep of wall. "Stop!" he cried. "Stay here. I do not go to the school at once."

"But what is to pay me for this coming and recoming?" said the driver petulantly. "Is the boy mad? Last time it was a dancing-girl. This time it is a priest."

Kim was in the road headlong, patting the dusty feet beneath the dirty yellow robe.

"I have waited here a day and a half," the lama's level voice began. "Nay, I had a disciple with me. He that was my friend at the Temple of the Tirthankers gave me a guide for this journey. I came from Benares in the train, when thy letter was given me. Yes, I am well fed. I need nothing."

"But why didst thou not stay with the Kulu woman, O Holy One? In what way didst thou get to Benares? My heart has been heavy since we parted."

"The woman wearied me by constant flux of talk and requiring charms for children. I separated myself from that company, permitting her to acquire merit by gifts. She is at least a woman of open hands, and I made a promise to return to her house if need arose. Then, perceiving myself alone in this great and terrible world, I bethought me of the *te-rain* to Benares, where I knew one abode in the Tirthankers' Temple who was a Seeker, even as I."

"Ah! Thy River," said Kim. "I had forgotten the River."

"So soon, my *chela?* I have never forgotten it; but when I had left thee it seemed better that I should go to the temple and take counsel, for, look you, India is very large, and it may be that wise men before us, some two or three, have left a record of the place of our River. There is debate in the Temple of the Tirthankers on this matter; some saying one thing, and some another. They are courteous folk."

"So be it; but what dost thou do now?"

"I acquire merit in that I help thee, my *chela,* to wisdom. The priest of that body of men who serve the Red Bull wrote me that all should be as I desired for thee. I sent the money to suffice for one year, and then I came, as thou seest me, to watch for thee going up into the Gates of Learning. A day and a half have I waited—not because I was led by any affection towards thee—that is no part of the Way—but, as they said at the Tirthankers' Temple, because, money having been paid for learning, it was right that I should oversee the end of the matter. They resolved my doubts most clearly. I had a fear that, perhaps, I came because I wished to see thee—misguided by the red mist of affection. It is not so. . . . Moreover, I am troubled by a dream."

"But surely, Holy One, thou hast not forgotten the road and all that befell on it. Surely it was a little to see me that thou didst come?"

"The horses are cold, and it is past their feeding-time," whined the driver.

"Go to Jehannum and abide there with thy reputationless aunt!" Kim snarled over his shoulder. "I am all alone in this land; I know not where I go nor what shall befall me. My heart was in that letter I sent thee. Except for Mahbub Ali, and he is a Pathan, I have no friend save thee, Holy One. Do not altogether go away."

"I have considered that also," the lama replied, in a shaking voice. "It is manifest that from time to time I shall acquire merit—if before that I have not found my River—by assuring myself that thy feet are set on wisdom. What they will teach thee I do not know, but the priest wrote me that no son of a Sahib in all India will be better taught than thou. So from time to time, therefore, I will come again. Maybe thou wilt be such a Sahib as he who gave me these spectacles"—the lama wiped them elaboratley—"in the Wonder House at Lahore. That is my hope, for he was a Fountain of Wisdom—wiser than many abbots. . . . Again, maybe thou wilt forget me and our meetings."

"If I eat thy bread," cried Kim passionately, "how shall I ever forget thee?"

"No—no." He put the boy aside. "I must go back to Benares. From time to time, now that I know the customs of letter-writers in this land, I will send thee a letter, and from time to time I will come and see thee."

"But whither shall I send my letters?" wailed Kim, clutching at the robe, all forgetful that he was a Sahib.

"To the Temple of the Tirthankers at Benares. That is the place I have chosen till I find my River. Do not weep; for, look you, all Desire is illusion and a new binding upon the Wheel. Go up to the Gates of Learning. Let me see thee go. . . . Dost thou love me? Then go, or my heart cracks. . . . I will come again. Surely I will come again."

The lama watched the *ticca-garri* rumble into the compound, and strode off, snuffing between each long stride.

"The Gates of Learning" shut with a clang.

. . . .

The country-born and bred boy has his own manners and customs, which do not resemble those of any other land; and his teachers approach him by roads which an English master would not understand. Therefore, you would scarcely be interested in Kim's experiences as a St. Xavier's boy among two or three hundred precocious youths, most of whom had never seen the sea. He suffered the usual penalties for breaking out of bounds when there was cholera in the city. This was before he had learned to write fair English, and so was obliged to find a bazar letter-writer. He was, of course, indicted for smoking and for the use of abuse more full-flavored than even St. Xavier's had ever heard. He learned to wash himself with the Levitical scrupulosity of the native-born, who in his heart considers the Englishman rather dirty. He played the usual tricks on the patient coolies pulling the punkahs in the sleeping-rooms where the boys thrashed through the hot nights telling tales till the dawn; and quietly he measured himself against his self-reliant mates.

They were sons of subordinate officials in the Railway, Telegraph, and Canal services; of warrant-officers, sometimes retired and sometimes acting as commanders-in-chief to a feudatory Rajah's army; of captains of the Indian Marine, Government pensioners, planters, Presidency shopkeepers, and missionaries. A few were cadets of the old Eurasian houses that have taken strong root in Dhurrumtollah–Pereiras, De Souzas, and D'Silvas. Their parents could well have educated them in England, but they loved the school that had served their own youth, and generation followed sallow-hued generation at St. Xavier's. Their homes ranged from Howrah of the railway people to abandoned cantonments like Monghyr and Chunar; lost tea-gardens Shillong-way; villages where their fathers were large landholders in Oudh or the Deccan; Mission-stations a week from the nearest railway line; seaports a thousand miles south, facing the brazen Indian surf; and cinchonaplantations south of all. The mere story of their adventures, which to them were no adventures, on their road to and from school would have crisped a Western boy's hair. They were used to jogging off alone through a hundred miles of jungle, where there was always the delightful chance of being delayed by tigers; but they would no more have bathed in the English Channel in an English August than their brothers across the world would have lain still while a leopard snuffed at their palanquin. There were boys of fifteen who had spent a day and a half on an islet in the middle of a flooded river, taking charge, as by right, of a camp of frantic pilgrims returning from a shrine; there were seniors who had requisitioned a chance-met Rajah's elephant, in the name of St. Francis Xavier, when the rains once blotted out the cart-track that led to their father's estate, and had all but lost the huge beast in a quicksand. There was a boy who, he said, and none doubted, had helped his father to beat off with rifles from the verandah a rush of Akas in the days when those head-hunters were bold against lonely plantations.

And every tale was told in the even, passionless voice of the native-born, mixed with quaint reflections, borrowed unconsciously from native foster-mothers, and turns of speech that showed they had been that instant translated from the vernacular. Kim watched, listened, and approved. This was not insipid, single-word talk of drummer-boys. It dealt with a life he knew and in part understood. The atmosphere suited him, and he throve by inches. They gave him a white drill suit as the weather warmed, and he rejoiced in the new-found bodily comforts as he rejoiced to use his sharpened mind over the tasks they set him. His quickness would have delighted an English master; but at St. Xavier's they know the first rush of minds developed by sun and surroundings, as they know the half-collapse that sets in at twenty-two or twenty-three.

None the less he remembered to hold himself lowly. When tales were told of hot nights, Kim did not sweep the board with his reminiscences; for St. Xavier's looks down on boys who "go native altogether." One must never forget that one is a Sahib, and that some day, when examinations are passed, one will command natives. Kim made a note of this, for he began to understand where examinations led.

Then came the holidays from August to October—the long holidays imposed by the heat and the rains. Kim was informed that he would go north to some station in the hills behind Umballa, where Father Victor would arrange for him.

"A barrack school?" said Kim, who had asked many questions and thought more.

"Yes, I suppose so," said the master. "It will not do you any harm to keep you out of mischief. You can go up with young DeCastro as far as Delhi."

Kim considered it in every possible light. He had been diligent, even as the Colonel advised. A boy's holiday was his own property,—of so much the talk of his companions had advised him,—and a barrack school would be torment after St. Xavier's. Moreover—this was magic worth anything else—he could write. In three months he had discovered how men can speak to each other without a third party, at the cost of half an anna and a little knowledge. No word had come from the lama, but there remained the Road. Kim yearned for the caress of soft mud squishing up between the toes, as his mouth watered from mutton stewed with butter and cabbages, for rice speckled with strong-scented cardamoms, for the saffron-tinted rice, garlic and onions, and the forbidden greasy sweetmeats of the bazars. They would feed him raw beef on a platter at the barrack school, and he must smoke by stealth. But again, he was a Sahib and was at St. Xavier's, and that pig Mahbub Ali . . . No, he would not test Mahbub's hospitality—and yet . . . He thought it out alone in the dormitory, and came to the conclusion he had been unjust to Mahbub.

The school was empty; nearly all the masters had gone away; Colonel Creighton's railway pass lay in his hand, and Kim puffed himself that he had not spent Colonel Creighton's or Mahbub's money in riotous living. He was still lord of two rupees seven annas. His new bullock-trunk, marked "K. O'H.," and bedding-roll lay in the empty sleeping-room. "Sahibs are always tied to their baggage," said Kim, nodding at them. "You will stay here." He went out into the warm rain, smiling sinfully, and sought a certain house whose outside he had noted down some time before. . . .

"Arré! Dost thou know what manner of women we be in this quarter? O shame!"

"Was I born yesterday?" Kim squatted native fashion on the cushions of that upper room. "A little dye-stuff and three yards of cloth to help out a jest. Is it much to ask?"

"Who is *she?* Thou art full young, as Sahibs go, for this devilry."

"Oh, she? She is the daughter of a certain schoolmaster of a regiment in the cantonments. He has beaten me twice because I went over their wall in these clothes. Now I would go as a gardener's boy. Old men are very jealous."

"That is true. Hold thy face still while I dab on the juice."

"Not too black, *Naikan.* I would not appear to her as a *hubshi* (nigger)."

"Oh, love makes nought of these things. And how old is she?"

"Twelve years, I think," said the shameless Kim. "Spread it also on the breast. It may be her father will tear my cothes off me and if I am piebald—" he laughed.

The girl worked busily, dabbing a twist of cloth into a little saucer of brown dye that holds longer than any walnut juice.

"Now send out and get me a cloth for the turban. Woe is me, my head is all unshaved! And he will surely knock off my turban."

"I am not a barber, but I will make shift. Thou wast born to be a breaker of hearts! All this disguise for one evening? Remember, the stuff does not wash away." She shook with laughter till her bracelets and anklets jingled. "But who is to pay me for this? Huneefa herself could not have given thee better stuff."

"Trust in the Gods, my sister," said Kim gravely, screwing his face round as the stain dried. "Besides, hast thou ever helped to paint a Sahib thus before?"

"Never indeed. But a jest is not money."

"It is worth much more."

"Child, thou art beyond all dispute the most shameless son of Shaitan that I have ever known to take up a poor girl's time with this play, and then to say: 'Is not the jest enough?' Thou wilt go very far in this world." She gave the dancing-girls' salutation in mockery.

"All one. Make haste and rough-cut my head." Kim shifted from foot to foot, his eyes ablaze with mirth as he thought of the fat days before him. He gave the girl four annas, and ran down the stairs in the likeness of a lowcaste Hindu boy–perfect in every detail. A cookshop was his next point of call, where he feasted in extravagance and greasy luxury.

On Lucknow station platform he watched young De Castro, all covered with prickly-heat, get into a second-class compartment. Kim patronised a third, and was the life and soul of it. He explained to the company that he was assistant to a juggler who had left him behind sick with fever, and that he would pick up his master at Umballa. As the occupants of the carriage changed, he varied this tale, or adorned it with all the shoots of a budding fancy, the more rampant for being held off native speech so long. In all India that night was no human being so joyful as Kim. At Umballa he got out and headed eastward, plashing over the sodden fields to the village where the old soldier lived.

About this time Colonel Creighton at Simla was advised from Lucknow by wire that young O'Hara had disappeared. Mahbub Ali was in town selling horses, and to him the Colonel confided the affair one morning cantering round Annandale race-course.

"Oh, that is nothing," said the horse-dealer. "Men are like horses. At certain times they need salt, and if that salt is not in the managers they will lick it up from the earth. He has gone back to the Road again for awhile. The *madrissah* wearied him. I knew it would. Another time, I will take him upon the Road myself. Do not be troubled, Creighton Sahib. It is as though a polo-pony, breaking loose, ran out to learn the game alone."

"Then he is not dead, think you?"

"Fever might kill him. I do not fear for the boy otherwise. A monkey does not fall among trees."

Next morning, on the same course, Mahbub's stallion ranged alongside the Colonel.

"It is as I had thought," said the horse-dealer. "He has come through Umballa at least, and there he has written a letter to me, having learned in the bazar that I was here."

"Read," said the Colonel, with a sigh of relief. It was absurd that a man of his position should take an interest in a little country-bred vegabond; but the Colonel remembered the conversation in the train, and often in the past few months had caught himself thinking of the queer, silent, self-possessed boy. His evasion, of course, was the height of insolence, but it argued some resource and nerve.

Mahbub's eyes twinkled as he reined out into the centre of the cramped little plain, where none could come near unseen.

"*'The Friend of the Stars, who is the Friend of all the World–'*"

"What is this?"

"A name we give him in Lahore city. *'The Friend of all the World takes leave to go to his own places. He will come back upon the appointed day. Let the box and the bedding-roll be sent for; and if there has been a fault, let the Hand of Friendship turn aside the Whip of Calamity.'* There is yet a little more, but–"

"No matter, read."

" *'Certain things are not known to those who eat with forks. It is better to eat with both hands for awhile. Speak soft words to those who do not understand this, that the return may be propitious.'* Now the manner in which that was cast is of course the work of the letter-writer, but see how wisely the boy has devised the matter of it so that no hint is given except to those who know!"

"Is this the Hand of Friendship to avert the Whip of Calamity?" laughed the Colonel.

"See how wise is the boy. He would go back to the Road again, as I said. Not knowing yet thy trade–"

"I am not quite sure of that," the Colonel muttered.

"He turns to me to make a peace between you. Is he not wise? He says he will return. He is but perfecting his knowledge. Think, Sahib! He has been three months at the school. And he is not mouthed to that bit. For my part, I rejoice: the pony learns the game."

"Ay, but another time he must not go alone."

"Why? He went alone before he came under the Colonel Sahib's protection. When he comes to the Great Game he must go alone–alone, and at peril of his head. *Then,* if he spits, or sneezes, or sits down other than as the people do whom he watches, he may be slain. Why hinder him now? Remember how the Persians say: The jackal that lives in the wilds of Mazanderan can only be caught by the hounds of Mazanderan."

"True. It is true, Mahbub Ali. And if he comes to no harm, I do not desire anything better. But it is great insolence on his part."

"He does not tell me, even, whither he goes," said Mahbub. "He is no fool. When his time is accomplished he will come to me. It is time the healer of pearls took him in hand. He ripens too quickly–as Sahibs reckon."

This prophecy was fulfilled to the letter a month letter. Mahbub had gone down to Umballa to bring up a fresh consignment of horses, and Kim met him on the Kalka road at dusk riding alone, begged an alms of him, was sworn at, and replied in English. There was nobody within earshot to hear Mahbub's gasp of amazement.

"Oho! And where hast thou been?"

"Up and down–down and up."

"Come under a tree, out of the wet, and tell."

"I stayed for awhile with an old man near Umballa; anon with a household of my acquaintance in Umballa. With one of these I went as far as Delhi to the southward. That is a wondrous city. Then I drove a bullock for a *teli* (an oilman) coming north; but I heard of a great feast forward in Patiala, and thither went I in the company of a fireworkmaker. It was a great feast" (Kim rubbed his stomach). "I saw Rajahs, and elephants with gold and silver trappings; and they lit all the fireworks at once, whereby eleven men were killed, my firework-maker among them, and I was blown across a tent but took no harm. Then I came back to the *rêl* with a Sikh horseman, to whom I was groom for my bread; and so here."

"*Shabash!*" said Mahbub Ali.

"But what does the Colonel Sahib say? I do not wish to be beaten."

"The Hand of Friendship has averted the Whip of Calamity; but another time, when thou takest the Road it will be with me.This is too early."

"Late enough for me. I have learned to read and to write English a little at the *madrissah.* I shall soon be altogether a Sahib."

"Hear him!" laughed Mahbub, looking at the little drenched figure dancing in the wet. "Salaam–Sahib," and he saluted ironically. "Well, art tired of the Road, or wilt thou come on to Umballa with me and work back with the horses?"

"I come with thee, Mahbub Ali."

Chapter Eight

Something I owe to the soil that grew–
More to the life that fed–
But most to Allah Who gave me two
Separate sides to my head.

I would go without shirts or shoes,
Friends, tobacco or bread
Sooner than for an instant lose
Either side of my head.

"THEN IN GOD'S Name take blue for red," said Mahbub, alluding to the Hindu color of Kim's disreputable turban.

Kim countered with the old proverb, "I will change my faith and my bedding, but *thou* must pay for it."

The dealer laughed till he nearly fell from his horse. At a shop on the outskirts of the city the change was made, and Kim stood up, externally at least, a Mohammedan.

Mahbub hired a room over against the railway station, sent for a cooked meal of the finest, with almond-curd sweetmeats (*balushai* we call it) and fine-chopped Lucknow tobacco.

"This is better than some other meat that I ate with the Sikh," said Kim, grinning as he squatted, "and assuredly they give no such victuals at my *madrissah.*"

"I have a desire to hear of that same *madrissah.*" Mahbub stuffed himself with great boluses of spiced mutton fried in fat with cabbage and golden-brown onions. "But tell me first, altogether and truthfully, the manner of thy escape. For, O Friend of all the World,"–he loosed his cracking belt,–"I do not think it is often that a Sahib and the son of a Sahib runs away from there."

"How should they? They do not know the land. It was nothing," said Kim, and began his tale. When he came to the disguisement and the interview with the girl in the bazar, Mahbub Ali's gravity went from him. He laughed aloud and beat his hand on his thigh.

"*Shabash! Shabash!* Oh, well done, little one! What will the healer of turquoises say to this? Now, slowly, let us hear what befell afterwards–step by step, omitting nothing."

Step by step then, Kim told his adventures between coughs as the full-flavoured tobacco caught his lungs.

"I said," growled Mahbub Ali to himself, "I *said* it was the pony breaking out to play polo. The fruit is ripe already–except that he must learn his distances and his pacings, and his rods and his compasses. Listen now. I have turned aside the Colonel's whip from thy skin, and that is no small service."

"True." Kim puffed serenely. "That is all true."

"But it is not to be thought that this running out and in is any way good."

"It was my holiday, Hajji. I was a slave for many weeks. Why should I not run away when the school was shut? Look, too, how I, living upon my friends or working for my bread, as I did with the Sikh, have saved the Colonel Sahib a great expense."

Mahbub's lips twitched under his well-pruned Mohammedan moustache.

"What are a few rupees"–the Pathan threw out his open hand carelessly–"to the Colonel Sahib? He spends them for a purpose, not in any way for love of thee."

"That," said Kim slowly, "I knew a very long time ago."

"Who told?"

"The Colonel Sahib himself. Not in those many words, but plainly enough for one who is not altogether a mudhead. Yea, he told me in the *te-rain* when we went down to Lucknow."

"Be it so. Then I will tell thee more, Friend of all the World, though in the telling I lend thee my head."

"It was forfeit to me," said Kim, with deep relish, "in Umballa, when thou didst pick me up on the horse after the drummer-boy beat me."

"Speak a little plainer. All the world may tell lies save thou and I. For equally is thy life forefeit to me if I chose to raise my finger here."

"And this is known to me also," said Kim, readjusting the live charcoal-ball on the weed. "It is a very sure tie between us. Indeed thy hold is surer even than mine; for who would miss a boy beaten to death, or, it may be, thrown into a well by the roadside? Many people here and in Simla and across the passes behind the Hills would, on the other hand, say: 'What has come to Mahbub Ali?' if he were found dead among his horses. Surely too the Colonel Sahib would make inquiries. But again,"–Kim's face puckered with cunning,–"he would not make overlong inquiry, lest people should ask: 'What has this Colonel Sahib to do with that horse-dealer?' But I–if I lived–"

"As thou wouldst surely die–"

"It may be; but I say, *if* I lived, I, and I alone, would know that one had come by night, as a common thief perhaps, to Mahbub Ali's bulkhead in the serai, and there had slain him, either before or after that thief had made a full search into his saddle-bags and between the soles of his slippers. Is that news to tell to the Colonel, or would he say to me–(I have not forgotten when he sent me back for a cigar-case that he had *not* left behind him)–'What is Mahbub Ali to me?' "

Up went a gout of heavy smoke. There was a long pause; then Mahbub Ali spoke in admiration: "And with these things on thy mind, dost thou lie down and rise again among all the Sahibs' little sons at the *madrissah* and meekly take instruction from thy teachers?"

"It is an order," said Kim blandly. "Who am I to dispute an order?"

"A most finished son of Eblis," said Mahbub Ali. "But what is this tale of the thief and the search?"

"That which I saw," said Kim, "the night that my lama and I lay next thy place in the Kashmir Serai. The door was left unlocked, which I think is not thy custom, Mahbub. He came in as one assured that thou wouldst not soon return. My eye was against a knot-hole in the plank. He searched as it were for something–not a rug, not stirrups, nor a bridle, nor brass pots–something little and most carefully hid. Else why did he prick with an iron between the soles of thy slippers?"

"Ha!" Mahbub Ali smiled gently. "And seeing these things, what tale didst thou fashion to thyself, Well of the Truth?"

"None. I put my hand upon my amulet, which lies always next to my skin, and, remembering the pedigree of a white stallion that I had bitten out of a piece of Mussalmani bread, I went away to Umballa perceiving that a heavy trust was laid upon me. At that hour, had I chosen, thy head was forfeit. It needed only to say to that man, 'I have here a paper concerning a horse which I cannot read.' And then?" Kim peered at Mahbub under his eyebrows.

"Then thou wouldst have drunk water twice–perhaps thrice, afterwards. I do not think more than thrice," said Mahbub simply.

"It is true. I thought of that a little, but most I thought that I loved thee, Mahbub. Therefore I went to Umballa, as thou knowest, but (and this thou dost not know) I lay hid in the garden-grass to see what Colonel Creighton Sahib might do upon reading the white stallion's pedigree."

"And what did he?" for Kim had bitten off the conversation.

"Dost *thou* give news for love, or dost thou sell it?" Kim asked.

"I sell and–I buy." Mahbub took a four-anna piece out of his belt and held it up.

"Eight!" said Kim, mechanically following the huckster instinct of the East.

Mahbub laughed, and put away the coin. "It is too easy to deal in that market, Friend of all the World. Tell me for love. Our lives lie in each other's hand."

"Very good. I saw the Jang-i-Lat Sahib come to a big dinner. I saw him in Creighton Sahib's office. I saw the two read the white stallion's pedigree. I heard the very orders given for the opening of a great war."

"Hah!" Mahbub nodded with deepest eyes afire. "The game is well played. That war is done now, and the evil, we hope, nipped before the flower–thanks to me–and thee. What dids't thou later?"

"I made the news as it were a hook to catch me victual and honor among the villagers in a village whose priest drugged my lama. But I bore away the old man's purse, and the Brahmin found nothing. So next morning he was angry. Ho! Ho! And I also used the news when I fell into the hands of that white regiment with their Bull!"

"That was foolishness." Mahbub scowled. "News is not meant to be thrown about like dung-cakes, but used sparingly–like *bhang.*"

"So I think now, and moreover, it did me no sort of good. But that was very long ago,"–he made as to brush it all away with a thin brown hand,–"and since then, and especially in the nights under the punkah at the *madrissah,* I have thought very greatly."

"Is it permitted to ask whither the Heaven-born's thought might have led?" said Mahbub, with an elaborate sarcasm, smoothing his scarlet beard.

"It is permitted," said Kim, and threw back the very tone. "They say at Nucklao that no Sahib must tell a black man that he has made a fault."

Mahbub's hand shot into his bosom, for to call a Pathan a "black man" *(kala admi)* is a blood-insult. Then he remembered and laughed. "Speak, Sahib: thy black man hears."

"But," said Kim, "I am *not* a Sahib, and I say I made a fault when I cursed thee, Mahbub Ali, on the day at Umballa I thought I was betrayed by a Pathan. I was senseless; for I was but newly caught, and I wished to kill that low-caste drummer-boy. I saw now, Hajji, that it was well done; and I see my road all clear before me to a good service. I will stay in the *madrissah* till I am ripe."

"Well said. Especially are distances and numbers and the manner of using compasses to be learned in that game. One waits in the Hills above to show thee."

"I will learn their teaching upon a condition–that my time is given to me without question when the *madrissah* is shut. Ask that for me of the Colonel."

"But why not ask the Colonel in the Sahib's tongue?"

"The Colonel is the servant of the Government. He is sent hither and yon at a word, and must consider his own advancement. (See how much I have already learned at Nucklao!) Moreover, the Colonel I know since three months only. I have known one Mahbub Ali for six years. So! To the *madrissah* I will go. At the *madrissah* I will learn. In the *madrissah* I will be a Sahib. But when the *madrissah* is shut, then must I be free and go among my people. Otherwise I die."

"And who are thy people, Friend of all the World?"

"This great and beautiful land," said Kim, waving his paw round the little clay-walled room where the oil lamp in its niche burned heavily through the tobacco-smoke. "And further, I would see my lama again. And further, I need money."

"That is the need of every one," said Mahbub ruefully. "I will give thee eight annas, for much money is not picked out of horses' hooves, and it must suffice for many days. As to all the rest, I am well pleased, and no further talk is needed. Make haste to learn, and in three years, or it may be less, thou wilt be an aid—even to me."

"Have I been such a hindrance till now?" said Kim, with a boy's giggle.

"Do not give answers," Mahbub grunted. "Thou art my new horse-boy. Go and bed among my men. They are near the north end of the station, with the horses."

"They will beat me to the south end of the station if I come without authority."

Mahbub felt in his belt, wetted his thumb on a cake of Chinese ink, and dabbed the impression on a piece of soft native paper. From Balkh to Bombay men know that rough-ridged print with the old scar running diagonally across it.

"That is enough to show my headman. I come in the morning."

"By which road?" said Kim.

"By the road from the City. There is but one. And then we return to Creighton Sahib. I have saved thee a beating."

"Allah! What is a beating when the very head is loose on the shoulders?"

Kim slid out quietly into the night, walked half round the house, keeping close to the walls, and headed away from the station for a mile or so. Then, fetching a wide compass, he worked back at leisure, for he needed time to invent a story if any of Mahbub's retainers asked questions.

They were camped on a piece of waste ground beside the railway, and, being natives, had not, of course, unloaded the two trucks in which Mahbub's animals stood among a consignment of country-breds bought by the Bombay tram-company. The headman, a broken-down, consumptive-looking Mohammedan, promptly challenged Kim, but was pacified at sight of Mahbub's sign-manual.

"The Hajji has of his favor give me service," said Kim testily. "If this is doubted, wait till he comes in the morning. Meantime, a place by the fire."

Followed the usual aimless babble that every low-caste native must raise on every occasion. It died down, and Kim lay out behind the little knot of Mahbub's followers, almost under the wheels of a horse-truck, a borrowed blanket for covering. Now a bed among brickbats and ballast-refuse on a damp night, between overcrowded horses and unwashen Baltis, would not appeal to many white boys; But Kim was utterly happy. Change of scene, service, and surroundings were the breath of his little nostrils, and thinking of the neat white cots of St. Xavier's all arow under the punkah gave him joy as keen as the repetition of the multiplication-table in English.

"I am very old," he thought sleepily. "Every month I become a year more old. I was very young, and a fool to boot, when I took Mahbub's message to Umballa. Even when I was with that white regiment I was very young and small and had no wisdom. But now I learn every day, and in three years the Colonel will take me out of the *madrissah* and let me go upon the Road with Mahbub hunting for horses' pedigrees, or maybe I shall go by myself; or maybe I shall find the lama and go with him. Yes; that is best. To walk again as a *chela* with my lama when he comes back to Benares." The thoughts came more slowly and disconnectedly. He was plunging into a beautiful dreamland when his ears caught a whisper, thin and sharp, above the monotonous babble round the fire. It came from behind the iron-skinned horse-truck.

"He is not here then?"

"Where should he be but roystering in the City? Who looks for a rat in a frog-pond? Come away. He is not our man."

"He must not go back beyond the Passes a second time. It is the order."

"Hire some woman to drug him. It is a few rupees only, and there is no evidence."

"Except the woman. It must be more certain; and remember the price upon his head."

"Ay, but the police have a long arm, and we are far from the Border. If it were in Peshawur now!"

"Yes–in Peshawur," the second voice sneered. "Peshawur, full of his blood-kin–full of bolt-holes and women behind whose clothes he will hide. Yes, Peshawur or Jehannum would suit us equally well."

"Then what is the plan?"

"O fool, have I not told it a hundred times? Wait till he comes to lie down, and then one sure shot. The trucks are between us and pursuit. We have but to run back over the lines and go our way. They will not see whence the shot came. Wait here at least till the dawn. What manner of *faquir* art thou to shiver at a little watching?"

"Oho!" thought Kim behind close-shut eyes.

"Once again it is Mahbub. Indeed a white stallion's pedigree is not a good thing to peddle to Sahibs! Oh maybe Mahbub has been selling other news. Now what is to do, Kim? I know not where Mahbub houses, and if he comes here before the dawn they will shoot him. That would be no profit for thee, Kim. And this is not a matter for the police. That would be no profit for Mahbub; and," he giggled almost aloud, "I do not remember any lesson at Nucklao which will help me. Allah! Here is Kim and yonder are they. First then, Kim must wake and go away, so that they shall not suspect. A bad dream wakes a man–thus–"

He threw the blanket off his face, and raised himself suddenly with the terrible, bubbling meaningless yell of the Asiatic roused by nightmare.

"Urr-urr-urr-urr! Ya-la-la-la-la! *Narain!* The *churel!* The *churel!*"

A *churel* is the peculiarly malignant ghost of a woman who has died in child-bed. She haunts lonely roads, her feet are turned backwards on the ankles, and she leads men to torment.

Louder rose Kim's quavering howl, till at last he leaped to his feet and staggered off sleepily, while the camp cursed him for waking them. Some twenty yards farther up the line he lay down again, taking care that the whisperers should hear his grunts and groans as he recomposed himself. After a few minutes he rolled towards the road and stole away into the thick darkness.

He paddled along swiftly till he came to a culvert, and dropped behind it, his chin on a level with the coping-stone. Here he could command all the night-traffic, himself unseen.

Two or three carts passed, jingling out to the suburbs; a coughing policeman and a hurrying foot-passenger or two who sang to keep off evil spirits. Then rapped the shod feet of a horse.

"Ah! This is more like Mahbub," thought Kim, as the beast shied at the little head above the culvert.

"Ohé, Mahbub Ali," he whispered, "have a care!"

The horse was reined back almost on its haunches, and forced towards the culvert.

"Never again," said Mahbub, "will I take a shod horse for night-work. They pick up all the bones and nails in the city." He stooped to lift its forefoot, and that brought his head within a foot of Kim's. "Down–keep down," he muttered. "The night is full of eyes."

"Two men wait thy coming behind the horse-trucks. They will shoot thee at thy lying down, because there is a price on thy head. I heard, sleeping near the horses."

"Didst thou see them? . . . Hold still, Sire of Devils!" This furiously to the horse.

"No."

"Was one dressed belike as a *faquir?*"

"One said to the other, 'What manner of a *faquir* art thou to shiver at a little watching?'"

"Good. Go back to the camp and lie down. I do not die to-night."

Mahbub wheeled his horse and vanished. Kim tore back down the ditch till he reached a point opposite his second resting-place, slipped across the road like a weasel, and re-coiled himself in the blanket.

"At least Mahbub knows," he thought contentedly. "And certainly he spoke as one expecting it. I do not think those two men will profit by to-night's watch."

An hour passed, and, with the best will in the world to keep awake all night, he slept deeply. Now and again a night train roared along the metals within twenty feet of him; but he had all the Oriental's indifference to mere noise, and it did not even weave a dream through his slumber.

Mahbub was anything but asleep. It annoyed him vehemently that people outside his tribe and unaffected by his casual amours should pursue him for the life. His first and natural impulse was to cross the line lower down, work up again, and, catching his well-wishers from behind, summarily slay them. Here, he reflected with sorrow, another branch of the Government, totally unconnected with Colonel Creighton, might demand explanations which would be hard to supply; and he knew that south the Border a perfectly ridiculous fuss is made about a corpse or so. He had not been troubled in this way since he sent Kim to Umballa with the message, and hoped that suspicion had been finally averted.

Then a most brilliant notion struck him.

"The English do eternally tell the truth," he said, "therefore we of this country are eternally made foolish. By Allah, I will tell the truth to an Englishman! Of what use is the Government police if a poor Cabuli be robbed of his horses in their very trucks? This is as bad as Peshawur! I should lay a complaint at the station. Better still, some young Sahib on the Railway! They are zealous, and if they catch thieves it is remembered to their honor."

He tied up his horse outside the station, and strode on to the platform.

"Hulo, Mahbub Ali!" said a young Assistant District Traffic Superintendent who was waiting to go down the line–a tall, tow-haired, horsey youth in dingy white linen. "What are you doing here? Selling weeds–eh?"

"No; I am not troubled for my horses. I could to look for Lutuf Ullah. I have a truck-load up the line. Could any one take them out without the Railway's knowledge?"

" 'Shouldn't think so, Mahbub. You can claim against us if they do."

"I have seen two men crouching under the wheels of one of the trucks nearly all the night. *Faquirs* do not steal horses, so I gave them no more thought. I would find Lutuf Ullah, my partner."

"The deuce you did? And you didn't bother your head about it? 'Pon my word, it's just almost as well that I met you. What were they like, eh?"

"They were only *faquirs*. They will no more than take a little grain perhaps from one of the trucks. There are many up the line. The State will never miss the dole. I came here seeking for my partner, Lutuf Ullah–"

"Never mind your partner. Where are your horse-trucks?"

"A little to this side of the farthest place where they make lamps for the trains."

"The signal-box. Yes."

"And upon the rail nearest to the road upon the right-hand side–looking up the line thus. But as regards Lutuf Ullah–a tall man with a broken nose, and a Persian greyhound–Aie!"

The boy had hurried off to wake up a young and enthusiastic policeman; for, as he said, the Railway had suffered much from depredations in the goods-yard. Mahbub Ali chuckled in his dyed beard.

"They will walk in their boots, making a noise, and then they will wonder why there are no *faquirs*. They are very clever boys–Barton Sahib and Young Sahib."

He waited idly for a few minutes, expecting to see them hurry up the line girt for action. A light engine slid through the station, and he caught a glimpse of young Barton in the cab.

"I did that child an injustice. He is not altogether a fool," said Mahbub Ali. "To take a fire-carriage for a thief is a new game!"

When Mahbub Ali came to his camp in the dawn, no one thought it worth while to tell him any news of the night. No one, at least, but one small horse-boy, newly advanced to the great man's service, whom Mahbub called to his tiny tent to assist in some packing.

"It is all known to me," whispered Kim, bending above saddle-bags. "Two Sahibs came up on a *te-rain*. I was running to and fro in the dark on this side of the trucks as the *te-rain* moved up and down slowly. They fell upon two men sitting under this truck–Hajji, what shall I do with this lump of tobacco? Wrap it in paper and put it under the salt-bag? Yes–and struck them down. But one man struck at a Sahib with a *faquir's* buck's horn" (Kim meant the conjoined black-buck horns, which are a *faquir's* sole temporal weapon)–"the blood came. So the other Sahib, first smiting his own man senseless, smote the stabber with a short gun which had rolled from the first man's hand. They all raged as though mad together."

Mahbub smiled with heavenly resignation. "No! That is not so much *dewanee* (madness, or a case for the civil court–the word can be punned upon both ways) as *nizamut* (a criminal case). A gun sayest thou? Ten good years in jail."

"Then they both lay still, but I think they were nearly dead when they were put on the *te-rain*. Their heads moved thus. And there is much blood on the line. Come and see?"

"I have seen blood before. Jail is the sure place–and assuredly they will give false names, and assuredly no man will find them for a long time. They were unfriends of mine. Thy Fate and mine seem on one string. What a tale for the healer of pearls! Now swiftly with the saddle-bags and the cooking-platter. We will take out the horses and away to Simla."

Swiftly,–as Orientals understood speed,–with long explanations, with abuse and windy talk, carelessly, amid a hundred checks for little things forgotten, the untidy camp broke up and led the half-dozen stiff and fretful horses along the Kalka road in the fresh of the rain-swept dawn. Kim, regarded as Mahbub Ali's favorite by all who wished to stand well with the Pathan, was not called upon to work. They strolled on by the easiest of stages, halting every few hours at a wayside shelter. Very many Sahibs travel along the Kalka road; and, as Mahbub Ali says, every young Sahib must needs esteem himself a judge of a horse, and, though he be over head in debt to the money-lender, must make as if to buy. That was the reason that Sahib after Sahib, rolling along in a stage-carriage, would stop and open talk. Some would even descend from their vehicles and feel the horses' legs; asking inane questions, or, through sheer ignorance of the vernacular, grossly insulting the imperturbable trader.

"When first I dealt with Sahibs, and that was when Colonel Soady Sahib was Governor of Fort Abazi and flooded the Commissioner's camping-ground for spite," Mahbub confided to Kim as the boy filled his pipe under a tree, "I did not know how greatly they were fools, and this made me wroth. As thus—" and he told Kim a tale of an expression, misused in all innocence, that doubled Kim up with mirth. "Now I see, however,"—he exhaled smoke slowly,—"that it is with them as with all men—in certain matters they are wise, and in others most foolish. Very foolish it is to use the wrong word to a stranger; for though the heart may be clean of offense, how is the stranger to know that? He is more like to search truth with a dagger."

"True. True talk," said Kim solemnly. "Fools speak of a cat when a woman is brought to bed, for instance. I have heard them."

"Therefore, in one situate as thou art, it particularly behooves thee to remember this with both kinds of faces. Among Sahibs, never forgetting thou art a Sahib; among the folk of Hind, always remembering thou art—" he paused, with a puzzled smile.

"What am I? Mussalman, Hindu, Jain, or Buddhist? That is a hard nut."

"Thou art beyond question an unbeliever, and therefore thou wilt be damned. So says my Law—or I think it does. But thou art also Little Friend of all the World, and I love thee. So says my heart. This matter of creeds is like horse-flesh. The wise man knows horses are good—that there is a profit to be made from all; and for myself—but that I am a good Sunni and hate the men of Tirah—I could believe the same of all the Faiths. Now manifestly a Katti-war mare taken from the sands of her birthplace and removed to the west of Bengal founders—nor is even a Balkh stallion (and there are no better horses than those of Balkh, were they not so heavy in the shoulder) of any account in the great Northern deserts beside the snow-camels I have seen. Therefore I say in my heart the Faiths are like the horses. Each has merit in its own country."

"But my lama said altogether a different thing."

"Oh, he is an old dreamer of dreams from Bhotiyal. My heart is a little angry, O Friend of all the World, that thou shouldst see such worth in a man so little known."

"It is true, Hajji; but that worth do I see; and to him my heart is drawn."

"And his to thine, I hear. Hearts are like horses. They come and they go against bit or spur. Shout Gul Sher Khan yonder to drive in that bay stallion's pickets more firmly. We do not want a horse-fight at every resting-stage, and the dun and the black will be locked in a little. . . . Now hear me. Is it necessary to the comfort of thy heart to see that lama?"

"It is one part of my bond," said Kim. "If I do not see him, and if he is taken from me, I will go out of that *madrissah* in Nucklao, and, and—once gone, who is to find me again?"

"It is true. Never was colt held on a lighter heel-rope than thou." Mahbub nodded his head.

"Do not be afraid." Kim spoke as though he could have evanished on the moment. "My lama has said that he will come to see me at the *madrissah*—"

"A beggar and his bowl in the presence of those young Sa—"

"Not all!" Kim cut in with a snort. "Their eyes are blued and their nails are blackened with low-caste blood, many of them. Sons of *metheeranes*—brothers-in-law to the *bhungi* (sweeper)."

We need not follow the rest of the pedigree; but Kim made his little point clearly and without heat, chewing a piece of sugar-cane the while.

"Friend of all the World," said Mahbub, pushing over the pipe for the boy to clean, "I have met many men, women, and boys, and not a few Sahibs. I have never in all my days met such an imp as thou art."

"And why? When I always tell thee the truth."

"Perhaps the very reason, for this is a world of danger to honest men." Mahbub Ali hauled himself off the ground, girt in his belt, and went over to the horses.

"Or sell it?"

There was that in the tone that made Mahbub halt and turn. "What new devilry?"

"Eight annas, and I will tell," said Kim, grinning. "It touches thy peace."

"O Shaitan!" Mahbub gave the money.

"Rememberest thou the little business of the thieves in the dark, down yonder at Umballa?"

"Seeing they sought my life, I have not altogether forgotten. Why?"

"Rememberest thou the Kashmir Serai?"

"I will twist thy ears in a moment, Sahib."

"No need—Pathan. Only, the second *faquir,* whom the Sahibs beat senseless, was the man who came to search thy bulkhead at Lahore. I saw his face as they helped him on the engine. The very same man."

"Why didst thou not tell before?"

"Oh, he will go to jail, and be safe for some years. There is no need to tell more than is necessary at any one time. Besides, I did not then need money for sweetmeats."

"Allah kerim!" said Mahbub Ali. "Wilt thou some day sell my head for a few sweetmeats if the fit takes thee?"

Kim will remember till he dies that long, lazy journey from Umballa, through Kalka and the Pinjore Gardens near by, up to Simla. A sudden spate in the Gugger River swept down one horse (the most valuable, be sure), and nearly drowned Kim among the dancing boulders. Farther up the road the horses were stampeded by a Government elephant, and being in high condition of grass food, it cost a day and a half to get them together again. Then they met Sikandar Khan coming down with a few unsaleable screws,—remnants of his string,—and Mahbub, who has more of horse-coping in his little finger-nail than Sikandar Khan in all his tents, must needs buy two of the worst, and that meant eight hours' laborious diplomacy and untold tobacco. But it was all pure delight—the wandering road, climbing, dipping, and sweeping about the growing spurs; the flush of the morning laid along the distant snows; the branched cacti, tier upon tier on the stony hillsides; the voices of a thousand water-channels; the chatter of the monkeys; the solemn deodars, climbing one after another with down-drooped branches; the vista of the Plains rolled out far beneath them; the incessant twanging of the tonga-horns and the wild rush of the led-horses when a tonga swung round a curve; the halts for prayers (Mahbub was very religious in dry-washings and bellowings when time did not press); the evening conferences by the halting-places, when camels and bullocks chewed solemnly together and the stolid drivers told the news of the Road—all these things lifted Kim's heart to song within him.

"But, when the singing and dancing is done," said Mahbub Ali, "comes the Colonel Sahib's, and that is not so sweet."

"A fair land—a most beautiful land is this of Hind—and the land of the

Five Rivers is fairer than all," Kim half chanted. "Into it I will go again if Mahbub Ali or the Colonel lift hand or foot against me. Once gone, who shall find me? Look, Hajji, is yonder the city of Simla? Allah, what a city!"

"My father's brother, and he was an old man when Mackerson Sahib's well was new at Peshawur, could recall when there were but two houses in it."

He led the horses below the main road into the lower Simla bazar—the crowded rabbit-warren that climbs up from the valley to the Town Hall at an angle of forty-five. A man who knows his way there can defy all the police of India's summer capital; so cunningly does verandah communicate with verandah, alley-way with alley-way, and bolt-hole with bolt-hole. Here live those who minister to the wants of the glad city—jhampanis who pull the pretty ladies' rickshaws by night and gamble till the dawn; grocers, oil-sellers, curio-venders, firewood-dealers, priests, pickpockets, and native employees of the Government: here are discussed by courtesans the things which are supposed to be profoundest secrets of the India Council; and here gather all the sub-sub-agents of half of the native States. Here, too, Mahbub Ali rented a room, much more securely locked than his bulkhead at Lahore, in the house of a Mohammedan cattle-dealer. It was a place of miracles, too, for there went in at twilight a Mohammedan horse-boy, and there came out an hour later a Eurasian lad—the Lucknow girl's dye was of the best—in badly fitting shop-clothes.

"I have spoken with Creighton Sahib," quoth Mahbub Ali, "and a second time has the Hand of Friendship averted the Whip of Calamity. He says that thou hast altogether wasted sixty days upon the Road, and it is too late, therefore, to send thee to any hill-school."

"I have said that my holidays are my own. I do not go to school twice over. That is part of my bond."

"The Colonel Sahib is not yet aware of the contract. Thou art to lodge in Lurgan Sahib's house till it is time to go again to Nucklao."

"I had sooner lodge with thee, Mahbub."

"Thou dost not know the honor. Lurgan Sahib himself asked for thee. Thou wilt go up the hill and along the road atop, and there thou must forget for awhile that thou hast ever seen or spoken to me, Mahbub Ali, who sells horses to Creighton Sahib, whom thou dost not know. Remember this order."

Kim nodded. "Good," said he, "and who is Lurgan Sahib? Nay"—he caught Mahbub's sword-keen glance—"indeed I have never heard his name. Is he by chance"—he lowered his voice—"one of us?"

"What talk is this of *us*, Sahib?" Mahbub Ali returned, in the tone he used toward Europeans. "I am a Pathan; thou art a Sahib and the son of a Sahib. Lurgan Sahib has a shop among the European shops. All Simla knows it. Ask there . . . and, Friend of all the World, he is one to be obeyed to the last wink of his eyelashes. Men say he does magic, but that should not touch thee. Go up the hill and ask. Here begins the Great Game."

Chapter Nine

S'doaks was a son of Yelth the wise–
    Chief of the Raven clan.
Itswoot the Bear had him in care
    To make him a medicine-man.

He was quick and quicker to learn–
    Bold and bolder to dare:
He danced the dread Kloo-Kwallie Dance
    To tickle Itswoot the Bear!

Oregon Legend.

KIM FLUNG HIMSELF whole-heartedly upon the next turn of the wheel. He would be a Sahib again for awhile. In that idea, so soon as he had reached the broad road under Simla Town Hall, he cast about for one to impress. A Hindu child, some ten years old, squatted under a lamp-post.

"Where is Mr. Lurgan's house?" demanded Kim.

"I do not understand English," was the answer, and Kim shifted his speech accordingly.

"I will show."

Together they set off through the mysterious dusk, full of the noises of a city below the hillside, and the breath of a cool wind in deodar-crowned Jakko, shouldering the stars. The house-lights, scattered on every level, made, as it were, a double firmament. Some were fixed, others belonged to the rickshaws of careless, open-spoken English folk, going out to dinner.

"It is here," said Kim's guide, and halted in a verandah flush with the main road. No door stayed them, but a curtain of beaded reeds that split up the lamp-light beyond.

"He is come," said the boy, in a voice little louder than a sigh, and vanished. Kim felt sure that the boy had been posted to guide him from the first, but putting a bold face on it, parted the curtain. A black-bearded man, with a green shade over his eyes, sat at a table, and, one by one, with short, white hands, picked up globules of light from a tray before him, threaded them on a glancing silken string, and hummed to himself the while. Kim was conscious that beyond the circle of light the room was full of things that smelt like the temples of all the East. A whiff of musk, a puff of sandal-wood, and a breath of sickly jessamine-oil caught his opened nostrils.

"I am here," said Kim at last, speaking in the vernacular: the smells made him forget that he was to be a Sahib.

"Seventy-nine, eighty, eighty-one," the man counted to himself, stringing pearl after pearl so quickly that Kim could scarcely follow his fingers. He slid off the green shade and looked fixedly at Kim for a full half-minute. The pupils of the eye dilated and closed to pin-pricks, as if at will. There was a *faquir* by the Taksali Gate who had just this gift and made money by it, especially when cursing silly women. Kim stared with interest. His disreputable friend could further twitch his ears, almost like a goat, and Kim was disappointed that this new man could not imitate him.

"Do not be afraid," said Mr. Lurgan suddenly.

"Why should I fear?"

"Thou wilt sleep here to-night, and stay with me till it is time to go again to Nucklao. It is an order."

"It is an order," Kim repeated. "But where shall I sleep?"

"Here, in this room." Lurgan Sahib waved his hand towards the darkness behind him.

"So be it," said Kim composedly. "Now?"

He nodded and held the lamp above his head. As the light swept them, there leaped out from the walls a collection of Tibetan devil-dance masks, hanging above the fiend-embroidered draperies of those ghastly functions—horned masks, scowling masks, and masks of idiotic terror. In a corner, a Japanese warrior, mailed and plumed, menaced him with a halberd, and a score of lances and *khandas* and *kuttars* gave back the unsteady gleam. But what interested Kim more than all these things—he had seen devil-dance masks at the Lahore Museum—was a glimpse of the soft-eyed Hindu child who had left him in the doorway, sitting cross-legged under the table of pearls with a little smile on his scarlet lips.

"I think that Lurgan Sahib wished to make me afraid. And I am sure that the devil's brat below the table wishes to see me afraid. This place," he said aloud, "is like a Wonder House. Where is my bed?"

Lurgan Sahib pointed to a native quilt in a corner by the loathsome masks, picked up the lamp, and left the room black.

"Was that Lurgan Sahib?" Kim asked as he cuddled down. No answer. He could hear the Hindu boy breathing, however, and, guided by the sound, crawled across the floor, and cuffed into the darkness, crying: "Give answer, devil! Is this the way to lie to a Sahib?"

From the darkness he fancied he could hear the echo of a chuckle. It could not be his soft-fleshed companion, because he was weeping. So Kim lifted up his voice and called aloud: "Lurgan Sahib! O Lurgan Sahib! Is it an order that thy servant does not speak to me?"

"It is an order." The voice came from behind him, and he started.

"Very good. But remember," he muttered, as he resought the quilt, "I will beat thee in the morning. I do not love Hindus."

That was no cheerful night; the room being overfull of voices and music. Kim was waked twice by some one calling his name. The second time he set out in search, and ended by bruising his nose against a box that certainly spoke with a human tongue, but in no sort of human accent. It seemed to end in a tin trumpet and to be joined by wires to a smaller box on the floor—so far, at least, as he could judge by touch. And the voice, very hard and whirring, came out of the trumpet. Kim rubbed his nose and grew furious, thinking, as usual, in Hindu.

"This with a beggar from the bazar might be good, but—I am a Sahib and the son of a Sahib and, which is twice as much more beside, a student of Nucklao. Yess" (here he turned to English), "a boy of St. Xavier's. Damn Mr. Lurgan's eyes!—It is some sort of machinery like a sewing-machine. Oh, it is a *great* cheek of him—we are not frightened that way at Lucknow—Now!" Then in Hindi: "But what does *he* gain? He is only a trader—I am in his shop. But Creighton Sahib is a Colonel—and I think Creighton Sahib gave orders that it should be done. *How* I will beat that Hindu in the morning! What is this?"

The trumpet-box was pouring out a string of the most elaborate abuse that even Kim had ever heard, in a high uninterested voice, that for a moment lifted the short hairs of his neck. When the vile thing drew breath, Kim was reassured by the soft, sewing-machine-like whirr.

"Chûp!" (be still) he cried, and again he heard a chuckle and something lifted with a click. He had evidently raised a lid. If there was a devil inside,

now was its time for–he sniffed–thus did the sewing-machines of the bazar smell. He would clean the *shaitan.* He slipped off his jacket, and plunged it into the box's mouth. Something long and round bent under the pressure, there was a whirr and the voice stopped–as voices must if you ram a thrice-doubled coat on to the wax cylinder and into the works of an expensive phonograph. Kim finished his slumbers with a serene mind.

In the morning he was aware of Lurgan Sahib looking down on him.

"Oah!" said Kim, firmly resolved to cling to his Sahib-dom. "There was a box in the night that gave me bad talk. So I stopped it. Was it your box?"

The man held out his hand.

"Shake hands, O'Hara," he said. "Yes, it was my box. I keep such things because my friends the Rajahs like them. That one is broken, but it was cheap at the price. Yes, my friends the Kings are very fond of toys–and so am I sometimes."

Kim looked him over out of the corners of his eyes. He was a Sahib in that he wore Sahib's clothes; the accent of his Urdu, the intonation of his English, showed that he was anything but a Sahib. He seemed to understand what moved in Kim's mind ere the boy opened his mouth, and he took no pains to explain himself as did Father Victor or the Lucknow masters. Sweetest of all–he treated Kim as an equal on the Asiatic side.

"I am sorry you cannot beat my boy this morning. He says he will kill you with a knife or poison. He is jealous, so I have put him in the corner and I shall not speak to him to-day. He has just tried to kill me. You must help me with the breakfast. He is almost too jealous to trust, just now."

Now a genuine imported Sahib from English would have made a great to-do over this tale. Lurgan Sahib stated it as simply as Mahbub Ali was used to record his little affairs in the North.

The back verandah of the shop was built out over the sheer hillside, and they looked down into their neighbors' chimney-pots, as is the custom of Simla. But even more than the purely Persian meal cooked by Lurgan Sahib with his own hands, the shop fascinated Kim. The Lahore Museum was larger, but here were more wonders–ghost-daggers and prayer-wheels from Tibet; turquoise and raw amber necklaces; green jade bangles; curiously packed incense-sticks in jars crusted over with raw garnets; the devil-masks of overnight and a wall full of peacock-blue draperies; gilt figures of Buddha, and little portable lacquer altars; Russian samovars with turquoises on the lid; eggshell china sets in quaint octagonal cane boxes; yellow ivory crucifixes–from Japan of all places in the world, so Lurgan Sahib said; carpets in dusty bales, smelling atrociously, pushed back behind torn and rotten screens of geometrical work; Persian water-jugs for the hands after meals; dull copper incense-burners, neither Chinese nor Persian, with friezes of fantastic devils running around them; tarnished silver belts that knotted like raw hide; hair-pins of jade, ivory, and plasma; arms of all sorts and kinds, and a thousand other oddments were cased, or piled, or merely thrown into the room, leaving a clear space only round the rickety deal table, where Lurgan Sahib worked.

"Those things are nothing," said his host, following Kim's glance. "I buy them because they are pretty, and sometimes I sell–if I like the buyer's look. My work is on the table–some of it."

It blazed in the morning light–all red and blue and green flashes, picked out with the vicious blue-white spurt of a diamond here and there. Kim opened his eyes.

"Oh, they are quite well, those stones. It will not hurt them to take the sun. Besides, they are cheap. But with sick stones it is very different." He piled Kim's plate anew. "There is no one but *me* can doctor a sick pearl and re-blue turquoises. I grant you opals–any fool can cure an opal–but for a sick pearl there is only me. Suppose I were to die! Then there would be no one. . . . Oh no! *You* cannot do anything with jewels. It will be quite enough if you understand a little about the Turquoise–some day."

He moved to the end of the verandah to refill the heavy, porous clay water-jug from the filter.

"Do you want drink?"

Kim nodded. Lurgan Sahib, fifteen feet off, laid one hand on the jar. Next instant, it stood at Kim's elbow, full to within half an inch of the brim–the white cloth only showing, by a small wrinkle, where it had slid into place.

"Wah!" said Kim in most utter amazement. "That is magic." Lurgan Sahib's smile showed that the compliment had gone home.

"Throw it back."

"It will break."

"I say, throw it back."

Kim pitched it at random. It fell short and crashed into fifty pieces, while the water dripped through the rough verandah boarding.

"I said it would break."

"All one. Look at it. Look at the largest piece."

That lay with a sparkle of water in its curve, as it were a star on the floor. Kim looked intently; Lurgan Sahib laid one hand gently on the nape of his neck, stroked it twice or thrice, and whispered: "Look! It shall come to life again, piece by piece. First the big piece shall join itself to two others on the right and the left–on the right and the left. Look!"

To save his life, Kim could not have turned his head. The light touch held him as in a vice, and his blood tingled pleasantly through him. There was one large piece of the jar where there had been three, and above them the shadowy outline of the entire vessel. He could see the verandah through it, but it was thickening and darkening with each beat of his pulse. Yet the jar–how slowly the thoughts came!–the jar had been smashed before his eyes. Another wave of prickling fire raced down his neck, as Lurgan Sahib moved his hand.

"Look! It is coming into shape," said Lurgan Sahib.

So far Kim had been thinking in Hindi, but a tremor came on him, and with an effort like that of a swimmer before sharks, who hurls himself half out of the water, his mind leaped up from a darkness that was swallowing it and took refuge in–the multiplication-table in English!

"Look! It is coming into shape," whispered Lurgan Sahib.

The jar had been smashed–yes, smashed–not the native word, he would not think of that–but smashed–into fifty pieces, and twice three was six, and thrice three was nine, and four times three was twelve. He clung desperately to the repetition. The shadow-outline of the jar cleared like a mist after rubbing eyes. There were the broken shards; there was the spilt water drying in the sun, and through the cracks of the verandah showed, all ribbed, the white house-wall below–and thrice twelve was thirty-six!

"Look! Is it coming into shape?" asked Lurgan Sahib.

"But it *is* smashed–smashed," he gasped–Lurgan Sahib had been muttering softly for the last half-minute. Kim wrenched his head aside. "Look! *Dekho!* It is there as it was there."

"It is there as it was there," said Lurgan, watching Kim closely while the boy rubbed his neck. "But you are the first of many who have ever seen it so." He wiped his broad forehead.

"Was that more magic?" Kim asked suspiciously. The tingle had gone from his veins; he felt unusually wide awake.

"No, that was not magic. It was only to see if there was–a flaw in a jewel. Sometimes very fine jewels will fly all to pieces if a man holds them in his hands, and knows the proper way. That is why one must be careful before one sets them. Tell me, did you see the shape of the pot?"

"For a little time. It began to grow like a flower from the ground."

"And then what did you do? I mean, how did you think?"

"Oah! I knew it was broken, and so, I think, that was what I thought–and it *was* broken."

"Hm! Has any one ever done that sort of magic to you before?"

"If it was," said Kim, "do you think I should let it again? I should run away."

"And now you are not afraid–eh?"

"Not now."

Lurgan Sahib looked at him more closely than ever. "I shall ask Mahbub Ali–not now, but some day later," he muttered. "I am pleased with you–yes; and I am pleased with you–no. You are the first that ever saved himself. I wish I knew what it was that . . . But you are right. You should not tell that–not even to me."

He turned into the dusky gloom of the shop, and sat down at the table, rubbing his hands softly. A small, husky sob came from behind a pile of carpets. It was the Hindu child obediently facing towards the wall: his thin shoulders worked with grief.

"Ah! He is jealous, so jealous. I wonder if he will try to poison me again in my breakfast, and make me cook it twice."

"Kubbee–kubbee nahin," came the broken answer.

"And whether he will kill this other boy?"

"Kubbee–kubbee nahin" (never–never. No!).

"What do *you* think he will do?" He turned suddenly on Kim.

"Oah! I do not know. Let him go, perhaps. Why did he want to poison you?"

"Because he is so fond of me. Suppose you were fond of some one, and you saw some one come, and the man you were fond of was more pleased with him than he was with you, what would you do?"

Kim thought. Lurgan repeated the sentence slowly in the vernacular.

"I should not poison that man," said Kim reflectively, "but I should beat that boy–*if* that boy was fond of my man. But first I would ask that boy if it were true."

"Ah! He thinks everyone must be fond of me."

"Then I think he is a fool."

"Hearest thou?" said Lurgan Sahib to the shaking shoulders. "The Sahib's son thinks thou art a fool. Come out, and next time thy heart is troubled, do not try white arsenic quite so openly. Surely the Devil Dasim was lord of our table-cloth that day! It might have made me ill, child, and then a stranger would have guarded the jewels. Come!"

The child, heavy-eyed with much weeping, crept out from behind the bale and flung himself passionately at Lurgan Sahib's feet, with an extravagance of remorse that impressed even Kim.

"I will look into the ink-pools–I will faithfully guard the jewels! Oh, my father and my mother, send *him* away!" He indicated Kim with a backward jerk of his bare heel.

"Not yet–not yet. In a little while he will go away again. But now he is at school–at a new *madrissah*–and thou shalt be his teacher. Play the Play of the Jewels against him. I will keep tally."

The child dried his tears at once, and dashed to the back of the shop, whence he returned with a copper tray.

"Give me!" he said to Lurgan Sahib. "Let them come from thy hand, for he may say that I knew them before."

"Gently–gently," the man replied, and from a drawer under the table dealt a half handful of clattering trifles into the tray.

"Now," said the child, waving an old newspaper. "Look on them as long as thou wilt, stranger. Count and, if need be, handle. One look is enough for *me.*" He turned his back proudly.

"But what is the game?"

"When thou hast counted and handled and art sure that thou canst remember tham all, I cover them with this paper, and thou must tell over the tally to Lurgan Sahib. *I* will write mine."

"Oah!" The instinct of competition waked in his breast. He bent over the tray. There were but fifteen stones on it. "That is easy," he said after a minute. The child slipped the paper over the winking jewels and scribbled in a native account-book.

"There are under that paper five blue stones–one big, one smaller, and three small," said Kim, all in haste. "There are four green stones, and one with a hole in it; there is one yellow stone that I can see through, and one like a pipe-stem. There are two red stones, and–and–I made the count fifteen, but two I have forgotten. No! Give me time. One was of ivory, little and brownish; and–and–give me time . . ."

"One–two"–Lurgan Sahib counted him out up to ten. Kim shook his head.

"Hear my count!" the child burst in, trilling with laughter. "First, are two flawed sapphires–one of two ruttees and one of four as I should judge. The four-ruttee sapphire is chipped at the edge. There is one Turkestan turquoise, plain with black veins, and there are two inscribed–one with a Name of God in gilt, and the other being cracked across, for it came out of an old ring, I cannot read. We have now all five blue stones. Four flawed emeralds there are, but one is drilled in two places, and one is a little carven–"

"Their weights?" said Lurgan Sahib impassively.

"Three–five–five–and four ruttees as I judged it. There is one piece of old greenish pipe amber, and a cut topaz from Europe. There is one ruby of Burma, of two ruttees, without a flaw, and there is a balas-ruby, flawed, of two ruttees. There is a carved ivory from China representing a rat sucking an egg; and there is last–ah ha!–a ball of crystal as big as a bean set in a gold leaf."

He clapped his hands at the close.

"He is thy master," said Lurgan Sahib, smiling.

"Huh! He knew the names of the stones," said Kim flushing. "Try again! With common things such as he and I both know."

They heaped the tray again with odds and ends gathered from the shop, and even the kitchen, and every time the child won, till Kim marvelled. "Bind my eyes–let me feel once with my fingers, and even *then* I will leave thee open-eyed behind," he challenged.

Kim stamped with vexation when the lad made his boast good. "If it were men–or horses," he said, "I could do better. This playing with tweezers and knives and scissors is too little."

"Learn first–teach later," said Lurgan Sahib. "Is he thy master?"

"Truly. But how is it done?"

"By doing it many times over till it is done perfectly–for it is worth doing."

The Hindu boy, in highest feather, actually patted Kim on the back.

"Do not despair," he said. "I myself will teach thee."

"And I will see that thou art well taught," said Lurgan Sahib, still speaking in the vernacular, "for except my boy here–it was foolish of him to buy so much white arsenic when, if he had asked, I could have given it–except my boy here I have not in a long time met with one better worth teaching. And there are ten days more ere thou canst return to Nucklao, where they teach nothing–at the long price. We shall, I think, be friends."

They were a most mad ten days, but Kim enjoyed himself too much to reflect on their craziness. In the morning they played the Jewel Game—sometimes with veritable stones, sometimes with piles of swords and daggers, sometimes with photographs of natives. Through the afternoons he and the Hindu boy would mount guard in the shop, sitting dumb behind a carpet-bale or a screen and watching Mr. Lurgan's many and very curious visitors. There were small Rajahs, escorts coughing in the verandah, who came to buy curiosities—such as phonographs and mechanical toys. There were ladies in search of necklaces, and men, it seemed to Kim—but his mind may have been vitiated by early training—in search of the ladies; natives from independent and feudatory courts whose ostensible business was the repair of broken necklaces—rivers of light poured out upon the table—but whose true end seemed to be to raise money for angry Maharanees or young Rajahs. There were Babus to whom Lurgan Sahib talked with austerity and authority, but at the end of each interview he gave them money in coined silver and currency notes. There were occasional gatherings of long-coated theatrical natives who discussed metaphysics in English and Bengali, to Mr. Lurgan's great edification. He was always interested in religion. At the end of the day, Kim and the Hindu boy—whose name varied at Lurgan's pleasure—were expected to give a detailed account of all they had seen and heard—their view of each man's character, as shown in his face, talk, and manner, and their notions of his real errand. After dinner, Lurgan Sahib's fancy turned more to what might be called dressing-up, in which game he took a most informing interest. He could paint faces to a marvel; with a brush-dab here and a line there changing them past recognition. The shop was full of all manner of dresses and turbans, and Kim was apparelled variously as a young Mohammedan of good family, an oilman, and once—which was a joyous evening—as the son of an Oudh landholder in the fullest of full dress. Lurgan Sahib had a hawk's eye to detect the least flaw in the make-up; and lying on a worn teak-wood couch, would explain by the half-hour together how such and such a caste talked, or walked, or coughed, or spat, or sneezed, and, since "hows" matter in this world, the "why" of everything. The Hindu child played this game clumsily. That little mind, keen as an icicle where tally of jewels was concerned, could not temper itself to enter another's soul; but a demon in Kim woke up and sang with joy as he put on the changing dresses, and changed speech and gesture therewith.

Carried away by enthusiasm, he volunteered to show Lurgan Sahib one evening how the disciples of a certain caste of *faquir,* old Lahore acquaintances, begged doles by the roadside; and what sort of language he would use to an Englishman, to a Punjabi farmer going to a fair, and to a woman without a veil. Lurgan Sahib laughed immensely, and begged Kim to stay as he was, immobile for half an hour—cross-legged, ash-smeared, and wild-eyed, in the back room. At the end of that time entered hulking, obese Babu whose stockinged legs shook with fat, and Kim opened on him with a shower of wayside charm. Lurgan Sahib—this annoyed Kim—watched the Babu and not the play.

"I think," said the Babu heavily, lighting a cigarette, "I am of opeenion that it is most extraordinary and effeecient performance. Except that you had told me I should have opined that—that—that you were pulling my legs. How soon can he become approximately effeecient chain-man? Because *then* I shall indent for him."

"That is what he must learn at Lucknow."

"Then order him to be jolly dam-quick. Good-night, Lurgan." The Babu swung out with the gait of a bogged cow.

When they were telling over the day's list of visitors, Lurgan Sahib asked Kim who he thought the man might be.

"God knows!" said Kim cheerily. The tone might almost have deceived

Mahbub Ali, but it failed entirely with the healer of sick pearls.

"That is true. God He knows; but I wish to know what you think."

Kim glanced sideways at his companion, whose eye had a way of compelling truth. "I—I think he will want me when I come from the school, but"—confidentially, as Lurgan Sahib nodded approval—"I do not understand how *he* can wear many dresses and talk many tongues."

"Thou wilt understand many things later. He is a writer of tales for a certain Colonel. His honor is great only in Simla, and it is noticeable that he has no name, but only a number and a letter—that is a custom among us."

"And is there a price upon his head too—as upon Mah—all the others."

"Not yet; but if a boy rose up who is now sitting here and went—look, the door is open!—as far as a certain house with a red-painted verandah, behind that which was the old theatre in the Lower Bazar, and whispered through the shutters: 'Hurree Chunder Mookerjee bore the bad news of last month,' that boy might take away a belt full of rupees."

"How many?" said Kim promptly.

"Five hundred—a thousand—as many as he might ask for."

"Good. And how long might such a boy live after the news was told?" He smiled merrily at Lurgan Sahib's very beard.

"Ah! That is to be well thought of. Perhaps if he were very clever, he might live out the day—but not the night. By no means the night."

"Then what is the Babu's pay if so much is put upon his head?"

"Eighty—perhaps a hundred—perhaps a hundred and fifty rupees; but the pay is the least part of the work. From time to time, God causes men to be born—and thou art one of them—who have a lust to go abroad at the risk of their lives and discover news—to-day it may be of far-off things, to-morrow of some hidden mountain, and the next day of some near-by men who have done a foolishness against the State. These souls are very few; and of these few, not more then ten are of the best. Among these ten I count the Babu, and that is curious. How great therefore and desirable must be a business that brazens the heart of a Bengali!"

"True. But the days go slowly for me. I am yet a boy, and it is only within two months I learned to write Angrezi. Even now I cannot read it well. And there are yet years and years and long years before I can be even a chain-man."

"Have patience, Friend of all the World"—Kim started at the title. "Would I had a few of the years that so irk thee. I have proved thee in several small ways. This will not be forgotten when I make my report to the Colonel Sahib." Then, changing suddenly into English with a deep laugh:—

"By Jove! O'Hara, I think there is a great deal in you; but you must not be proud and you must not talk. You must go back to Lucknow and be a good little boy and mind your book, as the English say, and perhaps next holidays, if you care you can come back to me!" Kim's face fell. "Oh, I mean *if* you like. I know where you want to go."

Four days later a seat was booked for Kim and his small trunk at the rear of a Kalka tonga. His companion was the whale-like Babu, who, with a fringed shawl wrapped round his head, and his fat open-work-stockinged left leg tucked under him, shivered and grunted in the morning chill.

"How comes it that this man is one of *us?*" thought Kim, considering the jelly-back as they jolted down the road; and the reflection threw him into the most pleasant day-dreams. Lurgan Sahib had given him five rupees—a splendid sum—as well as the assurance of his protection if he worked. Unlike Mahbub, Lurgan Sahib had spoken most explicitly of the reward that would follow obedience, and Kim was content. If only, like the Babu, he could enjoy the dignity of a letter and a number—and a price upon his head! Some day he would be all that and more. Some day he might be almost as great as

Mahbub Ali! The housetops of his search should be half India; he would follow Kings and ministers, as in the old days he had followed *vakils* and lawyers' touts across Lahore city for Mahbub Ali's sake. Meantime, there was the present, and not at all unpleasant, fact of St. Xavier's immediately before him. There would be new boys to condescend to, and there would be tales of holiday adventures to hear. Young Martin, son of the tea-planter at Manipur, had boasted that he would go to war, with a rifle, against the head-hunters. That might be, but it was certain young Martin had not been blown half across the forecourt of a Patiala palace by an explosion of fireworks; nor had he . . . Kim fell to telling himself the story of his own adventures through the last three months. He could paralyse St. Xavier's—even the biggest boys who shaved—with the recital, were that permitted. But it was, of course, out of the question. There would be a price upon his head in good time, as Lurgan Sahib had assured him; and if he talked foolishly now, not only would that price never be set, but Colonel Creighton would cast him off—and he would be left to the wrath of Lurgan Sahib and Mahbub Ali—for the short space of life that would remain to him.

"So I should lose Delhi for the sake of a fish," was his proverbial philosophy. It behooved him to forget his holidays (there would always remain the fun of inventing imaginary adventures), and, as Lurgan Sahib had said, to work.

Of all the boys hurrying back to St. Xavier's, from Sukkur in the sands to Galle beneath the palms, none was so filled with virtue as Kimball O'Hara, jigetting down to Umballa behind Hurree Chunder Mookerjee, whose name on the books of one section of the Ethnological Survey was R.17.

And if additional spur were needed, the Babu supplied it. After a huge meal at Kalka, he spoke uninterruptedly. Was Kim going to school? Then he, an M.A. of Calcutta University, would explain the advantages of education. There were marks to be gained by due attention to Latin and Wordsworth's *Excursion* (all this was Greek to Kim). French, too, was vital, and the best was to be picked up in Chandernagore, a few miles from Calcutta. Also a man might go far, as he himself had done, by strict attention to plays called *Lear* and *Julius Caesar,* both much in demand by examiners. *Lear* was not so full of historical allusions as *Julius Caesar;* The book cost four annas, but could be bought second-hand in Bow Bazar for two. Still more important than Wordsworth, or the eminent authors Burke and Hare, was the art and science of mensuration. A boy who had passed his examination in these branches—for which, by the way, there were no cram-books—could, by merely marching over a country with a compass and a level and a straight eye, carry away a picture of that country which might be sold for large sums in coined silver. But as it was occasionally inexpedient to carry about measuring-chains, a boy would do well to know the precise length of his own foot-pace, so that when he was deprived of what Hurree Chunder called "adventitious aids" he might still tread his distances. To keep count of thousands of paces, Hurree Chunder's experience had shown him nothing more valuable than a rosary of eighty-one or a hundred and eight beads, for "it was divisible and subdivisible into many multiples and sub-multiples." Through the volleying drifts of English, Kim caught the general trend of the talk, and it interested him very much. Here was a new craft that a man could tuck away in his head; and by the look of the large wide world unfolding itself before him, it seemed that the more a man knew the better for him.

Said the Babu when he had talked for an hour and a half, "I hope some day to enjoy your offeecial acquaintance. *Ad interim,* if I may be pardoned that expression, I shall give you this betel-box, which is highly valuable article and cost me two rupees only four years ago." It was a cheap, heart-shaped brass thing with three compartments for carrying the eternal betel-nut, lime, and *pan*-leaf; but it was filled with little tabloid-bottles. "That is reward of merit for your performance in character of that holy man. You see, you are so young you think you will last for ever and not take care of your body. It is great nuisance to go sick in the middle of business. I am fond of drugs myself, and they are handy to cure poor people too. These are good departmental drugs—quinine and so on. I give it you for souvenir. Now good-bye. I have urgent private business here by the roadside."

He slipped out noiselessly as a cat, on the Umballa road, hailed a passing ekka and jingled away, while Kim, tongue-tied, twiddled the brass betel-box in his hands.

The record of a boy's education interests few save his parents, and, as you know, Kim was an orphan. It is written in the books of St. Xavier in Partibus that a report of Kim's progress was forwarded at the end of each term to Colonel Creighton and to Father Victor, from whose hands duly came the money for his schooling. It is further recorded in the same books that he showed a great aptitude for mathematical studies as well as map-making, and carried away a prize *(The Life of Lord Lawrence,* tree-calf, two vols., nine rupees eight annas) for proficiency therein; and the same term played in St. Xavier's eleven against the Allyghur Mohammedan College, his age being fourteen years and ten months. He was also re-vaccinated (from which we may assume that there had been another epidemic of small-pox at Lucknow) about the same time. Pencil notes on the edge of an old muster-roll record that he was punished several times for "conversing with improper persons," and it seems that he was once sentenced to heavy pains for "absenting himself for a day in the company of a street beggar." That was when he got over the gate and pleaded with the lama through a whole day down the banks of the Goomtee to accompany him on the road next holidays—for one month—for a little week; and the lama set his face as a flint against it, averring that the time had not yet come. Kim's business, said the old man as they ate cakes together, was to get all the wisdom of the Sahibs and then he would see. The hand of friendship must in some way have averted the whip of calamity, for six weeks later Kim seems to have passed an examination in elementary surveying "with great credit," his age being fifteen years and eight months. From this date the record is silent. His name does not appear in the year's batch of those who entered for the subordinate Survey of India, but against it stands the words "removed on appointment."

Several times in those three years, cast up at the Temple of the Tirthankers in Benares the lama, a little thinner and a shade yellower, if that were possible, but gentle and untainted as ever. Sometimes it was from the South that he came—from south of Tuticorin, whence the wonderful fire-boats go to Ceylon where are priests who know Pali; sometimes it was from the wet green West and the thousand cotton-factory chimneys that ring Bombay; and once from the North, where he had doubled back eight hundred miles to talk a day with the Keeper of the Images in the Wonder House. He would stride to his cell in the cool, cut marble—the priests of the temple were good to the old man—wash off the dust of travel, make prayer, and depart for Lucknow, well accustomed now to the ways of the rail, in a third-class carriage. Returning, it was noticeable, as his friend the Seeker pointed out to the head-priest, that he ceased for awhile to mourn the loss of his River, or to draw wondrous pictures of the Wheel of Life, but preferred to talk of the beauty and wisdom of a certain mysterious *chela* whom no man of the temple had ever seen. Yes, he had followed the traces of the Blessed Feet throughout all India. (The curator has still in his possession a most marvellous account of his wanderings and meditations.) There remained nothing more in life but to find the River of the Arrow. Yet it was shown to him in dreams that it was a matter not to be undertaken with any hope of success unless that seeker had with him the one *chela* appointed to bring the event to a happy issue, and versed in great wisdom–such wisdom as white-haired Keepers of Images possess. For example (here came out the snuff-gourd, and the kindly Jain priests made haste to be silent):–

"Long and long ago, when Devadatta was King of Benares–let all listen to the *Jâtaka!*–an elephant was captured for a time by the King's hunters and, ere he broke free, beringed with a grievous leg-iron. This he strove to remove with hate and frenzy in his heart, and hurrying up and down the forests, besought his brother-elephants to wrench it asunder. One by one, with their strong trunks, they tried and failed. At the last they gave it as their opinion that the ring was not to be broken by any bestial power. And in a thicket, new-born, wet with the moisture of birth, lay a day-old calf of the herd whose mother had died. The fettered elephant, forgetting his own agony, said: 'If I do not help this suckling it will perish under our feet.' So he stood above the young thing, making his legs buttresses against the uneasily moving herd; and he begged milk of a virtuous cow, and the calf throve, and the ringed elephant was the calf's guide and defence. Now the days of an elephant–let all listen to the *Jâtaka!*–are thirty-five years to his full strength, and through thirty-five Rains the ringed elephant befriended the younger, and all the while the fetter ate into the flesh.

"Then one day the young elephant saw the half-buried iron, and turning to the elder said: 'What is this?' 'It is even my sorrow,' said he who had befriended him. Then that other put out his trunk and in the twinkling of an eyelash abolished the ring, saying: 'The appointed time has come.' So the virtuous elephant who had waited temperately and done kind acts was relieved, at the appointed time, by the very calf whom he had turned aside to cherish–let all listen to the *Jâtaka!*–for the Elephant was Ananda, and the Calf that broke the ring was none other than The Lord Himself. . . ."

Then he would shake his head benignly, and over the ever-clicking rosary point out how free that elephant calf was from the sin of pride. He was as humble as a *chela* who, seeing his master sitting in the dust outside the Gates of Learning, overleapt the gates (though they were locked) and took his master to his heart in the presence of the proud-stomached city. Rich would be the reward of such a master and such a *chela* when the time came for them to seek freedom together!

So did the lama speak, coming and going across India as softly as a bat. A sharp-tongued old woman in a house among the fruit-trees behind Saharunpore honored him as the woman honored the prophet, but his chamber was by no means upon the wall. In an apartment of the forecourt overlooked by cooing doves he would sit, while she laid aside her useless veil and chattered of spirits and fiends of Kulu, of grandchildren unborn, and of the free-tongued brat who had talked to her in the resting-place. Once, too, he strayed alone from the Grand Trunk Road below Umballa to the very village whose priest had tried to drug him; but the kind heaven that guards lamas sent him at twilight through the crops, absorbed and unsuspicious, to the ressaldar's door. Here was like to have been a grave misunderstanding, for the old soldier asked him why the Friend of the Stars had gone that way only six days before.

"That may not be," said the lama. "He has gone back to his own people."

"He sat in that corner telling a hundred merry tales five nights ago," his host insisted. "True, he vanished somewhat suddenly in the dawn after foolish talk with my granddaughter. He grows apace, but he is the same Friend of the Stars as brought me true word of the war. Have ye parted?"

"Yes–and No," the lama replied. "We–we have not altogether parted, but the time is not ripe that we should take the Road together. He acquires wisdom in another place. We must wait."

"All one—but if it were not the boy how did he come to speak so continually of thee?"

"And what said he?" asked the lama eagerly.

"Sweet words—an hundred thousand—that thou art his father and mother and such all. Pity that he does not take the Queen's service. He is fearless."

This news amazed the lama, who did not then know how religously Kim kept to the contract made with Mahbub Ali, and perforce ratified by Colonel Creighton. . . .

"There is no holding the young pony from the Game," said the horse-dealer when the Colonel pointed out that vagabonding over India in holiday-time was absurd. "If permission be refused to go and come as he chooses, he will make light of the refusal. Then who is to catch him? Colonel Sahib, only once in a thousand years is a horse born so well fitted for the Game as this our colt. And we need men."

Chapter Ten

Your tiercel's too long at hack, Sire. He's no eyass
But a passage-hawk that footed ere we caught him,
Dangerously free o' the air. Faith! were he mine
(As mine's the glove he binds to for his tirings)
I'd fly him with a make-hawk. He's in yarak
Plumed to the very point—so manned so weathered . . .
Give him the firmament God made him for,
And what shall take the air of him?

Old Play.

LURGAN SAHIB DID not use as direct speech, but his advice tallied with Mahbub's; and the upshot was good for Kim. He knew better now than to leave Lucknow city in native garb, and if Mahbub were anywhere within reach of a letter, it was to Mahbub's camp he headed, and made his change under the Pathan's wary eye. Could the little Survey paint-box that he used for map-tinting in term-time have found a tongue to tell of holiday doings, he might have been expelled. Once Mahbub and he went together as far as the beautiful city of Bombay, with three truck-loads of tram-horses, and Mahbub nearly melted when Kim proposed a sail in a dhow across the Indian Ocean to buy Gulf Arabs, which he understood, from a hanger-on of the dealer Abdul Rahman, fetched better prices than mere Cabulis.

He dipped his hand into the dish with that great trader when Mahbub and a few co-religionists were invited to a big Haj dinner. They came back by way of Karachi by sea, when Kim took his first experience of sea-sickness sitting on the fore-hatch of a coasting-steamer, well persuaded he had been poisoned. The Babu's famous drug-box proved useless, though Kim had restocked it at Bombay. Mahbub had business at Quetta, and there Kim, as Mahbub admitted, earned his keep, and perhaps a little over, by spending four curious days as scullion in the house of a fat Commissariat sergeant, from whose office-box, in an auspicious moment, he removed a little vellum ledger which he copied out—it seemed to deal entirely with cattle and camel sales—by moonlight, he returned the ledger to its place, and, at Mahbub's word, left that service unpaid, rejoining him six miles down the road, the clean copy in his bosom.

"That soldier is a small fish," Mahbub Ali explained, "but in time we shall catch the larger one. He only sells oxen at two prices–one for himself and one for the Government–which I do not think is a sin."

"Why could not I take away the little book and be done with it?"

"Then he would have been frightened, and he would have told his master. Then we should miss, perhaps, a great number of new rifles which seek their way up from Quetta to the North. The Game is so large that one sees but a little at a time."

"Oho!" said Kim, and held his tongue. That was in the monsoon holidays, after he had taken the prize for mathematics. The Christmas holidays he spent–deducting ten days for private amusements–with Lurgan Sahib, where he sat for the most part in front of a roaring wood-fire–Jakko-road was four feet deep in snow that year–and–the small Hindu had gone away to be married–helped Lurgan to thread pearls. He made Kim learn whole chapters of the Koran by heart, till he could deliver them with the very roll and cadence of a mullah. Moreover, he told Kim the names and properties of many native drugs, as well as the runes proper to recite when you administer them. And in the evenings he wrote charms on parchment–elaborate pentagrams crowned with the names of devils–Murra, and Awan the Companion of Kings–all fantastically written in the corners. More to the point, he advised Kim as to the care of his own body, the cure of fever-fits, and simple remedies of the Road. A week before it was time to go down, Colonel Creighton Sahib–this was unfair–sent Kim a written examination-paper that concerned itself solely with rods and chains and links and angles.

Next holidays he was out with Mahbub, and here, by the way, he nearly died of thirst, plodding through the sand on a camel to the mysterious city of Bikaneer, where the wells are four hundred feet deep, and lined throughout with camel-bone. It was not an amusing trip from Kim's point of view, because–in defiance of the contract–the Colonel ordered him to make a map of that wild, walled city; and since Mohammedan horse-boys and pipe-tenders are not expected to drag Survey-chains round the capital of an independent native State, Kim was forced to pace all his distances by means of a bead rosary. He used the compass for bearings as occasion served–after dark chiefly, when the camels had been fed–and by the help of his little Survey paint-box of six color-cakes and three brushes, he achieved something not remotely unlike the city of Jeysalmir. Mahbub laughed a great deal, and advised him to make up a written report as well; and in the back of the big account-book that lay under the flap of Mahbub's pet saddle Kim fell to work.

"It must hold everything that thou hast seen or touched or considered. Write as though the Jang-i-Lat Sahib himself had come by stealth with a vast army outsetting to war."

"How great an army?"

"Oh, half a lakh of men."

"Folly! Remember how few and bad were the wells in the sand. Not a thousand thirsty men could come near by here."

"Then write that down–also all the old breaches in the walls–and when the firewood is cut–and what is the temper and disposition of the King. I stay here till all my horses are sold. I will hire a room by the gateway, and thou shalt be my accountant. There is a good lock to the door."

The report in its unmistakable St. Xavier's running script, and the brown, yellow, and lake-daubed map, was on hand a few years ago (a careless clerk filed it with the rough notes of E.23's second seistan survey), but by now the pencil characters must be almost illegible. Kim translated it, sweating under the light of an oil-lamp, to Mahbub, the second day of their return journey. The Pathan rose and stooped over his dappled saddle-bags.

"I knew it would be worthy a dress of honor, and so I made one ready," he said smiling. "Were I Amir of Afghanistan (and some day we may see him), I would fill thy mouth with gold." He laid the garments formally at Kim's feet. There was a gold-embroidered Peshawur turban-cap, rising to a cone, and a big turban-cloth ending in a broad fringe of gold. There was a Delhi embroidered waistcoat to slip over a milky-white shirt, fastening to the right, ample and flowing; green pyjamas with twisted silk waist-string; and that nothing might be lacking, russia-leather slippers, smelling divinely, with arrogantly curled lips.

"Upon a Wednesday, and in the morning, to put on new clothes is auspicious," said Mahbub solemnly. "But we must not forget the wicked folk in the world. So!"

He capped all the splendour, that was taking Kim's delighted breath away, with a mother-of-pearl, nickel-plated, self-extracting .450 revolver.

"I had thought of a smaller bore, but reflected that this takes Government bullets. A man can always come by those–especially across the Border. Stand up and let me look." He clapped Kim on the shoulder. "May you never be tired, Pathan! Oh, the hearts to be broken! Oh, the eyes under the eyelashes looking sideways!"

Kim turned about, pointed his toes, stretched, and felt mechanically for the moustache that was just beginning. Then he stooped towards Mahbub's feet to make proper acknowledgment with fluttering, quick-patting hands; his heart too full for words. Mahbub forestalled and embraced him.

"My son," said he, "what need of words between us? But is not the little gun a delight? All six cartridges come out at one twist. It is borne in the bosom next the skin, which, as it were, keeps it oiled. Never put it elsewhere, and please God, thou shalt some day kill a man with it."

"Hai mai!" said Kim ruefully. "If a Sahib kills a man he is hung in the jail."

"True: but one pace beyond the Border, men are wiser. Put it away; but fill it first. Of what use is a gun unfed?"

"When I go back to the *madrissah* I must return it. They do not allow little guns. Thou wilt keep it for me?"

"Son, I am wearied of that *madrissah,* where they take the best years of a man to teach him what he can only learn upon the Road. The folly of the Sahibs has neither top nor bottom. No matter. Maybe thy written report shall save thee further bondage; and God He knows we need men more and more in the Game."

They marched, jaw-bound against blowing sand, across the salt desert to Jodhpore, where Mahbub and his handsome nephew Habib Ullah did much trading; and then sorrowfully, in European clothes, which he was fast outgrowing, Kim went second-class to St. Xavier's. Three weeks later, Colonel Creighton, pricing Tibetan ghost-daggers at Lurgan's shop, faced Mahbub Ali openly mutinous. Lurgan Sahib operated as support in reserve.

"The pony is made–finished–mouthed and paced, Sahib! From now on, day by day, he will lose his manners if he is kept at tricks. Drop the rein on his back and let go," said the horse-dealer. "We need him."

"But he is so young, Mahbub–not more than sixteen–is he?"

"When I was fifteen I had shot my man and begot my man, Sahib."

"You impenitent old heathen." Creighton turned to Lurgan. The black beard nodded assent to the wisdom of the Afghan's dyed scarlet.

"I should have used him long ago," said Lurgan. "The younger the better. That is why I always have my really valuable jewels watched by a child. You sent him to me to try. I tried him in every way: he is the only boy I could not make to see things."

"In the crystal–in the ink-pool?" demanded Mahbub.

"No. Under my hand, as I told you. That has never happened before. It means that he is strong enough–but you think it skittles, Colonel Creighton–to make any one do anything he wants. And that is three years ago. I have taught him a good deal since, Colonel Creighton. I think you waste him now."

"Hmm! Maybe you're right. But, as you know, there is no Survey work for him at present."

"Let him out–let him go," Mahbub interrupted. "Who expects any colt to carry heavy weight at first? Let him run with the caravans like our white camel-colts–for luck. I would take him myself, but–"

"There is a little business where he would be most useful–in the South," said Lurgan, with peculiar suavity, dropping his heavy blued eyelids.

"E. 23 has that in hand," said Creighton quickly. "He must not go down there. Besides, he knows no Turki."

"Only tell him the shape and the smell of the letters we want and he will bring them back," Lurgan insisted.

"No. That is a man's job," said Creighton.

It was a wry-necked matter of unauthorised and incendiary correspondence between a person who claimed to be the ultimate authority in all matters of the Mohammedan religion throughout the world, and a younger member of a royal house who had been brought to book for kidnapping women within British territory. The Moslem Archbishop had been emphatic and over-arrogant; the young prince was merely sulky at the curtailment of his privileges, but there was no need he should continue a correspondence which might some day compromise him. One letter indeed had been procured, but the finder was later found dead by the roadside in the habit of an Arab trader, as E.23, taking up the work, duly reported.

These facts, and a few others not to be published, made both Mahbub and Creighton shake their heads.

"Let him go out with his Red Lama," said the horse-dealer with visible effort. "He is fond of the old man. He can learn his paces by the rosary at least."

"I have had some dealings with the old man–by letter," said Colonel Creighton, smiling to himself. "Whither goes he?"

"Up and down the land, as he has these three years. He seeks a River of Healing. God's curse upon all–" Mahbub checked himself. "He beds down at the Temple of the Tirthankers or at Buddh Gaya when he is in from the Road. Then he goes to see the boy at the *madrissah,* as we know, for the boy was punished for it twice or thrice. He is quite mad, but a peaceful man. I have met him. The Babu also has had dealings with him. We have watched him for three years. Red Lamas are not so common in Hind that one loses track."

"Babus are very curious," said Lurgan meditatively. "Do you know what Hurree Babu really wants? He wants to be made a member of the Royal Society by taking ethnological notes. I tell you, I tell him about the lama everything that Mahbub and the boy have told me. Hurree Bubu goes down to Benares–at his own expense, I think."

"*I* don't," said Creighton briefly. He had paid Hurree's travelling expenses, out of a most lively curiosity to learn what the lama might be.

"And he applies to the lama for information on lamaism, and devil dances, and spells and charms, several times in these few years. Holy Virgin! I could have told him all that yee-ars ago. I think Hurree Babu is getting too old for the Road. He likes better to collect manners and customs information. Yes, he wants to be an F.R.S."

"Hurree thinks well of the boy, doesn't he?"

"Oh, very indeed–we have had some pleasant evenings at my little place–

but I think it would be waste to throw him away with Hurree on the Ethnological side."

"Not for a first experience. How does that strike you, Mahbub? Let the boy run with the lama for six months. After that we can see. He will get experience."

"He has it already, Sahib–as a fish controls the water he swims in; but for every reason it will be well to loose him from the school."

"Very good, then," said Creighton, half to himself. "He can go with the lama, and if Hurree Babu cares to keep an eye on them so much the better. He won't lead the boy into any danger as Mahbub would. Curious–his wish to be an F.R.S. Very human, too. He *is* best on the Ethnological side–Hurree."

No money and no preferment would have drawn Creighton from his work on the Indian Survey, but deep in his heart also lay the ambition to write "F.R.S." after his name. Honors of a sort he knew could be obtained by ingenuity and the help of friends, but, to the best of his belief, nothing save work–papers representing a life of it–took a man into the Society which he had bombarded for years with monographs on strange Asiatic cults and unknown customs. Nine men out of ten would flee from a Royal Society soirée in extremity of boredom; but Creighton was the tenth, and at times his soul yearned for the crowded rooms in easy London where silver-haired, bald-headed gentlemen who know nothing of the Army move among spectroscopic experiments, the lesser plants of the frozen tundras, electric flight-measuring machines, and apparatus for slicing into fractional millimetres the left eye of the female mosquito. By all right and reason, it was the Royal Geographical that should have appealed to him, but men are as chancy as children in their choice of playthings. So Creighton smiled, and thought the better of Hurree Babu, moved by like desire.

He dropped the ghost-dagger and looked up at Mahbub.

"How soon can we get the colt from the stable?" said the horse-dealer, reading his eyes.

"Hmm! If I withdraw him by order now–what will he do, think you? I have never before assisted at the teaching of such an one."

"He will come to me," said Mahbub promptly. "Lurgan Sahib and I will prepare him for the Road."

"So be it, then. For six months he shall run at his choice: but who will be his sponsor?"

Lurgan slightly inclined his head. "He will not tell anything, if that is what you are afraid of, Colonel Creighton."

"It's only a boy, after all."

"Ye-es; but first, he has nothing to tell; and secondly, he knows what would happen. Also, he is very fond of Mahbub, and of me a little."

"Will he draw pay?" demanded the practical horse-dealer.

"Food and water allowance only. Twenty rupees a month."

One advantage of the Secret Service is that it has no worrying audit. The service is ludicrously starved, of course, but the funds are administered by a few men who do not call for vouchers or present itemized accounts. Mahbub's eyes lighted with almost a Sikh's love of money. Even Lurgan's impassive face changed. He considered the years to come when Kim would have been entered and made to the Great Game that never ceases day and night, throughout India. He foresaw honor and credit in the mouths of a chosen few, coming to him from his pupil. Lurgan Sahib had made E.23 what E.23 was, out of a bewildered, impertinent, lying little North-West Province man.

But the joy of these masters was pale and smoky beside the joy of Kim when St. Xavier's Head called him aside, with word that Colonel Creighton had sent for him.

"I understand, O'Hara, that he has found you a place as an assistant chainman in the Canal Department: that comes of taking up mathematics. It is great luck for you, for you are only seventeen; but of course you understand that you do not become *pukka* (permanent) till you have passed the autumn examination. So you must not think you are going out into the world to enjoy yourself, or that your fortune is made. There is a great deal of hard work before you. Only, if you succeed in becoming *pukka,* you can rise, you know, to four hundred and fifty a month." Whereat the Principal gave him much good advice as to his conduct, and his manners, and his morals; and others, his elders, who had not been wafted into billets, talked, as only Anglo-Indian lads can, of favoritism and corruption. Indeed, young Cazalet, whose father was pensioner at Chunar, hinted very broadly that Colonel Creighton's interest in Kim was directly paternal; and Kim, instead of retaliating, did not even use language. He was thinking of the immense fun to come, of Mahbub's letter of the day before, all neatly written in English, making appointment for that afternoon in a house the very name of which would have crisped the Principal's hair with horror. . . .

Said Kim to Mahbub in Lucknow railway station that evening, above the luggage-scales–"I feared lest, at the last, the roof would fall upon me and cheat me. Is it indeed all finished, O my father?"

Mahbub snapped his fingers to show the utterness of that end, and his eyes blazed like red coals.

"Then where is the pistol that I may wear it?"

"Softly! A half-year, to run without heel-ropes. I begged that much from Colonel Creighton Sahib. At twenty rupees a month. Old Red Hat knows that thou art coming."

"I will pay thee *dustoorie* (commission) on my pay for three months," said Kim gravely. "Yea, two rupees a month. But first we must get rid of these." He plucked his thin linen trousers and dragged at his collar. "I have brought with me all that I need on the Road. My trunk has gone up to Lurgan Sahib's."

"Who sends his salaams to thee–Sahib."

"Lurgan Sahib is a very clever man. But what dost thou do?"

"I go North again, upon the Great Game. What else? Is thy mind still set on following old Red Hat?"

"Do not forget he made me what I am–though he did not know it. Year by year, he sent the money that taught me."

"I would have done as much–had it struck my thick head," Mahbub growled. "Come away. The lamps are lit now, and none will mark thee in the bazar. We go to Huneefa's house."

On the way thither, Mahbub gave him much the same sort of advice as his mother gave to Lemuel, and curiously enough, Mahbub was exact to point out how Huneefa and her likes destroyed Kings.

"And I remember," he quoted maliciously, "one who said, 'Trust a snake before a harlot, and a harlot before a Pathan, Mahbub Ali.' Now, excepting as to Pathans, of whom I am one, all that is true. Most true is it in the Great Game, for it is by means of women that all plans come to ruin and we lie out in dawning with our throats cut. So it happened to such a one,"–he gave the reddest particulars.

"Then why–?" Kim paused before a filthy staircase that climbed to the warm darkness of an upper chamber, in the ward that is behind Azim Ullah's tobacco-shop. Those who know it call it The Bird-cage–it is so full of whisperings and whistlings and chirrupings.

The room, with its dirty cushions and half-smoked hookahs, smelt abominably of stale tobacco. In one corner lay a huge and shapeless woman clad in greenish gauzes, and decked, brow, nose, ear, neck, wrist, arm, waist, and ankle, with heavy native jewelry. When she turned it was like the clashing of copper pots. A lean cat in the balcony outside the window mewed hungrily. Kim checked, bewildered, at the door-curtain.

"Is that the new stuff, Mahbub?" said Huneefa lazily, scarce troubling to remove the mouth-piece from her lips. "O Buktanoos!"–like most of her kind, she swore by the Djinns–"O Buktanoos! He is very good to look upon."

"That is part of the selling of the horse," Mahbub explained to Kim, who laughed.

"I have heard that talk since my Sixth Day," he replied, squatting by the light. "Whither does it lead?"

"To protection. To-night we change thy color. This sleeping under roofs has blanched thee like an almond. But Huneefa has the secret of a color that catches. No painting of a day or two. Also, we fortify thee against the chances of the Road. That is *my* gift to thee, my son. Take out all metals on thee and lay them here. Make ready, Huneefa."

Kim dragged forth his compass, Survey paint-box, and the new-filled medicine-box. They had all accompanied his travels, and boy-like he valued them immensely.

The woman rose slowly and moved with her hands a little spread before her. Then Kim saw that she was blind. "No, no," she muttered, "the Pathan speaks truth–my colour does not go in a week or a month, and those whom I protect are under strong guard."

"When one is far off and alone, it would not be well to grow blotched and leprous of a sudden," said Mahbub. "When thou wast with me I could oversee the matter. Besides, a Pathan is a fairskin. Strip to the waist now and look how thou art whitened." Huneefa felt her way back from an inner room. "It is no matter, she cannot see." He took a pewter bowl from her ringed hand.

The dye-stuff showed blue and gummy. Kim experimented on the back of his wrist, with a dab of cotton-wool; but Huneefa heard him.

"No, no," she cried, "the thing is not done thus, but with the proper ceremonies. The coloring is the least part. I give thee the full protection of the Road."

"Jadoo?" (magic), said Kim, with a half start. He did not like the white, sightless eyes. Mahbub's hand on his neck bowed him to the floor, nose within an inch of the boards.

"Be still. No harm comes to thee, my son. I am thy sacrifice!"

He could not see what the woman was about, but heard the clish-clash of her jewelry for many minutes. A match lit up the darkness; he caught the well-known purr and fizzle of grains of incense. Then the room filled with smoke–heavy, aromatic, and stupefying. Through growing drowse he heard the names of devils–of Zulbazan, Son of Eblis, who lives in bazars and *paraos,* making all the sudden lewd wickedness of wayside halts; of Dulhan, invisible about mosques, the dweller among the slippers of the Faithful, who hinders folk from their prayers; and Musboot, Lord of lies and panic. Huneefa, now whispering in his ear, now talking as from an immense distance, touched him with horrible soft fingers, but Mahbub's grip never shifted from his neck till, relaxing with a sigh, the boy lost his senses.

"Allah! How he fought! We should never have done it but for the drugs. That was his White blood, I take it," said Mahbub testily. "Go on with the *dawut* (invocation). Give him full Protection."

"O Hearer! Thou that hearest with ears, be present. Listen, O Hearer!" Huneefa moaned, her dead eyes turned to the west. The dark room filled with moanings and snortings.

From the outer balcony, a ponderous figure raised a round bullet head and coughed nervously.

"Do not interrupt this ventriloquial necromanciss, my friend," it said in English. "I opine that it is very disturbing to you, but no enlightened observer is jolly well upset."

"*. . . I will lay a plot for their ruin! O Prophet, bear with the unbelievers. Let them alone awhile!*" Huneefa's face, turned to the northward, worked horribly, and it was as though voices from the ceiling answered her.

Hurree Babu returned to his note-book, balanced on the window-sill, but his hand shook. Huneefa, in some sort of drugged ecstasy, wrenched herself to and fro as she sat cross-legged by Kim's still head and called upon devil after devil, in the ancient order of the ritual, binding them to avoid the boy's every action.

"*With Him are the keys of the Secret Things! None knoweth them beside Himself. He knoweth that which is in the dry land and in the sea!*" Again broke out the unearthly whistling responses.

"I–I apprehend it is not at all malignant in its operation?" said the Babu, watching the throat-muscles quiver and jerk as Huneefa spoke with tongues. "It–it is not likely that she has killed the boy? If so, I decline to be witness at the trial. . . . What was the last hypothetical devil mentioned?"

"Babuji," said Mahbub in the vernacular, "I have no regard for the devils of Hind, but the Sons of Eblis are far otherwise, and whether they be *jumalee* (well-affected) or *jullalee* (terrible) they love not Kafirs."

"Then you think I had better go?" said Hurree Babu, half rising. "They are, of course, dematerialized phenomena. Spencer says–"

Huneefa's crisis passed, as these things must, in a paroxysm of howling, with a touch of froth at the lips. She lay spent and motionless beside Kim, and the crazy voices ceased. "Wah! That work is done. May the boy be better for it; and Huneefa is surely a mistress of *dawut.* Help haul her aside, Babu. Do not be afraid."

"How am I to fear the absolutely non-existent?" said Hurree Babu, talking English to reassure himself. It is an awful thing still to dread the magic that you contemptuously investigate–to collect folk-lore for the Royal Society with a lively belief in all Powers of Darkness.

Mahbub chuckled. He had been out with Hurree on the Road ere now. "Let us finish the coloring," said he. "The boy is well protected if–if the Lords of the Air have ears to hear. I am a *sufi* (free-thinker), but when one can get blind-sides of a woman, a stallion, or a devil, why go round to invite a kick? Set him upon the way, Babu, and see that old Red Hat does not lead him beyond our reach. I must get back to my horses."

"All raight," said Hurree Babu. "He is at present a curious spectacle."

About a third cockcrow, Kim woke after a sleep of thousands of years. Huneefa, in her corner, snored heavily, but Mahbub was gone.

"I hope you were not frightened," said an oily voice at his elbow. "I superintended entire operation, which was most interesting from ethnological point of view. It was high-class *dawut.*"

"Huh!" said Kim, recognizing Hurree Babu, who smiled ingratiatingly.

"And also I had honor to bring down from Lurgan your present costume. I am not in the habit offeecially of carrying such gauds to subordinates, but"–he giggled–"your case is noted as exceptional on the books. I hope Mr. Lurgan will note my action."

Kim yawned and stretched himself. It was good to turn and twist within loose clothes once again.

"What is this?" He looked curiously at the heavy dufflestuff loaded with the scents of the far North.

"Oho! That is inconspicuous dress of *chela* attached to service of lamaistic lama. *Com*plete in every particular," said Hurree Babu, rolling into the balcony to clean his teeth at a goglet. "I am of opeenion it is not your old gentleman's precise religion, but rather sub-variant of same. I have contributed rejected notes to *Asiatic Quarterly Review* on these subjects. Now it is curious that the old gentleman himself is totally devoid of religiosity. He is not a dam particular."

"Do you know him?"

Hurree Babu held up his hand to show he was engaged in the prescribed rites that accompany tooth-cleaning and such things among decently bred Bengalis. Then he recited in English an Arya-Somaj prayer of a theistical nature, and stuffed his mouth with *pan* and betel.

"Oah yes. I have met him several times at Benares, and also at Buddh Gaya, to interrogate him on religious points and devil-worship. He is pure agnostic–same as me."

Huneefa stirred in her sleep, and Hurree Babu jumped nervously to the copper incense-burner, all black and discolored in morning-light, rubbed a finger in the accumulated lampblack, and drew it diagonally across his face.

"Who has died in thy house?" asked Kim in the vernacular.

"None. But she may have the Evil Eye–that sorceress," the Babu replied.

"What dost thou do now, then?"

"I will set thee on thy way to Benares, if thou goest thither, and tell thee what must be known by Us."

"I go. At what hour runs the *te-rain?*" He rose to his feet, looked round the desolate chamber and at the yellow-wax face of Huneefa as the low sun stole across the floor. "Is there money to be paid that witch?"

"No. She has charmed thee against all devils and all dangers–in the name of her devils. It was Mahbub's desire." In English: "He is highly obsolete, *I* think, to indulge in such supersteetion. Why, it is all ventri*lo*quy. Belly-speak–eh?"

Kim snapped his fingers mechanically to avert whatever evil–Mahbub, he knew, meditated none–might have crept in through Huneefa's ministrations; and Hurree giggled once more. But as he crossed the room he was careful not to step in Huneefa's blotched, squat shadow on the boards. Witches–when their time is on them–can lay hold of the heels of a man's soul if he does that.

"Now you must well listen," said the Babu when they were in the fresh air. "Part of these ceremonies which we witnessed they include supply of effeecient amulet to those of our Department. If you feel in your neck you will find one small silver amulet, verree cheap. That is *ours.* Do you understand?"

"Oah yes, *hawa-dilli* (a heart-lifter)," said Kim, feeling at his neck.

"Huneefa she makes them for two rupees twelve annas with–oh, all sorts of exorcisms. They are quite common, except they are partially black enamel, and there is a paper inside each one full of names of local saints and such things. *Thatt* is Huneefa's look-out, you see? Huneefa makes them onlee for us, but in case she does not, when we get them we put in, before issue, one small piece of turquoise. Mr. Lurgan he gives them. There is no other source of supply; but it was me invented all this. It is strictly unoffeecial of course, but convenient for subordinates. Colonel Creighton he does not know. He is European. The turquoise is wrapped in the paper. . . . Yes, that is road to railway station. . . . Now suppose you go with the lama, or with me, I hope, some day, or with Mahbub. Suppose we get into a dam-tight place. I am a fearful man–most fearful–but I tell you I have been in dam-tight places more than hairs on my head. You say: 'I am Son of the Charm.' Verree good."

"I do not understand quite. We must not be heard talking English here."

"That is all raight. I am only Babu showing off my English to you. All we Babus talk English to show off," said Hurree, flinging his shoulder-cloth jauntily. "As I was about to say, 'Son of the Charm' means that you may be member of the *Sat Bhai*–the Seven Brothers, which is Hindi *and* Tantric. It is popularly supposed to be extinct society, but I have written notes to show it is still extant. You see it is all my invention. Verree good. *Sat Bhai* has many members, and perhaps before they jolly-well-cut-your-throat they may give you just a chance for life. That is useful, anyhow. And moreover, these foolish natives–if they are not too excited–they always stop to think before they kill a man who says he belongs to any speecific organization. You see? You say then when you are in tight place, 'I am Son of the Charm,' and you get–perhaps–ah–your second wind. That is only in extreme instances, or to open negotiations with a stranger. Can you quite see? Verree good. But suppose now I, or any one of the Department, come to you dressed quite different. You would not know me at all unless I choose, I bet you. Some day I will prove it. I come as Ladakhi trader–oh anything–and I say to you: 'You want to buy precious stones?' You say: 'Do I look like a man who buys precious stones?' Then I say: 'Even verree poor man can buy a turqoise or *tarkeean.*' "

"That is *kichree*–vegetable curry," said Kim.

"Of course it is. You say: 'Let me see the *tarkeean.*' Then I say: 'It was cooked by a woman, and perhaps it is bad for your caste.' Then you say: 'There is no caste when men go to–look for *tarkeean.*' You stop a little between those words, 'to–look." That is thee whole secret. The little stop before the words."

Kim repeated the test-sentence.

"That is all raight. Then I will show you my turquoise if there is time, and then you know who I am, and then we exchange views and documents and those-all things. And so it is with any other man of us. We talk sometimes about turquoises and sometimes about *tarkeean,* but always with that little stop in the words. It is verree easy. First, 'Son of the Charm,' if you are in a tight place. Perhaps that may help you–perhaps not. Then what I have told you about the *tarkeean,* if you want to transact offeecial business with a strange man. Of curse, at present, you have no offeecial business. You are–ah ha!–supernumerary on probation. Quite unique specimen. If you were Asiatic of birth you might be employed right off; but this half-year of leave is to make you de-Englishized, you see? The lama, he expects you, because I have demi-offeecially informed him you have passed all your examinations, and will soon obtain Government appointment. Oh ho! You are on acting-allowance, you see: so if you are called upon to help Sons of the Charm, mind you jolly well try. Now I shall say good-bye, my dear fellow, and I hope you–ah–will come out topside all raight."

Hurree Babu stepped back a pace or two into the crowd at the entrance of Lucknow station and–was gone. Kim drew a deep breath and hugged himself all over. The nickel-plated revolver he could feel in the bosom of his sad-colored robe, the amulet was on his neck; begging-gourd, rosary, and ghost-dagger (Mr. Lurgan had forgotten nothing) were all to hand, with medicine, paint-box, and compass, and in a worn old purse-belt embroidered with porcupine-quill patterns lay a month's pay. Kings could be no richer. He bought sweetmeats in a leaf-cup from a Hindu trader, and ate them with glad rapture till a policeman ordered him off the steps.

Chapter Eleven

Give the man who is not made
    To his trade
Swords to fling and catch again,
Coins to ring and snatch again,
Men to harm and cure again,
Snakes to charm and lure again–
He'll be hurt by his own blade,
By his serpents disobeyed,
By his clumsiness bewrayed,
By the people mocked to scorn–
  So 'tis not with juggler born.
Pinch of dust or withered flower,
  Chance-flung fruit or borrowed staff,
Serve his need and shore his power,
Bind the spell, or loose the laugh!
But a man who, etc., Op. 15.

FOLLOWED A SUDDEN natural reaction.

"Now am I alone–all alone," he thought. "In all India is no one so alone as I! If I die to-day, who shall bring the news–and to whom? If I live and God is good, there will be a price upon my head, for I am a Son of the Charm–I, Kim."

A very few white people, but many Asiastics, can throw themselves into a mazement as it were by repeating their own names over and over again to themselves, letting the mind go free upon speculation as to what is called personal identity. When one grows older, the power, usually, departs, but while it lasts it may descend upon a man at any moment. "Who is Kim–Kim–Kim?"

He squatted in a corner of the clanging waiting-room, rapt from all other thoughts; hands folded in lap, and pupils contracted to pin-points. In a minute–in another half-second–he felt he would arrive at the solution of the tremendous puzzle; but here, as always happens, his mind dropped away from those heights with the rush of a wounded bird, and passing his hand before his eyes, he shook his head.

A long-haired Hindu *bairagi* (holy man), who had just bought a ticket, halted before him at that moment and stared intently.

"I also have lost it," he said sadly. "It is one of the Gates to the Way, but for me it has been shut many years."

"What is the talk?" said Kim, abashed.

"Thou wast wondering there in thy spirit what manner of thing thy soul might be. The seizure came of a sudden. *I* know. Who should know but I? Whither goest thou?"

"Toward Kashi (Benares)."

"There are no Gods there. I have proved them. I go to Prayag (Allahabad) for the fifth time–seeking the road to Enlightenment. Of what faith art thou?"

"I too am a Seeker," said Kim, using one of the lama's pet words. "Though"–he forgot his Northern dress for the moment–"though Allah alone knoweth what I seek."

The old fellow slipped the *bairagi's* crutch under his armpit and sat down on a patch of ruddy leopard's skin as Kim rose at the call for the Benares train.

"Go in hope, little brother," he said. "It is a long road to the feet of the One; but thither do we all travel."

Kim did not feel so lonely after this, and ere he had sat out twenty miles in the crowded compartment, was cheering his neighbors with a string of most wonderful yarns about his own and his master's magical gifts.

Benares struck him as a peculiarly filthy city, though it was pleasant to find how his cloth was respected. At least one-third of the population prays eternally to some group or other of the many million deities, and so revere every sort of holy man. Kim was guided to the Temple of the Tirthankers, about a mile outside the city, near Sarnath, by a chance-met Punjabi farmer–a Kamboh from Jullunder-way who had appealed in vain to every God of his homestead to cure his small son, and was trying Benares as a last resort.

"Thou art from the North?" he asked, shouldering through the press of the narrow, stinking streets much like his own pet bull at home.

"Ay, I know the Punjab. My mother was a Pahareen, but my father came from Amritzar–by Jandiala," said Kim, oiling his ready tongue for the needs of the Road.

"Jandiala–Jullunder? Oho! Then we be neighbors in some sort, as it were." He nodded tenderly to the wailing child in his arms. "Whom dost thou serve?"

"A most holy man at the Temple of the Tirthankers."

"They are all most holy and–most greedy," said the Jat with bitterness. "I have walked the pillars and trodden the temples till my feet are flayed, and the child is no whit better. And the mother being sick too. . . . Hush, then, little one. . . . We changed his name when the fever came. We put him into girl's clothes. There was nothing we did not do, except–I said to his mother when she bundled me off to Benares–she should have come with me–I *said* Sakhi Sarwar Sultan would serve us best. We know His generosity, but these down-country Gods are strangers."

The child turned on the cushion of the huge corded arms and looked at Kim through heavy eyelids. "And was it all worthless?" Kim asked, with easy interest.

"All worthless–all worthless," said the child, lips cracking with fever.

"The Gods have given him a good mind, at least," said the father proudly. "To think he should have listened so cleverly. Yonder is thy temple. Now I am a poor man,–many priests have dealt with me,–but my son is my son, and if a gift to thy master can cure him–I am at my very wits' end."

Kim considered for awhile, tingling with pride. Three years ago he would have made prompt profit on the situation and gone his way without a thought; but now, the very respect the Jat paid him proved that he was a man. Moreover, he had tasted fever once or twice already, and knew enough to recognize starvation when he saw it.

"Call him forth and I will give him a bond on my best yoke, so that the child is cured."

Kim halted at the carved outer door of the temple. A white-clad Oswal banker from Ajmir, his sins of usury new wiped out, asked him what he did.

"I am *chela* to Teshoo Lama, an Holy One from Bhotiyal–within there. He bade me come. I wait. Tell him."

"Do not forget the child," cried the importunate Jat over his shoulder, and then bellowed in Punjabi: "O Holy One–O disciple of the Holy One–O

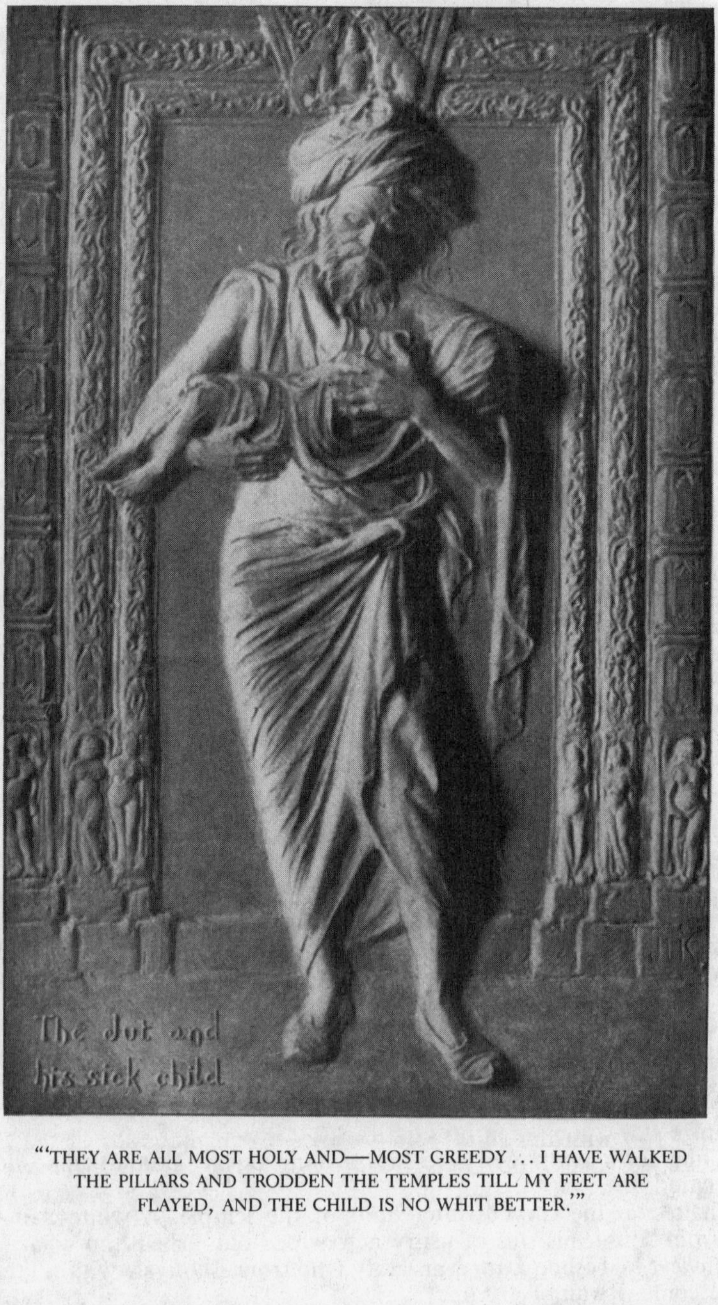

"'THEY ARE ALL MOST HOLY AND—MOST GREEDY . . . I HAVE WALKED THE PILLARS AND TRODDEN THE TEMPLES TILL MY FEET ARE FLAYED, AND THE CHILD IS NO WHIT BETTER.'"

Gods above all the Worlds—behold affliction sitting at the gate!" That cry is so common in Benares that the passers never turned their heads.

The Oswal, at peace with mankind, carried the message into the darkness behind him, and the easy, uncounted Eastern minutes slid by; for the lama was asleep in his cell, and no priest would wake him. When the click of his rosary again broke the hush of the inner court where the calm images of the Arhats stand, a novice whispered, "Thy *chela* is here," and the old man strode forth, forgetting the end of that prayer.

Hardly had the tall figure shown in the doorway than the Jat ran before him, and, lifting up the child, cried; "Look upon this, Holy One; and if the Gods will, he lives—he lives!"

He fumbled in his waist-belt and drew out a small silver coin.

"What is now?" The lama's eyes turned to Kim. It was noticeable he spoke far clearer Urdu than long ago, under Zam-Zammah; but the father would allow no private talk.

"It is no more than a fever," said Kim. "The child is not well fed."

"He sickens at everything, and his mother is not here."

"If it be permitted, I may cure, Holy One."

"What! Have they made thee a Healer? Wait here," said the lama, and he sat down by the Jat upon the lowest step of the temple, while Kim, looking out of the corner of his eyes, slowly opened the little betel-box. He had dreamed dreams at school of returning to the lama as a Sahib—of chaffing the old man before he revealed himself—boy's dreams all. There was more drama in this abstracted, brow-puckered search through the tabloid-bottles, with a pause here and there for thought and a muttered invocation between whiles. Quinine he had in tablets, and dark brown meat-lozenges—beef most probably, but that was not *his* business. The little thing would not eat, but it sucked at a lozenge greedily, and said it liked the salt taste.

"Take then these six." Kim handed them to the man. "Praise the Gods, and boil three in milk; other three in water. After he has drunk the milk give him this (it was the half of a quinine pill), and wrap him warm. Give him the water of the other three, and the other half of this white pill when he wakes. Meantime, here is another brown medicine that he may suck at on the way home."

"Gods, what wisdom!" said the Kamboh, snatching.

It was as much as Kim could remember of his own treatment in a bout of autumn malaria—if you except the patter that he added to impress the lama.

"Now go! Come again in the morning."

"But the price—the price," said the Jat, and threw back his sturdy shoulders. "My son is my son. Now that he will be whole again, how shall I go back to his mother and say I took help by the wayside and did not even give a bowl of curds in return?"

"They are alike, these Jats," said Kim softly. "The Jat stood on his dunghill and the King's elephants went by. 'O driver,' said he, 'what will you sell those little donkeys for?' "

The Jat burst into a roar of laughter, stifled with apologies to the lama. "It is the saying of my own country—the very talk of it. So are we Jats all. I will come to-morrow with the child; and the blessing of the Gods of the Homesteads—who are good little Gods—be on you both. . . Now, son, we grow strong again. Do not spit it out, little Princeling! King of my Heart, do not spit it out, and we shall be strong men, wrestlers and club-wielders, by morning."

He moved away, crooning and mumbling. The lama turned to Kim, and all the loving old soul of him looked out through his narrow eyes. "To heal the sick is to acquire merit; but first one gets knowledge. That was wisely done, O Friend of all the World."

"I was made wise by thee, Holy One," said Kim, forgetting the little play just ended; forgetting St. Xavier's; forgetting his white blood; forgetting even the Great Game as he stooped, Mohammedan fashion, to touch his master's feet in the dust of the Jain temple. "My teaching I owe to thee. I have eaten thy bread three years. My time is finished. I am loosed from the schools. I come to thee."

"Herein is my reward. Enter! Enter! And is all well?" They passed to the inner court, where the afternoon sun sloped golden across. "Stand that I may see. So!" He peered critically. "It is no longer a child, but a man, ripened in wisdom, walking as a physician. I did well—I did well when I gave thee up to the armed men on that black night. Dost thou remember our first day under Zam-Zammah?"

"Ay," said Kim. "Dost thou remember when I leapt off the carriage the first day I went to—"

"The Gates of Learning? Truly. And the day that we ate the cakes together at the back of the river by Nucklao. Aha! Many times hast thou begged for me, but that day I begged for thee."

"Good reason," quoth Kim. "I was then a scholar in the Gates of Learning, and attired as a Sahib. Do not forget, Holy One," he went on playfully, "I am still a Sahib—by thy favor."

"True. And a Sahib in most high esteem. Come to my cell, *chela.*"

"How is that known to thee?"

The lama smiled. "First by means of letters from the kindly priest whom we met in the camp of armed men; but he is now gone to his own country, and I sent the money to his brother." Colonel Creighton, who had succeeded to the trusteeship when Father Victor went to England with the Mavericks, was hardly the chaplain's brother. "But I do not well understand Sahibs' letters. They must be interpreted to me. I chose a surer way. Many times when I returned from my Search to this temple, which has always been a nest to me, there came one seeking Enlightenment—a man from Leh—that had been, he said, a Hindu, but wearied of all those Gods." The lama pointed to the Arhats.

"A fat man?" said Kim, a twinkle in his eye.

"Very fat; but I perceived in a little his mind was wholly given up to useless things—such as devils and charms and the form and fashion of our tea-drinkings in the monasteries, and by what road we initiated the novices. A man abounding in questions; but he was a friend of thine, *chela.* He told me that thou wast on the road to much honor as a scribe. And I see thou art a physician."

"Yes, that am I—a scribe, when I am a Sahib, but it is set aside when I come as thy disciple. I have accomplished the years appointed for a Sahib."

"As it were a novice?" said the lama, nodding his head. "Art thou freed from the schools? I would not have thee unripe."

"I am all free. In due time I take service under the Government as a scribe—"

"Not as a warrior. That is well."

"But first I come to wander—with thee. Therefore I am here. Who begs for thee, these days?" he went on quickly. The ice was thin.

"Very often I beg myself; but, as thou knowest, I am seldom here, except when I come to look again at my disciple. From one end to another of Hind have I travelled afoot and in the *te-rain.* A great and a wonderful land! But here, when I put in, is as though I were in my own Bhotiyal."

He looked round the little clean cell complacently. A low cushion gave him a seat, on which he had disposed himself in the cross-legged attitude of the Bodhisat emerging from meditation; a black teak-wood table, not twenty inches high, set with copper tea-cups, was before him. In one corner stood a tiny altar, also of heavily carved teak, bearing a copper-gilt image of the seated Buddha and fronted by a lamp, an incense-holder, and a pair of copper flower-pots.

"The Keeper of the Images in the Wonder House acquired merit by giving me these a year since," he said, following Kim's eye. "When one is far from one's own land such things carry remembrance; and we must reverence the Lord for that He showed the Way. See!" he pointed to a curiously built mound of colored rice crowned with a fantastic metal ornament. "When I was abbot in my own place–before I came to better knowledge–I made that offering daily. It is the Sacrifice of the Universe to the Lord. Thus do we of Bhotiyal offer all the world daily to the Excellent Law. And I do it even now though I know that the excellent One is beyond all pinchings and pattings." He snuffed from his gourd.

"It is well done, Holy One," Kim murmured, sinking at ease on the cushions, very happy and rather tired.

"And also," the old man chuckled, "I write pictures of the Wheel of Life. Three days to a picture. I was busied on it–or it may be I shut my eyes a little–when they brought word of thee. It is good to have thee here: I will show thee my art–not for pride's sake, but because thou must learn. The Sahibs have not *all* this world's wisdom."

He drew from under the table a sheet of strangely scented yellow Chinese paper, the brushes, and slab of India ink. In cleanest, severest outline he had traced the Great Wheel with its six spokes, whose center is the conjoined Hog, Snake, and Dove (Ignorance, Anger, and Lust), and whose compartments are all the heavens and hells, and all the chances of human life. Men say that the Bodhisat Himself first drew it with grains of rice upon dust, to teach His disciples the cause of things. Many ages have crystallized it into a most wonderful convention crowded with hundreds of little figures whose every line carries a meaning. Few can translate the picture-parable; there are not twenty in all the world who can draw it surely without a copy: of those who can both draw and expound are but three. "I have a little learned to draw," said Kim. "But this is a marvel beyond marvels."

"I have written it for many years," said the lama. "Time was when I could write it all between one lamp-lighting and the next. I will teach thee the art–after due preparation; and I will show thee the meaning of the Wheel."

"We take the Road, then?"

"The Road and our Search. I was but waiting for thee. It was made plain to me in a hundred dreams–notably one that came upon the night of the day that the Gates of learning first shut–that without thee I should never find my River. Again and again, as thou knowest, I put this from me, fearing an illusion. Therefore I would not take thee with me that day at Lucknow, when we ate the cakes. I would not take thee till the time was ripe and auspicious. From the Hills to the Sea, from the Sea to the Hills have I gone, but it was vain. Then I remembered the *Jâtaka.*"

He told Kim the story of the elephant with the leg-iron, as he had told it so often to the Jain priests.

"Further testimony is not needed," he ended serenely. "Thou wast sent for an aid. That aid removed, my Search came to nought. Therefore we will go out again together, and our Search is sure."

"Whither go we?"

"What matters, Friend of all the World? The Search, I say, is sure. If need be, the River will break from the ground before us. I acquired merit when I sent thee to the Gates of Learning, and gave thee the jewel that is Wisdom. Thou didst return, I saw even now, a follower of Sakyamuni, the Physician, whose altars are many in Bhotiyal. It is sufficient. We are together, and all things are as they were–Friend of all the World–Friend of the Stars–my *chela!*"

Then they talked of matters secular; but it was noticeable that the lama never demanded any details of life at St. Xavier's, nor showed the faintest curiosity as to the manners and customs of Sahibs. His mind moved all in the past, and he revived every step of their wonderful first journey together, rubbing his hands and chuckling, till it pleased him to curl himself up into the sudden sleep of old age.

Kim watched the last dusty sunshine fade out of the court, and played with his ghost-dagger and rosary. The clamor of Benares, oldest of all earth's cities awake before the Gods, day and night, beat round the walls as the sea's roar round a breakwater. Now and again, a Jain priest crossed the court, with some small offering to the images, and swept the path about him lest by chance he should take the life of a living thing. A lamp twinkled, and there followed the sound of a prayer. Kim watched the stars as they rose one after another in the still, sticky dark, till he fell asleep at the foot of the altar. That night he dreamed in Hindustanee, with never an English word. . . .

"Holy One, there is the child to whom we gave the medicine," he said, about three o'clock in the morning, when the lama, also waking from dreams, would have fared forth on pilgrimage. "The Jat will be here at the light."

"I am well answered. In my haste I would have done a wrong." He sat down on the cushions and returned to his rosary. "Surely old folk are as children," he said pathetically. "They desire a matter–behold, it must be done at once, or they fret and weep! Many times when I was upon the Road I have been ready to stamp with my feet at the hindrance of an ox-cart in the way, or a mere cloud of dust. It was not so when I was a man–a long time ago. None the less it is wrongful–"

"But thou art indeed old, Holy One."

"The thing was done. A Cause was put out into the world, and, old or young, sick or sound, knowing or unknowing, who can rein in the effect of that Cause? Does the Wheel hang still if a child spin it–or a drunkard? *Chela,* this is a great and a terrible world."

"I think it good," Kim yawned. "What is there to eat? I have not eaten since yesterday even."

"I had forgotten thy need. Yonder is good Bhotiyal tea and cold rice."

"We cannot walk far on such stuff." Kim felt all the European's lust for flesh-meat, which is not accessible in a Jain temple. Yet, instead of going out at once with the begging-bowl, he stayed his stomach on slabs of cold rice till the full dawn. It brought the farmer, voluble, stuttering with gratitude.

"In the night the fever broke and the sweat came," he cried. "Feel here–his skin is fresh and new! He esteemed the salt lozenges and took milk with greed." He drew the cloth from the child's face, and it smiled sleepily at Kim. A little knot of Jain priests, silent but all-observant, gathered by the temple door. They knew, and Kim knew that they knew, how the old lama had met his disciple. Being courteous folk, they had not obtruded themselves overnight by presence, word, or gesture. Wherefore Kim repaid them as the sun rose.

"Thank the Gods of the Jains, brother," he said, not knowing how those Gods were named. "The fever is indeed broken."

"Look! See!" The lama beamed in the background upon his hosts of three years. "Was there ever such a *chela?* He follows our Lord the Healer."

Now the Jains officially recognize all the Gods of the Hindu creed, as well as the Lingam and the Snake. They wear the Brahminical thread; they adhere to every claim of Hindu caste-law. But, because they knew and loved the lama, because he was an old man, because he sought the Way, because he was their guest, and because he collogued long of nights with the head-priest–as free-thinking a metaphysician as ever split one hair into seventy–they murmured assent.

"Remember,"–Kim bent over the child,–"this trouble may come again."

"Not if thou hast the proper spell," said the father.

"But in a little while we go away."

"True," said the lama to all the Jains. "We go now together upon the Search whereof I have often spoken. I waited till my *chela* was ripe. Behold him; We go North. Never again shall I look upon this place of my rest, O people of good will."

"But I am not a beggar." The cultivator rose to his feet, clutching the child.

"Be still. Do not trouble the Holy One," a priest cried.

"Go," Kim whispered. "Meet us again under the big railway bridge, and for the sake of all the Gods of our Punjab, bring food–curry, pulse, cakes fried in fat, and sweetmeats. Specially sweetmeats. Be swift!"

The pallor of hunger suited Kim very well as he stood, tall and slim, in his sad-colored, sweeping robes, one hand on his rosary and the other in the attitude of benediction, faithfully copied from the lama. An English observer might have said that he looked rather like the young saint of a stained-glass window, whereas he was but a growing lad faint with emptiness.

Long and formal were the farewells, thrice ended and thrice renewed. The Seeker–he who had invited the lama to that haven from far-away Tibet, a silver-faced, hairless ascetic–took no part in it, but meditated, as always, alone among the images. The others were very human; pressing small comforts upon the old man,–a betel-box, a fine new iron pencase, a food-bag, and such like,–warning him against the dangers of the world without, and prophesying a happy end to the Search. Meantime Kim, lonelier than ever, squatted on the steps, and swore to himself in the language of St. Xavier's.

"But it is my own fault," he concluded. "With Mahbub, I ate Mahbub's bread, or Lurgan Sahib's. At St. Xavier's, three meals a day. Here I must jolly well look out for myself. Besides, I am not in good training. *How* I could eat a plate of beef now! . . . Is it finished, Holy One?"

The lama, both hands raised, intoned a final blessing in ornate Chinese. "I must lean on thy shoulder," said he, as the temple-gates closed. "We grow stiff, I think."

The weight of a six-foot man is not light to steady through miles of crowded streets, and Kim, loaded down with bundles and packages for the way, was glad to reach the shadow of the railway bridge.

"Here we eat," he said resolutely, as the Kamboh, blue robed and smiling, hove in sight, a basket in one hand and the child on the other.

"Fall to, Holy Ones!" he cried from fifty yards. (They were by the shoal under the first bridge-span, out of sight of hungry priests.) "Rice and good curry, cakes all warm and well scented with *hing* (asafoetida), curds and sugar. King of my fields," this to the small son, "let us show these holy men that we Jats of Jullunder can pay a service. . . . I had heard the Jains would eat nothing that they had not cooked, but truly"–he looked away politely over the broad river–"where there is no eye there is no caste."

"And we," said Kim, turning his back and heaping a leaf-platter for the lama, "are beyond all castes."

They gorged themselves on the good food in silence. Nor till he had licked the last of the sticky sweet-stuff from his little finger did Kim note that the Kamboh too was girt for travel.

"If our roads lie together," he said roughly, "I go with thee. One does not often find a worker of miracles, and the child is still weak. But *I* am not altogether a reed." He picked up his *lathi*–a five-foot male-bamboo ringed with bands of polished iron–and flourished it in the air. "The Jats are called quarrelsome, but that is not true. Except when we are crossed, we are like our own buffaloes."

"So be it," said Kim. "A good stick is a good reason."

The lama gazed placidly up-stream, where in long, smudged perspective the ceaseless columns of smoke go up from the burning-ghats by the river. Now and again, despite all municipal regulations, the fragment of a half-burned body bobbed by on the full current.

"But for thee," said the Kamboh, drawing the child into his hairy breast, "I might to-day have gone thither–with this one. The priests tell us that Benares is holy–which none doubt–and desirable to die in. But I do not know their Gods, and they ask for money; and when one has done one worship a shaved-head vows it is of none effect except one do another. Wash here! Wash there! Pour, drink, lave, and scatter flowers–but always pay the priests. No, the Punjab for me, and the soil of the Jullunder-*doab* for the best soil in it."

"I have said many times–in the temple I think–that, if need be, the River will open at our feet. We will therefore go North," said the lama, rising. "I remember a pleasant place, set about with fruit-trees, where one can walk in meditation–and the air is cooler there. It comes from the Hills and the snow of the Hills."

"What is the name?" said Kim.

"How should I know? Didst thou–no, that was after the Army rose out of the earth and took thee away. I abode there in meditation in a room against the dovecot–except when she talked eternally."

"Oho! the woman from Kulu. That is by Saharunpore." Kim laughed.

"How does the spirit move thy master? Does he go afoot, for the sake of past sins?" the Jat demanded cautiously. "It is a far cry to Delhi."

"No," said Kim. "I will beg a *tikkut* for the *te-rain.*" One does not own to the possession of money in India.

"Then in the name of the Gods, let us take the fire-carriage. My son is best in his mother's arms. The Government has brought on us many taxes, but it gives us one good thing–the *te-rain* that joins friends and unites the anxious. A wonderful matter is the *te-rain.*"

They all piled into it a couple of hours later, and slept through the heat of the day. The Kamboh plied Kim with ten thousand questions as to the lama's walk and work in life, and received some curious answers. Kim was content to be where he was, to look out upon the flat North-Western landscape, and to talk to the changing mob of fellow-passengers. Even to-day, tickets and ticket-clipping are dark oppression to Indian rustics. They do not understand why, when they have paid for a magic piece of paper, strangers should punch great pieces out of the charm. So, long and furious are the debates between travellers and Eurasian ticket-collectors. Kim assisted at two or three with grave advice, meant to darken counsel and to show off his wisdom before the lama and the admiring Kambob. But at Somna Road the Fates sent him a matter to think upon. There tumbled into the compartment, as the train was moving off, a mean, lean little person–a Mahratta, so far as Kim could judge by the cock of the tight turban. His face was cut, his muslin upper-garment was badly torn, and one leg was bandaged. He told them that a country-cart had upset and nearly slain him: he was going to Delhi, where his son lived. Kim watched him closely. If, as he asserted, he had been rolled over and over on the earth, there should have been signs of gravel-rash on the skin. But all his injuries seemed clean cuts, and a mere fall from a cart could not cast a man into such extremity of terror. As, with shaking fingers, he knotted up the torn cloth about his neck he laid bare an amulet of the kind called a keeper up of the heart. Now, amulets are common enough, but they are not generally strung on square-plaited copper wire, and still fewer amulets bear black enamel on silver. There were none except the Kamboh and the lama in the compartment, which, luckily, was of an old type with solid ends. Kim made as to scratch in his bosom, and thereby lifted his own amulet. The Mahratta's face changed altogether at the sight, and he disposed the amulet fairly on his breast.

"Yes," he went on to the Kamboh, "I was in haste, and the cart, driven by a bastard, bound its wheel in a watercut, and besides the harm done to me there was lost a full dish of *tarkeean.* I was not a Son of the Charm (a lucky man) that day."

"That was a great loss," said the Kamboh, withdrawing interest. His experience of Benares had made him suspicious.

"Who cooked it?" said Kim.

"A woman." The Mahratta raised his eyes.

"But all women can cook *tarkeean,*" said the Kamboh. "It is a good curry, as I know."

"Oh yes, it is a good curry," said the Mahratta.

"And cheap," said Kim. "But what about caste?"

"Oh, there is no caste where men go to–look for *tarkeean,*" the Mahratta replied, in the prescribed cadence. "Of whose service art thou?"

"Of the service of this Holy One." Kim pointed to the happy, drowsy lama, who woke with a jerk.

"Ah, he was sent from Heaven to aid me. He is called the Friend of all the World. He is also called the Friend of the Stars. He walks as a physician–his time being ripe. Great is his wisdom."

"And a Son of the Charm," said Kim under his breath, as the Kamboh made haste to prepare a pipe lest the Mahratta should beg.

"And who is *that?*" the Mahratta asked, glancing sideways nervously.

"One whose child I–we have cured, who lies under great debt to us.–Sit by the window, man from Jullunder. Here is a sick one."

"Humph! *I* have no desire to mix with chance-met wastrels. *My* ears are not long. I am not a woman wishing to overhear secrets." The Jat slid himself into a far corner.

"Art thou anything of a healer? I am ten leagues deep in calamity," cried the Mahratta, picking up the cue.

"The man is cut and bruised all over. I go about to cure him," Kim retorted. "None interfered between thy babe and me."

"I am rebuked," said the Kamboh meekly. "I am thy debtor for the life of my son. Thou art a miracle-worker–I know it."

"Show me the cuts." Kim bent over the Mahratta's neck, his heart nearly choking him; for this was the Great Game with a vengeance. "Now, tell thy tale swiftly, brother, while I say a charm."

"I come from the South, where my work lay. One of us they slew by the roadside. Hast thou heard?" Kim shook his head. He, of course, knew nothing of E.23's predecessor, slain down South in the habit of an Arab trader. "Having found a certain letter which I was sent to seek, I came away. I escaped from the city and ran to Mhow. So sure was I that none knew, I did not change my face. At Mhow a woman brought charge against me of theft of jewellery in that city which I had left. Then I saw the cry was out against me. I ran from Mhow by night, bribing the police, who had been bribed to hand me over without question to my enemies in the South. Then I lay in old Chitor city a week, a penitent in a temple, but I could not get rid of the letter which was my charge. I buried it under the Queen's Stone, at Chitor, in the place known to us all."

Kim did not know, but not for worlds would he have broken the thread.

"At Chitor, look you, I was all in Kings' country; for Kotah to the east is beyond the Queen's law, and east again lie Jeypur and Gwalior. Neither love spies, and there is no justice. I was hunted like a wet jackal; but I broke through at Bandakui, where I heard there was a charge against me of murder in the city I had left–of the murder of a boy. They have both the corpse and the witnesses waiting."

"But cannot the Government protect?"

"We of the Game are beyond protection. If we die, we die. Our names are blotted from the book. That is all. At Bandakui, where lives one of us, I thought to slip the scent by changing my face, and so made me a Mahratta. Then I came to Agra, and would have turned back to Chitor to recover the letter. So sure I was I had slipped them. Therefore I did not send a *tar* (telegram) to any one saying where the letter lay. I wished the credit of it all."

Kim nodded. He understood that feeling well.

"But at Agra, walking in the streets, a man cried a debt against me, and approaching with many witnesses, would hale me to the courts then and there. Oh, they are clever in the South! He recognized me as his agent for cotton. May he burn in Hell for it!"

"And wast thou?"

"Oh fool! I was the man they sought for the matter of the letter! I ran into the Fleshers' Ward and came out by the House of the Jew, who feared a riot and pushed me forth. I came afoot to Somna Road–I had only money for my *tikkut* to Delhi–and there, while I lay in a ditch with a fever, one sprang out of the bushes and beat me and cut me and searched me from head to foot. Within earshot of the *te-rain* it was!"

"Why did he not slay thee out of hand?"

"They are not so foolish. If I am taken in Delhi at the instance of lawyers, upon a proven charge of murder, my body is handed over to the State that desires it. I go back guarded, and then–I die slowly for an example to the rest of us. The South is not my country. I run in circles–like a goat with one eye. I have not eaten for two days. I am marked"–he touched the filthy bandage on his leg–"so that they will know me at Delhi."

"Thou art safe in the *te-rain,* at least."

"Live a year at the Great Game and tell me that again! The wires will be out against me at Delhi, describing every tear and rag upon me. Twenty–a hundred, if need be–will have seen me slay that boy. And thou art useless!"

Kim knew enough of native methods of attack not to doubt that the case would be deadly complete–even to the corpse. The Mahratta twitched his fingers with pain from time to time. The Kamboh in his corner glared sullenly; the lama was busy over his beads; and Kim, fumbling doctor-fashion at the man's neck, thought out his plan between invocations.

"Hast thou a charm to change my shape? Else I am dead. Five–ten minutes alone, if I had not been so pressed, and I might–"

"Is he cured yet, miracle-worker?" said the Kamboh jealously. "Thou hast chanted long enough."

"Nay. There is no cure for his hurts, as I see, except he sit for three days in the habit of a *bairagi.*" This is a common penance, often imposed on a fat trader by his spiritual teacher.

"One priest always goes about to make another priest," was the retort. Like most grossly superstitious folk, the Kamboh could not keep his tongue from deriding his Church.

"Will thy son be a priest, then? It is time he took more of my quinine."

"We Jats are all buffaloes," said the Kamboh, softening anew.

Kim rubbed a finger-tip of bitterness on the child's trusting little lips. "I have asked for nothing," he said sternly to the father, "except food. Dost thou grudge me that? I go to heal another man. Have I thy leave–Prince?"

Up flew the man's huge paws in supplication. "Nay–nay. Do not mock me thus."

"It pleases me to cure this sick one. Thou shalt acquire merit by aiding. What color ash is there in thy pipe-bowl? White. That is auspicious. Was there raw turmeric among thy food-stuffs?"

"I–I–"

"Open thy bundle!"

It was the usual collection of small oddments: bits of cloth, quack medicines, cheap fairings, a clothful of *atta,*—grayish, rough-ground native flour,—twists of down-country tobacco, tawdry pipe-stems, and a packet of curry-stuff, all wrapped in a quilt. Kim turned it over with the air of a wise warlock, muttering a Mohammedan invocation.

"This is wisdom I learned from the Sahibs," he whispered to the lama; and here, when one thinks of his training at Lurgan's, he spoke no more than the truth. "There is a great evil in this man's fortune, as shown by the Stars, which—which troubles him. Shall I take it away?"

"Friend of the Stars, thou hast done well in all things. Let it be at thy pleasure. Is it another healing?"

"Quick! Be quick!" gasped the Mahratta. "The train may stop."

"A healing against the shadow of death," said Kim, mixing the Kamboh's flour with the mingled charcoal and tobaco ash in the red-earth bowl of the pipe. E.23, without a word, slipped off his turban and shook down his long black hair.

"That is my food—priest," the Jat growled.

"A buffalo in the temple! Hast thou dared to look even thus far?" said Kim. "I must do mysteries before fools; but have a care for thy eyes. Is there a film before them already? I save the babe, and for return thou—oh, shameless!" The man flinched at the direct gaze, for Kim was wholly in earnest. "Shall I curse thee, or shall I—" He picked up the outer cloth of the bundle and threw it over the bowed head. "Dare so much as to think a wish to see, and—and—even I cannot save thee. Sit! Be dumb!"

"I am blind—dumb. Forbear to curse! Co—come, child; we will play a game of hiding. Do not, for my sake, look from under the cloth."

"I see hope," said E.23. "What is thy scheme?"

"This comes next," said Kim, plucking the thin bodyshirt. E.23 hesitated, with all a North-West man's dislike of baring his body.

"What is caste to a cut-throat?" said Kim, rending it to the waist. "We must make thee a yellow Saddhu all over. Strip—strip swiftly, and shake thy hair over thy eyes while I scatter the ash. Now, a caste-mark on thy forehead." He drew from his bosom the little Survey paint-box and a cake of crimson lake.

"Art thou only a beginner?" said E.23, laboring literally for the dear life, as he slid out of his body-wrappings and stood clear in the loin-cloth while Kim splashed in a noble caste-mark on the ash-smeared brow.

"But two days entered to the Game, brother," Kim replied. "Smear more ash on the bosom."

"Hast thou met—a physician of sick pearls?" He switched out his long, tight-rolled turban-cloth and, with swiftest hands, rolled it over and under about his loins into the intricate devices of a Saddhu's cincture.

"Hah! Dost thou know his touch, then? He was my teacher for awhile. We must bar thy legs. Ash cures wounds. Smear it again."

"I was his pride once, but thou art almost better. The Gods are kind to us! Give me *that.*"

It was a tin box of opium pills among the rubbish of the Jat's bundle. E.23 gulped down a half handful. "They are good against hunger, fear, and chill. And they make the eyes red too," he explained. "Now I shall have heart to play the Game. We lack only a Saddhu's tongs. What of the old clothes?"

Kim rolled them small, and stuffed them into the slack folds of his tunic. With a yellow-ochre paint-cake he smeared the legs and the breast, great streaks against the background of flour, ash, and turmeric.

"The blood on them is enough to hang thee, brother."

"Maybe; but no need to throw them out of the window. . . . It is finished." His voice thrilled with a boy's pure delight in the Game. "Turn and look, O Jat!"

"The Gods protect us," said the hooded Kamboh, emerging like a buffalo from the reeds. "But–whither went the Mahratta? What hast thou done?"

Kim had been trained by Lurgan Sahib; and E.23, by virtue of his business, was no bad actor. In place of the tremulous, shrinking trader there lolled against the corner an all but naked, ash-smeared, ochre-barred, dusty-haired Saddhu, his swollen eyes–opium takes quick effect on an empty stomach–luminous with insolence and bestial lust, his legs crossed under him, Kim's brown rosary round his neck, and a scant yard of worn, flowered chintz on his shoulders. The child buried his face in his amazed father's arms.

"Look up, Princeling! We travel with warlocks, but they will not hurt thee. Oh, do not cry. . . . What is the sense of curing a child one day and killing him with fright the next?"

"The child will be fortunate all his life. He has seen a great healing. When I was a child I made clay men and horses."

"I have made them too. Sir Banás, he comes in the night and makes them all alive at the back of our kitchen-midden," piped the child.

"And so thou art not frightened at anything. Eh, Prince?"

"I was frightened because my father was frightened. I felt his arms shake."

"Oh, chicken-man," said Kim, and even the abashed Jat laughed. "I have done a healing on this poor trader. He must forsake his gains and his account-books, and sit by the wayside three nights to overcome the malignity of his enemies. The Stars are against him."

"The fewer money-lenders the better, say I; but, Saddhu or no Saddhu, he should pay for my stuff on his shoulders."

"So? But that is thy child on thy shoulder–given over to the burning-ghat not two days ago. There remains one thing more. I did this charm in thy presence because need was great. I changed his shape and his soul. None the less, if, by any chance, O man from Jullunder, thou rememberest what thou hast seen, either among the elders sitting under the village tree, or in thy own house, or in company of thy priest when he blesses thy cattle, a murrain will come among the buffaloes, and a fire in thy thatch, and rats in the corn-bin, and the curse of our Gods upon thy fields that they may be barren before thy feet and after thy ploughshare." This was part of an old curse picked up from a *faquir* by the Taksali Gate in the days of Kim's innocence. It lost nothing by repetition.

"Cease, Holy One! In mercy, cease!" cried the Jat. "Do not curse the household. I saw nothing! I heard nothing! I am thy cow!" and he made to grab at Kim's bare foot beating rhythmically on the carriage floor.

"But since thou hast been permitted to aid me in the matter of a pinch of flour and a little opium and such trifles as I have honored by using in my art, so will the Gods return a blessing," and he gave it at length, to the man's immense relief. It was one that he had learned from Lurgan Sahib.

The lama stared through his spectacles as he had not stared at the business of disguisement.

"Friend of the Stars," he said at last, "thou hast acquired great wisdom. Beware that it do not give birth to pride. No man having the Law before his eyes speaks hastily of any matter which he has seen or encountered."

"No–no–no indeed," cried the farmer, fearful lest the master should be minded to improve on the pupil. E.23, with relaxed mouth, gave himself up to the opium that is meat, tobacco, and medicine to the spent Asiatic.

So, in a silence of awe and great miscomprehension, they slid into Delhi about lamp-lighting time.

Chapter Twelve

Who hath desired the Sea—the sight of salt-water unbounded?
The heave and the halt and the hurl and the crash of the comber wind-hounded?
The sleek-barrelled swell before storm—gray, foamless, enormous, and growing?
Stark calm on the lap of the Line—or the crazy-eyed hurricane blowing?
His Sea in no showing the same—his Sea and the same 'neath all showing—
His Sea that his being fulfils?
So and no otherwise—so and no otherwise hillmen desire their hills!

"I HAVE FOUND my heart again," said E.23, under cover of the platform's tumult. "Hunger and fear make men dazed, or I might have thought of this escape before. I was right. They come to hunt for me. Thou hast saved my head."

A group of yellow-trousered Punjab policemen, headed by a hot and perspiring young Englishman, parted the crowd about the carriages. Behind them, inconspicuous as a cat, ambled a small fat person who looked like a lawyer's tout.

"See the young Sahib reading from a paper. My description is in his hand," said E.23. "They go carriage by carriage, like fisher-folk netting a pool."

When the procession reached their compartment, E.23 was counting his beads with a steady jerk of the wrist; while Kim jeered at him for being so drugged as to have lost the ringed fire-tongs which are the Saddhu's distinguishing mark. The lama, deep in meditation, stared straight before him; and the farmer, glancing furtively, gathered up his belongings.

"Nothing here but a parcel of holy-bolies," said the Englishman aloud, and passed on amid a ripple of uneasiness; for native police mean extortion to the native all India over.

"The trouble now," whispered E.23, "lies in sending a wire as to the place where I hid that letter I was sent to find. I cannot go to the *tar*-office in this guise."

"Is it not enough I have saved thy neck?"

"Not if the work be left unfinished. Did never the healer of sick pearls tell thee so? Comes another Sahib! Ah!"

This was a tallish, sallowish District Superintendent of Police,—belt, helmet, polished spurs and all,—strutting and twirling his dark moustache.

"What fools are these Police Sahibs!" said Kim genially.

E.23 glanced up under his eyelids. "It is well said," he muttered in a changed voice. "I go to drink water. Keep my place."

He blundered out almost into the Englishman's arms, and was bad-worded in clumsy Urdu.

"*Tum mut?* You drunk? You mustn't bang about as though Delhi station belonged to you, my friend."

E.23, not moving a muscle of his countenance, answered with a stream of the filthiest abuse, at which Kim naturally rejoiced. It reminded him of the drummer-boys and the barrack-sweepers at Umballa in the terrible time of his first schooling. "My good fool," the Englishman drawled. "*Nickle-jao!* Go back to your carriage."

Step by step, withdrawing deferentially, and dropping his voice, the yellow Saddhu climbed back to the carriage, cursing the D.S.P. to remotest posterity by–here Kim almost jumped–by the curse of the Queen's Stone, by the writing under the Queen's Stone, and by an assortment of Gods with wholly new names.

"I don't know what you're saying."–the Englishman flushed angrily,–"but it's some piece of blasted impertinence. Come out of that!"

E.23, affecting to misunderstand, gravely produced his ticket, which the Englishman wrenched angrily from his hand.

"Oh *zoolum!* What oppression!" growled the Jat from his corner. "All for the sake of a jest too." He had been grinning at the freedom of the Saddhu's tongue. "Thy charms do not work well to-day, Holy One!"

The Saddhu followed the policeman, fawning and supplicating. The ruck of passengers, busy with their babies and their bundles, had not noticed the affair. Kim slipped out behind him; for it flashed through his head that he had heard this angry, stupid Sahib discoursing loud personalities to an old lady near Umballa three years ago.

"It is well," the Saddhu whispered, jammed in the calling, shouting, bewildered press–a Persian greyhound between his feet and a cadgeful of yelling hawks under charge of a Rajput falconer in the small of his back. "He has gone now to send word of the letter which I hid. They told me he was in Peshawur. I might have known that he is like the crocodile–always at the other ford. He has saved me from present calamity, but I owe my life to thee."

"Is he also one of Us?" Kim ducked under a Mewar camel-driver's greasy armpit and cannoned off a covey of jabbering Sikh matrons.

"Not less than the greatest. We are both fortunate! I will make report to him of what thou hast done. I am safe under his protection."

He bored through the edge of the crowd besieging the carriages, and squatted by the bench near the telegraph-office. "Return, or they take thy place! Have no fear for the work, brother–or my life. Thou hast given me breathing-space, and Strickland Sahib has pulled me to land. We may work together at the Game yet. Farewell!"

Kim hurried to his carriage: elated, bewildered, but a little nettled in that he had no key to the secrets about him.

"I am only a beginner at the Game, that is sure. *I* could not have leaped into safety as did the Saddhu. He knew it was darkest under the lamp. *I* could not have thought to tell news under pretence of cursing . . . and how clever was the Sahib! No matter, I saved the life of one. . . . Where is the kamboh gone, Holy One?" he whispered, as he took his seat in the now crowded compartment.

"A fear gripped him," the lama replied, with a touch of tender malice. "He saw thee change the Mahratta to a Saddhu in the twinkling of an eye, as a protection against evil. That shook him. Then he saw the Saddhu fall sheer into the hands of the *polis*–all the effect of thy art. Then he gathered up his son and fled; for he said that thou didst change a quiet trader into an impudent bandier of words with the Sahibs, and he feared a like fate. Where is the Saddhu?"

"With the *polis,*" said Kim. . . . "Yet I saved the Kamboh's child."

The lama snuffed blandly. "Ah, *chela,* see how thou art overtaken! Thou didst cure the Kamboh's child solely to acquire merit. But thou didst put a spell on the Mahratta with prideful workings–I watched thee–and with sidelong glances to bewilder an old, old man and a foolish farmer: whence calamity and suspicion."

Kim controlled himself with an effort beyond his years. Not more than any other youngster did he like to eat dirt or to be misjudged, but he saw himself in a cleft stick. The train rolled out of Delhi into the night.

"It is true," he murmured. "Where I have offended thee I have done wrong."

"It is more, *chela.* Thou hast loosed an Act upon the world, and as a stone thrown into a pool so spread the consequences thou canst not tell how far."

This ignorance was well both for Kim's vanity and for the lama's peace of mind, when we think that there was then being handed in at Simla a code-wire reporting the arrival of E.23 at Delhi, and, more important, the whereabouts of a letter he had been commissioned to–abstract. Incidentally, an over-zealous policeman had arrested, on charge of murder done in a far southern State, a horribly indignant Ajmir cotton-broker, who was explaining himself to a Mr. Strickland on Delhi platform, while E.23 was paddling through byways into the locked heart of Delhi city. In two hours several telegrams had reached the angry minister of a southern State reporting that all trace of a somewhat bruised Mahratta had been lost; and by the time the leisurely train halted at Saharunpore the last ripple of the stone Kim had helped to heave was lapping against the steps of a mosque in far-away Roum–where it disturbed a pious man at prayers.

The lama made his in ample form near the dewy bougainvillea-trellis near the platform, cheered by the clear sunshine and the presence of his disciple. "We will put these things behind us," he said, indicating the brazen engine and the gleaming track. "The jolting of the *te-rain*–though a wonderful thing–has turned my bones to water. We will use clean air henceforward."

"Let us go to the Kulu woman's house." Kim stepped forth cheerily under the bundles. Early morning Saharunpore-way is clean and well scented. He thought of the other mornings at St. Xavier's, and it topped his already thrice-heaped contentment.

"Where is this new haste born from? Wise men do not run about like chickens in the sun. We have come hundreds upon hundreds of *kos* already, and, till now, I have scarcely been alone with thee an instant. How canst thou receive instruction all jostled of crowds? How can I, whelmed by a flux of talk, meditate upon the Way?"

"Her tongue grows no shorter with the years, then?" The disciple smiled.

"Nor her desire for charms. I remember once when I spoke of the Wheel of Life"–the lama fumbled in his bosom for his latest copy–"she was only curious about the devils that besiege children. She shall acquire mer't by entertaining us–in a little while–at an after-occasion–softly, softly. Now we will wander loose-foot, waiting upon the Chain of Things. The Search is sure."

So they travelled very easily across and among the broad bloomful fruit-gardens–by way of Aminabad, Sahaigunge, Akrola of the Ford, and little Phulesa–the line of the Sewaliks always to the north, and behind them again the snows. After long, sweet sleep under the dry stars came the lordly, leisurely passage through a waking village–begging-bowl held forth in silence, but eyes roving in defiance of the Law from sky's edge to sky's edge. Then would Kim return soft-footed through the soft dust to his master under the shadow of a mango-tree or the thinner shade of a white Doon *siris,* to eat and drink at ease. At mid-day, after talk and a little wayfaring, they slept; meeting the world refreshed when the air was cooler. Night found them adventuring into new territory–some chosen village spied three hours before across the fat land, and much discussed upon the road.

There they told their tale,–a new one each evening so far as Kim was concerned,–and there were they made welcome, either by priest or headman, after the custom of the kindly East.

When the shadows shortened and the lama leaned more heavily upon Kim, there was always the Wheel of Life to draw forth, to hold flat under wiped stones, and with a long straw to expound cycle by cycle. Here sat the Gods on high–and they were dreams of dreams. Here was our Heaven and the world of the demi-Gods–horsemen fighting among the hills. Here were the agonies done upon the beasts, souls ascending or descending the ladder and therefore not to be interfered with. Here were the Hells, hot and cold, and the abodes of tormented ghosts. Let the *chela* study the troubles that come from over-eating–bloated stomach and burning bowels. Obediently then, with bowed head and brown finger alert to follow the pointer, did the *chela* study; but when they came to the Human World, busy and profitless, that is just above the Hells, his mind was distracted; for by the roadside trundled the very Wheel itself, eating, drinking, trading, marrying, and quarrelling–all warmly alive. Often the lama made the living pictures the matter of his text, bidding Kim–too ready–note how the flesh takes a thousand thousand shapes, desirable or detestable as men reckon, but in truth of no account either way; and how the stupid spirit, bond-slave to the Hog, the Dove, and the Serpent–lusting after betel-nut, a new yoke of oxen, women, or the favor of kings–is bound to follow the body through all the Heavens and all the Hells, and strictly round again. Sometimes a woman or a poor man, watching the ritual–it was nothing less–when the great yellow chart was unfolded, would throw a few flowers or a handful of cowries upon its edge. It sufficed these humble ones they had met a Holy One who might be moved to remember them in his prayers.

"Cure them if they are sick," said the lama, when Kim's sporting instincts woke. "Cure them if they have fever, but by no means work charms. Remember what befell the Mahratta."

"Then all Doing is evil?" Kim replied, lying out under a big tree at the fork of the Doon road, watching the little ants run over his hand.

"To abstain from action is well–except to acquire merit."

"At the Gates of Learning we were taught that to abstain from action was unbefitting a Sahib. And I am a Sahib."

"Friend of all the World,"–the lama looked directly at Kim,–"I am an old man–pleased with shows as are children. To those who follow the Way there is neither black nor white, Hind nor Bhotiyal. We be all souls seeking escape. No matter what thy wisdom learned among Sahibs, when we come to my River thou wilt be freed from all illusion–at my side. Hai! my bones ache for that River, as they ached in the *te-rain;* but my spirit sits above my bones, waiting. The Search is sure!"

"I am answered. Is it permitted to ask a question?"

The lama inclined his stately head.

"I ate thy bread for three years–as thou knowest. Holy One, whence came–?"

"There is much wealth, as men count it, in Bhotiyal," the lama returned with composure. "In my own place I have the illusion of honor. I ask for that I need. I am not concerned with the account. That is for my monastery. Ai! The black high seats in the monastery, and the novices all in order!"

And he told stories, tracing with a finger in the dust, of the immense and sumptuous ritual of avalanche-guarded cathedrals; of processions and devil-dances; of the changing of monks and nuns into swine; of holy cities fifteen thousand feet in the air; of intrigue between monastery and monastery; of voices among the hills, and of that mysterious mirage that dances on dry snow. He spoke even of Lhassa and of the Dalai Lama, whom he had seen and adored.

Each long, perfect day rose behind Kim for a barrier to cut him off from his race and his mother-tongue. He slipped back to thinking and dreaming in the vernacular, and mechanically followed the lama's ceremonial observances at eating, drinking, and the like. The old man's mind turned more and more to his monastery as his eyes turned to the steadfast snows. His River troubled him nothing. Now and again, indeed, he would gaze long and long at a tuft or a twig, expecting, he said, the earth to cleave and deliver its blessing; but he was content to be with his disciple, at ease in the temperate wind that comes down from the Doon. This was not Ceylon, nor Buddh Gaya, nor Bombay, nor some grass-tangled ruins that he seemed to have stumbled upon two years ago. He spoke of those places as a scholar removed from vanity, as a Seeker walking in humility, as an old man, wise and temperate, illumining knowledge with brilliant insight. Bit by bit, disconnectedly, each tale called up by some wayside thing, he spoke of all his wanderings up and down Hind; till Kim, who had loved him without reason, now loved him for fifty good reasons. So they enjoyed themselves in high felicity, abstaining, as the Rule demands, from evil words, covetous desires; not over-eating, not lying on high beds, nor wearing rich clothes. Their stomach told them the time, and the people brought them their food, as the saying is. They were lords of the villages of Aminabad, Sahaigunge, Akrola of the Ford, and little Phulesa, where Kim gave the soulless woman a blessing.

But news travels fast in India, and too soon shuffled across the crop-land, bearing a basket of fruits with a box of Cabul grapes and gilt oranges, a white-whiskered servitor—a lean, dry Oorya—begging them to bring the honor of their presence to his mistress, distressed in her mind that the lama had neglected her so long.

"Now do I remember"—the lama spoke as though it were a wholly new proposition. "She is virtuous, but an inordinate talker."

Kim was sitting on the edge of a cow's manger, telling stories to a village smith's children.

"She will only ask for another son for her daughter. I have not forgotten her," he said. "Let her acquire merit. Send word that we will come."

They covered eleven miles through the fields in two days, and were overwhelmed with attentions at the end; for the old lady held a fine tradition of hospitality, to which she forced her son-in-law, who was under the thumb of his women-folk and bought peace by borrowing of the money-lender. Age had not weakened her tongue or her memory, and from a discreetly barred upper window, in the hearing of not less than a dozen servants, she paid Kim compliments that would have flung European audiences into unclean dismay.

"But thou art still the shameless beggar-brat of the *parao,*" she shrilled. "I have not forgotten thee. Wash ye and eat. The father of my daughter's son is gone away awhile. So we poor women are dumb and useless."

For proof, she harangued the entire household unsparingly till food and drink were brought; and in the evening—the smoke-scented evening, copper-dun and turquoise across the fields—it pleased her to order her palanquin to be set down in the untidy forecourt by smoky torch-light; and there, behind not too closely drawn curtains, she gossiped.

"Had the Holy One come alone, I should have received him otherwise; but with this rogue, who can be too careful?"

"Maharanee," said Kim, choosing as always the amplest title, "is it my fault that none other than a Sahib—a *polis*-sahib—called the Maharanee whose face he—"

"Chitt! That was on the pilgrimage. When we travel—thou knowest the proverb."

"Called the Maharanee a Breaker of Hearts and a Dispenser of Delights?"

"To remember that! It was true. So he did. That was in the time of the bloom of my beauty." She chuckled like a contented parrot above the sugar lump. "Now tell me of thy goings and comings—as much as may be without shame. How many maids, and whose wives, hang upon they eyelashes? Ye hail from Benares? I would have gone there again this year, but my daughter—we have only two sons. Phaii! Such is the effect of these low plains. Now in Kulu men are elephants. But I would ask thy Holy One—stand aside, rogue—a charm against most lamentable windy colics that in mango-time overtake my daughter's eldest. Two years back he gave me a powerful spell."

"Oh, Holy One!" said Kim, bubbling with mirth at the lama's rueful face.

"It is true. I gave her one against wind."

"Teeth—teeth—teeth," snapped the old woman.

"Cure them when they are sick," Kim quoted relishingly, "but by no means work charms. Remember what befell the Mahratta."

"That was two Rains ago; she wearied me with her continual importunity." The lama groaned as the Unjust Judge had groaned before him. "Thus it comes—take note, my *chela*—that even those who would follow the Way are thrust aside by idle women. Three days through, when the child was sick, she talked to me."

"Arre! and to whom else should I talk? The boy's mother knew nothing, and the father—in the nights of the cold weather it was—'Pray to the Gods,' said he, forsooth, and turning over, snored!"

"I gave her the charm. What is an old man to do?"

"'To abstain from action is well—except when we acquire merit.'"

"Ah, *chela,* if thou desertest me, I am all alone."

"He found his milk-teeth easily at any rate," said the old lady. "But all priests are alike."

Kim coughed severely. Being young, he did not approve of her flippancy. "To importune the wise out of season is to invite calamity."

"There is a talking *mynah*"—the thrust came back with the well-remembered snap of the jewelled forefinger—"over the stables which has picked up the very tone of the family-priest. Maybe I forget honor to my guests, but if ye had seen *him* double his fists into his belly, which was like a half-grown gourd, and cry: 'Here is the pain!' ye would forgive. I am half minded to take the *hakim's* medicine. He sells it cheap, and certainly it makes him fat as Shiv's own bull. *He* does not deny remedies, but I doubted for the child because of the inauspicious color of the bottles."

The lama, under cover of the monologue, had faded out into the darkness towards the room prepared.

"Thou hast angered him, belike," said Kim.

"Not he. He is wearied, and I forgot, being a grandmother. (None but a grandmother should ever oversee a child. Mothers are only fit for bearing.) To-morrow, when he sees how my daughter's son is grown, he will write the charm. Then, too, he can judge of the new *hakim's* drugs."

"Who is the *hakim,* Maharanee?"

"A wanderer, as thou art, but a most sober Bengali from Dacca—a master of medicine. He relieved me of an oppression after meat by means of a small pill that wrought like a devil unchained. He travels about now, vending preparations of great value. He has even papers, printed in Angrezi, telling what things he has done for weak-backed men and slack women. He has been here four days; but hearing ye were coming (*hakims* and priests are snake and tiger the world over) he has, as I take it, gone to cover."

While she drew breath after this volley, the ancient servant, sitting unrebuked on the edge of the torch-light, muttered: "This house is a cattle-pound, as it were, for all charlatans and—priests. Let the boy stop eating mangoes . . . but who can argue with a grandmother?" He raised his voice respectfully: "Sahiba, the *hakim* sleeps after his meat. He is in the quarters behind the dovecot."

Kim bristled like an expectant terrier. To outface and down-talk a Calcutta-taught Bengali, a voluble Dacca drug-vendor, would be a good game. It was not seemly that the lama, and incidentally himself, should be thrown aside for such an one. He knew those curious bastard English advertisements at the backs of native newspapers. St. Xavier's boys sometimes brought them in by stealth to snigger over among their mates; for the language of the grateful patient recounting his symptoms is most simple and revealing. The Oorya, not unanxious to play off one parasite against the other, slunk away towards the dovecot.

"Yes," said Kim, with measured scorn. "Their stock-in-trade is a little colored water and a very great shamelessness. Their prey are broken-down kings and over-fed Bengalis. Their profit is in children—who are not born."

The old lady chuckled. "Do not be envious. Charms are better, eh? *I* never gainsaid it. See that thy Holy One writes me a good amulet by the morning."

"None but the ignorant deny"—a thick, heavy voice boomed through the darkness, as a figure came to rest squatting—"none but the ignorant deny the value of charms. None but the ignorant deny the value of medicines."

"A rat found a piece of turmeric. Said he: 'I will open a grocer's shop,'" Kim retorted.

Battle was fairly joined now, and they heard the old lady stiffen to attention.

"The priest's son knows the names of his nurse and three Gods. Says he: 'Hear me, or I will curse you by the three million Great Ones.'" Decidedly this invisible had an arrow or two in his quiver. He went on: "I am but a teacher of the alphabet. I have learned all the wisdom of the Sahibs."

"The Sahibs never grow old. They dance and they play like children when they are grandfathers. A strong-backed breed," piped the voice inside the palanquin.

"I have, too, our drugs which loosen humours of the head in hot and angry men. *Sinà* well compounded when the moon stands in the proper House; yellow earths I have—*arplan* from China that makes a man renew his youth and astonish his household; saffron from Kashmir, and the best salep of Cabul. Many people have died before—"

"That I surely believe," said Kim.

"They knew the value of my drugs. I do not give *my* sick the mere ink in which a charm is written, but hot and rending drugs which descend and wrestle with the evil."

"Very mightily they do so," sighed the old lady.

The voice launched into an immense tale of misfortune and bankruptcy, studded with plentiful petitions to the Government. "But for my fate, which overrules all, I had been now in Government employ. I bear a degree from the great school at Calcutta—whither, maybe, the son of this house shall go."

"He shall indeed. If our neighbor's brat can in a few years be made an F.A." (First Arts—she used the English word, of which she had heard so often), "how much more shall children clever as some that I know bear away prizes at rich Calcutta."

"Never," said the voice, "have I seen such a child! Born in an auspicious hour, and—but for that colic which, alas! turning into black cholera, may carry him off like a pigeon—destined to many years, he is enviable."

"*Hai mai!*" said the old lady. "To praise children is inauspicious, or I could listen to this talk. But the back of the house is unguarded, and even in this soft air men think themselves to be men and women we know. . . . The child's father is away too, and I must be *chowkedar* (watchman) in my old age. Up! Up! Take up the palanquin. Let the *hakim* and the young priest settle between them whether charms or medicine most avail. Ho! worthless people, fetch tobacco for the guests, and—round the homestead go I!"

The palanquin reeled off, followed by straggling torches and a horde of dogs. Twenty villages knew the Sahiba—her failings, her tongue, and her large charity. Twenty villages cheated her after immemorial custom, but no man would have stolen or robbed within her jurisdiction for any gift under Heaven. None the less, she made great parade of her formal inspections, the riot of which could be heard halfway to Mussoorie.

Kim relaxed, as one augur must when he meets another. The *hakim,* still squatting, slid over his hookah with a friendly foot, and Kim pulled at the good weed. The hangers-on expected grave professional debate, and perhaps a little free doctoring.

"To discuss medicine before the ignorant is of one piece with teaching the peacock to sing," said the *hakim.*

"True courtesy," Kim echoed, "is very often inattention."

These, be it understood, were company-manners, designed to impress.

"Hi! I have an ulcer on my leg," cried a scullion. "Look at it!"

"Get hence! Remove!" said the *hakim.* "Is it the habit of the place to pester honored guests? Ye crowd in like buffaloes."

"If the Sahiba knew–" Kim began.

"Ai! Ai! Come away. They are meat for our mistress. When her young Shaitan's colics are cured perhaps we poor people may be suffered to–"

"The mistress fed thy wife when thou wast in jail for breaking the money-lender's head. Who speaks against her?" The old servitor curled his white moustaches savagely in the young moonlight. "*I* am responsible for the honour of this house. Go!" and he drove the underlings before him.

Said the *hakim,* hardly more than shaping the words with his lips: "How do you do, Mister O'Hara? I am jolly glad to see you again."

Kim's hand clenched about the pipe-stem. Anywhere on the open road, perhaps, he would not have been astonished; but here, in this quiet backwater of life, he was not prepared for Hurree Babu. It annoyed him, too, that he had been hoodwinked.

"Ah ha! I told you at Lucknow–*resurgam*–I shall rise again and you shall not know me. How much did you bet–eh?"

He chewed leisurely upon a few cardamom seeds, but he breathed uneasily. "But why come here, Babuji?"

"Ah! *Thatt* is the question, as Shakespeare hath said. I come to congratulate you on your extraordinary effecient performance at Delhi. Oah! I tell you we are all proud of you. It was verree neat and handy. Our mutual friend, he is old friend of mine. He has been in some dam-tight places. Now he will be in some more. He told me; I tell Mister Lurgan; and he is pleased you graduate so nicely. All the Department is pleased."

For the first time in his life, Kim thrilled to the clean pride (it can be a deadly pitfall, none the less) of Departmental praise–ensnaring praise from an equal of work appreciated by fellow-workers. Earth has nothing on the same plane to compare with it. But, cried the Oriental in him, Babus do not travel far to retail compliments.

"Tell thy tale, Babu," he said authoritatively.

"Oah, it is nothing. Onlee I was at Simla when the wire came in about what our mutual friend said he had hidden, and old Creighton–" He looked to see how Kim would take this piece of audacity.

"The Colonel Sahib," the boy from St. Xavier's corrected.

"*Of* course. He found me at a loose string, and I had to go down to Chitor to find that beastly letter. I do not like the South–too much railway travel; but I drew good travelling allowance. Ha! Ha! I meet our mutual at Delhi on the way back. He lies quiet just now, and says Saddhu-disguise suits him to the ground. Well, there I hear what you have done so well, so quickly, upon the instantaneous spur of the moment. I tell our mutual friend you take the bally bun, by Jove! It was splendid. I come to tell you so."

"Umm!"

The frogs were busy in the ditches, and the moon slid to her setting. Some happy servant had gone out to commune with the night and to beat upon a drum. Kim's next sentence was in the vernacular.

"How didst thou follow us?"

"Oah, thatt was nothing. I know from our mutual friend you go to Saharunpore. So I come on. Red lamas are not insconspicuous persons. I buy myself my drug-box, and I am very good doctor really. I go to Akrola by the Ford, and hear all about you, and I talk here and talk there. All the common people know what you do. I know when the hospitable old lady sent the *dooli.* They have great recollections of the old lama's visits here. I know old ladies cannot keep their hands from medicines. So I am a doctor and–you hear my talk? I think it is verree good. My word, Mister O'Hara, they know about you and the lama for fifty miles–the common people. So I come. Do you mind?"

"Babuji," said Kim, looking up at the broad, grinning face, "I am a Sahib."

"My dear Mister O'Hara–"

"And I hope to play the Great Game."

"You are subordinate to me departmentally at present."

"Then why talk like an ape in a tree? Men do not come after one from Simla and change their dress, for the sake of a few sweet words. I am not a child. Talk Hindi and let us get to the yolk of the egg. Thou art here–speaking not one word of truth in ten. Why art thou here? Give a straight answer."

"That is so verree disconcerting of the European, Mister O'Hara. *You* should know better at your time of life."

"But I want to know," said Kim, laughing. "If it is the Game, I may help. How can I do anything if you *bukh* (babble) all round the shop?"

Hurree Babu reached for the pipe, and sucked it till it guggled again.

"Now I will speak vernacular. You sit tight, Mister O'Hara. . . . It concerns the pedigree of a white stallion."

"Still? That was finished long ago."

"When every one is dead the Great Game is finished. Not before. Listen to me till the end. There were Five Kings who prepared a sudden war three years ago, when thou wast given the stallion's pedigree by Mahbub Ali. Upon them, because of that news, and ere they were ready, fell our Army."

"Ay–eight thousand men with guns. I remember that night."

"But the war was not pushed. That is the Government custom. The troops were recalled because the Government believed the Five Kings were cowed; and it is not cheap to feed men among the high Passes. Hilás and Bunár–Rajahs with guns–undertook for a price to guard the Passes against all coming from the North. They protested both fear and friendship." He broke off with a giggle into English: "Of course, I tell you this unoffeecially to elucidate political situation, Mister O'Hara. Offeecially, I am debarred from criticising any action of superior. Now I go on.–This pleased the Government, anxious to avoid expense, and a bond was made for so many rupees a month that Hilás and Bunár should guard the Passes as soon as the State's troops were withdrawn. At that time–it was after we two met–I, who had been selling tea in Leh, became a clerk of accounts in the Army. When the troops were withdrawn, I was left behind to pay the coolies who made new roads in the Hills. This road-making was part of the bond between Bunár, Hilás, and the Government."

"So; and then?"

"I tell you, it was jolly beastly cold up there too, after summer," said Hurree Babu confidentially. "I was afraid these Bunár men would cut my throat every night for thee pay-chest. My native sepoy-guard, they laughed at me! By Jove! I was such a fearful man. Nevar mind thatt. I go on colloquially. . . . I send word many times that these two Kings were sold to the North; and Mahbub Ali, who was yet farther north, amply confirmed it. Nothing was done. Only my feet were frozen, and a toe dropped off. I sent word that the roads for which I was paying money to the diggers were being made for the feet of strangers and enemies."

"For?"

"For the Russians. The thing was an open jest among the colies. Then I was called down to tell what I knew by speech of tongue. Mahbub came South too. See the end! Over the Passes this year after snow-melting"–he shivered afresh–"come two strangers under cover of shooting wild goats. They bear guns, but they bear also chains and levels and compasses."

"Oho! The thing gets clearer."

"They are well received by Hilás and Bunár. They make great promises; they speak as the mouthpiece of a Kaisar with gifts. Up the valleys, down the valleys go they, saying, 'Here is a place to build a breastwork; here can ye pitch a fort. Here can ye hold the road against an army'–the very roads for which I paid out the rupees monthly. The Government knows, but does nothing. The three other Kings, who were *not* paid for guarding the Passes, tell them by runner of the bad faith of Bunár and Hilás. When all the evil is done, look you–when these two strangers with the levels and the compasses make the Five Kings to believe that a great army will sweep the Passes to-morrow or the next day– Hill-people are all fools–comes the order to me, Hurree Babu, 'Go North and see what those strangers do.' I say to Creighton Sahib, 'This is not a lawsuit, that we go about to collect evidence,'" He returned to his English with a jerk: "'By Jove,' I said, 'why the dooce do you not issue demi-offecial orders to some brave man to poison them, for an example? It is, if you permit the observation, most reprehensible laxity on your part.' And Colonel Creighton, he laughed at me! It is all your beastly English pride. You think no one dare conspire! That is all tommy-rött."

Kim smoked slowly, revolving the business, so far as he understood it, in his quick mind.

"Then thou goest forth to follow the strangers?"

"No; to meet them. They are coming in to Simla to send down their horns and heads to be dressed at Calcutta. They are exclusively sporting gentlemen, and they are allowed special faceelities by the Government. Of course, we always do that. It is our British pride."

"Then what is to fear from them?"

"By Jove, they are not black people. I can do all sorts of things with black people, of course. They are Russians, and highly unscrupulous people. I–I do not want to consort with them without a witness."

"Will they kill thee?"

"Oah, thatt is nothing. I am good enough Herbert Spencerian, I trust, to meet little thing like death, which is all in my fate, you know. But–but they may beat me."

"Why?"

Hurree Babu snapped his fingers with irritation. "Of *course* I shall affeeliate myself to their camp in supernumerary capacity as perhaps interpreter, or person mentally impotent and hungree, or some such thing. And then I must pick up what I can, I suppose. That is as easy for me as playing Mister Doctor to the old lady. Onlee–onlee–you see, Mister O'Hara, I am unfortunately Asiatic, which is serious detriment in some respects. And *allso* I am Bengali–a fearful man."

"God made the Hare and the Bengali. What shame?" said Kim, quoting the proverb.

"It was process of Evolution, *I* think, from Primal Necessity, but the fact remains in all its *cui bono.* I am, oh, awfully fearful!–I remember once they wanted to cut off my head on the road to Lhassa. (No, I have never reached to Lhassa.) I sat down and cried, Mister O'Hara, anticipating Chinese tortures. I do not suppose these two gentlemen will torture me, but I like to provide for possible contingency with European assistance in emergency." He coughed and spat out the cardamoms. "It is purely unoffeecial indent, to which you can say 'No, Babu.' If you have no pressing engagement with your old man–perhaps you might divert him; perhaps I can seduce his fancies–I should like you to keep in Departmental touch with me till I find those sporting coves. I have great oppeenion of you since I met my friend at Delhi. And also I will embody your name in my offeecial report when matter is finally adjudicated. It will be a great feather in your cap. That is why I come really."

"Humph! The end of the tale, I think, is true; but what of the fore-part?"

"About the Five Kings? Oah! there is ever so much truth in it. A lots more than you would suppose," said Hurree earnestly. "You come–eh? I go from here straight into the Doon. It is verree verdant and painted meads. I shall go to Mussoorie–to good old Munsoorie Pahar, as the gentlemen and ladies say. Then by Rampur into Chini. That is the only way they can come. I do not like waiting in the cold, but we must wait for them. I want to walk with them to Simla. You see, one Russian is a Frenchman, and I know my French pretty well. I have friends in Chandernagore."

"*He* would certainly rejoice to see the Hills again," said Kim meditatively. "All his speech these ten days past has been of little else. If we go together–"

"Oah! We can be quite strangers on the road, if your lama prefers. I shall just be four or five miles ahead. There is no hurry for Hurree. That is an Europe pun, ha! ha! and you come after. There is plenty of time; they will plot and survey and map of course. I shall go to-morrow, and you the next day, if you choose. Eh? You go think on it till morning. By Jove, it is near morning now." He yawned ponderously, and with never a civil word lumbered off to his sleeping-place. But Kim slept little, and his thoughts ran in Hindustanee:

"Well is the Game called great! I was four days a scullion at Quetta, waiting on the wife of the man whose book I stole. And that was part of the Great Game! From the South–God knows how far–camp up the Mahratta, playing the Great Game in fear of his life. Now I shall go far and far into the North playing the Great Game. Truly, it runs like a shuttle throughout all Hind. And my share and my joy"–he smiled to the darkness–"I owe to the lama here. Also to Mahbub Ali–also to Creighton Sahib, but chiefly to the Holy One. He is right–a great and a wonderful world–and I am Kim–Kim–Kim–alone–one person–in the middle of it all. But I will see these strangers with their levels and chains . . ."

"What was the upshot of last night's babble?" said the lama, after his orisons.

"There came a strolling seller of drugs–a hanger-on of the Sahiba's. Him I abolished by arguments and prayers, proving that our charms are worthier than his colored waters."

"Alas! my charms. Is the virtuous woman still bent upon a new one?"

"Very strictly."

"Then it must be written, or she will deafen me with her clamour." He fumbled at his pencase.

"In the Plains," said Kim, "are always too many people. In the Hills, as I understand, there are fewer."

"Oh! the Hills, and the snow upon the Hills." The lama tore off a tiny square of paper fit to go in an amulet. "But what dost thou know of the Hills?"

"They are very close." Kim thrust open the door and looked at the long, peaceful line of the Himalayas flushed in the morning-gold. "Except in the dress of a Shaib, I have never set foot among them."

The lama snuffed the wind wistfully.

"If we go North,"–Kim put the question to the waking sunrise,–"would not much mid-day heat be avoided by walking among the lower hills at least? . . . Is the charm made, Holy One?"

"I have written the names of seven silly devils–not one of whom is worth a grain of dust in the eye. Thus do foolish women drag us from the Way!"

Hurree Babu came out from behind the dovecot, washing his teeth with ostentatious ritual. Full-fleshed, heavy-haunched, bull-necked, and deep-voiced, he did not look like "a fearful man." Kim signed almost imperceptibly that matters were in good train, and when the morning toilet was over Hurree Babu, in flowery speech, came to do honour to the lama. They ate, of course, apart, and afterwards the old lady, more or less veiled behind a window, returned to the vital business of green-mango colics in the young. The lama's knowledge of medicine was of course sympathetic only. He believed that the dung of a black horse, mixed with sulphur, and carried in a snake-skin, was a sound remedy for cholera; but the symbolism interested him far more than the science. Hurree Babu deferred to these views with enchanting politeness, so that the lama called him a courteous physician. Hurree Babu replied that he was no more than an inexpert dabbler in the mysteries; but at least–he thanked the Gods therefore–he knew when he sat in the presence of a master. He himself had been taught by the Shaibs, who do not consider expense, in the lordly halls of Calcutta; but, as he was ever first to acknowledge, there lay a wisdom behind earthly wisdom–the high and lonely lore of meditation. Kim looked on with envy. The Hurree Babu of his knowledge–oily, effusive, and nervous–was gone; gone too was the brazen drug-vendor of overnight. There remained–polished, polite, attentive–a sober, learned son of experience and adversity, gathering wisdom from the lama's lips. The old lady confided to Kim that these rare levels were beyond her. She liked charms with plenty of ink that one could wash off in water, swallow, and be done with. Else what was the use of the Gods? She liked men and women, and she spoke of them–of kinglets she had known in the past; of her own youth and beauty; of the depredations of leopards and the eccentricities of love Asiatic; of the incidence of taxation, rack-renting, funeral ceremonies, her son-in-law (this by allusion, easy to be followed), the care of the young, and the age's lack of decency. And Kim, as interested in the life of this world as she soon to leave it, squatted with his feet under the hem of his robe, drinking all in, while the lama demolished one after another every theory of body-curing put forward by Hurree Babu.

At noon the Babu strapped up his brass-bound drug-box, took his patent-leather shoes of ceremony in one hand, a gay blue and white umbrella in the other, and set off northwards to the Doon, where, he said, he was in demand among the lesser kings of those parts.

"We will go in the cool of the evening, *chela,*" said the lama. "That doctor, learned in physic and courtesy, affirms that the people among these lower hills are devout, generous, and much in need of a teacher. In a very short time–so says the *hakim*–we come to cool air and the smell of pines."

"Ye go to the Hills. And by Kulu-road? Oh, thrice happy!" shrilled the old lady. "But that I am a little pressed with the care of the homestead I would take palanquin . . . but that would be shameless, and my reputation would be cracked. Ho! Ho! I know the road–every march of the road I know. Ye will find charity throughout–it is not denied to the well-looking. I will give orders for provision. A servant to set you forth upon your journey? No. . . . Then I will at least cook ye good food."

"What a woman is the Sahiba!" said the white-bearded Oorya, when a

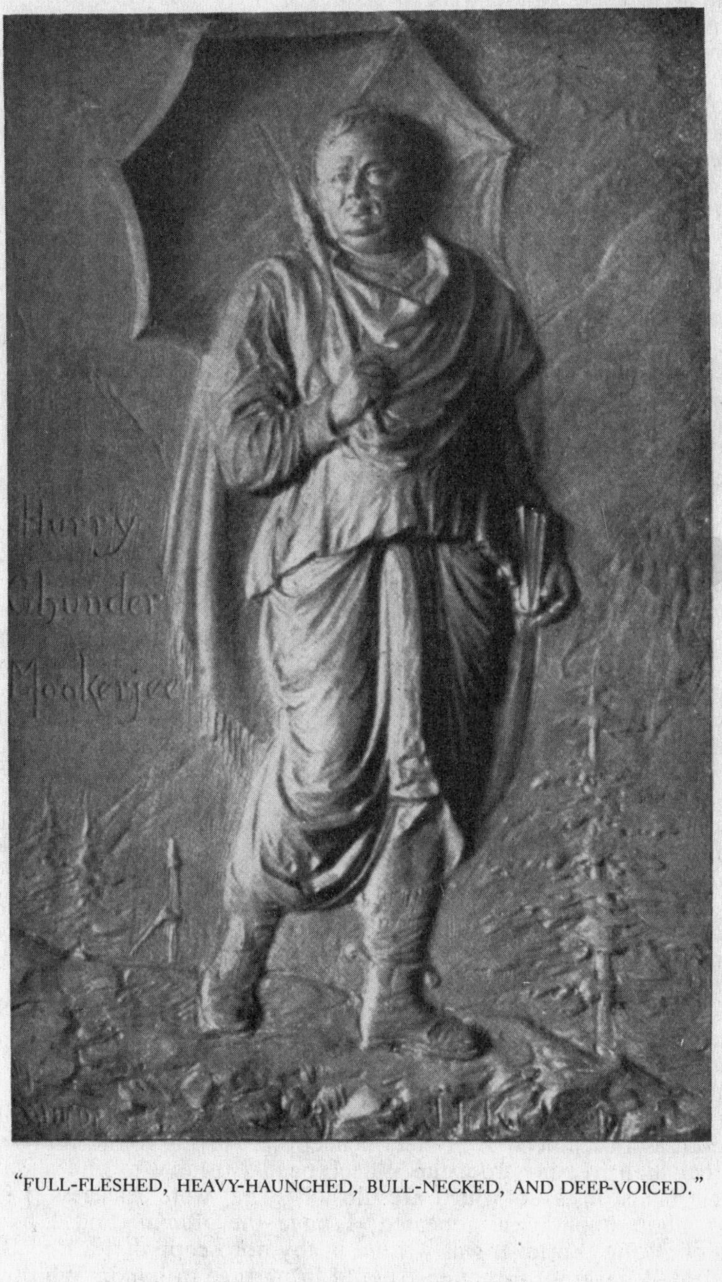

"FULL-FLESHED, HEAVY-HAUNCHED, BULL-NECKED, AND DEEP-VOICED."

tumult rose by the kitchen quarters. "She has never forgotten a friend: she has never forgotten an enemy in all her years. And her cookery–wah!" He rubbed his slim stomach.

There were cakes, there were sweetmeats, there was cold fowl stewed to rags with rice and prunes–enough to burden Kim like a mule.

"I am old and useless," she said. "None now love me–and none respect–but there are few to compare with me when I call on the Gods and squat to my cooking-pots. Come again, O people of good will. Holy One and disciple, come again. The room is always prepared; the welcome is always ready. . . . See the women do follow thy *chela* too openly. *I* know the women of Kulu. Take heed, *chela,* lest he run away when he smells his Hills again. . . . Hai! Do not tilt the rice-bag upside down. . . . Bless the household, Holy One, and forgive thy servant her stupidities."

She wiped her red old eyes on a corner of her veil, and clucked throatily.

"Women talk," said the lama at last, "but that is a woman's infirmity. I gave her a charm. She is upon the Wheel and wholly given over to the shows of this life, but none the less, *chela,* she is virtuous, kindly, hospitable–of a whole and zealous heart. Who shall say she does not acquire merit?"

"Not I, Holy One," said Kim, reslinging the bountiful provision on his shoulders. "In my mind–behind my eyes–I have tried to picture such an one altogether freed from the Wheel–desiring nothing, causing nothing–a nun, as it were."

"And, O imp?" The lama almost laughed aloud.

"I cannot make the picture."

"Nor I. But there are many, many millions of lives before her. She will get wisdom a little, it may be, in each one.

"And will she forget how to make stews with saffron upon that road?"

"Thy mind is set on things unworthy. But she has skill. I am refreshed all over. When we reach the lower hills I shall be yet stronger. The *hakim* spoke truly to me this morn when he said a breath from the snows blows away twenty years from the life of a man. We will go up into the Hills–the high hills–up to the sound of snow-water and the sound of the trees–for a little while. The *hakim* said that at any time we may return to the Plains, for we do no more than skirt the pleasant places. The *hakim* is full of learning; but he is in no way proud. I spoke to him–when thou wast talking to the Sahiba–of a certain dizziness that lays hold upon the back of my neck in the night, and he said it rose from excessive heat–to be cured by cool air. Upon consideration, I marvelled that I had not thought of such a simple remedy."

"Didst thou tell him of thy Search?" said Kim, a little jealously. He preferred to sway the lama by his own speech–not through the wiles of Hurree Babu.

"Assuredly. I told him of my dream, and of the manner by which I had acquired merit by causing thee to be taught wisdom."

"Thou didst not say I was a Sahib?"

"What need? I have told thee many times we be but two souls seeking escape. He said–and he is just herein–that the River of Healing will break forth even as I dreamed–at my feet if need be. Having found the Way, seest thou, that shall free me from the Wheel, need I trouble to find a way about the mere fields of earth–which are illusion? That were senseless. I have my dreams, night upon night repeated; I have the *Jâtaka;* and I have thee, Friend of all the World. It was written in thy horoscope that a Red Bull on a green field–I have not forgotten–should bring thee to honor. Who but I saw that prophecy accomplished? Indeed, I was the instrument. Thou shalt find me my River, being in return the instrument. The Search is sure!"

He set his ivory-yellow face, serene and untroubled, towards the beckoning Hills; his shadow shouldering far before him in the dust.

Chapter Thirteen

Who hath desired the Sea—the immense and contemptuous surges?
The shudder, the stumble, the swerve ere the star-stabbing bowsprit emerges—
The orderly clouds of the trade and the ridged roaring sapphire thereunder—
Unheralded cliff-lurking flaws and the head-sails' low-volleying thunder?
His Sea is no wonder the same—his Sea and the same in each wonder—
His Sea that his being fulfils?
So and no otherwise—so and no otherwise hillmen desire their hills!

"WHO GOES TO the Hills goes to his mother."

They had crossed the Sewaliks and the half-tropical Doon, left Mussoorie behind them, and headed north along the narrow hill-roads. Day after day they struck deeper into the huddled mountains, and day after day Kim watched the lama return to a man's strength. Among the terraces of the Doon he had leaned on the boy's shoulder, ready to profit by wayside halts. Under the great ramp to Mussoorie he drew himself together as an old hunter faces a well-remembered bank, and where he should have sunk exhausted swung his long draperies about him, drew a deep double-lungful of the diamond air, and walked as only a hillman can. Kim, plains-bred and plains-fed, sweated and panted astonished. "This is *my* country," said the lama. "Beside Such-zen, this is flatter than a rice-field"; and with steady, driving strokes from the loins he strode upwards. But it was on the steep downhill marches, three thousand feet in three hours, that he went utterly away from Kim, whose back ached with holding back, and whose big toe was nigh cut off by his grass sandal-string. Through the speckled shadow of the great deodar-forests; through oak feathered and plumed with ferns; birch, ilex, rhododendron, and pine, out on to the bare hillsides' slippery sunburnt grass, and back into the woodlands' coolth again, till oak gave way to bamboo and palm of the valley, he swung untiring.

Glancing back in the twilight at the huge ridges behind him and the faint, thin line of the road whereby they had come, he would lay out, with a hillman's generous breadth of vision, fresh marches for the morrow; or, halting in the neck of some uplifted pass that gave on Spiti and Kulu, would stretch out his hands yearningly towards the high snows of the horizon. In the dawns they flared windy-red above stark blue, as Kedarnath and Badrinath—kings of that wilderness—took the first sunlight. All day long they lay like molten silver under the sun, and at evening put on their jewels again. At first they breathed temperately upon the travellers, winds good to meet when one crawled over some gigantic hog-back; but in a few days, at a height of nine or ten thousand feet, those breezes bit; and Kim kindly allowed a village of hillmen to acquire merit by giving him a rough blanket-coat. The lama was mildly surprised that any one should object to the knife-edged breezes which had cut the years off his shoulders.

"These are but the lower hills, *chela.* There is no cold till we come to the true Hills."

"Air and water are good, and the people are devout enough, but the food is very bad," Kim growled; "and we walk as though we were mad—or English. It freezes at night, too."

"A little, maybe; but only enough to make old bones rejoice in the sun. We must not always delight in the soft beds and rich food."

"We might at the least keep to the road."

Kim had all a plainsman's affection for the well-trodden track, not six feet wide, that snaked among the mountains; but the lama, being Tibetan, could not refrain from short cuts over spurs and the rims of gravel-strewn slopes. As he explained to his limping disciple, a man bred among mountains can prophesy the course of a mountain-road, and though low-lying clouds might be a hindrance to a short-cutting stranger, they made no earthly difference to a thoughtful man. Thus, after long hours of what would be reckoned very fair mountaineering in civilised countries, they would pant over a saddle-back, sidle past a few land-slips, and drop through forest at an angle of forty-five on to the road again. Along their track lay the villages of the hill-folk—mud and earth huts, timbers now and then rudely carved with an axe—clinging like swallows' nests against the steeps, huddled on tiny flats half-way down a three-thousand-foot glissade; jammed into a corner between cliffs that funnelled and focussed every wandering blast; or, for the sake of summer pasture, cowering down on a neck that in winter would be ten feet deep in snow. And the people—the sallow, greasy, duffle-clad people, with short bare legs and faces almost Esquimaux—would flock out and adore. The Plains—kindly and gentle—had treated the lama as a holy man among holy men. But the Hills worshipped him as one in the confidence of all the devils. Theirs was an almost obliterated Buddhism, overlaid with a nature-worship fantastic as their own landscapes, elaborate as the terracing of their tiny fields; but they recognised the big hat, the clicking rosary, and the rare Chinese texts for great authority; and they respected the man under the hat.

"We saw thee come down over the black Breasts of Eua," said a Betah who gave them cheese, sour milk, and stone-hard bread one evening. "We do not use that often—except when calving cows stray in summer." There is a sudden wind among those stones that casts men down on the stillest day. But what should such folk care for the Devil of Eua!

Then did Kim, aching in every fibre, dizzy with looking down, footsore with cramping desperate toes into inadequate crannies, take joy in the day's march—such joy as a boy of St. Xavier's who had won the quarter-mile on the flat might take in the praises of his friends. The hills sweated the *ghi* and sugar suet off his bones; the dry air, taken sobbingly at the head of cruel passes, firmed and built out his upper ribs; and the tilted levels put new hard muscles into calf and thigh.

They meditated often on the Wheel of Life—the more so since, as the lama said, they were freed from its visible temptations. Except the gray eagle and an occasional far-seen bear grubbing and rooting on the hillside, the vision of a furious painted leopard met at dawn in a still valley devouring a goat, and now and again a bright-coloured bird, they were alone with the winds and the grass singing under the wind. The women of the smoky huts over whose roofs the two walked as they descended the mountains were unlovely and unclean, wives of many husbands, and afflicted with goitre. The men were wood-cutters when they were not farmers—meek, and of an incredible simplicity. But that suitable discourse might not fail, Fate sent them, overtaking and overtaken upon the road, the courteous Dacca physician, who paid for his food in ointments good for goitre and counsels that restore peace between men and women. He seemed to know these hills as well as he knew the hill dialects, and gave the lama the lie of the land toward Ladakh and Tibet. He said they could return to the Plains at any moment. Meantime, for such as loved mountains, yonder road might amuse. This was not all revealed in a breath, but at evening encounters on the stone threshing-floors, when, patients disposed of, the doctor would smoke and the lama snuff, while Kim watched the wee cows grazing on the housetops, or threw his soul after his eye across the deep blue gulfs between range and range. And there were talks apart in the dark woods, when the doctor would seek herbs, and Kim, as budding physician, must accompany him.

"You see, Mister O'Hara, I do not know what the deuce-an'all I shall do when I find our sporting friends; but if you will kindly keep within sight of my umbrella, which is fine fixed point for cadastral survey, I feel much better."

Kim looked out across the jungle of peaks. "This is not my country, *hakim.* Easier, I think, to find one louse in a bear-skin."

"Oah, thatt is my strong points. There is no hurry for Hurree. They were at Leh not so long ago. They said they had come down from the Kara Korum with their heads and horns and all. I am onlee afraid they will have sent back all their letters and compromising things from Leh into Russian territoree. Of course they will walk away as far to the East as possible—just to show that they were never among the Western States. You do not know the Hills?" He scratched with a twig on the earth. "Look! They should have come in by Srinagar or Abbottabad. *Thatt* is their short road—down the river by Bunji and Astor. But they have made mischief in the West. So"—he drew a furrow from left to right—"they march and they march away East to Leh (ah! it is cold there), and down the Indus to Han-lé (I know that road), and then down, you see, to Bushahr and Chini valley. That is ascertained by process of elimination, and also by asking questions from people that I cure so well. Our friends have been a long time playing about and producing impressions. So they are well known from far off. You will see me catch them somewhere in Chini valley. Please keep your eye on the umbrella."

It nodded like a wind-blown harebell down the valleys and round the mountain-sides, and in due time the lama and Kim, who steered by compass, would overhaul it, vending ointments and powders at eventide. "We came by such and such a way!" The lama would throw a careless finger backward at the ridges, and the umbrella would expend itself in compliments.

They crossed a snowy pass in cold moonlight, when the lama, mildly chaffing Kim, went through up to his knees, like a Bactrian camel—the snow-bred, shag-haired sort that come into the Kashmir Serai. They dipped across beds of light snow and snow-powdered shale, where they took refuge from a gale in a camp of Tibetans hurrying down tiny sheep, each laden with a bag of borax. They came out upon grassy shoulders still snow-speckled, and through forest, to grass anew. For all their marchings, Kedarnath and Badrinath were not impressed; and it was only after days of travel that Kim, uplifted upon some insignificant ten-thousand-foot hummock, could see that a shoulder-knot or horn of the two great lords had—ever so slightly—changed outline.

At last they entered a world within a world—a velley of leagues where the high hills were fashioned of the mere rubble and refuse from off the knees of the mountains. Here one day's march carried them no farther, it seemed, than a dreamer's clogged pace bears him in a nightmare.

They skirted a shoulder painfully for hours, and, behold, it was but an outlying boss in an outlying buttress of the main pile! A rounded meadow revealed itself, when they had reached it, for a vast tableland running far into the valley. Three days later, it was a dim fold in the earth to southward.

"Surely the Gods live here," said Kim, beaten down by the silence and the appalling sweep and dispersal of the cloud-shadows after rain. "This is no place for men!"

"Long and long ago," said the lama, as to himself, "it was asked of the Lord whether the world were everlasting. To this the Excellent One returned no answer. . . . When I was in Ceylon, a wise Seeker confirmed that from the gospel which is written in Pali. Certainly, since we know the way to Freedom, the question were unprofitable, but—look, and know illusion, *chela!* These are the true Hills! They are like my hills by Such-zen. Never were such hills!"

Above them, still enormously above them, earth towered away towards the snow-line, where from east to west across hundreds of miles, ruled as with a ruler, the last of the bold birches stopped. Above that, in scarps and blocks upheaved, the rocks strove to fight their heads above the white smother. Above these again, changeless since the world's beginning, but changing to every mood of sun and cloud, lay out the eternal snow. They could see blots and blurs on its face where storm and wandering williwaw got up to dance. Below them, as they stood, the forest slid away in a sheet of blue-green for mile upon mile; below the forest was a village in its sprinkle of terraced fields and steep grazing-grounds; below the village they knew, though a thunderstorm worried and growled there for the moment, a pitch of twelve or fifteen hundred feet gave to the moist valley where the streams gather that are the mothers of young Sutluj.

As usual, the lama had led Kim by cow-track and by-road, far from the main route along which Hurree Babu, that "fearful man," had bucketed three days before through a storm to which nine Englishmen out of ten would have given full right of way. Hurree was no game-shot,—the snick of a trigger made him change color,—but, as he himself would have said, he was "fairly effeecient stalker," and he had raked the huge valley with a pair of cheap binoculars to some purpose. Moreover, the white of worn canvas tents against green carries far. Hurree Babu had seen all he wanted to see when he sat on the threshing-floor of Ziglaur, twenty miles away as the eagle flies, and forty by road—that is to say, two small dots which one day were just below the snow-line, and the next had moved downward perhaps six inches on the hillside. Once cleaned out and set to the work, his fat bare legs could cover a surprising amount of ground, and this was the reason why, while Kim and the lama lay in a leaky hut at Ziglaur till the storm should be overpassed, an oily, wet, but always smiling Bengali, talking the best of English with the vilest of phrases, was ingratiating himself with two sodden and rather rheumatic foreigners. He had arrived, revolving many wild schemes, on the heels of a thunderstorm which had split a pine over against their camp, and so convinced a dozen or two forcibly impressed baggage-coolies the day was inauspicious for farther travel that with one accord they had thrown down their loads and jibbed. They were subjects of a Hill-Rajah who farmed out their services, as is the custom, for his private gain; and, to add to their personal distresses, the strange Sahibs had already threatened them with rifles. The most of them knew rifles and Sahibs of old: they were trackers and *shikarris* of the Northern valleys, keen after bear and wild goat; but they had never been thus treated in their lives. So the forest took them to her bosom, and, for all oaths and clamor, refused to restore. There was no need to feign madness or—the Babu had thought of another means of securing a welcome. He wrung out his wet clothes, slipped on his patent-leather shoes, opened the blue and white umbrella, and with mincing gait and a heart beating against his tonsils appeared as "agent for His Royal Highness, the Rajah of Rampur, gentlemen. What can I do for you, please?"

The gentlemen were delighted. One was visibly French, the other Russian, but they spoke English not much inferior to the Babu's. They begged his kind offices. Their native servants had gone sick at Leh. They had hurried on because they were anxious to bring the spoils of the chase to Simla ere the skins grew moth-eaten. They bore a general letter of introduction (the Babu salaamed to it orientally) to all Government officials. No, they had not met any other shooting-parties *enroute.* They did for themselves. They had plenty of supplies. They only wished to push on as soon as might be. At this he waylaid a cowering hillman among the trees, and after three minutes' talk and a little silver (one cannot be economical upon State service, though Hurree's heart bled at the waste) the eleven coolies and the three hangers-on reappeared. At least the Babu would be a witness to oppression.

"My royal master, he will be much annoyed, but these people are onlee common people and grossly ignorant. If your honours will kindly overlook unfortunate affair, I shall be much pleased. In a little while rain will stop and we can then proceed. You have been shooting, eh? That is fine performance!"

He skipped nimbly from one *kilta* to the next, making pretence to adjust each conical basket. The Englishman is not, as a rule, familiar with the Asiatic, but he would not strike across the wrist a kindly Babu who had accidentally upset a *kilta* with a red oil-skin top. On the other hand, he would not press drink upon a Babu were he never so friendly, nor would he invite him to meat. The strangers did all these things, and asked many questions,–about women mostly,–to which Hurree returned gay and unstudied answers. They gave him a glass of whitish fluid like to gin, and then more; and in a little time his gravity departed from him. He became thickly treasonous, and spoke in terms of sweeping indecency of a Government which had forced upon him a white man's education and neglected to supply him with a white man's salary. He babbled tales of oppression and wrong till the tears ran down his cheeks for the miseries of his land. Then he staggered off, singing love-songs of Lower Bengal, and collapsed upon a tree-trunk. Never was so unfortunate a product of English rule in India more unhappily thrust upon aliens.

"They are all just of that pattern," said one sportsman to the other in French. "When we get into India proper thou wilt see. I should like to visit his Rajah. One might speak the good word there. It is possible that he has heard of us and wishes to signify his good will."

"We have not time. We must get into Simla as soon as may be," his companion replied. "For my own part, I wish our reports had been sent back from Hilás or even Leh."

"The English post is better and safer. Remember we are given all facilities–and name of God!–they give them to us too! Is it unbelievable stupidity?"

"It is pride–pride that deserves and will receive punishment."

"Yes! To fight a fellow-Continental in our game is something. There is a risk attached, but these people–bah! It is too easy."

"Pride–all pride, my friend."

"Now what the deuce is good of Chandernagore being so close to Calcutta and all," said Hurree, snoring open-mouthed on the sodden moss, "if I cannot understand their French? They talk so par*tic*ularly fast! It would have been much better to cut their beastly throats."

When he presented himself again he was racked with a headache–penitent, and volubly afraid that in his drunkenness he might have been indiscreet. He loved the British Government–it was the source of all prosperity and honour, and his master at Rampur held the very same opinion. Upon this the men began to deride him and to quote past words, till step by step, with deprecating smirks, oily grins, and leers of infinite cunning, the poor Babu was beaten out of his defences and forced to speak–truth. When Lurgan was told the tale later, he mourned aloud that he could not have been in the place of the stubborn, inattentive coolies, who, with grass mats over their heads and the raindrops puddling in their footprints, waited on the weather. All the Sahibs of their acquaintance–rough-clad men joyously returning year after year to their chosen gullies–had servants and cooks and orderlies, very often hillmen. These Sahibs travelled without any retinue. Therefore they were poor Sahibs, and ignorant; for no Sahib in his senses would follow a

Bengali's advice. But the Bengali, appearing from somewhere, had given them money, and would make shift with their dialect. Used to comprehensive ill-treatment from their own color, they suspected a trap somewhere, and stood by to run if occasion offered.

Then through the new-washed air, streaming with delicious earth-smells, the Babu led the way down the slopes–walking ahead of the coolies in pride; walking behind the foreigners in humility. His thoughts were many and various. The least of them would have interested his companions beyond words. But he was an agreeable guide, ever keen to point out the beauties of his royal master's domain. He peopled the hills with anything they had a mind to slay–thar, ibex, or markhor, and bears by Elisha's allowance. He discoursed of botany and ethnology with unimpeachable inaccuracy, and his store of local legends–he had been a trusted agent of the State for fifteen years, remember–was inexhaustible.

"Decidedly this fellow is an original," said the taller of the two foreigners. "He is like the nightmare of a Viennese courier."

"He represents *in petto* India in transition–the monstrous hybridism of East and West," the Russian replied. "It is *we* who can deal with Orientals."

"He has lost his own country and has not acquired any other. But he has a most complete hatred of his conquerors. Listen. He confides to me last night," etc.

Under the striped umbrella Hurree Babu was straining ear and brain to follow the quick-poured French, and keeping both eyes on a *kilta* full of maps and documents–an extra large one with a double red oil-skin cover. He did not wish to steal anything. He only desired to know what to steal, and, incidentally, how to get away when he had stolen it. He thanked all the Gods of Hindustan, and Herbert Spencer, that there remained some valuables to steal.

On the second day the road rose steeply to a grass spur above the forest; and it was here, about sunset, that they came across an aged lama–but they called him a bonze–sitting cross-legged above a mysterious chart held down by stones, which he was explaining to a young man, evidently a neophyte, of singular, though unwashen, beauty. The striped umbrella had been sighted half a march away, and Kim had suggested a halt till it came up to them.

"Ha!" said Hurree Babu, resourceful as Puss-in-boots. "That is eminent local holy man. Probably subject of my royal master."

"What is he doing? It is very curious."

"He is expounding holy picture–*all* hand-worked."

The two men stood bare-headed in the wash of the afternoon sunlight low across the gold-colored grass. The sullen coolies, glad of the check, halted and slid down their loads.

"Look!" said the Frenchman. "It is like a picture for the birth of a religion–the first teacher and the first disciple. Is he a Buddhist?"

"Of some debased kind," the other answered. "There are no true Buddhists among the Hills. But look at the folds of the drapery. Look at his eyes–how insolent! Why does this make one feel that we are so young a people?" The speaker struck passionately at a tall weed. "We have nowhere left our mark yet. Nowhere! *That,* do you understand, is what disquiets me." He scowled at the placid face, and the monumental calm of the pose.

"Have patience. We shall make your mark together–we and you young people. Meantime, draw his picture."

The Babu advanced loftily; his back out of all keeping with his deferential speech, or his wink towards Kim.

"Holy One, these be Sahibs. My medicines cured one of a flux, and I go into Simla to oversee his recovery. They wish to see thy picture–"

"To heal the sick is always good. This is the Wheel of Life," said the lama, "the same I showed thee in the hut at Ziglaur when the rain fell."

"And to hear thee expound it."

The lama's eyes lighted at the prospect of new listeners. "To expound the Most Excellent Way is good. Have they any knowledge of Hindi, such as had the Keeper of Images?"

"A little, maybe."

Hereat, simply as a child engrossed with a new game, the lama threw back his head and began the full-throated invocation of the Doctor of Divinity ere he opens the full doctrine. The strangers leaned on their alpenstocks and listened. Kim, squatting humbly, watched the red sunlight on their faces, and the blend and parting of their long shadows. They wore un-English leggings and curious girt-in belts that reminded him hazily of the pictures in a book at St. Xavier's library: *The Adventures of a Young Naturalist in Mexico* was its name. Yes, they looked very like the wonderful M. Sumichrast of that tale, and very unlike the "highly unscrupulous folk" of Hurree Babu's imagining. The coolies, earth-colored and mute, crouched reverently some twenty or thirty yards away, and the Babu, the slack of his thin gear snapping like a marking-flag in the chill breeze, stood by with an air of happy proprietorship.

"These are the men," Hurree whispered, as the ritual went on and the two whites followed the grass blade sweeping from Hell to Heaven and back again. "All their books are in the large *kilta* with the reddish top,—books and reports and maps,—and I have seen a King's letter that either Hilás or Bunár has written. They guard it most carefully. They have sent nothing back from Hilás or Leh. That is sure."

"Who is with them?"

"Only the *beggar*-coolies. They have no servants. They are so close they cook their own food."

"But what am I to do?"

"Wait and see. Only if any chance comes to me thou wilt know where to seek for the papers."

"This were better in Mahbub Ali's hands than a Bengali's," said Kim scornfully.

"There are more ways of getting to a sweetheart than butting down a wall."

"See here the Hell appointed for avarice and greed. Flanked upon the one side by Desire and on the other by Weariness." The lama warmed to his work, and one of the strangers sketched him in the quick-fading light.

"That is enough," the man said at last brusquely. "I cannot understand him, but I want that picture. He is a better artist than I. Ask him if he will sell it."

"He says 'No, Sar,' " the Babu replied. The lama, of course, would no more have parted with his chart to a casual wayfarer than an archbishop would pawn the holy vessels of a cathedral. All Tibet is full of cheap reproductions of the Wheel; but the lama was an artist, as well as a wealthy abbot in his own place.

"Perhaps in three days, or four, or ten, if I perceive that the Sahib is a Seeker and of good understanding, I may myself draw him another. But *this* was used for the initiation of a novice. Tell him so, *hakim*."

"He wishes it now—for money."

The lama shook his head slowly and began to fold up the Wheel. The Russian, on his side, saw no more than an unclean old man haggling over a dirty piece of paper. He drew out a handful of rupees, and snatched half-jestingly at the chart, which tore in the lama's grip. A low murmur of horror went up from the coolies—some of whom were Spiti men and, by their lights, good Buddhists. The lama rose at the insult; his hand went to the heavy iron pencase that is the priest's weapon, and the Babu danced in agony.

"Now you see–you see why I wanted witnesses. They are highly unscrupulous people. Oh Sar! Sar! You must *not* hit holy man!"

"*Chela!* He has defiled the Written Word!"

It was too late. Before Kim could ward him off, the Russian struck the old man full on the face. Next instant he was rolling over and over down hill with Kim at his throat. The blow had waked every unknown Irish devil in the boy's blood, and the sudden fall of his enemy did the rest. The lama dropped to his knees, half-stunned; the coolies under their loads fled up the hill as fast as plainsmen run across the level. They had seen sacrilege unspeakable, and it behoved them to get away before the Gods and devils of the hills took vengeance. The Frenchman ran towards the lama, fumbling at his revolver with some notion of making him a hostage for his companion. A shower of cutting stones–hillmen are very straight shots–drove him away, and a coolie from Ao-chung snatched the lama into the stampede. All came about as swiftly as the sudden mountain-darkness.

"They have taken the baggage and all the guns," yelled the Frenchman, firing blindly into the twilight.

"All right, Sar! All right! Don't shoot. I go to rescue," and Hurree, pounding down the slope, cast himself bodily upon the delighted and astonished Kim, who was banging his breathless foe's head against a boulder.

"Go back to the coolies," whispered the Babu in his ear. "They have the baggage. The papers are in the *kilta* with the red top, but look through all. Take their papers, and specially the *murasla* (King's letter). Go! The other man comes!"

Kim tore up hill. A revolver-bullet rang on a rock by his side, and he cowered partridge-wise.

"If you shoot," shouted Hurree, "they will descend and annihilate us. I have rescued the gentleman, Sar. This is par*tic*ularly dangerous."

"By Jove!" Kim was thinking hard in English. "This is dam-tight place, but *I* think it is self-defence." He felt in his bosom for Mahbub's gift, and uncertainly–save for a few practice shots in the Bikaner desert, he had never used the little gun–pulled trigger.

"What did I say, Sar!" The Babu seemed to be in tears. "Come down here and assist to resuscitate. We are all up a tree, I tell you."

The shots ceased. There was a sound of stumbling feet, and Kim hurried upward through the gloom, swearing like a cat–or a country-bred.

"Did they wound thee, *chela?*" called the lama above him.

"No. And thou?" He dived into a clump of stunted firs.

"Unhurt. Come away. We go with these folk to Shamlegh-under-the-Snow."

"But not before we have done justice," a voice cried. "I have got the Sahibs' guns–all four. Let us go down."

"He struck the Holy One–we saw it! Our cattle will be barren–our wives will cease to bear! The snows will slide upon us as we go home. . . . On top of all other oppression too!"

The little fir-clump filled with clamoring coolies–panic-stricken, and in their terror capable of anything. The man from Ao-chung clicked the breech-bolt of his gun impatiently, and made as to go down hill. "Wait a little, Holy One; they cannot go far: wait till I return."

"It is this person who has suffered wrong," said the lama, his hand over his brow.

"For that very reason," was the reply.

"If this person overlooks it, your hands are clean. Moreover, ye acquire merit by obedience."

"Wait, and we will all go to Shamlegh together," the man insisted.

For a moment, for just so long as it needs to stuff a cartridge into a breechloader, the lama hesitated. Then he rose to his feet, and laid a finger on the man's shoulder.

"Hast thou heard? *I* say there shall be no killing–I who was Abbot of Such-zen. Is it any lust of thine to be re-born as a rat, or a snake under the eaves–a worm in the belly of the most mean beast? Is it thy wish to–"

The man from Ao-chung fell to his knees, for the voice boomed like a Tibetan devil-gong.

"Ai! ai!" cried the Spiti men. "Do not curse us–do not curse him. It was but his zeal, Holy One! . . . Put down the rifle, fool!"

"Anger on anger! Evil on evil! There will be no killing. Let the priest-beaters go in bondage to their own acts. Just and sure is the Wheel, swerving not a hair! They will be born many times–in torment." His head drooped, and he leaned heavily on Kim's shoulder.

"I have come near to great evil, *chela,*" he whispered in that dead hush under the pines. "I was tempted to loose the bullet; and truly, in Tibet there would have been a heavy and a slow death for them. . . . He struck me across the face . . . upon the flesh . . ." He slid to the ground, breathing heavily, and Kim could hear the over-driven heart bump and check.

"Have they hurt him to the death?" said the Ao-chung man, while the others stood mute.

Kim knelt over the body in deadly fear. "Nay," he cried passionately, "this is only a weakness." Then he remembered that he was a white man, with a white man's camp-fittings at his service. "Open the *kiltas!* The Sahibs may have a medicine."

"Oho! Then I know it," said the Ao-chung man with a laugh. "Not for five years was I Yankling Sahib's *shikarri* without knowing that medicine. I too have tasted it. Behold!" He drew from his breast a bottle of cheap whisky–such as is sold to explorers at Leh–and cleverly forced a little between the lama's teeth.

"So I did when Yankling Sahib twisted his foot beyond Astor. Aha! I have already looked into their baskets–but we will make fair division at Shamlegh. Give him a little more. It is good medicine. Feel! His heart goes better now. Lay his head down and rub a little on the chest. If he had waited quietly while I accounted for the Sahibs this would never have come. But perhaps the Sahibs may chase us here. Then it would not be wrong to shoot them with their own guns, heh?"

"One is paid, I think, already," said Kim between his teeth. "I kicked him in the groin as we went down hill. Would I had killed him!"

"It is well to be brave when one does not live in Rampur," said one whose hut lay within a few miles of the Rajah's rickety palace. "If we get a bad name among the Sahibs, none will employ us as *Shikarris* any more."

"Oh, but there are not Angrezi Sahibs–not merry-minded men like Fostum Sahib or Yankling Sahib. They are foreigners–they cannot speak Angrezi as do Sahibs."

Here the lama coughed and sat up, groping for the rosary.

"There shall be no killing," he murmured. "Just is the Wheel! Evil on evil–"

"Nay, Holy One. We are all here." The Ao-chung man timidly patted his feet. "Except by thy order, no one shall be slain. Rest awhile. We will make a little camp here, and later, as the moon rises, we go to Shamlegh-under-the-Snow."

"After a blow," said a Spiti man sententiously, "It is best to sleep."

"There is, as it were, a dizziness at the back of my neck, and a pinching in it. Let me lay my head on thy lap, *chela.* I am an old man, but not free from passion. . . . We must think of the Cause of Things."

"Give him a blanket. We dare not light a fire lest the Sahibs see."

"Better get away to Shamlegh. None will follow us to Shamlegh." This was the nervous Rampur man.

"I have been Fostum Sahib's *shikarri,* and I am Yankling Sahib's *shikarri.* I should have been with Yankling Sahib now but for this cursed beegar (the *corvée*). Let two men watch below with the guns lest the Sahibs do more foolishness. *I* shall not leave this Holy One."

They sat down a little apart from the lama, and, after listening awhile, passed round a water-pipe whose receiver was an old Day and Martin blacking-bottle. The glow of the red charcoal as it went from hand to hand lit up the narrow, blinking eyes, the high Chinese cheek-bones, and the bull-throats that melted away into the dark duffle folds round the shoulders. They looked like kobolds from some magic mine–gnomes of the hills in conclave. And while they talked, the voices of the snow-waters round them diminished one by one as the night-frost choked and clogged the runnels.

"How he stood up against us!" said a Spiti man admiring. "I remember an old ibex, out Ladakh-way, that Dupont Sahib missed on a shoulder-shot, seven seasons back, standing up just like him. Dupont Sahib was a good *shikarri.*"

"Not as good as Yankling Sahib." The Ao-chung man took a pull at the whisky-bottle and passed it over. "Now hear me–unless any other man thinks he knows more."

The challenge was not taken up.

"We go to Shamlegh when the moon rises. There we will fairly divide the baggage between us. I am content with this new little rifle and all its cartridges."

"Are the bears only bad on thy holding?" said a mate, sucking at the pipe.

"No; but musk-pods are worth six rupees apiece now, and thy women can have the canvas of the tents and some of the cooking-gear. We will do all that at Shamlegh before dawn. Then we all go our ways, remembering that we have never seen or taken service with these Sahibs, who may, indeed, say that we have stolen their baggage."

"That is well for thee, but what will our Rajah say?"

"Who is to tell him? Those Sahibs, who cannot speak our talk, or the Babu, who for his own ends gave us money? Will *he* lead an army against us? What evidence will remain? That we do not need we shall throw on Shamlegh midden, where no man has yet set foot."

"Who is at Shamlegh this summer?" The place was only a grazing centre of three or four huts.

"The Woman of Shamlegh. *She* has no love for Sahibs, as we know. The others can be pleased with little presents; and here is enough for us all." He patted the fat sides of the nearest basket.

"But–but–"

"I have said they are not true Sahibs. All their skins and heads were bought in the bazar at Leh. *I* know the marks. I showed them to ye last march."

"True. They were all bought skins and heads. Some had even the moth in them."

That was a shrewd argument, and the Ao-chung man knew his fellows.

"If the worst comes to the worst, I shall tell Yankling Sahib, who is a man of a merry mind, and he will laugh. We are not doing any wrong to any Sahibs whom we know. *They* are priest-beaters. They frightened us. We fled! Who knows where we dropped the baggage? Do ye think Yankling Sahib will permit down-country police to wander all over the hills, disturbing his game? It is a far cry from Simla to Chini, and farther from Shamlegh to Shamlegh midden."

"So be it, but I carry the big *kilta.* The basket with the red top that the

Sahibs pack themselves every morning."

"Thus it is proved," said the Shamlegh man adroitly, "that they are Sahibs of no account. Who ever heard of Fostum Sahib, or Yankling Sahib, or even the little Peel Sahib that sits up of nights to shoot serow–I saw, who ever heard of these Sahibs coming into the hills without a down-country cook, and a bearer, and–and all manner of well-paid, high-handed and oppressive folk in their tail? How can they make trouble? What of the *kilta?*"

"Nothing, but that it is full of the Written Word–books and papers in which they wrote, and strange instruments, as of worship."

"Shamlegh midden will take them all."

"True! But how if we insult the Sahib's Gods thereby? I do not like to handle the Written Word in that fashion. And their brass idols are beyond my comprehension. It is no plunder for simple hill-folk."

"The old man still sleeps. Hst! We will ask his *chela.*" The Ao-chung man refreshed himself, and swelled with pride of leadership.

"We have here," he whispered, "a *kilta* whose nature we do not know."

"But I do," said Kim cautiously. The lama drew breath in natural, easy sleep, and Kim had been thinking of Hurree's last words. As a player of the Great Game, he was disposed just then to reverence the Babu. "It is a *kilta* with a red top full of very wonderful things, not to be handled by fools."

"I said it; I said it," cried the bearer of that burden. "Thinkest thou it will betray us?"

"Not if it be given to me. I will draw out its magic. Otherwise it will do great harm."

"A priest always takes his share." Whisky was demoralising the Ao-chung man.

"It is no matter to me," Kim answered, with the craft of his mother-country. "Share it among you, and see what comes!"

"Not I. I was only jesting. Give the order. There is more than enough for us all. We go our way from Shamlegh in the dawn."

They arranged and re-arranged their artless little plans for another hour, while Kim shivered with cold and pride. The humor of the situation tickled the Irish and the Oriental in his soul. Here were the emissaries of the dread Power of the North, very possibly as great in their own land as Mahbub or Colonel Creighton, suddenly smitten helpless. One of them, he privately knew, would be lame for a time. They had made promises to Kings. To-night they lay out somewhere below him, chartless, foodless, tentless, gunless,–except for Hurree Babu, guideless. And this collapse of their Great Game (Kim wondered to whom they would report it), this panicky bolt into the night, had come about through no craft of Hurree's or contrivance of Kim's, but simply, beautifully, and inevitably as the capture of Mahbub's *faquir*-friends by the zealous young policeman at Umballa.

"They are there–with nothing; and, by Jove, it is cold! I am here with all their things. Oh, they will be angry! I am sorry for Hurree Babu."

Kim might have saved his pity, for though at that moment the Bengali suffered acutely in the flesh, his soul was puffed and lofty. A mile down the hill, on the edge of the pine-forest, two half-frozen men–one powerfully sick at intervals–were varying mutual recriminations with the most poignant abuse of the Babu, who seemed distraught with terror. They demanded a plan of action. He explained that they were very lucky to be alive; that their coolies, if not then stalking them, had passed beyond recall; that the Rajah, his master, was ninety miles away, and, so far from lending them money and a retinue for the Simla journey, would surely cast them into prison if he heard that they had hit a priest. He enlarged on this sin and its consequences till they bade him change the subject. Their one hope, said he, was unostentatious flight from village to village till they reached civilisation; and, for the hundredth time dissolved in tears, he demanded of the high stars why the Sahibs "had beaten holy man."

Ten steps would have taken Hurree into the creaking gloom utterly beyond their reach—to the shelter and food of the nearest village, where glib-tongued doctors were scarce. But he preferred to endure cold, belly-pinch, bad words, and occasional blows in the company of his honored employers. Crouched against a tree-trunk, he sniffed dolefully.

"And have you thought," said the uninjured man hotly, "what sort of spectacle we shall present wandering through these hills among these aborigines?"

Hurree Babu had thought of little else for some hours, but the remark was not to his address.

"We cannot wander! I can hardly walk," groaned Kim's victim.

"Perhaps the holy man will be merciful in loving-kindness, Sar, otherwise—"

"I promise myself a peculiar pleasure in emptying my revolver into that young bonze when next we meet," was the unchristian answer.

"Revolvers! Vengeance! Bonzes!" Hurree crouched lower. The war was breaking out afresh. "Have you no consideration for our loss? The baggage! The baggage!" He could hear the speaker literally dancing on the grass. "Everything we bore! Everything we have secured! Our gains! Eight months' work! Do you know what that means? 'Decidedly it is we who can deal with Orientals!' Oh, you have done well."

They fell to it in several tongues, and Hurree smiled. Kim was with the *kiltas,* and in the *kiltas* lay eight months of good diplomacy. There was no means of communicating with the boy, but he could be trusted. For the rest, he could so stage-manage the journey through the hills that Hilás, Bunár, and four hundred miles of hill-roads should tell the tale for a generation. Men who cannot control their own coolies are little respected in the Hills, and the hillman has a very keen sense of humor.

"If I had done it myself," thought Hurree, "it would not have been better; and, by Jove, now I think of it, of course I arranged it myself. How quick I have been! Just when I ran down hill I thought it! Thee outrage was accidental, but onlee me could have worked it—ah—for all it was dam well worth. Consider the moral effect upon these ignorant peoples! No treaties—no papers—no written documents at all—and *me* to interpret for them. How I shall laugh with the Colonel! I wish I had their papers also: but you cannot occupy two places simultaneously. Thatt is axiomatic."

Chapter Fourteen

My brother kneels (so saith Kabir)
    To stone and brass in heathenwise,
But in my brother's voice I hear
    My own unanswered agonies.
His God is as his Fates assign—
His prayer is all the world's—and mine.
KABIR.

AT MOONRISE THE cautious coolies got under way. The lama, refreshed by his sleep and the spirit, needed no more than Kim's shoulder to bear him along—a silent, swift-striding man. They held the shale-sprinkled grass for an hour, swept round the shoulder of an immortal cliff, and climbed into a new country entirely blocked off from all sight of Chini valley. A huge pasture-ground ran up fan-shaped to the living snow. At its base was perhaps half an acre of flat land, on which stood a few soil and timber huts. Behind them—for, hill-fashion, they were perched on the edge of all things—the ground fell sheer two thousand feet to Shamlegh midden, where never yet man has set foot.

The men made no motion to divide the plunder till they had seen the lama bedded down in the best room in the place, with Kim shampooing his feet, Mohammedan fashion.

"We will send food," said the Ao-chung man, "and the red-topped *kilta.* By dawn there will be none to give evidence, one way or the other. If anything is not needed in the *kilta*—see here!"

He pointed through the window—opening into space that was filled with moonlight reflected from the snow—and threw out an empty whisky-bottle.

"No need to listen for the fall. This is the world's end," he said, and swung off. The lama looked forth, a hand on either sill, with eyes that shone like yellow opals. From the enormous pit before him white peaks lifted themselves yearning to the moonlight. The rest was as the darkness of interstellar space.

"These," he said slowly, "are indeed my Hills. Thus should a man abide, perched above the world, separated from delights, considering vast matters."

"Yes; if he has a *chela* to prepare tea for him, and to fold a blanket for his head, and to chase out calving cows."

A smoky lamp burned in a niche, but the full moonlight beat it down; and by the mixed light, stooping above the food-bag and cups, Kim moved like a tall ghost.

"Ai! But now I have let the blood cool, my head still beats and drums, and there is a cord round the back of my neck."

"No wonder. It was a strong blow. May he who dealt it—"

"But for my own passions there would have been no evil."

"What evil? Thou hast saved the Sahibs from death they deserved a hundred times."

"The lesson is not well learnt, *chela.*" The lama came to rest on a folded blanket, as Kim went forward with his evening routine. "The blow was but a shadow upon a shadow. Evil in itself—my legs weary apace these latter days!–it met evil in me–anger, rage, and a lust to return evil. These wrought in my blood, woke tumult in my stomach, and dazzled my ears." Here he drank scalding block-tea ceremonially, taking the hot cup from Kim's hand. "Had I been passionless, the evil blow would have done only bodily evil–a scar, or a bruise–which is illusion. But my mind was *not* abstracted, for rushed in straightway a lust to let the Spiti men kill. In fighting that lust, my soul was torn and wrenched beyond a thousand blows. Not till I had repeated the Blessings (he meant the Buddhist Beatitudes) did I achieve calm. But the evil planted in me by that moment's carelessness works out to its end. Just is the Wheel, swerving not a hair! Learn the lesson, *chela.*"

"It is too high for me," Kim muttered. "I am still all shaken. I am glad I hurt the man."

"I felt that sleeping upon thy knees, in the wood below. It disquieted me in my dreams–the evil in thy soul working through to mine. Yet on the other hand"–he loosed his rosary–"I have acquired merit by saving two lives–the lives of those that wronged me. Now I must see into the Cause of Things. The boat of my soul staggers."

"Sleep, and be strong. That is wisest."

"I meditate: there is a need greater than thou knowest."

Till the dawn, hour after hour, as the moonlight paled on the high peaks, and that which had been belted blackness on the sides of the far hills showed as tender green forest, the lama stared fixedly at the wall. From time to time he groaned. Outside the barred door, where discomfited kine came to ask for their old stable, Shamlegh and the coolies gave itself up to plunder and riotous living. The Ao-chung man was their leader, and once they had opened the Sahibs' tinned foods and found that they were very good they dared not turn back. Shamlegh kitchen-midden took the dunnage.

When Kim, after a night of bad dreams, stole forth to brush his teeth in the morning chill, a fair-colored woman with turquoise-studded head-gear drew him aside.

"The others have gone. They left thee this *kilta* as the promise was. I do not love Sahibs, but thou wilt make us a charm in return for it. We do not wish little Shamlegh to get a bad name on account of the –accident. I am the Woman of Shamlegh." She looked him over with bold, bright eyes, unlike the usual furtive glance of hillwomen.

"Assuredly. But it must be done in secret."

She raised the heavy *kilta* like a toy and slung it into her own hut. "Out and bar the door! Let none come near till it is finished."

"But afterwards–we may talk?"

Kim tilted the *kilta* on the floor-a cascade of Survey-instruments, books, diaries, letters, maps, and queerly scented native correspondence. At the very bottom was an embroidered bag covering a sealed, gilded, and illuminated document such as one King sends to another. Kim caught his breath with delight, and reviewed the situation from a Sahib's point of view.

"The books I do not want. Besides, they are logarithms–Survey, I suppose." He laid them aside. "The letters I do not understand, but Colonel Creighton will. They must all be kept. The maps–they draw better maps than me–*of* course. All the native letters–oho!–and particularly the *murasla.*" He sniffed the embroidered bag. "That must be from Hilás or Bunár, and Hurree Babu spoke truth. By Jove! It is a fine haul. I wish Hurree could know. . . . The rest must go out of the window." He fingered a superb prismatic compass and the shiny top of a theodolite. But after all, a Sahib cannot very well steal, and the things might be inconvenient evidence later. He sorted out every scrap of manuscript, every map, and the native letters. They made one softish slab. The three locked ferril-backed books, with five worn pocket-books, he put aside.

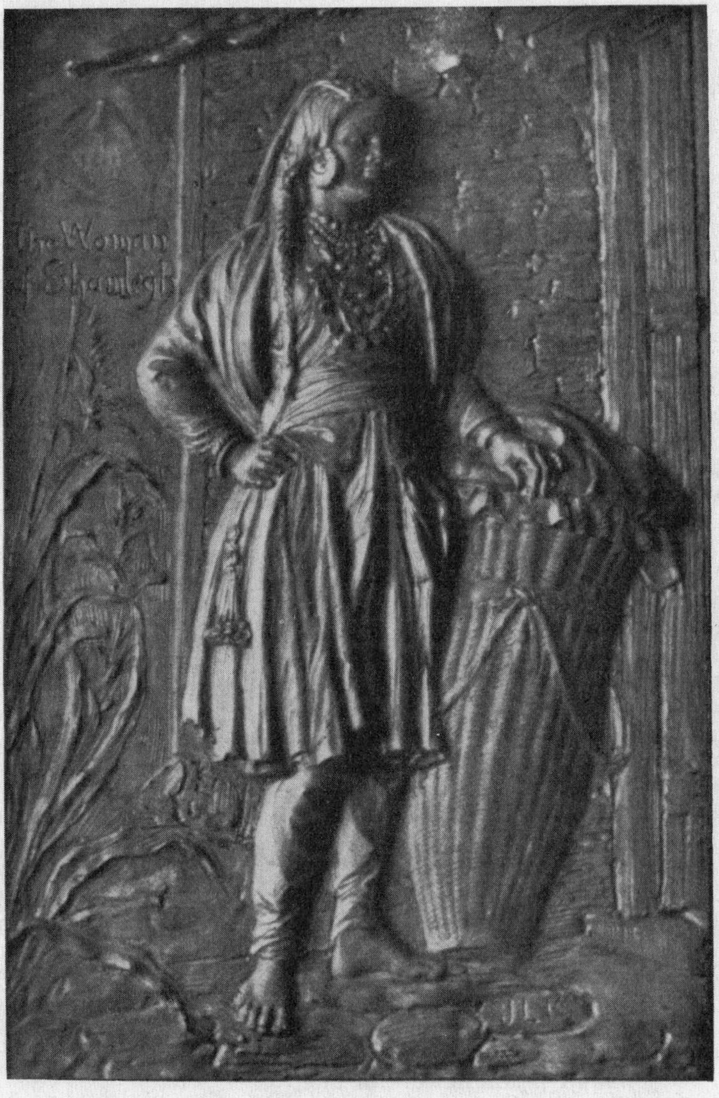

"'I AM THE WOMAN OF SHAMLEGH.'"

"The letter and the *murasla* I must carry inside my coat and under my belt, and the hand-written books I must put into the food-bag. It will be very heavy. No, I do not think there is anything more. If there is, the coolies have thrown it down the *khud,* so *thatt* is all right. Now you go too." He repacked the *kilta* with all he meant to lose, and hove it up on to the window-sill. A thousand feet below lay a long, lazy, round-shouldered bank of mist, as yet untouched by the morning sun. A thousand feet below that was an hundred-year-old pine-forest. He could see the green tops looking like a bed of moss when a wind-eddy thinned the cloud.

"No! I don't think any one will go after *you!*"

The wheeling basket vomited its contents as it dropped. The theodolite hit a jutting cliff-ledge and exploded like a shell; the books, inkstands, paint-boxes, compasses, and rulers showed for a few seconds like a swarm of bees. Then they vanished; and though Kim, hanging half out of window, strained his young ears, never a sound came up from the gulf.

"Five hundred–a thousand rupees could not buy them," he thought sorrowfully. "It was verree wasteful, but I have all their other stuff–everything they did–I hope. Now how the deuce am I to tell Hurree Babu, and *whatt* the deuce am I to do? And my old man is sick. I must tie up the letters in oilcloth. That is something to do first–else they will get all sweated. . . . And I am all alone!" He bound them into a neat packet, swedging down the stiff, sticky oilcloth at the corners, for his roving life had made him as methodical as an old hunter in matters of the road. Then with double care he packed away the books at the bottom of the food-bag.

The woman rapped at the door.

"But thou hast made no charm," she said, looking about.

"There is no need." Kim had completely overlooked the necessity for a little patter-talk. The woman laughed at his confusion irreverently.

"None–for thee. Thou canst cast a spell by the mere winking of an eye. But think of us poor people when thou art gone! They were all too drunk last night to hear a woman. Thou art not drunk?"

"I am a priest." Kim had recovered himself, and, the woman being aught but unlovely, thought best to stand on his office.

"I warned them that the Sahibs will be angry and will make an inquisition and a report to the Rajah. There is also the Babu with them. Clerks have long tongues."

"Is that all thy trouble?" The plan rose fully formed in Kim's mind, and he smiled ravishingly.

"Not all," quoth the woman, putting out a hard brown hand all covered with torquoises set in silver.

"I can finish that in a breath," he went on quickly. "The Babu is the very *hakim* (thou hast heard of him?) who was wandering among the hills by Ziglaur. I know him."

"He will tell for the sake of a reward. Sahibs cannot distinguish one hillman from another, but Babus have eyes for men–and women."

"Carry a word to him from me."

"There is nothing I would not do for thee."

He accepted the compliment calmly, as men must in lands where women make the love, tore a leaf from a note-book, and with a patent indelible pencil wrote in gross Shikast–the script that bad little boys use when they write dirt on walls: *"I have everything that they have written: their pictures of the country, and many letters. Especially the* murasla. *Tell me what to do. I am at Shamlegh-under-the-Snow. The old man is sick."*

"Take this to him. It will altogether shut his mouth. He cannot have gone far."

"Indeed no. They are still in the forest across the spur. Our children went to watch them when the light came, and have cried the news as they moved."

Kim looked his astonishment; but from the edge of the sheep-pasture floated a shrill, kite-like trill. A child tending cattle had picked it up from a brother or sister on the far side of the slope that commanded Chini valley.

"My husbands are also out there gathering wood." She drew a handful of walnuts from her bosom, split one neatly, and began to eat. Kim affected blank ignorance.

"Dost thou not know the meaning of the walnut–priest?" she said coyly, and handed him the half-shells.

"Well thought of." He slipped the piece of paper between them quickly. "Hast thou a little wax to close them on this letter?"

The woman sighed aloud, and Kim relented. "There is no payment till service has been rendered. Carry this to the Babu, and say it was sent by the Son of the Charm."

"Ai! Truly! Truly! By a magician–who is like a Sahib."

"Nay, son of the Charm: and ask if there be any answer."

"But if he offer a rudeness? I–I am afraid."

Kim laughed. "He is, I have no doubt, very tired and very hungry. The Hills make cold bed-fellows. Hai, my"–it was on the tip of his tongue to say Mother, but he turned it to Sister–"thou art a wise and witty woman. By this time all the villages know what has befallen the Sahibs–eh?"

"True. News was at Ziglaur by midnight, and by to-morrow should be at Kotgarth. The villages are both afraid and angry."

"No need. Tell the villages to feed the Sahibs and pass them on, in peace. We must get them quietly away from our valleys. To steal is one thing–to kill another. The Babu will understand, and there will be no after-complaints. Be swift. I must tend my master when he wakes."

"So be it. After service–thou hast said?–comes the reward. I am the Woman of Shamlegh, and I hold from the Rajah. I am no common bearer of babes. Shamlegh is thine: hoof and horn and hide, milk and butter. Take or leave."

She turned resolutely up hill, her silver necklaces clicking on her broad breast, to meet the morning sun fifteen hundred feet above them. This time Kim thought in the vernacular as he waxed down the oil-skin edges of the packets.

"How can a man follow the Way or the Great Game when he is eternally pestered by women? There was that girl at Akrola by the Ford; and there was the scullion's wife behind the dovecot–not counting the others–and now comes this one! When I was a child it was well enough, but now I am a man and they will not regard me as a man. Walnuts indeed! Ho! ho! It is almonds in the Plains!"

He went out to levy on the village–not with a begging-bowl, which might do for down-country, but in the manner of a prince. Shamlegh's summer population is only three families–four women and eight or nine men. They were all full of tinned meats–and mixed drinks, from ammoniated quinine to white vodka–for they had taken their full share in the overnight loot. The neat Continental tents had been cut up and shared long ago, and there were patent aluminum sauce-pans abroad.

But they considered the lama's presence a perfect safeguard against all consequences, and impenitently brought Kim of their best–even to drink of *chang*–the barley-beer that comes from Ladakh-way. Then they thawed out in the sun, and sat with their legs hanging over infinite abysses, chattering, laughing, and smoking. They judged India and its Government solely from their experience of wandering Sahibs who had employed them or their friends as *shikarris.* Kim heard tales of shots missed upon ibex, serow, or markhor, by Sahibs twenty years in their graves–every detail lighted from behind like twigs on tree-tops seen against lightning. They told him of their little diseases, and, more important, the diseases of their tiny, sure-footed cattle; of trips as far as Katgarh, where the strange missionaries live, and beyond even to marvelous Simla, where the streets are paved with silver, and any one, look you, can get service with the Sahibs, who ride about in two-wheeled carts and spend money with a spade. Presently, grave and aloof, walking very heavily, the lama joined himself to the chatter under the eaves, and they gave him great room. The thin air refreshed him, and he sat on the edge of precipices with the best of them, and, when talk languished, flung pebbles into the void. Thirty miles away, as the eagle flies, lay the next range, seamed and channelled and pitted with little patches of brush–forests, each a day's dark march. Behind the village, Shamlegh hill itself cut off all view to southward. It was like sitting in a swallow's nest under the eaves of the roof of the world.

From time to time the lama stretched out his hand, and with a little, low-voiced prompting would point out the road to Spiti and north across the Parungla.

"Beyond, where the hills lie thickest, lies Dech'en" (he meant Han-lé), "the great Monastery. s'Tag-stan-ras-ch'en built it, and of him there runs this tale." Whereupon he told it: a fantastic piled narrative of bewitchment and miracles that set Shamlegh agasping. Turning west a little, he speered for the green hills of Kulu, and sought Kailung under the glaciers. "For thither came I in the old, old days. From Leh I came, over the Baralachi."

"Yes, yes; we know it," said the far-faring people of Shamlegh.

"And I slept two nights with the priests of Kailung. These are the Hills of my delight! Shadows blessed above all other shadows! There my eyes opened to this world; there I found Enlightenment; and there I girt my loins for my Search. Out of the Hills I came–the high Hills and the strong winds. Oh, just is the Wheel!" He blessed them in detail–the great glaciers, the naked rocks, the piled moraines and tumbled shale; dry upland, hidden salt-lake, age-old timber and fruitful water-shot valley one after the other, as a dying man blesses his folk, and Kim marveled at his passion.

"Yes–yes. There is no place like our Hills," said the people of Shamlegh. And they fell to wondering how a man could live in the hot terrible Plains where the cattle run as big as elephants, unfit to plough on a hillside; where village touches village, they had heard, for a hundred miles; where folk went about stealing in gangs, and what the robbers spared the Police carried utterly away.

So the still forenoon wore through, and at the end of it Kim's messenger dropped from the steep pasture as unbreathed as when she had set out.

"I sent a word to the *hakim,*" Kim explained, while she made reverence.

"He joined himself to the idolators? Nay, I remember he did a healing upon one of them. He has acquired merit, though the healed employed his strength for evil. Just is the Wheel! What of the *hakim?*"

"I feared that thou hadst been bruised and–and I knew he was wise." Kim took the waxed walnut-shell and read in English on the back of his note: "*Your favor received. Cannot get away from present company at present, but shall take them into Simla. After which, hope to rejoin you. Inexpedient to follow angry gentlemen. Return by same road you came, and will overtake. Highly gratified about correspondence due to my forethought.*" "He says, Holy One, that he will escape from the idolators, and will return to us. Shall we wait awhile at Shamlegh, then?"

The lama looked long and lovingly upon the Hills, and shook his head.

"That may not be, *chela.* From my bones outward I do desire it, but it is forbidden. I have seen the Cause of Things."

"Why? When the Hills gave thee back thy strength day by day? Remember we were weak and fainting down below there in the Doon."

"I became strong to do evil and to forget. A brawler and a swashbuckler upon the hillsides was I." Kim bit back a smile. "Just and perfect is the Wheel, swerving not a hair. When I was a man—a long time ago—I did pilgrimage to Guru Ch'wan among the poplars" (he pointed Bhotanwards), "where they keep the Sacred Horse."

"Quiet, be quiet!" said Shamlegh, all arow. "He speaks of Jam-lin-nin-k'or, the Horse That Can Go Round The World In a Day."

"I speak to my *chela* only," said the lama, in gentle reproof, and they scattered like frost on south eaves of a morning. "I did not seek truth in those days, but the talk of doctrine. All illusion! I drank the beer and ate the bread of Guru Ch'wan. Next day one said: 'We got out to fight Sangor Gutok down the valley to discover (mark again how Lust is tied to Anger!) which abbot shall bear rule in the valley, and take the profit of the prayers they print at Sangor Gutok.' I went, and we fought a day."

"But how, Holy One?"

"With our long pencases as I could have shown. . . . I say, we fought under the poplars, both abbots and all the monks, and one laid open my forehead to the bone. See!" He tilted back his cap and showed a puckered silvery scar. "Just and perfect is the Wheel! Yesterday the scar itched, and after fifty years I recalled how it was dealt and the face of him who dealt it; dwelling a little in illusion. Followed that which thou didst see—strife and stupidity. Just is the Wheel! The idolater's blow fell upon the scar. Then I was shaken in my soul: my soul was darkened, and the boat of my soul rocked upon the waters of illusion. Not till I came to Shamlegh could I meditate upon the Cause of Things, or trace the running grass-roots of Evil. I strove all the long night."

"But, Holy One, thou art innocent of all evil. May I be thy sacrifice!"

Kim was genuinely distressed at the old man's sorrow, and Mahbub Ali's phrase slipped out unawares.

"In the dawn," he went on more gravely, ready rosary clicking between the slow sentences, "came enlightenment. It is here. . . . I am an old man . . . hill-bred, hill-fed, never to sit down among my Hills. Three years I travelled through Hind, but—can earth be stronger than Mother Earth? My stupid body yearned to the Hills and the snow of the Hills, from below there. I said, and it is true, my Search is sure. So, at the Kulu woman's house I turned hillward, over-persuaded by myself. There is no blame to the *hakim*. He—following Desire—foretold that the Hills would make me strong. They strengthened me to do evil, to forget my Search. I delighted in life and the lust of life. I desired strong slopes to climb. I cast about to find them. I measured the strength of my body, which is evil, against the high Hills. I made a mock of thee when thy breath came short under Jamnotri. I jested when thou wouldst not face the snow of the pass."

"But what harm? I *was* afraid. It was just. I am not a hillman; and I loved thee for thy new strength."

"More than once I remember," he rested his cheek dolefully on his hand, "I sought thy praise and the *hakim's* for the mere strength of my legs. Thus evil followed evil till the cup was full. Just is the Wheel! All Hind for three years did me all honor. From the Fountain of Wisdom in the Wonder House to"—he smiled—"a little child playing by a big gun—the world prepared my road. And why?"

"Because we loved thee. It is only the fever of the blow. I myself am still sick and shaken."

"No! It was because I was upon the Way—tuned as are *si-nen* (cymbals) to the purpose of the Law. I departed from that ordinance. The tune was broken: followed the punishment. In my own Hills, on the edge of my own country, in the very place of my evil desire, comes the buffet—here!" (He touched his brow.) "As a novice is beaten when he misplaces the cups, so am I beaten, who was Abbot of Such-zen. No word, look you, but a blow, *chela.*"

"But were well matched. Ignorance and Lust met Ignorance and Lust upon the road, and they begat Anger. The blow was a sign to me, who am no better than a strayed yak, that my place is not here. Who can read the Cause of an act is half-way to Freedom! 'Back to the path,' says the Blow. 'The Hills are not for thee. Thou canst not choose Freedom and go in bondage to the delight of life.' "

"If we had never met that thrice-cursed Russian!"

"Our Lord Himself cannot make the Wheel swing backward. And for my merit that I had acquired I gain yet another sign." He put his hand in his bosom, and drew forth the Wheel of Life. "Look! I considered this after I had meditated. There remains untorn by the idolator no more than the breadth of my finger-nail."

"I see."

"So much, then, is the span of my life in this body. I have served the Wheel all my days. Now the Wheel serves me. But for the merit I have acquired in guiding thee upon the Way, there would have been added to me yet another like ere I had found my River. Is it plain, *chela?*"

Kim stared at the brutally disfigured chart. From left to right diagonally the rent ran—from the Eleventh House where Desire gives birth to the Child (as it is drawn by Tibetans)—across the human and animal worlds, to the Fifth House—the empty House of the Senses. The logic was unanswerable.

"Before our Lord won enlightenment," the lama folded all away with reverence, "He was tempted. I too have been tempted, but it is finished. The Arrow fell in the Plains—not in the Hills. Therefore, what make we here?"

"Shall we at least wait for the *hakim?*"

"I know how long I live in this body. What can a *hakim* do?"

"But thou art all sick and shaken. Thou canst not walk."

"How can I be sick if I see Freedom?" He rose unsteadily to his feet.

"Then I must get food from the village. Oh, the weary Road!" Kim felt that he too needed rest.

"That is lawful. Let us eat and go. The Arrow fell in the Plains . . . but I yielded to Desire. Make ready, *chela.*"

Kim turned to the woman with the torquoise head-gear, who had been idly pitching pebbles over the cliff. She smiled very kindly.

"I found him like a strayed buffalo in a corn-field—the Babu; snorting and sneezing with cold. He was so hungry that he forgot his dignity and gave me sweet words. The Sahibs have nothing." She flung out an empty palm. "One is very sick about the stomach. Thy work?"

Kim nodded, with a bright eye.

"I spoke to the Bengali first—and to the people of a nearby village after. The Sahibs will be given food as they need it—nor will the people ask money. The plunder is already distributed. That Babu makes lying speeches to the Sahibs. Why does he not leave them?"

"Out of the greatness of his heart."

"Was never a Bengali yet had one bigger than a dried walnut. But it is no matter. . . . Now as to walnuts. After service comes reward. I have said the village is thine."

"It is my loss," Kim began. "Even now I had planned desirable things in my heart which"—there is no need to go through the compliments proper to these occasions. He sighed deeply. . . . "But my master, led by a vision—"

"Huh! What can old eyes see except a full begging-bowl?"

"—turns from this village to the Plains again."

"Bid him stay."

Kim shook his head. "I know my Holy One, and his rage if he be crossed. His curses shake the Hills."

"Pity they did not save him from a broken head! I heard that thou wast the tiger-hearted one who smote the Sahib. Let him dream a little longer. Stay!"

"Hillwoman," said Kim, with austerity that could not harden the outlines of his young oval face, "these matters are too high for thee."

"The Gods be good to us! Since when have men and women been other than men and women?"

"A priest is a priest. He says he will go upon this hour. I am his *chela,* and I go with him. We need food for the Road. He is an honored guest in all the villages, but"—he broke into a pure boy's grin—"the food here is good. Give me some."

"What if I do not give it thee? I am the woman of this village."

"Then I curse thee—a little—not greatly, but enough to remember." He could not help smiling.

"Thou hast cursed me already by the down-dropped eyelash and the uplifted chin. Curses? What should I care for mere words?" She clenched her hands upon her bosom. . . . "But I would not have thee to go in anger, thinking hardly of me—a gatherer of cow-dung and grass at Shamlegh, but still a woman of substance."

"I think nothing," said Kim, "but that I am grieved to go, for I am tired, and that we need food. Here is the bag."

The woman snatched it angrily. "I was foolish," said she. "Who is thy woman in the Plains? Fair or black? I was fair once. Laughest thou? Once, long ago, if thou canst believe, a Sahib looked on me with favor. Once, long ago, I wore European clothes at the Mission-house yonder." She pointed towards Kotgarth. "Once, long ago, I was *Ker-lis-ti-an* and spoke English—as the Sahibs speak it. Yes. My Sahib said he would return and wed me—yes, wed me. He went away—I had nursed him when he was sick—but he never returned. Then I saw that the Gods of the Kerlistians lied, and I went back to my own people. . . . I have never set eyes on a Sahib since. (Do not laugh at me. The fit is past, little priestling.) Thy face and thy walk and thy fashion of speech put me in mind of my Sahib, though thou art only a wandering mendicant to whom I give a dole. Curse me? Thou canst neither curse nor bless!" She set her hands on her hips and laughed bitterly. "Thy Gods are lies; thy works are lies; thy words are lies. There are no Gods under all the heavens. I know it. . . . But for awhile I thought it was my Sahib come back, and he was my God. Yes, once I made music on a *pianno* in the Mission-house at Kotgarth. Now I give alms to priests who are *heatthen."* She wound up with the English word, and tied the mouth of the brimming bag.

"I wait for thee, *chela,"* said the lama, leaning against the door-post.

The woman swept the tall figure with her eyes. "He walk! He cannot cover half a mile. Whither would old bones go?"

At this Kim, already perplexed by the lama's collapse and foreseeing the weight of the bag, fairly lost his temper.

"What is it to thee, woman of ill-omen, where he goes?"

"Nothing—but something to thee, priest with a Sahib's face. Wilt thou carry him on thy shoulders?"

"I go to the Plains. None must hinder my return. I have wrestled with my soul till I am strengthless. The stupid body is spent, and we are far from the Plains."

"Behold!" she said simply, and drew aside to let Kim see his own utter helplessness. "Curse me. Maybe it will give him strength. Make a charm! Call on thy great God. Thou art a priest." She turned away.

The lama had squatted limply, still holding by the door-post. One cannot strike down an old man that he recovers again like a boy in a night. Weakness bowed him to the earth, but his eyes that hung on Kim were alive and imploring.

"It is all well," said Kim. "It is the thin air that weakens thee. In a little while we go! It is the mountain-sickness. I too am a little sick at stomach," . . . and he knelt and comforted with such poor words as came first to his lips. Then the woman returned, more erect than ever.

"Thy Gods useless, heh? Try mine. *I* am the Woman of Shamlegh." She hailed hoarsely, and there came out of a cow-pen her two husbands and three others with a *dooli,* the rude native litter of the Hills, that they use for carrying the sick and for visits of state. "These cattle," she did not condescend to look at them, "are thine for so long as thou shalt need."

"But we will not go Simla-way. We will not go near the Sahibs," cried the first husband.

"They will not run away as the others did, nor will they steal baggage. Two I know for weaklings. Stand to the rear-pole, Sonoo and Taree." They obeyed swiftly. "Lower now, and lift in that holy man. I will see to the village and your virtuous wives till ye return."

"When will that be?"

"Ask the priests. Do not pester me. Lay the food-bag at the foot, it balances better so."

"Oh, Holy One, thy Hills are kinder than our Plains!" cried Kim, relieved, as the lama tottered to the litter. "It is a very king's bed–a place of honor and ease. And we owe it to–"

"A woman of ill-omen. I need they blessings as much as I do thy curses. It is *my* order and none of thine. Lift and away! Here! Hast thou money for the road?"

She beckoned Kim to her hut, and stooped above a battered English cash-box under her cot.

"I do not need anything," said Kim, angered where he should have been grateful. "I am already rudely loaded with favors."

She looked up with a curious smile and laid a hand on his shoulder. "At least, thank me. I am foul-faced and a hill-woman, but, as thy talk goes, I have acquired merit. Shall I show thee how the Sahibs render thanks?" and her hard eyes softened.

"I am but a wandering priest," said Kim, his eyes lighting in answer. "Thou needest neither my blessings nor my curses."

"Nay. But for one little moment–thou canst overtake the *dooli* in ten strides–*if* thou wast a Sahib, shall I show thee what thou wouldst do?"

"How if I guess, though?" said Kim, and putting his arm round her waist, he kissed her on the cheek, adding in English: "Thank you verree much, my dear."

Kissing is practically unknown among Asiatics, which may have been the reason that she leaned back with wide-open eyes and a face of panic.

"Next time," Kim went on, "you must not be so sure of your heathen priests. Now I say good-bye." He held out his hand English-fashion. She took it mechanically. "Good-bye, my dear."

"Good-bye, and–and"–she was remembering her English words one by one–"you will come back again? Good-bye, and–thee God bless you."

Half an hour later, as the creaking litter jolted up the hill path that leads south-easterly from Shamlegh, Kim saw a tiny figure at the hut door waving a white rag.

"She has acquired merit beyond all others," said the lama. "For to set a man upon the way to Freedom is half as great as though she had herself found it."

"Umm," said Kim thoughtfully, considering the past. "It may be that I have acquired merit also. . . . At least she did not treat me like a child." He hitched the front of his robe, where lay the slab of documents and maps, restowed the precious food-bag at the lama's feet, laid his hand on the litter edge, and buckled down to the slow pace of the grunting husbands.

"These also acquire merit," said the lama, after three miles.

"More than that, they shall be paid in silver," quoth Kim. The Woman of Shamlegh had given it to him; and it was only fair, he argued, that her men should earn it back again.

Chapter Fifteen

I'd not give room for an Emperor–
    I'd hold my road for a King.
To the Triple Crown I'd not bow down–
    But this is a different thing!
I'll not fight with the Powers of Air–
    Sentries pass him through!
Drawbridge let fall–He's the Lord of us all–
    The Dreamer whose dream came true!

The Siege of the Fairies.

TWO HUNDRED MILES north of Chini, on the blue shale of Ladakh, lies Yankling Sahib, the merry-minded man, spy-glassing wrathfully across the ridges for some sign of his pet tracker–a man from Ao-chung. But that renegade, with a new Männlicher rifle and two hundred cartridges, is elsewhere, shooting musk-deer for the market, and Yankling Sahib will learn next season how very ill he has been.

Up the valleys of Bushahr–the far-beholding eagles of the Himalayas swerve at his new blue and white gored umbrella–hurries a Bengali, once fat and well-looking, now lean and weather-worn. He had received the thanks of two foreigners of distinction, piloted not unskillfully to Mashobra tunnel, which leads to the great and gay capital of India. It was not his fault that, blanketed by wet mists, he conveyed them past the telegraph-station and European colony of Kotgarth. It was not his fault, but that of the Gods, of whom he discoursed so engagingly, that he led them into the borders of Nahan, where the Rajah of that State mistook them for deserting British soldiery. Hurree Babu explained the greatness and glory, in their own country, of his companions, till the drowsy kinglet smiled. He explained it to every one who asked–many times–aloud–variously. He begged food, arranged accommodation, proved a skilful leech for an injury of the groin–such a blow as one may receive rolling down a rock-covered hillside in the dark–and in all things indispensable. The reason of his friendliness did him credit. With millions of fellow-serfs, he had learned to look upon Russia as the great deliverer from the North. He was a fearful man. He had been afraid that he could not save his illustrious employers from the anger of an excited peasantry. He himself would just as lief hit a holy man as not, but . . . He was deeply grateful and sincerely rejoiced that he had done his "little possible" towards bringing their venture to–barring the lost baggage–a successful issue. He had forgotten the blows; denied that any blows had been dealt that unseemly first night under the pines. He asked neither pension nor retaining fee, but, if they deemed him worthy, would they write him a testimonial? It might be useful to him later, if others, their friends, came over the Passes. He begged them to remember him in their future greatnesses, for he "opined subtly" that he, even he, Mohendro Lal Dutt, M.A. of Calcutta, had "done the State some service."

They gave him a certificate praising his courtesy, helpfulness, and unerring skill as a guide. He put it in his waistbelt and sobbed with emotion; they had endured so many dangers together. He led them at high noon along crowded Simla Mall to the Alliance Bank of Simla, where they wished to establish their identity. Thence he vanished like a dawn-cloud on Jakko.

Behold him, too fine-drawn to sweat, too pressed to vaunt the drugs in his little brass-bound box, ascending Shamlegh slope, a just man made perfect. Watch him, all Babudom laid aside, smoking at noon on a cot, while a woman with turquoise-studded head-gear points south-easterly across the bare grass. Litters, she says, do not travel as fast as single men, but his birds should now be in the Plains. The holy man would not stay though Lispeth pressed him. The Babu groans heavily, girds up his huge loins, and is off again. He does not care to travel after dusk; but his days' marches—there is none to enter them in a book—would astonish folk who mock at his race. Kindly villagers, remembering the Dacca drug-vendor of two months ago, give him shelter against evil spirits of the wood. He dreams of Bengali Gods, University text-books of education, and the Royal Society, London, England. Next dawn the bobbing blue and white umbrella goes forward.

On the edge of the Doon, Mussoorie well behind them and the Plains spread out in golden dust before, rests a worn litter in which—all the Hills know it—lies a sick lama who seeks a River for his healing. Villages have almost come to blows over the honor of bearing it, for not only has the lama given them blessings, but his disciple good money—full one-third Sahib's prices. Twelve miles a day has the *dooli* traveled, as the greasy, rubbed pole-ends show, and by roads that few Sahibs use. Over the Nilang Pass in storm, when the driven snow-dust filled every fold of the impassive lama's drapery; between the black horns of Raieng, where they heard the whistle of the wild goats through the clouds; pitching and strained on the shale below; hard-held between shoulder and clenched jaw when they rounded the hideous curves of the Cut Road under Bhagirati; swinging and creaking to the steady jog-trot of the descent into the Valley of the Waters; pressed along the steamy levels of that locked valley; up, up and out again, to meet the roaring gusts off Kedarnath; set down of mid-days in the dun-gloom of kindly oak-forests; passed from village to village in dawn-chill, when even devotees may be forgiven for swearing at impatient holy men; or by torth-light, when the least fearful think of ghosts—the *dooli* has reached her last stage. The little hillfolk sweat in the modified heat of the lower Sewaliks, and gather round the priests for their blessing and their wage.

"Ye have acquired merit," says the lama. "Merit greater than your knowing. And ye will return to the Hills," he sighs.

"Surely. The high Hills as soon as may be." The bearer rubs his shoulder, drinks water, spits it out again, and readjusts his grass sandal. Kim—his face is drawn and tired—pays very small silver from his belt, heaves out the food-bag, crams an oil-skin packet—they are holy writings—into his bosom, and helps the lama to his feet. The peace has come again into the old man's eyes, and he does not look for the hills to fall down and crush him as he did that terrible night when they were delayed by the flooded river.

The men pick up the *dooli* and swing out of sight between the scrub clumps.

The lama raises a hand towards the rampart of the Himalayas. "Not with you, O blessed among all hills, fell the Arrow of Our Lord! And never shall I breathe your air again!"

"But thou art ten times the stronger man in this good air," says Kim, for to his wearied soul appeal the well-cropped, kindly plains. "Here, or hereabouts, fell the Arrow, yes. We will go very softly, perhaps a *kos* a day, for the Search is sure. But the bag weighs heavy."

"Ay, our Search is sure. I have come out of great temptation."

It was never more than a couple of miles a day now, and Kim's shoulders bore all the weight of it—the burden of an old man, the burden of the heavy food-bag with the locked books, the load of the writings on his heart, and the details of the daily routine. He begged in the dawn, set blankets for the lama's meditation, held the weary head on his lap through the noonday heats, fanning away the flies till his wrist ached, begged again in the evenings, and rubbed the lama's feet, who rewarded him with promise of Freedom—to-day, to-morrow, or, at furthest, the next day.

"Never was such a *chela.* I doubt at times whether Ananda more faithfully nursed Our Lord. And thou art a Sahib? When I was a man—a long time ago—I forgot that. Now I look upon thee often, and every time I remember that thou art a Sahib. It is strange."

"Thou hast said there is neither black nor white. Why plague me with this talk, Holy One? Let me rub the other foot. It vexes me, I am *not* a Sahib. I am thy *chela,* and my head is heavy on my shoulders."

"Patience a little! We reach Freedom together. Then thou and I, upon the far bank of the River, will look back upon our lives as in the Hills we saw our day's marches laid out behind us. Perhaps I was once a Sahib."

" 'Was never a Sahib like thee, I swear it."

"I am certain the Keeper of the Images in the Wonder House was in past life a very wise abbot. But even his spectacles do not make my eyes see. There fall shadows when I would look steadily. No matter—we know the tricks of the poor stupid carcass—shadow changing to another shadow. I am bound by the illusion of Time and Space. How far came we to-day in the flesh?"

"Perhaps half a *kos."* Three quarters of a mile, and it was a weary march.

"Half a *kos.* Ha! I went ten thousand thousand in the spirit. How we are all lapped and swathed and swaddled in these senseless things." He looked at his thin blue-veined hand that found the beads so heavy. *"Chela,* has thou never a wish to leave me?"

Kim thought of the oil-skin packet and the books in the food-bag. If some one duly authorised would only take delivery of them the Great Game might play itself for aught he then cared. He was tired and hot in his head, and a cough that came from the stomach worried him.

"No," he said almost sternly. "I am not a dog or a snake to bite when I have learned to love."

"Thou art too tender for me."

"Not that either. I have moved in one matter without consulting thee. I have sent a message to the Kulu woman by that woman who gave us the goat's milk this morn, saying that thou wast a little feeble and would need a litter. I beat myself in my mind that I did not do it when we entered the Doon. We stay in this place till the litter returns."

"I am content. She is a woman with a heart of gold, as thou sayest, but a talker—something of a talker."

"She will not weary thee. I have looked to that also. Holy One, my heart is very heavy for my many carelessnesses towards thee." An hysterical catch rose in his throat. "I have walked thee too far; I have not picked good food always for thee; I have not considered the heat, I have talked to people on the road and left thee alone. . . . I have—I have . . . *Hai mai!* But I love thee . . . and it is all too late. . . . I was a child. . . . Oh why was I not a man! . . ." Overborne by strain, fatigue, and the weight beyond his years,

Kim broke down and sobbed at the lama's feet.

"What a to-do is here," said the old man gently. "Thou hast never stepped a hair's breadth from the Way of Obedience. Neglect me? Child, I have lived on thy strength as an old tree lives on the lime of a new wall. Day by day, since Shamlegh down, I have stolen strength from thee. *Therefore,* not through any sin of thine, art thou weakened. It is the Body–the silly, stupid Body–that speaks now. Not the assured Soul! Be comforted! Know at least the devils that thou fightest. They are earth-born–children of illusion. We will go to the woman from Kulu. She shall acquire merit in housing us, and specially in tending me. Thou shalt run free till strength returns. I had forgotten the stupid Body. If there be any blame, I bear it. But we are too close to the gates of deliverance to weigh blame. I could praise thee, but what need? In a little–in a very little–we shall sit beyond all needs."

And so he petted and comforted Kim with wise saws and grave texts on that little understood beast, our Body, who, being but a delusion, insists on posing as the Soul, to the darkening of the Way, and the immense multiplication of unnecessary devils.

"Hai! hai! Let us talk of the woman from Kulu. Think you she will ask another charm for her grandsons? When I was a young man, a very long time ago, I was plagued with these vapors, and some others, and I went to an abbot–a very holy man and a seeker after truth, though then I knew it not. Sit up and listen, child of my soul! My tale was told. Said he to me, '*Chela,* know this. There are many lies in the world, and not a few liars, but there are no liars like our bodies, except it be the sensations of our bodies.' Considering this I was comforted, and of his great favor he suffered me to drink tea in his presence. Suffer me now to drink tea, for I am thirsty."

With a laugh above his tears, Kim kissed the lama's feet, and went about tea-making.

"Thou leanest on me in the body, Holy One, but I lean on thee for some other things. Dost know it?"

"I have guessed maybe," and the lama's eyes twinkled. "We must change that."

So, when with scufflings and scrapings and a hot air of importance, paddled up nothing less than the Sahib's pet palanquin sent twenty miles, with that same grizzled old Oorya servant in charge, and when they reached the disorderly order of the long white rambling house behind Saharunpore, the lama took his own measures.

Said the Sahib cheerfully from an upper window, after compliments: "What is the good of an old woman's advice to an old man? I told thee–I *told* thee, Holy One, to keep an eye upon the *chela.* How didst thou do it? Never answer me! *I* know. He has been running among the women. Look at his eyes–hollow and sunk–and the Betraying Line from the nose down! He has been sifted out! Fie! Fie! And a priest, too!"

Kim looked up over-weary to smile, shaking his head in denial.

"Do not jest," said the lama. "That time is done. We are here upon great matters. A sickness of soul took me in the Hills, and him a sickness of the body. Since then I have lived upon his strength–eating him."

"Children together–young and old," she sniffed, but forbore to make any new jokes. "May this present hospitality restore ye. Hold awhile and I will come to gossip of the high good Hills."

At evening time–her son-in-law was returned, so she did not need to go on inspection round the farm–she won to the meat of the matter, explained low-voicedly by the lama. The two old heads nodded wisely together. Kim had reeled to a room with a cot in it, and was dozing soddenly. The lama had forbidden him to set blankets or get food.

"I know–I know. Who but I?" she cackled. "We who go down to the burning-ghats clutch at the hands of those coming from the River of Life with full water-jars—yes, brimming water-jars. I did the boy wrong. He lent thee his strength? It is true that the old eat the young daily. 'Stands now we must restore him."

"Thou has many times acquired merit—"

"*My* merit. What is it? Old bag of bones making curries for men who do not ask 'Who cooked this?' Now if it were stored up for my grandson—"

"He that had the belly-pain?"

"To think the Holy One remembers *that!* I must tell his mother. It is most singular honor! 'He that had the belly-pain'—straightway the Holy One remembered. She will be proud."

"My *chela* is to me as is a son to the unenlightened."

"Say grandson, rather. Mothers have not the wisdom of our years. If a child cries they say the heavens are falling. Now a grandmother is far enough separated from the pain of bearing and the pleasure of giving the breast to consider whether a cry is wickedness pure or the wind. And since thou speakest once again of wind, when last the Holy One was here, maybe I offended in pressing for charms."

"Sister," said the lama, using that form of address a Buddhist monk may sometimes employ towards a nun, "if charms comfort thee—"

"They are better than ten thousand doctors."

"I say, if they comfort thee, I, who was Abbot of Suchzen, will make as many as thou mayest desire. I have never seen thy face—"

"*That* even the monkeys who steal our loquats count for a gain. Hee! hee!"

"But as he who sleeps there said," he nodded at the shut door of the guest-chamber across the forecourt, "thou hast a heart of gold. . . . And he is in the spirit my very 'grandson' to me."

"Good! I am the Holy One's cow." This was pure Hinduism, but the lama never heeded. "I am old. I have borne sons in the body. Oh once I could please men! Now I can cure them." He heard her armlets tinkle as though she bared arms for action. "I will take over the boy and dose him, and stuff him, and make him all whole. Hai! hai! We old people know something yet."

Wherefore when Kim, aching in every bone, opened his eyes, and would go to to the cook-house to get his master's food, he found strong coercion about him, and a veiled old figure at the door, flanked by the manservant, who told him precisely the things that he was on no account to do.

"Thou must have—thou shalt have nothing. What? A locked box in which to keep holy books? Oh, that is another matter. Heavens forbid I should come between a priest and his prayers! It shall be brought, and thou shalt keep the key."

They pushed the coffer under his cot, and Kim shut away Mahbub's pistol, the oil-skin packet of letters, and the locked books and diaries, with a groan of relief. For some absurd reason their weight on his shoulders was nothing to their weight on his poor mind. His neck ached under it of nights.

"Thine is a sickness uncommon in youth these days: since young folk have given up tending their betters. The remedy is sleep, and certain drugs," said the Sahiba; and he was glad to give himself up to the blankness that half menaced and half soothed him.

She brewed drinks, in some mysterious Asiatic equivalent to the still-room—drenches that smelt pestilently and tasted worse. She stood over Kim till they went down, and inquired exhaustively after they had come up. She laid a taboo upon the forecourt, and enforced it by means of an armed man. It is true he was seventy odd, that his scabbarded sword ceased at the hilt; but he represented the authority of the Sahiba, and loaded wains, chattering servants, calves, dogs, hens, and the like, fetched a wide compass by those parts. Best of all, when the body was cleared, she cut out from the mass of poor relations that crowded the back of the buildings—household dogs, we name them—a cousin's widow, skilled in what Europeans, who know nothing about it, call massage. And the two of them, laying him east and west, that the mysterious earth-currents which thrill the clay of our bodies might help and not hinder, took him to pieces all one long afternoon—bone by bone, muscle by muscle, ligament by ligament, and lastly, nerve by nerve. Kneaded to irresponsible pulp, half hypnotised by the perpetual flick and readjustment of the uneasy *chudders* that veiled their eyes, Kim slid ten thousand miles into slumber—thirty-six hours of it—sleep that soaked like rain after drought.

Then she fed him, and the house spun to her clamor. She caused fowls to be slain; she sent for vegetables, and the sober, slow-thinking gardener, nigh as old as she, sweated for it; she took spices, and milk, and onion, with little fish from the brooks—anon limes for sherbets, quails of the pit, then chicken-livers upon a skewer, with sliced ginger between.

"I have seen something of this world," she said over the crowded trays, "and there are but two sorts of women in it—those who take the strength out of a man and those who put it back. Once I was that one, and now I am this. Nay—do not play the priestling with me. Mine was but a jest. If it does not hold good now, it will when thou takest the road again. Cousin"—this to the poor relation, never wearied of extolling her patroness's charity—"he is getting a bloom on the skin of a new-curried horse. Our work is like polishing jewels to be thrown to a dance-girl—eh?"

Kim sat up and smiled. The terrible weakness had dropped from him like an old shoe. His tongue itched for free speech again, and but a week back the lightest word clogged it like ashes. The pain in his neck (he must have caught it from the lama) had gone with the heavy dengueaches and the evil taste in the mouth. The two old women, a little, but not much more careful about their veils now, clucked as merrily as the hens that had entered picking through the open door.

"Where is my Holy One?" he demanded.

"Hear him! Thy Holy One is well," she snapped viciously. "Though that is none of *his* merit. Knew I a charm to make him wise, I'd sell my jewels and buy it. To refuse good food that I cooked myself—and go roving into the fields for two nights on an empty belly—and to tumble into a brook at the end of it—call you *that* holiness? Then, when he has nearly broken what thou hast left of my heart with anxiety he tells me that he has acquired merit. Oh, how like are all men! No, that was not it—he tells me he is freed from all sin. *I* could have told him that before he wetted himself all over. He is well now—this happened a week ago—but burn me such holiness! A babe of three would do better. Do not fret thyself for the Holy One. He keeps both eyes on thee when he is not wading our brooks."

"I do not remember to have seen him. I remember that the days and nights passed like bars of white and black, opening and shutting. I was not sick: I was only tired."

"A lethargy that comes by right some few score years later. But it is all done now."

"Maharanee," Kim began, but led by the look in her eye, changed it to the title of plain love—"Mother, I owe my life to thee. How shall I make thanks? Ten thousand blessings upon thy house and—"

"The house be unblessed." (It is impossible to give exactly the old lady's word.) "Thank the Gods as a priest if thou wilt, but thank me if thou carest as a son. Heavens above! Have I shifted thee and lifted thee and slapped and twisted thy ten toes to find texts flung at my head? Somewhere a mother must have borne thee to break her heart. What used thou to her—son?"

"I had no mother, my mother," said Kim. "She died, they tell me, when I was young."

"Hai mai! Then none can say I have robbed her of any right if—when thou takest the road again and this house is but one of a thousand used for shelter and forgotten, after an easy-flung blessing. No matter. I need no blessings, but—but—" She stamped her foot at the poor relation: "Take up the trays to the house. What is the good of stale food in the room, oh woman of ill-omen?"

"I ha—have borne a son in my time too, but he died," whimpered the bowed sister-figure behind the *chudder.* "Thou knowest he died! I only waited for the order to take away the tray."

"It is I that am the woman of ill-omen," cried the old lady penitently. "We that go down to the *chattris* (the big umbrellas above the burning-ghats where the priests take their last dues) clutch hard at the bearers of the *chattis* (water-jars—young folk full of the pride of life, she meant; but the pun is clumsy). When one cannot dance in the festival one must e'en look out of the window, and grandmothering takes all a woman's time. The master gives me all the charms I now desire for my daughter's eldest, by reason—is it?—that he is wholly free from sin. The *hakim* is brought very low these days. He goes about poisoning my servants for lack of their betters."

"What *hakim,* mother?"

"That very Dacca man who gave me the pill which rent me in three pieces. He cast up like a strayed camel a week ago, vowing that he and thou had been blood-brothers together up Kulu-way, and feigning great anxiety for thy health. He was very thin and hungry, so I gave orders to have him stuffed too—him and his anxiety!"

"I would see him if he is here."

"He eats five times a day, and lances boils for my hinds to save himself from an apoplexy. He is so full of anxiety for thy health that he sticks to the cook-house door and stays himself with scraps. He will keep. We shall never get rid of him."

"Send him here, mother"—the twinkle returned to Kim's eye for a flash—"and I will try."

"I'll send him, but to chase him off is an ill turn. At least he had the sense to fish the Holy One out of the brook; thus, as the Holy One did *not* say, acquiring merit."

"He is a very wise *hakim.* Send him, mother."

"Priest praising priest? A miracle! If he is any friend of thine (ye squabbled at your last meeting) I'll hale him here with horse-ropes and—and give him a caste-dinner afterwards, my son. . . . Get up and see the world! This lying abed is the mother of seventy devils . . . my son! my son!"

She trotted forth to raise a typhoon off the cook-house, and almost on her shadow rolled in the Babu, robed as to the shoulders like a Roman emperor, jowled like Titus, bareheaded, with new patent-leather shoes, in highest condition of fat, exuding joy and salutations.

"By Jove, Master O'Hara, but I *am* jolly glad to see you. I will kindly shut the door. It is a pity you are sick. Are you very sick?"

"The papers—the papers from the *kilta.* The maps and the *murasla!"* He held out the key impatiently; for the present need on his soul was to get rid of the loot.

"You are quite right. That is correct Departmental view to take. You have got everything?"

"All that was handwritten in the *kilta* I took. The rest I threw down the hill." He could hear the key's grate in the lock, the sticky pull of the slow-rending oil-cloth, and a quick shuffling of papers. He had been annoyed out of all reason by the knowledge that they lay below him through the sick idle days—a burden incommunicable. For that reason the blood tingled through his body, when Hurree, skipping elephantinely, shook hands again.

"This is fine! This is finest! Mister O'Hara! You have–ha! ha!–swiped the whole bag of tricks–locks, stocks, and barrels. They told me it was eight months' work gone up the spouts! By Jove, how they beat me! . . . Look, here is the letter from Hilás!" He intoned a line or two of Court Persian, which is the language of authorised and unauthorised diplomacy. "Mister Rajah Sahib has just about put his foot in the holes. He will have to explain to the Czar. He will have to explain offeecially how the deuce-an'-all he is writing love-letters to the Czar. And they are very cunning maps . . . and there is three or four Prime Ministers of these parts implicated by the correspondence. By Gad, Sar! The British Government will change the succession in Hilás and Bunár, and nominate new heirs to the throne. 'Trea-son most base' . . . but you do not understand? Eh?"

"Are they in thy hands?" said Kim. It was all he cared for.

"Just you jolly well bet yourself they are." He stowed the entire trove about his body, as only Orientals can. "They are going to the office, too. The old lady thinks I am permanent fixture here, but I shall go away with these straight off–immediately. Mister Lurgan will be proud man. You are offeecially subordinate to me, but I shall embody your name in my verbal report. It is a pity we are not allowed written reports. We Bengalis excel in the exact science." He tossed back the key and showed the box empty.

"Good. That is good. I was very tired. My Holy One was sick, too. And did he fall into–"

"Oah yess. I am his good friend, I tell you. He was behaving very strange when I came down after you, and I thought perhaps he might have the papers. I followed him on his meditations, and to discuss ethnological points also. You see, I am verree small person here nowadays, in comparison with all his charms. By Jove, O'Hara, do you know, he is afflicted with infirmity of fits. Yess, I tell you. Cataleptic, too, if not also epileptic. I found him in such a state under a tree *in articulo mortem,* and he jumped up and walked into a brook, and he was nearly drowned but for me. I pulled him out."

"Because I was not there!" said Kim. "He might have died."

"Yes, he might have died, but he is dry now, and asserts he had undergone transfiguration." The Babu tapped his forehead knowingly. "I took notes of his statements for Royal Society–*in posse.* You must make haste and be quite well and come back to Simla, and I will tell you all my tale at Lurgan's. It was splendid. The bottoms of their trousers were *quite* torn, and old Nahan Rajah, he thought they were European soldiers deserting."

"Oh, the Russians? How long were they with thee?"

"One was a Frenchman. Oh, days and days and days! Now all the hill-people believe all Russians are all beggars. By Jove! they had not one dam-thing that I did not get them. And I told the common people–oah, *such* tales and anecdotes! I will tell you at old Lurgan's when you come up. We will have–ah–a night out! It is feather in both our caps! Yess, and they gave me a certificate. That is creaming joke. You should have seen them at the Alliance Bank identifying themselves! And thank Almighty God you got their papers so well! You do not laugh verree much, but you shall laugh when you are well. Now I will go straight to the railway and get out. You shall have all sorts of credits for your game. When do you come along? We are very proud of you though you gave us great frights. And especially Mahbub."

"Ay, Mahbub. And where is he?"

"Selling horses in this vi-cinity, course."

"Here! Why? Speak slowly. There is a thickness in my head still."

The Babu looked shyly down his nose. "Well, you see, I am fearful man, and I do not like responsibility. You were sick, you see, and I did not know where deuce-an'-all the papers were, and if so, how many. So when I had come down here I slipped in private wire to Mahbub–he was at Meerut for races—and I tell him how case stands. He comes up with his men and he consorts with the lama, and then he calls me a fool, and is very rude—"

"But wherefore—wherefore?"

"That is what *I* ask. I only suggest that if any one steals the papers I should like some good, strong, brave men to rob them back again. You see they are vitally important, and Mahbub Ali he did not know where you were."

"Mahbub Ali to rob the Sahiba's house? Thou art mad, Babu," said Kim with indignation.

"I wanted the papers. Suppose she had stole them? It was only practical suggestion, *I* think. You are not pleased, eh?"

A native proverb—unquotable—showed the blackness of Kim's disapproval.

"Well,"—Hurree shrugged his shoulders,—"there is no accounting for thee taste. Mahbub was angry too. He has sold horses all about here, and he says old lady is *pukka* (thorough) old lady and would not condescend to such ungentlemanly things. *I* do not care. I have got the papers, and I was very glad of moral support from Mahbub. I tell you I am fearful man, but, somehow or other, the more fearful I am the more dam-tight places I get into. So I was glad you came with me to Chini, and I am glad Mahbub was close by. The old lady she is sometimes very rude to me and my beautiful pills."

"Allah be merciful," said Kim on his elbow, rejoicing. "What a beast of wonder is a Babu! And that man walked alone—if he did walk—with robbed and angry foreigners!"

"Oah, thatt was nothing, after they had done beating me; but if I lost the papers it was pretty jolly serious. Mahbub he nearly beat me too, and he went and consorted with the lama no end. I shall stick to ethnological investigations henceforward. Now good-bye, Mister O'Hara. I can catch 4.25 P.M. to Umballa if I am quick. It will be good times when we all tell thee tale up at Mister Lurgan's. I shall report you offeecially better. Good-bye, my dear fallow, and when next you are under thee emotions please do not use the Mohammedan terms with the Tibet dress."

He shook hands twice—a Babu to his boot-heels—and opened the door. With the fall of the sunlight upon his still triumphant face he returned to the humble Dacca quack.

"He robbed them," thought Kim, forgetting his own share in the game. "He tricked them. He lied to them like a Bengali. They gave him a *chit* (a testimonial). He makes them a mock at the risk of his life—*I* never would have gone down to them after the pistol-shots—and then he says he is a fearful man. . . . And he *is* a fearful man. I must get into the world again."

At first his legs bent like bad pipe-stems, and the flood and rush of the sunlit air dazzled him. He squatted by the white wall, the mind rummaging among the incidents of the long *dooli* journey, the lama's weaknesses, and, now that the stimulus of talk was removed, his own self-pity, of which, like the sick, he had great store. The unnerved brain edged away from all the outside, as a raw horse, once rowelled, sidles from the spur. It was enough, amply enough, that the spoil of the *kilta* was away—off his hands—out of his possession. He tried to think of the lama,—to wonder why he had tumbled into a brook,—but the bigness of the world, seen between the forecourt gates, swept linked thought aside. Then he looked upon the trees and the broad fields, with the thatched huts hidden among crops—looked with strange eyes unable to take up the size and proportions and use of things—stared for a still half-hour. All that while he felt, though he could not put it into words, that his soul was out of gear with its surroundings—a cog-wheel unconnected with any machinery, just like the idle cog-wheel of a cheap Beheea sugar-crusher laid by in a corner. The breezes fanned over him, the parrots shrieked at him, the noises of the populated house behind–squabbles, orders, and reproofs–hit on dead ears.

"I am Kim. I am Kim. And what is Kim?" His soul repeated it again and again.

He did not want to cry,–had never felt less like crying in his life,–but of a sudden easy, stupid tears trickled down his nose, and with an almost audible click he felt the wheels of his being lock up anew on the world without. Things that rode meaningless on the eyeball an instant before slid into proper proportions. Roads were meant to be walked upon, houses to be lived in, cattle to be driven, fields to be tilled, and men and women to be talked to. They were all real and true–solidly planted upon the feet–perfectly comprehensible–clay of his clay, neither more nor less. He shook himself like a dog with a flea in his ear, and rambled out of the gate. Said the Sahiba, to whom watchful eyes reported this move: "Let him go. I have done my share. Mother Earth must do the rest. When the Holy One comes back from meditation, tell him."

There stood an empty bullock-cart on a little knoll half a mile away, with a young banian-tree behind–a look-out, as it were, above some new-ploughed levels; and his eyelids, bathed in soft air, grew heavy as he neared it. The ground was good clean dust–no new herbage that, living, is halfway to death already, but the hopeful dust that hold the seed of all life. He felt it between his toes, patted it with his palms, and joint by joint, sighing luxuriously, laid him down full length along in the shadow of the wooden-pinned cart. And Mother Earth was as faithful as the Sahiba. She breathed through him to restore the poise he had lost lying so long on a cot off from her good currents. His head lay powerless upon her breast, and his opened hands surrendered to her strength. The many-rooted tree above him, and even the dead man-handled wood beside, knew what he sought, as he himself did not know. Hour upon hour he lay deeper than sleep.

Towards evening, when the dust of returning kine made all the horizons smoke, came the lama and Mahbub Ali, both afoot, walking cautiously, for the house had told them where he had gone.

"Allah! What a fool's trick to play in open country," muttered the horse-dealer. "He could be shot a hundred times–but this not the Border."

"And," said the lama, repeating a many-times-told tale, "never was such a *chela.* Temperate, kindly, wise, of ungrudging disposition, a merry heart upon the road, never forgetting, learned, truthful, courteous. Great in his reward!"

"I know the boy–as I have said."

"And he was all those things?"

"Some of them–but I have not yet found a Red Hat's charm for making him overly truthful. He has certainly been well nursed."

"The Sahiba is a heart of gold," said the lama earnestly. "She looks upon him as her son."

"Hmph! Half Hind seems that-way disposed. I only wished to see that the boy had come to no harm and was a free agent. As thou knowest, he and I were old friends in the first days of your pilgrimage together."

"That is a bond between us." The lama sat down. "We are at the end of the pilgrimage."

"No thanks to thee thine was not cut off for good and all a week back. I heard what the Sahiba said to thee when we bore thee up on the cot." Mahbub laughed, and tugged his new-dyed beard.

"I was meditating upon other matters that tide. It was the *hakim* from Dacca broke my meditations."

"Otherwise"–this was in Pashtu for decency's sake–"thou wouldst have ended thy meditations upon the sultry side of Hell–being an unbeliever and an idolator for all thy child's simplicity. But now, Red Hat, what is to be done?"

"This very night,"–the words came slowly, vibrating with triumph,–"this very night he will be as free as I am from all taint of sin–assured as I am when he quits this body of Freedom from the Wheel of Things. I have a sign," he laid his hand above the torn chart in his bosom, "that my time is short; but I shall have safe-guarded him throughout the years. Remember, I have reached Knowledge, as I told thee only three nights back."

"It must be true, as the Tirah priest said when I stole his cousin's wife, but I am a *sufi* (a free-thinker); for here I sit," said Mahbub to himself, drinking in blasphemy unthinkable. ". . . I remember the tale. On that, then, he goes to *Jannatu l'Adn* (the Gardens of Eden). But how? Wilt thou slay him or drown him in that wonderful river from which the Babu dragged thee?"

"I was dragged from no river," said the lama simply. "Thou hast forgotten what befell. I found it by Knowledge."

"Oh, ay. True," stammered Mahbub, divided between high indignation and enormous mirth. "I had forgotten the exact run of what happened. Thou didst find it knowingly."

"And to say that I would take life is–not a sin, but a madness simple. My *chela* aided me to the River. It is his right to be cleansed from sin–with me."

"Ay, he needs cleansing. But afterwards, old man–afterwards?"

"What matter under all the heavens? He is sure of Nibban–enlightened–as I am."

"Well said. I had a fear he might mount Mohammed's Horse and fly away."

"Nay–he must go forth as a teacher."

"Aha! Now I see! That is the right gait for the colt. Certainly he must go forth as a teacher. He is somewhat urgently needed as a scribe by the State, for instance."

"To that end he was prepared. I acquired merit in that I gave alms for his sake. A good deed does not die. He aided me in my Search. I aided him in his. Just is the Wheel, O horse-seller from the North. Let him be a teacher; let him be a scribe–what matter? He will have attained Freedom at the end. The rest is illusion."

"What matter? When I must have him with me beyond Balkh in six months! I come up with ten lame horses and three strong-backed men–thanks to that chicken of a Babu–to break a sick boy by force out of an old trot's house. It seems that I stand by while a young Sahib is hoisted into Allah knows what of an idolator's heaven by means of old Red Hat. And I am reckoned something of a player of the Game myself! But the madman is fond of the boy; and I must be very reasonably mad too."

"What is the prayer?" said the lama, as the rough Pashtu rumbled into the red beard.

"No matter at all; but now I understand that the boy, sure of Paradise, can yet enter Government service, my mind is easier. I must get to my horses. It grows dark. Do not wake him. I have no wish to hear him call thee master."

"But he *is* my disciple. What else?"

"He has told me." Mahbub choked down his touch of spleen and rose laughing. "I am not altogether of thy faith, Red Hat–if so small a matter concern thee."

"It is nothing," said the lama.

"I thought not. Therefore it will not move thee, sinless, new-washed and three parts drowned to boot, when I call thee a good man–a very good man. We have talked together some four or five evenings now, and for all I am a horse-coper I can still, as the saying is, see holiness beyond the legs of a horse. Yea, can see, too, how our Friend of all the World put his hand in thine at the first. Use him well, and suffer him to return to the world as a teacher, when thou hast–bathed his legs, if that be the proper medicine for the colt."

"Why not follow the Way thyself, and so accompany the boy?"

Mahbub stared stupefied at the magnificent insolence of the demand, which across the Border he would have paid with more than a blow. Then the humor of it touched his worldly soul.

"Softly–softly–one foot at a time, as the lame gelding went over the Umballa jumps. I may come to Paradise later–I have workings that way–great motions–and I owe them to thy simplicity. Thou hast never lied?"

"What need?"

"O Allah, hear him! 'What need' in this Thy world! Nor ever harmed a man?"

"Once–with a pencase–before I was wise."

"So? I think the better of thee. Thy teachings are good. Thou hast turned one man that I know from the path of strife." He laughed immensely. "He came here open-minded to commit a *dacoity* (a house-robbery with violence). Yes, to cut, rob, kill, and carry off what he desired."

"A great foolishness!"

"Oh! black shame too. So he thought after he had seen thee–and a few others, male and female. So he abandoned it; and now he goes to beat a big fat Babu man."

"I do not understand."

"Allah forbid it! Some men are strong in knowledge, Red Hat. Thy strength is stronger still. Keep it–I think thou wilt. If the boy be not a good servant, pull his ears off."

With a hitch of his broad Bokhariot belt the Pathan swaggered off into the gloaming, and the lama came down from his clouds so far as to look at the broad back.

"That person lacks courtesy, and is deceived by the shadow of appearances. But he spoke well of my *chela,* who now enters upon his reward. Let me make the prayer! . . . Wake, O fortunate above all born of women. Wake! It is found!"

Kim came up from those deep wells, and the lama attended his yawning pleasure; duly snapping fingers to head off evil spirits.

"I have slept a hundred years. Where–? Holy One, hast *thou* been here long? I went out to look for thee, but"–he laughed drowsily–"I slept by the way. I am all well now. Hast thou eaten? Let us go to the house. It is many days since I tended thee. And the Sahiba fed thee well? Who shampooed thy legs? What of the weaknesses–the belly and the neck, and the beating in the ears?"

"Gone–all gone. Dost thou not know?"

"I know nothing, but that I have not seen thee in a monkey's age. Know what?"

"Strange the knowledge did not reach out to thee, when all my thoughts were theeward."

"I cannot see the face, but the voice is like a gong. Has the Sahiba made a young man of thee by her cookery?"

He peered at the cross-legged figure, outlined jet-black against the lemon-colored drift of light. So does the stone Bodhisat sit who looks down upon the patent self-registering turnstiles of the Lahore Museum.

The lama held his peace. Except for the click of the rosary and a faint *clop-clop* of Mahbub's retreating feet, the soft, smoky silence of evening in India wrapped them close.

"Hear me! I bring news."

"But let us–"

Out shot the long yellow hand compelling silence. Kim tucked his feet under his robe-edge obediently.

"Hear me! I bring news! The Search is finished. Comes now the Reward. . . . Thus. When we were among the Hills, I lived on thy strength till the young branch bowed and nigh broke. When we came out of the Hills, I was troubled for thee and for other matters which I held in my heart. The boat of my soul lacked direction; I could not see into the Cause of Things. So I gave thee over to the virtuous woman altogether. I took no food. I drank no water. Still I saw not the Way. They pressed food upon me and cried at my shut door. So I removed myself to a hollow under a tree. I took no food. I took no water. I sat in meditation two days and two nights, abstracting my mind; inbreathing and outbreathing in the required manner. . . . Upon the second night—so great was my reward—the wise Soul loosed itself from the silly Body and went free. This I have never before attained, though I have stood on the threshold of it. Consider, for it is a marvel!"

"A marvel indeed. Two days and two nights without food! Where was the Sahiba?" said Kim under his breath.

"Yes, my Soul went free, and, wheeling like an eagle, saw indeed that there was no Teshoo Lama nor any other soul. As a drop draws to water, so my soul drew near to the Great Soul which is beyond all things. At that point, exalted in contemplation, I saw all Hind, from Ceylon in the sea to the Hills, and my own Painted Rocks at Such-zen; I saw every camp and village, to the least, where we have ever rested. I saw them at one time and in one place; for they were within the Soul. By this I knew the Soul had passed beyond the illusion of Time and Space and of Things. By this I knew that I was free. I saw thee lying in thy cot, and I saw thee falling down hill under the idolater—at one time, in one place, in my Soul, which, as I say, had touched the Great Soul. Also I saw the stupid body of Teshoo Lama lying down, and the *hakim* from Dacca kneeled beside, shouting in its ear. Then my Soul was all alone, and I saw nothing, for I was all things, having reached the Great Soul. And I meditated a thousand years, passionless, well aware of the Causes of all Things. Then a voice cried: 'What shall come to the boy if thou art dead?' and I was shaken back and forth in myself with pity for thee; and I said: 'I will return to my *chela,* lest he miss the Way.' Upon this my Soul, which is the soul of Teshoo Lama, withdrew itself from the Great Soul with strivings and yearnings and retchings and agonies not to be told. As the egg from the fish, as the fish from the water, as the water from the cloud, as the cloud from the thick air, so put forth, so leaped out, so drew away, so fumed up the soul of Teshoo Lama from the Great Soul. Then a voice cried: 'The River! Take heed to the River!' and I looked down upon all the world, which was as I had seen it before—one in time, one in place—and I saw plainly the River of the Arrow at my feet. At that hour my Soul was hampered by some evil or other whereof I was not wholly cleansed, and it lay upon my arms and coiled round my waist; but I put it aside, and I cast forth as an eagle in my flight for the very place of the River. I pushed aside world upon world for thy sake. I saw the River below me—the River of the Arrow—and, descending, the waters of it closed over me; and behold I was again in the body of Teshoo Lama, but free from sin, and the *hakim* from Dacca bore up my head in the waters of the River. It is here! It is behind the mango-tope here—even here!"

"Allah Kerim! Oh, well that the Babu was by! Wast thou very wet?"

"Why should I regard? I remember the *hakim* was concerned for the body of Teshoo Lama. He haled it out of the holy water in his hands, and there came afterwards thy horse-seller from the North with a cot and men, and they put the body on the cot and bore it up to the Sahiba's house."

"What said the Sahiba?"

"I was meditating in that body, and did not hear. So thus the Search is ended. For the merit that I have acquired, the River of the Arrow is here. It broke forth at our feet, as I have said. I have found it. Son of my Soul, I have wrenched my Soul back from the Threshold of Freedom to free thee from all sin—as I am free, and sinless. Just is the Wheel! Certain is our deliverance. Come!"

He crossed his hands on his lap and smiled, as a man may who has won Salvation for himself and his beloved.

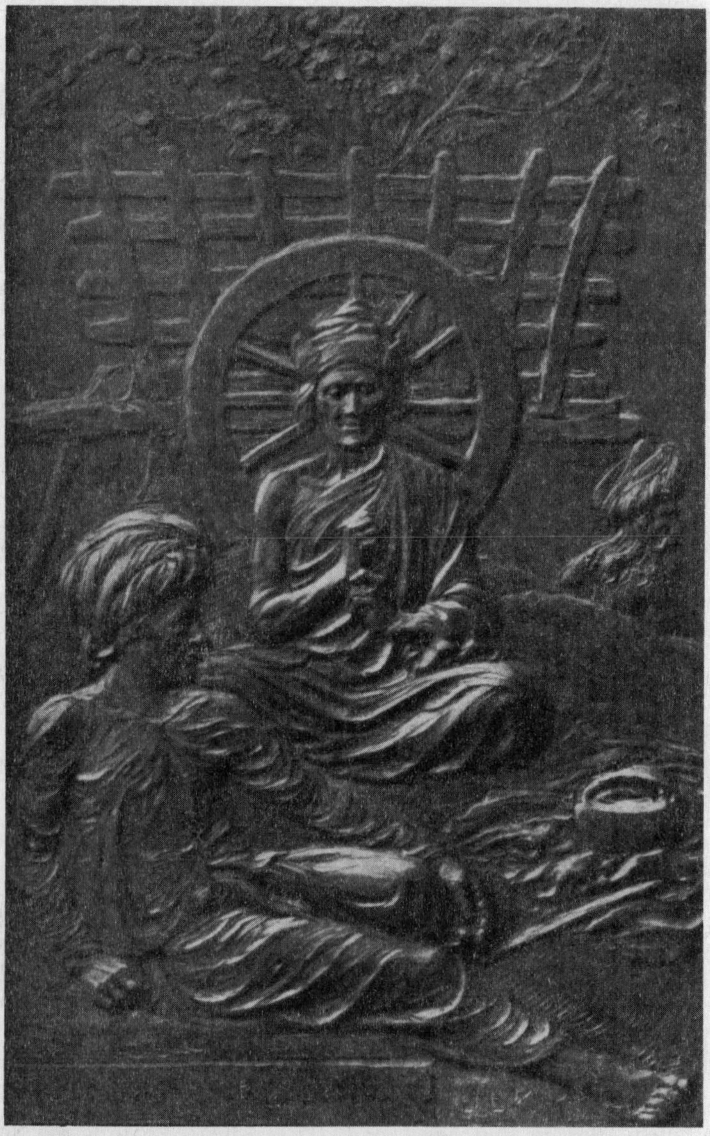

"HE CROSSED HIS HANDS ON HIS LAP AND SMILED, AS A MAN WHO HAS WON SALVATION FOR HIMSELF AND HIS BELOVED."

Plain Tales from the Hills

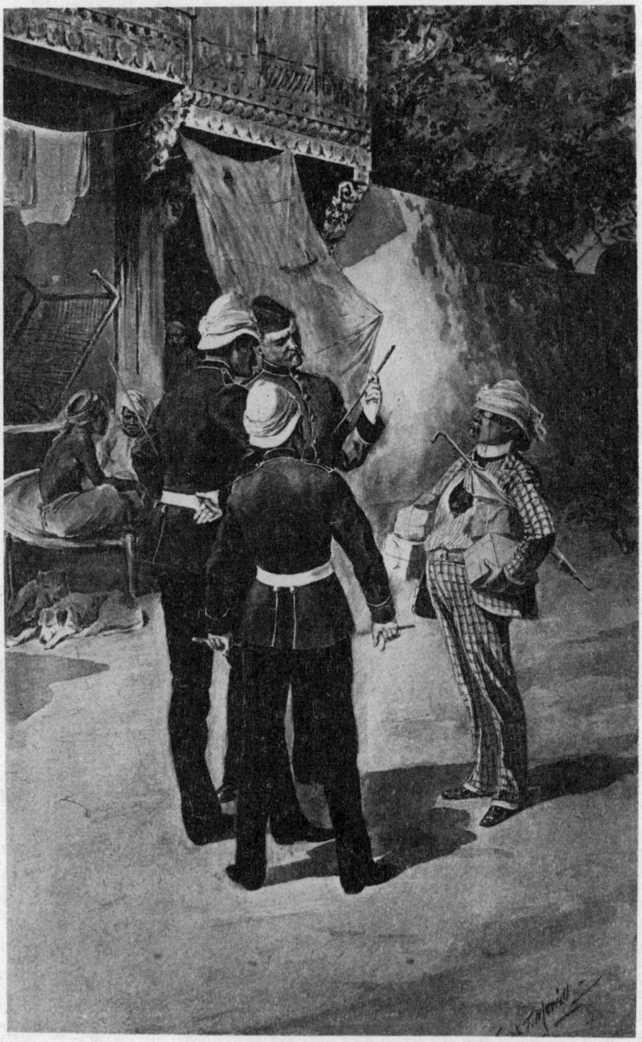

THE THREE MUSKETEERS.

Lispeth

Look, you have cast out Love! What Gods are these
You bid me please?
The Three in One, the One in Three? Not so!
To my own Gods I go.
It may be they shall give me greater ease
Than your cold Christ and tangled Trinities.
The Convert.

SHE WAS THE daughter of Sonoo, a Hill-man, and Jadéh his wife. One year their maize failed, and two bears spent the night in their only poppy-field just above the Sutlej Valley on the Kotgarh side; so, next season, they turned Christian, and brought their baby to the Mission to be baptized. The Kotgarh Chaplain christened her Elizabeth, and "Lispeth" is the Hill or *pahari* pronunciation.

Later, cholera came into the Kotgarh Valley and carried off Sonoo and Jadéh, and Lispeth became half-servant, half-companion, to the wife of the then Chaplain of Kotgarh. This was after the reign of the Moravian missionaries, but before Kotgarh had quite forgotten her title of "Mistress of the Northern Hills."

Whether Christianity improved Lispeth, or whether the gods of her own people would have done as much for her under any circumstances, I do not know; but she grew very lovely. When a Hill girl grows lovely, she is worth traveling fifty miles over bad ground to look upon. Lispeth had a Greek face–one of those faces people paint so often, and see so seldom. She was of a pale, ivory color and, for her race, extremely tall. Also, she possessed eyes that were wonderful; and, had she not been dressed in the abominable print-cloths affected by Missions, you would, meeting her on the hillside unexpectedly, have thought her the original Diana of the Romans going out to slay.

Lispeth took to Christianity readily, and did not abandon it when she reached womanhood, as do some Hill girls. Her own people hated her because she had, they said, become a *memsahib* and washed herself daily; and the Chaplain's wife did not know what to do with her. Somehow, one cannot ask a stately goddess, five foot ten in her shoes, to clean plates and dishes. So she played with the Chaplain's children and took classes in the Sunday School, and read all the books in the house, and grew more and more beautiful, like the Princesses in fairy tales. The Chaplain's wife said that the girl ought to take service in Simla as a nurse or something "genteel." But Lispeth did not want to take service. She was very happy where she was.

When travelers–there were not many in those years–came into Kotgarh, Lispeth used to lock herself into her own room for fear they might take her away to Simla, or somewhere out into the unknown world.

One day, a few months after she was seventeen years old, Lispeth went out for a walk. She did not walk in the manner of English ladies–a mile and a half out, and a ride back again. She covered between twenty and thirty miles in her little constitutionals, all about and about, between Kotgarh and Narkunda. This time she came back at full dusk, stepping down the break-neck descent into Kotgarh with something heavy in her arms. The Chaplain's wife was dozing in the drawing-room when Lispeth came in breathing hard and very exhausted with her burden. Lispeth put it down on the sofa, and said simply:—"This is my husband. I found him on the Bagi Road. He has hurt himself. We will nurse him, and when he is well, your husband shall marry him to me."

This was the first mention Lispeth had ever made of her matrimonial views, and the Chaplain's wife shrieked with horror. However, the man on the sofa needed attention first. He was a young Englishman, and his head had been cut to the bone by something jagged. Lispeth said she had found him down the *khud,* so she had brought him in. He was breathing queerly and was unconscious.

He was put to bed and tended by the Chaplain, who knew something of medicine; and Lispeth waited outside the door in case she could be useful. She explained to the Chaplain that this was the man she meant to marry; and the Chaplain and his wife lectured her severely on the impropriety of her conduct. Lispeth listened quietly, and repeated her first proposition. It takes a great deal of Christianity to wipe out uncivilized Eastern instincts, such as falling in love at first sight. Lispeth, having found the man she worshiped, did not see why she should keep silent as to her choice. She had no intention of being sent away, either. She was going to nurse that Englishman until he was well enough to marry her. This was her little program.

After a fortnight of slight fever and inflammation, the Englishman recovered coherence and thanked the Chaplain and his wife, and Lispeth—especially Lispeth—for their kindness. He was a traveler in the East, he said—they never talked about "globe-trotters" in those days, when the P. & O. fleet was young and small—and had come from Dehra Dun to hunt for plants and butterflies among the Simla hills. No one at Simla, therefore, knew anything about him. He fancied he must have fallen over the cliff while stalking a fern on a rotten tree-trunk, and that his coolies must have stolen his baggage and fled. He thought he would go back to Simla when he was a little stronger. He desired no more mountaineering.

He made small haste to go away, and recovered his strength slowly. Lispeth objected to being advised either by the Chaplain or his wife; so the latter spoke to the Englishman, and told him how matters stood in Lispeth's heart. He laughed a good deal, and said it was very pretty and romantic, a perfect idyl of the Himalayas; but, as he was engaged to a girl at Home, he fancied that nothing would happen. Certainly he would behave with discretion. He did that. Still he found it very pleasant to talk to Lispeth, and walk with Lispeth, and say nice things to her, and call her pet names while he was getting strong enough to go away. It meant nothing at all to him, and everything in the world to Lispeth. She was very happy while the fortnight lasted, because she had found a man to love.

Being a savage by birth, she took no trouble to hide her feelings, and the Englishman was amused. When he went away, Lispeth walked with him, up the Hill as far as Narkunda, very troubled and very miserable. The Chaplain's wife, being a good Christian and disliking anything in the shape of fuss or scandal—Lispeth was beyond her management entirely—had told the Englishman to tell Lispeth that he was coming back to marry her. "She is but a child you know, and, I fear, at heart a heathen," said the Chaplain's wife. So all the twelve miles up the hill the Englishman, with his arm around Lispeth's waist, was assuring the girl that he would come back and marry her; and Lispeth made him promise over and over again. She wept on the Narkunda Ridge till he had passed out of sight along the Muttiani path.

Then she dried her tears and went in to Kotgarh again, and said to the Chaplain's wife: "He will come back and marry me. He has gone to his own people to tell them so." And the Chaplain's wife soothed Lispeth and said: "He will come back." At the end of two months, Lispeth grew impatient, and was told that the Englishman had gone over the seas to England. She knew where England was, because she had read little geography primers; but, of course, she had no conception of the nature of the sea, being a Hill girl. There was an old puzzle-map of the World in the house. Lispeth had played with it when she was a child. She unearthed it again, and put it together of evenings, and cried to herself, and tried to imagine where her Englishman was. As she had no ideas of distance or steamboats, her notions were somewhat erroneous. It would not have made the least difference had she been perfectly correct; for the Englishman had no intention of coming back to marry a Hill girl. He forgot all about her by the time he was butterfly-hunting in Assam. He wrote a book on the East afterwards. Lispeth's name did not appear.

At the end of three months, Lispeth made daily pilgrimage to Narkunda to see if her Englishman was coming along the road. It gave her comfort, and the Chaplain's wife finding her happier thought that she was getting over her "barbarous and most indelicate folly." A little later the walks ceased to help Lispeth and her temper grew very bad. The Chaplain's wife thought this a profitable time to let her know the real state of affairs–that the Englishman had only promised his love to keep her quiet–that he had never meant anything, and that it was "wrong and improper" of Lispeth to think of marriage with an Englishman, who was of a superior clay, besides being promised in marriage to a girl of his own people. Lispeth said that all this was clearly impossible because he had said he loved her, and the Chaplain's wife had, with her own lips, asserted that the Englishman was coming back.

"How can what he and you said be untrue?" asked Lispeth.

"We said it as an excuse to keep you quiet, child," said the Chaplain's wife.

"Then you have lied to me," said Lispeth, "you and he?"

The Chaplain's wife bowed her head, and said nothing. Lispeth was silent, too, for a little time; then she went out down the valley, and returned in the dress of a Hill girl–infamously dirty, but without the nose and earrings. She had her hair braided into the long pig-tail, helped out with black thread, that Hill women wear.

"I am going back to my own people," said she. "You have killed Lispeth. There is only left old Jadéh's daughter–the daughter of a *pahari* and the servant of *Tarka Devi.* You are all liars, you English."

By the time that the Chaplain's wife had recovered from the shock of the announcement that Lispeth had 'verted to her mother's gods, the girl had gone; and she never came back.

She took to her own unclean people savagely, as if to make up the arrears of the life she had stepped out of; and, in a little time, she married a wood-cutter who beat her, after the manner of *paharis,* and her beauty faded soon.

"There is no law whereby you can account for the vagaries of the heathen," said the Chaplain's wife, "and I believe that Lispeth was always at heart an infidel." Seeing she had been taken into the Church of England at the mature age of five weeks, this statement does not do credit to the Chaplain's wife.

Lispeth was a very old woman when she died. She always had a perfect command of English, and when she was sufficiently drunk, could sometimes be induced to tell the story of her first love-affair.

It was hard then to realize that the bleared, wrinkled creature, so like a wisp of charred rag, could ever have been "Lispeth of the Kotgarh Mission."

Three and—an Extra

"When halter and heel ropes are slipped, do not give chase with sticks but with *gram.*"

Punjabi Proverb.

AFTER MARRIAGE ARRIVES a reaction, sometimes a big, sometimes a little one; but it comes sooner or later, and must be tided over by both parties if they desire the rest of their lives to go with the current.

In the case of the Cusack-Bremmils this reaction did not set in till the third year after the wedding. Bremmil was hard to hold at the best of times; but he was a beautiful husband until the baby died and Mrs. Bremmil wore black, and grew thin, and mourned as if the bottom of the Universe had fallen out. Perhaps Bremmil ought to have comforted her. He tried to do so, I think; but the more he comforted the more Mrs. Bremmil grieved, and, consequently, the more uncomfortable Bremmil grew. The fact was that they both needed a tonic. And they got it. Mrs. Bremmil can afford to laugh now, but it was no laughing matter to her at the time.

You see, Mrs. Hauksbee appeared on the horizon; and where she existed was fair chance of trouble. At Simla her by-name was the "Stormy Petrel." She had won that title five times to my own certain knowledge. She was a little, brown, thin, almost skinny, woman, with big, rolling, violet-blue eyes, and the sweetest manners in the world. You had only to mention her name at afternoon teas for every woman in the room to rise up, and call her—well—*not*—blessed. She was clever, witty, brilliant, and sparkling beyond most of her kind; but possessed of many devils of malice and mischievousness. She could be nice, though, even to her own sex. But that is another story.

Bremmil went off at score after the baby's death and the general discomfort that followed, and Mrs. Hauksbee annexed him. She took no pleasure in hiding her captives. She annexed him publicly, and saw that the public saw it. He rode with her, and walked with her, and talked with her, and picnicked with her, and tiffined at Peliti's with her, till people put up their eyebrows and said: "Shocking!" Mrs. Bremmil stayed at home turning over the dead baby's frocks and crying into the empty cradle. She did not care to do anything else. But some eight dear, affectionate lady-friends explained the situation at length to her in case she should miss the cream of it. Mrs. Bremmil listened quietly, and thanked them for their good offices. She was not as clever as Mrs. Hauksbee, but she was no fool. She kept her own counsel, and did not speak to Bremmil of what she had heard. This is worth remembering. Speaking to, or crying over, a husband never did any good yet.

When Bremmil was at home, which was not often, he was more affectionate than usual; and that showed his hand. The affection was forced partly to soothe his own conscience and partly to soothe Mrs. Bremmil. It failed in both regards.

Then "the A.-D.-C. in Waiting was commanded by Their Excellencies, Lord and Lady Lytton, to invite Mr. and Mrs. Cusack-Bremmil to Peterhoff on July 26th at 9-30 P.M."—"Dancing" in the bottom-left-hand corner.

"I can't go," said Mrs. Bremmil, "it is too soon after poor little Florrie . . . but it need not stop you, Tom."

She meant what she said then, and Bremmil said that he would go just to put in an appearance. Here he spoke the thing which was not; and Mrs. Bremmil knew it. She guessed—a woman's guess is much more accurate than a man's certainty—that he had meant to go from the first, and with Mrs. Hauksbee. She sat down to think, and the outcome of her thoughts was that the memory of a dead child was worth considerably less than the affections of a living husband. She made her plan and staked her all upon it. In that hour she discovered that she knew Tom Bremmil thoroughly, and this knowledge she acted on.

"Tom," said she, "I shall be dining out at the Longmores' on the evening of the 26th. You'd better dine at the Club."

This saved Bremmil from making an excuse to get away and dine with Mrs. Hauksbee, so he was grateful, and felt small and mean at the same time—which was wholesome. Bremmil left the house at five for a ride. About half-past five in the evening a large leather-covered basket came in from Phelps' for Mrs. Bremmil. She was a woman who knew how to dress; and she had not spent a week on designing that dress and having it gored, and hemmed, and herring-boned, and tucked and rucked (or whatever the terms are) for nothing. It was a gorgeous dress—slight mourning. I can't describe it, but it was what *The Queen* calls "a creation"—a thing that hit you straight between the eyes and made you gasp. She had not much heart for what she was going to do; but as she glanced at the long mirror she had the satisfaction of knowing that she had never looked so well in her life. She was a large blonde and, when she chose, carried herself superbly.

After the dinner at the Longmores, she went on to the dance—a little late—and encountered Bremmil with Mrs. Hauksbee on his arm. That made her flush, and as the men crowded round her for dances she looked magnificent. She filled up all her dances except three, and those she left blank. Mrs. Hauksbee caught her eye once; and she knew it was war—real war—between them. She started handicapped in the struggle, for she had ordered Bremmil about just the least little bit in the world too much; and he was beginning to resent it. Moreover, he had never seen his wife look so lovely. He stared at her from doorways, and glared at her from passages as she went about with her partners; and the more he stared, the more taken was he. He could scarcely believe that this was the woman with the red eyes and the black stuff gown who used to weep over the eggs at breakfast.

Mrs. Hauksbee did her best to hold him in play, but, after two dances, he crossed over to his wife and asked for a dance.

"I'm afraid you've come too late, *Mister* Bremmil," she said with her eyes twinkling.

Then he begged her to give him a dance, and, as a great favor, she allowed him the fifth waltz. Luckily 5 stood vacant on his program. They danced it together, and there was a little flutter round the room. Bremmil had a sort of a notion that his wife could dance, but he never knew she danced so divinely. At the end of that waltz he asked for another—as a favor, not as a right; and Mrs. Bremmil said: "Show me your program, dear!" He showed it as a naughty little schoolboy hands up contraband sweets to a master. There was a fair sprinkling of "H" on it besides "H" at supper. Mrs. Bremmil said nothing, but she smiled contemptuously, ran her pencil through 7 and 9—two "H's"—and returned the card with her own name written above—a pet name that only she and her husband used. Then she shook her finger at him, and said, laughing: "Oh, you silly, *silly* boy!"

Mrs. Hauksbee heard that, and—she owned as much—felt she had the worst of it. Bremmil accepted 7 and 9 gratefully. They danced 7, and sat out 9 in one of the little tents. What Bremmil said and what Mrs. Bremmil did is no concern of any one's.

When the band struck up "The Roast Beef of Old England," the two went out into the veranda, and Bremmil began looking for his wife's dandy (this was before 'rickshaw days) while she went into the cloak-room. Mrs. Hauksbee came up and said: "You take me in to supper, I think, Mr. Bremmil!" Bremmil turned red and looked foolish: "Ah—h'm! I'm going home with my wife, Mrs. Hauksbee. I think there has been a little mistake." Being a man, he spoke as though Mrs. Hauksbee were entirely responsible.

Mrs. Bremmil came out of the cloak-room in a swansdown cloak with a white "cloud" round her head. She looked radiant; and she had a right to.

The couple went off into the darkness together, Bremmil riding very close to the dandy.

Then says Mrs. Hauksbee to me—she looked a trifle faded and jaded in the lamplight: "Take my word for it, the silliest woman can manage a clever man; but it needs a very clever woman to manage a fool."

Then we went in to supper.

Thrown Away

"And some are sulky, while some will plunge;
  [*So ho! Steady! Stand still, you!*]
Some you must gentle, and some you must lunge.
  [*There! There! Who wants to kill you?*]
Some—there are losses in every trade—
Will break their hearts ere bitted and made,
Will fight like fiends as the rope cuts hard,
And die dumb-mad in the breaking-yard."

Toolungala Stockyard Chorus.

TO REAR A boy under what parents call the "sheltered life system" is, if the boy must go into the world and fend for himself, not wise. Unless he be one in a thousand he has certainly to pass through many unnecessary troubles; and may, possibly, come to extreme grief simply from ignorance of the proper proportions of things.

Let a puppy eat the soap in the bath-room or chew a newly-blacked boot. He chews and chuckles until, by and by, he finds out that blacking and Old Brown Windsor made him very sick; so he argues that soap and boots are not wholesome. Any old dog about the house will soon show him the unwisdom of biting big dogs' ears. Being young, he remembers and goes abroad, at six months, a well-mannered little beast with a chastened appetite. If he had been kept away from boots, and soap, and big dogs till he came to the trinity full-grown and with developed teeth, just consider how fearfully sick and thrashed he would be! Apply that motion to the "sheltered life," and see how it works. It does not sound pretty, but it is the better of two evils.

There was a Boy once who had been brought up under the "sheltered life" theory; and the theory killed him dead. He stayed with his people all his days, from the hour he was born till the hour he went into Sandhurst nearly at the top of the list. He was beautifully taught in all that wins marks by a private tutor, and carried the extra weight of "never having given his parents an hour's anxiety in his life." What he learnt at Sandhurst beyond the regular routine is of no great consequence. He looked about him, and he found soap and blacking, so to speak, very good. He ate a little, and came out of Sandhurst not so high as he went in. Then there was an interval and a scene with his people, who expected much from him. Next a year of living "unspotted from the world" in a third-rate depot battalion where all the juniors were children, and all the seniors old women; and lastly he came out to India where he was cut off from the support of his parents, and had no one to fall back on in time of trouble except himself.

Now India is a place beyond all others where one must not take things too seriously–the midday sun always excepted. Too much work and too much energy kill a man just as effectively as too much assorted vice or too much drink. Flirtation does not matter, because every one is being transferred and either you or she leave the Station, and never return. Good work does not matter, because a man is judged by his worst output and another man takes all the credit of his best as a rule. Bad work does not matter, because other men do worse and incompetents hang on longer in India than anywhere else. Amusements do not matter, because you must repeat them as soon as you have accomplished them once, and most amusements only mean trying to win another person's money. Sickness does not matter, because it's all in the day's work, and if you die another man takes over your place and your office in the eight hours between death and burial. Nothing matters except Home-furlough and acting allowances, and these only because they are scarce. This is a slack, *kutcha* country where all men work with imperfect instruments; and the wisest thing is to take no one and nothing in earnest, but to escape as soon as ever you can to some place where amusement is amusement and a reputation worth the having.

But this Boy–the tale is as old as the Hills–came out, and took all things seriously. He was pretty and was petted. He took the pettings seriously, and fretted over women not worth saddling a pony to call upon. He found his new free life in India very good. It *does* look attractive in the beginning, from a Subaltern's point of view–all ponies, partners, dancing, and so on. He tasted it as the puppy tastes the soap. Only he came late to the eating, with a growing set of teeth. He had no sense of balance–just like the puppy–and could not understand why he was not treated with the consideration he received under his father's roof. This hurt his feelings.

He quarreled with other boys and, being sensitive to the marrow, remembered these quarrels, and they excited him. He found whist, and gymkhanas, and things of that kind (meant to amuse one after office) good; but he took them seriously too, just as he took the "head" that followed after drink. He lost his money over whist and gymkhanas because they were new to him.

He took his losses seriously, and wasted as much energy and interest over a two-goldmohur race for maiden *ekka*-ponies with their manes hogged, as if it had been the Derby. One half of this came from inexperience–much as the puppy squabbles with the corner of the hearthrug–and the other half from the dizziness bred by stumbling out of his quiet life into the glare and excitement of a livelier one. No one told him about the soap and the blacking, because an average man takes it for granted that an average man is ordinarily careful in regard to them. It was pitiful to watch The Boy knocking himself to pieces, as an over-handled colt falls down and cuts himself when he gets away from the groom.

This unbridled license in amusements not worth the trouble of breaking line for, much less rioting over, endured for six months–all through one cold weather–and then we thought that the heat and the knowledge of having lost his money and health and lamed his horses would sober The Boy down, and he would stand steady. In ninety-nine cases out of a hundred this would have happened. You can see the principle working in any Indian Station. But this particular case fell through because The Boy was sensitive and took things seriously—as I may have said some seven times before. Of course, we couldn't tell how his excesses struck him personally. They were nothing very heart-breaking or above the average. He might be crippled for life financially, and want a little nursing. Still the memory of his performances would wither away in one hot weather, and the *shroff* would help him to tide over the money-troubles. But he must have taken another view altogether and have believed himself ruined beyond redemption. His Colonel talked to him severely when the cold weather ended. That made him more wretched than ever; and it was only an ordinary "Colonel's wigging!"

What follows is a curious instance of the fashion in which we are all linked together and made responsible for one another. *The* thing that kicked the beam in The Boy's mind was a remark that a woman made when he was talking to her. There is no use in repeating it, for it was only a cruel little sentence, rapped out before thinking, that made him flush to the roots of his hair. He kept himself to himself for three days, and then put in for two days' leave to go shooting near a Canal Engineer's Rest House about thirty miles out. He got his leave, and that night at Mess was noisier and more offensive than ever. He said that he was "going to shoot big game," and left at half-past ten o'clock in an *ekka.* Partridge—which was the only thing a man could get near the Rest House—is not big game; so every one laughed.

Next morning one of the Majors came in from short leave, and heard that The Boy had gone out to shoot "big game." The Major had taken an interest in The Boy, and had, more than once, tried to check him in the cold weather. The Major put up his eyebrows when he heard of the expedition and went to The Boy's rooms, where he rummaged.

Presently he came out and found me leaving cards on the Mess. There was no one else in the ante-room.

He said: "The Boy has gone out shooting. *Does* a man shoot *tetur* with a revolver and a writing-case!"

I said: "Nonsense, Major!" for I saw what was in his mind.

He said: "Nonsense or no nonsense, I'm going to the Canal now—at once. I don't feel easy."

Then he thought for a minute, and said: "Can you lie?"

"You know best," I answered. "It's my profession."

"Very well," said the Major; "you must come out with me now—at once—in an *ekka* to the Canal to shoot black-buck. Go and put on *shirkar*-kit—*quick*—and drive here with a gun."

The Major was a masterful man; and I knew that he would not give orders for nothing. So I obeyed, and on return found the Major packed up in an *ekka*—gun-cases and food slung below—all ready for a shooting-trip.

He dismissed the driver and drove himself. We jogged along quietly while in the station; but as soon as we got to the dusty road across the plains, he made that pony fly. A country-bred can do nearly anything at a pinch. We covered the thirty miles in under three hours, but the poor brute was nearly dead.

Once I said:—"What's the blazing hurry, Major?"

He said, quietly: "The Boy has been alone, by himself for—one, two, five,—fourteen hours now! I tell you, I don't feel easy."

This uneasiness spread itself to me, and I helped to beat the pony.

When we came to the Canal Engineer's Rest House the Major called for The Boy's servant; but there was no answer. Then we went up to the house, calling for The Boy by name; but there was no answer.

"Oh, he's out shooting," said I.

Just then I saw through one of the windows a little hurricane-lamp burning. This was at four in the afternoon. We both stopped dead in the veranda, holding our breath to catch every sound; and we heard, inside the room, the *"brr—brr—brr"* of a multitude of flies. The Major said nothing, but he took off his helmet and we entered very softly.

The Boy was dead on the *charpoy* in the center of the bare, lime-washed room. He had shot his head nearly to pieces with his revolver. The gun-cases were still strapped, so was the bedding, and on the table lay The Boy's writing-case with photographs. He had gone away to die like a poisoned rat!

The Major said to himself softly:—"Poor Boy! Poor, *poor* devil!" Then he turned away from the bed and said:—"I want your help in this business."

Knowing The Boy was dead by his own hand, I saw exactly what that help would be, so I passed over to the table, took a chair, lit a cheroot, and began to go through the writing-case; the Major looking over my shoulder and repeating to himself: "We came too late!—Like a rat in a hole!—Poor, *poor* devil!"

The Boy must have spent half the night in writing to his people, and to his Colonel, and to a girl at Home; and as soon as he had finished, must have shot himself, for he had been dead a long time when we came in.

I read all that he had written, and passed over each sheet to the Major as I finished it.

We saw from his accounts how very seriously he had taken everything. He wrote about "disgrace which he was unable to bear"—"indelible shame"—"criminal folly"—"wasted life," and so on; besides a lot of private things to his Father and Mother much too sacred to put into print. The letter to the girl at Home was the most pitiful of all; and I choked as I read it. The Major made no attempt to keep dry-eyed. I respected him for that. He read and rocked himself to and fro, and simply cried like a woman without caring to hide it. The letters were so dreary and hopeless and touching. We forgot all about The Boy's follies, and only thought of the poor Thing on the *charpoy* and the scrawled sheets in our hands. It was utterly impossible to let the letters go Home. They would have broken his Father's heart and killed his Mother after killing her belief in her son.

At last the Major dried his eyes openly, and said:—"Nice sort of thing to spring on an English family! What shall we do?"

I said, knowing what the Major had brought me out for:—"The Boy died of cholera. We were with him at the time. We can't commit ourselves to half-measures. Come along."

Then began one of the most grimly comic scenes I have ever taken part in—the concoction of a big, written lie, bolstered with evidence, to soothe The Boy's people at home. I began the rough draft of the letter, the Major throwing in hints here and there while he gathered up all the stuff that The Boy had written and burnt it in the fireplace. It was a hot, still evening when we began, and the lamp burned very badly. In due course I got the draft to my satisfaction, setting forth how The Boy was the pattern of all virtues, beloved by his regiment, with every promise of a great career before him, and so on; how we had helped him through the sickness—it was no time for little lies you will understand—and how he had died without pain. I choked while I was putting down these things and thinking of the poor people who would read them. Then I laughed at the grotesqueness of the affair, and the laughter mixed itself up with the choke—and the Major said that we both wanted drinks.

I am afraid to say how much whisky we drank before the letter was finished. It had not the least effect on us. Then we took off The Boy's watch, locket, and rings.

Lastly, the Major said:—"We must send a lock of hair too. A woman values that."

But there were reasons why we could not find a lock fit to send. The Boy was black-haired, and so was the Major, luckily. I cut off a piece of the Major's hair above the temple with a knife, and put it into the packet we were making. The laughing-fit and the chokes got hold of me again, and I had to stop. The Major was nearly as bad; and we both knew that the worst part of the work was to come.

We sealed up the packet, photographs, locket, seals, ring, letter, and lock of hair with The Boy's sealing-wax and The Boy's seal.

Then the Major said:–"For God's sake let's get outside–away from the room–and think!"

We went outside, and walked on the banks of the Canal for an hour, eating and drinking what we had with us, until the moon rose. I know now exactly how a murderer feels. Finally, we forced ourselves back to the room with the lamp and the Other Thing in it, and began to take up the next piece of work. I am not going to write about this. It was too horrible. We burned the bedstead and dropped the ashes into the Canal; we took up the matting of the room and treated that in the same way. I went off to a village and borrowed two big hoes,–I did not want the villagers to help,–while the Major arranged—the other matters. It took us four hours' hard work to make the grave. As we worked, we argued out whether it was right to say as much as we remembered of the Burial of the Dead. We compromised things by saying the Lord's Prayer with a private unofficial prayer for the peace of the soul of The Boy. Then we filled in the grave and went into the veranda–not the house–to lie down to sleep. We were dead-tired.

When we woke the Major said, wearily:–"We can't go back till to-morrow. We must give him a decent time to die in. He died early *this* morning, remember. That seems more natural." So the Major must have been lying awake all the time, thinking.

I said:–"Then why didn't we bring the body back to cantonments?"

The Major thought for a minute:–"Because the people bolted when they heard of the cholera. And the *ekka* has gone!"

That was strictly true. We had forgotten all about the *ekka*-pony, and he had gone home.

So, we were left there alone, all that stifling day, in the Canal Rest House, testing and re-testing our story of The Boy's death to see if it was weak in any point. A native turned up in the afternoon, but we said that a *Sahib* was dead of cholera, and he ran away. As the dusk gathered, the Major told me all his fears about The Boy, and awful stories of suicide or nearly-carried-out suicide–tales that made one's hair crisp. He said that he himself had once gone into the same Valley of the Shadow as The Boy, when he was young and new to the country; so he understood how things fought together in The Boy's poor jumbled head. He also said that youngsters, in their repentant moments, consider their sins much more serious and ineffaceable than they really are. We talked together all through the evening and rehearsed the story of the death of The Boy. As soon as the moon was up, and The Boy, theoretically, just buried, we struck across country for the Station. We walked from eight till six o'clock in the morning; but though we were dead-tired, we did not forget to go to The Boy's rooms and put away his revolver with the proper amount of cartridges in the pouch. Also to set his writing-case on the table. We found the Colonel and reported the death, feeling more like murderers than ever. Then we went to bed and slept the clock round; for there was no more in us.

The tale had credence as long as was necessary, for every one forgot about The Boy before a fortnight was over. Many people, however, found time to say that the Major had behaved scandalously in not bringing in the body for a regimental funeral. The saddest thing of all was the letter from The Boy's mother to the Major and me–with big inky blisters all over the sheet. She wrote the sweetest possible things about our great kindness, and the obligation she would be under to us as long as she lived.

All things considered, she *was* under an obligation; but not exactly as she meant.

Miss Youghal's Sais

When Man and Woman are agreed, what can the Kazi do?
Mahomedan Proverb.

SOME PEOPLE SAY that there is no romance in India. Those people are wrong. Our lives hold quite as much romance as is good for us. Sometimes more.

Strickland was in the Police, and people did not understand him; so they said he was a doubtful sort of a man and passed by on the other side. Strickland had himself to thank for this. He held the extraordinary theory that a Policeman in India should try to know as much about the natives as the natives themselves. Now, in the whole of Upper India, there is only *one* man who can pass for Hindu or Mahomedan, *chamar* or *faquir,* as he pleases. He is feared and respected by the natives from the Ghor Kathri to the Jamma Musjid; and he is supposed to have the gift of invisibility and executive control over many Devils. But what good has this done him with the Government? None in the world. He has never got Simla for his charge; and his name is almost unknown to Englishmen.

Strickland was foolish enough to take that man for his model; and, following out his absurd theory, dabbled in unsavory places no respectable man would think of exploring–all among the native riff-raff. He educated himself in this peculiar way for seven years, and people could not appreciate it. He was perpetually "going Fantee" among natives, which, of course, no man with any sense believes in. He was initiated into the *Sat Bhai* at Allahabad once, when he was on leave; he knew the Lizard-Song of the Sansis, and the *Hálli-Hukk* dance, which is a religious *can-can* of a startling kind. When a man knows who dances the *Hálli-Hukk,* and how, and when, and where, he knows something to be proud of. He has gone deeper than the skin. But Strickland was not proud, though he had helped once, at Jagadhri, at the Painting of the Death Bull, which no Englishman must even look upon; had mastered the thieves'-patter of the *chángars;* had taken a Eusufzai horse-thief alone near Attock; and had stood under the *mimbar*-board of a Border mosque and conducted service in the manner of a Sunni Mollah.

His crowning achievement was spending eleven days as a *faquir* in the gardens of Baba Atal at Amritsar, and there picking up the threads of the great Nasiban Murder Case. But people said, justly enough:–"Why on earth can't Strickland sit in his office and write up his diary, and recruit, and keep quiet, instead of showing up the incapacity of his seniors?" So the Nasiban Murder Case did him no good departmentally; but, after his first feeling of wrath, he returned to his outlandish custom of prying into native life. By the way, when a man once acquires a taste for this particular amusement, it abides with him all his days. It is the most fascinating thing in the world; Love not excepted. Where other men took ten days to the Hills, Strickland took leave for what he called *shikar,* put on the disguise that appealed to him at the time, stepped down into the brown crowd, and was swallowed up for a while. He was a quiet, dark young fellow–spare, black eyes–and, when he was not thinking of something else, a very interesting companion. Strickland on Native Progress as he had seen it was worth hearing. Natives hated Strickland; but they were afraid of him. He knew too much.

When the Youghals came into the station, Strickland—very gravely, as he did everything—fell in love with Miss Youghal; and she, after a while, fell in love with him because she could not understand him. Then Strickland told the parents; but Mrs. Youghal said she was not going to throw her daughter into the worst paid Department in the Empire, and old Youghal said, in so many words, that he mistrusted Strickland's ways and works, and would thank him not to speak or write to his daughter any more. "Very well," said Strickland, for he did not wish to make his lady-love's life a burden. After one long talk with Miss Youghal he dropped the business entirely.

The Youghals went up to Simla in April.

In July, Strickland secured three months' leave on "urgent private affairs." He locked up his house—though not a native in the Province would wittingly have touched "Estreekin Sahib's" gear for the world—and went down to see a friend of his, an old dyer, at Tarn Taran.

Here all trace of him was lost, until a *sais* met me on the Simla Mall with this extraordinary note:—

> *"Dear old man,*
>
> *"Please give bearer a box of cheroots—Supers, No.* 1, *for preference. They are freshest at the Club. I'll repay when I reappear; but at present I'm out of Society.*
>
> *"Yours,*
>
> "E. STRICKLAND."

I ordered two boxes, and handed them over to the *sais* with my love. That *sais* was Strickland, and he was in old Youghal's employ, attached to Miss Youghal's Arab. The poor fellow was suffering for an English smoke, and knew that whatever happened I should hold my tongue till the business was over.

Later on, Mrs. Youghal, who was wrapped up in her servants, began talking at houses where she called of her paragon among *saises*—the man who was never too busy to get up in the morning and pick flowers for the breakfast-table, and who blacked—actually *blacked*—the hoofs of his horse like a London coachman! The turnout of Miss Youghal's Arab was a wonder and a delight. Strickland—Dulloo, I mean—found his reward in the pretty things that Miss Youghal said to him when she went out riding. Her parents were pleased to find she had forgotten all her foolishness for young Strickland and said she was a good girl.

Strickland vows that the two months of his service were the most rigid mental discipline he has ever gone through. Quite apart from the little fact that the wife of one of his fellow *saises* fell in love with him and then tried to poison him with arsenic because he would have nothing to do with her, he had to school himself into keeping quiet when Miss Youghal went out riding with some man who tried to flirt with her, and he was forced to trot behind carrying the blanket and hearing every word! Also, he had to keep his temper when he was slanged in "Benmore" porch by a policeman—especially once when he was abused by a Naik he had himself recruited from Isser Jang village—or, worse still, when a young subaltern called him a pig for not making way quickly enough.

But the life had its compensations. He obtained great insight into the ways and thefts of *saises*—enough, he says, to have summarily convicted half the *châmar* population of the Punjab if he had been on business. He became one of the leading players at knuckle-bones, which all *jhampânis* and many *saises* play while they are waiting outside the Government House or the Gaiety Theater of nights; he learned to smoke tobacco that was three-fourths cow-dung; and he heard the wisdom of the grizzled Jemadar of the Government

House *saises,* whose words are valuable. He saw many things which amused him; and he states, on honor, that no man can appreciate Simla properly, till he has seen it from the *sais's* point of view. He also says that, if he chose to write all he saw, his head would be broken in several places.

Strickland's account of the agony he endured on wet nights, hearing the music and seeing the lights in "Benmore," with his toes tingling for a waltz and his head in a horse-blanket, is rather amusing. One of these days, Strickland is going to write a little book on his experiences. That book will be worth buying; and even more worth suppressing.

Thus, he served faithfully as Jacob served for Rachel; and his leave was nearly at an end when the explosion came. He had really done his best to keep his temper in the hearing of the flirtations I have mentioned; but he broke down at last. An old and very distinguished General took Miss Youghal for a ride, and began that specially offensive "you're-only-a-little-girl" sort of flirtation—most difficult for a woman to turn aside deftly, and most maddening to listen to. Miss Youghal was shaking with fear at the things he said in the hearing of her *sais.* Dulloo—Strickland—stood it as long as he could. Then he caught hold of the General's bridle, and, in most fluent English, invited him to step off and be heaved over the *cliff.* Next minute, Miss Youghal began crying; and Strickland saw that he had hopelessly given himself away, and everything was over.

The General nearly had a fit, while Miss Youghal was sobbing out the story of the disguise and the engagement that wasn't recognized by the parents. Strickland was furiously angry with himself and more angry with the General for forcing his hand: so he said nothing, but held the horse's head and prepared to thrash the General as some sort of satisfaction, but when the General had thoroughly grasped the story, and knew who Strickland was, he began to puff and blow in the saddle, and nearly rolled off with laughing. He said Strickland deserved a V.C., if it were only for putting on a *sais's* blanket. Then he called himself names, and vowed that he deserved a thrashing, but he was too old to take it from Strickland. Then he complimented Miss Youghal on her lover. The scandal of the business never struck him; for he was a nice old man, with a weakness for flirtations. Then he laughed again, and said that old Youghal was a fool. Strickland let go of the cob's head, and suggested that the General had better help them, if that was his opinion. Strickland knew Youghal's weakness for men with titles and letters after their names and high official position. "It's rather like a forty-minute farce," said the General, "but begad, I *will* help, if it's only to escape that tremendous thrashing I deserved. Go along to your home, my *sais*-Policeman, and change into decent kit and I'll attack Mr. Youghal. Miss Youghal, may I ask you to canter home and wait?"

. . . .

About seven minutes later, there was a wild hurroosh at the Club. A *sais,* with blanket and headrope, was asking all the men he knew: "For Heaven's sake lend me decent clothes!" As the men did not recognize him, there were some peculiar scenes before Strickland could get a hot bath, with soda in it, in one room, a shirt here, a collar there, a pair of trousers elsewhere, and so on. He galloped off, with half the Club wardrobe on his back, and an utter stranger's pony under him, to the house of old Youghal. The General, arrayed in purple and fine linen, was before him. What the General had said Strickland never knew, but Youghal received Strickland with moderate civility; and Mrs. Youghal, touched by the devotion of the transformed Dulloo, was almost kind. The General beamed and chuckled, and Miss Youghal came in, and almost before old Youghal knew where he was, the parental consent had been wrenched out, and Strickland had departed with Miss Youghal to the Telegraph Office to wire for his kit. The final embarrassment was when an utter stranger attacked him on the Mall and asked for the stolen pony.

So, in the end, Strickland and Miss Youghal were married, on the strict understanding that Strickland should drop his old ways, and stick to Departmental routine which pays best and leads to Simla. Strickland was far too fond of his wife, just then, to break his word, but it was a sore trial to him; for the streets and the bazars, and the sounds in them, were full of meaning to Strickland, and these called to him to come back and take up his wanderings and his discoveries. Some day, I will tell you how he broke his promise to help a friend. That was long since, and he has, by this time, been nearly spoilt for what he would call *shikar*. He is forgetting the slang, and the beggar's cant, and the marks, and the signs, and the drift of the under-currents, which, if a man would master, he must always continue to learn.

But he fills in his Departmental returns beautifully.

"Yoked with an Unbeliever"

I am dying for you, and you are dying for another.
Punjabi Proverb.

WHEN THE GRAVESEND tender left the P. & O. steamer for Bombay and went back to catch the train to Town, there were many people in it crying. But the one who wept most, and most openly, was Miss Agnes Laiter. She had reason to cry, because the only man she ever loved—or ever could love, so she said—was going out to India; and India, as every one knows, is divided equally between jungle, tigers, cobras, cholera and sepoys.

Phil Garron, leaning over the side of the steamer in the rain, felt very unhappy too; but he did not cry. He was sent out to "tea." What "tea" meant he had not the vaguest idea, but fancied that he would have to ride on a prancing horse over hills covered with tea-vines, and draw a sumptuous salary for doing so; and he was very grateful to his uncle for getting him the berth. He was really going to reform all his slack, shiftless ways, save a large proportion of his magnificent salary yearly, and, in a very short time, return to marry Agnes Laiter. Phil Garron had been lying loose on his friends' hands for three years, and, as he had nothing to do, he naturally fell in love. He was very nice; but he was not strong in his views and opinions and principles, and though he never came to actual grief his friends were thankful when he said good-by, and went out to this mysterious "tea" business near Darjiling. They said:—"God bless you, dear boy! Let us never see your face again,"—or at least that was what Phil was given to understand.

When he sailed, he was very full of a great plan to prove himself several hundred times better than any one had given him credit for—to work like a horse, and triumphantly marry Agnes Laiter. He had many good points besides his good looks; his only fault being that he was weak, the least little bit in the world weak. He had as much notion of economy as the Morning

Sun; and yet you could not lay your hand on any one item, and say:—"Herein Phil Garron is extravagant or reckless." Nor could you point out any particular vice in his character; but he was "unsatisfactory" and as workable as putty.

Agnes Laiter went about her duties at home—her family objected to the engagement—with red eyes, while Phil was sailing to Darjiling—"a port on the Bengal Ocean," as his mother used to tell her friends. He was popular enough on board ship, made many acquaintances and a moderately large liquor-bill, and sent off huge letters to Agnes Laiter at each port. Then he fell to work on this plantation, somewhere between Darjiling and Kangra, and, though the salary and the horse and the work were not quite all he had fancied, he succeeded fairly well, and gave himself much unnecessary credit for his perseverance.

In the course of time, as he settled more into collar, and his work grew fixed before him, the face of Agnes Laiter went out of his mind and only came when he was at leisure, which was not often. He would forget all about her for a fortnight, and remember her with a start, like a school-boy who has forgotten to learn his lesson. She did not forget Phil, because she was of the kind that never forgets. Only, another man—a really desirable young man—presented himself before Mrs. Laiter; and the chance of a marriage with Phil was as far off as ever; and his letters were so unsatisfactory; and there was a certain amount of domestic pressure brought to bear on the girl; and the young man really was an eligible person as incomes go; and the end of all things was that Agnes married him, and wrote a tempestuous whirlwind of a letter to Phil in the wilds of Darjiling, and said she should never know a happy moment all the rest of her life. Which was a true prophecy.

Phil got that letter, and held himself ill-treated. This was two years after he had come out; but by dint of thinking fixedly of Agnes Laiter, and looking at her photograph, and patting himself on the back for being one of the most constant lovers in history, and warming to the work as he went on, he really fancied that he had been very hardly used. He sat down and wrote one final letter—a really pathetic "world without end, amen," epistle; explaining how he would be true to Eternity, and that all women were very much alike, and he would hide his broken heart, etc., etc.; but if, at any future time, etc., etc., he could afford to wait, etc., etc., unchanged affections, etc., etc., return to her old love, etc., etc., for eight closely-written pages. From an artistic point of view, it was very neat work, but an ordinary Philistine, who knew the state of Phil's real feelings—not the ones he rose to as he went on writing—would have called it the thoroughly mean and selfish work of a thoroughly mean and selfish, weak man. But this verdict would have been incorrect. Phil paid for the postage, and felt every word he had written for at least two days and a half. It was the last flicker before the light went out.

That letter made Agnes Laiter very unhappy, and she cried and put it away in her desk, and became Mrs. Somebody Else for the good of her family. Which is the first duty of every Christian maid.

Phil went his ways, and thought no more of his letter, except as an artist thinks of a neatly touched-in sketch. His ways were not bad, but they were not altogether good until they brought him across Dunmaya, the daughter of a Rajput ex-Subadar-Major of our Native Army. The girl had a strain of Hill blood in her, and, like the Hill women, was not a *purdah nashin.* Where Phil met her, or how he heard of her, does not matter. She was a good girl and handsome, and, in her way, very clever and shrewd; though, of course, a little hard. It is to be remembered that Phil was living very comfortably, denying himself no small luxury, never putting by an anna, very satisfied with himself and his good intentions, was dropping all his English correspondents one by one, and beginning more and more to look upon this land as his home. Some men fall this way; and they are of no use afterwards. The climate where he was stationed was good, and it really did not seem to him that there was anything to go Home for.

He did what many planters have done before him—that is to say, he made up his mind to marry a Hill-girl and settle down. He was seven and twenty then, with a long life before him, but no spirit to go through with it. So he married Dunmaya by the forms of the English Church, and some fellow-planters said he was a fool, and some said he was a wise man. Dunmaya was a thoroughly honest girl, and, in spite of her reverence for an Englishman, had a reasonable estimate of her husband's weaknesses. She managed him tenderly, and became, in less than a year, a very passable imitation of an English lady in dress and carriage. [It is curious to think that a Hill-man, after a lifetime's education, is a Hill-man stiff; but a Hill-woman can in six months master most of the ways of her English sisters. There was a coolie-woman once. But that is another story.] Dunmaya dressed by preference in black and yellow, and looked well.

Meantime the letter lay in Agnes's desk, and now and again she would think of poor, resolute, hard-working Phil among the cobras and tigers of Darjiling, toiling in the vain hope that she might come back to him. Her husband was worth ten Phils, except that he had rheumatism of the heart. Three years after he was married,—and after he had tried Nice and Algeria for his complaint—he went to Bombay, where he died, and set Agnes free. Being a devout woman, she looked on his death and the place of it, as a direct interposition of Providence, and when she had recovered from the shock she took out and re-read Phil's letter with the "etc., etc.," and the big dashes, and the little dashes, and kissed it several times. No one knew her in Bombay; she had her husband's income, which was a large one, and Phil was close at hand. It was wrong and improper, of course, but she decided, as heroines do in novels, to find her old lover, to offer him her hand and her gold, and with him spend the rest of her life in some spot far from unsympathetic souls. She sat for two months, alone in Watson's Hotel, elaborating this decision, and the picture was a pretty one. Then she set out in search of Phil Garron, Assistant on a tea plantation with a more than usually unpronounceable name.

. . . . . .

She found him. She spent a month over it, for his plantation was not in the Darjiling district at all, but nearer Kangra. Phil was very little altered, and Dunmaya was very nice to her.

Now the particular sin and shame of the whole business is that Phil, who really is not worth thinking of twice, was and is loved by Dunmaya, and more than loved by Agnes, the whole of whose life he seems to have spoilt.

Worst of all, Dunmaya is making a decent man of him; and he will be ultimately saved from perdition through her training.

Which is manifestly unfair.

False Dawn

To-night God knows what thing shall tide,
The Earth is racked and faint–
Expectant, sleepless, open-eyed;
And we, who from the Earth were made,
Thrill with our Mother's pain.
In Durance.

NO MAN WILL ever know the exact truth of this story; though women may sometimes whisper it to one another after a dance, when they are putting up their hair for the night and comparing lists of victims. A man, of course, cannot assist at these functions. So the tale must be told from the outside–in the dark–all wrong.

Never praise a sister to a sister, in the hope of your compliments reaching the proper ears, and so preparing the way for you later on. Sisters are women first, and sisters afterwards; and you will find that you do yourself harm.

Saumarez knew this when he made up his mind to propose to the elder Miss Copleigh. Saumarez was a strange man, with few merits, so far as men could see, though he was popular with women, and carried enough conceit to stock a Viceroy's Council and leave a little over for the Commander-in-Chief's Staff. He was a Civilian. Very many women took an interest in Saumarez, perhaps, because his manner to them was offensive. If you hit a pony over the nose at the outset of your acquaintance, he may not love you, but he will take a deep interest in your movements ever afterwards. The elder Miss Copleigh was nice, plump, winning, and pretty. The younger was not so pretty, and, from men disregarding the hint set forth above, her style was repellent and unattractive. Both girls had, practically, the same figure, and there was a strong likeness between them in look and voice; though no one could doubt for an instant which was the nicer of the two.

Saumarez made up his mind, as soon as they came into the station from Behar, to marry the elder one. At least, we all made sure that he would, which comes to the same thing. She was two-and-twenty, and he was thirty-three, with pay and allowances of nearly fourteen hundred rupees a month. So the match, as we arranged it, was in every way a good one. Saumarez was his name, and summary was his nature, as a man once said. Having drafted his Resolution, he formed a Select Committee of One to sit upon it, and resolved to take his time. In our unpleasant slang, the Copleigh girls "hunted in couples." That is to say, you could do nothing with one without the other. They were very loving sisters; but their mutual affection was sometimes inconvenient. Saumarez held the balance-hair true between them, and none but himself could have said to which side his heart inclined; though every one guessed. He rode with them a good deal and danced with them, but he never succeeded in detaching them from each other for any length of time.

Women said that the two girls kept together through deep mistrust, each fearing that the other would steal a march on her. But that has nothing to do with a man. Saumarez was silent for good or bad, and as business-likely attentive as he could be, having due regard to his work and his polo. Beyond doubt both girls were fond of him.

As the hot weather drew nearer, and Saumarez made no sign, women said that you could see their trouble in the eyes of the girls—that they were looking strained, anxious, and irritable. Men are quite blind in these matters unless they have more of the woman than the man in their composition, in which case it does not matter what they say or think. I maintain it was the hot April days that took the color out of the Copleigh girls' cheeks. They should have been sent to the Hills early. No one—man or woman—feels an angel when the hot weather is approaching. The younger sister grew more cynical—not to say acid—in her ways; and the winningness of the elder wore thin. There was more effort in it.

Now the Station wherein all these things happened was, though not a little one, off the line of rail, and suffered through want of attention. There were no gardens or bands or amusements worth speaking of, and it was nearly a day's journey to come into Lahore for a dance. People were grateful for small things to interest them.

About the beginning of May, and just before the final exodus of Hill-goers, when the weather was very hot and there were not more than twenty people in the Station, Saumarez gave a moonlight riding-picnic at an old tomb, six miles away, near the bed of the river. It was a "Noah's Ark" picnic; and there was to be the usual arrangement of quarter-mile intervals between each couple, on account of the dust. Six couples came altogether, including chaperons. Moonlight picnics are useful just at the very end of the season, before all the girls go away to the Hills. They lead to understandings, and should be encouraged by chaperons; especially those whose girls look sweetest in riding habits. I knew a case once. But that is another story. That picnic was called the "Great Pop picnic," because every one knew Saumarez would propose then to the eldest Miss Copleigh; and, beside his affair, there was another which might possibly come to happiness. The social atmosphere was heavily charged and wanted clearing.

We met at the parade-ground at ten: the night was fearfully hot. The horses sweated even at walking-pace, but anything was better than sitting still in our own dark houses. When we moved off under the full moon we were four couples, one triplet, and Mr. Saumarez rode with the Copleigh girls, and I loitered at the tail of the procession wondering with whom Saumarez would ride home. Every one was happy and contented; but we all felt that things were going to happen. We rode slowly; and it was nearly midnight before we reached the old tomb, facing the ruined tank, in the decayed gardens where we were going to eat and drink. I was late in coming up; and before I went into the garden, I saw that the horizon to the north carried a faint, dun-colored feather. But no one would have thanked me for spoiling so well-managed an entertainment as this picnic—and a dust-storm, more or less, does no great harm.

We gathered by the tank. Some one had brought out a banjo—which is a most sentimental instrument—and three or four of us sang. You must not laugh at this. Our amusements in out-of-the-way Stations are very few indeed. Then we talked in groups or together, lying under the trees, with the sun-baked roses dropping their petals on our feet, until supper was ready. It was a beautiful supper, as cold and as iced as you could wish; and we stayed long over it.

I had felt that the air was growing hotter and hotter; but nobody seemed to notice it until the moon went out and a burning hot wind began lashing the orange-trees with a sound like the noise of the sea. Before we knew where we were, the dust-storm was on us, and everything was roaring, whirling darkness. The supper-table was blown bodily into the tank. We were afraid of staying anywhere near the old tomb for fear it might be blown down. So we felt our way to the orange-trees where the horses were picketed and waited for the storm to blow over. Then the little light that was left vanished, and you could not see your hand before your face. The air was heavy with dust and sand from the bed of the river, that filled boots and pockets and drifted down necks and coated eyebrows and mustaches. It was one of the worst dust-storms of the year. We were all huddled together close to the trembling horses, with the thunder chattering overhead, and the lightning spurting like water from a sluice, all ways at once. There was no danger, of course, unless the horses broke loose. I was standing with my head downwind and my hands over my mouth, hearing the trees thrashing each other. I could not see who was next me till the flashes came. Then I found that I was packed near Saumarez and the eldest Miss Copleigh, with my own horse just in front of me. I recognized the eldest Miss Copleigh, because she had a *pagri* round her helmet, and the younger had not. All the electricity in the air had gone into my body and I was quivering and tingling from head to foot–exactly as a corn shoots and tingles before rain. It was a grand storm. The wind seemed to be picking up the earth and pitching it to leeward in great heaps; and the heat beat up from the ground like the heat of the Day of Judgment.

The storm lulled slightly after the first half-hour, and I heard a despairing little voice close to my ear, saying to itself, quietly and softly, as if some lost soul were flying about with the wind:"O my God!" Then the younger Miss Copleigh stumbled into my arms, saying: "Where is my horse? Get my horse. I want to go home. I *want* to go home. Take me home."

I thought that the lightning and the black darkness had frightened her; so I said there was no danger, but she must wait till the storm blew over. She answered: "It is not *that!* It is not *that!* I want to go home! O take me away from here!"

I said that she could not go till the light came; but I felt her brush past me and go away. It was too dark to see where. Then the whole sky was split open with one tremendous flash, as if the end of the world were coming, and all the women shrieked.

Almost directly after this, I felt a man's hand on my shoulder and heard Saumarez bellowing in my ear. Through the rattling of the trees and howling of the wind, I did not catch his words at once, but at last I heard him say:– "I've proposed to the wrong one! What shall I do?" Saumarez had no occasion to make this confidence to me. I was never a friend of his, nor am I now; but I fancy neither of us were ourselves just then. He was shaking as he stood with excitement, and I was feeling queer all over with the electricity. I could not think of anything to say except:–"More fool you for proposing in a dust-storm." But I did not see how that would improve the mistake.

Then he shouted:–"Where's Edith–Edith Copleigh?" Edith was the younger sister. I answered out of my astonishment:–"What do you want with *her?*" Would you believe it, for the next two minutes, he and I were shouting at each other like maniacs,–he vowing that it was the younger sister he had meant to propose to all along, and I telling him till my throat was hoarse that he must have made a mistake! I can't account for this except, again, by the fact that we were neither of us ourselves. Everything seemed to me like a bad dream–from the stamping of the horses in the darkness to Saumarez telling me the story of his loving Edith Copleigh since the first. He was still clawing my shoulder and begging me to tell him where Edith Copleigh was, when another lull came and brought light with it, and we saw the dust-cloud forming on the plain in front of us. So we knew the worst was over. The moon was low down, and there was just the glimmer of the false dawn that comes about an hour before the real one. But the light was very faint, and the dun cloud roared like a bull. I wondered where Edith Copleigh had gone; and as I was wondering I saw three things together: First Maud Copleigh's face come smiling out of the darkness and moved towards Saumarez who was standing by me. I heard the girl whisper:—"George," and slide her arm through the arm that was not clawing my shoulder, and I saw that look on her face which only comes once or twice in a lifetime—when a woman is perfectly happy and the air is full of trumpets and gorgeous-colored fire and the Earth turns into cloud because she loves and is loved. At the same time, I saw Saumarez's face as he heard Maud Copleigh's voice, and fifty yards away from the clump of orange-trees, I saw a brown holland habit getting upon a horse.

It must have been my state of over-excitement that made me so quick to meddle with what did not concern me. Saumarez was moving off to the habit; but I pushed him back and said:—"Stop here and explain. I'll fetch her back!" And I ran out to get at my own horse. I had a perfectly unnecessary notion that everything must be done decently and in order, and that Saumarez's first care was to wipe the happy look out of Maud Copleigh's face. All the time I was linking up the curb-chain I wondered how he would do it.

I cantered after Edith Copleigh, thinking to bring her back slowly on some pretense or another. But she galloped away as soon as she saw me, and I was forced to ride after her in earnest. She called back over her shoulder—"Go away! I'm going home. Oh, go *away!*" two or three times; but my business was to catch her first, and argue later. The ride just fitted in with the rest of the evil dream. The ground was very bad, and now and again we rushed through the whirling, choking "dust-devils" in the skirts of the flying storm. There was a burning hot wind blowing that brought up a stench of stale brick-kilns with it; and through the half light and through the dust-devils, across that desolate plain, flickered the brown holland habit on the gray horse. She headed for the Station at first. Then she wheeled round and set off for the river through beds of burnt down jungle-grass, bad even to ride pig over. In cold blood I should never have dreamed of going over such a country at night, but it seemed quite right and natural with the lightning crackling overhead, and a reek like the smell of the Pit in my nostrils. I rode and shouted, and she bent forward and lashed her horse, and the aftermath of the dust-storm came up and caught us both, and drove us down wind like pieces of paper.

I don't know how far we rode; but the drumming of the horse-hoofs and the roar of the wind and the race of the faint blood-red moon through the yellow mist seemed to have gone on for years and years, and I was literally drenched with sweat from my helmet to my gaiters when the gray stumbled, recovered himself, and pulled up dead lame. My brute was used up altogether. Edith Copleigh was in a sad state, plastered with dust, her helmet off, and crying bitterly. "Why can't you let me alone?" she said. "I only wanted to get away and go home. Oh, *please* let me go!"

"You have got to come back with me, Miss Copleigh. Saumarez has something to say to you."

It was a foolish way of putting it; but I hardly knew Miss Copleigh, and, though I was playing Providence at the cost of my horse, I could not tell her in as many words what Saumarez had told me. I thought he could do that better himself. All her pretense about being tired and wanting to go home broke down, and she rocked herself to and fro in the saddle as she sobbed, and the hot wind blew her black hair to leeward. I am not going to repeat what she said, because she was utterly unstrung.

This, if you please, was the cynical Miss Copleigh. Here was I, almost an utter stranger to her, trying to tell her that Saumarez loved her and she was to come back to hear him say so? I believe I made myself understood, for she gathered the gray together and made him hobble somehow, and we set off for the tomb, while the storm went thundering down to Umballa and a few big drops of warm rain fell. I found out that she had been standing close to

Saumarez when he proposed to her sister, and had wanted to go home to cry in peace, as an English girl should. She dabbed her eyes with her pocket-handkerchief as we went along, and babbled to me out of sheer lightness of heart and hysteria. That was perfectly unnatural; and yet, it seemed all right at the time and in the place. All the world was only the two Copleigh girls, Saumarez and I, ringed in with the lightning and the dark; and the guidance of this misguided world seemed to lie in my hands.

When we returned to the tomb in the deep, dead stillness that followed the storm, the dawn was just breaking and nobody had gone away. They were waiting for our return. Saumarez most of all. His face was white and drawn. As Miss Copleigh and I limped up, he came forward to meet us, and, when he helped her down from her saddle, he kissed her before all the picnic. It was like a scene in a theater, and the likeness was heightened by all the dust-white, ghostly-looking men and women under the orange-trees, clapping their hands—as if they were watching a play—at Saumarez's choice. I never knew anything so un-English in my life.

Lastly, Saumarez said we must all go home or the Station would come out to look for us, and *would* I be good enough to ride home with Maud Copleigh? Nothing would give me greater pleasure, I said.

So, we formed up, six couples in all, and went back two by two; Saumarez walking at the side of Edith Copleigh, who was riding his horse.

The air was cleared; and little by little, as the sun rose, I felt we were all dropping back again into ordinary men and women and that the "Great Pop Picnic" was a thing altogether apart and out of the world—never to happen again. It had gone with the dust-storm and the tingle in the hot air.

I felt tired and limp, and a good deal ashamed of myself as I went in for a bath and some sleep.

There is a woman's version of this story, but it will never be written . . . unless Maud Copleigh cares to try.

The Rescue of Pluffles

Thus, for a season, they fought it fair—
She and his cousin May—
Tactful, talented, debonnaire,
Decorous foes were they;
But never can battle of man compare
With merciless feminine fray.
Two and One.

MRS. HAUKSBEE WAS sometimes nice to her own sex. Here is a story to prove this; and you can believe just as much as ever you please.

Pluffles was a subaltern in the "Unmentionables." He was callow, even for a subaltern. He was callow all over—like a canary that had not finished fledging itself. The worst of it was he had three times as much money as was good for him; Pluffles' Papa being a rich man and Pluffles being the only son. Pluffles' Mamma adored him. She was only a little less callow than Pluffles, and she believed everything he said.

Pluffles' weakness was not believing what people said. He preferred what he called "trusting to his own judgment." He had as much judgment as he had seat or hands; and this preference tumbled him into trouble once or twice. But the biggest trouble Pluffles ever manufactured came about at Simla–some years ago, when he was four-and-twenty.

He began by trusting to his own judgment, as usual, and the result was that, after a time, he was bound hand and foot to Mrs. Reiver's 'rickshaw wheels.

There was nothing good about Mrs. Reiver, unless it was her dress. She was bad from her hair–which started life on a Brittany girl's head–to her boot-heels which were two and three-eighth inches high. She was not honestly mischievous like Mrs. Hauksbee; she was wicked in a business-like way.

There was never any scandal–she had not generous impulses enough for that. She was the exception which proved the rule that Anglo-Indian ladies are in every way as nice as their sisters at Home. She spent her life in proving that rule.

Mrs. Hauksbee and she hated each other fervently. They heard far too much to clash; but the things they said of each other were startling–not to say original. Mrs. Hauksbee was honest–honest as her own front-teeth–and, but for her love of mischief, would have been a woman's woman. There was no honesty about Mrs. Reiver; nothing but selfishness. And at the beginning of the season, poor little Pluffles fell a prey to her. She laid herself out to that end, and who was Pluffles to resist? He went on trusting to his judgment, and he got judged.

I have seen Hayes argue with a tough horse–I have seen a tonga-driver coerce a stubborn pony–I have seen a riotous setter broken to gun by a hard keeper–but the breaking-in of Pluffles of the "Unmentionables" was beyond all these. He learned to fetch and carry like a dog, and to wait like one, too, for a word from Mrs. Reiver. He learned to keep appointments which Mrs. Reiver had no intention of keeping. He learned to take thankfully dances which Mrs. Reiver had no intention of giving him. He learned to shiver for an hour and a quarter on the windward side of Elysium while Mrs. Reiver was making up her mind to come for a ride. He learned to hunt for a 'rickshaw, in a light dress-suit under pelting rain, and to walk by the side of that 'rickshaw when he had found it. He learned what it was to be spoken to like a coolie and ordered about like a cook. He learned all this and many other things besides. And he paid for his schooling.

Perhaps, in some hazy way, he fancied that it was fine and impressive, that it gave him a status among men, and was altogether the thing to do. It was nobody's business to warn Pluffles that he was unwise. The pace that season was too good to inquire; and meddling with another man's folly is always thankless work. Pluffles' Colonel should have ordered him back to his regiment when he heard how things were going. But Pluffles had got himself engaged to a girl in England the last time he went home; and if there was one thing more than another which the Colonel detested, it was a married subaltern. He chuckled when he heard of the education of Pluffles, and said it was "good training for the boy." But it was not good training in the least. It led him into spending money beyond his means, which were good: above that the education spoilt an average boy and made it a tenth-rate man of an objectionable kind. He wandered into a bad set, and his little bill at Hamilton's was a thing to wonder at.

Then Mrs. Hauksbee rose to the occasion. She played her game alone, knowing what people would say of her; and she played it for the sake of a girl she had never seen. Pluffles' *fiancée* was to come out, under chaperonage of an aunt, in October, to be married to Pluffles.

At the beginning of August, Mrs. Hauksbee discovered that it was time to interfere. A man who rides much knows exactly what a horse is going to do next before he does it. In the same way, a woman of Mrs. Hauksbee's experience knows accurately how a boy will behave under certain circumstances—notably when he is infatuated with one of Mrs. Reiver's stamp. She said that, sooner or later, little Pluffles would break off that engagement for nothing at all—simply to gratify Mrs. Reiver, who, in return, would keep him at her feet and in her service just so long as she found it worth her while. She said she knew the signs of these things. If she did not, no one else could.

Then she went forth to capture Pluffles under the guns of the enemy; just as Mrs. Cusack-Bremmil carried away Bremmil under Mrs. Hauksbee's eyes.

This particular engagement lasted seven weeks—we called it the Seven Weeks' War—and was fought out inch by inch on both sides. A detailed account would fill a book, and would be incomplete then. Any one who knows about these things can fit in the details for himself. It was a superb fight—there will never be another like it as long as Jakko stands—and Pluffles was the prize of victory. People said shameful things about Mrs. Hauksbee. They did not know what she was playing for. Mrs. Reiver fought, partly because Pluffles was useful to her, but mainly because she hated Mrs. Hauksbee, and the matter was a trial of strength between them. No one knows what Pluffles thought. He had not many ideas at the best of times, and the few he possessed made him conceited. Mrs. Hauksbee said:—"The boy must be caught; and the only way of catching him is by treating him well."

So she treated him as a man of the world and of experience so long as the issue was doubtful. Little by little, Pluffles fell away from his old allegiance and came over to the enemy, by whom he was made much of. He was never sent on out-post duty after 'rickshaws any more, nor was he given dances which never came off, nor were the drains on his purse continued. Mrs. Hauksbee held him on the snaffle; and, after his treatment at Mrs. Reiver's hands, he appreciated the change.

Mrs. Reiver had broken him of talking about himself, and made him talk about her own merits. Mrs. Hauksbee acted otherwise, and won his confidence, till he mentioned his engagement to the girl at Home, speaking of it in a high and mighty way as a "piece of boyish folly." This was when he was taking tea with her one afternoon, and discoursing in what he considered a gay and fascinating style. Mrs. Hauksbee had seen an earlier generation of his stamp bud and blossom, and decay into fat Captains and tubby Majors.

At a moderate estimate there were about three and twenty sides to that lady's character. Some men say more. She began to talk to Pluffles after the manner of a mother, and as if there had been three hundred years, instead of fifteen, between them. She spoke with a sort of throaty quaver in her voice which had a soothing effect, though what she said was anything but soothing. She pointed out the exceeding folly, not to say meanness, of Pluffles' conduct, and the smallness of his views. Then he stammered something about "trusting to his own judgment as a man of the world;" and this paved the way for what she wanted to say next. It would have withered up Pluffles had it come from any other woman; but in the soft cooing style in which Mrs. Hauksbee put it, it only made him feel limp and repentant—as if he had been in some superior kind of church. Little by little, very softly and pleasantly, she began taking the conceit out of Pluffles, as you take the ribs out of an umbrella before re-covering it. She told him what she thought of him and his judgment and his knowledge of the world; and how his performances had made him ridiculous to other people; and how it was his intention to make love to herself if she gave him the chance. Then she said that marriage would be the making of him; and drew a pretty little picture—all rose and opal—of the Mrs. Pluffles of the future going through life relying on the "judgment" and "knowledge of the world" of a husband who had nothing to reproach himself with. How she reconciled these two statements she alone knew. But they did not strike Pluffles as conflicting.

Hers was a perfect little homily—much better than any clergyman could have given—and it ended with touching allusions to Pluffles' Mamma and Papa, and the wisdom of taking his bride Home.

Then she sent Pluffles out for a walk, to think over what she had said. Pluffles left, blowing his nose very hard and holding himself very straight. Mrs. Hauksbee laughed.

What Pluffles had intended to do in the matter of the engagement only Mrs. Reiver knew, and she kept her own counsel to her death. She would have liked it spoiled as a compliment, I fancy.

Pluffles enjoyed many talks with Mrs. Hauksbee during the next few days. They were all to the same end, and they helped Pluffles in the path of Virtue.

Mrs. Hauksbee wanted to keep him under her wing to the last. Therefore she discountenanced his going down to Bombay to get married. "Goodness only knows what might happen by the way!" she said. "Pluffles is cursed with the curse of Reuben, and India is no fit place for him!"

In the end, the *fiancée* arrived with her aunt; and Pluffles, having reduced his affairs to some sort of order—here again Mrs. Hauksbee helped him—was married.

Mrs. Hauksbee gave a sigh of relief when both the "I wills" had been said, and went her way.

Pluffles took her advice about going Home. He left the Service, and is now raising speckled cattle inside green painted fences somewhere at Home. I believe he does this very judiciously. He would have come to extreme grief out here.

For these reasons if any one says anything more than usually nasty about Mrs. Hauksbee, tell him the story of the Rescue of Pluffles.

Cupid's Arrows

Pit where the buffalo cooled his hide,
By the hot sun emptied, and blistered and dried;
Log in the *reh*-grass, hidden and alone;
Bund where the earth-rat's mounds are strown:
Cave in the bank where the sly stream steals;
Aloe that stabs at the belly and heels,
Jump if you dare on a steed untried—
Safer it is to go wide—go wide!
Hark, from in front where the best men ride:
"Pull to the off, boys! Wide! Go wide!"

The Peora Hunt.

ONCE UPON A time there lived at Simla a very pretty girl, the daughter of a poor but honest District and Sessions Judge. She was a good girl, but could not help knowing her power and using it. Her Mamma was very anxious about her daughter's future, as all good Mammas should be.

When a man is a Commissioner and a bachelor and has the right of wearing open-work jam-tart jewels in gold and enamel on his clothes, and of going through a door before every one except a Member of Council, a Lieutenant-Governor, or a Viceroy, he is worth marrying. At least, that is what ladies say. There was a Commissioner in Simla, in those days, who was, and wore, and did, all I have said. He was a plain man—an ugly man—the ugliest man in Asia, with two exceptions. His was a face to dream about and try to carve on a pipe-head afterwards. His name was Saggott—Barr-Saggott—Anthony Barr-Saggott and six letters to follow. Departmentally, he was one of the best men the Government of India owned. Socially, he was like a blandishing gorilla.

When he turned his attentions to Miss Beighton, I believe that Mrs. Beighton wept with delight at the reward Providence had sent her in her old age.

Mr. Beighton held his tongue. He was an easy-going man.

Now a Commissioner is very rich. His pay is beyond the dreams of avarice—is so enormous that he can afford to save and scrape in a way that would almost discredit a Member of Council. Most Commissioners are mean; but Barr-Saggott was an exception. He entertained royally; he horsed himself well; he gave dances, he was a power in the land; and he behaved as such.

Consider that everything I am writing of took place in an almost prehistoric era in the history of British India. Some folk may remember the years before lawn-tennis was born when we all played croquet. There were seasons before that, if you will believe me, when even croquet had not been invented, and archery—which was revived in England in 1844—was as great a pest as lawn-tennis is now. People talked learnedly about "holding" and "loosing," "steles," "reflexed bows," "56-pound bows," "backed" or "self-yew bows," as we talk about "rallies," "volleys," "smashes," "returns," and "16-ounce rackets."

Miss Beighton shot divinely over ladies' distance—60 yards, that is—and was acknowledged the best lady archer in Simla. Men called her "Diana of Tara-Devi."

Barr-Saggott paid her great attention; and, as I have said, the heart of her mother was uplifted in consequence. Kitty Beighton took matters more calmly. It was pleasant to be singled out by a Commissioner with letters after his name, and to fill the hearts of other girls with bad feelings. But there was no denying the fact that Barr-Saggott was phenomenally ugly; and all his attempts to adorn himself only made him more grotesque. He was not christened "The *Langur*"—which means gray ape—for nothing. It was pleasant, Kitty thought, to have him at her feet, but it was better to escape from him and ride with the graceless Cubbon—the man in a Dragoon Regiment at Umballa—the boy with a handsome face, and no prospects. Kitty liked Cubbon more than a little. He never pretended for a moment that he was anything less than head over heels in love with her; for he was an honest boy. So Kitty fled, now and again, from the stately wooings of Barr-Saggott to the company of young Cubbon, and was scolded by her Mamma in consequence. "But, Mother," she said, "Mr. Saggott is such—such a—is so *fearfully* ugly, you know!"

"My dear," said Mrs. Beighton, piously, "we cannot be other than an all-ruling Providence has made us. Besides, you will take precedence of your own Mother, you know! Think of that and be reasonable."

Then Kitty put up her little chin and said irreverent things about precedence, and Commissioners, and matrimony. Mr. Beighton rubbed the top of his head; for he was an easy-going man.

Late in the season, when he judged that the time was ripe, Barr-Saggott developed a plan which did great credit to his administrative powers. He arranged an archery-tournament for ladies with a most sumptuous diamond-studded bracelet as prize. He drew up his terms skilfully, and every one saw that the bracelet was a gift to Miss Beighton; the acceptance carrying with it the hand and the heart of Commissioner Barr-Saggott. The terms were a St. Leonard's Round—thirty-six shots at sixty yards—under the rules of the Simla Toxophilite Society.

All Simla was invited. There were beautifully arranged tea-tables under the deodars at Annandale, where the Grand Stand is now; and, alone in its glory, winking in the sun, sat the diamond bracelet in a blue velvet case. Miss Beighton was anxious–almost too anxious–to compete. On the appointed afternoon, all Simla rode down to Annandale to witness the Judgment of Paris turned upside down. Kitty rode with young Cubbon, and it was easy to see that the boy was troubled in his mind. He must be held innocent of everything that followed. Kitty was pale and nervous, and looked long at the bracelet. Barr-Saggott was gorgeously dressed, even more nervous than Kitty, and more hideous than ever.

Mrs. Beighton smiled condescendingly, as befitted the mother of a potential Commissioneress, and the shooting began; all the world standing a semicircle as the ladies came out one after the other.

Nothing is so tedious as an archery competition. They shot, and they shot, and they kept on shooting, till the sun left the valley, and little breezes got up in the deodars, and people waited for Miss Beighton to shoot and win. Cubbon was at one horn of the semicircle round the shooters, and Barr-Saggott at the other. Miss Beighton was last on the list. The scoring had been weak, and the bracelet, *plus* Commissioner Barr-Saggott, was hers to a certainty.

The Commissioner strung her bow with his own sacred hands. She stepped forward, looked at the bracelet, and her first arrow went true to a hair–full into the heart of the "gold"–counting nine points.

Young Cubbon on the left turned white, and his Devil prompted Barr-Saggott to smile. Now horses used to shy when Barr-Saggott smiled. Kitty saw that smile. She looked to her left-front, gave an almost imperceptible nod to Cubbon, and went on shooting.

I wish I could describe the scene that followed. It was out of the ordinary and most improper. Miss Kitty fitted her arrows with immense deliberation, so that every one might see what she was doing. She was a perfect shot; and her 46-pound bow suited her to a nicety. She pinned the wooden legs of the target with great care four successive times. She pinned the wooden top of the target once, and all the ladies looked at each other. Then she began some fancy shooting at the white, which, if you hit it, counts exactly one point. She put five arrows into the white. It was wonderful archery; but, seeing that her business was to make "golds" and win the bracelet, Barr-Saggott turned a delicate green like young water-grass. Next, she shot over the target twice, then wide to the left twice–always with the same deliberation–while a chilly hush fell over the company, and Mrs. Beighton took out her handkerchief. Then Kitty shot at the ground in front of the target, and split several arrows. Then she made a red–or seven points–just to show what she could do if she liked, and she finished up her amazing performance with some more fancy shooting at the target-supports. Here is her score as it was pricked off:–

	Gold.	Red.	Blue.	Black.	White.	Total Hits.	Total Score.
Miss Beighton	1	1	0	0	5	7	21

Barr-Saggott looked as if the last few arrowheads had been driven into his legs instead of the target's, and the deep stillness was broken by a little snubby, mottled, half-grown girl saying in a shrill voice of triumph,–"Then *I've* won!"

Mrs. Beighton did her best to bear up; but she wept in the presence of the people. No training could help her through such a disappointment. Kitty unstrung her bow with a vicious jerk, and went back to her place, while Barr-Saggott was trying to pretend that he enjoyed snapping the bracelet on the snubby girl's raw, red wrist. It was an awkward scene–most awkward. Every one tried to depart in a body and leave Kitty to the mercy of her Mamma.

But Cubbon took her away instead, and–the rest isn't worth printing.

The Three Musketeers

An' when the war began, we chased the bold Afghan,
An' we made the bloomin' Ghazi for to flee, boys O!
An' we marched into *Kabul,* and we tuk the Balar 'Issar
An' we taught 'em to respec' the British Soldier.

Barrack Room Ballad.

MULVANEY, ORTHERIS AND Learoyd are Privates in B Company of a Line Regiment, and personal friends of mine. Collectively, I *think,* but am not certain, they are the worst men in the regiment, so far as genial blackguardism goes.

They told me this story, the other day, in the Umballa Refreshment Room while we were waiting for an up-train. I supplied the beer. The tale was cheap at a gallon and a half.

Of course you know Lord Benira Trig. He is a Duke, or an Earl, or something unofficial; also a Peer; also a Globe-trotter. On all three counts, as Ortheris says, " 'e didn't deserve no consideration." He was out here for three months collecting materials for a book on "Our Eastern Impedimenta," and quartering himself upon everybody, like a Cossack in evening-dress.

His particular vice–because he was a Radical, I suppose–was having garrisons turned out for his inspection. He would then dine with the Officer Commanding, and insult him, across the Mess table, about the appearance of the troops. That was Benira's way.

He turned out troops once too often. He came to Helanthami Cantonment on a Tuesday. He wished to go shopping in the bazars on Wednesday, and he "desired" the troops to be turned out on a Thursday. *On–a–Thursday!* The Officer Commanding could not well refuse; for Benira was a Lord. There was an indignation-meeting of subalterns in the Mess Room, to call the Colonel pet names.

"But the rale dimonstrashin," said Mulvaney, "was in B Comp'ny barrick; we three headin' it."

Mulvaney climbed on to the refreshment-bar, settled himself comfortably by the beer, and went on:–"Whin the row was at ut's foinest an' B Comp'ny was fur goin' out to murther this man Thrigg on the p'rade-groun', Learoyd here takes up his helmut an' sez–fwhat was ut ye said?"

"Ah said," said Learoyd, "gie us t' brass. Tak oop a subscripshun, lads, for to put off t' p'rade, an' if t' p'rade's not put off, ah'll gie t'brass back agean. Thot's wot ah said. All B Coomp'ny knawed me. Ah took oop a big subscripshun–fower rupees eight annas 'twas–an' ah went oot too turn t' job over. Mulvaney an' Orth'ris coom with me."

"We three raises the Divil in couples gin'rally," explained Mulvaney.

Here Ortheris interrupted. " 'Ave you read the papers?" said he.

"Sometimes," I said.

"We 'ad read the papers, an' we put hup a faked decoity, a—a sedukshun."

"*Ab*dukshin, ye cockney," said Mulvaney.

"*Ab*dukshun or *se*dukshun—no great odds. Any'ow, we arrange to taik an' put Mister Benhira out o' the way till Thursday was hover, or 'e too busy to rux 'isself about p'raids. *Hi* was the man wot said: 'We'll make a few rupees off o' the business.' "

"We hild a Council av War," continued Mulvaney, "walkin' roun' by the Artill'ry Lines. I was Prisidint, Learoyd was Minister av Finance, an' little Orth'ris here was—"

"A bloomin' Bismarck! *Hi* made the 'ole show pay."

"This interferin' bit av a Benira man," said Mulvaney, "did the thrick for us himself; for, on me sowl, we hadn't a notion av what was to come afther the next minut. He was shoppin' in the bazar on fut. 'Twas dhrawin' dusk thin, an' we stud watchin' the little man hoppin' in an' out av the shops, thryin' to injuce the naygurs to *mallum* his *bat.* Prisintly he sthrols up, his arrums full av thruck, an' he sez in a consiquinshal way, shticking out his little belly:—'Me good men,' sez he, 'have ye seen the Kernel's b'roosh?' 'B'roosh?' says Learoyd. 'There's no b'roosh here—nobbut a *hekka.*' 'Fwhat's that?' sez Thrigg. Learoyd shows him wan down the sthreet, an' he sez:—'How thruly Orientil! I will ride on a *hekka.*' I saw thin that our Rigimintal Saint was for givin' Thrigg over to us neck an' brisket. I purshued a *hekka,* an' I sez to the dhriver-divil, I sez—'Ye black limb, there's a *Sahib* comin' for this *hekka.* He wants to go *jildi* to the Padsahi Jhil'—'twas about tu moiles away—to shoot snipe—*chirria.* 'You dhrive *Jehannum ke marfik, mallum?* 'Tis no manner av *faider bukkin'* to the *Sahib,* bekaze he doesn't *samjao* your *bat.* Av he *bolos* anything, just you *choop* and *chel. Dekker?* Go *arsty* for the first *arder*-mile from cantonmints. Then *chel, Shaitan ke marfik,* an' the *chooper* you *choops* an' the *jilder* you *chels* the better *kooshy* will that *Sahib* be; an' here's a rupee for ye.'

"The *hekka*-man knew there was somethin' out av the common in the air. He grinned and sez:—'*Bote achee!* I goin' damn fast.' I prayed that the Kernel's b'roosh wudn't arrive till me darlin' Benira by the grace av God was undher weigh. The little man puts his thruck into the *hekka* an' scuttles in like a fat guinea-pig; niver offerin' us the price of a dhrink for our services in helpin' him home. 'He's off to the Padsahi *jhil,*' sez I to the others."

Ortheris took up the tale:—

"Jist then, little Buldoo kim up, 'oo was the son of one of the Artillery *Saises*—'e would 'av made a 'evinly newspaper-boy in London, bein' sharp and fly to all manner o' games. 'E'ad bin watchin' us puttin' Mister Benhira into 's temporary baroush, an' 'e sez:—'What *'ave* you been a doin' of, *Sahibs?*' sez 'e. Learoyd 'e caught 'im by the ear an' 'e sez—"

"Ah says," went on Learoyd: " 'Young mon, that mon's gooin' to have 't 'goons out o' Thursday—*kul*—an' thot's more work for you, young mon. Now, sitha, tak a *tat* an' a *lookri,* an' ride tha domdest to t' Padsahi Jhil. Cotch thot there *hekka,* and tell t' driver in your lingo tho you've coom to tak' his place. T' *Sahib* doesn't speak t' *bat,* an' he's a little mon. Drive t' *hekka* into t' Padsahi Jhil into t' watter. Leave t' *Sahib* theer an' roon hoam; an' here's a rupee for tha.' "

Then Mulvaney and Ortheris spoke together in alternate fragments: Mulvaney leading [You must pick out the two speakers as best you can.]:—"He was a knowin' little divil was Bhuldoo,—'e sez *bote achers* an' cuts—wid a wink in his oi—but *Hi* sez there's money to be made—an' I want to see the end av the campaign—so *Hi* says we'll double hout to the Padsahi Jhil—and save the little man from bein' dacoited by the murtherin' Bhuldoo—an' turn hup like reskoors in a Ryle Victoria Theayter Melodrama—so we doubled for the *jhil,* an' prisintly there was the divil of a hurroosh behind us an' three bhoys on grasscuts' *tats* come by, pounding along for the dear life–s'elp me Bob, hif Bhuldoo 'adn't raised a regular *harmy* of dacoits–to do the job in shtile. An' we ran, and they ran, shplittin' with laughin', till we gets near the *jhil*–and 'ears sounds of distress floatin' molloncally on the heavenin' hair." [Ortheris was growing poetical under the influence of the beer. The duet recommenced; Mulvaney leading again.]

"Thin we heard Bhuldoo, the dacoit, shoutin' to the *hekka* man, an' wan of the young divils brought his *lakri* down on the top av the *hekka*-cover, an' Benira Thrigg inside howled 'Murther an' Death.' Bhuldoo takes the reins and dhrives like mad for the *jhil,* havin' dishpersed the *hekka*-driver–'oo cum up to us an' 'e sez, sez 'eh:–'That *Sahib's* nigh *gawbry* with funk! Wot devil's work 'ave you led me into?' 'Hall right,' sez we, 'you *puckrow* thate there pony an' come along. This *Sahib's* been decoited, an' we're going to resky 'im!' Says the driver: 'Decoits! Wot decoits? That's Bhuldoo the *budmash'*– 'Bhuldoo be shot!' sez we. ' 'Tis a woild dissolute Pathan frum the hills. There's about eight av 'im coercin' the *Sahib.* You remimber that an' you'll get another rupee!' Then we heard the *whop-whop-whop* av the *hekka* turnin' over, an' a splash av watter an' the voice av Benira Thrigg callin' upon God to forgive his sins–an' Bhuldoo an' 'is friends squotterin' in the water like boys in the Serpentine."

Here the Three Musketeers retired simultaneously into the beer.

"Well? What came next?" said I.

"Fwhat nex'?" answered Mulvaney, wiping his mouth. "Wud you let three bould sodger-bhoys lave the ornamint av the House av Lords to be dhrowned an' dacoited in a *jhil?* We formed line av quarther-column an' we desinded upon the inimy. For the better part av tin minutes you could not hear yerself spake. The *tattoo* was screamin' in chune wid Benira Thrigg an' Bhuldoo's army, an' the shticks was whistlin' roun' the *hekka,* an' Orth'ris was beatin' the *hekka*-cover wid his fistes, an' Learoyd yellin':–'Look out for their knives!' an' me cuttin' into the dark, right an' lef', dishpersin' arrmy corps av Pathans. Holy Mother av Moses! 'twas more disp'rit than Ahmid Kheyl wid Maiwund thrown in. Afther a while Bhuldoo an' his bhoys flees. Have ye iver seen a rale live Lord thryin' to hide his nobility undher a fut an' a half av brown *jhil* wather? 'Tis the livin' image av a *bhisti's mussick* wid the shivers. It tuk toime to pershuade me friend Benira he was not disimbowiled: an' more toime to get out the *hekka.* The dhriver come up afther the battle, swearin' he tuk a hand in repulsin' the inimy. Benira was sick wid the fear. We escorted him back, very slow, to cantonmints, for that an' the chill to soak into him. *It suk!* Glory be to the Rigimintil Saint, but it suk to the marrow av Lord Benira Thrigg!"

Here Ortheris, slowly, with immense pride:–" 'E sez:–'You har my noble preservers,' sez 'e. 'You har a *h*onor to the British Harmy,' sez e'. With that 'e describes the hawful band of decoits wot set on 'im. There was about forty of 'em an' 'e was hoverpowered by numbers, so 'e was; but 'e never lost 'is presence of mind, so 'e didn't. 'E guv the *hekka*-driver five rupees for 'is noble hassistance, an' 'e said 'e would see to us after 'e 'ad spoken to the Kernul. For we was a *h*onor to the Regiment, we was."

"An' we three," said Mulvaney, with a seraphic smile, "have dhrawn the par-ti-cu-lar attinshin av Bobs Bahadur more than wanst. But he's a rale good little man is Bobs. Go on, Orth'ris, me son."

"Then we leaves 'im at the Kernul's 'ouse, werry sick, an' we cuts over to B Comp'ny barrick an' we sez we 'ave saved Benira from a bloody doom, an' the chances was agin there bein' p'raid on Thursday. About ten minutes later come three envelicks, one for each of us. S'elp me Bob, if the old blike 'adn't guv us a fiver apiece–sixty-four dibs in the vazar! On Thursday 'e was in 'orspital recoverin' from 's sanguinary encounter with a gang of Pathans, an'

B Comp'ny was drinkin' 'emselves inter clink by squads. So there never was no Thursdy p'raid. But the Kernul, when 'e 'eard of our galliant conduct, 'e sez:–'Hi know there's been some devilry somewheres,' sez 'e, 'but hi can't bring it 'ome to you three.' "

"An' my privit imprisshin is," said Mulvaney, getting off the bar and turning his glass upside down, "that, av they had known they wudn't have brought ut home. 'Tis flyin' in the face, firstly av Nature, second, av the Rig'lations, an' third, the will av Terrence Mulvaney, to hold p'rades av Thursdays."

"Good, ma son!" said Learoyd: "but, young mon, what's t' notebook for?"

"Let be," said Mulvaney; "this time next month we're in the *Sherapis.* 'Tis immortial fame the gentleman's goin' to give us. But kape it dhark till we're out av the range av me little frind Bobs Bahadur."

And I have obeyed Mulvaney's order.

His Chance in Life

Then a pile of heads be laid–
Thirty thousand heaped on high–
All to please the Kafir maid,
Where the Oxus ripples by.
Grimly spake Atulla Khan:–
"Love hath made this thing a Man."
Oatta's Story.

IF YOU GO straight away from Levées and Government House Lists, past Trades' Balls–far beyond everything and everybody you ever knew in your respectable life–you cross, in time, the Borderline where the last drop of White blood ends and the full tide of Black sets in. It would be easier to talk to a new-made Duchess on the spur of the moment than to the Borderline folk without violating some of their conventions or hurting their feelings. The Black and the White mix very quaintly in their ways. Sometimes the White shows in spurts of fierce, childish pride–which is Pride of Race run crooked–and sometimes the Black in still fiercer abasement and humility, half heathenish customs and strange, unaccountable impulses to crime. One of these days, this people–understand they are far lower than the class whence Derozio, the man who imitated Byron, sprung–will turn out a writer or a poet; and then we shall know how they live and what they feel. In the meantime, any stories about them cannot be absolutely correct in fact or inference.

Miss Vezzis came from across the Borderline to look after some children who belonged to a lady until a regularly ordained nurse could come out. The lady said Miss Vezzis was a bad, dirty nurse and inattentive. It never struck her that Miss Vezzis had her own life to lead and her own affairs to worry over, and that these affairs were the most important things in the world to Miss Vezzis. Very few mistresses admit this sort of reasoning. Miss Vezzis was as black as a boot, and to our standard of taste, hideously ugly. She wore cotton-print gowns and bulged shoes; and when she lost her temper with the children, she abused them in the language of the Borderline–which is part

English, part Portuguese, and part Native. She was not attractive; but she had her pride, and she preferred being called "Miss Vezzis."

Every Sunday she dressed herself wonderfully and went to see her Mamma, who lived, for the most part, on an old cane chair in a greasy *tussur*-silk dressing-gown and a big rabbit-warren of a house full of Vezzises, Pereiras, Ribieras, Lisboas and Gonsalveses, and a floating population of loafers; besides fragments of the day's *bazar,* garlic, stale incense, clothes thrown on the floor, petticoats hung on strings for screens, old bottles, pewter crucifixes, dried *immortelles,* pariah puppies, plaster images of the Virgin, and hats without crowns. Miss Vezzis drew twenty rupees a month for acting as nurse, and she squabbled weekly with her Mamma as to the percentage to be given towards housekeeping. When the quarrel was over, Michele D'Cruze used to shamble across the low mud wall of the compound and make love to Miss Vezzis after the fashion of the Borderline, which is hedged about with much ceremony. Michele was a poor, sickly weed and very black; but he had his pride. He would not be seen smoking a *huqa* for anything; and he looked down on natives as only a man with seven-eighths native blood in his veins can. The Vezzis Family had their pride too. They traced their descent from a mythical plate-layer who had worked on the Sone Bridge when railways were new in India, and they valued their English origin. Michele was a Telegraph Signaler on Rs. 35 a month. The fact that he was in Government employ made Mrs. Vezzis lenient to the shortcomings of his ancestors.

There was a compromising legend–Dom Anna the tailor brought it from Poonani–that a black Jew of Cochin had once married into the D'Cruze family; while it was an open secret that an uncle of Mrs. D'Cruze was at that very time doing menial work, connected with cooking, for a Club in Southern India! He sent Mrs. D'Cruze seven rupees eight annas a month; but she felt the disgrace to the family very keenly all the same.

However, in the course of a few Sundays, Mrs. Vezzis brought herself to overlook these blemishes and gave her consent to the marriage of her daughter with Michele, on condition that Michele should have at least fifty rupees a month to start married life upon. This wonderful prudence must have been a lingering touch of the mythical plate-layer's Yorkshire blood; for across the Borderline people take a pride in marrying when they please–not when they can.

Having regard to his departmental prospects, Miss Vezzis might as well have asked Michele to go away and come back with the Moon in his pocket. But Michele was deeply in love with Miss Vezzis, and that helped him to endure. He accompanied Miss Vezzis to Mass one Sunday, and after Mass, walking home through the hot stale dust with her hand in his, he swore by several Saints whose names would not interest you, never to forget Miss Vezzis; and she swore by her Honor and the Saints–the oath runs rather curiously; *"In nomine Sanctis-simae–"* (whatever the name of the she-Saint is) and so forth, ending with a kiss on the forehead, a kiss on the left cheek, and a kiss on the mouth–never to forget Michele.

Next week Michele was transferred, and Miss Vezzis dropped tears upon the window-sash of the "Intermediate" compartment as he left the Station.

If you look at the telegraph-map of India you will see a long line skirting the coast from Backergunge to Madras. Michele was ordered to Tibasu, a little Sub-office one-third down this line, to send messages on from Berhampur to Chicacola, and to think of Miss Vezzis and his chances of getting fifty rupees a month out of office-hours. He had the noise of the Bay of Bengal and a Bengali Babu for company; nothing more. He sent foolish letters, with crosses tucked inside the flaps of the envelopes, to Miss Vezzis.

When he had been at Tibasu for nearly three weeks his chance came.

Never forget that unless the outward and visible signs of Our Authority are always before a native he is as incapable as a child of understanding what authority means, or where is the danger of disobeying it. Tibasu was a forgotten little place with a few Orissa Mahomedans in it. These, hearing nothing of the Collector-*Sahib* for some time and heartily despising the Hindu Sub-Judge, arranged to start a little Mohurrum riot of their own. But the Hindus turned out and broke their heads; when finding lawlessness pleasant, Hindus and Mahomedans together raised an aimless sort of Donnybrook just to see how far they could go. They looted each other's shops, and paid off private grudges in the regular way. It was a nasty little riot, but not worth putting in the newspapers.

Michele was working in his office when he heard the sound that a man never forgets all his life–the "*ah-yah*" of an angry crowd. [When that sound drops out three tones, and changes to a thick, droning *ut*, the man who hears it had better go away if he is alone.] The Native Police Inspector ran in and told Michele that the town was in an uproar and coming to wreck the Telegraph Office. The Babu put on his cap and quietly dropped out of the window; while the Police Inspector, afraid, but obeying the old race-instinct which recognizes a drop of White blood as far as it can be diluted, said:– "What orders does the *Sahib* give?"

"The "*Sahib*" decided Michele. Though horribly frightened, he felt that, for the hour, he, the man with the Cochin Jew and the menial uncle in his pedigree, was the only representative of English authority in the place. Then he thought of Miss Vezzis and the fifty rupees, and took the situation on himself. There were seven native policemen in Tibasu, and four crazy smooth-bore muskets among them. All the men were gray with fear, but not beyond leading. Michele dropped the key of the telegraph instrument, and went out, at the head of his army, to meet the mob. As the shouting crew came round a corner of the road, he dropped and fired; the men behind him loosing instinctively at the same time.

The whole crowd–curs to the backbone–yelled and ran; leaving one man dead, and another dying in the road. Michele was sweating with fear, but he kept his weakness under, and went down into the town, past the house where the Sub-Judge had barricaded himself. The streets were empty. Tibasu was more frightened than Michele, for the mob had been taken at the right time.

Michele returned to the Telegraph-Office, and sent a message to Chicacola asking for help. Before an answer came, he received a deputation of the elders of Tibasu, telling him that the Sub-Judge said his actions generally were "unconstitutional," and trying to bully him. But the heart of Michele D'Cruze was big and white in his breast, because of his love for Miss Vezzis, the nurse-girl, and because he had tasted for the first time Responsibility and Success. Those two make an intoxicating drink, and have ruined more men than ever has Whisky. Michele answered that the Sub-Judge might say what he pleased, but, until the Assistant Collector came, the Telegraph Signaler was the Government of India in Tibasu, and the elders of the town would be held accountable for further rioting. Then they bowed their heads and said:– "Show mercy!" or words to that effect, and went back in great fear; each accusing the other of having begun the rioting.

Early in the dawn, after a night's patrol with his seven policemen, Michele went down the road, musket in hand, to meet the Assistant Collector who had ridden in to quell Tibasu. But, in the presence of this young Englishman, Michele felt himself slipping back more and more into the native, and the tale of the Tibasu Riots ended, with the strain on the teller, in an hysterical outburst of tears, bred by sorrow that he had killed a man, shame that he could not feel as uplifted as he had felt through the night, and childish anger that his tongue could not do justice to his great deeds. It was the White drop in Michele's veins dying out, though he did not know it.

But the Englishman understood; and, after he had schooled those men of

Tibasu, and had conferred with the Sub-Judge till that excellent official turned green, he found time to draught an official letter describing the conduct of Michele. Which letter filtered through the proper Channels, and ended in the transfer of Michele up-country once more, on the Imperial salary of sixty-six rupees a month.

So he and Miss Vezzis were married with great state and ancientry; and now there are several little D'Cruzes sprawling about the verandas of the Central Telegraph Office.

But, if the whole revenue of the Department he serves were to be his reward, Michele could never, never repeat what he did at Tibasu for the sake of Miss Vezzis the nurse-girl.

Which proves that, when a man does good work out of all proportion to his pay, in seven cases out of nine there is a woman at the back of the virtue.

The two exceptions must have suffered from sunstroke.

Watches of the Night

What is in the Brahmin's books that is in the Brahmin's heart. Neither you nor I knew there was so much evil in the world.

Hindu Proverb.

THIS BEGAN IN a practical joke; but it has gone far enough now, and is getting serious.

Platte, the Subaltern, being poor, had a Waterbury watch and a plain leather guard.

The Colonel had a Waterbury watch also, and for guard, the lip-strap of a curb-chain. Lip-straps make the best watch guards. They are strong and short. Between a lip-strap and an ordinary leather guard there is no great difference; between one Waterbury watch and another none at all. Every one in the station knew the Colonel's lip-strap. He was not a horsey man, but he liked people to believe he had been one once; and he wove fantastic stories of the hunting-bridle to which this particular lip-strap had belonged. Otherwise he was painfully religious.

Platte and the Colonel were dressing at the Club—both late for their engagements, and both in a hurry. That was *Kismet.* The two watches were on a shelf below the looking-glass—guards hanging down. That was carelessness. Platte changed first, snatched a watch, looked in the glass, settled his tie, and ran. Forty seconds later, the Colonel did exactly the same thing; each man taking the other's watch.

You may have noticed that many religious people are deeply suspicious. They seem—for purely religious purposes, of course—to know more about iniquity than the Unregenerate. Perhaps they were specially bad before they became converted? At any rate, in the imputation of things evil, and in putting the worst construction on things innocent, a certain type of good people may be trusted to surpass all others. The Colonel and his Wife were of that type. But the Colonel's Wife was the worst. She manufactured the Station scandal, and—*talked to her ayah!* Nothing more need be said. The Colonel's Wife broke up the Laplace's home. The Colonel's Wife stopped the Ferris-Haughtrey engagement. The Colonel's Wife induced young Buxton to keep his wife down in the Plains through the first year of the marriage. Whereby little Mrs. Buxton died, and the baby with her. These things will be remembered against the Colonel's Wife so long as there is a regiment in the country.

But to come back to the Colonel and Platte. They went their several ways from the dressing-room. The Colonel dined with two Chaplains, while Platte went to a bachelor-party, and whist to follow.

Mark how things happen! If Platte's *sais* had put the new saddle-pad on the mare, the butts of the territs would not have worked through the worn leather, and the old pad into the mare's withers, when she was coming home at two o'clock in the morning. She would not have reared, bolted, fallen into a ditch, upset the cart, and sent Platte flying over an aloe-hedge on to Mrs. Larkyn's well-kept lawn; and this tale would never have been written. But the mare did all these things, and while Platte was rolling over and over on the turf, like a shot rabbit the watch and guard flew from his waistcoat—as an Infantry Major's sword hops out of the scabbard when they are firing a *feu de joie*—and rolled and rolled in the moonlight, till it stopped under a window.

Platte stuffed his handkerchief under the pad, put the cart straight, and went home.

Mark again how *Kismet* works! This would not happen once in a hundred years. Towards the end of his dinner with the two Chaplains, the Colonel let out his waistcoat and leaned over the table to look at some Mission Reports. The bar of the watch-guard worked through the buttonhole, and the watch—Platte's watch—slid quietly on to the carpet. Where the bearer found it next morning and kept it.

Then the Colonel went home to the wife of his bosom; but the driver of the carriage was drunk and lost his way. So the Colonel returned at an unseemly hour and his excuses were not accepted. If the Colonel's Wife had been an ordinary "vessel of wrath appointed for destruction," she would have known that when a man stays away on purpose, his excuse is always sound and original. The very baldness of the Colonel's explanation proved its truth.

See once more the workings of *Kismet!* The Colonel's watch, which came with Platte hurriedly on to Mrs. Larkyn's lawn, chose to stop just under Mrs. Larkyn's window, where she saw it early in the morning, recognized it, and picked it up. She had heard the crash of Platte's cart at two o'clock that morning, and his voice calling the mare names. She knew Platte and liked him. That day she showed him the watch and heard his story. He put his head on one side, winked and said:—"How disgusting! Shocking old man! With his religious training, too! I should send the watch to the Colonel's Wife and ask for explanations."

Mrs. Larkyn thought for a minute of the Laplaces—whom she had known when Laplace and his wife believed in each other—and answered:—"I will send it. I think it will do her good. But, remember, we must *never* tell her the truth."

Platte guessed that his own watch was in the Colonel's possession, and thought that the return of the lip-strapped Waterbury with a soothing note from Mrs. Larkyn would merely create a small trouble for a few minutes. Mrs. Larkyn knew better. She knew that any poison dropped would find good holding-ground in the heart of the Colonel's Wife.

The packet, and a note containing a few remarks on the Colonel's calling-hours, were sent over to the Colonel's Wife, who wept in her own room and took counsel with herself.

If there was one woman under Heaven whom the Colonel's Wife hated with holy fervor, it was Mrs. Larkyn. Mrs. Larkyn was a frivolous lady, and called the Colonel's Wife "old cat." The Colonel's Wife said that somebody in Revelations was remarkably like Mrs. Larkyn. She mentioned other Scripture people as well. From the Old Testament. [But the Colonel's Wife was the only person who cared or dared to say anything against Mrs. Larkyn. Every one else accepted her as an amusing, honest little body.] Wherefore, to believe that her husband had been shedding watches under that "Thing's" window at ungodly hours, coupled with the fact of his late arrival on the previous night, was. . . .

At this point she rose up and sought her husband. He denied everything except the ownership of the watch. She besought him, for his Soul's sake, to speak the truth. He denied afresh, with two bad words. Then a stony silence held the Colonel's Wife, while a man could draw his breath five times.

The speech that followed is no affair of mine or yours. It was made up of wifely and womanly jealousy; knowledge of old age and sunken cheeks; deep mistrust born of the text that says even little babies' hearts are as bad as they make them; rancorous hatred of Mrs. Larkyn, and the tenets of the creed of the Colonel's Wife's upbringing.

Over and above all, was the damning lip-strapped Waterbury, ticking away in the palm of her shaking, withered hand. At that hour, I think, the Colonel's Wife realized a little of the restless suspicion she had injected into old Laplace's mind, a little of poor Miss Haughtrey's misery, and some of the canker that ate into Buxton's heart as he watched his wife dying before his eyes. The Colonel stammered and tried to explain. Then he remembered that his watch had disappeared; and the mystery grew greater. The Colonel's Wife talked and prayed by turns till she was tired, and went away to devise means for "chastening the stubborn heart of her husband." Which translated, means, in our slang, "tail-twisting."

You see, being deeply impressed with the doctrine of Original Sin, she could not believe in the face of appearances. She knew too much, and jumped to the wildest conclusions.

But it was good for her. It spoilt her life, as she had spoilt the life of the Laplaces. She had lost her faith in the Colonel, and–here the creed-suspicion came in–he might, she argued, have erred many times, before a merciful Providence, at the hands of so unworthy an instrument as Mrs. Larkyn, had established his guilt. He was a bad, wicked, gray-haired profligate. This may sound too sudden a revulsion for a long-wedded wife; but it is a venerable fact that, if a man or woman makes a practise of, and takes a delight in, believing and spreading evil of people indifferent to him or her, he or she will end in believing evil of folk very near and dear. You may think, also, that the mere incident of the watch was too small and trivial to raise this misunderstanding. It is another aged fact that, in life as well as racing, all the worst accidents happen at little ditches and cut-down fences. In the same way, you sometimes see a woman who would have made a Joan of Arc in another century and climate, threshing herself to pieces over all the mean worry of housekeeping. But that is another story.

Her belief only made the Colonel's Wife more wretched, because it insisted so strongly on the villainy of men. Remembering what she had done, it was pleasant to watch her unhappiness, and the penny-farthing attempts she made to hide it from the Station. But the Station knew and laughed heartlessly; for they had heard the story of the watch, with much dramatic gesture, from Mrs. Larkyn's lips.

Once or twice Platte said to Mrs. Larkyn, seeing that the Colonel had not cleared himself:–"This thing has gone far enough. I move we tell the Colonel's Wife how it happened." Mrs. Larkyn shut her lips and shook her head, and vowed that the Colonel's Wife must bear her punishment as best she could. Now Mrs. Larkyn was a frivolous woman, in whom none would have suspected deep hate. So Platte took no action, and came to believe gradually from the Colonel's silence, that the Colonel must have "run off the line" somewhere that night, and, therefore, preferred to stand sentence on the lesser count of rambling into other people's compounds out of calling-hours. Platte forgot about the watch business after a while, and moved down-country with his regiment. Mrs. Larkyn went home when her husband's tour of Indian service expired. She never forgot.

But Platte was quite right when he said that the joke had gone too far. The mistrust and the tragedy of it—which we outsiders cannot see and do not believe in—are killing the Colonel's Wife, and are making the Colonel wretched. If either of them read this story, they can depend upon its being a fairly true account of the case, and can "kiss and make friends."

Shakespeare alludes to the pleasure of watching an Engineer being shelled by his own Battery. Now this shows that poets should not write about what they do not understand. Any one could have told him that Sappers and Gunners are perfectly different branches of the Service. But, if you correct the sentence, and substitute Gunner for Sapper, the moral comes just the same.

The Other Man

When the earth was sick and the skies were gray,
And the woods were rotted with rain,
The Dead Man rode through the autumn day
To visit his love again.

Old Ballad.

FAR BACK IN the "seventies," before they had built any Public Offices at Simla, and the broad road around Jakko lived in a pigeon-hole in the P. W. D. hovels, her parents made Miss Gaurey marry Colonel Schriederling. He could not have been *much* more than thirty-five years her senior; and, as he lived on two hundred rupees a month and had money of his own, he was well off. He belonged to good people, and suffered in the cold weather from lung complaints. In the hot weather he dangled on the brink of heat-apoplexy; but it never quite killed him.

Understand, I do not blame Schreiderling. He was a good husband according to his lights, and his temper only failed him when he was being nursed. Which was some seventeen days in each month. He was almost generous to his wife about money matters, and that, for him, was a concession. Still Mrs. Schreiderling was not happy. They married her when she was this side of twenty and had given all her poor little heart to another man. I have forgotten his name, but we will call him the Other Man. He had no money and no prospects. He was not even good-looking; and I think he was in the Commissariat or Transport. But, in spite of all these things, she loved him very badly; and there was some sort of an engagement between the two when Schreiderling appeared and told Mrs. Gaurey that he wished to marry her daughter. Then the other engagement was broken off—washed away by Mrs. Gaurey's tears, for that lady governed her house by weeping over disobedience to her authority and the lack of reverence she received in her old age. The daughter did not take after her mother. She never cried. Not even at the wedding.

The Other Man bore his loss quietly, and was transferred to as bad a station as he could find. Perhaps the climate consoled him. He suffered from intermittent fever, and that may have distracted him from his other trouble. He was weak about the heart also. Both ways. One of the valves was affected, and the fever made it worse. This showed itself later on.

Then many months passed, and Mrs. Schreiderling took to being ill. She did not pine away like people in story books, but she seemed to pick up every form of illness that went about a station, from simple fever upwards. She was never more than ordinarily pretty at the best of times; and the illness made her ugly. Schreiderling said so. He prided himself on speaking his mind.

When she ceased being pretty, he left her to her own devices, and went back to the lairs of his bachelordom. She used to trot up and down Simla Mall in a forlorn sort of way, with a gray Terai hat well on the back of her head, and a shocking bad saddle under her. Schreiderling's generosity stopped at the horse. He said that any saddle would do for a woman as nervous as Mrs. Schreiderling. She never was asked to dance, because she did not dance well; and she was so dull and uninteresting, that her box very seldom had any cards in it. Schreiderling said that if he had known that she was going to be such a scare-crow after her marriage, he would never have married her. He always prided himself on speaking his mind, did Schreiderling!

He left her at Simla one August, and went down to his regiment. Then she revived a little, but she never recovered her looks. I found out at the Club that the Other Man is coming up sick—very sick—on an off chance of recovery. The fever and the heart-valves had nearly killed him. She knew that, too, and she knew—what I had no interest in knowing—when he was coming up. I suppose he wrote to tell her. They had not seen each other since a month before the wedding. And here comes the unpleasant part of the story.

A late call kept me down at the Dovedell Hotel till dusk one evening. Mrs. Schreiderling had been flitting up and down the Mall all the afternoon in the rain. Coming up along the Cart-road, a tonga passed me, and my pony, tired with standing so long, set off at a canter. Just by the road down to the Tonga Office Mrs. Schreiderling, dripping from head to foot, was waiting for the tonga. I turned up-hill, as the tonga was no affair of mine; and just then she began to shriek. I went back at once and saw, under the Tonga Office lamps, Mrs. Schreiderling kneeling in the wet road by the back seat of the newly-arrived tonga, screaming hideously. Then she fell face down in the dirt as I came up.

Sitting in the back seat, very square and firm, with one hand on the awning-stanchion and the wet pouring off his hat and mustache, was the Other Man—dead. The sixty-mile up-hill jolt had been too much for his valve, I suppose. The tonga-driver said:—"The Sahib died two stages out of Solon. Therefore, I tied him with a rope, lest he should fall out by the way, and so came to Simla. Will the Sahib give me *bukshish?* It," pointing to the Other Man, "should have given one rupee."

The Other Man sat with a grin on his face, as if he enjoyed the joke of his arrival; and Mrs. Schreiderling, in the mud, began to groan. There was no one except us four in the office and it was raining heavily. The first thing was to take Mrs. Schreiderling home, and the second was to prevent her name from being mixed up with the affair. The tonga-driver received five rupees to find a bazar 'rickshaw for Mrs. Schreiderling. He was to tell the tonga Babu afterwards of the Other Man, and the Babu was to make such arrangements as seemed best.

Mrs. Schreiderling was carried into the shed out of the rain, and for three-quarters of an hour we two waited for the 'rickshaw. The Other Man was left exactly as he had arrived. Mrs. Schreiderling would do everything but cry, which might have helped her. She tried to scream as soon as her senses came back, and then she began praying for the Other Man's soul. Had she not been as honest as the day, she would have prayed for her own soul too. I waited to hear her do this, but she did not. Then I tried to get some of the mud off her habit. Lastly, the 'rickshaw came, and I got her away—partly by force. It was a terrible business from beginning to end; but most of all when the 'rickshaw had to squeeze between the wall and the tonga, and she saw by the lamp-light that thin, yellow hand grasping the awning-stanchion.

She was taken home just as every one was going to a dance at Viceregal Lodge—"Peterhoff" it was then—and the doctor found out that she had fallen from her horse, that I had picked her up at the back of Jakko, and really deserved great credit for the prompt manner in which I had secured medical aid. She did not die—men of Schreiderling's stamp marry women who don't die easily. They live and grow ugly.

She never told of her one meeting, since her marriage, with the Other Man; and, when the chill and cough following the exposure of that evening, allowed her abroad, she never by word or sign alluded to having met me by the Tonga Office. Perhaps she never knew.

She used to trot up and down the Mall, on that shocking bad saddle, looking as if she expected to meet some one round the corner every minute. Two years afterward, she went Home, and died—at Bournemouth, I think.

Schreiderling, when he grew maudlin at Mess, used to talk about "my poor dear wife." He always set great store on speaking his mind, did Schreiderling!

Consequences

Rosicrucian subtleties
In the Orient had rise;
Ye may find their teachers still
Under Jacatala's Hill.
Seek ye Bombast Paracelsus,
Read what Flood the Seeker tells us
Of the Dominant that runs
Through the cycles of the Suns—
Read my story last and see
Luna at her apogee.

THERE ARE YEARLY appointments, and two-yearly appointments, and five-yearly appointments at Simla, and there are, or used to be, permanent appointments, whereon you stayed up for the term of your natural life and secured red cheeks and a nice income. Of course, you could descend in the cold weather; for Simla is rather dull then.

Tarrion came from goodness knows where—all away and away in some forsaken part of Central India, where they call Pachmari a "Sanitarium," and drive behind trotting bullocks, I believe. He belonged to a regiment; but what he really wanted to do was to escape from his regiment and live in Simla forever and ever. He had no preference for anything in particular, beyond a good horse and a nice partner. He thought he could do everything well; which is a beautiful belief when you hold it with all your heart. He was clever in many ways, and good to look at, and always made people round him comfortable—even in Central India.

So he went up to Simla, and, because he was clever and amusing, he gravitated naturally to Mrs. Hauksbee, who could forgive everything but stupidity. Once he did her great service by changing the date on an invitation-card for a big dance which Mrs. Hauksbee wished to attend, but couldn't because she had quarreled with the A.-D.-C., who took care, being a mean man, to invite her to a small dance on the 6th instead of the big Ball of the 26th. It was a very clever piece of forgery; and when Mrs. Hauksbee showed the A.-D.-C. her invitation-card, and chaffed him mildly for not better managing his vendettas, he really thought that he had made a mistake; and—which was wise—realized that it was no use to fight with Mrs. Hauksbee. She was grateful to Tarrion and asked what she could do for him. He said simply: "I'm a Freelance up here on leave, on the look-out for what I can loot. I haven't a square inch of interest in all Simla. My name isn't known to any man with an appointment in his gift, and I want an appointment—a good, sound, *pukka* one. I believe you can do anything you turn yourself to. Will you help me?" Mrs. Hauksbee thought for a minute, and passed the lash of her riding-whip through her lips, as was her custom when thinking. Then her eyes sparkled and she said:—"I will;" and she shook hands on it. Tarrion, having perfect confidence in this great woman, took no further thought of the business at all. Except to wonder what sort of an appointment he would win.

Mrs. Hauksbee began calculating the prices of all the Heads of Departments and Members of Council she knew, and the more she thought the more she laughed, because her heart was in the game and it amused her. Then she took a Civil List and ran over a few of the appointments. There are some beautiful appointments in the Civil List. Eventually, she decided that, though Tarrion was too good for the Political Department, she had better begin by trying to get him in there. What were her own plans to this end, does not matter in the least, for Luck or Fate played into her hands and she had nothing to do but to watch the course of events and take the credit of them.

All Viceroys, when they first come out, pass through the "Diplomatic Secrecy" craze. It wears off in time; but they all catch it in the beginning, because they are new to the country. The particular Viceroy who was suffering from the complaint just then—this was a long time ago, before Lord Dufferin ever came from Canada, or Lord Ripon from the bosom of the English Church—had it very badly; and the result was that men who were new to keeping official secrets went about looking unhappy; and the Viceroy plumed himself on the way in which he had instilled notions of reticence into his Staff.

Now, the Supreme Government have a careless custom of committing what they do to printed papers. These papers deal with all sorts of things—from the payment of Rs. 200 to a "secret" service native, up to rebukes administered to Vakils and Motamids of Native States, and rather brusque letters to Native Princes, telling them to put their houses in order, to refrain from kidnapping women, or filling offenders with pounded red pepper, and eccentricities of that kind. Of course, these things could never be made public, because Native Princes never err officially, and their States are, officially, as well administered as Our territories. Also, the private allowances to various queer people are not exactly matters to put into newspapers, though they give quaint reading sometimes. When the Supreme Government is at Simla, these papers are prepared there, and go round to the people who ought to see them in office-boxes or by post. The principle of secrecy was to that Viceroy quite as important as the practise, and he held that a benevolent despotism like Ours should never allow even little things, such as appointments of subordinate clerks, to leak out till the proper time. He was always remarkable for his principles.

There was a very important batch of papers in preparation at that time. It had to travel from one end of Simla to the other by hand. It was not put into an official envelope, but a large, square, pale-pink one; the matter being in MS. on soft crinkly paper. It was addressed to "The Head Clerk, etc., etc." Now, between "The Head Clerk, etc., etc.," and "Mrs. Hauksbee" and a flourish, is no very great difference if the address be written in a very bad hand, as this was. The *chaprassi* who took the envelope was not more of an idiot than most *chaprassis.* He merely forgot where this most unofficial cover was to be delivered, and so asked the first Englishman he met, who happened to be a man riding down to Annandale in a great hurry. The Englishman hardly looked, said: *"Hauksbee Sahib ki Mem,"* and went on. So did the *chaprassi,* because that letter was the last in stock and he wanted to get his work over. There was no book to sign; he thrust the letter into Mrs. Hauksbee's bearer's hands and went off to smoke with a friend. Mrs. Hauksbee was expecting some cut-out pattern things in flimsy paper from a friend. As soon as she got the big square packet, therefore, she said, "Oh, the *dear* creature!" and tore it open with a paper-knife, and all the MS. enclosures tumbled out on the floor.

Mrs. Hauksbee began reading. I have said the batch was rather important. That is quite enough for you to know. It referred to some correspondence, two measures, a peremptory order to a native chief, and two dozen other things. Mrs. Hauksbee gasped as she read, for the first glimpse of the naked machinery of the Great Indian Government, stripped of its casings, and lacquer, and paint, and guard-rails, impresses even the most stupid man. And Mrs. Hauksbee was a clever woman. She was a little afraid at first, and felt as if she had laid hold of a lightning-flash by the tail, and did not quite know what to do with it. There were remarks and initials at the side of the papers; and some of the remarks were rather more severe than the papers. The initials belonged to men who are all dead or gone now; but they were great in their day. Mrs. Hauksbee read on and thought calmly as she read. Then the value of her trove struck her, and she cast about for the best method of using it. Then Tarrion dropped in, and they read through all the papers together, and Tarrion, not knowing how she had come by them, vowed that Mrs. Hauksbee was the greatest woman on earth. Which I believe was true, or nearly so.

"The honest course is always the best," said Tarrion after an hour and a half of study and conversation. "All things considered, the Intelligence Branch is about my form. Either that or the Foreign Office. I go to lay siege to the High Gods in their Temples."

He did not seek a little man, or a little big man, or a weak Head of a strong Department, but he called on the biggest and strongest man that the Government owned, and explained that he wanted an appointment at Simla on a good salary. The compound insolence of this amused the Strong Man, and, as he had nothing to do for the moment, he listened to the proposals of the audacious Tarrion. "You have, I presume, some special qualifications, besides the gift of self-assertion, for the claims you put forward?" said the Strong Man. "That, Sir," said Tarrion, "is for you to judge." Then he began, for he had a good memory, quoting a few of the more important notes in the papers–slowly and one by one as a man drops chlorodyne into a glass. When he had reached the peremptory order–and it *was* a peremptory order–the Strong Man was troubled.

Tarrion wound up:–"And I fancy that special knowledge of this kind is at least as valuable for, let us say, a berth in the Foreign Office, as the fact of being the nephew of a distinguished officer's wife." That hit the Strong Man hard, for the last appointment to the Foreign Office had been by black favor, and he knew it. "I'll see what I can do for you," said the Strong Man. "Many thanks," said Tarrion. Then he left, and the Strong Man departed to see how the appointment was to be blocked.

. . . . . .

Followed a pause of eleven days; with thunders and lightnings and much telegraphing. The appointment was not a very important one, carrying only between Rs. 500 and Rs. 700 a month; but, as the Viceroy said, it was the principle of diplomatic secrecy that had to be maintained, and it was more likely that a boy so well supplied with special information would be worth translating. So they translated him. They must have suspected him, though he protested that his information was due to singular talents of his own. Now, much of this story, including the after-history of the missing envelope, you must fill in for yourself, because there are reasons why it cannot be written. If you do not know about things Up Above, you won't understand how to fill it in, and you will say it is impossible.

What the Viceroy said when Tarrion was introduced to him was:—"So, this is the boy who 'rushed' the Government of India, is it? Recollect, Sir, that is not done *twice.*" So he must have known something.

What Tarrion said when he saw his appointment gazetted was:—"If Mrs. Hauksbee were twenty years younger, and I her husband, I should be Viceroy of India in fifteen years."

What Mrs. Hauksbee said, when Tarrion thanked her, almost with tears in his eyes, was first:—"I told you so!" and next, to herself:—"What fools men are!"

The Conversion of Aurelian McGoggin

Ride with an idle whip, ride with an unused heel.
But, once in a way, there will come a day
When the colt must be taught to feel
The lash that falls, and the curb that galls, and the sting of the roweled steel.

Life's Handicap.

THIS IS NOT a tale exactly. It is a Tract; and I am immensely proud of it. Making a Tract is a Feat.

Every man is entitled to his own religious opinions; but no man—least of all a junior—has a right to thrust these down other men's throats. The Government sends out weird Civilians now and again; but McGoggin was the queerest exported for a long time. He was clever—brilliantly clever—but his cleverness worked the wrong way. Instead of keeping to the study of the vernaculars, he had read some books written by a man called Comte, I think, and a man called Spencer, and a Professor Clifford. [You will find these books in the Library.] They deal with people's insides from the point of view of men who have no stomachs. There was no order against his reading them; but his Mamma should have smacked him. They fermented in his head, and he came out to India with a rarefied religion over and above his work. It was not much of a creed. It only proved that men had no souls, and there was no God and no hereafter, and that you must worry along somehow for the good of Humanity.

One of its minor tenets seemed to be that the one thing more sinful than giving an order was obeying it. At least, that was what McGoggin said; but I suspect he had misread his primers.

I do not say a word against this creed. It was made up in Town, where there is nothing but machinery and asphalt and building—all shut in by the fog. Naturally, a man grows to think that there is no one higher than himself, and that the Metropolitan Board of Works made everything. But in this country, where you really see humanity—raw, brown, naked humanity—with nothing between it and the blazing sky, and only the used-up, over-handled earth underfoot, the notion somehow dies away, and most folk come back to simpler theories. Life, in India, is not long enough to waste in proving that there is no one in particular at the head of affairs. For this reason. The Deputy is above the Assistant, the Commissioner above the Deputy, the Lieutenant-Governor above the Commissioner, and the Viceroy above all four, under the orders of the Secretary of State who is responsible to the Empress. If the Empress be not responsible to her Maker—if there is no Maker for her to be responsible to—the entire system of Our administration must be wrong. Which is manifestly impossible. At Home men are to be excused. They are stalled up a good deal and get intellectually "beany." When you take a gross, "beany" horse to exercise, he slavers and slobbers over the bit till you can't see the horns. But the bit is there just the same. Men do not get "beany" in India. The climate and the work are against playing bricks with words.

If McGoggin had kept his creed, with the capital letters and the endings in "isms," to himself, no one would have cared: but his grandfathers on both sides had been Wesleyan preachers, and the preaching strain came out in his mind. He wanted every one at the Club to see that they had no souls too, and to help him to eliminate his Creator. As a good many men told him, *he* undoubtedly had no soul, because he was so young, but it did not follow that his seniors were equally undeveloped; and, whether there was another world or not, a man still wanted to read his papers in this. "But that is not the point—that is not the point!" Aurelian used to say. Then men threw sofa-cushions at him and told him to go to any particular place he might believe in. They christened him the "Blastoderm,"—he said he came from a family of that name somewhere, in the pre-historic ages,—and, by insult and laughter strove to choke him dumb, for he was an unmitigated nuisance at the Club; besides being an offense to the older men. His Deputy Commissioner, who was working on the Frontier when Aurelian was rolling on a bedquilt, told him that, for a clever boy, Aurelian was a very big idiot. And, you know, if he had gone on with his work, he would have been caught up to the Secretariat in a few years. He was just the type that goes there—all head, no physique and a hundred theories. Not a soul was interested in McGoggin's soul. He might have had two, or none, or somebody else's. His business was to obey orders and keep abreast of his files instead of devastating the Club with "isms."

He worked brilliantly; but he could not accept any order without trying to better it. That was the fault of his creed. It made men too responsible and left too much to their honor. You can sometimes ride an old horse in a halter; but never a colt. McGoggin took more trouble over his cases than any of the men of his year. He may have fancied that thirty-page judgments on fifty-rupee cases—both sides perjured to the gullet—advanced the cause of Humanity. At any rate, he worked too much, and worried and fretted over the rebukes he received, and lectured away on his ridiculous creed out of office, till the Doctor had to warn him that he was overdoing it. No man can toil eighteen annas in the rupee in June without suffering. But McGoggin was still intellectually "beany" and proud of himself and his powers, and he would take no hint. He worked nine hours a day steadily.

"Very well," said the doctor, "you'll break down because you are over-engined for your beam." McGoggin was a little chap.

One day, the collapse came–as dramatically as if it had been meant to embellish a Tract.

It was just before the Rains. We were sitting in the veranda in the dead, hot, close air, gasping and praying that the black-blue clouds would let down and bring the cool. Very, very far away, there was a faint whisper, which was the roar of the Rains breaking over the river. One of the men heard it, got out of his chair, listened, and said, naturally enough:–"Thank God!"

Then the Blastoderm turned in his place and said:–

"Why? I assure you it's only the result of perfectly natural causes–atmospheric phenomena of the simplest kind. Why you should, therefore, return thanks to a Being who never did exist–who is only a figment–"

"Blastoderm," grunted the man in the next chair, "dry up, and throw me over the *Pioneer*. We know all about your figments." The Blastoderm reached out to the table, took up one paper, and jumped as if something had stung him. Then he handed the paper over.

"As I was saying," he went on slowly and with an effort–"due to perfectly natural causes–perfectly natural causes. I mean–"

"Hi! Blastoderm, you've given me the *Calcutta Mercantile Advertiser*."

The dust got up in little whorls, while the tree-tops rocked and the kites whistled. But no one was looking at the coming of the Rains. We were all staring at the Blastoderm who had risen from his chair and was fighting with his speech. Then he said, still more slowly:–

"Perfectly conceivable—dictionary—red oak—amenable—cause—retaining—shuttlecock—alone."

"Blastoderm's drunk," said one man. But the Blastoderm was not drunk. He looked at us in a dazed sort of way, and began motioning with his hands in the half light as the clouds closed overhead. Then–with a scream:–

"What is it?—Can't—reserve—attainable—market—obscure—"

But his speech seemed to freeze in him, and–just as the lightning shot two tongues that cut the whole sky into three pieces and the rain fell in quivering sheets–the Blastoderm was struck dumb. He stood pawing and champing like a hard-held horse, and his eyes were full of terror.

The Doctor came over in three minutes, and heard the story. "It's *aphasia,*" he said. "Take him to his room. I *knew* the smash would come." We carried the Blastoderm across, in the pouring rain to his quarters, and the Doctor gave him bromide of potassium to make him sleep.

Then the Doctor came back to us and told us that *aphasia* was like all the arrears of "Punjab Head" falling in a lump; and that only once before–in the case of a sepoy–had he met with so complete a case. I myself have seen mild *aphasia* in an overworked man, but this sudden dumbness was uncanny–though, as the Blastoderm himself might have said, due to "perfectly natural causes."

"He'll have to take leave after this," said the Doctor; "He won't be fit for work for another three months. No; it isn't insanity or anything like it. It's only complete loss of control over the speech and memory. I fancy it will keep the Blastoderm quiet, though."

Two days later, the Blastoderm found his tongue again. The first question he asked was:–"What was it?" The Doctor enlightened him. "But I can't understand it!" said the Blastoderm; "I'm quite sane; but I can't be sure of my mind, it seems–my *own* memory–can I?"

"Go up into the Hills for three months, and don't think about it," said the Doctor.

"But I can't understand it," repeated the Blastoderm. "It was my *own* mind and memory."

"I can't help it," said the Doctor; "there are a good many things you can't understand; and, by the time you have put in my length of service, you'll know exactly how much a man dare call his own in this world."

The stroke cowed the Blastoderm. He could not understand it. He went into the Hills in fear and trembling, wondering whether he would be permitted to reach the end of any sentence he began.

This gave him a wholesome feeling of mistrust. The legitimate explanation, that he had been overworking himself, failed to satisfy him. Something had wiped his lips of speech, as a mother wipes the milky lips of her child, and he was afraid—horribly afraid.

So the Club had rest when he returned; and if ever you come across Aurelian McGoggin laying down the law on things Human—he doesn't seem to know as much as he used to about things Divine—put your forefinger on your lip for a moment, and see what happens.

Don't blame me if he throws a glass at your head!

The Taking of Lungtungpen

"So we loosed a bloomin' volley,
And we made the beggars cut,
An' when our pouch was emptied out,
We used the bloomin' butt,
Ho! My!
Don't yer come anigh,
When Tommy is a playin' with the baynit an' the butt."
Barrack Room Ballad.

MY FRIEND PRIVATE Mulvaney told me this, sitting on the parapet of the road to Dagshai, when we were hunting butterflies together. He had theories about the Army, and colored clay pipes perfectly. He said that the young soldier is the best to work with, "on account av the surpassing innocince av the child."

"Now, listen!" said Mulvaney, throwing himself full length on the wall in the sun. "I'm a born scutt av the barrick-room! The Army's mate an' dhrink to me, bekase I'm wan av the few that can't quit ut. I've put in sivinteen years, an' the pipeclay's in the marrow av me. Av I cud have kept out av wan big dhrink a month, I wud have been a Hon'ry Lift'nint by this time—a nuisince to my betthers, a laughin'-shtock to my equils, an' a curse to meself. Bein' fwhat I am, I'm Privit Mulvaney, wid no good-conduc' pay an' a devourin' thirst. Always barrin' me little frind Bobs Bahadur, I know as much about the Army as most men."

I said something here.

"Wolseley be shot! Betune you an' me an' that butterfly-net, he's a ramblin', incoherint sort av a divil, wid wan oi on the Quane an' the Coort, and the other on his blessed silf—everlastin'ly playing Saysar an' Alexandrier rowled into a lump. Now Bobs is a sinsible little man. Wid Bobs an' a few three-year-olds, I'd swape any army av the earth into a *jhairum,* an' throw it away afterwards. Faith, I'm not jokin'! 'Tis the bhoys—the raw bhoys—that don't know fwhat a bullut manes, an' wudn't care av they did—that dhu the work. They're crammed wid bullmate till they fairly *ramps* wid good livin'; and thin, av they don't fight, they blow each other's hids off. 'Tis the trut' I'm tellin' you. They shold be kept on *dal-bhat* an' *kijri* in the hot weather; but there'd be a mut'ny av 'twas done.

"Did ye iver hear how Privit Mulvaney tuk the town av Lungtungpen? I thought not! 'Twas the Lift'nint got the credit; but 'twas me planned the schame. A little before I was inviladed from Burma, me an' four an' twenty young wans undher a Lift'nint Brazenose, was ruinin' our dijeshins thryin' to catch dacoits. An' such double-ended divils I niver knew! 'Tis only a *dah* an' a Snider that makes a dacoit. Widout thim, he's a paceful cultivator, an' felony for to shoot. We hunted, an' we hunted, an' tuk fever an' elephints now an' again; but no dacoits. Evenshually, we *puckarowed* wan man. 'Trate him tinderly,' sez the Lift'nint. So I tuk him away into the jungle, wid the Burmese Interprut'r an' my clanin'-rod. Sez I to the man:–'My peaceful squireen,' sez I, 'you shquot on your hunkers an' dimonstrate to *my* frind here, where *your* frinds are whin they're at home?' Wid that I introjuced him to the clanin'-rod, and he comminst to jabber; the Interprut'r interprutin' in betweens, an' me helpin' the Intilligince Departmint wid my clanin'-rod whin the man misremimbered.

"Prisintly, I learned that, acrost the river, about nine miles away, was a town just *dhrippin'* wid dahs, an' bohs an' arrows, an' dacoits, an' elephints, an' *jingles.* 'Good,' sez I. 'This office will now close!'

"That night, I went to the Lift'nint an' communicates my information. I never thought much of Lift'nint Brazenose till that night. He was shtiff wid books an' the-*ouries,* an' all manner av thrimmin's no manner av use. 'Town did ye say?' sez he. 'Accordin' to the the-*ouries* av War, we shud wait for reinforcemints.' 'Faith!' thinks I, 'we'd betther dig our graves thin;' for the nearest throops was up to their shtocks in the marshes out Mimbu way. 'But,' says the Lift'nint, 'since 'tis a speshil case, I'll make an excepshin. We'll visit this Lungtungpen to-night.'

"The bhoys was fairly woild wid deloight whin I tould 'em; an' by this an' that, they wint through the jungle like buck-rabbits. About midnight we come to the shtrame which I had clane forgot to minshin to my orficer. I was on, ahead, wid four bhoys, an' I thought that the Lift'nint might want to the-*ourize.* 'Shtrip, bhoys!' sez I. 'Shtrip to the buff, an' shwim in where glory waits!' 'But I *can't* shwim!' sez two av thim. 'To think I should live to hear that from a bhoy wid a board-school edukashin!' sez I. 'Take a lump av thimber, an' me an' Conolly here will ferry ye over, ye young ladies!'

"We got an ould tree-trunk, an' pushed off wid the kits an' the rifles on it. The night was chokin' dhark, an' just as we was fairly embarked, I heard the Lift'nint behind av me callin' out. 'There's a bit av a *nullah* here, Sorr,' sez I, 'but I can feel the bottom already.' So I cud, for I was not a yard from the bank.

" 'Bit av a *nullah!* Bit av an eshtuary!' sez the Lift'nint. 'Go on, ye mad Irishman! Shtrip, bhoys!' I heard him laugh; an' the bhoys begun shtrippin' an' rollin' a log into the water to put their kits on. So me an' Conolly shtruck out through the warm wather wid our log, an' the rest come on behind.

"That shtrame was miles woide! Orth'ris, on the rear-rank log, whispers we had got into the Thames below Sheerness by mistake. 'Kape on shwimmin', ye little blayguard,' sez I, 'an don't go pokin' your dirty jokes at the Irriwaddy.' 'Silince, men!' sings out the Lift'nint. So we shwum on into the black dhark, wid our chests on the logs, trustin' in the Saints an' the luck av the British Army.

"Evenshually, we hit ground–a bit av sand—an' a man. I put my heel on the back av him. He skreeched an' ran.

" '*Now* we've done it!' sez Lift'nint Brazenose. 'Where the Divil *is* Lungtungpen?' There was about a minute and a half to wait. The bhoys laid a hould av their rifles an' some thried to put their belts on; we was marchin' wid fixed baynits av coorse. *Thin* we knew where Lungtungpen was; for we had hit the river-wall av it in the dhark, an' the whole town blazed wid thim messin' *jingles* an Sniders like a cat's back on a frosty night. They was firin' all ways at wanst; but over our hids into the shtrame.

"'Have you got your rifles?' sez Brazenose. 'Got 'em!' sez Orth'ris, 'I've got that thief Mulvaney's for all my back-pay, an' she'll kick my heart sick wid that blunderin' long shtock av hers.' 'Go on!' yells Brazenose, whippin' his sword out. 'Go on an' take the town! An' the Lord have mercy on our sowls!'

"Thin the bhoys gave wan divastatin' howl, an' pranced into the dhark, feelin' for the town, an' blindin' an' stiffin' like Cavalry Ridin' Masters whin the grass pricked their bare legs. I hammered wid the butt at some bamboo thing that felt wake, an' the rest come an' hammerd contagious, while the *jingles* was jingling, an' feroshus yells from inside was shplittin' our ears. We was too close under the walls for them to hurt us.

"Evenshually, the thing, whatever ut was, bruk; an' the six and twinty av us tumbled, wan afther the other, naked as we was borrun, into the town of Lungtungpen. There was a *melly* av a sumpshus kind for a whoile; but whether they tuk us, all white an' wet, for a new breed av divil, or a new kind av dacoit, I don't know. They ran as though we was both, an' we wint into thim, baynit an' butt, shriekin' wid laughin'. There was torches in the shtreets, an' I saw little Orth'ris rubbin' his showlther ivry time he loosed my long-shtock Martini; an' Brazenose walkin' into the gang wid his sword, like Diarmid av the Golden Collar–barring he hadn't a stitch av clothin' on him. We diskivered elephints wid dacoits under their bellies, an', what wid wan thing an' another, we was busy till mornin' takin' possession av the town of Lungtungpen.

"Thin we halted an' formed up, the wimmen howlin' in the houses an' Lift'nint Brazenose blushin' pink in the light av the mornin' sun. 'Twas the most ondasint p'rade I iver tuk a hand in. Foive and twenty privits an' a orficer av the line in review ordher, an' not as much as wud dust a fife betune 'em all in the way of clothin'! Eight av us had their belts an' pouches on; but the rest had gone in wid a handful av cartridges an' the skin God gave him. *They* was as nakid as Vanus.

"'Number off from the right!' sez the Lift'nint. 'Odd numbers fall out to dress; even numbers pathrol the town till relieved by the dressing party.' Let me tell you, pathrolin' a town wid nothing on is an ex*pay*rience. I pathroled for tin minutes, an' begad, before 'twas over, I blushed. The women laughed so. I niver blushed before or since; but I blushed all over my carkiss thin. Orth'ris didn't pathrol. He sez only:–'Porthsmith Barricks an' the 'Ard av a Sunday!' Thin he lay down an' rowled anyways wid laughin'.

"When we was all dhressed, we counted the dead–sivinty-foive dacoits besides wounded. We tuk five elephints, a hunder' an' sivinty Sniders, two hunder' dahs, and a lot av other burglarious thruck. Not a man av us was hurt–excep' may be the Lift'nint, an' he from the shock to his dasincy.

"The Headman av Luntungpen, who surrinder'd himself, asked the Interprut'r:–'Av the English fight like that wid their clo'es off, what in the wurruld do they do wid their clo'es on?' Orth'ris began rowlin' his eyes an' crackin' his fingers an' dancin' a step-dance for to impress the Headman. He ran to his house; an' we spint the rest av the day carryin' the Lift'nint on our showlthers round the town, an' playin' wid the Burmese babies–fat, little, brown little divils, as pretty as pictures.

"Whin I was inviladed for the dysent'ry to India, I sez to the Lift'nint:–'Sorr,' sez I, 'you've the makin's in you av a great man; but, av you'll let an ould sodger spake, you're too fond of the-*ourizin'*. He shuk hands wid me and sez:–'Hit high, hit low, there's no plasin' you, Mulvaney. You've seen me waltzin' through Lungtungpen like a Red Injin widout the war-paint, an' you say I'm too fond av the-*ourizin'?*' 'Sorr,' sez I, for I loved the bhoy; 'I wud waltz wid you in that condishin through *Hell,* an' so wud the rest av the men!' Thin I wint downshtrame in the flat an' left him my blessin'. May the Saints cary ut where ut shud go, for he was a fine upstandin' young orficer.

"To reshume! Fwhat I've said jist shows the use av three-year-olds. Wud fifty seasoned sodgers have taken Lungtungpen in the dhark that way? No! They'd know the risk av fever an chill. Let alone the shootin'. Two hundher' might have done ut. But the three-year-olds know little an' care less; an' where there's no fear, there's no danger. Catch them young, feed them high, an' by the honor av that great little man Bobs, behind a good orficer 'tisn't only dacoits they'd smash wid their clo'es off–'ts Con-ti-nental Ar-r-r-mies! They tuk Lungtungpen nakid; an' they'd take St. Pethersburg in their dhrawers! Begad, they would that!

"Here's your pipe, Sorr! Shmoke her tinderly wid honey-dew, afther letting the reek av the Canteen plug die away. But 'tis no good, thanks to you all the same, fillin' my pouch wid your chopped *bhoosa.* Canteen baccy's like the army. It sphoils a man's taste for moilder things."

So saying, Mulvaney took up his butterfly-net, and returned to barracks.

A Germ Destroyer

> Pleasant it is for the Little Tin Gods,
> When great Jove nods;
> But Little Tin Gods make their little mistakes
> In missing the hour when great Jove wakes.

As a general rule, it is inexpedient to meddle with questions of State in a land where men are highly paid to work them out for you. This tale is a justifiable exception.

Once in every five years, as you know, we indent for a new Viceroy; and each Viceroy imports, with the rest of his baggage, a Private Secretary, who may or may not be the real Viceroy, just as Fate ordains. Fate looks after the Indian Empire because it is so big and so helpless.

There was a Viceroy once, who brought out with him a turbulent Private Secretary–a hard man with a soft manner and a morbid passion for work. This Secretary was called Wonder–John Fennil Wonder. The Viceroy possessed no name–nothing but a string of counties and two-thirds of the alphabet after them. He said, in confidence, that he was the electro-plated figure-head of a golden administration, and he watched in a dreamy, amused way Wonder's attempts to draw matters which were entirely outside his province into his own hands. "When we are all cherubims together," said His Excellency once, "my dear, good friend Wonder will head the conspiracy for plucking out Gabriel's tailfeathers or stealing Peter's keys. *Then* I shall report him."

But, though the Viceroy did nothing to check Wonder's officiousness, other people said unpleasant things. May be the Members of Council began it; but, finally, all Simla agreed that there was "too much Wonder, and too little Viceroy" in the *régime.* Wonder was always quoting "His Excellency." It was "His Excellency this," "His Excellency that," "In the opinion of his Excellency," and so on. The Viceroy smiled; but he did not heed. He said that, so long as his old men squabbled with his "dear, good Wonder," they might be induced to leave the "Immemorial East" in peace.

"No wise man has a policy," said the Viceroy. "A Policy is the blackmail levied on the Fool by the Unforeseen. I am not the former, and I do not believe in the latter."

I do not quite see what this means, unless it refers to an Insurance Policy. Perhaps it was the Viceroy's way of saying:—"Lie low."

That season, came up to Simla one of these crazy people with only a single idea. These are the men who make things move; but they are not nice to talk to. This man's name was Mellish, and he had lived for fifteen years on land of his own, in Lower Bengal, studying cholera. He held that cholera was a germ that propagated itself as it flew through a muggy atmosphere; and stuck in the branches of trees like a woolflake. The germ could be rendered sterile, he said, by "Mellish's Own Invincible Fumigatory"—a heavy violet-black powder—"the result of fifteen years' scientific investigation, Sir!"

Inventors seem very much alike as a caste. They talk loudly, especially about "conspiracies of monopolists;" they beat upon the table with their fists; and they secrete fragments of their inventions about their persons.

Mellish said that there was a Medical "Ring" at Simla, headed by the Surgeon-General, who was in league, apparently, with all the Hospital Assistants in the Empire. I forget exactly how he proved it, but it had something to do with "skulking up to the Hills;" and what Mellish wanted was the independent evidence of the Viceroy—"Steward of our Most Gracious Majesty the Queen, Sir." So Mellish went up to Simla, with eighty-four pounds of Fumigatory in his trunk, to speak to the Viceroy and to show him the merits of the invention.

But it is easier to see a Viceroy than to talk to him, unless you chance to be as important as Mellishe of Madras. He was a six-thousand-rupee man, so great that his daughters never "married." They "contracted alliances." He himself was not paid. He "received emoluments," and his journeys about the country were "tours of observation." His business was to stir up the people in Madras with a long pole—as you stir up tench in a pond—and the people had to come up out of their comfortable old ways and gasp:—"This is Enlightenment and progress. Isn't it fine!" Then they gave Mellish statues and jasmine garlands, in the hope of getting rid of him.

Mellish came up to Simla "to confer with the Viceroy." That was one of his perquisites. The Viceroy knew nothing of Mellishe except that he was "one of those middle-class deities who seem necessary to the spiritual comfort of this Paradise of the Middle-classes," and that, in all probability, he had "suggested, designed, founded, and endowed all the public institutions in Madras." Which proves that His Excellency, though dreamy, had experience of the ways of six-thousand-rupee men.

Mellishe's name was E. Mellishe and Mellish's was E. S. Mellish, and they were both staying at the same hotel, and the Fate that looks after the Indian Empire ordained that Wonder should blunder and drop the final "*e;*" that the Chaprassi should help him, and that the note which ran: *"Dear Mr. Mellish.—Can you set aside your other engagements, and lunch with us at two to-morrow? His Excellency has an hour at your disposal then,"* should be given to Mellish with the Fumigatory. He nearly wept with pride and delight, and at the appointed hour cantered to Peterhoff, a big paper-bag full of the Fumigatory in his coat-tail pockets. He had his chance, and he meant to make the most of it. Mellishe of Madras had been so portentously solemn about his "conference," that Wonder had arranged for a private tiffin,—no A.-D.-C.'s, no Wonder, no one but the Viceroy, who said plaintively that he feared being left alone with unmuzzled autocrats like the great Mellishe of Madras.

But his guest did not bore the Viceroy. On the contrary, he amused him. Mellish was nervously anxious to go straight to his Fumigatory, and talked at random until tiffin was over and His Excellency asked him to smoke. The

Viceroy was pleased with Mellish because he did not talk "shop."

As soon as the cheroots were lit, Mellish spoke like a man; beginning with his cholera-theory, reviewing his fifteen years' "scientific labors," the machinations of the "Simla Ring," and the excellence of his Fumigatory, while the Viceroy watched him between half-shut eyes and thought: "Evidently, this is the wrong tiger; but it is an original animal." Mellish's hair was standing on end with excitement, and he stammered. He began groping in his coat-tails and, before the Viceroy knew what was about to happen, he had tipped a bagful of his powder into the big silver ash-tray.

"J-j-judge for yourself, Sir," said Mellish. "Y' Excellency shall judge for yourself! Absolutely infallible, on my honor."

He plunged the lighted end of his cigar into the powder, which began to smoke like a volcano, and send up fat, greasy wreaths of copper-colored smoke. In five seconds the room was filled with a most pungent and sickening stench–a reek that took fierce hold of the trap of your windpipe and shut it. The powder then hissed and fizzed, and sent out blue and green sparks, and the smoke rose till you could neither see, nor breathe, nor gasp. Mellish, however, was used to it.

"Nitrate of strontia," he shouted; "baryta, bonemeal, *et cetera!* Thousand cubic feet smoke per cubic inch. Not a germ could live–not a germ, Y' Excellency!"

But His Excellency had fled, and was coughing at the foot of the stairs, while all Peterhoff hummed like a hive. Red Lancers came in, and the Head Chaprassi who speaks English, came in, and mace-bearers came in, and ladies ran down-stairs screaming, "fire;" for the smoke was drifting through the house and oozing out of the windows, and bellying along the verandas, and wreathing and writhing across the gardens. No one could enter the room where Mellish was lecturing on his Fumigatory, till that unspeakable powder had burned itself out.

Then an Aide-de-Camp, who desired the V. C., rushed through the rolling clouds and hauled Mellish into the hall. The Viceroy was prostrate with laughter, and could only waggle his hands feebly at Mellish, who was shaking a fresh bagful of powder at him.

"Glorious! Glorious!" sobbed His Excellency. "Not a germ, as you justly observe, could exist! I can swear it. A magnificent success!"

Then he laughed till the tears came, and Wonder, who had caught the real Mellishe snorting on the Mall, entered and was deeply shocked at the scene. But the Viceroy was delighted, because he saw that Wonder would presently depart. Mellish with the Fumigatory was also pleased, for he felt that he had smashed the Simla Medical "Ring."

. . . .

Few men could tell a story like His Excellency when he took the trouble, and the account of "my dear, good Wonder's friend with the powder" went the round of Simla, and flippant folk made Wonder unhappy by their remarks.

But His Excellency told the tale once too often–for Wonder. As he meant to do. It was at a Seepee Picnic. Wonder was sitting just behind the Viceroy.

"And I really thought for a moment," wound up His Excellency, "that my dear good Wonder had hired an assassin to clear his way to the throne!"

Every one laughed; but there was a delicate subtinkle in the Viceroy's tone which Wonder understood. He found that his health was giving way; and the Viceroy allowed him to go, and presented him with a flaming "character" for use at Home among big people.

"My fault entirely," said His Excellency, in after seasons, with a twinkling in his eye. "My inconsistency must always have been distasteful to such a masterly man."

Kidnapped

There is a tide in the affairs of men,
Which, taken any way you please, is bad,
And strands them in forsaken guts and creeks
No decent soul would think of visiting.
You cannot stop the tide; but now and then,
You may arrest some rash adventurer
Who–h'm–will hardly thank you for your pains.
Vibart's Moralities.

WE ARE A high-caste and enlightened race, and infant-marriage is very shocking and the consequences are sometimes peculiar; but, nevertheless, the Hindu notion–which is the Continental notion, which is the aboriginal notion–of arranging marriages irrespective of the personal inclinations of the married, is sound. Think for a minute, and you will see that it must be so; unless, of course, you believe in "affinities." In which case you had better not read this tale. How can a man who has never married; who cannot be trusted to pick up at sight a moderately sound horse; whose head is hot and upset with visions of domestic felicity, go about the choosing of a wife? He cannot see straight or think straight if he tries; and the same disadvantages exist in the case of a girl's fancies. But when mature, married and discreet people arrange a match between a boy and a girl, they do it sensibly, with a view to the future, and the young couple live happily ever afterwards. As everybody knows.

Properly speaking, Government should establish a Matrimonial Department, efficiently officered, with a Jury of Matrons, a Judge of the Chief Court, a senior Chaplain, and an Awful Warning, in the shape of a love-match that has gone wrong, chained to the trees in the courtyard. All marriages should be made through the Department, which might be subordinate to the Educational Department, under the same penalty as that attaching to the transfer of land without a stamped document. But Government won't take suggestions. It pretends that it is too busy. However, I will put my notion on record, and explain the example that illustrates the theory.

Once upon a time there was a good young man–a first-class officer in his own Department–a man with a career before him and, possibly, a K. C. I. E. at the end of it. All his superiors spoke well of him, because he knew how to hold his tongue and his pen at the proper times. There are to-day only eleven men in India who possess this secret; and they have all, with one exception, attained great honor and enormous incomes.

This good young man was quiet and self-contained–too old for his years by far. Which always carries its own punishment. Had a Subaltern, or a Tea-Planter's Assistant, or anybody who enjoys life and has no care for to-morrow, done what he tried to do not a soul would have cared. But when Peythroppe–the estimable, virtuous, economical, quiet, hard-working, young Peythroppe–fell, there was a flutter through five Departments.

The manner of his fall was in this way. He met a Miss Castries–d'Castries it was originally, but the family dropped the d' for administrative reasons–and he fell in love with her even more energetically than he worked. Understand clearly that there was not a breath of a word to be said against Miss Castries–not a shadow of a breath. She was good and very lovely–possessed what innocent people at home call a "Spanish" complexion, with thick blue-black hair growing low down on the forehead, into a "widow's peak," and big violet eyes under eyebrows as black and as straight as the borders of a *Gazette Extraordinary*, when a big man dies. But—but—but—. Well, she was a *very* sweet girl and very pious, but for many reasons she was "impossible." Quite so. All good Mammas know what "impossible" means. It was obviously absurd that Peythroppe should marry her. The little opal-tinted onyx at the base of her finger-nails said this as plainly as print. Further, marriage with Miss Castries meant marriage with several other Castries–Honorary Lieutenant Castries her Papa, Mrs. Eulalie Castries her Mamma, and all the ramifications of the Castries family, on incomes ranging from Rs. 175 to Rs. 470 a month, and *their* wives and connections again.

It would have been cheaper for Peythroppe to have assaulted a Commissioner with a dog-whip, or to have burned the records of a Deputy Commissioner's Office, than to have contracted an alliance with the Castries. It would have weighted his after-career less–even under a Government which never forgets and *never* forgives. Everybody saw this but Peythroppe. He was going to marry Miss Castries, he was–being of age and drawing a good income–and woe betide the house that would not afterwards receive Mrs. Virginie Saulez Peythroppe with the deference due to her husband's rank. That was Peythroppe's ultimatum, and any remonstrance drove him frantic.

These sudden madnesses most afflict the sanest men. There was a case once–but I will tell you of that later on. You cannot account for the mania, except under a theory directly contradicting the one about the Place wherein marriages are made. Peythroppe was burningly anxious to put a millstone round his neck at the outset of his career; and argument had not the least effect on him. He was going to marry Miss Castries, and the business was his own business. He would thank you to keep your advice to yourself. With a man in this condition, mere words only fix him in his purpose. Of course he cannot see that marriage out here does not concern the individual but the Government he serves.

Do you remember Mrs. Hauksbee–the most wonderful woman in India? She saved Pluffles from Mrs. Reiver, won Tarrion his appointment in the Foreign Office, and was defeated in open field by Mrs. Cusack-Bremmil. She heard of the lamentable condition of Peythroppe, and her brain struck out the plan that saved him. She had the wisdom of the Serpent, the logical coherence of the Man, the fearlessness of the Child, and the triple intuition of the Woman. Never–no, never–as long as a tonga buckets down the Solon dip, or the couples go a-riding at the back of Summer Hill, will there be such a genius as Mrs. Hauksbee. She attended the consultation of Three Men on Peythroppe's case; and she stood up with the lash of her riding whip between her lips and spake.

. . . .

Three weeks later, Peythroppe dined with the Three Men, and the *Gazette of India* came in. Peythroppe found to his surprise that he had been gazetted a month's leave. Don't ask me how this was managed. I believe firmly that if Mrs. Hauksbee gave the order, the whole Great Indian Administration would stand on its head. The Three Men had also a month's leave each. Peythroppe put the *Gazette* down and said bad words. Then there came from the compound the soft "pad-pad" of camels–"thieves' camels," the Bikaneer breed that don't bubble and howl when they sit down and get up.

After that I don't know what happened. This much is certain. Peythroppe disappeared–vanished like smoke–and the long foot-rest chair in the house of the Three Men was broken to splinters. Also a bedstead departed from one of the bedrooms.

Mrs. Hauksbee said that Mr. Peythroppe was shooting in Rajputana with the Three Men; so we were compelled to believe her.

At the end of the month, Peythroppe was gazetted twenty days' extension of leave; but there was wrath and lamentation in the house of Castries. The marriage-day had been fixed, but the bridegroom never came: and the D'Silvas, Pereiras and Ducketts lifted their voices and mocked Honorary Lieutenant Castries as one who had been basely imposed upon. Mrs. Hauksbee went to the wedding, and was much astonished when Peythroppe did not appear. After seven weeks, Peythroppe and the Three Men returned from Rajputana. Peythroppe was in hard, tough condition, rather white, and more self-contained than ever.

One of the Three Men had a cut on his nose, caused by the kick of a gun. Twelve-bores kick rather curiously.

Then came Honorary Lieutenant Castries, seeking for the blood of his perfidious son-in-law to be. He said things—vulgar and "impossible" things, which showed the raw rough "ranker" below the "Honorary," and I fancy Peythroppe's eyes were opened. Anyhow, he held his peace till the end; when he spoke briefly. Honorary Lieutenant Castries asked for a "peg" before he went away to die or bring a suit for breach of promise.

Miss Castries was a very good girl. She said that she would have no breach of promise suits. She said that, if she was not a lady, she was refined enough to know that ladies kept their broken hearts to themselves; and, as she ruled her parents, nothing happened. Later on, she married a most respectable and gentlemanly person. He traveled for an enterprising firm in Calcutta, and was all that a good husband should be.

So Peythroppe came to his right mind again, and did much good work, and was honored by all who knew him. One of these days he will marry; but he will marry a sweet pink-and-white maiden, on the Government House List, with a little money and some influential connections, as every wise man should. And he will never, all his life, tell her what happened during the seven weeks of his shooting-tour in Rajputana.

But just think how much trouble and expense—for camel hire is not cheap, and those Bikaneer brutes had to be fed like humans—might have been saved by a properly conducted Matrimonial Department, under the control of the Director-General of Education, but corresponding direct with the Viceroy.

The Arrest of Lieutenant Golightly

" 'I've forgotten the countersign,' sez 'e.
'Oh! You 'ave, 'ave you?' sez I.
'But I'm the Colonel,' sez 'e.
'Oh! You are, are you?' sez I. 'Colonel nor no Colonel, you waits 'ere till I'm relieved, an' the Sarjint reports on your ugly old mug. *Coop!'* sez I.

. . . .

An' s'elp me soul, 'twas the Colonel after all! But I was a recruity then."

The Unedited Autobiography of Private Ortheris.

IF THERE WAS one thing on which Golightly prided himself more than another, it was looking like "an Officer and a Gentleman." He said it was for the honor of the Service that he attired himself so elaborately; but those who knew him best said that it was just personal vanity. There was no harm about Golightly—not an ounce. He recognized a horse when he saw one, and could do more than fill a cantle. He played a very fair game at billiards, and was a sound man at the whist-table. Every one liked him; and nobody ever dreamed of seeing him handcuffed on a station platform as a deserter. But this sad thing happened.

He was going down from Dalhousie, at the end of his leave–riding down. He had cut his leave as fine as he dared, and wanted to come down in a hurry.

It was fairly warm at Dalhousie, and knowing what to expect below, he descended in a new *khaki* suit–tight fitting–of a delicate olive-green; a peacock-blue tie, white collar, and a snowy white *solah* helmet. He prided himself on looking neat even when he was riding post. He did look neat, and he was so deeply concerned about his appearance before he started that he quite forgot to take anything but some small change with him. He left all his notes at the hotel. His servants had gone down the road before him, to be ready in waiting at Pathankote with a change of gear. That was what he called traveling in "light marching-order." He was proud of his faculty of organization–what we call *bundobust.*

Twenty-two miles out of Dalhousie it began to rain–not a mere hill-shower but a good, tepid monsoonish downpour. Golightly bustled on, wishing that he had brought an umbrella. The dust on the roads turned into mud, and the pony mired a good deal. So did Golightly's *khaki* gaiters. But he kept on steadily and tried to think how pleasant the coolth was.

His next pony was rather a brute at starting, and Golightly's hands being slippery with the rain, contrived to get rid of Golightly at a corner. He chased the animal, caught it, and went ahead briskly. The spill had not improved his clothes or his temper, and he had lost one spur. He kept the other one employed. By the time that stage was ended, the pony had had as much exercise as he wanted, and, in spite of the rain, Golightly was sweating freely. At the end of another miserable half-hour, Golightly found the world disappear before his eyes in clammy pulp. The rain had turned the pith of his huge and snowy *solah-topee* into an evil-smelling dough, and it had closed on his head like a half-opened mushroom. Also the green lining was beginning to run.

Golightly did not say anything worth recording here. He tore off and squeezed up as much of the brim as was in his eyes and plowed on. The back of the helmet was flapping on his neck and the sides stuck to his ears, but the leather band and green lining kept things roughly together, so that the hat did not actually melt away where it flapped.

Presently, the pulp and the green stuff made a sort of slimy mildew which ran over Golightly in several directions–down his back and bosom for choice. The *khaki* color ran too–it was really shockingly bad dye–and sections of Golightly were brown, and patches were violet, and contours were ochre, and streaks were ruddy red, and blotches were nearly white according to the nature and peculiarities of the dye. When he took out his handkerchief to wipe his face and the green of the hat lining and the purple stuff that had soaked through on to his neck from the tie became thoroughly mixed, the effect was amazing.

Near Dhar the rain stopped and the evening sun came out and dried him up slightly. It fixed the colors, too. Three miles from Pathankote the last pony fell dead lame, and Golightly was forced to walk. He pushed on into Pathankote to find his servants. He did not know then that his *khitmatgar* had stopped by the roadside to get drunk, and would come on the next day saying that he had sprained his ankle. When he got into Pathankote, he couldn't find his servants, his boots were stiff and ropy with mud, and there were large quantities of dirt about his body. The blue tie had run as much as the *khaki.* So he took it off with the collar and threw it away. Then he said something about servants generally and tried to get a peg. He paid eight annas for the drink, and this revealed to him that he had only six annas more in his pocket—or in the world as he stood at that hour.

He went to the Station-Master to negotiate for a first-class ticket to Khasa, where he was stationed. The booking-clerk said something to the Station-Master, the Station-Master said something to the Telegraph Clerk, and the three looked at him with curiosity. They asked him to wait for half an hour, while they telegraphed to Umritsar for authority. So he waited and four constables came and grouped themselves picturesquely round him. Just as he was preparing to ask them to go away, the Station-Master said that he would give the *Sahib* a ticket to Umritsar, if the *Sahib* would kindly come inside the booking-office. Golightly stepped inside, and the next thing he knew was that a constable was attached to each of his legs and arms, while the Station-Master was trying to cram a mail-bag over his head.

There was a very fair scuffle all round the booking-office, and Golightly received a nasty cut over his eye through falling against a table. But the constables were too much for him, and they and the Station-Master handcuffed him securely. As soon as the mail-bag was slipped, he began expressing his opinions, and the head-constable said:—"Without doubt this is the soldier-Englishman we required. Listen to the abuse!" Then Golightly asked the Station-Master what the this and the that the proceedings meant. The Station-Master told him he was "Private John Binkle of the——Regiment, 5 ft. 9 in., fair hair, gray eyes, and a dissipated appearance, no marks on the body," who had deserted a fortnight ago. Golightly began explaining at great length: and the more he explained the less the Station-Master believed him. He said that no Lieutenant could look such a ruffian as did Golightly, and that his instructions were to send his capture under proper escort to Umritsar. Golightly was feeling very damp and uncomfortable, and the language he used was not fit for publication, even in an expurgated form. The four constables saw him safe to Umritsar in an "intermediate" compartment, and he spent the four-hour journey in abusing them as fluently as his knowledge of the vernaculars allowed.

At Umritsar he was bundled out on the platform into the arms of a Corporal and two men of the——Regiment. Golightly drew himself up and tried to carry off matters jauntily. He did not feel too jaunty in handcuffs, with four constables behind him, and the blood from the cut on his forehead stiffening on his left cheek. The Corporal was not jocular either. Golightly got as far as:—"This is a very absurd mistake, my men," when the Corporal told him to "stow his lip" and come along. Golightly did not want to come along. He desired to stop and explain. He explained very well indeed, until the Corporal cut in with:—"*You* a orficer! It's the like o' *you* as brings disgrace on the likes of *us*. Bloomin' fine orficer you are! I know your regiment. The Rogue's March is the quickstep where you come from. You're a black shame to the Service."

Golightly kept his temper, and began explaining all over again from the beginning. Then he was marched out of the rain into the refreshment-room and told not to make a qualified fool of himself. The men were going to run him up to Fort Govindghar. And "running up" is a performance almost as undignified as the Frog March.

Golightly was nearly hysterical with rage and the chill and the mistake and the handcuffs and the headache that the cut on his forehead had given him. He really laid himself out to express what was in his mind. When he had quite finished and his throat was feeling dry, one of the men said:—"I've 'eard a few beggars in the click blind, stiff and crack on a bit; but I've never 'eard any one to touch this ere 'orficer.'" They were not angry with him. They rather admired him. They had some beer at the refreshment-room, and offered Golightly some too, because he had "swore won'erful." They asked him to tell them all about the adventures of Private John Binkle while he was loose on the country-side; and that made Golightly wilder than ever. If he had kept his wits about him he would have kept quiet until an officer came; but he attempted to run.

Now the butt of a Martini in the small of your back hurts a great deal, and rotten, rain-soaked *khaki* tears easily when two men are jerking at your collar.

Golightly rose from the floor feeling very sick and giddy, with his shirt ripped open all down his breast and nearly all down his back. He yielded to his luck, and at that point the down-train from Lahore came in carrying one of Golightly's Majors.

This is the Major's evidence in full:—

"There was the sound of a scuffle in the second-class refreshment-room, so I went in and saw the most villainous loafer that I ever set eyes on. His boots and breeches were plastered with mud and beer-stains. He wore a muddy-white dunghill sort of thing on his head, and it hung down in slips on his shoulders which were a good deal scratched. He was half in and half out of a shirt as nearly in two pieces as it could be, and he was begging the guard to look at the name on the tail of it. As he had rucked the shirt all over his head, I couldn't at first see who he was, but I fancied that he was a man in the first stage of D. T. from the way he swore while he wrestled with his rags. When he turned round, and I had made allowance for a lump as big as a pork-pie over one eye, and some green warpaint on the face, and some violet stripes round the neck, I saw that it was Golightly. He was very glad to see me," said the Major, "and he hoped I would not tell the Mess about it. *I* didn't, but you can, if you like, now that Golightly has gone Home."

Golightly spent the greater part of that summer in trying to get the Corporal and the two soldiers tried by Court-Martial for arresting an "officer and a gentleman." They were, of course, very sorry for their error. But the tale leaked into the regimental canteen, and thence ran about the Province.

In the House of Suddhoo

A stone's throw out on either hand
From that well-ordered road we tread,
  And all the world is wild and strange;
Churel and ghoul and *Djinn* and sprite
Shall bear us company to-night,
For we have reached the Oldest Land
  Wherein the Powers of Darkness range,
From the Dusk to the Dawn.

THE HOUSE OF Suddhoo, near the Taksali Gate is two-storied, with four carved windows of old brown wood, and a flat roof. You may recognize it by five red hand-prints arranged like the Five of Diamonds on the whitewash between the upper windows. Bhagwan Dass, the bunnia, and a man who says he gets his living by seal-cutting, live in the lower story with a troop of wives, servants, friends, and retainers. The two upper rooms used to be occupied by Janoo and Azizun and a little black-and-tan terrier that was stolen from an Englishman's house and given to Janoo by a soldier. To-day, only Janoo lives in the upper rooms. Suddhoo sleeps on the roof generally, except when he sleeps in the street. He used to go to Peshawar in the cold weather to visit his son, who sells curiosities near the Edwardes' Gate, and then he slept under a real mud roof. Suddhoo is a great friend of mine, because his cousin had a son who secured, thanks to my recommendation, the post of head-messenger to a big firm in the Station. Suddhoo says that God will make me a Lieutenant-Governor one of these days. I daresay his prophecy will come true. He is very, very old, with white hair and no teeth worth showing, and he has outlived his wits–outlived nearly everything except his fondness for his son at Peshawar. Janoo and Azizun are Kashmiris, Ladies of the City, and theirs was an ancient and more or less honorable profession; but Azizun has since married a medical student from the North-West and has settled down to a most respectable life somewhere near Bareilly. Bhagwan Dass is an extortionate and an adulterator. He is very rich. The man who is supposed to get his living by seal-cutting pretends to be very poor. This lets you know as much as is necessary of the four principal tenants in the house of Suddhoo. Then there is Me, of course; but I am only the chorus that comes in at the end to explain things. So I do not count.

Suddhoo was not clever. The man who pretended to cut seals was the cleverest of them all–Bhagwan Dass only knew how to lie–except Janoo. She was also beautiful, but that was her own affair.

Suddhoo's son at Peshawar was attacked by pleurisy, and old Suddhoo was troubled. The seal-cutter man heard of Suddhoo's anxiety and made capital out of it. He was abreast of the times. He got a friend in Peshawar to telegraph daily accounts of the son's health. And here the story begins.

Suddhoo's cousin's son told me, one evening, that Suddhoo wanted to see me; that he was too old and feeble to come personally, and that I should be conferring an everlasting honor on the House of Suddhoo if I went to him. I went; but I think, seeing how well-off Suddhoo was then, that he might have sent something better than an *ekka,* which jolted fearfully, to haul out a future Lieutenant-Governor to the City on a muggy April evening. The *ekka* did not run quickly. It was full dark when we pulled up opposite the door of Ranjit Singh's Tomb near the main gate of the Fort. Here was Suddhoo and he said that, by reason of my condescension, it was absolutely certain that I should become a Lieutenant-Governor while my hair was yet black. Then we talked about the weather and the state of my health, and the wheat crops, for fifteen minutes, in the Huzuri Bagh, under the stars.

Suddhoo came to the point at last. He said that Janoo had told him that there was an order of the *Sirkar* against magic, because it was feared that magic might one day kill the Empress of India. I didn't know anything about the state of the law; but I fancied that something interesting was going to happen. I said that so far from magic being discouraged by the Government it was highly commended. The greatest officials of the State practised it themselves. (If the Financial Statement isn't magic, I don't know what is.) Then, to encourage him further, I said that, if there was any *jadoo* afoot, I had not the least objection to giving it my countenance and sanction, and to seeing that it was clean *jadoo*–white magic, as distinguished from the unclean *jadoo* which kills folk. It took a long time before Suddhoo admitted that this was just what he had asked me to come for. Then he told me, in jerks and quavers, that the man who said he cut seals was a sorcerer of the cleanest kind; that every day he gave Suddhoo news of the sick son in Peshawar more quickly than the lightning could fly, and that this news was always corroborated by the letters. Further, that he had told Suddhoo how a great danger was threatening his son, which could be removed by clean *jadoo;* and, of course, heavy payment. I began to see exactly how the land lay, and told Suddhoo that *I* also understood a little *jadoo* in the Western line, and would go to his house to see that everything was done decently and in order. We set off together; and on the way Suddhoo told me that he had paid the seal-cutter between one hundred and two hundred rupees already; and the *jadoo* of that night would cost two hundred more. Which was cheap, he said, considering the greatness of his son's danger; but I do not think he meant it.

The lights were all cloaked in the front of the house when we arrived. I could hear awful noises from behind the seal-cutter's shop-front, as if some one were groaning his soul out. Suddhoo shook all over, and while we groped our way up-stairs told me that the *jadoo* had begun. Janoo and Azizun met us at the stair-head, and told us that the *jadoo*-work was coming off in their rooms, because there was more space there. Janoo is a lady of a free-thinking turn of mind. She whispered that the *jadoo* was an invention to get money out of Suddhoo, and that the seal-cutter would go to a hot place when he died. Suddhoo was nearly crying with fear and old age. He kept walking up and down the room in the half light, repeating his son's name over and over again, and asking Azizun if the seal-cutter ought not to make a reduction in the case of his own landlord. Janoo pulled me over to the shadow in the recess of the carved bow-windows. The boards were up, and the rooms were only lit by one tiny oil-lamp. There was no chance of my being seen if I stayed still.

Presently, the groans below ceased, and we heard steps on the staircase. That was the seal-cutter. He stopped outside the door as the terrier barked and Azizun fumbled at the chain, and he told Suddhoo to blow out the lamp. This left the place in jet darkness, except for the red glow from the two *huqas* that belonged to Janoo and Azizun. The seal-cutter came in, and I heard Suddhoo throw himself down on the floor and groan. Azizun caught her breath, and Janoo backed on to one of the beds with a shudder. There was a clink of something metallic, and then shot up a pale blue-green flame near the ground. The light was just enough to show Azizun, pressed against one corner of the room with the terrier between her knees; Janoo, with her hands clasped, leaning forward as she sat on the bed; Suddhoo, face down, quivering, and the seal-cutter.

I hope I may never see another man like that seal-cutter. He was stripped to the waist, with a wreath of white jasmine as thick as my wrist round his forehead, a salmon-colored loin-cloth round his middle, and a steel bangle on each ankle. This was not awe-inspiring. It was the face of the man that turned me cold. It was blue-gray in the first place. In the second, the eyes were rolled back till you could only see the whites of them; and, in the third, the face was the face of a demon—a ghoul—anything you please except of the sleek, oily old ruffian who sat in the daytime over his turning-lathe downstairs. He was lying on his stomach with his arms turned and crossed behind him, as if he had been thrown down pinioned. His head and neck were the only parts of him off the floor. They were nearly at right angles to the body, like the head of a cobra at spring. It was ghastly. In the center of the room, on the bare earth floor, stood a big, deep, brass basin, with a pale blue-green light floating in the center like a night-light. Round that basin the man on the floor wriggled himself three times. How he did it I do not know. I could see the muscles ripple along his spine and fall smooth again; but I could not see any other motion. The head seemed the only thing alive about him, except that slow curl and uncurl of the laboring back-muscles. Janoo from the bed was breathing seventy to the minute; Azizun held her hands before her eyes; and old Suddhoo, fingering at the dirt that had got into his white beard, was crying to himself. The horror of it was that the creeping, crawly thing made no sound—only crawled! And remember, this lasted for ten minutes, while the terrier whined, and Azizun shuddered, and Janoo gasped and Suddhoo cried.

I felt the hair lift at the back of my head, and my heart thump like a thermantidote paddle. Luckily, the seal-cutter betrayed himself by his most impressive trick and made me calm again. After he had finished that unspeakable triple crawl, he stretched his head away from the floor as high as he could, and sent out a jet of fire from his nostrils. Now I knew how fire-spouting is done—I can do it myself—so I felt at ease. The business was a fraud. If he had only kept to that crawl without trying to raise the effect, goodness knows what I might not have thought. Both the girls shrieked at the jet of fire and the head dropped, chin-down, on the floor with a thud; the whole body lying then like a corpse with its arms trussed. There was a pause of five full minutes after this, and the blue-green flame died down. Janoo stooped to settle one of her anklets, while Azizun turned her face to the wall and took the terrier in her arms. Suddhoo put out an arm mechanically to Janoo's *huqa,* and she slid it across the floor with her foot. Directly above the body and on the wall, were a couple of flaming portraits, in stamped paper frames, of the Queen and the Prince of Wales. They looked down on the performance, and, to my thinking, seemed to heighten the grotesqueness of it all.

Just when the silence was getting unendurable, the body turned over and rolled away from the basin to the side of the room, where it lay stomach-up. There was a faint "plop" from the basin—exactly like the noise a fish makes when it takes a fly—and the green light in the center revived.

I looked at the basin, and saw, bobbing in the water, the dried, shriveled, black head of a native baby—open eyes, open mouth and shaved scalp. It was worse, being so very sudden, than the crawling exhibition. We had no time to say anything before it began to speak.

Read Poe's account of the voice that came from the mesmerized dying man, and you will realize less than one-half of the horror of that head's voice.

There was an interval of a second or two between each word and a sort of "ring, ring, ring," in the note of the voice, like the timbre of a bell. It pealed slowly, as if talking to itself, for several minutes before I got rid of my cold sweat. Then the blessed solution struck me. I looked at the body lying near the doorway, and saw, just where the hollow of the throat joins on the shoulders, a muscle that had nothing to do with any man's regular breathing, twitching away steadily. The whole thing was a careful reproduction of the Egyptian teraphin that one reads about sometimes; and the voice was as clever and as appalling a piece of ventriloquism as one could wish to hear. All this time the head was "lip-lip-lapping" against the side of the basin, and speaking. It told Suddhoo, on his face again whining, of his son's illness and of the state of the illness up to the evening of that very night. I always shall respect the seal-cutter for keeping so faithfully to the time of the Peshawar telegrams. It went on to say that skilled doctors were night and day watching over the man's life; and that he would eventually recover if the fee to the potent sorcerer, whose servant was the head in the basin, were doubled.

Here the mistake from the artistic point of view came in. To ask for twice your stipulated fee in a voice that Lazarus might have used when he rose from the dead, is absurd. Janoo, who is really a woman of masculine intellect, saw this as quickly as I did. I heard her say *"Asli nahin! Fareib!"* scornfully under her breath; and just as she said so, the light in the basin died out, the head stopped talking, and we heard the room door creak on its hinges. Then Janoo struck a match, lit the lamp, and we saw that head, basin, and seal-cutter were gone. Suddhoo was wringing his hands and explaining to any one who cared to listen, that, if his chances of eternal salvation depended on it, he could not raise another two hundred rupees. Azizun was nearly in hysterics in the corner; while Janoo sat down composedly on one of the beds to discuss the probabilities of the whole thing being a *bunao,* or "make-up."

I explained as much as I knew of the seal-cutter's way of *jadoo;* but her argument was much more simple:—"The magic that is always demanding gifts is no true magic," said she. "My mother told me that the only potent love spells are those which are told you for love. This seal-cutter man is a liar and a devil. I dare not tell, do anything, or get anything done, because I am in debt to Bhagwan Dass the *bunnia* for two gold rings and a heavy anklet. I must get my food from his shop. The seal-cutter is the friend of Bhagwan Dass, and he would poison my food. A fool's *jadoo* has been going on for ten days, and has cost Suddhoo many rupees each night. The seal-cutter used black hens and lemons and *mantras* before. He never showed us anything like this till to-night. Azizun is a fool, and will be a *pur dahnashin* soon. Suddhoo has lost his strength and his wits. See now! I had hoped to get from Suddhoo many rupees while he lived, and many more after his death; and behold, he is spending everything on that offspring of a devil and a she-ass, the seal-cutter!"

Here I said:–"But what induced Suddhoo to drag me into the business? Of course I can speak to the seal-cutter, and he shall refund. The whole thing is child's talk–shame–and senseless."

"Suddhoo *is* an old child," said Janoo. "He has lived on the roofs these seventy years and is as senseless as a milch-goat. He brought you here to assure himself that he was not breaking any law of the *Sirkar,* whose salt he ate many years ago. He worships the dust off the feet of the seal-cutter, and that cow-devourer has forbidden him to go and see his son. What does Suddhoo know of your laws or the lightning-post? I have to watch his money going day by day to that lying beast below."

Janoo stamped her foot on the floor and nearly cried with vexation; while Suddhoo was whimpering under a blanket in the corner, and Azizun was trying to guide the pipe-stem to his foolish old mouth.

. . . . . .

Now the case stands thus. Unthinkingly, I have laid myself open to the charge of aiding and abetting the seal-cutter in obtaining money under false pretenses, which is forbidden by Section 420 of the Indian Penal Code. I am helpless in the matter for these reasons, I cannot inform the Police. What witnesses would support my statement? Janoo refuses flatly, and Azizun is a veiled woman somewhere near Bareilly–lost in this big India of ours. I care not again to take the law into my own hands, and speak to the seal-cutter; for certain am I that, not only would Suddhoo disbelieve me, but this step would end in the poisoning of Janoo, who is bound hand and foot by her debt to the *bunnia.* Suddhoo is an old dotard; and whenever we meet mumbles my idiotic joke that the *Sirkar* rather patronizes the Black Art than otherwise. His son is well now; but Suddhoo is completely under the influence of the seal-cutter, by whose advice he regulates the affairs of his life. Janoo watches daily the money that she hoped to wheedle out of Suddhoo taken by the seal-cutter, and becomes daily more furious and sullen.

She will never tell, because she dare not; but unless something happens to prevent her, I am afraid that the seal-cutter will die of cholera–the white arsenic kind–about the middle of May. And thus I shall have to be privy to a murder in the House of Suddhoo.

His Wedded Wife

Cry "Murder!" in the market-place, and each
Will turn upon his neighbor anxious eyes
That ask:—"Art thou the man?" We hunted Cain,
Some centuries ago, across the world,
That bred the fear our own misdeeds maintain
Today.

Vibart's Moralities.

SHAKESPEARE SAYS SOMETHING about worms, or it may be giants or beetles, turning if you tread on them too severely. The safest plan is never tread on a worm—not even on the last new subaltern from Home, with his buttons hardly out of their tissue paper, and the red of sappy English beef in his cheeks. This is the story of the worm that turned. For the sake of brevity, we will call Henry Augustus Ramsay Faizanne, "The Worm," although he really was an exceedingly pretty boy, without a hair on his face, and with a waist like a girl's when he came out to the Second "Shikarris" and was made unhappy in several ways. The "Shikarris" are a high-caste regiment, and you must be able to do things well—play a banjo or ride more than a little, or sing, or act—to get on with them.

The Worm did nothing except fall off his pony, and knock chips out of gate-posts with his trap. Even that became monotonous after a time. He objected to whist, cut the cloth at billiards, sang out of tune, kept very much to himself, and wrote to his Mamma and sisters at Home. Four of these five things were vices which the "Shikarris" objected to and set themselves to eradicate. Every one knows how subalterns are, by brother subalterns, softened and not permitted to be ferocious. It is good and wholesome, and does no one any harm, unless tempers are lost; and then there is trouble. There was a man once—but that is another story.

The "Shikarris" *shikarred* The Worm very much, and he bore everything without winking. He was so good and so anxious to learn, and flushed so pink, that his education was cut short, and he was left to his own devices by every one except the Senior Subaltern who continued to make life a burden to The Worm. The Senior Subaltern meant no harm; but his chaff was coarse, and he didn't quite understand where to stop. He had been waiting too long for his Company; and that always sours a man. Also he was in love, which made him worse.

One day, after he had borrowed The Worm's trap for a lady who never existed, had used it himself all the afternoon, had sent a note to The Worm, purporting to come from the lady, and was telling the Mess all about it, The Worm rose in his place and said, in his quiet ladylike voice:—"That was a very pretty sell; but I'll lay you a month's pay to a month's pay when you get your step, that I work a sell on you that you'll remember for the rest of your days, and the Regiment after you when you're dead or broke." The Worm wasn't angry in the least, and the rest of the Mess shouted. Then the Senior Subaltern looked at The Worm from the boots upwards, and down again and said, "Done, Baby." The Worm took the rest of the Mess to witness that the bet had been taken, and retired into a book with a sweet smile.

Two months passed, and the Senior Subaltern still educated The Worm, who began to move about a little more as the hot weather came on. I have said that the Senior Subaltern was in love. The curious thing is that a girl was in love with the Senior Subaltern. Though the Colonel said awful things, and the Majors snorted, and married Captains looked unutterable wisdom, and the juniors scoffed, those two were engaged.

The Senior Subaltern was so pleased with getting his Company and his acceptance at the same time that he forgot to bother The Worm. The girl was a pretty girl, and had money of her own. She does not come into this story at all.

One night, at beginning of the hot weather, all the Mess, except The Worm, who had gone to his own room to write Home letters, were sitting on the platform outside the Mess House. The Band had finished playing, but no one wanted to go in. And the Captains' wives were there also. The folly of a man in love is unlimited. The Senior Subaltern had been holding forth on the merits of the girl he was engaged to, and the ladies were purring approval, while the men yawned, when there was a rustle of skirts in the dark, and a tired, faint voice lifted itself:

"Where's my husband?"

I do not wish in the least to reflect on the morality of the "Shikarris;" but it is on record that four men jumped up as if they had been shot. Three of them were married men. Perhaps they were afraid that their wives had come from Home unbeknownst. The fourth said that he had acted on the impulse of the moment. He explained this afterwards.

Then the voice cried:–"Oh, Lionel!" Lionel was the Senior Subaltern's name. A woman came into the little circle of light by the candles on the peg-tables, stretching out her hands to the dark where the Senior Subaltern was, and sobbing. We rose to our feet, feeling that things were going to happen and ready to believe the worst. In this bad, small world of ours, one knows so little of the life of the next man–which, after all, is entirely his own concern–that one is not surprised when a crash comes. Anything might turn up any day for any one. Perhaps the Senior Subaltern had been trapped in his youth. Men are crippled that way occasionally. We didn't know; we wanted to hear; and the Captains' wives were as anxious as we. If he *had* been trapped, he was to be excused; for the woman from nowhere, in the dusty shoes, and gray traveling dress, was very lovely, with black hair and great eyes full of tears. She was tall, with a fine figure, and her voice had a running sob in it pitiful to hear. As soon as the Senior Subaltern stood up, she threw her arms round his neck, and called him "my darling," and said she could not bear waiting alone in England, and his letters were so short and cold, and she was his to the end of the world, and would he forgive her? This did not sound quite like a lady's way of speaking. It was too demonstrative.

Things seemed black indeed, and the Captains' wives peered under their eyebrows at the Senior Subaltern, and the Colonel's face set like the Day of Judgment framed in gray bristles, and no one spoke for a while.

Next the Colonel said, very shortly:–"Well, sir?" and the woman sobbed afresh. The Senior Subaltern was half choked with the arms round his neck, but he gasped out:–"It's a d–d lie! I never had a wife in my life!" "Don't swear," said the Colonel. "Come into the Mess. We must sift this clear somehow," and he sighed to himself, for he believed in his "Shikarris," did the Colonel.

We trooped into the anteroom, under the full lights, and there we saw how beautiful the woman was. She stood up in the middle of us all, sometimes choking with crying, then hard and proud, and then holding out her arms to the Senior Subaltern. It was like the fourth act of a tragedy. She told us how the Senior Subaltern had married her when he was Home on leave eighteen months before; and she seemed to know all that we knew, and more too, of his people and his past life. He was white and ashy gray, trying now and again to break into the torrent of her words; and we, noting how lovely she was and what a criminal he looked, esteemed him a beast of the worst kind.

We felt sorry for him though.

I shall never forget the indictment of the Senior Subaltern by his wife. Nor will he. It was so sudden, rushing out of the dark, unannounced, into our dull lives. The Captains' wives stood back; but their eyes were alight, and you could see that they had already convicted and sentenced the Senior Subaltern. The Colonel seemed five years older.

One Major was shading his eyes with his hand and watching the woman from underneath it. Another was chewing his mustache and smiling quietly as if he were witnessing a play. Full in the open space in the center, by the whist-tables, the Senior Subaltern's terrier was hunting for fleas. I remember all this as clearly as though a photograph were in my hand. I remember the look of horror on the Senior Subaltern's face. It was rather like seeing a man hanged; but much more interesting. Finally, the woman wound up by saying that the Senior Subaltern carried a double F.M. in tattoo on his left shoulder. We all knew that, and to our innocent minds it seemed to clinch the matter. But one of the Bachelor Majors said very politely:–"I presume that your marriage certificate would be more to the purpose?"

That roused the woman. She stood up and sneered at the Senior Subaltern for a cur, and abused the Major and the Colonel and all the rest. Then she wept, and then she pulled a paper from her breast, saying imperially:–"Take that! And let my husband–my lawfully wedded husband–read it aloud–if he dare!"

There was a hush, and the men looked into each other's eyes as the Senior Subaltern came forward in a dazed and dizzy way, and took the paper. We were wondering as we stared, whether there was anything against any one of us that might turn up later on. The Senior Subaltern's throat was dry; but, as he ran his eye over the paper, he broke out into a hoarse cackle of relief, and said to the woman:–"You young blackguard!"

But the woman had fled through the door, and on the paper was written:– "This is to certify that I, The Worm, have paid in full my debts to the Senior Subaltern, and, further, that the Senior Subaltern is my debtor, by agreement on the 23d of February, as by the Mess attested, to the extent of one month's Captain's pay, in the lawful currency of the India Empire."

Then a deputation set off for The Worm's quarters and found him, betwixt and between, unlacing his stays, with the hat, wig, serge dress, etc., on the bed. He came over as he was, and the "Shikarris" shouted till the Gunners' Mess sent over to know if they might have a share of the fun. I think we were all, except the Colonel and the Senior Subaltern, a little disappointed that the scandal had come to nothing. But that is human nature. There could be no two words about The Worm's acting. It leaned as near to a nasty tragedy as anything this side of a joke can. When most of the Subalterns sat upon him with sofa-cushions to find out why he had not said that acting was his strong point, he answered very quietly:"I don't think you ever asked me. I used to act at Home with my sisters." But no acting with girls could account for The Worm's display that night. Personally I think it was in bad taste. Besides being dangerous. There is no sort of use playing with fire, even for fun.

The "Shikarris" made him President of the Regimental Dramatic Club; and, when the Senior Subaltern paid up his debt, which he did at once, The Worm sank the money in scenery and dresses. He was a good Worm; and the "Shikarris" are proud of him. The only drawback is that he has been christened "Mrs. Senior Subaltern;" and as there are now two Mrs. Senior Subalterns in the Station, this is sometimes confusing to strangers.

Later on, I will tell you of a case something like this, but with all the jest left out and nothing in it but real trouble.

The Broken-Link Handicap

While the snaffle holds, or the "long-neck" stings,
While the big beam tilts, or the last bell rings,
While horses are horses to train and to race,
Then women and wine take a second place
    For me—for me—
    While a short "ten-three"
Has a field to squander or fence to face!

Song of the G.R.

THERE ARE MORE ways of running a horse to suit your book than pulling his head off in the straight. Some men forget this. Understand clearly that all racing is rotten—as everything connected with losing money must be. Out here, in addition to its inherent rottenness, it has the merit of being two-thirds sham; looking pretty on paper only. Every one knows every one else far too well for business purposes. How on earth can you rack and harry and post a man for his losing, when you are fond of his wife, and live in the same Station with him? He says, "on the Monday following," "I can't settle just yet." You say, "All right, old man, and think yourself lucky if you pull off nine hundred out of a two-thousand-rupee debt. Any way you look at it, Indian racing is immoral, and expensively immoral. Which is much worse. If a man wants your money, he ought to ask for it, or send round a subscription-list, instead of juggling about the country, with an Australian larrikin; a "brumby," with as much breed as the boy; a brace of *chumars* in gold-laced caps; three or four *ekka*-ponies with hogged manes, and a switch-tailed demirep of a mare called Arab because she has a kink in her flag. Racing leads to the *shroff* quicker than anything else. But if you have no conscience and no sentiments, and good hands, and some knowledge of pace, and ten years' experience of horses, and several thousand rupees a month, I believe that you can occasionally contrive to pay your shoeing-bills.

Did you ever know Shackles—b. w.g., 15. 13-8—coarse, loose, mule-like ears—barrel as long as a gate-post—tough as a telegraph-wire—and the queerest brute that ever looked through a bridle? He was of no brand, being one of an ear-nicked mob taken into the *Buchephalus* at £4–10s. a head to make up freight, and sold raw and out of condition at Calcutta for Rs. 275. People who lost money on him called him a "brumby;" but if ever any horse had Harpoon's shoulders and The Gin's temper, Shackles was that horse. Two miles was his own particular distance. He trained himself, ran himself, rode himself; and, if his jockey insulted him by giving him hints, he shut up at once and bucked the boy off. He objected to dictation. Two or three of his owners did not understand this, and lost money in consequence. At last he was bought by a man who discovered that, if a race was to be won, Shackles, and Shackles only, would win it in his own way, so long as his jockey sat still. This man had a riding-boy called Brunt—a lad from Perth, West Australia—and he taught Brunt, with a trainer's whip, the hardest thing a jock can learn—to sit still, and to keep on sitting still. When Brunt fairly grasped this truth, Shackles devastated the country. No weight could stop him at his own distance; and the fame of Shackles spread from Ajmir in the South, to

Chedputter in the North. There was no horse like Shackles, so long as he was allowed to do his work in his own way. But he was beaten in the end; and the story of his fall is enough to make angels weep.

At the lower end of the Chedputter race-course, just before the turn into the straight, the track passes close to a couple of old brick-mounds enclosing a funnel-shaped hollow. The big end of the funnel is not six feet from the railings on the offside. The astounding peculiarity of the course is that, if you stand at one particular place, about half a mile away, inside the course, and speak at ordinary pitch, your voice just hits the funnel of the brick mounds and makes a curious whining echo there. A man discovered this one morning by accident while out training with a friend. He marked the place to stand and speak from with a couple of bricks, and he kept his knowledge to himself. *Every* peculiarity of a course is worth remembering in a country where rats play the mischief with the elephant-litter, and Stewards build jumps to suit their own stables. This man ran a very fairish country-bred, a long, racking high mare with the temper of a fiend, and the paces of an airy wandering seraph—a drifty, glidy stretch. The mare was, as a delicate tribute to Mrs. Reiver, called "The Lady Regula Baddun"—or for short, Regula Baddun.

Shackles' jockey, Brunt, was a quiet well-behaved boy, but his nerves had been shaken. He began his career by riding jump-races in Melbourne, where a few Stewards want lynching, and was one of the jockeys who came through the awful butchery—perhaps you will recollect it—of the Maribyrnong Plate. The walls were colonial ramparts—logs of *jarrah* spiked into masonry—with wings as strong as Church buttresses. Once in his stride, a horse had to jump or fall. He couldn't run out. In the Maribyrnong Plate, twelve horses were jammed at the second wall. Red Hat, leading, fell this side, and threw out The Glen, and the ruck came up behind and the space between wing and wing was one struggling, screaming, kicking shambles. Four jockeys were taken out dead; three were very badly hurt, and Brunt was among the three. He told the story of the Maribyrnong Plate sometimes; and when he described how Whalley on Red Hat, said, as the mare fell under him:—"God ha' mercy, I'm done for!" and how, next instant, Sithee There and White Otter had crushed the life out of poor Whalley, and the dust hid a small hell of men and horses, no one marveled that Brunt had dropped jump-races and Australia together. Regula Baddun's owner knew that story by heart. Brunt never varied it in the telling. He had no education.

Shackles came to the Chedputter Autumn races one year, and his owner walked about insulting the sportsmen of Chedputter generally, till they went to the Honorary Secretary in a body and said:—"Appoint Handicappers, and arrange a race which shall break Shackles and humble the pride of his owner." The Districts rose against Shackles and sent up of their best; Ousel who was supposed to be able to do his mile in 1-53; Petard, the stud-bred, trained by a cavalry regiment who knew how to train; Gringalet, the ewe-lamb of the 75th; Bobolink, the pride of Peshawar; and many others.

They called that race The Broken-Link Handicap, because it was to smash Shackles; and the Handicappers piled on the weights, and the Fund gave eight hundred rupees, and the distance was "round the course for all horses." Shackles' owner said:—"You can arrange the race with regard to Shackles only. So long as you don't bury him under weightcloths, I don't mind." Regula Baddun's owner said:—"I throw in my mare to fret Ousel. Six furlongs is Regula's distance, and she will then lie down and die. So also will Ousel, for his jockey doesn't understand a waiting race." Now, this was a lie, for Regula had been in work for two months at Dehra, and her chances were good, always supposing that Shackles broke a blood-vessel—*or Brunt moved on him.*

The plunging in the lotteries was fine. They filled eight thousand-rupee lotteries on the Broken-Link Handicap, and the account in the *Pioneer* said that "favoritism was divided." In plain English, the various contingents were wild on their respective horses; for the Handicappers had done their work well. The Honorary Secretary shouted himself hoarse through the din; and the smoke of the cheroots was like the smoke, and the rattling of the dice-box like the rattle of small-arm fire.

Ten horses started—very level—and Regula Baddun's owner cantered out on his hack to a place inside the circle of the course, where two bricks had been thrown. He faced towards the brick-mounds at the lower end of the course and waited.

The story of the running is in the *Pioneer*. At the end of the first mile, Shackles crept out of the ruck, well on the outside, ready to get round the turn, lay hold of the bit and spin up the straight before the others knew he had got away. Brunt was sitting still, perfectly happy, listening to the *"drum, drum, drum"* of the hoofs behind, and knowing that, in about twenty strides, Shackles would draw one deep breath and go up the last half-mile like the "Flying Dutchman." As Shackles went short to take the turn and came abreast of the brick-mound, Brunt heard, above the noise of the wind in his ears, a whining, wailing voice on the offside, saying:—"God ha' mercy, I'm done for!" In one stride, Brunt saw the whole seething smash of the Maribyrnong Plate before him, started in his saddle and gave a yell of terror. The start brought the heels into Shackles' side, and the scream hurt Shackles' feelings. He couldn't stop dead; but he put out his feet and slid along for fifty yards, and then, very gravely and judicially, bucked off Brunt—a shaking, terror-stricken lump, while Regula Baddun made a neck-and-neck race with Bobolink up the straight, and won by a short head—Petard a bad third. Shackles' owner, in the Stand, tried to think that his field-glasses had gone wrong. Regula Baddun's owner, waiting by the two bricks, gave one deep sigh of relief, and cantered back to the stand. He had won, in lotteries and bets, about fifteen thousand.

It was a broken-link Handicap with a vengeance. It broke nearly all the men concerned, and nearly broke the heart of Shackles' owner. He went down to interview Brunt. The boy lay, livid and gasping with fright, where he had tumbled off. The sin of losing the race never seemed to strike him. All he knew was that Whalley had "called" him, that the "call" was a warning; and, were he cut in two for it, he would never get up again. His nerve had gone altogether, and he only asked his master to give him a good thrashing, and let him go. He was fit for nothing, he said. He got his dismissal, and crept up to the paddock, white as chalk, with blue lips, his knees giving way under him. People said nasty things in the paddock; but Brunt never heeded. He changed into tweeds, took his stick and went down the road, still shaking with fright, and muttering over and over again:—"God ha' mercy, I'm done for!" To the best of my knowledge and belief he spoke the truth.

So now you know how the Broken-link Handicap was run and won. Of course you don't believe it. You would credit anything about Russia's designs on India, or the recommendations of the Currency Commission; but a little bit of sober fact is more than you can stand!

Beyond the Pale

"Love heeds not caste nor sleep a broken bed. I went in search of love and lost myself."
Hindu Proverb.

A MAN SHOULD, whatever happens, keep to his own caste, race and breed. Let the White go to the White and the Black to the Black. Then, whatever trouble falls is in the ordinary course of things–neither sudden, alien nor unexpected.

This is the story of a man who wilfully stepped beyond the safe limits of decent every-day society, and paid for it heavily.

He knew too much in the first instance; and he saw too much in the second. He took too deep an interest in native life; but he will never do so again.

Deep away in the heart of the City, behind Jitha Megji's *bustee,* lies Amir Nath's Gully, which ends in a dead-wall pierced by one grated window. At the head of the Gully is a big cowbyre, and the walls on either side of the Gully are without windows. Neither Suchet Singh nor Gaur Chand approve of their women-folk looking into the world. If Durga Charan had been of their opinion, he would have been a happier man to-day, and little Bisesa would have been able to knead her own bread. Her room looked out through the grated window into the narrow dark Gully where the sun never came and where the buffaloes wallowed in the blue slime. She was a widow, about fifteen years old, and she prayed the Gods, day and night, to send her a lover; for she did not approve of living alone.

One day, the man–Trejago his name was–came into Amir Nath's Gully on an aimless wandering; and, after he had passed the buffaloes, stumbled over a big heap of cattle-food.

Then he saw that the Gully ended in a trap, and heard a little laugh from behind the grated window. It was a pretty little laugh, and Trejago, knowing that, for all practical purposes, the old *Arabian Nights* are good guides, went forward to the window, and whispered that verse of "The Love Song of Har Dyal" which begins:

Can a man stand upright in the face of the naked Sun; or a Lover in the Presence of his Beloved?
If my feet fail me, O Heart of my Heart, am I to blame, being blinded by the glimpse of your beauty?

There came the faint *tchinks* of a woman's bracelets from behind the grating, and a little voice went on with the song at the fifth verse:

Alas! alas! Can the Moon tell the Lotus of her love when the Gate of Heaven is shut and the clouds gather for the rains?
They have taken my Beloved, and driven her with the pack-horses to the North.
There are iron chains on the feet that were set on my heart.
Call to the bowman to make ready——

The voice stopped suddenly, and Trejago walked out of Amir Nath's Gully, wondering who in the world could have capped "The Love Song of Har Dyal" so neatly.

Next morning as he was driving to office, an old woman threw a packet into his dog-cart. In the packet was the half of a broken glass bangle, one flower of the blood-red *dhak,* a pinch of *bhusa* or cattle-food, and eleven cardamoms. That packet was a letter–not a clumsy compromising letter, but an innocent unintelligible lover's epistle.

Trejago knew far too much about these things, as I have said. No Englishman should be able to translate object-letters. But Trejago spread all the trifles on the lid of his office-box and began to puzzle them out.

A broken glass-bangle stands for a Hindu widow all India over; because, when her husband dies, a woman's bracelets are broken on her wrists. Trejago saw the meaning of the little bit of the glass. The flower of the *dhak* means diversely "desire," "come," "write," or "danger," according to the other things with it. One cardamom means "jealousy;" but when any article is duplicated in an object-letter, it loses its symbolic meaning and stands merely for one of a number indicating time, or, if incense, curds, or saffron be sent also, place. The message ran then:–"A widow–*dhak* flower and *bhusa*–at eleven o'clock." The pinch of *bhusa* enlightened Trejago. He saw–this kind of letter leaves much to instinctive knowledge–that the *bhusa* referred to the big heap of cattle-food over which he had fallen in Amir Nath's Gully, and that the message must come from the person behind the grating; she being a widow. So the message ran then:–"A widow, in the Gully in which is the heap of *bhusa,* desires you to come at eleven o'clock."

Trejago threw all the rubbish into the fireplace and laughed. He knew that men in the East do not make love under windows at eleven in the forenoon, nor do women fix appointments a week in advance. So he went, that very night at eleven, into Amir Nath's Gully, clad in a *boorka,* which cloaks a man as well as a woman. Directly the gongs in the City made the hour, the little voice behind the grating took up "The Love Song of Har Dyal" at the verse where the Panthan girl calls upon Har Dyal to return. The song is really pretty in the Vernacular. In English you miss the wail of it. It runs something like this:–

Alone upon the housetops, to the North
  I turn and watch the lightning in the sky,–
The glamour of thy footsteps in the North,
  Come back to me, Beloved, or I die!

Below my feet the still bazar is laid
  Far, far below the weary camels lie,–
The camels and the captives of thy raid,
  Come back to me, Beloved, or I die!

My father's wife is old and harsh with years,
  And drudge of all my father's house am I.–
My bread is sorrow and my drink is tears,
  Come back to me, Beloved, or I die!

As the song stopped, Trejago stepped up under the grating and whispered:–"I am here."

Bisesa was good to look upon.

That night was the beginning of many strange things, and of a double life so wild that Trejago to-day sometimes wonders if it were not all a dream. Bisesa or her old handmaiden who had thrown the object-letter had detached the heavy grating from the brick-work of the wall; so that the window slid inside, leaving only a square of raw masonry into which an active man might climb.

In the daytime, Trejago drove through his routine of office-work, or put on his calling-clothes and called on the ladies of the Station; wondering how long they would know him if they knew of poor little Bisesa. At night, when all the City was still, came the walk under the evil-smelling *boorka,* the patrol through Jitha Megji's *bustee,* the quick turn into Amir Nath's Gully between the sleeping cattle and the dead walls, and then, last of all, Bisesa, and the deep, even breathing of the old woman who slept outside the door of the bare little room that Durga Charan allotted to his sister's daughter. Who or what Durga Charan was, Trejago never inquired; and why in the world he was not discovered and knifed never occurred to him till his madness was over, and Bisesa. . . . But this comes later.

Bisesa was an endless delight to Trejago. She was as ignorant as a bird; and her distorted versions of the rumors from the outside world that had reached her in her room, amused Trejago almost as much as her lisping attempts to pronounce his name–"Christopher." The first syllable was always more than she could manage, and she made funny little gestures with her roseleaf hands, as one throwing the name away, and then, kneeling before Trejago asked him, exactly as an Englishwoman would do, if he were sure he loved her. Trejago swore that he loved her more than any one else in the world. Which was true.

After a month of this folly, the exigencies of his other life compelled Trejago to be especially attentive to a lady of his acquaintance. You may take it for a fact that anything of this kind is not only noticed and discussed by a man's own race but by some hundred and fifty natives as well. Trejago had to walk with this lady and talk to her at the Band-stand, and once or twice to drive with her; never for an instant dreaming that this would affect his dearer out-of-the-way life. But the news flew, in the usual mysterious fashion, from mouth to mouth, till Bisesa's duenna heard of it and told Bisesa. The child was so troubled that she did the household work evilly, and was beaten by Durga Charan's wife in consequence.

A week later, Bisesa taxed Trejago with the flirtation. She understood no gradations and spoke openly. Trejago laughed and Bisesa stamped her little feet–little feet, light as marigold flowers, that could lie in the palm of a man's one hand.

Much that is written about "Oriental passion and impulsiveness" is exaggerated and compiled at second-hand, but a little of it is true; and when an Englishman finds that little, it is quite as startling as any passion in his own proper life. Bisesa raged and stormed, and finally threatened to kill herself if Trejago did not at once drop the alien *Memsahib* who had come between them. Trejago tried to explain, and to show her that she did not understand these things from a Western standpoint. Bisesa drew herself up, and said simply:

"I do not. I know only this–it is not good that I should have made you dearer than my own heart to me, *Sahib.* You are an Englishman. I am only a black girl–" she was fairer than bar-gold in the Mint,–"and the widow of a black man."

Then she sobbed and said: "But on my soul and my Mother's soul, I love you. There shall no harm come to you, whatever happens to me."

Trejago argued with the child, and tried to soothe her, but she seemed quite unreasonably disturbed. Nothing would satisfy her save that all relations between them should end. He was to go away at once. And he went. As he dropped out at the window, she kissed his forehead twice, and he walked home wondering.

A week, and then three weeks, passed without a sign from Bisesa. Trejago, thinking that the rupture had lasted quite long enough, went down to Amir Nath's Gully for the fifth time in the three weeks, hoping that his rap at the sill of the shifting grating would be answered. He was not disappointed.

There was a young moon, and one stream of light fell down into Amir Nath's Gully, and struck the grating which was drawn away as he knocked.

From the black dark, Bisesa held out her arms into the moonlight. Both hands had been cut off at the wrists, and the stumps were nearly healed.

Then, as Bisesa bowed her head between her arms and sobbed, some one in the room grunted like a wild beast, and something sharp–knife, sword or spear,–thrust at Trejago in his *boorka.* The stroke missed his body, but cut into one of the muscles of the groin, and he limped slightly from the wound for the rest of his days.

The grating went into its place. There was no sign whatever from inside the house,–nothing but the moonlight strip on the high wall, and the blackness of Amir Nath's Gully behind.

The next thing Trejago remembers, after raging and shouting like a madman between those pitiless walls, is that he found himself near the river as the dawn was breaking, threw away his *boorka* and went home bareheaded.

. . . .

What the tragedy was–whether Bisesa had in a fit of causeless despair told everything, or the intrigue had been discovered and she tortured to tell; whether Durga Charan knew his name and what became of Bisesa–Trejago does not know to this day. Something horrible had happened, and the thought of what it must have been comes upon Trejago in the night now and again, and keeps him company till the morning. One special feature of the case is that he does not know where lies the front of Durga Charan's house. It may open on to a courtyard common to two or more houses, or it may lie behind any one of the gates of Jitha Megji's *bustee.* Trejago cannot tell. He cannot get Bisesa–poor little Bisesa–back again. He has lost her in the City where each man's house is as guarded and as unknowable as the grave; and the grating that opens into Amir Nath's Gully has been walled up.

But Trejago pays his calls regularly, and is reckoned a very decent sort of man.

There is nothing peculiar about him, except a slight stiffness, caused by a riding-strain, in the right leg.

In Error

They burnt a corpse upon the sand
The light shone out afar;
It guided home the plunging boats
That beat from Zanzibar.
Spirit of Fire, where'er Thy altars rise,
Thou art Light of Guidance to our eyes!
Salsette Boat-Song.

THERE IS HOPE for a man who gets publicly and riotously drunk more often than he ought to do; but there is no hope for the man who drinks secretly and alone in his own house–the man who is never seen to drink.

This is a rule; so there must be an exception to prove it. Moriarty's case was that exception.

He was a Civil Engineer, and the Government, very kindly, put him quite by himself in an out-district, with nobody but natives to talk to and a great deal of work to do. He did his work well in the four years he was utterly alone; but he picked up the vice of secret and solitary drinking, and came up out of the wilderness more old and worn and haggard than the dead-alive life had any right to make him. You know the saying that a man who has been alone in the jungle for more than a year is never quite sane all his life after. People credited Moriarty's queerness of manner and moody ways to the solitude, and said that it showed how Government spoilt the futures of its best men. Moriarty had built himself the plinth of a very good reputation in the bridge-dam-girder line. But he knew, every night of the week, that he was taking steps to undermine that reputation with L. L. L. and "Christopher" and little nips of liqueurs, and filth of that kind. He had a sound constitution and a great brain, or else he would have broken down and died like a sick camel in the district, as better men have done before him.

Government ordered him to Simla after he had come out of the desert; and he went up meaning to try for a post then vacant. That season, Mrs. Reiver—perhaps you will remember her—was in the height of her power, and many men lay under her yoke. Everything bad that could be said has already been said about Mrs. Reiver, in another tale. Moriarty was heavily-built and handsome, very quiet and nervously anxious to please his neighbors when he wasn't sunk in a brown study. He started a good deal at sudden noises or if spoken to without warning; and, when you watched him drinking his glass of water at dinner, you could see the hand shake a little. But all this was put down to nervousness, and the quiet, steady, "sip-sip-sip, fill and sip-sip-sip, again," that went on in his own room when he was by himself, was never known. Which was miraculous, seeing how everything in a man's private life is public property out here.

Moriarty was drawn, not into Mrs. Reiver's set, because they were not his sort, but into the power of Mrs. Reiver, and he fell down in front of her and made a goddess of her. This was due to his coming fresh out of the jungle to a big town. He could not scale things properly or see who was what.

Because Mrs. Reiver was cold and hard, he said she was stately and dignified. Because she had no brains, and could not talk cleverly, he said she was reserved and shy. Mrs. Reiver shy! Because she was unworthy of honor or reverence from any one, he reverenced her from a distance and dowered her with all the virtues in the Bible and most of those in Shakespeare.

The big, dark, abstracted man who was so nervous when a pony cantered behind him, used to moon in the train of Mrs. Reiver, blushing with pleasure when she threw a word or two his way. His admiration was strictly platonic: even other women saw and admitted this. He did not move out in Simla, so he heard nothing against his idol: which was satisfactory. Mrs. Reiver took no special notice of him, beyond seeing that he was added to her list of admirers, and going for a walk with him now and then, just to show that he was her property, claimable as such. Moriarty must have done most of the talking, for Mrs. Reiver couldn't talk much to a man of his stamp; and the little she said could not have been profitable. What Moriarty believed in, as he had good reason to, was Mrs. Reiver's influence over him, and, in that belief, set himself seriously to try to do away with the vice that only he himself knew of.

His experiences while he was fighting with it must have been peculiar, but he never described them. Sometimes he would hold off from everything except water for a week. Then, on a rainy night, when no one had asked him out to dinner, and there was a big fire in his room, and everything comfortable, he would sit down and make a big night of it by adding little nip to little nip, planning big schemes of reformation meanwhile, until he threw himself on his bed hopelessly drunk. He suffered next morning.

One night, the big crash came. He was troubled in his own mind over his attempts to make himself "worthy of the friendship" of Mrs. Reiver. The past ten days had been very bad ones, and the end of it all was that he received the arrears of two and three quarter years of sipping in one attack of *delirium tremens* of the subdued kind; beginning with suicidal depression, going on to fits and starts and hysteria, and ending with downright raving. As he sat in a chair in front of the fire, or walked up and down the room picking a handkerchief to pieces, you heard what poor Moriarty really thought of Mrs. Reiver, for he raved about her and his own fall for the most part; though he raveled some P. W. D. accounts into the same skein of thought. He talked and talked, and talked in a low dry whisper to himself, and there was no stopping him. He seemed to know that there was something wrong, and twice tried to pull himself together and confer rationally with the Doctor; but his mind ran out of control at once, and he fell back to a whisper and the story of his troubles. It is terrible to hear a big man babbling like a child of all that a man usually locks up, and puts away in the deep of his heart. Moriarty read out his very soul for the benefit of any one who was in the room between ten-thirty that night and two-forty-five next morning.

From what he said, one gathered how immense an influence Mrs. Reiver held over him, and how thoroughly he felt for his own lapse. His whispering cannot, of course, be put down here; but they were very instructive as showing the errors of his estimates.

. . . .

When the trouble was over, and his few acquaintances were pitying him for the bad attack of jungle-fever that had so pulled him down, Moriarty swore a big oath to himself and went abroad again with Mrs. Reiver till the end of the season, adoring her in a quiet and deferential way as an angel from heaven. Later on he took to riding–not hacking but honest riding–which was good proof that he was improving, and you could slam doors behind him without his jumping to his feet with a gasp. That, again, was hopeful.

How he kept his oath, and what it cost him in the beginning nobody knows. He certainly managed to compass the hardest thing that a man who has drank heavily can do. He took his peg and wine at dinner but he never drank alone, and never let what he drank have the least hold on him.

Once he told a bosom-friend the story of his great trouble, and how the "influence of a pure honest woman, and an angel as well" had saved him. When the man–startled at anything good being laid to Mrs. Reiver's door–laughed, it cost him Moriarty's friendship. Moriarty, who is married now to a woman ten thousand times better than Mrs. Reiver–a woman who believes that there is no man on earth as good and clever as her husband–will go down to his grave vowing and protesting that Mrs. Reiver saved him from ruin in both worlds.

That she knew anything of Moriarty's weakness nobody believed for a moment. That she would have cut him dead, thrown him over, and acquainted all her friends with her discovery, if she had known of it, nobody who knew her doubted for an instant.

Moriarty thought her something she never was, and in that belief saved himself. Which was just as good as though she had been everything that he had imagined.

But the question is, what claim will Mrs. Reiver have to the credit of Moriarty's salvation, when her day of reckoning comes?

A Bank Fraud

He drank strong waters and his speech was coarse;
He purchased raiment and forebore to pay;
He struck a trusting junior with a horse,
And won Gymkhanas in a doubtful way..
Then, 'twixt a vice and folly, turned aside
To do good deeds and straight to cloak them, lied.
The Mess Room.

IF REGGIE BURKE were in India now, he would resent this tale being told; but as he is in Hongkong and won't see it, the telling is safe. He was the man who worked the big fraud on the Sind and Sialkote Bank. He was manager of an up-country Branch, and a sound practical man with a large experience of native loan and insurance work. He could combine the frivolities of ordinary life with his work, and yet do well. Reggie Burke rode anything that would let him get up, danced as neatly as he rode, and was wanted for every sort of amusement in the Station.

As he said himself, and as many men found out rather to their surprise, there were two Burkes, both very much at your service. "Reggie Burke," between four and ten, ready for anything from a hot-weather gymkhana to a riding-picnic; and, between ten and four, "Mr. Reginald Burke, Manager of the Sind and Sialkote Branch Bank." You might play polo with him one afternoon and hear him express his opinions when a man crossed; and you might call on him next morning to raise a two-thousand-rupee loan on a five hundred-pound insurance policy, eighty pounds paid in premiums. He would recognize you, but you would have some trouble in recognizing him.

The Directors of the Bank–it had its headquarters in Calcutta and its General Manager's word carried weight with the Government–picked their men well. They had tested Reggie up to a fairly severe breaking-strain. They trusted him just as much as Directors ever trust Managers. You must see for yourself whether their trust was misplaced.

Reggie's Branch was in a big Station, and worked with the usual staff–one Manager, one Accountant, both English, a Cashier, and a horde of native clerks; besides the Police patrol at nights outside. The bulk of its work, for it was in a thriving district, was *hoondi* and accommodation of all kinds. A fool has no grip of this sort of business; and a clever man who does not go about among his clients, and know more than a little of their affairs, is worse than a fool. Reggie was young-looking, clean-shaved, with a twinkle in his eye, and a head that nothing short of a gallon of the Gunners' Madeira could make any impression on.

One day, at a big dinner, he announced casually that the Directors had shifted on to him a Natural Curiosity, from England, in the Accountant line. He was perfectly correct. Mr. Silas Riley, Accountant, was a *most* curious animal–a long, gawky, rawboned Yorkshireman, full of the savage self-conceit that blossoms only in the best county in England. Arrogance was a mild word for the mental attitude of Mr. S. Riley. He had worked himself up, after seven years, to a Cashier's position in a Huddersfield Bank; and all his experience lay among the factories of the North. Perhaps he would have done better on the Bombay side, where they are happy with one-half per cent profits, and money is cheap. He was useless for Upper India and a wheat

Province, where a man wants a large head and a touch of imagination if he is to turn out a satisfactory balance-sheet.

He was wonderfully narrow-minded on business, and, being new to the country, had no notion that Indian banking is totally distinct from Home work. Like most clever self-made men, he had much simplicity in his nature; and, somehow or other, had construed the ordinarily polite terms of his letter of engagement into a belief that the Directors had chosen him on account of his special and brilliant talents, and that they set great store by him. This notion grew and crystallized; thus adding to his natural North-country conceit. Further, he was delicate, suffered from some trouble in his chest, and was short in his temper.

You will admit that Reggie had reason to call his new Accountant a Natural Curiosity. The two men failed to hit it off at all. Riley considered Reggie a wild, feather-headed idiot, given to Heaven only knew what dissipation in low places called "Messes," and totally unfit for the serious and solemn vocation of banking. He could never get over Reggie's look of youth and "you-be-damned" air; and he couldn't understand Reggie's friends—clean-built, careless men in the Army—who rode over to big Sunday breakfasts at the Bank, and told sultry stories till Riley got up and left the room. Riley was always showing Reggie how the business ought to be conducted, and Reggie had more than once to remind him that seven years' limited experience between Huddersfield and Beverly did not qualify a man to steer a big up-country business. Then Riley sulked and referred to himself as a pillar of the Bank and a cherished friend of the Directors, and Reggie tore his hair. If a man's English subordinates fail him in this country, he comes to a hard time indeed, for native help has strict limitations. In the winter Riley went sick for weeks at a time with his lung complaint, and this threw more work on Reggie. But he preferred it to the everlasting friction when Riley was well.

One of the Traveling Inspectors of the Bank discovered these collapses and reported them to the Directors. Now Riley had been foisted on the Bank by an M. P. who wanted the support of Riley's father, who, again, was anxious to get his son out to a warmer climate because of those lungs. The M. P. had interest in the Bank; but one of the Directors wanted to advance a nominee of his own; and, after Riley's father had died, he made the rest of the Board see that an Accountant who was sick for half the year, had better give place to a healthy man. If Riley had known the real story of his appointment, he might have behaved better; but knowing nothing, his stretches of sickness alternated with restless, persistent, meddling irritation of Reggie, and all the hundred ways in which conceit in a subordinate situation can find play. Reggie used to call him striking and hair-curling names behind his back as a relief to his own feelings; but he never abused him to his face, because he said:—"Riley is such a frail beast that half of his loathsome conceit is due to pains in the chest."

Late one April, Riley went very sick indeed. The doctor punched him and thumped him, and told him he would be better before long. Then the doctor went to Reggie and said:—"Do you know how sick your Accountant is?" "No!" said Reggie—"The worse the better, confound him! He's a clacking nuisance when he's well. I'll let you take away the Bank safe if you can drug him silent for this hot weather."

But the doctor did not laugh—"Man, I'm not joking," he said. "I'll give him another three months in his bed and a week or so more to die in. On my honor and reputation that's all the grace he has in this world. Consumption has hold of him to the marrow."

Reggie's face changed at once into the face of "Mr. Reginald Burke," and he answered:—"What can I do?"

"Nothing," said the doctor. "For all practical purposes the man is dead already. Keep him quiet and cheerful and tell him he's going to recover. That's all. I'll look after him to the end, of course."

The doctor went away, and Reggie sat down to open the evening mail. His first letter was one from the Directors, intimating for his information that Mr. Riley was to resign, under a month's notice, by the terms of his agreement, telling Reggie that their letter to Riley would follow and advising Reggie of the coming of a new Accountant, a man whom Reggie knew and liked.

Reggie lit a cheroot, and, before he had finished smoking, he had sketched the outline of a fraud. He put away–"burked"–the Directors' letter, and went in to talk to Riley, who was as ungracious as usual, and fretting himself over the way the Bank would run during his illness. He never thought of the extra work on Reggie's shoulders, but solely of the damage to his own prospects of advancement. Then Reggie assured him that everything would be well, and that he, Reggie, would confer with Riley daily on the management of the Bank. Riley was a little soothed, but he hinted in as many words that he did not think much of Reggie's business capacity. Reggie was humble. And he had letters in his desk from the Directors that a Gilbarte or a Hardie might have been proud of!

The days passed in the big darkened house, and the Directors' letter of dismissal to Riley came and was put away by Reggie who every evening brought the books to Riley's room, and showed him what had been going forward, while Riley snarled. Reggie did his best to make statements pleasing to Riley, but the Accountant was sure that the Bank was going to rack and ruin without him. In June, as the lying in bed told on his spirit, he asked whether his absence had been noted by the Directors, and Reggie said that they had written most sympathetic letters, hoping that he would be able to resume his valuable services before long. He showed Riley the letters: and Riley said that the Directors ought to have written to him direct. A few days later, Reggie opened Riley's mail in the half-light of the room, and gave him the sheet–not the envelope–of a letter to Riley from the Directors. Riley said he would thank Reggie not to interfere with his private papers, specially as Reggie knew he was too weak to open his own letters. Reggie apologized.

Then Riley's mood changed, and he lectured Reggie on his evil ways: his horses and his bad friends. "Of course, lying here on my back, Mr. Burke, I can't keep you straight; but when I'm well, I *do* hope you'll pay some heed to my words." Reggie, who had dropped polo, and dinners, and tennis, and all to attend to Riley, said that he was penitent and settled Riley's head on the pillow and heard him fret and contradict in hard, dry, hacking whispers, without a sign of impatience. This at the end of a heavy day's office work, doing double duty, in the latter half of June.

When the new Accountant came, Reginald told him the facts of the case, and announced to Riley that he had a guest staying with him. Riley said that he might have had more consideration than to entertain his "doubtful friends" at such a time. Reggie made Carron, the new Accountant, sleep at the Club in consequence. Carron's arrival took some of the heavy work off his shoulders, and he had time to attend to Riley's exactions–to explain, soothe, invent, and settle and resettle the poor wretch in bed, and to forge complimentary letters from Calcutta. At the end of the first month, Riley wished to send some money home to his mother. Reggie sent the draft. At the end of the second month, Riley's salary came in just the same. Reggie paid it out of his own pocket; and, with it, wrote Riley a beautiful letter from the Directors.

Riley was very ill indeed, but the flame of his life burnt steadily. Now and then he would be cheerful and confident about the future, sketching plans for going Home and seeing his mother. Reggie listened patiently when the office work was over, and encouraged him.

At other times Riley insisted on Reggie's reading the Bible and grim

"Methody" tracts to him. Out of these tracts he pointed morals directed at his Manager. But he always found time to worry Reggie about the working of the Bank, and to show him where the weak points lay.

This in-door, sick-room life and constant strains wore Reggie down a good deal, and shook his nerves, and lowered his billiard-playing by forty points. But the business of the Bank, and the business of the sick-room, had to go on, though the glass was 1160 in the shade.

At the end of the third month, Riley was sinking fast, and had begun to realize that he was very sick. But the conceit that made him worry Reggie, kept him from believing the worst. "He wants some sort of mental stimulant if he is to drag on," said the doctor. "Keep him interested in life if you care about his living." So Riley, contrary to all the laws of business and the finance, received a 25-per-cent rise of salary from the Directors. The "mental stimulant" succeeded beautifully. Riley was happy and cheerful, and, as is often the case in consumption, healthiest in mind when the body was weakest. He lingered for a full month, snarling and fretting about the Bank, talking of the future, hearing the Bible read, lecturing Reggie on sin, and wondering when he would be able to move abroad.

But at the end of September, one mercilessly hot evening, he rose up in his bed with a little gasp, and said quickly to Reggie:—"Mr. Burke, I am going to die. I know it in myself. My chest is all hollow inside, and there's nothing to breathe with. To the best of my knowledge I have done nowt,"—he was returning to the talk of his boyhood—"to lie heavy on my conscience. God be thanked, I have been preserved from the grosser forms of sin; and I counsel *you,* Mr. Burke. . . ."

Here his voice died down, and Reggie stooped over him.

"Send my salary for September to my mother . . . done great things with the Bank if I had been spared . . . mistaken policy . . . no fault of mine. . . ."

Then he turned his face to the wall and died.

Reggie drew the sheet over Its face, and went out into the veranda, with his last "mental stimulant"—a letter of condolence and sympathy from the Directors—unused in his pocket.

"If I'd been only ten minutes earlier," thought Reggie, "I might have heartened him up to pull through another day."

Tods' Amendment

The World hath set its heavy yoke
Upon the old white-bearded folk
    Who strive to please the King.
God's mercy is upon the young,
God's wisdom in the baby tongue
    That fears not anything.
    The Parable of Chaiju Bhagat.

NOW TODS' MAMMA was a singularly charming woman, and every one in Simla knew Tods. Most men had saved him from death on occasions. He was beyond his *ayah's* control altogether, and periled his life daily to find out what would happen if you pulled a Mountain Battery mule's tail. He was an utterly fearless young Pagan, about six years old, and the only baby who ever broke the holy calm of the supreme Legislative Council.

It happened this way: Tods' pet got loose, and fled up the hills, off the

Boileaugunge Road, Tods after it, until it burst into the Viceregal Lodge lawn, then attached to "Peterhoff." The Council were sitting at the time, and the windows were open because it was warm. The Red Lancer in the porch told Tods to go away; but Tods knew the Red Lancer and most of the Members of Council personally. Moreover, he had firm hold of the kid's collar, and was being dragged all across the flower-beds. "Give my *salaam* to the long Councilor *Sahib,* and ask him to help me take *Moti* back!" gasped Tods. The Council heard the noise through the open windows; and, after an interval, was seen the shocking spectacle of a Legal Member and a Lieutenant-Governor helping, under the direct patronage of a Commander-in-Chief and a Viceroy, one small and very dirty boy in a sailor's suit and a tangle of brown hair, to coerce a lively and rebellious kid. They headed it off down the path to the Mall, and Tods went home in triumph and told his Mamma that *all* the Councilor *Sahibs* had been helping him to catch *Moti.* Whereat his Mamma smacked Tods for interfering with the administration of the Empire; but Tods met the Legal Member the next day, and told him in confidence that if the Legal Member ever wanted to catch a goat, he, Tods, would give him all the help in his power, "Thank you, Tods," said the Legal Member.

Tods was the idol of some eighty *jhampanis,* and half as many *saises.* He saluted them all as "O Brother." It never entered his head that any living human being could disobey his orders; and he was the buffer between the servants and his Mamma's wrath. The working of that household turned on Tods, who was adored by every one from the *dhoby* to the dog-boy. Even Futteh Khan, the villainous loafer *khit* from Mussoorie, shirked risking Tods' displeasure for fear his co-mates should look down on him.

So Tods had honor in the land from Boileaugunge to Chota Simla, and ruled justly according to his lights. Of course, he spoke Urdu, but he had also mastered many queer side-speeches like the *chotee bolee* of the women, and held grave converse with shopkeepers and Hill-coolies alike. He was precocious for his age, and his mixing with natives had taught him some of the more bitter truths of life; the meanness and the sordidness of it. He used, over his bread and milk, to deliver solemn and serious aphorisms, translated from the vernacular into the English, that made his Mamma jump and vow that Tods *must* go home next hot weather.

Just when Tods was in the bloom of his power, the Supreme Legislature were hacking out a Bill, for the Sub-Montane Tracts, a revision of the then Act, smaller than the Punjab Land Bill but affecting a few hundred thousand people none the less. The Legal Member had built, and bolstered, and embroidered, and amended that Bill, till it looked beautiful on paper. Then the Council began to settle what they called the "minor details." As if any Englishman legislating for natives knows enough to know which are the minor and which are the major points, from the native point of view, of any measure! That Bill was a triumph of "safe guarding the interests of the tenant." One clause provided that land should not be leased on longer terms than five years at a stretch; because, if the landlord had a tenant bound down for, say, twenty years, he would squeeze the very life out of him. The notion was to keep up a stream of independent cultivators in the Sub-Montane Tracts; and ethnologically and politically the notion was correct. The only drawback was that it was altogether wrong. A native's life in Indian implies the life of his son. Wherefore, you cannot legislate for one generation at a time. You must consider the next from the native point of view. Curiously enough, the native now and then, and in Northern India more particularly, hates being over-protected against himself. There was a Naga village once, where they lived on dead *and* buried Commissariat mules. . . . But that is another story.

For many reasons, to be explained later, the people concerned objected to the Bill. The Native Member in Council knew as much about Punjabis as he knew about Charing Cross. He had said in Calcutta that "the Bill was entirely in accord with the desires of that large and important class, the cultivators;" and so on, and so on. The legal Member's knowledge of natives was limited to English-speaking Durbaris, and his own red *chaprassis,* the Sub-Montane Tracts concerned no one in particular, the Deputy Commissioners were a good deal too driven to make representations, and the measure was one which dealt with small landholders only. Nevertheless, the Legal Member prayed that it might be correct, for he was a nervously conscientious man. He did not know that no man can tell what natives think unless he mixes with them with the varnish off. And not always then. But he did the best he knew. And the measure came up to the Supreme Council for the final touches, while Tods patroled the Burra Simla Bazar in his morning rides, and played with the monkey belonging to Ditta Mull, the *bunnia,* and listened, as a child listens, to all the stray talk about this new freak of the *Lat Sahib's.*

One day there was a dinner-party, at the house of Tods' Mamma, and the Legal Member came. Tods was in bed, but he kept awake till he heard the bursts of laughter from the men over the coffee. Then he paddled out in his little red flannel dressing-gown and his night-suit and took refuge by the side of his father, knowing that he would not be sent back. "See the miseries of having a family!" said Tods' father, giving Tods three prunes, some water in a glass that had been used for claret, and telling him to sit still. Tods sucked the prunes slowly, knowing that he would have to go when they were finished, and sipped the pink water like a man of the world, as he listened to the conversation. Presently, the Legal Member, talking "shop" to the Head of a Department, mentioned his Bill by its full name–"The Sub Montane Tracts *Ryotwari* Revised Enactment." Tods caught the one native word and lifting up his small voice said:–

"Oh, I know *all* about that! Has it been *murramutted* yet, Councilor *Sahib?"*

"How much?" said the Legal Member.

"Murramutted–mended.–Put *theek,* you know–made nice to please Ditta Mull!"

The Legal Member left his place and moved up next to Tods.

"What do you know about *Ryotwari,* little man?" he said.

"I'm not a little man, I'm Tods, and I know *all* about it. Ditta Mull, and Choga Lall, and Amir Nath, and–oh, *lakhs* of my friends tell me about it in the bazars when I talk to them."

"Oh, they do–do they? What do they say, Tods?"

Tods tucked his feet under his red flannel dressing-gown and said:–"I must *fink."*

The Legal Member waited patiently. Then Tods, with infinite compassion:

"You don't speak my talk, do you, Councilor *Sahib?"*

"No; I am sorry to say I do not," said the Legal Member.

"Very well," said Tods, "I must *fink* in English."

He spent a minute putting his ideas in order, and began very slowly, translating in his mind from the vernacular to English, as many Anglo-Indian children do. You must remember that the Legal Member helped him on by questions when he halted, for Tods was not equal to the sustained flight of oratory that follows.

"Ditta Mull says:–'This thing is the talk of a child, and was made up by fools.' But *I* don't think you are a fool, Councilor *Sahib,"* said Tods, hastily. "You caught my goat. This is what Ditta Mull says:–'I am not a fool, and why should the Sirkar say I am a child? I can see if the land is good and if the landlord is good. If I am a fool, the sin is upon my own head. For five years I take my ground for which I have saved money, and a wife I take too, and a little son is born.' Ditta Mull has one daughter now, but he *says* he will have a son, soon. And he says: 'At the end of five years, by this new *bundobust,* I must go. If I do not go, I must get fresh seals and *takkus*-stamps on the papers, perhaps in the middle of the harvest, and to go to the law-courts once is wisdom, but go twice is *Jehannum.'* That is *quite* true," explained Tods, gravely. "All my friends say so. And Ditta Mull says:–'Always fresh *takkus* and paying money to *vakils* and *chaprassis* and law-courts every five years, or else the landlord makes me go. Why do I want to go? Am I a fool? If I am a fool and do not know, after forty years, good land when I see it, let me die! But if the new *bundobust* says for *fifteen* years, that is good and wise. My little son is a man, and I am burnt, and he takes the ground or another ground, paying only once for the *takkus*-stamps on the papers, and his little son is born, and at the end of fifteen years is a man too. But what profit is there in five years and fresh papers? Nothing but *dikh,* trouble, *dikh.* We are not young men who take these lands, but old ones–not *jais,* but tradesmen with a little money–and for fifteen years we shall have peace. Nor are we children that the Sirkar should treat us so."

Here Tods stopped short, for the whole table were listening. The Legal Member said to Tods: "Is that all?"

"All I can remember," said Tods. "But you should see Ditta Mull's big monkey. It's just like a Councilor *Sahib."*

"Tods! Go to bed," said his father.

Tods gathered up his dressing-gown tail and departed.

The Legal Member brought his hand down on the table with a crash–"By Jove!" said the Legal Member, "I believe the boy is right. The short tenure *is* the weak point."

He left early, thinking over what Tods had said. Now, it was obviously impossible for the Legal Member to play with a *bunnia's* monkey, by way of getting understanding; but he did better. He made inquiries, always bearing in mind the fact that the real native–not the hybrid, University-trained mule–is as timid as a colt, and, little by little, he coaxed some of the men to give in their views, which squared very closely with Tods' evidence.

So the Bill was amended in that clause; and the Legal Member was filled with an uneasy suspicion that Native Members represent very little except the Orders they carry on their bosoms. But he put the thought from him as illiberal. He was a most Liberal Man.

After a time, the news spread through the bazars that Tods had got the Bill recast in the tenure-clause, and if Tods' Mamma had not interfered, Tods would have made himself sick on the baskets of fruit and pistachio nuts and Cabuli grapes and almonds that crowded the veranda. Till he went Home, Tods ranked some few degrees before the Viceroy in popular estimation. But for the little life of him Tods could not understand why.

In the Legal Member's private-paper-box still lies the rough draft of the Sub-Montane Tracts *Ryotwari* Revised Enactment; and, opposite the twenty-second clause, penciled in blue chalk, and signed by the Legal Member, are the words *"Tods' Amendment."*

The Daughter of the Regiment

Jain 'Ardin' was a Sarjint's wife,
  A Sarjint's wife wus she.
She married of 'im in Orldershort
  An' comed acrost the sea.
(Chorus) 'Ave you never 'eard tell o' Jain 'Ardin'?
  Jain 'Ardin'?
  Jain 'Ardin'?
'Ave you never 'eard tell o' Jain 'Ardin'?
The pride o' the Compan*ee?*

Old Barrack-Room Ballad.

"A GENTLEMAN WHO doesn't know the Circassian Circle ought not to stand up for it—puttin' everybody out." That was what Miss McKenna said, and the Sergeant who was my *vis-a-vis* looked the same thing. I was afraid of Miss McKenna. She was six feet high, all yellow freckles and red hair, and was simply clad in white satin shoes, a pink muslin dress, an apple-green stuff sash and black silk gloves, with yellow roses in her hair. Wherefore I fled from Miss McKenna and sought my friend Private Mulvaney who was at the cant—refreshment-table.

"So you've been dancin' with little Jhansi McKenna, Sorr—she that's goin' to marry Corp'ril Slane? Whin you next conversh wid your lorruds an' your ladies, tell thim you've danced with little Jhansi. 'Tis a thing to be proud av."

But I wasn't proud. I was humble. I saw a story in Private Mulvaney's eye; and, besides, if he stayed too long at the bar, he would, I knew, qualify for more pack-drill. Now to meet an esteemed friend doing pack-drill outside the guard-room, is embarrassing, especially if you happen to be walking with his Commanding Officer.

"Come on to the parade-ground, Mulvaney, it's cooler there, and tell me about Miss McKenna. What is she, and who is she, and why is she called 'Jhansi'?"

"D'ye mane to say you've never heard av Ould Pummeloe's daughter? An' you thinkin' you know things! I'm wid ye in a minut' whin me poipe's lit."

We came out under the stars. Mulvaney sat down on one of the artillery bridges, and began in the usual way: his pipe between his teeth, his big hands clasped and dropped between his knees, and his cap well on the back of his head:

"Whin Mrs. Mulvaney that is, was Miss Shad that was, you were a dale younger than you are now, an' the Army was dif'rint in sev'ril e-senshuls. Bhoys have no call fer to marry nowadays, an' that's why the Army has so few rale, good, honust, swearin', strapagin', tinder-hearted, heavy-futted wives as ut used to hav whin I was a Corp'ril. I was rejuced afterwards—but no mather—I was a Corp'ril wanst. In thim times, a man lived *an'* died wid his rigimint; an' by natur', he married whin he was a *man.* Whin I was Corp'ril—Mother av Hivin, how the rigimint has died an' been borrun since that day!—my Color-Sar'jint was Ould McKenna, an' a married man tu. An' his woife—his first woife, for he married three times did McKenna—was

Bridget McKenna, from Portarlington like mesilf. I've misremembered fwhat her first name was; but in B Comp'ny we called her 'Ould Pummeloe' by reason av her figure, which was entirely cir-cum-fe-renshil. Like the big dhrum! Now that woman–God rock her sowl to rest in glory!–was for everlastin' havin' childher; an' McKenna, whin the fifth or sixth come squallin' on to the musther-roll, swore he wud number them off in future. But Ould Pummeloe she prayed av him to christen thim after the names of the stations they was borrun in. So there was Colaba McKenna an' Muttra McKenna, an' a whole Presidincy av other McKennas, an' little Jhansi, dancin' over yonder. Whin the children wasn't bornin', they was dying; for, av our childer die like sheep in these days, they died like flies thin. I lost me own little Shad–but no matther. 'Tis long ago, and Mrs. Mulvaney niver had another.

"I'm digresshin. Wan divil's hot summer, there come an order from some mad ijjit, whose name I misremember, for the rigimint to go up-country. May be they wanted to know how the new rail carried throops. They knew! On me sowl, they knew before they was done! Ould Pummeloe had just buried Muttra McKenna; an' the season bein' onwholesim, only little Jhansi McKenna, who was four year ould thin, was left on hand.

"Five children gone in fourteen months. 'Twas harrd, wasn't ut?

"So we wint up to our new station in that blazin' heat–may the curse av Saint Lawrence conshume the man who gave the ordher! Will I ivir forget that move? They gave us two wake thrains to the rigimint; an' we was eight hundher' and sivinty strong. There was A, B, C, an' D Companies in the secon' thrain, wid twelve women, no orficers' ladies, an' thirteen childher. We was to go six hundher' miles, an' railways was new in thim days. Whin we had been a night in the belly av the thrain–the men ragin' in their shirts an' dhrinkin' anything they could find, an' eatin' bad fruit-stuff whin they cud, for we cudn't stop em–I was a Corp'ril thin–the cholera bruk out wid the dawnin' av the day.

"Pray to the Saints, you may niver see cholera in a throop-thrain! 'Tis like the judgmint av God hittin' down from the nakid sky! We run into a rest-camp–as ut might have been Ludianny, but not by any means so comfortable. The Orficer Commandin' sent a telegrapt up the line, three hundher' mile up, askin' for help. Faith, we wanted ut, for ivry sowl av the followers ran for the dear life as soon as the thrain stopped; an' by the time that telegrapt was writ, there wasn't a naygur in the station exceptin' the telegrapt-clerk–an' he only bekaze he was held down to his chair by the scruff av his sneakin' black neck. Thin the day began wid the noise in the carr'ges, an the rattle av the men on the platform fallin' over, arms an' all, as they stud for to answer the Comp'ny muster-roll before goin' over to the camp. 'Tisn't for me to say what like the cholera was like. Maybe the Doctor cud ha' tould, av he hadn't dropped on to the platform from the door av a carriage where we was takin' out the dead. He died wid the rest. Some bhoys had died in the night. We tuk out siven, and twinty more was sickenin' as we tuk thim. The women was huddled up any ways, screamin' wid fear.

"Sez the Commandin' Officer, whose name I misremember:–'Take the women over to that tope av trees yonder. Get thim out av the camp. 'Tis no place for thim.'

"Ould Pummeloe was sittin' on her beddin'-rowl, tryin' to kape little Jhansi quiet. 'Go off to that tope!' sez the Orficer. 'Go out av the men's way!'

" 'Be damned av I do!' sez Ould Pummeloe, an' little Jhansi, squattin' by her mother's side, squeaks out:–'Be damned av I do,' tu. Thin Ould Pummeloe turns to the women an' she sez:–'Are ye goin' to let the bhoys die while you're picnickin', ye sluts?' sez she. ' 'Tis wather they want. Come on an' help.'

"Wid that, she turns up her sleeves an' steps out for a well behind the rest-camp—little Jhansi trottin' behind wid a *lotah* an' string, an' the other women followin' like lambs, wid horse-buckets and cookin' *degchies.* Whin all the things was full, Ould Pummeloe marches back into camp—'twas like a battlefield wid all the glory missin'—at the hid av the rigimint av women.

" 'McKenna, me man!' she sez, wid a voice on her like grand-roun's challenge, 'tell the bhoys to be quiet, Ould Pummeloe's acomin' to look afther thim—wid free dhrinks.'

"Thin we cheered, and the cheerin' in the lines was louder than the noise av the poor divils wid the sickness on thim. But not much.

"You see, we was a new an' raw rigimint in those days, an' we cud make neither head nor tail av the sickness; an' so we was useless. The men was goin' roun' an' about like dumb sheep, waitin' for the nex' man to fall over, an' sayin' undher their spache:—'Fwhat is ut? In the name av God *fwhat* is ut?' 'Twas horrible. But through ut all, up an' down, an' down an' up, wint Ould Pummeloe an' little Jhansi—all we cud see av the baby, undher a dead man's helmet wid the chin-strap swingin' about her little stummick—up an' down wid the wather and fwhat brandy there was.

"Now an' thin, Ould Pummeloe, the tears runnin' down her fat, red face, sez:—'Me bhoys, me poor, dead darlin' bhoys!' But, for the most, she was thryin' to put heart into the men an' kape thim stiddy; and little Jhansi was tellin' thim all they wud be 'better in the mornin'.' 'Twas a thrick she'd picked up from hearing Ould Pummeloe whin Muttra was burnin' out wid fever. In the mornin'! 'Twas the iverlastin' mornin' at St. Peter's Gate, was the mornin' for seven an' twenty good men; an' twenty more was sick to the death in that bitter, burnin' sun. But the women worked like angils, as I've said, an' the men like divils, till two doctors come down from above, an' we was rescued.

"But, just before that, Ould Pummeloe, on her knees over a bhoy in my squad—right-cot man to me he was in the barrick—tellin' him the worrud av the Church that niver failed a man yet, sez:—'Hould me up, bhoys! I'm feelin' bloody sick!' 'Twas the sun, not the cholera, did ut. She misremembered she was only wearin' her ould black bonnet, an she died wid 'McKenna, me man,' houldin' her up, an' the bhoys howled whin they buried her.

"That night, a big wind blew, an' blew, an' blew, an' blew the tents flat. But it blew the cholera away an' niver another case there was all the while we was waitin'—ten days in quarintin'. Av you will belave me, the thrack of the sickness in the camp was for all the worruld the thrack of a man walkin' four times in a figur-av-eight through the tents. They say 'tis the Wandherin' Jew takes the cholera wid him. I believe ut.

"An, *that*," said Mulvaney, illogically, "is the cause why little Jhansi McKenna is fwhat she is. She was brought up by the Quarter-Master Sergeant's wife whin McKenna died, but she b'longs to B Comp'ny; an' this tale I'm tellin' you—*wid* a proper appreciashin av Jhansi McKenna—I've belted into every recruity av the Comp'ny as he was drafted. Faith, 'twas me belted Corp'ril Slane into askin' the girl!"

"Not really?"

"Man, I did! She's no beauty to look at, but she's Ould Pummeloe's daughter, an' 'tis my juty to provide for her. Just before Slane got his waneight a day, I sez to him:—'Slane,' sez I, 'to-morrow 'twill be insubordinashin av me to chastise you; but, by the sowl av Ould Pummeloe, who is now in glory, av you don't give me your worrud to ask Jhansi McKenna at wanst, I'll peel the flesh off yer bones wid a brass huk to-night. 'Tis a disgrace to B Comp'ny she's been single so long!' sez I. Was I goin' to let a three-year-ould preshume to discoorse wid me, my will bein' set? No! Slane wint an' asked her. He's a good bhoy is Slane. Wan av these days he'll get into the

Com'ssariat an dhrive a boggy wid his—savin's. So I provided for Ould Pummeloe's daughter; an' now you go along an' dance again wid her."

And I did.

I felt a respect for Miss Jhansi McKenna; and I went to her wedding later on.

Perhaps I will tell you about that one of these days.

In the Pride of His Youth

"Stopped in the straight when the race was his own!
Look at him cutting it–cur to the bone!"
"Ask, ere the youngster be rated and chidden,
What did he carry and how was he ridden?
Maybe they used him too much at the start;
Maybe Fate's weight-cloths are breaking his heart."

Life's Handicap.

WHEN I WAS telling you of the joke that The Worm played off on the Senior Subaltern, I promised a somewhat similar tale, but with all the jest left out. This is that tale.

Dicky Hatt was kidnapped in his early, early youth–neither by landlady's daughter, housemaid, barmaid, nor cook, but by a girl so nearly of his own caste that only a woman could have said she was just the least little bit in the world below it. This happened a month before he came out to India, and five days after his one-and-twentieth birthday. The girl was nineteen–six years older than Dicky in the things of this world, that is to say–and, for the time, twice as foolish as he.

Excepting, always, falling off a horse there is nothing more fatally easy than marriage before the Registrar. The ceremony costs less than fifty shillings, and is remarkably like walking into a pawnshop. After the declarations of residence have been put in, four minutes will cover the rest of the proceedings–fees, attestation, and all. Then the Registrar slides the blotting-pad over the names, and says grimly with his pen between his teeth:–"Now you're man and wife;" and the couple walk out into the street, feeling as if something were horribly illegal somewhere.

But that ceremony holds and can drag a man to his undoing just as thoroughly as the "long as ye both shall live" curse from the altar-rails, with the bridesmaids giggling behind and *"The Voice that breathed o'er Eden"* lifting the roof off. In this manner was Dicky Hatt kidnapped, and he considered it vastly fine, for he had received an appointment in India which carried a magnificent salary from the Home point of view. The marriage was to be kept secret for a year. Then Mrs. Dicky Hatt was to come out and the rest of life was to be a glorious golden mist. That was how they sketched it under the Addison Road Station lamps; and, after one short month, came Gravesend and Dicky steaming out to his new life, and the girl crying in a thirty-shillings a week bed-and-living-room, in a back-street off Montpelier Square near the Knightsbridge Barracks.

But the country that Dicky came to was a hard land where "men" of twenty-one were reckoned very small boys indeed, and life was expensive. The salary that loomed so large six thousand miles away did not go far. Particularly when Dicky divided it by two, and remitted more than the fair half, at 1-6, to Montpelier Square. One hundred and thirty-five rupees out of three hundred and thirty is not much to live on; but it was absurd to suppose that Mrs. Hatt could exist forever on the £20 held back by Dicky, from his outfit allowance. Dicky saw this and remitted at once; always remembering that Rs. 700 were to be paid, twelve months later, for a first-class passage out for a lady. When you add to these trifling details the natural instincts of a boy beginning a new life in a new country and longing to go about and enjoy himself, and the necessity for grappling with strange work—which, properly speaking, should take up a boy's undivided attention—you will see that Dicky started handicapped. He saw it himself for a breath or two; but he did not guess the full beauty of his future.

As the hot weather began, the shackles settled on him and ate into his flesh. First would come letters—big, crossed, seven sheet letters—from his wife, telling him how she longed to see him, and what a Heaven upon earth would be their property when they met. Then some boy of the chummery wherein Dicky lodged would pound on the door of his bare little room, and tell him to come out to look at a pony—the very thing to suit him. Dicky could not afford ponies. He had to explain this. Dicky could not afford living in the chummery, modest as it was. He had to explain this before he moved to a single room next the office where he worked all day. He kept house on a green oil-cloth table-cover, one chair, one *charpoy,* one photograph, one tooth-glass, very strong and thick, a seven-rupee eight-anna filter, and messing by contract at thirty-seven rupees a month. Which last item was extortion. He had no punkah, for a punkah costs fifteen rupees a month; but he slept on the roof of the office with all his wife's letters under his pillow. Now and again he was asked out to dinner where he got both a punkah and an iced drink. But this was seldom, for people objected to recognizing a boy who had evidently the instincts of a Scotch tallow-chandler, and who lived in such a nasty fashion. Dicky could not subscribe to any amusement, so he found no amusement except the pleasure of turning over his Bank-book and reading what it said about "loans on approved security." That cost nothing. He remitted through a Bombay Bank, by the way, and the Station knew nothing of his private affairs.

Every month he sent Home all he could possibly spare for his wife—and for another reason which was expected to explain itself shortly and would require more money.

About this time, Dicky was overtaken with the nervous, haunting fear that besets married men when they are out of sorts. He had no pension to look to. What if he should die suddenly, and leave his wife unprovided for? The thought used to lay hold of him in the still, hot nights on the roof, till the shaking of his heart made him think that he was going to die then and there of heart-disease. Now this is a frame of mind which no boy has a right to know. It is a strong man's trouble; but, coming when it did, it nearly drove poor punkahless, perspiring Dicky Hatt mad. He could tell no one about it.

A certain amount of "screw" is as necessary for a man as for a billiard-ball. It makes them both do wonderful things. Dicky needed money badly, and he worked for it like a horse. But, naturally, the men who owned him knew that a boy can live very comfortably on a certain income—pay in India is a matter of age not merit, you see, and, if their particular boy wished to work like two boys, Business forbid that they should stop him! But Business forbid that they should give him an increase of pay at his present ridiculously immature age! So Dicky won certain rises of salary—ample for a boy—not enough for a wife and a child—certainly too little for the seven-hundred-rupee passage that he and Mrs. Hatt had discussed so lightly once upon a time. And with this he was forced to be content.

Somehow, all his money seemed to fade away in Home drafts and the crushing Exchange, and the tone of the Home letters changed and grew querulous. "Why wouldn't Dicky have his wife and the baby out? Surely he had a salary—a fine salary—and it was too bad of him to enjoy himself in India. But would he—could he—make the next draft a little more elastic?" Here followed a list of baby's kit, as long as a Parsee's bill. Then Dicky, whose heart yearned to his wife and the little son he had never seen—which, again, is a feeling no boy is entitled to—enlarged the draft and wrote queer half-boy, half-man letters, saying that life was not so enjoyable after all and would the little wife wait yet a little longer? But the little wife, however much she approved of money, objected to waiting, and there was a strange, hard sort of ring in her letters that Dicky didn't understand. How could he, poor boy?

Later on still—just as Dicky had been told—*a propos* of another youngster who had "made a fool of himself" as the saying is—that matrimony would not only ruin his further chances of advancement, but would lose him his present appointment—came the news that the baby, his own little, little son, had died and, behind this, forty lines of an angry woman's scrawl, saying that death might have been averted if certain things all costing money, had been done, or if the mother and the baby had been with Dicky. The letter struck at Dicky's naked heart; but, not being officially entitled to a baby, he could show no sign of trouble.

How Dicky won through the next four months, and what hope he kept alight to force him into his work, no one dare say. He pounded on, the seven-hundred-rupee passage as far away as ever, and his style of living unchanged, except when he launched into a new filter. There was the strain of his office-work, and the strain of his remittances, and the knowledge of his boy's death, which touched the boy more, perhaps, than it would have touched a man; and, beyond all, the enduring strain of his daily life. Gray-headed seniors who approved of his thrift and his fashion of denying himself everything pleasant, reminded him of the old saw that says:—

"If a youth would be distinguished in his art, art, art,
He must keep the girls away from his heart, heart, heart."

And Dicky, who fancied he had been through every trouble that a man is permitted to know, had to laugh and agree; with the last line of his balanced Bank book jingling in his head day and night.

But he had one more sorrow to digest before the end. There arrived a letter from the little wife—the natural sequence of the others if Dicky had only known it—and the burden of that letter was "gone with a handsomer man than you." It was a rather curious production, without stops, something like this:—"She was not going to wait forever and the baby was dead and Dicky was only a boy and he would never set eyes on her again and why hadn't he waved his handkerchief to her when he left Gravesend and God was her judge she was a wicked woman but Dicky was worse enjoying himself in India and this other man loved the ground she trod on and would Dicky ever forgive her for she would never forgive Dicky; and there was no address to write to."

Instead of thanking his stars that he was free, Dicky discovered exactly how an injured husband feels—again, not at all the knowledge to which a boy is entitled—for his mind went back to his wife as he remembered her in the thirty-shilling "suite" in Montpelier Square, when the dawn of his last morning in England was breaking, and she was crying in the bed. Whereat he rolled about on his bed and bit his fingers. He never stopped to think whether, if he had met Mrs. Hatt after those two years, he would have discovered that he and she had grown quite different and new persons. This, theoretically, he ought to have done. He spent the night after the English Mail came in rather severe pain.

Next morning, Dicky Hatt felt disinclined to work. He argued that he had missed the pleasure of youth. He was tired, and he had tasted all the sorrow in life before three and twenty. His Honor was gone—that was the man; and now he, too, would go to the Devil—that was the boy in him. So he put his head down on the green oil-cloth table-cover, and wept before resigning his post, and all it offered.

But the reward of his services came. He was given three days to reconsider himself, and the Head of the establishment, after some telegraphings, said that it was a most unusual step, but, in view of the ability that Mr. Hatt had displayed at such and such a time, at such and such junctures, he was in a position to offer him an infinitely superior post—first on probation, and later, in the natural course of things, on confirmation. "And how much does the post carry?" said Dicky. "Six hundred and fifty rupees," said the Head slowly, expecting to see the young man sink with gratitude and joy.

And it came then! The seven hundrd rupee passage, and enough to have saved the wife, and the little son, and to have allowed of assured and open marriage, came then. Dicky burst into a roar of laughter—laughter he could not check—nasty, jangling merriment that seemed as if it would go on forever. When he had recovered himself he said, quite seriously:—"I'm tired of work. I'm an old man now. It's about time I retired. And I will."

"The boy's mad!" said the Head.

I think he was right; but Dicky Hatt never reappeared to settle the question.

Pig

Go, stalk the red deer o'er the heather,
Ride, follow the fox if you can!
But, for pleasure and profit together,
Allow me the hunting of Man,—
The chase of the Human, the search for the Soul
To its ruin,—the hunting of man.
The Old Shikarri.

I BELIEVE THE difference began in the matter of a horse, with a twist in his temper, whom Pinecoffin sold to Nafferton and by whom Nafferton was nearly slain. There may have been other causes of offense; the horse was the official stalking-horse. Nafferton was very angry; but Pinecoffin laughed and said that he had never guaranteed the beast's manners. Nafferton laughed, too, though he vowed that he would write off his fall against Pinecoffin if he waited five years. Now, a Dalesman from beyond Skipton will forgive an injury when the Strid lets a man live; but a South Devon man is as soft as a Dartmoor bog. You can see from their names that Nafferton had the race-advantage of Pinecoffin. He was a peculiar man, and his notions of humor were cruel. He taught me a new and fascinating form of *shikar.* He hounded Pinecoffin from Mithankot to Jagadri, and from Gurgaon to Abbottabad—up and across the Punjab, a large province and in places remarkably dry. He said that he had no intention of allowing Assistant Commissioners to "sell him pups," in the shape of ramping, screaming, countrybreds, without making their lives a burden to them.

Most Assistant Commissioners develop a bent for some special work after their first hot weather in the country. The boys with digestions hope to write their names large on the Frontier, and struggle for dreary places like Bannu and Kohat. The bilious ones climb into the Secretariat. Which is very bad for the liver. Others are bitten with a mania for District work, Ghuznivide coins or Persian poetry; while some, who come of farmers' stock, find that the smell of the Earth after the Rains gets into their blood, and calls them to "develop the resources of the Province." These men are enthusiasts. Pinecoffin belonged to their class. He knew a great many facts bearing on the cost of bullocks and temporary wells, and opium-scrapers, and what happens if you burn too much rubbish on a field, in the hope of enriching used-up soil. All the Pinecoffins come of a landholding breed, and so the land only took back her own again. Unfortunately–most unfortunately for Pinecoffin–he was a Civilian, as well as a farmer. Nafferton watched him, and thought about the horse. Nafferton said:–"See me chase that boy till he drops!" I said:–"You can't get your knife into an Assistant Commissioner." Nafferton told me that I did not understand the administration of the Province.

Our Government is rather peculiar. It gushes on the agricultural and general information side, and will supply a moderately respectable man with all sorts of "economic statistics," if he speaks to it prettily. For instance, you are interested in gold-washing in the sands of the Sutlej. You pull the string, and find that it wakes up half a dozen Departments, and finally communicates, say, with a friend of yours in the Telegraph, who once wrote some notes on the customs of the gold-washers when he was on construction-work in their part of the Empire. He may or may not be pleased at being ordered to write out everything he knows for your benefit. This depends on his temperament. The bigger man you are, the more information and the greater trouble can you raise.

Nafferton was not a big man; but he had the reputation of being very "earnest." An "earnest" man can do much with a Government. There was an earnest man once who nearly wrecked . . . but all India knows *that* story. I am not sure what real "earnestness" is. A very fair imitation can be manufactured by neglecting to dress decently, by mooning about in a dreamy, misty sort of way, by taking office-work home after staying in office till seven, and by receiving crowds of native gentlemen on Sundays. That is one sort of "earnestness."

Nafferton cast about for a peg whereon to hang his earnestness, and for a string that would communicate with Pinecoffin. He found both. They were Pig. Nafferton became an earnest inquirer after Pig. He informed the Government that he had a scheme whereby a very large percentage of the British Army in India could be fed, at a very large saving, on Pig. Then he hinted that Pinecoffin might supply him with the "varied information necessary to the proper inception of the scheme." So the Government wrote on the back of the letter:–"Instruct Mr. Pinecoffin to furnish Mr. Nafferton with any information in his power." Government is very prone to writing things on the backs of letters which, later, lead to trouble and confusion.

Nafferton had not the faintest interest in Pig, but he knew that Pinecoffin would flounce into the trap. Pinecoffin was delighted at being consulted about Pig. The Indian Pig is not exactly an important factor in agricultural life; but Nafferton explained to Pinecoffin that there was room for improvement, and corresponded direct with that young man.

You may think that there is not much to be evolved from Pig. It all depends how you set to work. Pinecoffin being a Civilian and wishing to do things thoroughly, began with an essay on the Primitive Pig, the Mythology of the Pig, and the Dravidian Pig. Nafferton filed that information–twenty-seven foolscap sheets–and wanted to know about the distribution of the Pig in the Punjab, and how it stood the Plains in the hot weather. From this point onwards, remember that I am giving you only the barest outlines of the affair–the guy-ropes, as it were, of the web that Nafferton spun round Pinecoffin.

Pinecoffin made a colored Pig-population map, and collected observations on the comparative longevity of Pig *(a)* in the sub-montane tracts of the Himalayas, and *(b)* in the Rechna Doab. Nafferton filed that, and asked what sort of people looked after Pig. This started an ethnological excursus on swineherds, and drew from Pinecoffin long tables showing the proportion per thousand of the caste in the Derajat. Nafferton filed that bundle, and explained that the figures which he wanted referred to the Cis-Sutlej states, where he understood that Pigs were very fine and large, and where he proposed to start a Piggery. By this time, Government had quite forgotten their instructions to Mr. Pinecoffin. They were like the gentlemen, in Keats' poem, who turned well-oiled wheels to skin other people. But Pinecoffin was just entering into the spirit of the Pig-hunt, as Nafferton well knew he would do. He had a fair amount of work of his own to clear away; but he sat up of nights reducing Pig to five places of decimals for the honor of his Service. He was not going to appear ignorant of so easy a subject as Pig.

Then Government sent him on special duty to Kohat, to "inquire into" the big, seven-foot, ironshod spades of that District. People had been killing each other with those peaceful tools; and Government wished to know "whether a modified form of agricultural implement could not, tentatively and as a temporary measure, be introduced among the agricultural population without needlessly or unduly exasperating the existing religious sentiments of the peasantry."

Between those spades and Nafferton's Pig, Pinecoffin was rather heavily burdened.

Nafferton now began to take up "*(a)* The food-supply of the indigenous Pig, with a view to the improvement of its capacities as a flesh-former. *(b)* The acclimatization of the exotic Pig, maintaining its distinctive peculiarities." Pinecoffin replied exhaustively that the exotic Pig would become merged in the indigenous type; and quoted horse-breeding statistics to prove this. The side-issue was debated, at great length on Pinecoffin's side, till Nafferton owned that he had been in the wrong, and moved the previous question. When Pinecoffin had quite written himself out about flesh-formers, and fibrins, and glucose and the nitrogenous constituents of maize and lucerne, Nafferton raised the question of expense. By this time Pinecoffin, who had been transferred from Kohat, had developed a Pig theory of his own, which he stated in thirty-three folio pages—all carefully filed by Nafferton. Who asked for more.

These things took ten months, and Pinecoffin's interest in the potential Piggery seemed to die down after he had stated his own views. But Nafferton bombarded him with letters on "the Imperial aspect of the scheme, as tending to officialize the sale of pork, and thereby calculated to give offense to the Mahomedan population of Upper India." He guessed that Pinecoffin would want some broad, free-hand work after his niggling, stippling, decimal details. Pinecoffin handled the latest development of the case in masterly style, and proved that no "popular ebullition of excitement was to be apprehended." Nafferton said that there was nothing like Civilian insight in matters of this kind, and lured him up a bye path—"the possible profits to accrue to the Government from the sale of hogbristles." There is an extensive literature of hogbristles, and the shoe, brush, and colorman's trades recognize more varieties of bristles than you would think possible. After Pinecoffin had wondered a little at Nafferton's rage for information, he sent back a monograph, fifty-one pages, on "Products of the Pig." This led him, under Nafferton's tender handling, straight to the Cawnpore factories, the trade in hogskin for saddles—and thence to the tanners. Pinecoffin wrote that pomegranate-seed was the best cure for hogskin, and suggested—for the past fourteen months had wearied him—that Nafferton should "raise his pigs before he tanned them."

Nafferton went back to the second section of his fifth question. How could the exotic Pig be brought to give as much pork as it did in the West and yet "assume the essentially hirsute characteristics of its oriental congener?" Pinecoffin felt dazed, for he had forgotten what he had written sixteen months before, and fancied that he was about to reopen the entire question. He was too far involved in the hideous tangle to retreat, and, in a weak moment, he wrote:—"Consult my first letter." Which related to the Dravidian Pig. As a matter of fact, Pinecoffin had still to reach the acclimatization stage; having gone off on a side-issue on the merging of types.

Then Nafferton really unmasked his batteries! He complained to the Government, in stately language, of "the paucity of help accorded to me in my earnest attempts to start a potentially remunerative industry, and the flippancy with which my requests for information are treated by a gentleman whose pseudo-scholarly attainments should at least have taught him the primary differences between the Dravidian and the Berkshire variety of the genus *Sus.* If I am to understand that the letter to which he refers me contains his serious views on the acclimatization of a valuable, though possibly uncleanly, animal, I am reluctantly compelled to believe," etc., etc.

There was a new man at the head of the Department of Castigation. The wretched Pinecoffin was told that the Service was made for the Country, and not the Country for the Service, and that he had better begin to supply information about Pigs.

Pinecoffin answered insanely that he had written everything that could be written about Pig, and that some furlough was due to him.

Nafferton got a copy of that letter, and sent it, with the essay on the Dravidian Pig, to a down-country paper which printed both in full. The essay was rather high-flown; but if the Editor had seen the stacks of paper, in Pinecoffin's handwriting, on Nafferton's table, he would not have been so sarcastic about the "nebulous discursiveness and blatant self-sufficiency of the modern Competition-*wallah,* and his utter inability to grasp the practical issues of a practical question." Many friends cut out these remarks and sent them to Pinecoffin.

I have already stated that Pinecoffin came of a soft stock. This last stroke frightened and shook him. He could not understand it; but he felt that he had been, somehow, shamelessly betrayed by Nafferton. He realized that he had wrapped himself up in the Pigskin without need, and that he could not well set himself right with his Government. All his acquaintances asked after his "nebulous discursiveness" or his "blatant self-sufficiency," and this made him miserable.

He took a train and went to Nafferton, whom he had not seen since the Pig business began. He also took the cutting from the paper, and blustered feebly and called Nafferton names, and then died down to a watery, weak protest of the "I-say-it's-too-bad-you-know" order.

Nafferton was very sympathetic.

"I'm afraid I've given you a good deal of trouble, haven't I?" said he.

"Trouble!" whimpered Pinecoffin; "I don't mind the trouble so much, though that was bad enough; but what I resent is this showing up in print. It will stick to me like a burr all through my service. And I *did* do my best for your interminable swine. It's too bad of you, on my soul it is!"

"I don't know," said Nafferton; "have you ever been stuck with a horse? It isn't the money I mind, though that is bad enough; but what I resent is the chaff that follows, especially from the boy who stuck me. But I think we'll cry quits now."

Pinecoffin found nothing to say save bad words; and Nafferton smiled ever so sweetly, and asked him to dinner.

The Rout of the White Hussars

It was not in the open fight
We threw away the sword,
But in the lonely watching
In the darkness by the ford.
The waters lapped, the night-wind blew,
Full-armed the Fear was born and grew,
And we were flying ere we knew
From panic in the night.

Beoni Bar.

SOME PEOPLE HOLD that an English Cavalry regiment cannot run. This is a mistake. I have seen four hundred and thirty-seven sabers flying over the face of the country in abject terror, have seen the best Regiment that ever drew bridle, wiped off the Army List for the space of two hours. If you repeat this tale to the White Hussars they will, in all probability, treat you severely. They are not proud of the incident.

You may know the White Hussars by their "side" which is greater than that of all the Cavalry Regiments on the roster. If this is not a sufficient mark, you may know them by their old brandy. It has been sixty years in the Mess and is worth going far to taste. Ask for the "McGaire" old brandy, and see that you get it. If the Mess Sergeant thinks that you are uneducated, and that the genuine article will be lost on you, he will treat you accordingly. He is a good man. But, when you are at Mess, you must never talk to your hosts about forced marches or long-distance rides. The Mess are very sensitive; and, if they think that you are laughing at them, will tell you so.

As the White Hussars say, it was all the Colonel's fault. He was a new man, and he ought never to have taken the Command. He said that the Regiment was not smart enough. This to the White Hussars, who knew they could walk round any Horse and through any Guns, and over any Foot on the face of the earth! That insult was the first cause of offense.

Then the Colonel cast the Drum-Horse—the Drum-Horse of the White Hussars! Perhaps you do not see what an unspeakable crime he had committed. I will try to make it clear. The soul of the Regiment lives in the Drum-Horse who carries the silver kettle-drums. He is nearly always a big piebald Waler. That is a point of honor; and a Regiment will spend anything you please on a piebald. He is beyond the ordinary laws of casting. His work is very light, and he only maneuvers at a foot-pace. Wherefore, so long as he can step out and look handsome, his well-being is assured. He knows more about the Regiment than the Adjutant, and could not make a mistake if he tried.

The Drum-Horse of the White Hussars was only eighteen years old, and perfectly equal to his duties. He had at least six years' more work in him, and carried himself with all the pomp and dignity of a Drum-Major of the Guards. The Regiment had paid Rs. 1,200 for him.

But the Colonel said that he must go, and he was cast in due form and replaced by a washy, bay beast as ugly as a mule, with a ewe-neck, rat-tail, and cow-hocks. The Drummer detested that animal, and the best of the

Band-horses put back their ears and showed the whites of their eyes at the very sight of him. They knew him for an upstart and no gentleman. I fancy that the Colonel's ideas of smartness extended to the Band, and that he wanted to make it take part in the regular parade movements. A Cavalry Band is a sacred thing. It only turns out for Commanding Officers' parades, and the Band Master is one degree more important than the Colonel. He is a High Priest and the *"Keel Row"* is his holy song. The *"Keel Row"* is the Cavalry Trot; and the man who has never heard that tune rising, high and shrill, above the rattle of the Regiment going past the saluting-base, has something yet to hear and understand.

When the Colonel cast the Drum-Horse of the White Hussars, there was nearly a mutiny.

The officers were angry, the Regiment were furious, and the Bandsmen swore–like troopers. The Drum-Horse was going to be put up to auction–public auction–to be bought, perhaps, by a Parsee and put into a cart! It was worse than exposing the inner life of the Regiment to the whole world, or selling the Mess Plate to a Jew–a black Jew.

The Colonel was a mean man and a bully. He knew what the Regiment thought about his action; and, when the troopers offered to buy the Drum-Horse, he said that their offer was mutinous and forbidden by the Regulations.

But one of the Subalterns–Hogan-Yale, an Irishman–bought the Drum-Horse for Rs. 160 at the sale; and the Colonel was wroth. Yale professed repentance–he was unnaturally submissive–and said that, as he had only made the purchase to save the horse from possible ill-treatment and starvation, he would now shoot him and end the business. This appeared to soothe the Colonel, for he wanted the Drum-Horse disposed of. He felt that he had made a mistake, and could not of course acknowledge it. Meantime, the presence of the Drum-Horse was an annoyance to him.

Yale took to himself a glass of the old brandy, three cheroots, and his friend, Martyn; and they all left the Mess together. Yale and Martyn, conferred for two hours in Yale's quarters; but only the bull-terrier who keeps watch over Yale's boot-trees knows what they said. A horse, hooded and sheeted to his ears, left Yale's stables and was taken very unwillingly, into the Civil Lines. Yale's groom went with him. Two men broke into the Regimental theater and took several paint-pots and some large scenery brushes. Then night fell over the Cantonments, and there was a noise as of a horse kicking his loose-box to pieces in Yale's stables. Yale had a big, old, white Waler trap-horse.

The next day was a Thursday, and the men, hearing that Yale was going to shoot the Drum-Horse in the evening, determined to give the beast a regular regimental funeral–a finer one than they would have given the Colonel had he died just then. They got a bullock-cart and some sacking, and mounds and mounds of roses, and the body, under sacking, was carried out to the place where the anthrax cases were cremated; two-thirds of the Regiment followed. There was no Band, but they all sang *"The Place where the old Horse died"* as something respectful and appropriate to the occasion. When the corpse was dumped into the grave and the men began throwing down armfuls of roses to cover it, the Farrier-Sergeant ripped out an oath and said aloud:–"Why, it ain't the Drum-Horse any more than it's me!" The Troop-Sergeant-Majors asked him whether he had left his head in the Canteen. The Farrier-Sergeant said that he knew the Drum-Horse's feet as well as he knew his own; but he was silenced when he saw the regimental number burnt in on the poor stiff, upturned near-fore.

Thus was the Drum-Horse of the White Hussars buried; the Farrier-Sergeant grumbling. The sacking that covered the corpse was smeared in places with black paint; and the Farrier-Sergeant drew attention to this fact.

But the Troop-Sergeant-Major of E Troop kicked him severely on the shin, and told him that he was undoubtedly drunk.

On the Monday following the burial, the Colonel sought revenge on the White Hussars. Unfortunately, being at that time temporarily in Command of the Station, he ordered a Brigade field-day. He said that he wished to make the regiment "sweat for their damned insolence," and he carried out his notion thoroughly. That Monday was one of the hardest days in the memory of the White Hussars. They were thrown against a skeleton-enemy, and pushed forward, and withdrawn, and dismounted, and "scientifically handled" in every possible fashion over dusty country, till they sweated profusely. Their only amusement came late in the day when they fell upon the battery of Horse Artillery and chased it for two miles. This was a personal question, and most of the troopers had money on the event; the Gunners saying openly that they had the legs of the White Hussars. They were wrong. A march-past concluded the compaign, and when the Regiment got back to their Lines, the men were coated with dirt from spur to chin-strap.

The White Hussars have one great and peculiar privilege. They won it at Fontenoy, I think.

Many Regiments possess special rights such as wearing collars with undress uniform, or a bow of ribbon between the shoulders, or red and white roses in their helmets on certain days of the year. Some rights are connected with regimental saints, and some with regimental successes. All are valued highly; but none so highly as the right of the White Hussars to have the Band playing when their horses are being watered in the Lines. Only one tune is played, and that tune never varies. I don't know its real name, but the White Hussars call it:–*"Take me to London again."* It sounds very pretty. The Regiment would sooner be struck off the roster than forego their distinction.

After the "dismiss" was sounded, the officers rode off home to prepare for stables; and the men filed into the lines, riding easy. That is to say, they opened their tight buttons, shifted their helmets, and began to joke or to swear as the humor took them; the more careful slipping off and easing girths and curbs. A good trooper values his mount exactly as much as he values himself, and believes, or should believe, that the two together are irresistible where women or men, girls or guns, are concerned.

Then the Orderly-Officer gave the order:–"Water horses," and the Regiment loafed off to the squadron-troughs which were in rear of the stables and between these and the barracks. There were four huge troughs, one for each squadron, arranged *en echelon,* so that the whole Regiment could water in ten minutes if it liked. But it lingered for seventeen, as a rule, while the Band played.

The Band struck up as the squadrons filed off the troughs, and the men slipped their feet out of the stirrups and chaffed each other. The sun was just setting in a big, hot bed of red cloud, and the road to the Civil Lines seemed to run straight into the sun's eye. There was a little dot on the road. It grew and grew till it showed as a horse, with a sort of gridiron thing on his back. The red cloud glared through the bars of the gridiron. Some of the troopers shaded their eyes with their hands and said:–"What the mischief 'as that there 'orse got on 'im!"

In another minute they heard a neigh that every soul–horse and man–in the Regiment knew, and saw, heading straight towards the Band, the dead Drum-Horse of the White Hussars!

On his withers banged and bumped the kettle-drum draped in crape, and on his back, very stiff and soldierly sat a bareheaded skeleton.

The Band stopped playing, and for a moment, there was a hush.

Then some one in E troop–men said it was the Troop-Sergeant-Major–swung his horse round and yelled. No one can account exactly for what happened afterwards; but it seems that, at least, one man in each troop set an example of panic, and the rest followed like sheep. The horses that had barely put their muzzles into the troughs reared and capered; but, as soon as the Band broke, which it did when the ghost of the Drum-Horse was about a furlong distant, all hooves followed suit, and the clatter of the stampede—quite different from the orderly throb and roar of a movement on parade, or the rough horseplay of watering in camp—made them only more terrified. They felt that the men on their backs were afraid of something. When horses once know *that,* all is over except the butchery.

Troop after troop turned from the troughs and ran—anywhere, and everywhere—like spilt quick-silver. It was a most extraordinary spectacle, for men and horses were in all stages of easiness, and the carbine-buckets flopping against their sides urged the horses on. Men were shouting and cursing, and trying to pull clear of the Band which was being chased by the Drum-Horse whose rider had fallen forward and seemed to be spurring for a wager.

The Colonel had gone over to the Mess for a drink. Most of the Officers were with him, and the Subaltern of the Day was preparing to go down to the lines, and receive the watering reports from the Troop-Sergeant-Majors. When *"Take me to London again"* stopped after twenty bars every one in the Mess said:—"What on earth has happened?" A minute later, they heard unmilitary noises, and saw, far across the plain, the White Hussars scattered, and broken, and flying.

The Colonel was speechless with rage, for he thought that the Regiment had risen against him or was unanimously drunk. The Band, a disorganized mob, tore past, and at its heels labored the Drum-Horse—the dead and buried Drum-Horse—with the jolting, clattering skeleton. Hogan-Yale whispered softly to Martyn:—"No wire will stand that treatment," and the Band, which had doubled like a hare, came back again. But the rest of the Regiment was gone, was rioting all over the Province, for the dusk had shut in and each man was howling to his neighbor that the Drum-Horse was on his flank. Troop-Horses are far too tenderly treated as a rule. They can, on emergencies, do a great deal, even with seventeen stone on their backs. As the troopers found out.

How long this panic lasted I cannot say. I believe that when the moon rose the men saw they had nothing to fear, and, by twos and threes and half-troops, crept back into Cantonments very much ashamed of themselves. Meantime, the Drum-Horse, disgusted at his treatment by old friends, pulled up, wheeled round, and trotted up to the Mess veranda-steps for bread. No one like to run; but no one cared to go forward till the Colonel made a movement and laid hold of the skeleton's foot. The Band had halted some distance away, and now came back slowly. The Colonel called it, individually and collectively, every evil name that occurred to him at the time; for he had set his hand on the bosom of the Drum-Horse and found flesh and blood. Then he beat the kettle-drums with his clenched fist, and discovered that they were but made of silvered paper and bamboo. Next, still swearing, he tried to drag the skeleton out of the saddle, but found that it had been wired into the cantle. The sight of the Colonel, with his arms round the skeleton's pelvis and his knee in the old Drum-Horse's stomach, was striking. Not to say amusing. He worried the thing off in a minute or two, and threw it down on the ground, saying to the Band:—"Here, you curs, that's what you're afraid of." The skeleton did not look pretty in the twilight. The Band-Sergeant seemed to recognize it, for he began to chuckle and choke. "Shall I take it away, sir?" said the Band-Sergeant. "Yes," said the Colonel, "take it to Hell, and ride there yourselves!"

The Band-Sergeant saluted, hoisted the skeleton across his saddle-bow, and led off to the stables. Then the Colonel began to make inquiries for the rest of the Regiment, and the language he used was wonderful. He would disband the Regiment—he would court-martial every soul in it—he would not command such a set of rabble, and so on, and so on. As the men dropped in, his language grew wilder, until at last it exceeded the utmost limits of free speech allowed even to a Colonel of Horse.

Martyn took Hogan-Yale aside and suggested compulsory retirement from the service as a necessity when all was discovered. Martyn was the weaker man of the two, Hogan-Yale put up his eyebrows and remarked, firstly, that he was the son of a Lord, and secondly, that he was as innocent as the babe unborn of the theatrical resurrection of the Drum-Horse.

"My instructions," said Yale, with a singularly sweet smile, "were that the Drum-Horse should be sent back as impressively as possible. I ask you, *am* I responsible if a mule-headed friend sends him back in such a manner as to disturb the peace of mind of a regiment of Her Majesty's Cavalry?"

Martyn said:—"You are a great man, and will in time become a General; but I'd give my chance of a troop to be safe out of this affair."

Providence saved Martyn and Hogan-Yale. The Second-in-Command led the Colonel away to the little curtained alcove wherein the Subalterns of the White Hussars were accustomed to play poker of nights; and there, after many oaths on the Colonel's part, they talked together in low tones. I fancy that the Second-in-Command must have represented the scare as the work of some trooper whom it would be hopeless to detect; and I know that he dwelt upon the sin and the shame of making a public laughing-stock of the scare.

"They will call us," said the Second-in-Command, who had really a fine imagination, "they will call us the 'Fly-by-Nights;' they will call us the 'Ghost Hunters;' they will nickname us from one end of the Army list to the other. All the explanations in the world won't make outsiders understand that the officers were away when the panic began. For the honor of the Regiment and for your own sake keep this thing quiet."

The Colonel was so exhausted with anger that soothing him down was not so difficult as might be imagined. He was made to see, gently and by degrees, that it was obviously impossible to court-martial the whole Regiment, and equally impossible to proceed against any subaltern who, in his belief, had any concern in the hoax.

"But the beast's alive! He's never been shot at all!" shouted the Colonel. "It's flat, flagrant disobedience! I've known a man broke for less, d—d side less. They're mocking me, I tell you, Mutman! They're mocking me!"

Once more, the Second-in-Command set himself to soothe the Colonel, and wrestled with him for half-an-hour. At the end of that time, the Regimental Sergeant-Major reported himself. The situation was rather novel to him; but he was not a man to be put out by circumstances. He saluted and said: "Regiment all come back, Sir." Then, to propitiate the Colonel:—"An' none of the horses any the worse, Sir."

The Colonel only snorted and answered—"You'd better tuck the men into their cots, then, and see that they don't wake up and cry in the night." The Sergeant withdrew.

His little stroke of humor pleased the Colonel, and, further, he felt slightly ashamed of the language he had been using. The Second-in-Command worried him again, and the two sat talking far into the night.

Next day but one, there was a Commanding Officer's parade, and the Colonel harangued the White Hussars vigorously. The pith of his speech was that, since the Drum-Horse in his old age had proved himself capable of cutting up the whole Regiment, he should return to his post of pride at the head of the Band, *but* the Regiment were a set of ruffians with bad consciences.

The White Hussars shouted, and threw everything movable about them into the air, and when the parade was over, they cheered the Colonel till they couldn't speak. No cheers were put up for Lieutenant Hogan-Yale who smiled very sweetly in the background.

Said the Second-in-Command to the Colonel, unofficially:–

"These little things ensure popularity, and do not the least affect discipline."

"But I went back on my word," said the Colonel.

"Never mind," said the Second-in-Command. "The White Hussars will follow you anywhere from to-day. Regiments are just like women. They will do anything for trinketry."

A week later, Hogan-Yale received an extraordinary letter from some one who signed himself "Secretary, *Charity and Zeal,* 3709, E. C.," and asked for "the return of our skeleton which we have reason to believe is in your possession."

"Who the deuce is this lunatic who trades in bones?" said Hogan-Yale.

"Beg your pardon, Sir," said the Band-Sergeant, "but the skeleton is with me, and I'll return it if you'll pay the carriage into the Civil Lines. There's a coffin with it, Sir."

Hogan-Yale smiled and handed two rupees to the Band-Sergeant, saying:– "Write the date on the skull, will you?"

If you doubt this story, and know where to go, you can see the date on the skeleton. But don't mention the matter to the White Hussars.

I happen to know something about it, because I prepared the Drum-Horse for his resurrection. He did not take kindly to the skeleton at all.

The Bronckhorst Divorce-Case

> In the daytime, when she moved about me,
> In the night, when she was sleeping at my side,–
> I was wearied, I was wearied of her presence,
> Day by day and night by night I grew to hate her–
> Would God that she or I had died!
>
> *Confessions.*

THERE WAS A man called Bronckhorst–a three-cornered, middle-aged man in the Army–gray as a badger, and, some people said, with a touch of country blood in him. That, however, cannot be proved. Mrs. Bronckhorst was not exactly young, though fifteen years younger than her husband. She was a large, pale, quiet woman, with heavy eyelids, over weak eyes, and hair that turned red or yellow as the lights fell on it.

Bronckhorst was not nice in any way. He had no respect for the pretty public and private lies that make life a little less nasty than it is. His manner towards his wife was coarse. There are many things–including actual assault with the clenched fist–that a wife will endure; but seldom a wife can bear–as Mrs. Bronckhorst bore–with a long course of brutal, hard chaff, making light of her weaknesses, her headaches, her small fits of gayety, her dresses, her queer little attempts to make herself attractive to her husband when she knows that she is not what she has been, and–worst of all–the love that she spends on her children. That particular sort of heavy-handed jest was specially dear to Bronckhorst. I suppose that he had first slipped into it, meaning no harm, in the honeymoon, when folk find their ordinary stock of endearments run short, and so go to the other extreme to express their feelings. A similar impulse makes a man say:—"Hutt, you old beast!" when a favorite horse nuzzles his coat-front. Unluckily, when the reaction fo marriage sets in, the form of speech remains, and, the tenderness having died out, hurts the wife more than she cares to say. But Mrs. Bronckhorst was devoted to her "Teddy" as she called him. Perhaps that was why he objected to her. Perhaps—this is only a theory to account for his infamous behavior later on—he gave way to the queer, savage feeling that sometimes takes by the throat a husband twenty years' married, when he sees, across the table, the same face of his wedded wife, and knows that, as he has sat facing it, so must he continue to sit until day of its death or his own. Most men and all women know the spasm. It only lasts for three breaths as a rule, must be a "throw-back" to times when men and women were rather worse than they are now, and is too unpleasant to be discussed.

Dinner at the Bronckhorsts' was an infliction few men cared to undergo. Bronckhorst took a pleasure in saying things that made his wife wince. When their little boy came in at dessert, Bronckhorst used to give him half a glass of wine, and naturally enough, the poor little mite got first riotous, next miserable, and was removed screaming. Bronckhorst asked if that was the way Teddy usually behaved, and whether Mrs. Bronckhorst could not spare some of her time to teach the "little beggar decency." Mrs. Bronckhorst, who loved the boy more than her own life, tried not to cry—her spirit seemed to have been broken by her marriage. Lastly, Bronckhorst used to say:—"There! That'll do, that'll do. For God's sake try to behave like a rational woman. Go into the drawing-room." Mrs. Bronckhorst would go, trying to carry it all off with a smile; and the guest of the evening would feel angry and uncomfortable.

After three years of this cheerful life—for Mrs. Bronckhorst had no woman-friends to talk to—the Station was startled by the news that Bronckhorst had instituted proceedings *on the criminal count,* against a man called Biel, who certainly had been rather attentive to Mrs. Bronckhorst whenever she had appeared in public. The utter want of reserve with which Bronckhorst treated his own dishonor helped us to know that the evidence against Biel would be entirely circumstantial and native. There were no letters; but Bronckhorst said openly that he would rack Heaven and Earth until he saw Biel superintending the manufacture of carpets in the Central Jail. Mrs. Bronckhorst kept entirely to her house, and let charitable folks say what they pleased. Opinions were divided. Some two-thirds of the Station jumped at once to the conclusion that Biel was guilty; but a dozen men who knew and liked him held by him. Biel was furious and surprised. He denied the whole thing, and vowed that he would thrash Bronckhorst within an inch of his life. No jury, we knew, could convict a man on the criminal count on native evidence in a land where you can buy a murder-charge, including the corpse, all complete for fifty-four rupees; but Biel did not care to scrape through by the benefit of a doubt. He wanted the whole thing cleared: but as he said one night:—"He can prove anything with servants' evidence, and I've only my bare word." This was about a month before the case came on; and beyond agreeing with Biel, we could do little. All that we could be sure of was that the native evidence would be bad enough to blast Biel's character for the rest of his service; for when a native begins perjury he perjures himself thoroughly. He does not boggle over details.

Some genius at the end of the table whereat the affair was being talked over, said:—"Look here! I don't believe lawyers are any good. Get a man to wire to Strickland, and beg him to come down and pull us through."

Strickland was about a hundred and eighty miles up the line. He had not long been married to Miss Youghal, but he scented in the telegram a chance of return to the old detective work that his soul lusted after, and next night he came in and heard our story. He finished his pipe and said oracularly:—"We must get at the evidence. *Oorya* bearer, Mussulman *khit* and *methraniayah,* I suppose, are the pillars of the charge. I am on in this piece; but I'm afraid I'm getting rusty in my talk."

He rose and went into Biel's bedroom where his trunk had been put, and shut the door. An hour later, we heard him say:—"I hadn't the heart to part with my old makeups when I married. Will this do?" There was a lothely *faquir* salaaming in the doorway.

"Now lend me fifty rupees," said Strickland, "and give me your Words of Honor that you won't tell my Wife."

He got all that he asked for, and left the house while the table drank his health. What he did only he himself knows. A *faquir* hung about Bronckhorst's compound for twelve days. Then a *mehter* appeared, and when Biel heard of *him,* he said that Strickland was an angel full-fledged. Whether the *mehter* made love to Janki, Mrs. Bronckhorst's *ayah,* is a question which concerns Strickland exclusively.

He came back at the end of three weeks, and said quietly:—"You spoke the truth, Biel. The whole business is put up from beginning to end. Jove! It almost astonishes *me!* That Bronckhorst-beast isn't fit to live."

There was uproar and shouting, and Biel said:—"How are you going to prove it? You can't say that you've been trespassing on Bronckhorst's compound in disguise!"

"No," said Strickland. "Tell your lawyer-fool, whoever he is, to get up something strong about 'inherent improbabilities' and 'discrepancies of evidence.' He won't have to speak, but it will make him happy. *I'm* going to run this business."

Biel held his tongue, and the other men waited to see what would happen. They trusted Strickland as men trust quiet men. When the case came off the Court was crowded. Strickland hung about in the veranda of the Court, till he met the Mohammedan *khitmatgar.* Then he murmured a *faquir's* blessing in his ear, and asked him how his second wife did. The man spun round, and, as he looked into the eyes of "Estreeken *Sahib,"* his jaw dropped. You must remember that before Strickland was married, he was, as I have told you already, a power among natives. Strickland whispered a rather coarse vernacular proverb to the effect that he was abreast of all that was going on, and went into the Court armed with a gut trainer's-whip.

The Mohammedan was the first witness and Strickland beamed upon him from the back of the Court. The man moistened his lips with his tongue and, in his abject fear of "Estreeken *Sahib"* the *faquir*, went back on every detail of his evidence—said he was a poor man and God was his witness that he had forgotten everything that Bronckhorst *Sahib* had told him to say. Between his terror of Strickland, the Judge, and Bronckhorst he collapsed, weeping.

Then began the panic among the witnesses. Janki, the *ayah,* leering chastely behind her veil, turned gray, and the bearer left the Court. He said that his Mamma was dying and that it was not wholesome for any man to lie unthriftily in the presence of "Estreeken *Sahib."*

Biel said politely to Bronckhorst:—"Your witnesses don't seem to work. Haven't you any forged letters to produce?" But Bronckhorst was swaying to and fro in his chair, and there was a dead pause after Biel had been called to order.

Bronckhorst's Counsel saw the look on his client's face, and without more ado, pitched his papers on the little green baize table, and mumbled something about having been misinformed. The whole Court applauded wildly, like soldiers at a theater, and the Judge began to say what he thought.

. . . .

Biel came out of the place, and Strickland dropped a gut trainer's-whip in the veranda. Ten minutes later, Biel was cutting Bronckhorst into ribbons behind the old Court cells, quietly and without scandal. What was left of Bronckhorst was sent home in a carriage; and his wife wept over it and nursed it into a man again.

Later on, after Biel had managed to hush up the counter-charge against Bronckhorst of fabricating false evidence, Mrs. Bronckhorst, with her faint watery smile, said that there had been a mistake, but it wasn't her Teddy's fault altogether. She would wait till her Teddy came back to her. Perhaps he had grown tired of her, or she had tried his patience, and perhaps we wouldn't cut her any more, and perhaps the mothers would let their children play with "little Teddy" again. He was so lonely. Then the Station invited Mrs. Bronckhorst everywhere, until Bronckhorst was fit to appear in public, when he went Home and took his wife with him. According to the latest advices, her Teddy did "come back to her," and they are moderately happy. Though, of course, he can never forgive her the thrashing that she was the indirect means of getting for him.

. . . .

What Biel wants to know is:–"Why didn't I press home the charge against the Bronckhorst-brute, and have him run in?"

What Mrs. Strickland wants to know is:–How *did* my husband bring such a lovely, lovely Waler from your Station? I know *all* his money-affairs; and I'm *certain* he didn't *buy* it."

What I want to know is:–"How do women like Mrs. Bronckhorst come to marry men like Bronckhorst?"

And my conundrum is the most unanswerable of the three.

Venus Annodomini

And the years went on as the years must do;
But our great Diana was always new–
Fresh, and blooming, and blonde, and fair,
With azure eyes and with aureate hair;
And all the folk, as they came or went,
Offered her praise to her heart's content.

Diana of Ephesus.

SHE HAD NOTHING to do with Number Eighteen in the Braccio Nuovo of the Vatican, between Visconti's Ceres and the God of the Nile. She was purely an Indian deity–an Anglo-Indian deity, that is to say–and we called her *the* Venus Annodomini, to distinguish her from other Annodominis of the same everlasting order. There was a legend among the Hills that she had once been young; but no living man was prepared to come forward and say boldly that the legend was true. Men rode up to Simla, and stayed, and went away and made their name and did their life's work, and returned again to find the Venus Annodomini exactly as they had left her. She was as immutable as the Hills. But not quite so green. All that a girl of eighteen could do in the way of riding, walking, dancing, picnicking and over-exertion generally, the Venus Annodomini did, and showed no sign of fatigue or trace of weariness. Besides perpetual youth, she had discovered, men said, the secret of perpetual health; and her fame spread about the land. From a mere woman, she grew to be an

Institution, insomuch that no young man could be said to be properly formed who had not, at some time or another, worshiped at the shrine of the Venus Annodomini. There was no one like her, though there were many imitations. Six years in her eyes were no more than six months to ordinary women; and ten made less visible impression on her than does a week's fever on an ordinary woman. Every one adored her, and in return she was pleasant and courteous to nearly every one. Youth had been a habit of hers for so long, that she could not part with it—never realized, in fact, the necessity of parting with it—and took for her more chosen associates young people.

Among the worshipers of the Venus Annodomini was young Gayerson. "Very Young" Gayerson, he was called to distinguish him from his father "Young" Gayerson, a Bengal Civilian, who affected the customs—as he had the heart—of youth. "Very Young" Gayerson was not content to worship placidly and for form's sake, as the other young men did, or to accept a ride or a dance, or a talk from the Venus Annodomini in a properly humble and thankful spirit. He was exacting, and, therefore, the Venus Annodomini repressed him. He worried himself nearly sick in a futile sort of way over her; and his devotion and earnestness made him appear either shy or boisterous or rude, as his mood might vary, by the side of the older men who, with him, bowed before the Venus Annodomini. She was sorry for him. He reminded her of a lad who, three-and-twenty years ago, had professed a boundless devotion for her, and for whom in return she had felt something more than a week's weakness. But that lad had fallen away and married another woman less than a year after he had worshiped her; and the Venus Annodomini had almost—not quite—forgotten his name. "Very Young" Gayerson had the same big blue eyes and the same way of pouting his underlip when he was excited or troubled. But the Venus Annodomini checked him sternly none the less. Too much zeal was a thing that she did not approve of; preferring instead, a tempered and sober tenderness.

"Very Young" Gayerson was miserable, and took no trouble to conceal his wretchedness. He was in the Army—a Line regiment I think, but am not certain—and, since his face was a looking-glass and his forehead an open book, by reason of his innocence, his brothers in arms made his life a burden to him and embittered his naturally sweet disposition. No one except "Very Young" Gayerson, and he never told his views, knew how old "Very Young" Gayerson believed the Venus Annodomini to be. Perhaps he thought her five-and-twenty, or perhaps she told him that she was this age. "Very Young" Gayerson would have forded the Gugger in flood to carry her lightest word, and had implicit faith in her. Every one liked him, and every one was sorry when they saw him so bound a slave of the Venus Annodomini. Every one, too, admitted that it was not her fault; for the Venus Annodomini differed from Mrs. Hauksbee and Mrs. Reiver in this particular—she never moved a finger to attract any one; but, like Ninon de l'Enclos, all men were attracted to her. One could admire and respect Mrs. Hauksbee, despise and avoid Mrs. Reiver, but one was forced to adore the Venus Annodomini.

"Very Young" Gayerson's papa held a Division or a Collectorate or something administrative in a particularly unpleasant part of Bengal—full of Babus who edited newspapers proving that "Young" Gayerson was a "Nero" and a "Scylla" and a "Charybdis"; and, in addition to the Babus, there was a good deal of dysentery and cholera abroad for nine months of the year. "Young" Gayerson—he was about five and forty—rather liked Babus, they amused him, but he objected to dysentery, and when he could get away, went to Darjilling for the most part. This particular season he fancied that he would come up to Simla, and see his boy. The boy was not altogether pleased. He told the Venus Annodomini that his father was coming up, and she flushed a little and said that she should be delighted to make his acquaintance. Then she looked long and thoughtfully at "Very Young" Gayerson, because she was very, very sorry for him, and he was a very, very big idiot.

"My daughter is coming out in a fortnight, Mr. Gayerson," she said.

"Your *what?*" said he

"Daughter," said the Venus Annodomini. "She's been out for a year at Home already, and I want her to see a little of India. She is nineteen and a very sensible, nice girl I believe."

"Very Young" Gayerson, who was a short twenty-two years old, nearly fell out of his chair with astonishment; for he had persisted in believing, against all belief, in the youth of the Venus Annodomini. She, with her back to the curtained window, watched the effect of her sentences and smiled.

"Very Young" Gayerson's papa came up twelve days later, and had not been in Simla four and twenty hours, before two men, old acquaintances of his, had told him how "Very Young" Gayerson had been conducting himself.

"Young" Gayerson laughed a good deal, and inquired who the Venus Annodomini might be. Which proves that he had been living in Bengal where nobody knows anything except the rate of Exchange. Then he said "boys will be boys," and spoke to his son about the matter. "Very Young" Gayerson said that he felt wretched and unhappy; and "Young" Gayerson said that he repented of having helped to bring a fool into the world. He suggested that his son had better cut his leave short and go down to his duties. This led to an unfilial answer, and relations were strained, until "Young" Gayerson demanded that they should call on the Venus Annodomini. "Very Young" Gayerson went with his papa, feeling, somehow, uncomfortable and small.

The Venus Annodomini received them graciously and "Young" Gayerson said:—"By Jove! It's Kitty!" "Very Young" Gayerson would have listened for an explanation, if his time had not been taken up with trying to talk to a large, handsome, quiet, well-dressed girl—introduced to him by the Venus Annodomini as her daughter. She was far older in manners, style and repose than "Very Young" Gayerson; and, as he realized this thing, he felt sick.

Presently, he heard the Venus Annodomini saying:—"Do you know that your son is one of my most devoted admirers?"

"I don't wonder," said "Young" Gayerson. Here he raised his voice:—"He follows his father's footsteps. Didn't I worship the ground you trod on, ever so long ago, Kitty—and you haven't changed since then. How strange it all seems!"

"Very Young" Gayerson said nothing. His conversation with the daughter of the Venus Annodomini was, through the rest of the call, fragmentary and disjointed.

. . . . . .

"At five to-morrow then," said the Venus Annodomini. "And mind you are punctual."

"At five punctually," said "Young" Gayerson. "You can lend your old father a horse I dare say, youngster, can't you? I'm going for a ride tomorrow afternoon."

"Certainly," said "Very Young" Gayerson. "I am going down to-morrow morning. My ponies are at your service, Sir."

The Venus Annodomini looked at him across the half-light of the room, and her big gray eyes filled with moisture. She rose and shook hands with him.

"Good-by, Tom," whispered the Venus Annodomini.

The Bisara of Pooree

Little Blind Fish, thou art marvelous wise,
Little Blind Fish, who put out thy eyes?
Open thine ears while I whisper my wish—
Bring me a lover, thou little Blind Fish.
The Charm of the Bisara.

SOME NATIVES SAY that it came from the other side of Kulu, where the eleven-inch Temple Sapphire is. Others that it was made at the Devil-Shrine of Ao-Chung in Thibet, was stolen by a Kafir, from him by a Gurkha, from him again by a Lahouli, from him by a *khitmatgar,* and by this latter sold to an Englishman, so all its virtue was lost: because, to work properly, the Bisara of Pooree must be stolen—with bloodshed if possible, but, at any rate, stolen.

These stories of the coming into India are all false. It was made at Pooree ages since—the manner of its making would fill a small book—was stolen by one of the Temple dancing-girls there, for her own purposes, and then passed on from hand to hand, steadily northward, till it reached Hanlá: always bearing the same name—the Bisara of Pooree. In shape it is a tiny, square box of silver, studded outside with eight small balas-rubies. Inside the box, which opens with a spring, is a little eyeless fish, carved from some sort of dark, shiny nut and wrapped in a shred of faded gold-cloth. That is the Bisara of Pooree, and it were better for a man to take a king cobra in his hand than to touch the Bisara of Pooree.

All kinds of magic are out of date, and done away with except in India, where nothing changes in spite of the shiny, toy-scum stuff that people call "civilization." Any man who knows about the Bisara of Pooree will tell you what its powers are—always supposing that it has been honestly stolen. It is the only regularly working, trustworthy love-charm in the country, with one exception.

[The other charm is in the hands of a trooper of the Nizam's Horse, at a place called Tuprani, due north of Hyderabad.] This can be depended upon for a fact. Some one else may explain it.

If the Bisara be not stolen, but given or bought or found, it turns against its owner in three years, and leads to ruin or death. This is another fact which you may explain when you have time. Meanwhile, you can laugh at it. At present, the Bisara is safe on an *ekka*-pony's neck, inside the blue bead-necklace that keeps off the Evil-eye. If the *ekka*-driver ever finds it, and wears it, or gives it to his wife, I am sorry for him.

A very dirty hill-cooly woman, with goiter, owned it at Theog in 1884. It came into Simla from the north before Churton's *khitmatgar* bought it, and sold it, for three times its silver-value, to Churton, who collected curiosities. The servant knew no more what he had bought than the master; but a man looking over Churton's collection of curiosities—Churton was an Assistant Commissioner by the way—saw and held his tongue. He was an Englishman; but he knew how to believe. Which shows that he was different from most Englishmen. He knew that it was dangerous to have any share in the little box when working or dormant; for unsought Love is a terrible gift.

Pack—"Grubby" Pack, as we used to call him—was, in every way, a nasty little man who must have crawled into the Army by mistake. He was three inches taller than his sword, but not half so strong. And the sword was a fifty-shilling, tailor-made one. Nobody liked him, and, I suppose, it was his wizenedness and worthlessness that made him fall so hopelessly in love with Miss Hollis, who was good and sweet, and five foot seven in her tennis shoes. He was not content with falling in love quietly, but brought all the strength of his miserable little nature into the business. If he had not been so objectionable, one might have pitied him. He vapored, and fretted, and fumed, and trotted up and down, and tried to make himself pleasing in Miss Hollis's big, quiet, gray eyes, and failed. It was one of the cases that you sometimes meet, even in this country where we marry by Code, of a really blind attachment all on one side, without the faintest possibility of return. Miss Hollis looked on Pack as some sort of vermin running about the road. He had no prospect beyond Captain's pay, and no wits to help that out by one anna. In a large-sized man, love like his would have been touching. In a good man it would have been grand. He being what he was, it was only a nuisance.

You will believe this much. What you will not believe is what follows: Churton, and The Man who Knew that the Bisara was, were lunching at the Simla Club together. Churton was complaining of life in general. His best mare had rolled out of stable down the hill and had broken her back; his decisions were being reversed by the upper Courts, more than an Assistant Commissioner of eight years' standing has a right to expect; he knew liver and fever, and, for weeks past, had felt out of sorts. Altogether, he was disgusted and disheartened.

Simla Club dining-room is built, as all the world knows, in two sections, with an arch-arrangement dividing them. Come in, turn to your own left, take the table under the window, and you cannot see any one who has come in, turned to the right, and taken a table on the right side of the arch. Curiously enough, every word that you say can be heard, not only by the other diner, but by the servants beyond the screen through which they bring dinner. This is worth knowing: an echoing-room is a trap to be forewarned against.

Half in fun, and half hoping to be believed, The Man who Knew told Churton the story of the Bisara of Pooree at rather greater length than I have told it to you in this place; winding up with a suggestion that Churton might as well throw the little box down the hill and see whether all his troubles would go with it. In ordinary ears, English ears, the tale was only an interesting bit of folk-lore. Churton laughed, said that he felt better for his tiffin, and went out. Pack had been tiffining by himself to the right of the arch, and had heard everything. He was nearly mad with his absurd infatuation for Miss Hollis that all Simla had been laughing about.

It is a curious thing that, when a man hates or loves beyond reason, he is ready to go beyond reason to gratify his feelings. Which he would not do for money or power merely. Depend upon it, Solomon would never have built altars to Ashtaroth and all those ladies with queer names, if there had not been trouble of some kind in his *zenana,* and nowhere else. But this is beside the story. The facts of the case are these: Pack called on Churton next day when Churton was out, left his card, and *stole* the Bisara of Pooree from its place under the clock on the mantelpiece! Stole it like the thief he was by nature. Three days later, all Simla was electrified by the news that Miss Hollis had accepted Pack—the shriveled rat, Pack! Do you desire clearer evidence than this? The Bisara of Pooree had been stolen, and it worked as it had always done when won by foul means.

There are three or four times in a man's life when he is justified in meddling with other people's affairs to play Providence.

The Man who Knew felt that he *was* justified; but believing and acting on a belief are quite different things. The insolent satisfaction of Pack as he ambled by the side of Miss Hollis, and Churton's striking release from liver, as soon as the Bisara of Pooree had gone, decided the Man. He explained to Churton and Churton laughed, because he was not brought up to believe that men on the Government House List steal——at least little things. But the miraculous acceptance by Miss Hollis of that tailor, Pack, decided him to take steps on suspicion. He vowed that he only wanted to find out where his ruby-studded silver box had vanished to. You cannot accuse a man on the Government House List of stealing. And if you rifle his room you are a thief yourself. Churton, prompted by The Man who Knew, decided on burglary. If he found nothing in Pack's room . . . but it is not nice to think of what would have happened in that case.

Pack went to a dance at Benmore–Benmore *was* Benmore in those days, and not an office–and danced fifteen waltzes out of twenty-two with Miss Hollis. Churton and The Man took all the keys that they could get their hands on, and went to Pack's room in the hotel, certain that his servants would be away. Pack was a cheap soul. He had not purchased a decent cash-box to keep his papers in, but one of those native imitations that you buy for ten rupees. It opened to any sort of key, and there at the bottom, under Pack's Insurance Policy, lay the Bisara of Pooree!

Churton called Pack names, put the Bisara of Pooree in his pocket, and went to the dance with The Man. At least, he came in time for supper, and saw the beginning of the end in Miss Hollis's eyes. She was hysterical after supper, and was taken away by her Mamma.

At the dance, with the abominable Bisara in his pocket, Churton twisted his foot on one of the steps leading down to the old Rink, and had to be sent home in a rickshaw, grumbling. He did not believe in the Bisara of Pooree any the more for this manifestation, but he sought out Pack and called him some ugly names; and "thief" was the mildest of them. Pack took the names with the nervous smile of a little man who wants both soul and body to resent an insult, and went his way. There was no public scandal.

A week later, Pack got his definite dismissal from Miss Hollis. There had been a mistake in the placing of her affections, she said. So he went away to Madras, where he can do no great harm even if he lives to be a Colonel.

Churton insisted upon The Man who Knew taking the Bisara of Pooree as a gift. The Man took it, went down to the Cart-Road at once, found an *ekka*-pony with a blue bead-necklace, fastened the Bisara of Pooree inside the necklace with a piece of shoestring and thanked Heaven that he was rid of a danger. Remember, in case you ever find it, that you must destroy the Bisara of Pooree. I have not time to explain why just now, but the power lies in the little wooden fish. Mister Gubernatis or Max Muller could tell you more about it than I.

You will say that all this story is made up. Very well. If ever you come across a little, silver, ruby-studded box, seven-eighths of an inch long by three-quarters wide, with a dark-brown wooden fish, wrapped in gold cloth, inside it, keep it. Keep it for three years, and then you will discover for yourself whether the story is true or false.

Better still, steal it as Pack did, and you will be sorry that you had not killed yourself in the beginning.

The Gate of a Hundred Sorrows

"If I can attain Heaven for a pice, why should you be envious?"
Opium Smoker's Proverb.

THIS IS NO work of mine. My friend, Gabral Misquitta, the half-caste, spoke it all, between moon-set and morning, six weeks before he died; and I took it down from his mouth as he answered my questions so:–

It lies between the Coppersmith's Gully and the pipestem sellers' quarter, within a hundred yards, too, as the crow flies, of the Mosque of Wazir Khan. I don't mind telling any one this much, but I defy him to find the Gate, however well he may think he knows the City. You might even go through the very gully it stands in a hundred times, and be none the wiser. We used to call the gully, "the Gully of the Black Smoke," but its native name is altogether different of course. A loaded donkey couldn't pass between the walls; and, at one point, just before you reach the Gate, a bulged house-front makes people go along all sideways.

It isn't really a gate though. It's a house. Old Fung-Tching had it first five years ago. He was a boot-maker in Calcutta. They say that he murdered his wife there when he was drunk. That was why he dropped bazar-rum and took to the Black Smoke instead. Later on, he came up north and opened the Gate as a house where you could get your smoke in peace and quiet. Mind you, it was a *pukka,* respectable opium-house, and not one of those stifling, sweltering *chandoo-khanas,* that you can find all over the City. No; the old man knew his business thoroughly, and he was most clean for a Chinaman. He was a one-eyed little chap, not much more than five feet high, and both his middle fingers were gone. All the same, he was the handiest man at rolling black bills I have ever seen. Never seemed to be touched by the Smoke, either; and what he took day and night, night and day, was a caution. I've been at it five years, and I can do my fair share of the Smoke with any one; but I was a child to Fung-Tching that way. All the same, the old man was keen on his money, very keen; and that's what I can't understand. I heard he saved a good deal before he died, but his nephew has got all that now; and the old man's gone back to China to be buried.

He kept the big upper room, where his best customers gathered, as neat as a new pin. In one corner used to stand Fung-Tching's Joss–almost as ugly as Fung-Tching–and there were always sticks burning under his nose: but you never smelt 'em when the pipes were going thick. Opposite the Joss was Fung-Tching's coffin. He had spent a good deal of his savings on that, and whenever a new man came to the Gate he was always introduced to it. It was lacquered black, with red and gold writings on it, and I've heard that Fung-Tching brought it out all the way from China. I don't know whether that's true or not, but I know that, if I came first in the evening, I used to spread my mat just at the foot of it. It was a quiet corner, you see, and a sort of breeze from the gully came in at the window now and then. Besides the mats, there was no other furniture in the room–only the coffin, and the old Joss all green and blue and purple with age and polish.

Fung-Tching never told us why he called the place "The Gate of a Hundred Sorrows." (He was the only Chinaman I know who used bad-sounding fancy names. Most of them are flowery. As you'll see in Calcutta.) We used to find that out for ourselves. Nothing grows on you so much, if you're white, as the Black Smoke. A yellow man is made different. Opium doesn't tell on him scarcely at all; but white and black suffer a good deal. Of course, there are some people that the Smoke doesn't touch any more than tobacco would at first. They just doze a bit, as one would fall asleep naturally, and next morning they are almost fit for work. Now, I was one of that sort when I began, but I've been at it for five years pretty steadily, and it's different now. There was an old aunt of mine, down Agra way, and she left me a little at her death. About sixty rupees a month secured. Sixty isn't much. I can recollect a time, seems hundreds and hundreds of years ago, that I was getting my three hundred a month, and pickings, when I was working on a big timber contract in Calcutta.

I didn't stick to that work for long. The Black Smoke does not allow of much other business; and even though I am very little affected by it, as men go, I couldn't do a day's work now to save my life. After all, sixty rupees is what I want. When old Fung-Tching was alive he used to draw the money for me, give me about half of it to live on (I eat very little), and the rest he kept himself. I was free of the Gate at any time of the day and night, and could smoke and sleep there when I liked, so I didn't care. I know the old man made a good thing out of it; but that's no matter. Nothing matters much to me; and, besides, the money always came fresh and fresh each month.

There was ten of us met at the Gate when the place was first opened. Me, and two Baboos from a Government Office somewhere in Anarkulli, but they got the sack and couldn't pay (no man who has to work in the daylight can do the Black Smoke for any length of time straight on); a Chinaman that was Fung-Tching's nephew; a bazar-woman that had got a lot of money somehow; an English loafer—Mac-Somebody I think, but I have forgotten—that smoked heaps, but never seemed to pay anything (they said he had saved Fung-Tching's life at some trial in Calcutta when he was a barrister); another Eurasian, like myself, from Madras; a half caste woman, and a couple of men who said they had come from the North. I think they must have been Persians or Afghans or something. There are not more than five of us living now, but we come regular. I don't know what happened to the Baboos; but the bazar-woman she died after six months of the Gate, and I think Fung-Tching took her bangles and nose-ring for himself. But I'm not certain. The Englishman, he drank as well as smoked, and he dropped off. One of the Persians got killed in a row at night by the big well near the mosque a long time ago, and the Police shut up the well, because they said it was full of foul air. They found him dead at the bottom of it. So, you see, there is only me, the Chinaman, the half-caste woman that we call the *Memsahib* (she used to live with Fung-Tching), the other Eurasian, and one of the Persians. The *Memsahib* looks very old now. I think she was a young woman when the Gate was opened; but we are all old for the matter of that. Hundreds and hundreds of years old. It is very hard to keep count of time in the Gate, and besides, time doesn't matter to me. I draw my sixty rupees fresh and fresh every month. A very, very long while ago, when I used to be getting three hundred and fifty rupees a month, and pickings, on a big timber-contract at Calcutta, I had a wife of sorts. But she's dead now. People said that I killed her by taking to the Black Smoke. Perhaps I did, but it's so long since it doesn't matter. Sometimes when I first came to the Gate, I used to feel sorry for it; but that's all over and done with long ago, and I draw my sixty rupees fresh and fresh every month, and am quite happy. Not *drunk* happy, you know, but always quiet and soothed and contented.

How did I take to it? It began at Calcutta. I used to try it in my own house, just to see what it was like. I never went very far, but I think my wife must have died then. Anyhow, I found myself here, and got to know Fung-Tching.

I don't remember rightly how that came about; but he told me of the Gate and I used to go there, and, somehow, I have never got away from it since. Mind you, though, the Gate was a respectable place in Fung-Tching's time where you could be comfortable, and not at all like the *chandoo-khanas* where the niggers go. No; it was clean and quiet, and not crowded. Of course, there were others besides us ten and the man; but we always had a mat apiece with a wadded woolen headpiece, all covered with black and red dragons and things; just like a coffin in the corner.

At the end of one's third pipe the dragons used to move about and fight. I've watched 'em, many and many a night through. I used to regulate my Smoke that way, and now it takes a dozen pipes to make 'em stir. Besides, they are all torn and dirty, like the mats, and old Fung-Tching is dead. He died a couple of years ago, and gave me the pipe I always use now–a silver one, with queer beasts crawling up and down the receiver-bottle below the cup. Before that, I think, I used a big bamboo stem with a copper cup, a very small one, and a green jade mouthpiece. It was a little thicker than a walking-stick stem, and smoked sweet, very sweet. The bamboo seemed to suck up the smoke. Silver doesn't, and I've got to clean it out now and then, that's a great deal of trouble, but I smoke it for the old man's sake. He must have made a good thing out of me, but he always gave me clean mats and pillows, and the best stuff you could get anywhere.

When he died, his nephew Tsin-ling took up the Gate, and he called it the "Temple of the Three Posessions;" but we old ones speak of it as the "Hundred Sorrows," all the same. The nephew does things very shabbily, and I think the *Memsahib* must help him. She lives with him; same as she used to do with the old man. The two let in all sorts of low people, niggers and all, and the Black Smoke isn't as good as it used to be. I've found burnt bran in my pipe over and over again. The old man would have died if that had happened in his time. Besides, the room is never cleaned, and all the mats are torn and cut at the edges. The coffin has gone–gone to China again–with the old man and two ounces of smoke inside it, in case he should want 'em on the way.

The Joss doesn't get so many sticks burnt under his nose as he used to; that's a sign of ill-luck, as sure as Death. He's all brown, too, and no one ever attends to him. That's the *Memsahib's* work, I know; because, when Tsin-ling tried to burn gilt paper before him, she said it was a waste of money, and, if he kept a stick burning very slowly, the Joss wouldn't know the difference. So now we've got the sticks mixed with a lot of glue, and they take half-an-hour longer to burn, and smell stinky. Let alone the smell of the room by itself. No business can get on if they try that sort of thing. The Joss doesn't like it. I can see that. Late at night, sometimes, he turns all sorts of queer colors–blue and green and red–just as he used to do when old Fung-Tching was alive; and he rolls his eyes and stamps his feet like a devil.

I don't know why I don't leave the place and smoke quietly in a little room of my own in the bazar. Most like, Tsin-ling would kill me if I went away–he draws my sixty rupees now–and besides, it's so much trouble, and I've grown to be very fond of the Gate. It's not much to look at. Not what it was in the old man's time, but I couldn't leave it. I've seen so many come in and out. And I've seen so many die here on the mats that I should be afraid of dying in the open now. I've seen some things that people would call strange enough; but nothing is strange when you're on the Black Smoke, except the Black Smoke. And if it was, it wouldn't matter. Fung-Tching used to be very particular about his people, and never got in any one who'd give trouble by dying messy and such. But the nephew isn't half as careful. He tells everywhere that he keeps a "first-chop" house. Never tries to get men in quietly, and make them comfortable like Fung-Tching did. That's why the Gate is getting a little bit more known than it used to be. Among the niggers of course. The nephew daren't get a white, or, for matter of that, a mixed skin into the place. He has to keep us three of course—me and the *Memsahib* and the other Eurasian. We're fixtures. But he wouldn't give us credit for a pipeful—not for anything.

One of these days, I hope, I shall die in the Gate. The Persian and the Madras man are terrible shaky now. They've got a boy to light their pipes for them. I always do that myself. Most like, I shall see them carried out before me. I don't think I shall ever outlive the *Memsahib* or Tsin-ling. Women last longer than men at the Black Smoke, and Tsin-ling has a deal of the old man's blood in him, though he *does* smoke cheap stuff. The bazar-woman knew when she was going two days before her time; and *she* died on a clean mat with a nicely wadded pillow, and the old man hung up her pipe just above the Joss. He was always fond of her, I fancy. But he took her bangles just the same.

I should like to die like the bazar-woman—on a clean, cool mat with a pipe of good stuff between my lips. When I feel I'm going, I shall ask Tsin-ling for them, and he can draw my sixty rupees a month, fresh and fresh, as long as he pleases. Then I shall lie back, quiet and comfortable, and watch the black and red dragons have their last big fight together; and then. . . .

Well, it doesn't matter. Nothing matters much to me—only I wish Tsin-ling wouldn't put bran into the Black Smoke.

Bimi

THE ORANG-OUTANG in the big iron cage lashed to the sheep-pen began the discussion. The night was stiflingly hot, and as Hans Breitmann and I passed him, dragging our bedding to the fore-peak of the steamer, he roused himself and chattered obscenely. He had been caught somewhere in the Malayan Archipelago, and was going to England to be exhibited at a shilling a head. For four days he had struggled, yelled, and wrenched at the heavy iron bars of his prison without ceasing, and had nearly slain a Lascar incautious enough to come within reach of the great hairy paw.

"It would be well for you, mine friend, if you was a liddle seasick," said Hans Breitmann, pausing by the cage. "You haf too much Ego in your Cosmos."

The orang-outang's arm slid out negligently from between the bars. No one would have believed that it would make a sudden snake-like rush at the German's breast. The thin silk of the sleeping-suit tore out: Hans stepped back unconcernedly, to pluck a banana from a bunch hanging close to one of the boats.

"Too much Ego," said he, peeling the fruit and offering it to the caged devil, who was rending the silk to tatters.

Then we laid out our bedding in the bows, among the sleeping Lascars, to catch any breeze that the pace of the ship might give us. The sea was like smoky oil, except where it turned to fire under our forefoot and whirled back into the dark in smears of dull flame. There was a thunder-storm some miles away: we could see the glimmer of the lightning. The ship's cow, distressed by the heat and the smell of the ape-beast in the cage, lowed unhappily from time to time in exactly the same key as the lookout man at the bows answered the hourly call from the bridge. The trampling tune of the engines was very distinct, and the jarring of the ash-lift, as it was tipped into the sea, hurt the procession of hushed noise. Hans lay down by my side and lighted a good-night cigar. This was naturally the beginning of conversation. He owned a voice as soothing as the wash of the sea, and stores of experiences as vast as the sea itself; for his business in life was to wander up and down the world, collecting orchids and wild beasts and ethnological specimens for German and American dealers. I watched the glowing end of his cigar wax and wane in the gloom, as the sentences rose and fell, till I was nearly asleep. The orang-outang, troubled by some dream of the forests of his freedom, began to yell like a soul in purgatory, and to wrench madly at the bars of the cage.

"If he was out now dere would not be much of us left hereabouts," said Hans, lazily. "He screams good. See, now, how I shall tame him when he stops himself."

There was a pause in the outcry, and from Hans' mouth came an imitation of a snake's hiss, so perfect that I almost sprung to my feet. The sustained murderous sound ran along the deck, and the wrenching at the bars ceased. The orang-outang was quaking in an ecstasy of pure terror.

"Dot stop him," said Hans. "I learned dot trick in Mogoung Tanjong when I was collecting liddle monkeys for some peoples in Berlin. Efery one in der world is afraid of der monkeys–except der snake. So I blay snake against monkey, and he keep quite still. Dere was too much Ego in his Cosmos. Dot is der soul-custom of monkeys. Are you asleep, or will you listen, and I will tell a dale dot you shall not pelief?"

"There's no tale in the wide world that I can't believe," I said.

"If you have learned pelief you haf learned somedings. Now I shall try your pelief. Good! When I was collecting dose liddle monkeys–it was in '79 or '80, und I was in der islands of der Archipelago–over dere in der dark"–he pointed southward to New Guinea generally–"Mein Gott! I would sooner collect life red devils than liddle monkeys. When dey do not bite off your thumbs dey are always dying from nostalgia–homesick–for dey haf der imperfect soul, which is midway arrested in defelopment–und too much Ego. I was dere for nearly a year, und dere I found a man dot was called Bertran. He was a Frenchman, und he was a goot man–naturalist to the bone. Dey said he was an escaped convict, but he was a naturalist, and dot was enough for me. He would call all der life beasts from der forests, und dey would come. I said he was St. Francis of Assisi in a new dransmigration produced, und he laughed und said he haf never preach to der fishes. He sold them for tripang–*bêche-de-mer.*

"Und dot man, who was king of beasts-tamer men, he had in der house shush such anoder as dot devil-animal in der cage–a great orang-outang dot thought he was a man. He haf found him when he was a child–der orang-outang–und he was child and brother and opera comique all round to Bertran. He had his room in dot house–not a cage, but a room–mit a bed and sheets, and he would go to bed and get up in der morning and smoke his cigar und eat his dinner mit Bertran, und walk mit him hand-in-hand, which was most horrible. Herr Gott! I haf seen dot beast throw himself back in his chair and laugh when Bertran haf made fun of me. He was *not* a beast; he was a man, and he talked to Bertran, und Bertran comprehended, for I have seen dem. Und he was always politeful to me except when I talk too long to Bertran und say nodings at all to him. Den he would pull me away–dis great, dark devil, mit his enormous paws–shush as if I was a child. He was not a beast, he was a man. Dis I saw before I know him three months, und Bertran he haf saw the same; and Bimi, der orang-outang, haf understood us both, mit his cigar between his big-dog teeth und der blue gum.

"I was dere a year, dere und at dere oder islands somedimes for monkeys and somedimes for butterflies und orchits. One time Bertran says to me dot he will be married, because he haf found a girl dot was goot, and he inquire if this marrying idea was right. I would not say, pecause it was not me dot was going to be married. Den he go off courting der girl–she was a half-caste

French girl–very pretty. Haf you got a new light for my cigar? Oof! Very pretty. Only I say: 'Haf you thought of Bimi? If he pulls me away when I talk to you, what will he do to your wife? He will pull her in pieces. If I was you, Bertran, I would gif my wife for wedding present der stuff figure of Bimi.' By dot time I had learned somedings about der monkey peoples. 'Shoot him?' says Bertran. 'He is your beast,' I said; 'if he was mine he would be shot now."

"Den I felt at der back of my neck der fingers of Bimi. Mein Gott! I tell you dot he talked through dose fingers. It was der deaf-and-dumb alphabet all gomplete. He slide his hairy arm round my neck and he tilt up my chin und look into my face, shust to see if I understood his talk so well as he understood mine.

"'See now dere!' says Bertran, 'und you would shoot him while he is cuddling you? Dot is der Teuton ingrate?'

"But I knew dot I had made Bimi a life's enemy, pecause his fingers haf talk murder through the back of my neck. Next dime I see Bimi dere was a pistol in my belt, und he touch it once, und I open der breech to show him it was loaded. He haf seen der liddle monkeys killed in der woods, and he understood.

"So Bertran he was married, and he forgot clean about Bimi dot was skippin' alone on der beach mit der half of a human soul in his belly. I was see him skip, und he took a big bough and thrash der sand till he haf made a great hole like a grave. So I says to Bertran: 'For any sakes, kill Bimi. He is mad mit der jealousy.'

"Bertran haf said: 'He is not mad at all. He haf obey and love my wife, und if she speaks he will get her slippers,' und he looked at his wife across der room. She was a very pretty girl.

"Den I said to him: 'Dost thou pretend to know monkeys und dis beast dot is lashing himself mad upon der sands, pecause you do not talk to him? Shoot him when he comes to der house, for he haf der light in his eyes dot mean killing–und killing.' Bimi come to der house, but dere was no light in his eyes. It was all put away, cunning–so cunning–und he fetch der girl her slippers, and Bertran turn to me und say: 'Dost thou know him in nine months more dan I haf known him in twelve years? Shall a child stab his fader? I have fed him, und he was my child. Do not speak this nonsense to my wife or to me any more.'

"Dot next day Bertran came to my house to help me make some wood cases for der specimens, und he tell me dot he haf let his wife a liddle while mit Bimi in der garden. Den I finish my cases quick, und I say: 'Let us go to your house und get a trink.' He laugh und say: 'Come along, dry mans.'

"His wife was not in der garden, und Bimi did not come when Bertran called. Und his wife did not come when he called, und he knocked at her bedroom door und dot was shut tight–locked. Den he look at me, und his face was white. I broke down der door mit my shoulder, und der thatch of der roof was torn into a great hole, und der sun came in upon der floor. Haf you ever seen paper in der waste-basket, or cards at whist on der table scattered? Dere was no wife dot could be seen. I tell you dere was noddings in dot room dot might be a woman. Dere was stuff on der floor, und dot was all. I looked at dese things und I was very sick; but Bertran looked a liddle longer at what was upon the floor und der walls, und der hole in der thatch. Den he pegan to laugh, soft and low, und I knew und thank Gott dot he was mad. He nefer cried, he nefer prayed. He stood still in der doorway und laugh to himself. Den he said: 'She haf locked herself in dis room, and he haf torn up der thatch. *Fi donc*. Dot is so. We will mend der thatch und wait for Bimi. He will surely come.'

"I tell you we waited ten days in dot house, after der room was made into a room again, and once or twice we saw Bimi comin' a liddle way from der woods. He was afraid pecause he haf done wrong. Bertran called him when he was come to look on the tenth day, und Bimi come skipping along der beach und making noises, mit a long piece of black hair in his hands. Den Bertran laugh and say, *'Fi donc!'* shust as if it was a glass broken upon der table; und Bimi come nearer, und Bertran was honey-sweet in his voice and laughed to himself. For three days he made love to Bimi, pecause Bimi would not let himself be touched. Den Bimi come to dinner at der same table mit us, und der hair on his hands was all black und thick mit–mit what had dried on his hands. Bertran gave him sangaree till Bimi was drunk and stupid, und den–"

Hans paused to puff at his cigar.

"And then?" said I.

"Und den Bertran kill him with his hands, und I go for a walk upon der beach. It was Bertran's own piziness. When I come back der ape he was dead, und Bertran he was dying abofe him; but still he laughed a liddle und low, and he was quite content. Now you know der formula of der strength of der orang-outang–it is more as seven to one in relation to man. But Bertran, he haf killed Bimi mit sooch dings as Gott gif him. Dot was der mericle."

The infernal clamor in the cage recommenced. "Aha! Dot friend of ours haf still too much Ego in his Cosmos. Be quiet, thou!"

Hans hissed long and venomously. We could hear the great beast quaking in his cage.

"But why in the world didn't you help Bertran instead of letting him be killed?" I asked.

"My friend," said Hans, composedly stretching himself to slumber, "it was not nice even to mineself dot I should lif after I had seen dot room wit der hole in der thatch. Und Bertran, he was her husband. Goot-night, und sleep well."

Namgay Doola

ONCE UPON A time there was a king who lived on the road to Thibet, very many miles in the Himalaya Mountains. His kingdom was 11,000 feet above the sea, and exactly four miles square, but most of the miles stood on end, owing to the nature of the country. His revenues were rather less than £400 yearly, and they were expended on the maintenance of one elephant and a standing army of five men. He was tributary to the Indian government, who allowed him certain sums for keeping a section of the Himalaya-Thibet road in repair. He further increased his revenues by selling timber to the railway companies, for he would cut the great deodar trees in his own forest and they fell thundering into the Sutlej River and were swept down the Plains, 300 miles away, and became railway ties. Now and again this king, whose name does not matter, would mount a ring-streaked horse and ride scores of miles to Simlatown to confer with the lieutenant-governor on matters of state, or assure the viceroy that his sword was at the service of the queen-empress. Then the viceroy would cause a ruffle of drums to be sounded and the ring-streaked horse and the cavalry of the state–two men in tatters–and the herald who bore the Silver Stick before the king would trot back to their own place, which was between the tail of a heaven-climbing glacier and a dark birch forest.

Now, from such a king, always remembering that he possessed one veritable elephant and could count his descent for 1,200 years, I expected, when it was my fate to wander through his dominions, no more than mere license to live.

The night had closed in rain, and rolling clouds blotted out the lights of the villages in the valley. Forty miles away, untouched by cloud or storm, the white shoulder of Dongo Pa—the Mountain of the Council of the Gods—upheld the evening star. The monkeys sung sorrowfully to each other as they hunted for dry roots in the fern-draped trees, and the last puff of the day-wind brought from the unseen villages the scent of damp wood smoke, hot cakes, dripping undergrowth, and rotting pine-cones. That smell is the true smell of the Himalayas, and if it once gets into the blood of a man he will, at the last, forgetting everything else, return to the Hills to die. The clouds closed and the smell went away, and there remained nothing in all the world except chilling white mists and the bloom of the Sutlej River.

A fat-tailed sheep, who did not want to die, bleated lamentably at my tent-door. He was scuffling with the prime minister and the director-general of public education, and he was a royal gift to me and my camp servants. I expressed my thanks suitably and inquired if I might have audience of the king. The prime minister readjusted his turban—it had fallen off in the struggle—and assured me that the king would be very pleased to see me. Therefore I dispatched two bottles as a foretaste, and when the sheep had entered upon another incarnation, climbed up to the king's palace through the wet. He had sent his army to escort me, but it stayed to talk with my cook. Soldiers are very much alike all the world over.

The palace was a four-roomed, whitewashed mud-and-timber house, the finest in all the Hills for a day's journey. The king was dressed in a purple velvet jacket, white muslin trousers, and a saffron-yellow turban of price. He gave me audience in a little carpeted room opening off the palace courtyard, which was occupied by the elephant of state. The great beast was sheeted and anchored from trunk to tail, and the curve of his back stood out against the sky line.

The prime minister and the director-general of public instruction were present to introduce me; but all the court had been dismissed lest the two bottles aforesaid should corrupt their morals. The king cast a wreath of heavy, scented flowers round my neck as I bowed, and inquired how my honored presence had the felicity to be. I said that through seeing his auspicious countenance the mists of the night had turned into sunshine, and that by reason of his beneficent sheep his good deeds would be remembered by the gods. He said that since I had set my magnificent foot in his kingdom the crops would probably yield seventy per cent more than the average. I said that the fame of the king had reached to the four corners of the earth, and that the nations gnashed their teeth when they heard daily of the glory of his realm and the wisdom of his moon-like prime minister and lotus-eyed director-general of public education.

Then we sat down on clean white cushions, and I was at the king's right hand. Three minutes later he was telling me that the condition of the maize crop was something disgraceful, and that the railway companies would not pay him enough for his timber. The talk shifted to and fro with the bottles. We discussed very many quaint things, and the king became confidential on the subject of government generally. Most of all he dwelt on the shortcomings of one of his subjects, who, from what I could gather, had been paralyzing the executive.

"In the old days," said the king, "I could have ordered the elephant yonder to trample him to death. Now I must e'en send him seventy miles across the hills to be tried, and his keep for that time would be upon the state. And the elephant eats everything."

"What be the man's crimes, Rajah Sahib?" said I.

"Firstly, he is an 'outlander,' and no man of mine own people. Secondly, since of my favor I gave him land upon his coming, he refuses to pay revenue. Am I not the lord of the earth, above and below—entitled by right and custom to one eighth of the crop? Yet this devil, establishing himself, refused to pay a single tax . . . and he brings a poisonous spawn of babes."

"Cast him into jail," I said.

"Sahib," the king answered, shifting a little on the cushions, "once and only once in these forty years sickness came upon me so that I was not able to go abroad. In that hour I made a vow to my God that I would never again cut man or woman from the light of the sun and the air of God, for I perceived the nature of the punishment. How can I break my vow? Were it only the lopping off of a hand or a foot, I should not delay. But even that is impossible now that the English have rule. One or another of my people"—he looked obliquely at the director-general of public education—"would at once write a letter to the viceroy, and perhaps I should be deprived of that ruffle of drums."

He unscrewed the mouthpiece of his silver waterpipe, fitted a plain amber one, and passed the pipe to me. "Not content with refusing revenue," he continued, "this outlander refuses also to beegar" (this is the corvee or forced labor on the roads), "and stirs my people up to the like treason. Yet he is, if so he wills, an expert log-snatcher. There is none better or bolder among my people to clear a block of the river when the logs stick fast."

"But he worships strange gods," said the prime minister, deferentially.

"For that I have no concern," said the king, who was as tolerant as Akbar in matters of belief. "To each man his own god, and the fire or Mother Earth for us at the last. It is the rebellion that offends me."

"The king has an army," I suggested. "Has not the king burned the man's house, and left him naked to the night dews?"

"Nay. A hut is a hut, and it holds the life of a man. But once I sent my army against him when his excuses became wearisome. Of their heads he brake three across the top with a stick. The other two men ran away. Also the guns would not shoot."

I had seen the equipment of the infantry. One third of it was an old muzzle-loading fowling-piece with ragged rust holes where the nipples should have been; one third a wirebound match-lock with worm-eaten stock, and one third a four-bore flint duck-gun, without a flint.

"But it is to be remembered," said the king, reaching out for the bottle, "that he is a very expert log-snatcher and a man of a merry face. What shall I do to him, Sahib?"

This was interesting. The timid hill-folk would as soon have refused taxes to their king as offerings to their gods. The rebel must be a man of character.

"If it be the king's permission," I said, "I will not strike my tents till the third day, and I will see this man. The mercy of the king is godlike, and rebellion is like unto the sin of witchcraft. Moreover, both the bottles, and another, be empty."

"You have my leave to go," said the king.

Next morning the crier went through the state proclaiming that there was a log-jam on the river and that it behooved all loyal subjects to clear it. The people poured down from their villages to the moist, warm valley of poppy fields, and the king and I went with them.

Hundreds of dressed deodar logs had caught on a snag of rock, and the river was bringing down more logs every minute to complete the blockade. The water snarled and wrenched and worried at the timber, while the population of the state prodded at the nearest logs with poles, in the hope of easing the pressure. Then there went up a shout of "Namgay Doola! Namgay Doola!" and a large, red-haired villager hurried up, stripping off his clothes as he ran.

"That is he. That is the rebel!" said the king. "Now will the dam be cleared."

"But why has he red hair?" I asked, since red-hair among hill-folk is as uncommon as blue or green.

"He is an outlander," said the king. "Well done! Oh, well done!"

Namgay Doola had scrambled on the jam and was clawing out the butt of a log with a rude sort of a boat-hook. It slid forward slowly, as an alligator moves, and three or four others followed it. The green water spouted through the gaps. Then the villagers howled and shouted and leaped among the logs, pulling and pushing the obstinate timber, and the red head of Namgay Doola was chief among them all. The logs swayed and chafed and groaned as fresh consignments from up-stream battered the now weakening dam. It gave way at last in a smother of foam, racing butts, bobbing black heads, and a confusion indescribable, as the river tossed everything before it. I saw the red head go down with the last remnants of the jam and disappear between the great grinding tree trunks. It rose close to the bank, and blowing like a grampus, Namgay Doola wiped the water out of his eyes and made obeisance to the king.

I had time to observe the man closely. The virulent redness of his shock head and beard was most startling, and in the thicket of hair twinkled above high cheek-bones two very merry blue eyes. He was indeed an outlander, but yet a Thibetan in language, habit and attire. He spoke the Lepcha dialect with an indescribable softening of the gutturals. It was not so much a lisp as an accent.

"Whence comest thou?" I asked, wondering.

"From Thibet." He pointed across the hills and grinned. That grin went straight to my heart. Mechanically I held out my hand, and Namgay Doola took it. No pure Thibetan would have understood the meaning of the gesture. He went away to look for his clothes, and as he climbed back to his village, I heard a joyous yell that seemed unaccountably familiar. It was the whooping of Namgay Doola.

"You see now," said the king, "why I would not kill him. He is a bold man among my logs, but," and he shook his head like a schoolmaster, "I know that before long there will be complaints of him in the court. Let us return to the palace and do justice."

It was the king's custom to judge his subjects every day between eleven and three o'clock. I heard him do justice equitably on weighty matters of trespass, slander, and a little wife-stealing. Then his brow clouded and he summoned me.

"Again it is Namgay Doola," he said despairingly. "Not content with refusing revenue on his own part, he has bound half his village by an oath to the like treason. Never before has such a thing befallen me! Nor are my taxes heavy."

A rabbit-faced villager, with a blush-rose stuck behind his ear, advanced trembling. He had been in Namgay Doola's conspiracy, but had told everything and hoped for the king's favor.

"Oh, king!" said I, "if it be the king's will, let this matter stand over till the morning. Only the gods can do right in a hurry, and it may be that yonder villager has lied."

"Nay, for I know the nature of Namgay Doola; but since a guest asks, let the matter remain. Wilt thou, for my sake, speak harshly to this red-headed outlander? He may listen to thee."

I made an attempt that very evening, but for the life of me I could not keep my countenance. Namgay Doola grinned so persuasively and began to tell me about a big brown bear in a poppy field by the river. Would I care to shoot that bear? I spoke austerely on the sin of detected conspiracy and the certainty of punishment. Namgay Doola's face clouded for a moment. Shortly afterward he withdrew from my tent, and I heard him singing softly among the pines. The words were unintelligible to me, but the tune, like his liquid, insinuating speech seemed the ghost of something strangely familiar.

"Dir hane mard-i-yemen dir
To weeree ala gee."

crooned Namgay Doola again and again, and I racked my brain for that lost tune. It was not till after dinner that I discovered some one had cut a square foot of velvet from the center of my best camera-cloth. This made me so angry that I wandered down the valley in the hope of meeting the big brown bear. I could hear him grunting like a discontented pig in the poppy field as I waited shoulder deep in the dew-dripping Indian corn to catch him after his meal. The moon was at full and drew out the scent of the tasseled crop. Then I heard the anguished bellow of a Himalayan cow—one of the little black crummies no bigger than Newfoundland dogs. Two shadows that looked like a bear and her cub hurried past me. I was in the act of firing when I saw that each bore a brilliant red head. The lesser animal was trailing something rope-like that left a dark track on the path. They were within six feet of me, and the shadow of the moonlight lay velvet-black on their faces. Velvet-black was exactly the word, for by all the powers of moonlight they were masked in the velvet of my camera-cloth. I marveled, and went to bed.

Next morning the kingdom was in an uproar. Namgay Doola, men said, had gone forth in the night and with a sharp knife had cut off the tail of a cow belonging to the rabbit-faced villager who had betrayed him. It was sacrilege unspeakable against the holy cow! The state desired his blood, but he had retreated into his hut, barricaded the doors and windows with big stones, and defied the world.

The king and I and the populace approached the hut cautiously. There was no hope of capturing our man without loss of life, for from a hole in the wall projected the muzzle of an extremely well-cared-for gun—the only gun in the state that could shoot. Namgay Doola had narrowly missed a villager just before we came up.

The standing army stood.

It could do no more, for when it advanced pieces of sharp shale flew from the windows. To these were added from time to time showers of scalding water. We saw red heads bobbing up and down within. The family of Namgay Doola were aiding their sire. Blood-curdling yells of defiance were the only answer to our prayers.

"Never," said the king, puffing, "has such a thing befallen my state. Next year I will certainly buy a little cannon." He looked at me imploringly.

"Is there any priest in the kingdom to whom he will listen?" said I, for a light was beginning to break upon me.

"He worships his own gods," said the prime minister. "We can but starve him out."

"Let the white man approach," said Namgay Doola from within. "All others I will kill. Send me the white man."

The door was thrown open and I entered the smoky interior of a Thibetan hut crammed with children. And every child had flaming red hair. A fresh-gathered cow's tail lay on the floor, and by its side two pieces of black velvet—my black velvet—rudely hacked into the semblance of masks.

"And what is this shame, Namgay Doola?" I asked.

He grinned more charmingly than ever. "There is no shame," said he. "I did but cut off the tail of that man's cow. He betrayed me. I was minded to shoot him, sahib, but not to death. Indeed, not to death; only in the legs."

"And why at all, since it is the custom to pay revenue to the king? Why at all?"

"By the god of my father, I cannot tell," said Namgay Doola.

"And who was thy father?"

"The same that had this gun." He showed me his weapon, a Tower musket, bearing date 1832 and the stamp of the Honorable East India Company.

"And thy father's name?" said I.

"Timlay Doola," said he. "At the first, I being then a little child, it is in my mind that he wore a red coat."

"Of that I have no doubt; but repeat the name of thy father twice or thrice."

He obeyed, and I understood whence the puzzling accent in his speech came. "Thimla Dhula!" said he, excitedly. "To this hour I worship his god."

"May I see that god?"

"In a little while—at twilight time."

"Rememberest thou aught of thy father's speech?"

"It is long ago. But there was one word which he said often. Thus, ' 'Shun!' Then I and my brethren stood upon our feet, our hands to our sides, thus."

"Even so. And what was thy mother?"

"A woman of the Hills. We be Lepchas of Darjiling, but me they call an outlander because my hair is as thou seest."

The Thibetan woman, his wife, touched him on the arm gently. The long parley outside the fort had lasted far into the day. It was now close upon twilight—the hour of the Angelus. Very solemnly the red-headed brats rose from the floor and formed a semicircle. Namgay Doola laid his gun aside, lighted a little oil-lamp, and set it before a recess in the wall. Pulling back a whisp of dirty cloth, he revealed a worn brass crucifix leaning against the helmet badge of a long-forgotten East India Company's regiment. "Thus did my father," he said, crossing himself clumsily. The wife and children followed suit. Then, all together, they struck up the wailing chant that I heard on the hill-side:

"Dir hane mard-i-yemen dir
To weeree ala gee."

I was puzzled no longer. Again and again they sung, as if their hearts would break, their version of the chorus of "The Wearing of the Green":

"They're hanging men and women, too,
For the wearing of the green."

A diabolical inspiration came to me. One of the brats, a boy about eight years old—could he have been in the fields last night?—was watching me as he sung. I pulled out a rupee, held the coin between finger and thumb, and looked—only looked—at the gun leaning against the wall. A grin of brilliant and perfect comprehension overspread his porringer-like face. Never for an instant stopping the song, he held out his hand for the money, and then slid the gun to my hand. I might have shot Namgay Doola dead as he chanted, but I was satisfied. The inevitable blood-instinct held true. Namgay Doola drew the curtain across the recess. Angelus was over.

"Thus my father sung. There was much more but I have forgotten, and I do not know the purport of even these words, but it may be that the god will understand. I am not of this people, and I will not pay revenue."

"And why?"

Again that soul-compelling grin. "What occupation would be to me between crop and crop? It is better than scaring bears. But these people do not understand."

He picked the masks off the floor and looked in my face as simply as a child.

"By what road didst thou attain knowledge to make those deviltries?" I said, pointing.

"I can not tell. I am but a Lepcha of Darjiling, and yet the stuff——"

"Which thou has stolen," said I.

"Nay, surely. Did I steal? I desired it so. The stuff—the stuff. What else should I have done with the stuff?" He twisted the velvet between his fingers.

"But the sin of maiming the cow—consider that."

"Oh, sahib, the man betrayed me; the heifer's tail waved in the moonlight, and I had my knife. What else should I have done? The tail came off ere I was aware. Sahib, thou knowest more than I."

"That is true," said I. "Stay within the door. I go to speak to the king." The population of the state were ranged on the hillside. I went forth and spoke.

"Oh, king," said I, "touching this man, there be two courses open to thy wisdom. Thou canst either hang him from a tree—he and his brood—till there remains no hair that is red within thy land."

"Nay," said the king. "Why should I hurt the little children?"

They had poured out of the hut and were making plump obeisances to everybody. Namgay Doola waited at the door with his gun across his arm.

"Or thou canst, discarding their impiety of the cow-maiming, raise him to honor in thy army. He comes of a race that will not pay revenue. A red flame is in his blood which comes out at the top of his head in that glowing hair. Make him chief of thy army. Give him honor as may befall and full allowance of work, but look to it, oh, king, that neither he nor his hold a foot of earth from thee henceforth. Feed him with words and favor and also liquor from certain bottles that thou knowest of, and he will be a bulwark of defense. But deny him even a tuftlet of grass for his own. This is the nature that God has given him. Moreover, he has brethren—"

The state groaned unanimously.

"But if his brethren come they will surely fight with each other till they die; or else the one will always give information concerning the other. Shall he be of thy army, oh, king? Choose."

The king bowed his head, and I said: "Comeforth, Namgay Doola, and command the king's army. Thy name shall no more be Namgay in the mouths of men, but Patsay Doola, for, as thou hast truly said, I know."

Then Namgay Doola, new-christened Patsay Doola, son of Timlay Doola—which is Tim Doolan—clasped the king's feet, cuffed the standing army, and hurried in an agony of contrition from temple to temple making offerings for the sin of the cattle-maiming.

And the king was so pleased with my perspicacity that he offered to sell me a village for £20 sterling. But I buy no village in the Himalayas so long as one red head flares between the tail of the heaven-climbing glacier and the dark birch forest.

I know that breed.

Moti Guj—Mutineer

ONCE UPON A time there was a coffee-planter in India who wished to clear some forest land for coffee-planting. When he had cut down all the trees and burned the underwood, the stumps still remained. Dynamite is expensive and slow fire slow. The happy medium for stump-clearing is the lord of all beasts, who is the elephant. He will either push the stump out of the ground with his tusks, if he has any, or drag it out with ropes. The planter, therefore, hired elephants by ones and twos and threes, and fell to work. The very best of all the elephants belonged to the very worst of all the drivers or mahouts; and this superior beast's name was Moti Guj. He was the absolute property of his mahout, which would never have been the case under native rule: for Moti Guj was a creature to be desired by kings, and his name, being translated, meant the Pearl Elephant. Besides the British government was in the land, Deesa, the mahout, enjoyed his property undisturbed. He was dissipated. When he had made much money through the strength of his elephant, he would get extremely drunk and give Moti Guj a beating with a tent-peg over the tender nails of the forefeet. Moti Guj never trampled the life out of Deesa on these occasions, for he knew that after the beating was over, Deesa would embrace his trunk and weep and call him his love and his life and the liver of his soul, and give him some liquor. Moti Guj was very fond of liquor–arrack for choice, though he would drink palm-tree toddy if nothing better offered. Then Deesa would go to sleep between Moti Guj's forefeet, and as Deesa generally chose the middle of the public road, and as Moti Guj mounted guard over him, and would not permit horse, foot, or cart to pass by, traffic was congested till Deesa saw fit to wake up.

There was no sleeping in the day-time on the planter's clearing: the wages were too high to risk. Deesa sat on Moti Guj's neck and gave him orders, while Moti Guj rooted up the stumps–for he owned a magnificent pair of tusks; or pulled at the end of a rope–for he had a magnificent pair of shoulders–while Deesa kicked him behind the ears and said he was the king of elephants. At evening time Moti Guj would wash down his three hundred pounds' weight of green food with a quart of arrack, and Deesa would take a share, and sing songs between Moti Guj's legs till it was time to go to bed. Once a week Deesa led Moti Guj down to the river, and Moti Guj lay on his side luxuriously in the shallows, while Deesa went over him with a coir swab and a brick. Moti Guj never mistook the pounding blow of the latter for the smack of the former that warned him to get up and turn over on the other side. Then Deesa would look at his feet and examine his eyes, and turn up the fringes of his mighty ears in case of sores or budding ophthalmia. After inspection the two would "come up with a song from the sea," Moti Guj, all black and shining, waving a torn tree trunk twelve feet long in his trunk, and Deesa knotting up his own long wet hair.

It was a peaceful, well-paid life till Deesa felt the return of the desire to drink deep. He wished for an orgy. The little draughts that led nowhere were taking the manhood out of him.

He went to the planter, and "My mother's dead," said he, weeping.

"She died on the last plantation two months ago, and she died once before that when you were working for me last year," said the planter, who knew something of the ways of nativedom.

"Then it's my aunt, and she was just the same as a mother to me," said Deesa, weeping more than ever. "She has left eighteen small children entirely without bread, and it is I who must fill their little stomachs," said Deesa, beating his head on the floor.

"Who brought you the news?" said the planter.

"The post," said Deesa.

"There hasn't been a post for the past week. Get back to your lines!"

"A devastating sickness has fallen on my village, and all my wives are dying," yelled Deesa, really in tears this time.

"Call Chihun, who comes from Deesa's village," said the planter. "Chihun, has this man got a wife?"

"He?" said Chihun. "No. Not a woman of our village would look at him. They'd sooner marry the elephant."

Chihun snorted. Deesa wept and bellowed.

"You will get into a difficulty in a minute," said the planter. "Go back to your work!"

"Now I will speak Heaven's truth," gulped Deesa, with an inspiration. "I haven't been drunk for two months. I desire to depart in order to get properly drunk afar off and distant from this heavenly plantation. Thus I shall cause no trouble."

A flickering smile crossed the planter's face. "Deesa," said he, "you've spoken the truth, and I'd give you leave on the spot if anything could be done with Moti Guj while you're away. You know that he will only obey your orders."

"May the light of the heavens live forty thousand years. I shall be absent but ten little days. After that, upon my faith and honor and soul, I return. As to the inconsiderable interval, have I the gracious permission of the heaven-born to call up Moti Guj?"

Permission was granted, and in answer to Deesa's shrill yell, the mighty tusker swung out of the shade of a clump of trees where he had been squirting dust over himself till his master should return.

"Light of my heart, protector of the drunken, mountain of might, give ear!" said Deesa, standing in front of him.

Moti Guj gave ear, and saluted with his trunk. "I am going away," said Deesa.

Moti Guj's eyes twinkled. He liked jaunts as well as his master. One could snatch all manner of nice things from the road-side then.

"But you, you fussy old pig, must stay behind and work."

The twinkle died out as Moti Guj tried to look delighted. He hated stump-hauling on the plantation. It hurt his teeth.

"I shall be gone for ten days, oh, delectable one! Hold up your near forefoot and I'll impress the fact upon it, warty toad of a dried mud-puddle." Deesa took a tent-peg and banged Moti Guj ten times on the nails. Moti Guj grunted and shuffled from foot to foot.

"Ten days," said Deesa, "You will work and haul and root the trees as Chihun here shall order you. Take up Chihun and set him on your neck!" Moti Guj curled the tip of his trunk, Chihun put his foot there, and was swung on to the neck. Deesa handed Chihun the heavy *ankus*—the iron elephant goad.

Chihun thumped Moti Guj's bald head as a paver thumps a curbstone.

Moti Guj trumpeted.

"Be still, hog of the backwoods! Chihun's your mahout for ten days. And now bid me good-by, beast after mine own heart. Oh, my lord, my king! Jewel of all created elephants, lily of the herd, preserve your honored health; be virtuous. Adieu!"

Moti Guj lapped his trunk round Deesa and swung him into the air twice. That was his way of bidding him good-by.

"He'll work now," said Deesa to the planter. "Have I leave to go?"

The planter nodded, and Deesa dived into the woods. Moti Guj went back to haul stumps.

Chihun was very kind to him, but he felt unhappy and forlorn for all that. Chihun gave him a ball of spices, and tickled him under the chin, and Chihun's little baby cooed to him after work was over, and Chihun's wife called him a darling; but Moti Guj was a bachelor by instinct, as Deesa was. He did not understand the domestic emotions. He wanted the light of his universe back again—the drink and the drunken slumber, the savage beatings and the savage caresses.

None the less he worked well, and the planter wondered. Deesa had wandered along the roads till he met a marriage procession of his own caste, and, drinking, dancing, and tippling, had drifted with it past all knowledge of the lapse of time.

The morning of the eleventh day dawned, and there returned no Deesa.

Moti Guj was loosed from his ropes for the daily stint. He swung clear, looked round, shrugged his shoulders, and began to walk away, as one having business elsewhere.

"Hi! ho! Come back you!" shouted Chihun. "Come back and put me on your neck, misborn mountain! Return, splendor of the hill-sides! Adornment of all India, heave to, or I'll bang every toe off your fat forefoot!"

Moti Guj gurgled gently, but did not obey. Chihun ran after him with a rope and caught him up. Moti Guj put his ears forward, and Chihun knew what that meant, though he tried to carry it off with high words.

"None of your nonsense with me," said he. "To your pickets, devil son!"

"Hrrump!" said Moti Guj, and that was all–that and the forebent ears.

Moti Guj put his hands in his pockets, chewed a branch for a toothpick, and strolled about the clearing, making fun of the other elephants who had just set to work.

Chihun reported the state of affairs to the planter, who came out with a dog-whip and cracked it furiously. Moti Guj paid the white man the compliment of charging him nearly a quarter of a mile across the clearing and "Hrrumphing" him into his veranda. Then he stood outside the house, chuckling to himself and shaking all over with the fun of it as an elephant will.

"We'll thrash him," said the planter. "He shall have the finest thrashing ever elephant received. Give Kala Nag and Nazim twelve foot of chain apiece, and tell them to lay on twenty."

Kala Nag–which means Black Snake–and Nazim were two of the biggest elephants in the lines, and one of their duties was to administer the graver punishment, since no man can beat an elephant properly.

They took the whipping-chains and rattled them in their trunks as they sidled up to Moti Guj, meaning to hustle him between them. Moti Guj had never, in all his life of thirty-nine years, been whipped, and he did not intend to begin a new experience. So he waited, waving his head from right to left, and measuring the precise spot in Kala Nag's fat side where a blunt tusk could sink deepest. Kala Nag had no tusks; the chain was the badge of his authority; but for all that, he swung wide of Moti Guj at the last minute, and tried to appear as if he had brought the chain out for amusement. Nazim turned round and went home early. He did not feel fighting fit that morning and so Moti Guj was left standing alone with his ears cocked.

That decided the planter to argue no more, and Moti Guj rolled back to his amateur inspection of the clearing. An elephant who will not work and is not tied up is about as manageable as an eighty-one-ton gun loose in a heavy seaway. He slapped old friends on the back and asked them if the stumps were coming away easily; he talked nonsense concerning labor and the inalienable rights of elephants to a log "nooning;" and, wandering to and fro, he thoroughly demoralized the garden till sundown, when he returned to his picket for food.

"If you won't work, you shan't eat," said Chihun, angrily. "You're a wild elephant, and no educated animal at all. Go back to your jungle."

Chihun's little brown baby was rolling on the floor of the hut, and stretching out its fat arms to the huge shadow in the doorway. Moti Guj knew well that it was the dearest thing on earth to Chihun. He swung out his trunk with a fascinating crook at the end, and the brown baby drew itself, shouting, upon it. Moti Guj made fast and pulled up till the brown baby was crowing in the air twelve feet above his father's head.

"Great Lord!" said Chihun. "Flour cakes of the best, twelve in number, two feet across and soaked in rum, shall be yours on the instant, and two hundred pounds weight of fresh-cut young sugar-cane therewith. Deign only to put down safely that insignificant brat who is my heart and my life to me!"

Moti Guj tucked the brown baby comfortably between his forefeet, that could have knocked into toothpicks all Chihun's hut, and waited for his food.

He eat it, and the brown baby crawled away. Moti Guj dozed and thought of Deesa. One of many mysteries connected with the elephant is that his huge body needs less sleep than anything else that lives. Four or five hours in the night suffice–two just before midnight, lying down on one side; two just after one o'clock, lying down on the other. The rest of the silent hours are filled with eating and fidgeting, and long grumbling soliloquies.

At midnight, therefore, Moti Guj strode out of his pickets, for a thought had come to him that Deesa might be lying drunk somewhere in the dark forest with none to look after him. So all that night he chased through the undergrowth, blowing and trumpeting and shaking his ears. He went down to the river and blared across the shallows where Deesa used to wash him, but there was no answer. He could not find Deesa, but he disturbed all the other elephants in the lines, and nearly frightened to death some gypsies in the woods.

At dawn Deesa returned to the plantation. He had been very drunk indeed, and he expected to get into trouble for outstaying his leave. He drew a long breath when he saw that the bungalow and the plantation were still uninjured, for he knew something of Moti Guj's temper, and reported himself with many lies and salaams. Moti Guj had gone to his pickets for breakfast. The night exercise had made him hungry.

"Call up your beast," said the planter; and Deesa shouted in the mysterious elephant language that some mahouts believe came from China at the birth of the world, when elephants and not men were masters. Moti Guj heard and came. Elephants do not gallop. They move from places at varying rates of speed. If an elephant wished to catch an express train he could not gallop, but he could catch the train. So Moti Guj was at the planter's door almost before Chihun noticed that he had left his pickets. He fell into Deesa's arms trumpeting with joy, and the man and beast wept and slobbered over each other, and handled each other from head to heel to see that no harm had befallen.

"Now we will get to work," said Deesa. "Lift me up, my son and my joy!"

Moti Guj swung him up, and the two went to the coffee-clearing to look for difficult stumps.

The planter was too astonished to be very angry.

Short Stories

CONTENTS

The Drums of the Fore and Aft

"And a little child shall lead them."

IN THE ARMY List they still stand as "The Fore and Fit Princess Hohenzollern-Sigmaringen-Auspach's Merther-Tydfilshire Own Royal Loyal Light Infantry, Regimental District 329A," but the Army through all its barracks and canteens knows them now as the "Fore and Aft." They may in time do something that shall make their new title honorable, but at present they are bitterly ashamed, and the man who calls them "Fore and Aft" does so at the risk of the head which is on his shoulders.

Two words breathed into the stables of a certain Cavalry Regiment will bring the men out into the streets with belts and mops and bad language; but a whisper of "Fore and Aft" will bring out this regiment with rifles.

Their one excuse is that they came again and did their best to finish the job in style. But for a time all their world knows that they were openly beaten, whipped, and dumb-cowed, shaking and afraid. The men know it; their officers know it; the Horse Guards know it, and when the next war comes the enemy will know it also. There are two or three regiments of the Line that have a black mark against their names which they will then wipe out, and it will be excessively inconvenient for the troops upon whom they do their wiping.

The courage of the British soldier is officially supposed to be above proof, and, as a general rule, it is so. The exceptions are decently shoveled out of sight, only to be referred to in the freshet of unguarded talk that occasionally swamps a Mess-table at midnight. Then one hears strange and horrible stories of men not following their officers, of orders being given by those who had no right to give them, and of disgrace, that, but for the standing luck of the British Army, might have ended in brilliant disaster. These are unpleasant stories to listen to, and the Messes tell them under their breath, sitting by the big wood fires, and the young officer bows his head and thinks to himself, please God, his men shall never behave unhandily.

The British soldier is not altogether to be blamed for occasional lapses; but this verdict he should not know. A moderately intelligent General will waste six months in mastering the craft of the particular war that he may be waging; a Colonel may utterly misunderstand the capacity of his regiment for three months after it has taken the field; and even a Company Commander may err and be deceived as to the temper and temperament of his own handful: wherefore the soldier, and the soldier of to-day more particularly, should not be blamed for falling back. He should be shot or hanged afterward—*pour encourager les autres;* but he should not be vilified in newspapers, for that is want of tact and waste of space.

He has, let us say, been in the service of the Empress for, perhaps, four years. He will leave in another two years. He has no inherited morals, and four years are not sufficient to drive toughness into his fibre, or to teach him how holy a thing is his Regiment. He wants to drink, he wants to enjoy himself–in India he wants to save money–and he does not in the least like getting hurt. He has received just sufficient education to make him understand half the purport of the orders he receives, and to speculate on the nature of clean, incised, and shattering wounds. Thus, if he is told to deploy under fire preparatory to an attack, he knows that he runs a very great risk of being killed while he is deploying, and suspects that he is being thrown away to gain ten minutes' time. He may either deploy with desperate swiftness, or he may shuffle, or bunch, or break, according to the discipline under which he has lain for four years.

Armed with imperfect knowledge, cursed with the rudiments of an imagination, hampered by the intense selfishness of the lower classes, and unsupported by any regimental associations, this young man is suddenly introduced to an enemy who in eastern lands is always ugly, generally tall and hairy, and frequently noisy. If he looks to the right and the left and sees old soldiers–men of twelve years' service, who, he knows, know what they are about–taking a charge, rush, or demonstration without embarrassment, he is consoled and applies his shoulder to the butt of his rifle with a stout heart. His peace is the greater if he hears a senior, who has taught him his soldiering and broken his head on occasion, whispering:–"They'll shout and carry on like this for five minutes. Then they'll rush in, and then we've got 'em by the short hairs!"

But, on the other hand, if he sees only men of his own term of service, turning white and playing with their triggers and saying:–"What the Hell's up now?" while the Company Commanders are sweating into their sword-hilts and shouting:–"Front-rank, fix bayonets. Steady there–steady! Sight for three hundred–no, for five! Lie down, all! Steady! Front-rank, kneel!" and so forth, he becomes unhappy; and grows acutely miserable when he hears a comrade turn over with the rattle of fire-irons falling into the fender, and the grunt of a pole-axed ox. If he can be moved about a little and allowed to watch the effect of his own fire on the enemy he feels merrier, and may be then worked up to the blind passion of fighting, which is, contrary to general belief, controlled by a chilly Devil and shakes men like ague. If he is not moved about, and begins to feel cold at the pit of the stomach, and in that crisis is badly mauled and hears orders that were never given, he will break, and he will break badly; and of all things under the sight of the Sun there is nothing more terrible than a broken British regiment. When the worst comes to the worst and the panic is really epidemic, the men must be e'en let go, and the Company Commanders had better escape to the enemy and stay there for safety's sake. If they can be made to come again they are not pleasant men to meet, because they will not break twice.

About thirty years from this date, when we have succeeded in half-educating everything that wears trousers, our Army will be a beautifully unreliable machine. It will know too much and it will do too little. Later still, when all men are at the mental level of the officer of to-day it will sweep the earth. Speaking roughly, you must employ either blackguards or gentlemen, or, best of all, blackguards commanded by gentlemen, to do butcher's work with efficiency and despatch. The ideal soldier should, of course, think for himself–the *Pocketbook* says so. Unfortunately, to attain this virtue, he has to pass through the phase of thinking of himself, and that is misdirected genius. A blackguard may be slow to think for himself, but he is genuinely anxious to kill, and a little punishment teaches him how to guard his own skin and perforate another's. A powerfully prayerful Highland Regiment, officered by rank Presbyterians, is, perhaps, one degree more terrible in action than a hard-bitten thousand of irresponsible Irish ruffians led by most improper young unbelievers. But these things prove the rule—which is that the midway men are not to be trusted alone. They have ideas about the value of life and an upbringing that has not taught them to go on and take the chances. They are carefully unprovided with a backing of comrades who have been shot over, and until that backing is re-introduced, as a great many Regimental Commanders intend it shall be, they are more liable to disgrace themselves than the size of the Empire or the dignity of the Army allows. Their officers are as good as good can be, because their training begins early, and God has arranged that a clean-run youth of the British middle classes shall, in the matter of backbone, brains, and bowels, surpass all other youths. For this reason a child of eighteen will stand up, doing nothing, with a tin sword in his hand and joy in his heart until he is dropped. If he dies, he dies like a gentleman. If he lives, he writes Home that he has been "potted," "sniped," "chipped" or "cut over," and sits down to besiege Government for a wound-gratuity until the next little war breaks out, when he perjures himself before a Medical Board, blarneys his Colonel, burns incense round his Adjutant, and is allowed to go to the Front once more.

Which homily brings me directly to a brace of the most finished little fiends that ever banged drum or tootled fife in the Band of a British Regiment. They ended their sinful career by open and flagrant mutiny and were shot for it. Their names were Jakin and Lew—Piggy Lew—and they were bold, bad drummer-boys, both of them frequently birched by the Drum-Major of the Fore and Aft.

Jakin was a stunted child of fourteen, and Lew was about the same age. When not looked after, they smoked and drank. They swore habitually after the manner of the Barrack-room, which is cold-swearing and comes from between clinched teeth; and they fought religiously once a week. Jakin had sprung from some London gutter and may or may not have passed through Dr. Barnado's hands ere he arrived at the dignity of drummer-boy. Lew could remember nothing except the regiment and the delight of listening to the Band from his earliest years. He hid somewhere in his grimy little soul a genuine love for music, and was most mistakenly furnished with the head of a cherub: insomuch that beautiful ladies who watched the Regiment in church were wont to speak of him as a "darling." They never heard his vitriolic comments on their manners and morals, as he walked back to barracks with the Band and matured fresh causes of offence against Jakin.

The other drummer-boys hated both lads on account of their illogical conduct. Jakin might be pounding Lew, or Lew might be rubbing Jakin's head in the dirt, but any attempt at aggression on the part of an outsider was met by the combined forces of Lew and Jakin; and the consequences were painful. The boys were the Ishmaels of the corps, but wealthy Ishmaels, for they sold battles in alternate weeks for the sport of the barracks when they were not pitted against other boys; and thus amassed money.

On this particular day there was dissension in the camp. They had just been convicted afresh of smoking, which is bad for little boys who use plug-tobacco, and Lew's contention was that Jakin had "stunk so 'orrid bad from keepin' the pipe in pocket," that he and he alone was responsible for the birching they were both tingling under.

"I tell you I'd the pipe back o' barricks," said Jakin, pacifically.

"You're a bloomin' liar," said Lew, without heat.

"You're a bloomin' little bastard," said Jakin, strong in the knowledge that his own ancestry was unknown.

Now there is one word in the extended vocabulary of barrack-room abuse that cannot pass without comment. You may call a man a thief and risk nothing. You may even call him a coward without finding more than a boot whiz past your ear, but you must not call a man a bastard untill you are prepared to prove it on his front teeth.

"You might ha' hep' that till I wasn't so sore," said Lew, sorrowfully, dodging round Jakin's guard.

"I'll make you sorer," said Jakin, genially, and got home on Lew's alabaster forehead. All would have gone well and this story, as the books say, would never have been written, had not his evil fate prompted the Bazar-Sergeant's son, a long, employless man of five and twenty, to put in an appearance after the first round. He was eternally in need of money, and knew that the boys had silver.

"Fighting again," said he. "I'll report you to my father, and he'll report you to the Color-Sergeant."

"What's that to you?" said Jakin, with an unpleasant dilation of the nostrils.

"Oh! nothing to *me.* You'll get into trouble and you've been up too often to afford that."

"What the Hell do you know about what we've done?" asked Lew the Seraph. "*You* aren't in the Army, you lousy, cadging civilian."

He closed in on the man's left flank.

"Jes' 'cause you find two gentlemen settlin' their diff'rences with their fistes you stick in your ugly nose where you aren't wanted. Run 'ome to your 'arf-caste slut of a Ma—or we'll give you what-for," said Jakin.

The man attempted reprisals by knocking the boys' heads together. The scheme would have succeeded had not Jakin punched him vehemently in the stomach, or had Lew refrained from kicking his shins. They fought together, bleeding and breathless, for half an hour, and after heavy punishment, triumphantly pulled down their opponent as terriers pull down a jackal.

"Now," gasped Jakin, "I'll give you whatfor." He proceeded to pound the man's features while Lew stamped on the outlying portions of his anatomy. Chivalry is not a strong point in the composition of the average drummer-boy. He fights, as do his betters, to make his mark.

Ghastly was the ruin that escaped, and awful was the wrath of the Bazar-Sergeant. Awful too was the scene in Orderly-room when the two reprobates appeared to answer the charge of half-murdering a "civilian." The Bazar-Sergeant thirsted for a criminal action, and his son lied. The boys stood to attention while the black clouds of evidence accumulated.

"You little devils are more trouble than the rest of the Regiment put together," said the Colonel, angrily. "One might as well admonish thistledown, and I can't well put you in cells or under stoppages. You must be flogged again."

"Beg y' pardon, Sir. Can't we say nothin' in our own defence, Sir?" shrilled Jakin.

"Hey! What? Are you going to argue with me?" said the Colonel.

"No, Sir," said Lew. "But if a man come to you, Sir, and said he was going to report you, Sir, for 'aving a bit of a turn-up with a friend, Sir, an' wanted to get money out o' *you,* Sir"—

The Orderly-room exploded in a roar of laughter. "Well?" said the Colonel.

"That was what that measly *Jarnwar* there did, Sir, and 'e'd 'a' *done* it, Sir, if we 'adn't prevented 'im. We didn't 'it 'im much, Sir. 'E 'adn't no manner o' right to interfere with us, Sir. I don't mind bein' flogged by the Drum-Major, Sir, nor yet reported by *any* Corp'ral, but I'm—but I don't think it's fair, Sir, for a civilian to come an' talk over a man in the Army."

A second shout of laughter shook the Orderly-room, but the Colonel was grave.

"What sort of characters have these boys?" he asked of the Regimental Sergeant-Major.

"Accordin' to the Bandmaster, Sir," returned that revered official—the only soul in the regiment whom the boys feared—"they do everything *but* lie, Sir."

"Is it like we'd go for that man for fun, Sir?" said Lew, pointing to the plaintiff.

"Oh, admonished,—admonished!" said the Colonel, testily, and when the boys had gone he read the Bazar-Sergeant's son a lecture on the sin of unprofitable meddling, and gave orders that the Bandmaster should keep the Drums in better discipline.

"If either of you come to practice again with so much as a scratch on your two ugly little faces," thundered the Bandmaster, "I'll tell the Drum-Major to take the skin off your backs. Understand that, you young devils."

Then he repented of his speech for just the length of time that Lew, looking like a Seraph in red worsted embellishments, took the place of one of the trumpets —in hospital—and rendered the echo of a battle-piece. Lew certainly was a musician, and had often in his more exalted moments expressed a yearning to master every instrument of the Band.

"There's nothing to prevent your becoming a Bandmaster, Lew," said the Bandmaster, who had composed waltzes of his own, and worked day and night in the interests of the Band.

"What did he say?" demanded Jakin, after practice.

" 'Said I might be a bloomin' Bandmaster, an' he asked in to 'ave a glass o' sherry-wine on Mess-nights."

"Ho! 'Said you might be a bloomin' non-combatant, did 'e! That's just about wot 'e would say. When I've put in my boy's service—it's a bloomin' shame that doesn't count for pension—I'll take on a privit. Then I'll be a Lance in a year—knowin' what I know about the ins an' outs o' things. In three years I'll be a bloomin' Sergeant. I won't marry then, not I! I'll 'old on and learn the orf'cers' ways an' apply for exchange into a reg'ment that doesn't know all about me. Then I'll be a bloomin' orf'cer. Then I'll ask you to 'ave a glass o' sherry-wine, *Mister* Lew, an' you'll bloomin' well 'ave to stay in the hanty-room while the Mess-Sergeant brings it to your dirty 'ands."

" 'S'pose *I*'m going to be a Bandmaster? Not I, quite. I'll be a orf'cer too. There's nothin' like taking to a thing an' stickin' to it, the Schoolmaster says. The reg'ment don't go 'ome for another seven years. I'll be a Lance then or near to."

Thus the boys discussed their futures, and conducted themselves with exemplary piety for a week. That is to say, Lew started a flirtation with the Color-Sergeant's daughter, aged thirteen,—"not," as he explained to Jakin, "with any intention o' matrimony, but by way o' keepin' my 'and in." And the black-haired Cris Delighan enjoyed that flirtation more than previous ones, and the other drummer-boys raged furiously together, and Jakin preached sermons on the dangers of "bein' tangled along o' petticoats."

But neither love nor virtue would have held Lew long in the paths of propriety had not the rumor gone abroad that the Regiment was to be sent on active service, to take part in a war which, for the sake of brevity, we will call "The War of the Lost Tribes."

The barracks had the rumor almost before the Mess-room, and of all the nine hundred men in barracks not ten had seen a shot fired in anger. The Colonel had, twenty years ago, assisted at a Frontier expedition; one of the Majors had seen service at the Cape; a confirmed deserter in E Company had helped to clear streets in Ireland; but that was all. The Regiment had been put by for many years. The overwhelming mass of its rank and file had from three to four years' service; the non-commissioned officers were under thirty years old; and men and sergeants alike had forgotten to speak of the stories written in brief upon the Colors—the New Colors that had been formally blessed by an Archbishop in England ere the Regiment came away.

They wanted to go to the Front—they were enthusiastically anxious to go—but they had no knowledge of what war meant, and there was none to tell them. They were an educated regiment, the percentage of school-certificates in their ranks was high, and most of the men could do more than read and write. They had been recruited in loyal observance of the territorial idea; but they themselves had no notion of that idea. They were made up of drafts from an overpopulated manufacturing district. The system had put flesh and muscle upon their small bones, but it could not put heart into the sons of those who for generations had done overmuch work for overscanty pay, had sweated in drying-rooms, stooped over looms, coughed among white-lead and shivered on lime-barges. The men had found food and rest in the Army, and now they were going to fight "niggers"—people who ran away if you shook a stick at them. Wherefore they cheered lustily when the rumor ran, and the shrewd, clerkly non-commissioned officers speculated on the chances of batta and of saving their pay. At Headquarters, men said:—"The Fore and Fit have never been under fire within the last generation. Let us, therefore, break them in easily by setting them to guard lines of communication." And this would have been done but for the fact that British Regiments were wanted—badly wanted—at the Front, and there were doubtful Native Regiments that could fill the minor duties. "Brigade 'em with two strong Regiments," said Headquarters. "They may be knocked about a bit, but they'll learn their business before they come through. Nothing like a night-alarm and a little cutting-up of stragglers to make a Regiment smart in the field. Wait till they've had half a dozen sentries' throats cut."

The Colonel wrote with delight that the temper of his men was excellent, that the Regiment was all that could be wished and as sound as a bell. The Majors smiled with a sober joy, and the subalterns waltzed in pairs down the Mess-room after dinner and nearly shot themselves at revolver practice. But there was consternation in the hearts of Jakin and Lew. What was to be done with the drums? Would the Band go to the Front? How many of the drums would accompany the Regiment?

They took council together, sitting in a tree and smoking.

"It's more than a bloomin' toss-up they'll leave us be'ind at the Depôt with the women. You'll like that," said Jakin, sarcastically.

" 'Cause o' Cris, y' mean? Wot's a woman, or a 'old bloomin' depôt o' women, 'longside o' the chanst of field-service? You know I'm as keen on goin' as you," said Lew.

" 'Wish I was a bloomin' bugler," said Jakin, sadly. "They'll take Tom Kidd along, that I can plaster a wall with, an' like as not they won't take us."

"Then let's go an' make Tom Kidd so bloomin' sick 'e can't bugle no more. You 'old 'is 'ands an' I'll kick him," said Lew, wriggling on the branch.

"That ain't no good neither. We ain't the sort o' characters to presoon on our rep'tations—they're bad. If they had the Band at the Depôt we don't go, and no error *there*. If they take the Band we may get cast for medical unfitness. Are you medical fit, Piggy?" said Jakin, digging Lew in the ribs with force.

"Yus," said Lew, with an oath. "The Doctor says your 'eart's weak through smokin' on an empty stummick. Throw a chest an' I'll try yer."

Jakin threw out his chest, which Lew smote with all his might. Jakin turned very pale, gasped, crowed, screwed up his eyes and said,—"That's all right."

"You'll do," said Lew. "I've 'eard o' men dyin' when you 'it 'em fair on the breast-bone."

" 'Don't bring us no nearer goin', though," said Jakin. "Do you know where we're ordered?"

"Gawd knows, an' 'e won't split on a pal. Somewheres up to the Front to kill Paythans—hairy big beggars that turn you inside out if they get 'old o' you. They say their women are good-looking, too."

"Any loot?" asked the abandoned Jakin.

"Not a bloomin' ana, they say, unless you dig up the ground an' see what the niggers 'ave 'id. They're a poor lot." Jakin stood upright on the branch and gazed across the plain.

"Lew," said he, "there's the Colonel coming. 'Colonel's a good old beggar. Let's go an' talk to 'im."

Lew nearly fell out of the tree at the audacity of the suggestion. Like Jakin he feared not God neither regarded he Man, but there are limits even to the audacity of drummer-boy, and to speak to a Colonel was . . .

But Jakin had slid down the trunk and doubled in the direction of the Colonel. That officer was walking wrapped in thought and visions of a C. B.–yes, even a K. C. B., for had he not at command one of the best Regiments of the Line–the Fore and Fit? And he was aware of two small boys charging down upon him. Once before it had been solemnly reported to him that "the Drums were in a state of mutiny"; Jakin and Lew being the ringleaders. This looked like an organized conspiracy.

The boys halted at twenty yards, walked to the regulation four paces, and saluted together as well set-up as a ramrod and a little taller.

The Colonel was in a genial mood; the boys appeared very forlorn and unprotected on the desolate plain, and one of them was handsome.

"Well!" said the Colonel, recognizing them. "Are you going to pull me down in the open? I'm sure I never interfere with you, even though"–he sniffed suspiciously–"you have been smoking."

It was time to strike while the iron was hot. Their hearts beat tumultuously.

"Beg y' pardon, Sir," began Jakin. "The Reg'ment's ordered on active service, Sir?"

"So I believe," said the Colonel, courteously.

"Is the Band goin', Sir?" said both together. Then, without pause, "We're goin', Sir, ain't we?"

"You!" said the Colonel, stepping back the more fully to take in the two small figures. "You! You'd die in the first march."

"No, we wouldn't, Sir. We can march with the Regiment anywheres–p'rade an' anywhere else," said Jakin.

"If Tom Kidd goes 'e'll shut up like a claspknife," said Lew. "Tom 'as very close veins in both 'is legs, Sir."

"Very how much?"

"Very close veins, Sir. That's why they swells after long p'rade, Sir. If 'e can go, we can go, Sir."

Again the Colonel looked at them long and intently.

"Yes, the Band is going," he said, as gravely as though he had been addressing a brother officer. "Have you any parents, either of you two?"

"No, Sir," rejoicingly from Lew and Jakin. "We're both orphans, Sir. There's no one to be considered of our accounts, Sir."

"You poor little sprats, and you want to go up to the Front with the Regiment, do you? Why?"

"I've wore the Queen's Uniform for two years," said Jakin. "It's very 'ard, Sir, that a man don't get no recompense for doin' 'is dooty, Sir."

"An'–an' if I don't go, Sir," interrupted Lew, "the Bandmaster 'e says 'e'll catch an' make a bloo–a blessed musician o' me, Sir. Before I've seen any service, Sir."

The Colonel made no answer for a long time. Then he said quietly:–"If you're passed by the Doctor I dare say you can go. I shouldn't smoke if I were you."

The boys saluted and disappeared. The Colonel walked home and told the story to his wife, who nearly cried over it. The Colonel was well pleased. If that was the temper of the children, what would not the men do?

Jakin and Lew entered the boys' barrack-room with great stateliness, and refused to hold any conversation with their comrades for at least ten minutes. Then, bursting with pride, Jakin drawled:–"I've bin intervooin' the Colonel.

Good old beggar is the Colonel. Says I to 'im, 'Colonel,' says I, 'let me go the Front, along o' the Reg'ment.' 'To the Front you shall go,' says 'e, 'an' I only wish there was more like you among the dirty little devils that bang the bloomin' drums.' Kidd, if you throw your 'coutrements at me for tellin' you the truth to your own advantage, your legs 'll swell."

None the less there was a Battle-Royal in the barrack-room, for the boys were consumed with envy and hate, and neither Jakin nor Lew behaved in conciliatory wise.

"I'm goin' out to say adoo to my girl," said Lew, to cap the climax. "Don't none o' you touch my kit because it's wanted for active service, me bein' specially invited to go by the Colonel."

He strolled forth and whistled in the clump of trees at the back of the Married Quarters till Cris came to him, and, the preliminary kisses being given and taken, Lew began to explain the situation.

"I'm goin' to the Front with the Reg'ment," he said, valiantly.

"Piggy, you're a little liar," said Cris, but her heart misgave her, for Lew was not in the habit of lying.

"Liar yourself, Cris," said Lew, slipping an arm round her. "I'm goin'. When the Reg'ment marches out you'll see me with 'em, all galliant and gay. Give us another kiss, Cris, on the strength of it."

"If you'd on'y a-stayed at the Depôt–where you *ought* to ha' bin–you could get as many of 'em as–as you dam please," whimpered Cris, putting up her mouth.

"Its 'ard, Cris. I grant you it's 'ard. But what's a man to do? If I'd a-stayed at the Depôt, you wouldn't think anything of me."

"Like as not, but I'd 'ave you with me, Piggy. An' all the thinkin' in the world isn't like kissin'."

"An' all the kissin' in the world isn't like 'avin' a medal to wear on the front o' your coat."

"*You* won't get no medal."

"Oh, yus, I shall though. Me an' Jakin are the only acting-drummers that'll be took along. All the rest is full men, an' we'll get our medals with them."

"They might ha' taken anybody but you, Piggy. You'll get killed–you're so venturesome. Stay with me, Piggy, darlin', down at the Depôt, an' I'll love you true forever."

"Ain't you goin' to do that *now,* Cris? You said you was."

"O' course I am, but th' other's more comfortable. Wait till you've growed a bit, Piggy. You aren't no taller than me now."

"I've bin in the army for two years an' I'm not goin' to get out of a chanst o' seein' service an' don't you try to make me do so. I'll come back, Cris, an' when I take on as a man I'll marry you–marry you when I'm a Lance."

"Promise, Piggy?"

Lew reflected on the future as arranged by Jakin a short time previously, but Cris's mouth was very near to his own.

"I promise, s'elp me Gawd!" said he.

Cris slid an arm round his neck.

"I won't 'old you back no more, Piggy. Go away an' get your medal, an' I'll make you a new button-bag as nice as I know how," she whispered.

"Put some o' your 'air into it, Cris, an' I'll keep it in my pocket so long's I'm alive."

Then Cris wept anew, and the interview ended. Public feeling among the drummer-boys rose to fever pitch and the lives of Jakin and Lew became unenviable. Not only had they been permitted to enlist two years before the regulation boy's age–fourteen–but, by virtue, it seemed, of their extreme youth, they were allowed to go to the Front–which thing had not happened to acting-drummers within the knowledge of boy. The Band which was to accompany the Regiment had been cut down to the regulation twenty men, the surplus returning to the ranks. Jakin and Lew were attached to the Band as supernumeraries, though they would much have preferred being Company buglers.

" 'Don't matter much," said Jakin, after the medical inspection. "Be thankful that we're 'lowed to go at all. The Doctor 'e said that if we could stand what we took from the Bazar-Sergeant's son we'd stand pretty nigh anything."

"Which we will," said Lew, looking tenderly at the ragged and ill-made housewife that Cris had given him, with a lock of her hair worked into a sprawling "L" upon the cover.

"It was the best I could," she sobbed. "I wouldn't let mother nor the Sergeant's tailor 'elp me. Keep it always, Piggy, an' remember I love you true."

They marched to the railway station, nine hundred and sixty strong, and every soul in cantonments turned out to see them go. The drummers gnashed their teeth at Jakin and Lew marching with the Band, the married women wept upon the platform, and the Regiment cheered its noble self black in the face.

"A nice level lot," said the Colonel to the Second-in-Command, as they watched the first four companies entraining.

"Fit to do anything," said the Second-in-Command, enthusiastically. "But it seems to me they're a thought too young and tender for the work in hand. It's bitter cold up at the Front now."

"They're sound enough," said the Colonel. "We must take our chance of sick casualties."

So they went northward, ever northward, past droves and droves of camels, armies of camp followers, and legions of laden mules, the throng thickening day by day, till with a shriek the train pulled up at a hopelessly congested junction where six lines of temporary track accommodated six forty-wagon trains; where whistles blew, Babus sweated and Commissariat officers swore from dawn till far into the night amid the wind-driven chaff of the fodder-bales and the lowing of a thousand steers.

"Hurry up–you're badly wanted at the Front," was the message that greeted the Fore and Aft, and the occupants of the Red Cross carriages told the same tale.

" 'Tisn't so much the bloomin' fightin'," gasped a headbound trooper of Hussars to a knot of admiring Fore and Afts. " 'Tisn't so much the bloomin' fightin', though there's enough o' that. It's the bloomin' food an' the bloomin' climate. Frost all night 'cept when it hails, and biling sun all day, and the water stinks fit to knock you down. I got my 'ead chipped like a egg; I've got pneumonia too, an' my guts is all out o' order. 'Tain't no bloomin' picnic in those parts, I can tell you."

"Wot are the niggers like?" demanded a private.

"There's some prisoners in that train yonder. Go on look at 'em. They're the aristocracy o' the country. The common folk are a dashed sight uglier. If you want to know what they fight with, reach under my seat an' pull out the long knife that's there."

They dragged out and beheld for the first time the grim, bone-handled, triangular Afghan knife. It was almost as long as Lew.

"That's the thing to jint ye," said the trooper, feebly.

"It can take off a man's arm at the shoulder as easy as slicing butter. I halved the beggar that used that 'un, but there's more of his like up above. They don't understand thrustin', but they're devils to slice."

The men strolled across the tracks to inspect the Afghan prisoners. They were unlike any "niggers" that the Fore and Aft had ever met–these huge, black-haired, scowling sons of the Beni-Israel. As the men stared the Afghans spat freely and muttered one to another with lowered eyes.

"My eyes! Wot awful swine!" said Jakin, who was in the rear of the procession. "Say, old man, how you got *packrowed,* eh? *Kiswasti* you wasn't hanged for your ugly face, hey?"

The tallest of the company turned, his leg-irons, clanking at the movement, and stared at the boy. "See!" he cried to his fellows in Pushto. "They send children against us. What a people, and what fools!"

"Hya!" said Jakin, nodding his head cheerily. "You go down-country. *Khana* get, *peenikapanee* get–live like a bloomin' Raja *ke marfik.* That's a better *bandobust* than baynit get it in your innards. Good-bye, ole man. Take care o' your beautiful figure-'ed, an' try to look *kushy.*"

The men laughed and fell in for their first march when they began to realize that a soldier's life was not all beer and skittles. They were much impressed with the size and bestial ferocity of the niggers whom they had now learned to call "Paythans," and more with the exceeding discomfort of their own surroundings. Twenty old soldiers in the corps would have taught them how to make themselves moderately snug at night, but they had no old soldiers, and, as the troops on the line of march said, "they lived like pigs." They learned the heart-breaking cussedness of camp-kitchens and camels and the depravity of an E. P. tent and wither-wrung mule. They studied animalculae in water, and developed a few cases of dysentery in their study.

At the end of their third march they were disagreeably surprised by the arrival in their camp of a hammered iron slug which, fired from a steadyrest at seven hundred yards, flicked out the brains of a private seated by the fire. This robbed them of their peace for a night, and was the beginning of a long-range fire carefully calculated to that end. In the daytime they saw nothing except an occasional puff of smoke from a crag above the line of march. At night there were spurts of flame and occasional casualties, which set the whole camp blazing into the gloom, and, occasionally, into opposite tents. Then they swore vehemently and vowed that this was magnificent but not war.

Indeed it was not. The Regiment could not halt for reprisals against the *franctireurs* of the countryside. Its duty was to go forward and make connection with the Scotch and Gurkha troops with which it was brigaded. The Afghans knew this, and knew too, after their first tentative shots, that they were dealing with a raw regiment. Thereafter they devoted themselves to the task of keeping the Fore and Aft on the strain. Not for anything would they have taken equal liberties with a seasoned corps–with the wicked little Gurkhas, whose delight it was to lie out in the open on a dark night and stalk their stalkers–with the terrible, big men dressed in women's clothes, who could be heard praying to their God in the night-watches, and whose peace of mind no amount of "sniping" could shake–or with those vile Sikhs, who marched so ostentatiously unprepared and who dealt out such grim reward to those who tried to profit by that unpreparedness. This white regiment was different–quite different. It slept like a hog, and, like a hog, charged in every direction when it was roused. Its sentries walked with a footfall that could be heard for a quarter of a mile; would fire at anything that moved–even a driven donkey–and when they had once fired, could be scientifically "rushed" and laid out a horror and an offence against the morning sun. Then there were camp-followers who straggled and could be cut up without fear. Their shrieks would disturb the white boys, and the loss of their services would inconvenience them sorely.

Thus, at every march, the hidden enemy became bolder and the regiment writhed and twisted under attacks it could not avenge. The crowning triumph was a sudden night-rush ending in the cutting of many tent-ropes, the collapse of the sodden canvas and a glorious knifing of the men who struggled and kicked below. It was a great deed, neatly carried out, and it shook the already shaken nerves of the Fore and Aft. All the courage that they had been required to exercise up to this point was the "two o'clock in the morning courage"; and they, so far, had only succeeded in shooting their comrades and losing their sleep.

Sullen, discontented, cold, savage, sick, with their uniforms dulled and unclean, the "Fore and Aft" joined their Brigade.

"I hear you had a tough time of it coming up," said the Brigadier. But when he saw the hospital-sheets his face fell.

"This is bad," said he to himself. "They're as rotten as sheep." And aloud to the Colonel,–"I'm afraid we can't spare you just yet. We want all we have, else I should have given you ten days to recruit in."

The Colonel winced. "On my honor, Sir," he returned, "there is not the least necessity to think of sparing us. My men have been rather mauled and upset without a fair return. They only want to go in somewhere where they can see what's before them."

"'Can't say I think much of the Fore and Fit," said the Brigadier, in confidence, to his Brigade-Major. "They've lost all their soldiering, and, by the trim of them, might have marched through the country from the other side. A more fagged-out set of men I never put eyes on."

"Oh, they'll improve as the work goes on. The parade glass has been rubbed off a little, but they'll put on field polish before long," said the Brigade-Major. "They've been mauled, and they quite don't understand it."

They did not. All the hitting was on one side, and it was cruelly hard hitting with accessories that made them sick. There was also the real sickness that laid hold of a strong man and dragged him howling to the grave. Worst of all, their officers knew just as little of the country as the men themselves, and looked as if they did. The Fore and Aft were in a thoroughly unsatisfactory condition, but they believed that all would be well if they could once get a fair go-in at the enemy. Pot-shots up and down the valleys were unsatisfactory, and the bayonet never seemed to get a chance. Perhaps it was as well, for a long-limbed Afghan with a knife had a reach of eight feet, and could carry away enough lead to disable three Englishmen. The Fore and Fit would like some rifle-practice at the enemy–all seven hundred riflex blazing together. That wish showed the mood of the men.

The Gurkhas walked into their camp, and in broken, barrack-room English strove to fraternize with them; offered them pipes of tobacco and stood them treat at the canteen. But the Fore and Aft, not knowing much of the nature of the Gurkhas, treated them as they would treat any other "niggers," and the little men in green trotted back to their firm friends the Highlanders, and with many grins confided to them:–"That dam white regiment no dam use. Sulky–ugh! Dirty–ugy! Hya, any tot for Johnny?" Whereat the Highlanders smote the Burkhas as to the head, and told them not to vilify a British Regiment, and the Gurkhas grinned cavernously, for the Highlanders were their elder brothers and entitled to the privileges of kinship. The common soldier who touches a Gurkha is more than likely to have his head sliced open.

Three days later the Brigadier arranged a battle according to the rules of war and the peculiarity of the Afghan temperament. The enemy were massing in inconvenient strength among the hills, and the moving or many green standards warned him that the tribes were "up" in aid of the Afghan regular troops. A squadron and a half of Bengal Lancers represented the available Cavalry, and two screw-guns borrowed from a column thirty miles away, the Artillery at the General's disposal.

"If they stand, as I've a very strong notion that they will, I fancy we shall see an infantry fight that will be worth watching," said the Brigadier. "We'll do it in style. Each regiment shall be played into action by its Band, and we'll hold the Cavalry in reserve."

"For *all* the reserve?" somebody asked.

"For all the reserve; because we're going to crumple them up," said the Brigadier, who was an extraordinary Brigadier, and did not believe in the value of a reserve when dealing with Asiatics. And, indeed, when you come to think of it, had the British Army consistently waited for reserves in all its little affairs, the boundaries of Our Empire would have stopped at Brighton beach.

That battle was to be a glorious battle.

The three regiments debouching from three separate gorges, after duly crowning the heights above, were to converge from the centre, left and right upon what we will call the Afghan army, then stationed toward the lower extremity of a flat-bottomed valley. This it will be seen that three sides of the valley practically belonged to the English, while the fourth was strictly Afghan property. In the event of defeat the Afghans had the rocky hills to fly to, where the fire from the guerilla tribes in aid would cover their retreat. In the event of victory these same tribes would rush down and lend their weight to the rout of the British.

The screw-guns were to shell the head of each Afghan rush that was made in close formation, and the Cavalry, held in reserve in the right valley, were to gently stimulate the break-up which would follow on the combined attack. The Brigadier, sitting upon a rock overlooking the valley, would watch the battle unrolled at his feet. The Fore and Aft would debouch from the central gorge, the Gurkhas from the left, and the Highlanders from the right, for the reason that the left flank of the enemy seemed as though it required the most hammering. It was not every day that an Afghan force would take ground in the open, and the Brigadier was resolved to make the most of it.

"If we only had a few more men," he said, plaintively, "we could surround the creatures and crumble 'em up thoroughly. As it is, I'm afraid we can only cut them up as they run. It's a great pity."

The Fore and Aft had enjoyed unbroken peace for five days, and were beginning, in spite of dysentery, to recover their nerve. But they were not happy, for they did not know the work in hand, and had they known, would not have known how to do it. Throughout those five days in which old soldiers might have taught them the craft of the game, they discussed together their misadventures in the past–how such an one was alive at dawn and dead ere the dusk, and with what shrieks and struggles such another had given up his soul under the Afghan knife. Death was a new and horrible thing to the sons of mechanics who were used to die decently of zymotic disease; and their careful conservation in barracks had done nothing to make them look upon it with less dread.

Very early in the dawn the bugles began to blow, and the Fore and Aft, filled with a misguided enthusiasm, turned out without waiting for a cup of coffee and a biscuit; and were rewarded by being kept under arms in the cold while the other regiments leisurely prepared for the fray. All the world knows that it is ill taking the breeks off a Highlander. It is much iller to try to make him stir unless he is convinced of the necessity for haste.

The Fore and Aft awaited, leaning upon their rifles and listening to the protests of their empty stomachs. The Colonel did his best to remedy the default of lining as soon as it was borne in upon him that the affair would not begin at once, and so well did he succeed that the coffee was just ready when–the men moved off, their Band leading. Even then there had been a mistake in time, and the Fore and Aft came out into the valley ten minutes before the proper hour. Their Band wheeled to the right after reaching the open, and retired behind a little rocky knoll still playing while the regiment went past.

It was not a pleasant sight that opened on the unobstructed view, for the lower end of the valley appeared to be filled by an army in position–real and actual regiments attired in red coats, and–of this there was no doubt–firing

Martini-Henry bullets which cup up the ground a hundred yards in front of the leading company. Over that pock-marked ground the regiment had to pass, and it opened the ball with a general and profound courtesy to the piping pickets; ducking in perfect time, as though it had been brazed on a rod. Being half-capable of thinking for itself, it fired a volley by the simple process of pitching its rifle into its shoulder and pulling the trigger. The bullets may have accounted for some of the watchers on the hillside, but they certainly did not affect the mass of enemy in front, while the noise of the rifles drowned any orders that might have been given.

"Good God!" said the Brigadier, sitting on the rock high above all. "That regiment has spoiled the whole show. Hurry up the others, and let the screw-guns get off."

But the screw-guns, in working round the heights, had stumbled upon a wasp's nest of a small mud fort which they incontinently shelled at eight hundred yards, to the huge discomfort of the occupants, who were unaccustomed to weapons of such devilish precision.

The Fore and Aft continued to go forward but with shortened stride. Where were the other regiments, and why did these niggers use Martinis? They took open order instinctively, lying down and firing at random, rushing a few paces forward and lying down again, according to the regulations. Once in this formation, each man felt himself desperately alone, and edged in toward his fellow for comfort's sake.

Then the crack of his neighbor's rifle at his ear led him to fire as rapidly as he could—again for the sake of the comfort of the noise. The reward was not long delayed. Five volleys plunged the files in banked smoke impenetrable to the eye, and the bullets began to take ground twenty or thirty yards in front of the firers, as the weight of the bayonet dragged down, and to the right arms wearied with holding the kick of the leaping Martini. The Company Commanders peered helplessly through the smoke, the more nervous mechanically trying to fan it away with their helmets.

"High and to the left!" bawled a Captain till he was hoarse. "No good! Cease firing, and let it drift away a bit."

Three and four times the bugles shrieked the order, and when it was obeyed the Fore and Aft looked that their foe should be lying before them in mown swaths of men. A light wind drove the smoke to leeward, and showed the enemy still in position and apparently unaffected. A quarter of a ton of lead had been buried a furlong in front of them, as the ragged earth attested.

That was not demoralizing. They were waiting for the mad riot to die down, and were firing quietly into the heart of the smoke. A private of the Fore and Aft spun up his company shrieking with agony, and another was kicking the earth and gasping, and a third, ripped through the lower intestines by a jagged bullet, was calling aloud on his comrades to put him out of his pain. These were the casualties, and they were not soothing to hear or see. The smoke cleared to a dull haze.

Then the foe began to shout with a great shouting and a mass—a black mass—detached itself from the main body, and rolled over the ground at horrid speed. It was composed of, perhaps, three hundred men, who would shout and fire and slash if the rush of their fifty comrades who were determined to die carried home. The fifty were Ghazis, half-maddened with drugs and wholly mad with religious fanaticism. When they rushed the British fire ceased, and in the lull the order was given to close ranks and meet them with the bayonet.

Any one who knew the business could have told the Fore and Aft that the only way of dealing with a Ghazi rush is by volleys at long ranges; because a man who means to die, who desires to die, who will gain heaven by dying, must, in nine cases out of ten, kill a man who has a lingering prejudice in favor of life if he can close with the latter. Where they should have closed and gone forward, the Fore and Aft opened out and skirmished, and where they should have opened out and fired, they closed and waited.

A man dragged from his blankets half awake and unfed is never in a pleasant frame of mind. Nor does his happiness increase when he watches the whites of the eyes of three hundred six-foot fiends upon whose beards the foam is lying, upon whose tongues is a roar of wrath, and in whose hands are three-foot knives.

The Fore and Aft heard the Gurkha bugles bringing that regiment forward at the double, while the neighing of the Highland pipes came from the left. They strove to stay where they were, though the bayonets wavered down the line like the oars of a ragged boat. Then they felt body to body the amazing physical strength of their foes; a shriek of pain ended the rush, and the knives fell amid scenes not to be told. The men clubbed together and smote blindly–as often as not at their own fellows. Their front crumpled like paper, and the fifty Ghazis passed on; their backers, now drunk with success, fighting as madly as they.

Then the rear-ranks were bidden to close up, and the subalterns dashed into the stew–alone. For the rear-rank had heard the clamor in front, the yells and the howls of pain, and had seen the dark stale blood that makes afraid. They were not going to stay. It was the rushing of the camps over again. Let their officers go to Hell, if they chose; they would get away from the knives.

"Come on!" shrieked the subalterns, and their men, cursing them, drew back, each closing into his neighbor and wheeling round.

Charteris and Devlin, subalterns of the last company, faced their death alone in the belief that their men would follow.

"You've killed me, you cowards," sobbed Devlin and dropped, cut from the shoulder-strap to the centre of the chest, and a fresh detachment of his men retreating, always retreating, trampled him under foot as they made for the pass whence they had emerged.

> I kissed her in the kitchen and I kissed her in the hall.
> Child'un, child'un, follow me!
> Oh Golly, said the cook, is he gwine to kiss us all?
> Halla–Halla–Halla Halleujah!

The Gurkhas were pouring through the left gorge and over the heights at the double to the invitation of their regimental Quickstep. The black rocks were crowned with dark green spiders as the bugles gave tongue jubilantly:

> In the morning! In the morning by the bright light!
> When Gabriel blows his trumpet in the morning!

The Gurkha rear-companies tripped and blundered over loose stones. The front-files halted for a moment to take stock of the valley and to settle stray boot-laces. Then a happy little sigh of contentment soughed down the ranks, and it was as though the land smiled, for behold there below was the enemy, and it was to meet them that the Gurkhas had doubled so hastily. There was much enemy. There would be amusement. The little men hitched their *kukris* well to hand, and gaped expectantly at their officers as terriers grin ere the stone is cast for them to fetch. The Gurkhas' ground sloped downward to the valley, and they enjoyed a fair view of the proceedings. They sat upon the bowlders to watch, for their officers were not going to waste their wind in assisting to repulse a Ghazi rush more than half a mile away. Let the white men look to their own front.

"Hi! yi!" said the Subadar-Major, who was sweating profusely. "Dam fools yonder, stand close-order! This is no time for close order, it's time for volleys. Ugh!"

Horrified, amused, and indignant, the Gurkhas beheld the retirement–let us be gentle–of the Fore and Aft with a running chorus of oaths and commentaries. "They run! The white men run! Colonel Sahib, may *we* also do a little running?" murmured Runbir Thappa, the Senior Jemadar.

But the Colonel would have none of it. "Let the beggars be cut up a little," said he wrathfully. "Serves 'em right. They'll be prodded into facing round in a minute." He looked through his field-glasses, and caught the glint of an officer's sword.

"Beating 'em with the flat–damned conscripts! How the Ghazis are walking into them!" said he.

The Fore and Aft, heading back, bore with their officers. The narrowness of the pass forced the mob into solid formation, and the rear-rank delivered some sort of a wavering volley. The Ghazis drew off, for they did not know what reserves the gorge might hide. Moreover, it was never wise to chase white men too far. They returned as wolves return to cover, satisfied with the slaughter that they had done, and only stopping to slash at the wounded on the ground. A quarter of a mile had the Fore and Aft retreated, and now, jammed in the pass, was quivering with pain, shaken and demoralized with fear, while the officers, maddened beyond control, smote the men with the hilts and the flats of their swords.

"Get back! Get back, you cowards–you women! Right about face–column of companies, form–you hounds!" shouted the Colonel, and the subalterns swore aloud. But the Regiment wanted to go–to go anywhere out of the range of those merciless knives. It swayed to and fro irresolutely with shouts and outcries, while from the right the Gurkhas dropped volley after volley of cripple-stopper Snider bullets at long range into the mob of the Ghazis returning to their own troops.

The Fore and Aft Band, though protected from direct fire by the rocky knoll under which it had sat down, fled at the first rush. Jakin and Lew would have fled also, but their short legs left them fifty yards in the rear, and by the time the Band had mixed with the regiment, they were painfully aware that they would have to close in alone and unsupported.

"Get back to that rock," gasped Jakin. "They won't see us there."

And they returned to the scattered instruments of the Band; their hearts nearly bursting their ribs.

"Here's a nice show for *us,*" said Jakin, throwing himself full length on the ground. "A bloomin' fine show for British Infantry! Oh, the devils! They've gone an' left us alone here! Wot'll we do?"

Lew took possession of a cast-off water bottle, which naturally was full of canteen rum, and drank till he coughed again.

"Drink," said he, shortly. "They'll come back in a minute or two–you see."

Jakin drank, but there was no sign of the regiment's return. They could hear a dull clamor from the head of the valley of retreat, and saw the Ghazis slink back, quickening their pace as the Gurkhas fired at them.

"We're all that's left of the Band, an' we'll be cut up as sure as death," said Jakin.

"I'll die game, then," said Lew, thickly, fumbling with his tiny drummer's sword. The drink was working on his brain as it was on Jakin's.

" 'Old on! I know something better than fightin'," said Jakin, "stung by the splendor of a sudden thought" due chiefly to rum. "Tip our bloomin' cowards to come back. The Paythan beggars are well away. Come on, Lew! We won't get hurt. Take the fife an' give me the drum. The Old Step for all your bloomin' guts are worth! There's a few of our men coming back now. Stand up, ye drunken little defaulter. By your right–quick march!"

He slipped the drum-sling over his shoulder, thrust the fife into Lew's hand, and the two boys marched out of the cover of the rock into the open, making a hideous hash of the first bars of the "British Grenadiers."

As Lew had said, a few of the Fore and Aft were coming back sullenly and shamefacedly under the stimulus of blows and abuse; their red coats shone at the head of the valley, and behind them were wavering bayonets. But between this shattered line and the enemy, who with Afghan suspicion feared that the hasty retreat meant an ambush, and had not moved therefore, lay half a mile of a level ground dotted only by the wounded.

The tune settled into full swing and the boys kept shoulder to shoulder, Jakin banging the drum as one possessed. The one fife made a thin and pitiful squeaking, but the tune carried far, even to the Gurkhas.

"Come on, you dogs!" muttered Jakin, to himself. "Are we to play forhever?" Lew was staring straight in front of him and marching more stiffly than ever he had done on parade.

And in bitter mockery of the distant mob, the old tune of the Old Line shrilled and rattled:

> Some talk of Alexander,
> And some of Hercules;
> Of Hector and Lysander,
> And such great names as these!

There was a far-off clapping of hands from the Gurkhas, and a roar from the Highlanders in the distance, but never a shot was fired by British or Afghan. The two little red dots moved forward in the open parallel to the enemy's front.

> But of all the world's great heroes
> There's none that can compare,
> With a tow-row-row-row-row-row,
> To the British Grenadier!

The men of the Fore and Aft were gathering thick at the entrance into the plain. The Brigadier on the heights far above was speechless with rage. Still no movement from the enemy. The day stayed to watch the children.

Jakin halted and beat the long roll of Assembly, while the fife squealed despairingly.

"Right about face! Hold up, Lew, you're drunk," said Jakin. They wheeled and marched back:

> Those heroes of antiquity
> Ne'er saw a cannon'ball,
> Nor knew the force o' powder,

"Here they come!" said Jakin. "Go on, Lew:"

> To scare their foes withal!

The Fore and Aft were pouring out of the valley. What officers had said to men in that time of shame and humiliation will never be known; for neither officers nor men speak of it now.

"They are coming anew!" shouted a priest among the Afghans. "Do not kill the boys! Take them alive, and they shall be of our faith."

But the first volley had been fired, and Lew dropped on his face. Jakin stood for a minute, spun around and collapsed, as the Fore and Aft came forward, the maledictions of their officers in their ears, and in their hearts the shame of open shame.

Half the men had seen the drummers die, and they made no sign. They did not even shout. They doubled out straight across the plain in open order, and they did not fire.

"This," said the Colonel of the Gurkhas, softly, "is the real attack, as it ought to have been delivered. Come on, my children."

"Ulu-lu-lu-lu!" squealed the Gurkhas, and came down with a joyful clicking of *kukris*—those vicious Gurkha knives.

On the right there was no rush. The Highlanders, cannily commending their souls to God (for it matters as much to a dead man whether he has been shot in a Border scuffle or at Waterloo) opened out and fired according to their custom, that is to say without heat and without intervals, while the screw-guns, having disposed of the impertinent mud fort aforementioned, dropped shell after shell into the clusters round the flickering green standards on the heights.

"Charrging is an unfortunate necessity," murmured the Color-Sergeant of the right company of the Highlanders.

"It makes the men sweer so, but I am thinkin' that it will come to a charrge if these black devils stand much longer. Stewarrt, man, you're firing into the eye of the sun, and he'll not take any harm for Government ammuneetion. A foot lower and a great deal slower! What are the English doing? They're very quiet there in the centre. Running again?"

The English were not running. They were hacking and hewing and stabbing, for though one white man is seldom physically a match for an Afghan in a sheep-skin or wadded coat, yet, through the pressure of many white men behind, and a certain thirst for revenge in his heart, he becomes capable of doing much with both ends of his rifle. The Fore and Aft held their fire till one bullet could drive through five or six men, and the front of the Afghan force gave on the volley. They then selected their men, and slew them with deep gasps and short hacking coughs, and groanings of leather belts against strained bodies, and realized for the first time that an Afghan attacked is far less formidable than an Afghan attacking; which fact old soldiers might have told them.

But they had no old soldiers in their ranks.

The Gurkhas' stall at the bazar was the noisiest, for the men were engaged—to a nasty noise as of beef being cut on the block—with the *kukri,* which they preferred to the bayonet; well knowing how the Afghan hates the half-moon blade.

As the Afghans wavered, the green standards on the mountain moved down to assist them in a last rally. Which was unwise. The Lancers chafing in the right gorge had thrice despatched their only subaltern as galloper to report on the progress of affairs. On the third occasion he returned, with a bullet-graze on his knee, swearing strange oaths in Hindoostani, and saying that all things were ready. So that Squadron swung round the right of the Highlanders with a wicked whistling of wind in the pennons of its lances, and fell upon the remnant just when, according to all the rules of war, it should have waited for the foe to show more signs of wavering.

But it was a dainty charge, deftly delivered, and it ended by the Cavalry finding itself at the head of the pass by which the Afghans intended to retreat; and down the track that the lances had made streamed two companies of the Highlanders, which was never intended by the Brigadier. The new development was successful. It detached the enemy from his base as a sponge is torn from a rock, and left him ringed about with fire in that pitiless plain. And as a sponge is chased around the bath-tub by the hand of the bather, so were the Afghans chased till they broke into little detachments much more difficult to dispose of than large masses.

"See!" quoth the Brigadier. "Everything has come as I arranged. We've cut their base, and now we'll bucket 'em to pieces."

A direct hammering was all that the Brigadier had dared hope for, considering the size of the force at his disposal; but men who stand or fall by the errors of their opponents may be forgiven for turning Chance into Design. The bucketing went forward merrily. The Afghan forces were upon the run—the run of wearied wolves who snarl and bite over their shoulders. The red lances dipped by twos and threes, and, with a shriek, up rose the lance-butt, like a spar on a stormy sea, as the trooper cantering forward cleared his point. The Lancers kept between their prey and the steep hills, for all who could were trying to escape from the valley of death. The Highlanders gave the fugitives two hundred yards' law, and then brought them down, gasping and choking ere they could reach the protection of the bowlders above. The Gurkhas followed suit; but the Fore and Aft were killing on their own account, for they had penned a mass of men between their bayonets and a wall of rock, and the flash of the rifles was lighting the wadded coats.

"We cannot hold them, Chaptan Sahib!" panted a Ressaidar of Lancers. "Let us try the carbine. The lance is good, but it wastes time."

They tried the carbine, and still the enemy melted away—fled up the hills by hundreds when there were only twenty bullets to stop them. On the heights the screw-guns ceased firing—they had run out of ammunition—and the Brigadier groaned, for the musketry fire could not sufficiently smash the retreat. Long before the last volleys were fired, the litters were out in force looking for the wounded. The battle was over, and, but for want of fresh troops, the Afghans would have been wiped off the earth. As it was they counted their dead by hundreds, and nowhere were the dead thicker than in the track of the Fore and Aft.

But the Regiment did not cheer with the Highlanders, nor did they dance uncouth dances with the Gurkhas among the dead. They looked under their brows at the Colonel as they leaned upon their rifles and panted.

"Get back to camp, you. Haven't you disgraced yourself enough for one day! Go and look to the wounded. It's all you're fit for," said the Colonel. Yet for the past hour the Fore and Aft had been doing all that mortal commander could expect. They had lost heavily because they did not know how to set about their business with proper skill, but they had borne themselves gallantly, and this was their reward.

A young and sprightly Color-Sergeant, who had begun to imagine himself a hero, offered his water-bottle to a Highlander, whose tongue was black with thirst. "I drink with no cowards," answered the youngster, huskily, and, turning to a Gurkha, said, "Hya, Johnny! Drink water got it?" The Gurkha grinned and passed his bottle. The Fore and Aft said no word.

They went back to camp when the field of strife had been a little mopped up and made presentable, and the Brigadier, who saw himself a Knight in three months, was the only soul who was complimentary to them. The Colonel was heart-broken and the officers were savage and sullen.

"Well," said the Brigadier, "they are young troops of course, and it was not unnatural that they should retire in disorder for a bit."

"Oh, my only Aunt Maria!" murmured a junior Staff Officer. "Retire in disorder! It was a bally run!"

"But they came again as we all know," cooed the Brigadier, the Colonel's ashy-white face before him, "and they behaved as well as could possibly be expected. Behaved beautifully, indeed. I was watching them. It's not a matter to take to heart, Colonel. As some German General said of his men, they wanted to be shooted over a little, that was all." To himself he said: "Now they're blooded I can give 'em responsible work. It's as well that they got what they did. 'Teach 'em more than half a dozen rifle flirtations, that will—

later—run alone and bite. Poor old Colonel, though."

All that afternoon the heliograph winked and flickered on the hills, striving to tell the good news to a mountain forty miles away. And in the evening there arrived, dusty, sweating, and sore, a misguided Correspondent who had gone out to assist at a trumpery village-burning and who had read off the message from afar, cursing his luck the while.

"Let's have the details somehow—as full as ever you can, please. It's the first time I've ever been left this campaign," said the Correspondent to the Brigadier; and the Brigadier, nothing loath, told him how an Army of Communication had been crumpled up, destroyed, and all but annihilated by the craft, strategy, wisdom, and foresight of the Brigadier.

But some say, and among these be the Gurkhas who watched on the hillside, that that battle was won by Jakin and Lew, whose little bodies were borne up just in time to fit two gaps at the head of the big ditch-grave for the dead under the heights of Jagai.

Wee Willie Winkie

"An officer and a gentleman."

HIS FULL NAME was Percival William Williams, but he picked up the other name in a nursery-book, and that was the end of the christened titles. His mother's *ayah* called him Willie-*Baba,* but as he never paid the faintest attention to anything that the *ayah* said, her wisdom did not help matters.

His father was the Colonel of the 195th, and as soon as Wee Willie Winkie was old enough to understand what Military Discipline meant, Colonel Williams put him under it. There was no other way of managing the child. When he was good for a week, he drew good-conduct pay; and when he was bad, he was deprived of his good-conduct stripe. Generally he was bad, for India offers so many chances to little six-year-olds of going wrong.

Children resent familiarity from strangers, and Wee Willie Winkie was a very particular child. Once he accepted an acquaintance, he was graciously pleased to thaw. He accepted Brandis, a subaltern of the 195th, on sight. Brandis was having tea at the Colonel's, and Wee Willie Winkie entered strong in the possession of a good-conduct badge won for not chasing the hens round the compound. He regarded Brandis with gravity for at least ten minutes, and then delivered himself of his opinion.

"I like you," said he, slowly, getting off his chair and coming over to Brandis. "I like you. I shall call you Coppy, because of your hair. Do you *mind* being called Coppy? it is because of ve hair, you know."

Here was one of the most embarrassing of Wee Willie Winkie's peculiarities. He would look at a stranger for some time, and then, without warning or explanation, would give him a name. And the name stuck. No regimental penalties could break Wee Willie Winkie of this habit. He lost his good-conduct badge for christening the Commissioner's wife "Pobs"; but nothing that the Colonel could do made the Station forego the nickname, and Mrs. Collen remained Mrs. "Pobs" till the end of her stay. So Brandis was christened "Coppy," and rose, therefore, in the estimation of the regiment.

If Wee Willie Winkie took an interest in any one, the fortunate man was envied alike by the mess and the rank and file. And in their envy lay no suspicion of self-interest. "The Colonel's son" was idolized on his own merits entirely. Yet Wee Willie Winkie was not lovely. His face was permanently freckled, as his legs were permanently scratched, and in spite of his mother's almost tearful remonstrances he had insisted upon having his long yellow locks cut short in the military fashion. "I want my hair like Sergeant Tummil's," said Wee Willie Winkie, and, his father abetting, the sacrifice was accomplished.

Three weeks after the bestowal of his youthful affections on Lieutenant Brandis–henceforward to be called "Coppy" for the sake of brevity–Wee Willie Winkie Winkie was destined to behold strange things and far beyond his comprehension.

Coppy returned his liking with interest. Coppy had let him wear for five rapturous minutes his own big sword–just as tall as Wee Willie Winkie. Coppy had promised him a terrier pup; and Coppy had permitted him to witness the miraculous operation of shaving. Nay, more–Coppy had said that even he, Wee Willie Winkie, would rise in time to the ownership of a box of shiny knives, a silver soap-box and a silver-handled "sputter-brush," as Wee Willie Winkie called it. Decidedly, there was no one except his father, who could give or take away good-conduct badges at pleasure, half so wise, strong, and valiant as Coppy with the Afghan and Egyptian medals on his breast. Why, then, should Coppy be guilty of the unmanly weakness of kissing–vehemently kissing–a "big girl," Miss Allardyce to wit? In the course of a morning ride, Wee Willie Winkie had seen Coppy so doing, and, like the gentleman he was, had promptly wheeled round and cantered back to his groom, lest the groom should also see.

Under ordinary circumstances he would have spoken to his father, but he felt instinctively that this was a matter on which Coppy ought first to be consulted.

"Coppy," shouted Wee Willie Winkie, reining up outside that subaltern's bungalow early one morning–"I want to see you, Coppy!"

"Come in, youn' 'un," returned Coppy, who was at early breakfast in the midst of his dogs. "What mischief have you been getting into now?"

Wee Willie Winkie had done nothing notoriously bad for three days, and so stood on a pinnacle of virtue.

"I've been doing nothing bad," said he, curling himself into a long chair with a studious affectation of the Colonel's languor after a hot parade. He buried his freckled nose in a tea-cup and, with eyes staring roundly over the rim, asked:–"I say, Coppy, is it pwoper to kiss big girls?"

"By Jove! You're beginning early. Who do you want to kiss?"

"No one. My muvver's always kissing me if I don't stop her. If it isn't pwoper, how was you kissing Major Allardyce's big girl last morning, by ve canal?"

Coppy's brow wrinkled. He and Miss Allardyce had with great craft managed to keep their engagement secret for a fortnight. There were urgent and imperative reasons why Major Allardyce should not know how matters stood for at least another month, and this small marplot had discovered a great deal too much.

"I saw you," said Wee Willie Winkie, calmly. "But ve groom didn't see. I said, *'Hut jao.'* "

"Oh, you had that much sense, you young Rip," groaned poor Coppy half amused and half angry. "And how many people may have you told about it?"

"Only me myself. You didn't tell when I twied to wide ve buffalo ven my pony was lame; and I fought you wouldn't like."

"Winkie," said Coppy, enthusiastically, shaking the small hand, "you're the best of good fellows. Look here, you can't understand all these things. One of these days–hang it, how can I make you see it!–I'm going to marry Miss Allardyce, and then she'll be Mrs. Coppy, as you say. If your young mind is so scandalized at the idea of kissing big girls, go and tell your father."

"What will happen?" said Wee Willie Winkie, who firmly believed that his father was omnipotent.

"I shall get into trouble," said Coppy, playing his trump card with an appealing look at the holder of the ace.

"Ven I won't," said Wee Willie Winkie, briefly. "But my faver says it's un-man-ly to be always kissing, and I didn't fink *you'd* do vat, Coppy."

"I'm not always kissing, old chap. It's only now and then, and when you're bigger you'll do it too. Your father meant it's not good for little boys."

"Ah!" said Wee Willie Winkie, now fully enlightened. "It's like ve sputter-brush?"

"Exactly," said Coppy, gravely.

"But I don't fink I'll ever want to kiss big girls, nor no one, 'cept my muvver. And I *must* vat, you know."

There was a long pause, broken by Wee Willie Winkie.

"Are you fond of vis big girl, Coppy?"

"Awfully!" said Coppy.

"Fonder van you are of Bell or ve Butcha–or me?"

"It's in a different way," said Coppy. "You see, one of these days Miss Allardyce will belong to me, but you'll grow up and command the Regiment and–all sorts of things. It's quite different, you see."

"Very well," said Wee Willie Winkie, rising. "If you're fond of ve big girl, I won't tell any one. I must go now."

Coppy rose and escorted his small guest to the door, adding: "You're the best of little fellows, Winkie. I tell you what. In thirty days from now you can tell if you like–tell any one you like."

Thus the secret of the Brandis-Allardyce engagement was dependent on a little child's word. Coppy, who knew Wee Willie Winkie's idea of truth, was at ease, for he felt that he would not break promises. Wee Willie Winkie betrayed a special and unusual interest in Miss Allardyce, and, slowly revolving round that embarrassed young lady, was used to regard her gravely with unwinking eye. He was trying to discover why Coppy should have kissed her. She was not half so nice as his own mother. On the other hand, she was Coppy's property, and would in time belong to him. Therefore it behooved him to treat her with as much respect as Coppy's big sword or shiny pistol.

The idea that he shared a great secret in common with Coppy kept Wee Willie Winkie unusually virtuous for three weeks. Then the Old Adam broke out, and he made what he called a "camp-fire" at the bottom of the garden. How could he have foreseen that the flying sparks would have lighted the Colonel's little hayrick and consumed a week's store for the horses? Sudden and swift was the punishment–deprivation of the good-conduct badge and, most sorrowful of all, two-days' confinement to barracks–the house and veranda–coupled with the withdrawal of the light of his father's countenance.

He took the sentence like the man he strove to be, drew himself up with a quivering under-lip, saluted, and, once clear of the room, ran to weep bitterly in his nursery–called by him "my quarters." Coppy came in the afternoon and attempted to console the culprit.

"I'm under awwest," said Wee Willie Winkie, mournfully, "and I didn't ought to speak to you."

Very early the next morning he climbed on to the roof of the house–that was not forbidden–and beheld Miss Allardyce going for a ride.

"Where are you going?" cried Wee Willie Winkie.

"Across the river," she answered, and trotted forward.

Now the cantonment in which the 195th lay was bounded on the north by a river–dry in the winter. From his earliest years, Wee Willie Winkie had been forbidden to go across the river, and had noted that even Coppy–the almost almighty Coppy–had never set foot beyond it. Wee Willie Winkie had once been read to, out of a big blue book, the history of the Princess and the

Goblins—a most wonderful tale of a land where the Goblins were always warring with the children of men until they were defeated by one Curdie. Ever since that date it seemed to him that the bare black and purple hills across the river were inhabited by Goblins, and, in truth, every one had said that there lived the Bad Men. Even in his own house the lower halves of the windows were covered with green paper on account of the Bad Men who might, if allowed clear view, fire into peaceful drawing-rooms and comfortable bedrooms. Certainly, beyond the river, which was the end of all the Earth, lived the Bad Men. And here was Major Allardyce's big girl, Coppy's property, preparing to venture into their borders! What would Coppy say if anything happened to her? If the Goblins ran off with her as they did with Curdie's Princess? She must at all hazards be turned back.

The house was still. Wee Willie Winkie reflected for a moment on the terrible wrath of his father; and then—broke his arrest! It was a crime unspeakable. The low sun threw his shadow, very large and very black, on the trim garden-paths, as he went down to the stables and ordered his pony. It seemed to him in the hush of the dawn that all the big world had been bidden to stand still and look at Wee Willie Winkie guilty of mutiny. The drowsy groom handed him his mount, and, since the one great sin made all others insignificant, Wee Willie Winkie said that he was going to ride over to Coppy Sahib, and went out at a footpace, stepping on the soft mould of the flower-borders.

The devastating track of the pony's feet was the last misdeed that cut him off from all sympathy of Humanity. He turned into the road, leaned forward, and rode as fast as the pony could put foot to the ground in the direction of the river.

But the liveliest of twelve-two ponies can do little against the long canter of a Waler. Miss Allardyce was far ahead, and passed through the crops beyond, the Police-post, when all the guards were asleep, and her mount was scattering the pebbles of the river bed as Wee Willie Winkie left the cantonment and British India behind him. Bowed forward and still flogging, Wee Willie Winkie shot into Afghan territory, and could just see Miss Allardyce a black speck, flickering across the stony plain. The reason of her wandering was simple enough. Coppy, in a tone of too-hastily-assumed authority, had told her over night that she must not ride out by the river. And she had gone to prove her own spirit and teach Coppy a lesson.

Almost at the foot of the inhospitable hills, Wee Willie Winkie saw the Waler blunder and come down heavily. Miss Allardyce struggled clear, but her ankle had been severely twisted, and she could not stand. Having thus demonstrated her spirit, she wept copiously, and was surprised by the apparition of a white, wide-eyed child in khaki, on a nearly spent pony.

"Are you badly, badly hurted?" shouted Wee Willie Winkie, as soon as he was within range. "You didn't ought to be here."

"I don't know," said Miss Allardyce, ruefully ignoring the reproof. "Good gracious, child, what are *you* doing here?"

"You said you was going acwoss ve wiver," panted Wee Willie Winkie, throwing himself off his pony. "And nobody—not even Coppy—must go acwoss ve wiver, and I came after you ever so hard, but you wouldn't stop, and now you've hurted yourself, and Coppy will be angwy wiv me, and—I've broken my awwest! I've bwoken my awwest!"

The future Colonel of the 195th sat down and sobbed. In spite of the pain in her ankle the girl was moved.

"Have you ridden all the way from cantonments, little man? What for?"

"You belonged to Coppy. Coppy told me so!" wailed Wee Willie Winkie, disconsolately. "I saw him kissing you, and he said he was fonder of you van Bell or ve Butcha or me. And so I came. You must get up and come back. You didn't ought to be here. Vis is a bad place, and I've bwoken my awwest."

"I can't move, Winkie," said Miss Allardyce, with a groan. "I've hurt my foot. What shall I do?"

She showed a readiness to weep afresh, which steadied Wee Willie Winkie, who had been brought up to believe that tears were the depth of unmanliness. Still, when one is as great a sinner as Wee Willie Winkie, even a man may be permitted to break down.

"Winkie," said Miss Allardyce, "when you've rested a little, ride back and tell them to send out something to carry me back in. It hurts fearfully."

The child sat still for a little time and Miss Allardyce closed her eyes; the pain was nearly making her faint. She was roused by Wee Willie Winkie tying up the reins on his pony's neck and setting it free with the vicious cut of his whip that made it whicker. The little animal headed toward the cantonments.

"Oh, Winkie! What are you doing?"

"Hush!" said Wee Willie Winkie. "Vere's a man coming–one of ve Bad Men. I must stay wiv you. My faver says a man must *always* look after a girl. Jack will go home, and ven vey'll come and look for us. Vat's why I let him go."

Not one man but two or three had appeared from behind the rocks of the hills, and the heart of Wee Willie Winkie sank within him, for just in this manner were the Goblins wont to steal out and vex Curdie's soul. Thus had they played in Curdie's garden, he had seen the picture, and thus had they frightened the Princess's nurse. He heard them talking to each other, and recognized with joy the bastard Pushto that he had picked up from one of his father's grooms lately dismissed. People who spoke that tongue could not be the Bad Men. They were only natives after all.

They came up to the bowlders on which Miss Allardyce's horse had blundered.

Then rose from the rock Wee Willie Winkie, child of the Dominant Race, aged six and three-quarters, and said briefly and emphatically *"Jao!"* The pony had crossed the river-bed.

The men laughed, and laughter from natives was the one thing Wee Willie Winkie could not tolerate. He asked them what they wanted and why they did not depart. Other men with most evil faces and crooked-stocked guns crept out of the shadows of the hills, till, soon, Wee Willie Winkie was face to face with an audience some twenty strong. Miss Allardyce screamed.

"Who are you?" said one of the men.

"I am the Colonel Sahib's son, and my order is that you go at once. You black men are frightening the Miss Sahib. One of you must run to cantonments and take the news that Miss Sahib has hurt herself, and that the Colonel's son is here with her."

"Put our feet into the trap?" was the laughing reply. "Hear this boy's speech!"

"Say that I sent you–I, the Colonel's son. They will give you money."

"What is the use of this talk? Take up the child and the girl, and we can at least ask for the ransom. Ours are the villages on the heights," said a voice in the background.

These *were* the Bad Men–worse than Goblins–and it needed all Wee Willie Winkie's training to prevent him from bursting into tears. But he felt that to cry before a native, excepting only his mother's *ayah,* would be an infamy greater than any mutiny. Moreover, he, as future Colonel of the 195th, had that grim regiment at his back.

"Are you going to carry us away?" said Wee Willie Winkie, very blanched and uncomfortable.

"Yes, my little *Sahib Bahadur,"* said the tallest of the men, "and eat you afterward."

"That is child's talk," said Wee Willie Winkie. "Men do not eat men."

A yell of laughter interrupted him, but he went on firmly,–"And if you do carry us away, I tell you that all my regiment will come up in a day and kill you all without leaving one. Who will take my message to the Colonel Sahib?"

Speech in any vernacular–and Wee Willie Winkie had a colloquial acquaintance with three–was easy to the boy who could not manage his "r's" and "th's" aright.

Another man joined the conference, crying:–"O foolish men! What this babe says is true. He is the heart's heart of those white troops. For the sake of peace let them go both, for if he be taken, the regiment will break loose and gut the valley. *Our* villages are in the valley, and we shall not escape. That regiment are devils. They broke Khoda Yar's breast-bone with kicks when he tried to take the rifles; and if we touch this child they will fire and rape and plunder for a month, till nothing remains. Better to send a man back to take the message and get a reward. I say that this child is their God, and that they will spare none of us, nor our women, if we harm him."

It was Din Mahommed, the dismissed groom of the Colonel, who made the diversion, and an angry and heated discussion followed. Wee Willie Winkie, standing over Miss Allardyce, waited the upshot. Surely his "wegiment," his own "wegiment," would not desert him if they knew of his extremity.

. . . .

The riderless pony brought the news to the 195th, though there had been consternation in the Colonel's household for an hour before. The little beast came in through the parade ground in front of the main barracks, where the men were settling down to play Spoil-five till the afternoon. Devlin, the Color Sergeant of E Company, glanced at the empty saddle and tumbled through the barrack-rooms, kicking up each Room Corporal as he passed. "Up, ye beggars! There's something happened to the Colonel's son," he shouted.

"He couldn't fall off! S'elp me, *'e couldn't* fall off," blubbered a drummer-boy. "Go an' hunt acrost the river. He's over there if he's anywhere, an' maybe those Pathans have got 'im. For the love o' Gawd don't look for 'im in the nullahs! Let's go over the river."

"There's sense in Mott yet," said Devlin. "E Company, double out to the river–sharp!"

So E Company, in its shirt-sleeves mainly, doubled for the dear life, and in the rear toiled the perspiring Sergeant, adjuring it to double yet faster. The cantonment was alive with the men of the 195th hunting for Wee Willie Winkie, and the Colonel finally overtook E Company, far too exhausted to swear, struggling in the pebbles of the river-bed.

Up the hill under which Wee Willie Winkie's Bad Men were discussing the wisdom of carrying off the child and the girl, a look-out fired two shots.

"What have I said?" shouted Din Mahommed. "There is the warning! The *pulton* are out already and are coming across the plain! Get away! Let us not be seen with the boy!"

The men waited for an instant, and then, as another shot was fired, withdrew into the hills, silently as they had appeared.

"The wegiment is coming," said Wee Willie Winkie, confidently, to Miss Allardyce, "and it's all wight. Don't cwy!"

He needed the advice himself, for ten minutes later, when his father came up, he was weeping bitterly with his head in Miss Allardyce's lap.

And the men of the 195th carried him home with shouts and rejoicings; and Coppy, who had ridden a horse into a lather, met him, and, to his intense disgust, kissed him openly in the presence of the men.

But there was balm for his dignity. His father assured him that not only would the breaking of arrest be condoned, but that the good-conduct badge would be restored as soon as his mother could sew it on his blouse-sleeve. Miss Allardyce had told the Colonel a story that made him proud of his son.

"She belonged to you, Coppy," said Wee Willie Winkie, indicating Miss Allardyce with a grimy forefinger. "I *knew* she didn't ought to go acwoss de wiver, and I knew ve wegiment would come to me if I sent Jack home."

"You're a hero, Winkie," said Coppy–" a *pukka* hero!"

"I don't know what vat means," said Wee Willie Winkie, "but you mustn't call me Winkie any no more. I'm Percival Will'am Will'ams."

And in this manner did Wee Willie Winkie enter into his manhood.

My Own True Ghost Story

As I came through the Desert thus it was–
As I came through the Desert.
–*The City of Dreadful Night.*

SOMEWHERE IN THE Other World, where there are books and pictures and plays and shop-windows to look at, and thousands of men who spend their lives in building up all four, lives a gentleman who writes real stories about the real insides of people; and his name is Mr. Walter Besant. But he will insist upon treating his ghosts–he has published half a workshopful of them–with levity. He makes his ghost-seers talk familiarly, and, in some cases, flirt outrageously, with the phantoms. You may treat anything, from a Viceroy to a Vernacular Paper, with levity; but you must behave reverently toward a ghost, and particularly an Indian one.

There are, in this land, ghosts who take the form of fat, cold, pobby corpses, and hide in trees near the roadside till a traveler passes. Then they drop upon his neck and remain. There are also terrible ghosts of women who have died in child-bed. These wander along the pathways at dusk, or hide in the crops near a village, and call seductively. But to answer their call is death in this world and the next. Their feet are turned backward that all sober men may recognize them. There are ghosts of little children who have been thrown into wells. These haunt well-curbs and the fringes of jungles, and wail under the stars, or catch women by the wrist and beg to be taken up and carried. These and the corpse-ghosts, however, are only vernacular articles and do not attack Sahibs. No native ghost has yet been authentically reported to have frightened an Englishman; but many English ghosts have scared the life out of both white and black.

Nearly every other Station owns a ghost. There are said to be two at Simla, not counting the woman who blows the bellows at Syree dâk-bungalow on the Old Road; Mussoorie has a house haunted of a very lively Thing; a White Lady is supposed to do night-watchman round a house in Lahore; Dalhousie says that one of her houses "repeats" on autumn evenings all the incidents of a horrible horse-and-precipice accident; Murree has a merry ghost, and, now that she has been swept by cholera, will have room for a sorrowful one; there are Officers' Quarters in Mian Mir whose doors open without reason, and whose furniture is guaranteed to creak, not with the heat of June but with the weight of Invisibles who come to lounge in the chair; Peshawur possesses houses that none will willingly rent; and there is something–not fever–wrong with a big bungalow in Allahabad. The older Provinces simply bristle with haunted houses, and march phantom armies along their main thoroughfares.

Some of the dâk-bungalows on the Grand Trunk Road have handy little cemeteries in their compound–witnesses to the "changes and chances of this mortal life" in the days when men drove from Calcutta to the Northwest. These bungalows are objectionable places to put up in. They are generally very old, always dirty, while the *khansamah* is as ancient as the bungalow. He either chatters senilely, or falls into the long trances of age. In both moods he is useless. If you get angry with him, he refers to some Sahib dead and buried these thirty years, and says that when he was in that Sahib's service not a *khansamah* in the Province could touch him. Then he jabbers and mows and trembles and fidgets among the dishes, and you repent of your irritation.

In these dâk-bungalows, ghosts are most likely to be found, and when found, they should be made a note of. Not long ago it was my business to live in dâk-bungalows. I never inhabited the same house for three nights running, and grew to be learned in the breed. I lived in Government-built ones with red brick walls and rail ceilings, an inventory of the furniture posted in every room, and an excited snake at the threshold to give welcome. I lived in "converted" ones–old houses officiating as dâk-bungalows–where nothing was in its proper place and there wasn't even a fowl for dinner. I lived in second-hand palaces where the wind blew through open-work marble tracery just as uncomfortably as through a broken pane. I lived in dâk-bungalows where the last entry in the visitors' book was fifteen months old, and where they slashed off the curry-kid's head with a sword. It was my good-luck to meet all sorts of men, from sober traveling missionaries and deserters flying from British Regiments, to drunken loafers who threw whiskey bottles at all who passed; and my still greater good-fortune just to escape a maternity case. Seeing that a fair proportion of the tragedy of our lives out here acted itself in dâk-bungalows, I wondered that I had met no ghosts. A ghost that would voluntarily hang about a dâk-bungalow would be mad of course; but so many men have died mad in dâk-bungalows that there must be a fair percentage of lunatic ghosts.

In due time I found my ghost, or ghosts rather, for there were two of them. Up till that hour I had sympathized with Mr. Besant's method of handling them, as shown in *"The Strange Case of Mr. Lucraft and Other Stories."* I am now in the Opposition.

We will call the bungalow Katmal dâk-bungalow. But *that* was the smallest part of the horror. A man with a sensitive hide has no right to sleep in dâk-bungalows. He should marry. Katmal dâk-bungalow was old and rotten and unrepaired. The floor was of worn brick, the walls were filthy, and the windows were nearly black with grime. It stood on a bypath largely used by native Sub-Deputy Assistants of all kinds, from Finance to Forests; but real Sahibs were rare. The *khansamah,* who was nearly bent double with old age, said so.

When I arrived, there was a fitful, undecided rain on the face of the land, accompanied by a restless wind, and every gust made a noise like the rattling of dry bones in the stiff toddy-palms outside. The *khansamah* completely lost his head on my arrival. He had served a Sahib once. Did I know that Sahib. He gave me the name of a well-known man who has been buried for more than a quarter of a century, and showed me an ancient daguerreotype of that man in his prehistoric youth. I had seen a steel engraving of him at the head of a double volume of Memoirs a month before, and I felt ancient beyond telling.

The day shut in and the *khansamah* went to get me food. He did not go through the pretence of calling it *"khana"*–man's victuals. He said *"ratub,"* and that means, among other things, "grub"–dog's rations. There was no insult in his choice of the term. He had forgotten the other word, I suppose.

While he was cutting up the dead bodies of animals, I settled myself down, after exploring the dâk-bungalow. There were three rooms, beside my own, which was a corner kennel, each giving into the other through dingy white doors fastened with long iron bars. The bungalow was a very solid one, but the partition-walls of the rooms were almost jerry-built in their flimsiness. Every step or bang of a trunk echoed from my room down the other three, and every footfall came back tremulously from the far walls. For this reason I shut the door. There were no lamps—only candles in long glass shades. An oil wick was set in the bath-room.

For bleak, unadulterated misery that dâk-bungalow was the worst of the many that I had ever set foot in. There was no fireplace, and the windows would not open; so a brazier of charcoal would have been useless. The rain and the wind splashed and gurgled and moaned round the house, and the toddy-palms rattled and roared. Half a dozen jackals went through the compound singing, and a hyena stood afar off and mocked them. A hyena would convince a Sadducee of the Resurrection of the Dead—the worst sort of Dead. Then came the *ratub*—a curious meal, half native and half English in composition—with the old *khansamah* babbling behind my chair about dead and gone English people, and the wind-blown candles playing shadow-bo-peep with the bed and the mosquito-curtains. It was just the sort of dinner and evening to make a man think of every single one of his past sins, and of all the others that he intended to commit if he lived.

Sleep, for several hundred reasons, was not easy. The lamp in the bath-room threw the most absurd shadows into the room, and the wind was beginning to talk nonsense.

Just when the reasons were drowsy with blood-sucking I heard the regular—"Let-us-take-and-heave-him-over" grunt of doolie-bearers in the compound. First one doolie came in, then a second, and then a third. I heard the doolies dumped on the ground, and the shutter in front of my door shook. "That's some one trying to come in," I said. But no one spoke, and I persuaded myself that it was the gusty wind. The shutter of the room next to mine was attacked, flung back, and the inner door opened. "That's some Sub-Deputy Assistant," I said, "and he has brought his friends with him. Now they'll talk and spit and smoke for an hour."

But there were no voices and no footsteps. No one was putting his luggage into the next room. The door shut, and I thanked Providence that I was to be left in peace. But I was curious to know where the doolies had gone. I got out of bed and looked into the darkness. There was never a sign of a doolie. Just as I was getting into bed again, I heard, in the next room, the sound that no man in his senses can possibly mistake—the whir of a billiard ball down the length of the slates when the striker is stringing for break. No other sound is like it. A minute afterward there was another whir, and I got into bed. I was not frightened—indeed I was not. I was very curious to know what had become of the doolies. I jumped into bed for that reason.

Next minute I heard the double click of a cannon and my hair sat up. It is a mistake to say that hair stands up. The skin of the head tightens and you can feel a faint, prickly bristling all over the scalp. That is the hair sitting up.

There was a whir and a click, and both sounds could only have been made by one thing—a billiard ball. I argued the matter out at great length with myself; and the more I argued the less probable it seemed that one bed, one table, and two chairs—all the furniture of the room next to mine—could so exactly duplicate the sounds of a game of billiards. After another cannon, a three-cushion one to judge by the whir, I argued no more. I had found my ghost and would have given worlds to have escaped from that dâk-bungalow. I listened, and with each listen the game grew clearer. There was whir on whir and click on click. Sometimes there was a double click and a whir and another click. Beyond any sort of doubt, people were playing billiards in the next room. And the next room was not big enough to hold a billiard table!

Between the pauses of the wind I heard the game go forward–stroke after stroke. I tried to believe that I could not hear voices; but that attempt was a failure.

Do you know what fear is? Not ordinary fear of insult, injury or death, but abject, quivering dread of something that you cannot see–fear that dries the inside of the mouth and half of the throat–fear that makes you sweat on the palms of the hands, and gulp in order to keep the uvula at work? This is a fine Fear–a great cowardice, and must be felt to be appreciated. The very improbability of billiards in a dâk-bungalow proved the reality of the thing. No man–drunk or sober–could imagine a game at billiards, or invent the splitting crack of a "screw-cannon."

A severe course of dâk-bungalows has this disadvantage–it breeds infinite credulity. If a man said to a confirmed dâk-bungalow-haunter:–"There is a corpse in the next room, and there's a mad girl in the next but one, and the woman and man on that camel have just eloped from a place sixty miles away," the hearer would not disbelieve because he would know that nothing is too wild, grotesque, or horrible to happen in a dâk-bungalow.

This credulity, unfortunately, extends to ghosts. A rational person fresh from his own house would have turned on his side and slept. I did not. So surely as I was given up as a bad carcass by the scores of things in the bed because the bulk of my blood was in my heart, so surely did I hear every stroke of a long game at billiards played in the echoing room behind the iron-barred door. My dominant fear was that the players might want a maker. It was an absurd fear; because creatures who could play in the dark would be above such superfluities. I only know that that was my terror; and it was real.

After a long long while, the game stopped, and the door banged. I slept because I was dead tired. Otherwise I should have preferred to have kept awake. Not for everything in Asia would I have dropped the doorbar and peered into the dark of the next room.

When the morning came, I considered that I had done well and wisely, and inquired for the means of departure.

"By the way, *khansamah,*" I said, "what were those three doolies doing in my compound in the night?"

"There were no doolies," said the *khansamah.*

I went into the next room and the daylight streamed through the open door. I was immensely brave. I would, at that hour, have played Black Pool with the owner of the big Black Pool down below.

"Has this place always been a dâk-bungalow?" I asked.

"No," said the *khansamah.* "Ten or twenty years ago, I have forgotten how long, it was a billiard-room."

"A how much?"

"A billiard-room for the Sahibs who built the Railway. I was *khansamah* then in the big house where all the Railway-Sahibs lived, and I used to come across with brandy-*shrab.* These three rooms were all one, and they held a big table on which the Sahibs played every evening. But the Sahibs are all dead now, and the Railway runs, you say, nearly to Kabul."

"Do you remember anything about the Sahibs?"

"It is long ago, but I remember that one Sahib, a fat man and always angry, was playing here one night, and he said to me:–'Mangal Khan, brandy-*pani do,*' and I filled the glass, and he bent over the table to strike, and his head fell lower and lower till it hit the table, and his spectacles came off, and when we–the Sahibs and I myself–ran to lift him he was dead. I helped to carry him out. Aha, he was a strong Sahib! But he is dead and I, old Mangal Khan, am still living, by your favor."

That was more than enough! I had my ghost–a first-hand, authenticated article. I would write to the Society for Psychical Research–I would paralyze the Empire with the news! But I would, first of all, put eighty miles of assessed crop-land between myself and that dâk-bungalow before nightfall. The Society might send their regular agent to investigate later on.

I went into my own room and prepared to pack after noting down the facts of the case. As I smoked I heard the game begin again—with a miss in balk this time, for the whir was a short one.

The door was open and I could see into the room. *Click—click!* That was a cannon. I entered the room without fear, for there was sunlight within and a fresh breeze without. The unseen game was going on at a tremendous rate. And well it might, when a restless little rat was running to and fro inside the dingy ceiling-cloth, and a piece of loose window-sash was making fifty breaks off the window-bolt as it shook in the breeze!

Impossible to mistake the sound of billiard balls! Impossible to mistake the whir of a ball over the slate! But I was to be excused. Even when I shut my enlightened eyes the sound was marvelously like that of a fast game.

Entered angrily the faithful partner of my sorrows, Kadir Baksh.

"This bungalow is very bad and low-caste! No wonder the Presence was disturbed and is speckled. Three sets of doolie-bearers came to the bungalow late last night when I was sleeping outside, and said that it was their custom to rest in the rooms set apart for the English people! What honor has the *khansamah?* They tried to enter, but I told them to go. No wonder, if these *Oorias* have been here, that the Presence is sorely spotted. It is shame, and the work of a dirty man!"

Kadir Baksh did not say that he had taken from each gang two annas for rent in advance, and then, beyond my earshot, had beaten them with the big green umbrella whose use I could never before divine. But Kadir Baksh has no notions of morality.

There was an interview with the *khansamah,* but as he promptly lost his head, wrath gave place to pity, and pity led to a long conversation, in the course of which he put the fat Engineer-Sahib's tragic death in three separate stations—two of them fifty miles away. The third shift was to Calcutta, and there the Sahib died while driving a dog-cart.

If I had encouraged him the *khansamah* would have wandered all through Bengal with his corpse.

I did not go away as soon as I intended. I stayed for the night, while the wind and the rat and the sash and the window-bolt played a ding-dong "hundred and fifty up." Then the wind ran out and the billiards stopped, and I felt that I had ruined my one genuine, hall-marked ghost story.

Had I only stopped at the proper time, I could have made *anything* of it. That was the bitterest thought of all!

The Solid Muldoon

Did ye see John Malone, wid his shinin', brand-new hat?
Did ye see how he walked like a grand aristocrat?
There was flags an' banners wavin' high, an' dhress and shtyle were shown,
But the best av all the company was Misther John Malone.

—*John Malone.*

THERE HAD BEEN a royal dog-fight in the ravine at the back of the rifle-butts, between Learoyd's *Jock* and Ortheris's *Blue Rot*—both mongrel Rampur hounds, chiefly ribs and teeth. It lasted for twenty happy, howling minutes, and then *Blue Rot* collapsed and Ortheris paid Learoyd three rupees, and we were all very thirsty. A dog-fight is a most heating entertainment, quite apart from the shouting, because Rampurs fight over a couple of acres of ground. Later, when the sound of belt-badges clicking against the necks of beer-bottles had died away, conversation drifted from dog to man-fights of all kinds. Humans resemble red-deer in some respects. Any talk of fighting seems to wake up a sort of imp in their breasts, and they bell one to the other, exactly like challenging bucks. This is noticeable even in men who consider themselves superior to Privates of the Line: it shows the Refining Influence of Civilization and the March of Progress.

Tale provoked tale, and each tale more beer. Even dreamy Learoyd's eyes began to brighten, and he unburdened himself of a long history in which a trip to Malham Cove, a girl at Pateley Brigg, a ganger, himself and a pair of clogs were mixed in drawling tangle.

"An' so Ah coot's yead oppen from t' chin to t' hair, an' he was abed for t' matter o' a month," concluded Learoyd, pensively.

Mulvaney came out a revery—he was lying down—and flourished his heels in the air. "You're a man, Learoyd," said he, critically, "but you've only fought wid men, an' that's an ivry-day expayrience; but I've stud up to a ghost, an' that was *not* an ivry-day expayrience."

"No?" said Ortheris, throwing a cork at him. "You git up an' address the 'ouse—you an' yer expayriences. Is it a bigger one nor usual?"

" 'Twas the livin' trut'!" answered Mulvaney, stretching out a huge arm and catching Ortheris by the collar. "Now where are ye, me son? Will ye take the wurrud av the Lorrd out av my mouth another time?" He shook him to emphasize the question.

"No, somethin' else, though," said Ortheris, making a dash at Mulvaney's pipe, capturing it and holding it at arm's length; "I'll chuck it acrost the ditch if you don't let me go!"

"You maraudin' hathen! 'Tis the only cutty I iver loved. Handle her tinder or I'll chuck *you* acrost the nullah. If that poipe was bruk—Ah! Give her back to me, sorr!"

Ortheris had passed the treasure to my hand. It was an absolutely perfect clay, as shiny as the black ball at Pool. I took it reverently, but I was firm.

"Will you tell us about the ghost-fight if I do?" I said.

"Is ut the shtory that's troublin' you? Av course I will. I mint to all along. I was only gettin' at ut my own way, as Popp Doggle said whin they found him thrying to ram a cartridge down the muzzle. Orth'ris, fall away!"

He released the little Londoner, took back his pipe, filled it, and his eyes twinkled. He has the most eloquent eyes of any one that I know.

"Did I iver tell you," he began, "that I was wanst the divil of a man?"

"You did," said Learoyd, with a childish gravity that made Ortheris yell with laughter, for Mulvaney was always impressing upon us his great merits in the old days.

"Did I iver tell you," Mulvaney continued, calmly, "that I was wanst more av a divil than I am now?"

"Mer—ria! You don't mean it?" said Ortheris.

"Whin I was Corp-ril—I was rejuced aftherward—but, as I say, *whin* I was Corp-ril, I was a divil of a man."

He was silent for nearly a minute, while his mind rummaged among old memories and his eye glowed. He bit upon the pipe-stem and charged into his tale.

"Eyah! They was great times. I'm ould now; me hide's wore off in patches; sinthrygo has disconceited me, an' I'm a married man tu. But I've had my day—I've had my day, an' nothin' can take away the taste av that! Oh my time past, whin I put me fut through ivry livin' wan av the Tin Command-mints between Revelly and Lights Out, blew the froth off a pewter, wiped me moustache wid the back av me hand, an' slept on ut all as quiet as a little child! But ut's over–ut's over, an' 'twill niver come back to me; not though I prayed for a week av Sundays. Was there *any* wan in the Ould Rig'mint to touch Corp'ril Terence Mulvaney whin that same was turned out for sed-ukshin? I niver met him. Ivry woman that was not a witch was worth the runnin' afther in those days, an' ivry man was my dearest frind or–I had stripped to him an' we knew which was the betther av the tu.

"Whin I was Corp'ril I wud not ha' changed wid the Colonel–no, nor yet the Commandher-in-Chief. I wud be a Sargint. There was nothin' I wud not be! Mother av Hivin, look at me! Fwhat am I *now?*

"We was quartered in a big cantonmint–'tis no manner av use namin' names, for ut might give the barricks disrepitation–an' I was the Imperor av the Earth to my own mind, an' wan or tu women though the same. Small blame to thim. Afther we had lain there a year, Bragin, the Color Sargint av E Comp'ny, wint an' took a wife that was lady's maid to some big lady in the Station. She's dead now is Annie Bragin–died in child-bed at Kirpa Tal, or ut may ha' been Almorah–seven–nine years gone, an' Bragin he married agin. But she was a pretty woman whin Bragin inthrojuced her to cantonmint society. She had eyes like the brown av a buttherfly's wing whin the sun catches ut, an' a waist no thicker than my arm, an' a little sof' button av a mouth I would ha' gone through all Asia bristlin' wid bay'nits to get the kiss av. An' her hair was as long as the tail av the Colonel's charger–forgive me mentionin' that blunderin' baste in the same mouthful with Annie Bragin–but 'twas all shpun gold, an' time was when ut was more than di'monds to me. There was niver pretty woman yet, an' I've had thruck wid a few, cud open the door to Annie Bragin.

" 'Twas in the Cath'lic Chapel I saw her first, me oi rolling round as usual to see fwhat was to be seen. 'You're too good for Bragin, my love,' thinks I to me-silf, 'but that's a mistake I can put straight, or my name is not Terence Mulvaney.'

"Now take my wurrd for ut, you Orth'ris there an' Learoyd, an' kape out av the Married Quarters–as I did not. No good iver comes av ut, an' there's always the chance av your bein' found wid your face in the dirt, a long picket in the back av your head, an' your hands playing the fifes on the tread av another man's doorstep. 'Twas so we found O'Hara, he that Rafferty killed six years gone, when he wint to his death wid his hair oiled, whistlin' *Larry O'Rourke* betune his teeth. Kape out av the Married Quarters, I say, as I did not. 'Tis onwholesim, 'tis dangerous, an' 'tis ivrything else that's bad, but–O my sowl, 'tis swate while ut lasts!

"I was always hangin' abóut there whin I was off duty an' Bragin wasn't, but niver a sweet word beyon' ordinar' did I get from Annie Bragin. ' 'Tis the pervarsity av the sect,' sez I to mesilf, an' gave my cap another cock on my head an' straightened my back–'twas the back av a Dhrum Major in those days–an' wint off as tho' I did not care, wid all the women in the Married Quarters laughin'. I was pershuaded–most bhoys *are* I'm thinkin'–that no women born av woman cud stand against me av I hild up my little finger. I had reason fer thinkin' that way–till I met Annie Bragin.

"Time an' agin whin I was blandandherin' in the dusk a man wud go past me as quiet as a cat. 'That's quare,' thinks I, 'for I am, or I should be, the only man in these parts. Now what divilment can Annie be up to?' Thin I called myself a blayguard for thinkin' such things; but I thought thim all the same. An' that, mark you, is the way av a man.

"Wan evenin' I said:–'Mrs. Bragin, manin' no disrespect to you, who is that Corp'ril man'–I had seen the stripes though I cud niver get sight av his face–'*who* is that Corp'ril man that comes in always whin I'm goin' away?'

" 'Mother av God!' sez she, turnin' as white as my belt; 'have *you* seen him too?'

" 'Seen him!' sez I; 'av coorse I have. Did ye want me not to see him, for'–we were standin' talkin' in the dhark, outside the veranda av Bragin's quarters–'you'd betther tell me to shut me eyes. Onless I'm mistaken, he's come now.'

"An', sure enough, the Corp'ril man was walkin' to us, hangin' his head down as though he was ashamed av himsilf.

" 'Good-night, Mrs. Bragin,' sez I, very cool; ' 'tis not for me to interfere wid your *a-moors;* but you might manage some things wid more dacincy. I'm off to canteen,' I sez.

"I turned on my heel an' wint away, swearin' I wud give that man a dhressin' that wud shtop him messin' about the Married Quarters for a month an' a week. I had not tuk ten paces before Annie Bragin was hangin' on to my arm, an' I cud feel that she was shakin' all over.

" 'Stay wid me, Mister Mulvaney,' sez she; 'you're flesh an' blood, at the least–are ye not?'

" 'I'm *all* that,' sez I, an' my anger wint away in a flash. 'Will I want to be asked twice, Annie?'

"Wid that I slipped my arm round her waist, for, begad, I fancied she had surrindered at discretion, an' the honors av war were mine.

" 'Fwhat nonsinse is this?' sez she, dhrawin' hersilf up on the tips av her dear little toes. 'Wid the mother's milk not dhry on your impident mouth? Let go!' she sez.

" 'Did ye not say just now that I was flesh and blood?' sez I. 'I have not changed since,' I sez; an' I kep' my arm where ut was.

" 'Your arms to yourself!' sez she, an' her eyes sparkild.

" 'Sure, 'tis only human nature,' sez I, an' I kep' my arm where ut was.

" 'Nature or no nature,' sez she, 'you take your arm away or I'll tell Bragin, an' he'll alter the nature av your head. Fwhat d'you take me for?' she sez.

" 'A woman,' sez I; 'the prettiest in barricks.'

" 'A *wife,'* sez she; 'the straightest in cantonmints!'

"Wid that I dropped my arm, fell back tu paces, an' saluted, for I saw that she mint fwhat she said,"

"Then you know something that some men would give a good deal to be certain of. How could you tell?" I demanded in the interests of Science.

"Watch the hand," said Mulvaney; "av she shut her hand tight, thumb down over the knuckle, take up your hat an' go. You'll only make a fool av yoursilf av you shtay. But av the hand lies opin on the lap, or av you see her thryin' to shut ut, an' she can't,–go on! She's not past reasonin' wid.

"Well, as I was sayin', I fell back, saluted, an' was goin' away.

" 'Shtay wid me,' she sez. 'Look! He's comin' again.' She pointed to the veranda, an' by the Hoight av Impart'nince, the Corp'ril man was comin' out av Bragin's quarters.

" 'He's done that these five evenin's past,' sez Annie Bragin. 'Oh, fwhat will I do!'

" 'He'll not do ut again,' sez I, for I was fightin' mad.

"Kape way from a man that has been a thrifle crossed in love till the fever's died down. He rages like a brute beast. I wint up to the man in the veranda, manin', as sure as I sit, to knock the life out av him. He slipped into the open. 'Fwhat are you doin' philanderin' about here, ye scum av the gutter?' sez I polite, to give him his warnin', for I wanted him ready.

"He niver lifted his head, but sez, all mournful an' melancolius, as if he thought I wud be sorry for him: 'I can't find her,' sez he.

" 'My troth,' sez I, 'you've lived too long–you an' your seekin's an findin's in a dacint married woman's quarters! Hould up your head, ye frozen thief av Genesis,' sez I, 'an' you'll find all you want an' more!'

"But he niver hild up, an' I let go from the shoulder to where the hair is short over the eyebrows.

" 'That'll do your business,' sez I, but it nearly did mine instid. I put my bodyweight behind the blow, but I hit nothing at all, an' near put my shoulther out. The Corp'ril man was not there, an' Annie Bragin, who had been watchin' from the veranda, throws up her heels, an' carries on like a cock whin his neck's wrung by the dhrummer-bhoy. I wint back to her, for a livin' woman, an' a woman like Annie Bragin, is more than a p'rade-groun' full av ghosts. I'd never seen a woman faint before, an' I stud like a shtuck calf, askin' her whether she was dead, an' prayin' her for the love av me, an' the love av her husband, an' the love av the Virgin, to opin her blessed eyes again, an' callin' mesilf all the names undher the canopy av Hivin for plaguin' her wid my miserable *a-moors* whin I ought to ha' stud betune her an' this Corp'ril man that had lost the number av his mess.

"I misremimber fwhat nonsinse I said, but I was not so far gone that I cud not hear a fut on the dirt outside. 'Twas Bragin comin' in, an' by the same token Annie was comin' to. I jumped to the far end av the veranda an' looked as if butter wudn't melt in my mouth. But Mrs. Quinn, the Quarter-Master's wife that was, had tould Bragin about my hangin' round Annie.

" 'I'm not pleased wid you, Mulvaney,' sez Bragin, unbucklin' his sword, for he had been on duty.

" 'That's bad hearin',' I sez, an' I knew that the pickets were dhriven in. 'What for, Sargint?' sez I.

" 'Come outside,' sez he, 'an' I'll show you why.'

" 'I'm willin',' I sez; 'but my stripes are none so ould that I can afford to lose thim. Tell me now, *who* do I go out wid?' sez I.

"He was a quick man an' a just, an' saw fwhat I wud be afther. 'Wid Mrs. Bragin's husband,' sez he. He might ha' known by me askin' that favor that I had done him no wrong.

"We wint to the back av the arsenal an' I stripped to him, an' for ten minutes 'twas all I cud do to prevent him killin' himself against my fistes. He was mad as a dumb dog—just frothing wid rage; but he had no chanst wid me in reach, or learnin', or anything else.

" 'Will ye hear reason?' sez I, whin his first wind was run out.

" 'Not whoile I can see,' sez he. Wid that I gave him both, one after the other, smash through the low gyard that he'd been taught whin he was a boy, an' the eyebrow shut down on the cheek-bone like the wing av a sick crow.

" 'Will you hear reason now, ye brave man?' sez I.

" 'Not whoile I can speak,' sez he, staggerin' up blind as a stump. I was loath to do ut, but I wint round an' swung into the jaw side-on an' shifted ut a half pace to the lef'.

" 'Will ye hear reason now?' sez I; 'I can't keep my timper much longer, an' 'tis like I will hurt you."

" 'Not whoile I can stand,' he mumbles out av one corner av his mouth. So I closed an' threw him—blind, dumb, an' sick, an' jammed the jaw straight.

" 'You're an ould fool, *Mister* Bragin,' sez I.

" 'You're a young thief,' sez he, 'an' you've bruk my heart, you an' Annie betune you!'

"Thin he began cryin' like a child as he lay. I was sorry as I had niver been before. 'Tis an awful thing to see a strong man cry.

" 'I'll swear on the Cross!' sez I.

" 'I care for none av your oaths,' sez he.

" 'Come back to your quarters,' sez I, 'an' if you don't believe the livin', begad, you shall listen to the dead,' I sez.

"I hoisted him an' tuk him back to his quarters. 'Mrs. Brargin,' sez I, 'here's a man that you can cure quicker than me.'

" 'You've shamed me before my wife,' he whimpers.

" 'Have I so?' sez I. 'By the look on Mrs. Bragin's face I think I'm for a dhressin'-down worse than I gave you.'

"An' I was! Annie Bragin was woild wid indignation. There was not a name that a dacint woman cud use that was not given my way. I've had my Colonel walk roun' me like a cooper roun' a cask for fifteen minutes in Ord'ly Room, bekaze I wint into the Corner Shop an unstrapped lewnatic; but all that I iver tuk from his rasp av a tongue was ginger-pop to fwhat Annie tould me. An' that, mark you, is the way av a woman.

"Whin ut was done for want av breath, an' Annie was bendin' over her husband, I sez: ''Tis all thrue, an' I'm a blayguard an' you're an honest woman; but will you tell him of wan service that I did you?'

"As I finished speakin' the Corp'ril man came up to the veranda, an' Annie Bragin shquealed. The moon was up, an' we cud see his face.

"'I can't find her,' sez the Corp'ril man, an' wint out like the puff av a candle.

"'Saints stand betune us an' evil!' sez Bragin, crossin' himself; 'that's Flahy av the Tyrone.'

"'Who was he?' I sez, 'for he was given me a dale av fightin' this day.'

"Bragin tould us that Flahy was a Corp'ril who lost his wife av cholera in those quarters three years gone, an' wint mad, an' *walked* afther they buried him, huntin' for her.

"'Well,' sez I to Bragin, 'he's been hookin' out av Purgathory to kape company wid Mrs. Bragin ivry evenin' for the last fortnight. You may tell Mrs. Quinn, wid my love, for I know that she's been talkin' to you, an' you've been listenin', that she ought to ondherstand the differ 'twixt a man an' a ghost. She's had three husbands,' sez I, 'an' *you've* got a wife too good for you. Instid av which you lave her to be boddered by ghosts an'—an' all manner av evil spirruts. I'll niver go talkin' in the way av politeness to a man's wife again. Good-night to you both,' sez I; an' wid that I wint away, havin' fought wid woman, man and Divil all in the heart av an hour. By the same token I gave Father Victor wan rupee to say a mass for Flahy's soul, me havin' discommoded him by shticking my fist into his systim."

"Your ideas of politeness seem rather large, Mulvaney," I said.

"That's as you look at ut," said Mulvaney, calmly; "Annie Bragin niver cared for me. For all that, I did not want to leave anything behin' me that Bragin could take hould av to be angry wid her about—whin an honust wurrd cud ha' cleared all up. There's nothing like opin-speakin'. Orth'ris, ye scutt, let me put me oi to that bottle, for my throat's as dhry as whin I thought I wud get a kiss from Annie Bragin. An' that's fourteen years gone! Eyah! Cork's own city an' the blue sky about ut—an' the times that was—the times that was!"

Baa Baa, Black Sheep

Baa baa, black sheep,
Have you any wool?
Yes, sir; yes, sir; three bags full.
One for the master, one for the dame—
None for the little boy that cries down the lane.
—*Nursery Rhyme*

The First Bag

"When I was in my father's house I was in a better place."

THEY WERE PUTTING Punch to bed—the *ayah* and the *hamal* and Meeta, the big *Surti* boy with *the* red-and-gold turban. Judy, already tucked inside her mosquito-curtains, was nearly asleep. Punch had been allowed to stay up for dinner. Many privileges had been accorded to Punch within the last ten days, and a greater kindness from the people of his world had encompassed his ways and works, which were mostly obstreperous. He sat on the edge of his bed and swung his bare legs defiantly.

"Punch-*baba* going to bye-lo?" said the *ayah,* suggestively.

"No," said Punch. "Punch-*baba* wants the story about the Ranee that was turned into a tiger. Meeta must tell it, and the *hamal* shall hide behind the door and make tiger-noises at the proper time."

"But Judy-*baba* will wake up," said the *ayah.*

"Judy-*baba* is waking," piped a small voice from the mosquito-curtains. "There was a Ranee that lived at Delhi. Go on, Meeta," and she fell fast asleep again while Meeta began the story.

Never had Punch secured the telling of that tale with so little opposition. He reflected for a long time. The *hamal* made the tiger-noises in twenty different keys.

"Top!" said Punch, authoritatively. "Why doesn't papa come in and say he is going to give me *put-put?*"

"Punch-*baba* is going away," said the *ayah.* "In another week there will be no Punch-*baba* to pull my hair any more." She sighed softly, for the boy of the household was very dear to her heart.

"Up the Ghauts in a train?" said Punch, standing on his bed. "All the way to Nassick, where the Ranee tiger lives?"

"Not to Nassick this year, little sahib," said Meeta, lifting him on his shoulder. "Down to the sea, where the cocoanuts are thrown, and across the sea in a big ship. Will you take Meeta with you to *Belait?*"

"You shall all come," said Punch, from the height of Meeta's strong arms. "Meeta, and the *ayah,* and the *hamal,* and Bhini-in-the-garden, and the salaam-captain-sahib-snake-man."

There was no mockery in Meeta's voice when he replied: "Great is the sahib's favor," and laid the little man down in the bed, while the *ayah,* sitting in the moonlight at the doorway, lulled him to sleep with an interminable canticle such as they sing in the Roman Catholic Church at Parel. Punch curled himself into a ball and slept.

Next morning, Judy shouted that there was a rat in the nursery; and thus he forgot to tell her the wonderful news. It did not much matter, for Judy was only three and she would not have understood. But Punch was five, and he knew that going to England would be much more nicer than a trip to Nassick.

. . . .

And papa and mamma sold the brougham and the piano, and stripped the house, and curtailed the allowance of crockery for the daily meals, and took long counsel together over a bundle of letters bearing the Rocklington postmark.

"The worst of it is that one can't be certain of anything," said papa, pulling his mustache. "The letters in themselves are excellent, and the terms are moderate enough."

"The worst of it is that the children will grow up away from me," thought mamma; but she did not say it aloud.

"We are only one case among hundreds," said papa, bitterly. "You shall go home again in five years, dear."

"Punch will be ten then—and Judy eight. Oh, how long and long and long the time will be! And we have to leave them among strangers."

"Punch is a cheery little chap. He's sure to make friends wherever he goes."

"And who could help loving my Ju?"

They were standing over the cots in the nursery late at night, and I think that mamma was crying softly. After papa had gone away she knelt down by the side of Judy's cot. The *ayah* saw her and put up a prayer that the *memsahib* might never find the love of her children taken away from her and given to a stranger.

Mamma's own prayer was a slightly illogical one. Summarized it ran: "Let strangers love my children, and be as good to them as I should be; but let *me* preserve their love and their confidence forever and ever. Amen." Punch scratched himself in his sleep, and Judy moaned a little. That seems to be the only answer to the prayer; and, next day, they all went down to the sea, and there was a scene at the Apollo Bunder when Punch discovered that Meeta could not come, too, and Judy learned that the *ayah* must be left behind. But Punch found a thousand fascinating things in the rope, block, and steam-pipe line on the big P. and O. steamer long before Meeta and the *ayah* had dried their tears.

"Come back, Punch-*baba,"* said the *ayah.*

"Come back," said Meeta, "and be a *Burra sahib."*

"Yes," said Punch, lifted up in his father's arms to wave good-bye. "Yes, I will come back, and I will be a *Burra sahib Baha dur!"*

At the end of the first day, Punch demanded to be set down in England, which he was certain must be close at hand. Next day, there was a merry breeze, and Punch was very sick. "When I come back to Bombay," said Punch, on his recovery, "I will come by the road—in a broom-*gharri.* This is a very naughty ship."

The Swedish boatswain consoled him, and he modified his opinions as the voyage went on. There was so much to see, and to handle, and ask questions about that Punch nearly forgot the *ayah,* and Meeta, and the *hamal,* and with difficulty remembered a few words of the Hindoostanee, once his second speech.

But Judy was much worse. The day before the steamer reached Southampton, mamma asked her if she would not like to see the *ayah* again. Judy's blue eyes turned to the stretch of sea that had swallowed all her tiny past, and she said: *"Ayah!* What *ayah?"*

Mamma cried over her and Punch marveled. It was then that he heard, for the first time, mamma's passionate appeal to him never to let Judy forget mamma. Seeing that Judy was young, ridiculously young, and that mamma, every evening for four weeks past, had come into the cabin to sing her and

Punch to sleep with a mysterious tune that he called "Sonny, my soul," Punch could not understand what mamma meant. But he strove to do his duty; for, the moment mamma left the cabin, he said to Judy:

"Ju, you remember mamma?"

" 'Torse I do," said Judy.

"Then *always* remember mamma, else I won't give you the paper ducks that the red-haired Captain Sahib cut out for me."

So Judy promised always to "bemember mamma."

Many and many a time was mamma's command laid upon Punch, and papa would say the same thing with an insistence that awed the child.

"You must make haste and learn to write, Punch," said papa, "and then you'll be able to write letters to us in Bombay."

"I'll come into your room," said Punch, and papa choked.

Papa and mamma were always choking in those days. If Punch took Judy to task for not "bemembering," they choked. If Punch sprawled on the sofa in the Southampton lodging-house and sketched his future in purple and gold, they choked; and so they did if Judy put up her mouth for a kiss.

Through many days all four were vagabonds on the face of the earth—Punch with no one to give orders to, Judy too young for anything, and papa and mamma grave, distracted, and choking.

"Where," demanded Punch, wearied of a loathsome contrivance on four wheels with a mound of luggage atop—"*where* is our broom-*gharri?* This thing talks so much that *I* can't talk. Where is our *own* broom-*gharri?* When I was at Bandstand, before we comed away, I asked Inverarity Sahib why he was sitting in it, and he said it was his own. and I said, 'I will *give* it you'—I like Inverarity Sahib—and I said, 'Can you put your legs through the pully-wag loops by the window?' And Inverarity Sahib said 'No,' and laughed. *I* can put my legs through the pully-wag loops. I can put my legs through *these* pully-wag loops. Look! Oh, mamma's crying again! I didn't know. I wasn't not to do *so.*"

Punch drew his legs out of the loops of the four-wheeler; the door opened and he slid to the earth, in a cascade of parcels, at the door of an austere little villa whose gates bore the legend, "Downe Lodge." Punch gathered himself together and eyed the house with disfavor. It stood on a sandy road, and a cold wind tickled his knickerbockered legs.

"Let us go away," said Punch. "This is not a pretty place."

But mamma and papa and Judy had quitted the cab, and all the luggage was being taken into the house. At the door-step stood a woman in black, and she smiled largely, with dry, chapped lips. Behind her was a man—big, bony, gray, and lame as to one leg—behind him a boy of twelve, black-haired and oily in appearance. Punch surveyed the trio, and advanced without fear, as he had been accustomed to do in Bombay when callers came and he happened to be playing in the veranda.

"How do you do?" said he. "I am Punch." But they were all looking at the luggage—all except the gray man, who shook hands with Punch and said he was "a smart little fellow." There was much running about and banging of boxes, and Punch curled himself up on the sofa in the dining-room and considered things.

"I don't like these people," said Punch. "But never mind. We'll go away soon. We have always went away soon from everywhere. I wish we was gone back to Bombay *soon.*"

The wish bore no fruit. For six days mamma wept at intervals, and showed the woman in black all Punch's clothes—a liberty which Punch resented. "But p'r'aps she's a new white *ayah,*" he thought. "I'm to call her Antirosa, but she doesn't call *me* sahib. She says just Punch," he confided to Judy. "What is Antirosa?"

Judy didn't know. Neither she nor Punch had heard anything of an animal called an aunt. Their world had been papa and mamma, who knew everything, permitted everything, and loved everybody—even Punch when he used to go into the garden at Bombay and fill his nails with mold after the weekly nail-cutting, because, as he explained, between two strokes of the slipper, to his sorely tried father, his fingers "felt so new at the ends."

In an undefined way, Punch judged it advisable to keep both parents between himself and the woman in black and the boy in black hair. He did not approve of them. He liked the gray man, who had expressed a wish to be called "Uncleharri." They nodded at each other when they met, and the gray man showed him a little ship with rigging that took up and down.

"She is a model of the *Brisk*—the little *Brisk* that was sore exposed that day at Navarino." The gray man hummed the last words and fell into a reverie. "I'll tell you about Navarino, Punch, when we go for walks together; and you mustn't touch the ship, because she's the *Brisk*."

Long before that walk, the first of many, was taken, they roused Punch and Judy in the chill dawn of a February morning to say good-bye, and of all people in the wide earth, to papa and mamma—both crying this time. Punch was very sleepy, and Judy was cross.

"Don't forget us," pleaded mamma. "Oh, my little son, don't forget us, and see that Judy remembers us, too."

"I've told Judy to bemember," said Punch, wriggling, for his father's beard tickled his neck. "I've told Judy—ten—forty—'leven thousand times. But Ju's so young—quite a baby—isn't she?"

"Yes," said papa, "quite a baby, and you must be good to Judy, and make haste to learn to write and—and—and—"

Punch was back in his bed again. Judy was fast asleep, and there was the rattle of a cab below. Papa and mamma had gone away. Not to Nassick; that was across the sea. To some place much nearer, of course, and equally of course they would return. They came back after dinner-parties, and papa had come back after he had been to a place called "The Snows," and mamma with him, to Punch and Judy at Mrs. Inverarity's house in Marine Lines. Assuredly they would come back again. So Punch fell asleep till the true morning, when the black-haired boy met him with the information that papa and mamma had gone to Bombay, and that he and Judy were to stay at Downe Lodge "forever." Antirosa, tearfully appealed to for a contradiction, said that Harry had spoken the truth, and that it behooved Punch to fold up his clothes neatly on going to bed. Punch went out and wept bitterly with Judy, into whose fair head he had driven some ideas of the meaning of separation.

When a matured man discovers that he has been deserted by Providence, deprived of his God, and cast without help, comfort, or sympathy, upon a world which is new and strange to him, his despair, which may find expression in evil-living, the writing of his experiences, or the more satisfactory diversion of suicide, is generally supposed to be impressive. A child, under exactly similar circumstances, as far as its knowledge goes, can not very well curse God and die. It howls till its nose is red, its eyes are sore, and its head aches. Punch and Judy, through no fault of their own, had lost all their world. They sat in the hall and cried; the black-haired boy looking on from afar.

The model of the ship availed nothing, though the gray man assured Punch that he might pull the rigging up and down as much as he pleased; and Judy was promised free entry into the kitchen. They wanted papa and mamma, gone to Bombay beyond the seas, and their grief, while it lasted, was without remedy.

When the tears ceased, the house was very still. Antirosa had decided it was much better to let the children "have their cry out," and the boy had gone to school. Punch raised his head from the floor and sniffled mournfully.

Judy was nearly asleep. Three short years had not taught her how to bear sorrow with full knowledge. There was a distant dull boom in the air—a repeated heavy thud. Punch knew that sound in Bombay in the monsoon. It was the sea—the sea that must be traversed before any one could get to Bombay.

"Quick, Ju!" he cried, "we're close to the sea. I can hear it! Listen! That's where they've went. P'r'aps we can catch them, if we was in time. They didn't mean to go without us. They've only forgot."

"Iss," said Judy. "They've only forgotted. Less go to the sea."

The hall door was opened and so was the garden gate.

"It's very, very big, this place," he said, looking cautiously down the road, "and we will get lost; but I will find a man and order him to take me back to my house—like I did in Bombay."

He took Judy by the hand, and the two fled hatless in the direction of the sound of the sea. Downe Villa was almost the last of a range of newly built houses running out, through a chaos of brick-mounds, to a heath where gypsies occasionally camped, and where the Garrison Artillery of Rocklington practiced. There were few people to be seen, and the children might have been taken for those of the soldiery who ranged far. Half an hour the wearied little legs tramped across heath, potato-field, and sand-dune.

"I'se so tired," said Judy, "and mamma will be angry."

"Mamma's *never* angry. I suppose she is waiting at the sea now while papa gets tickets. We'll find them and go along with. Ju, you mustn't sit down. Only a little more and we'll come to the sea. Ju, if you sit down I'll *thmack* you!" said Punch.

They climbed another dune, and came upon the great gray sea at low tide. Hundreds of crabs were scuttling about the beach, but there was no trace of papa and mamma, not even of a ship upon the waters—nothing but sand and mud for miles and miles.

And "Uncleharri" found them by chance—very muddy and very forlorn—Punch dissolved in tears, but trying to divert Judy with an "ickle trab," and Judy wailing to the pitiless horizon for "mamma, mamma!" and again "mamma!"

The Second Bag

> Ah, well-a-day, for we are souls bereaved!
> Of all the creatures under heaven's wide scope
> We are most hopeless, who had once most hope,
> And most beliefless, who had most believed.
>
> —*The City of Dreadful Night.*

All this time not a word about Black Sheep. He came later, and Harry, the black-haired boy, was mainly responsible for his coming.

Judy—who could help loving little Judy?—passed, by special permit, into the kitchen and thence straight to Aunty Rosa's heart. Harry was Aunty Rosa's one child, and Punch was the extra boy about the house. There was no special place for him or his little affairs, and he was forbidden to sprawl on sofas and explain his ideas about the manufacture of this world and his hopes for his future. Sprawling was lazy and wore out sofas, and little boys were not expected to talk. They were talked to, and the talking to was intended for the benefit of their morals. As the unquestioned despot of the house at Bombay, Punch could not quite understand how he came to be of no account in this his new ife.

Harry might reach across the table and take what he wanted; Judy might point and get what she wanted. Punch was forbidden to do either. The gray man was his great hope and stand-by for many months after papa left, and he had forgotten to tell Judy to "bemember mamma."

This lapse was excusable, because, in the interval, he had been introduced by Aunty Rosa to two very impressive things—an abstraction called God, the intimate friend and ally of Aunty Rosa, generally believed to live behind the kitchen-range, because it was hot there—and a dirty brown book filled with unintelligible dots and marks. Punch was always anxious to oblige everybody. He, therefore, welded the story of the Creation on to what he could recollect of his Indian fairy tales, and scandalized Aunty Rosa by repeating the result to Judy. It was a sin, a grievous sin, and Punch was talked to for a quarter of an hour. He could not understand where the iniquity came in, but was careful not to repeat the offense, because Aunty Rosa told him that God had heard every word he had said and was very angry. If this were true, why didn't God come and say so, thought Punch, and dismissed the matter from his mind. Afterward he learned to know the Lord as the only thing in the world more awful than Aunty Rosa—as a creature that stood in the background and counted the strokes of the cane.

But the reading was, just then, a much more serious matter than any creed. Aunty Rosa sat him upon a table and told him that A B meant ab.

"Why?" said Punch. "A is a and B is bee. *Why* does A B mean ab?"

"Because I tell you it does," said Aunty Rosa, "and you've got to say it."

Punch said it accordingly, and for a month hugely against his will, stumbled through the brown book, not in the least comprehending what it meant. But Uncle Harry, who walked much, and generally alone, was wont to come into the nursery and suggest to Aunty Rosa that Punch should walk with him. He seldom spoke, but he showed Punch all Rocklington, from the mud-banks and the sand of the back-bay to the great harbors where ships lay at anchor, and the dockyards where the hammers are never still, and the marine-store shops, and the shiny brass counters in the offices where Uncle Harry went once every three months with a slip of blue paper and received sovereigns in exchange; for he held a wound-pension. Punch heard, too, from his lips, the story of the Battle of Navarino, where the sailors of the fleet, for three days afterward, were deaf as posts and could only sign to each other. "That was because of the noise of the guns," said Uncle Harry, "and I have got the wadding of a bullet somewhere inside me now."

Punch regarded him with curiosity. He had not the least idea what wadding was, and his notion of a bullet was a dock-yard cannon-ball bigger than his own head. How could Uncle Harry keep a cannon-ball inside him? He was ashamed to ask, for fear Uncle Harry might be angry.

Punch had never known what anger—real anger—meant until one terrible day when Harry had taken his paint-box to paint a boat with, and Punch had protested with a loud and lamentable voice. Then Uncle Harry had appeared on the scene, and, muttering something about "strangers' children," had, with a stick, smitten the black-haired boy across the shoulders till he wept and yelled, and Aunty Rosa came in and abused Uncle Harry for cruelty to his own flesh and blood, and Punch shuddered to the tips of his shoes. "It wasn't my fault," he explained to the boy, but both Harry and Aunty Rosa said that it was, and that Punch had told tales, and for a week there were no more walks with Uncle Harry.

But that week brought a great joy to Punch.

He had repeated, till he was thrice weary, the statement that "the cat lay on the mat and the rat came in."

"Now I can truly read," said Punch, "and now I will never read anything in the world."

He put the brown book in the cupboard where his school-books lived, and accidentally tumbled out a venerable volume, without covers, labeled "Sharpe's Magazine." There was the most portentous picture of a griffin on the first page, with verses below. The griffin carried off one sheep a day from a German village, till a man came with a "falchion" and split the griffin open. Goodness only knew what a falchion was, but there was the griffin, and his history was an improvement upon the eternal cat.

"This," said Punch, "means thiongs, and now I will know all about everything in all the world." He read till the light failed, not understanding a tithe of the meaning, but tantalized by glimpses of new worlds hereafter to be revealed.

"What is a 'falchion?' What is a 'wee lamb?' What is a 'base *uss*urper?' What is a 'verdant me-ad?' " he demanded, with flushed cheeks, at bed-time of the astonished Aunt Rosa.

"Say your prayers and go to sleep," she replied, and that was all the help Punch then or afterward found at her hands in the new and delightful exercise of reading.

"Aunt Rosa only knows about God and things like that," argue Punch. "Uncle Harry will tell me."

The next walk proved that Uncle Harry could not help either; but he allowed Punch to talk, and even sat down on a bench to hear about the griffin. Other walks brought other stories as Punch ranged farther afield, for the house held a large store of old books that no one ever opened–from Frank Fairlegh, in serial numbers, and the earlier poems of Tennyson, contributed anonymously to "Sharpe's Magazine," to '62 Exhibition Catalogues, gay with colors and delightfully incomprehensible, and odd leaves of "Gulliver's Travels."

As soon as Punch could string a few pot-books together he wrote to Bombay, demanding by return of post "all the books in all the world." Papa could not comply with this modest indent, but sent "Grimm's Fairy Tales" and a "Hans Andersen." That was enough. If he were only left alone Punch could pass, at any hour he chose, into a land of his own, beyond reach of Aunty Rosa and her God, Harry and his teasements, and Judy's claims to be played with.

"Don't disturve me, I'm reading. Go and play in the kitchen," grunted Punch. "Aunty Rosa lets *you* go there." Judy was cutting her second teeth and was fretful. She appealed to Aunty Rosa, who descended on Punch.

"I was reading," he explained, "reading a book. I *want* to read."

"You're only doing that to show off," said Aunty Rosa. "But we'll see. Play with Judy now, and don't open a book for a week."

Judy did not pass a very enjoyable playtime with Punch, who was consumed with indignation. There was a pettiness at the bottom of the prohibition which puzzled him.

"It's what I like to do," he said, "and she's found out that and stopped me. Don't cry, Ju–it wasn't your fault–*please* don't cry, or she'll say I made you."

Ju loyally mopped up her tears, and the two played in their nursery, a room in the basement and half underground, to which they were regularly sent after the midday dinner while Aunty Rosa slept. She drank wine–that is to say, something from a bottle in the cellaret–for her stomach's sake; but if she did not fall asleep she would sometimes come into the nursery to see that the children were really playing. Now, bricks, wooden hoops, nine-pins, and china-ware can not amuse forever, especially when all fairyland is to be won by the mere opening of a book, and, as often as not, Punch would be discovered reading to Judy or telling her interminable tales. That was an offense in the eyes of the law, and Judy would be whisked off by Aunty Rosa, while Punch was left to play alone, "and be sure that I hear you doing it."

It was not a cheering employ, for he had to make a playful noise. At last, with infinite craft, he devised an arrangement whereby the table could be supported as to three legs on toy bricks, leaving the fourth clear to bring down on the floor. He could work the table with one hand and hold a book with the other. This he did till an evil day when Aunty Rosa pounced upon him unawares and told him that he was "acting a lie."

"If you're old enough to do that," she said—her temper was always worst after dinner—"you're old enough to be beaten."

"But—I'm—I'm not a animal!" said Punch, aghast. He remembered Uncle Harry and the stick, and turned white. Aunty Rosa had hidden a light cane behind her, and Punch was beaten then and there over the shoulders. It was a revelation to him. The room-door was shut, and he was left to weep himself into repentance and work out his own gospel of life.

Aunty Rosa, he argued, had the power to beat him with many stripes. It was unjust and cruel, and mamma and papa would never have allowed it. Unless, perhaps, as Aunty Rosa seemed to imply, they had sent secret orders, in which case he was abandoned, indeed. It would be discreet in the future to propitiate Aunty Rosa; but, then, again, even in matters in which he was innocent, he had been accused of wishing to "show off." He had "shown off" before visitors when he had attacked a strange gentleman—Harry's uncle, not his own—with requests for information about the griffin and the falchion, and the precise nature of the tilbury in which Frank Fairlegh rode; all points of paramount interest which he was bursting to understand. Clearly it would not do to pretend to care for Aunty Rosa.

At this point Harry entered and stood afar off, eyeing Punch, a disheveled heap in the corner of the room, with disgust.

"You're a liar—a young liar," said Harry, with great unction, "and you're to have tea down here because you're not fit to speak to us. And you're not to speak to Judy again till mother gives you leave. You'll corrupt her. You're only fit to associate with the servant. Mother says so."

Having reduced Punch to a second agony of tears, Harry departed downstairs with the news that Punch was still rebellious.

Uncle Harry sat uneasily in the dining-room. "Rosa," said he, at last,"can't you leave the child alone? He's a good enough little chap when I met him."

"He puts on his best manners with you, Henry," said Aunty Rosa, "but I'm afraid, I'm very much afraid, that he is the black sheep of the family."

Harry heard and stored up the name for future use. Judy cried till she was bidden to stop, her brother not being worth tears; and the evening concluded with the return of Punch to the upper regions and a private sitting at which all the blinding horrors of hell were revealed to Punch with such store of imagery as Aunty Rosa's narrow mind possessed.

Most grievous of all was Judy's round-eyed reproach, and Punch went to bed in the depths of the Valley of Humiliation. He shared his room with Harry and knew the torture in store. For an hour and a half he had to answer that young gentleman's question as to his motives for telling a lie, and a grievous lie, the precise quantity of punishment inflicted by Aunt Rosa, and had also to profess his deep gratitude for such religious instruction as Harry thought fit to impart.

From that day began the downfall of Punch, now Black Sheep.

"Untrustworthy in one thing, untrustworthy in all," said Aunty Rosa, and Harry felt that Black Sheep was delivered into his hands. He would wake him up in the night to ask him why he was such a liar.

"I don't know," Punch would reply.

"Then don't you think you ought to get up and pray to God for a new heart?"

"Y-yess."

"Get out and pray, then!" And Punch would get out of bed with raging hate in his heart against all the world, seen and unseen. He was always tumbling into trouble. Harry had a knack of cross-examining him as to his day's doings, which seldom failed to lead him, sleepy and savage, into half-a-dozen contradictions—all duly reported to Aunty Rosa next morning.

"But it *wasn't* a lie," Punch would begin, charging into a labored explanation that landed him more hopelessly in the mire. "I said that I didn't say my prayers *twice* over in the day, and *that* was on Tuesday. *Once* I did. I *know* I did, but Harry said I didn't," and so forth till the tension brought tears, and he was dismissed from the table in disgrace.

"You usen't to be as bad as this!" said Judy, awestricken at the catalogue of Black Sheep's crimes. "Why are you so bad now?"

"I don't know," Black Sheep would reply. "I'm not, if I only wasn't bothered upside down. I knew what I *did,* and I want to say so; but Harry always makes it out different somehow, and Aunty Rosa doesn't believe a word I say. Oh, Ju! don't you say I'm bad too."

"Aunty Rosa says you are," said Judy. "She told the vicar so when he came yesterday."

"Why does she tell all the people outside the house about me? It isn't fair," said Black Sheep. "When I was in Bombay, and was bad–*doing* bad, not made-up bad like this–mamma told papa, and papa told me he knew, and that was all. *Outside* people didn't know, too–even Meeta didn't know."

"I don't remember," said Judy, wistfully. "I was all little then. Mamma was just as fond of you as she was of me, wasn't she?"

" 'Course she was. So was papa. So was everybody."

"Aunty Rosa likes me more than she does you. She says that you are a trial and a black sheep, and I'm not to speak to you more than I can help."

"Always? Not outside of the times when you mustn't speak to me at all?"

Judy nodded her head mournfully. Black Sheep turned away in despair, but Judy's arms were round his neck.

"Never mind, Punch," she whispered. "I *will* speak to you just the same as ever and ever. You're my own, own brother, though you are–though Aunty Rosa says you're bad, and Harry says you're a little coward. He says that if I pulled your hair hard, you'd cry."

"Pull, then," said Punch.

Judy pulled gingerly.

"Pull harder–as hard as you can! There! I don't mind how much you pull it *now.* If you'll speak to me the same as ever, I'll let you pull it as much as you like–pull it out if you like. But I know if Harry came and stood by and made you do it, I'd cry."

So the two children sealed the compact with a kiss, and Black Sheep's heart was cheered within him, and by extreme caution and careful avoidance of Harry, he acquired virtue, and was allowed to read undisturbed for a week. Uncle Harry took him for walks and consoled him with rough tenderness, never calling him Black Sheep. "It's good for you, I suppose, Punch," he used to say. "Let us sit down. I'm getting tired." His steps led him now, not to the beach, but to the cemetery of Rocklington, amid the potato fields. For hours the gray man would sit on a tombstone, while Black Sheep read epitaphs, and then, with a sigh would stump home again.

"I shall lie there soon," said he to Black Sheep, one winter evening, when his face showed white as a worn silver coin under the lights of the chapel lodge. "You needn't tell Aunty Rosa."

A month later, he turned sharp round, ere half a morning walk was completed, and stumped back to the house. "Put me to bed, Rosa," he muttered. "I've walked my last. The wadding has found me out."

They put him to bed, and for a fortnight the shadow of his sickness lay upon the house, and Black Sheep went to and fro unobserved. Papa had sent him some new books, and he was told to keep quiet. He retired into his own world, and was perfectly happy. Even at night his felicity was unbroken. He could lie in bed and string himself tales of travel and adventure while Harry was down-stairs.

"Uncle Harry's going to die," said Judy, who now lived almost entirely with Aunty Rosa.

"I'm very sorry," siad Black Sheep, soberly. "He told me that a long time ago."

Aunty Rosa heard the conversation. "Will nothing check your wicked tongue?" she said, angrily. There were blue circles round her eyes.

Black Sheep retreated to the nursery and read "Cometh Up as a Flower" with deep and uncomprehending interest. He had been forbidden to read it on account of its "sinfulness," but the bonds of the universe were crumbling, and Aunty Rosa was in great grief.

"I'm glad," said Black Sheep. "She's unhappy now. It wasn't a lie, though. *I* knew. He told me not to tell."

That night Black Sheep woke with a start. Harry was not in the room, and there was a sound of sobbing on the next floor. Then the voice of Uncle Harry, singing the song of the Battle of Navarino, cut through the darkness:

" 'Our vanship was the Asia–
The Albion and Genoa!' "

"He's getting well," thought Black Sheep, who knew the song through all its seventeen verses. But the blood froze at his little heart as he thought. The voice leaped an octave and rang shrill as a boatswain's pipe:

" 'And next came on the lovely Rose,
The Philomel, her fire-ship, closed,
And the little Brisk was sore exposed
That day at Navarino.' "

"That day at Navarino, Uncle Harry!" shouted Black Sheep, half wild with excitement and fear of he knew not what.

A door opened, and Aunty Rosa screamed up the stair-case: "Hush! For God's sake, hush, you little devil! Uncle Harry is *dead!*"

The Third Bag

"Journeys end in lovers' meeting,
Every wise man's son doth know."

"I wonder what will happen to me now," thought black Sheep, when the semi-pagan rites, peculiar to the burial of the dead in middle-class houses, had been accomplished, and Aunty Rosa, awful in black crape, had returned to this life. "I don't think I've done anything bad that she knows of. I suppose I will soon. She will be very cross after Uncle Harry's dying, and Harry will be cross, too. I'll keep in the nursery."

Unfortunately for Punch's plans, it was decided that he should be sent to a day-school which Harry attended. This meant a morning walk with Harry, and, perhaps, an evening one; but the prospect of freedom in the interval was refreshing. "Harry'll tell everything I do, but I won't do anything," said Black Sheep. Fortified with this virtuous resolution, he went to school only to find that Harry's version of his character had preceded him, and that life was a burden in consequence. He took stock of his associates. Some of them were unclean, some of them talked in dialect, many dropped their *h's,* and there were two Jews and a negro, or someone quite as dark, in the assembly. "That's a *hubshi,*" said Black Sheep to himself. "Even Meeta used to laugh at a *hubshi.* I don't think this is a proper place." He was indignant for at least an hour, till he reflected that any expostulation on his part would be by Aunty Rosa construed into "showing off," and that Harry would tell the boys.

"How do you like school?" said Aunty Rosa at the end of the day.

"I think it is a very nice place," said Punch, quietly.

"I suppose you warned the boys of Black Sheep's character?" said Aunty Rosa to Harry.

"Oh, yes," said the censor of Black Sheep's morals. "They all know about him."

"If I was with my father," said Black Sheep, stung to the quick, "I shouldn't *speak* to those boys. He wouldn't let me. They live in shops. I saw them go into shops—where their fathers live and sell things."

"You're too good for that school, are you?" said Aunty Rosa, with a bitter smile. "You ought to be grateful, Black Sheep, that those boys speak to you at all. It isn't every school that takes little liars."

Harry did not fail to make much capital out of Black Sheep's ill-considered remark, with the result that several boys, including the *hubshi,* demonstrated to Black Sheep the eternal equality of the human race by smacking his head, and his consolation from Aunty Rosa was that it "served him right for being vain." He learned, however, to keep his opinions to himself, and by propitiating Harry in carrying books and the like to secure a little peace. His existence was not too joyful. From nine till twelve he was at school, and from two to four, except on Saturdays. In the evenings he was sent down into the nursery to prepare his lessons for the next day, and every night came the dreaded cross-questionings at Harry's hand. Of Judy, he saw but little. She was deeply religious—at six years of age religion is easy to come by—and sorely divided between her natural love for Black Sheep and her love for Aunty Rosa, who could do no wrong.

The lean woman returned that love with interest, and Judy, when she dared, took advantage of this for the remission of Black Sheep's penalties. Failures in lessons at school were punished at home by a week without reading other than school books, and Harry brought the news of such a failure with glee. Further, Black Sheep was then bound to repeat his lessons at bed-time to Harry, who generally succeeded in making him break down, and consoled him by gloomiest forebodings for the morrow. Harry was at once spy, practical joker, inquisitor, and Aunty Rosa's deputy executioner. He filled his many posts to admiration. From his actions, now that Uncle Harry was dead, there was no appeal. Black Sheep had not been permitted to keep any self-respect at school; at home he was of course utterly discredited, and grateful for any pity that the servant-girls—they changed frequently at Downe Lodge because they, too, were liars—might show. "You're just fit to row in the same boat with Black Sheep," was a sentiment that each new Jane or Eliza might expect to hear, before a month was over, from Aunty Rosa's lips; and Black Sheep was used to ask new girls whether they had yet been compared to him. Harry was "Master Harry" in their mouths; Judy was officially "Miss Judy;" but Black Sheep was never anything more than Black sheep *tout court.*

As time went on and the memory of papa and mamma became wholly overlaid by the unpleasant task of writing them letters, under Aunty Rosa's eye, each Sunday, Black Sheep forgot what manner of life he had led in the beginning of things. Even Judy's appeals to "try and remember about Bombay" failed to quicken him.

"I can't remember," he said. "I know I used to give orders and mamma kissed me."

"Aunty Rosa will kiss you if you are good," pleaded Judy.

"Ugh! I don't want to be kissed by Aunty Rosa. She'd say I was doing it to get something more to eat."

The weeks lengthened into months, and the holidays came; but just before the holidays Black Sheep fell into deadly sin.

Among the many boys whom Harry had incited to "punch Black Sheep's head because he daren't hit back," was one more aggravating than the rest, who, in an unlucky moment, fell upon Black Sheep when Harry was not near. The blows stung, and Black Sheep struck back at random with all the power at his command. The boy dropped and whimpered. Black Sheep was astounded at his own act, but, feeling the unresisting body under him, shook it with both his hands in blind fury, and then began to throttle his enemy, meaning honestly to slay him. There was a scuffle, and Black Sheep was torn off the body by Harry and some colleagues, and cuffed home, tingling but exultant. Aunty Rosa was out; pending her arrival, Harry set himself to lecture Black Sheep on the sin of murder–which he described as the offense of Cain.

"Why didn't you fight him fair? What did you hit him when he was down for, you little cur?"

Black Sheep looked up at Harry's throat, and then at a knife on the dinner-table.

"I don't understand," he said, wearily. "You always set him on me, and told me I was a coward when I blubbered. Will you leave me alone until Aunty Rosa comes in? She'll beat me if you tell her I ought to be beaten; so it's all right."

"It's all wrong," said Harry, magisterially. "You nearly killed him, and I shouldn't wonder if he dies."

"Will he die?" said Black Sheep.

"I dare say," said Harry, "and then you'll be hanged."

"All right," said Black Sheep, possessing himself of the table-knife. "Then I'll kill you now. You say things and do things, and . . . and *I* don't know how things happen, and you never leave me alone–and I don't care *what* happens!"

He ran at the boy with the knife, and Harry fled upstairs to his room, promising Black Sheep the finest thrashing in the world when Aunty Rosa returned. Black Sheep sat at the bottom of the stairs, the table-knife in his hand, and wept for that he had not killed Harry. The servant-girl came up from the kitchen, took the knife away, and consoled him. But Black Sheep was beyond consolation. He would be badly beaten by Aunty Rosa; then there would be another beating at Harry's hands; then Judy would not be allowed to speak to him; then the tale would be told at school, and then. . . .

There was no one to help and no one to care, and the best way out of the business was by death. A knife would hurt; but Aunty Rosa had told him, a year ago, that if he sucked paint he would die. He went into the nursery, unearthed the now disused Noah's Ark, and sucked the paint off as many animals as remained. It tasted abominable, but he had licked Noah's dove clean by the time Aunty Rosa and Judy returned. He went upstairs and greeted them with: "Please, Aunty Rosa, I believe I've nearly killed a boy at school, and I've tried to kill Harry, and when you've done all about God and hell, will you beat me and get it over?"

The tale of the assault as told by Harry could only be explained on the ground of possession by the devil. Wherefore Black Sheep was not only most excellently beaten, one by Aunty Rosa, and once, when thoroughly cowed down, by Harry, but he was further prayed for at family prayers, together with Jane, who had stolen a cold *rissole* from the pantry and snuffled audibly as her enormity was brought before the Throne of Grace. Black Sheep was sore and stiff, but triumphant. He would die that very night and be rid of them all. No, he would ask for no forgiveness from Harry, and at bed-time would stand no questioning at Harry's hands, even though addressed as "Young Cain."

"I've been beaten," said he, "and I've done other things. I don't care what I do. If you speak to me tonight, Harry, I'll get out and try to kill you. Now, you can kill me if you like."

Harry took his bed into the spare room, and Black Sheep lay down to die.

It may be that the makers of Noah's arks know that their animals are likely to find their way into young mouths, and paint them accordingly. Certain it is that the common, weary next morning broke through the windows and found Black Sheep quite well and a good deal ashamed of himself, but richer by the knowledge that he could, in extremity, secure himself against Harry for the future.

When he descended to breakfast on the first day of the holidays, he was greeted with the news that Harry, Aunty Rosa, and Judy were going away to Brighton, while Black Sheep was to stay in the house with the servant. His latter outbreak suited Aunty Rosa's plans admirably. It gave her good excuse for leaving the extra boy behind. Papa in Bombay, who really seemed to know a young sinner's wants to the hour, sent, that week, a package of new books. And with these, and the society of Jane on board-wages, Black Sheep was left alone for a month.

The books lasted for ten days. They were eaten too quickly, in long gulps of four-and-twenty hours at a time. Then came days of doing absolutely nothing, of dreaming dreams and marching imaginary armies up and down stairs, of counting the number of banisters, and of measuring the length and breadth of every room in hand-spans–fifty down the side, thirty across, and fifty back again. Jane made many friends, and, after receiving Black Sheep's assurance that he would not tell of her absences, went out daily for long hours. Black Sheep would follow the rays of the sinking sun from the kitchen to the dining-room, and thence upward to his own bed-room, until all was gray dark, and he ran down to the kitchen fire and read by its light. He was happy in that he was left alone and could read as much as he pleased. But, later, he grew afraid of the shadows of window-curtains and the flapping of doors and the creaking of shutters. He went out into the garden, and the rustling of the laurel bushes frightened him.

He was glad when they all returned–Aunty Rosa, Harry, and Judy–full of news, and Judy laden with gifts. Who could help loving loyal little Judy. In return for all her merry babblement, Black Sheep confided to her that the distance from the hall door to the top of the first landing was exactly one hundred and eighty-four hand-spans. He had found it out himself.

Then the old life recommenced; but with a difference, and a new sin. To his other iniquities Black Sheep had now added a phenomenal clumsiness–was as unfit to trust in action as he was in word. He himself could not account for spilling everything he touched, upsetting glasses as he put his hand out, and bumping his head against doors that were manifestly shut. There was a gray haze upon all his world, and it narrowed month by month, until at last it left Black Sheep almost alone with the flapping curtains that were so like ghosts, and the nameless terrors of broad daylight that were only coats on pegs, after all.

Holidays came and holidays went, and Black Sheep was taken to see many people whose faces were all exactly alike; was beaten when occasion demanded, and tortured by Harry on all possible occasions; but defended by Judy through good and evil report, though she thereby drew upon herself the wrath of Aunty Rosa.

The weeks were interminable, and papa and mamma were clean forgotten. Harry had left school and was a clerk in a banking-office. Freed from his presence, Black Sheep resolved that he should no longer be deprived of his allowance of pleasure-reading. Consequently when he failed at school he reported that all was well, and conceived a large contempt for Aunty Rosa as he saw how easy it was to deceive her. "She says I'm a little liar when I don't tell lies, and now I do, she doesn't know," thought Black Sheep. Aunty Rosa had credited him in the past with petty cunning and stratagem that had never entered into his head. By the light of the sordid knowledge that she had revealed to him, he paid her back full tale. In a household where the most innocent of his motives—his natural yearning for a little affection—had been interpreted into a desire for more bread and jam, or to ingratiate himself with strangers and so put Harry into the background, his work was easy. Aunty Rosa could penetrate certain kinds of hypocrisy, but not all. He set his child's wits against hers and was no more beaten. It grew monthly more and more of a trouble to read the school-books, and even the pages of the open-print story-books danced and were dim. So Black Sheep brooded in the shadows that fell about him and cut him off from the world, inventing horrible punishments for "dear Harry," or plotting another line of the tangled web of deception that he wrapped round Aunty Rosa. Then the crash came and the cobwebs were broken. It was impossible to foresee everything. Aunty Rosa made personal inquiries as to Black Sheep's progress and received information that startled her. Step by step, with a delight as keen as when she convicted an under-fed house-maid of the theft of cold meats, she followed the trail of Black Sheep's delinquencies. For weeks and weeks, in order to escape banishment from the book-shelves, he had made a fool of Aunty Rosa, of Harry, of God, of all the world! Horrible, most horrible, and evidence of an utterly depraved mind.

Black Sheep counted the cost. "It will only be one big beating and then she'll put a card with 'Liar' on my back, same as she did before. Harry will whack me at prayers and tell me I'm a child of the devil, and give me hymns to learn. But I've done all my reading and she never knew. She'll say she knew all along. She's an old liar, too," said he.

For three days Black Sheep was shut in his own bedroom—to prepare his heart. "That means two beatings. One at school and one here. *That* one will hurt most." And it fell even as he thought. He was thrashed at school before the Jews and the *hubshi,* for the heinous crime of bringing home false reports of progress. He was thrashed at home by Aunty Rosa on the same account, and then the placard was produced. Aunty Rosa stitched it between his shoulders and bade him go for a walk with it upon him.

"If you make me do that," said Black Sheep, very quietly, "I shall burn this house down, and perhaps I'll kill you. I don't know whether I *can* kill you—you're so bony—but I'll try."

No punishment followed this blasphemy, though Black Sheep held himself ready to work his way to Aunty Rosa's withered throat, and grip there till he was beaten off. Perhaps Aunty Rosa was afraid, for Black sheep, having reached the Nadir of Sin, bore himself with a new recklessness.

In the midst of all the trouble, there came a visitor from over the seas to Downe Lodge, who knew papa and mamma, and was commissioned to see Punch and Judy. Black Sheep was sent to the drawing-room and charged into a solid tea-table laden with china.

"Gently, gently, little man," said the visitor, turning Black Sheep's face to the light, slowly. "What's that big bird on the palings?"

"What bird?" asked Black Sheep.

The visitor looked deep down into Black Sheep's eyes for half a minute, and then said, suddenly: "Good God, the little chap's nearly blind!"

It was a most business-like visitor. He gave orders, on his own responsibility, that Black Sheep was not to go to school or open a book until mamma came home. "She'll be here in three weeks, as you know, of course," said he; "and I'm Inverarity Sahib. I ushered you into this wicked world, young man, and a nice use you seem to have made of your time. You must do nothing whatever. Can you do that?"

"Yes," said Punch, in a dazed way. He had known that mamma was coming. There was a chance, then, of another beating. Thank Heaven, papa wasn't coming, too. Aunty Rosa had said of late that he ought to be beaten by a man.

For the next three weeks Black Sheep was strictly allowed to do nothing. He spent his time in the old nursery looking at the broken toys, for all of which account must be rendered to mamma. Aunty Rosa hit him over the hands if even a wooden boat were broken. But that sin was of small importance compared to the other revelations, so darkly hinted at by Aunty Rosa. "When your mother comes, and hears what I have to tell her, she may appreciate you properly," she said, grimly, and mounted guard over Judy lest that small maiden should attempt to comfort her brother, to the peril of her own soul.

And mamma came–in a four-wheeler and a flutter of tender excitement. Such a mamma! She was young, frivolously young, and beautiful, with delicately flushed cheeks, eyes that shone like stars, and a voice that needed no additional appeal of outstretched arms to draw little ones to her heart. Judy ran straight to her, but Black Sheep hesitated. Could this wonder be "showing off?" She would not put out her arms when she knew of his crimes. Meantime, was it possible that by fondling she wanted to get anything out of Black Sheep? Only all his love and all his confidence; but that Black Sheep did not know. Aunty Rosa withdrew and left mamma kneeling between her children, half laughing, half crying, in the very hall where Punch and Judy had wept five years before.

"Well, chicks, do you remember me?"

"No," said Judy, frankly, "but I said 'God bless papa and mamma' ev'vy night."

"A little," said Black Sheep. "Remember I wrote to you every week, anyhow. That isn't to show off, but 'cause of what comes afterward."

"What comes after! What should come after, my darling boy?" And she drew him to her again. He came awkwardly, with many angles. "Not used to petting," said the quick mother-soul. "The girl is."

"She's too little to hurt anyone," thought Black Sheep, "and if I said I'd kill her, she'd be afraid. I wonder what Aunty Rosa will tell."

There was a constrained late dinner, at the end of which mamma picked up Judy and put her to bed with endearments manifold. Faithless little Judy had shown her defection from Aunty Rosa already; and that lady resented it bitterly. Black Sheep rose to leave the room.

"Come and say good-nignt," said Aunty Rosa, offering a withered cheek.

"Huh!" said Black Sheep. "I never kiss you, and I'm not going to show off. Tell that woman what I've done, and see what she says."

Black Sheep climbed into bed feeling that he had lost Heaven after a glimpse through the gates. In half an hour "that woman" was bending over him. It wasn't fair to come and hit him in the dark. Even Aunty Rosa never tried that. But no blow followed.

"Are you showing off? I won't tell you anything more than Aunty Rosa has, and *she* doesn't know everything," said Black Sheep, as clearly as he could for the arms round his neck.

"Oh, my son–my little, little son! It was my fault–*my* fault, darling–and yet how could we help it? Forgive me, Punch." The voice died out in a broken whisper, and two hot tears fell on Black Sheep's forehead.

"Has she been making you cry, too?" he asked. "You should see Jane cry. But you're nice, and Jane is a born liar–Aunty Rosa says so."

"Hush, Punch, hush! My boy, don't talk like that. Try to love me a little bit–a little bit. You don't know how I want it. Punch-*baba,* come back to me! I am your mother–your own mother–and never mind the rest. I know–yes, I know, dear. It doesn't matter now. Punch, won't you care for me a little?"

It is astonishing how much petting a big boy of ten can endure when he is quite sure that there is no one to laugh at him. Black Sheep had never been made much of before, and here was this beautiful woman treating him—Black Sheep, the Child of the Devil and the Inheritor of Undying Flame—as though he were a small god.

"I care for you a great deal, mother dear," he whispered at last, "and I'm glad you've come back; but are you sure Aunty Rosa told you everything?"

"Everything. What *does* it matter? But"—the voice broke with a sob that was also laughter—"Punch, my poor, dear, half-blind darling, don't you think it was a little foolish of you?"

"*No.* It saved a lickin'."

Mamma shuddered and slipped away in the darkness to write a long letter to papa. Here is an extract:

". . . Judy is a dear, plump little prig who adores the woman, and wears, with as much gravity as her religious opinions—only eight, Jack!—a venerable horse-hair atrocity which she calls her bustle! I have just burned it, and the child is asleep in my bed as I write. She will come to me at once. Punch I can not quite understand. He is well nourished, but seems to have been worried into a system of small deceptions which the woman magnifies into deadly sins. Don't you recollect our own up-bringing, dear, when the fear of the Lord was so often the beginning of falsehood? I shall win Punch to me before long. I am taking the children away into the country to get them to know me, and, on the whole, I am content, or shall be when you come home, dear boy; and then, thank God, we shall be all under one roof again at last!"

Three months later, Punch, no longer Black Sheep, has discovered that he is the veritable owner of a real live, lovely mamma, who is also a sister, comforter, and friend, and that he must protect her till the father comes home. Deception does not suit the part of a protector, and when one can do anything without question, where is the use of deception?

"Mother would be awfully cross if you walked through that ditch," says Judy, continuing a conversation.

"Mother's never angry," says Punch. "She'd just say, 'You're a little *pagal';* and that's not nice, but I'll show."

Punch walks through the ditch and mires himself to the knees. "Mother dear," he shouts, "I'm as dirty as I can pos-*sib*-ly be!"

"Then change your clothes as quickly as you pos-*sib*-ly can!" rings out mother's clear voice from the house. "And don't be a little *pagal!*"

"There! Told you so," said Punch. "It's all different now, and we are just as much mother's as if she had never gone."

Not altogether, oh Punch, for when young lips have drunk deep of the bitter waters of Hate, Suspicion, and Despair, all the love in the world will not wholly take away that knowledge; though it may turn darkened eyes for awhile to the light, and teach Faith where no Faith was.

The Phantom 'Rickshaw

May no ill dreams disturb my rest,
Nor Powers of Darkness me molest.
—*Evening Hymn.*

ONE OF THE few advantages that India has over England is a great Knowability. After five years' service a man is directly or indirectly acquainted with the two or three hundred Civilians in his Province, all the Messes of ten or twelve Regiments and batteries, and some fifteen hundred other people of the non-official caste. In ten years his knowledge should be doubled, and at the end of twenty he knows, or knows something about, every Englishman in the Empire, and may travel anywhere and everywhere without paying hotel-bills.

Globe-trotters who expect entertainment as a right, have, even within my memory, blunted this openheartedness, but none the less to-day, if you belong to the Inner Circle and are neither a Bear nor a Black Sheep, all houses are open to you, and our small world is very, very kind and helpful.

Rickett of Kamartha stayed with Polder of Kumaon some fifteen years ago. He meant to stay two nights, but was knocked down by rheumatic fever, and for six weeks disorganized Polder's establishment, stopped Polder's work, and nearly died in Polder's bedroom. Polder behaved as though he had been placed under eternal obligation by Rickett, and yearly sends the little Ricketts a box of presents and toys. It is the same everywhere. The men who do not take the trouble to conceal from you their opinion that you are an incompetent ass, and the women who blacken your character and misunderstand your wife's amusements, will work themselves to the bone in your behalf if you fall sick or into serious trouble.

Heatherlegh, the Doctor, kept, in addition to his regular practice, a hospital on his private account–an arrangement of loose boxes for Incurables, his friend called it–but it was really a sort of fitting-up shed for craft that had been damaged by stress of weather. The weather in India is often sultry, and since the tale of bricks is always a fixed quantity, and the only liberty allowed is permission to work overtime and get no thanks, men occasionally break down and become as mixed as the metaphors in this sentence.

Heatherlegh is the dearest doctor that ever was, and his invariable prescription to all his patients is, "lie low, go slow, and keep cool."

He says that more men are killed by overwork than the importance of this world justifies. He maintains that three years ago. He has, of course, the right to speak authoritatively, and he laughs at my theory that there was a crack in Pansay's head and a little bit of the Dark World came through and pressed him to death. "Pansay went off the handle," says Heatherlegh, "after the stimulus of long leave at Home. He may or he may not have behaved like a blackguard to Mrs. Keith-Wessington. My notion is that the work of the Katabundi Settlement ran him off his legs, and that he took to brooding and making much of an ordinary P. & O. flirtation. He certainly was engaged to Miss Mannering, and she certainly broke off the engagement. Then he took a feverish chill and all that nonsense about ghosts developed. Overwork started his illness, kept it alight, and killed him, poor devil. Write him off to the System–one man to take the work of two and a half men."

I do not believe this. I used to sit up with Pansay sometimes when Heatherlegh was called out to patients, and I happened to be within claim. The man would make me most unhappy by describing in a low, even voice, the procession that was always passing at the bottom of his bed. He had a sick man's command of language. When he recovered I suggested that he should write out the whole affair from beginning to end, knowing that ink might assist him to ease his mind. When little boys have learned a new bad word they are never happy till they have chalked it up on a door. And this also is Literature.

He was in a high fever while he was writing, and the blood-and-thunder Magazine diction he adopted did not calm him. Two months afterward he was reported fit for duty, but, in spite of the fact that he was urgently needed to help an undermanned Commission stagger through a deficit, he preferred to die; vowing at last that he was hag-ridden. I got his manuscript before he died, and this is his version of the affair, dated 1885:

My doctor tells me that I need rest and change of air. It is not improbable that I shall get both ere long–rest that neither the red-coated messenger nor the midday gun can break, and change of air far beyond that which any homeward-bound steamer can give me. In the meantime I am resolved to stay where I am; and, in flat defiance of my doctor's orders, to take all the world into my confidence. You shall learn for yourselves the precise nature of my malady; and shall, too, judge for yourselves whether any man born of woman on this weary earth was ever so tormented as I.

Speaking now as a condemned criminal might speak ere the drop-bolts are drawn, my story, wild and hideously improbable as it may appear, demands at least attention. That it will ever receive credence I utterly disbelieve. Two months ago I should have scouted as mad or drunk the man who had dared tell me the like. Two months ago I was the happiest man in India. To-day, from Peshawur to the sea, there is no one more wretched. My doctor and I are the only two who know this. His explanation is, that my brain, digestion, and eyesight are all slightly affected; giving rise to my frequent and persistent "delusions." Delusions, indeed! I call him a fool; but he attends me still with the same unwearied smile, the same bland professional manner, the same neatly trimmed red whiskers, till I begin to suspect that I am an ungrateful, evil-tempered invalid. But you shall judge for yourselves.

Three years ago it was my fortune—my great misfortune—to sail from Gravesend to Bombay, on return from long leave, with one Agnes Keith-Wessington, wife of an officer on the Bombay side. It does not in the least concern you to know what manner of woman she was. Be content with the knowledge that, ere the voyage had ended, both she and I were desperately and unreasoningly in love with one another. Heaven knows that I can make the admission now without one particle of vanity. In matters of this sort there is always one who gives and another who accepts. From the first day of our ill-omened attachment, I was conscious that Agnes's passion was a stronger, a more dominant, and—if I may use the expression—a purer sentiment than mine. Whether she recognized the fact then, I do not know. Afterward it was bitterly plain to both of us.

Arrived at Bombay in the spring of the year, we went our respective ways, to meet no more for the next three or four months, when my leave and her love took us both to Simla. There we spent the season together; and there my fire of straw burned itself out to a pitiful end with the closing year. I attempt no excuse. I make no apology. Mrs. Wessington had given up much for my sake, and was prepared to give up all. From my own lips, in August, 1882, she learned that I was sick of her presence, tired of her company, and weary of the sound of her voice. Ninety-nine women out of a hundred would have wearied of me as I wearied of them; seventy-five of that number would have promptly avenged themselves by active and obtrusive flirtation with other men. Mrs. Wessington was the hundredth. On her neither my openly expressed aversion nor the cutting brutalities with which I garnished our interviews had the least effect.

"Jack, darling!" was her one eternal cuckoo cry: "I'm sure it's all a mistake—a hideous mistake; and we'll be good friends again some day. *Please* forgive me, Jack, dear."

I was the offender, and I knew it. That knowledge transformed my pity into passive endurance, and, eventually, into blind hate—the same instinct, I suppose, which prompts a man to savagely stamp on the spider he has but half killed. And with this hate in my bosom the season of 1882 came to an end.

Next year we met again at Simla—she with her montonous face and timid attempts at reconciliation, and I with loathing of her in every fibre of my frame. Several times I could not avoid meeting her alone; and on each occasion her words were identically the same. Still the unreasoning wail that it was all a "mistake"; and still the hope of eventually "making friends." I might have seen had I cared to look, that that hope only was keeping her alive. She grew more wan and thin month by month. You will agree with me, at least, that such conduct would have driven any one to despair. It was uncalled for; childish; unwomanly. I maintain that she was much to blame. And again, sometimes, in the black, fever-stricken night-watches, I have begun to think that I might have been a little kinder to her. But that really *is* a "delusion." I could not have continued pretending to love her when I didn't; could I? It would have been unfair to us both.

Last year we met again—on the same terms as before. The same weary appeals, and the same curt answers from my lips. At least I would make her see how wholly wrong and hopeless were her attempts at resuming the old relationship. As the season wore on, we fell apart—that is to say, she found it difficult to meet me, for I had other and more absorbing interests to attend to. When I think it over quietly in my sickroom, the season of 1884 seems a confused nightmare wherein light and shade were fantastically intermingled—my courtship of little Kitty Mannering; my hopes, doubts, and fears; our long rides together; my trembling avowal of attachment; her reply; and now and again a vision of a white face flitting by in the 'rickshaw with the black and white liveries I once watched for so earnestly; the wave of Mrs. Wessington's gloved hand; and, when she met me alone, which was but seldom, the irksome monotony of her appeal. I loved Kitty Mannering; honestly, heartily loved her, and with my love for her grew my hatred for Agnes. In August Kitty and I were engaged. The next day I met those accursed "magpie" *jhampanies* at the back of Jakko, and, moved by some passing sentiment of pity, stopped to tell Mrs. Wessington everything. She knew it already.

"So I hear you're engaged, Jack dear." Then, without a moment's pause:—"I'm sure it's all a mistake—a hideous mistake. We shall be as good friends some day, Jack, as we ever were."

My answer might have made even a man wince. It cut the dying woman before me like the blow of a whip. "Please forgive me, Jack; I didn't mean to make you angry; but it's true, it's true!"

And Mrs. Wessington broke down completely. I turned away and left her to finish her journey in peace, feeling, but only for a moment or two, that I had been an unutterably mean hound. I looked back, and saw that she had turned her 'rickshaw with the idea, I suppose, of overtaking me.

The scene and its surroundings were photographed on my memory. The rain-swept sky (we were at the end of the wet weather), the sodden, dingy pines, the muddy road, and the black powder-riven cliffs formed a gloomy background against which the black and white liveries of the *jhampanies,* the yellow-paneled 'rickshaw and Mrs. Wessington's down-bowed golden head stood out clearly. She was holding her handkerchief in her left hand and was leaning back exhausted against the 'rickshaw cushions. I turned my horse up a bypath near the Sanjowlie Reservoir and literally ran away. Once I fancied I heard a faint call of "Jack!" This may have been imagination. I never stopped to verify it. Ten minutes later I came across Kitty on horseback; and, in the delight of a long ride with her, forgot all about the interview.

A week later Mrs. Wessington died, and the inexpressible burden of her existence was removed from my life. I went Plainsward perfectly happy. Before three months were over I had forgotten all about her, except that at times the discovery of some of her old letters reminded me unpleasantly of our bygone relationship. By January I had disinterred what was left of our correspondence from among my scattered belongings and had burned it. At the beginning of April of this year, 1885, I was at Simla—semideserted Simla—once more, and was deep in lover's talks and walks with Kitty. It was decided that we should be married at the end of June. You will understand, therefore, that, loving Kitty as I did, I am not saying too much when I pronounce myself to have been, at that time, the happiest man in India.

Fourteen delightful days passed almost before I noticed their flight. Then, aroused to the sense of what was proper among mortals circumstanced as we were, I pointed out to Kitty that an engagement ring was the outward and visible sign of her dignity as an engaged girl; and that she must forthwith come to Hamilton's to be measured for one. Up to that moment, I give you my word, we had completely forgotten so trivial a matter. To Hamilton's we accordingly went on the 15th of April, 1885. Remember that–whatever my doctor may say to the contrary–I was then in perfect health, enjoying a well-balanced mind and an *absolutely* tranquil spirit. Kitty and I entered Hamilton's shop together, and there, regardless of the order of affairs, I measured Kitty for the ring in the presence of the amused assistant. The ring was a sapphire with two diamonds. We then rode out down the slope that leads to the Combermere Bridge and Peliti's shop.

While my Waler was cautiously feeling his way over the loose shale, and Kitty was laughing and chattering at my side–while all Simla, that is to say as much of it as had then come from the Plains, was grouped round the Reading-room and Peliti's veranda,–I was aware that some one, apparently at a vast distance, was calling me by my Christian name. It struck me that I had heard the voice before, but when and where I could not at once determine. In the short space it took to cover the road between the path from Hamilton's shop and the first plank of the Combermere Bridge I had thought over half a dozen people who might have committed such a solecism, and had eventually decided that it must have been singing in my ears. Immediately opposite Peliti's shop my eye was arrested by the sight of four *jhampanies* in "magpie" livery, pulling a yellow-paneled, cheap, bazar 'rickshaw. In a moment my mind flew back to the previous season and Mrs. Wessington with a sense of irritation and disgust. Was it not enough that the woman was dead and done with, without her black and white servitors reappearing to spoil the day's happiness? Whoever employed them now I thought I would call upon, and ask as a personal favor to change her *jhampanies'* livery. I would hire the men myself, and, if necessary, buy their coats from off their backs. It is impossible to say here what a flood of undesirable memories their presence evoked.

"Kitty," I cried, "there are poor Mrs. Wessington's *jhampanies* turned up again! I wonder who has them now?"

Kitty had known Mrs. Wessington slightly last season, and had always been interested in the sickly woman.

"What? Where?" she asked. "I can't see them anywhere."

Even as she spoke, her horse, swerving from a laden mule, threw himself directly in front of the advancing 'rickshaw. I had scarcely time to utter a word of warning when, to my unutterable horror, horse and rider passed *through* men and carriage as if they had been thin air.

"What's the matter?" cried Kitty; "what made you call out so foolishly, Jack? If I *am* engaged I don't want all creation to know about it. There was lots of space between the mule and the veranda; and, if you think I can't ride– There!"

Whereupon wilful Kitty set off, her dainty little head in the air, at a hand-gallop in the direction of the Bandstand; fully expecting, as she herself afterward told me, that I should follow her. What was the matter? Nothing indeed. Either that I was mad or drunk, or that Simla was haunted with devils. I reined in my impatient cob, and turned round. The 'rickshaw had turned too, and now stood immediately facing me near the left railing of the Combermere Bridge.

"Jack! Jack, darling!" (There was no mistake about the words this time: they rang through my brain as if they had shouted in my ear.) "It's some hideous mistake, I'm sure. *Please* forgive me, Jack, and let's be friends again."

The rickshaw-hood had fallen back, and inside, as I hope and pray daily for the death I dread by night, sat Mrs. Keith-Wessington, handkerchief in hand, and golden head bowed on her breast.

How long I stared motionless I do not know. Finally, I was aroused by my syce taking the Waler's bridle and asking whether I was ill. From the horrible to the commonplace is but a step. I tumbled off my horse and dashed, half fainting, into Peliti's for a glass of cherry-brandy. There two or three couples were gathered round the coffee-tables discussing the gossip of the day. Their trivialities were more comforting to me just then than the consolations of religion could have been. I plunged into the midst of the conversation at once; chatted, laughed, and jested with a face (when I caught a glimpse of it in a mirror) as white and drawn as that of a corpse. Three or four men noticed my condition; and, evidently setting it down to the results of overmany pegs, charitably endeavored to draw me apart from the rest of the loungers. But I refused to be led away. I wanted the company of my kind–as a child rushes into the midst of the dinner-party after a fright in the dark. I must have talked for about ten minutes or so, though it seemed an eternity to me, when I heard Kitty's clear voice outside inquiring for me. In another minute she had entered the shop, prepared to roundly upbraid me for failing so signally in my duties. Something in my face stopped her.

"Why, Jack," she cried, "what *have* you been doing? What *has* happened? Are you ill?" Thus driven into a direct lie, I said that the sun had been a little too much for me. It was close upon five o'clock of a cloudy April afternoon, and the sun had been hidden all day. I saw my mistake as soon as the words were out of my mouth: attempted to recover it; blundered hopelessly and followed Kitty in a regal rage, out of doors, amid the smiles of my acquaintances. I made some excuse (I have forgotten what) on the score of my feeling faint; and cantered away to my hotel, leaving Kitty to finish the ride by herself.

In my room I sat down and tried calmly to reason out the matter. Here was I, Theobald Jack Pansay, a well-educated Bengal Civilian in the year of grace 1885, presumably sane, certainly healthy, driven in terror from my sweetheart's side by the apparition of a woman who had been dead and buried eight months ago. These were facts that I could not blink. Nothing was further from my thought than any memory of Mrs. Wessington when Kitty and I left Hamilton's shop. Nothing was more utterly commonplace than the stretch of wall opposite Peliti's. It was broad daylight. The road was full of people; and yet here, look you, in defiance of every law of probability, in direct outrage of Nature's ordinance, there had appeared to me a face from the grave.

Kitty's Arab had gone *through* the 'rickshaw: so that my first hope that some woman marvelously like Mrs. Wessington had hired the carriage and the coolies with their old livery was lost. Again and again I went round this treadmill of thought; and again and again gave up baffled and in despair. The voice was as inexplicable as the apparition. I had originally some wild notion of confiding it all to Kitty; of begging her to marry me at once; and in her arms defying the ghostly occupant of the 'rickshaw. "After all," I argued, "the presence of the 'rickshaw is in itself enough to prove the existence of a spectral illusion. One may see ghosts of men and women, but surely never of coolies and carriages. The whole thing is absurd. Fancy the ghost of a hillman!"

Next morning I sent a penitent note to Kitty, imploring her to overlook my strange conduct of the previous afternoon. My Divinity was still very wroth, and a personal apology was necessary. I explained, with a fluency born of night-long pondering over a falsehood, that I had been attacked with a sudden palpitation of the heart–the result of indigestion. This eminently practical solution had its effect; and Kitty and I rode out that afternoon with the shadow of my first lie dividing us.

Nothing would please her save a canter round Jakko. With my nerves still unstrung from the previous night I feebly protested against the notion, suggesting Observatory Hill, Jutogh, the Boileaugunge road–anything rather than the Jakko round. Kitty was angry and a little hurt: so I yielded from fear of provoking further misunderstanding, and we set out together toward Chota Simla. We walked a greater part of the way, and, according to our custom, cantered from a mile or so below the Convent to the stretch of level road by the Sanjowlie Reservoir. The wretched horses appeared to fly, and my heart beat quicker and quicker as we neared the crest of the ascent. My mind had been full of Mrs. Wessington all the afternoon; and every inch of the Jakko road bore witness to our old-time walks and talks. The bowlders were full of it; the pines sang it aloud overhead; the rain-fed torrents giggled and chuckled unseen over the shameful story; and the wind in my ears chanted the iniquity aloud.

As a fitting climax, in the middle of the level men call the Ladies' Mile the Horror was awaiting me. No other 'rickshaw was in sight–only the four black and white *jhampanies,* the yellow-paneled carriage, and the golden head of the woman within–all apparently just as I had left them eight months and one fortnight ago! For an instant I fancied that Kitty *must* see what I saw–we were so marvelously sympathetic in all things. Her next words undeceived me–"Not a soul in sight! Come along, Jack, and I'll race you to the Reservoir buildings!" Her wiry little Arab was off like a bird, my Waler following close behind, and in this order we dashed under the cliffs. Half a minute brought us within fifty yards of the 'rickshaw. I pulled my Waler and fell back a little. The 'rickshaw was directly in the middle of the road; and once more the Arab passed through it, my horse following. "Jack! Jack dear! *Please* forgive me," rang with a wail in my ears, and, after an interval:–"It's all a mistake, a hideous mistake!"

I spurred my horse like a man possessed. When I turned my head at the Reservoir works, the black and white liveries were still waiting–patiently waiting–under the gray hillside, and the wind brought me a mocking echo of the words I had just heard. Kitty bantered me a good deal on my silence throughout the remainder of the ride. I had been talking up till then wildly and at random. To save my life I could not speak afterward naturally, and from Sanjowlie to the Church wisely held my tongue.

I was to dine with the Mannerings that night, and had barely time to canter home to dress. On the road to Elysium Hill I overheard two men talking together in the dusk.–"It's a curious thing," said one, "how completely all trace of it disappeared. You know my wife was insanely fond of the woman ('never could see anything in her myself), and wanted me to pick up her old 'rickshaw and coolies if they were to be got for love or money. Morbid sort of fancy I call it; but I've got to do what the *Memsahib* tells me. Would you believe that the man she hired it from tells me that all four of the men–they were brothers–died of cholera on the way to Hardwar, poor devils; and the 'rickshaw has been broken up by the man himself. 'Told me he never used a dead *Memsahib's* 'rickshaw. 'Spoiled his luck. Queer notion, wasn't it? Fancy poor little Mrs. Wessington spoiling any one's luck except her own!" I laughed aloud at this point; and my laugh jarred on me as I uttered it. So there *were* ghosts of 'rickshaws after all, and ghostly employments in the other world! How much did Mrs. Wessington give her men? What were their hours? Where did they go?

And for visible answer to my last question I saw the infernal Thing blocking my path in the twilight. The dead travel fast, and by short cuts unknown to ordinary coolies. I laughed aloud a second time and checked my laughter suddenly, for I was afraid I was going mad. Mad to a certain extent I must have been, for I recollect that I reined in my horse at the head of the 'rickshaw, and politely wished Mrs. Wessington "Good-evening." Her answer was one I knew only too well. I listened to the end; and replied that I had heard it all before, but should be delighted if she had anything further to say. Some malignant devil stronger than I must have entered into me that evening, for I have a dim recollection of talking the commonplaces of the day for five minutes to the Thing in front of me.

"Mad as a hatter, poor devil—or drunk. Max, try and get him to come home."

Surely *that* was not Mrs. Wessington's voice! The two men had overheard me speaking to the empty air, and had returned to look after me. They were very kind and considerate, and from their words evidently gathered that I was extremely drunk. I thanked them confusedly and cantered away to my hotel, there changed, and arrived at the Mannerings' ten minutes late. I pleaded the darkness of the night as an excuse; was rebuked by Kitty for my unlover-like tardiness; and sat down.

The conversation had already become general; and under cover of it, I was addressing some tender small talk to my sweetheart when I was aware that at the further end of the table a short red-whiskered man was describing, with much broidery, his encounter with a mad unknown that evening.

A few sentences convinced me that he was repeating the incident of half an hour ago. In the middle of the story he looked round for applause, as professional story-tellers do, caught my eye, and straightway collapsed. There was a moment's awkward silence, and the red-whiskered man muttered something to the effect that he had "forgotten the rest," thereby sacrificing a reputation as a good story-teller which he had built up for six seasons past. I blessed him from the bottom of my heart, and—went on with my fish.

In the fulness of time that dinner came to an end; and with genuine regret I tore myself away from Kitty—as certain as I was of my own existence that it would be waiting for me outside the door. The red-whiskered man, who had been introduced to me as Doctor Heatherlegh of Simla, volunteered to bear me company as far as our roads lay together. I accepted his offer with gratitude.

My instinct had not deceived me. It lay in readiness in the Mall, and, in what seemed devilish mockery of our ways, with a lighted headlamp. The red-whiskered man went to the point at once, in a manner that showed he had been thinking over it all dinner time.

"I say, Pansay, what the deuce was the matter with you this evening on the Elysium road?" The suddenness of the question wrenched an answer from me before I was aware.

"That!" said I, pointing to It.

"*That* may be either D. T. or Eyes for aught I know. Now you don't liquor. I saw as much at dinner, so it can't be *D. T.* There's nothing whatever where you're pointing, though you're sweating and trembling with fright like a scared pony. Therefore, I conclude that it's Eyes. And I ought to understand all about them. Come along home with me. I'm on the Blessington lower road."

To my intense delight the 'rickshaw instead of waiting for us kept about twenty yards ahead—and this, too, whether we walked, trotted, or cantered. In the course of that long night ride I had told my companion almost as much as I have told you here.

"Well, you've spoiled one of the best tales I've ever laid tongue to," said he, "but I'll forgive you for the sake of what you've gone through. Now come home and do what I tell you; and when I've cured you, young man, let this be a lesson to you to steer clear of women and indigestible food till the day of your death."

The 'rickshaw kept steady in front; and my red whiskered friend seemed to derive great pleasure from my account of its exact whereabouts.

"Eyes, Pansay—all Eyes, Brain, and Stomach. And the greatest of these three is Stomach. You've too much conceited Brain, too little Stomach and thoroughly unhealthy Eyes. Get your Stomach straight, and the rest follows. And all that's French for a liver pill. I'll take sole medical charge of you from this hour! for you're too interesting a phenomenon to be passed over."

By this time we were deep in the shadow of the Blessington lower road and the 'rickshaw came to a dead stop under a pine-clad, overhanging shale cliff. Instinctively I halted too, giving my reason. Heatherlegh rapped out an oath.

"Now, if you think I'm going to spend a cold night on the hillside for the sake of a Stomach-*cum*-Brain-*cum*-Eye illusion . . . Lord, ha' mercy! What's that?"

There was a muffled report, a blinding smother of dust just in front of us, a crack, the noise of rent boughs, and about ten yards of the cliff-side—pines, undergrowth, and all—slid down into the road below, completely blocking it up. The uprooted trees swayed and tottered for a moment like drunken giants in the gloom, and then fell prone among their fellows with a thunderous crash. Our two horses stood motionless and sweating with fear. As soon as the rattle of falling earth and stone had subsided, my companion muttered:—"Man, if we'd gone forward we should have been ten feet deep in our graves by now. 'There are more things in heaven and earth.' . . . Come home, Pansay, and thank God. I want a peg badly."

We retraced our way over the Church Ridge, and I arrived at Dr. Heatherlegh's house shortly after midnight.

His attempts toward my cure commenced almost immediately, and for a week I never left his sight. Many a time in the course of that week did I bless the good-fortune which had thrown me in contact wiht Simla's best and kindest doctor. Day by day my spirits grew lighter and more equable. Day by day, too, I became more and more inclined to fall in with Heatherlegh's "spectral illusion" theory, implicating eyes, brain, and stomach. I wrote to Kitty, telling her that a slight sprain caused by a fall from my horse kept me indoors for a few days; and that I should be recovered before she had time to regret my absence.

Heatherlegh's treatment was simple to a degree. It consisted of liver pills, cold-water baths, and strong exercise, taken in the dusk or at early dawn—for, as he sagely observed:—"A man with a sprained ankle doesn't walk a dozen miles a day, and your young woman might be wondering if she saw you."

At the end of the week, after much examination of pupil and pulse, and strict injunctions as to diet and pedestrianism, Heatherlegh dismissed me as brusquely as he had taken charge of me. Here is his parting benediction:—"Man, I certify to your mental cure, and that's as much as to say I've cured most of your bodily ailments. Now, get your traps out of this as soon as you can; and be off to make love to Miss Kitty."

I was endeavoring to express my thanks for his kindness. He cut me short.

"Don't think I did this because I like you. I gather that you've behaved like a blackguard all through. But, all the same, you're a phenomenon, and as queer a phenomenon as you are a blackguard. No!"—checking me a second time—"not a rupee please. Go out and see if you can find the eyes-brain-and-stomach business again. I'll give you a lakh for each time you see it."

Half an hour later I was in the Mannerings' drawing-room with Kitty—drunk with the intoxication of present happiness and the foreknowledge that I should never more be troubled with Its hideous presence. Strong in the sense of my new-found security, I proposed a ride at once; and, by preference, a canter round Jakko.

Never had I felt so well, so overladen with vitality and mere animal spirits, as I did on the afternoon of the 30th of April. Kitty was delighted at the change in my appearance, and complimented me on it in her delightfully frank and outspoken manner. We left the Mannerings' house together, laughing and talking, and cantered along the Chota Simla road as of old.

I was in haste to reach the Sanjowlie Reservoir and there make my assurance doubly sure. The horses did their best, but seemed all too slow to my impatient mind. Kitty was astonished at my boisterousness. "Why, Jack!" she cried at last, "you are behaving like a child. What are you doing?"

We were just below the Convent, and from sheer wantonness I was making my Waler plunge and curvet across the road as I tickled it with the loop of my riding-whip.

"Doing?" I answered; "nothing, dear. That's just it. If you'd been doing nothing for a week except lie up, you'd be as riotous as I.

"'Singing and murmuring in your feastful mirth,
Joying to feel yourself alive;
Lord over Nature, Lord of the visible Earth,
Lord of the senses five.'"

My quotation was hardly out of my lips before we had rounded the corner above the Convent; and a few yards further on could see across to Sanjowlie. In the centre of the level road stood the black and white liveries, the yellow-paneled 'rickshaw, and Mrs. Keith-Wessington. I pulled up, looked, rubbed my eyes, and, I believe, must have said something. The next thing I knew was that I was lying face downward on the road, with Kitty kneeling above me in tears.

"Has it gone, child!" I gasped. Kitty only wept more bitterly.

"Has what gone, Jack, dear? what does it all mean? There must be a mistake somewhere, Jack. A hideous mistake." Her last words brought me to my feet–mad–raving for the time being.

"Yes, there *is* a mistake somewhere," I repeated, "a hideous mistake. Come and look at It."

I have an indistinct idea that I dragged Kitty by the wrist along the road up to where It stood, and implored her for pity's sake to speak to It; to tell It that we were betrothed; that neither Death nor Hell could break the tie between us: and Kitty only knows how much more to the same effect. Now and again I appealed passionately to the Terror in the 'rickshaw to bear witness to all I had said, and to release me from a torture that was killing me. As I talked I suppose I must have told Kitty of my old relations with Mrs. Wessington, for I saw her listen intently with white face and blazing eyes.

"Thank you, Mr. Pansay," she said, "that's *quite* enough. *Syce ghora láo."*

The syces, impassive as Orientals always are, had come up with the recaptured horses; and as Kitty sprang into her saddle I caught hold of the bridle, entreating her to hear me out and forgive. My answer was the cut of her riding-whip across my face from mouth to eye, and a word or two of farewell that even now I cannot write down. So I judged, and judged rightly, that Kitty knew all; and I staggered back to the side of the 'rickshaw. My face was cut and bleeding, and the blow of the riding-whip had raised a livid blue wheal on it. I had no self-respect. Just then, Heatherlegh, who must have been following Kitty and me at a distance, cantered up.

"Doctor," I said, pointing to my face, "here's Miss Mannering's signature to my order of dismissal and . . . I'll thank you for that lakh as soon as convenient."

Heatherlegh's face, even in my abject misery, moved me to laughter.

"I'll stake my professional reputation"–he began. "Don't be a fool," I whispered. "I've lost my life's happiness and you'd better take me home."

As I spoke the 'rickshaw was gone. Then I lost all knowledge of what was passing. The crest of Jakko seemed to heave and roll like the crest of a cloud and fall in upon me.

Seven days later (on the 7th of May, that is to say) I was aware that I was lying in Heatherlegh's room as weak as a little child. Heatherlegh was watching me intently from behind the papers on his writing-table. His first words were not encouraging; but I was too far spent to be much moved by them.

"Here's Miss Kitty has sent back your letters. You correspond a good deal, you young people. Here's a packet that looks like a ring, and a cheerful sort of a note from Mannering Papa, which I've taken the liberty of reading and burning. The old gentleman's not pleased with you."

"And Kitty?" I asked, dully.

"Rather more drawn than her father from what she says. By the same token you must have been letting out any number of queer reminiscences just before I met you. 'Says that a man who would have behaved to a woman as you did to Mrs. Wessington ought to kill himself out of sheer pity for his kind. She's a hot-headed little virago, your mash. 'Will have it too that you were suffering from *D.T.* when that row on the Jakko road turned up. 'Says she'll die before she ever speaks to you again."

I groaned and turned over on the other side.

"Now you've got your choice, my friend. This engagement has to be broken off; and the Mannerings don't want to be too hard on you. Was it broken through *D.T.* or epileptic fits? Sorry I can't offer you a better exchange unless you'd prefer hereditary insanity. Say the word and I'll tell 'em it's fits. All Simla knows about that scene on the Ladies' Mile. Come! I'll give you five minutes to think over it."

During those five minutes I believe that I explored thoroughly the lowest circles of the Inferno which it is permitted man to tread on earth. And at the same time I myself was watching myself faltering through the dark labyrinths of doubt, misery, and utter despair. I wondered, as Heatherlegh in his chair might have wondered, which dreadful alternative I should adopt. Presently I heard myself answering in a voice that I hardly recognized,–

"They're confoundedly particular about morality in these parts. Give 'em fits, Heatherlegh, and my love. Now let me sleep a bit longer."

Then my two selves joined, and it was only I (half crazed, devil-driven I) that tossed in my bed, tracing step by step the history of the past month.

"But I am in Simla," I kept repeating to myself. "I, Jack Pansay, am in Simla, and there are no ghosts here. It's unreasonable of that woman to pretend there are. Why couldn't Agnes have left me alone? I never did her any harm. It might just as well have been me as Agnes. Only I'd never have come back on purpose to kill *her*. Why can't I be left alone–left alone and happy?"

It was high noon when I first awoke: and the sun was low in the sky before I slept–slept as the tortured criminal sleeps on his rack, too worn to feel any further pain.

Next day I could not leave my bed. Heatherlegh told me in the morning that he had received an answer from Mr. Mannering, and that, thanks to his (Heatherlegh's) friendly offices, the story of my affliction had traveled through the length and breadth of Simla, where I was on all sides much pitied.

"And that's rather more than you deserve," he concluded, pleasantly, "though the Lord knows you've been going through a pretty severe mill. Never mind; we'll cure you yet, you perverse phenomenon."

I declined firmly to be cured. "You've been much too good to me already, old man," said I; "but I don't think I need trouble you further."

In my heart I knew that nothing Heatherlegh could do would lighten the burden that had been laid upon me.

With that knowledge came also a sense of hopeless, impotent rebellion against the unreasonableness of it all. There were scores of men no better than I whose punishments had at least been reserved for another world; and

I felt that it was bitterly, cruelly unfair that I alone should have been singled out for so hideous a fate. This mood would in time give place to another where it seemed that the 'rickshaw and I were the only realities in a world of shadows; that Kitty was a ghost; that Mannering, Heatherlegh, and all the other men and women I knew were all ghosts; and the great, gray hills themselves but vain shadows devised to torture me. From mood to mood I tossed backward and forward for seven weary days; my body growing daily stronger and stronger, until the bedroom looking-glass told me that I had returned to everyday life, and was as other men once more. Curiously enough my face showed no signs of the struggle I had gone through. It was pale indeed, but as expressionless and commonplace as ever. I had expected some permanent alteration—visible evidence of the disease that was eating me away. I found nothing.

On the 15th of May I left Heatherlegh's house at eleven o'clock in the morning; and the instinct of the bachelor drove me to the Club. There I found that every man knew my story as told by Heatherlegh, and was, in clumsy fashion, abnormally kind and attentive. Nevertheless I recognized that for the rest of my natural life I should be among but not of my fellows; and I envied very bitterly indeed the laughing coolies on the Mall below. I lunched at the Club, and at four o'clock wandered aimlessly down the Mall in the vague hope of meeting Kitty. Close to the Band-stand the black and white liveries joined me; and I heard Mrs. Wessington's old appeal at my side. I had been expecting this ever since I came out; and was only surprised at her delay. The phantom 'rickshaw and I went side by side along the Chola Simla road in silence. Close to the bazar, Kitty and a man on horseback overtook and passed us. For any sign she gave I might have been a dog in the road. She did not even pay me the compliment of quickening her pace; though the rainy afternoon had served for an excuse.

So Kitty and her companion, and I and my ghostly Light-o'-Love, crept round Jakko in couples. The road was streaming with water; the pines dripped like roof-pipes on the rocks below, and the air was full of fine, driving rain. Two or three times I found myself saying to myself almost aloud: "I'm Jack Pansay on leave at Simla—*at Simla!* Everyday, ordinary Simla. I mustn't forget that—I mustn't forget that." Then I would try to recollect some of the gossip I had heard at the Club: the price of So-and-So's horses—anything, in fact, that related to the workaday Anglo-Indian world I knew so well. I even repeated the multiplication-table rapidly to myself, to make quite sure that I was not taking leave of my senses. It gave me much comfort; and must have prevented my hearing Mrs. Wessington for a time.

Once more I wearily climbed the Convent slope and entered the level road. Here Kitty and the man started off at a canter, and I was left alone with Mrs. Wessington. "Agnes," said I, "will you put back your hood and tell me what it all means?" The hood dropped noiselessly, and I was face to face with my dead and buried mistress. She was wearing the dress in which I had last seen her alive; carried the same tiny handkerchief in her right hand; and the same cardcase in her left. (A woman eight months dead with a cardcase!) I had to pin myself down to the multiplication-table, and to set both hands on the stone parapet of the road, to assure myself that that at least was real.

"Agnes," I repeated, "for pity's sake tell me what it all means." Mrs. Wessington leaned forward, with that odd, quick turn of the head I used to know so well, and spoke.

If my story had not already so madly overleaped the bounds of all human belief I should apologize to you now. As I know that no one—no, not even Kitty, for whom it is written as some sort of justification of my conduct—will believe me, I will go on. Mrs. Wessington spoke and I walked with her from the Sanjowlie road to the turning below the Commander-in-Chief's house as I might walk by the side of any living woman's 'rickshaw, deep in conversation.

The second and most tormenting of my moods of sickness had suddenly laid hold upon me, and like the Prince in Tennyson's poem, "I seemed to move amid a world of ghosts." There had been a garden-party at the Commander-in-Chief's, and we two joined the crowd of homeward-bound folk. As I saw them then it seemed that *they* were the shadows–impalpable, fantastic shadows–that divided for Mrs. Wessington's 'rickshaw to pass through. What we said during the course of that weird interview I cannot–indeed, I dare not–tell. Heatherlegh's comment would have been a short laugh and a remark that I had been "mashing a brain-eye-and-stomach chimera." It was ghastly and yet in some indefinable way a marvelously dear experience. Could it be possible, I wondered, that I was in this life to woo a second time the woman I had killed by my own neglect and cruelty?

I met Kitty on the homeward road–a shadow among shadows.

If I were to describe all the incidents of the next fortnight in their order, my story would never come to an end; and your patience would be exhausted. Morning after morning and evening after evening the ghostly 'rickshaw and I used to wander through Simla together. Wherever I went there the four black and white liveries followed me and bore me company to and from my hotel. At the Theatre I found them amid the crowd of yelling *jhampanies;* outside the Club veranda, after a long evening of whist; at the Birthday Ball, waiting patiently for my reappearance; and in broad daylight when I went calling. Save that it cast no shadow, the 'rickshaw was in every respect as real to look upon as one of wood and iron. More than once, indeed, I have had to check myself from warning some hard-riding friend against cantering over it. More than once I have walked down the Mall deep in conversation with Mrs. Wessington to the unspeakable amazement of the passers-by.

Before I had been out and about a week I learned that the "fit" theory had been discarded in favor of insanity. However, I made no change in my mode of life. I called, rode, and dined out as freely as ever. I had a passion for the society of my kind which I had never felt before; I hungered to be among the realities of life; and at the same time I felt vaguely unhappy when I had been separated too long from my ghostly companion. It would be almost impossible to describe my varying moods from the 15th of May up to to-day.

The presence of the 'rickshaw filled me by turns with horror, blind fear, a dim sort of pleasure, and utter despair. I dared not leave Simla; and I knew that my stay there was killing me. I knew, moreover, that it was my destiny to die slowly and a little every day. My only anxiety was to get the penance over as quietly as might be. Alternately I hungered for a sight of Kitty and watched her outrageous flirtations with my successor–to speak more accurately, my successors–with amused interest. She was as much out of my life as I was out of hers. By day I wandered with Mrs. Wessington almost content. By night I implored Heaven to let me return to the world as I used to know it. Above all these varying moods lay the sensation of dull, numbing wonder that the Seen and the Unseen should mingle so strangely on this earth to hound one poor soul to its grave.

. . . .

August 27.–Heatherlegh has been indefatigable in his attendance on me; and only yesterday told me that I ought to send in an application for sick leave. An application to escape the company of a phantom! A request that the Government would graciously permit me to get rid of five ghosts and an airy 'rickshaw by going to England! Heatherlegh's proposition moved me to almost hysterical laughter. I told him that I should await the end quietly at Simla; and I am sure that the end is not far off. Believe me that I dread its advent more than any word can say; and I torture myself nightly with a thousand speculations as to the manner of my death.

Shall I die in my bed decently and as an English gentleman should die; or, in one last walk on the Mall, will my soul be wrenched from me to take its place forever and ever by the side of that ghastly phantasm? Shall I return to my old lost allegiance in the next world, or shall I meet Agnes loathing her and bound to her side through all eternity? Shall we two hover over the scene of our lives till the end of Time? As the day of my death draws nearer, the intense horror that all living flesh feels toward escaped spirits from beyond the grave grows more and more powerful. It is an awful thing to go down quick among the dead with scarcely one-half of your life completed. It is a thousand times more awful to wait as I do in your midst, for I know not what unimaginable terror. Pity me, at least on the score of my "delusion," for I know you will never believe what I have written here. Yet as surely as ever a man was done to death by the Powers of Darkness I am that man.

In justice, too, pity her. For as surely as ever woman was killed by man, I killed Mrs. Wessington. And the last portion of my punishment is even now upon me.

The Madness of Private Ortheris

Oh! Where would I be when my froat was dry?
Oh! Where would I be when the bullets fly?
Oh! Where would I be when I come to die?
Why,
Somewheres anigh my chum.
If 'e's liquor 'e'll give me some,
If I'm dyin' 'e'll 'old my 'ead,
An' 'e'll write 'em 'Ome when I'm dead.–
Gawd send us a trusty chum!
–*Barrack Room Ballad.*

MY FRIENDS MULVANEY and Ortheris had gone on a shooting-expedition for one day. Learoyd was still in hospital, recovering from fever picked up in Burma. They sent me an invitation to join them, and were genuinely pained when I brought beer–almost enough beer to satisfy two Privates of the Line . . . and Me.

" 'Twasn't for that we bid you welkim, sorr," said Mulvaney, sulkily. " 'Twas for the pleasure av your comp'ny."

Ortheris came to the rescue with–"Well, 'e won't be none the worse for bringin' liquor with 'im. We ain't a file o' Dooks. We're bloomin' Tommies, ye cantankris Hirishman; an' 'eres your very good 'ealth!"

We shot all the forenoon, and killed two pariah-dogs, four green parrots, sitting, one kite by the burning-ghaut, one snake flying, one mud-turtle, and eight crows. Game was plentiful. Then we sat down to tiffin–"bull-mate an' bran-bread," Mulvaney called it–by the side of the river, and took pot shots at the crocodiles in the intervals of cutting up the food with our only pocket-knife. Then we drank up all the beer, and threw the bottles into the water and fired at them. After that, we eased belts and stretched ourselves on the warm sand and smoked. We were too lazy to continue shooting.

Ortheris heaved a big sigh, as he lay on his stomach with his head between his fists. Then he swore quietly into the blue sky.

"Fwhat's that for?" said Mulvaney. "Have ye not drunk enough?"

"Tott'nim Court Road, an' a gal I fancied there. Wot's the good of sodgerin'?"

"Orth'ris, me son," said Mulvaney, hastily, " 'tis more than likely you've got throuble in your inside wid the beer. I feel that way mesilf whin my liver gets rusty."

Ortheris went on slowly, not heeding the interruption–

"I'm a Tommy–a bloomin', eight-anna, dog-stealin' Tommy, with a number instead of a decent name. Wot's the good o' me? If I 'ad a stayed at 'Ome, I might a married that gal and a kep' a little shorp in the 'Ammersmith 'Igh.–'S. Orth'ris, Prac-ti-cal Taxi-der-mist.' With a stuff fox, like they 'as in the Haylesbury Dairies, in the winder, an' a little case of blue and yaller glass-heyes, an' a little wife to call 'shorp!' 'shorp!' when the door-bell rung. As it *his,* I'm on'y a Tommy–a Bloomin', Gawd-forsaken, Beer-swillin' Tommy. 'Rest on your harms–*'versed,* Stan' at–*hease; 'Shun.* 'Verse–*harms.* Right an' lef'–*tarrn.* Slow–*march.* 'Alt–*front.* Rest on your harms–*'versed.* With blank-cartridge–*load.'* An' that's the end o' me." He was quoting fragments from Funeral Parties' Orders.

"Stop ut!" shouted Mulvaney. "Whin you've fired into nothin' as often as me, over a better man than yoursilf, you will not make a mock av thim orders. 'Tis worse than whistlin' the *Dead March* in barricks. An' you full as a tick, an' the sun cool, an' all an' all! I take shame for you. You're no better than a Pagin–you an' your firin'-parties an' your glass-eyes. Won't *you* stop ut, sorr?"

What could I do? Could I tell Ortheris anything that he did not know of the pleasures of his life? I was not a Chaplain nor a Subaltern, and Ortheris had a right to speak as he thought fit.

"Let him run, Mulvaney," I said. "It's the beer."

"No! 'Tisn't the beer," said Mulvaney. "I know fwhat's comin'. He's tuk this way now an' agin, an' it's bad–it's bad–for I'm fond av the bhoy."

Indeed, Mulvaney seemed needlessly anxious; but I knew that he looked after Ortheris in a fatherly way.

"Let me talk, let me talk," said Ortheris, dreamily. "D'you stop your parrit screamin' of a 'ot day, when the cage is a-cookin' 'is pore little pink toes orf, Mulvaney?"

"Pink toes! D'ye mane to say you've pink toes undher your bullswools, ye blandanderin',"–Mulvaney gathered himself together for a terrific denunciation–"school-misthress! Pink toes! How much Bass wid the label did that ravin' child dhrink?"

" 'Tain't Bass," said Ortheris. "It's a bitterer beer nor that. It's 'omesickn!"

"Hark to him! An' he goin' Home in the *Sherapis* in the inside av four months!"

"I don't care. It's all one to me. 'Ow d'you know I ain't 'fraid o' dyin' 'fore I gets my discharge paipers?" He recommenced, in a sing-song voice, the Orders.

I had never seen this side of Ortheris' character before, but evidently Mulvaney had, and attached serious importance to it. While Ortheris babbled, with his head on his arms, Mulvaney whispered to me–

"He's always tuk this way whin he's been checked overmuch by the childher they make Sarjints nowadays. That an' havin' nothin' to do. I can't make ut out anyways."

"Well, what does it matter? Let him talk himself through."

Ortheris began singing a parody of "The Ramrod Corps," full of cheerful allusions to battle, murder, and sudden death. He looked out across the river as he sang; and his face was quite strange to me. Mulvaney caught me by the elbow to ensure attention.

"Matther? It matthers everything! 'Tis some sort av fit that's on him. I've seen ut. 'Twill hould him all this night, an' in the middle av it he'll get out av his cot an' go rakin' in the rack for his 'coutremints. Thin he'll come over to me an' say, 'I'm goin' to Bombay. Answer for me in the mornin'.' Thin me an' him will fight as we've done before–him to go an' me to hould him–an' so we'll both come on the books for disturbin' in barricks. I've belted him, an' I've bruk his head, an' I've talked to him, but 'tis no manner av use whin the fit's on him. He's as good a bhoy as ever stepped whin his mind's clear. I know fwhat's comin', though, this night in barricks. Lord send he doesn't loose on me whin I rise to knock him down. 'Tis that that's in my mind day an' night."

This put the case in a much less pleasant light, and fully accounted for Mulvaney's anxiety. He seemed to be trying to coax Ortheris out of the fit; for he shouted down the bank where the boy was lying–

"Listen now, you wid the 'pore pink toes' an' the glass-eyes! Did you shwim the Irriwaddy at night, behin' me, as a bhoy shud; or were you hidin' under a bed, as you was at Ahmid Kheyl?"

This was at once a gross insult and a direct lie, and Mulvaney meant it to bring on a fight. But Ortheris seemed shut up in some sort of trance. He answered slowly, without a sign of irritation, in the same cadenced voice as he had used for his firing-party orders–

"*Hi* swum the Irriwaddy in the night, as you know, for to take the town of Lungtungpen, nakid an' without fear. *Hand* where I was at Ahmed Kheyl you know, and four bloomin' Pathans know too. But that was summat to do, an' I didn't think o' dyin'. Now I'm sick to go 'Ome–go 'Ome–go 'Ome! No, I ain't mammy-sick, because my uncle brung me up, but I'm sick for London again; sick for the sounds of 'er, an' the sights of 'er, and the stinks of 'er; orange peel and hasphalte an' gas comin' in over Vaux'all Bridge. Sick for the rail goin' down to Box'ill, with your gal on your knee an' a new clay pipe in your face. That, an' the Stran' lights where you knows ev'ry one, an' the Copper that takes you up is a old friend that tuk you up before, when you was a little, smitchy boy lying loose 'tween the Temple an' the Dark Harches. No bloomin' guard-mountin', no bloomin' rotten-stone, nor khaki, an' yourself your own master with a gal to take an' see the Humaners practicin' a-hookin' dead corpses out of the Serpentine o' Sundays. An' I lef' all that for to serve the Widder beyond the seas, where there ain't no women and there ain't no liquor worth 'avin', and there ain't nothin' to see, nor do, nor say, nor feel, nor think. Lord love you, Stanley Orth'ris, but you're a bigger bloomin' fool than the rest o' the reg'ment and Mulvaney wired together! There's the Widder sittin' at 'Ome with a gold crownd on 'er 'ead; and 'ere am Hi, Stanley Orth'ris, the Widder's property, a rottin' FOOL!"

His voice rose at the end of the sentence, and he wound up with a six-shot Anglo-Vernacular oath. Mulvaney said nothing, but looked at me as if he expected that I could bring peace to poor Ortheris' troubled brain.

I remembered once at Rawal Pindi having seen a man, nearly mad with drink, sobered by being made a fool of. Some regiments may know what I mean. I hoped that we might slake off Ortheris in the same way, though he was perfectly sober. So I said–

"What's the use of grousing there, and speaking against The Widow?"

"I didn't!" said Ortheris. "S'elp me, Gawd, I never said a word agin 'er, an' I wouldn't–not if I was to desert this minute!"

Here was my opening. "Well, you meant to, anyhow. What's the use of cracking-on for nothing? Would you slip it now if you got the chance?"

"On'y try me!" said Ortheris, jumping to his feet as if he had been stung.

Mulvaney jumped too. "Fwhat are you going to do?" said he.

"Help Ortheris down to Bombay or Karachi, whichever he likes. You can report that he separated from you before tiffin, and left his gun on the bank here!"

"I'm to report that–am I?" said Mulvaney, slowly. "Very well. If Orth'ris manes to desert now, and will desert now, an' you, sorr, who have been a frind to me an' to him, will help him to ut, I, Terence Mulvaney, on my oath which I've never bruk yet, will report as you say. But"—here he stepped up to Ortheris, and shook the stock of the fowling-piece in his face—"your fists help you, Stanley Orth'ris, if ever I come across you agin!"

"I don't care!" said Ortheris. "I'm sick o' this dorg's life. Give me a chanst. Don't play with me. Le' me go!"

"Strip," said I, "and change with me, and then I'll tell you what to do."

I hoped that the absurdity of this would check Ortheris; but he had kicked off his ammunition-boots and got rid of his tunic almost before I had loosed my shirt-collar. Mulvaney gripped me by the arm—

"The fit's on him: the fit's workin' on him still! By my Honor and Sowl, we shall be accessiry to a desartion yet. Only, twenty-eight days, as you say, sorr, or fifty-six, but think o' the shame—the black shame to him an' me!" I had never seen Mulvaney so excited.

But Ortheris was quite calm, and, as soon as he had exchanged clothes with me, and I stood up a Private of the Line, he said shortly, "Now! Come on. What nex'? D'ye mean fair. What must I do to get out o' this 'ere a-Hell?"

I told him that, if he would wait for two or three hours near the river, I would ride into the Station and come back with one hundred rupees. He would, with that money in his pocket, walk to the nearest side-station on the line, about five miles away, and would there take a first-class ticket for Karachi. Knowing that he had no money on him when he went out shooting, his regiment would not immediately wire to the seaports, but would hunt for him in the native villages near the river. Further, no one would think of seeking a deserter in a first-class carriage. At Karachi, he was to buy white clothes and ship, if he could, on a cargo-steamer.

Here he broke in. If I helped him to Karachi, he would arrange all the rest. Then I ordered him to wait where he was until it was dark enough for me to ride into the station without my dress being noticed. Now God in His wisdom has made the heart of the British Soldier, who is very often an unlicked ruffian, as soft as the heart of a little child, in order that he may believe in and follow his officers into tight and nasty places. He does not so readily come to believe in a "civilian," but, when he does, he believes implicitly and like a dog. I had had the honor of the friendship of Private Ortheris, at intervals, for more than three years, and we had dealt with each other as man by man. Consequently, he considered that all my words were true, and not spoken lightly.

Mulvaney and I left him in the high grass near the river-bank, and went away, still keeping to the high grass, toward my horse. The shirt scratched me horribly.

We waited nearly two hours for the dusk to fall and allow me to ride off. We spoke of Ortheris in whispers, and strained our ears to catch any sound from the spot where we had left him. But we heard nothing except the wind in the plume-grass.

"I've bruk his head," said Mulvaney, earnestly, "time an' agin. I've nearly kilt him wid the belt, an' *yet* I can't knock thim fits out av his soft head. No! An' he's not soft, for he's reasonable an' likely by natur'. Fwhat is ut? Is ut his breedin' which is nothin', or his edukashin which he niver got? You that think ye know things, answer me that."

But I found no answer. I was wondering how long Ortheris, in the bank of the river, would hold out, and whether I should be forced to help him to desert, as I had given my word.

Just as the dusk shut down and, with a very heavy heart, I was beginning to saddle up my horse, we heard wild shouts from the river.

The devils had departed from Private Stanley Ortheris, No. 22639, B

Company. The loneliness, the dusk, and the waiting had driven them out as I had hoped. We set off at the double and found him plunging about wildly through the grass, with his coat off–my coat off, I mean. He was calling for us like a madman.

When we reached him he was dripping with perspiration, and trembling like a startled horse. We had great difficulty in soothing him. He complained that he was in civilian kit, and wanted to tear my clothes off his body. I ordered him to strip, and we made a second exchange as quickly as possible. The rasp of his own "grayback" shirt and the squeak of his boots seemed to bring him to himself. He put his hands before his eyes and said–

"Wot was it? I ain't mad, I ain't sunstrook, an' I've bin an' gone an' said, an' bin an' gone an' done. . . . *Wot* 'ave I bin an' done!"

"Fwhat have you done?" said Mulvaney. "You've dishgraced yourself–though that's no matter. You've dishgraced B Comp'ny, an' worst av all, you've dishgraced *Me!* Me that taught you how for to walk abroad like a man–whin you was a dhirty little, fish-backed little, whimperin' little recruity. As you are now, Stanley Orth'ris!"

Ortheris said nothing for a while. Then he unslung his belt, heavy with the badges of half a dozen regiments that his own had lain with, and handed it over to Mulvaney.

"I'm too little for to mill you, Mulvaney," said he, "an' you've strook me before; but you can take an' cut me in two with this 'ere if you like."

Mulvaney turned to me.

"Lave me to talk to him, sorr," said Mulvaney.

I left, and on my way home thought a good deal over Ortheris in particular, and my friend Private Thomas Atkins whom I love, in general.

But I could not come to any conclusion of any kind whatever.

The Story of Muhammad Din

Who is the happy man? He that sees in his own house at home, little children crowned with dust, leaping and falling and crying.

–*Munichandra,* translated by Professor Peterson.

THE POLO-BALL was an old one, scarred, chipped, and dinted. It stood on the mantelpiece among the pipe-stems which Imam Din, *khitmatgar,* was cleaning for me.

"Does the Heaven-born want this ball?" said Imam Din, deferentially.

The Heaven-born set no particular store by it; but of what use was a polo-ball to a *khitmatgar?*

"By your Honor's favor, I have a little son. He has seen this ball, and desires it to play with. I do not want it for myself."

No one would for an instant accuse portly old Imam Din of wanting to play with polo-balls. He carried out the battered thing into the veranda; and there followed a hurricane of joyful squeaks, a patter of small feet, and the *thud-thud-thud* of the ball rolling along the ground. Evidently the little son had been waiting outside the door to secure his treasure. But how had he managed to see that polo-ball?

Next day, coming back from office half an hour earlier than usual, I was aware of a small figure in the dining-room—a tiny, plump figure in a ridiculously inadequate shirt which came, perhaps, half-way down the tubby stomach. It wandered round the room, thumb in mouth, crooning to itself as it took stock of the pictures. Undoubtedly this was the "little son."

He had no business in my room, of course; but was so deeply absorbed in his discoveries that he never noticed me in the doorway. I stepped into the room and startled him nearly into a fit. He sat down on the ground with a gasp. His eyes opened, and his mouth followed suit. I knew what was coming, and fled, followed by a long, dry howl which reached the servants' quarters far more quickly than any command of mine had ever done. In ten seconds Imam Din was in the dining-room. Then despairing sobs arose, and I returned to find Imam Din admonishing the small sinner who was using most of his shirt as a handkerchief.

"This boy," said Imam Din, judicially, "is a *budmash*—a big *budmash.* He will, without doubt, go to the *jail-khana* for his behavior." Renewed yells from the penitent, and an elaborate apology to myself from Imam Din.

"Tell the baby," said I, "that the *Sahib* is not angry, and take him away." Imam Din conveyed my forgiveness to the offender, who had now gathered all his shirt round his neck, stringwise, and the yell subsided into a sob. The two set off for the door. "His name," said Imam Din, as though the name were part of the crime, "is Muhammad Din, and he is a *budmash.*" Freed from present danger, Muhammad Din turned round in his father's arms, and said gravely, "It is true that my name is Muhammad Din, *Tahib,* but I am not a *budmash.* I am a *man!*"

From that day dated my acquaintance with Muhammad Din. Never again did he come into my dining-room, but on the neutral ground of the garden, we greeted each other with much state, though our conversation was confined to *"Talaam, Tahib"* from his side, and *"Salaam, Muhammad Din"* from mine. Daily on my return from office, the little white shirt, and the fat little body used to rise from the shade of the creeper-covered trellis where they had been hid; and daily I checked my horse here, that my salutation might not be slurred over or given unseemly.

Muhammad Din never had any companions. He used to trot about the compound, in and out of the castor-oil bushes, on mysterious errands of his own. One day I stumbled upon some of his handiwork far down the grounds. He had half buried the polo-ball in dust, and stuck six shriveled old marigold flowers in a circle round it. Outside that circle again was a rude square, traced out in bits of red brick alternating with fragments of broken china; the whole bounded by a little bank of dust. The water-man from the well-curb put in a plea for the small architect, saying that it was only the play of a baby and did not much disfigure my garden.

Heaven knows that I had no intention of touching the child's work then or later; but, that evening, a stroll through the garden brought me unawares full on it; so that I trampled, before I knew, marigold-heads, dust-bank, and fragments of broken soap-dish into confusion past all hope of mending. Next morning, I came upon Muhammad Din crying softly to himself over the ruin I had wrought. Some one had cruelly told him that the *Sahib* was very angry with him for spoiling the garden, and had scattered his rubbish, using bad language the while. Muhammad Din labored for an hour at effacing every trace of the dust-bank and pottery fragments, and it was with a tearful and apologetic face that he said *"Talaam, Tahib,"* when I came home from office. A hasty inquiry resulted in Imam Din informing Muhammad Din that, by my singular favor, he was permitted to disport himself as he pleased. Whereat the child took heart and fell to tracing the ground-plan of an edifice which was to eclipse the marigold-polo-ball creation.

For some months, the chubby little eccentricity revolved in his humble orbit among the castor-oil bushes and in the dust; always fashioning magnificent palaces from stale flowers thrown away by the bearer, smooth water-worn pebbles, bits of broken glass, and feathers pulled, I fancy, from my fowls—always alone, and always crooning to himself.

A gaily-spotted sea-shell was dropped one day close to the last of his little buildings; and I looked that Muhammad Din should build something more than ordinarily splendid on the strength of it. Nor was I disappointed. He meditated for the better part of an hour, and his crooning rose to a jubilant song. Then he began tracing in the dust. It would certainly be a wondrous palace, this one, for it was two yards long and a yard broad in ground-plan. But the palace was never completed.

Next day there was no Muhammad Din at the head of the carriage-drive, and no *"Talaam, Tahib"* to welcome my return. I had grown accustomed to the greeting, and its omission troubled me. Next day Imam Din told me that the child was suffering slightly from fever and needed quinine. He got the medicine, and an English Doctor.

"They have no stamina, these brats," said the Doctor, as he left Imam Din's quarters.

A week later, though I would have given much to have avoided it, I met on the road to the Mussulman burying-ground Imam Din, accompanied by one other friend, carrying in his arms, wrapped in a white cloth all that was left of little Muhammad Din.

The Big Drunk Draf'

We're goin' 'ome, we're goin' 'ome—
  Our ship is *at* the shore,
An' you mus' pack your 'aversack,
  For we won't come back no more.
Ho, don't you grieve for me,
  My lovely Mary Ann,
For I'll marry you yet on a fourp'ny bit,
  As a time-expired ma-a-an!
      —*Barrack Room Ballad.*

AN AWFUL THING has happened! My friend, Private Mulvaney, who went home in the *Serapis,* time-expired, not very long ago, has come back to India as a civilian! It was all Dinah Shadd's fault. She could not stand the poky little lodgings, and she missed her servant Abdullah more than words could tell. The fact was that the Mulvaneys had been out here too long, and had lost touch of England.

Mulvaney knew a contractor on one of the new Central India lines, and wrote to him for some sort of work. The contractor said that if Mulvaney could pay the passage he would give him command of a gang of coolies for old sake's sake. The pay was eighty-five rupees a month, and Dinah Shadd said that if Terence did not accept she would make his life a "basted purgathory." Therefore the Mulvaneys came out as "civilians," which was a great and terrible fall; though Mulvaney tried to disguise it, by saying that he was 'Ker'nel on the railway line, an' a consequinshal man."

He wrote me an invitation, on a tool-indent form, to visit him; bungalow at the side of the line. Dinah Shadd had planted peas about and about, and nature had spread all manner of green stuff around the place. There was no change in Mulvaney except the change of clothing, which was deplorable, but could not be helped. He was standing upon his trolly, haranguing a gang-man, and his shoulders were as well drilled, and his big, thick chin was as clean-shaven as ever.

"I'm a civilian now," said Mulvaney. "Cud you tell that I was iver a martial man? Don't answer, sorr, av you're strainin' betune a complimint an' a lie. There's no houldin' Dinah Shadd now she's got a house av her own. Go inside, an' dhrink tay out av chiny in the drrrrawin'-room, an' thin we'll dhrink like Christians undher the tree here. Scutt, ye naygur-folk! There's a Sahib come to call on me, an' that's more than he'll iver do for you onless you run! Get out, an' go on pilin' up the earth, quick, till sundown."

When we three were comfortably settled under the big *sisham* in front of the bungalow, and the first rush of questions and answers about Privates Ortheris and Learoyd and old times and places had died away, Mulvany said, reflectively–"Glory be there's no p'rade tomorrow, an' no bun-headed Corp'ril-bhoy to give you his lip. An' yit I don't know. 'Tis harrd to be something ye niver were an' niver meant to be, an' all the ould days shut up along wid your papers. Eyah! I'm growin' rusty, an' 'tis the will av God that a man mustn't serve his Quane for time an' all."

He helped himself to a fresh peg, and sighed furiously.

"Let your beard grow, Mulvaney," said I, "and then you won't be troubled with those notions. You'll be a real civilian."

Dinah Shadd had told me in the drawing-room of her desire to coax Mulvaney into letting his beard grow. " 'Twas so civilian-like," said poor Dinah, who hated her husband's hankering for his old life.

"Dinah Shadd, you're a dishgrace to an honust, clane-scraped man!" said Mulvaney, without replying to me. "Grow a beard on your own chin, darlint, and lave my razors alone. They're all that stand betune me and disris-pect-ability. Av I didn't shave, I wud be torminted wid an outrajis thurrst; for there's nothin' so dhryin' to the throat as a big billy-goat beard waggin' undher the chin. Ye wudn't have me dhrink *always,* Dinah Shadd? By the same token, you're kapin' me crool dhry now. Let me look at that whiskey."

The whiskey was lent and returned, but Dinah Shadd, who had been just as eager as her husband in asking after old friends, rent me with–

"I take shame for you, sorr, coming down here–though the Saints know you're as welkim as the daylight whin you *do* come–an' upsettin' Terence's head wid your nonsense about–about fwhat's much better forgotten. He bein' a civilian now, an' you niver was aught else. Can you not let the Arrmy rest? 'Tis not good for Terence."

I took refuge by Mulvaney, for Dinah Shadd has a temper of her own.

"Let be–let be," said Mulvaney. " 'Tis only wanst in a way I can talk about the ould days." Then to me:–"Ye say Dhrumshticks is well, an' his lady tu? I niver knew how I liked the grey garron till I was shut av him an' Asia."–"Dhrumshticks" was the nickname of the Colonel commanding Mulvaney's old regiment.–"Will you be seein' him again? You will. Thin tell him"–Mulvaney's eyes began to twinkle–"tell him wid Privit"–

"*Mister,* Terence," interrupted Dinah Shadd.

"Now the Divil an' all his angils an' the Firmament av Hiven fly away wid the 'Mister,' an' the sin av making me swear be on your confession, Dinah Shadd! *Privit,* I tell ye. Wid *Privit* Mulvaney's best obedience, that but for me the last time-expired wud be still pullin' hair on their way to the sea."

He threw himself back in the chair, chuckled, and was silent.

"Mrs. Mulvaney," I said, "please take up the whiskey, and don't let him have it until he has told the story."

Dinah Shadd dexterously whipped the bottle away, saying at the same time, " 'Tis nothing to be proud av," and thus captured by the enemy, Mulvaney spake:–

" 'Twas on Chuseday week. I was behaderin' round wid the gangs on the 'bankmint–I've taught the hoppers how to kape step an' stop screechin'– whin a head-gangman comes up to me, wid about two inches av shirt-tail hanging round his neck an' a disthressful light in his oi. 'Sahib,' sez he, 'there's a reg'ment an' a half av soldiers up at the junction, knockin' red cinders out av ivrything an' ivrybody! They thried to hang me in my cloth,' he sez, 'an' there will be murder an' ruin an' rape in the place before nightfall! They say they're comin' down here to wake us up. What will we do wid our women-folk?"

" 'Fetch my throlly!' sez I; 'my heart's sick in my ribs for a wink at anything wid the Quane's uniform on ut. Fetch my throlly, an' six av the jildiest men, and run me up in shtyle.' "

"He tuk his best coat," said Dinah Shadd, reproachfully.

" 'Twas to do honor to the Widdy. I cud ha' done no less, Dinah Shadd. You and your digresshins interfere wid the coorse av the narrative. Have you iver considhered fwhat I wud look like wid me *head* shaved as well as my chin? You bear that in your mind, Dinah darlin'.

"I was throllied up six miles, all to get a shquint at that draf'. I *knew* 'twas a spring draf' goin' home, for there's no rig'mint hereabouts, more's the pity."

"Praise the Virgin!" murmured Dinah Shadd. But Mulvaney did not hear.

"Whin I was about three-quarters av a mile off the rest-camp, powtherin' along fit to burrst, I heard the noise av the men an', on my sowl, sorr, I cud catch the voice av Peg Barney bellowin' like a bison wid the belly-ache. You remimber Peg Barney that was in D Comp'ny–a red, hairy scraun, wid a scar on his jaw? Peg Barney that cleared out the Blue Lights' Jubilee meeting wid the cook-room mop last year?

"Thin I knew ut was a draf' of the ould rig'mint, an' I was conshumed wid sorrow for the bhoy that was in charge. We was harrd scrapin's at any time. Did I iver tell you how Horker Kelley went into clink nakid as Phoebus Apollonius, wid the shirts av the Corp'ril an' file undher his arrum? An' *he* was a moild man! But I'm digreshin'. 'Tis a shame both to the rig'mints and the Arrmy sendin' down little orf'cer bhoys wid a draf' av strong men mad wid liquor an' the chanst av gettin' shut av India, an' *niver a punishment that's fit to be given right down an' away from cantonmints to the dock!* 'Tis this nonsince. Whin I am servin' my time, I'm undher the Articles av War, an' can be whipped on the peg for *thim.* But whin I've *served* my time, I'm a Reserve man, an' the Articles av War haven't any hould on me. An orf'cer *can't* do anthin' to a time-expired savin' confinin' him to barricks. 'Tis a wise rig'lation bekaze a time-expired does *not* have any barricks; bein' on the move all the time. 'Tis a Solomon av a rig'lation, is that. I wud like to be inthroduced to the man that made ut. 'Tis easier to get colts from a Kibbereen horse-fair into Galway than to take a bad draf' over ten miles av country. Consiquintly that rig'lation–for fear that the men wud be hurt by the little orf'cer bhoy. No matther. The nearer my throlly came to the rest-camp, the woilder was the shine, an' the louder was the voice av Peg Barney. ' 'Tis good I am here,' thinks I to myself, 'for Peg alone is employmint for two or three.' He bein', I well knew, as copped as a dhrover.

"Faith, that rest-camp was a sight! The tent-ropes was all skew-nosed, an' the pegs looked as dhrunk as the men–fifty av thim–the scourin's, an' rinsin's, an' Divil's lavin's av the Ould Rig'mint. I tell you, sorr, they were dhrunker than any men you've ever seen in your mortial life. *How* does a draf' get dhrunk? How does a frog get fat? They suk ut in through their shkins.

"There was Peg Barney sittin' on the groun' in his shirt–wan shoe off an' wan shoe on—whackin' a tent-peg over the head wid his boot, an' singin' fit to wake the dead. 'Twas no clane song that he sung, though. 'Twas the Divil's Mass."

"What's that?" I asked.

"Whin a bad egg is shut av the Army, he sings the Divil's Mass for a good riddance; an' that manes swearin' at ivrything from the Commandher-in-Chief down to the Room Corp'ril, such as you niver in your days heard. Some men can swear so as to make green turf crack! Have you iver heard the Curse in an Orange Lodge? The Divil's Mass is ten times worse, an' Peg Barney was singin' ut, whackin' the tent-peg on the head wid his boot for each man that he cursed. A powerful big voice had Peg Barney, an' a hard swearer he was whin sober. I stood forninst him, an' 'twas not me oi alone that cud tell Peg was dhrunk as a coot.

" 'Good mornin', Peg,' I sez, whin he dhrew breath afther cursin' the Adj'tint Gen'ral; 'I've put on my best coat to see you, Peg Barney,' sez I.

" 'Thin take ut off again,' sez Peg Barney, latherin' away wid the boot; 'take ut off an' dance, ye lousy civilian!'

"Wid that he begins cursin' ould Dhrumshticks, being so full he clean disremimbers the Brigade-Major an' the Judge Advokit Gen'ral.

" 'Do you not know me, Peg?' sez I, though me blood was hot in me wid being called a civilian."

"An' him a decent married man!" wailed Dinah Shadd.

" 'I do not,' sez Peg, 'but dhrunk or sober I'll tear the hide off your back wid a shovel whin I've stopped singin'.'

" 'Say you so, Peg Barney?' sez I. ' 'Tis clear as mud you've forgotten me. I'll assist your autobiography.' Wid that I stretched Peg Barney, boot an' all, an' wint into the camp. An awful sight ut was!

" 'Where's the orf'cer in charge av the detachment?' sez I to Scrub Greene—the manest little worm that ever walked.

" 'There's no orf'cer, ye ould cook,' sez Scrub; 'we're a bloomin' Republic.'

" 'Are you that?' sez I; 'thin I'm O'Connell the Dictator, an' by this you will larn to keep a civil tongue in your rag-box.'

"Wid that I stretched Scrub Greene an' wint to the orf'cer's tent. 'Twas a new little bhoy—not wan I'd iver seen before. He was sittin' in his tent, purtendin' not to 'ave ear av the racket.

"I saluted—but for the life av me I mint to shake hands whin I went in. 'Twas the sword hangin' on the tent-pole changed my will.

" 'Can't I help, sorr?' sez I; ' 'tis a strong man's job they've given you, an' you'll be wantin' help by sundown.' He was a bhoy wid bowils, that child, an' a rale gintleman.

" 'Sit down,' sez he.

" 'Not before my orf'cer,' sez I; an' I tould him fwhat my service was.

" 'I've heard uv you,' sez he. 'You tuk the town av Lungtungpen nakid.'

" 'Faith,' thinks I, 'that's Honor an' Glory;' for 'twas Lift'nint Brazenose did that job. 'I'm wid ye, sorr,' sez I, 'if I'm av use. They shud niver ha' sent you down wid the draf'. Savin' your presince, sorr,' I sez, ' 'tis only Lift'nint Hackerston in the Ould Reg'mint can manage a Home draf'.'

" 'I've niver had charge of men like this before,' sez he, playin' wid the pens on the table; 'an' I see by the Rig'lations'—

" 'Shut your oi to the Rig'lations, sorr,' I sez, 'till the throoper's into blue wather. By the Rig'lations you've got to tuck thim up for the night, or they'll be runnin' foul av my coolies an' makin' a shiverarium half through the country. Can you trust your noncoms, sorr?'

" 'Yes,' sez he.

" 'Good,' sez I; 'there'll be throuble before the night. Are you marchin', sorr?'

" 'To the next station,' sez he.

" 'Better still,' sez I; 'there'll be big throuble.'

" 'Can't be too hard on a Home draf',' sez he; 'the great thing is to get thim in-ship.'

" 'Faith you've larnt the half av your lesson, sorr,' sez I, 'but av you shtick to the Rig'lations you'll niver get thim in-ship at all, at all. Or there won't be a rag av kit betune thim whin you do.'

" 'Twas a dear little orf'cer bhoy, an' by way av kapin' his heart up, I tould him fwhat I saw wanst in a draf' in Egypt."

"What was that, Mulvaney?" said I.

"Sivin an' fifty men sittin' on the bank av a canal, laughin' at a poor little squidgereen av an orf'cer that they'd made wade into the slush an' pitch the things out av the boats for their Lord High Mightinesses. That made me orf'cer bhoy woild wid indignation.

" 'Soft an' aisy, sorr,' sez I; 'you've niver had your draf' in hand since you left cantonmints. Wait till the night, an' your work will be ready to you. Wid your permission, sorr, I will investigate the camp, an' talk to my ould friends. 'Tis no manner av use thryin' to shtop the divilmint *now.*'

"Wid that I wint out into the camp an' inthrojuced mysilf to ivry man sober enough to remimber me. I was some wan in the ould days, an' the bhoys was glad to see me—all excipt Peg Barney wid a oi like a tomata five days in the bazar, an' a nose to match. They come round me an' shuk me, an' I tould thim I was in privit employ wid an income av me own, an' a drrrawin'-room fit to bate the Quane's; an' wid me lies an' me shtories an' nonsinse gin'rally, I kept 'em quiet in wan way an' another, knockin' roun' the camp. 'Twas *bad* even thin whin I was the Angil av Peace.

"I talked to me ould non-coms—*they* was sober—an' betune me an' thim we wore the draf' over into their tents at the proper time. The little orf'cer bhoy he comes round, decint an' civil-spoken as might be.

" 'Rough quarters, men,' sez he, 'but you can't look to be as comfortable as in barricks. We must make the best av things. I've shut my eyes to a dale av dog's tricks to-day, an' now there must be no more av ut.'

" 'No more we will. Come an' have a dhrink, me son,' sez Peg Barney, staggerin' where he stud. Me little orf'cer bhoy kep' his timper.

" 'You're a sulky swine, you are,' sez Peg Barney, an' at that the men in the tent began to laugh.

"I tould you me orf'cer bhoy had bowils. He cut Peg Barney as near as might be on the oi that I'd squshed whin we first met. Peg wint spinnin' acrost the tent.

" 'Peg him out, sorr,' sez I, in a whisper.

" 'Peg him out!' sez me orf'cer bhoy, up loud, just as if 'twas battalion-p'rade an' he pickin' his wurds from the Sargint.

"The non-coms tuk Peg Barney—a howlin' handful he was—an' in three minuts he was pegged out—chin down, tight-dhrawn—on his stummick, a tent-peg to each arm an' leg, swearin' fit to turn a naygur white.

"I tuk a peg an' jammed ut into his ugly jaw.—'Bite on that, Peg Barney,' I sez; 'the night is settin' frosty, an' you'll be wantin' divarsion before the mornin'. But for the Rig'lations you'd be bitin' on a bullet now at the thriangles, Peg Barney,' sez I.

"All the draf' was out av their tents watchin' Barney bein' pegged.

" ' 'Tis agin the Rig'lations! He strook him!' screeches out Scrub Greene, who was always a lawyer; an' some of the men tuk up the shoutin'.

" 'Peg out that man!' sez my orf'cer bhoy, niver losin' his timper; an' the non-coms wint in and pegged out Scrub Greene by the side av Peg Barney.

" 'I cud see that the draf' was comin' roun'. The men stud not knowin' fwhat to do.

" 'Get to your tents!' sez me orf'cer bhoy. 'Sargint, put a sintry over these two men.'

"The men wint back into the tents like jackals, an' the rest av the night there was no noise at all excipt the stip av the sintry over the two, an' Scrub Greene blubberin' like a child. 'Twas a chilly night, an' faith, ut sobered Peg Barney.

"Just before Revelly, my orf'cer bhoy comes out an' sez: 'Loose those men an' send thim to their tents!' Scrub Greene wint away widout a word, but Peg Barney, stiff wid the cowld, stud like a sheep, thryin' to make his orf'cer undershtand he was sorry for playin' the goat.

"There was no tucker in the draf' whin ut fell in for the march, an' divil a wurrd about 'illegality' cud I hear.

"I wint to the ould Color Sargint and I sez:—'Let me die in glory,' sez I. 'I've seen a man this day!'

" 'A man he is,' sez ould Hother; 'the draf's as sick as a herrin'. They'll all go down to the sea like lambs. That bhoy has the bowils av a cantonmint av Gin'rals.'

" 'Amin,' sez I, 'an' good luck go wid him, wheriver he be, by land or by sea. Let me know how the draf' gets clear.'

"An' do you know how they *did?* That bhoy, so I was tould by letter from Bombay, bullydamned 'em down to the dock, till they cudn't call their sowls their own. From the time they left me oi till they was 'tween decks, not wan av thim was more than dacintly dhrunk. An', by the Holy Articles av War, whin they wint abroad they cheered him till they cudn't spake, an' *that,* mark you, has not come about wid a draf' in the mim'ry av livin' man! You look to that little orf'cer bhoy. He has bowils. 'Tis not ivry child that wud chuck the Rig'lations to Flanders an' stretch Peg Barney on a wink from a brokin' an' dilapidated ould carkiss like mesilf. I'd be proud to serve"—

"Terence, you're a civilian," said Dinah Shadd, warningly.

"So I am—so I am. Is ut likely I wud forget ut? But he was a gran' bhoy all the same, an' I'm only a mudtipper wid a hod on my shoulthers. The whiskey's in the heel av your hand, sorr. Wid your good lave we'll dhrink to the Ould Rig'mint—three fingers—standin' up!"

And we drank.

His Majesty the King

"Where the word of a King is, there is power: And who may say unto him—What doest thou?"

"YETH! AND CHIMO to sleep at ve food of ve bed, and ve pink pikky-book, and ve bwead—'cause I will be hungwy in ve night—and vat's all, Miss Biddums. And now give me one kiss and I'll go to sleep.—So! Kite quiet. Ow! Ve pink pikky-book has slidded under ve pillow and ve bwead is cwumbling! Miss Biddums! Miss *Bid*dums! I'm *so* uncomfy! Come and tuck me up, Miss Biddums."

His Majesty the King was going to bed; and poor, patient Miss Biddums, who had advertised herself humbly as a "young person, European, accustomed to the care of little children," was forced to wait upon his royal caprices. The going to bed was always a lengthy process, because His Majesty had a convenient knack of forgetting which of his many friends, from the *mehter's* son to the Commissioner's daughter, he had prayed for, and, lest the Deity should take offence, was used to toil through his little prayers, in all reverence, five times in one evening. His Majesty the King believed in the efficacy of prayer as devoutly as he believed in Chimo the patient spaniel, or

Miss Biddums, who could reach him down his gun–"with cursuffun caps–*reel* ones"–from the upper shelves of the big nursery cupboard.

At the door of the nursery his authority stopped. Beyond lay the empire of his father and mother–two very terrible people who had no time to waste upon His Majesty the King. His voice was lowered when he passed the frontier of his own dominons, his actions were fettered, and his soul was filled with awe because of the grim man who lived among a wilderness of pigeon-holes and the most fascinating pieces of red tape, and the wonderful woman who was always getting into or stepping out of the big carriage.

To the one belonged the mysteries of the "*duftar*-room"; to the other the great, reflected wilderness of the "Memsahib's room" where the shiny, scented dresses hung on pegs, miles and miles up in the air, and the just-seen plateau of the toilet-table revealed an acreage of speckly combs, broidered "hanafitch bags," and "white-headed" brushes.

There was no room for His Majesty the King either in official reserve or mundane gorgeousness. He had discovered that, ages and ages ago–before even Chimo came to the house, or Miss Biddums had ceased grizzling over a packet of greasy letters which appeared to be her chief treasure on earth. His Majesty the King, therefore, wisely confined himself to his own territories, where only Miss Biddums, and she feebly, disputed his sway.

From Miss Biddums he had picked up his simple theology and welded it to the legends of gods and devils that he had learned in the servants' quarters.

To Miss Biddums he confided with equal trust his tattered garments and his more serious griefs. She would make everything whole. She knew exactly how the Earth had been born, and had reassured the trembling soul of His Majesty the King that terrible time in July when it rained continuously for seven days and seven nights, and–there was no Ark ready and all the ravens had flown away! She was the most powerful person with whom he was brought into contact–always excepting the two remote and silent people beyond the nursery door.

How was His Majesty the King to know that, six years ago, in the summer of his birth, Mrs. Austell, turning over her husband's papers, had come upon the intemperate letter of a foolish woman who had been carried away by the silent man's strength and personal beauty? How could he tell what evil the overlooked slip of note-paper had wrought in the mind of a desperately jealous wife? How could he, despite his wisdom, guess that his mother had chosen to make of it excuse for a bar and a division between herself and her husband, that strengthened and grew harder to break with each year; that she, having unearthed this skeleton in the cupboard, had trained it into a household God which should be about their path and about their bed, and poison all their ways?

These things were beyond the province of His Majesty the King. He only knew that his father was daily absorbed in some serious work for a thing called the *Sirkar* and that his mother was the victim alternately of the *Nautch* and the *Burrakhana.* To these entertainments she was escorted by a Captain-Man for whom His Majesty the King had no regard.

"He *doesn't* laugh," he argued with Miss Biddums, who would fain have taught him charity. "He only makes faces wiv his mouf, and when he wants to o-muse me I am *not* o-mused." And His Majesty the King shook his head as one who knew the deceitfulness of this world.

Morning and evening it was his duty to salute his father and mother–the former with a grave shake of the hand, and the latter with an equally grave kiss. Once, indeed, he had put his arms round his mother's neck, in the fashion he used toward Miss Biddums. The openwork of his sleeve-edge caught in an earring, and the last of His Majesty's little overture was a suppressed scream and summary dismissal to the nursery.

"It's w'ong," thought His Majesty the King, "to hug Memsahibs wiv fings in veir ears. I will amember." He never repeated the experiment.

Miss Biddums, it must be confessed, spoiled him as much as his nature admitted, in some sort of recompense for what she called "the hard ways of his Papa and Mamma." She, like her charge, knew nothing of the trouble between man and wife—the savage contempt for a woman's stupidity on the one side, or the dull, rankling anger on the other. Miss Biddums had looked after many little children in her time, and served in many establishments. Being a discreet woman, she observed little and said less, and, when her pupils went over the sea to the Great Unknown which she, with touching confidence in her hearers, called "Home," packed up her slender belongings and sought for employment afresh, lavishing all her love on each successive batch of ingrates. Only His Majesty the King had repaid her affection with interest; and in his uncomprehending ears she had told the tale of nearly all her hopes, her aspirations, the hopes that were dead, and the dazzling glories of her ancestral home in "*Cal*cutta, close to Wellington Square."

Everything above the average was in the eyes of His Majesty the King "Calcutta good." When Miss Biddums had crossed his royal will, he reversed the epithet to vex that estimable lady, and all things evil were, until the tears of repentance swept away spite, "Calcutta bad."

Now and again Miss Biddums begged for him the rare pleasure of a day in the society of the Commissioner's child—the wilful four-year-old Patsie, who, to the intense amazement of His Majesty the King, was idolized by her parents. On thinking the question out at length, by roads unknown to those who have left childhood behind, he came to the conclusion that Patsie was petted because she wore a big blue sash and yellow hair.

This precious discovery he kept to himself. The yellow hair was absolutely beyond his power, his own tousled wig being potato-brown; but something might be done toward the blue sash. He tied a large knot in his mosquito-curtains in order to remember to consult Patsie on their next meeting. She was the only child he had ever spoken to, and almost the only one that he had ever seen. The little memory and the very large and ragged knot held good.

"Patsie, lend me your blue wiband," said His Majesty the King.

"You'll bewy it," said Patsie, doubtfully, mindful of certain fearful atrocities committed on her doll.

"No, I won't—twoofanhonor. It's for me to wear."

"Pooh!" said Patsie. "Boys don't wear sa-ashes. Zey's only for dirls."

"I don't know." The face of His Majesty the King fell.

"Who wants ribands? Are you playing horses, chick-abiddies?" said the Commissioner's wife, stepping into the veranda.

"Toby wanted my sash," explained Patsie.

"I don't know," said His Majesty the King, hastily, feeling that with one of these terrible "grown-ups" his poor little secret would be shamelessly wrenched from him, and perhaps—most burning desecration of all—laughed at.

"I'll give you a cracker-cap," said the Commissioner's wife. "Come along with me," Toby, and we'll choose it."

The cracker-cap was still, three-pointed vermilion-and-tinsel splendor. His Majesty the King fitted it on his royal brow. The Commissioner's wife had a face that children instinctively trusted, and her action, as she adjusted the toppling middle spike, was tender.

"Will it do as well?" stammered His Majesty the King.

"As what, little one?"

"As ve wiban?"

"Oh, quite. Go and look at yourself in the glass."

The words were spoken in all sincerity and to help forward any absurb "dressing-up" amusement that the children might take into their minds. But the young savage has a keen sense of the ludicrous. His Majesty the King swung the great cheval-glass down, and saw his head crowned with the staring horror of a fool's cap–a thing which his father would rend to pieces if it ever came into his office. He plucked it off, and burst into tears."

"Toby," said the Commissioner's wife, gravely, "you shouldn't give way to temper. I am very sorry to see it. It's wrong."

His Majesty the King sobbed inconsolably, and the heart of Patsie's mother was touched. She drew the child on to her knee. Clearly it was not temper alone.

"What is it, Toby? Won't you tell me? Aren't you well?"

The torrents of sobs and speech met, and fought for a time, with chokings and gulpings and gasps. Then, in a sudden rush, His Majesty the King was delivered of a few inarticulate sounds, followed by the words:–"Go a–way you–dirty–little debbil!"

"Toby! What do you mean?"

"It's what he'd say. I *know* it is. He said vat when vere was only a little, little eggy mess, on my t-t-unic; and he'd say it again, and laugh, if I went in wif vat on my head."

"Who would say that?"

"M-m-my Papa! And I fought if I had ve blue wiban, he'd let me play in ve waste-paper basket under ve table."

"*What* blue riband, childie?"

"Ve same vat Patsie had–ve big blue wiban w-w-wound my t-ttummy!"

"What is it, Toby? There's something on your mind. Tell me all about it, and perhaps I can help."

"Isn't anyfing," sniffed His Majesty, mindful of his manhood, and raising his head from the motherly bosom upon which it was resting. "I only fought vat you–you petted Patsie 'cause she had ve blue wiban, and–and if I'd had ve blue wiban too, m-my Papa w-would pet me."

The secret was out, and His Majesty the King sobbed bitterly in spite of the arms round him, and the murmur of comfort on his heated little forehead.

Enter Patsie tumultuously, embarrassed by several lengths of the Commissioner's pet *mahseer-rod.* "Tum along, Toby! Zere's a *chu-chu* lizard in ze *chick,* and I've told Chimo to watch him till we tum. If we poke him wiz zis his tail will go *wiggle-wiggle* and fall off. Tum along! I can't weach."

"I'm coming," said His Majesty the King, climbing down from the Commissioner's wife's knee after a hasty kiss.

Two minutes later, the *chu-chu* lizard's tail was wriggling on the matting of the veranda, and the children were gravely poking it with splinters from the *chick,* to urge its exhausted vitality into "just one wiggle more, 'cause it doesn't hurt *chu-chu."*

The Commissioner's wife stood in the doorway and watched:–"Poor little mite! A blue sash . . . and my own precious Patsie! I wonder if the best of us, or we who love them best, ever understand what goes on in their topsy-turvy little heads."

A big tear splashed on the Commissioner's wife's wedding ring, and she went indoors to devise a tea for the benefit of His Majesty the King.

"Their souls aren't in their tummies at that age in this climate," said the Commissioner's wife, "but they are not far off. I wonder if I would make Mrs. Austell understand. Poor little fellow!"

With simple craft, the Commissioner's wife called on Mrs. Austell and spoke long and lovingly about children; inquiring specially for His Majesty the King.

"He's with his governess," said Mrs. Austell, and the tone intimated that she was not interested.

The Commissioner's wife, unskilled in the art of war, continued her questionings. "I don't know," said Mrs. Austell. "These things are left to Miss Biddums, and, of course, she does not ill-treat the child."

The Commissioner's wife left hastily. The last sentence jarred upon her nerves. "Doesn't *ill-treat* the child! As if that were all! I wonder what Tom would say if I only 'didn't ill-treat' Patsie!"

Thenceforward, His Majesty the King was an honored guest at the Commissioner's house, and the chosen friend of Patsie, with whom he blundered into as many scrapes as the compound and the servants' quarters afforded. Patsie's Mamma was always ready to give counsel, help, and sympathy, and, if need were and callers few, to enter into their games with an *abandon* that would have shocked the sleek-haired subalterns who squirmed painfully in their chairs when they came to call on her whom they profanely nick-named "Mother Bunch."

Yet, in spite of Patsie and Patsie's Mamma, and the love that these two lavished upon him, His Majesty the King fell grievously from grace, and committed no less a sin than that of theft–unknown, it is true, but burdensome.

There came a man to the door one day, when His Majesty was playing in the hall and the bearer had gone to dinner, with a packet for His Majesty's Mamma. And he put it upon the hall-table, said that there was no answer, and departed.

Presently, the pattern of the dado ceased to interest His Majesty, while the packet, a white, neatly wrapped one of fascinating shape, interested him very much indeed. His Mamma was out, so was Miss Biddums, and there was pink string round the packet. He greatly desired pink string. It would help him in many of his little businesses–the haulage across the floor of his small cane-chair, the torturing of Chimo, who could never understand harness–and so forth. If he took the string it would be his own, and nobody would be any the wiser. He certainly could not pluck up sufficient courage to ask Mamma for it. Wherefore, mounting upon a chair, he carefully untied the string and, behold, the stiff white paper spread out in four directions, and revealed a beautiful little leather box with gold lines upon it! He tried to replace the string, but that was a failure. So he opened the box to get full satisfaction for his iniquity, and saw a most beautiful Star that shone and winked, and was altogether lovely and desirable.

"Vat," said His Majesty, meditatively, "is a 'parkle cwown, like what I will wear when I go to heaven. I will wear it on my head–Miss Biddums says so. I would like to wear it *now*. I would like to play wiv it. I will take it away and play wiv it, very careful, until Mamma asks for it. I fink it was brought for me to play wiv–same as my cart."

His Majesty the King was arguing against his conscience, and he knew it, for he thought immediately after: "Never mind. I will keep it to play wiv until Mamma says where is it, and then I will say:–'I tookt it and I am sorry.' I will not hurt it because it is a 'parkle cwown. But Miss Biddums will tell me to put it back. I will not show it to Miss Biddums."

If Mamma had come in at that moment all would have gone well. She did not, and His Majesty the King stuffed paper, case, and jewel into the breast of his blouse and marched to the nursery.

"When Mamma asks I will tell," was the salve that he laid upon his conscience. But Mamma never asked, and for three whole days His Majesty the King gloated over his treasure. It was of no earthly use to him, but it was splendid, and, for aught he knew, something dropped from the heavens themselves. Still Mamma made no inquiries, and it seemed to him, in his furtive peeps, as though the shiny stones grew dim. What was the use of a 'parkle cwown if it made a little boy feel all bad in his inside? He had the pink string as well as the other treasure, but greatly he wished that he had not gone beyond the string. It was his first experience of iniquity, and it pained him after the flush of possession and secret delight in the " 'parkle cwown" had died away.

Each day that he delayed rendered confession to the people beyond the nursery doors more impossible. Now and again he determined to put himself in the path of the beautifully attired lady as she was going out, and explain that he and no one else was the possessor of a " 'parkle cwown," most beautiful and quite uninquired for. But she passed hurriedly to her carriage, and the opportunity was gone before His Majesty the King could draw the deep breath which clinches noble resolve. The dread secret cut him off from Miss Biddums, Patsie, and the Commissioner's wife, and–doubly hard fate–when he brooded over it Patsie, said, and told her mother, that he was cross.

The days were very long to His Majesty the King, and the nights longer still. Miss Biddums had informed him, more than once, what was the ultimate destiny of "fieves," and when he passed the interminable mud flanks of the Central Jail, he shook in his little strapped shoes.

But release came after an afternoon spent in playing boats by the edge of the tank at the bottom of the garden. His Majesty the King went to tea, and, for the first time in his memory, the meal revolted him. His nose was very cold, and his cheeks were burning hot. There was a weight about his feet, and he pressed his head several times to make sure that it was not swelling as he sat.

"I feel vevy funny," said His Majesty the King, rubbing his nose. "Vere's a buzz-buzz in my head."

He went to bed quietly. Miss Biddums was out and the bearer undressed him.

The sin of the " 'parkle cwown" was forgotten in the acuteness of the discomfort to which he roused after a leaden sleep of some hours. He was thirsty, and the bearer had forgotten to leave the drinking-water. "Miss Biddums! Miss Biddums! I'm so kirsty!"

No answer. Miss Biddums had leave to attend the wedding of a Calcutta schoolmate. His Majesty the King had forgotten that.

"I want a dwink of water!" he cried, but his voice was dried up in his throat. "I want a dwink! Vere is ve glass?"

He sat up in bed and looked round. There was a murmur of voices from the other side of the nursery door. It was better to face the terrible unknown than to choke in the dark. He slipped out of bed, but his feet were strangely wilful, and he reeled once or twice. Then he pushed the door open and staggered–a puffed and purple-faced little figure–into the brilliant light of the dining-room full of pretty ladies.

"I'm vevy hot! I'm vevy uncomfitivle," moaned His Majesty the King, clinging to the portière, "and vere's no water in ve glass, and I'm *so* kirsty. Give me a dwink of water."

An apparition in black and white–His Majesty the King could hardly see distinctly–lifted him up to the level of the table, and felt his wrists and forehead. The water came, and he drank deeply, his teeth chattering against the edge of the tumbler. Then every one seemed to go away–every one except the huge man in black and white, who carried him back to bed; the mother and father following. And the sin of the " 'parkle cwown" rushed back and took possession of the terrified soul.

"I'm a fief!" he gasped. "I want to tell Miss Biddums vat I'm a fief. Vere is Miss Biddums?"

Miss Biddums had come and was bending over him. "I'm a fief," he whispered. "A fief–like ve men in the pwison. But I'll tell now. I tookt . . . I tookt ve 'parkle cwown when the man that came left it in ve hall. I bwoke ve paper and ve little bwown box, and it looked shiny, and I tookt it to play wif, and I was afwaid. It's in ve dooly-box at ve bottom. No one *never* asked for it, but I was afwaid. Oh, go an' get ve dooly-box!"

Miss Biddums obediently stooped to the lowest shelf of the *almirah* and unearthed the big paper box in which His Majesty the King kept his dearest possessions. Under the tin soldiers, and a layer of mud pellets for a pellet-bow, winkled and blazed a diamond star, wrapped roughly in a half-sheet of note-paper whereon were a few words.

Somebody was crying at the head of the bed, and a man's hand touched the forehead of His Majesty the King, who grasped the packet and spread it on the bed.

"Vat is ve 'parkle cwown," he said, and wept bitterly; for now that he had made restitution he would fain have kept the shining splendor with him.

"It concerns you too," said a voice at the head of the bed. "Read the note. This is not the time to keep back anything."

The note was curt, very much to the point, and signed by a single initial. *"If you wear this to-morrow night I shall know what to expect."* The date was three weeks old.

A whisper followed, and the deeper voice returned: "And you drifted as far apart as *that!* I think it makes us quits now, doesn't it? Oh, can't we drop this folly once and for all? Is it worth it, darling?"

"Kiss me too," said His Majesty the king, dreamily. "You isn't *vevy* angwy, is you?"

The fever burned itself out, and His Majesty the King slept.

When he waked, it was in a new world—peopled by his father and mother as well as Miss Biddums: and there was much love in the world and no morsel of fear, and more petting than was good for several little boys. His Majesty the King was too young to moralize on the uncertainty of things human, or he would have been impressed with the singular advantages of crime—ay, black sin. Behold, he had stolen the " 'parkle cwown," and his reward was Love, and the right to play in the waste-paper basket under the table "for always."

. . . . . .

He trotted over to spend an afternoon with Patsie, and the Commissioner's wife would have kissed him. "No, not vere," said His Majesty the King, with superb insolence, fencing one corner of his mouth with his hand. "Vat's my Mamma's place—vere *she* kisses me."

"Oh!" said the Commissioner's wife, briefly. Then to herself; "Well, I suppose I ought to be glad for his sake. Children are selfish little grubs and—I've got my Patsie."

The Man Who Would Be King

"Brother to a Prince and fellow to a beggar if he be found worthy."

THE LAW, AS quoted, lays down a fair conduct of life, and one not easy to follow. I have been fellow to a beggar again and again under circumstances which prevented either of us finding out whether the other was worthy. I have still to be brother to a Prince, though I once came near to kinship with what might have been a veritable King and was promised the reversion of a Kingdom—army, lawcourts, revenue and policy all complete. But, to-day, I greatly fear that my King is dead, and if I want a crown I must go and hunt it for myself.

The beginning of everything was in a railway train upon the road to Mhow from Ajmir. There had been a Deficit in the Budget, which necessitated traveling, not Second-class, which is only half as dear as First-class, but by Intermediate, which is very awful indeed. There are no cushions in the Intermediate class, and the population are either Intermediate, which is Eurasian, or native, which for a long night journey is nasty, or Loafer, which is amusing though intoxicated. Intermediates do not patronize refreshment-rooms. They carry their food in bundles and pots, and buy sweets from the native sweetmeat-sellers, and drink the roadside water. That is why in the hot weather Intermediates are taken out of the carriages dead, and in all weathers are most properly looked down upon.

My particular Intermediate happened to be empty till I reached Nasirabab, when a huge gentleman in shirt-sleeves entered, and, following the custom of Intermediates, passed the time of day. He was a wanderer and a vagabond like myself, but with an educated taste for whiskey. He told tales of things he had seen and done, of out-of-the-way corners of the Empire into which he had penetrated, and of adventures in which he risked his life for a few days' food. "If India was filled with men like you and me, not knowing more than the crows where they'd get their next day's rations, it isn't seventy millions of revenue the land would be paying–it's seven hundred millions," said he; and as I looked at his mouth and chin I was disposed to agree with him. We talked politics–the politics of Loaferdom that sees things from the underside where the lath and plaster is not smoothed off–and we talked postal arrangements because my friend wanted to send a telegram back from the next station to Ajmir, which is the turning-off place from the Bombay to the Mhow line as you travel westward. My friend had no money beyond eight annas which he wanted for dinner, and I had no money at all, owing to the hitch in the Budget before mentioned. Further, I was going into a wilderness where, though I should resume touch with the Treasury, there were no telegraph offices. I was, therefore, unable to help him in any way.

"We might threaten a Station-master, and make him send a wire on tick," said my friend, "but that'd mean inquiries for you and me, and I've got my hands full these days. Did you say you are traveling back along this line within any days?"

"Within ten," I said.

"Can't you make it eight?" said he. "Mine is rather urgent business."

"I can send your telegram within ten days if that will serve you," I said.

"I couldn't trust the wire to fetch him now I think of it. It's this way. He leaves Delhi on the 23d for Bombay. That means he'll be running through Ajmir about the night of the 23d."

"But I'm going into the Indian Desert," I explained.

"Well *and* good," said he. "You'll be changing at Marwar Junction to get into Jodhpore territory–you must do that–and he'll be coming through Marwar Junction in the early morning of the 24th by the Bombay Mail. Can you be at Marwar Junction on that time? 'Twon't be inconveniencing you because I know that there's precious few pickings to be got out of these Central India States–even though you pretend to be correspondent of the *Backwoodsman.*"

"Have you ever tried that trick?" I asked.

"Again and again, but the Residents finds you out, and then you get escorted to the Border before you've time to get your knife into them. But about my friend here. I *must* give him a word o' mouth to tell him what's come to me or else he won't know where to go. I would take it more than kind of you if you was to come out of Central India in time to catch him at Marwar Junction, and say to him:–'He has gone South for the week.' He'll know what that means. He's a big man with a red beard, and a great swell he is. You'll find him sleeping like a gentleman with all his luggage round him in a Second-class compartment. But don't you be afraid. Slip down the window, and say:–'He has gone South for the week,' and he'll tumble. It's only cutting your time of stay in those parts by two days. I ask you as a stranger–going to the West," he said, with emphasis.

"Where have *you* come from?" said I.

"From the East," said he, "and I am hoping that you will give him the message on the Square–for the sake of my Mother as well as your own."

Englishmen are not usually softened by appeals to the memory of their mothers, but for certain reasons, which will be fully apparent, I saw fit to agree.

"It's more than a little matter," said he, "and that's why I ask you to do it–and now I know that I can depend on you doing it. A Second-class carriage at Marwar Junction, and a red-haired man asleep in it. You'll be sure to remember. I get out at the next station, and I must hold on there till he comes or sends me what I want."

"I'll give the message if I catch him," I said, "and for the sake of your Mother as well as mine I'll give you a word of advice. Don't try to run the Central India States just now as the correspondent of the *Backwoodsman.* There's a real one knocking about here, and it might lead to trouble."

"Thank you," said he, simply, "and when will the swine be gone? I can't starve because he's ruining my work. I wanted to get hold of the Degumber Rajah down here about his father's widow, and give him a jump."

"What did he do to his father's widow, then?"

"Filled her up with red pepper and slippered her to death as she hung from a beam. I found that out myself and I'm the only man that would dare going into the State to get hush-money for it. They'll try to poison me, same as they did in Chortumna when I went on the loot there. But you'll give the man at Marwar Junction my message?"

He got out at a little roadside station, and I reflected. I had heard, more than once, of men personating correspondents of newspapers and bleeding small Native States with threats of exposure, but I had never met any of the caste before. They lead a hard life, and generally die with great suddenness. The Native States have a wholesome horror of English newspapers, which may throw light on their peculiar methods of government, and do their best to choke correspondents with champagne, or drive them out of their mind with four-in-hand barouches. They do not understand that nobody cares a straw for the internal administration of Native States so long as oppression and crime are kept within decent limits, and the ruler is not drugged, drunk, or diseased from one end of the year to the other. Native States were created by Providence in order to supply picturesque scenery, tigers, and tall-writing. They are the dark places of the earth, full of unimaginable cruelty, touching the Railway and the Telegraph on one side, and, on the other, the days of Harun-al-Raschid. When I left the train I did business with divers Kings, and in eight days passed through many changes of life. Sometimes I wore dress-clothes and consorted with Princes and Politicals, drinking from crystal and eating from silver. Sometimes I lay out upon the ground and devoured what I could get, from a plate made of a flapjack, and drank the running water, and slept under the same rug as my servant. It was all in the day's work.

Then I headed for the Great Indian Desert upon the proper date, as I had promised, and the night Mail set me down at Marwar Junction, where a funny little, happy-go-lucky, native-managed railway runs to Jodhpore. The Bombay Mail from Delhi makes a short halt at Marwar. She arrived as I got in, and I had just time to hurry to her platform and go down the carriages. There was only one Second-class on the train. I slipped the window and looked down upon a flaming red beard, half covered by a railway rug. That was my man, fast asleep, and I dug him gently in the ribs. He woke with a grunt and I saw his face in the light of the lamps. It was a great and shining face.

"Tickets again?" said he.

"No," said I. "I am to tell you that he is gone South for the week. He is gone South for the week!"

The train had begun to move out. The red man rubbed his eyes. "He has gone South for the week," he repeated. "Now that's just like his impidence. Did he say that I was to give you anything?–'Cause I won't."

"He didn't," I said, and dropped away, and watched the red lights die out in the dark. It was horribly cold because the wind was blowing off the sands. I climbed into my own train–not an Intermediate Carriage this time–and went to sleep.

If the man with the beard had given me a rupee I should have kept it as a memento of a rather curious affair. But the consciousness of having done my duty was my only reward.

Later on I reflected that two gentlemen like my friends could not do any good if they foregathered and personated correspondents of newspapers, and might, if they "stuck up" one of the little rat-trap states of Central India or Southern Rajputana, get themselves into serious difficulties. I therefore took some trouble to describe them as accurately as I could remember to people who would be interested in deporting them: and succeeded, so I was later informed, in having them headed back from the Degumber borders.

Then I became respectable, and returned to an Office where they were no Kings and no incidents except the daily manufacture of a newspaper. A newspaper office seems to attract every conceivable sort of person, to the prejudice of discipline. Zenana-mission ladies arrive, and beg that the Editor will instantly abandon all his duties to describe a Christian prize-giving in a backslum of a perfectly inaccessible village; Colonels who have been overpassed for commands sit down and sketch the outline of a series of ten, twelve, or twenty-four leading articles on Seniority *versus* Selection; missionaries wish to know why they have not been permitted to escape from their regular vehicles of abuse and swear at a brother-missionary under special patronage of the editorial We; stranded theatrical companies troop up to explain that they cannot pay for their advertisements, but on their return from New Zealand or Tahiti will do so with interest; inventors of patent punkah-pulling machines, carriages couplings and unbreakable swords and axle-trees call with specifications in their pockets and hours at their disposal; tea-companies enter and elaborate their prospectuses with the office pens; secretaries of ball-committees clamor to have the glories of their last dance more fully expounded; strange ladies rustle in and say:"I want a hundred lady's cards printed *at once,* please," which is manifestly part of an Editor's duty; and every dissolute ruffian that ever tramped the Grand Turk Road makes it his business to ask for employment as a proof-reader. And, all the time, the telephone-bell is ringing madly, and Kings are being killed on the Continent, and Empires are saying–"You're another," and Mister Gladstone is calling down brimstone upon the British Dominions, and the little black copy-boys are whining, *"kaa-pi chay-ha-yeh"* (copy wanted) like tired bees, and most of the paper is as blank as Modred's shield.

But that is the amusing part of the year. There are other six months wherein none ever come to call, and the thermometer walks inch by inch up to the top of the glass, and the office is darkened to just above reading light, and the press machines are red-hot of touch, and nobody writes anything but accounts of amusements in the Hill-stations or obituary notices. Then the telephone becomes a tinkling terror, because it tells you of the sudden deaths of men and women that you knew intimately, and the prickly-heat covers you as with a garment, and you sit down and write:–"A slight increase of sickness is reported from the Khuda Janta Khan District. The outbreak is purely sporadic in its nature, and, thanks to the energetic efforts of the District authorities, is now almost at an end. It is, however, with deep regret we record the death, etc."

Then the sickness really breaks out, and the less recording and reporting the better for the peace of the subscribers. But the Empires and the Kings continue to divert themselves as selfishly as before, and the Foreman thinks that a daily paper really ought to come out once in twenty-four hours, and all the people at the Hill-stations in the middle of their amusements say:–"Good gracious! Why can't the paper be sparkling? I'm sure there's plenty going on up here."

That is the dark half of the moon, and, as the advertisements say, "must be experienced to be appreciated."

It was in that season, and a remarkably evil season, that the paper began running the last issue of the week on Saturday night, which is to say Sunday morning, after the custom of a London paper. This was a great convenience, for immediately after the paper was put to bed, the dawn would lower the thermometer from 96° to almost 84° for half an hour, and in that chill–you have no idea how cold is 84° on the grass until you begin to pray for it–a very tired man could set off to sleep ere the heat roused him.

One Saturday night it was my pleasant duty to put the paper to bed alone. A King or courtier or a courtesan or a community was going to die or get a new Constitution, or do something that was important on the other side of the world, and the paper was to be held open till the latest possible minute in order to catch the telegram. It was a pitchy black night, as stifling as a June night can be, and the *loo,* the red-hot wind from the westward, was booming among the tinder-dry trees and pretending that the rain was on its heels. Now and again a spot of almost boiling water would fall on the dust with the flop of a frog, but all our weary world knew that was only pretence. It was a shade cooler in the press-room than the office, so I sat there, while the type ticked and clicked, and the night-jars hooted at the windows, and the all but naked compositors wiped the sweat from their foreheads and called for water. The thing that was keeping us back, whatever it was, would not come off, though the *loo* dropped and the last type was set, and the whole round earth stood still in the choking heat, with its fingers on its lip, to wait the event. I drowsed, and wondered whether the telegraph was a blessing, and whether this dying man, or struggling people, was aware of the inconvenience the delay was causing. There was no special reason beyond the heat and worry to make tension, but as the clock hands crept up to three o'clock and the machines spun their fly-wheels two and three times to see that all was in order, before I said the word that would set them off, I could have shrieked aloud.

Then the roar and rattle of the wheels shivered the quiet into little bits. I rose to go away, but two men in white clothes stood in front of me. The first one said:–"It's him!" The second said:–"So it is!" And they both laughed almost as loudly as the machinery roared, and mopped their foreheads. "We see there was a light burning across the road and we were sleeping in that ditch there for coolness, and I said to my friend here, The office is open. Let's come along and speak to him as turned us back from the Degumber State," said the smaller of the two. He was the man I had met in the Mhow train, and his fellow was the red-bearded man of Marwar Junction. There was no mistaking the eyebrows of the one or the beard of the other.

I was not pleased, because I wished to go to sleep, not to squabble with loafers. "What do you want?" I asked.

"Half an hour's talk with you cool and comfortable, in the office," said the red-bearded man. "We'd *like* some drink–the Contrack doesn't begin yet, Peachey, so you needn't look–but what we really want is advice. We don't want money. We ask you as a favor, because you did us a bad turn about Degumber."

I led from the press-room to the stifling office with the maps on the walls, and the red-bearded man rubbed his hands. "That's something like," said he. "This was the proper shop to come to. Now, Sir, let me introduce to you Brother Peachey Carnehan, that's him, and Brother Daniel Dravot, that is *me,* and the less said about our professions the better, for we have been most things in our time. Soldier, sailor, compositor, photographer, proof-reader, street-preacher, and correspondents of the *Backwoodsman* when we thought the paper wanted one. Carnehan is sober, and so am I. Look at us first and see that's sure. It will save you cutting into my talk. We'll take one of your cigars apiece, and you shall see us light."

I watched the test. The men were absolutely sober, so I gave them each a tepid peg.

"Well *and* good," said Carnehan of the eyebrows, wiping the froth from his moustache. "Let me talk now, Dan. We have been all over India, mostly on foot. We have been boiler-fitters, engine-drivers, petty contractors, and all that, and we have decided that India isn't big enough for such as us."

They certainly were too big for the office. Dravot's beard seemed to fill half the room and Carnehan's shoulders the other half, as they sat on the big table. Carnehan continued:—"The country isn't half worked out because they that governs it won't let you touch it. They spend all their blessed time in governing it, and you can't lift a spade, nor chip a rock, nor look for oil, nor anything like that without all the Government saying—'Leave it alone and let us govern.' Therefore, such as it is, we will let it alone, and go away to some other place where a man isn't crowded and can come to his own. We are not little men, and there is nothing that we are afraid of except Drink, and we have signed a Contrack on that. *Therefore,* we are going away to be Kings."

"Kings in our own right," muttered Dravot.

"Yes, of course," I said. "You've been tramping in the sun, and it's a very warm night, and hadn't you better sleep over the notion? Come to-morrow."

"Neither drunk nor sunstruck," said Dravot. "We have slept over the notion half a year, and require to see Books and Atlases, and we have decided that there is only one place now in the world that two strong men can Sar-a-*whack*. They call it Kafiristan. But my reckoning it's the top right-hand corner of Afghanistan, not more than three hundred miles from Peshawur. They have two and thirty heathen idols there, and we'll be the thirty-third. It's a mountainous country, and the women of those parts are very beautiful."

"But that is provided against in the Contrack," said Carnehan. "Neither Women nor Liqu-or, Daniel."

"And that's all we know, except that no one has gone there, and they fight, and in any place where they fight a man who knows how to drill men can always be a King. We shall go to those parts and say to any King we find—'D' you want to vanquish your foes?' and we will show him how to drill men; for that we know better than anything else. Then we will subvert that King and seize his Throne and establish a Dynasty."

"You'll be cut to pieces before you're fifty miles across the border," I said. "You have to travel through Afghanistan to get to that country. It's one mass of mountains and peaks and glaciers, and no Englishman had been through it. The people are utter brutes, and even if you reached them you couldn't do anything."

"That's more like," said Carnehan. "If you could think us a little more mad we would be more pleased. We have come to you to know about this country, to read a book about it, and to be shown maps. We want you to tell us that we are fools and to show us your books." He turned to the bookcases.

"Are you at all in earnest?" I said.

"A little," said Dravot, sweetly. "As big a map as you have got, even if it's all blank where Kafiristan is, and any books you've got. We can read, through we aren't very educated."

I uncased the big thirty-two-miles-to-the-inch map of India, and two smaller Frontier maps, hauled down volume INF-KAN of the *Encyclopaedia Britannica,* and the men consulted them.

"See here!" said Dravot, his thumb on the map. "Up to Jagdallak, Peachey and me know the road. We was there with Roberts's Army. We'll have to turn off to the right at Jagdallak through Laghmann territory. Then we get among the hills–fourteen thousand feet–fifteen thousand–it will be cold work there, but it don't look very far on the map."

I handed him Wood on the *Sources of the Oxus.* Carnehan was deep in the *Encyclopaedia.*

"They're a mixed lot," said Dracot, reflectively; "and it won't help us to know the names of their tribes. The more tribes the more they'll fight, and the better for us. From Jagdallak to Ashang. H'mm!"

"But all the information about the country is as sketchy and inaccurate as can be," I protested. "No one knows anything about it really. Here's the file of the *United Services' Institute.* Read what Bellew says."

"Blow Bellew!" said Carnehan. "Dan, they're an all-fired lot of heathens, but this book here says they think they're related to us English."

I smoked while the men pored over *Raverty, Wood,* the maps and the *Encyclopaedia.*

"There is no use your waiting," said Dravot, politely. "It's about four o'clock now. We'll go before six o'clock if you want to sleep, and we won't steal any of the papers. Don't you sit up. We're two harmless lunatics, and if you come, to-morrow evening, down to the Serai we'll say good-bye to you."

"You *are* two fools," I answered. "You'll be turned back at the Frontier or cut up the minute you set foot in Afghanistan. Do you want any money or a recommendation down-country? I can help you to the chance of work next week."

"Next week we shall be hard at work ourselves, thank you," said Dravot. "It isn't so easy being a King as it looks. When we've got our Kingdom in going order we'll let you know, and you can come up and help us to govern it."

"Would two lunatics make a Contrack like that?" said Carnehan, with subdued pride, showing me a greasy half-sheet of note-paper on which was written the following. I copied it then and there, as a curiosity:

This Contract between me and you persuing witnesseth in the name of God–Amen and so forth.

(One) That me and you will settle this matter together: i.e., *to be Kings of Kafiristan.*

(Two) That you and me will not, while this matter is being settled, look at any Liquor, nor any woman, black, white or brown, so as to get mixed up with one or the other harmful.

(Three) That we conduct ourselves with dignity and discretion, and if one of us gets into trouble the other will stay by him.

Signed by you and me this day.
Peachey Taliaferro Carnehan.
Daniel Dravot.
Both Gentlemen at Large.

"There was no need for the last article," said Carnehan, blushing modestly; "but it looks regular. Now you know the sort of men that loafers are—we *are* loafers, Dan, until we get out of India—and *do* you think that we would sign a Contrack like that unless we was in earnest? We have kept away from the two things that make life worth having."

"You won't enjoy your lives much longer if you are going to try this idiotic adventure. Don't set the office on fire," I said, "and go away before nine o'clock."

I left them still poring over the maps and making notes on the back of the "Contrack." "Be sure to come down to the Serai to-morrow," were their parting words.

The Kumharsen Serai is the great four-square sink of humanity where the strings of camels and horses from the North load and unload. All the nationalities of Central Asia may be found there, and most of the folk of India proper. Balkh and Bokhara there meet Bengal and Bombay, and try to draw eye-teeth. You can buy ponies, turquoises, Persian pussy-cats, saddle-bags, fat-tailed sheep and musk in the Kumharsen Serai, and get many strange things for nothing. In the afternoon I went down there to see whether my friends intended to keep their word or were lying about drunk.

A priest attired in fragments of ribbons and rags stalked up to me, gravely twisting a child's paper whirligig. Behind him was his servant bending under the load of a crate of mud toys. The two were loading up two camels, and the inhabitants of the Serai watched them with shrieks of laughter.

"The priest is mad," said a horse-dealer to me. "He is going up to Kabul to sell toys to the Amir. He will either be raised to honor or have his head cut off. He came in here this morning and has been behaving madly ever since."

"The witless are under the protection of God," stammered a flat-cheeked Usbeg in broken Hindi. "They foretell future events."

"Would they could have foretold that my caravan would have been cut up by the Shinwaris almost within shadow of the Pass!" grunted the Eusufzai agent of a Rajputana trading-house whose goods had been feloniously diverted into the hands of other robbers just across the Border, and whose misfortunes were the laughing-stock of the bazaar. "Ohé, priest, whence come you and whither do you go?"

"From Roum have I come," shouted the priest, waving his whirligig; "from Roum, blown by the breath of a hundred devils across the sea! O thieves, robbers, liars, the blessings of Pir Khan on pigs, dogs, and perjurers! Who will take the Protected of God to the North to sell charms that are never still to the Amir? The camels shall not gall, the sons shall not fall sick, and the wives shall remain faithful while they are away, of the men who give me place in their caravan. Who will assist me to slipper the King of the Ross with a golden slipper with a silver heel? The protection of Pir Khan be upon his labors!" He spread out the skirts of his gaberdine and pirouetted between the lines of tethered horses.

"There starts a caravan from Peshawur to Kabul in twenty days, *Huzrut,*" said the Eusufzai trader. "My camels go therewith. Do thou also go and bring us good-luck."

"I will go even now!" shouted the priest. "I will depart upon my winged camels, and be at Pashawur in a day! Ho! Hazar Mir Khan," he yelled to his servant, "drive out the camels, but let me first mount my own."

He leaped on the back of his beast as it knelt, and, turning round to me, cried:—"Come thou also, Sahib, a little along the road, and I will sell thee a charm—an amulet that shall make thee King of Kafiristan."

Then the light broke upon me, and I followed the two camels out of the Serai till we reached the open road and the priest halted.

"What d' you think o' that?" said he in English. "Carnehan can't talk their patter, so I've made him my servant. He makes a handsome servant. 'Tisn't for nothing that I've been knocking about the country for fourteen years. Didn't I do that talk neat? We'll hitch on to a caravan at Peshawur till we get to Jagdallak, and then we'll see if we can get donkeys for our camels, and strike into Kafiristan. Whirligigs for the Amir, O Lor! Put your hand under the camel-bags and tell me what you feel."

I felt the butt of a Martini, and another and another.

"Twenty of 'em," said Dravot, placidly. "Twenty of 'em, and ammunition to correspond, under the whirligigs and the mud dolls."

"Heaven help you if you are caught with those things!" I said. "A Martini is worth her weight in silver among the Pathans."

"Fifteen hundred rupees of capital—every rupee we could beg, borrow, or steal—are invested on these two camels," said Dravot. "We won't get caught. We're going through the Khaiber with a regular caravan. Who'd touch a poor mad priest?"

"Have you got everything you want?" I asked, overcome with astonishment.

"Not yet, but we shall soon. Give us a memento of your kindness, *Brother*. You did me a service yesterday, and that time in Marwar. Half my Kingdom shall you have, as the saying is." I slipped a small charm compass from my watch-chain and handed it up to the priest.

"Good-bye," said Dravot, giving me hand cautiously. "It's the last time we'll shake hands with an Englishman these many days. Shake hands with him, Carnehan," he cried, as the second camel passed me.

Carnehan leaned down and shook hands. Then the camels passed away along the dusty road, and I was left alone to wonder. My eye could detect no failure in the disguises. The scene in Serai attested that they were complete to the native mind. There was just the chance, therefore, that Carnehan and Dravot wound be able to wander through Afghanistan without detection. But, beyond, they could find death, certain and awful death.

Ten days later a native friend of mine, giving me the news of the day from Peshawur, wound up his letter with:—"There has been much laughter here on account of a certain mad priest who is going in his estimation to sell petty gauds and insignificant trinkets which he ascribes as great charms to H.H. the Amir of Bokhara. He passed through Peshawur and associated himself to the Second Summer caravan that goes to Kabul. The merchants are pleased because through superstition they imagine that such mad fellows bring good-fortune."

The two, then, were beyond the Border. I would have prayed for them, but, that night, a real King died in Europe, and demanded an obituary notice.

. . . .

The wheel of the world swings through the same phases again and again. Summer passed and winter thereafter, and came and passed again. The daily paper continued and I with it, and upon the third summer there fell a hot night, a night-issue, and a strained waiting for something to be telegraphed from the other side of the world, exactly as had happened before. A few great men had died in the past two years, the machines worked with more clatter, and some of the trees in the Office garden were a few feet taller. But that was all the difference.

I passed over to the press-room, and went through just a scene as I have already described. The nervous tension was stronger than it had been two years before, and I felt the heat more acutely. At three o'clock I cried, "Print off," and turned to go, when there crept to my chair what was left of a man. He was bent into a circle, his head was sunk between his shoulders, and he moved his feet one over the other like a bear. I could hardly see whether he walked or crawled—this rag-wrapped, whining cripple who addressed me by name, crying that he was come back. "Can you give me a drink?" he whimpered. "For the Lord's sake, give me a drink!"

I went back to the office, the man following with groans of pain, and I turned up the lamp.

"Don't you know me?" he gasped, dropping into a chair, and he turned his drawn face, surmounted by a shock of gray hair, to the light.

I looked at him intently. Once before had I seen eyebrows that met over the nose in an inch-broad black band, but for the life of me I could not tell where.

"I don't know you," I said, handing him the whiskey. "What can I do for you?"

He took a gulp of the spirit raw, and shivered in spite of the suffocating heat.

"I've come back," he repeated; "and I was the King of Kafiristan–me and Dravot–crowned Kings we was! In this office we settled it–you setting there and giving us the books. I am Peachey–Peachey Taliaferro Carnehan, and you've been setting here ever since–O Lord!"

I was more than a little astonished, and expressed my feelings accordingly.

"It's true," said Carnehan, with a dry cackle, nursing his feet, which were wrapped in rags. "True as gospel. Kings we were, with crowns upon our heads–me and Dravot–poor Dan–oh, poor, poor Dan, that would never take advice, not though I begged of him!"

"Take the whiskey," I said, "and take your own time. Tell me all you can recollect of everything from beginning to end. You got across the border on your camels, Dravot dressed as a mad priest and you his servant. Do you remember that?"

"I ain't mad–yet, but I shall be that way soon. Of course I remember. Keep looking at me, or maybe my words will go all to pieces. Keep looking at me in my eyes and don't say anything."

I leaned forward and looked into his face as steadily as I could. He dropped one hand upon the table and I grasped it by the wrist. It was twisted like a bird's claw, and upon the back was a ragged, red, diamond-shaped scar.

"No, don't look there. Look at *me,"* said Carnehan.

"That comes afterward, but for the Lord's sake don't distrack me. We left with that caravan, me and Dravot playing all sorts of antics to amuse the people we were with. Dravot used to make us laugh in the evenings when all the people was cooking their dinners–cooking their dinners, and . . . what did they do then? They lit little fires with sparks that went into Dravot's beard, and we all laughed–fit to die. Little red fires they was, going into Dravot's red beard–so funny." His eyes left mine and he smiled foolishly.

"You went as far as Jagdallak with that caravan," I said, at a venture "after you had lit those fires. To Jagdallak, where you turned off to try to get into Kafiristan."

"No, we didn't neither. What are you talking about? We turned off before Jagdallak, because we heard the roads was bad. But they wasn't good enough for our two camels–mine and Dravot's. When we left the caravan, Dravot took off all his clothes and mine too, and said we would be heathen, because the Kafirs didn't allow Mohammedans to talk to them. So we dressed betwixt and between, and such a sight as Daniel Dravot I never saw yet nor expect to see again. He burned half his beard, and slung a sheep-skin over his shoulder, and shaved his head into patterns. He shaved mine, too, and made me wear outrageous things to look like a heathen. That was in a most mountainous country, and our camels couldn't go along any more because of the mountains. They were tall and black, and coming home I saw them fight like wild goats–there are lots of goats in Kafiristan. And these mountains, they never keep still, no more than the goats. Always fighting they are, and don't let you sleep at night."

"Take some more whiskey," I said, very slowly. "What did you and Daniel

Dravot do when the camels could go no further because of the rough roads that led into Kafiristan?"

"What did which do? There was a party called Peachey Taliaferro Carnehan that was with Dravot. Shall I tell you about him? He died out there in the cold. Slap from the bridge fell old Peachey, turning and twisting in the air like a penny whirligig that you can sell to the Amir.–No; they was two for three ha' pence, those whirligigs, or I am much mistaken and woful sore. And then these camels were no use, and Peachey said to Dravot–'For the Lord's sake, let's get out of this before our heads are chopped off,' and with that they killed the camels all among the mountains, not having anything in particular to eat, but first they took off their boxes with the guns and the ammunition, till two men came along driving four mules. Dravot up and dances in front of them, singing,–'Sell me four mules.' Says the first man,–'If you are rich enough to buy, you are rich enough to rob;' but before ever he could put his hand to his knife, Dravot breaks his neck over his knee, and the other party runs away. So Carnehan loaded the mules with the rifles that was taken off the camels, and together we starts forward into those bitter cold mountainous parts, and never a road broader than the back of your hand."

He paused for a moment, while I asked him if he could remember the nature of the country through which he had journeyed.

"I am telling you as straight as I can, but my head isn't as good as it might be. They drove nails through it to make me hear better how Dravot died. The country was mountainous and the mules were most contrary, and the inhabitants was dispersed and solitary. They went up and up, and down and down, and that other party, Carnehan, was imploring of Dravot not to sing and whistle so loud, for fear of bringing down the tremenjus avalanches. But Dravot says that if a King couldn't sing it wasn't worth being King, and whacked the mules over the rump, and never took no heed for ten cold days. We came to a big level valley all among the mountains, and the mules were near dead, so we killed them, not having anything in special for them or us to eat. We sat upon the boxes, and played odd and even with the cartridges that was jolted out.

"Then ten men with bows and arrows ran down that valley, chasing twenty men with bows and arrows, and the row was tremenjus. They was fair men–fairer than you or me–with yellow hair and remarkable well built. Says Dravot, unpacking the guns–'This is the beginning of the business. We'll fight for the ten men,' and with that he fires two rifles at the twenty men, and drops one of them at two hundred yards from the rock where we was sitting. The other men began to run, but Carnehan and Dravot sits on the boxes picking them off at all ranges, up and down the valley. Then we goes up to the ten men that had run across the snow too, and they fires a footy little arrow at us. Dravot he shoots above their heads and they all falls down flat. Then he walks over them and kicks them, and then he lifts them up and shakes hands all round to make them friendly like. He calls them and gives them the boxes to carry, and waves his hand for all the world as though he was King already. They take the boxes and him across the valley and up the hill into pine wood on the top, where there was half a dozen big stone idols. Dravot he goes to the biggest–a fellow they call Imbra–and lays a rifle and a cartridge at his feet, rubbing his nose respectfully with his own nose, patting him on the head, and saluting in front of it. He turns round to the men and nods his head, and says,–"That's all right. I'm in the know too, and all these old jim-jams are my friends.' Then he opens his mouth and points down it, and when the first man brings him food, he says–'No'; but when one of the old priests and the boss of the village brings him food, he says–'Yes'; very haughty, and eats it slow. That was how we came to our first village, without any trouble, just as though we had tumbled from the skies. But we tumbled from one of those damned rope-bridges, you see, and you couldn't expect a man to laugh much after that."

"Take some more whiskey and go on," I said. "That was the first village you came to. How did you get to be King?"

"I wasn't King," said Carnehan. "Dravot he was the King, and a handsome man he looked with the gold crown on his head and all. Him and the other party stayed in that village, and every morning Dravot sat by the side of old Imbra, and the people came and worshipped. That was Dravot's order. Then a lot of men came into the valley, and Carnehan and Dravot picks them off with the rifles before they knew where they was, and runs down into the valley and up again the other side, and finds another village, same as the first one, and the people all falls down flat on their faces, and Dravot says,– 'Now what is the trouble between you two villages?' and the people points to a woman, as fair as you or me, that was carried off, and Dravot takes her back to the first village and counts up the dead–eight there was. For each dead man Dravot pours a little milk on the ground and waves his arms like a whirligig and 'That's all right,' says he. Then he and Carnehan takes the big boss of each village by the arm and walks them down the valley, and shows them how to scratch a line with a spear right down the valley, and gives each a sod of turf from both sides o' the line. Then all the people comes down and shouts like the devil and all, and Dravot says,–'Go and dig the land, and be fruitful and multiply,' which they did, though they didn't understand. Then we asks the names of things in their lingo–bread and water and fire and idols and such, and Dravot leads the priest of each village up to the idol, and says he must sit there and judge the people, and if anything goes wrong he is to be shot.

"Next week they was all turning up the land in the valley as quiet as bees and much prettier, and the priests heard all the complaints and told Dravot in dumb show what it was about. 'That's just the beginning,' says Dravot. 'They think we're Gods.' He and Carnehan picks out twenty good men and shows them how to click off a rifle, and form fours, and advance in line, and they was very pleased to do so, and clever to see the hang of it. Then he takes out his pipe and his baccy-pouch and leaves one at one village and one at the other, and off we two goes to see what was to be done in the next village. That was all rock, and there was a little village there, and Carnehan says,– 'Send 'em to the old village to plant,' and takes 'em there and gives 'em some land that wasn't took before. They were a poor lot, and we blooded 'em with a kid before letting 'em into the new Kingdom. That was to impress the people, and then they settled down quiet, and Carnehan went back to Dravot who had got into another valley, all snow and ice and most mountainous. There was no people there and the Army got afraid, so Dravot shoots one of them, and goes on till he finds some people in a village, and the Army explains that unless the people wants to be killed they had better not shoot their little matchlock; for they had matchlocks. We makes friends with the priest and I stays there alone with two of the Army, teaching the men how to drill, and a thundering big Chief comes across the snow with kettle-drums and horns twanging, because he heard there was a new God kicking about. Carnehan sights for the brown of the men half a mile across the snow and wings one of them. Then he sends a message to the Chief that, unless he wished to be killed, he must come and shake hands with me and leave his arms behind. The Chief comes alone first, and Carnehan shakes hands with him and whirls his arms about, same as Dravot used, and very much surprised that Chief was, and strokes my eyebrows. Then Carnehan goes alone to the Chief, and asks him in dumb show if he had an enemy he hated. 'I have,' says the Chief. So Carnehan weeds out the pick of his men, and sets the two of the Army to show them drill and at the end of two weeks the army can maneuver about as well as Volunteers. So he marches with the Chief to a great big plain on the top of a mountain, and the Chief's men rushes into a village and takes it; we three Martinis firing into the brown of the enemy. So we took that village too, and I gives the Chief a rag from my coat and says, 'Occupy till I come:' which was scriptural. By way of a reminder, when me and the Army was eighteen hundred yards away, I drops a bullet near him standing on the snow, and all the people falls flat on their faces. Then I sends a letter to Dravot, wherever he be by land or by sea."

At the risk of throwing the creature out of train I interrupted,—"How could you write a letter up yonder?"

"The letter?—Oh!—The Letter! Keep looking at me between the eyes, please. It was a string-talk letter, that we'd learned the way of it from a blind beggar in the Punjab."

I remember that there had once come to the office a blind man with a knotted twig and a piece of string which he wound round the twig according to some cypher of his own. He could, after the lapse of days or hours, repeat the sentence which he had reeled up. He had reduced the alphabet to eleven primitive sounds; and tried to teach me his method, but failed.

"I sent the letter to Dravot," said Carnehan; "and told him to come back because this Kingdom was growing too big for me to handle, and then I struck for the first valley, to see how the priests were working. They called the village we took along with the Chief, Bashkai, and the first village we took, Er-Heb. The priests at Er-Heb was doing all right, but they had a lot of pending cases about land to show me, and some men from another village had been firing arrows at night. I went out and looked for that village and fired four rounds at it from a thousand yards. That used all the cartridges I cared to spend, and I waited for Dravot, who had been away two or three months, and I kept my people quiet.

"One morning I heard the devil's own noise of drums and horns, and Dan Dravot marches down the hill with his Army and a tail of hundreds of men, and, which was the most amazing—a great gold crown on his head. 'My Gord, Carnehan,' says Daniel, 'this is a tremenjus business, and we've got the whole country as far as it's worth having. I am the son of Alexander by Queen Semiramis, and you're my younger brother and a God too! It's the biggest thing we've ever seen. I've been marching and fighting for six weeks with the Army, and every footy little village for fifty miles has come in rejoiceful; and more than that, I've got the key of the whole show, as you'll see, and I've got a crown for you! I told 'em to make two of 'em at a place called Shu, where the gold lies in the rock like suet in mutton. Gold I've seen, and turquoise I've kicked out of the cliffs, and there's garnets in the sands of the river, and here's a chunk of amber that a man brought me. Call up all the priests and, here, take your crown.'

"One of the men opens a black hair bag and I slips the crown on. It was too small and too heavy, but I wore it for the glory. Hammered gold it was—five pound weight, like a hoop of a barrel.

" 'Peachey,' says Dravot, 'we don't want to fight no more. The Craft's the trick so help me!' and he brings forward that same Chief that I left at Bashkai—Billy Fish we called him afterward, because he was so like Billy Fish that drove the big tank-engine at Mach on the Bolan in the old days. 'Shake hands with him,' says Dravot, and I shook hands and nearly dropped, for Billy Fish gave me the Grip. I said nothing, but tried him with the Fellow Craft Grip. He answers, all right, and I tried the Master's Grip, but that was a slip. 'A Fellow Craft he is!' I says to Dan. 'Does he know the word?' 'He does,' says Dan, 'and all the priests know. It's a miracle! The Chiefs and the priests can work a Fellow Craft Lodge in a way that's very like ours, and they've cut the marks on the rocks, but they don't know the Third Degree, and they've come to find out. It's Gord's Truth. I've known these long years that the Afghans knew up to the Fellow Craft Degree, but this is a miracle. A God and a Grand-Master of the Craft am I, and a Lodge in the Third

Degree I will open, and we'll raise the head priests and the Chiefs of the villages.'

" 'It's against all the law,' I says, 'holding a Lodge without warrant from any one; and we never held office in any Lodge.'

" 'It's a master-stroke of policy,' says Dravot. 'It means running the country as easy as a four-wheeled bogy on a down grade. We can't stop to inquire now, or they'll turn against us. I've forty Chiefs at my heel, and passed and raised according to their merit they shall be. Billet these men on the villages and see that we run up a Lodge of some kind. The temple of Imbra will do for the Lodge-room. The women must make aprons as you show them. I'll hold a levee of Chiefs to-night and Lodge to-morrow.'

"I was fair run off my legs, but I wasn't such a fool as not to see what a pull this Craft business gave us. I showed the priests' families how to make aprons of the degrees, but for Dravot's apron the blue border and marks was made of turquoise lumps on white hide, not cloth. We took a great square stone in the temple for the Master's chair, and little stones for the officers' chairs, and painted the black pavement with white squares, and did what we could to make things regular.

"At the levee which was held that night on the hillside with big bonfires, Dravot gives out that him and me were Gods and sons of Alexander, and Past Grand-Masters in the Craft, and was come to make Kafiristan a country where every man should eat in peace and drink in quiet, and specially obey us. Then the Chiefs come round to shake hands, and they was so hairy and white and fair it was just shaking hands with old friends. We gave them names according as they was like men we had known in India–Billy Fish, Holly Dilworth, Pikky Kergan that was Bazar-master when I was at Mhow, and so on and so on.

"*The* most amazing miracle was at Lodge next night. One of the old priests was watching us continuous, and I felt uneasy, for I knew we'd have to fudge the Ritual, and I didn't know what the men knew. The old priest was a stranger come in from beyond the village of Bashkai. The minute Dravot puts on the Master's apron that the girls had made for him, the priest fetches a whoop and a howl, and tries to overturn the stone that Dravot was sitting on. 'It's all up now,' I says. 'That comes of meddling with the Craft without warrant!' Dravot never winked an eye, not when ten priests took and tilted over the Grand-Master's chair–which was to say the stone of Imbra. The priest begins rubbing the bottom end of it to clear away the black dirt, and presently he shows all the other priests the Master's Mark, same as was on Dravot's apron, cut into the stone. Not even the priests of the temple of Imbra knew it was there. The old chap falls flat on his face at Dravot's feet and kisses 'em. 'Luck again,' says Dravot, across the Lodge to me, 'they say it's the missing Mark that no one could understand the why of. We're more than safe now.' Then he bangs the butt of his gun for a gavel and says:–'By virtue of the authority vested in me by my own right hand and the help of Peachey, I declare myself Grand-Master of all Freemasonry in Kafiristan in this the Mother Lodge o' the country, and King of Kafiristan equally with Peachey!' At that he puts on his crown and I puts on mine–I was doing Senior Warden–and we opens the Lodge in most ample form. It was a amazing miracle! The priests moved in Lodge through the first two degrees almost without telling, as if the memory was coming back to them. After that, Peachey and Dravot raised such as was worthy–high priests and Chiefs of far-off villages. Billy Fish was the first, and I can tell you we scared the soul out of him. It was not in any way according to Ritual, but it served our turn. We didn't raise more than ten of the biggest men because we didn't want to make the Degree common. And they was clamoring to be raised.

" 'In another six months,' says Dravot, 'we'll hold another Communication and see how you are working.' Then he asks them about their villages, and learns that they was fighting one against the other and were fair sick and tired of it. And when they wasn't doing that they was fighting with the Mohammedans. 'You can fight those when they come into our country,' says Dravot. 'Tell off every tenth man of your tribes for a Frontier guard, and send two hundred at a time to this valley to be drilled. Nobody is going to be shot or speared any more so long as he does well, and I know that you won't cheat me because you're white people–sons of Alexander–and not like common, black Mohammedans. You are *my* people and by God,' says he, running off into English at the end–'I'll make a damned fine Nation of you, or I'll die in the making!'

"I can't tell all we did for the next six months because Dravot did a lot I couldn't see the hang of, and he learned their lingo in a way I never could. My work was to help the people plough, and now and again go out with some of the Army and see what the other villages were doing, and make 'em throw rope-bridges across the ravines which cut up the country horrid. Dravot was very kind to me, but when he walked up and down in the pine wood pulling that bloody red beard of his with both fists I knew he was thinking plans I could not advise him about, and I just waited for orders.

"But Dravot never showed me disrespect before the people. They were afraid of me and the Army, but they loved Dan. He was the best of friends with the priests and the Chiefs; but any one could come across the hills with a complaint and Dravot would hear him out fair, and call four priests together and say what was to be done. He used to call in Billy Fish from Bashkai, and Pikky Kergan from Shu, and an old Chief we called Kafuzelum–it was like enough to his real name–and hold councils with 'em when there was any fighting to be done in small villages. That was his Council of War, and the four priests of Bashkai, Shu, Khawak, and Madora was his Privy Council. Between the lot of 'em they sent me, with forty men and twenty rifles, and sixty men carrying turquoises, into the Ghorband country to buy those hand-made Martini rifles, that come out of the Amir's workshops at Kabul, from one of the Amir's Herati regiments that would have sold the very teeth out of their mouths for turquoises.

"I stayed in Ghorband a month, and gave the Governor there the pick of my baskets for hush-money, and bribed the Colonel of the regiment some more, and, between the two and the tribes-people, we got more than a hundred hand-made Martinis, a hundred good Kohat Jezails that'll throw to six hundred yards, and forty man-loads of very bad ammunition for the rifles. I came back with what I had, and distributed 'em among the men that the Chiefs sent to me to drill. Dravot was too busy to attend to those things, but the old Army that we first made helped me, and we turned out five hundred men that could drill, and two hundred that knew how to hold arms pretty straight. Even those cork-screwed, hand-made guns was a miracle to them. Dravot talked big about powder-shops and factories, walking up and down in the pine wood when the winter was coming on.

" 'I won't make a Nation,' says he. 'I'll make an Empire! These men aren't niggers; they're English! Look at their eyes–look at their mouths. Look at the way they stand up. They sit on chairs in their own houses. They're the Lost Tribes, or something like it, and they've grown to be English. I'll take a census in the spring if the priests don't get frightened. There must be a fair two million of 'em in these hills. The villages are full o' little children. Two million people–two hundred and fifty thousand fighting men–and all English! They only want the rifles and a little drilling. Two hundred and fifty thousand men, ready to cut in on Russia's right flank when she tries for India! Peachey, man,' he says, chewing his beard in great hunks, 'we shall be Emperors–Emperors of the Earth! Rajah Brooke will be a suckling to us. I'll treat with the Viceroy on equal terms. I'll ask him to send me twelve picked English–twelve that I know of–to help us govern a bit. There's Mackray,

Sergeant-pensioner at Segowli–many's the good dinner he's given me, and his wife a pair of trousers. There's Donkin, the Warder of Tounghoo Jail; there's hundreds that I could lay my hand on if I was in India. The Viceroy shall do it for me. I'll send a man through in the spring for those men, and I'll write for a dispensation from the Grand Lodge for what I've done as Grand-Master. That–and all the Sniders that'll be thrown out when the native troops in India take up the Martini. They'll be worn smooth, but they'll do for fighting in these hills. Twelve English, a hundred thousand Sniders run through the Amir's country in driblets–I'd be content with twenty thousand in one year–and we'd be an Empire. When everything was shipshape, I'd hand over the crown–this crown I'm wearing now–to Queen Victoria on my knees, and she'd say: "Rise up, Sir Daniel Dravot." Oh, it's big! It's big, I tell you! But there's so much to be done in every place–Bashkai, Khawak, Shu, and everywhere else.'

" 'What is it?' I says. 'There are no more men coming in to be drilled this autumn. Look at those fat, black clouds. They're bringing the snow.'

" 'It isn't that,' says Daniel, putting his hand very hard on my shoulder; 'and I don't wish to say anything that's against you, for no other living man would have followed me and made me what I am as you have done. You're a first-class Commander-in-Chief, and the people know you; but–it's a big country, and somehow you can't help me, Peachey, in the way I want to be helped.'

" 'Go to your blasted priests, then!' I said, and I was sorry when I made that remark, but it did hurt me sore to find Daniel talking so superior when I'd drilled all the men, and done all he told me.

" 'Don't let's quarrel, Peachey,' says Daniel, without cursing. 'You're a King too, and the half of this Kingdom is yours; but can't you see, Peachey, we want cleverer men than us now–three or four of 'em, that we can scatter about for our Deputies. It's a hugeous great State, and I can't always tell the right thing to do, and I haven't time for all I want to do, and here's the winter coming on and all.' He put half his beard into his mouth, and it was as red as the gold of his crown.

" 'I'm sorry, Daniel,' says I. 'I've done all I could. I've drilled the men and shown the people how to stack their oats better; and I've brought in those tinware rifles from Ghorband–but I know what you're driving at. I take it Kings always feel oppressed that way.'

" 'There's another thing, too,' says Dravot, walking up and down. 'The winter's coming and these people won't be giving much trouble, and if they do we can't move about. I want a wife.'

" 'For Gord's sake leave the women alone!' I says. 'We've both got all the work we can, though I *am* a fool. Remember the Contrack, and keep clear o' women.'

" 'The Contrack only lasted till such time as we was Kings; and Kings we have been these months past,' says Dravot, weighing his crown in his hand. 'You go get a wife too, Peachey–a nice, strappin', plump girl that'll keep you warm in the winter. They're prettier than English girls, and we can take the pick of 'em. Boil 'em once or twice in hot water, and they'll come as fair as chicken and ham.'

" 'Don't tempt me!' I says. 'I will not have any dealings with a woman not till we are a dam' side more settled than we are now. I've been doing the work o' two men, and you've been doing the work o' three. Let's lie off a bit, and see if we can get some better tobacco from Afghan country and run in some good liquor; but no women.'

" 'Who's talking o' *women?*' says Dravot. 'I said *wife*–a Queen to breed a King's son for the King. A Queen out of the strongest tribe, that'll make them your blood-brothers, and that'll lie by your side and tell you all the people thinks about you and their own affairs. That's what I want.'

" 'Do you remember that Bengali woman I kept at Mogul Serai when I was a plate-layer?' says I. 'A fat lot o' good she was to me. She taught me the lingo and one or two other things; but what happened? She ran away with the Station Master's servant and half my month's pay. Then she turned up at Dadur Junction in tow of a half-caste, and had the impidence to say I was her husband–all among the drivers in the running-shed!'

" 'We've done with that,' says Dravot. 'These women are whiter than you or me, and a Queen I will have for the winter months.'

" 'For the last time o' asking, Dan, do *not,'* I says. 'It'll only bring us harm. The Bible says that Kings ain't to waste their strength on women, 'specially when they've got a new raw Kingdom to work over.'

" 'For the last time of answering I will,' said Dravot, and he went away through the pine-trees looking like a big red devil. The low sun hit his crown and beard on one side and the two blazed like hot coals.

"But getting a wife was not as easy as Dan thought. He put it before the Council, and there was no answer till Billy Fish said that he'd better ask the girls. Dravot damned them all round. 'What's wrong with me?' he shouts, standing by the idol Imbra. 'Am I a dog or am I not enough of a man for your wenches? Haven't I put the shadow of my hand over this country? Who stopped the last Afghan raid?' It was me really, but Dravot was too angry to remember. 'Who brought your guns? Who repaired the bridges? Who's the Grand-Master of the sign cut in the stone?' and he thumped his hand on the block that he used to sit on in Lodge, and at Council, which opened like Lodge always. Billy Fish said nothing and no more did the others. 'Keep your hair on, Dan,' said I; 'and ask the girls. That's how it's done at Home, and these people are quite English.'

" 'The marriage of the King is a matter of State,' says Dan, in a white-hot rage, for he could feel, I hope, that he was going against his better mind. He walked out of the Council-room, and the others sat still, looking at the ground.

" 'Billy Fish,' says I to the Chief of Bashkai, 'what's the difficulty here? A straight answer to a true friend.' 'You know,' says Billy Fish. 'How should a man tell you who know everything? How can daughters of men marry Gods or Devils? It's not proper.'

"I remembered something like that in the Bible; but if, after seeing us as long as they had, they still believed we were Gods, it wasn't for me to undeceive them.

" 'A God can do anything,' says I. 'If the King is fond of a girl he'll not let her die.' 'She'll have to,' said Billy Fish. 'There are all sorts of Gods and Devils in these mountains, and now and again a girl marries one of them and isn't seen any more. Besides, you two know the Mark cut in the stone. Only the Gods know that. We thought you were men till you showed the sign of the Master.'

"I wished then that we had explained about the loss of the genuine secrets of a Master-Mason at the first go-off; but I said nothing. All that night there was a blowing of horns in a little dark temple half-way down the hill, and I heard a girl crying fit to die. One of the priests told us that she was being prepared to marry the King.

" 'I'll have no nonsense of that kind,' says Dan. 'I don't want to interfere with your customs, but I'll take my own wife.' 'The girl's a little bit afraid,' says the priest. 'She thinks she's going to die, and they are a-heartening of her up down in the temple.'

" 'Hearten her very tender, then,' says Dravot, 'or I'll hearten you with the butt of a gun so that you'll never want to be heartened again.' He licked his lips, did Dan, and stayed up walking about more than half the night, thinking of the wife that he was going to get in the morning. I wasn't any means comfortable, for I knew that dealings with a woman in foreign parts, though you was a crowned King twenty times over, could not but be risky. I got up very early in the morning while Dravot was asleep, and I saw the priests talking together in whispers, and the Chiefs talking together too, and they looked at me out of the corners of their eyes.

" 'What is up, Fish?' I says to the Bashkai man, who was wrapped up in his furs and looking splendid to behold.

" 'I can't rightly say,' says he; 'but if you can induce the King to drop all this nonsense about marriage, you'll be doing him and me and yourself a great service.'

" 'That I do believe,' says I. 'But sure, you know, Billy, as well as me, having fought against and for us, that the King and me are nothing more than two of the finest men that God Almighty ever made. Nothing more, I do assure you.'

" 'That may be,' says Billy Fish, 'and yet I should be sorry if it was.' He sinks his head upon his great fur cloak for a minute and thinks. 'King,' says he, 'be you man or God or Devil, I'll stick by you to-day. I have twenty of my men with me, and they will follow me. We'll go to Bashkai until the storm blows over.'

"A little snow had fallen in the night, and everything was white except the greasy fat clouds that blew down and down from the north. Dravot came out with his crown on his head, swinging his arms and stamping his feet, and looking more pleased than Punch.

" 'For the last time, drop it, Dan,' says I, in a whisper. 'Billy Fish here says that there will be a row.'

" 'A row among my people!' says Dravot. 'Not much. Peachey, you're a fool not to get a wife too. Where's the girl?' says he, with a voice as loud as the braying of a jackass. 'Call up all the Chiefs and priests, and let the Emperor see if his wife suits him.'

"There was no need to call any one. They were all there leaning on their guns and spears round the clearing in the centre of the pine wood. A deputation of priests went down to the little temple to bring up the girl, and the horns blew up fit to wake the dead. Billy Fish saunters round and gets as close to Daniel as he could, and behind him stood his twenty men with matchlocks. Not a man of them under six feet. I was next to Dravot, and behind me was twenty men of the regular Army. Up comes the girl, and a strapping wench she was, covered with silver and turquoises but white as death, and looking back every minute at the priests.

" 'She'll do,' said Dan, looking her over. 'What's to be afraid of, lass? Come and kiss me.' He puts his arm round her. She shuts her eyes, gives a bit of a squeak, and down goes her face in the side of Dan's flaming red beard.

" 'The slut's bitten me!' says he, clapping his hand to his neck, and, sure enough, his hand was red with blood. Billy Fish and two of his matchlock-men catches hold of Dan by the shoulders and drags him into the Bashkai lot, while the priests howl in their lingo,–'Neither God nor Devil but a man!' I was all taken aback, for a priest cut at me in front, and the Army behind began firing into the Bashkai men.

" 'God A-mighty!' says Dan. 'What is the meaning o' this?'

" 'Come back! Come away!' says Billy Fish. 'Ruin and Mutiny is the matter. We'll break for Bashkai if we can.'

"I tried to give some sort of orders to my men–the men o' the regular Army–but it was no use, so I fired into the brown of 'em with an English Martini and drilled three beggars in a line. The valley was full of shouting, howling creatures, and every soul was shrieking, 'Not a God nor a Devil but only a man!' The Bashkai troops stuck to Billy Fish all they were worth, but their matchlocks wasn't half as good as the Kabul breech-loaders, and four of them dropped. Dan was bellowing like a bull, for he was very wrathy; and Billy Fish had a hard job to prevent him running out at the crowd.

" 'We can't stand,' says Billy Fish. 'Make a run for it down the valley! The whole place is against us.' The matchlock-men ran, and we went down the valley in spite of Dravot's protestations. He was swearing horribly and crying out that he was a King. The priests rolled great stones on us, and the regular Army fired hard, and there wasn't more than six men, not counting Dan, Billy Fish, and Me, that came down to the bottom of the valley alive.

"Then they stopped firing and the horns in the temple blew again. 'Come away–for Gord's sake come away!' says Billy Fish. 'They'll send runners out to all the villages before ever we get to Bashkai. I can protect you there, but I can't do anything now.'

"My own notion is that Dan began to go mad in his head from that hour. He stared up and down like a stuck pig. Then he was all for walking back alone and killing the priests with his bare hands; which he could have done. 'An Emperor am I,' says Daniel, 'and next year I shall be a Knight of the Queen.'

" 'All right, Dan,' says I; 'but come along now while there's time.'

" 'It's your fault,' says he, 'for not looking after your Army better. There was mutiny in the midst, and you didn't know–you damned engine-driving, plate-laying, missionary's-pass-hunting hound!' He sat upon a rock and called me every foul name he could lay tongue to. I was too heart-sick to care, though it was all his foolishness that brought the smash.

" 'I'm sorry, Dan,' says I, 'but there's no accounting for natives. This business is our Fifty-Seven. Maybe we'll make something out of it yet, when we've got to Bashkai.'

" 'Let's get to Bashkai,' says Dan, 'and, by God, when I come back here again I'll sweep the valley so there isn't a bug in a blanket left!"

"We walked all that day, and all that night Dan was stumping up and down on the snow, chewing his beard and muttering to himself.

" 'There's no hope o' getting clear,' said Billy Fish. 'The priests will have sent runners to the villages to say that you are only men. Why didn't you stick on as Gods till things was more settled? I'm a dead man,' says Billy Fish, and he throws himself down on the snow and begins to pray to his Gods.

"Next morning we was in a cruel bad country–all up and down, no level ground at all, and no food either. The six Bashkai men looked at Billy Fish hungry-wise as if they wanted to ask something, but they said never a word. At noon we came to the top of a flat mountain all covered with snow, and when we climbed up into it, behold, there was an Army in position waiting in the middle!

" 'The runners have been very quick,' says Billy Fish, with a little bit of a laugh. 'They are waiting for us.'

"Three or four men began to fire from the enemy's side, and a chance shot took Daniel in the calf of the leg. That brought him to his senses. He looks across the snow at the Army, and sees the rifles that we had brought into the country.

" 'We're done for,' says he. 'They are Englishmen, these people,–and it's my blasted nonsense that has brought you to this. Get back, Billy Fish, and take your men away; you've done what you could, and now cut for it. Carnehan,' says he, 'shake hands with me and go along with Billy. Maybe they won't kill you. I'll go and meet 'em alone. It's me that did it. Me, the King!'

" 'Go!' says I. 'Go to hell, Dan. I'm with you here. Billy Fish, you clear out, and we two will meet those folk.'

" 'I'm a Chief,' says Billy Fish, quite quiet. 'I stay with you. My men can go.'

"The Bashkai fellows didn't wait for a second word but ran off, and Dan and Me and Billy Fish walked across to where the drums were drumming and the horns were horning. It was cold–awful cold. I've got that cold in the back of my head now. There's a lump of it there."

The punkah-coolies had gone to sleep. Two kerosene lamps were blazing in the office, and the perspiration poured down my face and splashed on the blotter as I leaned forward. Carnehan was shivering, and I feared that his mind might go. I wiped my face, took a fresh grip of the piteously mangled hands, and said:–"What happened after that?"

The momentary shift of my eyes had broken the clear current.

"What was you pleased to say?" whined Carnehan. "They took them without any sound. Not a little whisper all along the snow, not though the King knocked down the first man that set hand on him–not though old Peachey fired his last cartridge into the brown of 'em. Not a single solitary sound did those swines make. They just closed up tight, and I tell you their furs stunk. There was a man called Billy Fish, a good friend of us all, and they cut his throat, Sir, then and there, like a pig; and the King kicks up the bloody snow and says:–'We've had a dashed fine run for our money. What's coming next?' But Peachey, Peachey Taliaferro, I tell you, Sir, in confidence as betwixt two friends, he lost his head, Sir. No, he didn't neither. The King lost his head, so he did, all along o' one of those cunning rope-bridges. Kindly let me have the paper-cutter, Sir. It tilted this way. They marched him a mile across that snow to a rope-bridge over a ravine with a river at the bottom. You may have seen such. They prodded him behind like an ox. 'Damn your eyes!' says the King. 'D'you suppose I can't die like a gentleman?' He turns to Peachey–Peachey that was crying like a child. 'I've brought you to this, Peachey,' says he. 'Brought you out of your happy life to be killed in Kafiristan, where you was late Commander-in-Chief of the Emperor's forces. Say you forgive me, Peachey.' 'I do,' says Peachey. 'Fully and freely do I forgive you, Dan.' 'Shake hands, Peachey,' says he. 'I'm going now.' Out he goes, looking neither right nor left, and when he was plumb in the middle of those dizzy dancing ropes, 'Cut, you beggars,' he shouts; and they cut, and old Dan fell, turning round and round and round twenty thousand miles, for he took half an hour to fall till he struck the water, and I could see his body caught on a rock with the gold crown close beside.

"But do you know what they did to Peachey between two pine trees? They crucified him, Sir, as Peachey's hand will show. They used wooden pegs for his hands and his feet; and he didn't die. He hung there and screamed, and they took him down next day, and said it was a miracle that he wasn't dead. They took him down–poor old Peachey that hadn't done them any harm–that hadn't done them any . . ."

He rocked to and fro and wept bitterly, wiping his eyes with the back of his scarred hands and moaning like a child for some ten minutes.

"They was cruel enough to feed him up in the temple, because they said he was more of a God than old Daniel that was a man. Then they turned him out on the snow, and told him to go home, and Peachey came home in about a year, begging along the roads quite safe; for Daniel Dravot he walked before and said:–'Come along, Peachey. It's a big thing we're doing.' The mountains they danced at night, and the mountains they tried to fall on Peachey's head, but Dan he held up his hand, and Peachey came along bent double. He never let go of Dan's hand, and he never let go of Dan's head. They gave it to him as a present in the temple, to remind him not to come again, and though the crown was pure gold, and Peachey was starving, never would Peachey sell the same. You knew Dravot, Sir! You knew Right Worshipful Brother Dravot! Look at him now!"

He fumbled in the mass of rags round his bent waist; brought out a black horsehair bag embroidered with silver thread; and shook therefrom on to my table–the dried, withered head of Daniel Dravot! The morning sun that had long been paling the lamps struck the red beard and blind sunken eyes; struck, too, a heavy circlet of gold studded with raw turquoises, that Carnehan placed tenderly on the battered temples.

"You behold now," said Carnehan, "the Emperor in his habit as he lived–the King of Kafiristan with his crown upon his head. Poor old Daniel that was a monarch once!"

I shuddered, for, in spite of defacements, manifold, I recognized the head of the man of Marwar Junction. Carnehan rose to go. I attempted to stop him. He was not fit to walk abroad. "Let me take away the whiskey, and give me a little money," he gasped. "I was a King once. I'll go to the Deputy Commissioner and ask to set in the Poorhouse till I get my health. No, thank you, I can't wait till you get a carriage for me. I've urgent private affairs–in the south–at Marwar."

He shambled out of the office and departed in the direction of the Deputy Commissioner's house. That day at noon I had occasion to go down the blinding hot Mall, and I saw a crooked man crawling along the white dust of the roadside, his hat in his hand, quavering dolorously after the fashion of street-singers at Home. There was not a soul in sight, and he was out of all possible earshot of the houses. And he sang through his nose, turning his head from right to left:

"The Son of Man goes forth to war,
A golden crown to gain;
His blood-red banner streams afar–
Who follows in his train?"

I waited to hear no more, but put the poor wretch into my carriage and drove him off to the nearest missionary for eventual transfer to the Asylum. He repeated the hymn twice while he was with me whom he did not in the least recognize, and I left him singing it to the missionary.

Two days later I inquired after his welfare of the Superintendent of the Asylum.

"He was admitted suffering from sunstroke. He died early yesterday morning," said the Superintendent. "It is true that he was half an hour bareheaded in the sun at midday?"

"Yes," said I, "but do you happen to know if he had anything upon him by any chance when he died?"

"Not to my knowledge," said the Superintendent.

And there the matter rests.